Dvoretsky's Endgame Manual

Mark Dvoretsky

Second Edition

Foreword by
Artur Yusupov

Preface by
Jacob Aagaard

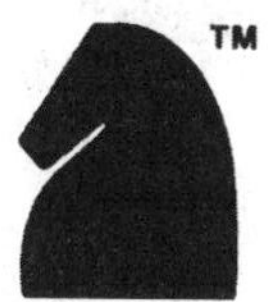

2006
Russell Enterprises, Inc.
Milford, CT USA

Dvoretsky's Endgame Manual

ISBN: 1-888690-19-4

Published by:
Russell Enterprises, Inc.
P.O. Box 5460
Milford, CT 06460 USA

http://www.chesscafe.com
info@chesscafe.com

Cover design by Pamela Terry, Opus 1 Design.
Cover photo by Charles Jones.
Chess piece courtesy of the House of Staunton.
http://www.houseofstaunton.com

Printed in the United States of America

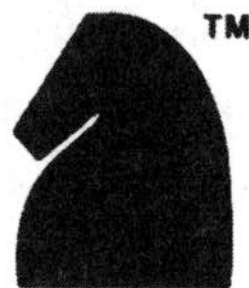

Table of Contents

Foreword

My cooperation and friendship with Mark Dvoretsky has already lasted almost 30 years. He was more than just a coach or second. He was my most important chess teacher. I owe my greatest victories to him and we are still in contact with each other quite often.

Mark has developed a method that can catapult a talented player from Elo 2200 to grandmaster level in 4 to 5 years. An important part of this procedure is the study of the endgame. Mark firmly believes that endgame technique is of universal value. He recognised this when he prepared several endgame sessions for the education of prospective Russian chess trainers. At first he thought that the job was routine work, only requiring him to write down what he already knew. But suddenly he realised that he was playing better!

I also believe in the *interactive* effect of endgame study. It makes it easier to judge and use the potential of the pieces and to understand their interaction. So not only our endgame technique, but also our intuition and positional understanding are refined. In the endgame, plans must be found all the time - so it sharpens our strategic eye as well.

So I was very happy when Mark told me two years ago, that he was planning to write an endgame manual. Now this work by one of the world's leading endgame specialists has appeared and you can enjoy the fruits of his labor. I am sure that those who study this work carefully will not only play the endgame better, but overall, their play will improve. One of the secrets of the Russian chess school is now before you, dear reader!

International Grandmaster Artur Yusupov
Weissenhorn, September 2003

Preface

The first time I heard about the book you are now holding in your hands was in the summer of 2000, when Mark Dvoretsky was giving lectures in Copenhagen for a group of the best Danish players. I had only just been able to put my jaw back in place after being rushed through a rook ending I was badly prepared to understand. What had fascinated me most was not that rook endings could be explained the way Mark explained them, but that the simplicity of dicta like *the rook should always be active* had such far reaching practical implications. *Hey, I can actually understand this!* was the thought running through my head. The game Flohr – Vidmar 1936 (p. 215) especially impressed me. Mark then told us that he was indeed working on a new book on the endgame, a comprehensive manual which would be finished within a year.

In fact it took far more than a year, and to be honest, I am not really sure that Mark will ever finish his work with this book - or that he should. In the summer of 2002 the German version, titled *Die Endspieluniversität,* was published. And I am the proud owner of the first ever signed copy of the book I called *The best chess book ever written* in a 10-page review in the Swedish chess magazine *Schacknytt.*

Since the book was released (and I wrote my review) I have worked with it, in both my own training and my work with juniors, and I have come to the following conclusion: Going through this book will certainly improve your endgame knowledge, but just as important, it will also greatly improve your ability to calculate variations. In particular, the section on pawn endings has convinced me that solving studies and pawn endings should be an important part of my pre-tournament training (and when am I not preparing for the next tournament?). So the book is practical indeed, more so than any other book in my extensive library.

But there is another point, just as important, regarding the general sense of aesthetics in the book. The studies, both those selected and those created by the author himself, are not just instructive, but some of the finest studies I have ever seen.

But what really impresses me is the deep level of analysis in the book. Rules and techniques are important for the practical player in the development of ability, but if the analysis is less than thorough, it is hard to really get into the text. Improvements have been found to the analysis of the German edition and incorporated into the English edition and Mark is always ready to discuss and improve his analysis with anyone. He understands fully that a book has a life and rights of its own. Greatness is possible, but perfection may not be. I must admit that I personally feel as if Shakespeare asked me to write a foreword to Hamlet, and yes, I must admit that I suffer from a lot of confusion as to why he did this. All I can say is: This is a great book. I hope it will bring you as much pleasure as it has me.

International Master Jacob Aagaard
Copenhagen, September 2003

From the Author (First Edition)

Endgame theory is not a complicated subject to study!

All one needs is thorough knowledge of a limited number of "precise" positions (as a rule, elementary ones) plus some of the most important principles, evaluations, and standard techniques. The question is, how to select the most important material from the thousands of endings analyzed in various handbooks? That is why this book was written: it offers the basic information you need as the foundation of your own personal endgame theory.

As long ago as 1970, when I was just a young chess master and a student at Moscow University, I was unexpectedly invited to give some endgame lectures to the chess faculty of the Moscow High School for Sports. It was then that I had to think about what exactly a practical chess player must study. I defined sound methods of studying endgame theory (from the point of view of logic, rather obvious ones) and prepared examples of the most important types of endgames (pawn, rook-and-pawn endgames, and those with opposite-colored bishops). I also prepared a series of lectures on the general principles of endgame play. By the way, the main ideas of that series became (with my permission) the basis of the popular book *Endgame Strategy* by Mikhail Shereshevsky (I recommend that book to my readers).

Later on, these materials, continually corrected and enlarged, were used in teaching numerous apprentices. They proved to be universal and useful for players of widely different levels: from ordinary amateurs to the world's leading grandmasters. My work with grandmasters, some of them belonging to the world's Top Ten, have convinced me that almost none of them had studied chess endings systematically. They either did not know or did not remember many important endgame positions and ideas, which can be absorbed even by those of relatively modest chess experience. As a result, even among grandmasters, grave errors occur even in elementary situations: you will find plenty of examples in this book. Some grandmasters asked me to help them, and our studies resulted usually in a substantial improvement of their tournament achievements. Two weeks of intensive study were usually more than enough to eliminate the gaps in their endgame education.

So, what will you find in this book?

Precise positions. This is our term for concrete positions – positions with a minimum number of pawns, which should be memorized and which will serve as guideposts again and again in your games.

The hardest part of preparing this book was deciding which positions to include and which to leave out. This required rejection of many examples that were intrinsically interesting and even instructive, but of little practical value. Common sense dictates that effort should be commensurate to the expected benefit. Human memory is limited, so there is no sense in filling it up with rarely-seen positions that will probably never occur in our actual games. One should study relatively few positions, the most important and most probable, but study and understand them perfectly. One should not remember long and perplexing analyses. We may never have an opportunity to reproduce them in our games, and we will certainly forget them sooner or later. Our basic theoretical knowledge must be easy to remember and comprehend. Some complicated positions are also important, but we may absorb their general evaluations and basic ideas, plus perhaps a few of their most important lines only.

The positions that I consider part of the basic endgame knowledge system are shown by diagrams and comments in blue print. If the explanatory notes are too complicated or less important the print is black; these positions are also useful but there is not much sense in committing them to memory.

Endgame ideas. These represent, of course, the most significant part of endgame theory. Study of certain endgame types can be almost fully reduced to absorbing ideas (general principles, standard methods and evaluations) rather than to memorizing precise positions.

When discussing precise positions, we will certainly point out the endgame ideas in them. But many standard ideas transcend any particular precise position. These ideas should be absorbed with the help of schemata – very simple positions where a technique or a tool works in a distilled form and our attention is not distracted by any analysis of side lines. Over the course of time we may forget the precise shape of a schema but will still remember the technique. Another method of absorbing endgame ideas is to study practical games or compositions where the ideas have occurred in the most attractive form.

The schemata and the most instructive endgames are represented by color diagrams as well. Plus, important rules, recommendations and names of the important tools are given in ***bold italics***.

As I am sure you realize, the choice of the ideas and precise positions included in this system of basic endgame knowledge is, to some extent, a subjective matter. Other authors might have made slightly different choices. Nevertheless I strongly recommend that you not ignore the information given in the colored font: it is very important. However you of course are free to examine it critically, and to enrich it with the other ideas in this book (those in black print), as well as with examples you already know, from other books or your own games.

Retention of the material. This book would have been rather thin if it included only a laconic list of positions and ideas related to the obligatory minimum of endgame knowledge. As you see, this is not so.

Firstly, the notes are definitely not laconic, after all, this is a manual, not a handbook. In a handbook, a solution of a position is all one needs; in a manual, it should be explained how one can discover the correct solution, which ideas are involved.

Secondly, in chess (as in any other sphere of human activity), a confident retention of theory cannot be accomplished solely by looking at one example: one must also get some practical training with it. For this purpose, additional examples (those with black diagrams and print) will be helpful.

You will see instructive examples where the basic theoretical knowledge you have just studied is applied in a practical situation. The connection between the theory and the practical case will not always be direct and obvious. It is not always easy to notice familiar theoretical shapes in a complicated position, and to determine which ideas should be applied in this concrete case. On the other hand, a position may resemble the theory very much but some unobvious details exist; one should discover them and find how this difference influences the course of the fight and its final outcome.

Some practical endings are introduced by the "tragicomedy" heading. These are examples of grave errors committed by various players (sometimes extremely strong ones). The point is not to laugh at them: you know that there are spots even on the sun. These cases are simply excellent warnings against ignoring endgame theory. Additionally, experience shows that these cases tend to be very well remembered by the student, and are therefore very helpful in absorbing and retaining endgame ideas.

Practical training, by which I mean solving appropriate exercises, is essential. You will find a large number and wide variety of exercises in this book, from easy to very difficult. Some solutions are given directly after the exercises, other are placed in the special chapter that concludes the book.

Some exercises do not involve a search for a single correct solution. They are designed for solving in the playing mode, when a series of contingent decisions is required. The best result can be achieved if a friend or coach assists you by referring to the book. But you can also play through the example without assistance, choosing moves for one side and taking the answering moves from the text of the book.

Of course, one need not study all these examples, nor must one solve all the exercises. But still, if you do, your knowledge of the basic theory will be more sound and reliable. Also, self-training develops one's ability to calculate lines deeply and precisely; this skill is essential for every player.

Analyses. When working on the manuscript, in addition to the large volume of material I had collected myself, I also – quite naturally – used endgame books by other authors. Checking their analyses, I found that an amazingly high number of endings, including many widely known and used in book after book, are analyzed badly and evaluated wrongly. In those cases I went deeper than the concept of the endgame manual required. I felt I had to do it. As I wrote above, studying endgame theory is not a very labor-intensive process, but analysis of a particular endgame, or practical play under time restriction in a tournament, can be a much more sophisticated and complicated matter. Therefore, my readers will find corrected versions of many interesting endgame analyses, plus some entirely new analyses that are important for endgame theory.

Presentation of the material. The material here is presented mainly in a traditional manner, classified according to the material relationships on the board. First pawn endings are analyzed, then those with minor pieces, then rook-and-pawn, etc. But this method is not followed too strictly. For example, the queen-versus-pawns section is in chapter 1, to demonstrate immediately what can arise in some sharp pawn endings.

In the chapter on pawn endings, you will meet some terms and techniques (such as "corresponding squares," "breakthrough," "shouldering" etc.) that are important for many kinds of endgame. Some of these techniques are illustrated by additional examples with more pieces on the board; as the book continues, we may refer to these cases again.

Some chapters (for example, those on pawn and rook-and-pawn endings) are quite long while others are rather short. Chapter length does not reflect the relative importance of a kind of endgame; rather it has to do with the richness of ideas and number of precise positions required for full understanding.

The final chapter deals with the most general principles, rules and methods of endgame play, such as king's activity, zugzwang, the fortress etc. Of course, these themes appear earlier in the book, but a review of already familiar ideas improves both understanding and retention.

What this book does not contain. Obviously, one cannot embrace the infinite. I have already described how the book's material has been selected. Now about other limitations.

My own formal definition of "endgame" is: the stage of a chess game when at least one side has no more than one piece (in addition to the king). Positions with more pieces are not discussed here (except for cases when the "extra" pieces are exchanged).

Our subject is endgame theory. Some problems of chess psychology that belong to "general endgame techniques" are beyond our discussion. Interested readers may turn to the aforementioned *Endgame Strategy* by Shereshevsky, or to *Technique for the Tournament Player*, a book by this writer and Yusupov.

Special signs and symbols. The role of colored fonts in this book is already explained. Now the time has come to explain special signs and symbols.

To the left of diagrams, you will find important information. First of all, the indication of who is on move: "W" means White and "B" Black.

If a question mark is shown, the position can be used as an exercise. Most often, there is no special explanation of what is expected from the reader – he must make a correct decision on his own, because in an actual game nobody will tell you whether you should play for a draw or for a win, calculate a lot or simply make a natural move. Sometimes, however, a certain hint is included in a verbal question.

Exercises with solutions that are given separately, in the end of the book, have two sets of numbers beside the diagrams. For example, diagram 1-14, the 14th diagram of chapter 1, also has the designation 1/1, meaning it is the first such exercise of chapter 1.

The combination "B?/Play" means that the position is designed for replaying, and that you are to take the black pieces.

Beside some black diagrams, the symbol "$" appears. This indicates that the position and the idea behind it have theoretical value, though less compared to those from basic theory (blue diagrams).

Many years ago the publication *Chess Informant* developed a system of symbols to describe the evaluation of a position or move. This system is widely used now and, with minimal changes, is applied in this book, too.

Finally, a work of this scope cannot be produced by a single individual. I am grateful to many others for their assistance during the many stages of producing this book. I would like to thank Artur Yusupov and Jacob Aagaard for their encouragement and eventual contributions, the Introduction and Preface respectively; Mark Donlan for his editing and layout work; Karsten Müller for his help proof-reading the text and checking the accuracy of variations; Taylor Kingston for his assistance editing the final version of the text; Jim Marfia and Valery Murakhveri for their translations of the original Russian text; Harold van der Heijden for his assistance checking sources; and Hanon Russell, the publisher, for coordinating the efforts of all concerned.

This book is an improved and expanded version of the German-language edition, and in that regard, it is also appropriate to thank Ulrich Dirr, who provided invaluable assistance in the preparation of the German edition and Jürgen Daniel, its publisher. Without their fine work, it would have been significantly more difficult to bring out this English-language edition.

Mark Dvoretsky
Moscow, September 2003

From the Author (Second Edition)

An author usually has a hard time predicting whether his book will be popular; in this case, however, I was confident that *Dvoretsky's Endgame Manual* would be a success. And it was, as witnessed by the almost uniformly favorable (and in some cases – ecstatic) reviews and the rapidly sold-out first edition. Now, only two years later, it is time to prepare a second edition.

The theory of the endgame is constantly evolving – although not, of course, as fast as opening theory. New instructive endgames are constantly being played and then analyzed; commentaries on endgames played earlier are corrected – in large measure, thanks to the use of rapidly improving computer programs. On the other hand, if we understand endgame theory, not as the mechanical accumulation of all the information we have, but as the results of our consideration of it, then the authors of endgame books (as opposed to the authors of opening books) have no need to be continuously expanding and reworking their texts, since very few new analyses have any practical value in forcing us to reexamine our approaches to the study and play of endgames.

In the past two years, very important discoveries have been made in the theory of one particular area of rook endgames – and I have completely reworked the corresponding chapter of this book. However, there have also been a number of corrections made in other chapters as well – perhaps not as fundamental, and some that are barely noticeable. A few of them involve corrections to the names of players and composers; but most of them, of course, are analytical. And here, the letters from readers to the author and to the publisher, Hanon Russell, have been most valuable. I am truly grateful to everyone who has written to us. All these notes have been considered in the preparation of the new edition – as a result, a number of new names now appear in the index of composers and analysts. Special thanks are due to that exacting aficionado of the endgame, Karsten Müller, who helped me eradicate of a number of inaccuracies and outright errors in the original text, just as he did with the preparation of the first edition.

Mark Dvoretsky
Moscow, March 2006

Other Signs, Symbols, and Abbreviations

!	a strong move
!!	a brilliant or unobvious move
?	a weak move, an error
??	a grave error
!?	a move worth consideration
?!	a dubious move
□	a forced move
=	an equal position
⩲	White stands slightly better
±	White has a clear advantage
+−	White has a winning position
⩱	Black stands slightly better
∓	Black has a clear advantage
−+	Black has a winning position
∞	an unclear position
△	with the threat or idea of
#	mate
⊙	zugzwang
*	in a game: a position that could arise but did not actually happen
*	in a study: a position that is not an initial one
m	match
wm	match for the world championship
zt	zonal tournament
izt	interzonal tournament
ct	candidates' tournament
cm	candidates' match
ch	championship
ch(1)	championship, 1st league
wch	world championship
ech	European championship
f	final
sf	semifinal
qf	quarterfinal
ol	Olympiad
tt	team tournament
jr	junior competitions
cr	correspondence game
simul	simultaneous display
bl	a blindfold game

Chapter 1

PAWN ENDGAMES

Pawn endings are very concrete - even the tiniest change in the position generally alters the shape and outcome of the struggle. Here you can rarely get along on "general principles" - you **must** know how to calculate accurately.

The study of pawn endings chiefly boils down, not to the memorization of exact positions, but to the assimilation of standard techniques, which considerably eases our search for a solution and the calculation of variations.

Many pawn endings are clearly defined tempo-battles. In these endgames, speed is everything: which pawn will queen first, will the king come in time to stop the passed pawn or get to the other side of the board in time. And there are other pawn endings in which a maneuvering war predominates, and in which zugzwang assumes paramount importance.

"Maneuvering" endgames are generally more complex than "rapid" ones, but we shall begin with them anyway, in order to acquire the vital concept of "corresponding squares." Then we shall switch to studying the ideas involved in "rapid" endgames, before returning once again to the "maneuvering."

Key Squares

Key Squares are what we call those squares whose occupation by the king assures victory, regardless of whose turn it is to move. In other types of endgames, we may also speak of key squares for other pieces besides the king.

1-1

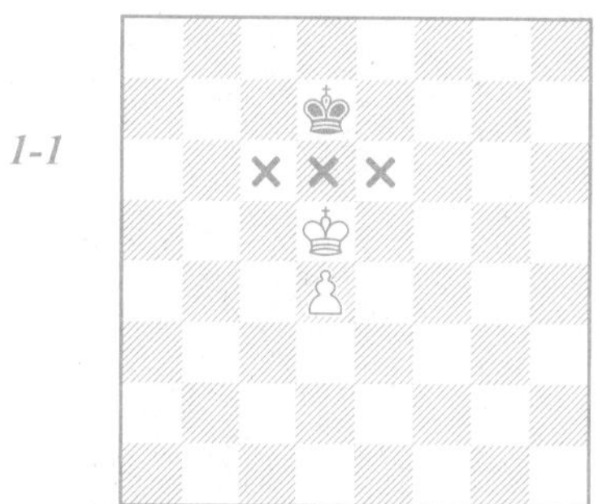

The d5-square on which the king now stands is not a key square - White to move does not win. The key squares are c6, d6 and e6. Black to move must retreat his king, allowing the enemy king onto one of the key squares. With White to move, the position is drawn, since he cannot move to any key square.

With the pawn on the 5th rank (see next diagram), the key squares are not only a7, b7 and c7, but also the similar 6th-rank squares a6, b6, and c6. White wins, even if he is on move.

1-2

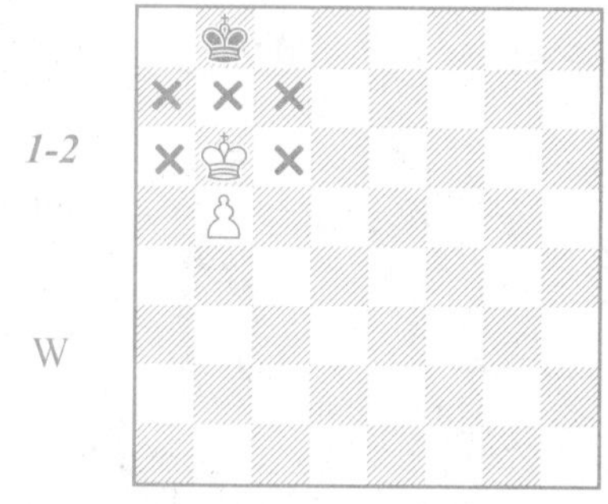

W

1 ♔a6! ♔a8 2 b6 ♔b8 3 b7+-

Note that 1 ♔c6?! is inaccurate, in view of 1...♔a7!, when White has to return to the starting position with 2 ♔c7 (2 b6+? ♔a8!⊙=) 2...♔a8 3 ♔b6 (again, 3 b6?? is stalemate) 3...♔b8 4 ♔a6!, etc.

1-3

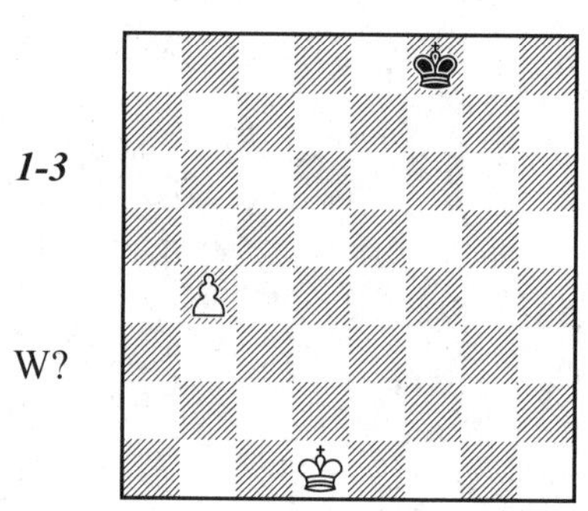

W?

The key squares are a6, b6 and c6. The sensible thing here is to head for the square farthest from the enemy king, since that will be the one hardest to defend.

1 ♔c2! ♔e7 2 ♔b3 ♔d6 3 ♔a4 (3 ♔c4? ♔c6=) **3...♔c6 4 ♔a5** (△ 5 ♔a6) **4...♔b7 5 ♔b5⊙+−.**

J. Moravec, 1952

1-4

W?

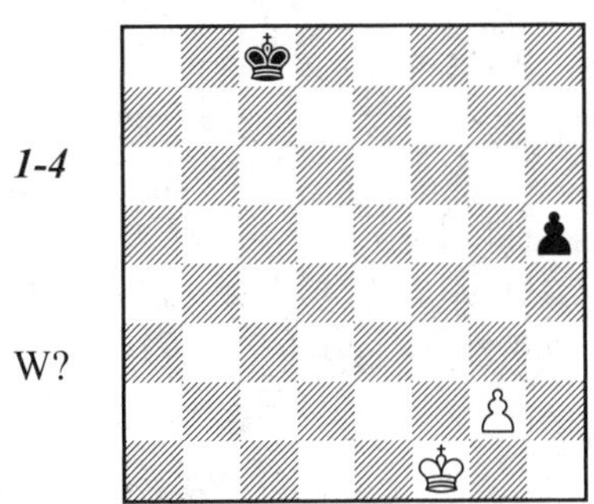

1 ♔f2!

On 1 ♔g1? ♔d7, Black's king successfully defends the pawn, whereas now, it is too late: 1...♔d7 2 ♔g3 ♔e6 3 ♔h4+−.

1...h4! 2 ♔g1!!

The natural 2 ♔f3? is refuted by 2...h3! If the pawn is taken, Black's king heads for h8. And if 3 g4, White cannot gain control of the key squares on the 6th rank: 3...♔d7 4 ♔g3 ♔e6 5 ♔×h3 ♔f6 6 ♔h4 ♔g6.

2...h3 3 g3!

The key squares for a pawn on g3 are on the 5th rank - closer to White's king.

3...♔d7 4 ♔h2 ♔e6 5 ♔×h3 ♔f5 6 ♔h4 ♔g6 7 ♔g4⊙+−.

Tragicomedies

Coull - Stanciu
Saloniki ol 1988

1-5

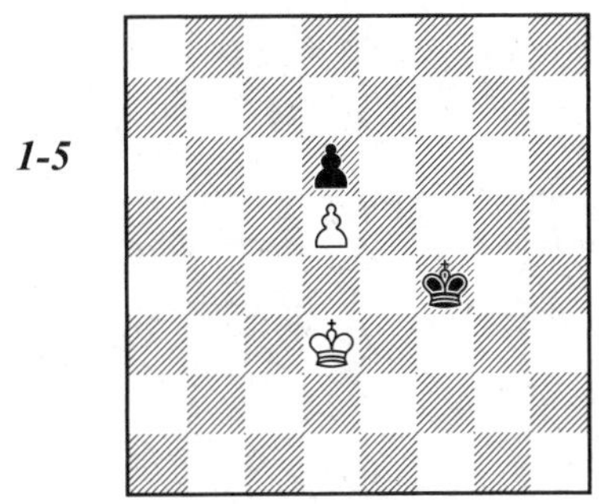

The lady playing White, Scotland's Board One, saw that she must lose the d5-pawn, and therefore resigned. What can I say, except: No comment needed!

Spielmann - Duras
Karlsbad 1907

1-6

W

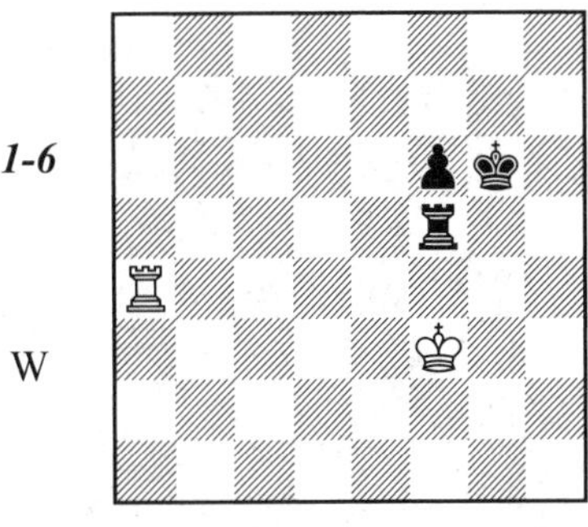

1 ♖f4?? ♔g5!
White resigned.

Corresponding Squares

Corresponding squares are squares of reciprocal zugzwang. We may speak of corresponding squares for kings, for kings with pawns, and with other material, we may speak of correspondence between any pairs of pieces.

The most commonly seen cases of corresponding squares are: ***the opposition, mined squares,*** *and* ***triangulation.***

Opposition

Opposition is the state of two kings standing on the same file with one square separating them ("close" opposition; three or five squares between is called "distant" opposition); the opposition may be vertical, horizontal, or diagonal.

"To get the opposition" means to achieve this standing of the kings one square apart with the opponent to move (that is, to place him in zugzwang); "to fall into opposition" means, conversely, to fall into zugzwang oneself.

Return to Diagram 1-1, where we see the simplest case of the opposition (close, vertical). With White to move, there is no win: 1 ♔c5 ♔c7⊙; or 1 ♔e5 ♔e7⊙. Black to move loses, because he must allow the enemy king onto one of the key squares: 1...♔c7 2 ♔e6; or 1...♔e7 2 ♔c6.

When we are speaking of the opposition, it is usually not just one pair of squares, but several, which are under consideration: c5 and c7, d5 and d7, e5 and e7.

The stronger side gets the opposition in order to execute an outflanking (where the enemy king retreats to one side, and our king then attacks the other way). ***The weaker side gets the opposition in order to prevent this outflanking.***

1-7

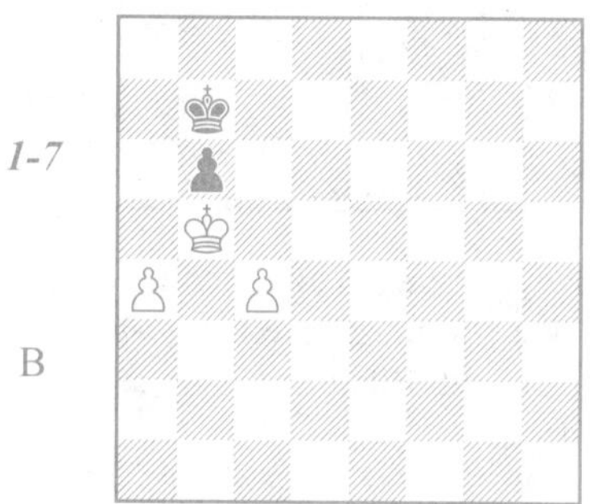

B

White has the opposition, but it's not enough to win.

1...♔c7!

1...♔a7? is a mistake, in view of 2 a5! ba 3 ♔×a5 (here, getting the opposition decides) 3...♔b7 4 ♔b5 ♔c7 5 ♔c5⊙+−.

2 ♔a6

Since 2 c5 would be useless, the king starts an outflanking maneuver. Black replies by getting the horizontal opposition.

2...♔c6 3 ♔a7 ♔c7! 4 ♔a8 ♔c8!= (but not 4...♔c6? 5 ♔b8 ♔c5 6 ♔b7+−).

If we moved the position one file to the right, White would win: 1...♔d7 is met by 2 d5!.

White would also win if he had a reserve tempo at his disposal. Let's move the a-pawn back to a3 - then, after 1...♔c7 2 ♔a6 ♔c6, he first recaptures the opposition by 3 a4!, and then performs the outflanking maneuver 3...♔c7 4 ♔a7 ♔c6 5 ♔b8! (outflanking!) 5...♔c5 6 ♔b7+−.

In the next diagram, White's king cannot move forward: on 1 ♔g3? there comes 1...♔e1! 2 ♔g2 ♔e2 3 ♔g3 ♔f1!−+.

White would like to take the opposition with 1 ♔f1, but this is a mistake, too. After 1...♔d2 2 ♔f2 ♔d3, the f3-square his king needs is occupied by his own pawn, and the opposition passes to his opponent: 3 ♔f1(or g3) ♔e3! 4 ♔g2 ♔e2, etc.

H. Neustadtl, 1890

1-8

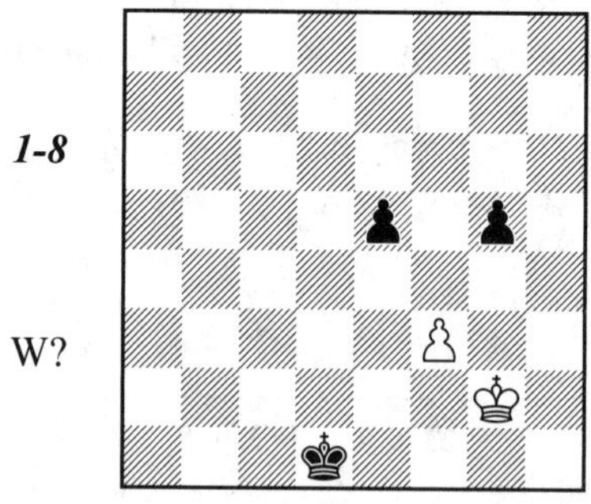

W?

The only thing that saves White is getting the distant opposition:

1 ♔h1!! ♔d2 (1...♔e1 2 ♔g1=; 1...g4 2 ♔g2! ♔d2 3 fg=) **2 ♔h2 ♔d3 3 ♔h3=**.

Now let's examine ***the mechanism by which the stronger side can exploit the distant opposition.*** It is, in fact, quite simple, and ***consists of the conversion of the distant opposition into close opposition by means of outflanking. If outflanking is not possible, then possession of the distant opposition is worthless.***

H. Mattison, 1918*

1-9

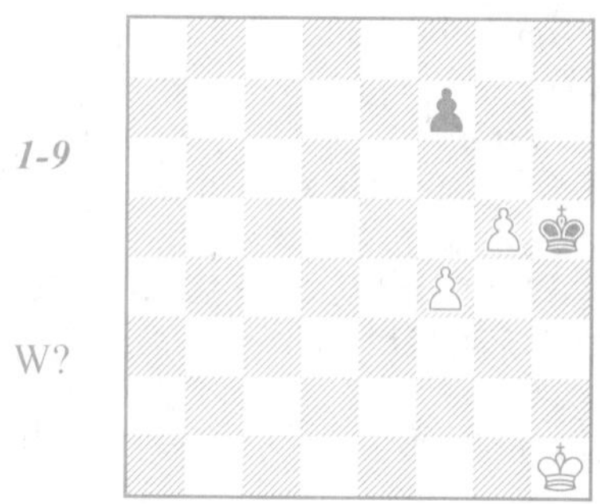

W?

The pawns are lost, after which Black's king will control the key squares in front of the f7-pawn. But White has a tactical resource at hand: he moves both pawns forward to lure Black's pawn nearer to his king allowing him to defend the new key squares.

1 g6! fg 2 f5!

2 ♔g2? ♔g4 3 f5 gf −+, and Black controls the opposition; also bad is 2 ♔h2? ♔g4 3 f5 ♔×f5! 4 ♔g3 ♔g5−+.

2...gf 3 ♔g1

Black controls the distant opposition, but he cannot convert it into close opposition. The problem is that after **2...♔g5 3 ♔f1**, outflanking with 3...♔h4 has no point; and on 3...♔f4 (g4), it is White who takes the close opposition by 4 ♔f2 (g2), and Black's king can't use the f5-square as it blocked by its own pawn. If the king and the pawn could both occupy this square simultaneously, then on the next move the outflanking would be decisive; unfortunately, the rules of chess don't allow such a thing.

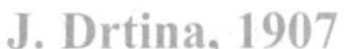

J. Drtina, 1907

1-10

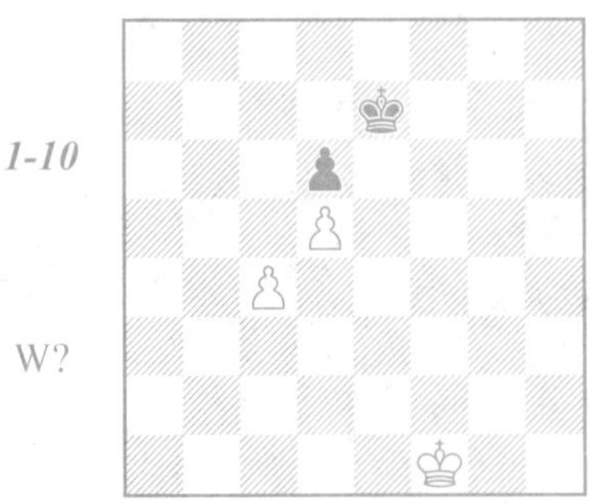

W?

Taking the distant opposition with 1 ♔e1? leads only to a draw. The opposition on the e-file is meaningless: 1...♔e8! 2 ♔e2 ♔e7 3 ♔e3 ♔e8 4 ♔e4 ♔e7, and White cannot get any closer, because the e5-square is off limits. And if the white king leaves the e-file, his opponent will take the opposition forever, i.e.: 2 ♔f2 ♔f8! 3 ♔g3 ♔g7! 4 ♔f3 ♔f7!, etc.

In such situations there is usually a "major" line, in which is it vitally important to capture the opposition. And when the enemy king retreats from it, you must outflank it. In this instance, that would be the f-file.

Imagine that Black's king was on f7, and moved to one side. White must move to outflank, thus: **1 ♔g2!**

It's pointless to stay on the e-file: White's king will reach the key square g6. So Black plays **1...♔f6**

As we have already noted, on the f-file it is necessary to maintain the opposition; therefore, **2 ♔f2!**

What's Black to do now? Moving the king forward is useless: 2...♔f5 3 ♔f3 ♔e5 4 ♔e3 ♔f5 5 ♔d4 and 6 c5. If we retreat the king to the right, White's king advances left and takes over the key squares on the queenside: 2...♔g6 3 ♔e3 ♔f7 4 ♔d4 (4 ♔f3 isn't bad, either) 4...♔e7 5 ♔c3 ♔d7 6 ♔b4 ♔c7 7 ♔a5! (diagonal opposition!) 7...♔b7 8 ♔b5⊙ ♔c7 9 ♔a6+−.

That leaves only **2...♔e7**; but then comes the algorithm we already know: **3 ♔g3! ♔f7 4 ♔f3! ♔e7 5 ♔g4 ♔f8 6 ♔f4! ♔e7 7 ♔g5! ♔f7 8 ♔f5**+−. The distant opposition has been successfully transformed into the close one.

F. Sackmann, 1913

1-11

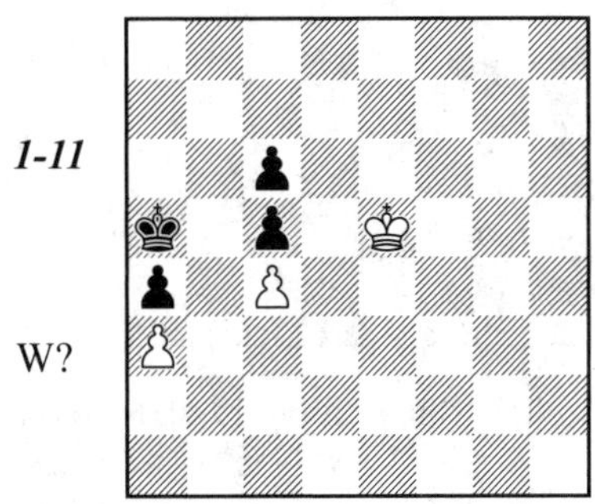

W?

The first thing White must do is seize the opposition.

1 ♔f5! ♔b6

Black's king must be the first one on the 6th rank. If it had been on a7 in the starting position, then 1...♔b7! would lead to a draw, since White could no longer seize the opposition: 2 ♔e6 ♔a6!=; or 2 ♔f6 ♔b6!=.

2 ♔f6!

The rest is the standard technique of converting distant opposition into close opposition. Here, the "major line" is the 7th rank.

2...♔b7 3 ♔f7! (3 ♔e5? ♔a7!=) **3...♔b6** (3...♔b8 4 ♔e6!) **4 ♔e8!** (outflanking!) **4...♔a7 5 ♔e7! ♔a8 6 ♔d6! ♔b7 7 ♔d7! ♔b6 8 ♔c8**+− (the final, decisive outflanking).

Instead of the easily winning 7 ♔d7!, White might also play 7 ♔×c5?! ♔c7 8 ♔b4 ♔b6 9 c5+! (9 ♔×a4? c5 10 ♔b3 ♔a5 11 ♔c3 ♔a4 12 ♔b2 ♔a5 13 ♔b3 ♔b6 14 ♔c3 ♔a5=) 9...♔a6 10 ♔×a4.

George Walker analyzed a similar position as far back as 1841. We shall return to it in our next section - mined squares.

Tragicomedies

Yates - Tartakower
Bad Homburg 1927

1-12

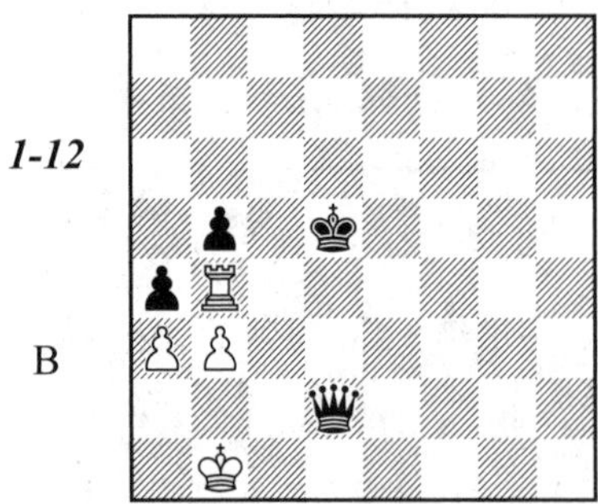

B

Black has a won position. 1...ab is possible; 1...♕c3!? 2 ♖×b5+ (2 ♔a2 ♕c2+; 2 ba ♕×a3) 2...♔c6 3 ba ♕×a3 is also strong. Tartakower, however, decided to transpose into a pawn ending, which he thought was won.

1...♕×b4?? 2 ab ab 3 ♔b2 ♔c4 4 ♔a3! b2 (4...♔c3 is stalemate) **5 ♔a2!**

Black had missed this move when he traded off his queen. He had hoped to win the b4-pawn and seize the opposition, but miscalculated. After 5...♔c3 6 ♔b1 ♔×b4 7 ♔×b2, the draw is obvious.

Yusupov - Ljubojevic
Linares 1992

1-13

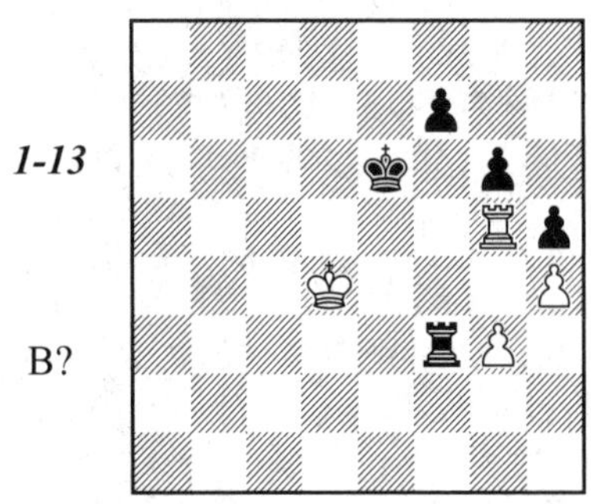

B?

White's rook is tied to the defense of the pawn at g3. Black would have won easily, if he had transferred his rook by 1...♖a3! (to prevent the white king from approaching the pawns: 2 ♔e4 f5+! and 3...♔f6 wins), followed by ...♔f6-g7 and ...f7-f6 (or ...f7-f5).

Instead, Black played **1...♖f5?? 2 ♔e4! ♖×g5 3 hg**

White has the opposition, but Ljubojevic had counted on **3...f6 4 gf ♔×f6 5 ♔f4 g5+**

Yusupov replied **6 ♔f3!**, and it became clear that the opposition on the f-file would give Black nothing, since 6...♔f5 is met by 7 g4+! hg+ 8 ♔g3=. And as soon as Black's king goes to the e-file, White's king immediately takes the opposition.

6...♔f7 7 ♔f2! ♔e6 8 ♔e2! ♔d6 9 ♔d2 ♔c5 10 ♔e3! Drawn.

Exercises

1-14

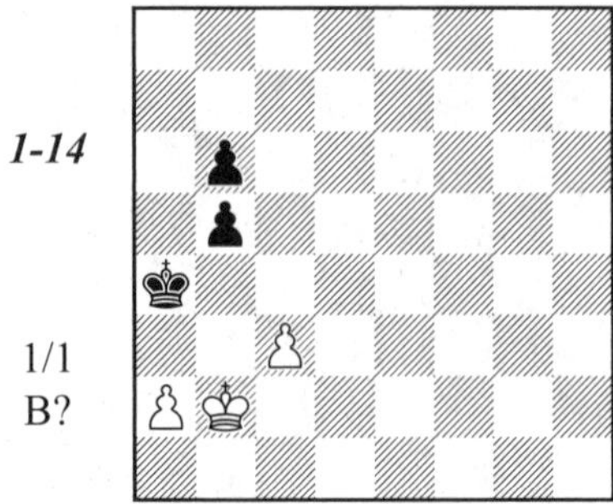

1/1
B?

1-15

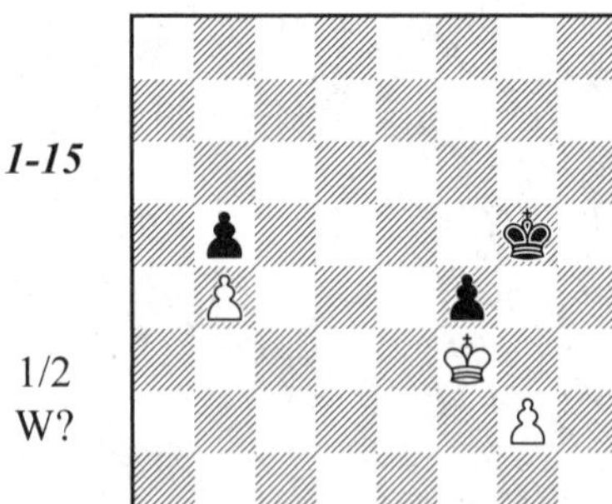

1/2
W?

1-16

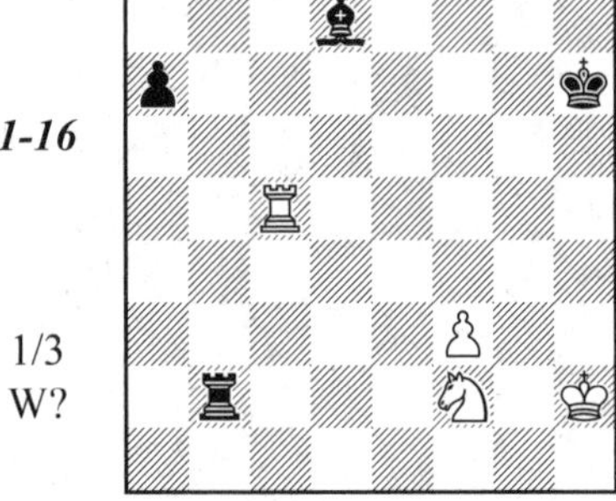

1/3
W?

1-17

1-4
W?/Play

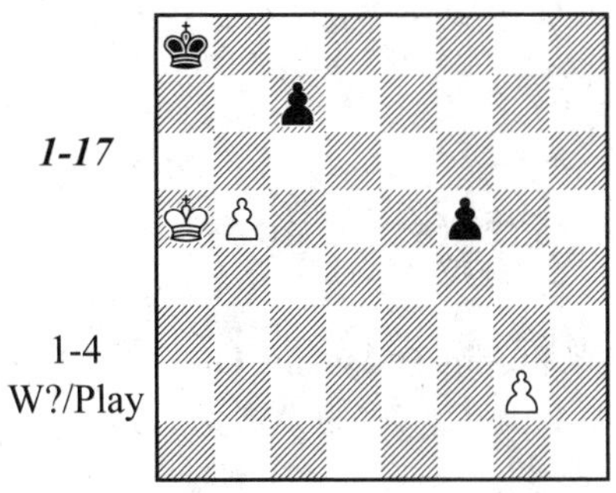

1-18

1-5
W?

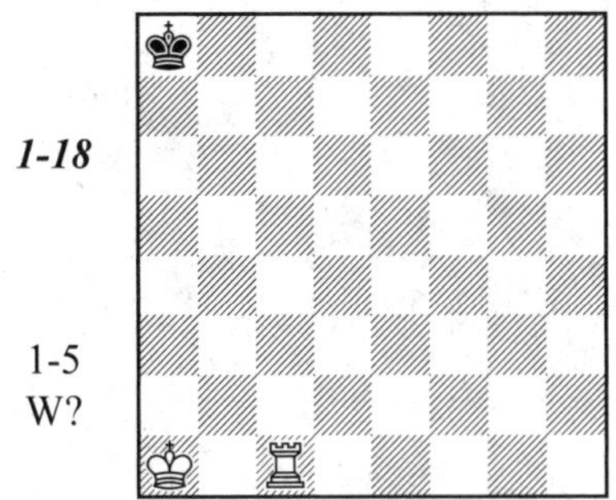

Mate Black with just one [mating] move by the rook.

Mined Squares

Sometimes, it is a single pair of squares that correspond; I refer to such squares as being "mined." Do not be the first to step on a mined square, or you'll be "blown up" - that is, fall into zugzwang. You must either first allow your opponent to step on the mined square, or move forward, accurately avoiding it.

Here are two quite typical examples of mined squares.

1-19

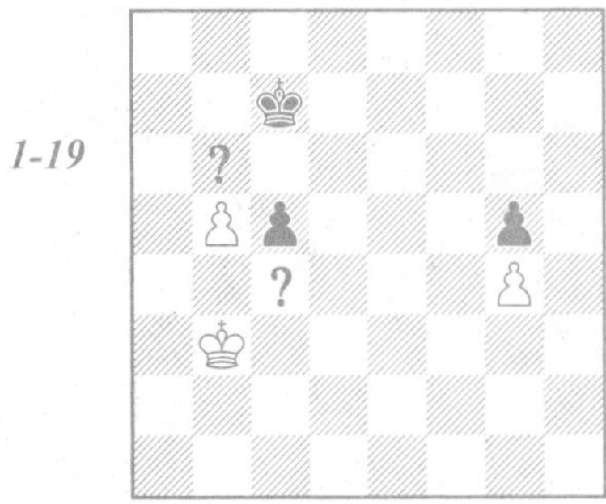

Here we have what I call "***untouchable pawns.***" White's king shuttles between b3, c3 and d3, while the black king goes from c7 to b7 to a7, neither of them able to attack the pawn - the squares c4 and b6 are mined.

1-20

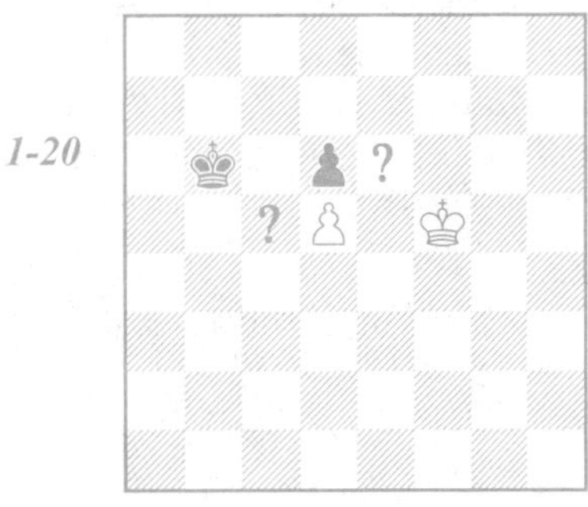

Here, kings at e6 and c5 result in reciprocal zugzwang. White wins by forcing his opponent to go to the mined square first.

1 ♔f6! ♔b5

Passive defense is hopeless too: 1...♔c7 2 ♔e7 ♔c8 3 ♔×d6 - the king captures the d6-pawn while simultaneously controlling the key square for the d5-pawn.

2 ♔e7! ♔c5 3 ♔e6!⊙+−

Black to move plays 1...♔b5! White, however, is better off than his opponent, in that the loss of a pawn does not mean the loss of the game: he replies 2 ♔e4 (but not 2 ♔f6? ♔c4! 3 ♔e6 ♔c5−+) 2...♔c4 3 ♔e3 ♔×d5 4 ♔d3, with a draw.

And now, let's return to a position we reached while analyzing F. Sackmann's study (Diagram 1-11).

1-21
$

B

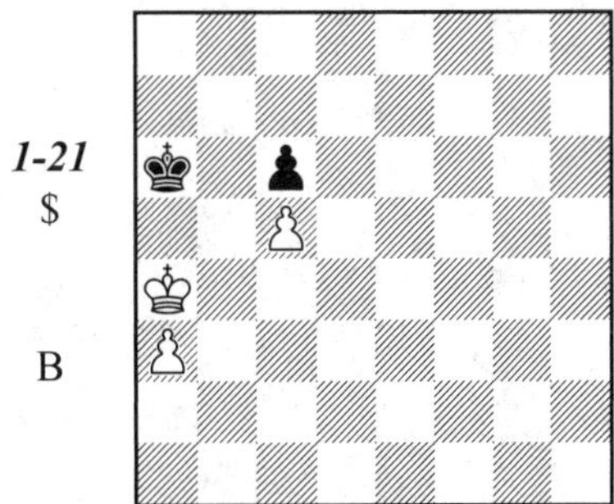

The only winning try is to get the king to the d6-square. To keep the opponent from counterattacking successfully on the queenside, it's important to begin the march with the black king as far away as possible. This consideration shows us the first pair of corresponding squares: a6 and b4.

1...♔b7 2 ♔b3! ♔a6 3 ♔b4!⊙ ♔b7

Now it's time to consider further action. Note the reciprocal zugzwang with the kings at d4 and b5; that means the d4-square is mined, and must be circumvented.

4 ♔c4 ♔a6 5 ♔d3!! ♔a5 6 ♔e4 ♔b5 7 ♔d4 (and Black is in zugzwang) **7...♔a4 8 ♔e5 ♔×a3 9 ♔d6+−.**

Alekhine - Yates
Hamburg 1910

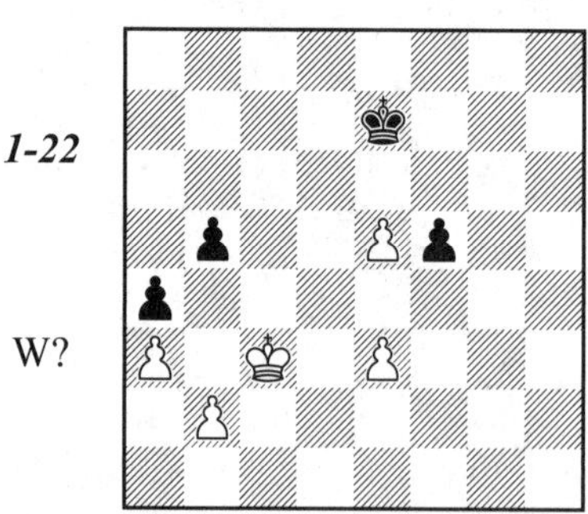

A mistake would be 1 ♔d4? ♔e6⊙; thus, the d4- and e6-squares are mined. And 1 ♔b4? ♔e6 2 ♔×b5 ♔×e5 3 ♔×a4 ♔e4 4 b4 ♔×e3 leads to a queen-and-rook-pawn vs. queen endgame, which is, according to theory, drawn.

1 ♔d3 ♔d7 (1...♔e6? 2 ♔d4+−) **2 e4! f4 3 ♔e2 ♔e6 4 ♔f2!!**, and Black resigned.

With a white pawn at e4 and a black one at f4, we already know the squares f3 and e5 are mined. White's king avoided entering the f3-square first, while his opposite number had no similar waiting move, since the e5-pawn was in the way.

Incidentally, White's moves could also have been transposed: 1 e4 f4 2 ♔d3 ♔e6 3 ♔e2!⊙ (3 ♔d4?! ♔e7).

Tragicomedies

Kobese - Tu Hoang Thai
Yerevan ol 1996

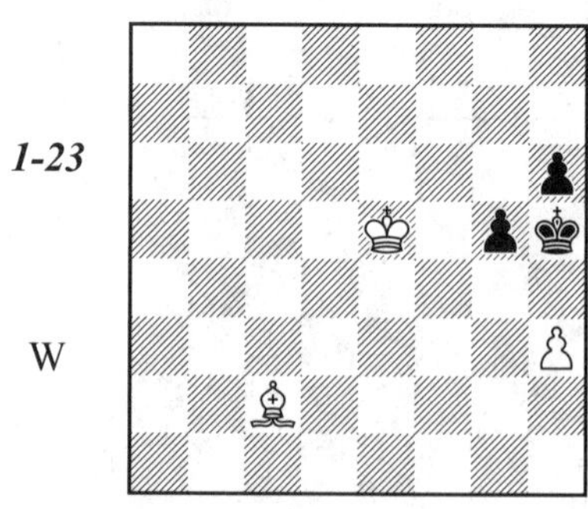

The position is drawn. White sets a last trap, which unexpectedly succeeds.

1 ♗d1+!? ♔h4??

1... ♔g6! was necessary, Δ 2...h5 and 3...g4=.

2 ♗g4 h5 3 ♔f5! hg 4 hg⊙ and Black resigned.

It is worth noting that 1 ♗f5!? must be met not with 1...♔h4?? 2 ♗g4+−, but with 1...g4! 2 ♗×g4+ (2 hg+ ♔g5 Δ 3...h5=) 2... ♔g6, with a draw (doubters are referred to the beginning of Chapter 4).

Exercises

The next pair of exercises are rather difficult. In each, you must judge whether Black ought to go into the pawn endgame.

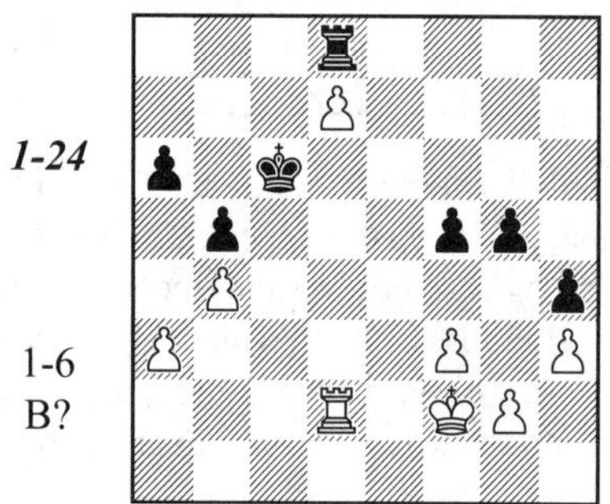

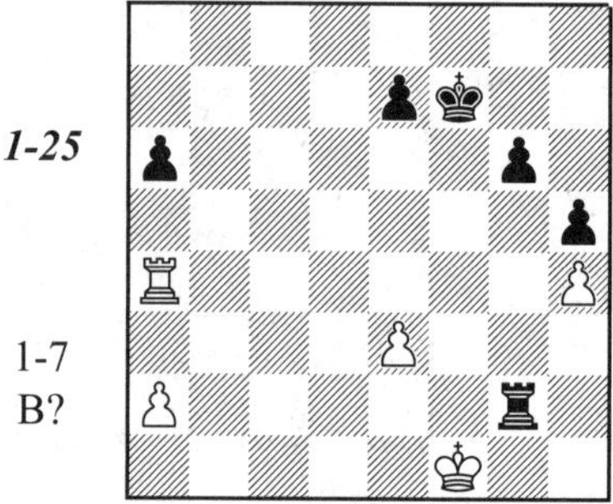

Triangulation

Triangulation refers to a king maneuver which aims to lose a tempo, and leave the opponent with the move.

1-26

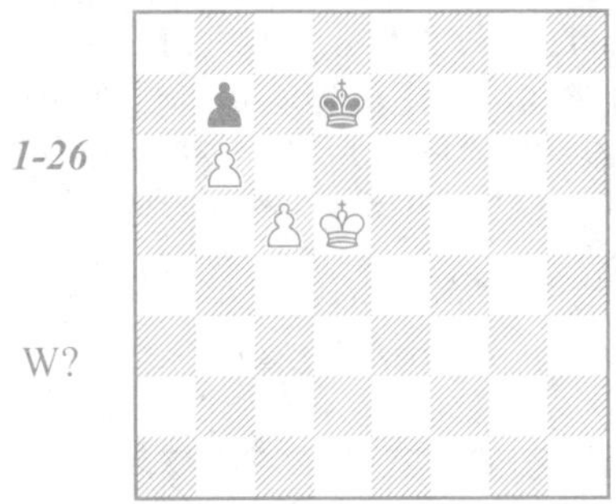

W?

The d5- and d7-squares are in correspondence. The mobility of Black's king is restricted: he must watch for the c5-c6 break, and also avoid being pressed to the edge of the board. It's not surprising, therefore, that White can easily "lose" a tempo and place his opponent in zugzwang.

1 ♔e5!

1 c6+? is mistaken here, in view of 1...♔c8! (but not 1...bc+? 2 ♔c5 ♔d8 3 ♔d6! ♔c8 4 ♔×c6 ♔b8 5 b7 +−) 2 ♔d6 ♔b8! 3 ♔d7 bc=.

1...♔c6 (1...♔e7 2 c6) **2 ♔d4 ♔d7 3 ♔d5**

White has achieved his aim, by describing a triangle with his king. The rest is simple.

3...♔c8 4 ♔e6! (diagonal opposition) **4...♔d8 5 ♔d6** (and now, vertical) **5...♔c8 6 ♔e7 ♔b8 7 ♔d7 ♔a8 8 c6+−.**

The following position is very important, both for itself and as an illustration of the characteristic logic of analyzing corresponding squares.

Fahrni - Alapin
1912

1-27

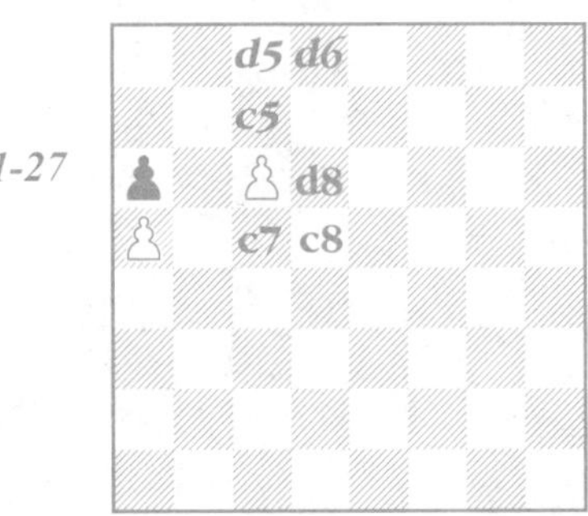

The kings were on d5 and c8 here; but we shall not place them on the board just yet - let's deal with the squares of correspondence first.

Two pairs of squares of reciprocal zugzwang are obvious right off: d6 - d8, and c5 - c7. The squares d6 and c5 border on d5; and for Black, the corresponding squares d8 and c7 border on c8. Thus, a standard means of identifying a new correspondence: that of the d5- and c8-squares.

Along with d5 and c5, White has two equally important squares: c4 and d4; while Black has, adjoining the corresponding squares c7 and c8, only one square: d8 (or b8). With Black's king on d8, White makes a waiting move with his king, from c4 to d4 (or the reverse). Black's king will be forced onto c7 or c8, when White occupies the corresponding square and wins.

1 ♔c4(d4)! ♔d8 2 ♔d4(c4)!⊙ ♔c8 3 ♔d5! ♔d8 (3...♔c7 4 ♔c5⊙ and 5 ♔b6) **4 ♔d6 ♔c8 5 c7⊙.**

H. Neustadtl, 1898

1-28

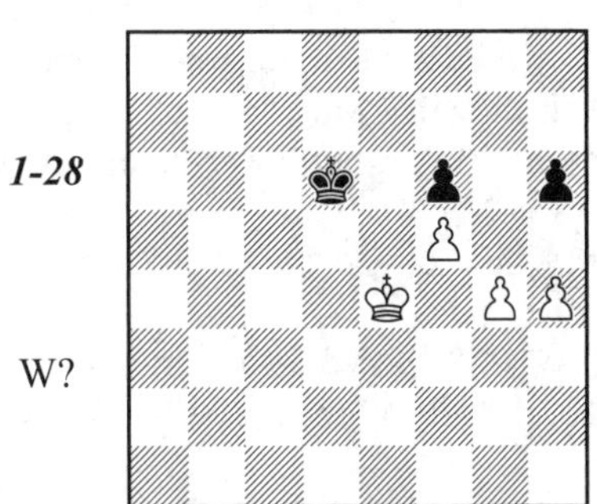

W?

Find two winning plans

The author's solution to this study involves the opposition, which White seizes with his very first move.

1 ♔d4 ♔c6 2 ♔c4 (2 g5? fg!= doesn't work) **2...♔d6 3 ♔b5!**

The opposition can only win if it leads to an outflanking. Here the outflanking looks risky, but it turns out to be playable, because of the line 3...♔e5 4 ♔c6 ♔f4 (4...h5 5 gh ♔×f5 6 ♔d5⊙) 5 ♔d6 ♔×g4 6 ♔e6+−.

3...♔d5! 4 ♔b6!

White takes the opposition again, thanks to his reserve tempo, h4-h5. But first, the enemy king must be decoyed to a bad position - as far as possible from the g4-pawn.

4...♔d6 5 ♔b7 ♔d7 6 h5! ♔d6 7 ♔c8

(another outflanking) **7...♔e5 8 ♔d7 ♔f4 9 ♔e6+−**.

In 1968, during a session of training in the calculation of variations (I find pawn endings quite useful for this), I discovered a second solution to this study, based on completely different logic.

The d5-square is key here (with White's king at d5, and Black's at d7, White wins by h4-h5). By the way, with the pawn already on h5, occupying the d5-square is no longer decisive: the key squares are now on the 6th rank - c6, d6 and e6. Which leads us to an important conclusion: ***when the pawn structure changes, the system of key squares associated with the position generally changes too, just as with the system of corresponding squares.***

With White's king at f4, Black must deal with the threat of g4-g5. It can be parried by putting the black king at e7 (but not f7, since then White will occupy the key square d5) - which immediately gives us two pairs of corresponding squares: f4 - e7 and e4 - d6. Next to these, White has two equivalent squares: f3 and e3. Black, meanwhile, has only one - d7. Thus, the winning mechanism becomes clear - triangulation!

1 ♔f4

1 ♔f3 - but not 1 ♔e3? ♔e5! 2 ♔f3 h5 3 ♔g3 ♔e4⊙.

1...♔e7 2 ♔f3 ♔d7 3 ♔e3! ♔d6

3...♔e7 4 ♔f4! ♔f7 5 ♔e4 ♔e7 6 ♔d5 ♔d7 7 h5+−.

4 ♔e4!⊙ ♔c6 5 ♔f4 ♔d6 6 g5+−.

Tragicomedies

Yudasin - Osnos
Leningrad 1987

1-29

B

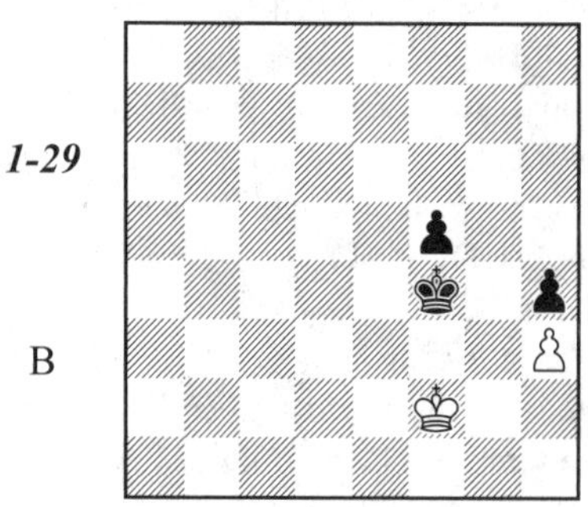

With his last move (1 ♔e2-f2), Yudasin offered a draw, adding that this position was a well-known draw, which one might find in any book. His opponent, an international master and an experienced trainer (he trained Viktor Korchnoi for many years) believed him, and accepted his offer!

After 1...♔e4 2 ♔e2 f4 3 ♔f2 f3, we reach a position which is, indeed, in all endgame books (Fahrni - Alapin), but it's a win. Black wins by triangulation: 4 ♔f1 ♔f5 5 ♔e1 ♔e5⊙ 6 ♔f1 ♔e4⊙.

Exercises

1-30
$

1/8
W?

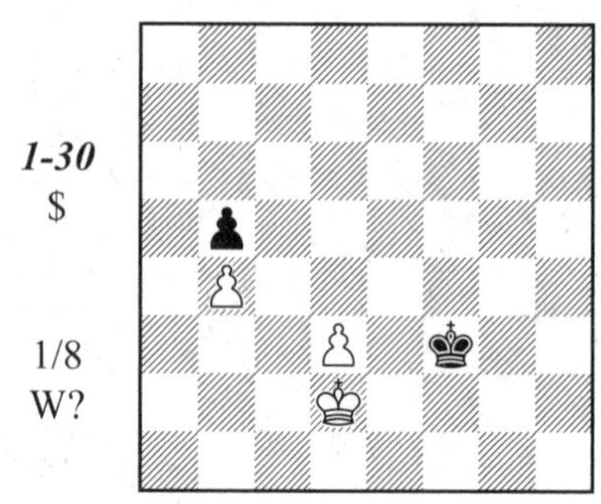

1-31

1/9
W?/Play

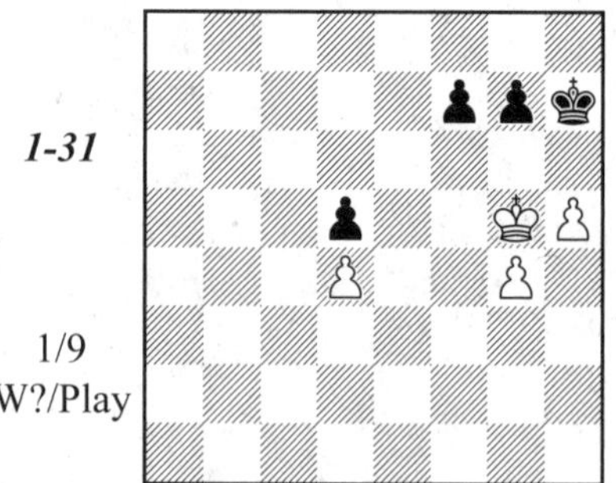

Other Cases of Correspondence

Situations with corresponding squares come in all shapes and sizes - from the most elementary to cases so complex that most of the unoccupied squares on the board turn out to be squares of reciprocal zugzwang.

How is the correspondence between squares determined? There is no special formula. The sensible way is to find key squares, examine the possible plans for both sides, and calculate the simplest variation. This preliminary analysis may uncover some reciprocal zugzwang situations; from there, you may go on to define an entire network of corresponding squares.

The following examples demonstrate how to make a logical analysis of a position.

N. Grigoriev, 1921

1-32

B

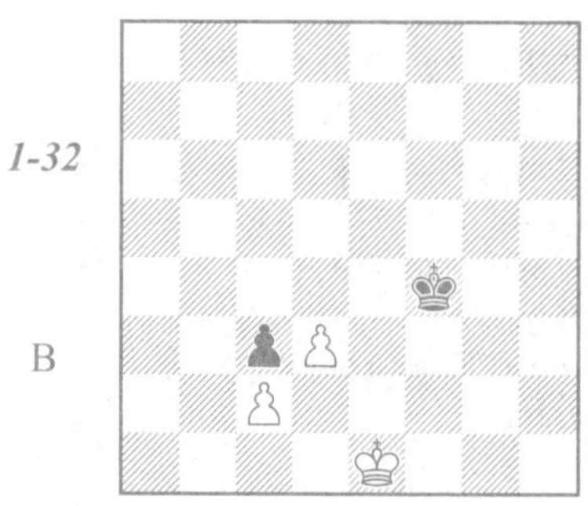

Black is obliged to defend the key squares e2 and f2, which he can do either by 1...♔e3 or 1...♔f3. The first appears more natural (the opposition!); but let's not be too hasty about drawing a conclusion.

White's king will attempt to break through on the queenside, by occupying the key square b3 - this too must be prevented. With White's king at a2, Black's king is obliged to occupy the b4-square (a4 would be too far from the kingside). Immediately, we have the whole packet of corresponding squares: a2 - b4, b1 - c5, c1 - d4, d1 - e3 and e1 - f3. As it turns out, the routine 1... ♔e3? loses - after 2 ♔d1, Black would be in zugzwang. But **1...♔f3! 2 ♔d1 ♔e3** draws easily.

I gave this example a blue diagram, not because it was especially important, but in order to underscore that a system of corresponding squares certainly does not have to always be "straightline," as with the opposition. Each case demands concrete analysis. You may only take the opposition after having ensured that this will place your opponent in zugzwang, not yourself.

And if, as in the present example, you must instead cede the opposition to your opponent, I call such cases of corresponding squares the ***"anti-opposition.***" This term seems more exact than the term, "knight's-move opposition" I have seen used (after all, the entire idea of "opposition" is for the kings to be standing on the same line, not on adjoining lines).

N. Grigoriev, 1922

1-33

W?

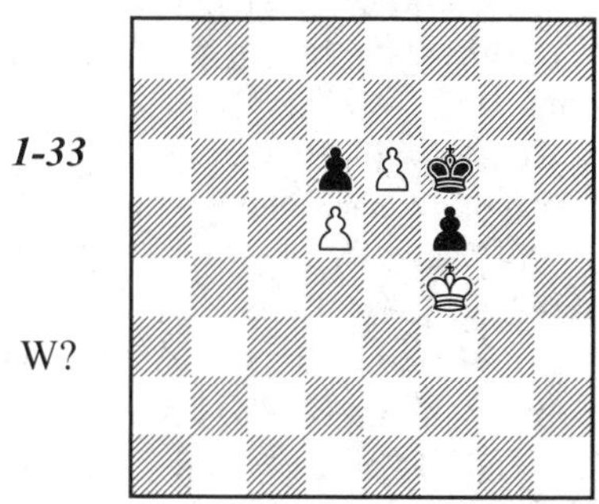

The correspondence of the squares f4 and f6 is obvious (on 1...♔g6 2 e7 ♔f7 3 ♔×f5 ♔×e7 4 ♔g6 decides). And when White's king appears on h4, Black must be on the g6-square (but not f6, because of ♔h5). The adjoining-squares principle permits us to define yet a third pair of corresponding squares: g3 - g7.

Let's go further. The square f3 adjoins both f4 and g3 - its obvious correspondent is g6. From h3, the king wants to go to g3 and h4 - thus, the corresponding square for Black is f6.

Let's pull back one rank, and look at the g2-square. From here, the king can go to f3 (the corresponding square: g6), g3 (g7), or h3 (f6). The only equivalent square for Black is f7 - but he can't go there.

Thus, the solution becomes clear. The g2-square is the key: White must simply retreat his king there, see where Black's king goes in response, and go to the corresponding square.

1 ♔f3 ♔g6! 2 ♔g2! ♔f6 (2...♔g7 3 ♔g3) **3 ♔h3! ♔g7 4 ♔g3! ♔f6** (4...♔g6 5 ♔h4 ♔f6 6 ♔h5) **5 ♔f4 ♔g6 6 e7 ♔f7 7 ♔×f5 ♔×e7 8 ♔g6+−.**

Gulko - Short
Riga 1995

1-34

W?

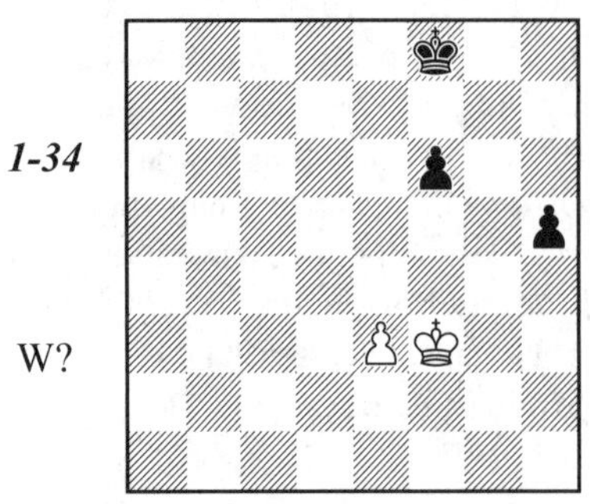

First, we must make sure that the direct attempt to force a draw by trading off the e-pawn does not work.

1 ♔f4? ♔e7! (it will become clear later why the king goes to this square, and not to f7) 2 ♔f5 ♔f7 3 e4 (3 ♔f4 ♔e6 4 ♔e4 h4 5 ♔f4 ♔d5!−+) 3...h4! 4 ♔g4 ♔e6 5 ♔xh4 ♔e5−+.

It's also worth noting that if it were White's move in the position after 3 e4, he would still lose after 4 e5 h4! 5 ♔g4 fe 6 ♔xh4 ♔e6 7 ♔g3 ♔d5 8 ♔f3 ♔d4. The move e4-e5 only saves the game with Black's king at g7 or e7 (since the threat is to take on f6 with check).

Now, what can White do against the black king's march to the center? The only possibility is to attack the h5-pawn. He can draw, if he can meet ♔e6 with ♔h4 (with the pawn still on e3).

But if Black's king goes to g6, then keeping the king at h4 becomes pointless - here, White must go to f4, with the idea of pushing the e-pawn.

Note that these paired squares we have found are not corresponding squares, since no zugzwangs exist; but our calculations now allow us to begin the search and analysis of correspondences.

From f7, Black's king is ready to move in two directions - to e6 or to g6. White's king must keep the same possibilities in hand. This clarifies the first, and most important pair of corresponding squares: f7 - g3. (And here is why 1 ♔f4? is to be met by 1...♔e7! - in order to meet 2 ♔g3!? with 2...♔f7!, placing White in zugzwang).

We are almost ready to make our first move. 1 ♔g3? ♔f7!⊙ is bad; and on 1 ♔f2? ♔e7! decides - the threat of 2...♔e6 forces White's king to approach h4 through the mined square g3.

1 ♔g2!! ♔g8

On 1...♔g7, White saves himself by 2 ♔f3! The black king can reach e6 only through f7. The white king will then be able to access g3 on its way to h4.

2 ♔f2 (2 ♔f3 leads to the same thing) **2...♔f8 3 ♔g2! ♔e7 4 ♔h3! ♔f7 5 ♔g3! ♔g6**

If 5...♔e6 6 ♔h4=; and if 5...f5, either 6 e4=, or 6 ♔f4 h4 7 e4 h3 8 ♔g3 fe 9 ♔xh3 ♔e6 10 ♔g3 ♔d5 11 ♔f2 ♔d4 12 ♔e2=.

6 ♔f4 ♔h6

On 6...♔f7, the only reply is 7 ♔g3! (7 ♔f5? ♔e7⊙), while on 6...♔g7, it's 7 ♔f3! (7 e4? ♔g6⊙, and 7 ♔f5? ♔f7 8 e4 h4−+ are two bad alternatives).

7 ♔f5 ♔h7

If 7...♔g7, then 8 ♔f4! (but not 8 e4? ♔f7 9 e5 h4−+) 8... ♔g6 9 e4!⊙ ♔h6 10 ♔f5 ♔g7 11 e5=.

8 e4 ♔h6 (8...♔g7 9 e5) **9 ♔xf6 h4** Draw.

Note that the game position is not new - in 1979, C. Costantini composed it as a study. Of course, GM Gulko didn't know it - but he was acquainted with the idea of corresponding squares and was able to put the method successfully into practice.

Exercises

1-35

1/10
W?

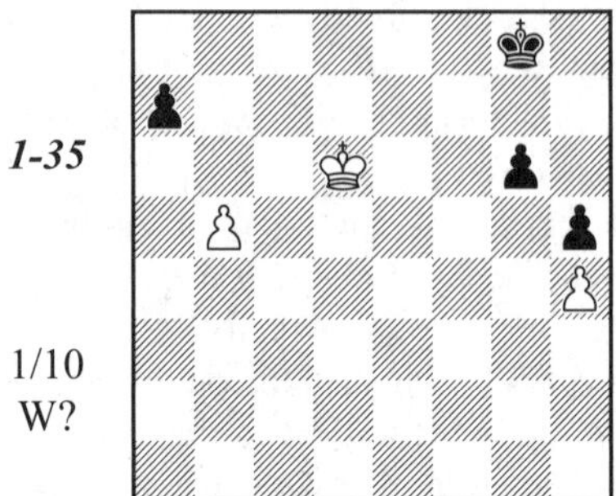

1-36

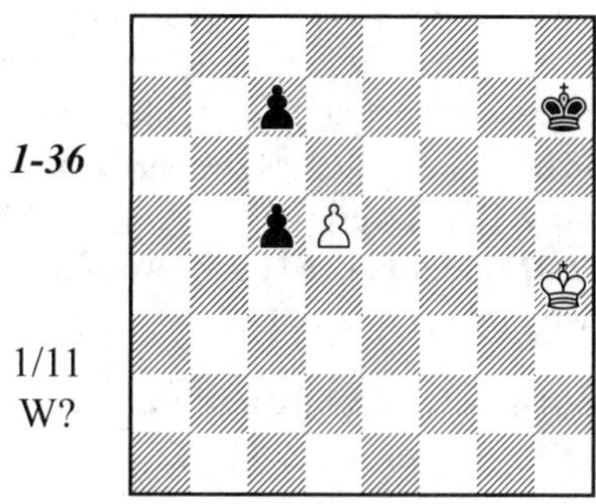

1/11
W?

King vs. Passed Pawns

The Rule of the Square

1-37

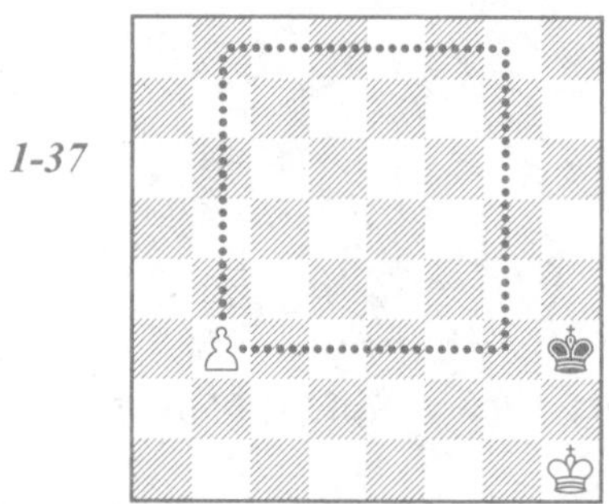

Imagine a square having for one of its sides the path from the pawn to its queening square. ***If the king stands within the square of the passed pawn, or can reach it on its move, the pawn can be stopped; otherwise, it will queen.***

Black to move gets inside the square and draws (1...♔g4 or 1...♔g3). If it's White's move, then after 1 b4 the side of the new square becomes the f-file, which Black's king cannot reach in time.

If the pawn stood on b2, then because the pawn can move two squares, the square should still be constructed from the b3-square.

Obstacles in the path of the king: It sometimes happens that even though the king is located within the square, it still can't stop the passed pawn, because its own pawns get in the way.

R. Bianchetti, 1925

1-38

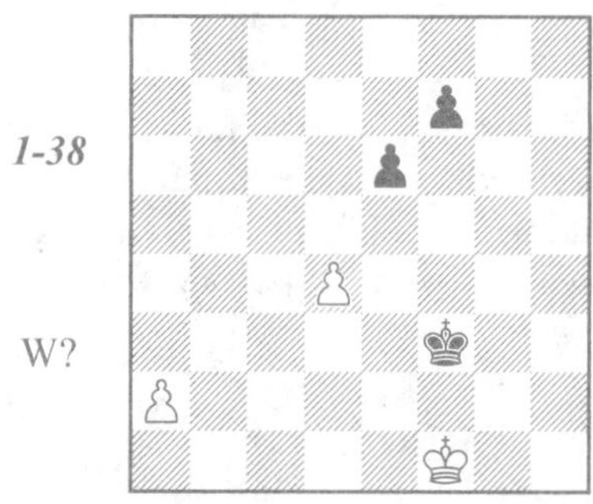

W?

1 d5! ed 2 a4 ♔e4 (2...d4 3 a5 d3 4 ♔e1) **3 a5+−**, as Black cannot play 3...♔d5.

1-39

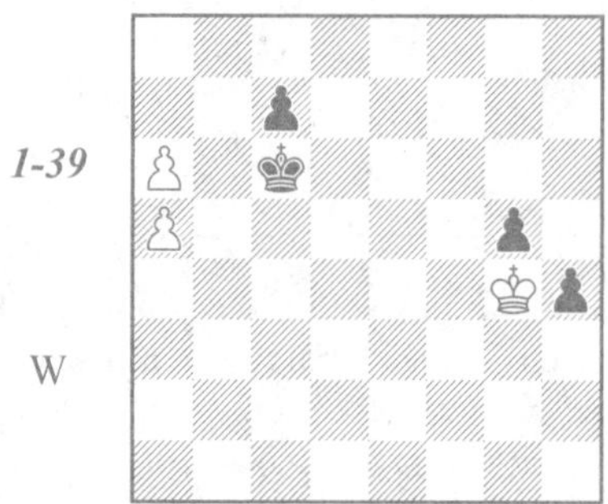

W

The waiting move **1 ♔h3** places Black in zugzwang - now he loses. Without the pawn at c7, the opposite result occurs.

An analogous zugzwang occurs if you move the pawn at a5 to c5. The only difference is that this time, without the pawn at c7, the position would be drawn.

Exercises

1-40

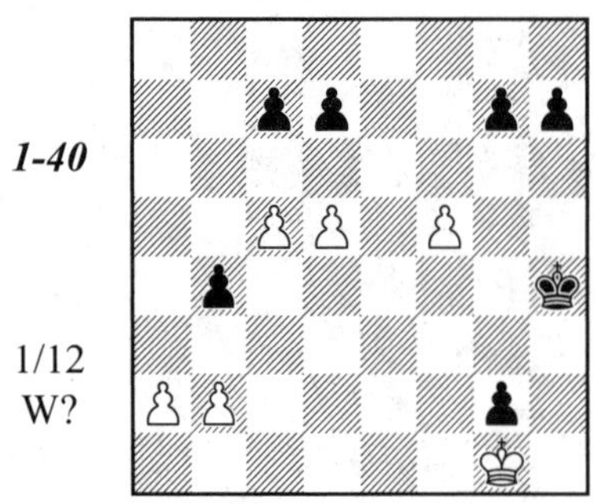

1/12
W?

Réti's Idea

It sometimes happens that a king outside the square of a passed pawn can still catch it. The win of the missing tempo (or even several tempi) is accomplished by the creation of accompanying threats, most often (though not exclusively) involved with supporting one's own passed pawn.

R. Réti, 1921

1-41

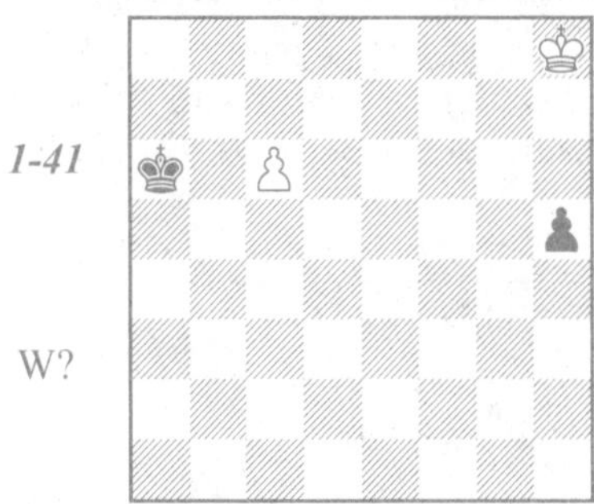

W?

Black's king lies within the square of the c6-pawn, while White is short two tempi needed to catch the h5-pawn. Nevertheless, he can save himself - the trick is "***to chase two birds at once.***" The king's advance is dual-purpose: he chases after the h-pawn, while simultaneously approaching the queen's wing.

1 ♔g7! h4 2 ♔f6! ♔b6

If 2...h3, then 3 ♔e7(or e6), and the pawns queen together.

3 ♔e5! ♔×c6

3...h3 4 ♔d6 h2 5 c7=.

4 ♔f4=

A miracle has come to pass: the king, even though two tempi behind, nevertheless has caught the pawn!

In 1928, Réti offered a different version of this study: move the white king to h5, and instead of the pawn at h5, put three (!) black pawns at f6, g7 and h6. The solution is similar: **1 ♔g6!**, and after any Black reply (1...f5, 2...h5, or 1...♔b6) - **2 ♔×g7!**, followed by the well-known "chasing two birds at once."

And now, a slightly different version of the same idea.

L. Prokeš, 1947

1-42

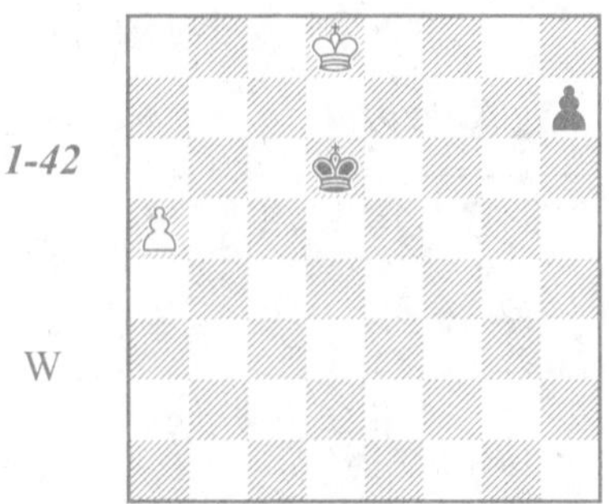

W

1 ♔c8 ♔c6 2 ♔b8! ♔b5 (else 3 a6) **3 ♔b7!**

Thanks to the threat of 4 a6, White wins a tempo and gets into the square of the h-pawn. 3 ♔c7? h5 is hopeless.

3...♔×a5 4 ♔c6=.

The study we shall now examine shows us that Réti's idea can be useful in more than just pawn endings.

A. & K. Sarychev, 1928

1-43

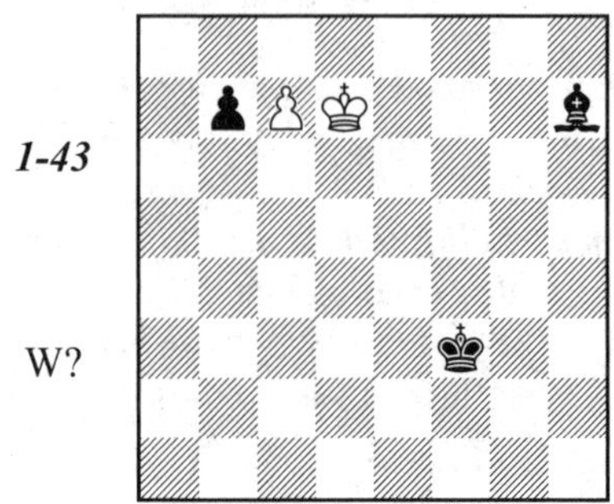

W?

1 c8♕? ♗f5+ 2 ♔c7 ♗×c8 is hopeless, as is 1 ♔d6? ♗f5 2 ♔c5 ♔e4 3 ♔b6 ♗c8 4 ♔a7 b5. The only saving line starts with a paradoxical move that forces the black pawn to advance.

1 ♔c8!! b5

As in Réti's study, White is short two tempi.

2 ♔d7 b4 3 ♔d6 ♗f5

Thanks to the threat of 4 c8♕, White wins one tempo; now he wins the other tempo by attacking the black bishop.

4 ♔e5! ♗c8 5 ♔d4=.

Tragicomedies

Yates - Marshall
Karlsbad 1929

1-44

W

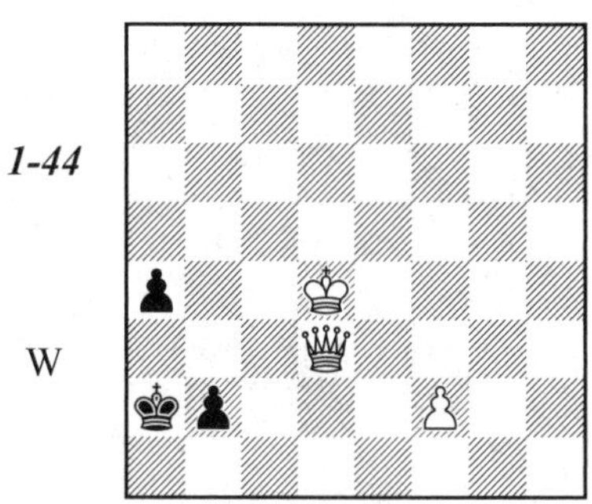

1 ♕c4+ ♔a3 2 ♕b5 (or c2)? is a mistake, in view of 2...b1♕! 3 ♕×b1 stalemate. But White wins easily after 1 ♕c2 a3 2 ♔c3 ♔a1 3 ♔b3 b1♕+ 4 ♕×b1+ ♔×b1 5 ♔×a3, when the black king can't reach the square (remember that when the pawn is on the 2nd rank, the square is constructed from f3, not from f2).

In the game, White chose a less accurate method of transposing into a pawn endgame.

1 ♔c3? b1♕ 2 ♕×b1+ ♔×b1 3 ♔b4

This is a situation known to us from the Prokeš study.

3...♔b2! 4 ♔×a4 ♔c3, with a draw.

Lasker - Tarrasch
St. Petersburg 1914

1-45

B?

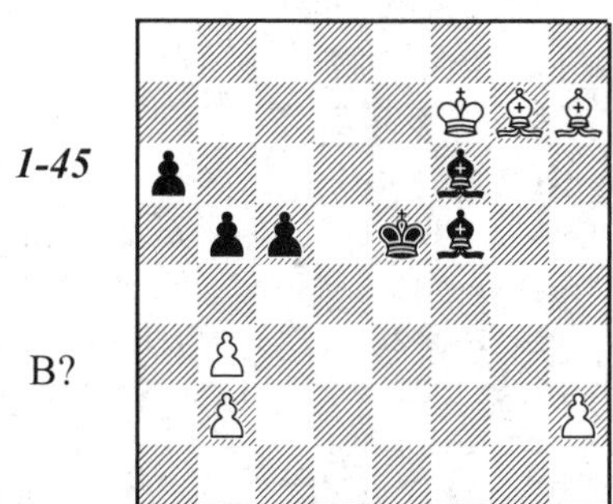

Black wins without trouble after 1...♗e6+ 2 ♔g6 ♗×g7 3 ♔×g7 ♗×b3 4 h4 ♗d1. Tarrasch decided that the pawn endgame would be simpler still. However, he overlooked the very same finesse as did Yates in the preceding example.

1...♗×g7? 2 ♗×f5! ♔×f5?!

I leave it to my readers to decide on their own if White could have saved himself after 2...♗h8 or 2...♗f6. Perhaps it would be worthwhile to return to this difficult question after we study the chapter on opposite-colored bishops.

3 ♔×g7 a5 4 h4 ♔g4

Tarrasch had expected to block White's king from stopping the passed pawn after 5 ♔f6? c4 6 bc bc 7 ♔e5 c3 8 bc a4 9 ♔d4 a3.

5 ♔g6! ♔×h4 6 ♔f5 ♔g3

6...c4 7 bc bc 8 ♔e4 c3 9 bc a4? 10 ♔d3 is now useless.

7 ♔e4 ♔f2 8 ♔d5 ♔e3 9 ♔×c5 ♔d3 10 ♔×b5 ♔c2 11 ♔×a5 ♔×b3 Draw.

Exercises

1-46

1/13
W?

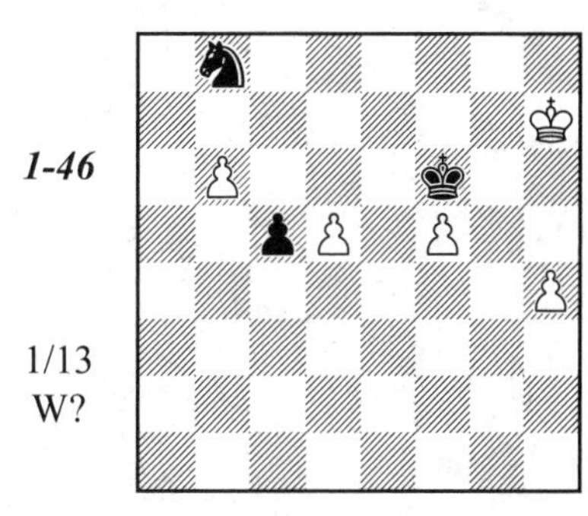

1-47

1/14
W?/Play

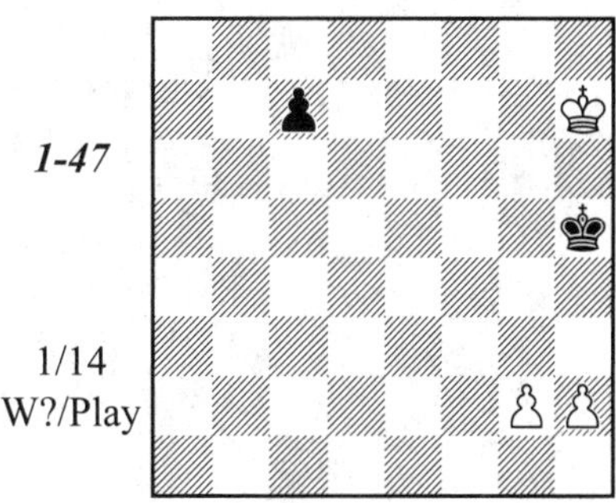

1-48

1/15
W?/Play

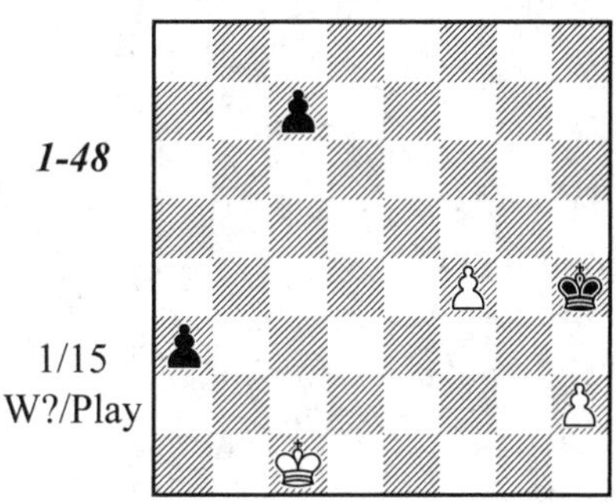

The Floating Square

There are cases in which the king must do battle with two separated passed pawns; in these cases, a useful rule is ***the floating-square rule***, suggested by Studenecki in 1939.

If a square whose two corners are occupied by pawns (on the same rank) reaches the edge of the board, then one of those pawns must queen.

If the square does not reach the edge of the board, then the king can hold the pawns. If there are two files between the pawns, the king can capture both; if the distance is any greater, he can only prevent their further advance.

1-49

B

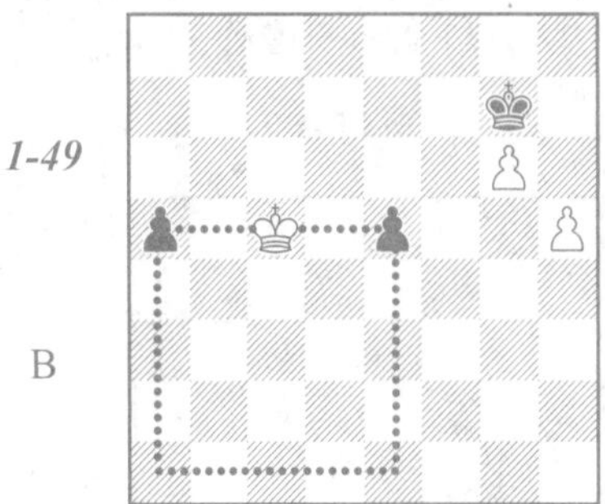

The square having reached the edge of the board, the pawns will queen, regardless of whose move it is.

1...a4 2 ♔b4 e4 3 ♔×a4 e3−+

Let's shift the pawns to a6 and e6. The square now reaches only to the 2nd rank, and the position becomes a draw. In fact, 1...a5? would be bad: 2 ♔b5 e5 3 ♔×a5+−; and so is 1...♔h6? 2 ♔d6! a5 3 ♔×e6 a4 4 ♔f7 a3 5 g7 a2 6 g8♕ a1♕ 7 ♕g6#. Black must play **1...♔f6 2 ♔c6** (but not 2 ♔b6? e5 3 ♔c5 a5−+) **2...♔g7** (2...e5 3 ♔d5 a5 4 g7 ♔×g7 5 ♔×e5= is possible, too) **3 ♔c5=.**

1-50

W

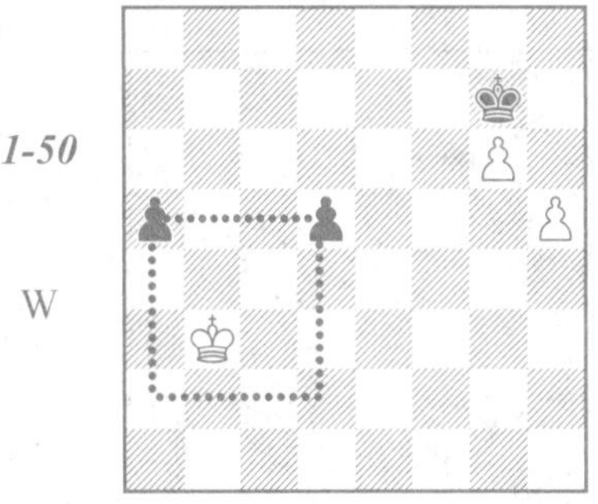

This square doesn't reach the edge of the board, and the distance between the pawns is the most unfavorable: two files. This means the pawns are lost, regardless of who is on move.

1 ♔a4 d4 2 ♔b3 ♔h6 3 ♔c4 a4 4 ♔×d4+−.

Let's examine one more substantive case.

1-51

W

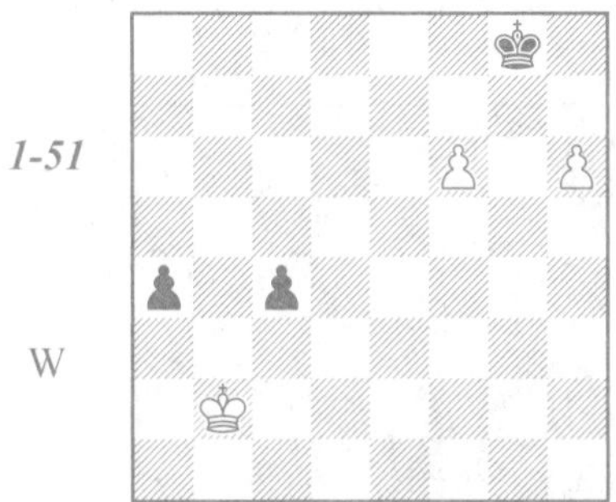

On the queenside, the square doesn't reach the edge of the board, so the pawns can be held: **1 ♔c3 a3 2 ♔c2.** On the kingside, however, the pawns are already quite far advanced. True, the king can prevent them from queening - so far; but because of zugzwang, he will soon be forced to let them through.

Khalifman - Belikov
Podolsk 1992

1-52

W

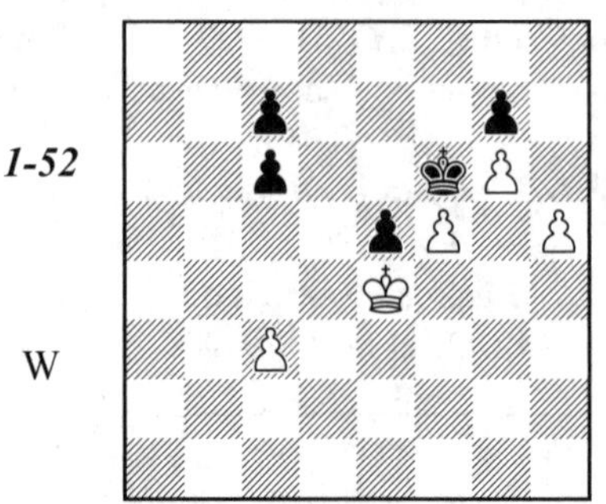

1 h6! gh 2 ♔f3 h5 3 ♔g3 c5

There are two files between the black passed pawns; the square doesn't reach the edge of the board - that means the pawns must be lost. The attempt to defend them with the king is doomed to failure: 3...♔g7 4 c4 c5 5 ♔h3 ♔h6 6 ♔h4 c6 7 ♔h3 ♔g7 8 ♔g3 (triangulation!) 8...♔h6 9 ♔h4⊙ e4 10 ♔g3 ♔g7 11 ♔f4+−

4 ♔h4 e4 5 ♔g3 Black resigned.

Tragicomedies

Stoltz - Nimzovitch
Berlin 1928

1-53

W

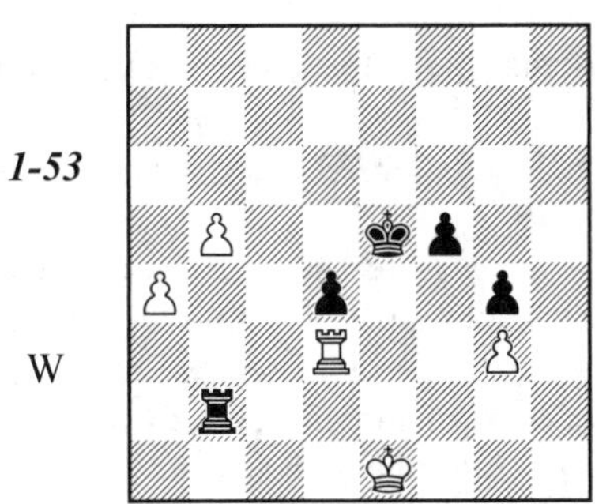

White would secure the draw by advancing his a-pawn and putting the rook behind it, thus: 1 a5! ♖×b5 2 ♖a3=, or by 1 ♖a3! ♔e4 2 a5 d3 3 a6 ♔e3 4 ♖×d3+ ♔×d3 5 a7=. Instead, Stoltz offered to trade rooks:

1 ♖d2?? ♖×d2! 2 ♔×d2 f4! 3 gf+ (3 a5 ♔d6 4 a6 ♔c7) **3...♔d6!**

The square of the d4- and g4-pawns reaches the edge of the board - that means it's impossible to prevent one of them from queening. The same could also be said of White's pawns - but they are much too late. Note the excellent move of the black king - from d6, it is prepared to stop either white pawn with a minimum of effort.

4 a5 g3 5 a6 ♔c7 6 ♔e2 d3+ 7 ♔×d3 g2 8 ♔e4 g1♕ 9 ♔f5 ♕b6 10 ♔g5 ♔d7 11 f5 ♔e7 White resigned.

We may add to our list of tragicomedies not just White's gross blunder, but also his stubborn refusal to end resistance in a completely hopeless situation.

Exercises

1-54

1/16
B?

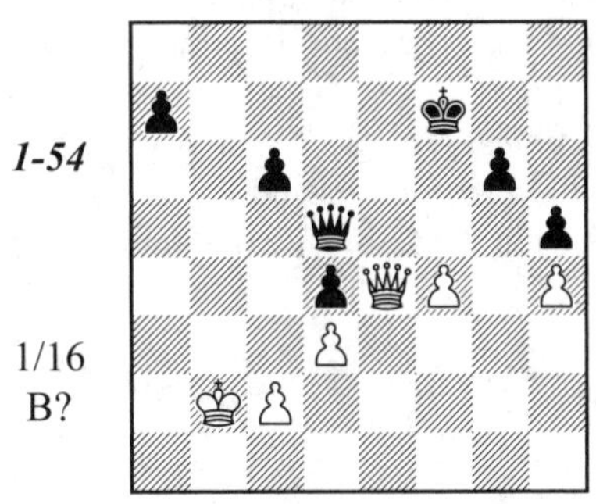

1-55

1/17
B?

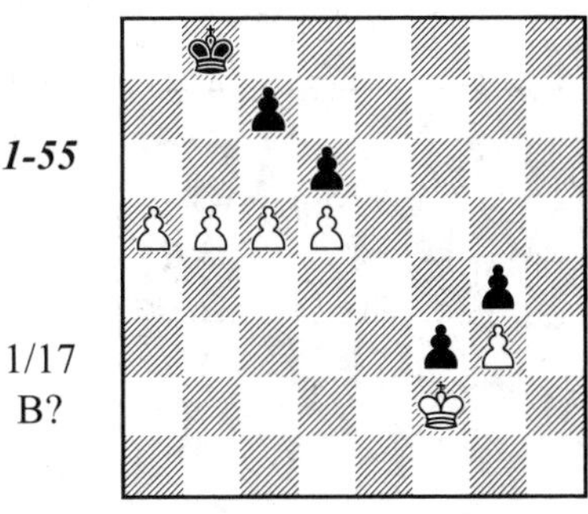

1-56

1/18
W?

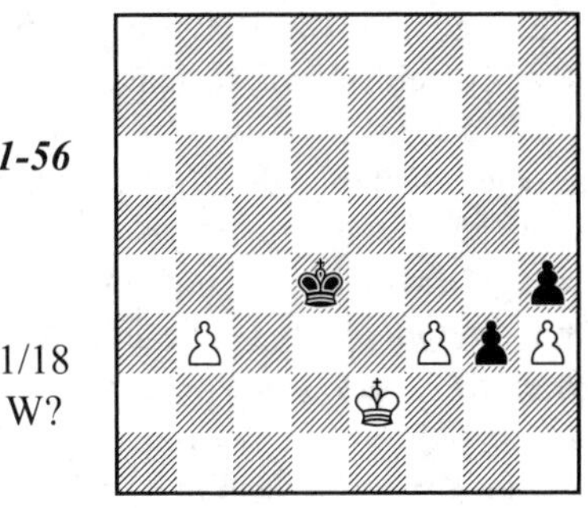

Three Connected Pawns

It's difficult for the king to fight three connected passed pawns. It has no chance at all, if the enemy has any moves in reserve. If not, then a situation of reciprocal zugzwang could arise.

1-57

W?

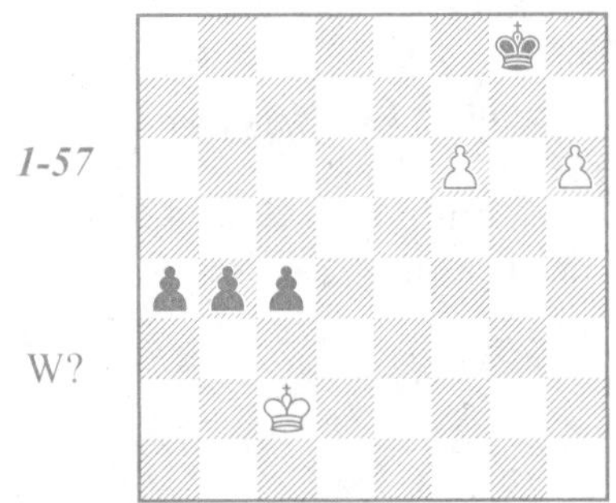

White to move wins by **1 ♔b1!** (1...b3 2 ♔b2⊙; 1...a3 2 ♔a2 c3 3 ♔b3⊙; 1...c3 2 ♔c2 a3 3 ♔b3⊙). Any other first move by White leads to the opposite result.

Nunn - Friedlander
Islington 1968

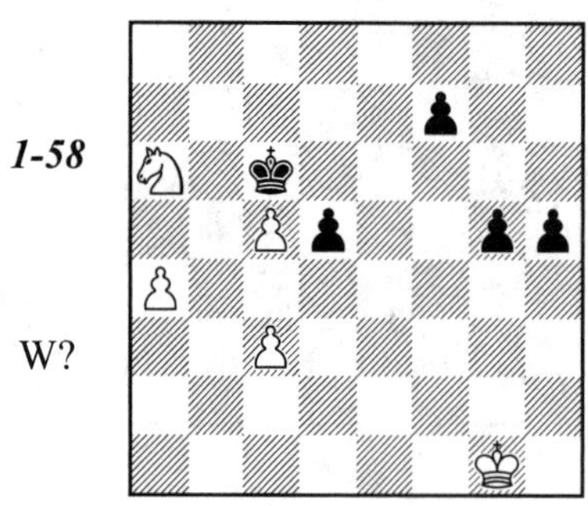

1-58

W?

On the queenside, we have equality: it would be bad for either side to make the first move there. The question is, who will fall into zugzwang, when the kingside pawn moves run out?

White would win by playing 1 ♔h2! (or 1 ♔g2!?); the important point is to be able to meet 1...h4 with 2 ♔h3!, for instance: 2...f5 (2...f6 3 ♔g4 f5+ 4 ♔h3 f4 5 ♔g4⊙) 3 ♔h2! g4 (3...f4 4 ♔g2) 4 ♔g2 f4 (4...h3+ 5 ♔g3 f4+ 6 ♔h2 f3 7 ♔g3⊙; 4...g3 5 ♔f3 f4 6 ♔g2⊙) 5 ♔g1!⊙ ♔b7 6 ♘b4.

Nothing would be changed by 1...g4 2 ♔g3 f5 (2...f6 3 ♔f4 f5 4 ♔g3) 3 ♔g2 f4 4 ♔f2(h2); or 1...f5 2 ♔g2! (or, with the king at g2 - 2 ♔g3 g4 3 ♔g2, etc.).

The actual game took an immediate wrong turn:

1 ♔f2?? h4! 2 ♔f3 (2 ♔g2 g4) **2...h3 3 ♔g3 g4 4 a5**

White has to be the first to upset the queenside equilibrium. He can no longer place his opponent in zugzwang, because the f-pawn retains the right of moving either one or two squares, according to circumstances (an important technique, to which we shall be returning).

4 ♔h2 f6! 5 ♔g3 f5⊙ 6 ♔h2 f4⊙.

4...f5 5 ♘b4+ ♔×c5 6 a6 ♔b6 7 ♘×d5+ ♔×a6 8 c4 ♔b7 Draw.

The section which follows is devoted to those cases in which both sides queen simultaneously. In such situations, the game sometimes turns into a "queen versus pawns" endgame - so it makes sense to get to know its theory first.

Queen vs. Pawns

The only cases which have significant practical importance are those elementary endings in which a queen plays against a pawn which has reached the next-to-last rank.

Knight or Center Pawn

The queen generally wins against either a center or knight pawn.

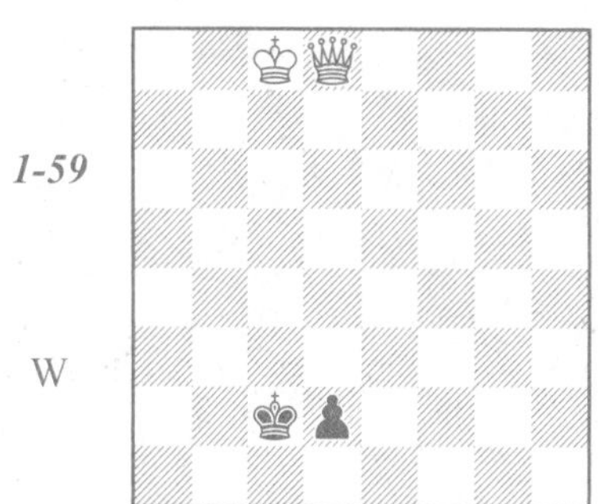

1-59

W

The algorithm is simple: the queen uses either checks or attacks on the pawn to get closer to the enemy king, and drive it onto the d1-square. This gives White's king a tempo to get closer to the pawn. This procedure is repeated as often as necessary.

1 ♕c7+ ♔b1 2 ♕b6+ ♔c2 3 ♕c5+ ♔b1 4 ♕b4+ (or 4 ♕d4) **4...♔c2 5 ♕c4+ ♔b2 6 ♕d3 ♔c1 7 ♕c3+ ♔d1 8 ♔c7 ♔e2 9 ♕c2** (or 9 ♕e5+) **9...♔e1 10 ♕e4+ ♔f2 11 ♕d3 ♔e1 12 ♕e3+ ♔d1 13 ♔c6**, etc.

A draw is only very rarely possible - when, for some reason, White is unable to execute this mechanism. An example would be if the white king in our previous diagram were at c7, c6 or c5.

Sometimes, the queen's approach is hindered by the presence of additional pawns on the board, as in the following diagram.

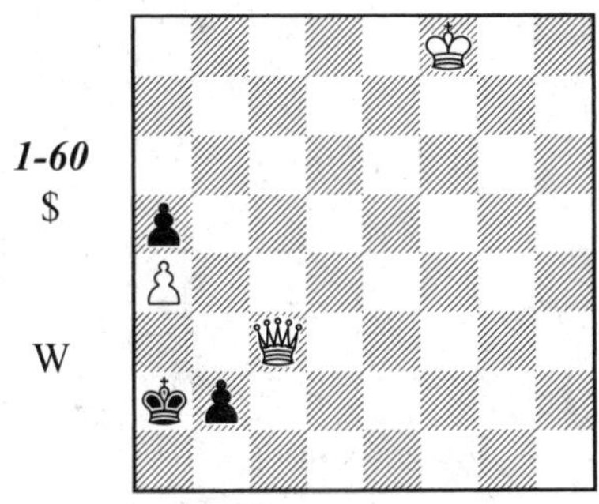

1-60
$
W

The king cannot be driven to b1, since White is unable to check on the a-file. The most White can achieve is a queen endgame with an extra rook pawn by 1 ♕×a5!? b1♕; but theory considers that endgame to be drawish. And the pawn endgame isn't won either: **1 ♕c2 ♔a1 2 ♔e7 b1♕ 3 ♕×b1+ ♔×b1 4 ♔d6 ♔c2 5 ♔c5 ♔d3 6 ♔b5 ♔d4 7 ♔×a5 ♔c5=**

However, with the white king at f7, the exchange of queens leads to victory.

1 ♕c2 ♔a1 2 ♔e6 b1♕ 3 ♕×b1+ ♔×b1 4 ♔d5 ♔c2 5 ♔c4! (the first, but not the last time we shall see "shouldering" used in this book) 5...♔d2 6 ♔b5+−.

Rook or Bishop's Pawn

With a rook or bishop's pawn, the above-described winning algorithm doesn't work - a stalemate defense appears.

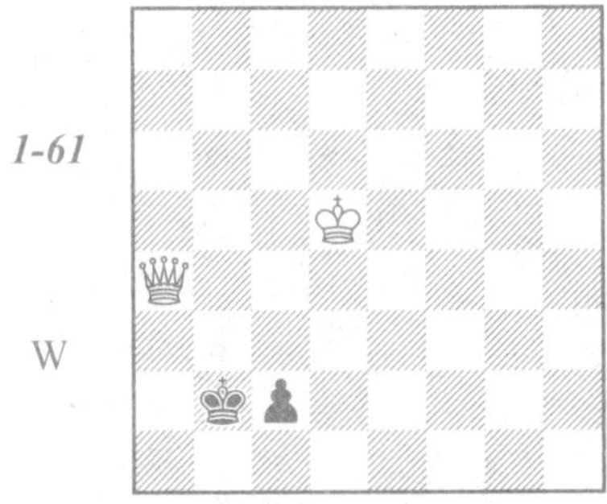

1-61
W

1 ♕b4+ ♔a2 2 ♕c3 ♔b1 3 ♕b3+ ♔a1! 4 ♕e3 ♔b1 5 ♕d3 ♔b2 6 ♕e2!? ♔a1!= (but not 6...♔b1? 7 ♔c4! c1♕+ 8 ♔b3+−).

The win is possible only if the white king stands so close that it can help the white queen mate the enemy king.

Let's put the black king on d2. Now, in order to reach its stalemate haven, it will have to cross the c1-square, giving White the tempo he needs to win:

1 ♕d4+ ♔e2 2 ♕c3 ♔d1 3 ♕d3+ ♔c1 4 ♔c4! ♔b2 5 ♕d2 ♔b1 6 ♔b3+−.

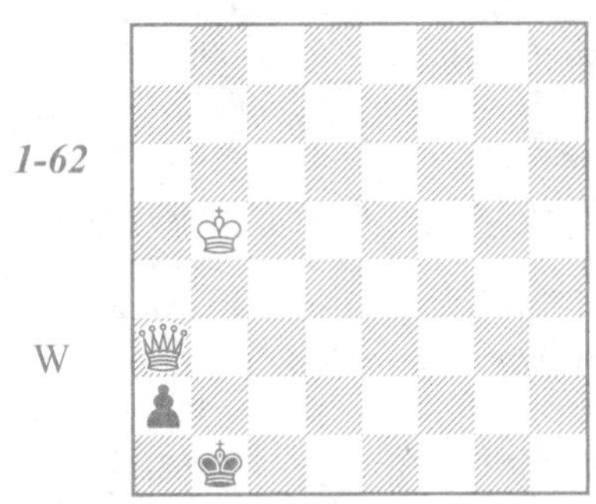

1-62
W

1 ♕b3+ ♔a1! 2 ♕d1+ ♔b2 3 ♕d2+ ♔b1 4 ♔b4! a1♕ 5 ♔b3+−

Starting with the white king at e4, the mate is delivered in somewhat different fashion: 1 ♕b3+ ♔a1 2 ♕c3+ ♔b1 3 ♔d3! a1♕ 4 ♕c2#.

With the king any farther from the pawn, there is no win. I shall limit myself to just that general observation - I don't think it makes any sense to reproduce the "winning zone" for each and every position of the black pawn that I have seen in other endgame texts. It's not worth memorizing - once you have mastered the winning and drawing mechanisms, you can easily figure out for yourself at the board what sort of position you're facing.

Of course, there are exceptions, in which the standard evaluations and techniques are no longer sufficient.

J. Timman, 1980

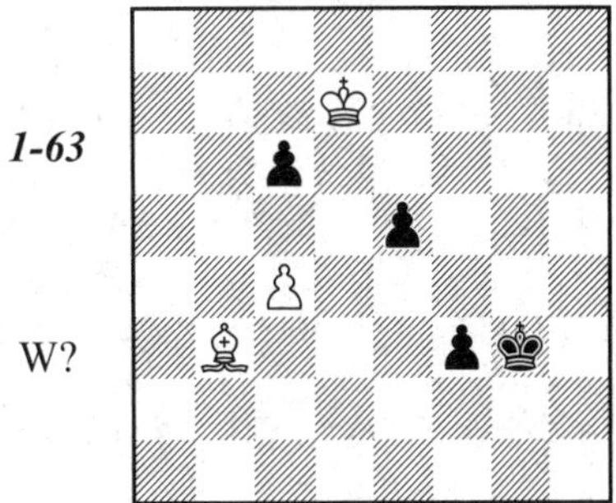

1-63
W?

1 c5! e4 (1...f2 2 ♗c4=) **2 ♗d1!! e3** (2...f2 3 ♗e2=) **3 ♗×f3 ♔×f3 4 ♔×c6 e2 5 ♔d7! e1♕ 6 c6** (△ 7 c7), and after 6...♕d1(d2)+ 7 ♔c8=, Black can't prevent 8 c7.

In the final position, it's very important that White's king is on d7. This is why 1 ♗d1? c5! would have been a mistake, since the king can't get to d7. And 1 ♗c2? f2 2 ♗d3 ♔f3! (2...e4? 3 ♗e2=) 3 ♔×c6 e4 4 ♗f1 e3 5 c5 e2−+ is also hopeless.

And Black's king must be drawn to f3 - with the king still on g3, Black wins by 6...♕d1+! 7 ♔c8 ♕g4+. After 1 c5! e4, the move 2 ♗d1!! solves this problem, while 2 ♔×c6? e3 3 ♗c4 e2 4 ♗×e2 fe 5 ♔d7 e1♕ leaves the black king on g3. White does no better with 3 ♗d5 e2 4 ♗×f3 e1♕ 5 ♔d7 - Black manages to bring up his king by: 5...♕d2+ 6 ♔c8 ♔f4! 7 c6 ♔e5 8 c7 ♕b4! 9 ♗b7 (9 ♔d7 ♕d6+ 10 ♔c8 ♕b6! 11 ♔d7 ♕e6+ 12 ♔d8 ♔d6−+) 9...♕f8+ 10 ♔d7 ♕d6+ 11 ♔c8 ♔e6 12 ♔b8 ♔d7 13 ♗c8+ ♔c6 14 ♗b7+ ♔b6−+.

N. Elkies, 1986

1-64

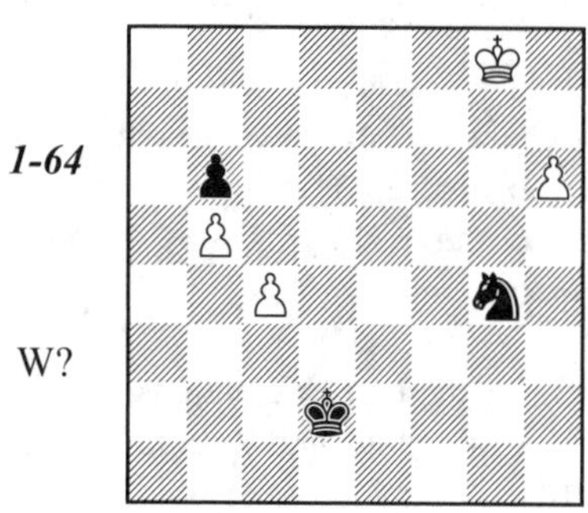

W?

When is the right time to break with c4-c5? Right now it would obviously be premature: 1 c5? ♘×h6+ 2 ♔f8 bc, or 2...♘f5 3 cb ♘d6, and draws.

And on 1 ♔g7? ♘×h6 2 ♔×h6 ♔e3! 3 c5 bc 4 b6 c4 5 b7 c3 6 b8♕ c2 7 ♔g5! (threatening the check at f4) 7...♔d2! the white king is too far from the pawn. The single tempo that White gets when Black's king occupies the c1-square is insufficient to win.

1 h7!! ♘f6+ 2 ♔g7 ♘×h7 3 ♔×h7

Now we have virtually the same position as in the preceding variation, with the king standing even farther from the queenside. But here, the h6-square is open!

3...♔e3! 4 c5 bc 5 b6 c4 6 b7 c3 7 b8♕ c2 8 ♕h2!! c1♕ (8...♔d3 9 ♕f4+−) **9 ♕h6+**.

Exercises

1-65

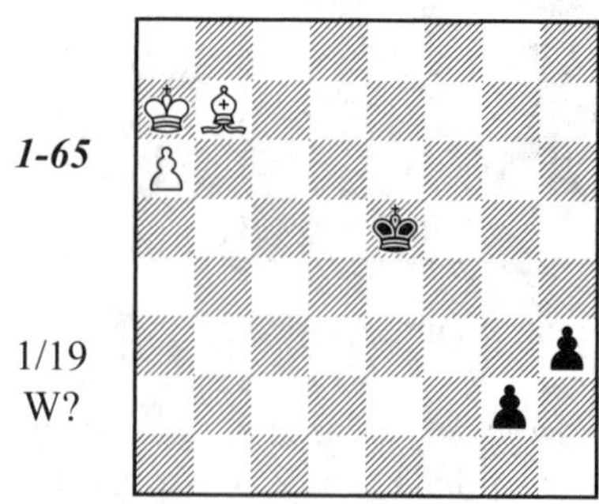

1/19
W?

1-66

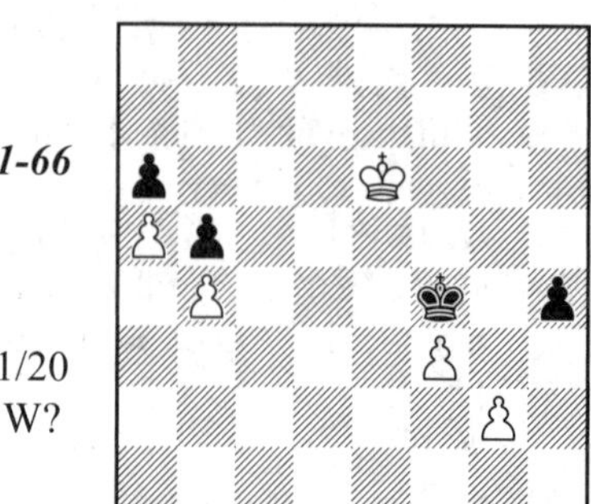

1/20
W?

1-67

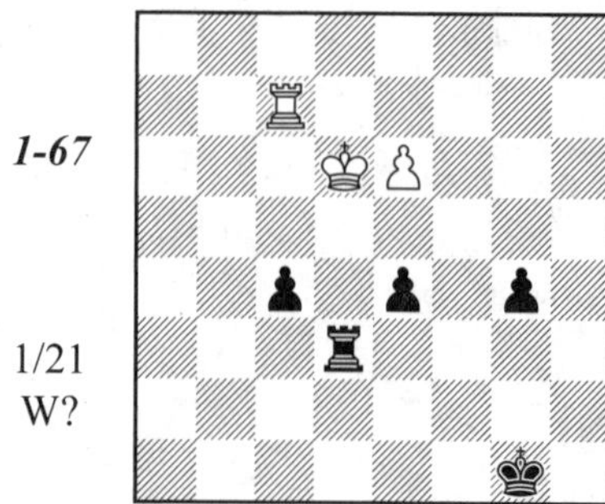

1/21
W?

1-68

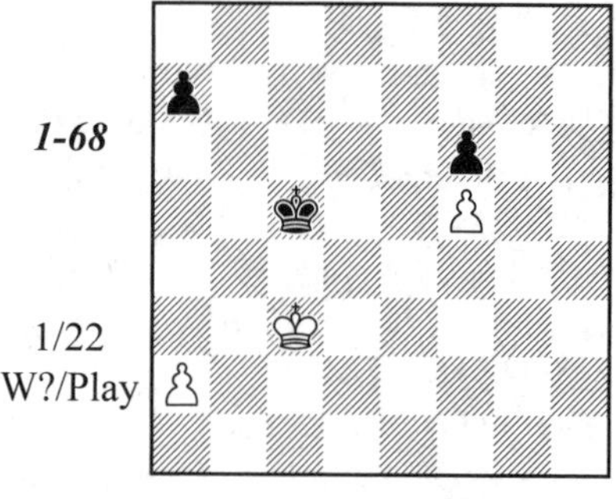

1/22
W?/Play

Pawn Races

Let's examine the sort of situation where both players advance simultaneously, and queen at the same time, or almost at the same time. Here, the following outcomes are possible:

1) One rook's pawn prevents the other rook's pawn from queening;

2) The pawn queens with check, and thereby prevents the enemy pawn from queening; or

3) We get a "queen vs. pawn (or pawns)" endgame.

Or, if both pawns queen, then:

4) One queen is lost to a "skewer" check along the file or diagonal;

5) Mate follows;

6) The queens are exchanged, after which we once again have a pawn ending; or

7) We get a queen ending (either an elementary one, or one with some play to it).

In order to get an idea of all these possibilities (except perhaps the last one), we shall present a sizeable number of examples. In the previous chapter we already saw an ending which transposed into a "queen vs. pawns" endgame; and earlier, we also saw cases where the king fell into check, or the queen was lost to a skewer check (see exercises 1/4, 1/7, 1/8, 1/10). Quite often, the chief problem of a position is either to draw the enemy king onto a bad square, or to avoid such a square with one's own king.

G. Walker, 1841

1-69

W

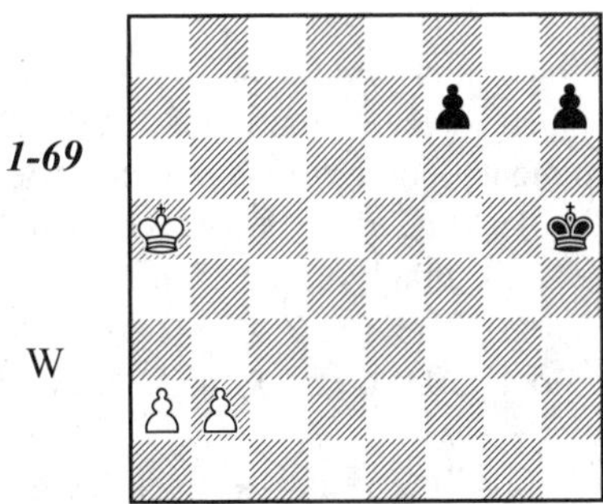

1 b4 f5 2 b5 f4 3 b6 f3 4 b7 f2 5 b8♕ f1♕ 6 ♕b5+! ♕×b5 7 ♔×b5 ♔g4 8 a4, and the h-pawn will never become a queen.

This simple example illustrates Points 1 and 6 of the above list; the following example is for Points 2 and 4 (perhaps the most important ones).

J. Moravec, 1925

1-70

W?

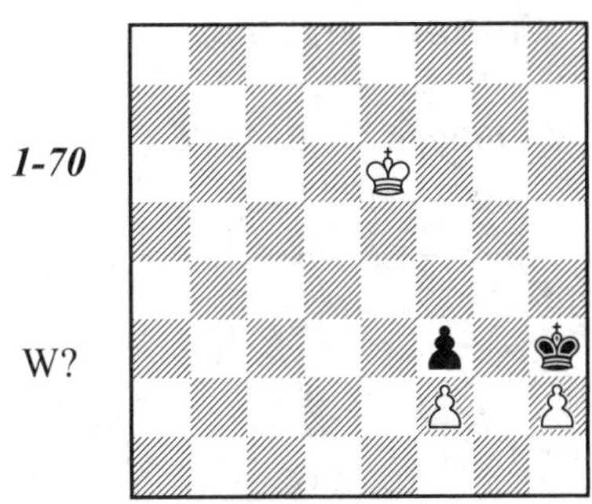

The only move to draw is **1 ♔d5! ♔g2!** (1...♔×h2? 2 ♔e4 ♔g2 3 ♔e3⊙+−) **2 h4**, and White's pawn queens immediately after Black's.

On 1 ♔f5? ♔g2! the black pawn queens with check; while on 1 ♔e5? ♔g2! White's queen will be lost after ...♕a1+.

N. Grigoriev, 1928

1-71

W?

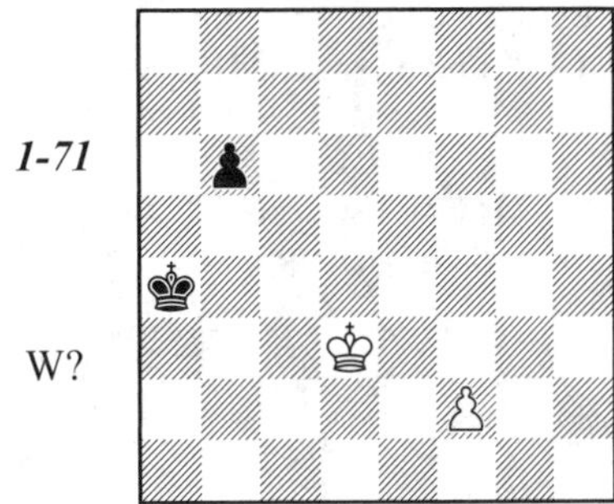

Black's king is in the square of the f-pawn, so the hasty 1 f4? ♔b5! leads only to a draw. White has to block the king's path to the kingside ("shouldering"!).

1 ♔d4! b5

The other defensive plan gets instructively refuted: 1...♔b5 2 ♔d5! ♔a6 3 f4 ♔b7 4 f5 ♔c7 5 ♔e6 ♔d8 6 ♔f7! b5 7 f6 b4 8 ♔g7 b3 9 f7 b2 10 f8♕+. In a practical game, nearly every pawn for some reason ends up queening with check; there are times, however, when you have to work a little bit for it!

Interestingly, if we place the pawn on b7 in the starting position, Black saves himself by 1...♔b5! 2 ♔d5 ♔b6! 3 ♔d6 ♔a7 4 f4 b5.

2 f4 b4 3 f5 b3

Now the enemy king must be drawn to a checkable square.

4 ♔c3! ♔a3 5 f6 b2 6 f7 b1♕ 7 f8♕+, mating or winning the queen.

Tragicomedies

Ljubojevic - Browne
Amsterdam 1972

1-72

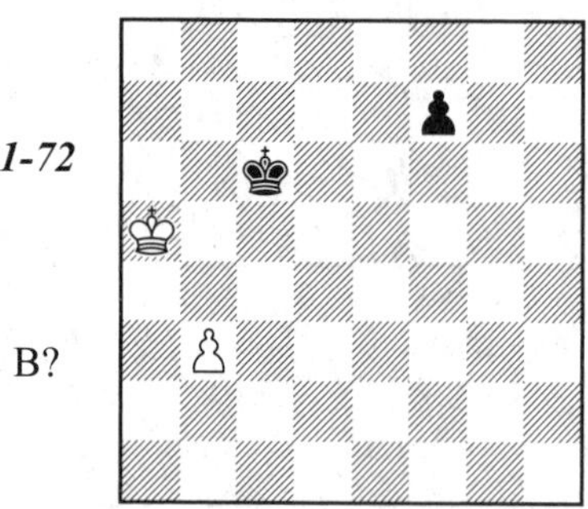

B?

Recognize this position? Yes, it's the Grigoriev study we just examined, except with colors reversed and the black king positioned differently (which has no meaning here). 1...♔d5! would have won; instead, GM Browne played **1...f5??**, and after **2 ♔b4**, a draw was agreed.

Mohr - Conquest
Gausdal 1989

1-73

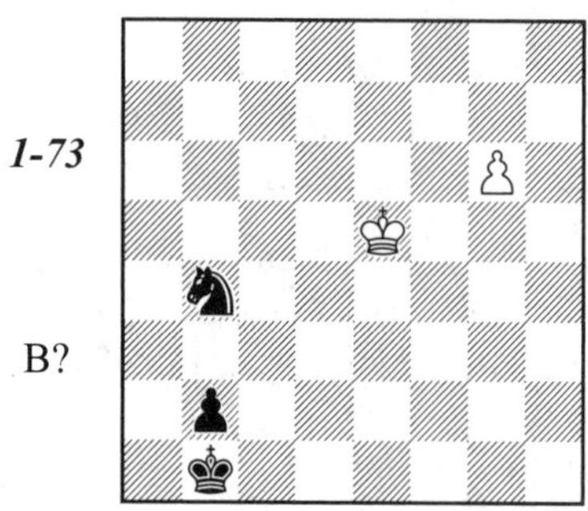

B?

After Conquest's move **1...♔c1?** the position became drawn: **2 g7 b1♕ 3 g8♕=.**

Black could have won by 1...♘d5! 2 ♔×d5 (2 g7 ♘e7 3 ♔e6 ♘g8 4 ♔f7 ♔c2 leads to a won "queen vs. knight's pawn" endgame) 2...♔c1 3 g7 b1♕ 4 g8♕ ♕b3+.

Gavrikov - Kharitonov
USSR ch(1), Sverdlovsk 1984

1-74

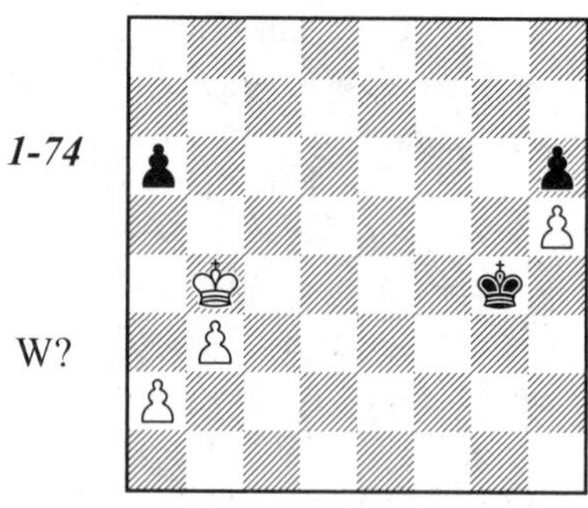

W?

The winning idea is 1 ♔c5! ♔×h5 2 b4 ♔g4 3 a4 h5 4 b5 ab 5 a5!, when the white pawn queens, while preventing the black one from doing so.

The game line was **1 ♔a5? ♔×h5 2 ♔×a6 ♔g4 3 b4 h5 4 b5 h4 5 b6 h3 6 b7 h2 7 b8♕ h1♕**, with a drawn queen endgame.

Golombek - Keres
Margate 1939

1-75

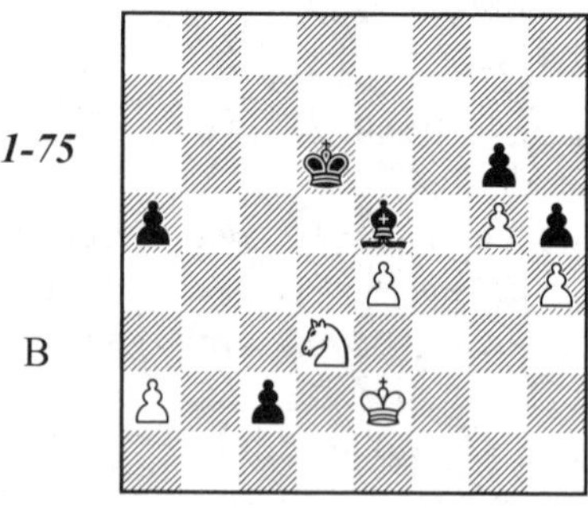

B

Black had an elementary win with 1...♗f4 or 1...♗g3. Instead, Keres continued **1...♗b2??**, and his opponent resigned, believing that after **2 ♔d2 c1♕+ 3 ♘×c1 ♗×c1+ 4 ♔×c1 ♔e5 5 ♔c2 ♔×e4**, his attack on the a5-pawn would come too late: 6 ♔b3 ♔f4 7 ♔a4 ♔g4 8 ♔×a5 ♔×h4 9 a4 ♔×g5 10 ♔b6 h4 11 a5 h3 12 a6 h2 13 a7 h1♕−+.

But White's king can also attack the other black pawn: **6 ♔c3! ♔f4 7 ♔d4 ♔g4 8 ♔e5 ♔×h4 9 ♔f6 ♔g4 10 ♔×g6 h4 11 ♔f6 h3 12 g6**, with a draw.

Exercises

1-76

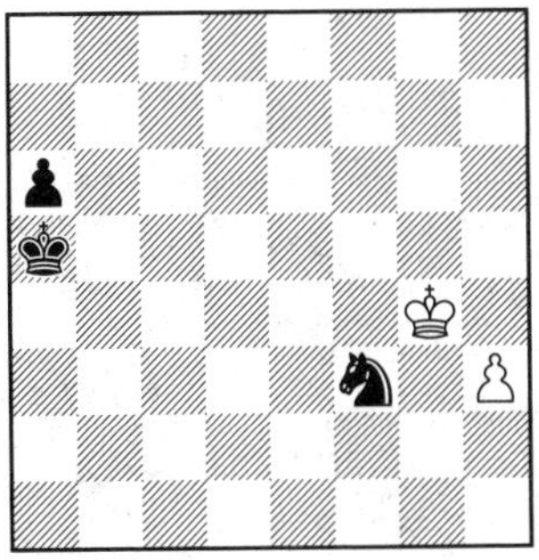

1/23
B?

1-79

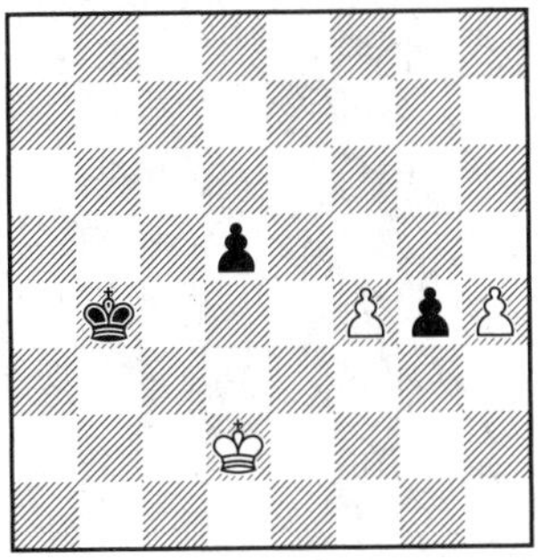

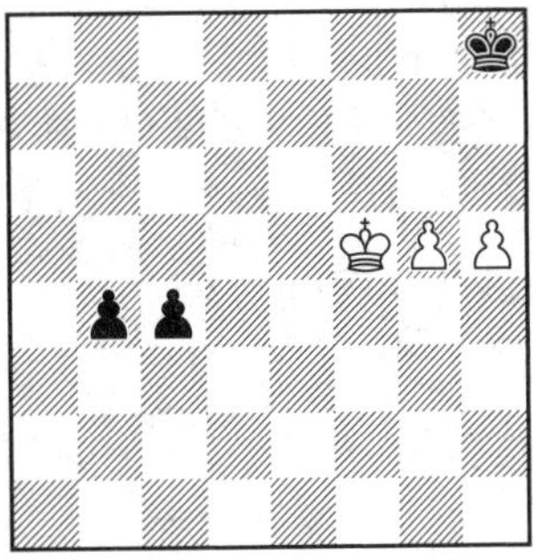

1/26
W?

1-77

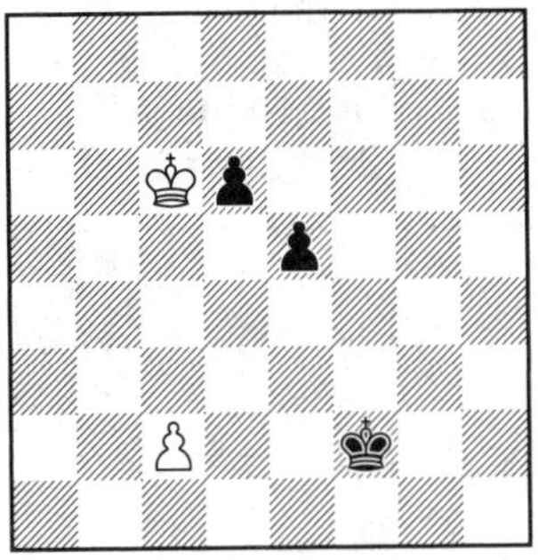

1/24
W?

1-80

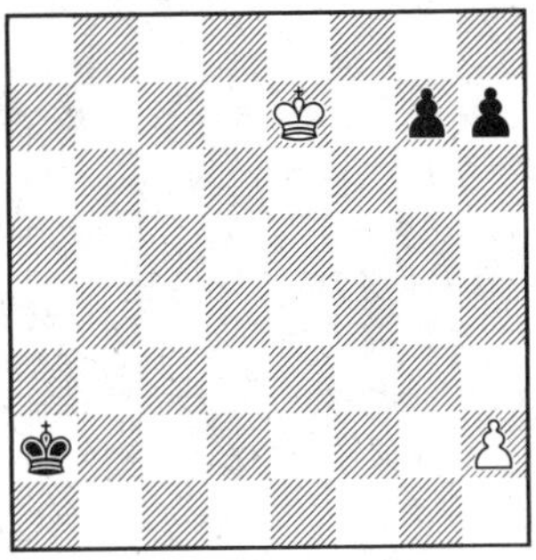

1/27
W?

1-78

1/25
W?

1-81

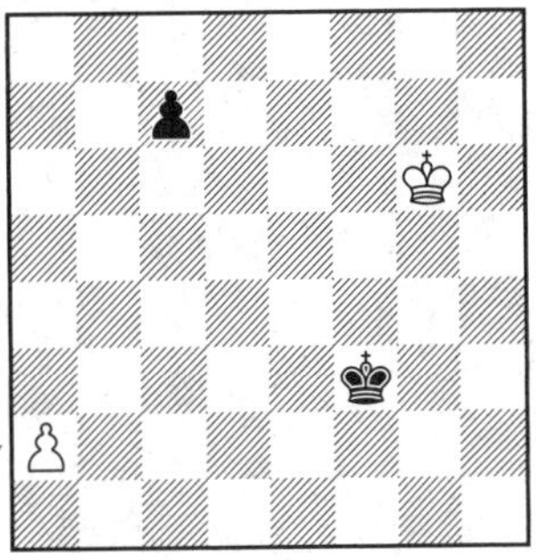

1/28
W?/Play

The Active King

King activity is the most important factor in the evaluation of position in a pawn endgame. In fact, not just in pawn endgames - in **any** endgame. But in pawn endgames, where there are no other pieces on the board, this is perhaps an especially important factor.

The influence the degree of king activity has on the battle's outcome is obvious in many of the preceding and succeeding examples. Here, we examine two vitally important means of exploiting an active king's position: playing for zugzwang, and the widening of the beachhead.

Zugzwang

M. Dvoretsky, 2000

1-82

W?

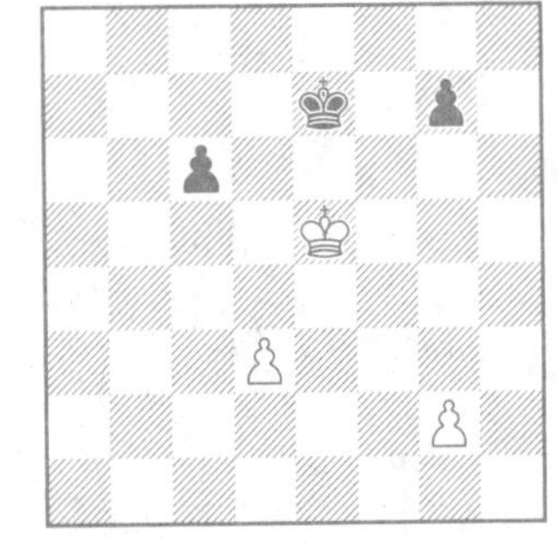

1 g3! ♔d7 2 g4 ♔e7 3 g5⊙

3 d4? ♔d7 4 ♔f5 ♔d6 5 ♔g6 ♔d5 6 ♔×g7 ♔×d4 would be less exact, as the pawns both queen. However, White could transpose moves by 3 ♔f5 ♔d6 4 g5! (4 ♔g6? ♔e5! 5 ♔×g7 ♔f4 6 ♔f6 ♔×g4=) 4...♔e7 (4...♔d5 5 ♔g6 ♔d4 6 ♔×g7 ♔×d3 7 g6 c5 8 ♔f6 c3 9 g7 c3 10 g8♕ c2 11 ♕g5+−) 5 ♔g6 etc.

Let's think about the position after 3 g5. White's king dominates the board - that's why zugzwang is unavoidable. In fact, whichever pawn Black moves is bound to be lost (3...c5 4 ♔d5, or 3...g6 4 d4⊙). Retreating the king to f7 clears the way for his opponent to go after the c6-pawn. That leaves just one move; but after that move, White finally executes his main plan - getting his king to h7.

3...♔d7 4 ♔f5 ♔e7 5 ♔g6 ♔f8 6 ♔h7 ♔f7 7 d4

One final, decisive zugzwang.

If it were Black's move in the starting position, then after 1...♔d7, 2 g4! would lead to the win. It makes quite a difference sometimes if you have a choice between moving a pawn one or two squares. For a more detailed examination of this, see "Steinitz's Rule," and the chapters which follow.

Widening the Beachhead

Hansen - Nimzovitch
Randers simul 1925

1-83

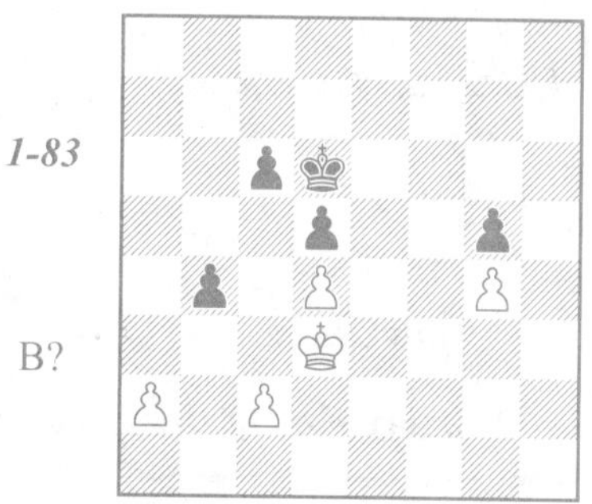

B?

Who stands better? White intends to play c2-c3, obtaining an outside passed pawn, which will secure him a decisive advantage (for example, after 1...c5? 2 dc+ ♔×c5 3 c3).

Nimzovitch hits upon the correct plan - he activates his king, even if it means sacrificing a pawn.

1...♔c7! 2 c3 ♔b6! 3 cb ♔b5 4 ♔c3 ♔a4⊙

As Black had foreseen, it's zugzwang. White resigned, since he has to lose all his queenside pawns: 5 ♔c2 ♔×b4 (White still has the outside passed pawn, but the activity of Black's king means far more here) 6 ♔d3 ♔a3 7 ♔c3 ♔×a2 8 ♔b4 ♔b2 9 ♔c5 ♔c3−+.

Let's look at **3 c4** (instead of 3 cb). White will continue by exchanging pawns at d5. It's not hard to see that b5-b3 and a4-b2 are corresponding squares; after that, we can establish a third pair of corresponding squares: a5-c2. Now we understand that Black must inevitably take advantage of this correspondence (since he can wait on either of the equivalent squares b6 and a6, while White cannot).

3...♔a6! 4 cd cd 5 ♔c2 ♔a5⊙ 6 ♔b2 ♔a4⊙ 7 ♔c2 ♔a3 8 ♔b1 b3 9 ♔a1 ♔b4 10 ♔b2 ba

In order to win, Black cleared a path for his king towards the center. This is, in fact, what "widening the beachhead" means - trading off pawns, with the idea of clearing a path for the king.

Let's examine another classic endgame.

Cohn - Rubinstein
St. Petersburg 1909

1-84

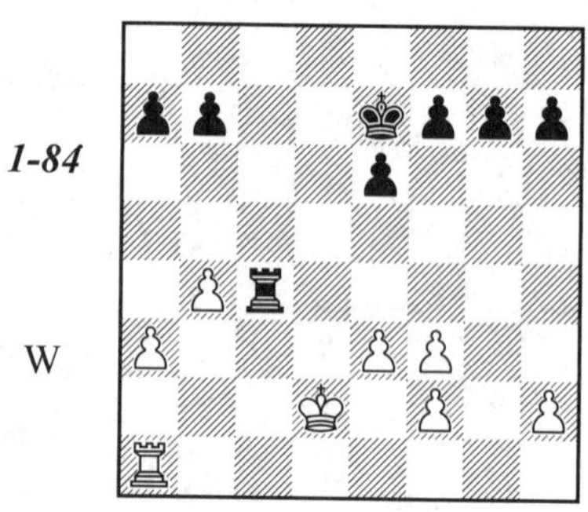

W

With 1 f4!, White would have had an inferior but defensible position. Instead, he decided to exchange rooks, because he had misjudged the pawn endgame.

1 ♖c1? ♖×c1 2 ♔×c1 ♔f6 3 ♔d2 ♔g5

Rubinstein sends his king to h3, in order to tie White's king to the defense of the weak pawn at h2. It's not hard to calculate that White's counterattack with 4 ♔d3 ♔h4 5 ♔c4 comes too late.

4 ♔e2 ♔h4 5 ♔f1 ♔h3 6 ♔g1 e5 7 ♔h1 b5!

It's useful to fix the queenside pawns, while Black also leaves himself the reserve tempo a7-

a6. White could have prevented this by playing 7 a4!?, but it would not have altered the assessment of the position.

8 ♔g1 f5

Black's further plan is to "widen the beachhead" - clear a path for his king to the queenside via pawn exchanges.

9 ♔h1 g5 10 ♔g1 h5 11 ♔h1 g4

11...h4 12 ♔g1 g4 13 fg ♔×g4 14 ♔g2 h3+ is also strong.

12 e4 fe! 13 fe

13 fg hg 14 ♔g1 e3 15 fe e4 16 ♔g1 g3 is no better.

13...h4 14 ♔g1 g3 15 hg hg White resigned.

12 fg (instead of 12 e4) 12...fg! 13 ♔g1 e4 14 ♔h1 h4 15 ♔g1 g3 changes nothing - Black still wins. However, taking with the other pawn - 12...hg?! - would have been a serious inaccuracy: 13 ♔g1 f4 14 ef ef 15 ♔h1.

1-85

B?

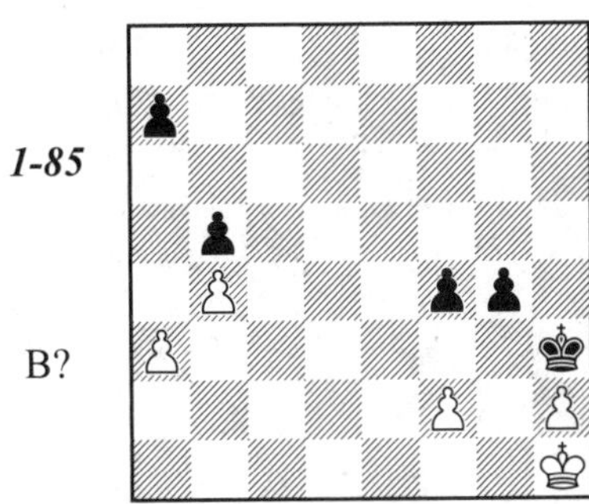

Here, widening the beachhead doesn't win anymore: 15...g3? 16 hg fg 17 fg (17 ♔g1=) 17...♔×g3 18 ♔g1 ♔f3 19 ♔f1 ♔e3 20 ♔e1 ♔d3 21 ♔d1 ♔c3 22 a4!=.

The right plan, 15...f3! 16 ♔g1 ♔h4 was pointed out by Jonathan Mestel.

17 ♔h1 ♔g5 18 h3 gh 19 ♔h2 ♔g4 20 ♔g1 ♔f4 21 ♔h2 ♔e4 22 ♔×h3 (22 ♔g3 h2!) 22...♔d3 23 ♔g4 ♔e2 24 ♔g3 a6−+ (here's where the reserve tempo comes in handy!)

17 ♔f1 ♔h5! 18 ♔e1 ♔g5⊙ 19 ♔f1 (19 ♔d2 ♔h4−+) 19...♔f4 20 ♔e1 ♔e4 21 ♔d2 ♔d4 22 ♔c2 ♔c4 23 ♔d2 ♔b3 24 ♔e3 ♔×a3 25 ♔f4 ♔×b4 26 ♔×g4 a5−+.

Tragicomedies

Horowitz - Denker
Philadelphia 1936

1-86

W?

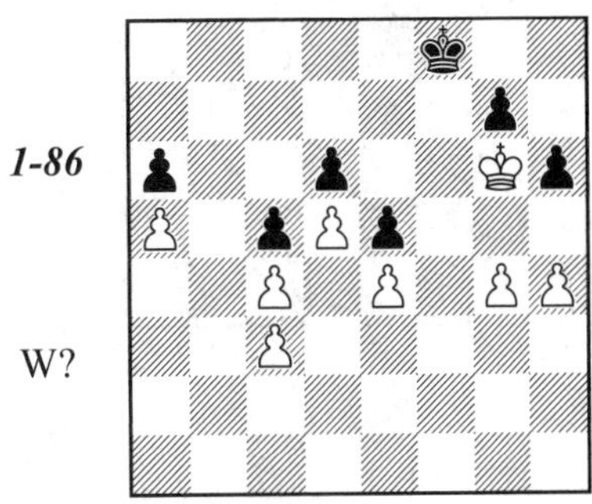

Here's how the game actually ended: **1 ♔h7 ♔f7 2 ♔h8 ♔f8 3 g5** Black resigned.

Zinar has shown that every move played by both sides was a mistake - except for the last one. His analysis follows:

1) White should not take his king into the corner. The correct plan to exploit his advantage is - widening the beachhead!

1 g5! hg 2 ♔×g5 ♔f7 3 h5 ♔e7 4 ♔g6 ♔f8 5 h6! ♔g8! 6 ♔h5! gh 7 ♔×h6 ♔f7 8 ♔h7 (the opposition) **8...♔f6 9 ♔g8** (now, an outflanking) **9...♔g5 10 ♔f7 ♔f4 11 ♔e6 ♔×e4 12 ♔×d6 ♔f4 13 ♔×c5 e4 14 d6 e3 15 d7 e2 16 d8♕ e1♕ 17 ♕f6+**, with an easily won queen endgame.

2) With 1...h5! (instead of 1...♔f7?), Black would have drawn: 2 g5 ♔f7 3 ♔h8 ♔g6! 4 ♔g8 stalemate; or 2 gh ♔f7 3 h6 g6! 6 ♔h8 ♔f8=.

3) But 2 ♔h8? lets slip the win. Also insufficient was 2 g5? h5! 3 g6+ (3 ♔h8 ♔g6!) 3...♔f6 4 ♔g8 ♔×g6 5 ♔f8 ♔f6 6 ♔e8 g5 7 hg+ ♔×g5 8 ♔e7 h4 9 ♔×d6 h3 10 ♔c7 h2 11 d6 h1♕ 12 d7 ♕h7 13 ♔c8 ♕h3=.

The right move was 2 h5! ♔f6 (we have already seen what happens after 2...♔f8 3 ♔g6 ♔g8 4 ♔f5 ♔f7 5 g5 hg 6 ♔×g5) 3 ♔g8 g6 (3...g5 4 ♔h7) 4 ♔f8! gh 5 gh ♔g5 6 ♔e7 ♔×h5 7 ♔×d6 ♔g4 8 ♔×e5+−.

4) And retreating the king to f8 was the decisive mistake. Black could still have drawn with 2...h5! 3 g5 ♔g6!, or 3 gh ♔f8 4 h6 g6!.

Exercises

1-87

1/29
W?

1-88

1/30
W?

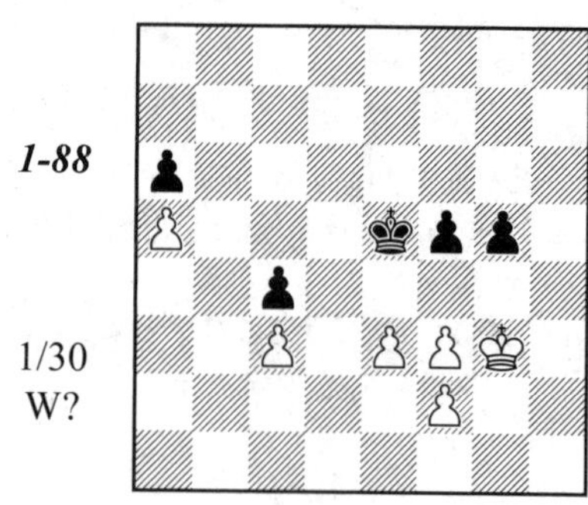

The King Routes

In this section, we shall examine some different types of king maneuvers.

Zigzag

The laws of geometry, as we have known them since grade school, have no relevance on the chessboard. There, a straight line is not the shortest distance between two points (or squares) - if the king follows a broken-line path, it is by no means longer. This phenomenon is exploited both in the Réti idea we have already examined, and in the "shoulder block" we shall learn later on.

Here, we shall speak of a technique closely connected with the simultaneous advance of pawns we just studied. To be more exact: we shall be speaking of two techniques, which look very similar. Let's call them "zigzag."

N. Grigoriev, 1928

1-89

W?

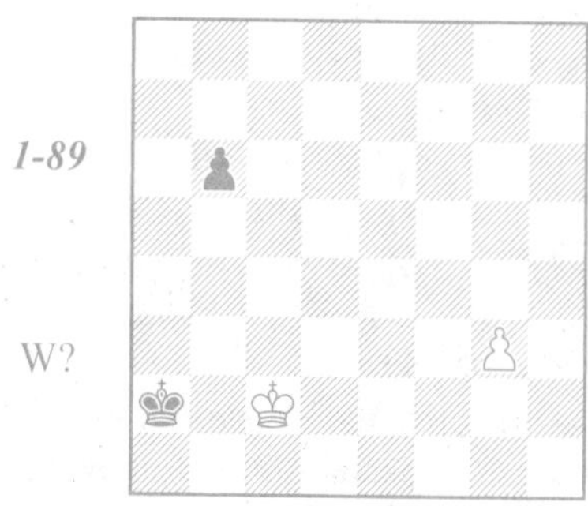

The direct 1 g4? leads only to a draw: 1...b5 2 g5 b4 3 g6 b3+ 4 ♔c3 b2 5 g7 b1♕ 6 g8♕+ ♔a1!=.

1 ♔c3! ♔a3 2 ♔c4 ♔a4 3 g4 b5+ 4 ♔d3!

Here's the zigzag! The king returns to c2, while avoiding the pawn check.

4...♔a3 5 g5 b4 6 g6 b3 7 g7 b2 8 ♔c2! (drawing the king into check) **8...♔a2 9 g8♕+.**

The other form of zigzag occurs when the king has to avoid a check from a newly-promoted queen.

J. Moravec, 1952

1-90

W?

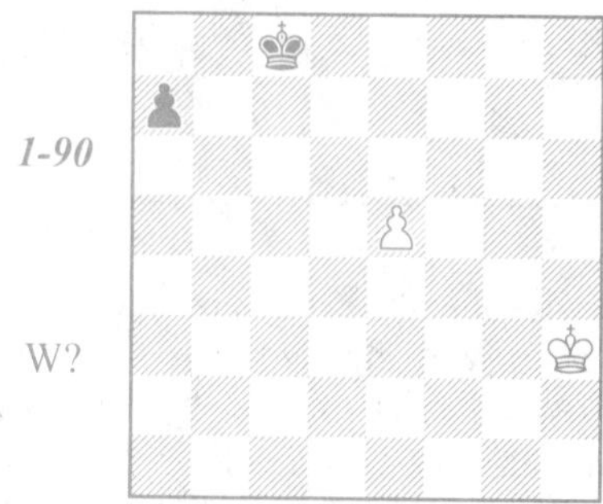

White is outside the square of the a-pawn. His only hope is Réti's idea.

1 ♔g4 a5 2 ♔f5! a4

Otherwise, the king gets into the square. Now White would lose by 3 e6? ♔d8 4 ♔f6 ♔e8; and 3 ♔f6? a3 4 e6 a2 5 e7 a1♕+ is also bad. The king must avoid the f6-square.

3 ♔g6! a3 4 e6 a2 5 e7 ♔d7 6 ♔f7=.

Exercises

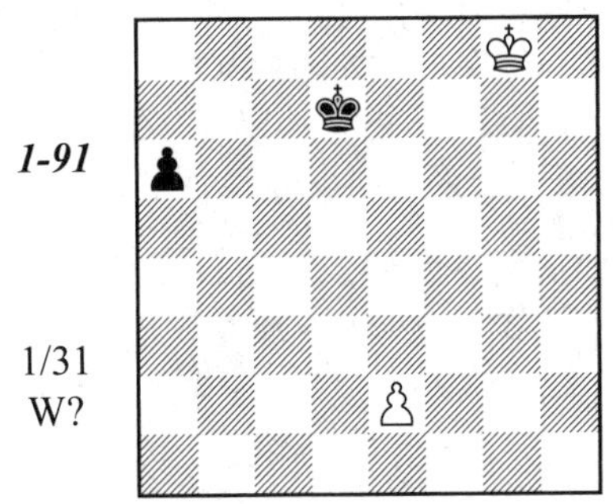

1-91

1/31
W?

How should this game end?

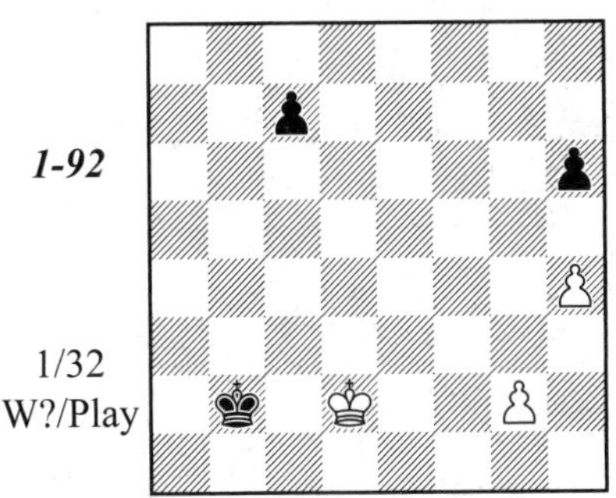

1-92

1/32
W?/Play

The Pendulum

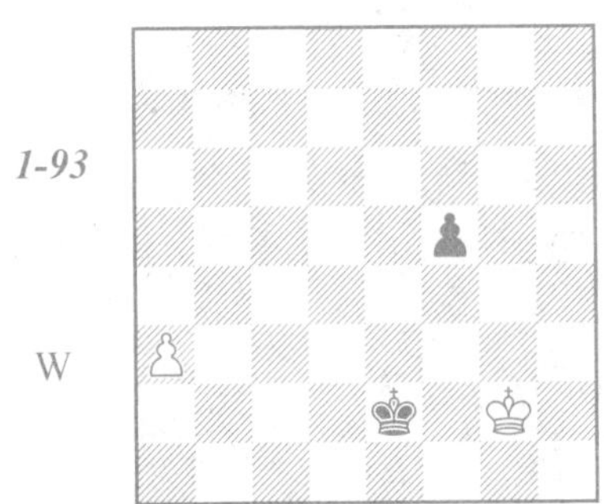

1-93

W

1 ♔g3! ♔e3 2 ♔g2! ♔e2 (2...f4 3 ♔f1) **3 ♔g3=**

This elementary defensive technique appears frequently.

Exercises

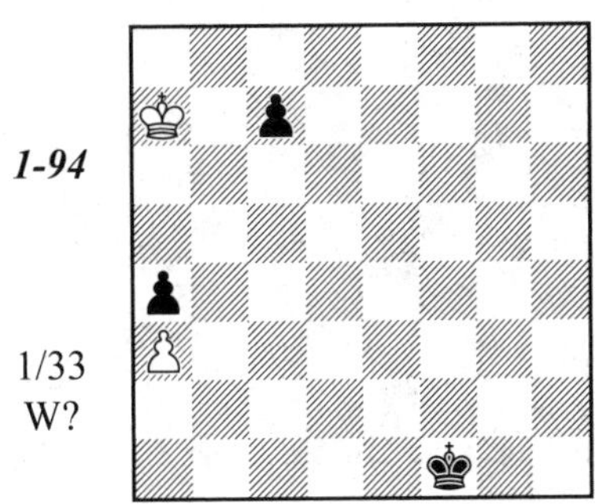

1-94

1/33
W?

Shouldering

Quite often, one must choose a route for the king that gives a "shouldering" to the enemy king - that is, it prevents the enemy from arriving in time at an important part of the board.

Schlage - Ahues
Berlin 1921

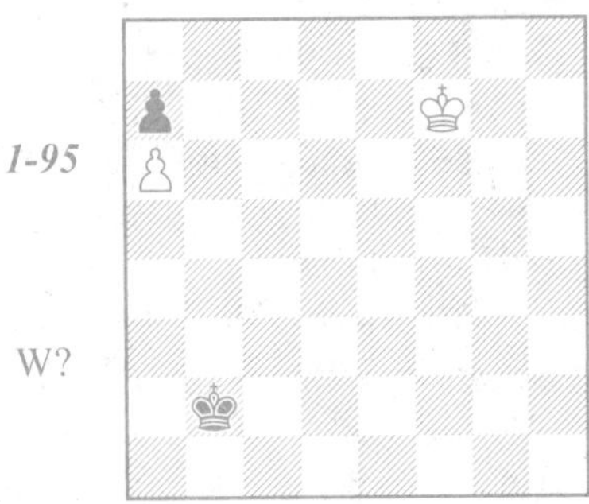

1-95

W?

White must inevitably win the pawn at a7. Black can save himself only if he can succeed in locking the white king into the corner with ...♔c7.

The game was drawn after 1 ♔e6 ♔c3 2 ♔d6? ♔d4 3 ♔c6 ♔e5 4 ♔b7 ♔d6 5 ♔xa7 ♔c7.

Maizelis demonstrated a win for White by **1 ♔e6! ♔c3 2 ♔d5!+−**

White's king approaches the a7-pawn while simultaneously "shouldering" the enemy king, keeping it from approaching the c7-square.

J. Moravec, 1940

1-96

W?

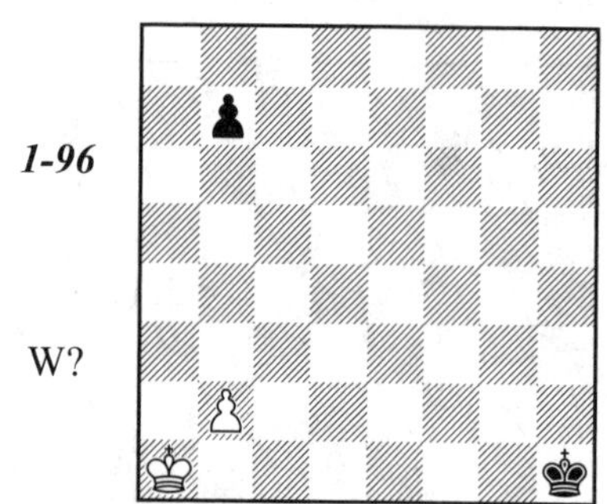

White only gets a draw out of 1 ♔a2? ♔g2 2 ♔b3 ♔f3 3 ♔c4 ♔e4 4 b4 ♔e5 5 ♔c5 (White's king does manage to shoulder the enemy king, but here this is insufficient) 5...♔e6 6 ♔b6 (6 b5 ♔d7 7 ♔b6 ♔c8=) 6...♔d5 7 ♔×b7 ♔c4=.

It's important to keep Black's king farther away from the pawns; and for this, White needs to meet him halfway.

1 ♔b1! ♔g2 2 ♔c2 ♔f3 3 ♔d3! ♔f4 4 ♔d4 ♔f5 5 ♔d5 ♔f6 6 ♔d6 ♔f7

If 6...♔f5, then 7 b4 ♔e4 8 b5 ♔d4 9 b6 with the idea of 10 ♔c7+−.

7 b4 ♔e8 8 ♔c7 b5 9 ♔c6+−.

Tragicomedies

Rogers - Shirov
Groningen 1990

1-97

B?

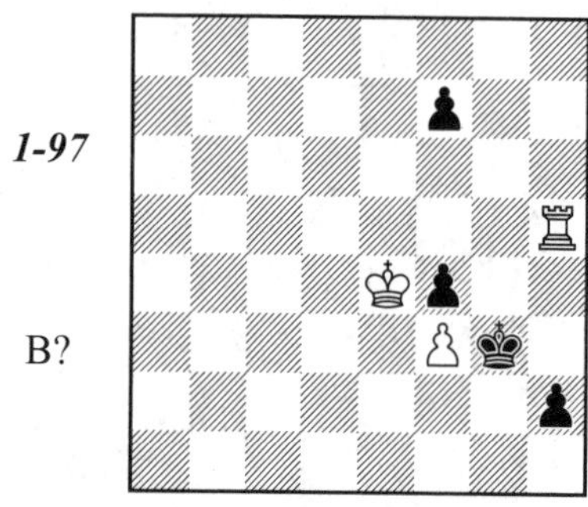

Black would have drawn, had he continued 1...f5+! 2 ♔×f5 (2 ♔d4 ♔g2) 2...♔×f3 3 ♖×h2 ♔g3 △ 4...f3. 1...f6! is also possible: 2 ♖h8 f5+ (or even 2...♔g2).

Shirov decided instead to pick up the rook for his h-pawn, but he misjudged the pawn ending.

1...♔g2?? 2 ♔×f4 h1♕ 3 ♖×h1 ♔×h1 4 ♔g3!

Black resigned. His king is squeezed into the corner, giving White time to push his f3-pawn forward, after which he can win Black's pawn. For example: 4...♔g1 5 f4 ♔f1 6 f5! (but not 6 ♔f3? f5!=) 6...♔e2 7 ♔f4 ♔d3 8 ♔e5 ♔e3 9 f6!+−.

Exercises

1-98

1/34
W?

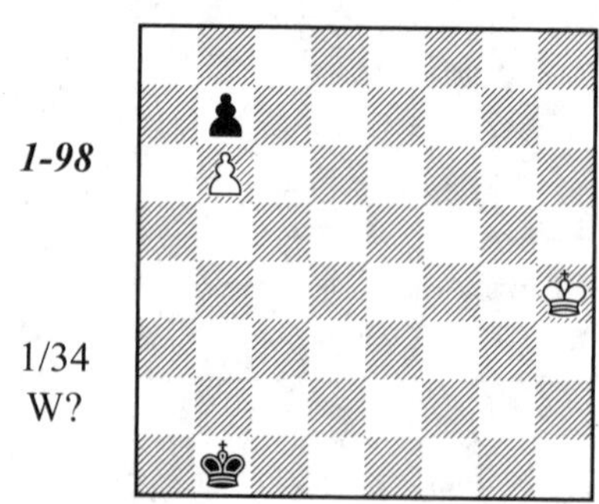

1-99

1/35
W?

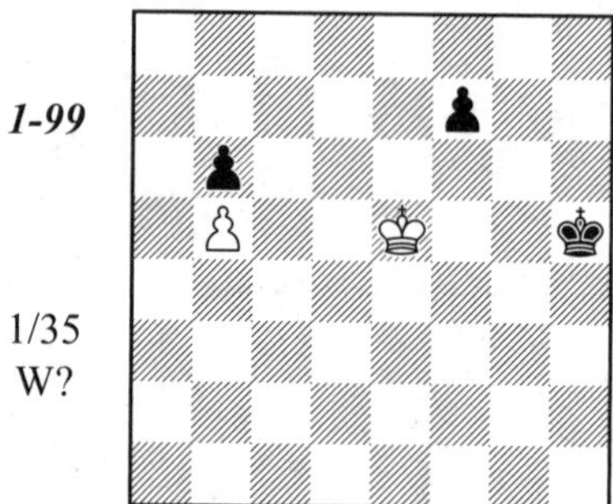

1-100

1/36
W?/Play

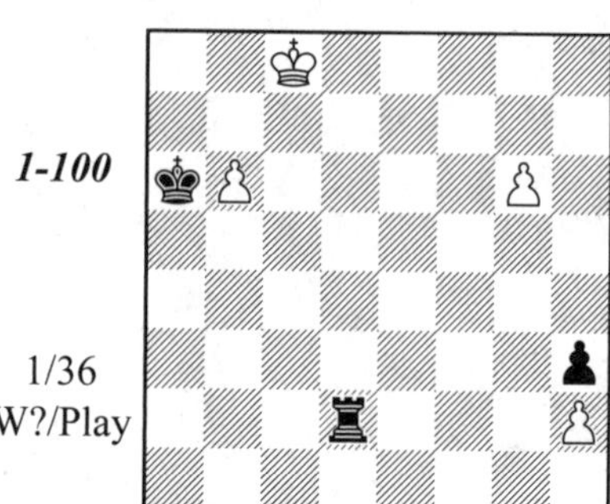

1-101

1/37
W?/Play

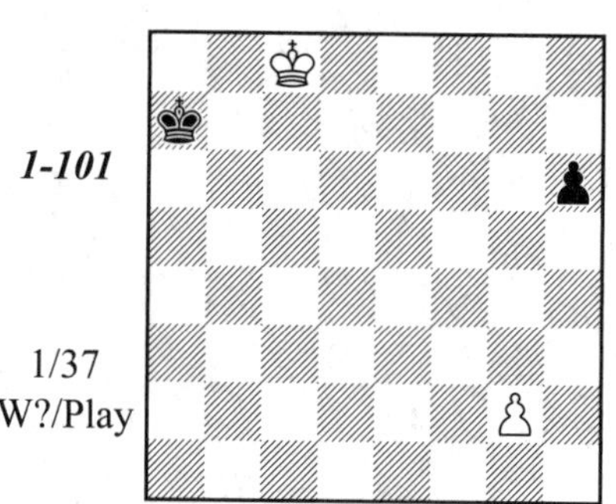

Breakthrough

A breakthrough occurs when one or more pawns are sacrificed in order to create a passed pawn and promote it.

Let's examine a few of the standard structures in which a pawn breakthrough is possible.

1-102

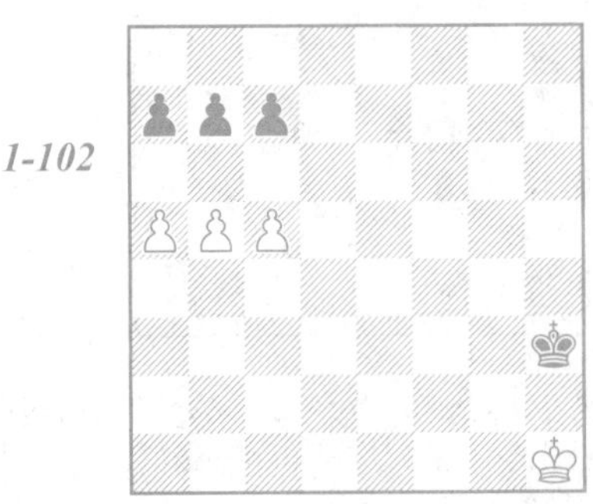

White to move wins by **1 b6! cb** (1...ab 2 c6) **2 a6! ba 3 c6**

Black to move has only one way to parry the threatened breakthrough: by **1...b6!** (both 1...a6? 2 c6! and 1...c6? 2 a6! are bad).

Let's add one more white pawn at c4. Now the move 1...b6 no longer works, because of 2 cb cb 3 c5.

Now let's move the a-pawn to a4. In this case, Black can stop the breakthrough for good by playing 1...c6! 2 a5 a6!

1-103

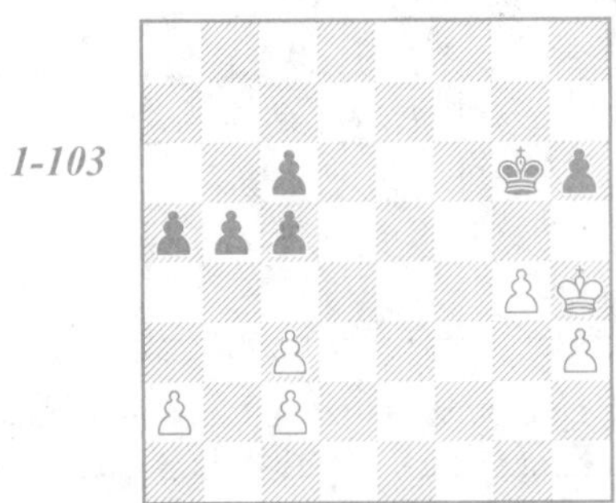

This is the sort of structure we find in the Ruy Lopez Exchange Variation. Black to move can create a passed pawn by 1...c4! 2 ♔g3 c5, followed by ...b5-b4, ...a5-a4 and ...b4-b3. (Formally the term "breakthrough" isn't really appropriate here, since no pawn sacrifice is involved; but the effect is just the same.)

White to move can stabilize the situation on the queenside by **1 c4!**, which guarantees him a decisive advantage, thanks to the outside passed pawn he will create on the opposite side of the board.

Maslov - Glebov
USSR 1936

1-104

B?

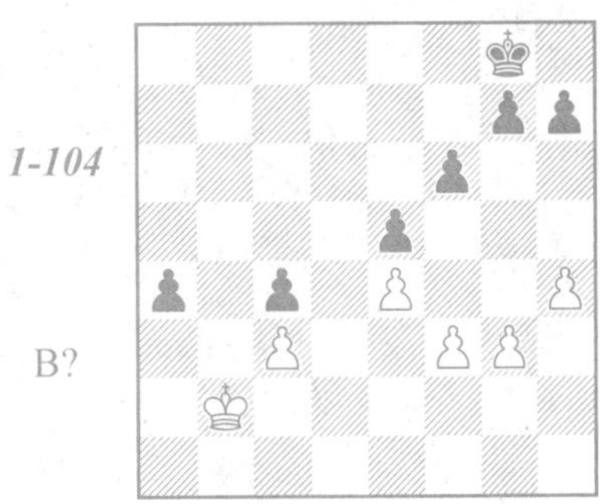

Black's position looks difficult, since the enemy king rules the queenside. But the possibility of a pawn breakthrough changes the evaluation of the position completely.

1...h5! 2 ♔a3 (2 g4 g5!) **2...g5 3 ♔×a4 f5! 4 ♔b5**

There is no defense: 4 hg f4!, or 4 ef g4! 5 fg e4.

4...f4 5 gf gh, and the h-pawn queens.

The errors committed in the following examples are quite instructive. They could have been put in the "Tragicomedies" section, except that I already had plenty of material for that section without them.

Havasi - Peko
Budapest 1976

1-105

B?

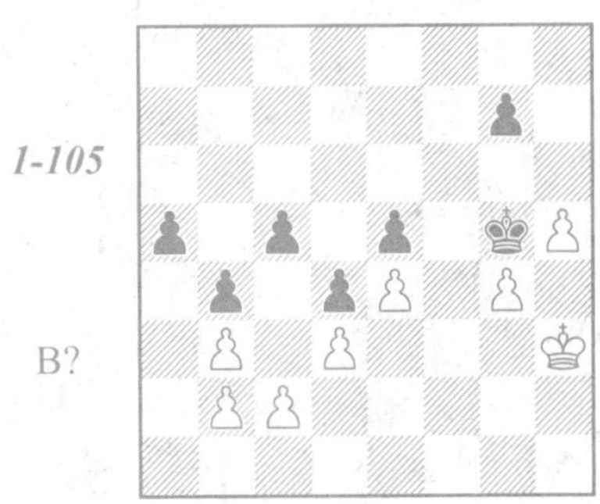

Black resigned, never suspecting that the queenside pawn structure contained the possibility of a breakthrough.

1...c4! 2 bc

If 2 dc, then 2...a4 3 ba b3 4 cb d3−+, while 2 ♔g3 is met by 2...a4! 3 ba b3 4 cb c3.

2...a4 3 c5 a3 4 ba ba 5 c6 a2 6 c7 a1♕ 7 c8♕

The pawns queen simultaneously; but Black has an easy win by once again obtaining a pawn ending. Note Black's working the queen up to h4 - a standard technique in these positions, ensuring that the g4-pawn is captured with check.

7...♕f1+ 8 ♔g3 ♕f4+ 9 ♔h3 ♕f3+ 10 ♔h2 ♕f2+! 11 ♔h3 ♕h4+ 12 ♔g2 ♕×g4+ 13 ♕×g4 ♔×g4 14 ♔f2 ♔×h5−+.

Capablanca - Ed. Lasker
London simul 1913

1-106

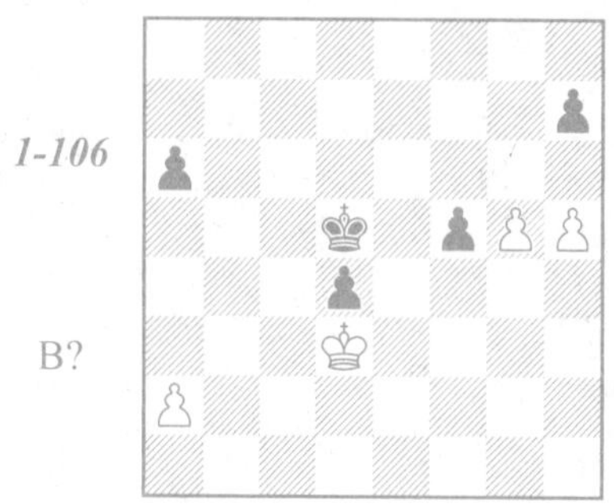

B?

1...♔e5?? 2 h6! (△ 3 g6) Black resigned.

The draw would have been assured after 1...♔e6! 2 ♔×d4 f4 3 ♔e4 f3 4 ♔×f3 ♔f5 5 g6 hg 6 h6 ♔f6=.

Kharlov - Ernst
Haninge 1992

1-107

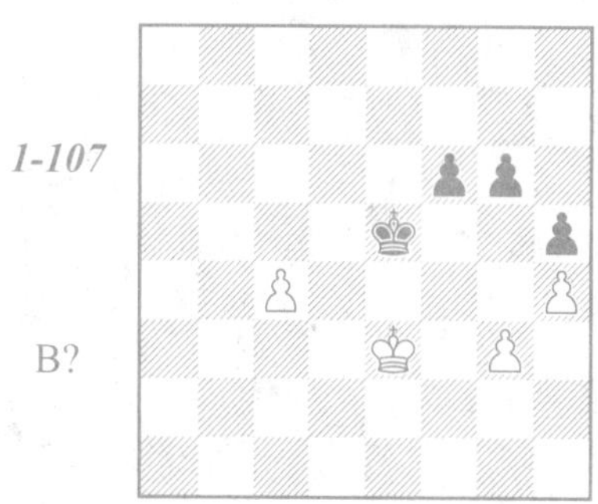

B?

The position is drawn: 1...♔d6! 2 ♔d4 ♔c6 3 c5 g5 4 ♔e4 gh 5 gh ♔×c5 6 ♔f5 ♔d6=.

In the game, Black played **1...g5?? 2 g4!+−**, and after a few more unnecessary moves (2...hg 3 h5 f5 4 h6 f4+ 5 ♔f2 g3+ 6 ♔g2 ♔e4 7 h7), he resigned.

Tragicomedies

Ed. Lasker - Moll
Berlin 1904

1-108

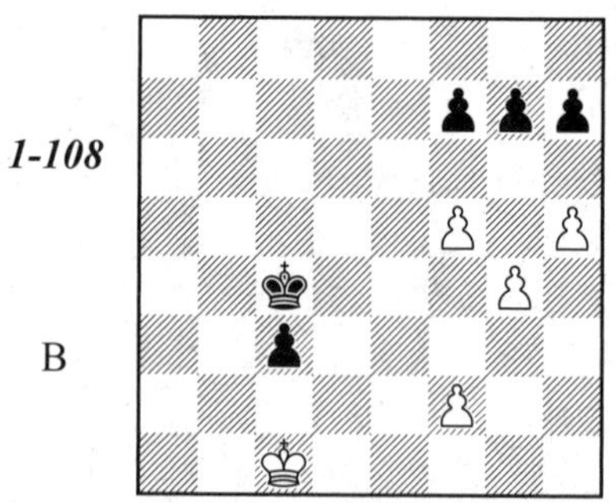

B

Black wins easily by 1...f6 2 g5 (2 h6 gh 3 f4 ♔d5) 2...h6; 1...♔d4 is also good.

1...h6??

A terrible blunder, allowing the breakthrough 2 f6! gf 3 f4 ♔d5 4 g5 fg 5 fg ♔e6 6 gh ♔f6 7 ♔c2⊙+−.

But White failed to exploit his unexpected opportunity, and lost after **2 f4?? f6! 3 g5 ♔d4.**

Svacina - Müller
Vienna 1941

1-109

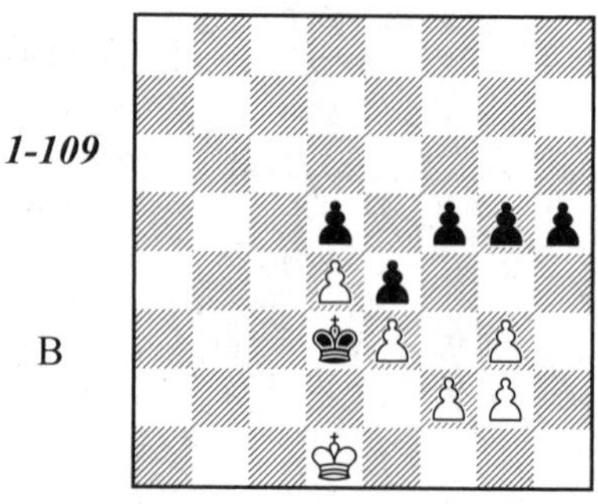

B

Black cannot capitalize on the active position of his king: 1...g4 2 ♔e1 ♔c2 3 ♔e2=; or 1...f4 2 gf gf 3 ef=. He thought up an amusing psychological trap: retreating his king instead.

1...♔c4 2 ♔c2 ♔b5 3 ♔b3 ♔c6 4 ♔b4 ♔d6 5 ♔b5 ♔d7 6 ♔c5 ♔e6 7 ♔c6?

And it worked! White, having no idea what his opponent was up to, naively marched his king deep into enemy territory - no doubt, he was already expecting to win. But now, Black plays the pawn breakthrough.

7...g4! 8 ♔c5 f4! 9 ef h4! 10 gh g3 11 fg e3 White resigned.

Nakagawa - Day
Buenos Aires ol 1978

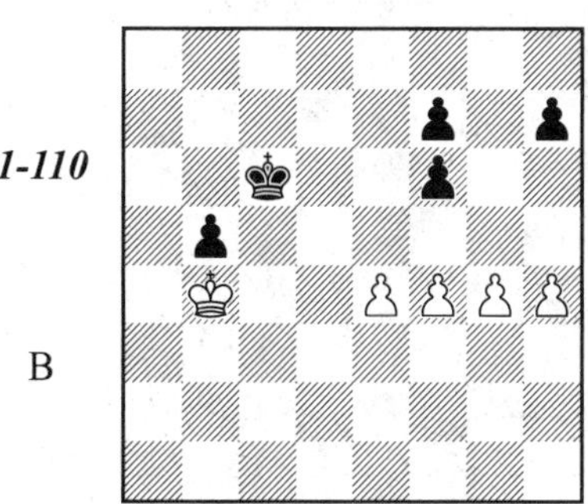

1-110
B

This position is drawn: the potential threat of a kingside breakthrough is counterbalanced by Black's outside passed pawn - but no more than that. Here is how matters should normally develop: 1...♔b6 2 h5 ♔c6 3 h6! ♔b6 4 e5 (4 f5 ♔c6 5 e5 ♔d5! 6 ♔xb5! ♔xe5 7 ♔c6=) 4...fe 5 fe (5 f5 e4 6 ♔c3! ♔c5 7 g5 is also possible.) 5...♔c6 6 e6! ♔d6 (6...fe? 7 g5+−) 7 ef ♔e7 8 ♔xb5 ♔xf7 9 ♔c4=.

But the game continued **1...h6??**, and now White could have won easily by 2 h5! (△ 3 g5). Instead, he chose **2 g5??**, which lost after **2...fg 3 fg h5! 4 e5 ♔d5**, etc.

Süss - Haakert
BRD ch, Kiel 1967

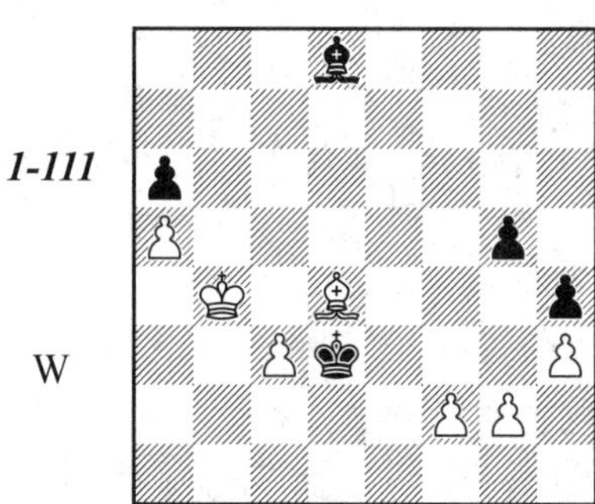

1-111
W

1 g4!? or 1 ♗b6!? would have retained excellent winning chances for White. However, he forgot about the possibility of a pawn breakthrough, and obtained the opposite result instead.

1 g3?? g4! 2 gh gh 3 ♗e5 ♗xh4 4 f3 ♗f6! 5 ♗h2 ♗xc3+ 6 ♔a4 ♔e3 7 f4 ♔e4 White resigned.

Averbakh - Bebchuk
Moscow 1964

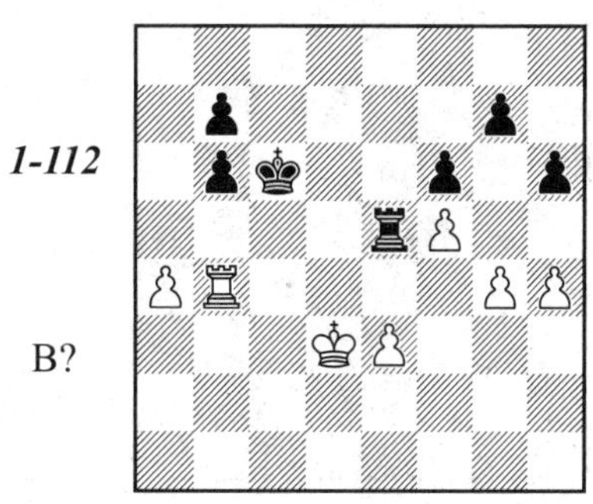

1-112
B?

Black has an inferior, but defensible endgame. Bebchuk, however, misjudged the pawn ending.

1...b5? 2 ♖xb5! ♖xb5 3 ab+ ♔xb5 4 e4 ♔c6 5 e5! fe

If 5...♔d5 6 e6 ♔d6, White brings his king to b6 (or, if Black plays ...b7-b6, to b5), and after Black replies ...♔c8, uses his reserve tempo h4-h5 to win.

6 g5 hg

Black finds no relief in 6...♔d6 7 f6 ♔e6 8 fg ♔f7 9 gh b5 (the floating square for Black's pawns doesn't reach the last rank, and the distance between the pawns is the unfavorable two files) 10 ♔e4 b4 11 ♔d3 and 12 ♔c4+−.

7 f6!

(Not, however, 7 h5? ♔d6 8 f6 ♔e6 9 fg ♔f7−+) Black resigned, in view of 7...gf 8 h5.

Black had a better defense in 1...h5!?, when White could have tried 2 ♖b5!. Here, too, the exchange of rooks leads to a loss: 2...♖xb5? 3 ab+ ♔xb5 4 e4! ♔c6 (4...hg 5 e5) 5 e5 ♔d7□ 6 e6+ ♔d6 7 gh b5 8 ♔c3 b6 (8...♔c7 9 ♔b4 ♔c6 10 ♔a5) 9 ♔b4 ♔c6 10 h6! gh 11 h5⊙ ♔d6 12 ♔xb5 ♔c7 13 e7+−. Black would have to play 2...♖e8! 3 gh ♖h8, with good drawing chances.

In the following diagram, after 1...♔h8! the draw is obvious. In the game, however, Black allowed the trade of queens.

1...♔f8?? 2 ♕f5+! ♕xf5 3 gf ♔g7 4 c4

A simpler way is 4 ♔g4 ♔h6 (4...♔f6 5 h6+−) 5 c4 f3 (5...♔g7 6 ♔f3⊙) 6 ♔xf3 ♔xh5 7 f6 (7 ♔g3 is good, too) 7...♔g6 (7...ef 8 c5+−) 8 fe ♔f7 9 ♔g4 ♔xe7 10 ♔xg5+−.

Gazik - Pétursson
Groningen ech jr 1978/79

1-113

B?

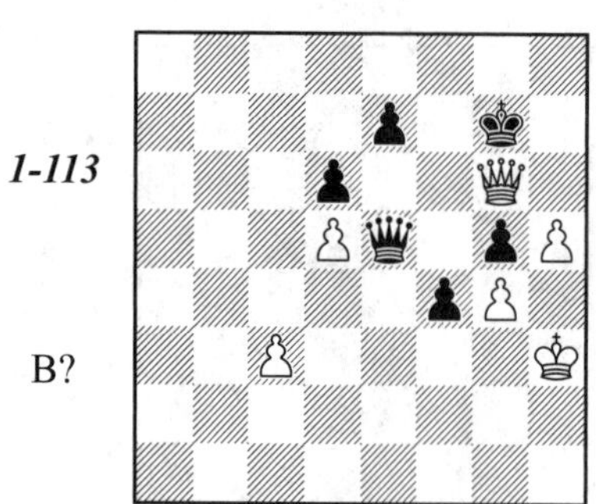

4...f3 5 h6+??

White returns the favor, by being in too much of a hurry for the breakthrough. The win was 5 ♔g3 g4 6 ♔f2!⊙ ♔h6 (6...♔f6 7 h6) 7 c5 (or 7 f6 ef 8 c5) 7...dc 8 f6 ef 9 d6.

5...♔×h6 6 c5 dc 7 f6 ♔g6! White resigned.

Wade - Korchnoi
Buenos Aires 1960

1-114

B?

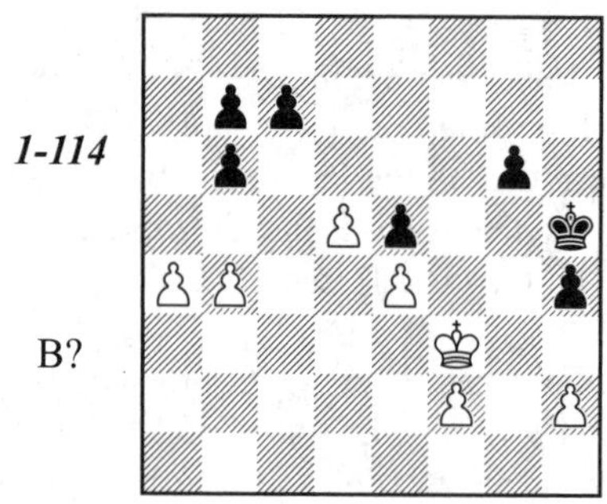

Korchnoi ignored the possible pawn breakthrough on the queenside.

1...♔g5?? 2 b5! ♔h5 3 a5!

Black resigned, in view of 3...ba 4 b6 cb 5 d6.

He would also have lost after 1...g5? 2 b5 g4+ 3 ♔e2 (3 ♔e3 ♔g5 4 f3 g3 5 hg hg 6 ♔e2! is also possible) 3...♔g5 (3...h3 4 a5!) 4 f3 or 4 h3. Black's king would be tied to the kingside, while White could break through on the queenside at the right moment.

The only way to ward off White's threat was by 1...b5! 2 ab b6, and we have a draw: 3 ♔e3 (3 h3 g5 4 ♔g2 g4?! 5 f4! g3!= is also good) 3...g5! (3...♔g5? 4 f4+! ef+ 5 ♔f3+−; or 3...♔g4? 4 f3+ ♔h3 5 f4 ef+ 6 ♔×f4 ♔×h2 7 e5+−) 4 h3 (4 f3 is weaker due to 4...g4 5 f4 h3!) 4...g4 5 f4! gh 6 ♔f3 ef 7 e5, etc.

Exercises

1-115

1/38
W?

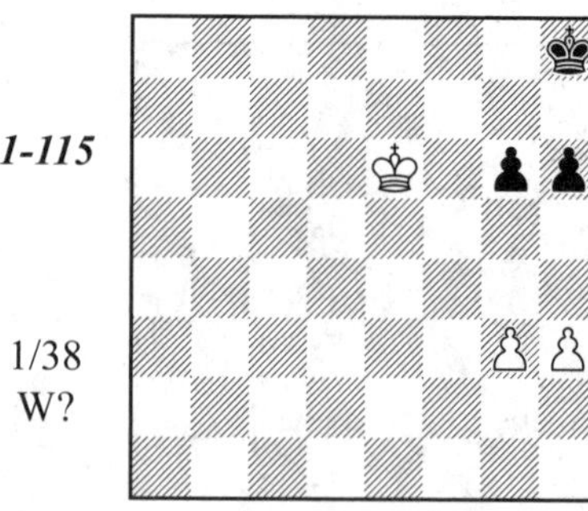

1-116

1/39
W?

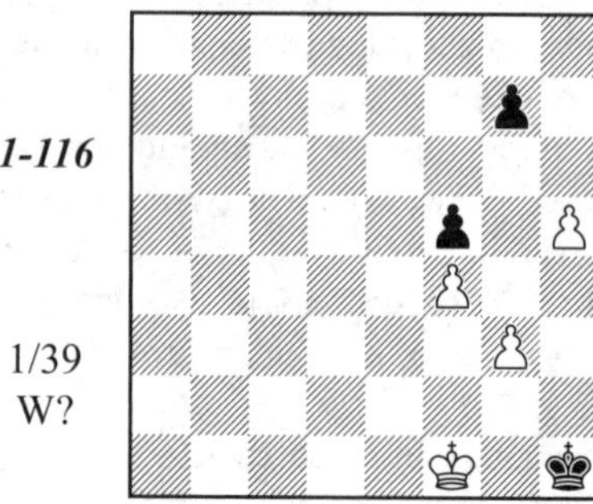

1-117

1/40
W?

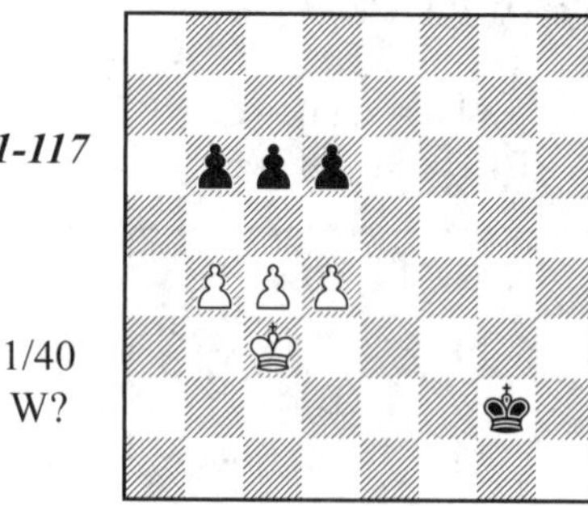

1-118

1/41
W?

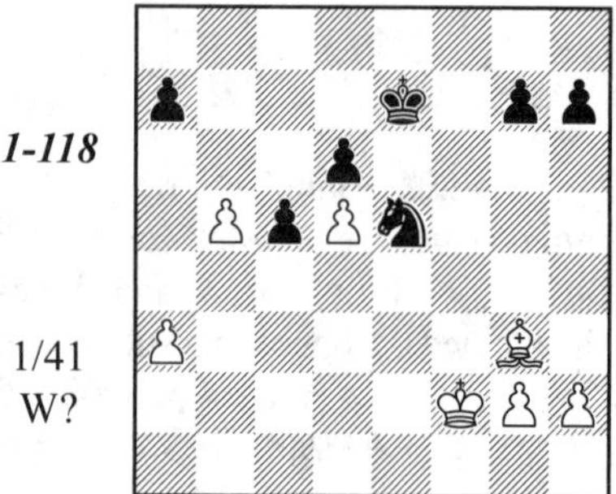

The Outside Passed Pawn

An outside passed pawn usually means a positional advantage sufficient to win. This pawn will draw off the enemy king, allowing the other king to be the first to attack the enemy pawns.

For example, in Diagram 1-103, after 1. c4!, stopping the threatened enemy breakthrough, we broke off our analysis, since the further exploitation of the outside passed pawn is elementary here.

Of course, that's not always the case. In the endgames Kharlov - Ernst (Diagram 1-107) or Nakagawa - Day (Diagram 1-110), the proper outcome would have been a draw, despite the presence of an outside passed pawn. And in the game Hansen - Nimzovitch (Diagram 1-83), Black met the threat of an outside passed pawn with the activation of his king, which even won for him.

Lombardy - Fischer
USA ch, New York 1960-61

1-119

W

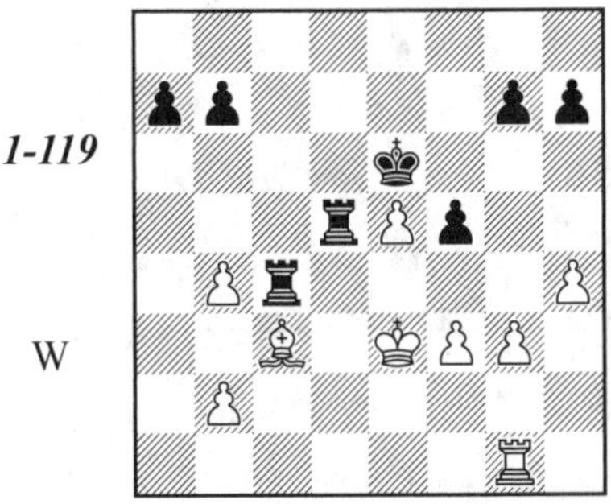

The game hangs in the balance after 1 ♖a1, despite Black's material advantage - it's not so easy to find a way to break through the enemy defenses. However, Lombardy committed "hara-kiri": he allowed Fischer to obtain an easily won pawn ending, based on the outside passed pawn.

1 ♖e1?? ♖×c3+! 2 bc ♖×e5+ 3 ♔d2 ♖×e1 4 ♔×e1 ♔d5 5 ♔d2 ♔c4 6 h5 b6

Black gets an outside passed a-pawn by force, which draws the white king to the edge of the board.

7 ♔c2 g5 8 h6 f4 9 g4 a5 10 ba ba 11 ♔b2 a4 12 ♔a3 ♔×c3 13 ♔×a4 ♔d4 14 ♔b4 ♔e3 White resigned.

In the following diagram, White had to play 1 ♖h1!, intending 2 ♖h5. After 1...♔c6! (neither 1...♖c7 2 b3, nor 1...♖e7 2 ♖h5 ♖e2 3 ♖×d5+ ♔c6 4 ♖a5= is dangerous) 2 ♖h5 ♖d6 3 f4!?∓,

Martynov - Ulybin
Daugavpils 1986

1-120

W?

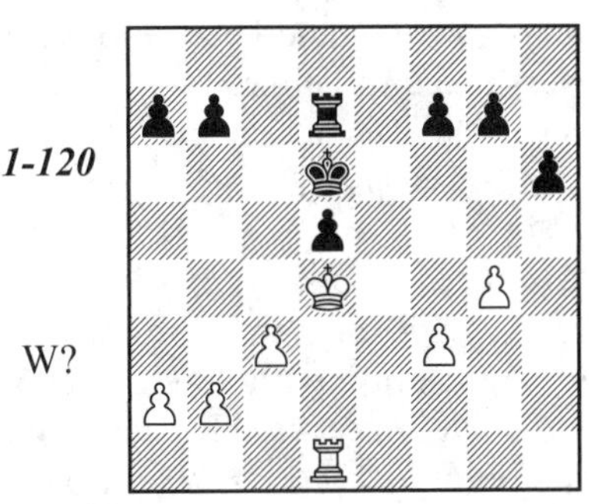

White's more active king and (even more important) rook positions assure him good compensation for the pawn minus.

In the game, he played **1 ♖e1?**, misjudging the force of the reply **1..♖e7!**

Ulybin allowed his opponent to reestablish material equality, because he knew that he would have a decisive positional advantage in the pawn endgame, thanks to his unstoppable threat to create an outside passed pawn.

2 ♖×e7 ♔×e7 3 ♔×d5 g6! 4 c4 h5 5 gh gh 6 ♔e5 h4 7 ♔f4 f5 8 b4 ♔d6 9 ♔e3 a5! 10 a3 ab 11 ab h3! 12 ♔f2 ♔e5 13 ♔g3 ♔d4

Here we see why Black exchanged a pair of pawns with 9...a5! In this way, he wins the queenside pawns quicker, and can queen his b-pawn before White gets anything going on the kingside.

14 ♔×h3 ♔×c4 15 ♔g3 ♔×b4 16 ♔f4 ♔c4 17 ♔×f5 b5 18 f4 b4 19 ♔e6 b3 White resigned.

Tragicomedies

Nimzovitch - Tarrasch
San Sebastian 1911

1-121

W?

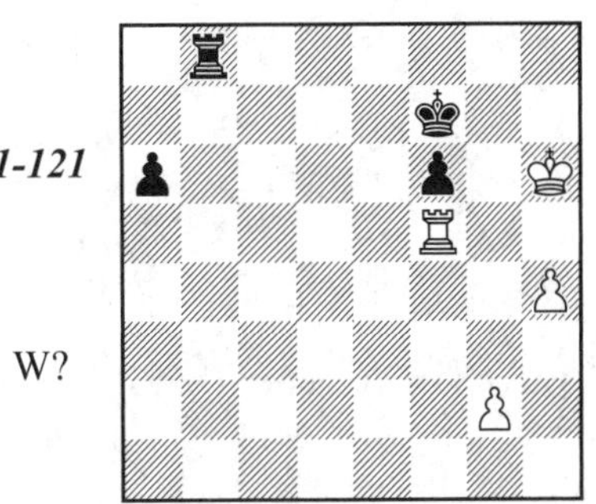

The actual move made, **1 ♔h5?**, lost: **1...♖b5! 2 ♔g4 ♖×f5 3 ♔×f5 a5 4 ♔e4**

The outside passed pawn draws the white king to the queenside - but Nimzovitch probably hoped that his pawns would be able to defend themselves, as in the variation 4...a4? 5 ♔d3 f5 6 g3! However, Tarrasch does not allow his opponent to connect his pawns.

4...f5+!

White resigned, since after 5 ♔d4 (5 ♔×f5 a4) 5...f4! 6 ♔c4 ♔g6, his pawns are lost.

White had a draw with 1 ♔h7! ♖b5 2 ♖×b5! (I suggest the reader establish for himself that White loses after 2 g4? ♖×f5 3 gf a5 4 h5 a4 5 h6 a3 6 ♔h8 a2 7 h7 ♔e7!) 2...ab 3 g4 b4 4 g5=.

Brüggemann - Darius
Botzov 1969

1-122

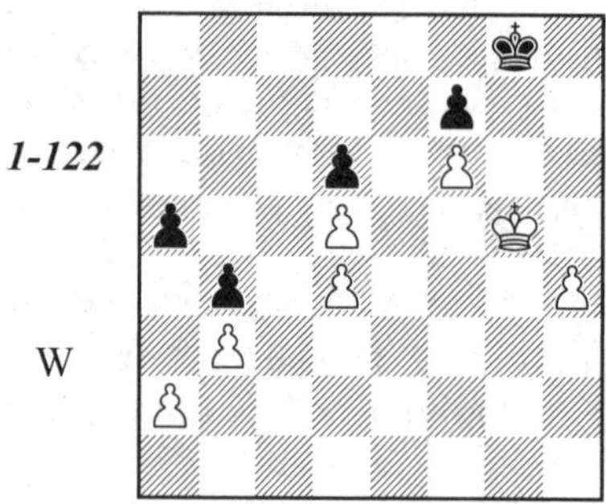

W

A draw was agreed here, but White can win.

1 ♔f5 ♔h7 2 ♔e4 ♔g6 3 ♔d3 ♔×f6

If Black doesn't take the pawn at once, White's king will capture Black's queenside, and still have enough time to get back to the kingside: 3...♔f5 4 ♔c4 ♔×f6 5 ♔b5 ♔g6 (or 5...♔f5 6 ♔×a5 ♔g4 7 ♔×b4 f5 8 a4 f4 9 a5, with a winning queen endgame) 6 ♔×a5 f5 7 ♔×b4 f4 (7...♔h5 8 a4 f4 9 a5+−) 8 ♔c3 ♔h5 9 ♔d3 ♔×h4 10 ♔e2 ♔g3 11 ♔f1+−.

4 ♔e4!

There isn't time to go after the queenside anymore; however, the situation on the kingside is now a simple win because of the outside passed pawn.

4...♔g6 5 ♔f4+− (after 5...♔h5, both 6 ♔g3 and 6 ♔f5 are good).

Exercises

1-123

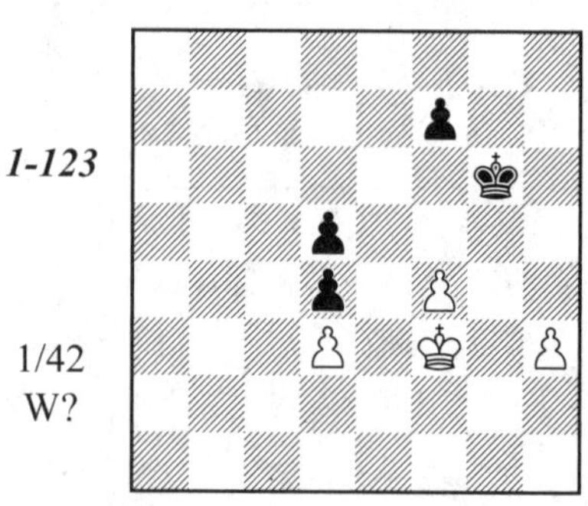

1/42
W?

Two Rook's Pawns with an Extra Pawn on the Opposite Wing

Positions in which two rook's pawns are facing each other, with one side having a distant passed pawn, are fairly common in practice; so it's useful to have a quick and accurate way of evaluating them. The plan to play for a win is obvious: the king will go after the rook's pawn. His opponent, meanwhile, must eliminate the pawn on the other wing, and then rush the king over to the corner where it can stop the rook's pawn. Under what circumstances can he succeed?

1-124

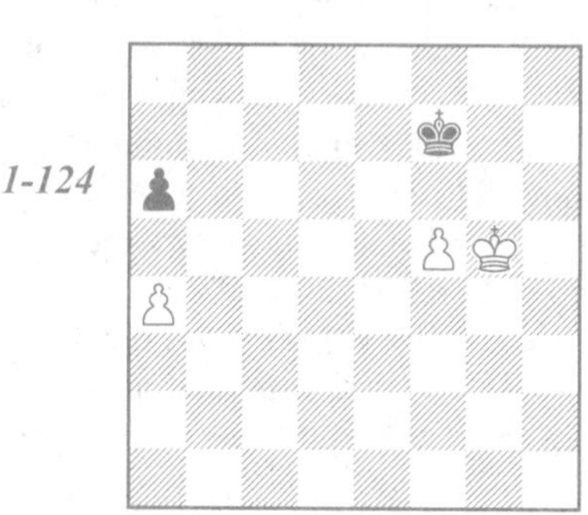

In the next diagram, White to move wins: **1 a5! ♔g7 2 ♔f4 ♔f6 3 ♔e4 ♔f7 4 ♔d5 ♔f6 6 ♔c6 ♔×f5 6 ♔b6 ♔e6 7 ♔×a6 ♔d7 8 ♔b7**

If it's Black to move, after **1...a5!** the position is drawn, as you may easily determine: Black's king has enough time to get to c8.

But let's say that we move the kings and the f-pawn one rank down, or one file to the left; then, once again, Black loses. But what if we also move the queenside pawns one rank down?

Of course, with the position standing in front of us, any question is easily answered. But in practice, such situations often occur at the end of long calculations, and extending such calculations a few moves further still could be most difficult. It would be good to have a definite evaluation of this position immediately, as soon as we lay eyes on it.

Bähr demonstrated such a means of quick appraisal in 1936. I did not find his rule very convenient for us; in addition, it wasn't designed to work when the king would be, not to one side, but ahead of the pawn. So therefore I offer a somewhat different method of quickly evaluating this sort of position.

1) The first rule is similar to Bähr's rule: ***If the rook's pawn of the stronger side has crossed the middle of the board, it's always a win.***

2) We shall designate a "normal" position, in which:

a) the rook's pawns, which block one another, are separated by the middle of the board; and

b) Black's king, aiming for the c8-square, can reach it without loss of time. This is because the passed pawn has either traversed the key diagonal h3-c8, or stands upon it.

The "normal" position is drawn.

3) For the kingside passed pawn, every square behind the h3-c8 diagonal is a reserve tempo for White. For example: the pawn at f4 means one reserve tempo; the pawn at e4 - two. And if the king is not beside the passed pawn, but in front of it, that's another reserve tempo.

And every square the queenside pawns are behind the "normal" position is a reserve tempo for the defending side. With pawns at a3/a4, Black has a reserve tempo in his favor; with pawns at a2/a3 - two.

White wins only if the relative number of tempi calculated by the means shown above is in his favor.

The formulation may seem a bit ungainly; but once memorized, it's quite easy to apply. For example:

In the following diagram, White of course is on move (if it were Black to move, the f-pawn would queen). White wins, because the count is 3:2 in his favor. Black has two tempi, because the queenside pawns are two squares behind the "normal" position; and White's f3-pawn being two squares behind the h3-c8 diagonal (the f5-square), and his king being in front of the pawn, gives him three tempi.

1-125

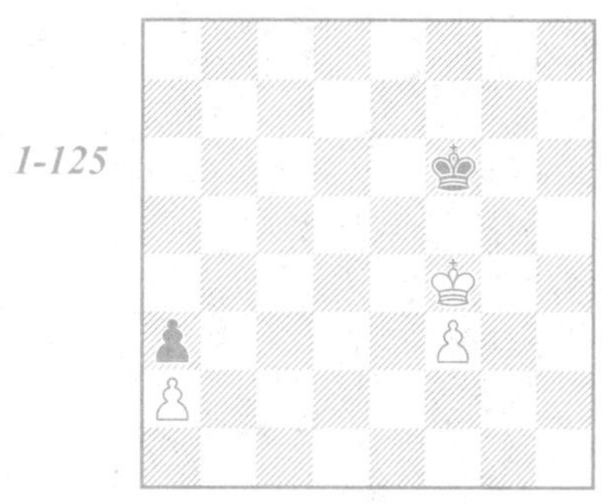

1 ♔e4! ♔e6 2 ♔d4(d3)+−

1 ♔e3? ♔e5(f5)= would be a terrible blunder, because then we would have a position where the tempi are 2:2 (White's king is no longer in front of the f-pawn, but next to it) - which makes it a draw.

One more useful addendum to the rule. Let's suppose that White's passed pawn is a rook's pawn, with the king in front of it, but the enemy king is boxing his opposite number in on the rook file. ***This situation is the same as the one in which the king is next to his pawn.***

1-126

B

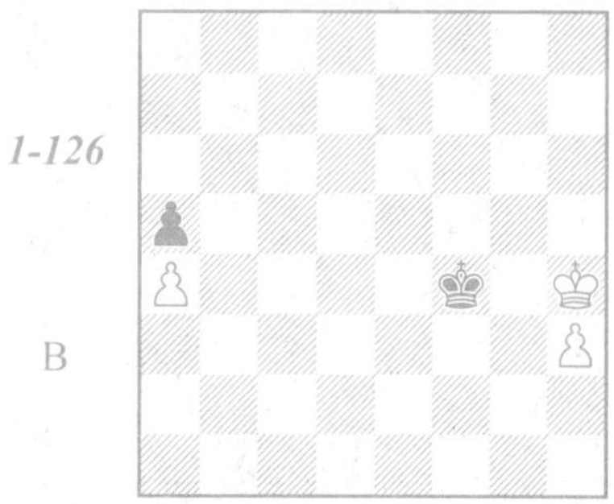

According to the rule formulated above, this is a draw. And in fact, after **1...♔f5 2 ♔h5** (2 ♔g3 ♔g5 is the "normal" position), Black does not play 2...♔f6? 3 ♔g4, when White has a reserve tempo, because his king is in front of his pawn, but **2...♔f4! 3 h4** (3 ♔g6 ♔g3) **3...♔f5 4 ♔h6 ♔f6 5 ♔h7 ♔f7(f5) 6 h5 ♔f6!**, etc.

It must be noted here that this last rule is inoperative with the pawn on its starting square.

In the following diagram, Black has one tempo (since the queenside pawns are one rank back), but if it's his move, he still loses. The problem lies in the fact that the standard 1...♔f3 is impossible, in view of 2 ♔g5 ♔g2 3 h4; while after 1...♔f5 2 ♔g3 ♔g5, White has not one, but two tempi (the pawn is below the c8-h3 diagonal, and the king is in front of the pawn).

1-127

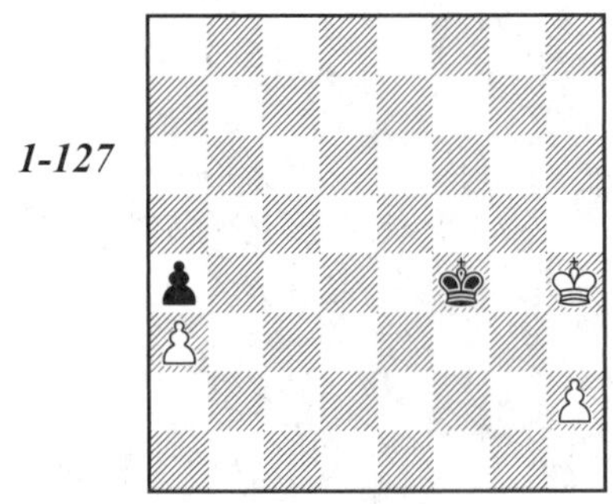

With White to move, the position is drawn, even if the queenside pawns are placed as in the "normal" position, because the h-pawn will have to go to h3: 1 ♔h5 ♔f5 2 h3 (2 ♔h6 ♔g4=) 2...♔f4!=.

Let's look at some more complex examples, in which understanding my proposed rule considerably simplifies the calculation of variations.

Privorotsky - Petersons
Riga 1967

1-128

W?

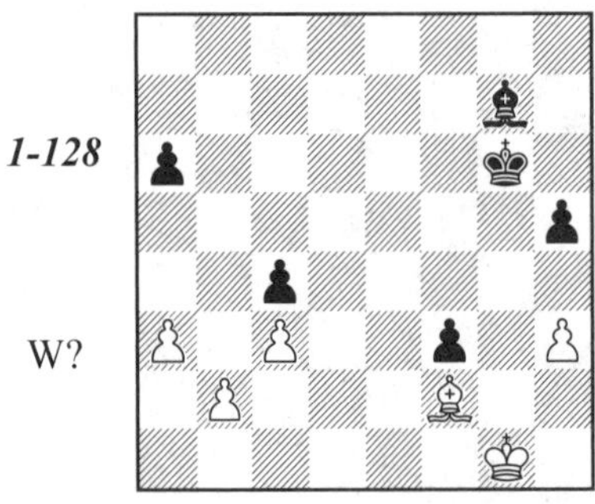

Black has an obvious positional plus. His plan is clear: ...♔g6-f5-e4, and then attack the queenside pawns with either bishop or king. This plan can be forestalled by offering a trade of bishops, but this requires accurate calculation.

1 ♗d4! ♗×d4+ (1...♗h6 2 ♔f2 ♗c1 3 ♔×f3 ♗×b2 4 a4=) **2 cd ♔f5 3 ♔f2 ♔e4 4 d5!** (otherwise 4...♔×d4 5 ♔×f3 ♔d3) **4...♔×d5 5 ♔×f3 ♔d4 6 ♔e2 c3**

On 6...h4 7 ♔d2 a5, White plays either 8 ♔c2 or 8 a4 .

7 bc+ ♔×c3 8 h4!!

Right! Otherwise, Black would play 8...h4! himself, and after picking up the a3-pawn, he wins, because his pawn on the opposite wing has crossed the center of the board. After the text, we have the "normal" - that is, the drawn - position.

8...♔b3 9 ♔d3 ♔×a3 10 ♔c3 a5 11 ♔c4! ♔a4 12 ♔c3 ♔b5 13 ♔b3 Drawn.

The calculation of this endgame resulted in positions we have examined in one form or another. If White had not been able to appraise them "mechanically," using the rule shown above, but had had to extend the variations to the end, he would have had to take each of his calculations a dozen moves further - certainly not a simple process.

The following endgame created even more complex problems for both sides.

Matanovic - Botvinnik
Belgrade 1969

1-129

W?

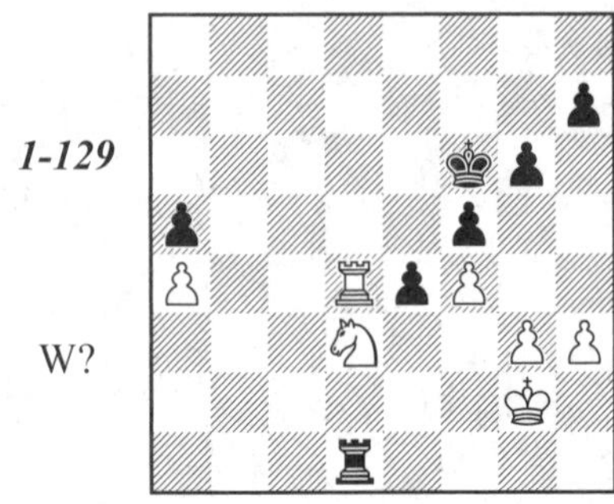

In his notes, Botvinnik analyzed two approaches for White: 1 ♖d5, and 1 ♖d6+ ♔e7 2 ♖a6. In fact, he had a third try: 1 ♔f2! For example, 1...ed 2 ♔e3 ♖a1 (2...♖g1 3 ♔f2) 3 ♖×d3 ♖×a4 4 ♖d6+ followed by 5 ♖a6, when White must draw.

But suppose we forget about this possibility, and try to choose the more exact of the two possible rook moves.

First, we must try some short variations, in order to establish the differences between them, to compare their advantages and their shortcomings.

On 1 ♖d6+ ♔e7 2 ♖a6, a clear draw follows 2...♖×d3 3 ♖×a5, or 2...♖d2+ 3 ♘f2 e3 4 ♔f3! (4 ♖×a5 ♖×f2+ 5 ♔g1 is also possible) 4...e2 (4...ef 5 ♔g2) 5 ♖a7+. However, the pawn capture on d3 is unpleasant: 2...ed! 3 ♖×a5 ♔d6. Now, 4 ♔f2? is bad, in view of 4...♖g1!; so White must continue 4 ♖a8, allowing the black king to get closer to his passed d-pawn. Is this rook ending lost or drawn? It's hard to say - which means that it's time to break off the calculation here, and look at the alternative.

1 ♖d5! ♖d2+!

Now this rook endgame, after 1...ed 2 ♖×a5, is harmless for White: 2...d2 3 ♖d5, or 2...♔e6 3 ♖e5+ ♔d6 4 ♔f2 d2 (4...♖g1 5 ♖e3) 5 ♔e2 ♖g1 6 ♔×d2 ♖×g3 7 ♖e3. And, thanks to the pin of the knight on the d-file, we have an in-between rook check, securing Black a transition into a favorable pawn endgame.

2 ♔f1 ♖×d3 3 ♖×d3

A forced exchange - otherwise, the g3-pawn is lost.

3...ed 4 ♔f2

1-130

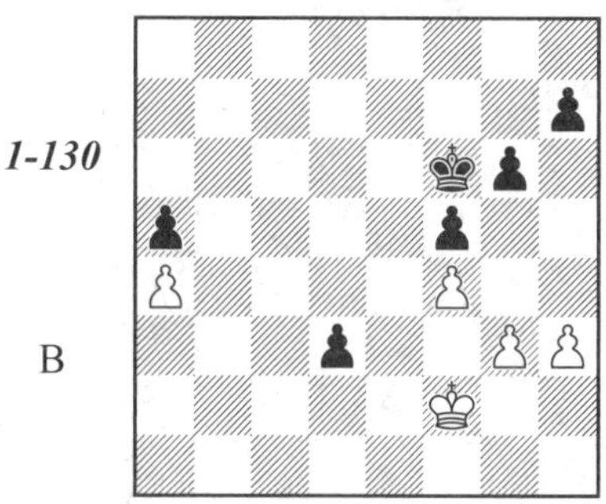

B

Unfortunately, here too it's not clear whether White can be saved. Nonetheless, pawn endings are generally of a more forcing nature than rook endings are. Here, as a rule, it's possible to obtain an accurate appraisal of the position, if you can take a variation to its conclusion. So it makes sense to concentrate our efforts on the calculation of this pawn endgame.

Black has two plans of action: bringing the king to the center, in the hope of putting his opponent in zugzwang; and the kingside break with g6-g5.

We can easily establish that the first plan is harmless: 4...♔e6 5 ♔e3 ♔d6 (5...♔d5 6 ♔×d3 h6 7 g4) 6 ♔×d3 ♔d5 7 g4 h6 (on 7...fg 8 hg h5, there is 9 f5!, although 9 gh gh 10 ♔e3 also does not lose) 8 g5! hg (8...h5 9 h4) 9 fg f4 10 h4 ♔e5 11 ♔e2, with equality.

4...g5! 4 fg+!

5 ♔e3? would be a mistake: 5...gf+ 6 gf ♔e6 7 h4 ♔d5 8 ♔×d3 h5⊙.

5...♔×g5 6 ♔e3 h5 7 ♔×d3 h4

We have already seen the situation occurring after 7...f4 8 gf+ ♔×f4 in the previous example. White's king can't attack the a-pawn - but this isn't necessary: it's enough to squeeze the enemy king onto the h-file. For example: 9 h4 (or 9 ♔d4) 9...♔g4 10 ♔e4 ♔×h4 11 ♔f4, with a draw.

8 gh+ ♔×h4

1-131

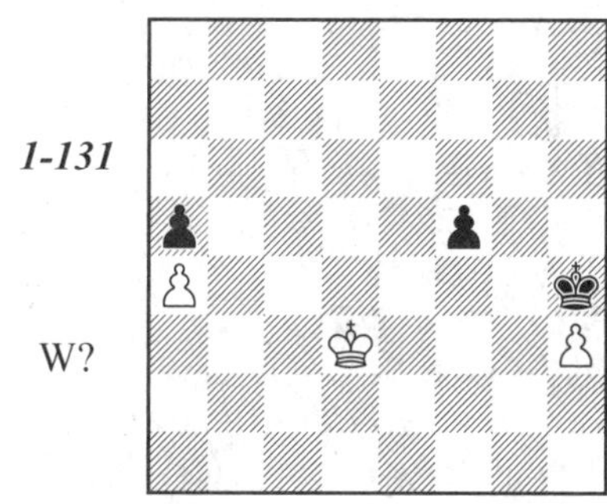

W?

Which of the two natural moves - 9 ♔e3 or 9 ♔e2 - should White make? Let's go back to the rule laid down above. After Black wins the h-pawn, our "arithmetic" shows that he will have one tempo, since the f-pawn is one square above the crucial c1-h6 diagonal. White can only save himself, if he can force that pawn forward to f4.

So clearly, 9 ♔e2? loses: 9...♔g3⊙ 10 h4 (10 ♔f1 ♔×h3 11 ♔f2 ♔g4, and Black now has two tempi) 10...♔×h4 11 ♔f3 ♔g5 12 ♔g3 ♔f6 13 ♔f4 ♔e6 14 ♔f3 ♔d5, etc.

9 ♔e3! ♔g3 10 ♔e2

Now it is Black who is in zugzwang: he must advance his pawn to f4, since 10...♔g2 11 ♔e3 ♔g3 12 ♔e2 is a useless "pendulum."

10...f4 11 ♔f1 ♔×h3 12 ♔f2 ♔g4 13 ♔g2

And we have the "normal" drawn position.

Matanovic was unable to calculate the pawn ending accurately, and so preferred to keep rooks on. Unfortunately for him, the rook ending turned out to be lost.

Let's return to Diagram 1-129.

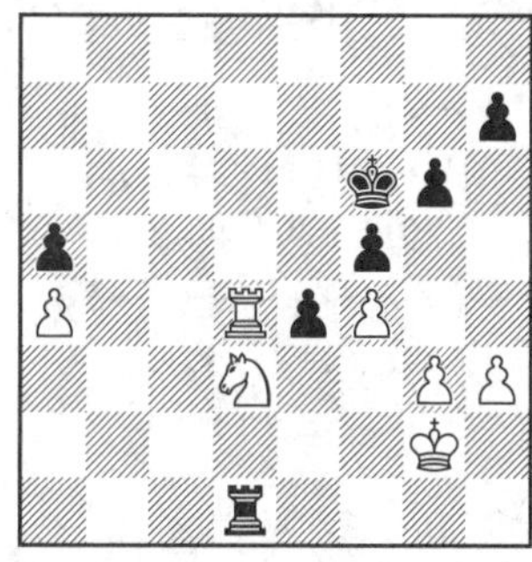

1 ♖d6+? ♔e7 2 ♖a6 ed! 3 ♖×a5 ♔d6 4 ♖a8 ♔c7 (Black repeats moves to gain thinking time) **5 ♖a5 ♔c6 6 ♖a8 ♔c5 7 ♔f2 ♖a1! 8 ♖d8** (8 ♔e3!? ♖g1 9 g4) **8...♔c4 9 ♔e3 ♖e1+** (9...♖g1? 10 ♖d4+) **10 ♔f2 ♖e2+ 11 ♔f3 ♖e6! 12 a5 ♔c3 13 ♖c8+ ♔d2! 14 h4**

According to Botvinnik's analysis, 14 ♖c7 wouldn't have saved White either: 14...h5 (14...♖e1? 15 a6 ♖a1 16 a7) 15 ♔f2 ♔d1 16 ♔f3 d2 17 ♔f2 ♖e2+! 18 ♔f1 ♖e3 19 a6 (19 ♔f2 ♖a3, followed by ...♖a1-c1) 19...♖×g3 20 a7 ♖a3 21 ♔f2 h4 22 ♔f1 ♖a4 23 ♔g2 ♔e2 24 ♖e7+ ♔d3 25 ♖d7+ ♔e3.

14...♖e1! 15 a6 ♖a1

Now on 16 ♖c6 ♔e1 is decisive: 17 ♖e6+ ♔f1 18 ♖d6 (18 ♔e3 ♖e1+) 18...d2 19 ♖×d2 ♖a3+, and White gets mated! The same thing happens after 16 ♖a8 ♔e1 17 a7 d2 18 ♖e8+ ♔f1 19 ♖d8 ♖a3+.

16 ♖c7 ♔e1 17 ♔g2 ♖×a6 18 ♖e7+ ♔d1 19 ♖×h7 ♖a2+ 20 ♔f1 d2 21 ♖c7 ♖a1 22 ♔f2 ♖c1 White resigned.

Tragicomedies

Colle - Grünfeld
Karlsbad 1929

1-132

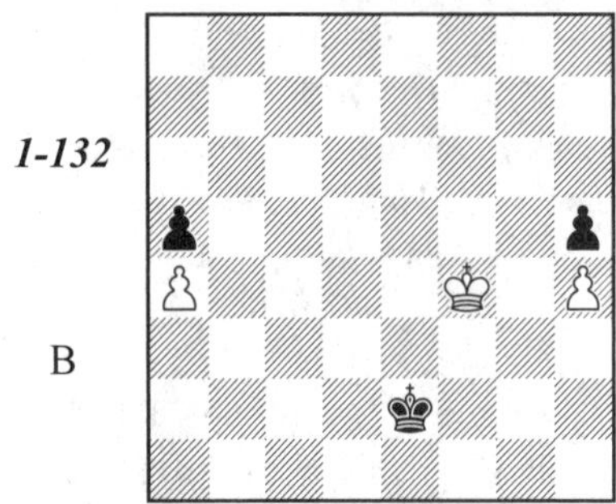

B

Grünfeld resigned, not realizing that, by squeezing the white king onto the h-file, he had an easy draw.

1...♔d3! 2 ♔g5 ♔e4 3 ♔×h5 ♔f5=, etc.

Winants - L. Hansen
Wijk aan Zee 1994

1-133

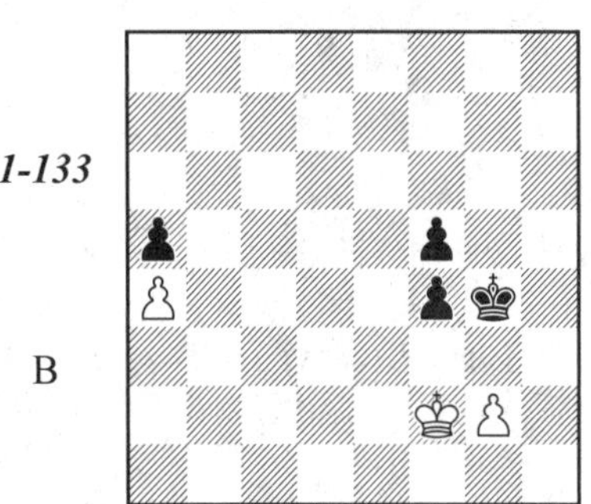

B

The position is drawn. Black tries one last chance:

1...f3!? 2 gf+??

The correct 2 g3! f4 3 gf ♔×f4 leads to the "normal" - i.e., drawn - position.

1...♔h3!

White resigned, since after 3 ♔e3 ♔g3 4 f4 ♔g4 5 ♔e2 ♔×f4 6 ♔f2, Black has two reserve tempi (even one would have been enough), since the pawn is above the c1-h6 diagonal and the king is in front of the pawn.

Exercises

1-134

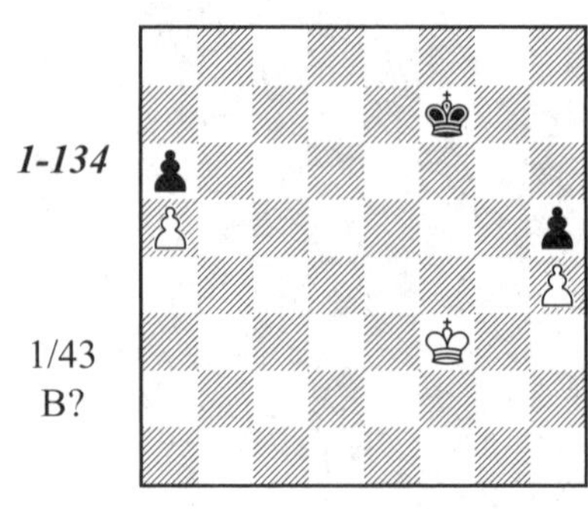

1/43
B?

1-135

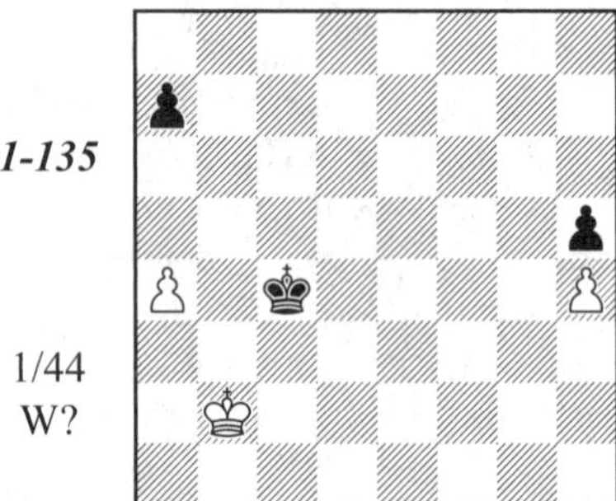

1/44
W?

1-136

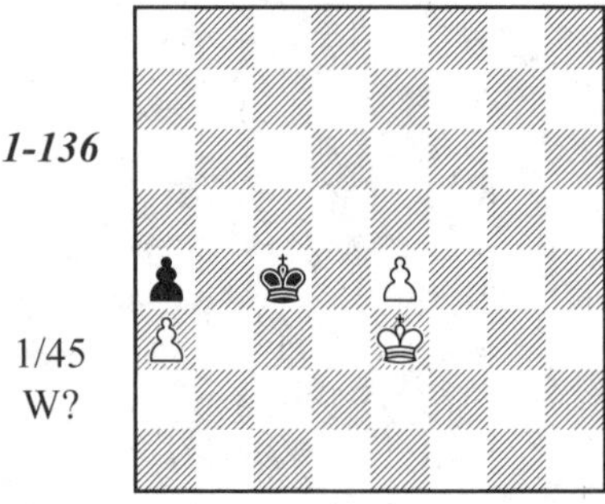

1/45
W?

The Protected Passed Pawn

The protected passed pawn, like the outside passed pawn, is usually a most definite positional advantage. The enemy king cannot leave its square, and cannot capture it, whereas our king has full freedom of movement.

Two Pawns to One

These positions are generally won.

1-137

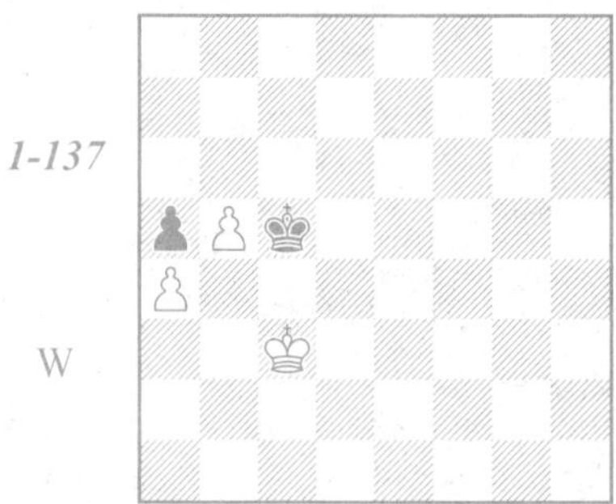

W

1 ♔d3 ♔d5 2 ♔e3 ♔e5 3 ♔f3 ♔d5 4 ♔f4 ♔d6 5 ♔e4 ♔e6 6 ♔d4 ♔d6 7 ♔c4 (Black must give up the opposition) **7...♔c7 8 ♔d5!**

8 ♔c5?! is inaccurate: 8...♔b7, and White cannot continue 9 b6? because of 9...♔a6! 10 ♔c6 stalemate.

8...♔b6 9 ♔d6 ♔b7 10 ♔c5⊙ ♔c7 11 b6+ ♔b7 12 ♔b5+−.

Now let's look at the two most important drawn positions. The first is an elementary one, but it comes up rather regularly. The second is less likely to occur, but it's very instructive.

1-138

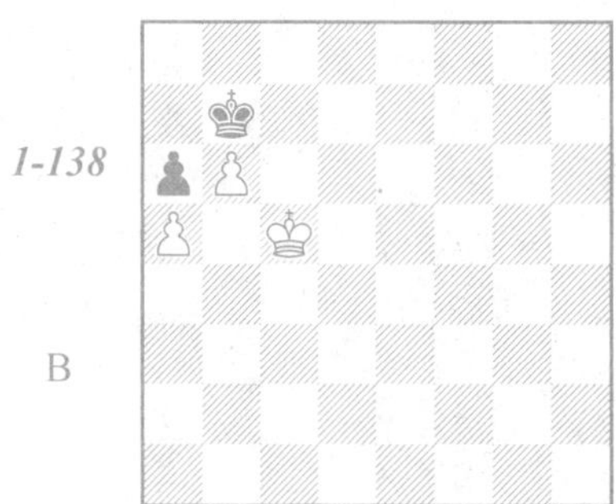

B

Black plays **1...♔b8 2 ♔c6 ♔c8=.**

Move the whole position one file to the right, and White wins easily by sacrificing the pawn and then winning the enemy's last pawn.

F. Dedrle, 1921

1-139

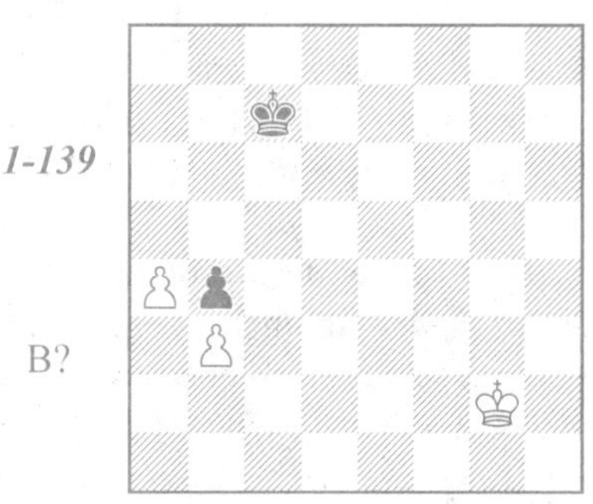

B?

The key squares are c4, d4, and e4. Black can protect them, if he can control the opposition when the enemy king approaches.

Let's determine the corresponding squares. With White's king on d3, f3 or h3, Black's king must occupy d5; the e3- and g3-squares correspond to e5. When the king advances farther, Black must keep the lateral opposition, maneuvering along the d- and e-files.

When White's king is on the second rank, Black's king must stay next to the d5- and e5-squares - specifically, on d6 or e6. So the first move - as well as all the play that follows - now becomes clear:

1...♔d6! (but not 1...♔c6? 2 ♔g3! ♔d6 3 ♔f4! ♔d5 4 ♔f5+−; or 2...♔c5 3 ♔g4! ♔d4 4 ♔f4+−) **2 ♔h3** (2 ♔f2 ♔e6! 3 ♔e2 ♔d6!) **2...♔d5! 3 ♔g3 ♔e5! 4 ♔h4 ♔d4! 5 ♔h5 ♔d5! 6 ♔g6 ♔e6!**, etc.

Multi-Pawn Endgames

The next example features a typical plan for exploiting the advantage.

I. Bottlik, 1952

1-140

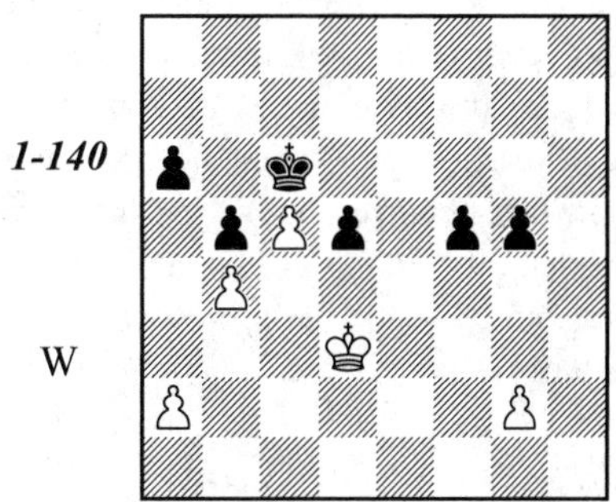

W

Black may have an extra pawn, but his position is difficult. How does he meet the threatened invasion of the white king?

1 ♔d4 f4 2 ♔e5 a5! 3 a3 a4

Black would prefer to exchange a pair of pawns; but after 3...ab 4 ab, he's in zugzwang.

4 ♔f5 d4! 5 ♔e4 d3 6 ♔×d3 ♔d5 7 g3!

A necessary undermining of the enemy kingside pawns (undermining, by the way, is the theme of our next section). It's only a draw after 7 ♔e2? g4 8 ♔d3 ♔e5 9 c6 ♔d6 10 ♔e4 ♔×c6 11 ♔×f4 ♔d5 12 ♔×g4 ♔c4, because both pawns will queen.

7...fg

No better is 7...♔e5 8 gf+ gf 9 ♔e2 ♔d5 10 ♔f3 ♔e5 11 c6 ♔d6 12 ♔×f4 ♔×c6 13 ♔e5+−. This would be a draw if Black had exchanged pawns on his 3rd move; but if he had, unfortunately, he wouldn't have gotten the draw then either.

8 ♔e2 (or 8 ♔e3 g4 9 ♔e2) **8...♔e5** (8...g4 9 ♔f1 changes nothing) **9 ♔f3 ♔e6 10 ♔×g3 ♔f5**

1-141

W

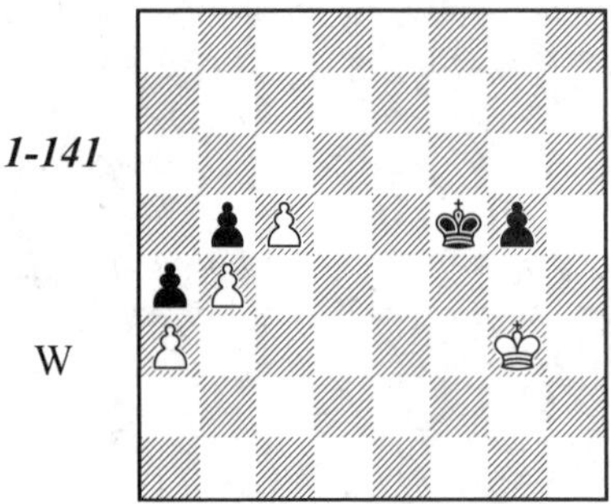

Here's a typical position with a protected passed pawn versus an outside passed pawn. The mined squares are g4 and f6. Most often (as here), the stronger side is unable to place his opponent in zugzwang. The only thing to be done then is to advance one's own passed pawn, and exchange it for the other side's passed pawn. Sometimes this wins; sometimes not. In the similar situation that occurred as one of the variations of the game Averbakh - Bebchuk (Diagram 1-112), we were able to lose a move to Black, making use of our reserve tempo (in that case, h4-h5).

11 ♔f3 ♔e5 12 ♔g4 ♔f6 13 c6 ♔e6 14 ♔×g5 ♔d6 15 ♔f5 ♔×c6 16 ♔e6+−.

Tragicomedies

Here we shall include examples of overestimating the power of the protected passed pawn.

Shirov - Timman
Wijk aan Zee 1996

1-142

W

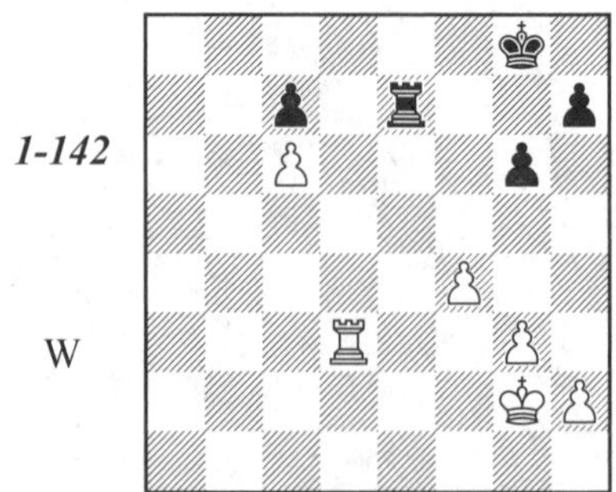

1 ♔f3! looks good. Black responds 1...♖e6, and if White defends the pawn by 2 ♖c3, then Black will have decent drawing chances, in view of the passive position of White's rook. White could trade off the rooks by playing 2 ♖d8+ ♔f7 3 ♖d7+ ♖e7 4 ♖×e7+ ♔×e7 - this leads by force to a queen endgame, where White has an extra g-pawn: 5 ♔g4 ♔d6 6 ♔g5 ♔×c6 7 ♔h6 ♔b7 8 ♔×h7 c5 9 ♔×g6 c4 10 f5 c3 11 f6 c2 12 f7 c1♕ 13 f8♕ ♕c2+ 14 ♕f5 ♕×h2. Objectively speaking, this position is won (see Chapter 12); however, converting this advantage is not easy, and would take another several dozen moves.

None of this appealed to Shirov. The grandmaster discovered what seemed to him like a more forcing means to the desired end.

1 g4? ♖e6 2 ♖d8+?! (2 ♖c3) **2...♔f7 3 ♖d7+ ♖e7 4 ♖×e7+ ♔×e7 5 g5!**

1-143

B

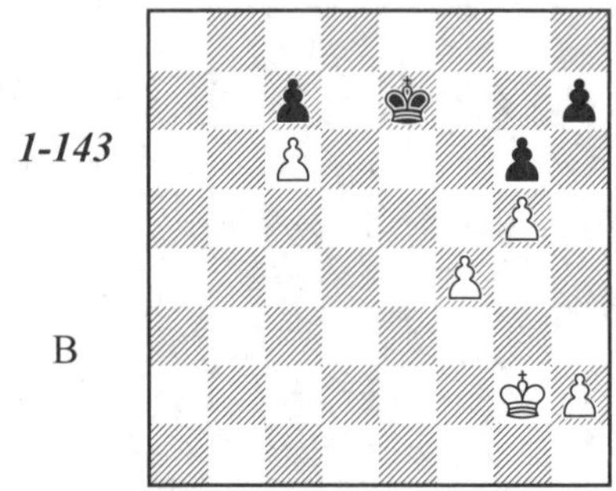

And in this position, Timman resigned. Both sides believed that 5...♔d6 was refuted by the pawn breakthrough 6 h4 ♔×c6 7 f5 gf 8 h5 ♔d7 9 g6 hg 10 h6+−.

But Black does not have to take on f5! He could draw with the continuation 7...♔d7 8 f6 ♔e6(e8). This is the same position as in our previous example (a protected passed pawn versus an outside passed pawn). The mined squares are c6 and d8. With kings at d5 and d7, Black plays 1...♔e8!, after which neither 2 ♔e6 ♔f8 3 f7 c5, nor 2 ♔c6 ♔d8⊙ 3 f7 ♔e7 4 ♔×c7 ♔×f7 will do better than draw If Black wants, he can even leave his pawn at c6, instead of c7.

Aronin - Smyslov
USSR ch, Moscow 1951

1-144

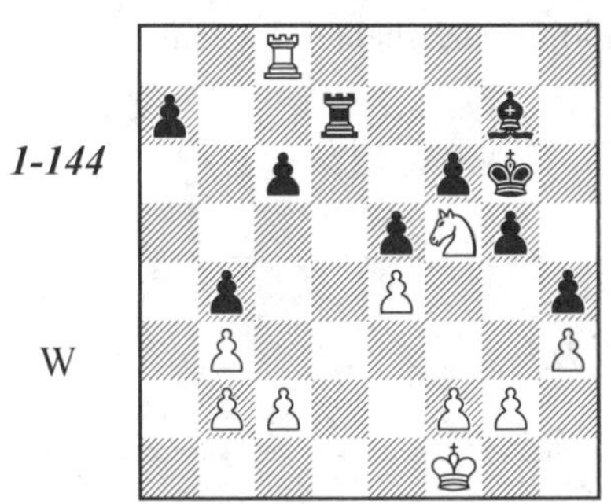

W

Black's position is quite hopeless. The simplest solution is 1 ♖×c6, or 1 ♖g8 ♔h7 2 ♖e8! △ 3 ♖e7. However, the game was adjourned here, and Aronin chose, after home analysis, to cash in his advantage by entering a pawn ending.

1 ♖g8 ♔h7 2 ♖×g7+?? ♖×g7 3 ♘×g7 ♔×g7 4 g4

Before marching his king over to the queenside, White wishes to close up the kingside, to prevent Black's potential counterplay by ...f6-f5 and ...g5-g4. Aronin examined the lengthy variation 4...♔f7 5 ♔e2 ♔e6 6 ♔d3 ♔d6 7 ♔c4 a5 (7...c5 8 ♔b5) 8 f3 ♔d7 9 ♔c5 ♔c7 10 c3 bc 11 bc ♔b7 12 ♔d6 ♔b6 13 c4 ♔b7 14 c5+−.

He didn't think the exchange on g3 was playable, since White then gets the possibility of creating an outside passed h-pawn. However, Smyslov found an elegant defense: he offered his opponent, not an outside passed pawn, but a **protected** passed pawn!

4...hg! 5 fg g4!! 6 h4 c5 7 ♔e2 ♔h7 8 ♔d3 ♔h6

1-145

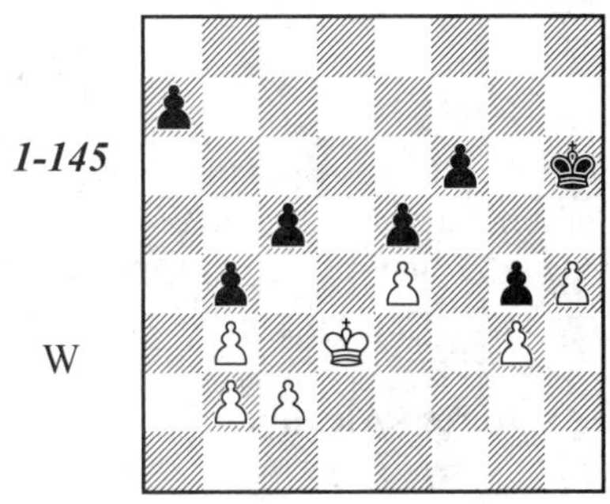

W

It turns out that the king can go no further: 9 ♔c4? f5! 10 ef (10 ♔d3 f4 11 gf ef 12 ♔e2 ♔h5 13 e5 ♔g6, and 14...♔f5−+) 10...e4⊙−+.

9 c3 a5 10 cb ab! Draw.

Exercises

1-146

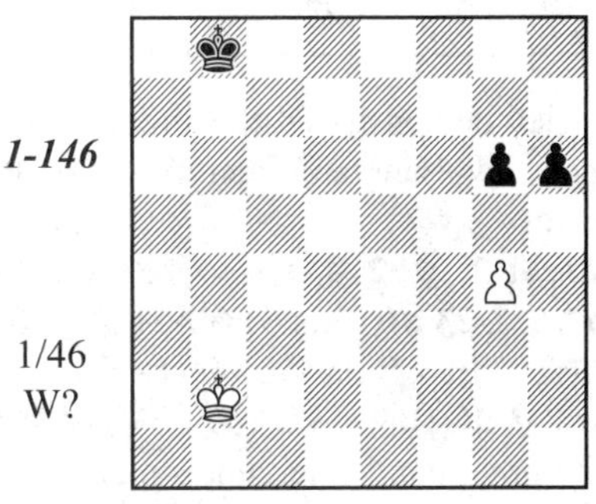

1/46
W?

1-147

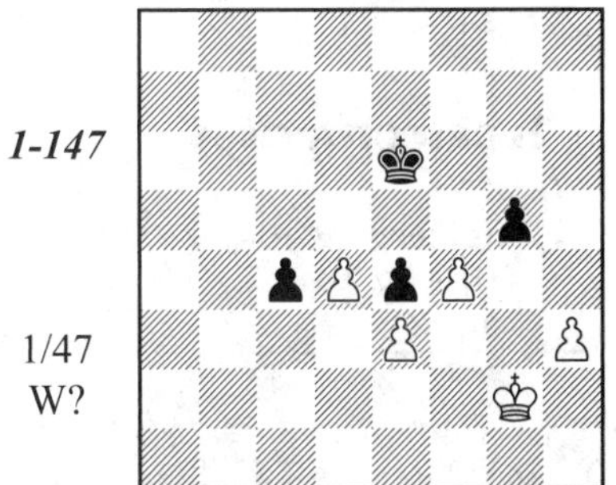

1/47
W?

Undermining

Sometimes the pawns are too strong to be successfully attacked by the king. In such cases, undermining can be used successfully - the exchange of a pair or two of pawns, with the aim of weakening the pawn chain.

Keres - Alekhine
Dresden 1936

1-148

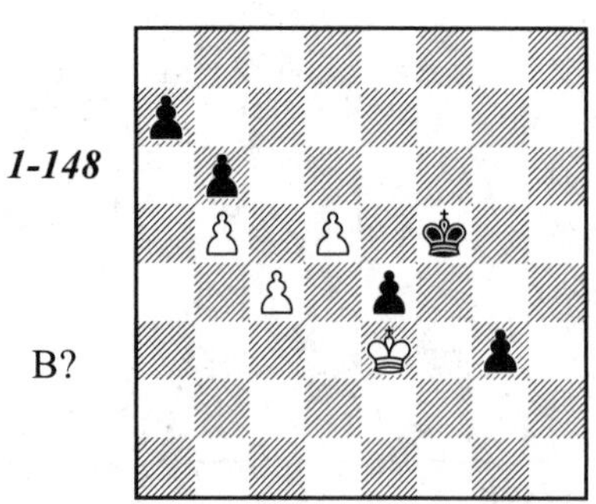

B?

Grigoriev demonstrated the simplest winning method, involving an undermining on the queenside.

1...♔e5! 2 ♔e2 ♔d6 3 ♔e3 ♔c7 4 ♔e2 ♔b7 5 ♔e3 a6 (5...a5) **6 ba+ ♔×a6 7 ♔e2 ♔b7** (7...b5?? 8 d6 ♔b6 9 cb=) **8 ♔e3 ♔c7 9 ♔e2 ♔d6 10 ♔e3 b5 11 cb ♔×d5−+**

On the other hand, Alekhine's plan of going into a queen endgame was also quite strong.

1...♔g4!? 2 d6 g2 3 ♔f2 ♔h3 4 d7 e3+! 5 ♔f3 g1♕ 6 d8♕ ♕f2+ 7 ♔e4 e2 8 ♕d7+ ♔g2 9 ♕g4+ ♔f1 White resigned.

Tragicomedies

Golberg - Zhuk
USSR 1934

1-149

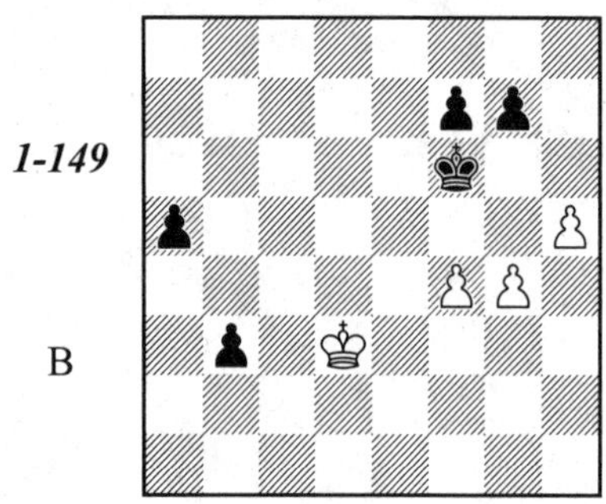

B

1...a4 (1...g6?? 2 h6 g5 3 f5 wins; 1...g5? 2 f5=) **2 g5+ ♔f5??**

The only winning plan was undermining with ...f7-f6. But first, Black had to bring his king to h7. As Grigoriev pointed out, the right way was 2...♔e7! 3 ♔c3 ♔f8 4 ♔b2 ♔g8 5 ♔a3 ♔h7 6 ♔b2 f6! 7 ♔a3 fg 8 fg ♔g8 9 ♔b2 ♔f7 10 ♔a3 ♔e6 11 ♔b2 ♔f5.

3 ♔c3 ♔e6?

Having let the win slip, Black now lets slip the draw, which he could have had by playing 3...f6! 4 g6 ♔e6.

4 h6 gh 5 gh ♔f6 6 f5⊙

Black resigned. We have already seen the final position in the chapter devoted to the rule of the square.

Sulipa - Gritsak
Lvov 1995

1-150

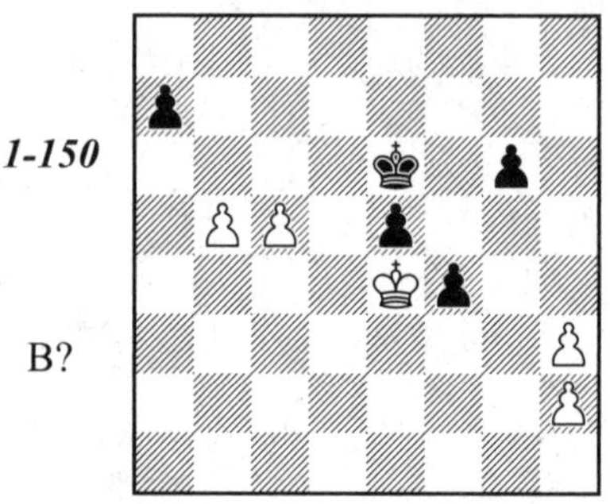

B?

1...g5??

Far from improving Black's position, this move actually degrades it significantly, by giving his opponent the possibility of exchanging a pair of kingside pawns, and creating a passed h-pawn.

White had no answer to the undermining plan with: 1...♔d7! 2 ♔f3 ♔c7 (2...♔e7 is also good: 3 ♔e4 ♔e6⊙ 4 ♔f3 ♔d5 5 c6 ♔d6 6 ♔e4 a6−+, or 4 h4 ♔d7! 5 ♔f3 ♔e7 6 ♔e4 ♔e6, triangulating again and again with the king, until the opponent runs out of pawn moves) 3 h4 ♔c8 (not 3...♔b7 4 ♔e4 a6? at once, in view of 5 ba+ ♔×a6 6 c6! ♔b6 7 ♔×e5 f3 8 ♔d6 f2 9 c7=) 4 ♔e4 ♔b7⊙ 5 h3 ♔c8 6 ♔f3 ♔c7 7 ♔e4 ♔b7⊙ 8 ♔f3 a6!−+

2 ♔f3??

The wrong order of moves. After 2 h4! gh 3 ♔f3 ♔d5 4 c6 ♔d6 5 ♔g4 a6 6 ba ♔×c6 7 ♔×h4 ♔b6 8 ♔g4 ♔×a6 9 h4, it's now White who wins.

2...♔d5 3 c6 ♔d6??

3...e4+! was necessary: 4 ♔g4 ♔d6−+.

4 ♔e4??

For the fourth time, the appraisal of the position is reversed. White wins with 4 h4! gh 5 ♔g4. **4...a6 5 ba ♔×c6 6 ♔f3 ♔b6 7 h4** (too late!) **7...gh 8 ♔g4 ♔×a6 9 ♔×h4 ♔b6 10 ♔g4 ♔c6 11 h4 ♔d6** White resigned.

Two Connected Passed Pawns

B. Horwitz, J. Kling, 1851

1-151

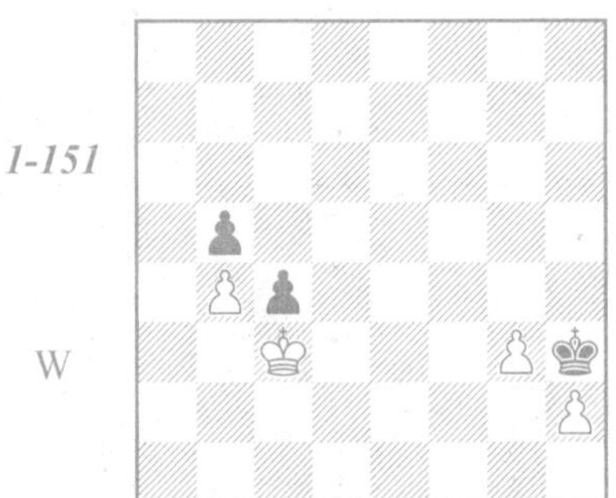

W

Here we have a typical situation with two connected passed pawns. The draw would appear to be inescapable, since the white king is tied to the square of the protected passed pawn at c4. But in fact, in such cases White can sometimes leave the square to help his pawns queen or checkmate his opponent.

White's plan usually consists of the following elements:

The farthest possible advance of the pawns;

The optimum placement of the pawns - "ready to roll";

Choosing the best time for the king's decisive advance.

Let's watch this plan in action. In the first stage the king, without leaving the square of the c4-pawn (which ends at f4), aids in the advance of its pawns.

1 ♔d4 ♔g4 2 h4 ♔h5 3 ♔e3 ♔g4 4 ♔e4 ♔h5 5 ♔f4 ♔h6 6 g4 ♔g6 7 h5+ ♔h6 8 ♔f3 ♔g5 9 ♔e4 ♔h6 10 ♔f4

Triangulation is White's most important weapon in this ending.

10...♔h7 11 g5 ♔g7 12 g6!

The ideal pawn array! The erroneous 12 h6+? would throw away the win.

12...♔f6 13 ♔e4 ♔g7 14 ♔f3 ♔f6 15 ♔f4 ♔g7

Now that White has strengthened his position to its utmost, it's time for the decisive advance!

16 ♔g5! c3 17 h6+ ♔g8 18 ♔f6 c2 19 h7+ ♔h8 20 g7+ (or 20 ♔f7 c1♕ 21 g7+) **20...♔×h7 21 ♔f7 c1♕ 22 g8♕+ ♔h6 23 ♕g6#.**

Tragicomedies

Potter - Zukertort
London m (5) 1875

1-152

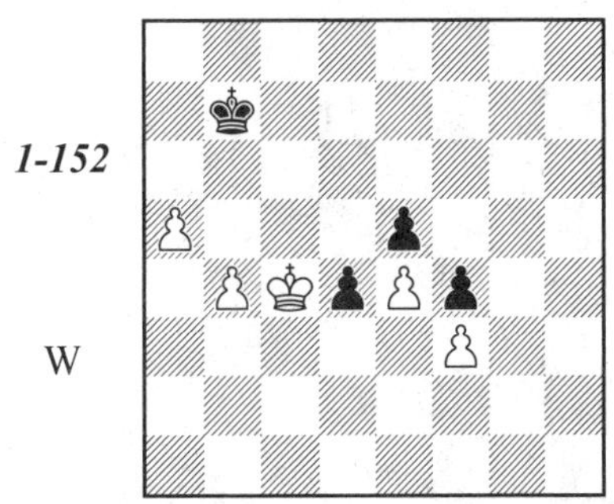

W

The position is in fact the same as in our preceding example, which was published a quarter of a century before this game. White, unacquainted with endgame theory, agreed to a draw here.

The win is elementary:

1 b5 ♔a7 2 b6+ ♔a6 3 ♔b4 ♔b7 4 ♔b5! d3 5 a6+ ♔b8 6 ♔c6 d2 7 a7+ ♔a8 8 b7+ ♔×a7 9 ♔c7 d1♕ 10 b8♕+ ♔a6 11 ♕b6#.

A century later, chessplayers, alas, continue to make the very same mistakes.

Bouaziz - Pomar
Siegen ol 1970

1-153

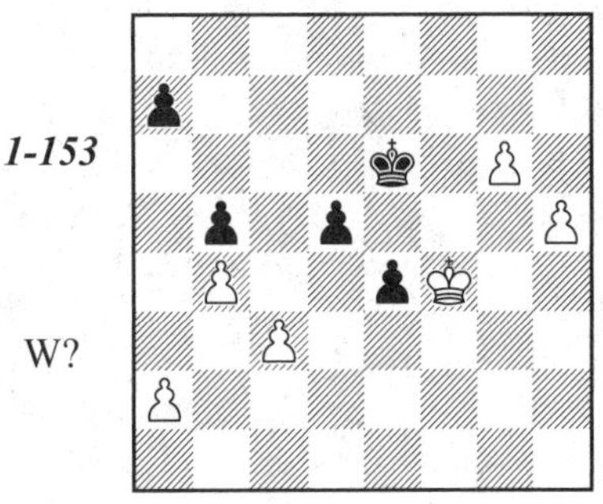

W?

The proper array of the pawns would be g6/ h7. So the win is: 1 h6! ♔f6 2 h7 ♔g7 3 ♔g4 (the immediate 3 ♔f5 e3 4 ♔e6 e2 5 h8♕+ ♔×h8 6 ♔f7 was also possible) 3...♔h8 4 ♔f5 e3 5 ♔f6 e2 6 g7+ ♔×h7 7 ♔f7.

White chose **1 g7?? ♔f7 2 h6 ♔g8**. Drawn, because 3 ♔f5(e5) is met by 3...♔f7!.

Exercises

1-154

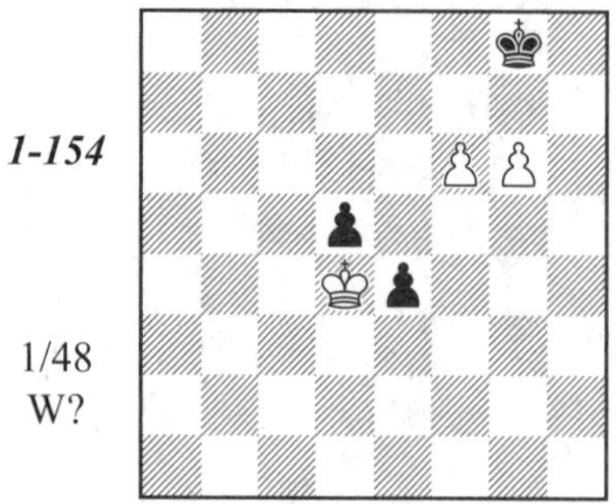

1/48
W?

1-155

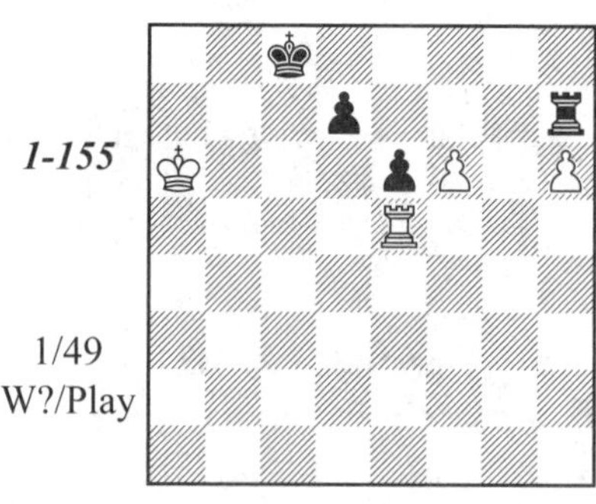

1/49
W?/Play

1-156

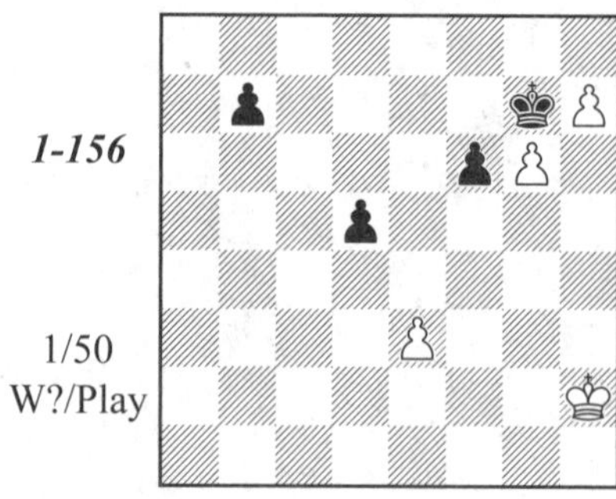

1/50
W?/Play

Stalemate

The Stalemate Refuge

When there are only a very few pieces left on the board, stalemate becomes one of the most important defensive resources - remember the "king and pawn vs. king" ending, if nothing else.

Out of the many possible stalemate situations, it's worth noting the following:

1-157

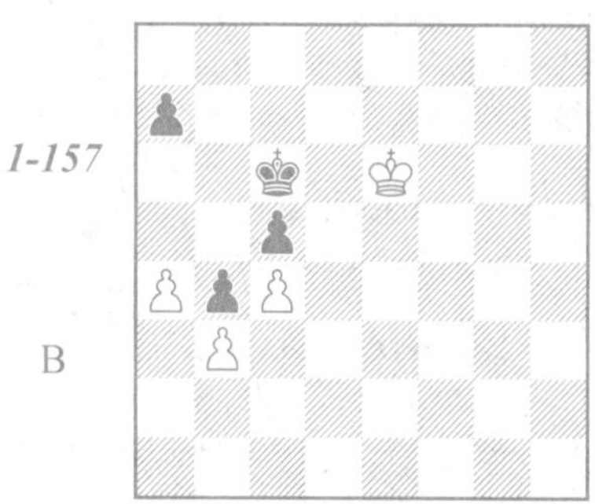

B

The loss of the c5-pawn appears inevitable; however, Black can still save himself.

1...♔b6! 2 ♔d5 a6! 3 ♔d6 ♔a5!, and the pawn is untouchable, because of the stalemate.

Transposition of moves by 1...a6?? would be a grievous error - White would reply 2 a5!, eliminating the king's stalemate refuge.

In the following endgame, we shall see, besides stalemate, other techniques we saw earlier.

Nikolaevsky - Taimanov
USSR ch, Tbilisi 1966

1-158

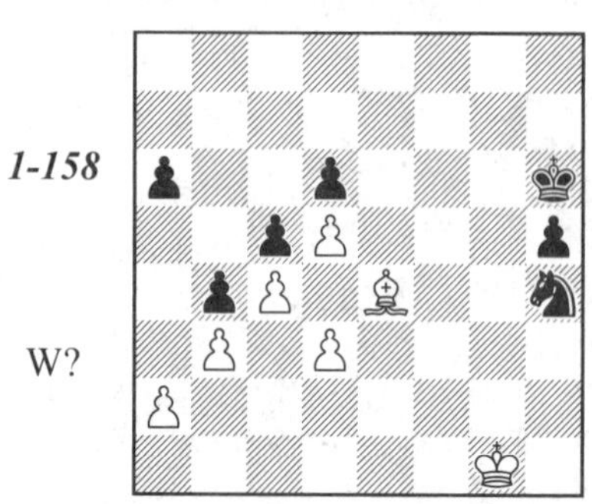

W?

How should this game end?

1 d4! (breakthrough) **1...♘g6!**

Of course not 1...cd? 2 c5, and a pawn queens.

2 dc dc 3 ♗×g6

3 d6?! ♘e5, and now it's White who must work for the draw.

3...♔×g6 4 ♔f2

Here's a position we know: the protected versus the outside passed pawn. White can't get a zugzwang position - kings at h4 and g6, with Black to move; therefore, he will have to trade his d-pawn for Black's h-pawn. This exchange would have led to victory, if Black's pawn were at a5 (instead of a6), or White's pawn at a4 (instead of a2). As it is, the upshot is a stalemate.

4...♔f6 5 ♔g3 ♔g5 6 ♔h3 ♔f5 (6...h4) **7 ♔h4 ♔g6 8 d6 ♔f6 9 ♔×h5 ♔e6 10 ♔g5 ♔×d6 11 ♔f5 ♔c6 12 ♔e5 ♔b6 13 ♔d5 ♔a5! 14 ♔×c5** Stalemate.

Tragicomedies

Chigorin - Tarrasch
Ostende 1905

1-159

W?

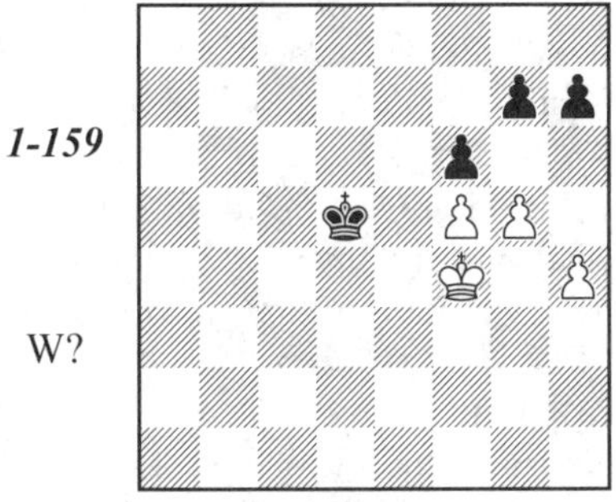

The draw is obtained by constructing a stalemate refuge: 1 ♔g4! (not 1 g6?? h5!−+) 1...♔e4 2 g6! h6 (2...hg 3 fg f5+ 4 ♔g5 f4 5 h5 f3 6 h6=) 3 ♔h5!=.

The game continuation was: **1 gf?? gf 2 ♔g4 ♔e4 3 ♔h3 ♔f4** White resigned. Also insufficient was 3 ♔h5 ♔×f5 4 ♔h6, when Black's simplest win is 4...♔g4 5 ♔×h7 ♔h5! (shouldering), but another possible win is 4...♔e6 5 ♔×h7 f5 6 ♔g6 f4 7 h5 f3 8 h6 f2 9 h7 f1♕ 10 h8♕ ♕f5+, with mate soon to follow.

Aronson - Mednis
USA 1953

1-160

W?

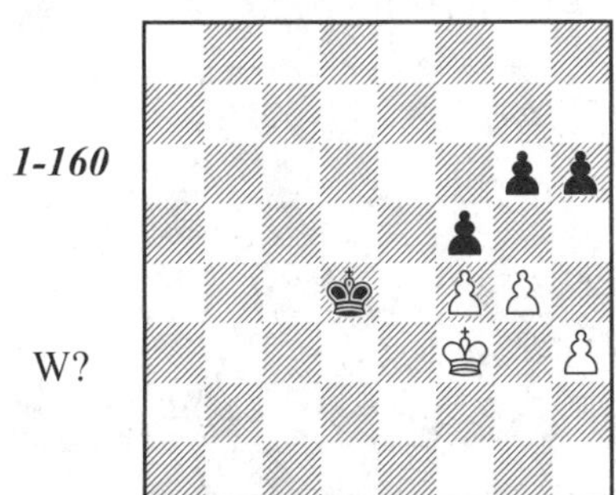

The exact same position as in the previous diagram, except with all the pieces one rank lower. Here, 1 ♔g3? ♔e4 2 g5 would be a mistake, in view of 2...hg! 3 fg ♔e3−+; on the other hand, 1 g5! h5 2 ♔g3 ♔e4 3 ♔h4!= is possible.

The game actually continued **1 h4?? h5−+**.

Exercises

1-161

1/51
B?

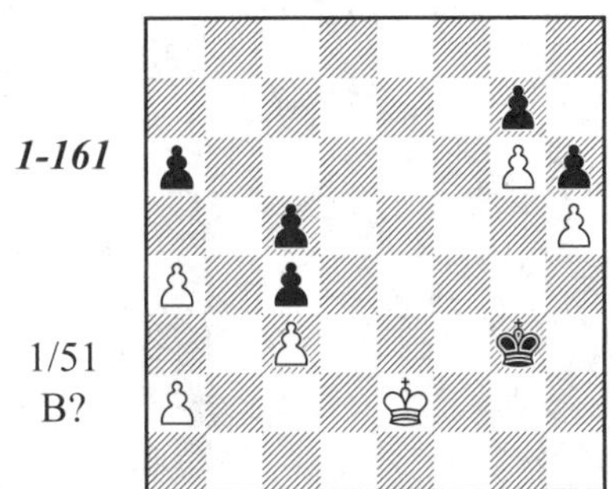

1-162

1/52
W?/Play

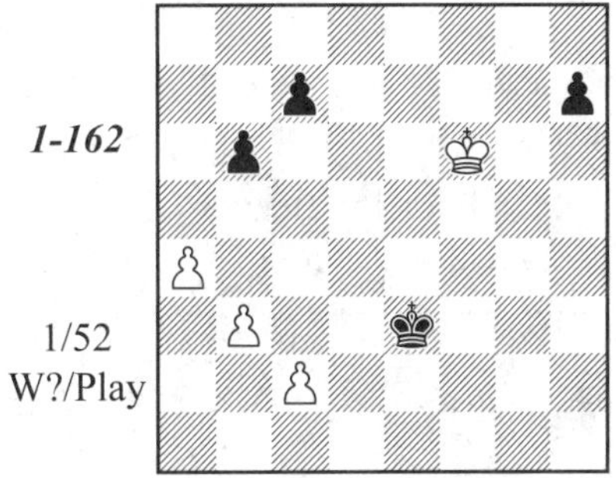

"Semi-Stalemate"

This is what I call the situation when the king is stalemated (on the edge or in the corner of the board), but there are still pawn moves left to make. Instead of stalemate, what we get is zugzwang - usually, a fatal one for the stalemated side.

Here are two simple examples:

Marshall - Réti
New York 1924*

1-163

W

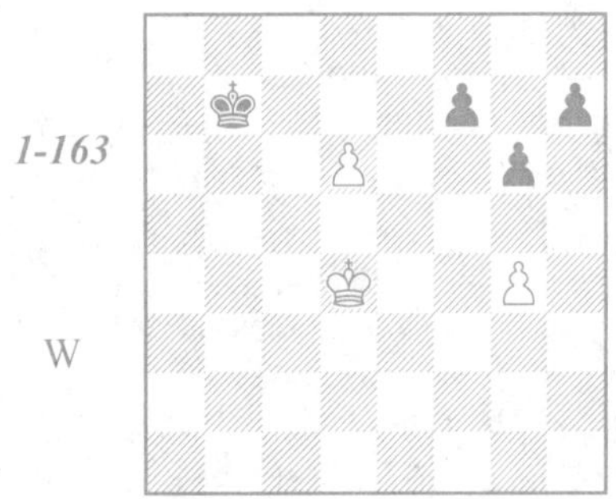

1 g5! (or 1 ♔e5 ♚c8 2 g5!) **1...♚c6 2 ♔e5 ♚d7 3 ♔d5!** (3 ♔f6?? ♚xd6 4 ♔xf7 ♚e5−+) **3...♚d8 4 ♔c6 ♚c8 5 d7+ ♚d8 6 ♔d6**⊙+−.

J. Kling, B. Horwitz, 1851

1-164

W?

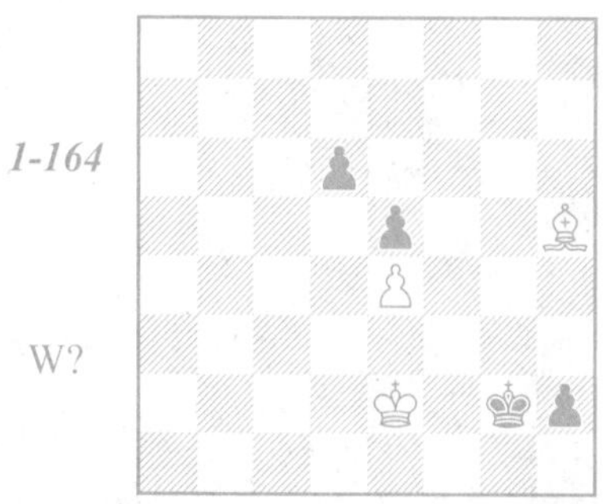

1 ♗f3+ ♚g1 2 ♗h1! ♚xh1 3 ♔f1!⊙ **d5 4 ed e4 5 d6 e3 6 d7 e2+ 7 ♔xe2 ♚g2 8 d8♕ h1♕ 9 ♕g5+ ♚h3 10 ♕h5+ ♚g2 11 ♕g4+ ♚h2 12 ♔f2**+−.

The next example is considerably more difficult and hence more interesting.

Mandler - Procházka
Czechoslovakia 1976

1-165

W?

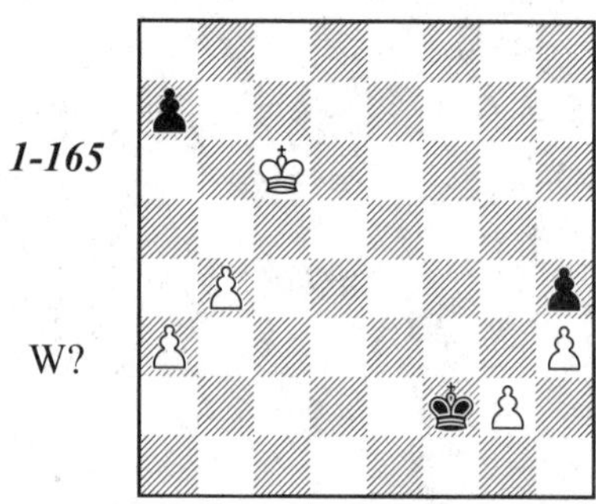

The straightforward 1 b5? leads to a drawn queen endgame with an extra rook's pawn: 1...♚xg2 2 ♔b7 ♚xh3 3 ♔xa7 ♚g4! 4 b6 h3 5 b7 h2 6 b8♕ h1♕.

The other, more promising plan is to squeeze the enemy king into the corner. However, it requires lengthy and accurate calculation.

1 ♔d5!! ♚xg2 2 ♔e4 ♚xh3 3 ♔f3 ♚h2 4 ♔f2!

After 4 b5? (or 4 a4?), Black's king can use Réti's idea to help him get to the queenside in time: 4...♚g1 5 ♔g4 ♚g2! 6 ♔xh4 ♚f3=.

4...h3

4...a6 is inferior: 5 a4 h3 6 a5! ♚h1 7 b5 h2 8 ♔f1!⊙+−.

5 b5!

5 a4? would be a mistake, in view of 5...a5! 6 ba ♚h1 7 a6 h2=.

5...♚h1 6 ♔f1!

Again, not 6 a4? a5!=. Now Black must stalemate his own king, since 6...♚h2 allows an easy win by 7 a4 ♚h1 8 a5 a6 (8...h2 9 ♔f2 a6 10 ♔f1) 9 ♔f2.

6...h2 7 b6!!

The only move! White only gets a draw after 7 a4? a5! or 7 ♔f2? a5!.

7...a5

7...ab 8 a4 b5 9 a5+−.

8 b7 a4 9 ♔e2! ♚g1 10 b8♕ h1♕ 11 ♕b6+

White wants mate. As can easily be seen, exchanging queens wins also.

11...♚h2 12 ♕d6+ ♚g1 13 ♕d4+ ♚h2 14 ♕h4+ ♚g2 15 ♕g4+ ♚h2 16 ♔f2 Black resigned.

Reserve Tempi

Exploiting Reserve Tempi

We have already seen more than once how the outcome of a game may hinge on one side's store of reserve pawn tempi. This is not surprising, considering that zugzwang is the fundamental weapon in the majority of pawn endings.

The rules involved in the use of reserve tempi are simple and self-evident:

1) Use every chance to accumulate reserve tempi and to deprive your opponent of his;

2) Hold onto them - don't waste them except under absolute necessity.

Let's observe these rules in action. The first is illustrated in the following two examples.

1-166

W?

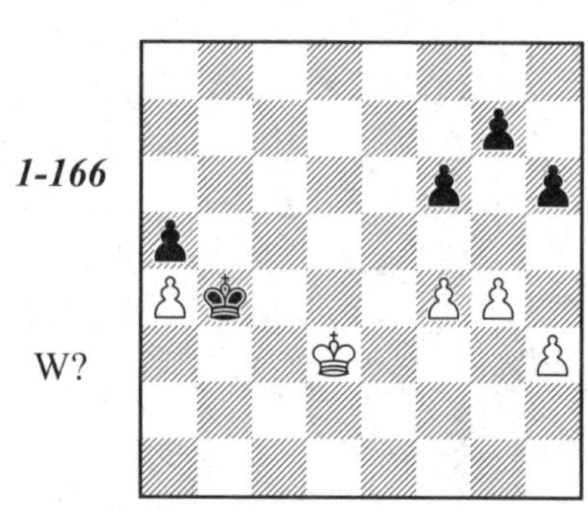

1 f5!

This move secures White two reserve pawn tempi - just enough to squeeze the enemy king at the edge of the board.

1...♔×a4 2 ♔c4 ♔a3 3 ♔c3 a4 4 h4 ♔a2 5 ♔c2 a3 (5...h5 6 gh a3 7 h6 gh 8 h5 is zugzwang) **6 h5⊙ ♔a1 7 ♔c1=.**

Despotovic - Dvoretsky
Moscow tt 1968

1-167

B?

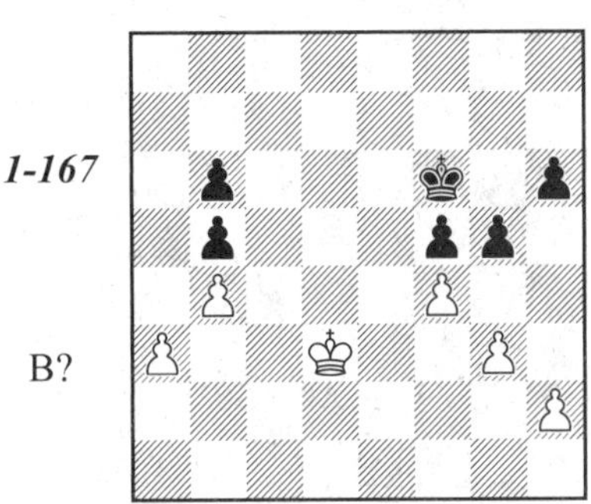

1...g4!

Now Black has the reserve tempo h6-h5. Here, the game was adjourned; White sealed the move 2 ♔c3?, but later resigned without continuing, in view of 2...♔e6 3 ♔d4 (3 ♔b3 ♔d5 4 a4 ba+ 5 ♔×a4 ♔c4–+) 3...♔d6 4 ♔c3 ♔d5 5 ♔d3 h5–+. Thanks to his reserve tempo, Black put his opponent into zugzwang, and his king broke through on the wing.

But White could have saved himself by playing **2 ♔e3! ♔e6 3 h3!**

Yes! White loses with either 3 h4? ♔d5 4 ♔d3 h5⊙ or 3 ♔f2? ♔d5 4 h3 h5!

But now what is Black to do? On 3...h5 4 h4 (or 4 hg), he loses his reserve tempo, and the position is now drawn: 4...♔d5 5 ♔d3⊙. And in the sharp variation **3...gh 4 ♔f2 ♔d5,** White has time to create kingside counterplay.

Karsten Müller noted that if, instead of 4...♔d5, Black were to try 4...♔f6 5 ♔g1 ♔g7!?, then the only move to draw would be 6 ♔h1! – the h2-square is mined. The problem is that after 6 ♔h2? ♔g6 7 ♔×h3 ♔h5⊙ 8 g4+, Black does not play 8...fg+? 9 ♔g3 ♔g6 10 ♔×g4⊙ ♔f6 (10...h5+ 11 ♔h4) 11 ♔h5 ♔f5 12 ♔×h6 ♔×f4 13 ♔g6, when the White king reaches the queenside in time, but 8...♔g6! 9 ♔h4 ♔f6! 10 ♔h5 fg 11 ♔×g4 ♔g6 – here, it is White who falls into zugzwang.

5 ♔g1 ♔c4 6 ♔h2 h5 (6...♔b3? 7 g4!) **7 ♔×h3 ♔b3 8 ♔h4 ♔×a3 9 ♔×h5** (9 ♔g5!?) **9...♔×b4 10 g4 fg 11 ♔×g4 ♔c3** (11...♔c5 12 ♔f3!) **12 f5 b4 13 f6 b3 14 f7 b2 15 f8♕ b1♕ 16 ♕f6+**, and the queen endgame is drawn.

N. Grigoriev, 1931

1-168
$

W?

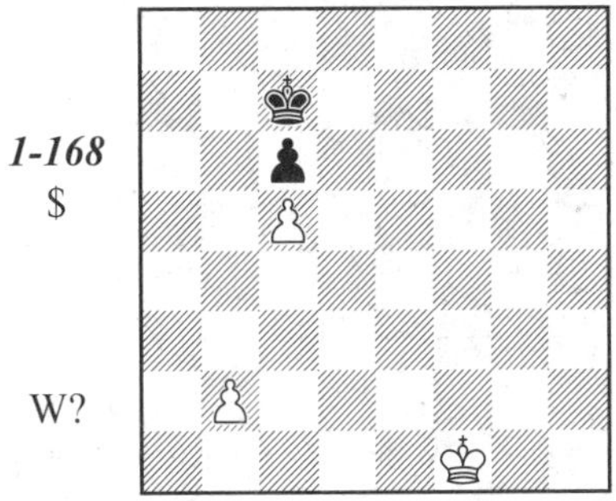

White's king has nothing to do on the kingside (with the kings on the 4th and 6th ranks, it's easy to establish that the opposition is meaningless, and therefore White cannot create zugzwang). The winning plan will be to feint with the king on the queenside, and then march over to the kingside. For this plan to succeed, White will need both of his reserve pawn tempi (with the pawn at b3, the position would be drawn); so it's important not to lose them on the way.

1 ♔e2 ♔d7

1...♔b7 2 ♔d3 ♔a6 would be senseless, in view of 3 b4 (3 ♔c4) 3...♔b5 4 ♔c3 ♔a6 5 ♔c4! ♔b7 6 ♔d4+–.

2 ♔d3 ♔e7! 3 ♔c3!

Both sides must keep in mind that the e6- and c4-squares are mined. After 2...♔e6 3 ♔c4, Black cannot play 3...♔e5 in view of 4 b4 ♔e6 5 b5; however, if he does not play this, White's king continues on his way to the queenside. Now on 2...♔e7 3 ♔c4? ♔e6, the line 4 ♔b4(b3) ♔d5= is bad; so is 4 ♔d4 ♔f6! 5 ♔c3 ♔e5! - therefore, White has to play 4 b3, prematurely using up one of his reserve tempi, which renders the win impossible.

3...♔e6 4 ♔c4 ♔d7 5 ♔b4 ♔c7 6 ♔a5 ♔b7 7 b3!

The first tempo is used up, in order to force the black king away from the kingside.

7...♔a7 8 ♔b4 ♔b7 (8...♔a6 9 ♔c3 ♔a5 10 ♔c4 ♔a6 11 b4+–) **9 ♔c4 ♔c7 10 ♔d4 ♔d7 11 ♔e5 ♔e7 12 b4⊙+–**

That's where we use the second tempo!

Tragicomedies

Kachiani - Maric
Kishinev izt 1995

1-169

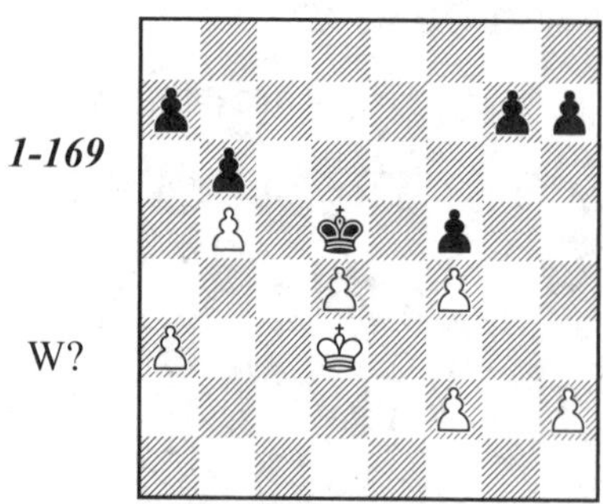

W?

On the kingside - equality (each side has three pawn moves). White has the reserve tempo a3-a4 on the queenside. Unfortunately, she was too eager to use it:

1 a4??

White wins by 1 ♔c3! ♔e6 (1...♔e4 2 ♔c4 ♔xf4 3 ♔d5+−) 2 ♔c4 ♔d6 3 d5 ♔d7 4 ♔d4 ♔d6 5 h3 h6 6 h4 h5 7 f3 g6 8 a4!⊙.

1...♔d6 2 ♔c4 ♔e6 3 d5+ ♔d7 4 ♔d4 ♔d6⊙

Here is where White could have used the reserve tempo - but alas, it's already gone.

5 ♔c4 ♔d7 6 ♔d3 ♔e7

Of course, Black will not be the first to go to the mined square d6. The game soon ended in a draw.

Exercises

1-170

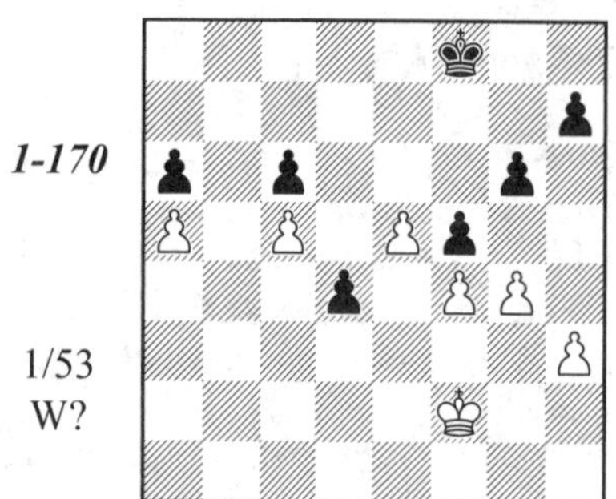

1/53
W?

1-171

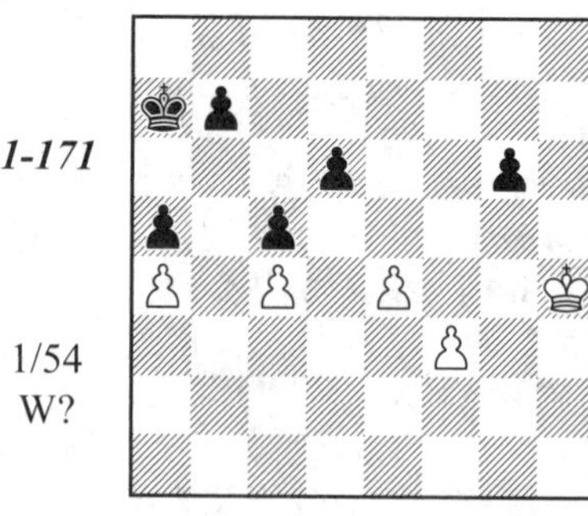

1/54
W?

1-172

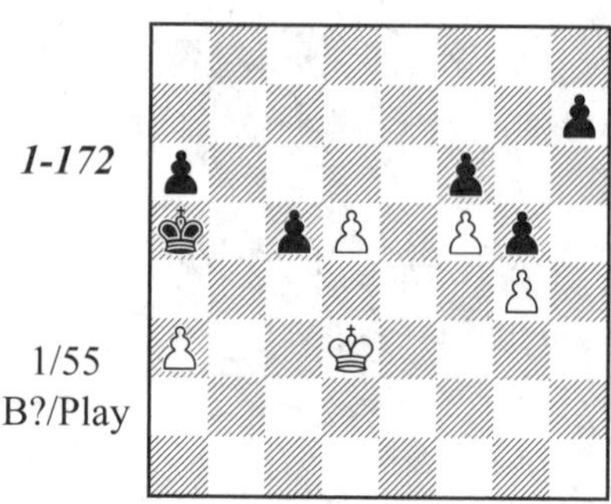

1/55
B?/Play

Steinitz's Rule

Wilhelm Steinitz, the first World Champion, put forth the following paradox: that the pawns stand best on their original squares. His explanation: ***In the endgame, it is useful to have a choice of whether to advance a pawn one or two squares.*** We shall see the point of his idea to its fullest extent in the following subchapters; so I shall limit myself to just one example of it here. The analysis given below was made by Artur Yusupov when he was still quite young, with the assistance of the author.

Yusupov - Ionov
Podolsk 1977*

1-173

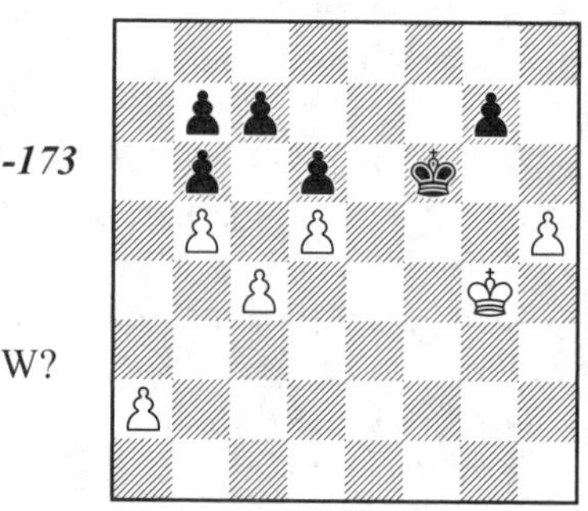

W?

We can see at once the idea of a pawn breakthrough on the queenside, after a2-a4 and c4-c5. Obviously, it will have no chance of succeeding unless the black king is taken far enough away.

First, it is necessary to put Black on move. It is also important to leave the a-pawn where it is, since from its original square, it has the choice of moving one or two squares forward.

1 ♔f4!

In playing this, White must be prepared for 1...g6 2 h6 g5+; however, now the pawn breakthrough works: 3 ♔e3! (the best square for the king to deal with the black pawns) 3...♔g6 4 a4 ♔×h6 5 c5! bc (5...dc 6 a5 ba 7 b6 cb 8 d6) 6 a5 c4 7 a6 ba 8 ba c3 9 a7 c2 10 ♔d2.

1...♔e7 2 ♔g5

The king goes inexorably to g6, after which White - thanks to the fact that his pawn is still on a2 - can execute the breakthrough at the ideal moment: when Black's king is on g8.

2...♔f8

2...♔f7 is met by 3 ♔f5 ♔e7 4 ♔g6 ♔f8 5 a4! ♔g8 6 c5!.

3 ♔g6 ♔g8

1-174

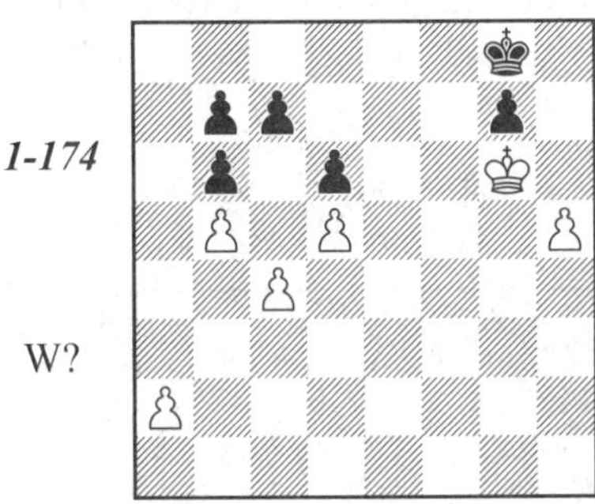

W?

4 a3! ♔f8 5 a4 ♔g8 6 c5! dc 7 a5 ba 8 b6 cb 9 d6 ♔f8 10 d7 ♔e7 11 ♔×g7 a4 12 h6 a3 13 h7 a2 14 d8♕+! ♔×d8 15 h8♕+

An incautious pawn advance on move one would have let the win slip. Black in response need only be careful which square he picks for his king. For example, after 1 a3? ♔f7? would be a mistake: 2 ♔f5 ♔e7 (otherwise 3 ♔e6) 3 ♔g6 ♔f8 4 a4⊙+−; but Black could play 1...♔e7! 2 ♔g5 (2 ♔f5 ♔f7!) 2...♔f8! 3 ♔g6 ♔g8 4 a4 ♔f8⊙, and the breakthrough doesn't work now, and the move-losing maneuver is no longer possible.

The g- and h-Pawns vs. the h-Pawn

1-175

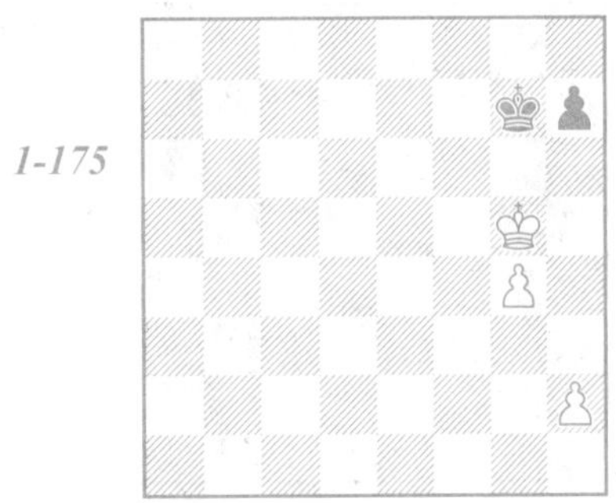

With Black's pawn on its starting square, the only winning plan becomes a king invasion at h6. Even the conquest of the h6-square, however, only guarantees victory in the event that one of White's pawns remains on the 2nd rank, in order to have the choice between moving one or two squares.

Black to move loses:

1...h6+ 2 ♔f5 ♔f7 3 h3 (3 h4 ♔g7 4 ♔e6 is possible, too) 3...♔g7 4 h4 ♔f7 5 h5+−;

1...♔f7 2 ♔h6 ♔g8 3 g5 ♔h8 4 h4! ♔g8 5 h5 ♔h8 6 g6 hg 7 hg ♔g8 8 g7+−;

1...♔g8 2 ♔h6! (2 ♔f6? ♔f8=) **2...♔h8 3 g5 ♔g8 4 h3! ♔h8 5 h4 ♔g8 6 h5 ♔h8 7 g6 hg 8 hg ♔g8 9 g7+−**

But with White to move, the position is drawn. 1 ♔f5 ♔f7 is useless, and on 1 ♔h5 h6! draws. After the h-pawn moves, Black only needs to select the right square for his king to retreat to.

1 h3 ♔g8! 2 ♔h6 ♔h8 3 g5 ♔g8 4 h4 ♔h8 5 h5 ♔g8 6 g6 hg 7 hg ♔h8=

Clearly, 1 h4 would be met by 1...♔f7! (or 1...♔h8!) 2 ♔h6 ♔g8, with the same outcome. We can see that the squares g8 and h8 correspond to the position of the pawn (at h3, h4 or h5); and with White's pawn at g4, there's one correspondence, but with the pawn at g5 - it's the opposite.

Matters are more complicated when the defending side's pawn has already left its starting square. Here everything depends on the nuances of king and pawn position. The ideas inherent in such positions are aptly illustrated by the following study.

R. Réti, A. Mandler, 1921

1-176
$
W?

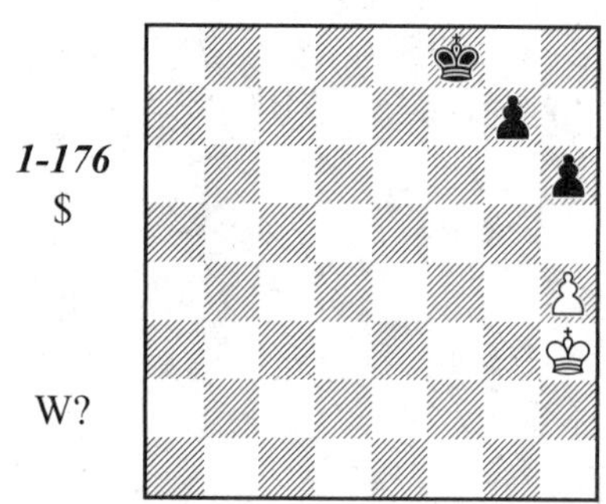

1 ♔g3!!

After 1 ♔g4? ♔f7, the position is lost. For example:

2 h5 ♔e6⊙ (the diagonal opposition);

2 ♔h5 ♔f6 3 ♔g4 ♔e5 4 ♔h5 ♔f4 5 ♔g6 ♔g4 6 ♔×g7 h5;

2 ♔f4 ♔e6! 3 ♔e4 g6 4 ♔f4 ♔d5 5 ♔f3 ♔e5 6 ♔e3 ♔f5 7 ♔f3 h5⊙. Note that with Black's pawn at g6 the opposition is important for both sides; with the pawn at g7, it's the anti-opposition that's important. This generalization is the mainspring driving this particular endgame.

2 ♔f5 g6+ 3 ♔e5 ♔e7 4 ♔d5 (4 h5 g5 5 ♔f5 ♔d6) 4...♔f6 5 ♔e4 ♔e6, etc.;

2 ♔f3 g6! (Black seizes the distant opposition, and then converts it into close opposition, as usual, with an outflanking) 3 ♔e3 ♔e7! 4 ♔f3 ♔d6! 5 ♔e4 ♔e6, etc.

1...♔e7

1...♔f7 is met by 2 ♔g4! Now 2..♔g6 3 h5+ would be useless; and after 2...♔e6 3 ♔f4! White, as should be done in positions with the pawn at g7, gives up the opposition to his opponent (3...♔f6 4 h5= or 3...g6 4 ♔e4=); while after 2...g6 he seizes the distant opposition with 3 ♔f3! All that remains is 2...♔f6, but then White is saved by the unexpectedly direct 3 ♔h5! ♔e5 (3...♔f5 is stalemate) 4 ♔g6 ♔f4 5 ♔×g7 h5 6 ♔f6! ♔g4 7 ♔e5 ♔×h4 8 ♔f4=.

2 ♔f3!

Of course not 2 ♔f4? ♔e6!−+.

2...♔f6

2...♔e6 3 ♔f4!; 2...g6 3 ♔e3!.

3 ♔e4!

Still the same principle at work - with the pawn on g7, anti-opposition.

3...♔f7!? 4 ♔e3! ♔e7 5 ♔f3!=.

Tragicomedies

Marshall - Schlechter
San Sebastian 1911

1-177
B?

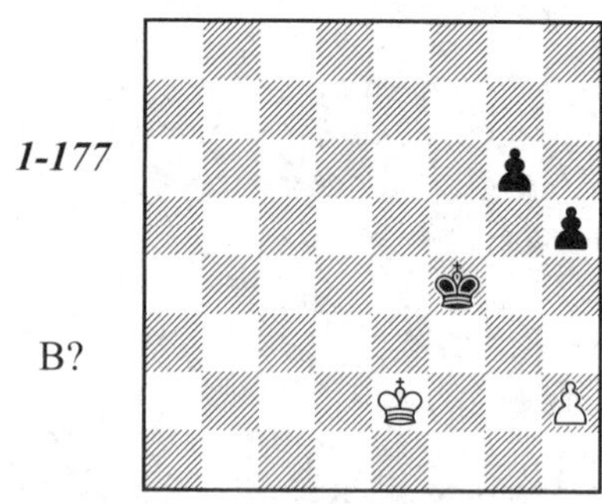

1...♔g4! 2 ♔f2 ♔h3 decides: 3 ♔g1 (White's king is on the wrong square: on h1, it would be a draw) 3...g5 4 ♔h1 g4 5 ♔g1 h4 6 ♔h1 g3 7 hg hg 8 ♔g1 g2−+.

Instead, Schlechter played **1...♔e4??**, when the position was drawn, because both black pawns have now left their starting rank; and if Black tries to get his king into h3 (there's no other plan), White's king can always choose the right square on the 1st rank.

2 ♔f2 ♔d3 3 ♔f3 g5 4 ♔f2 ♔e4 5 ♔e2 ♔f4 6 ♔f2 ♔g4 7 ♔g2 h4 8 h3+ (the simplest, although 8 ♔g1 was possible too) Draw.

Chiburdanidze - Watson
Brussels 1987

1-178
W

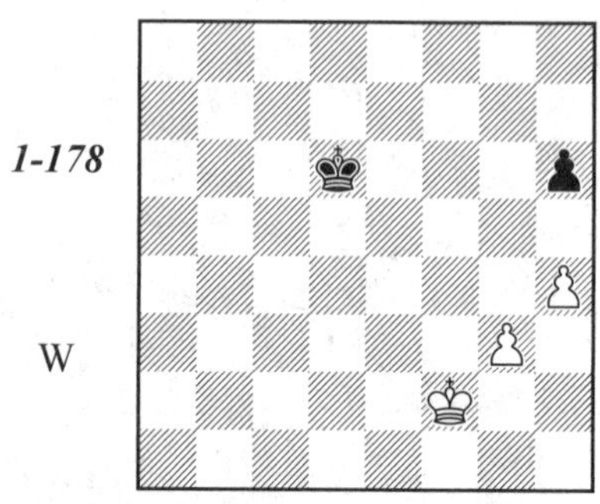

The position is almost the same as the Réti, Mandler study. White wins with either 1 g4! ♔e6 2 ♔e2! ♔f6 3 ♔d3, or 1 ♔e3! ♔e5 (1...♔e6 2 ♔f4! ♔f6 3 g4) 2 g4.

1 ♔f3?? ♔e7! 2 ♔f4 ♔e6! 3 g4 ♔f6 4 ♔f3 ♔e7??

An awful blunder in return. As long as the pawn stood on g3, Black ceded his opponent the right to control the opposition. But now, with the pawn on g4, he cannot give the opposition up! 4...♔f7!= was necessary.

5 ♔e3!+− ♔f7 6 ♔d4! ♔f6 7 ♔d5 ♔e7 8 ♔e5 ♔f7 9 ♔f5 ♔g7 10 ♔e6 ♔g6 11 h5+ ♔g5 12 ♔f7 ♔×g4 13 ♔g6 ♔f4 14 ♔×h6 Black resigned.

The f- and h-Pawns vs. the h-Pawn

We shall analyze the basic ideas of such positions by using the following study as an example.

N. Grigoriev, 1920

1-179

W?

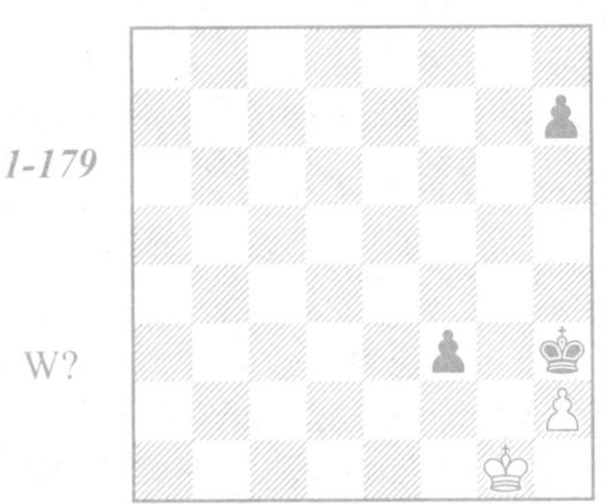

If White plays 1 ♔h1? (naively hoping for 1...f2?? stalemate) , then after 1...♔g4, his position is lost. Black's plan is elementary: his king goes to e3, and then he advances ...f3-f2, forcing the advance of White's h-pawn. The fact that Black can choose whether to move his h-pawn one or two squares forward allows him to place his opponent in zugzwang. For example: 2 ♔g1 ♔f4 3 ♔f2 ♔e4 4 ♔f1 (4 ♔e1 ♔e3 5 ♔f1 f2 6 h4 h5!) 4...♔e3 5 ♔e1 f2+ 6 ♔f1 ♔f3! 7 h3 h5! 8 h4 ♔g3, or 7 h4 h6! 8 h5 ♔g3.

1 ♔f2! ♔g4 2 ♔e3!⊙

Thanks to zugzwang, the pawn must leave the h7-square; the position is now a draw. White must only make sure he chooses the right back-rank square for his king (corresponding to the position of Black's h-pawn).

2...h6 3 ♔f2 ♔f4 4 ♔e1! ♔e3

Or 4...h5 5 ♔f2 ♔e4 6 ♔f1!.

5 ♔f1 h5

5...f2 6 h3! ♔f3 7 h4 ♔g3 8 h5⊙=.

6 ♔e1 f2+

6...h4 would be met by 7 ♔f1! f2 8 h3=. But not the hasty 7 h3?, which would be a terrible blunder here, leading to the Fahrni - Alapin ending we know so well (from Diagram 1-27). Just a reminder: Black wins by triangulating with his king: 7...♔e4 8 ♔f1 ♔e5 9 ♔e1 ♔f5! 10 ♔f1 ♔e4⊙.

7 ♔f1 ♔f3 8 h3! ♔g3 9 h4=

So the stronger side wins only if the rook's pawn is on the starting square. The only exception to this rule was found by Maizelis in 1955 (although it was seen even earlier, in a 1949 study by Valles).

1-180

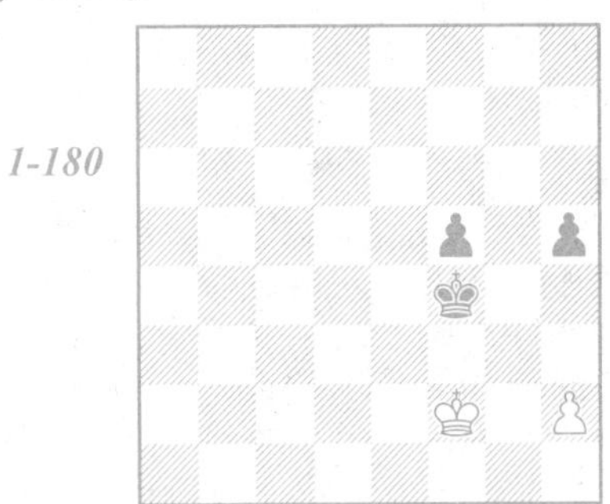

Here, everything depends on whose turn it is to move. Black to move wins.

1...♔e4 2 ♔e2 h4! (an exceptionally important position - reciprocal zugzwang!) **3 ♔f2 ♔d3!!**

Control of the opposition is exploited, as usual, by outflanking - although this time, a paradoxical one.

4 ♔f3 h3!⊙ 5 ♔f2

There is no help in either 5 ♔f4 ♔e2 6 ♔×f5 ♔f3! or 5 ♔g3 ♔e3(e2) 6 ♔×h3 f4.

5...♔d2! 6 ♔f3 (6 ♔f1 ♔e3 7 ♔e1 ♔f3 8 ♔f1 f4 9 ♔g1 ♔e2−+) **6...♔e1 7 ♔e3 ♔f1 8 ♔f3 ♔g1 9 ♔g3 f4+ 10 ♔f3** (10 ♔×h3 f3) **10...♔×h2 11 ♔f2 f3⊙−+**

With White to move, there is no win: 1 ♔e2 ♔e4 2 ♔f2 h4 (2...♔d3 3 ♔f3 h4 4 ♔f4 ♔e2 5 ♔×f5=) 3 ♔e2⊙ h3 4 ♔f2 ♔d3 5 ♔f3 ♔d2 6 ♔f2!=.

Maizelis' position serves as a most important guidepost in analyzing situations where one side has an advanced rook's pawn - the outcome of the battle depends on whether the stronger side can reach Maizelis' position and whose move it is.

Maizelis studied the following position, and considered it lost. His conclusion would appear to be supported by the result of this game.

1 ♔g3 h5! 2 ♔f3 (on 2 ♔g2, Black should play 2...♔f4!, and if 2 ♔f2, then 2...♔g4! 3 ♔e3 ♔h3, or 3 ♔g2 h4) 2...h4 3 ♔g2 ♔g4! 4 ♔f2

Vaganian - Sunye Neto
Rio de Janeiro izt 1979

1-181

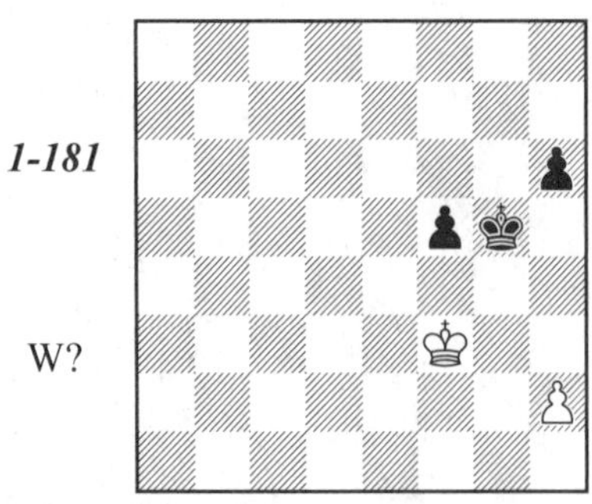

W?

♔f4 5 ♔e2 ♔e4 (White is in zugzwang) 6 ♔f2 ♔d3!! 7 ♔f3 h3! White resigned.

I was in Rio de Janeiro. Unfamiliar with Maizelis' analysis, and astounded that Black could win such a position, I focused on it intensely and quickly found the saving line. Pal Benko (who was Sunye Neto's second at the Interzonal) came to the same conclusion a bit earlier.

Since the central problem here is one of reciprocal zugzwang, let's analyze the corresponding squares. If Black's king moves to the 4th rank with the pawn at h4 or h6, White's king must respond by taking the opposition. If the pawn is at h5, the opposite is true - White must take the anti-opposition.

This means that neither 1 ♔g2? ♔g4! nor 1 ♔f2? ♔f4! is good. And we have already seen what happens to 1 ♔g3? So:

1 ♔e2!! ♔g4

After 1...♔f4 2 ♔f2, White's in fine shape - he has the opposition with the pawn at h6. The game might continue 2...h5 3 ♔e2 ♔e4 4 ♔f2 h4 (with the pawn at h5, the outflanking 4...♔d3 doesn't work) 5 ♔e2=. If 1...h5, then either 2 ♔e3 or 2 ♔f1.

2 ♔e3! h5 (2...♔h3 3 ♔f4) **3 ♔f2**

The goal is reached: White has the anti-opposition, with the pawn at h5.

3...♔f4 4 ♔e2 ♔e4 5 ♔f2 h4 6 ♔e2⊙=.

The following exceptionally complex example was first given in Fine's book (1941), but unfortunately with a completely erroneous analysis. Maizelis (1956) did a much better job on the position; and later his conclusions were refined and extended by other authors.

1-182

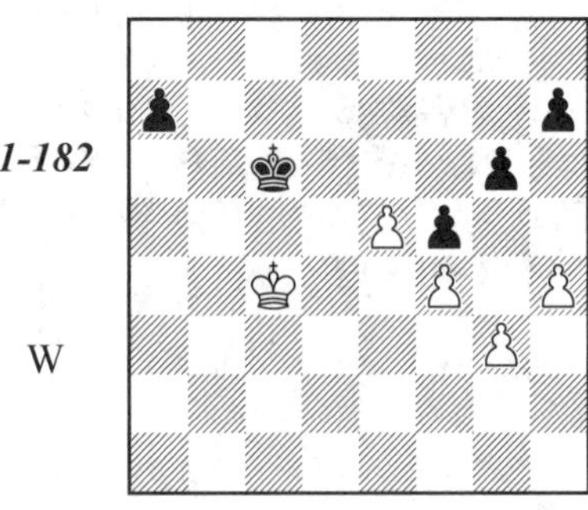

W

Here we have a protected passed pawn versus an outside passed pawn. Since White cannot win the a-pawn, he will have to trade it for his e-pawn. But what does this leave us with?

1 ♔b4

Or 1 ♔d4 ♔c7 2 ♔c5 a6 3 ♔c4 ♔c8 (but not 3...♔c6? 4 ♔d4⊙) 4 ♔b4 ♔b8 5 ♔a5 ♔b7.

1...♔b6

Black cannot close up the kingside with 1...h5, since then the trade of pawns will give White an easy win: 2 ♔a5 ♔b7 3 ♔b5 ♔c7 4 ♔a6 ♔b8 5 e6 ♔c7 6 ♔×a7 ♔d6 7 ♔b6 ♔×e6 8 ♔c6 (taking the lateral opposition decides) 8...♔e7 9 ♔c7 ♔e6 10 ♔d8 (outflanking) 10...♔d5 (10...♔f7 11 ♔d7 ♔f6 12 ♔e8 ♔g7 13 ♔e7 ♔h7 14 ♔f7 ♔h6 15 ♔g8⊙) 11 ♔e7 ♔e4 12 ♔f6 ♔f3 13 ♔×g6 ♔×g3 14 ♔g5!⊙.

2 ♔a4 a5

Equally good is 2...♔c6 3 ♔a5 ♔c7 4 ♔a6 ♔b8. Fine only examined 2...a6? 3 ♔b4 ♔c6 4 ♔c4 ♔b6 (4...a5 5 ♔d4!) 5 ♔d5! and White either queens his pawn or wins the pawn on a6.

3 h5!

Before exchanging pawns, it is necessary first to weaken the enemy kingside pawn chain. Because it's zugzwang, Black has no choice:

3...gh 4 e6! ♔c6 5 ♔×a5 ♔d6 6 ♔b6 ♔×e6

The pawn at f5 must fall. But if Black replies to the capture of the pawn with 1...h4 2 gh ♔e7, he will draw, because this will lead to Maizelis' position with White in zugzwang. But if the pawn is captured instead with the king at either e7 or g7, Black is the one in zugzwang, and he loses. So this is what the further course of the struggle will be about.

This conclusion allows us to discover the corresponding squares e5 and f7, d5 and e7 (g7). Continuing this analysis, we find more corresponding squares: e6 and g6(e8), f6 and f8.

7 ♔c6!

But not 7 ♔c5? ♔d7! (7...♔f7!) 8 ♔d5 ♔e7 9 ♔e5 ♔f7 10 ♔xf5 h4 11 gh ♔e7 12 ♔e5 ♔f7 13 h5 ♔e7⊙=.

1-183

B

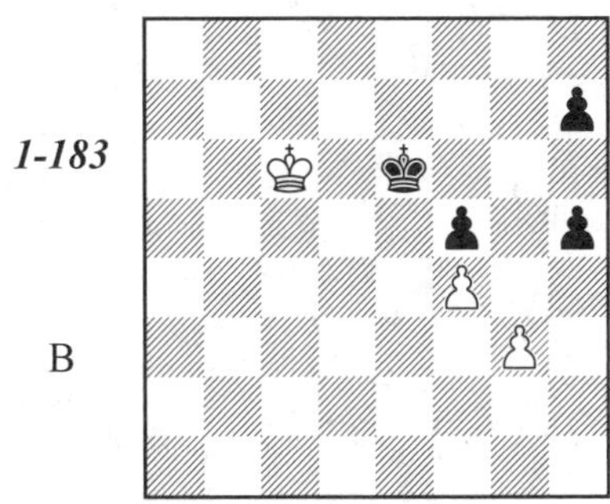

7...♔f7!

The most stubborn defense, pointed out by Euwe and Hooper (1958). Things are simpler for White after 7...♔e7 8 ♔d5 ♔f6 9 ♔d6 ♔f7 10 ♔e5 ♔g6 11 ♔e6 ♔g7 12 ♔xf5 h4 13 gh ♔f7 14 ♔e5 ♔e7 15 h5⊙+−.

But now, since 8 ♔d5? ♔e7! (8...♔g7!) and 8 ♔d6? ♔f6 9 ♔d5 ♔e7(g7)! do not work, there remains but one move:

8 ♔d7! ♔f8 9 ♔d6!!

9 ♔e6? would be a mistake: 9...♔e8 10 ♔f6 h4 (10...♔f8 11 ♔g5 h4! 12 ♔xh4 h6 is also possible, or 12 gh ♔f7!) 11 gh ♔f8 12 h5 (12 ♔xf5 ♔e7!) 12...♔g8 13 ♔xf5 ♔f7!=.

9...♔g7 10 ♔e7! ♔g8

10...♔g6 11 ♔e6 ♔g7 12 ♔xf5 h4 13 gh ♔f7 14 ♔e5 ♔e7 15 h5⊙+−.

11 ♔e6! ♔f8 12 ♔f6⊙ ♔g8 13 ♔xf5 h4 14 gh

White has achieved his aim - the enemy king cannot go to e7 now.

14...♔f7 15 ♔e5 ♔e7 16 h5!⊙ ♔f7 17 ♔d6!! ♔f6 18 h6!, etc.

The only defense left to examine involves Black holding on to both h-pawns: 10...♔g6 11 ♔e6 h6 12 ♔e5 ♔g7 13 ♔xf5 ♔f7 14 ♔e5 ♔e7 15 f5 ♔f7 16 f6.

1-184

B

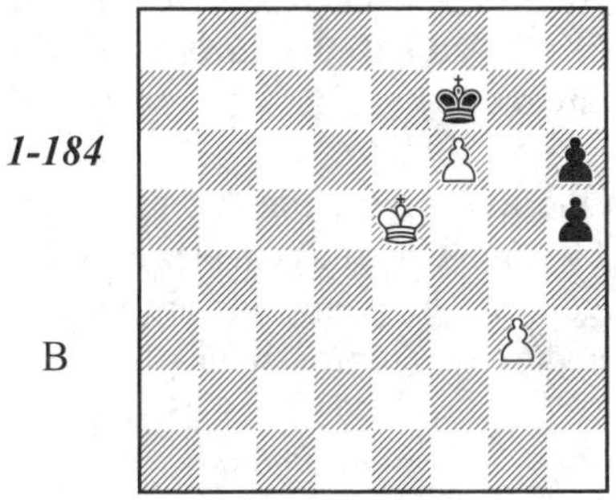

With the pawn pushed up to h6, 16...h4 17. gh is now useless: at a minimum, White gets the winning position from the game Fahrni - Alapin. On the other hand, we have practically the same situation on the board now - the only difference being that the e6-square, as is easily seen, corresponds to f8, not e8; and that means the e5-square corresponds to e8. So the familiar triangulation decides.

16...♔e8! 17 ♔f4 ♔f8 18 ♔e4! ♔e8 19 ♔e5!⊙ ♔f8 (19...♔f7 20 ♔f5) 20 ♔e6 ♔e8 21 f7+ ♔f8 22 ♔f6⊙ h4 23 gh h5 24 ♔g6+−.

Tragicomedies

Azmaiparashvili - Eolian
USSR ch tt 1979

1-185

W?

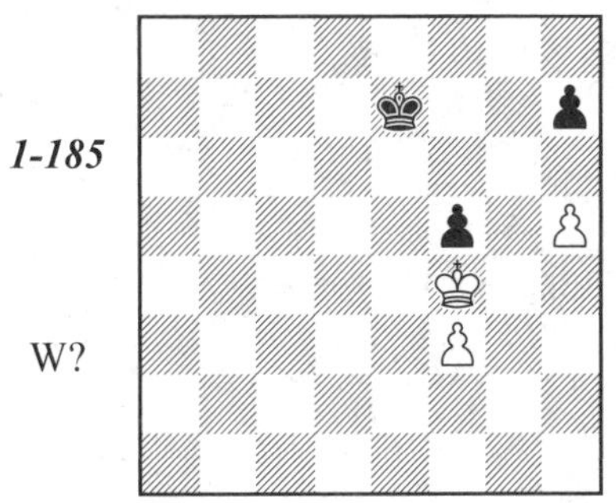

1 ♔g5??

White wins by 1 ♔xf5! ♔f7 2 f4 ♔e7 3 ♔e5⊙ ♔f7 4 ♔d6!!

1...♔f8 2 ♔xf5 ♔f7??

2...♔e7! 3 f4 ♔f7=

3 ♔g4??

The comedy of errors continues! Of course, either 3 f4 or 3 ♔e5 was correct.

3...♔f6??

The king steps upon a mined square - one he should only have gone to after f3-f4. Black draws after either 3...♔e6! (4 ♔g5 ♔f7!; 4 f4 ♔f6!), or 3...♔f8!

4 ♔f4

4 f4!⊙ was simpler: next move, the white king advances, seizing the opposition. For example: 4...♔e7 5 ♔g5! ♔f7 (5...♔e6 6 ♔h6) 6 ♔f5, etc.

4...♔f7?!

4...♔e6!? would not have helped, in view of 5 ♔g4!⊙ (5 ♔g5? ♔f7=) 5...♔f6 (5...♔e7 6 ♔f5!) 6 f4!+−.

5 ♔f5??

And once again, White misses the opportunity: 5 ♔e5! ♔e7 6 f4⊙+−.

5...♔e7 6 ♔e5 ♔f7 7 ♔d6 ♔f6 8 ♔d7 ♔f7

Black also draws after 8...♔g5 (or 8...♔f5 9 ♔e7 ♔g5!) 9 ♔e6 h6!⊙ 10 ♔e5 ♔×h5 11 f4 ♔g6 12 ♔e6 ♔g7! 13 ♔e7 ♔g6 (the pendulum).

9 h6 (9 f4 ♔f6 10 ♔e8 ♔f5 11 ♔f7 ♔×f4 12 ♔g7 ♔f5 13 ♔×h7 ♔f6=) **9...♔g6! 10 f4** (10 ♔e6 ♔×h6 11 f4 ♔g7 12 ♔e7 ♔g6!= - the pendulum) **10...♔f7!**⊙ (10...♔×h6? 11 f5+−) **11 f5 ♔f6** Draw

This example demonstrates how senseless the play of both sides can seem when they are unacquainted with the ideas behind a position.

Both Sides have Reserve Tempi

In many cases, it is not hard to establish the number of reserve tempi available for both sides (as it was, for example in the ending Kachiani - Maric, from Diagram 1-169). However, there are far more complex situations as well.

Šveida - Sika
Brno 1929

1-186

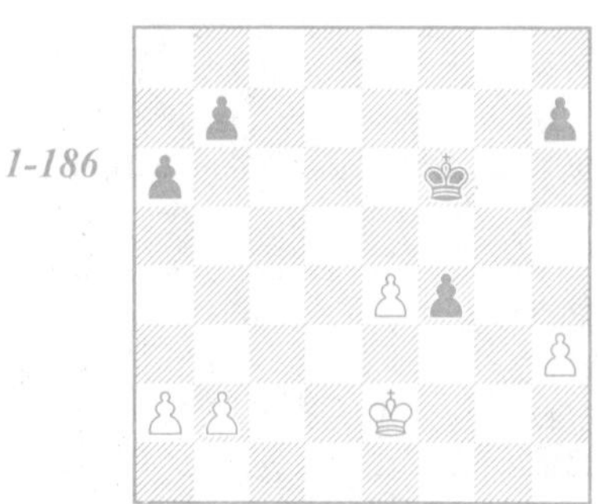

Steinitz's rule tells us that, as far as reserve tempi go, White stands better on the queenside, while Black is better on the kingside. The following bit of advice will help you select the optimal strategy for such situations: ***Try to equalize, as quickly as possible, the situation on your "unfavorable" side.***

Whoever has the move in the above position will succeed in executing the principle outlined above, and will win.

Let's suppose it's Black to move.

1...♔e5 2 ♔f3 a5!

The pawns retaining the right to move either one or two squares should be left alone.

3 h4

3 a4 h6! and 3 b3 b5! 4 h4 b4 5 h5 h6 are no better.

3...a4 4 h5 h6 5 b4 ab (5...a3 6 b5 b6) **6 ab b6! 7 b4 b5−+**

Now let's see what happens with White to move.

1 ♔f3 ♔e5 2 h4! (but not 2 b4? h6!) **2...a5 3 h5 a4** (3...h6 4 a4) **4 h6! b6** (4...a3 5 ba b5 6 a4 ba 7 a3) **5 b4! ab** (5...a3 6 b5) **6 ab b5 7 b4⊙ ♔e6** (7...♔f6 8 ♔×f4 ♔g6 9 ♔e5! ♔×h6 10 ♔f6+−) **8 ♔×f4 ♔f6 9 e5+ ♔g6 10 ♔e4 ♔×h6 11 ♔d5 ♔g7 12 ♔d6 h5 13 e6+−**.

Tragicomedies

Draško - Vratonjic
Yugoslavia tt 1997

1-187

W

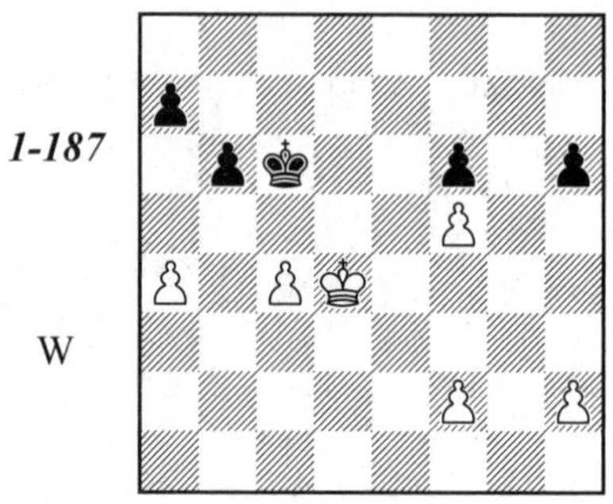

1 f4??

An awful move! Without any need, White gives away two reserve tempi. The obvious drawing line was 1 ♔d3 ♔c5 2 ♔c3 h5 3 h4 a6 4 f3 a5 5 f4=.

1...♔d6 2 ♔d3 ♔c5 3 ♔c3 h5 4 ♔b3 (4 h4 a5⊙) **4...h4 5 ♔c3 h3 6 ♔b3 a6**

After 6...♔d4? 7 ♔b4 a6 8 a5! ba+ 9 ♔×a5 ♔×c4 10 ♔×a6 ♔d4, White's king is just in time to get back to the kingside: 11 ♔b5 ♔e4 12 ♔c4 ♔×f5 13 ♔d3 ♔×f4 14 ♔e2=.

7 a5 (7 ♔c3 a5⊙−+) **7...ba 8 ♔a4 ♔×c4 9 ♔×a5 ♔d4 10 ♔×a6 ♔e4 11 ♔b5 ♔×f5** White resigned.

With the following difficult, but beautiful example, I wish to close this chapter devoted to pawn endgames. The comments are based on those of Lindgren in Informant 74.

Laveryd - Wikström
Umeå 1997

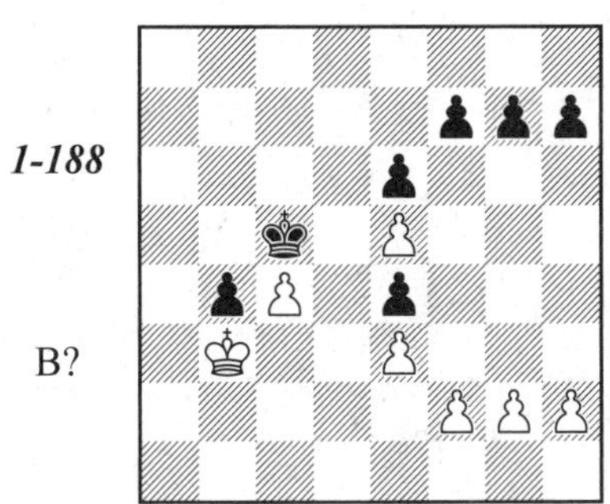

1-188 B?

How should this game end?

On the queenside, the two kings have already occupied the mined squares b3 and c5. It would seem that the side (let's say, Black) that first runs out of pawn moves will lose. So the correct answer - that the position is a draw - appears paradoxical.

The first question is: How is Black to avoid losing immediately? For 1...f6? (or 1...f5?) is completely hopeless, in view of 2 ef gf 3 g4!

1...h5!

It turns out that, after the natural 2 h4?, it is not White who places his opponent in zugzwang - he falls into it himself: 2...g5! 3 hg h4⊙.

(By the way, this example fully deserves to be placed in "tragicomedies," since the actual continuation was 1...h6?? 2 h3?? [2 g4! g6 3 h4+−; or 2...f5 3 ef gf 4 h4+−] 2...h5!−+ 3 h4 g5! 4 g3 g4, and White resigned.)

2 h3!

The only move! We already know that 2 h4? doesn't work; and 2 f4? ef 3 gf h4 4 h3 f6 (or 4...f5) and 2 g3? f6 (2...f5) are both bad. But now, Black once again faces a tough defensive task.

2...g5? loses at once to 3 g3, and 2...f5? to 3 h4. No better is 2...h4 3 g3! hg (3...g5 4 g4) 4 fg f5 5 ef gf 6 h4. And 2...g6? is elegantly refuted by 3 g4! (but not by 3 h4? g5!) 3...hg 4 h4!

So there's only one move left.

2...f6! 3 h4!

Of course not 3 ef? gf; and it's not difficult to see that White is the one in zugzwang. But now what does Black do?

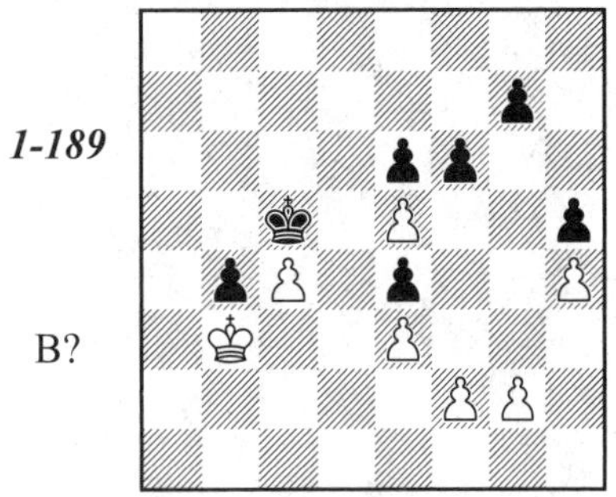

1-189 B?

3...fe is met by 4 g4!; and if 3...f5, then 4 f4! ef 5 gf g5 (5...f4 6 ef g6 7 f5) 6 hg h4 7 g6 h3 8 g7 h2 9 g8♕ h1♕ 10 ♕f8+ ♔c6 11 ♕d6+, with an easily won queen endgame.

One must have an unusual gift for the fantastic (or know some of Grigoriev's studies) to find the idea of a stalemate haven in the middle of the board!

3...fe! 4 g4! g6! (4...hg? 5 h5+−) **5 g5⊙ ♔b6!** (5...♔d6!) **6 ♔×b4 ♔c6 7 c5 ♔d5!! 8 ♔b5** Stalemate.

Chapter 2

KNIGHT VS. PAWNS

King in the Corner

Mate

If the defender's king is trapped in the corner, sometimes even a lone knight is able to mate.

A. Salvio, 1634

2-1

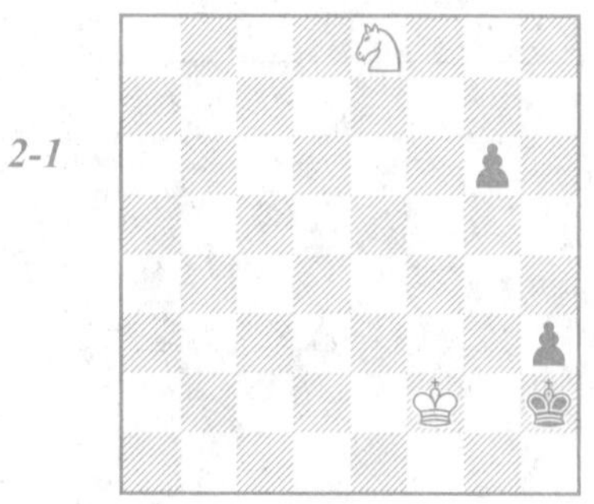

White to move wins by 1 ♘f6 ♔h1 2 ♘g4 g5 3 ♔f1⊙ h2 4 ♘f2#. But even with Black to move, the game lasts only a little longer.

1...♔h1

1...g5 2 ♘f6 g4 3 ♘×g4+ ♔h1 4 ♔f1⊙ h2 5 ♘f2#.

2 ♘f6 ♔h2

2...h2 3 ♘g4 g5 4 ♘e3! g4 5 ♘f1 g3+ 6 ♘×g3#; 2...g5 3 ♘g4⊙ h2 4 ♘e3!.

3 ♘g4+ ♔h1 4 ♔f1 g5 5 ♔f2⊙ h2 6 ♘e3 g4 7 ♘f1 g3+ 8 ♘×g3#.

Drawn Positions

Knight and pawn win easily against a lone king (that is, of course, so long as the pawn is not lost). But there are exceptions.

2-2

B?

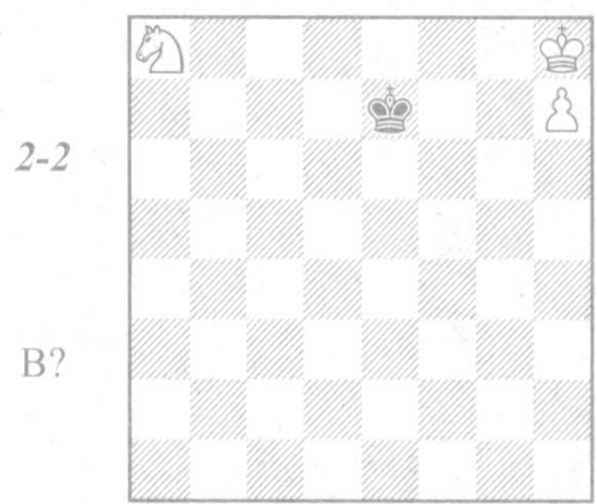

Black saves himself by squeezing the opposing king in the corner. He must only be careful to choose the correct square for his king. 1...♔f8? loses after 2 ♘c7 ♔f7 3 ♘e6⊙.

1...♔f7! 2 ♘c7 ♔f8 3 ♘e6+ ♔f7=

It's useful to note that ***the knight (unlike the other the pieces) cannot "lose" a move in order to give the move to the opponent*** - the knight can't triangulate.

We shall learn about other drawing situations by analyzing the following example:

V. Chekhover, 1952*

2-3

W?

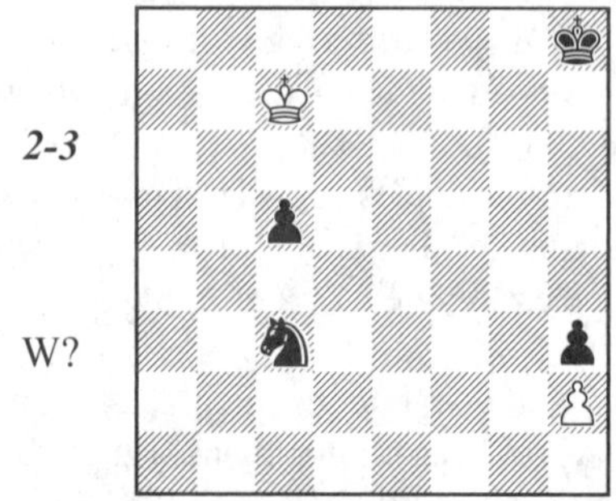

1 ♔c6! (1 ♔d6? ♘a4−+; 1 ♔b6? ♘e4−+) **1...♘e4 2 ♔d5 ♘g5 3 ♔×c5 ♘f3 4 ♔d5! ♘×h2 5 ♔e4 ♘g4 6 ♔f3 ♔g7 7 ♔g3 h2 8 ♔g2**

2-4

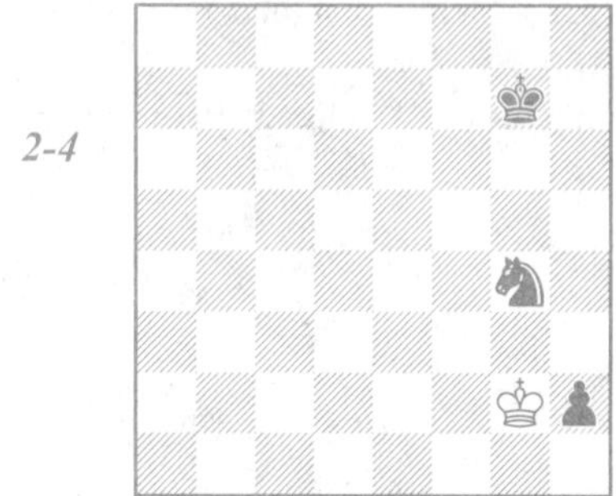

We may conclude that ***in those cases where the pawn has gone too far (in other words, to the next-to-last rank), the position is drawn.*** The knight could also be at f1 (5...♔g7 6 ♔f4 ♘f1 7 ♔f3 ♔g6 8 ♔f2 h2 9 ♔g2) without affecting the outcome.

Another try for Black is: 1...♔g7 2 ♔×c5 ♔f6 3 ♔d4 ♘d1 4 ♔d3 ♔f5 5 ♔e2 ♘c3+ 6 ♔f2 ♔f4 7 ♔g1

2-5

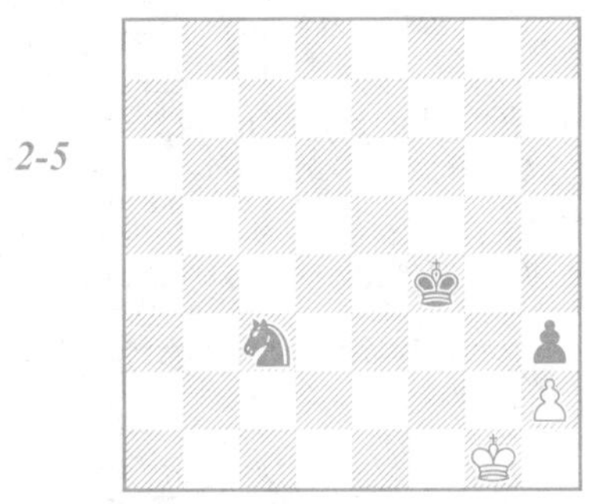

It's impossible either to drive the king from the corner or to mate him - the best Black can achieve is stalemate.

Exercises

2-6

2/1
W?

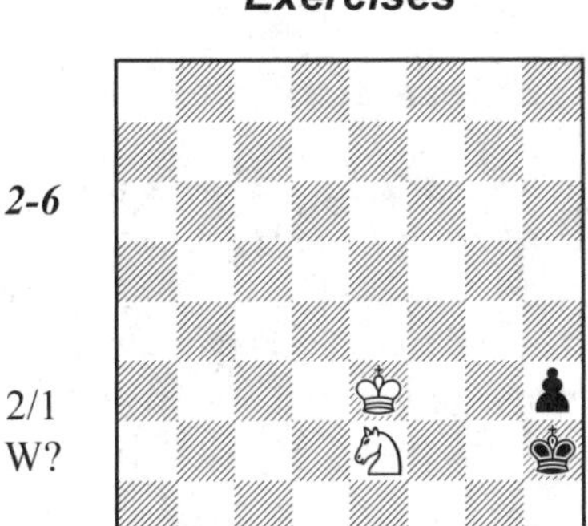

2-7

2/2
W?

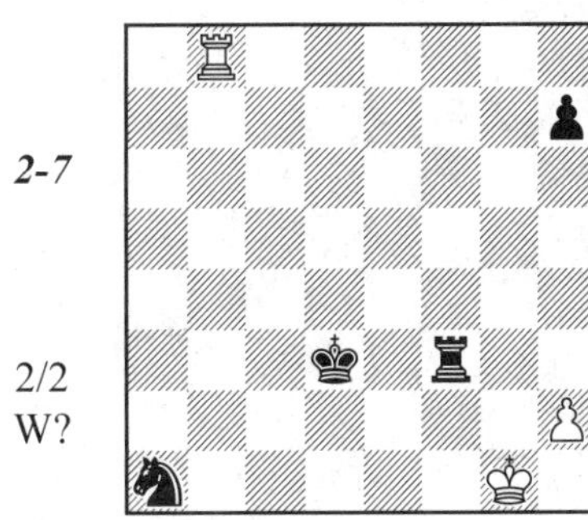

2-8

2/3
W?/Play

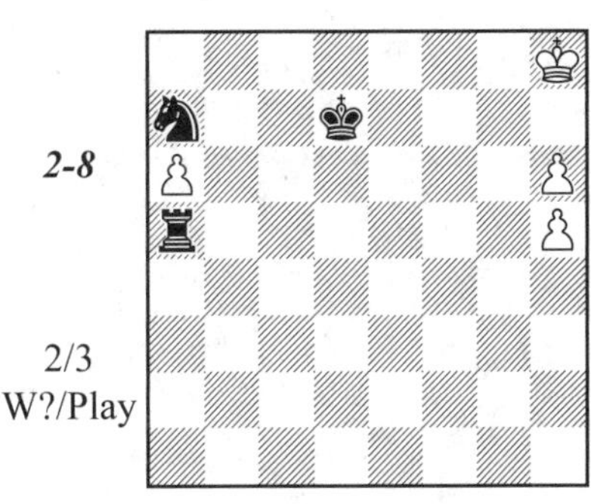

Knight vs. Rook Pawn

The closer the passed pawn to the edge of the board, the more difficulty the knight has dealing with it. The rook pawns are especially dangerous. Here is a simple, yet instructive example.

A. Chéron, 1952

2-9

W?

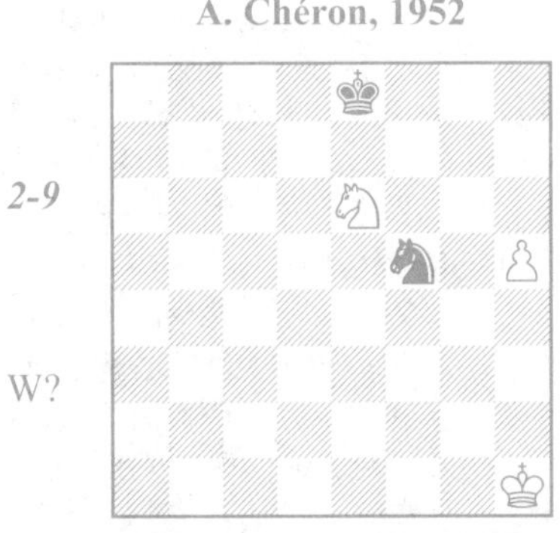

1 ♘g7+! ♘×g7 2 h6 ♔f7 3 h7+−.

Note, that with White's king at g2, the position would be drawn: the pawn is stopped after, for instance, 2...♘e6 3 h7 ♘f4+ and 4...♘g6. ***In many instances, the knight can win the necessary tempo with a check to the enemy king.***

The knight can hold a rook pawn without the king's help, if it "touches" any square in the pawn's path, except the final, corner square.

2-10

W?

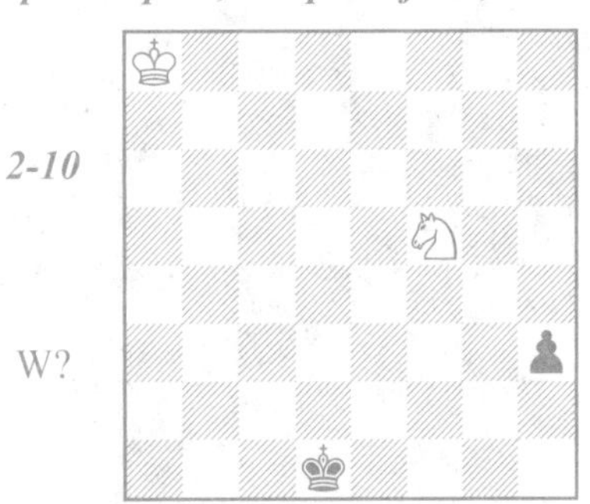

1 ♘g3? h2 2 ♔b7 ♔e1 3 ♔c6 ♔f2 is hopeless. The knight should aim for h2, not h1.

1 ♘e3+! ♔e2 2 ♘g4 ♔f3 3 ♘h2+ ♔g2 4 ♘g4 ♔g3 5 ♘e3! ♔f3 (5...h2 6 ♘f1+) **6 ♘f1**, etc.

I should also point out that even with the knight in the corner, the position is certainly not always hopeless. True, the knight can no longer deal with the pawn by itself; but sometimes the king can come to its rescue in time.

In the starting position, let's move the black king to d3. Now the knight cannot get to h2 (1 ♘h6? h2 2 ♘g4 h1♕+ - the pawn queens with check). So White has to play 1 ♘g3 (threatening 2 ♘f1) 1...h2 2 ♔b7.

2-11

B

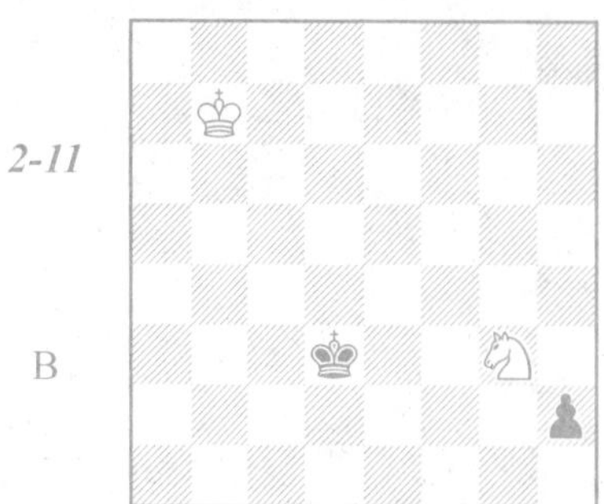

The knight has set up a ***barrier*** against the enemy king, who not only can't cross the e2- and e4-squares, but also is denied e3 and d2 (because of the forking ♘f1+). ***Knight forks are a vital technique in knight endgames.***

In order to attack the knight, the king will have to lose time with the outflanking ...♔c2-d1-e1-f2, or ...♔d4-e5-f4.

2...♔d4 3 ♔c6 ♔e5 4 ♔c5 ♔f4 5 ♘h1 ♔f3 6 ♔d4 ♔g2 7 ♔e3 ♔×h1 8 ♔f2=.

2...♔c2 3 ♔c6 ♔d1 4 ♔d5 ♔e1 5 ♔e4 ♔f2 6 ♔f4= (or 6 ♘h1+ ♔g2 6 ♔e3=).

N. Grigoriev, 1932

2-12

W?

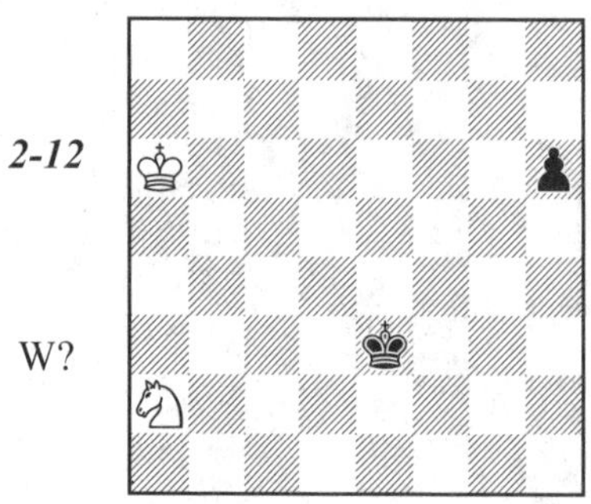

The knight goes after the h-pawn, while the black king stands athwart his path. Which side will win out?

1 ♘b4! h5 2 ♘c6!

2 ♘d5+? ♔f3! 3 ♘c7 h4 4 ♘e6 ♔g4! loses for White.

2...♔e4!

Certainly not 2...h4? 3 ♘e5 h3 (3...♔f4 4 ♘g6+ and 5 ♘×h4) 4 ♘g4+ ♔f4 5 ♘h2=. ***The king restricts the knight best from a distance of one square diagonally (and also two squares away on a file or a rank).*** This generalization may be illustrated by the variation 3 ♘d8? h4 4 ♘e6 ♔f5! 5 ♘d4+ ♔g4−+.

3 ♘a5!! h4 4 ♘c4 (4 ♘b3? ♔e3) **4...♔f3!?** (4...h3 5 ♘d2+ ♔e3 6 ♘f1+)

2-13

W?

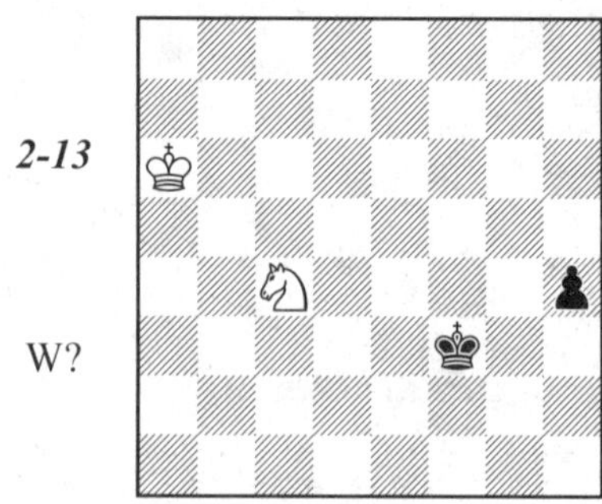

One last little task: to choose between 5 ♘d2+ and 5 ♘e5+. On 5 ♘d2+? Black responds 5...♔e2! (5...♔g2? 6 ♘c4! h3 7 ♘e3+) 6 ♘e4 h3 7 ♘g3+ ♔f2 - and since the knight cannot reach the h2-square, White loses.

5 ♘e5+! ♔g3

On 5...♔f4 White plays 6 ♘g6+, while other retreats allow the knight to get to g4.

6 ♘c4! h3 7 ♘e3=

It's interesting that the only way to refute 2 ♘c2+? (instead of 2 ♘c6!) is by 2...♔f2! The natural reply 2...♔e4? allows White the same sort of saving maneuver as in the main variation: 3 ♘a3! h4 (3...♔d3 4 ♔b5! h4 5 ♘c4 h3 6 ♘e5+) 4 ♘c4=.

Let's think about the strategic basis for White's saving plan. His knight goes to the h2-square via g4 or f1. Each of those routes individually might be interdicted by the king. The c4-square is key, because both routes intersect here: c4-e5-g4 and c4-d2-f1. Black cannot prevent the double threat.

Double attack is one of the most effective methods of struggle in chess. Along with tactical double attacks (such as knight forks), it is important to learn the use of "strategic double attacks" as well - moves which further two (or more) goals simultaneously.

In addition to the study we have just examined, this strategy might also be illustrated by some of the pawn endgames examined earlier, such as Weenink's position (Diagram 1-15) or B. Neuenschwander's position (Diagram 1-31).

Exercises

2-14

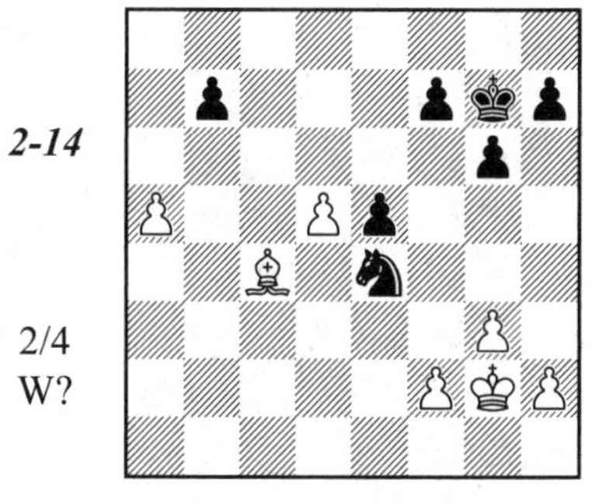

2/4
W?

2-16

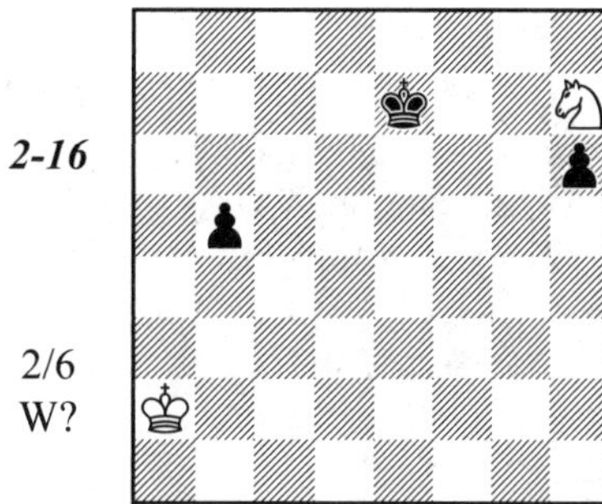

2/6
W?

2-15

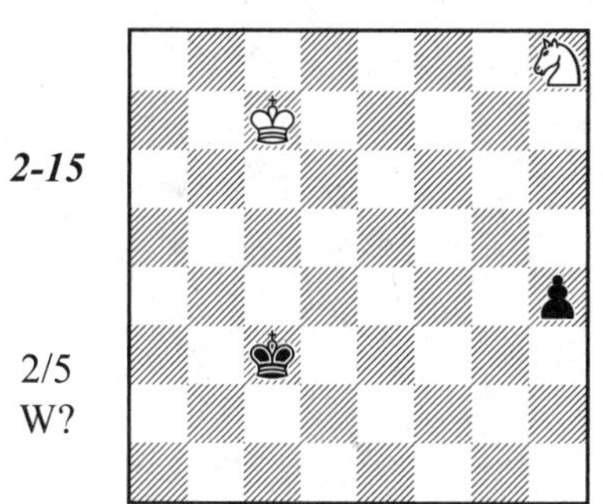

2/5
W?

2-17

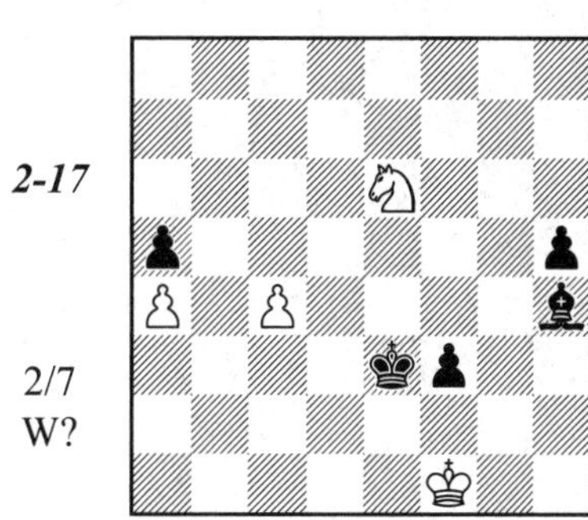

2/7
W?

The Knight Defends the Pawn

The best way for the knight to defend the passed pawn is from the rear. Here, the knight is immune from capture, since that would put the king outside the square of the passed pawn.

2-18

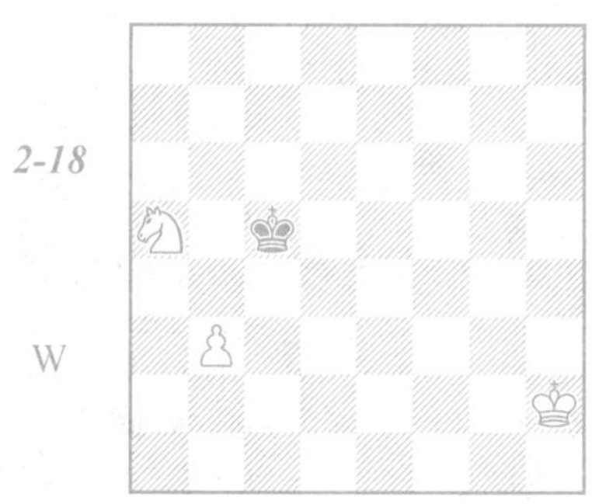

W

White parries the threat of 1...♔b4 with **1 ♘c4! ♔b4 2 ♘d2 ♔c3 3 ♔g3+–.**

The knight can easily defend its pawn if both white and black pawns are on the same file, and the pawns blockade one another.

M. Dvoretsky, 2000

2-19

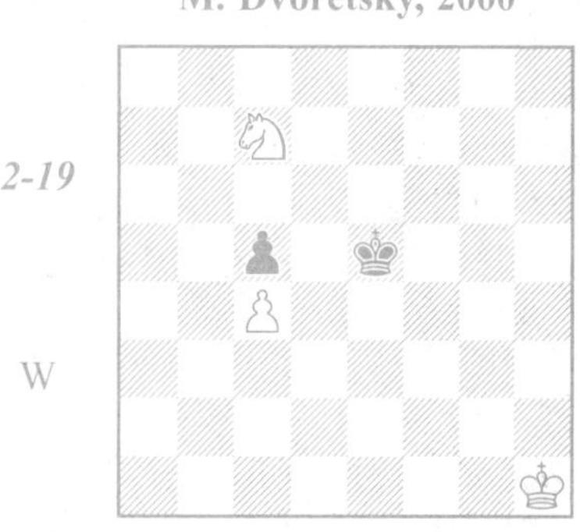

W

White can play either **1 ♘b5 ♔e4 2 ♔g2 ♔d3 3 ♘d6,** or **1 ♘d5 ♔d4 2 ♘b6** - in either case, the knight can handle it, without the king's assistance.

Let's move the pawn to c3. White's task is now more complex. He only gets a draw out of 1 ♔g2? ♔e4 2 ♔g3 ♔d3 3 ♘b5(d5) ♔c4, or 1 ♘b5? ♔d5 (1...♔e4? 2 c4) 2 ♘a3 ♔e4 3 ♔g2 ♔d3 4 c4 ♔c3 5 ♔f3 ♔b3 6 ♔e4 ♔×a3 (here, if the king were on e5, White would win with 7 ♔d6). But there is a solution: **1 ♘a8! ♔d5** (1...♔e4 2 c4) **2 ♘b6+ ♔c6 3 ♘c4 ♔d5**, and now the simplest is **4 ♘d2+–** (the barrier).

Understandably, if we moved the starting position one file to the left, there would be no win.

If White must defend the knight with his king, then the wins come far less often. Sometimes, we get a position of reciprocal zugzwang.

Ebralidze - Bondarevsky
USSR ch, Tbilisi 1937

2-20

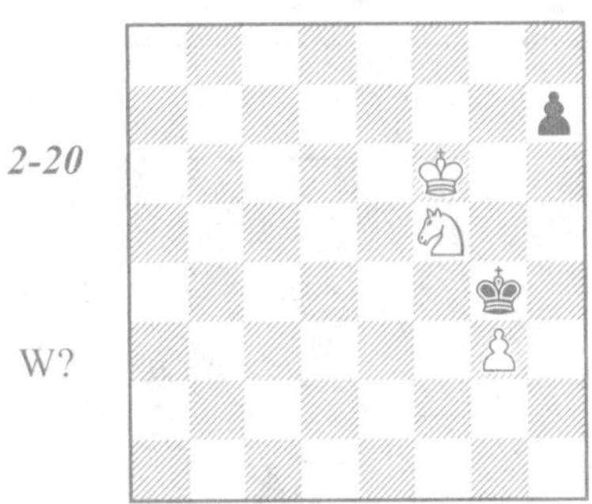

W?

1 ♔e5!

Seizing the opposition is important when the black pawn is at h5 - consequently, it follows that with the pawn at h7, White needs the anti-opposition. In the actual game, White erred, missing the win: 1 ♔e6? ♔g5! 2 ♔e5 h5 3 ♔e6 (3 ♔e4 ♔g4) 3...♔g6! 4 ♘e3 ♔g5. Drawn, in view of 5 ♔e5 h4 6 g4 h3.

1...♔g5

Other moves don't help either:

1...h5 2 ♔f6 (or 2 ♔e4);

1...h6 2 ♔f6! ♔h5 3 ♘×h6! ♔×h6 4 g4;

1...♔f3 2 ♔e6! ♔g4 3 ♔f6⊙ (the king triangulates) 3...♔h5 (3...h5 4 ♔g6) 4 ♘e3.

2 ♘e3 h5 3 ♔e4 (3 ♘f5) **3...h4 4 g4 h3 5 ♔f3**+−.

And now I offer for your enjoyment the analysis of a very deep and elegant study.

From the next diagram, let's first examine White's most natural plan: approaching the pawns with his king.

1 ♔c1? ♔g4 2 ♔d2 f3 3 ♘e3+ (3 ♔e3 f2! 4 ♔×f2 ♔f4=) 3...♔f4 4 ♔d3 f2 5 ♘f1 ♔f3 6 ♘d2+ ♔f4! We have reached the reciprocal zugzwang position fundamental to this endgame. Black to move loses (7...♔g3 8 ♔e2). But it's White's move here, and 7 ♔e2 is met by 7...f1♕+! 8 ♔×f1 ♔e3 9 ♔e1 ♔d3 10 ♔d1 ♔e3 11 ♔c2 ♔d4=.

D. Blundell, 1995

2-21

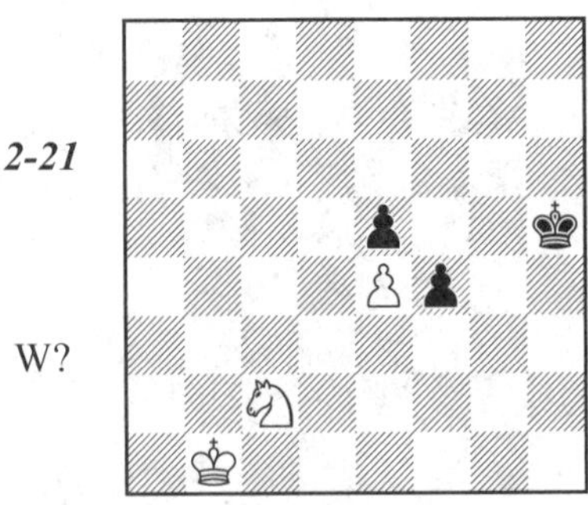

W?

Let's try 1 ♘a3? f3 2 ♘c4. Now the natural 2...♔g4? leads to a loss: 3 ♔c2 ♔g3 4 ♔c3!⊙ 4...♔g4 (4...f2 5 ♘d2 ♔f4 6 ♔d3⊙+−; 4...♔f4 5 ♔d3 f2 6 ♘d2⊙+−) 5 ♘×e5+! ♔f4 6 ♔d4.

White won here only because with his king at c3 the e5-pawn could be captured with check. That can be avoided by playing 2...♔g5(h4)!! 3 ♔c2 ♔g4! 4 ♔c3!? ♔g3! (there is also 4...♔g5!?, for example: 5 ♔d2!? f2 6 ♘e3 ♔f4 7 ♔d3 ♔g3! 8 ♘f1+ ♔f3! 9 ♘d2+ ♔f4). We have reached another reciprocal zugzwang position, this time with White to move. 5 ♘d2 runs into 5...♔f4 6 ♔d3 f2= (the main zugzwang); an equivalent line is 5 ♔d2 f2 6 ♔e2 ♔f4 7 ♘d2 (7 ♘d6 ♔g3) 7...f1♕+! or 5 ♔d3 f2 6 ♘d2 ♔f4!⊙.

Incidentally, looking at this variation leads us to the astonishing conclusion that **both** sides should maneuver so as not to be the first to approach the other. As soon as White plays either ♘d2 or ♔d3, he falls into zugzwang; and if Black is too hasty with either ...f2 or ...♔f4, the zugzwang position occurs with him to move instead. Thus, we have a case known to us from pawn endings: mined squares. However, this is the only case I know of where the squares are mined for four different pieces at once, and not for the usual two.

And now, for the solution. White must play much as in the last variation, except that he must place his knight, not on c4, but on b3, leaving the c4-square open for his king.

1 ♘a1!! f3 2 ♘b3 ♔g4 3 ♔c2 ♔g3 4 ♔c3! ♔g4 5 ♔c4!

Here is the point! Black can wait no longer: on 5...♔g3 6 ♔d5 f2 7 ♘d2 ♔f4 8 ♘f1+− decides. He must go to the mined square first, which of course puts him into zugzwang.

5...♔f4 6 ♔d3! (6 ♔d5? ♔e3; 6 ♘d2? ♔e3) **6...f2 7 ♘d2⊙ ♔g3 8 ♔e2** (8 ♔c4 ♔f4

9 ♔d5? is mistaken, in view of 9...♔e3 10 ♘f1+ ♔f4⊙=) **8...♔g2 9 ♘f1 ♔g1 10 ♘e3⊙+–**.

Tragicomedies

Nimzovitch - Rubinstein
Karlsbad 1911

2-22

W?

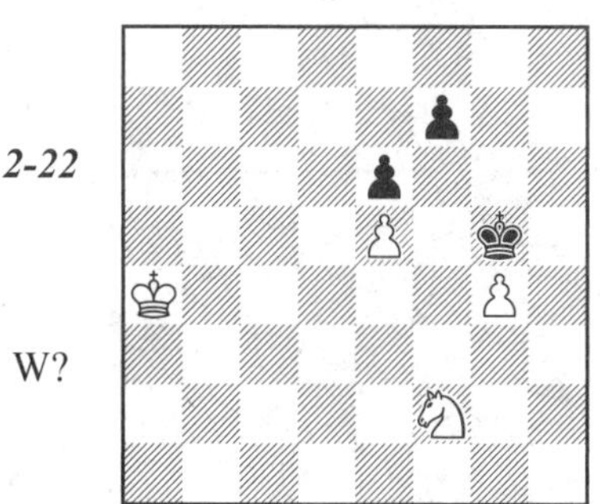

The best square for the knight would have been d7, from where it defends the e5-pawn and prevents the exchange ...f7-f6. This could easily have been achieved by 1 ♔b4(b3,b5)! ♔f4 2 ♘d3+ ♔×g4 (2...♔e4 3 ♔c4) 3 ♘c5! ♔f5 4 ♘d7+–. Unfortunately, Nimzovitch got too hasty.

1 ♘d3? f6! 2 ef ♔×f6 3 ♘f2 ♔g5

White's king is too far from the center of the action - Black has enough time to drive the knight from f2 by advancing his e-pawn.

4 ♔b4 e5 5 ♔c4 e4 Drawn, in view of 6 ♔d4 ♔f4 and 7...e3.

Trolldalen - Schüssler
Groningen ech jr 1975/76

2-23

W

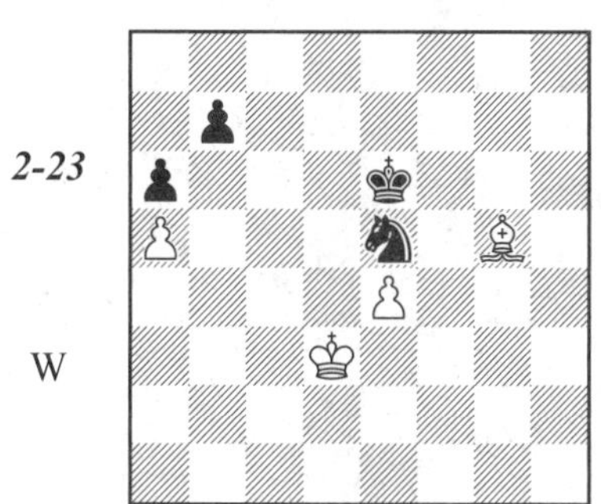

With 1 ♔c2 ♘c4 2 ♗d8 (stronger than 2 ♗d2 ♔e5 3 ♗e1! ♔×e4) 2...♔d7 3 ♔c3! ♘d6 4 ♗h4 ♘×e4+ 5 ♔d4, White would probably have drawn. An even simpler route to the same end was 1 ♔c3 ♘c6 2 ♔c4 ♘×a5+ 3 ♔c5 △ 4 ♔b6.

1 ♔d4? ♘f3+ 2 ♔c5 ♘×g5 3 ♔b6 ♘×e4 4 ♔×b7 ♘c5+ 5 ♔c6 ♘d3 6 ♔b6

Sacrificing his bishop, Trolldahlen assessed the position as drawn, and his opponent evidently agreed with him. Neither side suspected that this was now a position from a 1914 study by Kubbel (with colors and flanks reversed).

6...♘b4 7 ♔c5 ♘d5 8 ♔c6 ♔e5 9 ♔c5 ♔e4 10 ♔c4

2-24
$

B?

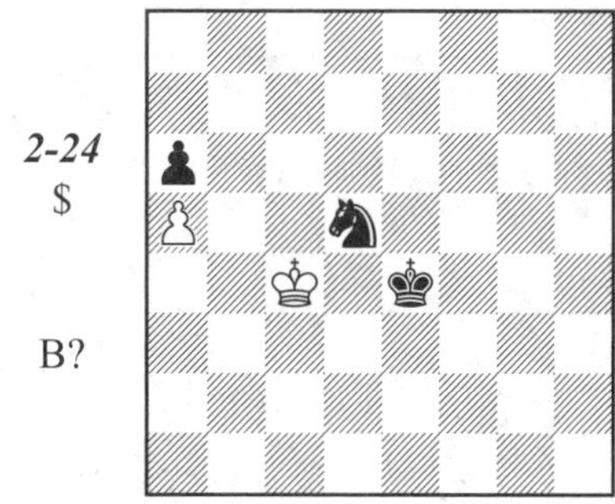

10...♘c7 11 ♔c5 ♔d3? doesn't work: 12 ♔b6 ♔c4 13 ♔×c7 ♔b5 14 ♔d6 ♔×a5 15 ♔c5=. Kubbel's solution was: 10...♘f6!! 11 ♔c5 ♘d7+ 12 ♔c6 ♘b8+ 13 ♔b7 ♔d5 14 ♔×b8 ♔c6! (shouldering) 15 ♔c8 ♔b5–+.

10...♘e3+ 11 ♔c5 ♘c2 12 ♔b6 ♘b4 13 ♔c5 ♘d5 14 ♔c4 ♔e5? (14...♘f6!!) **15 ♔c5 ♔e6 16 ♔c6** Draw. Even if Black had found the winning plan at that moment, he could no longer avoid the three-time repetition.

Keres - Lengyel
Luhacovice 1969

2-25

B

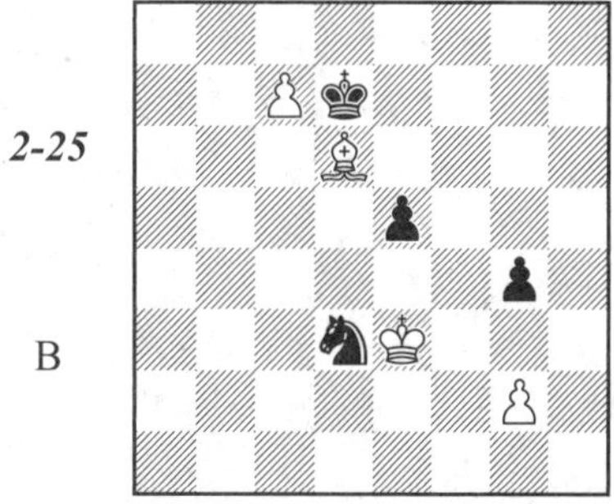

The game was adjourned here, and Lengyel resigned without continuing. Evidently, he assumed that his e- and g-pawns were doomed, and White must inevitably wind up two pawns ahead.

But this is not the case. As Keres pointed out, Black has a simple plan of defense which guarantees him the draw. First, he must force g2-

g3, after which he can defend the g4-pawn from h2 with his knight. White cannot break down this defensive setup: ♗g1 is met by ...♘f3 with tempo. And there is no possible zugzwang, either.

Simplest is **1...♘e1** at once. On 2 g3 ♘f3, we already have the indicated defensive position. And 2 ♔f2 is met by 2...♘d3+ 3 ♔f1 (3 ♔g3 e4 4 ♔×g4 e3 5 ♔f3 ♘e1+ 6 ♔g3 e2 7 ♔f2 ♘×g2=) 3...♔c8 4 g3 ♔d7 5 ♔e2 e4 6 ♔e3 ♘e1=.

1...♘f4 2 g3 ♘e6 is also possible (but not 2...♘d5+ 3 ♔e4 ♘f6+ 4 ♔f5!+−) **3 ♗×e5 ♘g5 4 ♔f4 ♘f3 5 ♗d6 ♘h2=.**

Exercises

2-26

2/8
W?

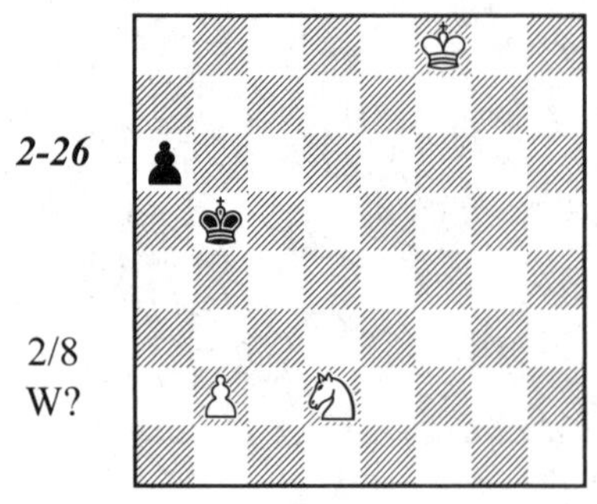

2-27

2/9
B?

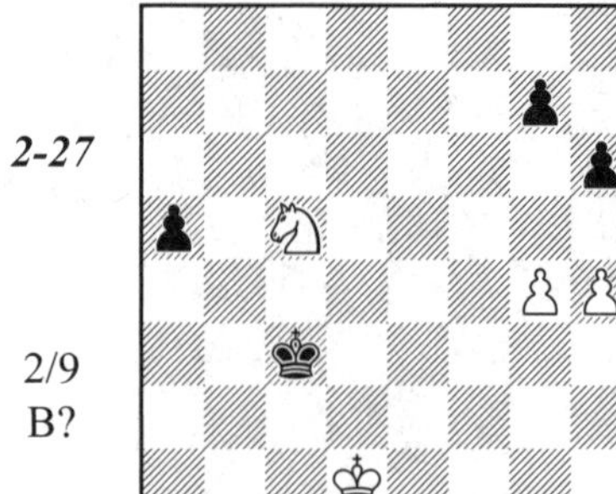

Chapter 3

KNIGHT ENDGAMES

In examining the "knight versus pawns" endgame, also we learned quite a bit that is useful about knight endgames. Firstly, because the peculiarites of the knight which we learned about there (such as its "distaste" for rook pawns, or its ability to fork or win tempi by checking the enemy king), also function here. And secondly, the knight must quite often be sacrificed in order to obtain a "knight versus pawns" endgame.

The Deflecting Knight Sacrifice

We shall not be making a systematic examination of the endgame in which a knight faces a knight and pawn: its theory is quite complex, and in my view, rather chaotic. There are no principles which are operative for many positions; the evaluation and the course of the struggle depend entirely upon the concrete details.

The deflecting knight sacrifice is the almost universally employed technique in such endings. And not only in these - there are many situations in which one side tries to queen its own passed pawn or to break into the enemy's camp with his king.

Eingorn - Beliavsky
USSR ch, Kiev 1986

3-1

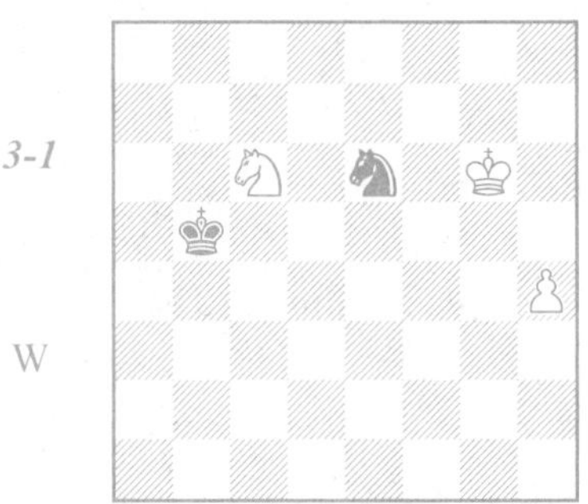

W

1 ♘d4+! ♘×d4 2 ♔f6!+−

The king goes, as we taught, one square diagonally away from the knight; which renders the h-pawn unstoppable.

2...♘c2 3 h5 ♘e3 4 ♔g5! (the same idea again) **4...♘c4 5 h6** Black resigned, in view of 5...♘e5 6 h7 ♘f7+ 7 ♔f6 ♘h8 8 ♔g7.

In the next diagram, Black may be a pawn down, but White's scattered pieces and more importantly the dangerous passed d-pawn, supported by the excellently centralized king and knight, assure him the advantage.

Barcza - Simagin
Moscow - Budapest m tt, 1949

3-2

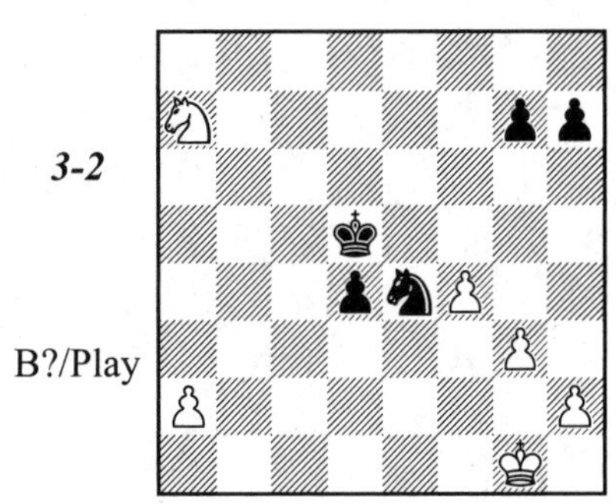

B?/Play

1...d3 2 ♔f1 ♘c3!

It's most important to deprive the white knight of the b5-square, which is exactly the square it needs to help the king battle the passed pawn, as shown by the following variations:

2...♔d4? 3 ♘b5+ ♔e3 4 ♘a3! d2 5 ♘c4+ ♔d3 6 ♘×d2!, when White draws without too much trouble, since the a-pawn will draw one of Black's pieces to the queenside;

2...♔c4? 3 a4! ♔b3 4 ♘b5 ♔×a4 5 ♘d4∓.

3 ♔e1! ♔d4 4 ♔d2 (4 ♘c6+? ♔e3−+) **4...♘e4+ 5 ♔c1□**

5 ♔e1? (or 5 ♔d1?) would lose at once to 5...♔e3. Here, that move would fall short after 6 ♘b5 d2+ 7 ♔c2 ♔e2 8 ♘d4+.

5...♘d6!!

The knight repositions itself more favorably, all the while maintaining control over that vital b5-square. Meanwhile, White's knight has no other way to reach the pawn: 6 ♘c6+ ♔c3 7 ♘e7 (7 ♘e5 d2+ 8 ♔d1 ♘e4) 7...d2+ 8 ♔d1 ♘e4 9 ♘d5+ ♔c4!−+.

6 ♔d2 ♘c4+ 7 ♔c1 d2+ 8 ♔c2 ♔e3 9 ♘b5 (9 ♘c6 ♘b2−+)

3-3

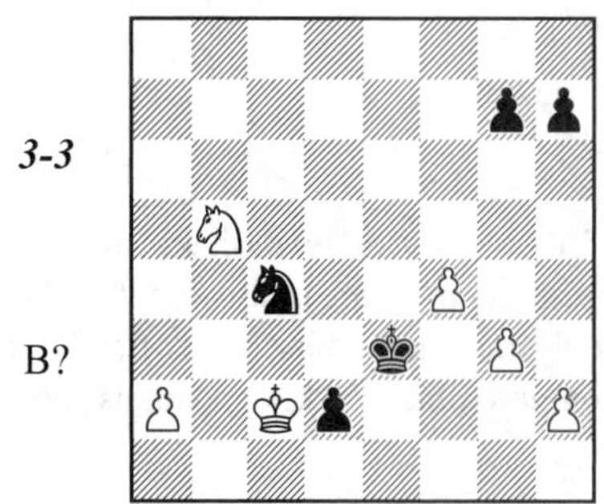

B?

9...♘a3+!

And in conclusion - a deflecting knight sacrifice (10 ♘×a3 ♔e2). White resigned.

Hernandez - Sula
Saloniki ol 1984

3-4

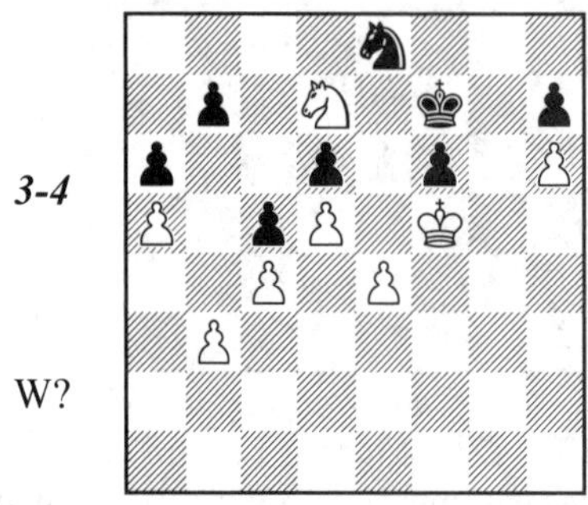

W?

1 ♘f8! ♔×f8 2 ♔e6

This knight sacrifice has allowed the king to invade the enemy camp. Black is in zugzwang: on 2...♔g8 3 ♔e7 decides.

2...♘g7+ 3 hg+ ♔×g7 4 ♔×d6 h5 5 ♔e7 h4 6 d6 h3 7 d7 h2 8 d8♕ h1♕ 9 ♕f8+ ♔h7 10 ♕f7+ ♔h8 11.♕×f6+ ♔h7 and Black resigned.

Exercises

3-5

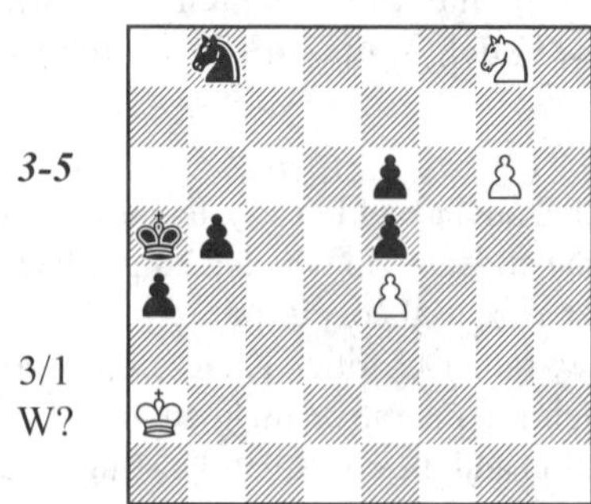

3/1
W?

3-6

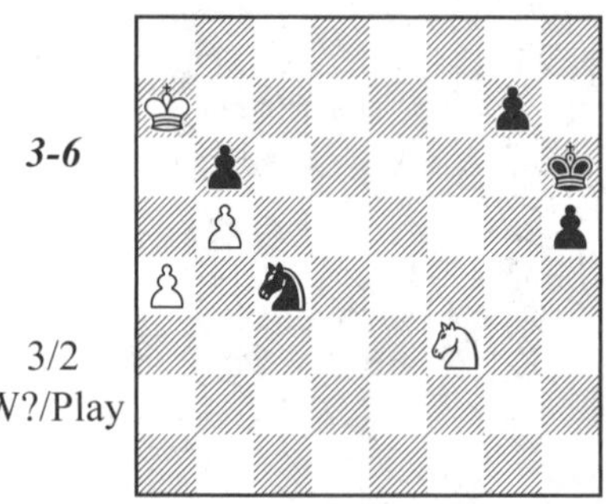

3/2
W?/Play

Botvinnik's Formula

"Knight endgames are pawn endgames": that's something Botvinnik once said. What he had in mind, is that many of the laws of pawn endings apply equally to knight endings. The same high value is given, for instance, to the active position of the king or the outside passed pawn. Such techniques as the pawn breakthrough, shouldering, the various methods of playing for zugzwang, and so forth, are seen constantly, not just in pawn endgames, but also in knight endgames. And we shall be convinced of this after studying a few practical examples.

Let's begin with a classic endgame.

Lasker - Nimzovitch
Zürich 1934

3-7

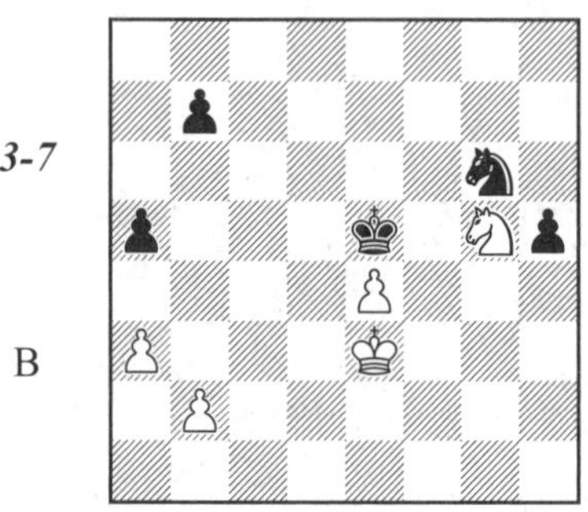

B

In the diagram, the pawn endgame would be an easy win for Black, in view of the outside passed h-pawn. In the knight endgame, he has considerably more complex problems to solve.

1...♔f6

A high degree of accuracy is required. The overhasty 1...h4? would allow the white knight to attack the queenside pawns by 2 ♘f7+ ♔f6 3 ♘d6 b6 4 ♘c4 h3 5 ♔f2!.

2 ♘h7+ ♔g7 3 ♘g5 ♔f6 4 ♘h7+ ♔e7!

The king retreats, but only briefly; now the e5-square can be occupied by the knight. On 5 ♔d4? Black forces a won pawn endgame by 5...♘f8! 6 ♘g5 ♘e6+!.

5 ♘g5 ♘e5 6 ♔d4

6 b3!? was worth considering, in order to prevent Black from fixing the queenside pawns by ...a5-a4, and retaining the option of moving the king either to d4 or to f4.

6...♔d6 7 ♘h3 a4 8 ♘f4 h4 9 ♘h3 b6!

"Steinitz's Rule" in action! Nimzovitch intends ...b7-b5 and ...♘c6+; however, the check would have been better delivered with the white knight on h3, as may be seen from the variation 9...b5 10 ♘f4 ♘c6+ 11 ♔c3!, when Black can't play 11...♔e5 in view of 12 ♘g6+. By making use of the choice of either the one-square or two-square move for this pawn, Black solves the problem - though it is true he had some help from his opponent.

10 ♘f4 b5⊙ 11 ♘h3?

The knight should not have left the f4-square, where it prevents the move ♔e5. White's best defense was 11 ♔c3! In reply, the deflecting knight sacrifice 11...♘g6?! 12 ♘xg6 h3 fails to 13 ♘h4! h2 14 ♘f5+ ♔e5 15 ♘g3 ♔f4 16 ♘h1 ♔xe4 17 ♔d2=. If 11...♘c6, then White can either wait with 12 ♔d3(d2), or exchange a pair of queenside pawns. After 12 b3, the tempting breakthrough 12...b4+!? will win in the line 13 ab? a3 14 b5 ♘b4 15 e5+ ♔xe5 16 ♘g6+ ♔e4 17 ♘xh4 ♘d3! However, White would answer 13 ♔b2!, for example: 13...ba+ (13...ab 14 ab) 14 ♔xa3 ab 15 ♔xb3 ♘e7 (otherwise, Black can't play ♔e5) 16 ♔c3 ♔e5 17 ♘h3 ♔xe4 18 ♔d2 ♔f3 19 ♔e1=.

Black could fight on with 11...♔c5!? 12 ♘e6+ ♔b6 13 ♘f4 ♘g6! 14 ♘h3 ♔c5. However, I am not sure that Black's positional advantage is sufficient for victory here.

11...♘c6+!

The straightforward attempt 11...♘c4 12 ♔c3 ♔e5 is erroneous in view of 13 b3! ab (13...♘xa3 14 ♔b2 ♘c4+ 15 bc bc 16 ♔c3 a3 17 ♘f2 ♔f4 18 ♔c2=) 16 ♔xb3 ♔xe4 17 ♔b4 △ 18 a4= (Müller, Lamprecht).

12 ♔e3

Emanuel Lasker probably rejected 12 ♔c3!?, because of 12...♔e5 13 ♔d3 ♘a5. Let us look what could happen: 14 ♘g1! ♔f4 15 e5 ♘c6! 16 e6 ♔f5 17 ♔c3(e3), and the pawn is invulnerable: 17...♔xe6? 18 ♘f3 h3 19 ♘g5+. However after 17 ♔c3 ♔f6! White is in zugzwang (18 ♔d3 ♘d8 or 18 b3 ab 19 ♔xb3 ♘d4+). 17 ♔e3 loses, too: 17...♔f6! 18 ♔e4 ♘d8 19 ♔d5 ♘xe6 20 ♔c6 ♔f5 21 ♔xb5 ♔g4 22 ♔xa4 ♔g3 (Müller, Lamprecht).

12...♔c5 13 ♔d3

On 13 ♔f4, Black has the strong 13...♔c4, or the equally strong 13...♔d4 △ 14...♘e5. Here, we see yet another technique borrowed from the arsenal of pawn endgames: widening the beachhead.

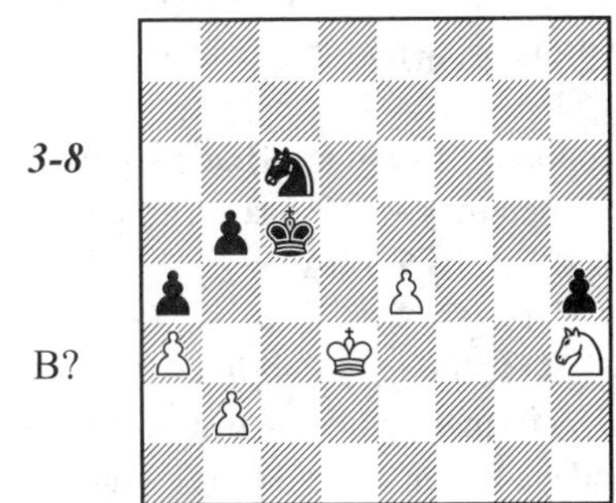

3-8

B?

13...b4! 14 ab+

If 14 ♘f4, then 14...♘e5+ 15 ♔c2 ba 16 ba ♔d4.

14...♔xb4 15 ♔c2 ♘d4+!

Nimzovitch displays outstanding technique. The point of widening the beachhead is to clear the king's path to the opposite wing; but the grandmaster is in no hurry to execute this plan. First, it is useful to reposition the knight to e6, where it hobbles the enemy knight. The consequences of the variation 15...♔c4 16 ♘g5 ♘e5 (16...♔d4? 17 ♘f3+) 17 ♘h3 ♔d4 18 b3 ab+ (18...a3 19 ♔b1) 19 ♔xb3 ♔xe4 20 ♔c2 are certainly not clear (even though this position, objectively, should be won).

16 ♔b1

16 ♔d3 ♘e6 17 ♔e3 ♔b3 is absolutely hopeless.

16...♘e6 17 ♔a2 (17 ♔c2 ♔c4⊙) **17...♔c4 18 ♔a3 ♔d4 19 ♔xa4 ♔xe4 20 b4 ♔f3 21 b5 ♔g2** White resigned.

On 22 b6 there follows 22...♔xh3 23 b7 (23 ♔b5 ♘d8) 23...♘c5+. Nimzovitch evidently calculated this whole variation when he played 15...♘d4+!.

Botvinnik - Kholmov
Moscow ch tt 1969

3-9
W

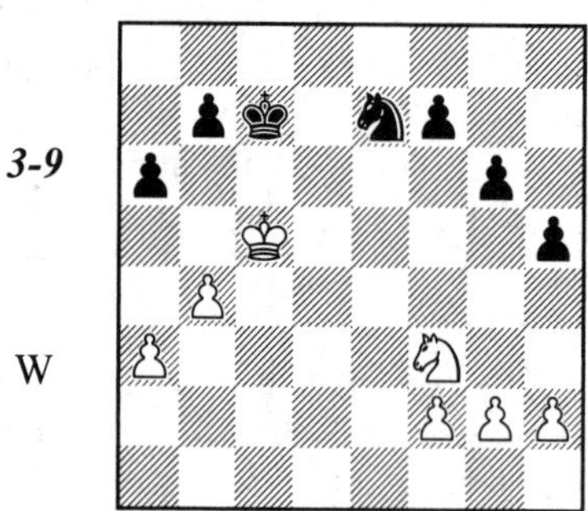

White's king is considerably more active than his opponent's, and that factor defines his great, and probably winning, advantage.

1 ♘g5!

It's important to induce Black's pawns to advance, as then they will be easier to attack.

1...f6 2 ♘h7 f5 3 h4

After 3...b6+ 4 ♔d4 ♔d6 5 ♘f8 ♘c6+ 6 ♔e3 ♘e5 7 ♔f4, the g6-pawn is lost. If White had played 3 f4? (instead of 3 h4), the king would not have had the f4-square, and Black would hold (by 6...♘e7).

3...f4

Waiting tactics must eventually result in zugzwang for Black, so he lashes out in a desperate attempt at counterattack on the kingside.

4 ♘f8 b6+

In Botvinnik's opinion, there were more practical chances after 4...f3!? 5 g3 (5 gf? b6+ 6 ♔d4 ♘f5+ 7 ♔e5 ♘xh4∞) 5...♘f5 6 ♘xg6 ♘xg3, although Black's position remains difficult after 7 ♔d4.

5 ♔d4 ♘f5+ 6 ♔e4 ♘xh4

6...f3 wouldn't have helped, in view of 7 ♔xf3 ♘xh4+ 8 ♔g3 ♘f5+ (8...g5 9 ♘e6+) 9 ♔f4.

7 ♘e6+ ♔c6 8 ♘xf4 ♔b5

On 8...g5, White replies 9 g3! gf 10 gh+−.

9 g3 ♘f5 10 ♘xg6 ♘h6

Now, from the next diagram, it's time to use the technique of defending the pawn with the knight that we learned in the "knight vs. pawns" chapter.

11 ♘e5! ♔a4 12 ♘c4 ♔b3

After 12...b5 13 ♘e5 ♔xa3 14 ♘c6!, the knight defends the pawn and prevents ...a6-a5. If 12...♔b5, then 13 ♘b2+− (barrier).

3-10
W

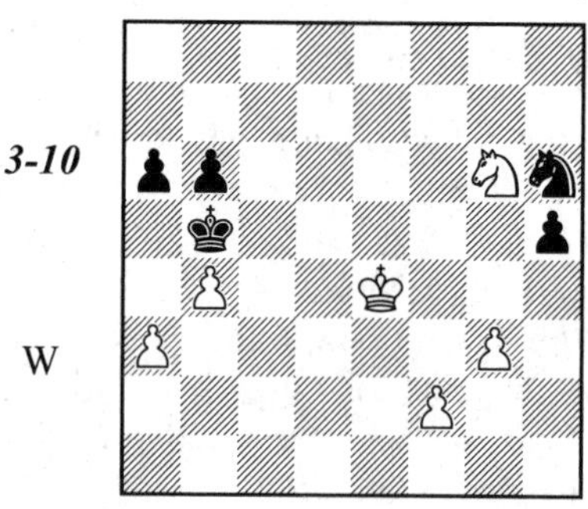

13 ♘xb6 ♔xa3 14 ♘d5 ♔b3 15 f4 ♔c4 16 ♘c7 ♔xb4 17 ♘xa6+ Black resigned.

The following is an example of zugzwang.

R. Réti, 1929

3-11
$
W?

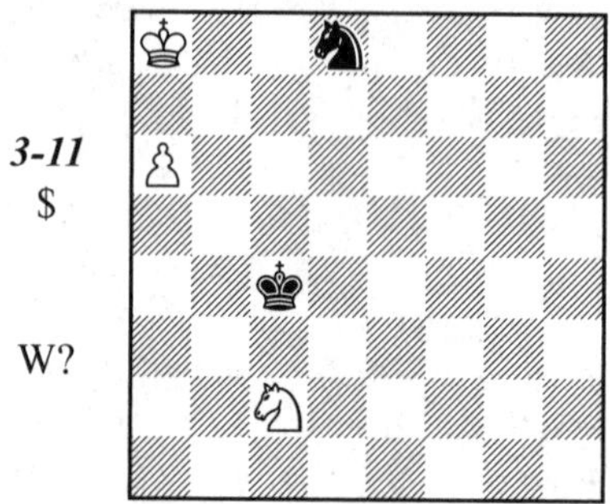

On 1 ♔b8? ♔b5! (1...♘c6+? 2 ♔b7 ♔c5 3 ♘d4! or 3 ♘b4! - a standard deflecting knight sacrifice) 2 ♘b4 ♘c6+ 3 ♔b7, Black forces the draw with 3...♘a5+! 4 ♔c7 ♘c6.

Before moving his king to b8, White must lose a move so as to force the enemy king, through zugzwang, to occupy the a5-square.

1 ♔a7! ♔b5

Black loses immediately with 1...♔c5 2 ♘d4! (zugzwang - but not 2 ♘b4? ♔b5 3 ♔b8 ♘c6+, with the drawing position we know already) 2...♔xd4 3 ♔b6+−.

2 ♘b4⊙ ♔a5

The goal is achieved! Black's king stands badly here - it deprives the knight of this square, and also fails to control c6.

3 ♔b8! ♘c6+ 4 ♔b7 (4 ♔c7?? ♘xb4 5 a7 ♘d5+) **4...♘d8+ 5 ♔c7 ♘e6+ 6 ♔b8(c6)**+−.

Alburt - Lerner
Kiev 1978

3-12

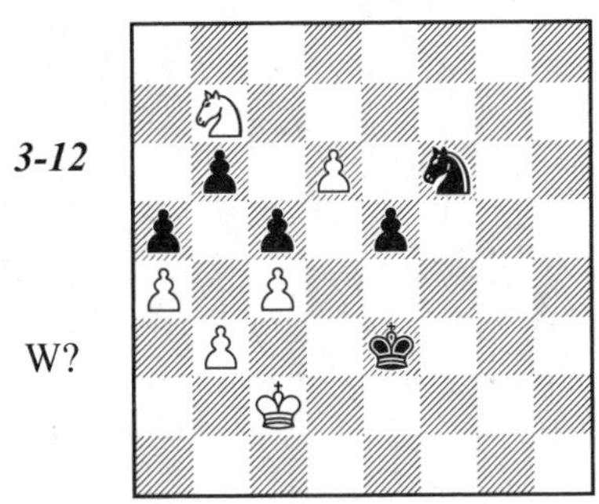

W?

Although Black might appear to be better, thanks to his more active king, White's spectacular pawn break completely changes the picture.

1 ♘×c5!! bc 2 b4 ab

Let's examine the other possibilities:

2...cb 3 c5 b3+ 4 ♔b2 (or 4 ♔×b3 ♘e4 5 ♔c4);

2...e4 3 bc ♔f2 4 c6 e3 5 d7 e2 6 d8♕;

2...♘d7 3 ba ♔f2 4 a6 e4 5 a7 e3 6 a8♕ e2 7 ♕e4 e1♕ 8 ♕×e1+ ♔×e1 9 a5.

3 a5 e4 4 a6 ♔f2 5 a7 e3 6 a8♕ e2 7 ♕f8 e1♕ 8 ♕×f6+ ♔g3

The queen ending is a win. White only has to get his queen to the d-file, where it will safeguard the king against checks and support the advance of his passed pawn.

9 ♕g5+ ♔h3

9...♔f3 10 ♕d5+ ♔g3 11 ♕d3+ ♔h4 12 d7+−.

10 ♕d2! ♕a1

10...♕e4+ 11 ♕d3+; 10...b3+ 11 ♔c3 ♕a1+ 12 ♔×b3 ♕b1+ 13 ♔a4+−.

11 d7 ♕a4+ 12 ♔b1 ♕b3+ 13 ♔c1 ♕a3+ (13...♕×c4+ 14 ♔b2) **14 ♔d1 ♕b3+ 15 ♔e2 ♔g4!**

The final trap: on 16 d8♕?? Black has a perpetual: 16...♕f3+ 17 ♔e1 ♕h1+ 18 ♔f2 ♕h2+ 19 ♔e3 ♕f4+ 20 ♔d3 ♕f5+. White replies with a typical trick for queen endgames: he utilizes the enemy king position to meet Black's check with a check of his own.

16 ♕d1! ♕×c4+ 17 ♔e3 Black resigned.

Exercises

3-13

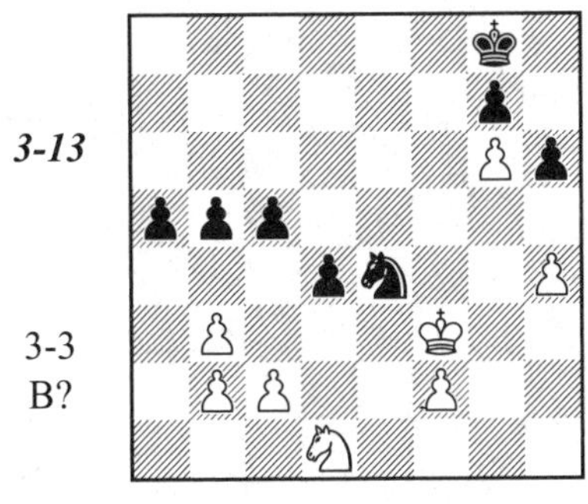

3-3
B?

3-15

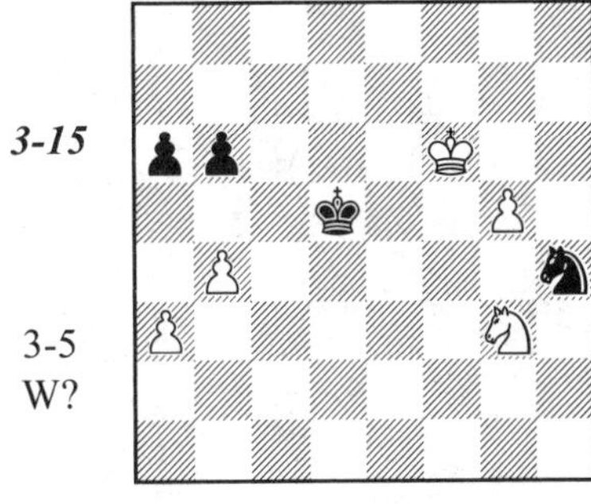

3-5
W?

3-14

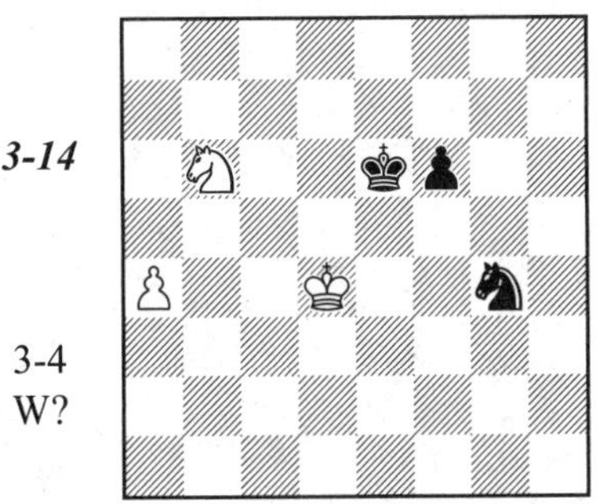

3-4
W?

3-16

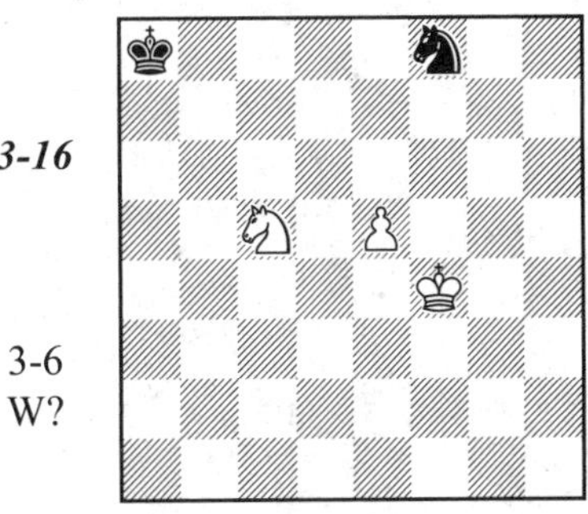

3-6
W?

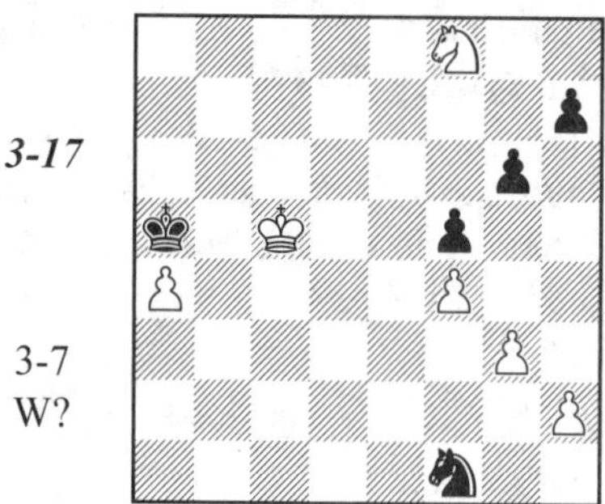
3-17

3-7
W?

Pawns on the Same Side

Is it possible to convert an extra pawn, if all the pawns are on the same side? Practice in such positions has shown, that with the exception of pawn endgames, a player's chances of success are greatest in knight endgames. For example, ***the "four vs. three" position is considered a win.***

R. Fine, 1941

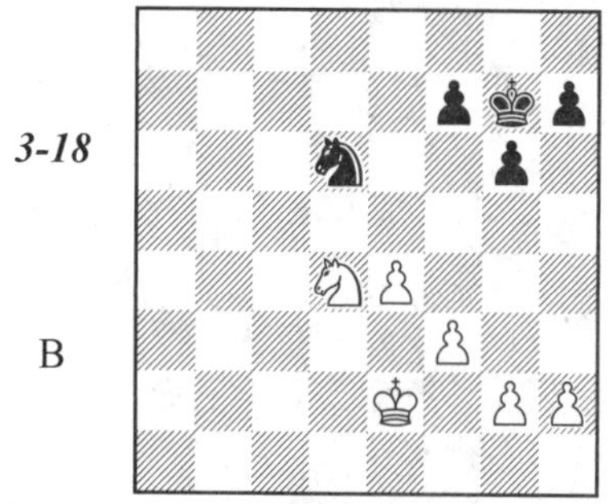
3-18

B

1...♔f6 2 g3 ♔e5 3 ♘c6+ ♔e6 4 ♔e3 f5

A reasonable plan, in principle: Black tries to trade off as many pawns as possible. Fine also examines other defensive plans:

4...♔d7 5 ♘d4 f6 6 f4 ♔e7 7 h4 (White strengthens his position to the maximum by advancing his kingside pawns) 7...♘f7 8 g4 ♔d7 9 ♔d3 ♔e7 10 ♔c4 ♔d6 11 g5! fg 12 hg h6 (otherwise, Black will soon run out of moves: 12...♔e7 13 e5 ♘d8 14 ♔d5 ♘f7 15 ♘c6+ ♔e8 16 e6 ♘h8 17 ♔e5 ♔f8 18 ♔f6+−) 13 e5+ ♔e7 14 gh ♘×h6 15 ♔d5 ♘g4 16 ♘c6+ ♔e8 (16...♔d7 17 e6+ ♔e8 18 ♔d6 ♘f6 19 ♘b4 ♘e4+ 20 ♔e5 ♘f2 21 ♘d5 ♘g4+ 22 ♔d6+−) 17 ♔e6 ♘e3 19 ♘b4 ♘g2 19 ♘d5, followed by 20 ♔f6+−;

4...g5 5 ♘d4+ ♔f6 6 f4! gf+ 7 gf ♘c4+ 8 ♔f2 (8 ♔f3 ♘d2+) 8...♔g7 9 e5 ♔g6 10 ♔e2 ♘b2 11 ♔f3 ♘c4 12 ♔e4 ♘d2+ 13 ♔d5 ♘f1 14 f5+ ♔g5 15 e6! fe+ 16 ♔×e6 ♘×h2 17 f6+−.

5 ♘d4+

5 e5? would be premature in view of 5...♘c4+ (but not 5...♔d5? 6 ed ♔×c6 7 ♔f4 ♔×d6 8 ♔g5) 6 ♔d4 ♘d2, or 6 ♔f4 ♔d5 (Dvoretsky). But on 5...♔e7 White can now play 6 e5 ♘c4+ 7 ♔f4 h6 8 h4 ♘b2 9 ♘×f5+! gf 10 ♔×f5, when three pawns outweigh the knight: 10...♔f7 11 f4 ♘d3 12 h5 ♘f2 13 g4 ♘h3 14 g5+−.

5...♔f6 6 ef gf 7 ♔f4 ♔g6 8 ♔e5 ♘f7+ 9 ♔e6 ♘d8+ 10 ♔e7 ♘b7

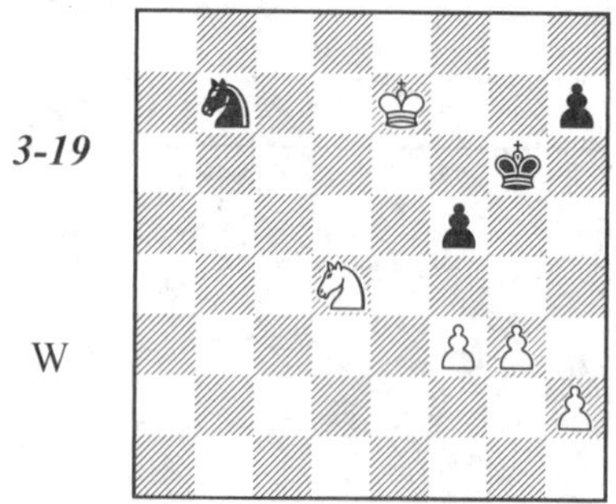
3-19

W

11 ♘e6!

Discovered by Chekhover. Fine examined 11 f4 ♘c5 12 ♘f3 (12 g4! is stronger: 12...fg 13 f5+ ♔h5 14 f6 ♘d3 15 ♘c6+− Müller) 12...♔h5 13 ♘e5, but then Black could play for stalemate: 13...h6! 14 ♔f6 ♘e4+ 15 ♔×f5 ♘g3+!, when the outcome remains unclear.

11...♘a5 12 ♘f4+ ♔g5 13 h4+ ♔h6 14 ♔f6+−

During the course of our analysis, we obtained a number of won positions involving a smaller number of pawns. Nevertheless, the configurations of "one pawn vs. two" and "two pawns vs. three" can frequently be saved; defending them, however, requires accuracy.

Tragicomedies

Fine - Najdorf
New York m (3) 1949

3-20

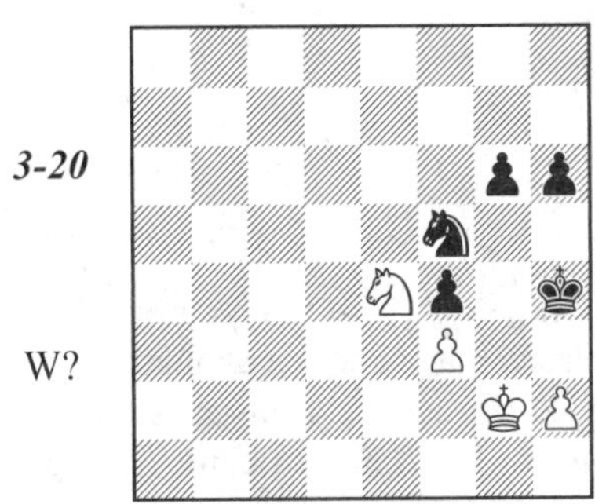

W?

White should hold the position. It is essential, however, not to move the pawn from h2: 1 ♘f2 ♘e3+ 2 ♔g1 ♘c2 3 ♘d3 g5 4 ♔f2 ♔h3 5 ♔g1 h5 (5...♘d4 6 ♘f2+ ♔h4 7 ♔g2) 6 ♘f2+ ♔h4 7 ♘d3, etc.

1 h3?

Now Black has a forced win. He executes a deflecting sacrifice of his knight, which allows him to snap off the pawn at h3, and thereby obtain a decisive passed h-pawn.

1...♘e3+ 2 ♔h2 ♘c2! 3 ♔g2 ♘e1+ 4 ♔f2 ♔×h3! 5 ♔×e1 ♔g2 6 ♔e2 h5 7 ♘g5 h4 8 ♘e6 g5!

White resigned, in view of 9 ♘×g5 h3 10 ♘×h3 ♔×h3 11 ♔d3 ♔g2−+.

Chapter 4

BISHOP VS. PAWNS

The Elementary Fortresses

There are many endgames in which the only way to defend consists of constructing a position impenetrable to the enemy. Such a position is called a fortress, and the method is called constructing a fortress.

I use the term "elementary fortress" to mean those theoretical positions with minimal material and a king usually placed on the edge or in a corner of the board, in which the stronger side proves unable to exploit a significant material advantage. We have already encountered such positions in the chapter on "Knight vs. Pawns" (Diagrams 2-2, 2-4, and 2-5). Here, and also in later chapters, you will learn other elementary fortresses which are important for the practical player.

Bishop and Rook Pawn

If the bishop does not control the rook pawn's queening square, then the weaker side has only to get his king into the corner (we call that the "safe" corner).

4-1

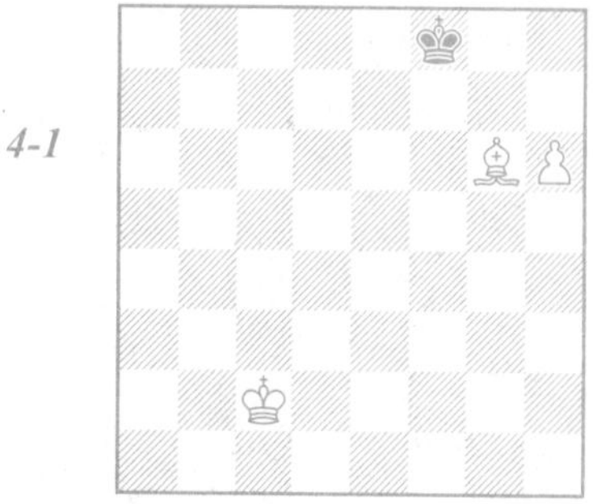

Black to move plays **1...♚g8!**, with an obvious draw.

Let's learn the techniques of cutting the king off from the safe corner. Let's suppose that it's White's move instead. If the bishop were on f5, he would win after 1 ♗e6! With Black's king on f6, a different standard cutoff maneuver - 1 ♗h5(e8)! - works instead. But in the diagrammed position, there is only one way to play for the win:

1 ♗h7 ♚f7 2 ♔d3 ♚f6 (△ 3...♚g5) **3 ♗f5 ♚f7** (△ 4...♚g8) **4 ♗h7** (4 ♗e6+ ♚g6) **4...♚f6=**

Relocate the white king to d2, and it can reach the pawn in time to help it queen: 1 ♗h7! ♚f7 2 ♔e3 ♚f6 3 ♔f4+−.

Everything we've said so far is elementary. Yet even strong players forget about these ideas surprisingly often, and make mistakes in the simplest positions. I had no difficulty finding examples for the "tragicomedies" section of this chapter.

Now let's look at a position with paired rook pawns (with the king cut off from the corner). The famous theoretician Vsevolod Rauzer did considerable analysis on this situation.

V. Rauzer, 1928

4-2

W

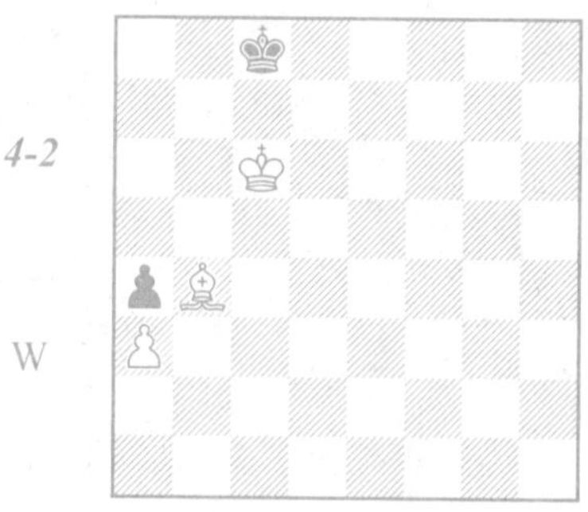

White cuts off and then drives the king away from the corner, yet still, he cannot win. ***The defensive method is simple: just keep the king in the upper half of the board.*** Then, any attempt to remove the a4-pawn will allow Black's king to get back to the safe corner a8.

1 ♗d6 ♚d8 2 ♔b7 ♚d7 3 ♗c7 ♚e6 4 ♔c6 ♚e7 5 ♗b6 ♚e6 6 ♗c5 ♚e5 7 ♗f8 ♚e6 8 ♗d6 ♚f7 9 ♔d7 ♚f6 10 ♗h2 ♚f7

10...♚f5 11 ♔e7 ♚g5 (but not 11...♚e4? 12 ♔e6+−) 12 ♔e6 ♚g6 is also possible.

11 ♗e5 ♚g6

Or 11...♚f8, but not 11...♚g8? 12 ♔c6! ♚f7 13 ♔b5 ♚e6 14 ♔×a4!+−.

12 ♔e6 (12 ♔c6 ♚f5!) **12...♚g5 13 ♗b2 ♚g6 14 ♗f6 ♚h6 15 ♔f7 ♚h7 16 ♗e5 ♚h6 17 ♗g7+ ♚h7 18 ♔f8 ♚g6 19 ♔g8 ♚f5 20 ♔f7 ♚g5 21 ♗f8 ♚f5 22 ♗e7**

White has managed to drive the king closer to the center; but now he has to keep him from returning to a8. As a result, the way is once again open to the upper half of the board.

22...♔e5 23 ♔e8 ♔e6 24 ♗f8 ♔f6 25 ♗b4 ♔g7, etc.

Now let's see what happens with the king in the lower half of the board instead: let's play 7...♔d4? (instead of 7...♔e6).

4-3
$

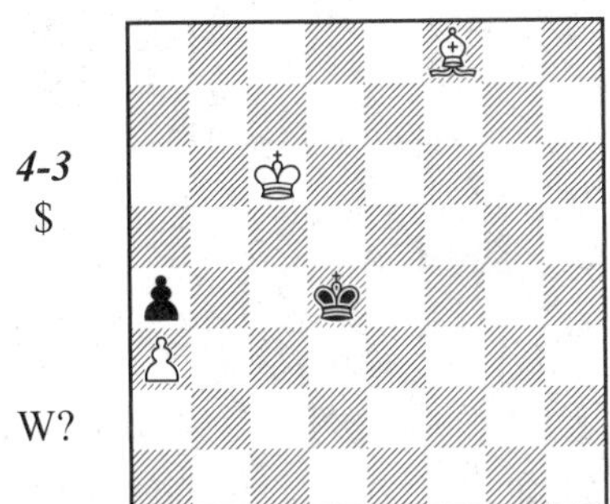

W?

8 ♗d6! ♔e4 (8...♔c4 9 ♗c5 ♔d3 10 ♔b5) 9 ♔b5 ♔d5 10 ♗h2⊙ ♔e6 11 ♔×a4 ♔d7 12 ♔b5 ♔c8 13 ♔b6+−. From this variation we can see how vital that h2-b8 diagonal is to the bishop. However, the only way the bishop can occupy it is if the black king gets too frisky. If he follows the above-cited rule of defense instead, then White will be unable to keep the bishop on the necessary diagonal and keep the king out at the same time.

Amazingly, in the last diagrammed position Averbakh examines only 8 ♗g7+?, allowing Black to gain the half-point by 8...♔e4! (after 8...♔c4? the quickest win is by 9 ♗b2 ♔b3 10 ♔b5!) 9 ♔d6 ♔f5 10 ♗e5, and now 10...♔g6 - again, not the "active" 10...♔e4? 11 ♔e6!+−. And yet, in the final position, it's still quite difficult to demonstrate a win for White. For example, after 11...♔f3! 12 ♔f5 ♔e3, he must find the exact move: 13 ♗b2!! I won't reproduce all of Rauzer's analysis here - those wishing to see it may find it in any endgame reference.

I might add (without giving the full proof, which is pretty weighty) that if, in Rauzer's starting position, we move the pawn on a3 back to a2, the evaluation changes. White will try to stalemate the enemy king (while still keeping him away from the corner, of course), in order to force the move a4-a3, after which the bishop can pick off the pawn. If Black tries to avoid this scenario, then he must move his king into the center, which will allow White, by playing a2-a3 at the right moment, to obtain the "bad" black king situation we have already seen.

Now for one more variation on Rauzer's position (analyzed by Horwitz and Averbakh). Let's add a black pawn at b5.

4-4
$

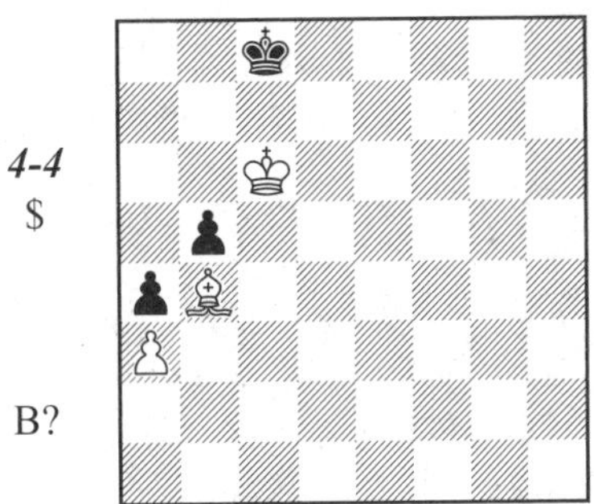

B?

Now the king's arrival in that left-hand upper corner is mortally dangerous. It will be stalemated, and be forced to play ...b5-b4, when the a3-pawn goes to the b-file. White to move wins quickly by 1 ♗a5 ♔b8 2 ♗b6 ♔a8 (2...♔c8 3 ♗c7⊙) 3 ♔c7⊙ b4 4 ab+−.

But Black to move renders the position drawn, since White can no longer stalemate the king. The move ...b5-b4 is no longer even fatal; in fact, at the right moment it will be Black's salvation.

1...♔d8! 2 ♔d6 ♔e8 3 ♔e6 ♔d8 4 ♗d6 (4 ♗a5+ ♔e8!) **4...♔c8** (4...♔e8? 5 ♗e7⊙) **5 ♗e5** (5 ♔e7 ♔b7 6 ♔d7 b4! 7 ab ♔b6=, but not 7...a3? 8 ♗c5! a2 9 ♗d4+−) **5...♔d8!**

Black loses after 5...♔b7? 6 ♔d6 ♔c8 (6...b4 7 ab ♔b6 8 ♗b2! ♔b5 9 ♗a3 ♔c4 10 ♔c6 ♔b3 11 b5; 6...♔b6 7 ♗d4+ ♔b7 8 ♔d7) 7 ♗f6 ♔b7 8 ♗d8 ♔c8 9 ♗b6 ♔b7 10 ♔c5 ♔c8 11 ♔c6 ♔b8 12 ♗a5 ♔a7 (12...♔c8 13 ♗c7; 12...♔a8 13 ♔c7 ♔a7 14 ♗b6+ ♔a6 15 ♔c6) 13 ♗c7 or 13 ♗b4.

6 ♗f6+ ♔c7! 7 ♗e7 ♔c6 8 ♗d6 b4!=

White can drive the enemy king to the kingside and try to stalemate it there. In order to avoid stalemate, the king will have to retreat to the lower half of the board; but that is less dangerous now than it was without the b5-pawn, in view of ...b5-b4! at the right moment, which now becomes a resource for Black.

Tragicomedies

Gutman - Mikenas
Riga 1969

4-5

W

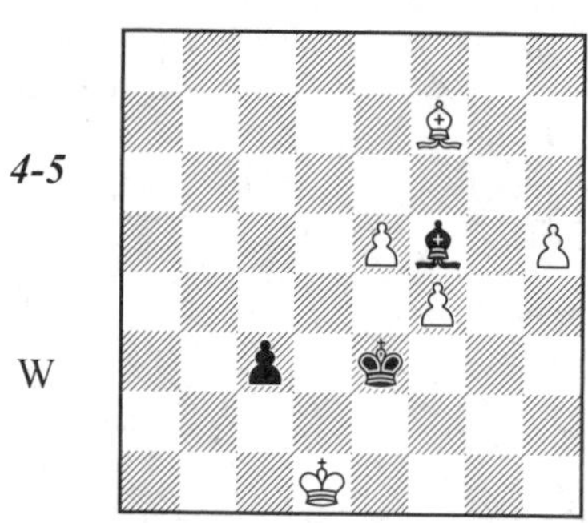

What could have been simpler than 1 e6 ♔×f4 2 e7 ♗d7 3 h6+−, or 1 h6 ♔×f4 2 e6+−?

1 ♗g6?? ♔×f4 2 ♗×f5

Gutman evidently expected 2...♔×f5? 3 h6 ♔g6 4 e6+−. However, it is more important for Black to take, not the bishop, but the e-pawn.

2...♔×e5! 3 h6 ♔f6 4 ♔c2 ♔f7 5 ♗h7 ♔f6 6 ♗g8 ♔g6 7 h7 ♔g7 Drawn.

Gershon - Thorhallsson
Bermuda 1999

4-6

W

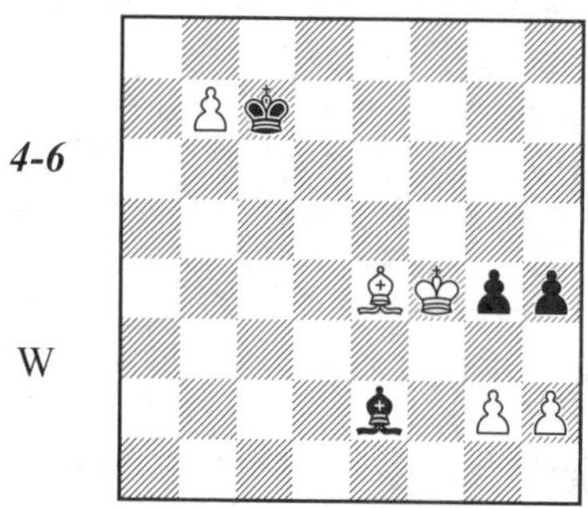

Here too, the win is elementary: 1 ♔g5 h3 2 g3, followed by 3 ♗f5 - White winds up two pawns ahead. Gershon chose a different way, making the same mistake Gutman did in the preceding example: he only expected Black to take his attacked bishop.

1 h3?? gh 2 gh ♗a6 3 ♔g5 ♗×b7 4 ♗×b7 ♔d7!

On 5 ♔×h4, the black king has time to get to h8; otherwise, we have Rauzer's drawn position. The game ended in a draw.

Where should Black put his king in the next diagram? As close as possible to h8, of course.

Fischer - Taimanov
Vancouver cmqf (2)

4-7

B

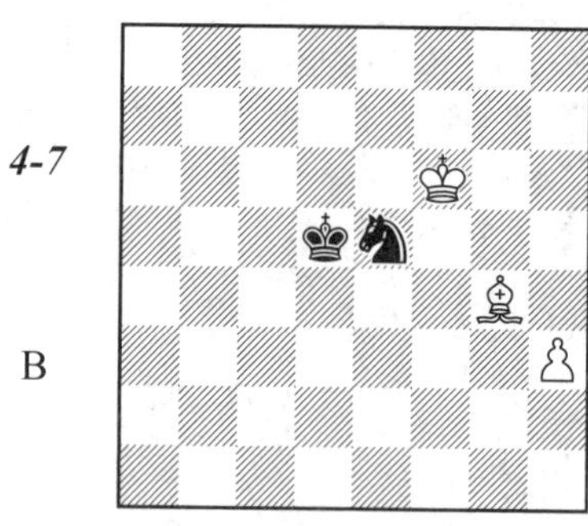

The most accurate way to draw was: 1...♘d3! 2 h4 ♘f4 3 ♔f5 ♔d6! 4 ♔×f4 ♔e7=. Also possible was 1...♔d6 2 ♗e2 ♘d7+ 3 ♔f7 ♔e5 4 h4 ♘f6=.

Amazingly, the highly experienced grandmaster sent his king off in the opposite direction.

1...♔e4?? 2 ♗c8! ♔f4 (2...♘f3 3 ♗b7+; 2...♘d3 3 ♗f5+) **3 h4**

Nothing can save him now: as you will recall, the knight has a difficult time with rook pawns.

3...♘f3 4 h5 ♘g5 5 ♗f5! ♘f3 6 h6 ♘g5 7 ♔g6 ♘f3 8 h7 ♘h4+ 9 ♔f6 Black resigned.

Dombrowska - Lyszowska
Polish ch 1988

4-8

W?

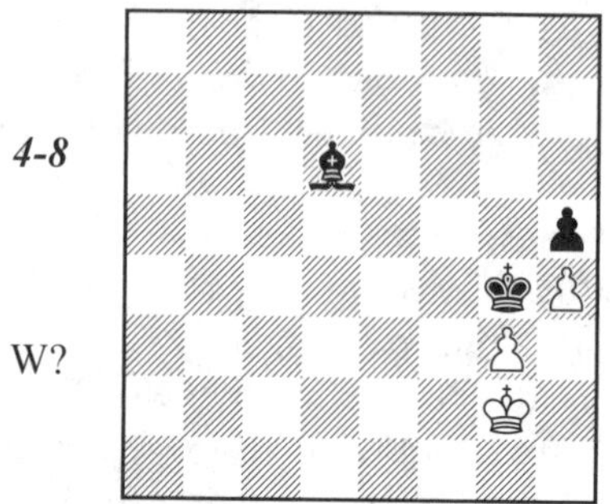

1 ♔g1?? ♔h3!

If 2 ♔h1, then 2...♗c5⊙ 2 g4 hg, and the rook pawn becomes a knight pawn. And on 2 ♔f1, either 2...♔h2 or 2...♗c5 decides. Therefore, White resigned.

White had to play 1 ♔h2! Black can neither drive White's king from the corner, nor put White in zugzwang. For example, 1...♔f3 2 ♔h3 ♗c5 3 ♔h2 ♗d4 4 ♔h1!= (but not 4 ♔h3?? ♗g1⊙).

Exercises

4-9

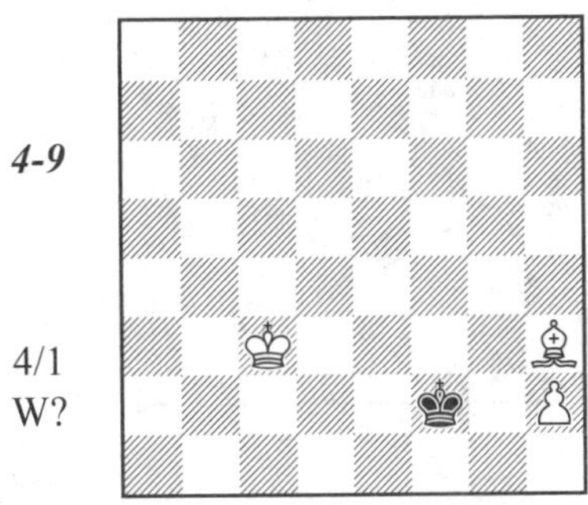

4/1
W?

4-10

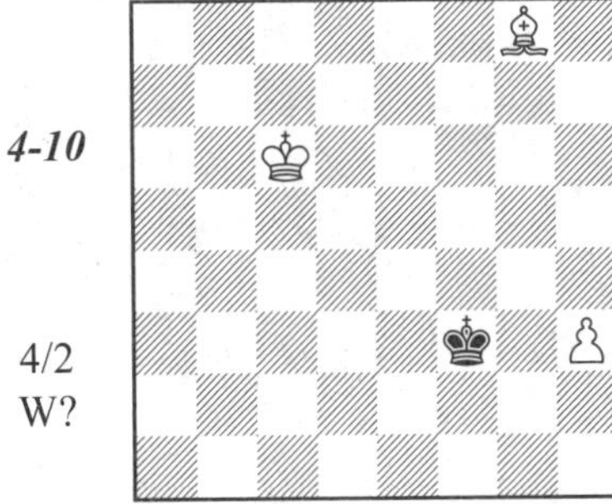

4/2
W?

4-11

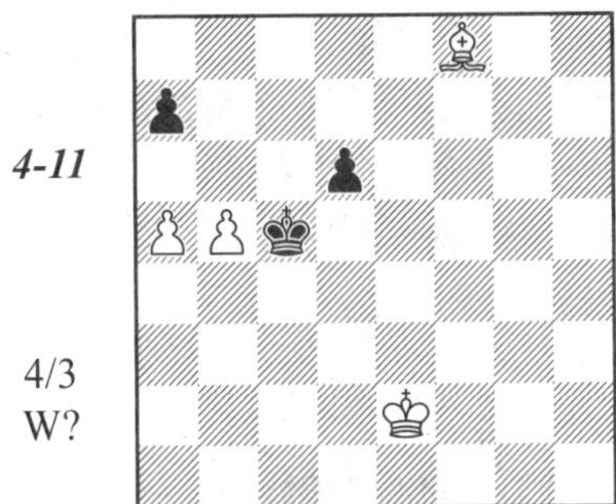

4/3
W?

Pawns at h6 and h7

4-12

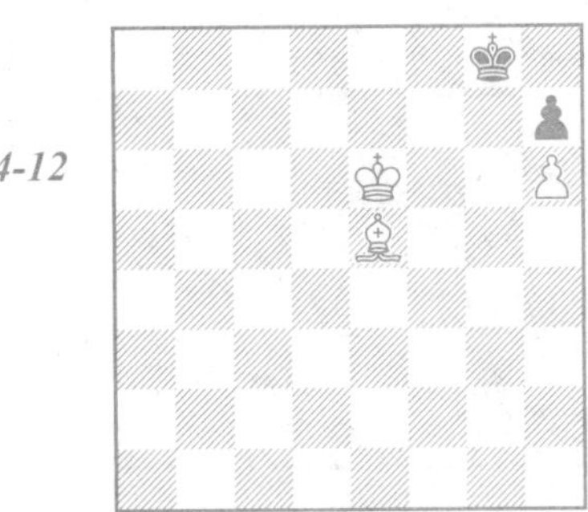

Even though the bishop controls the queening square, this position is still drawn. On **1 ♔f6**, Black of course replies **1...♔f8!=** (but not 1...♔h8?? 2 ♔f7#). The evaluation would not be changed, even if you added pawn pairs at g5/g6 and f4/f5.

Tragicomedies

Maiwald - Bischoff
German ch, Gladenbach 1997

4-13

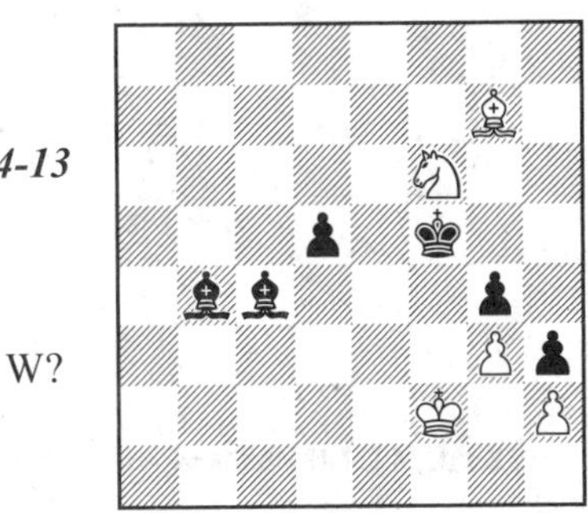

W?

1 ♘e8? ♗c5+ 2 ♔e1 ♔e4

White resigned, since the enemy king marches unhindered to g2.

He could have saved the game with a piece sacrifice: 1 ♘×d5! ♗×d5 (1...♗c5+ 2 ♘e3+ ♔e4 3 ♗h6=) 2 ♗d4 ♔e4 3 ♗a7. White keeps his king at g1, and his bishop on the g1-a7 diagonal. If the bishops are exchanged, we have the drawing position we already know.

Exercises

4-14

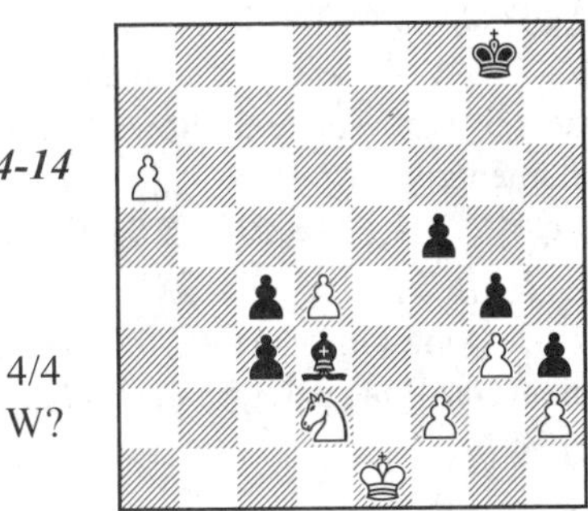

4/4
W?

Pawns at g6 and g7

4-15

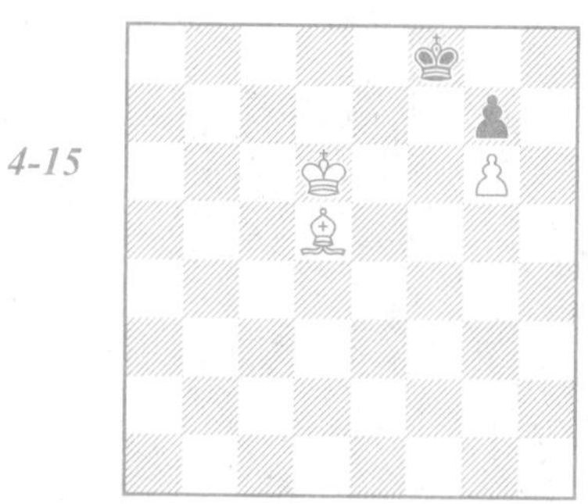

Here too the draw is obvious, and it would still be so if we added more pawn pairs at h5/h6, f5/f6, and e4/e5.

Tragicomedies

Polugaevsky - Zakharov
USSR ch, Leningrad 1963

4-16

B

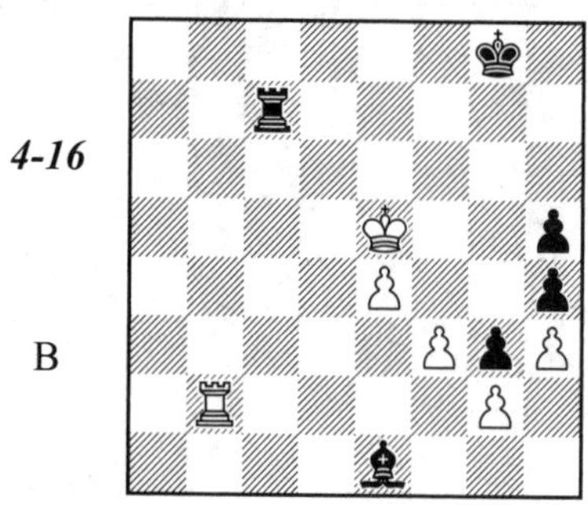

1...♗c3+ 2 ♔d6 ♗×b2?

After 2...♖a7, Black would soon have won with his extra bishop. The text allows White to set up an elementary fortress.

3 ♔×c7 ♔f7 4 ♔d6 ♔f6 5 ♔d5 ♔g5 6 ♔c4

Draw. The king has managed to get home in time from his far-flung peregrinations (6...♔f4 7 ♔d3=).

Exercises

4-17

4/5
W?

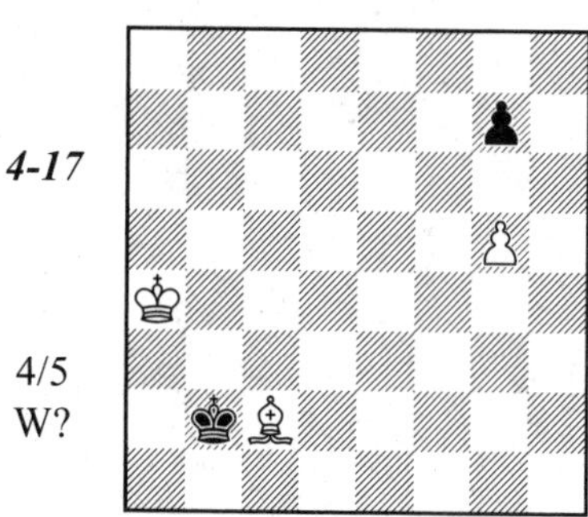

4-18

4/6
W?

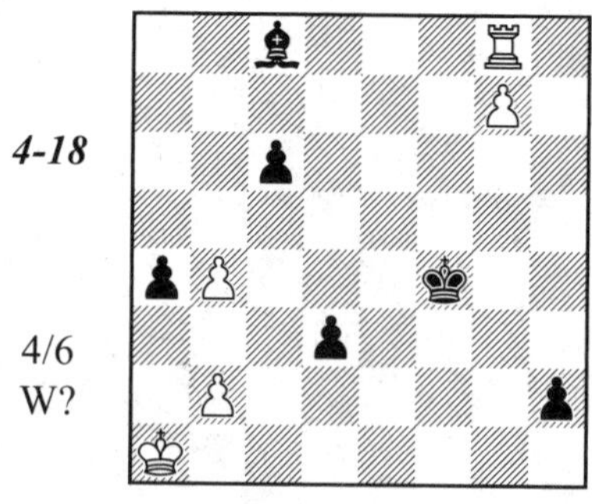

Bishop at h7 and Pawn at g6

D. Ponziani, 1782

4-19

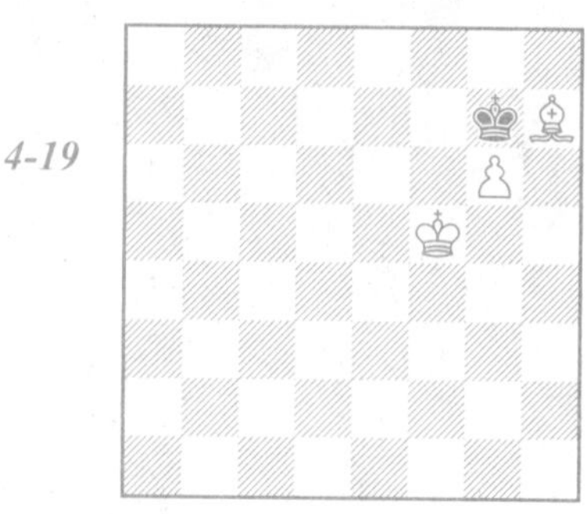

This drawing position has been known since the 18th century. The bishop cannot escape from its corner; and giving it up leads to a drawn pawn ending.

1 ♔g5 ♔h8 2 ♗g8 ♔×g8 3 ♔h6 ♔h8=.

Tragicomedies

Paulsen - Metger
Nürnberg 1888

4-20

W?

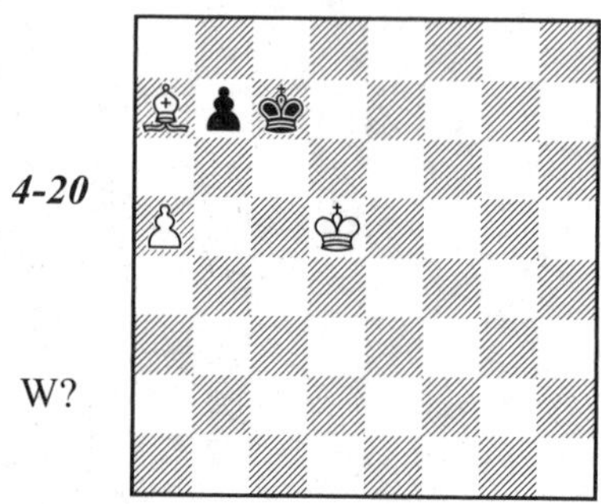

After **1 ♔c4?? b5+!** (but not 1...b6? 2 a6!+−), the draw would have been inescapable, since either Black's king reaches the corner not controlled by the bishop (2 ♔×b5 ♔b7), or Ponziani's position is reached (2 ab+ ♔b7).

The same result is reached after 1 ♔c5? b6+!.

The winning move was 1 ♔d4! ♔c6 (1...b5 2 a6 ♔c6 3 ♔c3 or 1...b6 2 a6 ♔c6 3 ♔c4) 2 ♗b6! (2 ♔c3? b6! 3 a6 ♔b5=) 2...♔d6 (2...♔b5 3 ♔d5 ♔a6 4 ♔d6) 3 ♔c4 ♔c6 4 ♔b4 ♔d7 5 ♔c5 ♔c8 6 ♗a7 ♔c7 7 ♔b5 ♔d7 8 ♗b8 ♔c8 9 ♗f4 ♔d7 10 ♔b6 ♔c8 11 ♗e5+−.

Sax - Kovacevic
Sarajevo 1982

4-21

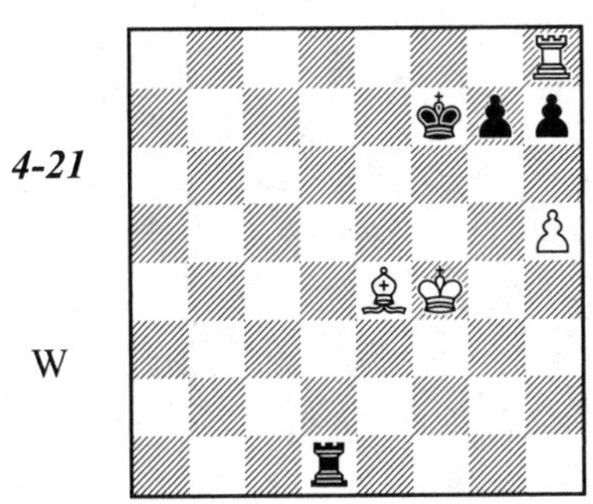

W

White has good chances for success. One very strong line is 1 ♔e5! ♖e1 2 ♖c8 ♖e2 3 ♖c7+ ♔f8 4 ♔d5 △ 5 ♗×h7. Another way of threatening the h7-pawn would be 1 ♔g3!.

But the immediate capture of this pawn is a terrible mistake.

1 ♗×h7? (1 ♖×h7? ♔g8=) **1...g5+!! 2 hg+** (2 ♔×g5 ♔g7=) **2...♔g7 3 ♖g8+ ♔h6**

It turns out that even adding rooks doesn't change the evaluation of Ponziani's position - White can neither queen the pawn nor free his bishop.

4 ♖c8 ♔g7 5 ♗g8 ♖f1+ 6 ♔e5 ♖e1+ 7 ♔d6 ♔×g6, and the game was soon drawn.

Exercises

4-22

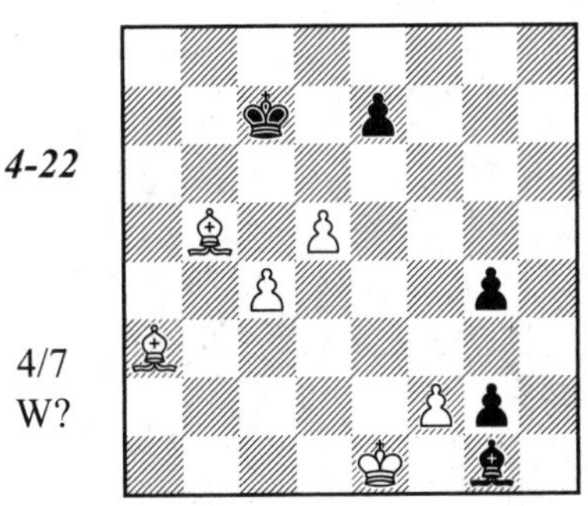

4/7
W?

4-23

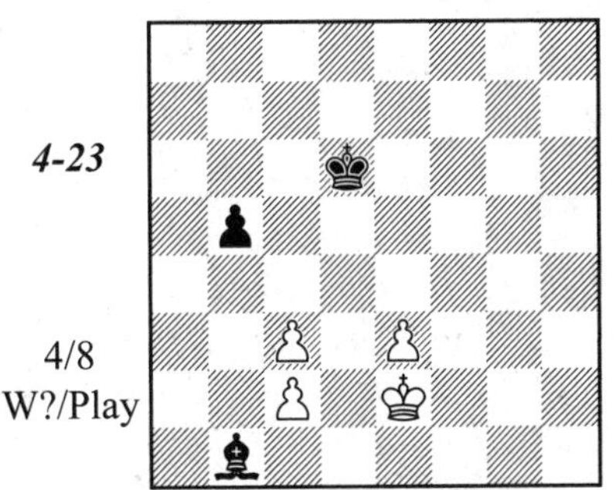

4/8
W?/Play

Bishop vs. Disconnected Pawns

M. Dvoretsky, 2000

4-24

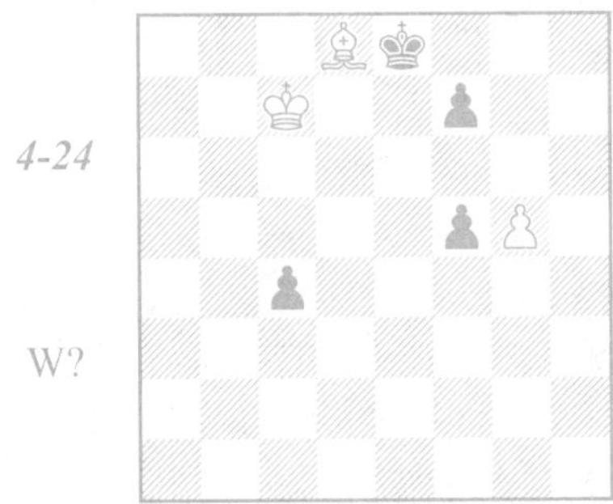

W?

The primitive 1 ♗f6? f4 2 ♔d6 f3 3 ♗d4 leads to a loss after 3...c3! In chess jargon, this situation is referred to as ***"the pants"***: the bishop stops pawns on two different diagonals, but advancing one of the pawns means the bishop must give up its guard over the other. This is the same sort of "pants" situation that could have arisen in the Gutman - Mikenas game (Diagram 4-5) after the correct 1 e6 or 1 h6.

Sometimes, the bishop is not holding a passed pawn on one of the two diagonals, but defending its own pawn, or some other important point. For all practical purposes, this is the same thing: advancing a pawn pulls the bishop away from fulfilling its other obligation. An example of this might be Smyslov's study (Exercise 4/4).

Keep in mind also that there are other ways to exploit a "torn" bishop. Sometimes, it may be driven away from the intersection of two diagonals by the king, or forced to move away by means of zugzwang.

Return to the position above. White saves himself with a pawn sacrifice:

1 g6! (△ 2 g7) **1...fg 2 ♗g5=**

The one-diagonal principle! The bishop

now fulfills both functions from a single diagonal, c1-h6, which allows White to draw without difficulty.

Rather than taking the pawn, Black could try 1...f6!?, hoping to get "the pants" after 2 ♗×f6? f4. But by continuing 2 ♔d6! ♔f8 (2...f4? is bad in view of 3 ♗e7! f3 4 ♔e6 f2 5 g7+−) 3 ♔d5(c5) instead, White draws.

Tragicomedies

Ilyin-Zhenevsky - Miasoedov
Leningrad 1932

4-25

W

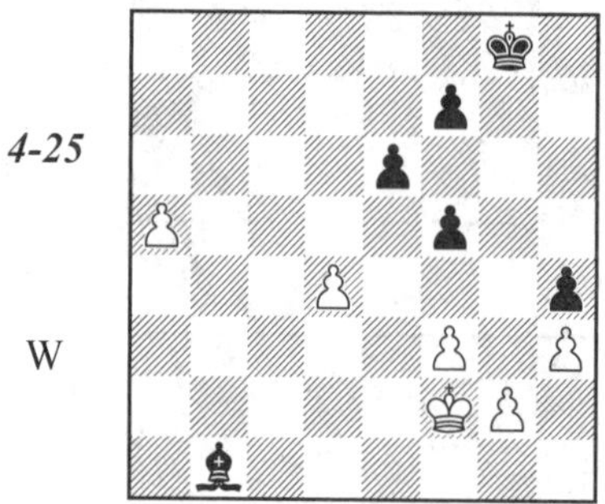

Black should have an uncomplicated win with his extra piece. For instance, on 1 ♔e3, he has the strong continuation 1...♗a2 2 ♔f4 f6! 3 g4 hg 4 ♔×g3 e5 5 de fe 6 ♔h4 e4 7 fe fe 8 ♔g3 ♗d5 (of course not 8...♗c4 9 ♔f4 ♗d3?? 10 a6=) 9 ♔f4 ♔g7 10 a6 ♔g6 11 a7 ♔h5. White is helpless in this variation, because the bishop holds the a-pawn while defending its own pawn on one diagonal, a8-h1.

Ilyin-Zhenevsky tries one last chance:

1 d5! ♗d3?

This error costs Black the win. Of course, 1...ed?? 2 a6 is bad, since the pawn cannot be stopped; but he had to fix the kingside with 1...f4! After 2 a6 ♗a2 3 de (3 d6 ♔f8) 3...fe 4 a7 ♗d5 5 ♔e2 e5, or 2 ♔e2 e5! 3 a6 ♗a2 4 d6 ♔f8, the struggle is over. Now, on the other hand, it's just beginning.

2 d6 ♔f8 3 g3!

Now in addition to the a-pawn, White will have a passed h-pawn, which the bishop will be helpless against ("the pants"!). The question now will be whether Black will have time to capture the d6-pawn, stop one rook pawn with his king, and the other with his bishop.

The solution is 3...hg+ 4 ♔×g3 ♔e8 5 h4 ♔d7 6 h5 ♔×d6 7 h6 (7 f4? ♔e7) 7...f4+! (7...♔e7? 8 a6+−; 7...♔c6? 8 f4+−) 8 ♔×f4 f6 9 ♔e3 ♗f5. But with 10 a6 ♔c6 11 a7 ♔b7 12 ♔d4 ♔×a7 13 ♔c5 ♔b7 14 ♔d6 ♔b6 15 ♔e7 ♔c5 16 ♔×f6 ♔d6 17 f4 ♔d5 18 ♔f7, White gets a draw. On 18...♔e4 there follows 19 h7 - the bishop is torn between two diagonals.

3...f4?? 4 gh ♔e8

4-26

W?

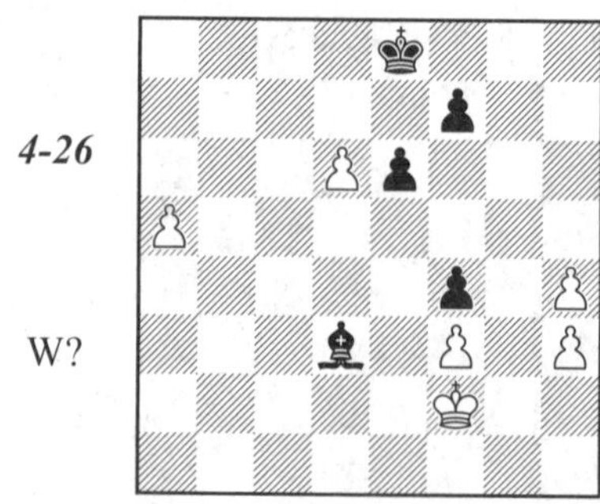

Black obviously had 5 h5? ♔d7 6 h6 ♔×d6 7 a6 ♔c6−+ in mind. Unfortunately, a major disappointment awaits him.

5 ♔e1!

The king can drive the bishop from the d3-square, the point of intersection of the two diagonals; this will inescapably result in one of the two pawns going on to queen.

5...e5 (5...♔d7 6 ♔d2 ♗a6 7 h5+−) **6 ♔d2 e4 7 h5 ♗b1 8 a6**, and White won.

Exercises

4-27

4/9
W?

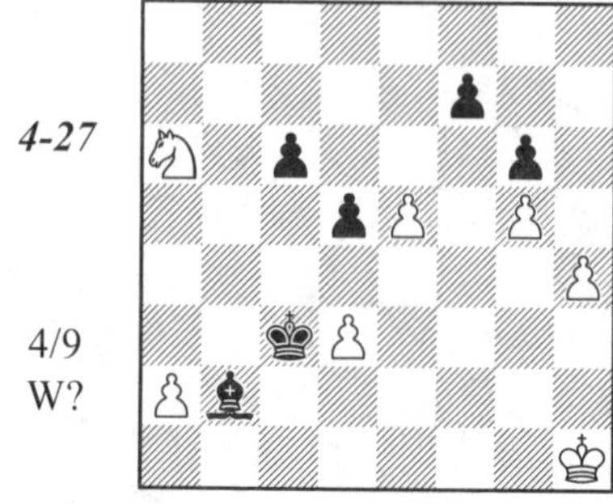

4-28

4/10
W?/Play

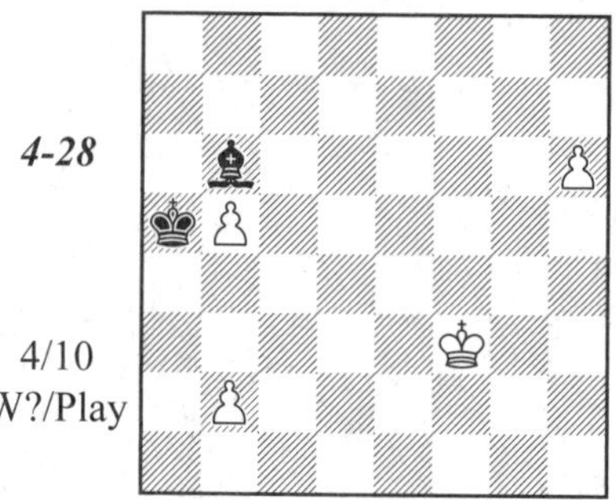

Bishop vs. Connected Pawns

The following instructive ending demonstrates the most important ideas for positions involving connected pawns.

Gavrikov - Chikovani
USSR 1979

4-29

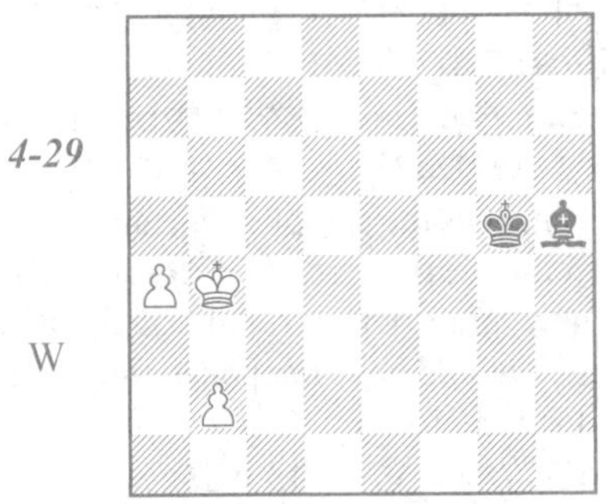

W

First, we examine 1 ♔c5 ♔f6 2 ♔d6 (shouldering). White's plan works after 2...♔f7? 3 b4 ♔e8 4 ♔c7 ♗d1 5 b5+−.

In response, Black employs a standard technique, which I call ***"pawns in the crosshairs"*** - attacking the enemy pawns with the bishop. The point to this attack is either to force the pawns to advance, which aids in the task of their subsequent blockade (as in the present example), or else to tie the king to their defense.

2...♗d1! 3 a5 ♗e2 4 b4 ♗f1 5 ♔c6 ♔e7 6 b5 ♔d8= (or 6...♗xb5+).

In the game, White tried a different plan.

1 ♔a5 ♔f6 2 b4

How does Black defend now? The attempt to put the king in front of the pawns (as he did after 1 ♔c5) no longer works: 2...♔e7 3 b5 ♔d7? (3...♗d1? 4 b6! ♔d7 5 ♔a6+−; 3...♔d6!) 4 ♔a6! (but not 4 ♔b6? ♗d1! 5 a5 ♗e2= - once again, "pawns in the crosshairs") 4...♔c8 5 ♔a7+−.

4-30

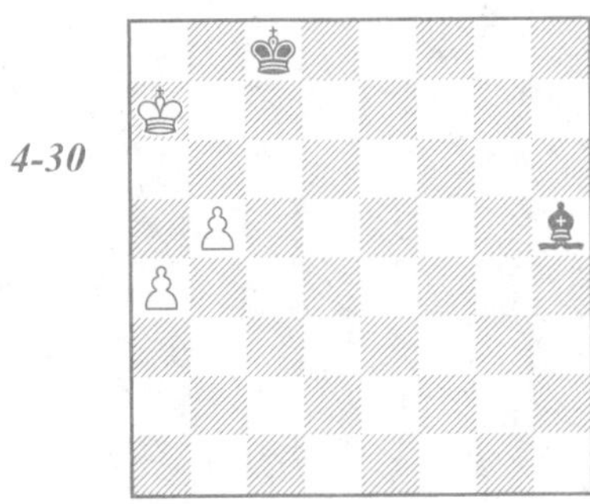

This scheme of interaction between king and pawns, securing their passage to the queening square, I suggest we label ***"autopilot"*** (later we shall have further reason to refer to it).

Black is saved by another, also quite widespread technique: ***"the tail-hook"*** - tying the king to the rearmost pawn from behind. We shall use this defensive method also in the endings of "rook vs. two connected passed pawns."

2...♔e5! 3 b5 ♔d4 4 ♔b6

White can no longer go on autopilot: 4 b6 ♗f3 5 ♔a6 ♔c5 6 a5 ♔b4!, or 5 ♔b5 ♗e2+ 6 ♔c6 ♔c4, followed by 7...♗f3+.

4...♗f3 (4...♔c4 transposes) **5 a5 ♔c4 6 a6 ♔b4 7 a7**

One last task for Black. Now the waiting 7...♗g2? fails to 8 ♔a6 ♔c5 9 b6 ♗f1+ 10 ♔b7 ♗g2+ 11 ♔c7+−.

7...♗a8!

Draw, in view of 8 ♔a6 ♔c5 9 b6 ♔c6=.

V. Zviagintsev, 1993

4-31

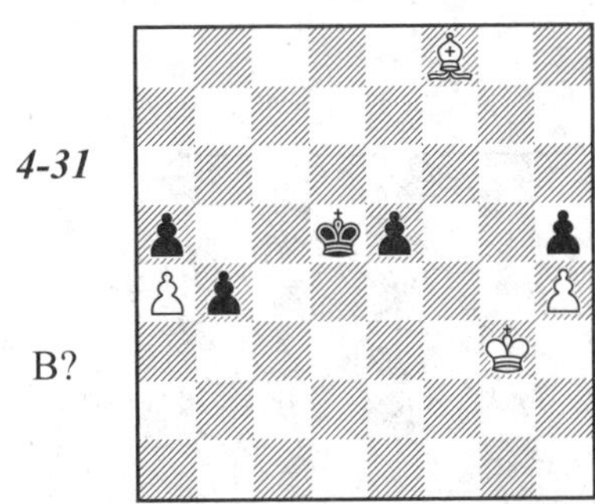

B?

Which should Black aim for: the separated passed pawns on the b- and e-files, or two connected passed pawns, after he captures the a-pawn? Let's examine both plans:

1) 1...♔c4 2 ♗d6□ (2 ♗g7? ♔d4 3 ♗f8 b3 4 ♗a3 ♔c3−+) 2...♔b3 3 ♗xe5 ♔xa4 4 ♔f4. If now 4...♔a3, then 5 ♔g5! b3 6 ♔xh5 a4 7 ♔g4 ♔a2 (7...b2 8 ♗xb2+ ♔xb2 9 h5) 8 h5 a3 9 h6=.

The attempt to save a tempo by playing 4...b3 only works after 4 ♔e3? ♔a3!−+ (autopilot) or 5 ♔g5? ♔b5! (indicated by Müller; 5...♔b4? 6 ♔xh5 a4 7 ♗d6+! gives only a draw) 6 ♔f4 (6 ♔xh5 a4−+) 6...a4 7 ♔e3 ♔b4! 8 ♔d2 ♔a3 and 9...♔a2−+. The correct way is 5 ♗b2! ♔b4 6 ♔e4, and now 6...a4? even loses after 7

♔d3 a3 (7...♔c5 8 ♔c3) 8 ♗g7+−. But the position remains drawn after 6...♔c4! 7 ♔e3 a4 8 ♔e4 ♔c5 9 ♔d3 ♔d5 10 ♔c3 ♔e4 11 ♔b4 ♔f5 △ 12...♔g4 (Black is just in time).

2) 1...♔d4 2 ♔f2□ (2 ♔f3 would be a mistake: 2...b3 3 ♗a3 ♔d3−+). If Black goes back to the first plan here, by 2...♔c3 3 ♗g7 ♔b3 4 ♗×e5 ♔×a4, it's already too late to attack the h5-pawn; on the other hand, White's king is a bit closer to the queenside, and therefore can "grab onto the tail" of the enemy pawns and prevent the autopilot: 5 ♔e3 ♔b3 6 ♔d4 ♔a2 7 ♔c4 b3 8 ♔b5=.

After 2...b3 3 ♗a3 ♔c3 4 ♗d6! (it's important to drive the e-pawn closer to the white king) 4...e4 5 ♔e3 b2 6 ♗e5+ ♔c2 7 ♗×b2 ♔×b2 8 ♔×e4 ♔b3 9 ♔d4 ♔×a4 10 ♔c4, we have a draw (remember the section "Two rook pawns with an extra pawn on the opposite wing," from the theory of pawn endgames). Nothing is changed by 3...♔d3 4 ♗b2 e4 5 ♗g7 ♔d2 6 ♗d4! (the bishop may be "torn" here, but it's impossible to put it in zugzwang - in other words, to obtain the same position, but with White to move) 6...b2 7 ♗×b2 e3+ 8 ♔f3 e2 9 ♗c3+ ♔×c3 10 ♔×e2 ♔b4 11 ♔d3 ♔×a4 12 ♔c4=.

When examining the Grigoriev study in Diagram 2-12, we spoke of "strategic double attacks" - we noted that those moves and plans which pursue not just one, but two aims, are usually the most effective. Here too, we must find a way to combine both strategies, selecting one or the other depending on what our opponent does.

1...♔c4! 2 ♗d6 e4!

The main line runs: **3 ♔f2 ♔b3! 4 ♔e3 ♔×a4 5 ♔×e4 ♔a3**

Black engages the autopilot; meanwhile, his opponent can neither counterattack on the kingside, nor "grab onto the tail" of the black pawns (which would have happened if the white bishop had stood on e5).

6 ♔d3 ♔a2 7 ♔c4 b3 8 ♗e5 (the decisive loss of tempo) **8...a4**−+

If we save a move in this variation by playing 3 ♗e5, then Black's king switches to the support of the e-pawn: 3...e3! (but not 3...♔d3? 4 ♔f2=) 4 ♔g2 ♔d3 5 ♔f1 ♔d2−+. And 3 ♔f4 ♔d3 is just as hopeless.

Exercises

4-32

4/11
B?

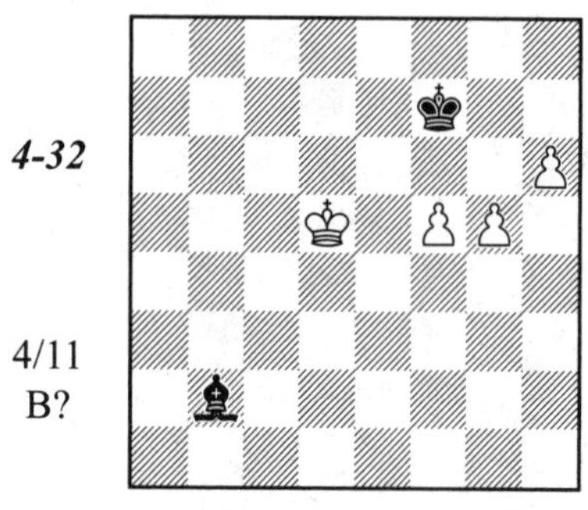

4-33

4/12
B?

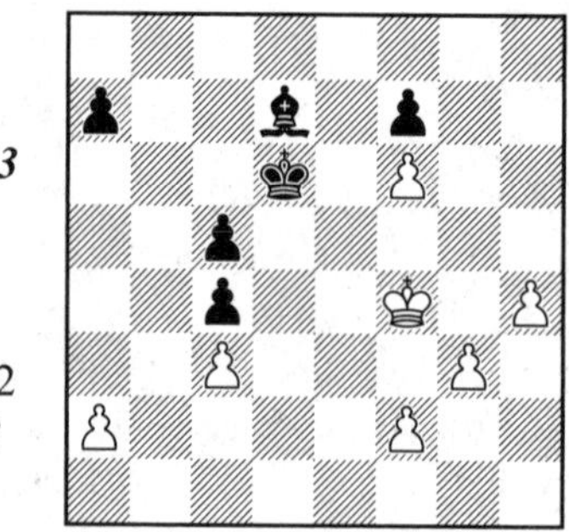

Chapter 5

OPPOSITE-COLORED BISHOPS

The Most Important Rules

Endings with opposite-colored bishops are perhaps the most "strategic" of them all. My studies of these endings have taught me some rules which will help you get your bearings in nearly all such endings.

I. Drawing Tendencies

Here it is frequently possible to save oneself even two or three pawns down. The consequences of this rule are obvious: ***the stronger side must be exceptionally alert, whether going into an opposite-colored bishops endgame, or playing one out - here it doesn't take long to stumble on a drawing counterchance. And for the weaker side, going into the opposite-bishop ending is sometimes the key to salvation, sharply increasing the chances for a favorable outcome.***

II. The Fortress

The main theme of opposite-colored bishop endings is that of the Fortress. The weaker side strives to create one, the stronger side strives to prevent its formation, or (if it already exists) to find a way to break through it.

An important factor in endgame play is the ability to analyze a position logically, to think through various plans and schemes. Logical thinking is of special importance in endings with opposite-colored bishops. In the majority of cases, such endings are not "played" as much as they are "constructed" – first it is necessary to determine the configuration of pawns and pieces which will render the position impenetrable; only then can we proceed with the calculation of variations which will prove whether or not we can attain the desired configuration, and whether it is impenetrable in fact.

The following rules show the most important techniques for setting up and breaking down fortresses.

III. Pawn Placement

In the next chapter, we discuss the principle that required us to place our pawns on the opposite color squares from that controlled by our bishop. In opposite-colored bishop endings, this principle only holds true for the stronger side - it's especially important with connected passed pawns.

But ***the weaker side must, contrary to the general rule, keep his pawns on the same color squares as his own bishop*** – in that event, he will usually be able to defend them. In fact, a pawn defended by its bishop can only be attacked by the enemy king - which renders it invulnerable. In other types of endgames, such a pawn could be attacked, not just by the king, but also by other pieces (such as a knight, or a bishop of the same color).

IV. Positional Nuances are Worth More than Material

When we are playing an opposite-bishop ending, the number of pawns on the board frequently has less significance than a small alteration in the placement of pieces or pawns - even an apparently insignificant one. Therefore, ***in opposite-colored bishop endgames, we quite frequently encounter positional pawn sacrifices.***

V. The One-Diagonal Principle

We have already met this principle in the "bishop vs. pawns" endgame (Chapter 4). ***For both the stronger and the weaker side it is very important that the bishop should both defend its own and stop the enemy pawns "without tearing" - that is, along one and the same diagonal.***

VI. "Pawns in the Crosshairs"

A typical means of defense is for the bishop to attack the enemy pawns. This will either force their advance, to the less favorable squares of the color of their own bishop, or tie the enemy king to the pawns' defense. This technique, like the previous one, was also studied in Chapter 4. In opposite-bishop endgames, both techniques are used frequently.

The logical thing would be to illustrate each of these rules by concrete examples. However, that would be difficult, only because they are rarely employed separately. Consider the following simple endgame, and you will see all of the rules we have been talking about, appearing simultaneously.

5-1

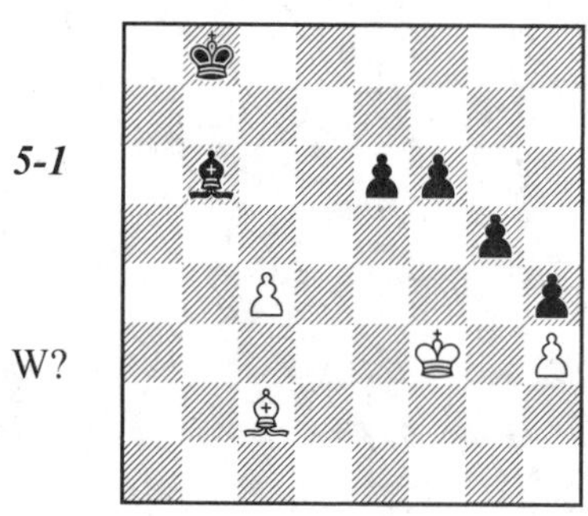

W?

1 c5! ♗×c5 2 ♗b3 e5 3 ♗e6 ♔c7 4 ♔e4

The draw is obvious – White need only run his bishop up and down the h3-c8 diagonal.

Thus, White was able to save himself - three (!) pawns down **(drawing tendency)**. The final position is a **fortress**, in which the **weaker side's only pawn is properly placed on the same color square as its own bishop.** The bishop defends its pawn at h3 and holds the enemy pawns at g5 and f6 **on the same diagonal**. White **sacrificed a pawn**, so that **by attacking the enemy's sole well-placed pawn at e6**, he could force it to advance to a dark square, after which the pawns could be easily blockaded.

Analyzing almost any endgame in this chapter, you will see some or all of our just-formulated rules in action.

Bishop and Two Connected Pawns vs. Bishop

Careful analysis of the following basic theoretical position will familiarize us with the characteristic ideas of such endgames.

5-2

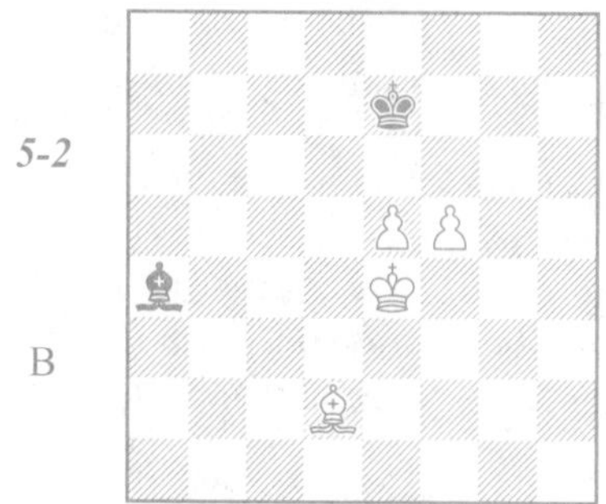

B

White threatens to continue e5-e6, followed by ♔e5 and f5-f6. To stop this plan, Black must take the e6-square under control with his bishop. But from d7 or from b3? Let's examine both choices.

On 1...♗b3? the position is lost. First, White gives a ***probing check***, to see which way the enemy king goes. ***It's important to have the bishop preventing him from getting between the pawns after e5-e6.*** Therefore, 2 ♗g5+!.

Then, ***the white king goes to help the e-pawn from the side opposite the one the enemy king went to***. For example: 2...♔f7 3 ♔d4 ♗a2 4 ♔c5 ♗b3 (4...♗b1 5 e6+ and 6 f6) 5 ♔d6 and 6 e6+. Or 2...♔d7 3 ♔f4 ♗a2 4 ♗h4 ♗f7 5 ♔g5 ♔e7 6 ♔h6+ ♔d7 7 ♔g7 ♗c4 8 ♔f6 and 9 e6+, winning.

Note that the bishop check from the other side is ineffective: 2 ♗b4+ ♔f7! 3 ♔d4? ♗c2! 4 e6+ ♔f6 5 e7 ♗a4, and draws. ***As soon as the pawns are blocked on the same color squares as their bishop, the draw becomes obvious.***

So with his bishop on b3, Black loses. But he gets an easy draw after **1...♗d7! 2 ♗g5+ ♔f7.** Now Black merely waits, shuttling the bishop back and forth between c8 and d7. In order to prepare e5-e6, White needs to maneuver his king left. But this is impossible, as long as the king is tied to the defense of the f5-pawn.

Which suggests a rule: ***The bishop must be placed where it prevents the advance of one of the pawns while simultaneously attacking the other.***

Let's use the ideas from the position we just looked at to analyze other positions.

Move all the pieces one rank further up. What has changed?

5-3

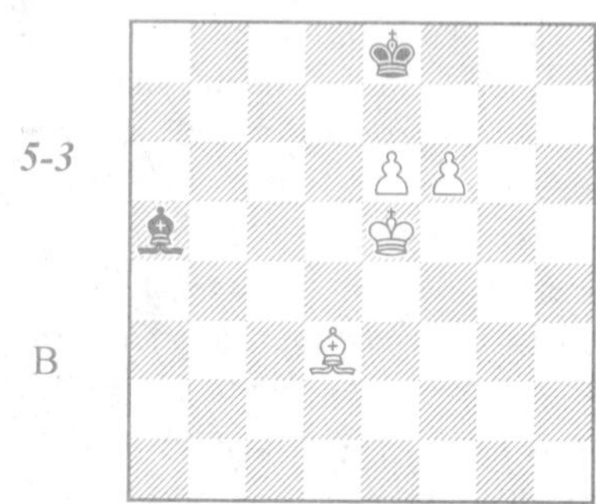

B

On 1...♗b4, nothing. White wins by the exact same method (check, followed by a king outflanking); here, both checks - from g6 or b5 - are equally good.

After **1...♗d8 2 ♗g6+** (or 2 ♗b5+) **2...♔f8 3 ♔f5**, Black loses because of zugzwang - compared to the previous position, he no longer has any waiting moves with his bishop.

5-4

B?

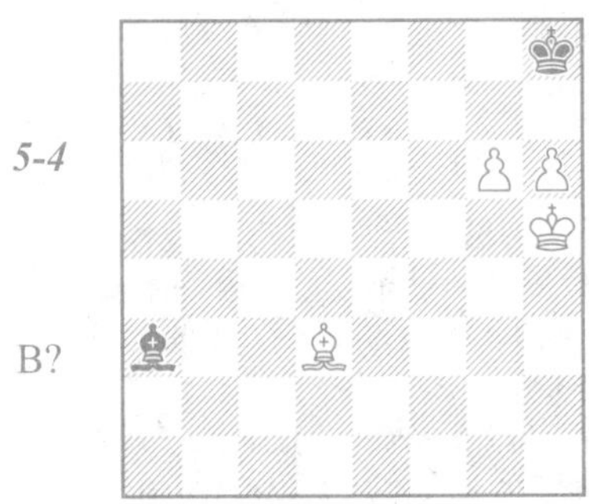

Being at the edge of the board introduces new elements into the assessment of the position. Let's try 1...♗b2. If Black could follow up with 2...♔g8 and 3...♔f8, the draw would be obvious. With the king on f8, White's only plan - an outflanking to the right with the king - is impossible, because the board's edge gets in the way.

But White to move locks the enemy king in the corner by 2 ♗c4!, and then carries out an outflanking to the left by ♔g4-f5-e6-f7.

After **1...♗f8!**, the outflanking is now impossible; but how about threatening zugzwang? In order to force the enemy into zugzwang, White must take away the g8-square from the king with **2 ♗c4**. However, after **2...♗×h6! 3 ♔×h6**, it's stalemate.

5-5

B?

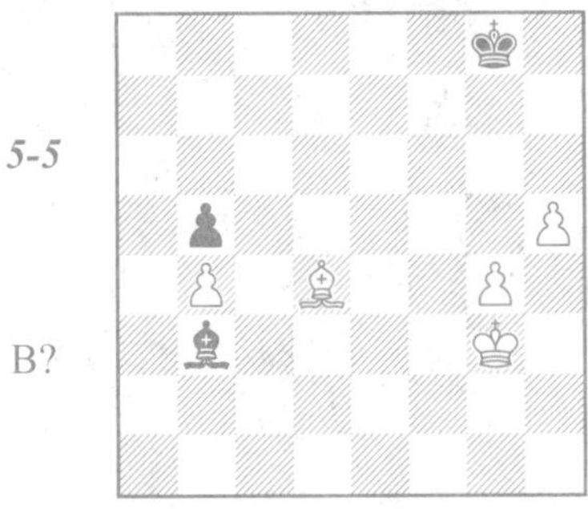

In all the endings we have so far analyzed, the defending side tried to give up its bishop for the two pawns. Here, this defensive plan is obviously insufficient. So does that mean that Black is doomed? As it turns out, no: the wing pawns can be stopped without recourse to a bishop sacrifice.

1...♗d1! ("pawns in the crosshairs") **2 ♔h4** (how else does he get in g4-g5?) **2...♔f7 3 g5 ♔e6! 4 g6 ♔f5!**

White cannot advance either his king (the edge of the board gets in the way), or the h-pawn. And on 5 g7 ♗b3 and 6...♗g8 blocks the enemy pawns securely on white squares.

Let's look at a more complex case.

M. Henneberger, 1916

5-6

$

W

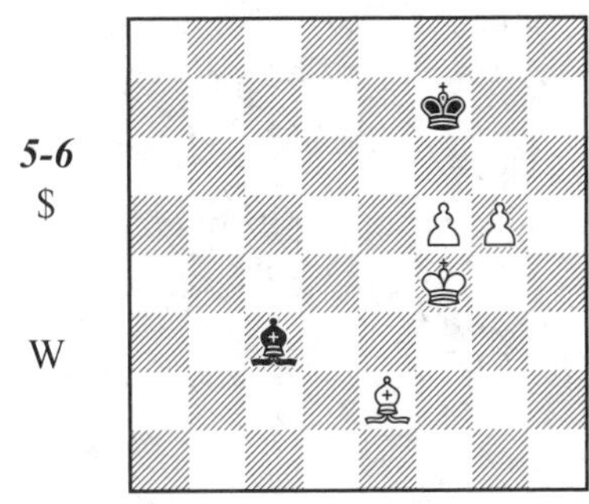

Black's bishop is not ideally posted - it should be at either e7 or d8. In the basic theoretical position we started with, White won easily against such a bishop. Proceeding logically, it would seem that only one circumstance could hinder the execution of the standard winning plan, and that is the nearness of the board's edge. Let's see:

"According to the rules", one should first check on h5, in order to control the g6-square. Black retreats his king to e7, forcing White's king to go on a right-hand outflanking, where there is little room to maneuver.

1 ♗h5+ ♔e7! (on 1...♔g7? 2 ♔e4, Black does not have the same resources to prevent a left-hand outflanking) 2 ♔g4 ♗b2 3 ♗g6 (there is no other way of making progress; but now the g6-square is not available to the king) 3...♗c3 4 ♔h5 (threatening 5 ♔h6, 6 ♗h5 etc.) 4...♗g7! 5 ♗h7 ♔f7! 6 ♗g6+ ♔e7, and White cannot reach his goal of preparing f5-f6+.

And the bishop check on the other diagonal we already know gives nothing: 1 ♗c4+ ♔g7! 2 ♔e4 ♗d2! 3 f6+ ♔g6.

However, White's resources for playing to win are not yet exhausted. We could decoy the king to g7 first, and then put the bishop on the e8-h5 diagonal, thus preparing a left-hand outflanking by the king.

1 ♔g4 ♗b2 2 ♔h5 ♔g7!

White threatened 3 ♔h6; 2...♗g7? is bad, because of 3 ♗c4+ and 4 ♔g6.

3 ♗b5 ♗c3 4 ♗e8 ♗d4 (4...♔f8 5 ♗g6 ♔g7 is the same thing) **5 ♗g6**

On 5 ♔g4 (threatening 6 ♗h5, 7 ♔f3, 8 ♔e4 etc.) Black's king has enough time to relocate to e7: 5...♔f8! 6 ♗h5 ♔e7, transposing to the first variation.

5...♗c3 6 ♔g4

White's plan appears triumphant: 6...♔f8 7 f6 is bad; and on other moves, White plays 7 ♗h5. But as Berger pointed out, at precisely this moment, the black bishop succeeds in reaching its destined spot.

6...♗a5!!

With White's bishop at g6, he no longer has 7 f6+.

7 ♗h5 ♗d8

And Black has set up the basic fortress draw of this type of ending.

Tragicomedies

Walther - Fischer
Zürich 1959

5-7

B?

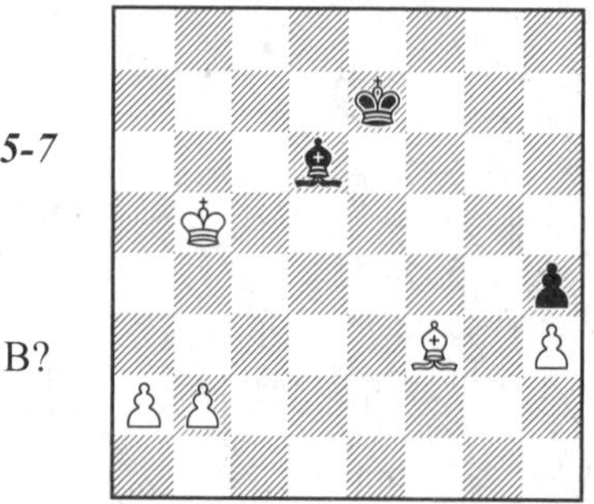

Black dreams of giving up his bishop for the queenside pawns. Then his king would go to h8, and even if it can't, we have Rauzer's drawing position (Diagram 4-2).

White's goal is to put his king at a6 and his pawn at b5. This situation ("autopilot") is known to us from the section on bishop vs. connected passed pawns from Chapter 4.

1...♔d7??

Black had to employ the "pawns in the crosshairs" technique: 1...♗f4! 2 b4 ♗d2 3 a3 ♗c1! 4 a4 ♗d2! 5 ♔c5 ♔d7 (pointed out by Solomon). After 6 a5 (6 b5 ♗e3+ 7 ♔c4 ♔d6 8 a5 ♗d2 9 a6 ♗e3=) 6...♔c7 7 ♔b5 ♗e1 8 ♔a4 ♗d2 9 b5, Black defends himself similarly to Diagram 5-5: 9...♔d6! 10 b6 ♔c5=.

2 a4??

White errs in return. The winning line was 2 b4! ♔c7 3 ♔a5! ♔b8 (3...♗g3 4 b5 ♗f2 5 ♔a6 △ a4-a5) 4 b5 (Black hasn't time to prevent b5-b6) 4...♗a3!? 5 b6 ♔c8 6 ♔a6 ♔b8 7 ♗e4⊙ ♔c8 (7...♗c5 8 a4) 8 ♔a7 ♗c5 9 a4+- (pointed out by the Swiss problemist Fontana).

2...♔c7

A simpler draw could probably have been obtained by 2...♗g3!? 3 ♔b6 (3 b4 ♗e1) 3...♗f2+! 4 ♔b7 ♗e1.

3 b4 ♔b8!

By tucking his king at a7, Fischer gains control of a6, which prevents his opponent from going on autopilot.

4 a5 ♔a7 5 ♔c4 ♗g3 (5...♗c7) **6 ♔b3**

If 6 b5, then 6...♗e1 7 b6+ ♔a6=.

6...♗e1 7 ♔a4 ♗d2 8 ♗h5 ♗e1 9 b5 ♗f2! 10 ♗e2

On 10 b6+ ♗xb6 11 ab+ ♔xb6, the king goes to h8. Also useless is 10 ♗f3 ♗e3 11 ♔b3 ♗d2.

10...♗e3 11 ♔b3 ♗d2!

Black allows his opponent to advance the pawn to b6, so as to reach the defensive position of Diagram 5-5.

12 b6+ ♔b7 13 ♔a4 ♔c6! 14 ♗b5+ ♔c5 15 ♗e8 ♗e1 Drawn.

Exercises

5-8

5/1
B?

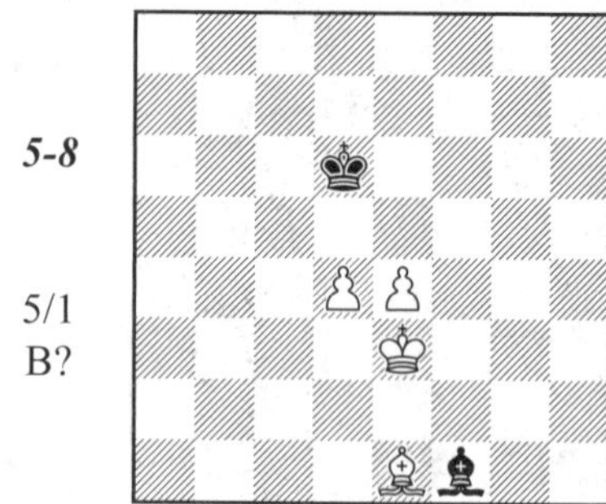

5-9

5/2
W?

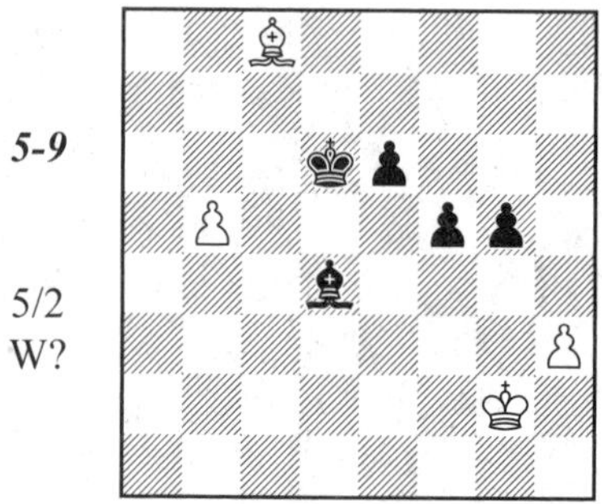

Separated Passed Pawns

With separated passed pawns, the stronger side's strategy is always one and the same: the king goes toward the pawn that the bishop is holding back.

C. Salvioli, 1887

5-10

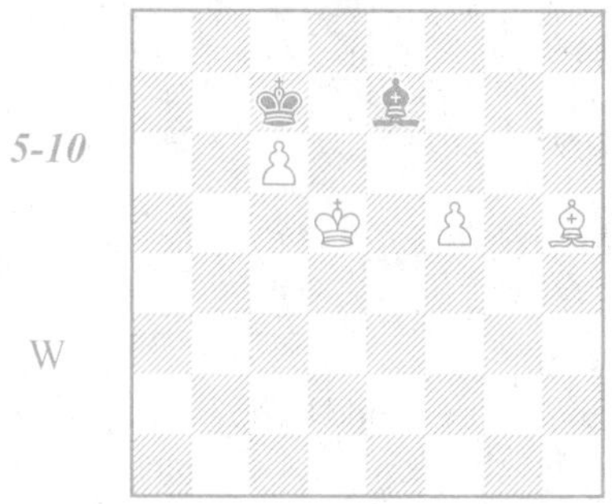

W

1 ♗f3 ♔d8 2 ♔e6 ♗b4 3 f6 ♗a5 4 f7 ♗b4 5 ♔f6 ♗c3+ 6 ♔g6 ♗b4 7 ♔g7+−.

It's interesting to analyze those situations where it's impossible to realize a material advantage. Here are some instances:

If one of the pawns is a rook pawn, and the bishop does not control the queening square, the draw can be secured by blocking that pawn with the king and sacrificing the bishop for the other.

If the pawns are separated by just one file, then the stronger side will only be able to win the bishop for the two pawns (imagine white pawns at c6 and e6 with the black king at d8, and the bishop restraining the pawn which is supported by white's king).

Sometimes the weaker side's king can help the bishop defend against both pawns at once. It ***"maintains the zone"*** (an expression borrowed from hockey), by shuttling to whichever flank it's needed to prevent the enemy king from invading its territory. This kind of defense is very important when the pawns are split.

The next diagram offers a very simple example.

Y. Averbakh, 1950

5-11

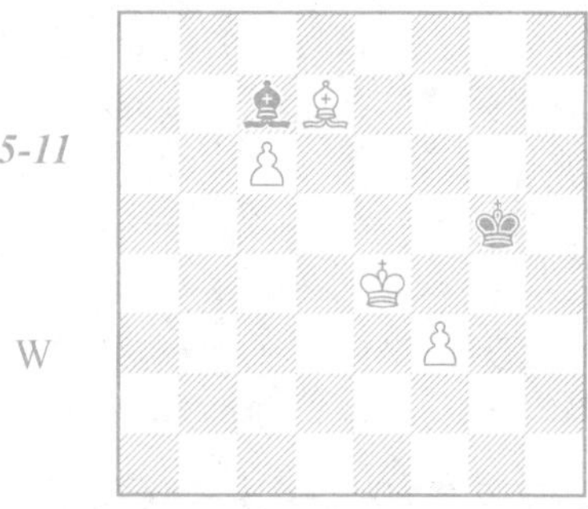

W

The draw is obvious: **1 ♔d5** is met by **1...♔f6**; if the king goes to b7, Black's king turns up at d8. Black can draw in large part because his bishop restrains both pawns along the b8-h2 diagonal.

And finally, the standard winning plan often does not work because the edge of the board is too close (for example, when one of the pawns is a knight pawn). The following position has great practical significance.

Berger - Kotlerman
Arkhangelsk 1948

5-12

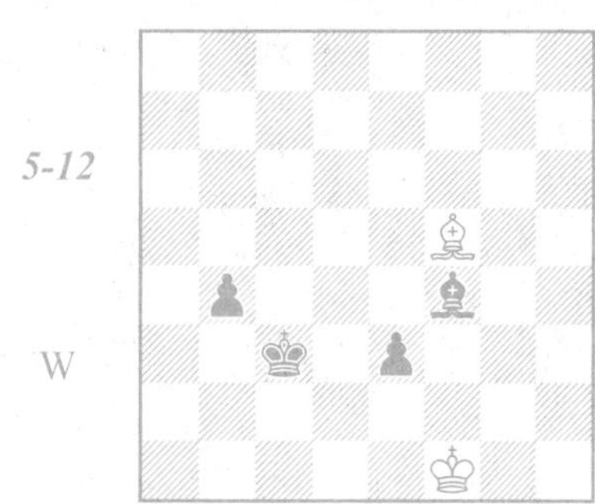

W

1 ♔e2 b3 2 ♔d1 ♔b4 3 ♗h7 ♔a3 4 ♗g6

If 4...b2 (threatening 5...♔a2), then 5 ♗b1! ♔b3 6 ♔e2.

4...♔b2 5 ♗f7!

Black threatened 5...♔a1 and 6...b2. White stops this plan by attacking the b3-pawn.

5...♔a2 6 ♗e6 ♔a3 (threatening 7...b2 8 ♗f5 ♔a2) **7 ♗f5!** Drawn.

The ideas we have examined thus far will help you orient yourself in the most varied kinds of situations with disconnected pawns - even with a large number of pawns on the board.

Y. Averbakh, 1954

5-13

B?

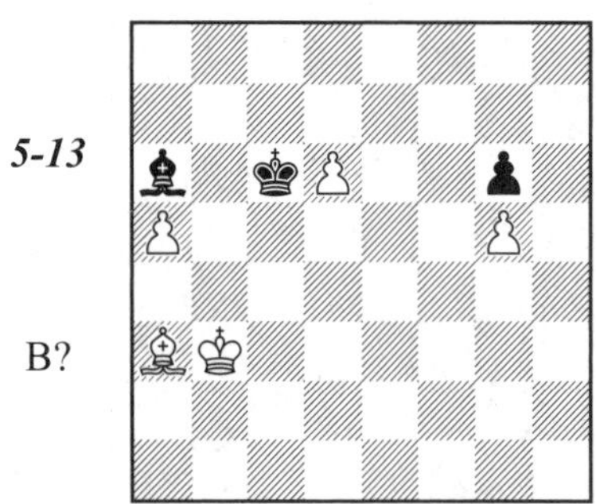

1...♔d7! 2 ♔c3 ♔e6 3 ♔d4 ♗e2

3...♗b7 4 ♔c5 ♔d7 is equivalent.

4 ♔c5 (△ ♔c6-c7+−) **4...♗f3!**

4...♔d7? would be a mistake: after 5 ♔d5 ♗f1 6 ♔e5 ♗e2, when the white king gets into the kingside. Now, White will get nothing out of 7 ♔f6 ♗d3 8 a6? ♗×a6 9 ♔×g6 ♔e8 - with the same drawing position as in the game Berger - Kotlerman (with opposite colors and reversed flanks).

The correct idea is to play for zugzwang. From d3, the bishop defends the g6-pawn on one diagonal, while on the other, it restrains the advance of the a-pawn; *ergo*, it has no moves. White's king cannot be allowed to get to e7 - that means that, in addition to d7, the black king has just two other squares: e8 and d8. We can take away the first one by putting the king on f7; the second, by moving the bishop to c7.

7 ♗c5 ♗f1 8 ♗b6 ♗e2 9 ♗c7 ♗d3 10 ♔f6 ♔e8 11 ♔g7⊙ ♔d7 12 ♔f7⊙+−.

5 a6 ♔d7 6 ♔b6 ♔c8! (the king maintains the zone: White threatened 7 ♔a7 ♔c8 8 d7+! ♔×d7 9 ♔b8+−) **7 ♔a7**

5-14

$

B?

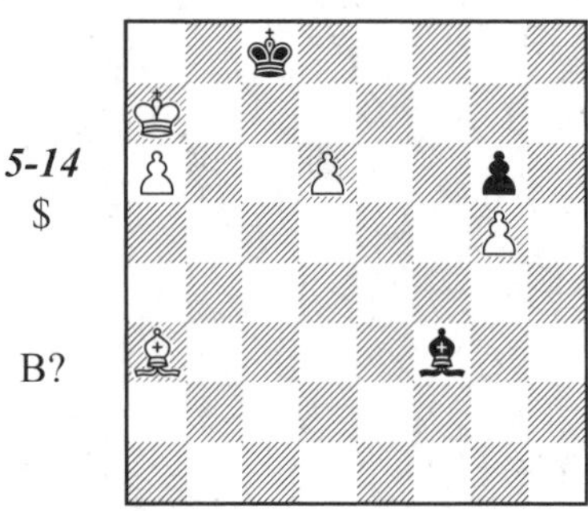

Once again, Black must be accurate. After 7...♗c6? 8 ♗b4, he gets into zugzwang: 8...♗d7 9 ♔b6 ♗f5 10 d7+! ♔×d7 11 ♔b7, or 10...♗×d7 11 a7.

7...♗g4! 8 ♔b6 ♗f3! 9 ♔c5 ♔d7! 10 ♔d4 ♔e6!=.

Topalov - Shirov

Linares 1998

5-15

B?

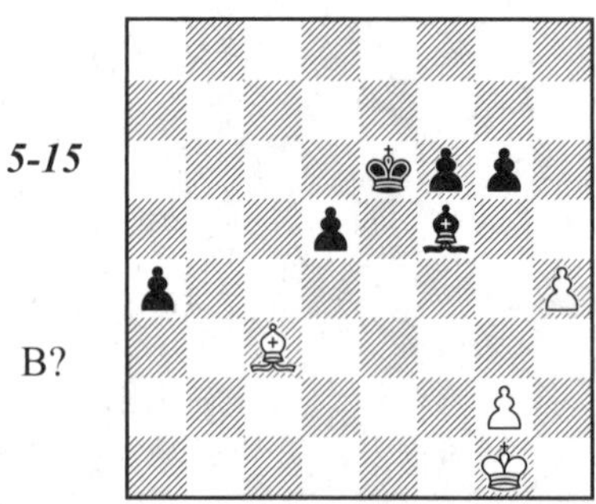

"Normal" play would bring White the draw without too much trouble, for instance:

1...♔d6? 2 ♔f2! (simplest - although White also does not lose after 2 ♗×f6 ♔c5 3 ♔f2 d4 4 ♔e2 ♔c4 5 ♗e7 ♔c3 6 ♔d1) 2...♔c5 3 ♔e3=;

1...♗e4? 2 ♔f2 ♔f5 3 g3! a3 4 ♔e3 ♔g4 5 ♗×f6 ♔×g3 6 ♔d2 ♔f4 (on 6...d4 7 ♗×d4 ♔×h4 8 ♔c1 g5 9 ♗c5 a2 10 ♔b2, White need only give up his bishop for the g-pawn) 7 ♗e7! (while there's time, it's useful to force the enemy pawn onto the same color square as his bishop) 7...a2 8 ♗f6 ♗f5 9 ♗g7 ♔e4 10 ♗a1 d4 11 ♗b2 (with the pawn at a3, White would risk falling into zugzwang here) 11...d3 12 ♗c3 ♔f4 13 ♗b2 ♔g4 14 ♗f6 a1♕ 15 ♗×a1 ♔×h4, and we have transposed into the Berger - Kotlerman ending.

Shirov found a fantastic resolution of the position.

1...♗h3!!

The bishop is sacrificed for a single tempo - the one needed for the king to get to e4.

2 gh

2 ♔f2 ♔f5 3 ♔f3 would not help in view of 3...♗×g2+! 4 ♔×g2 ♔e4−+.

2...♔f5 3 ♔f2 ♔e4! 4 ♗×f6

After 4 ♔e2 f5, Black has too many passed pawns.

4...d4 (△ 5...a3) **5 ♗e7 ♔d3** (threatening 6...♔c2 and 7...d3) **6 ♗c5 ♔c4!** (but not 6...♔c3? 7 ♔e2) **7 ♗e7 ♔b3** (7...♔c3 is just as good).

Now the king must reach c2, which gives us the "pants" situation we spoke of in Chapter Four. White resigned.

Tragicomedies

Marin - Slovineanu
Romania 1999

5-16

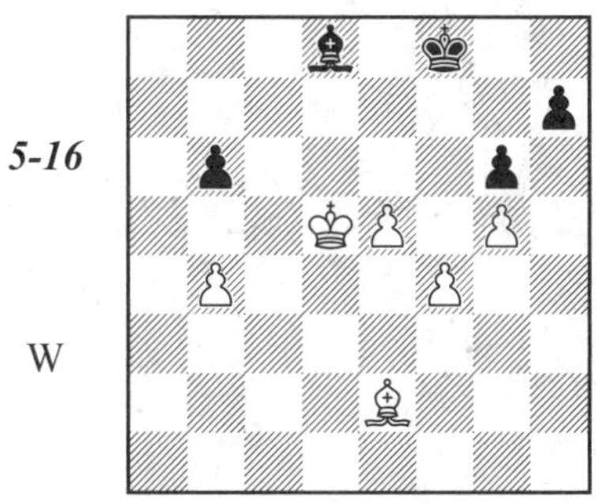

W

The game ended very quickly: **1 ♔c4?! ♗e7 2 ♔b5 ♔g7 3 ♗d3 h6** Drawn.

Marin, in Informant 75, gave his 1 ♔c4 two question marks. He assessed his position as winning, and demonstrated this with the following variation:

1 ♔c6 ♗e7 2 b5 ♗c5 3 ♔d7 ♗b4 4 e6 ♗c5 5 ♗d3 ♗e7 6 ♗e4 ♗c5 7 f5 gf 8 ♗×f5 ♗e7 9 ♔c6! (D. Rogozenko) - apparently it was this last move, later pointed out by his colleague, that the GM failed to notice during the game - 9...♗×g5 (9...♗d8 10 ♗×h7) 10 ♔×b6 ♔e7 11 ♔c6 ♗f4 12 b6 h5 13 ♔b7 ♗e3 14 ♔c7+−.

Evidently, neither Marin nor Rogozenko was aware of the Berger - Kotlerman endgame. Otherwise, they would clearly have seen that 12...♔d8! (instead of 12...h5??) would secure Black the draw. Actually, if he wishes, Black could even keep his h-pawn (which, in fact, has not the slightest value anyway) by playing 11...h5 (instead of 11...♗f4) 12 b6 (12 ♔c7 ♗f4+ 13 ♔c8 ♗e3) 12...♔d8 13 ♔b7 ♗e3!=, or 13 b7 ♗f4 14 ♔b6 ♗b8!=.

Cifuentes - Langeweg
El Vendrell 1996

5-17

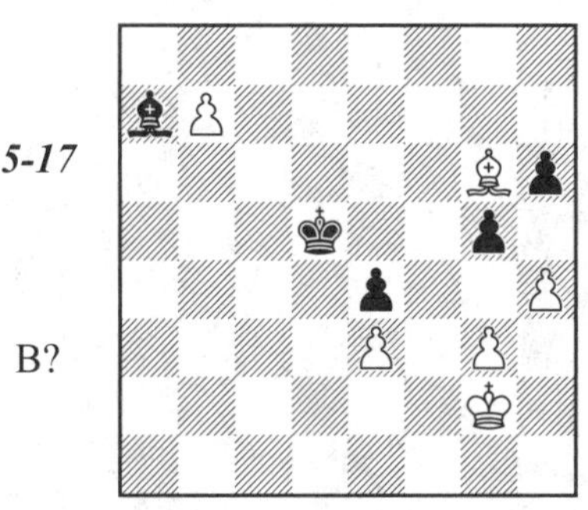

B?

1...♔e5?!

A strange move indeed! Common sense would indicate Black should exchange on h4. *The side that is down material should usually exchange pawns whenever possible.*

Cifuentes believes that Black would stand poorly then, and demonstrates this with the following variation: 1...gh 2 gh ♗b8 3 ♔h3 ♗a7 4 ♔g4 ♔e5 5 ♔h5⊙ ♔d5 6 ♗f5! (6 ♔×h6? would be premature: 6...♗×e3+ 7 ♔g7 ♗a7! 8 ♗×e4+ ♔×e4 9 h5 ♔d5 10 h6 ♔c6=) 6...♔e5 7 ♔g6 ♔d5 (7...h5 8 ♗h3 ♔d6 9 ♗g2 ♔e5 10 ♔×h5 ♔f5 11 ♗×e4+!) 8 h5 ♔e5 9 ♗×e4! ♔×e4 10 ♔×h6 ♗×e3+ 11 ♔g6+−.

Cifuentes' analysis is completely unconvincing. Why should Black allow White's king to attack his h-pawn? For example, he could try 3...h5!? 4 ♗×h5 ♔c6. It would be much simpler, however, to set up an impregnable fortress by giving up Black's main weakness - the e4-pawn - at once.

Let's continue: 3...♔e5 4 ♔g4 ♔f6! 5 ♗×e4 ♗c7. Now the h-pawn is untouchable - 6 ♔h5 is met by 6...♔g7. White has to bring his king to the queenside; but the most he can achieve there is the win of the bishop for his b- and e-pawns. But then Black's king goes to h8, with an elementary draw (the enemy bishop does not control the rook pawn's queening square). And this important defensive resource comes about precisely because of the exchange of pawns at h4.

Even in Cifuentes' line 3...♗a7 4 ♔g4 ♔e5 5 ♔h5, it's still not too late to return to the right plan: 5...♔f6!, since after 6 ♔×h6 (6 ♗×e4 ♔g7=) 6...♗×e3+ 7 ♔h7 ♗f4 8 ♗×e4 ♗b8, White is unable to queen the h-pawn: 9 ♗f3 ♗c7 10 h5 ♔g5 11 h6 ♗e5 12 ♗e2 ♗b8 13 ♔g7 ♗e5+.

Black's refusal to trade pawns probably stems from the fact that Langeweg did not want to free the g3-square for White's king. The king cannot approach through the h3-square, which can be seen from the line 2 ♔h3 ♔d6! 3 ♔g4 ♔c7 (3...gh) 4 h5 (4 hg hg 5 ♗×e4 ♗×e3=) 4...♗×e3 (4...♔×b7 5 ♗×e4+ ♔c7=) 5 ♗×e4 ♗d2 6 ♔f5 g4!=.

2 h5!? ♔d5?

This was, evidently, the decisive error! As Bologan pointed out, Black had a simple draw with 2...g4! followed by ...♗b8. Black's king easily defends the kingside pawns (3 ♗e8

♔f5); and the g3-pawn will drop as soon as the white king leaves its side.

3 g4!

After fixing the kingside, White can now direct his king to the opposite side of the board, restrict his opponent's movements, and finally break through the center to reach the weak pawn at h6.

3...♔e5 4 ♔f2 ♗b8 5 ♔e2 ♗a7 6 ♔d2 ♔d5 7 ♔c3⊙ ♗b8 8 ♗f7+ ♔c5 9 ♗g6 ♔d5 10 ♔b4! ♗g3 11 ♔b5 ♗c7 12 ♔a6 ♗b8 13 ♔b6⊙ ♔e5 14 ♔c6 ♔e6

Black had to give up the e4-pawn anyway (because of the mortal threat of ♔d7-c8), but in a far less favorable situation.

15 ♗×e4 ♗g3 16 ♗f5+ ♔e7 17 ♔b6 ♗b8 18 e4 ♔d6

5-18

W?

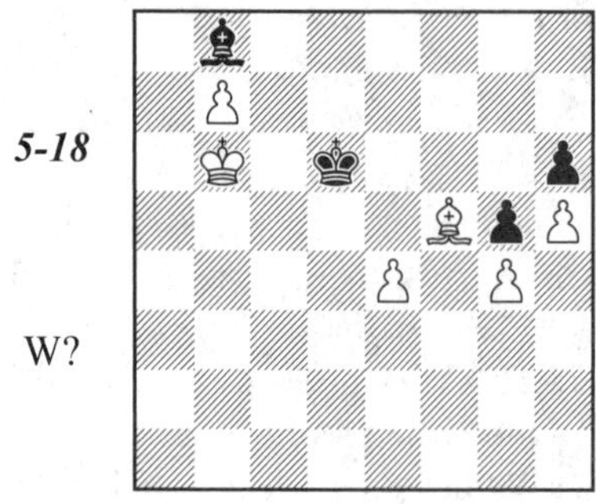

19 e5+! ♔e7

19...♔×e5 loses to 20 ♔c6; and if 19...♔d5, then 20 ♗c8 ♔×e5 21 ♔c6 ♔f6 22 ♔d7 ♔f7 23 ♔d8+−. Now imagine the same position, but without the g-pawns: Black could then simply capture on e5.

20 ♗c2 ♔e6 21 ♗b3+ ♔e7 22 ♗a2⊙ (if 22 ♔c6?? ♗×e5 23 ♔d5 ♔f6=) **22...♔d7 23 ♔c5! ♗×e5 24 ♔d5 ♗f4 25 ♔e4 ♔e7 26 ♔f5 ♗c7 27 ♔g6** Black resigned.

Exercises

5-19

5/3
B?

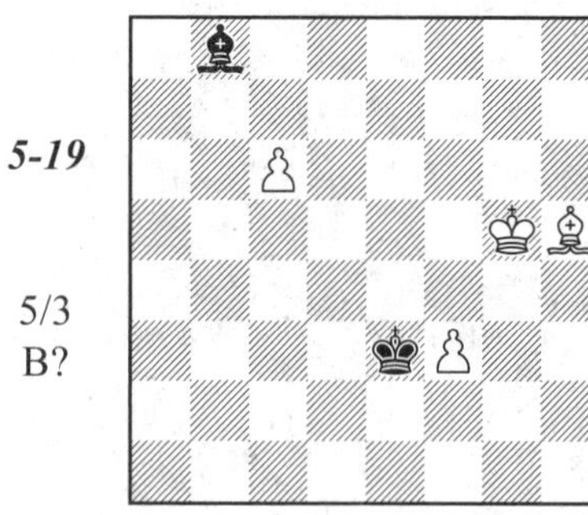

5-20

5/4
W?

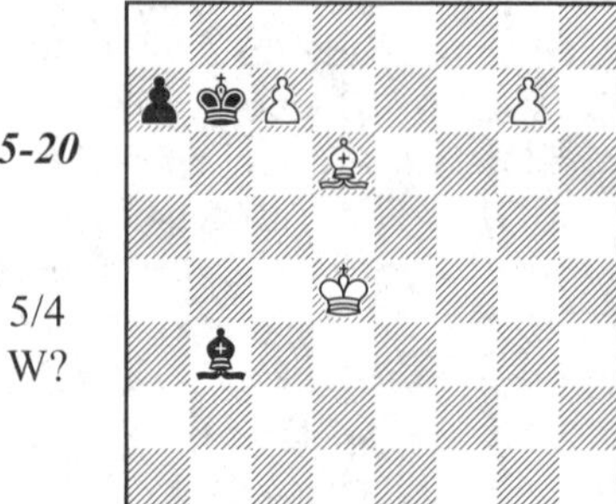

The King Blockades the Passed Pawn

Quite often the stronger side will have a passed pawn, which needs to be blockaded by either the king or the bishop.

The first defensive system: The king blockades the enemy passed pawn, while the bishop defends its own pawns. This is the basic and usually the most secure defensive arrangement.

Attempts to break down the first defensive system always involve the creation of a second passed pawn, frequently by means of a pawn breakthrough.

J. Speelman

5-21

W

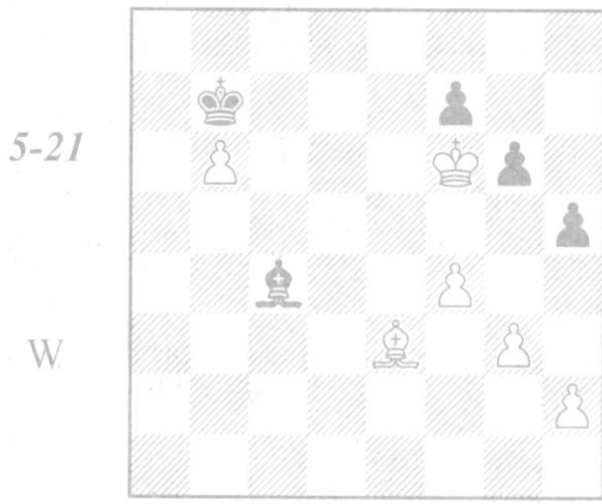

In such situations the bishop can easily handle the defense of the kingside, so a drawn outcome should come as no surprise.

1 f5 (the only try) **1...gf?!**

This move makes Black's task a bit more difficult. 1...♗d3!= is safer.

2 ♔×f5 ♗e6+! 3 ♔g5 ♗g4=

The assessment of the position would change if Black incautiously played 2...♔c6? (instead of 2...♗e6+!):

3 ♔g5 ♗e2 4 h3! (but not 4 ♔f6 ♗c4 5 h3?, in view of 5...♗f1! 6 g4 h4! 7 ♔×f7 ♗×h3 8 g5 ♗f1 - the advance of the h-pawn distracts the bishop from the defense of the b6-pawn).

4...♔b7 (4...♗f1 5 g4 hg 6 h4+−) 5 ♗d4 ♔c6 6 g4 hg 7 h4+−.

White has achieved his aim: the creation of a second passed pawn!

7...g3 8 ♔f4 (8 h5 f6+ 9 ♔g6?! is much less convincing: 9...f5 10 h6 f4 11 ♔g5 f3 12 h7 f2 - White's play might be strengthened, however, by 9 ♔h4!) 8...♗h5 (8...g2 9 ♔g5 △ 10 h5) 9 ♔×g3 f6 10 ♔f4 ♗g6 11 ♔g4 ♔b7 12 h5 ♗h7.

Black has set up a barrier, but one which can be overcome without much difficulty. White's king goes to a5, to free his bishop from the defense of the b6-pawn. The f6-pawn will then have to advance, and White's king will return to the kingside.

Kotov - Botvinnik
USSR ch, Moscow 1955

5-22

B?

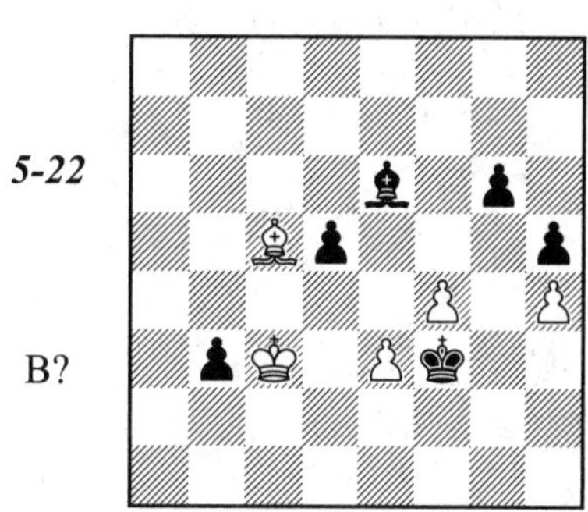

A classic example of the destruction of the first defensive system. The decisive breakthrough aims to create a second passed pawn.

1...g5!!

A mistake would be 1...♔g4? 2 ♗e7=, and if 2...♔f3 (this position occurred in the game: White played ♗c5?), then 3 ♔d2! b2 4 ♔c2 ♔×e3 5 ♔×b2 ♔×f4 6 ♔c3=.

2 fg

Hopeless is 2 hg h4 3 f5 (3 ♗d6 ♗f5 4 g6 ♗×g6 5 f5 ♗×f5 6 ♔×b3 ♔g2) 3...♗×f5 4 ♔×b3 h3 5 ♗d6 ♔×e3.

2...d4+!

The b3-pawn must be defended 2...♔g3? 3 ♔×b3=.

3 ed

An interesting sideline is 3 ♗×d4 ♔g3 4 g6 ♔×h4 5 ♔d2 ♔h3! (5...♔g3 6 ♗e5+ ♔g2 7 ♗f6) 6 ♗f6 (6 ♔e2 ♔g2! 7 ♗f6 h4) 6...h4 (threatening 7..♔g3) 7 ♔e2 ♔g2−+ ("pants").

3...♔g3

The careless 3...♔g4? would have led to a draw after 4 d5 ♗×d5 5 ♗f2.

4 ♗a3

Note the black bishop's excellent position in the variation 4 ♗e7 ♔×h4 5 g6+ ♔g4. It protects the b3-pawn and restrains both enemy pawns along the single diagonal a2-g8. White has no counterplay, so Black just advances his h-pawn and wins the bishop for it.

4...♔×h4 5 ♔d3 ♔×g5

Another strong line is 5...♔g3 6 ♔e4 h4 7 d5 h3 8 de h2 9 ♗d6+ ♔g4 10 ♗xh2 b2 11 e7 b1♕+.

6 ♔e4 h4 7 ♔f3 (7 d5 ♗xd5+) **7...♗d5+**

White resigned. After 8 ♔f2, Black's king goes after the b3-pawn. The bishop, meanwhile, defends the h-pawn, while restraining the d-pawn along the diagonal c8-h3.

Tragicomedies

Bellón - Minic
Siegen ol 1970

5-23

W?

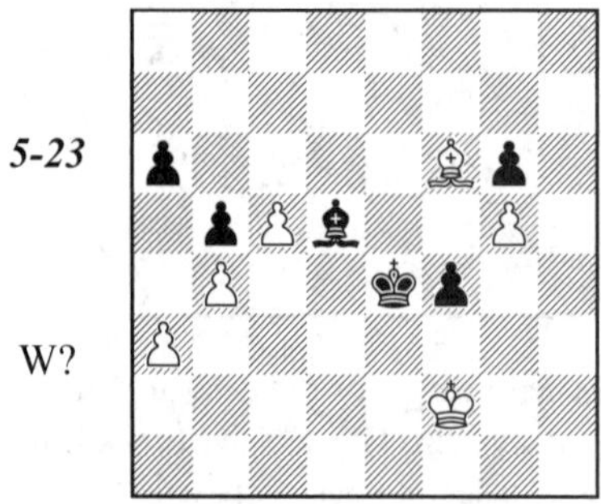

This was the adjourned position, in which White sealed his 41st move. After analyzing in their rooms, the players agreed to a draw without resumption. Black's positional advantage appeared insufficient for victory to Minic. Judging from his comments in the "Informant", he was convinced by the following line: 1 ♗d8 ♗c6 2 ♗c7 ♔f5 3 ♗d8 ♔g4 4 ♗e7 a5 5 ba ♔f5 6 a6 ♔e4 7 a7 ♔d4 8 a8♕ ♗xa8 9 c6 ♗xc6 10 ♗d6, when the a3-pawn is securely protected, and the draw is obvious.

It's surprising that even after home analysis, neither the players themselves nor their teammates were able to solve this rather simple position. In point of fact, its evaluation hinges on the sealed move.

After 1 ♗d8? ♗c6!, Black wins. To begin with, he must simply capture the a3-pawn (since the bishop cannot protect it), and then the threat of the ...a6-a5 breakthrough will become more serious. Taking the pawn at a5 would give Black his second passed pawn.

2 ♗c7 f3 3 ♗d8 ♔d3 4 ♗c7 ♔c2 5 ♗d8 ♔b3 6 ♗c7 ♔xa3 7 ♗a5 ♔b3

Having done its job, the king returns to the other side.

8 ♔e3 ♔c4 9 ♔f2 ♔d3 10 ♗d8 ♔e4 11 ♗c7 ♔f5 12 ♗d8

5-24

B

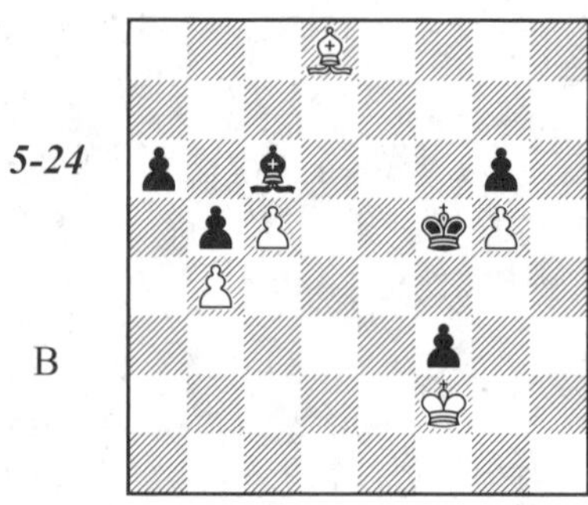

12...♔f4!

Zugzwang! White's bishop is torn apart: on the one diagonal, it protects the g5-pawn; on the other, it controls the a5-square. On 13 ♗c7+ ♔xg5, Black moves his king to d3 and plays ...g6-g5-g4-g3+, when ♗xg3 loses to ...a6-a5, and ♔xg3 to ...♔e2.

After 13 ♗e7 a5! 14 ba b4, the king goes to the queenside once again, to win the bishop for the b-pawn. White has no counterplay, since the black bishop does everything on the one diagonal a8-h1, defending the f3-pawn and stopping both enemy passers.

The king retreat is no help either.

13 ♔f1 ♔e3 14 ♗c7 a5! 15 ♗xa5 (15 ba b4) 15...♗d5, followed by 16...♗c4+ and 17...f2+.

After giving some thought to the final position of this variation, we come to understand that White's own pawn at c5 is in his way, because it blocks the important a7-g1 diagonal. So White must rid himself of it.

1 c6!!

The only saving line. In fact, Bellon probably sealed the other move instead. Otherwise, after the game ended, this line would have been revealed in the annotations.

1...♗xc6 2 ♗d8 ♔d3 3 ♗c7!

"Pawns in the crosshairs" - it's important to force them to move onto the same color squares as their bishop.

3...f3 4 ♗d8 ♔c2 5 ♗c7 ♔b3 6 ♗d8 ♔xa3 7 ♗a5 ♔b3 8 ♔e3 ♔c4 9 ♔f2 ♔d3 10 ♗c7 ♔e4 11 ♗b6 ♗d5 12 ♗c7 ♔f5 13 ♗d8

This is the same position as in the last diagram - except that there is no pawn at c5. Here Black gets nothing from 13...a5 14 ♗xa5 ♔xg5, since the connected passed pawns are easily blockaded on the dark squares. If White had not forced the timely advance of the f-pawn, with the pawn at f4 this position would be lost, of course.

13...♔f4 14 ♔f1!

Now on 14...♔e3, White has 15 ♗b6+ - this check was the reason behind the pawn sacrifice.

14...♗c4+ 15 ♔f2

On 15...♗d3, White cannot play either 16 ♔e1? ♔g3! 17 ♗c7+ ♔g2 or 16 ♔g1? ♔e3! 17 ♗b6+ ♔e2, followed by 18...a5. However, he does have 16 ♗c7+, exploiting the fact that the f3-pawn is not protected by the bishop (16...♔×g5 17 ♔×f3). On 15...♗e2, there follows 16 ♔g1! ♔e3 17 ♗b6+ (the e2-square is occupied). And if the bishop goes to g2, White plays ♔e1! (analysis by Dvoretsky).

Ljubojevic - Karpov

Milan 1975

5-25

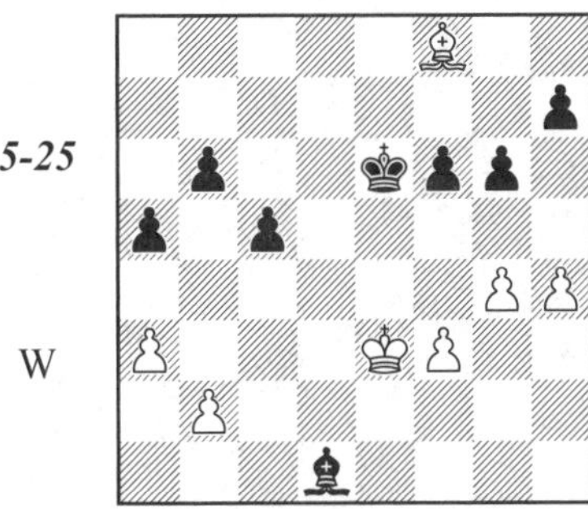

W

Of course, the position is drawn. All White need do is to take the kingside pawns off the light squares, and his bishop can defend them. This frees the king to counter Black's play on the queenside, where he wants to create a passed pawn.

The simplest solution to the problem is 1 g5! f5 (1...fg 2 hg △ f4=) 2 f4 ♔d5 3 ♗g7. Another reasonable line would be 1 h5!? g5 (1...gh 2 gh ♔d5 3 ♗g7 f5 4 h6 ♔c4 5 f4 ♔b3 6 ♔d2= Matanovic) 2 ♔e4 ♗c2+ 3 ♔e3 f5 4 gf+ ♔×f5 5 h6=.

1 ♔e4?! a4 2 h5?

White is doing all he possibly can to complicate his life. Here again, 2 g5! f5+ 3 ♔e3 would have secured an elementary draw.

2...gh 3 gh f5+ 4 ♔e3 ♔d5 5 h6 ♔c4 6 f4 ♔b3

5-26

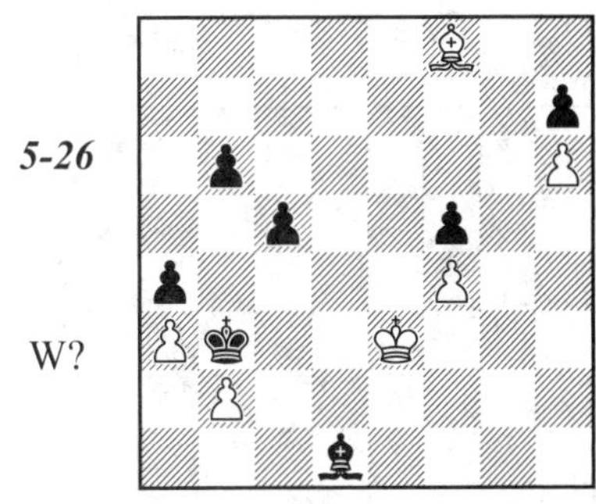

W?

White might still have saved the game by playing 7 ♔d2! ♗f3 8 ♔c1 (or 8 ♗g7). Evidently, Ljubojevic didn't feel like calculating the consequences of 7...♔×b2. However, as Villeneuve has established, the bishop sacrifice is insufficient: 8 ♔×d1 c4 (8...♔×a3 9 ♔c2 ♔b4 10 ♔b2=) 9 ♗g7+ c3 10 ♔e2! (10 ♗e5? b5 11 ♗d4 b4−+) 10...♔×a3 (10...♔c2 11 ♔e3 b5 12 ♔d4! ♔d2 13 ♔c5!) 11 ♗×c3 (11 ♔d3 b5 12 ♔c2!) 11...b5 12 ♗e5 b4 (△ 13...♔a2−+) 13 ♗d6!=.

7 ♗g7? ♔c2!

Only now, when the white king is cut off from the queenside, does his position become lost. Black's pawn advance will reach its goal - but only with the black bishop on b3, which is where Karpov is sending it now.

8 ♗e5 ♗h5 9 ♗f6

9 ♗c7 wouldn't help: 9...♔×b2 10 ♗×b6 c4 11 ♗d4+ (11 ♗c5 c3 12 ♗d4 ♔c2 13 ♗f6 ♗e8 followed by 14...♗b5 and 15...♔b3) 11...♔×a3 12 ♔d2 ♔b3 13 ♗f6 a3. Then Black will place his bishop at b1, pawn at a2, transfer his king to g6 and (with the white bishop at g7), trade the c4 and h6 pawns by means of ...c4-c3.

9...♗f7 10 ♗e5 ♗b3! 11 ♗g7 b5 12 ♗f8

Nothing would be changed with 12 ♗c3 b4! 13 ♗g7 (13 ab a3!; 13 ♗e1 ♔×b2 14 ab cb 15 ♗×b4 a3 16 ♔d4 a2 17 ♗c3+ ♔c2 18 ♗a1 ♔b1 19 ♗c3 ♗f7! 20 ♔e5 ♗g6−+) 13...c4.

12...c4 13 ♗g7 b4! 14 ♔d4

The main line of Karpov's idea runs 14 ab c3 15 ♗×c3 (15 bc ♗c4!) 15...a3 16 ♗e5 a2−+. Without the bishop at b3 in the final position, White could save himself with 17 b3.

14...c3 15 bc ba 16 c4 a2 17 ♔c5 ♔b1 18 ♔b4 a1♕ 19 ♗×a1 ♔×a1 20 c5 ♔b2 21 c6 a3 22 c7 ♗e6 23 ♔c5 a2 24 ♔d6 ♗c8 White resigned.

Exercises

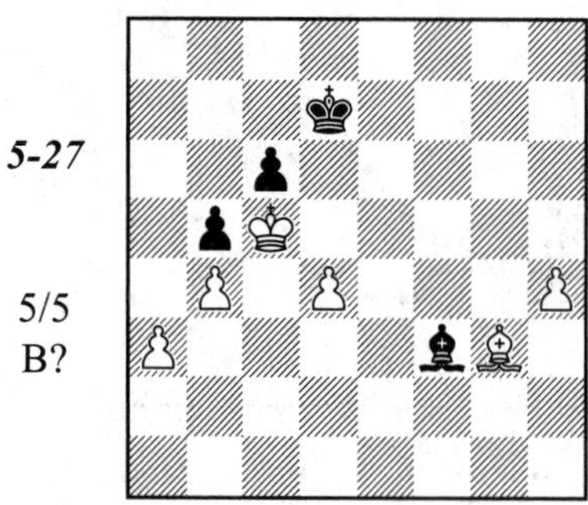

5-27

5/5
B?

The Bishop Restrains the Passed Pawn

Situations in which the bishop stops a passed pawn (and sometimes two - on the same diagonal) we call the ***second defensive system.*** The weaker side's king in these cases "maintains the zone" - that is, it defends its pawns, and limits the activity of the opposing king.

Attempts to break down the second defensive system invariably involve breaking through to the passed pawn with the king (often after a preliminary diversionary attack, and "widening the beachhead" on the other wing).

Euwe - Yanofsky
Groningen 1946

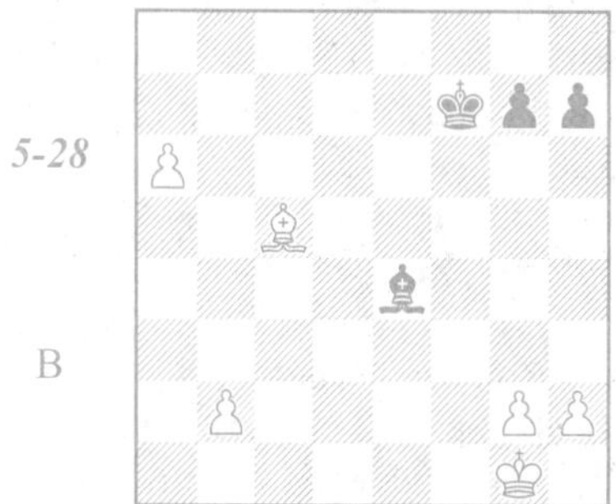

5-28

B

1...h5!

A typical move, ensuring the safety of the kingside pawns. On 1...♔e6?!, Black would have had to reckon not only with 2 g4!?, but also with 2 ♔f2 ♔d7? 3 ♗f8 g6 4 ♗h6!, when the h7-pawn becomes an attractive target for the white king.

2 ♔f2 ♗d3!

A technique we have already seen more than once: the a-pawn is forced onto a square of the same color as its bishop.

3 a7 ♗e4 4 g3 ♔e6 5 ♔e3

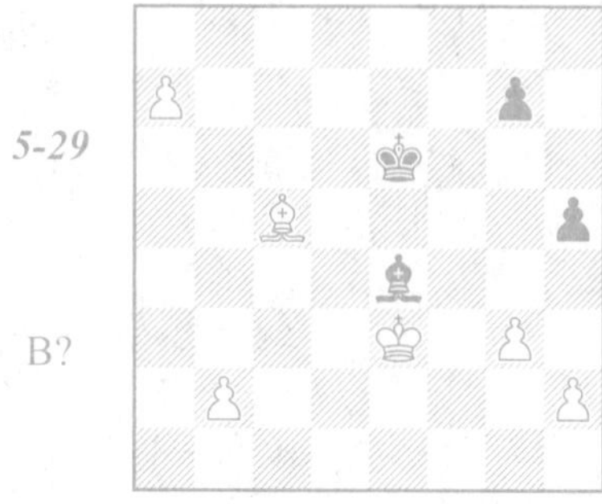

5-29

B?

5...♗g2?

An instructive error: the white king should not have been allowed near the pawns. The draw becomes unavoidable after 5...♔f5! 6 ♗f8 g6 7 ♔d4 ♗g2 8 ♔c5 ♔e6! 9 ♔b6 ♔d7 10 b4 ♗a8 11 b5 ♔c8!= (but not 11...♗g2? in view of 12 a8♕! ♗×a8 13 ♔a7 ♗f3 14 ♔b8+−, with the unstoppable threat of b5-b6-b7).

6 ♔f4! g6 7 g4!

The first step is to widen the kingside beachhead.

7...hg 8 ♔×g4 ♗h1 9 ♔g5 ♔f7 10 ♗d4 ♗g2 11 h4 ♗h1 12 b4 ♗g2 13 b5 ♗h1

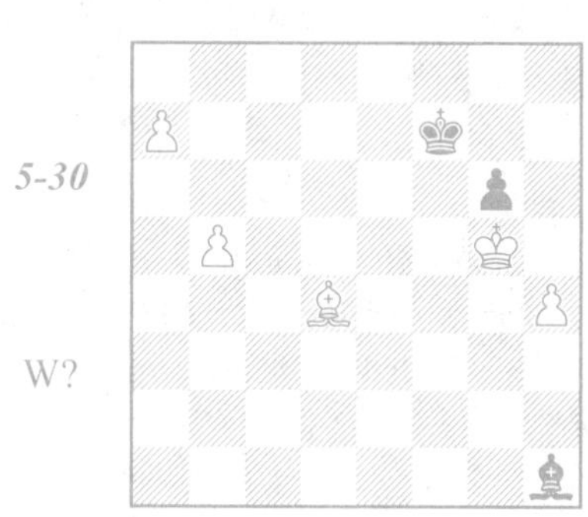

5-30

W?

14 ♗f6! ♗g2

On 14...♗e4, both 15 ♔f4 △ ♔e5 and 15 b6⊙ are strong.

15 h5! (the second, decisive step!) **15...gh 16 ♔f5** Black resigned.

If 16...♔e8, then 17 ♔e6 △ ♔d6-c7. White's bishop restrains the h-pawn and simultaneously deprives the enemy king of the squares e7 and d8 on the single diagonal d8-h4.

Makarychev - Averbakh
Lvov 1973

5-31

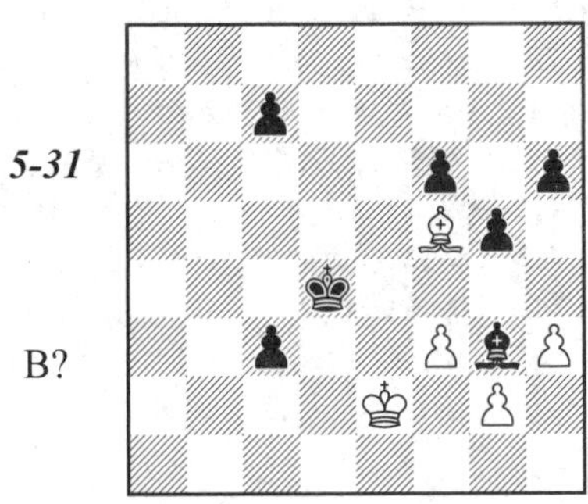

B?

Black's plan is the same as in the preceding example: first, the king invades the kingside; then, the beachhead is widened; and finally, the king breaks through to the c-pawn.

1...♔e5 2 ♗c2 ♔f4 3 ♗b1 ♗h2 4 ♔f2 ♗g1+! 5 ♔e2

5 ♔×g1 ♔e3 6 ♔f1 ♔d2 would lose immediately.

5...♔g3 6 ♔f1 ♗f2!

In order to prepare ...f7-f5, Black must first take control of the e1-square.

7 ♗c2 f5! 8 ♗b1

On 8 ♗×f5, the king gets through to his passed pawn: 8...♔f4 9 ♗c2 ♔e3−+ (it is important that White cannot reply 10 ♔e1).

8...f4 9 ♗g6 ♗e3 10 ♗c2 h5 11 ♗f5 c5 12 ♗g6 h4!

Black only gets a draw out of 12...g4? 13 hg hg (13...h4 14 ♗e4) 14 fg, for example: 14...♔×g4 15 ♔e2 ♔g3 16 ♔f1 (but not 16 ♗e4? c2 17 ♗×c2 ♔×g2) 16...♗f2 17 ♗e4! c4 18 ♔e2! c2 19 ♔d2=.

13 ♗f5 (13 ♗e4 c4⊙) **13...g4! 14 hg**

No better is 14 fg f3 15 gf ♔×h3−+.

14...h3 15 gh ♔×f3 16 g5 ♔g3 17 g6 ♗d4 18 h4 f3 19 h5 ♗g7 20 ♔e1 f2+

White resigned. After 21 ♔f1 ♔f3, the king marches unhindered to d2.

And now, let's examine a much more complex ending, excellently played and annotated by Kaidanov.

Kaidanov - Antoshin
RSFSR ch 1984

5-32

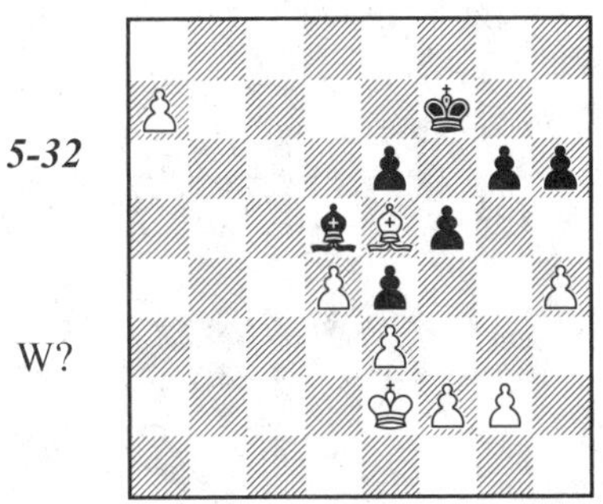

W?

What plan should White select? 1 ♗f4? (hoping to induce the reply 1...h5, giving his king invasion squares on the kingside) would be a gross blunder, in view of the pawn sacrifice 1...g5! 2 hg hg 3 ♗×g5 ♔e8. Black's king arrives at b7 (the "first defensive system"), and White is unable to create a second passed pawn on the kingside.

By the way, ...g6-g5 is not yet a threat - White replies h4-h5, fixing the h6-pawn. (With a light-squared bishop, for the weaker side to have his pawns on dark squares renders them weak, and is generally a serious positional defect.) But without exchanging off these pawns, it makes no sense to go into the first defensive position, because the bishop will be unable to defend its kingside.

White will not be able to get to the a-pawn through the queenside: the enemy king will "maintain the zone." But by doing so, he will be diverted from the f7-square, and then White can play ♗g7, induce ...h6-h5, and return with his king to the kingside. Let's try it: 1 ♔d2 ♗a8 2 ♔c3 ♗b7 3 ♔b4 ♔e7 4 ♗g7 h5 5 ♔c3. Is there a way to prevent White's king from going through h2 to e5? Yes there is - the black king can counterattack: 5...♔d6! 6 ♔d2 ♔d5 7 ♔e1 ♔c4 8 ♔f1 ♔d3 9 ♔g1 ♔e2=.

1 ♔f1! ♗a8 2 ♔g1 ♗d5 3 ♔h2 ♗a8 4 ♔g3!

Now let's examine 4 ♔h3 ♗d5 5 g4? fg+ 6 ♔×g4 ♗a8 7 ♔g3 ♗d5 8 ♔g2 ♗a8 9 ♔f1 ♗d5 10 ♔e2 ♗a8 11 ♔d2 ♗d5 12 ♔c3 ♗a8 13 ♔b4. Now, the defensive plan of marching the black king down to e2 (13...♔e7? 14 ♗g7 h5 15 ♔c3

♔d6 16 ♔d2 ♔d5) doesn't work, because his opponent will advance through the now open square g2. But there is another idea: Black can return to the first defensive position: 13...♗d5! 14 ♔c5 ♔e7 15 ♗g7 h5 15 ♔b4 ♔d6 17 ♔c3 ♔c7! 18 ♗e5+ ♔b7 19 ♗b8 ♔b6! 20 ♔d2 ♔b7 21 ♔e1 ♗c4!=, and White's king will not get to the kingside.

4...♗d5 5 ♗c7!

5-33

B

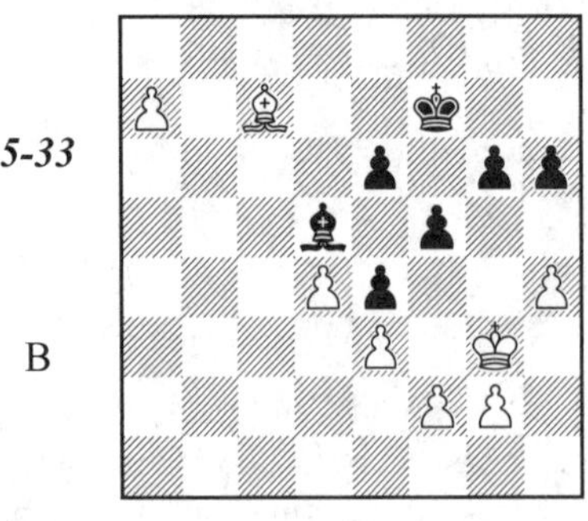

5...♔e7

Forced, because the temporizing 5...♗a8? allows White's king to get to its passed pawn: 6 ♔f4! g5+ 7 ♔e5! gh (7...♔e7 8 h5!+−) 8 ♔d6+−. With the king already on e7, 6 ♔f4? g5+!= no longer works for White; on the other hand, the bishop sacrifice now becomes strong.

6 ♗f4! g5! 7 ♗×g5+! hg 8 hg ♔f7 9 f4!

But not 9 ♔f4? ♔g6 10 f3 ♔f7 (or 10...♔h5) 11 fe fe=.

9...♔g6 (9...ef 10 gf △ ♔f4, e4+−) **10 ♔h4 ♗a8 11 g4! fg 12 ♔×g4 ♗d5 13 ♔g3**

Having strengthened his kingside position to the utmost, White brings the king over to the queenside. Black must send his king to meet it - but then the g-pawn charges ahead.

13...♔f7 14 ♔f2 ♔e7 15 ♔e1 ♔d6 16 ♔d2 ♗c6 (16...♔c7 17 g6 ♔b7 18 g7 e5 19 de ♔×a7 20 f5+−) **17 ♔c3 ♗a8 18 ♔b4 ♗d5 19 g6 ♔e7 20 ♔c5 ♔f6** (20...♗a8 21 f5 ef 22 d5+−) **21 f5! ♗a8 22 fe ♔×e6 23 d5+** Black resigned.

Exercises

Both of the following exercises are rather difficult. In the first, you must calculate variations accurately; in the second, you must find a far from obvious plan of action.

5-34

5/6
W?

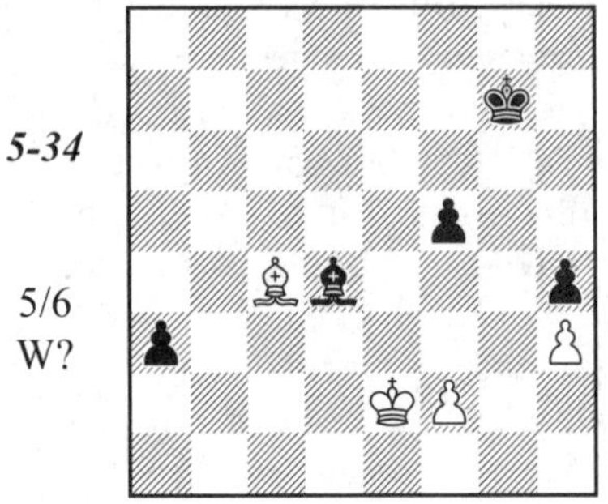

5-35

5/7
W?

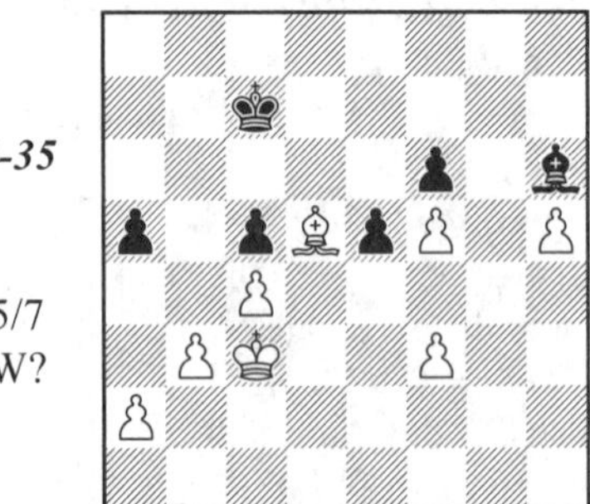

Chapter 6

BISHOPS OF THE SAME COLOR

Minimal Material

Bishop and Pawn vs. Bishop

These endgames were first subjected to thorough analysis in the mid-19th century by the Italian player Centurini. Later, significant additions to the theory were made by GM Averbakh.

6-1

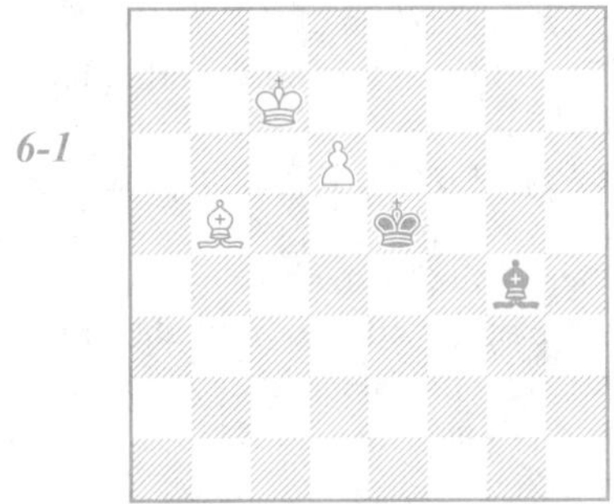

White to move wins, by ***driving off*** the enemy bishop from one diagonal, and then ***interfering*** along the other diagonal.

1 ♗d7 ♗d1 2 ♗h3 ♗a4 3 ♗g2 △ **4 ♗c6+–**

Can this plan be prevented? Yes, it can - provided Black's king can get to c5, preventing White's bishop from interfering along the diagonal. Black to move draws:

1...♔d4! (but not 1...♔d5? 2 ♗d7 ♗d1 3 ♗c6+ and 4 d7) **2 ♗d7 ♗d1 3 ♗h3 ♗a4 4 ♗g2 ♔c5!=**

Thus, if the weaker side's king cannot get in front of the pawn, then the basic defensive principle becomes: ***king behind the king!***

The short diagonal: even with the "right" king position, the draw is impossible, if one of the diagonals along which the bishop will restrain the pawn proves too short.

6-2

W

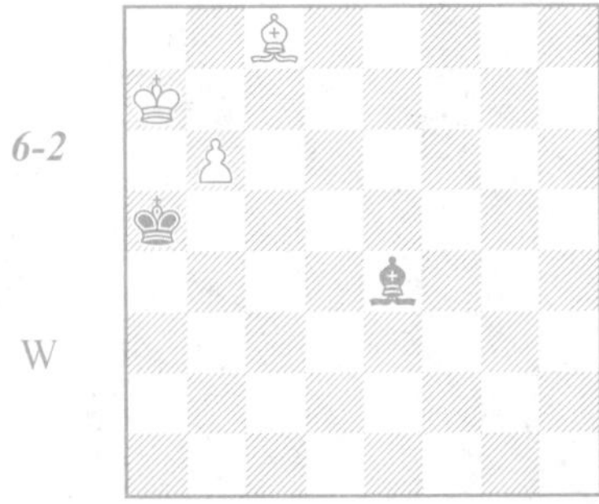

1 ♗b7 ♗f5 2 ♗f3 ♗c8 3 ♗e2⊙+–

All the squares on the c8-a6 diagonal, except c8, are under the control of White pieces - that's why we get a zugzwang. Now, if we were to move the entire position down one rank, the bishop would get another free square, and White could no longer win.

The following position of reciprocal zugzwang has some practical significance.

6-3

$

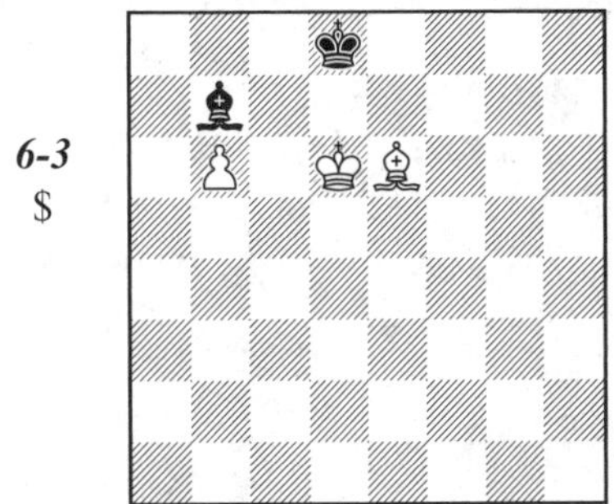

White to move draws. 1 ♗d5 ♔c8 (or 1...♗a6) is useless. On **1 ♗f5**, there follows **1...♗f3 2 ♗e6** (△ 3 ♗d5+–) **2...♗b7! 3 ♔c5 ♗f3** (3...♔e7? 4 ♗d5) **4 ♗d5 ♗e2** (△♔c8) **5 ♗b7 ♔d7=**

But what is Black to do, if it is his move? Any bishop retreat along the h1-a8 diagonal is refuted by 2 ♗d5; therefore, he must play **1...♗a6**. By the way (here's a tragicomedy!), in this won position, Botvinnik accepted a draw against Model in the 1931 Leningrad Championship.

The path to victory is uncomplicated: **2 ♔c6! ♗c8 3 ♗c4!⊙ ♗g4 4 ♔b7! ♗f3+ 5 ♔a7** △ ♗a6-b7+–.

Transposition to Positions with One Pawn

Charushin - Rosenholz
cr 1986

6-4

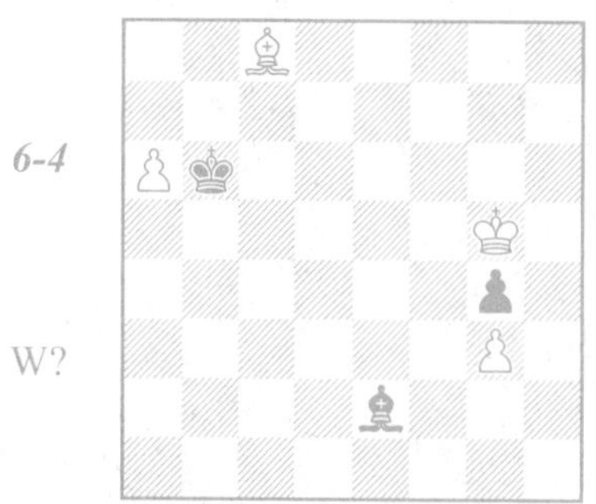

W?

A typical situation: White can take the g4-pawn only at the cost of his a6-pawn. The question is whether the enemy king can get back in time.

1 ♔f4!⊙

Excellently played! White improves his own king's position (now it no longer stands in the path of its pawn) while simultaneously using zugzwang to force the enemy king further away from the kingside. The hasty 1 ♗×g4? ♗×a6 2 ♔f4 ♔c7 3 ♗f3 ♔d6 4 g4 ♔e7 leads only to a draw.

1...♔a7□ (1...♔c7 2 a7 ♗f3 3 ♗×g4) **2 ♗×g4 ♗×a6 3 ♗f3 ♔b6**

No better is 3...♗c8 4 ♗e4 ♔b6 5 ♗f5.

4 g4 ♔c5 5 g5 ♔d6 6 g6 ♔e6

Nothing is altered by 6...♔e7 7 ♔g5 ♔f8 8 ♔h6 ♗c4 9 g7+ ♔g8 10 ♗e4 △ 11 ♗h7+.

7 ♔g5 ♗c4 8 g7

Black resigned, in view of 8...♔f7 9 ♔h6 ♔f6 10 ♔h7 ♔g5 11 ♔h8 ♔h6 12 ♗e4, followed by ♗h7-g8 (the h7-g8 diagonal, where the black bishop must move, is too short).

Capablanca - Janowsky
New York 1916

6-5

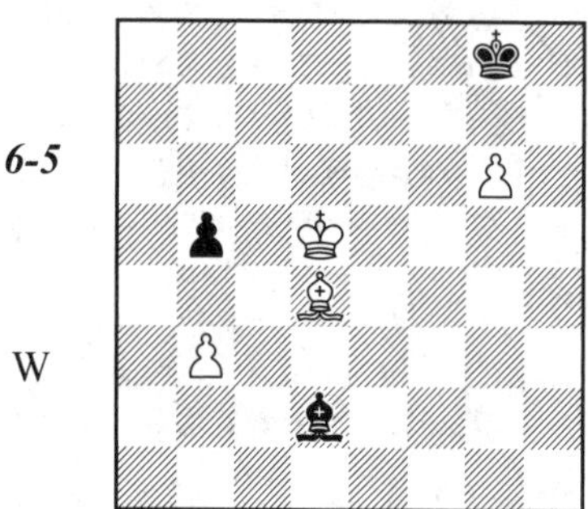

W

White has nothing to play for, other than to pick up the b-pawn in exchange for his g6-pawn. Unfortunately, this plan would not be enough to win. I present the main variation: 1 ♔c5 b4 2 ♔c4 ♗e1 3 ♗c5 ♔g7 4 ♗×b4 ♗g3! (Averbakh's analysis shows that 4...♗f2 also draws, but that 4...♗h4? loses) 5 ♗c3+ ♔×g6 6 b4 ♔f7 7 b5 ♗c7! 8 ♔d5 ♔e7 9 ♔c6 ♔d8 10 ♔b7 ♔d7=.

1 ♔e4

Capablanca is in no hurry to force matters - he maneuvers, hoping for a mistake by his opponent.

1...b4

By no means forced (1...♗e1 2 ♔d3 ♗b4 3 ♗c3 ♗e7 isn't bad); but, on the other hand, it doesn't spoil anything.

2 ♗e3 ♗c3 3 ♔d3 ♗e1 4 ♗d2 ♗f2 5 ♔e4 (5 ♗×b4 ♔g7=) **5...♗c5?**

And here's the mistake! Now White captures the b4-pawn, with a tempo ahead of the other variations. First Black had to lure the king away from the queenside: 5...♔g7! 6 ♔f5, and now he can defend the pawn (6...♗c5 7 ♗f4 ♗f2 8 ♗e5+ ♔g8=).

6 ♔d5! ♗e7

Still worse is 6...♗f2 7 ♗×b4 ♔g7 8 ♗c3+ ♔×g6 9 b4 ♔f7 10 ♗d4 ♗g3 11 b5 ♗c7 12 ♔c6 ♗a5 13 ♗e5 △ ♗c7+−.

7 ♔c4 ♔g7 8 ♗×b4 ♗d8 9 ♗c3+?

White errs in return - although it's not at all obvious. The win was 9 ♗d2! - a variation we shall examine later.

9...♔×g6 10 b4 ♔f5 11 ♔d5

6-6

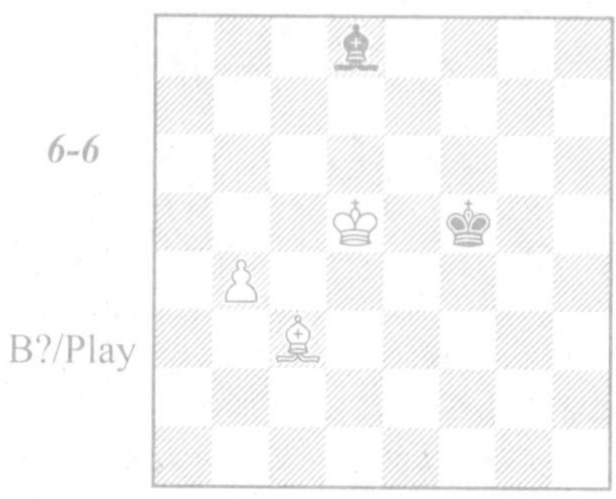

B?/Play

In this position, Janowsky resigned. And wrongly so - as Averbakh has shown, Black could get a draw by employing the basic defensive plan of "king behind king." Since White is going to put his king on c6, Black must hurry his king over to c4.

11...♔f4!! 12 ♗d4 (12 ♗e5+ ♔e3 13 b5 ♔d3 14 ♔c6 ♔c4=) **12...♔f3! 13 b5** (13 ♗c5

♔e2 14 ♔c6 ♔d3 15 ♔d7 ♗g5 16 b5 ♔c4) **13...♔e2! 14 ♔c6 ♔d3 15 ♗b6 ♗g5 16 ♗c7 ♗e3**

After 17 ♗d6 ♔c4, Black has time to prevent the interference along the diagonal at c5. But the struggle is not over yet.

17 ♔d5!

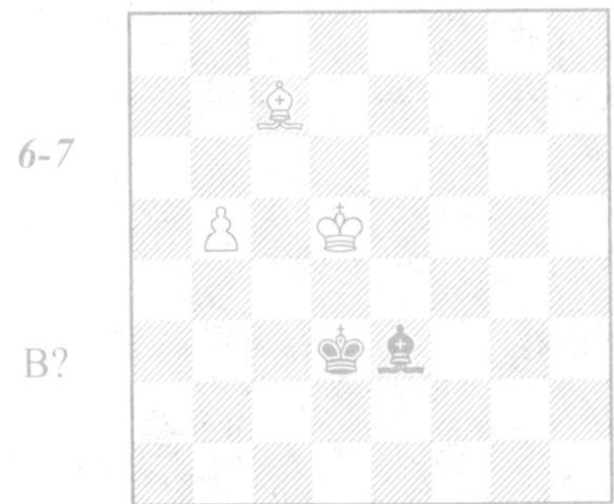
6-7

B?

The most dangerous continuation, as pointed out by Issler. If Black now plays 17...♔c3?, then 18 ♗d6 ♗b6 (18...♔b3 19 ♗c5 ♔a4 20 ♔c6) 19 ♔c6. Black hasn't time to play ♔c4 - White is ready to reply with either 20 ♗c7 or ♗c5, depending on where Black's bishop retreats.

Black is saved by a tactic, which is very useful to remember: it's a typical trick in bishop endgames.

17...♗d2!!

On 18 b6, the *pin* 18...♗a5 saves him.

18 ♗d8 ♗e3!

Now the threat of 19 b6 ♗a5 20 b7 forces Black to retreat. That's OK - White's bishop stands worse on d8 than it did on c7, and there is no longer any danger in 19 ♗e7 (△20 ♗c5) 19...♗b6! 20 ♔c6 ♗a5! (White no longer has 21 ♗c7) 21 ♗d6 ♔c4=.

White has just one final trap:

19 ♗c7 ♗d2! 20 ♔c6 ♗e3! 21 ♔b7! (21 ♗d6 ♔c4=) **21...♔c4 22 ♔a6 ♔b3!!**

Once again, the same technique of "king behind king": the black king heads for a4. He would lose after 22...♗f2? 23 ♗b6 ♗h4 24 ♗e3 ♗d8 25 ♗d2 △ ♗a5+−. And 22...♔b4? 23 ♗b6 ♗g5 24 ♗a5+ and 25 b6+− is wrong too.

23 ♗b6 ♗g5 24 ♗f2 ♗d8 25 ♗e1 ♔a4=

All that's left for us to see is what would have happened, had Capablanca played more exactly on his 9th move.

9 ♗d2! ♔×g6 10 b4 ♔f5 11 ♔d5

Now we are looking at the position from the next-to-last diagram, but with the bishop on d2 (instead of c3). Here Black's king is unable to get behind White's.

11...♔g4 12 b5 ♔f3 13 ♔c6 ♔e4 14 ♔b7!! ♔d3 15 ♗e1! ♔c4 16 ♔a6 ♔b3 17 ♗a5 ♗g5 18 b6+−.

Interference

We know that intereference is the primary instrument by which the stronger side secures (or attempts to secure) the queening of its pawn. In all the examples we have looked at thus far the bishop has done this work. But sometimes (although certainly not nearly as often), interference is carried out with the aid of the pawns. For instance, there is the following spectacular study.

P. Heuäcker, 1930

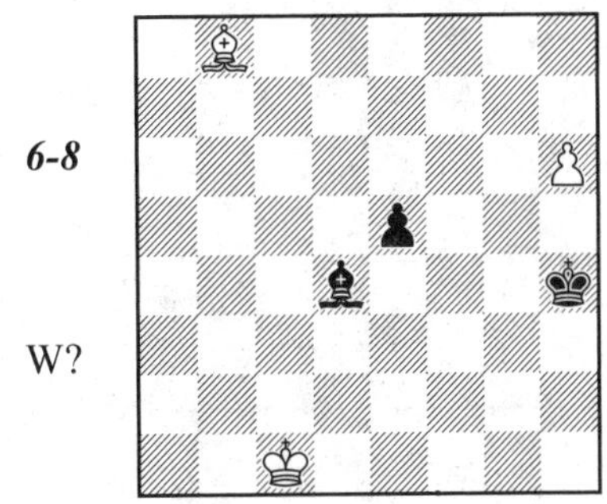
6-8

W?

1 ♗a7! (1 h7? e4=) **1...♗a1 2 ♔b1 ♗c3 3 ♔c2 ♗a1 4 ♗d4!! ♗×d4** (4...ed 5 ♔d3+−) **5 ♔d3 ♗b2 6 ♔e4+−**.

Tragicomedies

We have already seen the tragicomedies that occurred in the games Botvinnik - Model and Capablanca - Janowsky. I will add one more example.

Savchenko - Krivonosov
USSR 1989

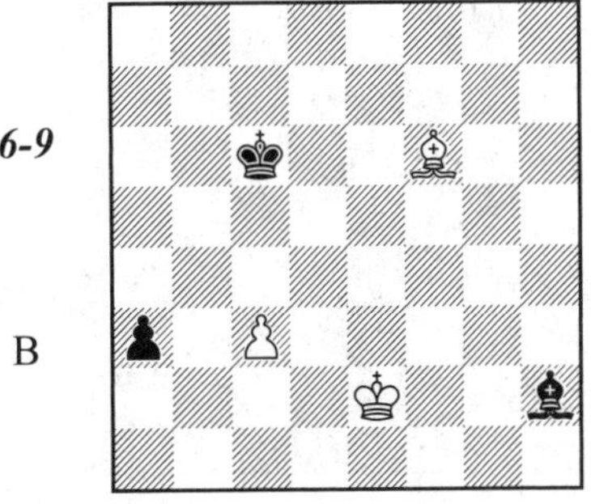
6-9

B

1...♗e5?? 2 ♗×e5 ♔d5 3 ♗g7?? ♔c4!, and Black won.

The same tactical idea of interference as in the Heuäcker study brought Black success here. However, this occurred only as a result of his opponent's gross blunder. After 3 ♔d3! ♔×e5 (3...a2? 4 ♗g7+−) 4 ♔c2, the king is in the square of the a-pawn.

Black should have carried out his interference in a more primitive form, by preparing ...♗e5. This could have been achieved either by 1...♔d5 2 ♔d3!? ♔e6! (but not 2...a2? 3 c4+) 3 ♗d4 a2 4 c4 ♗e5, or by 1...♔d6 2 c4 ♗e5 (2...a2; 2...♔e6) 3 c5+ ♔e6!−+ (3...♔d5? is a mistake, because of 4 c6=).

Exercises

6-10

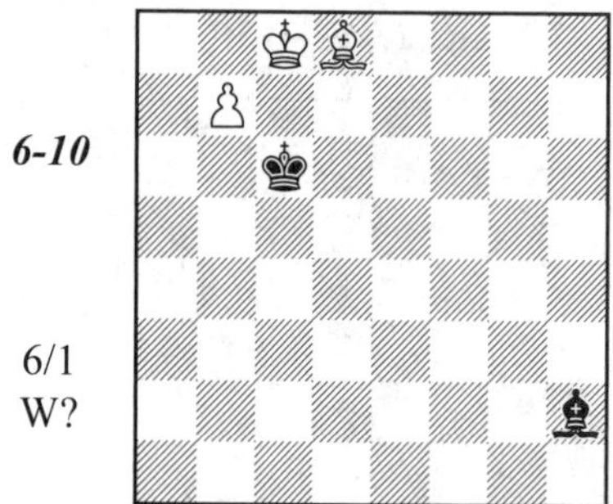

6/1
W?

6-11

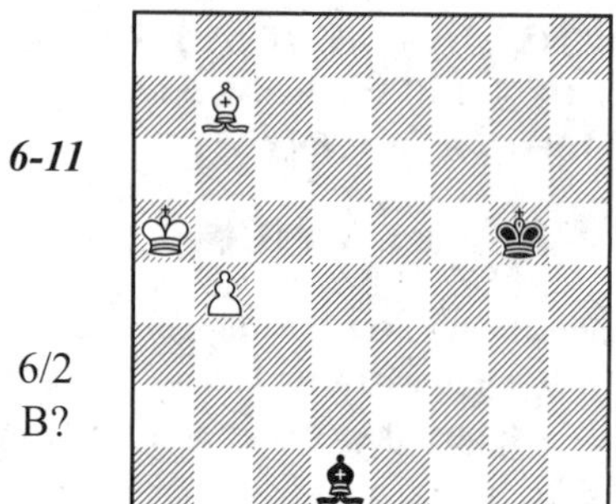

6/2
B?

6-12

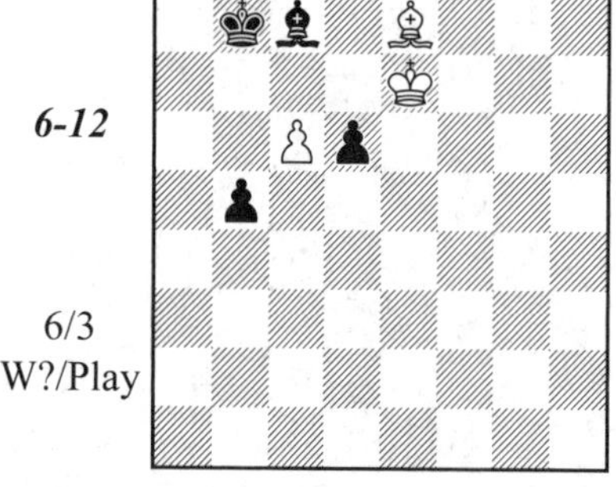

6/3
W?/Play

6-13

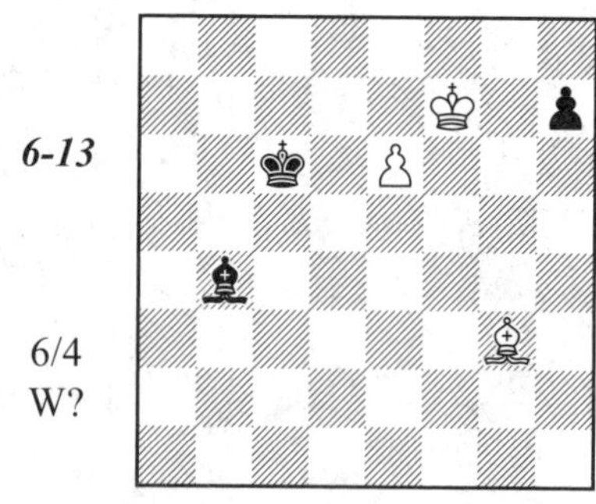

6/4
W?

6-14

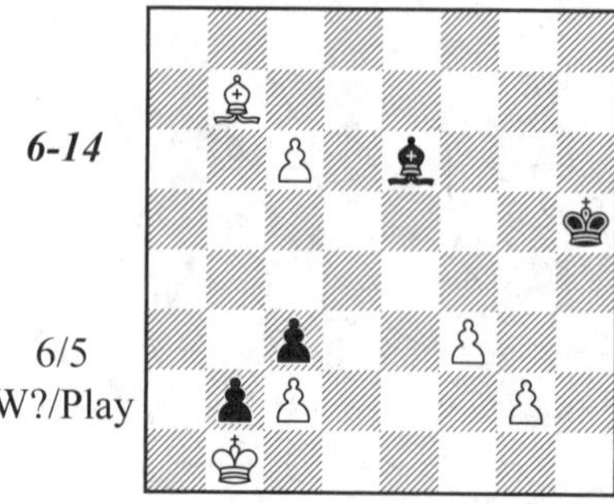

6/5
W?/Play

Bishops of the Same Color

The Bad Bishop

A vital principle of chess strategy (which is certainly applicable in more places than the endgame) requires us ***not to place our pawns on the same color squares as our own bishop.***

In the first place, pawns that are fixed on the same color squares as the bishop limit its mobility - this is why such a bishop is called "bad."

In the second place, a bad bishop is unable to attack the enemy pawns (which are usually placed on the opposite color squares), which dooms it to passive defense of its own pawns.

And third, since both pawns and bishop control only one color of squares, there will be "holes" in between those squares that the enemy pieces will occupy.

Fixing Pawns

Averbakh - Veresov
Moscow 1947

6-15

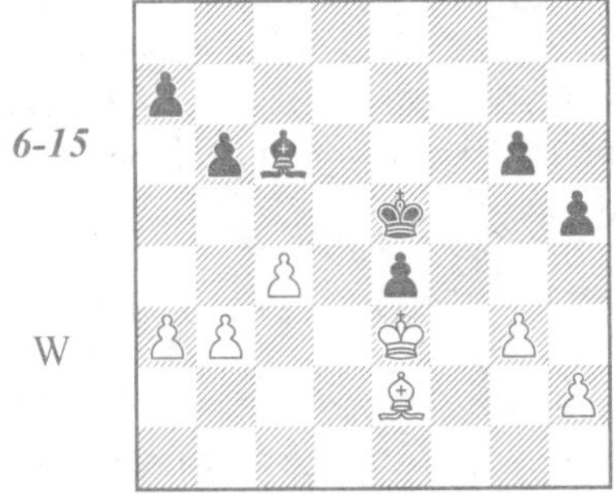

W

1 h4!

The experienced player makes such moves - fixing the enemy pawns on the same color squares as his bishop - without thinking.

White has a great positional advantage. After the necessary preparations, he will create an outside passed pawn on the queenside, which will divert the enemy forces, allowing White to fall upon the kingside pawns.

1...♗d7 2 ♗f1 a5 3 ♗g2 ♗c6 (3...♗f5 4 ♗h1⊙) **4 ♗h3!**

The bishop aims for d7, where it will support the queenside pawn advance while at the same time be ready to attack the pawn at g6. For example: 4...♗a8 5 ♗d7 ♗b7 6 b4 ab 7 ab ♗a8 8 c5 bc 9 bc ♔d5 10 ♗e8 g5! (10...♔xc5 11 ♗xg6 ♔d6 12 ♗xh5 ♔e5 13 ♗g6 ♗c6 14 g4+−) 11 hg ♔xc5 12 ♗g6! ♗d5 13 ♗xe4 ♗g8 14 ♔f4 ♔d6 15 ♔f5 ♔e7 16 ♔g6+−.

4...b5 6 cb ♗xb5 6 ♗c8 ♗c6 7 b4 ab 8 ab ♗b5 9 ♗b7 g5!

On 9...♗d3, 10 ♗c6 ♔f5 11 b5 (11 ♗d7+) 11...♔g4 (11...♗xb5 12 ♗xb5 ♔g4 13 ♔f2 e3+ 14 ♔g2+−) 12 b6 ♗a6 13 ♔f2 e3+ 14 ♔g2 is decisive.

10 ♗xe4 gh 11 gh ♗a4

11...♗e8 loses also: 12 ♗f3 ♔f5 13 ♗e2! (but not 13 ♔d4? ♔f4 and 14...♔g3) 13...♔e5 14 ♗d3!⊙ ♗d7 (14...♔d5 15 ♔f4 ♔d4 16 ♗e2+−) 15 ♗g6 ♔d5 16 ♗xh5 ♔c4 17 ♗e2+ ♔xb4 18 h5 ♗f5 19 ♗d3 ♗e6 20 h6 ♗g8 21 ♔d4.

12 ♗g6 ♗d1 13 b5 ♔d5 14 ♔f4 ♔c5 15 ♔g5 ♗e2! (15...♔xb5 16 ♗xh5 ♗c2 17 ♗e8+ ♔c5 18 h5 ♔d6 19 ♔f6!+−)

6-16

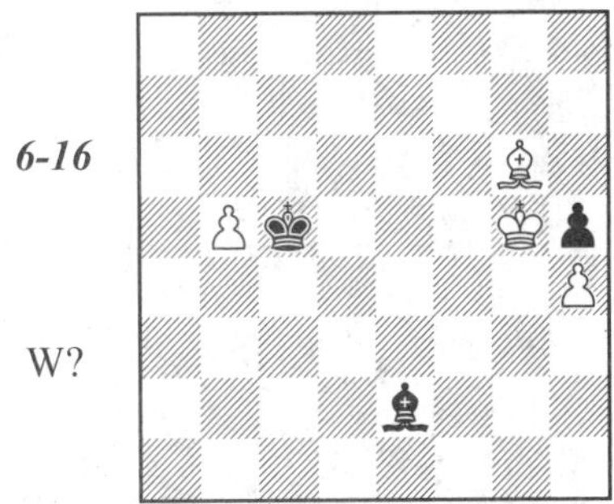

W?

16 ♗e8!⊙

We know this technique from the ending Charushin - Rosenholz (Diagram 6-4). Before taking the pawn, it is important to drive the black king back to b6 - as far as possible from the kingside. The hasty 16 ♗xh5? ♗xb5 17 ♗g4 ♗e8 18 ♗f5 ♔d6 19 ♗g6 ♔e7! leads only to a draw.

16...♔b6 17 ♗xh5 ♗xb5 18 ♗g4 ♗e8 19 ♗f5 ♔c7 20 ♗g6 ♔d8 21 ♔f6! Black resigned (analysis by Averbakh).

Zugzwang

With a bad bishop, the weaker side's defensive hopes often are destroyed through zugzwang. Here's the simplest example:

Y. Averbakh, 1954

6-17

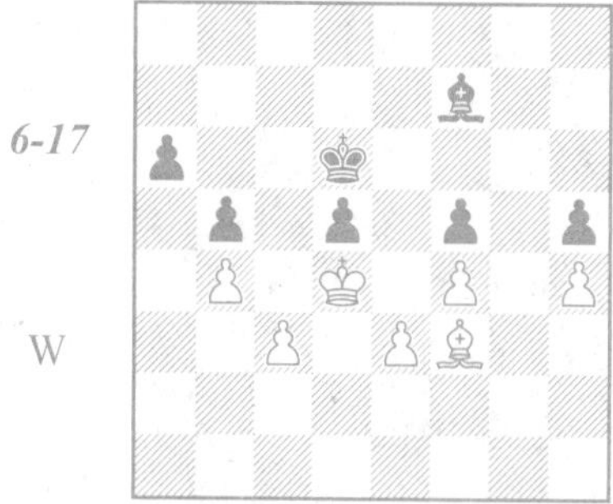

W

The correspondence between the f3- and f7-squares is obvious - to win, it is necessary only to give Black the move. If you like, you can also find other pairs of corresponding squares (for example, the f1- and b3-squares also correspond to f7), but there's no real need.

1 ♗e2 ♗e8

If 1...♗g6, then 2 ♗d3 ♗h7 3 ♗f1! ♗g6 (3...♗g8 4 ♗e2 ♗f7 5 ♗f3⊙) 4 ♗g2 ♗f7 5 ♗f3⊙.

2 ♗d3 ♗g6

2...♗d7 3 ♗c2 ♗e6 4 ♗d1 ♗f7 5 ♗f3⊙.

3 ♗c2 ♗h7 4 ♗b3! ♗g8 5 ♗d1 ♗f7 5 ♗f3+−.

Now, let's look at a considerably more complex endgame.

Shabalov - Varavin
Moscow 1986

6-18

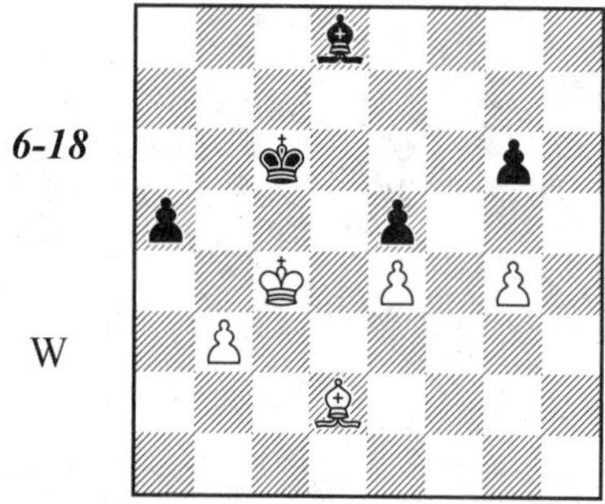

W

1 ♗e1 ♗b6

On 1...♗c7? 2 ♗c3, Black is in zugzwang, and must put another pawn on the same color as his bishop, making his opponent's winning task that much simpler. For example, 2...g5 3 ♗b2 ♗d6 4 ♗c1 ♗e7 5 ♗e3 ♗f6 (5...♗d8 6 ♗d2⊙) 6 ♗c5 ♗d8 7 ♗a3 ♗b6 (7...♗f6 8 ♗b2 △ ♗c3) 8 ♗b2 ♗c7 9 ♗c3⊙. White's bishop maneuvers here in roughly the same way as he did in the preceding example.

2 ♗h4! ♗e3

The c7-square turns out to correspond, not just to the c3-square, but also to g3. 2...♗c7? would be bad: 3 ♗g3! ♗b8 4 ♗e1 ♗c7 5 ♗c3. And on 2...♗d4 3 ♗d8 decides.

3 ♗g3 ♗d4

After 3...♗f4 4 ♗e1, Black must defend the a5-pawn with his king, and allow the enemy king to enter. This bodes nothing good for Black: 4...♔b6 5 ♔d5 ♔b5 6 ♗c3 g5 7 ♗xe5 ♗xe5 8 ♔xe5 ♔b4 9 ♔d5 ♔xb3 10 e5 a4 11 e6 a3 12 e7 a2 13 e8♕ a1♕ 14 ♕e3+ ♔c2 15 ♕e2+, forcing the exchange of queens.

4 ♗h2!⊙ ♗b2

4...♗a1 is even worse: 5 ♗g1 ♗b2 6 ♗f2 △ ♗e1+−.

5 ♗g1 ♗a3

On 5...♗c1, there follows 6 ♗f2 ♗g5 (6...♗d2 7 ♗g3) 7 ♗g3, and Black's bishop is forced onto the f6-h8 diagonal - a fate which also befalls him in the game continuation.

6 ♗f2 ♗e7

Otherwise, we get the basic zugzwang position: 6...♗d6 7 ♗e1 ♗c7 8 ♗c3⊙, or 6...♗b4 7 ♗g3 ♗d6 8 ♗e1, etc.

7 ♗g3! ♗f6

By means of a series of accurate maneuvers, Shabalov has achieved his aim - the bishop has been deflected onto a poor diagonal. On the other hand, there was no longer any choice: 7...♗d6 8 ♗e1 ♗c7 9 ♗c3⊙+−.

6-19

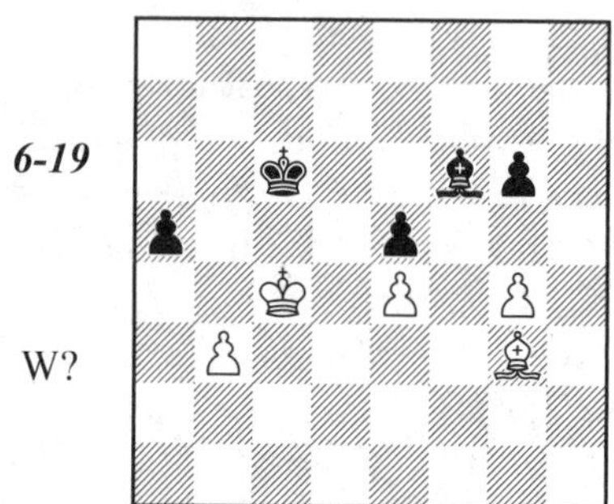

W?

8 ♗h2⊙ ♗g7 9 g5!

White "breaks the rule," by moving a pawn onto a square the same color as his own bishop - in order to restrict the enemy bishop's mobility still further. There is no other way to reach his goal.

9...♗f8

9...♗h8 10 ♗g3 ♗g7 11 ♗e1 is hopeless.

10 ♗×e5 ♗e7 11 ♗f6 ♗b4 12 ♗c3

Advancing the e-pawn does nothing for White: 12 e5 ♗d2 13 e6 ♔d6 14 e7 ♔d7. So he takes the a5-pawn in exchange for the g5-pawn.

12...♗e7 13 ♗×a5 ♗×g5 14 b4 ♗f4 15 b5+ ♔d6 16 ♗c3! g5 17 e5+ ♔c7

17...♗×e5 18 ♗×e5+ ♔×e5 19 b6! (but not 19 ♔c5? ♔e6) 19...♔d6 20 ♔b5 g4 21 ♔a6+−.

18 ♗a5+ ♔c8 19 ♔d5 g4 20 e6 g3 21 ♔c6! ♗g5 (22 e7 was threatened) **22 b6** Black resigned.

"Renegade" Pawns

In chess, there are no absolute laws. Even so important and generally useful an axiom as the unprofitability of placing one's pawns on the same color squares as one's bishop must occasionally be broken. Here are the possible reasons for doing so:

- To restrict the mobility of the enemy bishop using one's own pawns (as occurred in the preceding example);
- The need to undermine the enemy pawn chain; and
- The attempt to create an impregnable fortress around a "bad bishop."

The first and third points are illustrated by the following case:

Wojtkiewicz - Khalifman
Rakvere 1993

6-20

W?

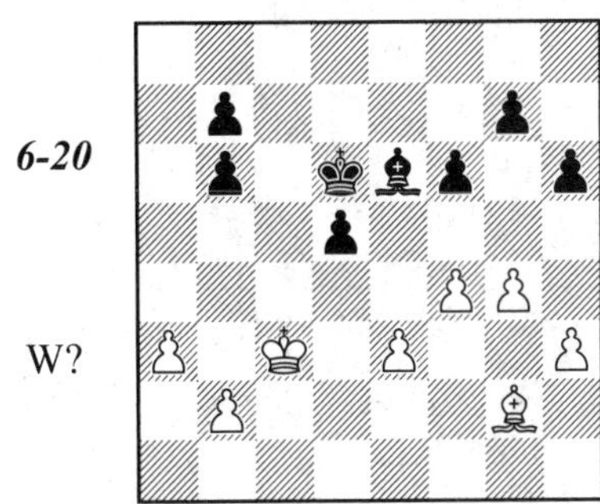

The hackneyed 1 ♔d4? would have allowed Black to set up an impregnable fortress by 1...b5!, followed by ...b7-b6. For example, 2 ♗f1 ♗d7 3 ♔c3 ♔c5! (not allowing the enemy king to get to b4) 4 b4+ ♔d6. Here there can be no zugzwang, since White's bishop is unable to attack two enemy pawns simultaneously (as in the endings examined earlier).

1 a4! g5

1...♗d7! was more stubborn. On 2 ♔d4? ♗×a4 3 ♗×d5 ♗c6 4 e4 g5 5 e5+ fe+ 6 fe+ ♔e7, Black should get a draw. The right line would be 2 b3 ♔c5 (2...b5 3 a5 ♔c5 4 b4+ ♔d6 5 ♔d4 is hopeless, in view of the weakness of the b7-pawn after the unavoidable e3-e4) 3 ♗f3! (3 b4+? ♔d6 is premature). And now: 3...g5 4 b4+ ♔d6 5 ♗d1!, with 6 ♔d4 to follow, leads to roughly the same position as in the game. While 3...h5!? gives reasonable chances to survive.

2 ♔d4 ♗f7 3 ♗f3 ♗e6 4 f5! ♗f7 5 b4 ♗e8 6 b5!

6-21

B

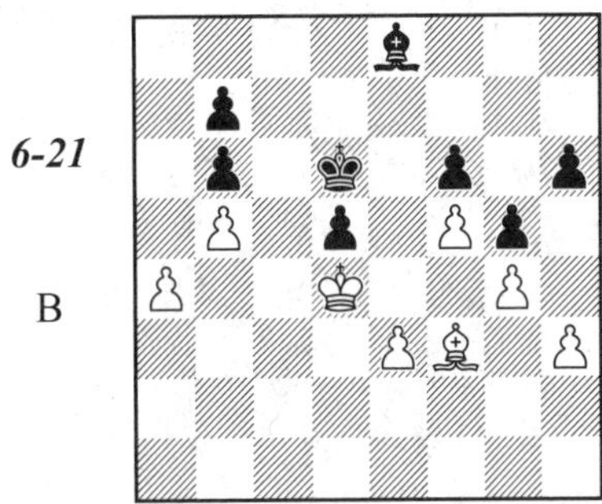

White's pawns have maximally restricted the enemy bishop. Now he brings his bishop around to b3, and plays e3-e4. When he thought up his plan, Wojtkiewicz had to calculate exactly the pawn endgame that now arises by force.

6...♗f7 7 ♗d1 ♗g8 8 ♗b3 ♗f7 9 e4 ♗g8 10 ♗a2 ♗f7 11 ♗×d5 ♗×d5 12 ed ♔c7 13 ♔c3! (△14 ♔b4, 15 a5) **13...♔d6 14 ♔c4 ♔e5**

Also losing was 14...♔d7 15 ♔b4 ♔d6 16 a5 ♔×d5 (16...ba+ 17 ♔×a5 ♔×d5 18 ♔b6 ♔c4 19 ♔×b7 ♔×b5 20 ♔c7+−) 17 a6 ba 18 ba ♔c6 19 ♔a4 b5+ 20 ♔a5.

15 a5! ba 16 ♔c5 a4 17 d6 b6+ 18 ♔c6 a3 19 d7 a2 20 d8♕ a1♕ 21 ♕d6+ ♔e4 22 ♔×b6 ♔f3 23 ♔b7 ♔g2 24 ♕d3 ♕c1 25 b6 ♕c5 26 ♕b3 ♔h2 27 ♕f3 ♕d4 28 ♕c6! ♔×h3 29 ♔c8 ♕b4 30 b7 ♕f8+ 31 ♔d7 ♔×g4 (31...♕f7+ 32 ♔d6 ♕f8+ 33 ♔e6) **32 ♕c8** Black resigned.

And now an example of the undermining theme:

Sveshnikov - Kasparov
USSR ch, Minsk 1979

6-22

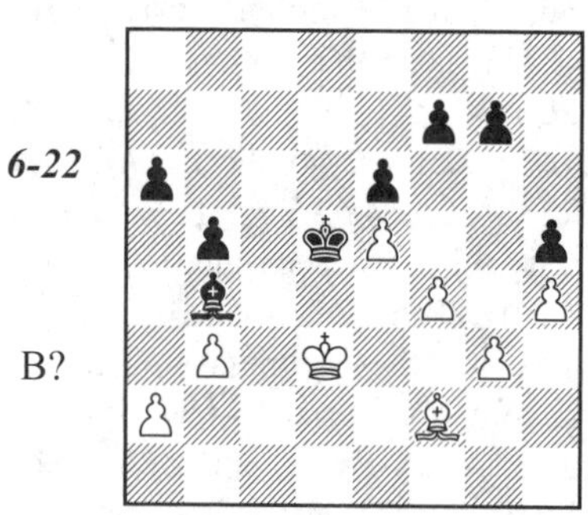

B?

First, let's evaluate what actually happened in the game.

1...g6⊙ **2 ♔e2** (the bishop can't retreat, owing to 2...♗e1) **2...♗c5 3 ♗×c5?** (the pawn ending is lost) **3...♔×c5 4 ♔d3 ♔b4 5 ♔c2 ♔a3 6 ♔b1 a5 7 ♔a1 a4!** (widening the beachhead) **8 ba ♔×a4 9 ♔b1** (9 ♔b2 b4) **9...♔a3 10 ♔a1 b4 11 ♔b1 b3** White resigned.

White could have drawn by avoiding the exchange of bishops. After 3 ♗e1! ♔e4 4 ♗a5, I can't see how Black can improve his position. And if 3...b4 (hoping for 4 ♗d2? ♔e4 5 ♗e1 a5 6 ♗d2 ♗d4 7 ♗e1 ♗e3, with zugzwang, or 7 ♗c1 ♗c3 8 ♗e3 ♗e1!), then simply 4 ♔f3!=.

But Black was the first to err here - the natural move 1...g6? was a mistake. The pawn should have been left on g7, in order to support the undermining with ...f7-f6! The right way to obtain a zugzwang was by making a waiting move with the bishop.

1...♗a5! 2 ♔e2 (after 2 a3!? followed by b3-b4, Black could also have tried for the win with the undermining ...f7-f6 and ...a6-a5) 2...♔e4 3 ♗c5 f6! (undermining!) 4 ef gf. Black continues by getting his bishop to c7 (or on 5 ♗d6 - to b6), his king to f5, and playing ...e6-e5 with a great and probably decisive advantage.

Tragicomedies

Teichmann - Marshall
San Sebastian 1911

6-23

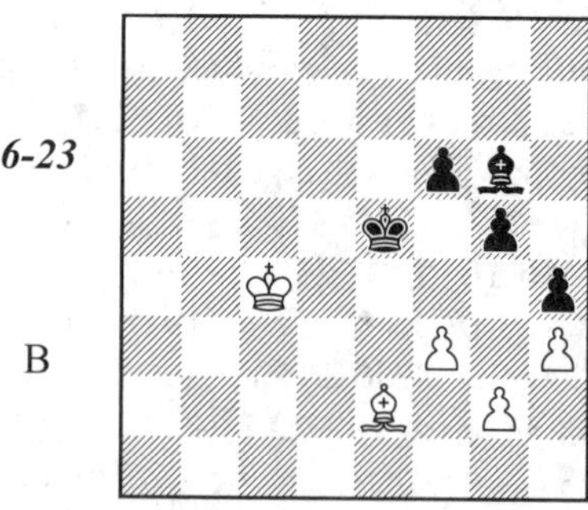

B

Even though Black has an overwhelming positional advantage, the endgame is not as simple as it seems. Both sides made many errors; nor did grandmaster Averbakh avoid errors in his commentaries.

1...♗f7+?

An unfortunate move, allowing the king to return to the defense of the kingside through the d3-square. Now the position becomes drawn.

2 ♔d3! ♔f4 3 ♗f1 ♔g3 4 ♔e3 ♗d5 5 ♔e2 f5 6 ♔e3 ♗e6

The bishop sacrifice is insufficient: 6...f4+ 7 ♔e2 ♗b7 8 ♔e1 ♗×f3 9 gf ♔×f3 10 ♗e2+ ♔g2 (10...♔g3 11 ♗g4 ♔g2 12 ♔e2) 11 ♗f1+ ♔g3 12 ♔e2=. The only remaining try at making progress is ...g5-g4, but this leads to the exchange of too many pawns.

7 ♔e2 g4

6-24

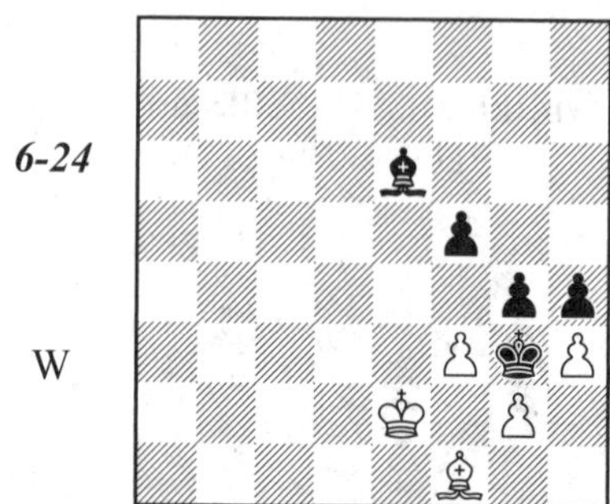

W

8 hg

Averbakh recommends 8 fg fg 9 ♔e3, which leads to an obvious draw after 9...gh 10 gh ♗d7 11 ♔e2 ♗b5+ 12 ♔e1 ♗c6 13 ♔e2=. And if 9...♗d7 then White replies either with Benko's recommendation of 10 ♔e2 ♗b5+ 11 ♔e1 ♗c6 12 ♗e2! (not 12 hg ♗×g2, when the h-pawn will queen with check). Or with 10 hg! ♗×g4 11 ♗b5!

(pointed out by Chéron), giving up the g2-pawn right away, but activating his bishop. For example: 11...♗e6 12 ♗c6 ♗c4 13 ♗e4 ♗f1 14 ♗d5 ♗×g2 15 ♗e6= (the attempted interference leads to a drawn pawn ending), or 11...♔×g2 12 ♔f4! (12 ♗c6+? ♔g3 △h3-h2, ♗h3-g2) 12...♗e6 13 ♗c6+ ♔f2 (after 13...♔h2 14 ♗b7 h3 15 ♗e4 ♔g1 16 ♔g3 h2 the interference on g2 is impossible) 14 ♗d5! ♗d7 (14...♗×d5 15 ♔g4) 15 ♗c6! ♗h3 16 ♗d5 ♗g2 17 ♗e6=.

Averbakh considers the text move the decisive error, but he's wrong.

8...fg 9 ♔e3?

9 fg! ♗×g4+ 10 ♔e1! was necessary (Averbakh only considers 10 ♔e3 ♗d7−+), leading to a curious position of reciprocal zugzwang. White to move loses: 11 ♗b5 ♔×g2 12 ♗c6+ ♔g1. But it's Black to move here, and after 10...♗d7 (10...♗h5 11 ♗b5 ♔×g2 12 ♗d7, or 12 ♗c6+ first) 11 ♗a6 ♔×g2 (11...♗c6 12 ♗c8 ♗×g2 13 ♗d7=) 12 ♗b7+ ♔g1, White has time to get his king to g3: 13 ♔e2! h3 14 ♔f3 h2 15 ♔g3=.

9...♗d7?

Black blunders in turn, allowing his opponent to force the draw by the same means indicated in the notes to move 8. The win was 9...gf! 10 gf ♗d7⊙ 11 ♔e2 (11 f4 ♗g4!⊙ 12 ♔e4 ♔f2−+) 11...♗b5+ 12 ♔e1 ♗c6 13 f4 ♗e4! (13...♗g2? 14 f5 h3 15 f6) 14 ♔e2 ♗f5! 15 ♔e1 ♗g4⊙.

10 fg! ♗×g4 11 ♔e4??

The loser is always the one who makes the last mistake! We already know that 11 ♗b5! would draw. But with the bishop on f1, White is helpless.

11...♗c8 12 ♔e3 ♗d7⊙ White resigned.

On 13 ♔e4 (or 13 ♔e2), Black wins by 13...♗c6+ 14 ♔e3 ♗×g2; while if 13 ♔d2 ♔f2! 14 ♗c4 ♔×g2 15 ♔e1 ♔g1! 16 ♗f1 ♗e6⊙ 17 ♗b5 h3 18 ♗c6 h2 19 ♗e4 ♗h3 △ ♗g2.

Let's go back to the starting position of this endgame. Averbakh recommends 1...♗b1!

On 2 ♗f1, ♔f4 decides, for instance: 3 ♔d4 f5!⊙ 4 ♔d5 ♔e3 5 ♔e6 ♔f2 6 ♗c4 ♔×g2, or 3 ♔d5 ♔g3 4 ♔e6 f5 5 ♔f6 ♔f2 6 ♗c4 ♔×g2 7 ♔×g5 ♔×h3 8 f4 ♔g3−+.

White has greater practical chances with 2 ♗d3!? ♗a2+! 3 ♔c5.

6-25

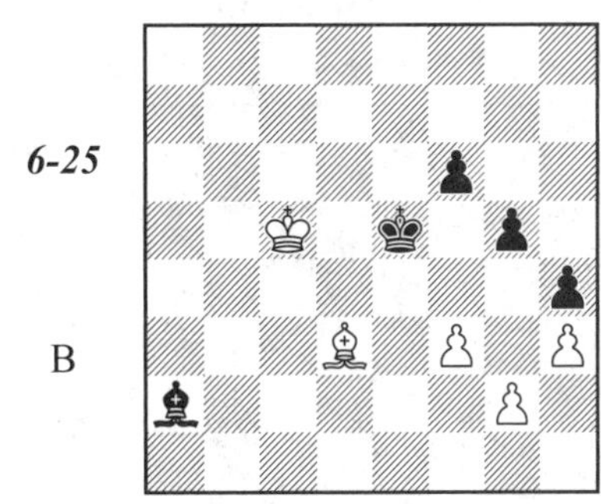

B

Averbakh contents himself with the single variation 3...♔f4 4 ♔d4 ♔g3−+. But I think that 3...♔f4? is an error, owing to 4 ♔d6!

a) 4...♔g3 5 ♔e7 ♔×g2 (5...f5 6 ♔f6!) 6 ♔×f6 ♔×f3 7 ♔×g5 ♔g3 8 ♔f5! (8 ♗f5? ♗c4, with ...♗f1×h3 to follow) 8...♗d5 (8...♔×h3 9 ♔f4=) 9 ♗f1! (9 ♗e4? ♗c4 or 9 ♔e5? ♗g2 10 ♔d4 ♗×h3 11 ♔e3 ♗c8 12 ♗f1 ♗b7 are both bad) 9...♗c6 10 ♔e5 ♗d7 11 ♔e4 ♔f2 12 ♔f4 ♗e6 13 ♗b5 ♗×h3 14 ♗c6 (reaching a position from Chéron's line) 14...♗c8 15 ♗b7! ♗e6 16 ♗d5!, etc.

b) 4...f5 5 ♔e7 ♗d5 6 ♗f1! (6 ♔f6? is a mistake, in view of 6...g4 7 fg fg 8 hg ♗×g2 9 g5 h3 10 g6 h2 11 g7 ♗d5−+) 6...g4 (6...♔e5 7 ♔d7 isn't dangerous either) 7 fg fg 8 hg ♔×g4 9 ♔f6 ♗e4 (9...♔g3 10 ♔g5 ♗c6 11 ♔h5=) 10 ♔e5! ♗a8 11 ♔f6 ♗b7 12 ♔g6 ♗e4+ 13 ♔h6!= (but not 13 ♔f6? ♔f4!, when White is in zugzwang).

Black's king stands very well on e5, where it shoulders aside the enemy king. Before attacking the g2-pawn, Black must first strengthen his position.

Simplest is 3...f5!, for example: 4 ♔c6 g4! 5 fg fg 6 hg ♗d5+ 7 ♔c5 ♗×g2 8 g5 h3 9 g6 ♔f6!−+ or 4 ♗f1 ♔f4 5 ♔d6 (5 ♔d4 ♗b1!⊙) 5..♔g3 6 ♔e5 ♗b1 7 ♔f6 ♔f2 8 ♗c4 ♔×g2 9 ♔×g5 ♔×h3−+.

And 3...♗e6! 4 ♗a6 f5 5 ♗f1 ♗c8!? or 5...♗d5 6 ♗e2 ♗b7 7 ♗f1 ♔f4 8 ♔d4 ♗c8!⊙−+ are not bad either. However, the hasty 5...g4? would let slip the win: 6 fg fg 7 hg ♗×g4 8 ♗a6! (on 8 ♔c4? ♗c8! 9 ♔c3 ♔f4 10 ♔d2 ♔g3 11 ♔e3 ♗d7!⊙−+ or 11 ♔e1 ♗g4!⊙−+, we get zugzwangs already familiar to us) 8...♗e6 (8...♗f5 9 ♔c4) 9 ♗b7! ♗f5 10 ♔c4 ♗e4 11 ♗c8=.

Euwe - Menchik
Hastings 1930/31

6-26

W?

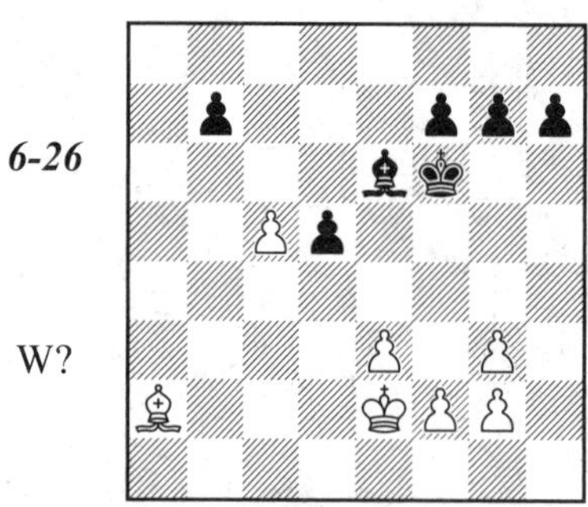

White's king wants to get to d4. Black will prevent that with ...♔e5; after White responds with f2-f4+, he will try to counterattack with ...♔f5 and ...♔g4.

The accurate prophylactic move, 1 ♗b3!! would allow White to realize his indisputable positional advantage convincingly. After 1...♔e5 there would then follow 2 f4+ ♔f5 3 ♗d1! (△ 4 ♔d3), arriving just in time to cover the g4-square. For example: 3...d4 4 ♗c2+! ♔g4 5 ed ♔×g3 6 ♔e3 f5 7 ♗d1 ♗d5 8 ♗f3+−; or 3...♔g4 4 ♔f2+ ♔f5 5 ♗f3! g5 (5...♔f6 6 ♔e2 ♔e7 7 ♔d3 ♔d7 8 ♔d4 ♔c6 9 f5 ♗×f5 10 ♗×d5+ ♔c7 11 ♗×f7+−) 6 g4+ ♔f6 7 ♔e2! (7 f5 is possible, too) 7...♗d7 8 ♔d3 ♗c6 9 ♔d4 gf 10 ef ♔e6 11 g5 ♔f5 12 g3+−.

In the game, Euwe played a less exact continuation, which placed his win in doubt.

1 ♔d3?! ♔e5 2 g4

If 2 f4+ ♔f5 3 ♔e2 (3 ♔d4 ♔g4 4 ♗×d5 ♗×d5 5 ♔×d5 ♔×g3=) 5...♔g4 6 ♔f2, then 6...d4! (6...h5 7 ♗b3 g6 is also possible) 7 ♗×e6+ fe 8 ed g6.

2...g5!

Black loses after 2...♗×g4? 3 f4+ ♔e6 4 e4 ♔e7 5 ♗×d5 ♗c8 6 ♔c4!

3 g3 ♗×g4 4 f4+ gf 5 gf+ (5 ef+ ♔e6 6 ♔d4 ♗f3=) **5...♔f6 6 ♗×d5 ♗c8**

6-27

W?

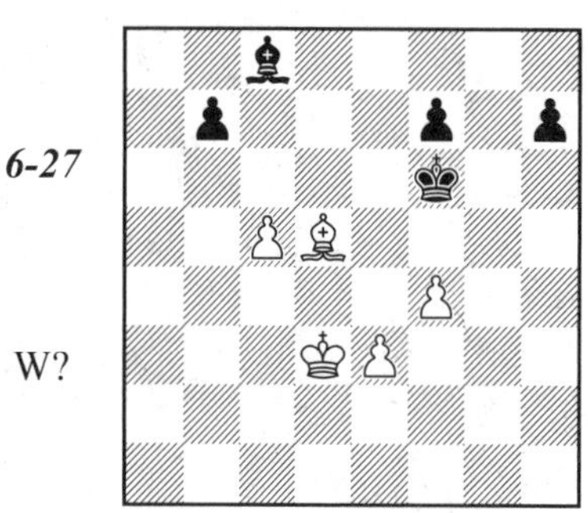

Comparing this position to the analogous position after 2...♗×g4?, here Black has a passed h-pawn. So this already rules out 7 ♔c4? ♗e6! On 7 ♔c3 ♔e7 8 ♔b4, advancing the h-pawn gives Black serious counterplay: 8...h5! 9 ♔b5 h4 10 ♔b6 h3 11 ♔c7 ♗e6 12 ♗×b7 ♗c4 △ ♗f1-g2.

White could still keep real winning chances by 7 e4!? ♔e7 8 ♔e3! △ f4-f5, ♔f4, and then either e4-e5 or ♔g4-h5.

7 ♗f3?

White restrains the passed pawn, but now Black's king is able to get to c7.

7...♔e7 8 ♔c4 ♔d8 (9 ♔b5 allows 9...♔c7) **9 ♔d5?! b6! 10 c6?**

Euwe fails to sense the danger. He had to accept the draw after 10 ♗h5.

10...♔c7 11 ♔e5 ♗e6 12 f5 ♗b3?! (12...♗c4 is both stronger and more logical) **13 ♔f6 b5 14 ♔g7?**

The decisive mistake. 14 e4! would have given White the draw.

14...b4−+ 15 ♔×h7 ♗c2 16 ♔g7 b3 17 ♗d5 b2 18 ♗a2 ♔×c6 19 f6 ♔d6 20 e4 ♗×e4 21 ♔×f7 ♗d5+ 22 ♗×d5 b1♕ 23 ♔g7 ♕g1+ 24 ♔f8 ♔×d5 White resigned.

Exercises

6-28

6/6
W?

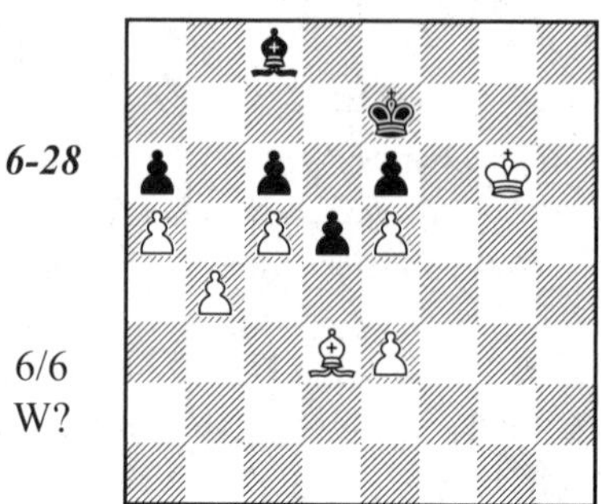

Barrier

Although there are occasional cases where a player can save himself with his pawns on the same color as his bishop, such a defensive method is not to be recommended in the majority of cases. The more secure defensive method is ***to control the squares of one color with the bishop, and of the other color, with pawns.*** This places a barrier in the path of the enemy king, making it difficult to invade our camp.

If the opponent has a passed pawn, the king must usually blockade it.

I. Ivanov - Christiansen
Pasadena 1983

6-29

W?

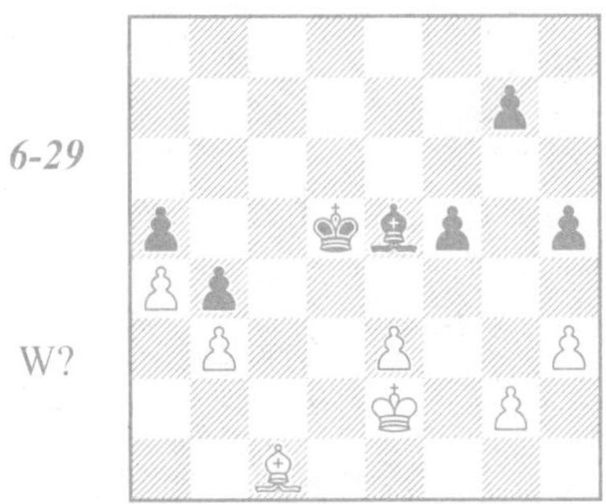

White's position is difficult. The e3-pawn greatly restricts the bishop's mobility; and on the other wing, the same role is played by the enemy pawns (White's bishop will not likely ever have the opportunity to attack them from behind.)

Nevertheless, as Christiansen pointed out, White has a comparatively simple way to draw - he must sacrifice a pawn, opening the diagonal for his bishop and erecting an impassable barrier before the black king.

1 ♔d3! ♗c3 2 e4+! fe+ 3 ♔e2=

It's worth mentioning that the pawn endgame after 2 ♗d2? ♗×d2 3 ♔×d2 is lost: 3...h4! (but not 3...♔e4? 4 h4! f4 5 ef ♔×f4 6 ♔d3 ♔g3 7 ♔c4=) 4 ♔d3 g6⊙ (4...♔e5? 5 ♔c4= ; 4...g5 5 ♔d2 ♔e4 6 ♔e2 f4 7 ef gf!−+) 5 ♔d2 ♔e4 6 ♔e2 f4 7 ef ♔×f4 8 ♔f2 ♔e4 9 ♔e2 ♔d4 10 ♔d2 g5⊙−+.

Ivanov failed to find the pawn sacrifice, and wound up in a hopeless position.

1 ♗d2? ♔e4 2 ♗e1 g5 3 h4

If 3 ♗f2, then 3...h4! 4 ♗e1 (4 ♗g1 ♗c7 5 ♗f2 ♗b6⊙ 6 ♔d2 f4 7 ♔e2 ♗×e3 8 ♗e1 ♔d4) 4...♗b2 5 ♗f2 (5 g3 g4! 6 gh gh 7 ♗g3 ♗c1; 5 ♗d2 ♗c3 6 ♗c1 g4) 5...♗c1 6 ♗g1 g4 7 ♗f2 g3 8 ♗g1 ♗b2 9 ♔d2 ♗e5 10 ♔e2 ♗c3⊙−+ (Or 10...♗c7 11 ♔d2 ♗b6 12 ♔e2 f4−+).

3...g4 4 g3

If 4 ♗f2 g3 5 ♗e1, Black "triangulates" with the bishop: 5...♗d6! 6 ♔d2 ♗c7! 7 ♔e2 ♗e5, and then wins the h4-pawn: 8 ♗d2 (8 ♔d2 ♗c3+) 8...♗f6 9 ♗e1 ♗×h4 10 ♔d2 f4−+. However, the text is no better.

4...♗d6 5 ♗f2 ♗c5 6 ♗g1 f4! 7 gf g3 8 f5 ♗e7 9 ♔f1 ♔f3! 10 e4 g2+ 11 ♔e1 ♗×h4+ 12 ♔d2 ♔×e4 13 ♔e2 ♗f6

White resigned (14 ♔f2 ♗d4+.)

In the following endgame, Dolmatov successfully resolved much more complex problems.

Sveshnikov - Dolmatov
Yerevan zt 1982

6-30

B?

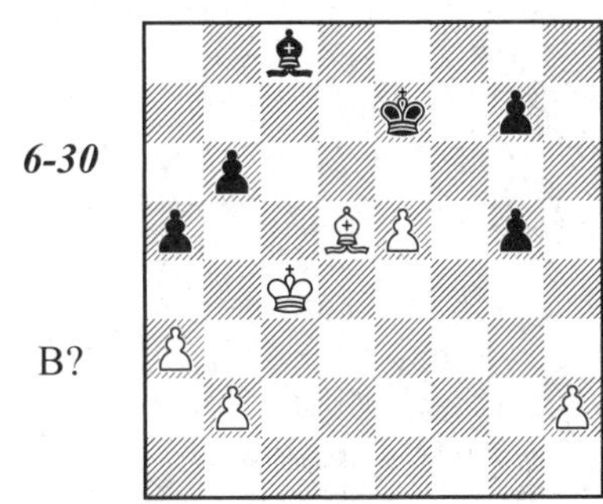

1...♗a6+!

The weaker 1...♗d7?! 2 ♗g2 ♗e8 3 ♔d5 ♗d7 4 ♗f3⊙ ♗e8 5 e6 would leave Black facing the difficult problem of how to deal with threats on both wings (♔d5-e5-f5 or b2-b3, a3-a4 and ♗f3-e2-b5).

2 ♔b3 ♗b5!

The king cannot be allowed to get to a4 - then White could secure the b5-square as well by continuing b2-b3 and ♗c4. Also risky is 2...♗c8 3 ♗c6 ♔e6 4 ♔a4 ♗a6 5 ♗b5 ♗c8 6 ♗c4+ ♔×e5 7 ♔b5.

3 ♔c3

6-31

B?

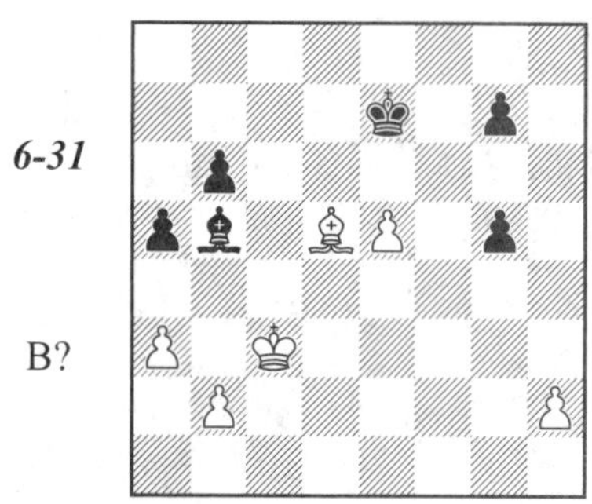

3...♔f8!!

A brilliant defensive move discovered through the method of exclusion. Let's follow the grandmaster's logic.

The position after 3...♗d7?! (or 3...♗e8?!) 4 ♔c4, with ♗g2 and ♔d5 to follow, we have already rated as unfavorable. In any event, it's better not to choose such a course, if we don't have to.

3...♗f1? loses to 4 b4! ab+ (otherwise, after the exchange of pawns on a5, White's king obtains the important square c5) 5 ♔xb4, and there is no defense against 6 ♗c4.

3...♔e8? is bad: 4 b4! ab+ 5 ♔xb4 ♗d7 6 e6 and 7 ♔b5. 3...♔d7? fails for the same reason.

Finally, on 3...♔d8?! there follows 4 ♗c4 ♗c6 5 ♗g8! (threatening 6 ♔c4) 5...♗b5 6 ♔d4, and the king gets in via c4 or d5.

But after 3...♔f8!! 4 ♗c4 ♗c6, the g8-square is covered, and 5 ♗a2 is not dangerous, in view of 5...♔e7 6 ♔c4 ♔e6.

4 b4

Before changing the contour of the game, White should have tried one more positional trap: 4 ♗e6 ♔e7 5 ♗c8!? (cleverer than 5 ♗f5 ♗a6! 6 ♔d4 ♗b7!). The simplistic 5...♔d8? 6 ♗f5 ♔e7 would leave Black in serious, perhaps insurmountable, difficulties after 7 ♔d4 ♗a6 (7...♗c6 8 ♗e4 and 9 ♔d5) 8 ♔e3! ♗b7 9 ♔f2, with the awful threat of ♔g3-g4. The threat of marching the king to g4 must be met by a timely transfer of the bishop to d5: 5...♗f1! 6 ♔d4 ♗g2 7 ♔e3 ♗d5!, and on 8 ♔f2 Black now has 8...♗e6.

4...ab+ 5 ♔xb4 ♗d7 6 ♗b3 (White also gets nothing from 6 e6 ♗e8 7 ♔c4 ♔e7 8 ♔d4 ♔d6) **6...♔e7**

White can only seize the b5-square with his king by playing ♗a4 first; and then Black's king can attack the e5-pawn.

7 ♗a4 ♗g4 8 ♗c6 ♔e6

Of course not 8...♗e2? 9 ♗d5 and 10 ♗c4.

9 ♔b5 ♔xe5 10 ♔xb6 ♗d1 11 h3

11 a4 ♗xa4 12 ♗xa4 ♔f4 13 ♗d7 g4=.

11...g4 12 hg ♗xg4 13 a4 g5 14 a5 ♗e2 Drawn.

Setting up a barrier is an effective defensive tool, but it too is not always sufficient. Sometimes the opponent can overcome the barrier by offering an exchange of bishops. When doing so, it is necessary to calculate the pawn ending accurately.

Donner - Smyslov
Havana 1964

6-32

B

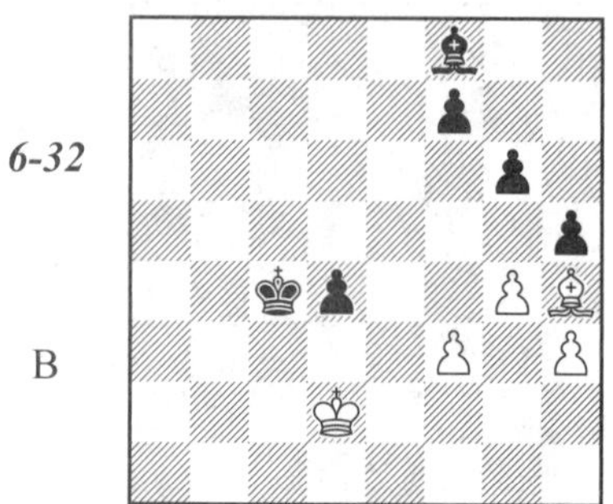

With the pawn on g2, Black could not have broken through the enemy defenses; but now it is possible, although with considerable difficulty - thanks to the weakness of the pawn at f3.

1...♗h6+ 2 ♔c2 d3+ 3 ♔d1 ♔d4 4 ♗f2+ ♔c3 5 ♗b6 d2! 6 ♗f2 ♔d3 7 ♗b6 ♗f4 8 ♗f2 ♗e5⊙ 9 ♗g1

If 9 gh gh 10 ♗g1, then 10...♗c3⊙ (premature would be 10...♗d4 11 ♗h2, when Black cannot play 11...♔e3 because of 12 ♗g1+ ♔xf3 13 ♗xd4=) 11 ♗b6 ♗d4 12 ♗a5 (12 ♗xd4 ♔xd4 13 ♔xd2 h4 14 ♔e2 f5 15 ♔d2 f4⊙) 12...♔e3 13 ♗xd2+ ♔xf3 14 ♔e1 ♔g2 15 ♔e2 ♗e5! △ ...f5-f4-f3.

9...h4!

Smyslov prepares the exchange of bishops. The immediate 9...♗d4? leads only to a draw: 10 ♗xd4 ♔xd4 11 ♔xd2 h4 12 g5!.

10 ♗f2 ♗c3⊙ 11 ♗g1 ♗d4! 12 ♗xd4

After 12 ♗h2 Black sacrifices the bishop: 12...♔e3! 13 ♗g1+ ♔xf3 14 ♗xd4 ♔g2 15 ♔xd2 ♔xh3 16 g5 ♔g2 17 ♗e5 h3 18 ♔e3 h2 19 ♗xh2 ♔xh2−+.

12...♔×d4 13 ♔×d2 ♔e5 14 ♔e3 g5

White resigned, in view of 15 f4+ (15 ♔e2 ♔f4 16 ♔f2 f6⊙) 15...gf+ 16 ♔f3 f6 17 ♔f2 ♔e4 18 ♔e2 f3+ 19 ♔f1 f2! (the standard triangulation maneuver, as seen in the game Fahrni - Alapin, doesn't work here, since Black's king doesn't have the f5-square available) 20 ♔×f2 (20 ♔e2 f1♕+) 20...♔f4⊙−+.

Tragicomedies

Matanovic - Uhlmann
Skopje 1976

6-33

B?

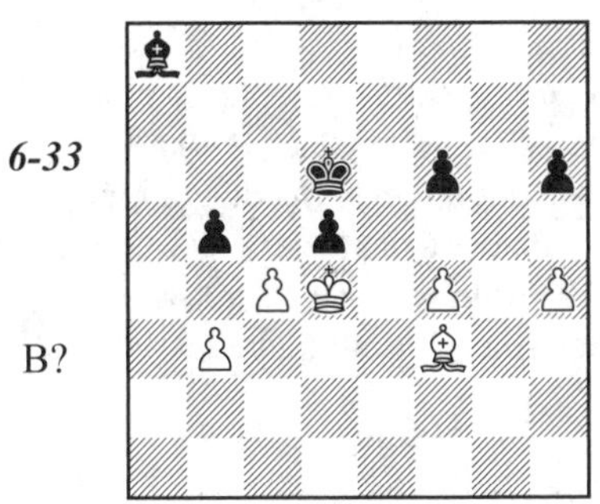

Black chose the desperate **1...dc? 2 ♗×a8 cb**, and after **3 ♗e4 b2 4 h5 b4 5 ♔c4**, he resigned.

As Matanovic pointed out, Black could have saved the game by playing 1...bc 2 bc ♗c6 3 ♗×d5 ♗e8 4 c5+ ♔c7. White's king cannot get through the barrier.

Exercises

6-34

6/7
B?

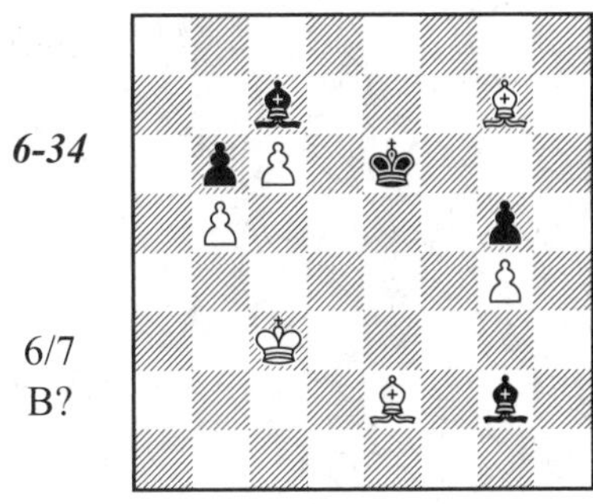

Chapter 7

BISHOP VS. KNIGHT

With this configuration of material there is not, in my opinion, a single fundamental theoretical position that would be worth memorizing. For the practical player, what's important is to become acquainted with the overall ideas, and with some concrete battle techniques.

Bishop and Pawn vs. Knight

V. Bron, 1955

7-1

W

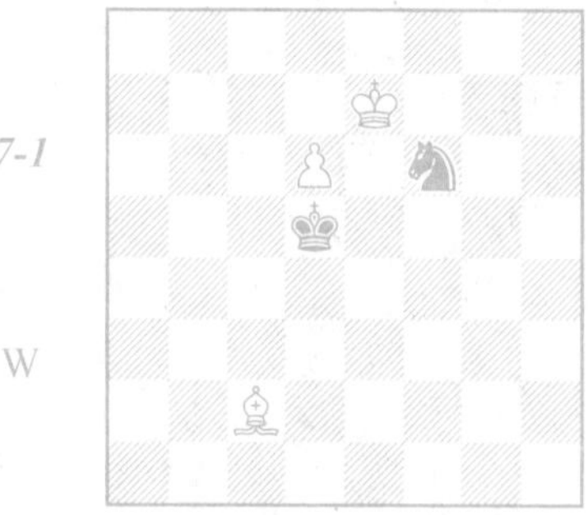

The outcome in all endgames of this sort depends wholly on whether the stronger side can place his opponent in zugzwang. In the present case, this is possible.

1 ♗b3+ ♔c5

On 1...♔e5 2 ♗e6⊙, the game ends at once.

2 ♗a2 ♔c6 (2...♘g4 3 ♔e6) **3 ♔e6 ♘h7** (3...♔c5 4 ♗b1 or 4 ♗d5) **4 ♗d5+ ♔c5 5 ♔e7 ♘f6**

5...♘f8 6 ♗e4⊙ is no better.

6 ♗f3 ♘g8+ 7 ♔e6 ♘f6 8 ♗e4!+−

The decisive zugzwang!

Let's put Black's king on e5. Now the variations are different, but the evaluation of the position doesn't change, as well as the goal of White's maneuvers - zugzwang.

1 ♗b3 ♔f5 2 ♗f7 ♔g5 (2...♔e5 3 ♗e6⊙) **3 ♗e6 ♔g6 4 ♔f8! ♘h7+** (4...♔h6 5 ♔f7 ♔g5 6 ♗h3⊙) **5 ♔e8! ♘f6+ 6 ♔e7⊙** (in order to give his opponent the move, White has triangulated with his king) **6...♔g7 7 ♗f7 ♘g4! 8 ♗d5** (but not 8 d7? ♘e5 9 d8♕ ♘c6+) **8...♘e5** (8...♘f6 9 ♗e4! ♘g8+ 10 ♔e6 ♘f6 11 ♗f5⊙) **9 ♗e4 ♔g8 10 ♔e6 ♘f7 11 d7 ♔f8 12 ♗d5 ♘d8+ 13 ♔d6⊙ ♔g7 14 ♔e7+−.**

Now, in the diagrammed position, let's move White's king to c7. It's not hard to see that Black can draw this - and not just with his knight on f6, but also on f8 or e5. Which brings us to the conclusion: *For a successful defense, it's important to keep the knight far away from the enemy king.*

But even for the knight placed close to the enemy king, zugzwang is not at all a sure thing. Let's return once again to the diagrammed position. Let's suppose that after 1 ♗b3+ ♔c5 White, instead of the waiting move 2 ♗a2!, chose 2 ♔e6? ♘h7! 3 ♔e7 (there's nothing better) 3...♘f8!

M. Mandelail, 1938

7-2

$

W

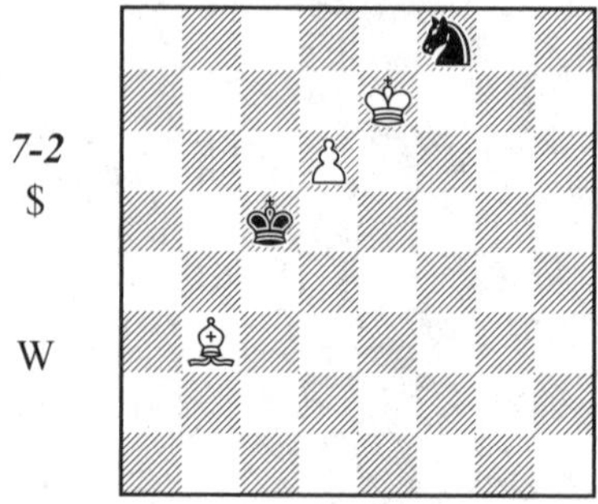

4 ♗c2 (White cannot allow the knight check at g6) **4...♔c6** (4...♔d5 is possible too) **5 ♗a4+**

With the bishop on the b1-h7 diagonal, the king will shuttle between c6 and d5, avoiding the mined squares c5 and e5. For example: 5 ♗b1 ♔d5! 6 ♗d3 ♔c6! (6...♔c5? 7 ♗e4⊙, 6...♔e5? 7 ♗e4⊙) 7 ♗e4+ ♔c5⊙.

5...♔c5 6 ♗e8 ♔d5 7 ♗f7+ ♔c6 8 ♗h5 ♔c5!=

8...♔d5? is a mistake, in view of 9 ♗f3+ ♔e5(c5) 10 ♗e4⊙+−. But now we have a position of reciprocal zugzwang, with White to move; and he cannot give the move back to his opponent.

It is not uncommon in such situations for Black to have a passed pawn, too. The stronger side's strategy remains unchanged: White must still play for zugzwang. The defender, however, now has a new resource: ***deflection***. Sometimes, the pawn distracts the bishop from controlling an important square, which the knight then immediately occupies. Or the reverse can happen: sometimes the knight is sacrificed to allow the pawn to queen.

Lisitsyn - Zagorovsky
Leningrad 1953

7-3

W?

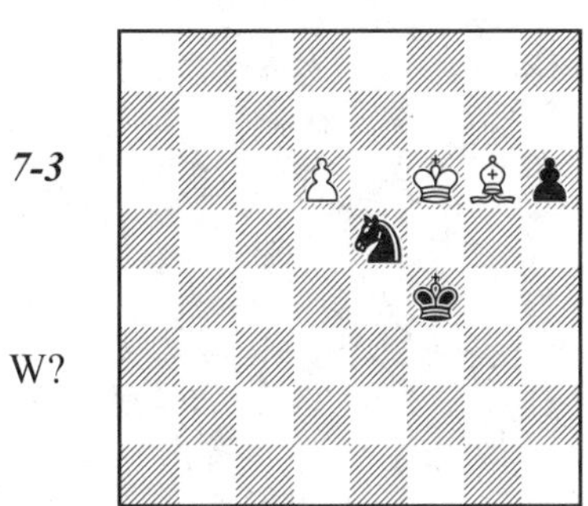

1 ♗e8? would be a mistake in view of 1...h5! (deflection) 2 ♗xh5 ♘d7+ 3 ♔e6 ♘b6. The knight stands far away from the king, and the position would be drawn.

1 ♗f5! h5 2 ♔e6 h4 3 ♔f6⊙ ♘c6

3...h3 is no better: 4 ♗xh3 ♔e4 5 ♔e6 ♔d4 6 ♗f5⊙.

4 d7 ♘d8 5 ♗e6 (△ ♗d5, ♔e7) **5...♔e4 6 ♗h3**

The most accurate move, threatening 7 ♗g2+ and 8 ♔e7. But the immediate 6 ♔e7 ♘b7 7 ♗c4 h3 8 ♗a6+− was also possible.

6...♔f3 7 ♔e7 ♘b7 (7...♘c6+ 8 ♔d6 ♘d8 9 ♔c7 ♘f7 10 ♗e6+−) **8 ♗f1 ♔g3 9 ♗a6 ♘c5 10 d8♕** Black resigned.

Now, here's a more complex example.

Nazarevsky - Simonenko
Kiev 1939

7-4
$

W

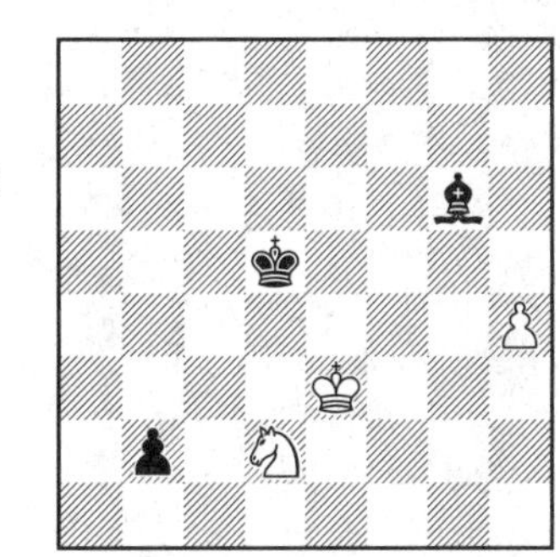

1 h5!

Exploiting the fact that the pawn is temporarily poisoned (1...♗xh5? 2 ♔d3=), to advance it further. On 1 ♔e2? ♔d4 the position is lost.

1...♗h7 2 h6 ♔c5 3 ♔e2 ♔d4 4 ♔d1 ♔c3

Let's examine the other attempts to play for zugzwang:

4...♗d3 5 ♔e1 ♔e3 works well if White plays 6 ♔d1? ♔f2⊙. But White saves himself if he sacrifices a pawn to deflect the bishop: 6 h7! ♗xh7 7 ♘c4+.

4...♔d3 5 ♔e1 ♔c3 6 ♔e2! (but not 6 ♔d1? ♗d3 7 ♔e1 ♔c2⊙). Now 6...♗g6 is met by 7 ♔e1!, leading back to the game line (7 ♔e3? ♗d3⊙ or 7 ♔d1? ♗d3 8 ♔e1 ♔c2⊙ would be a mistake). And if 6...♔c2 (counting on 7 ♔e1? ♗d3⊙ or 7 ♔e3? ♔d1⊙), then White saves himself with the knight sacrifice indicated by Konstantinopolsky: 7 ♘c4!! ♗d3+ 8 ♔e3 ♗xc4 9 h7 b1♕ 10 h8♕=.

5 ♔e1 ♔c2 6 ♔e2 ♗d3+ 7 ♔e1!

7 ♔e3? ♔c3⊙ is a mistake.

7...♔c1 8 ♘b3+ ♔b1 9 ♔d1!

The final touch. 9 ♘d2+? ♔c2⊙ or 9 ♔d2? ♔a2 10 ♘c1+ ♔a3 both lose.

9...♗c2+ 10 ♔e2 ♗h7 11 ♔d1 ♗c2+ 12 ♔e2 ♗g6 13 ♔d1 ♗h5+ 14 ♔d2 ♔a2 15 h7 b1♕ 16 ♘c1+ ♔a3 17 h8♕ Draw

Exercises

In the following exercises, you must answer the question, "What should be the result of this game?"

7-5

7/1
W?

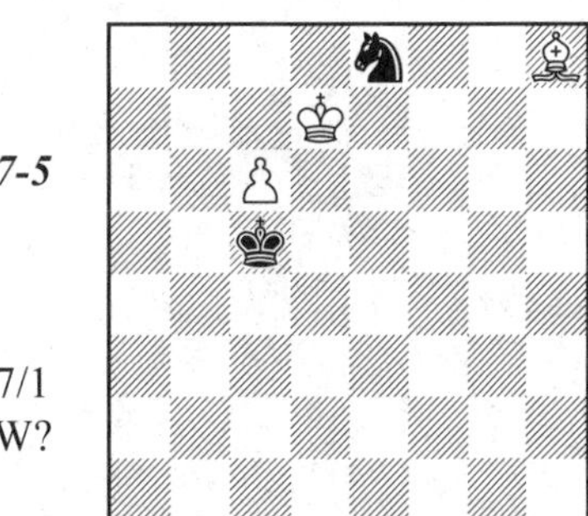

7-6

7/2
W?

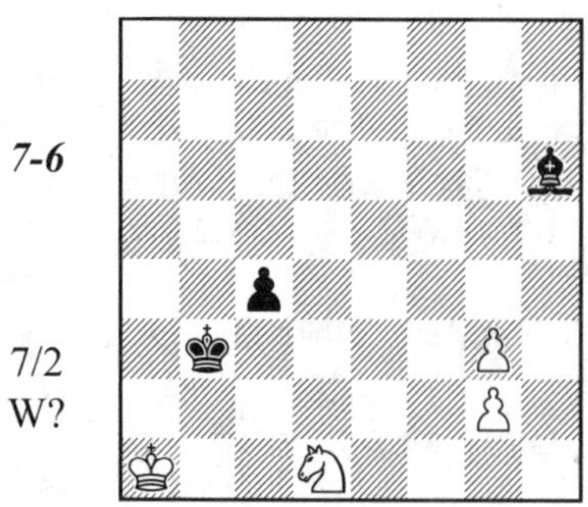

Knight and Pawn vs. Bishop

The bishop is a strong piece, sometimes capable of preventing a pawn from queening even without the king's help.

7-7

B

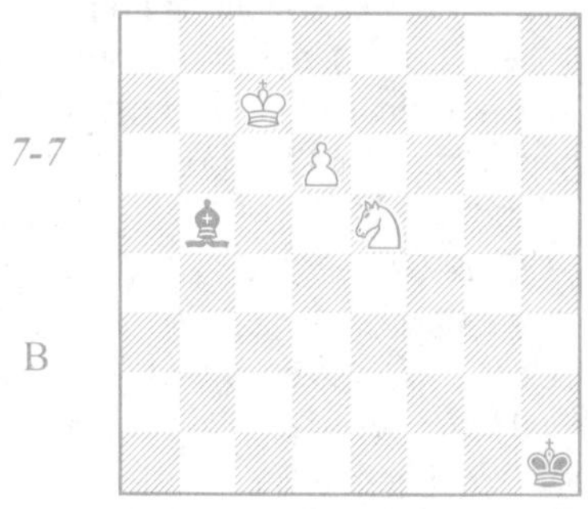

1...♗e8! (White threatened interference with 2 ♘c6) **2 ♘d7 ♔g2 3 ♔d8 ♗g6 4 ♔e7 ♗f5 5 ♘c5** (△♘e6) **5...♗c8!=**

Black was saved, first of all, because the pawn had not yet reached the 7th rank, and second, because the bishop's diagonal was sufficiently long: 5 squares. Knight and king are only capable of interdicting two squares apiece, which leaves the fifth square free.

If we move the position one file to the left, the diagonal grows shorter, and Black loses.

7-8

B

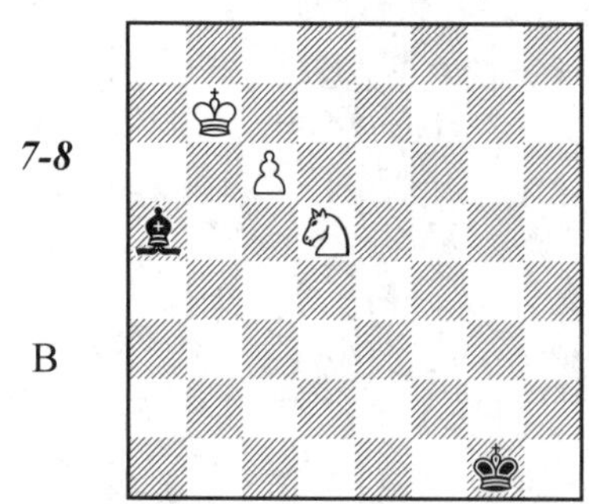

1...♗d8 2 ♘f4 ♔f2 3 ♘e6 ♗a5 4 ♔a6+−.

These examples show us the ***two basic techniques for promoting the pawn: driving the bishop off the diagonal, and interference.***

If the bishop can't handle the job on its own (which is what happens most often), then the outcome depends upon the position of the defending king: can it prevent the bishop from being interfered with or driven off?

Y. Averbakh, 1958

7-9

W

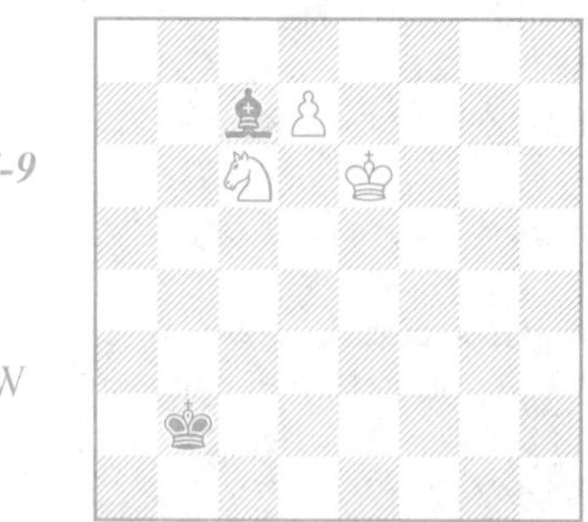

With the king at a1 or b1, White would win by ♔d5-c4-b5-a6-b7. But here (or with the king at c1, also), Black's king is in time to help the bishop: **1 ♔d5 ♔c3! 2 ♔c5 ♔d3! 3 ♔b5 ♔e4 4 ♔a6 ♔d5 5 ♔b7 ♔d6=**

Note Black's accurate first move: 1...♔a3? would be refuted by 2 ♔c4! ♔a4 3 ♔c5⊙+− (this is how White wins if the king is on a2 in the starting position). And if 1...♔b3? (hoping for 2 ♔c5? ♔a4, when White's the one in zugzwang), then 2 ♘d4+ ♔b4 3 ♘e6 ♗a5 4 ♔c6, with the unstoppable threat of interference by 5 ♘c7.

The other plan, 1 ♔e7 ♔c3(b3) 2 ♘d8 ♔c4 3 ♘e6 ♗a5 4 ♔d6 ♗b4+! doesn't win for White either. It's important that White doesn't have the 5 ♘c5 interference - the king covers that square.

But with the king at c1 in the starting position, this plan leads to the queening of the pawn: 1 ♔e7! ♔b2 (1...♔d2 2 ♘d4! ♔e3 3 ♘e6 ♗g3 4 ♔e8 ♗h4 5 ♘f8 ♔e4 6 ♘g6 △7 ♘e7) 2 ♘d4! ♗a5 3 ♘e6 ♔c3 4 ♔d6 ♗b4+ 5 ♘c5! ♗a5 6 ♘b7 ♗b6 ♔c6+−, or 3...♗b4+ 4 ♔f6! ♗c3+ 5 ♔f5 ♗a5 6 ♔e4 ♔b3 7 ♔d5 △♔c6, ♘c7+−.

Tragicomedies

Stein - Dorfman
USSR 1970

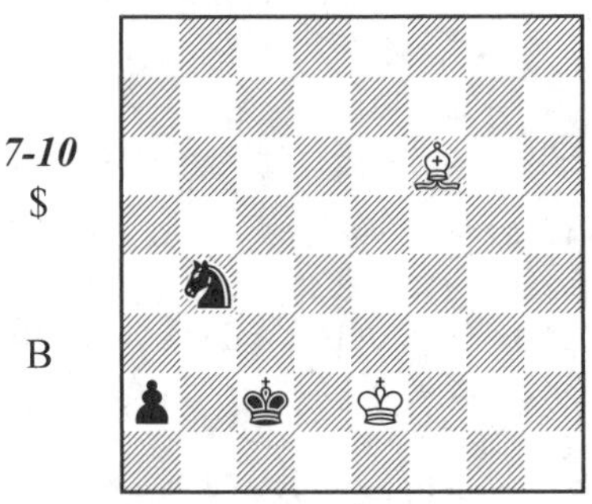

The bishop has a hard time with a rook's pawn, since it has only one diagonal to work with. However, Dorfman played too straightforwardly, and was unable to gain the point.

1...♘d3 2 ♗a1□ (Black threatened the interference 2...♘b2) **2...♘b2 3 ♔e1**

3 ♔e3 must be answered by 3...♘a4! 4 ♔e2 ♔c1! (see below), or 5 ♔d4 ♔b1 5 ♔d3 ♘c5+ 6 ♔c3 ♔xa1−+. Whereas, in the game Sakaev - Sunye Neto (Sao Paulo 1991), after 3...♔b1? 4 ♔d2! the win was gone.

3...♔b1 4 ♔d2 ♔xa1 5 ♔c1! ♘c4 6 ♔c2 Draw. We know the concluding position from the chapter "Knight vs. Pawns" (diagram 2-2).

The road to victory was noted as far back as the 19th century by Horwitz. Black should have played 3...♘a4! (instead of 3...♔b1?) 4 ♔e2 ♔c1. Possible variations are:

5 ♔d3 ♔b1 6 ♔d2 ♘b2⊙ 7 ♔c3 ♔xa1 8 ♔c2 ♘d3⊙−+;

5 ♔e3 ♔b1 6 ♔d3 (6 ♔d2 ♘b2⊙) 6...♘c5+! (of course not 6...♔xa1? 7 ♔c2=) 7 ♔c3 (7 ♔d2 ♘b3+) 7...♔xa1 8 ♔c2 ♘b3(d3)⊙−+;

5 ♔e1 ♘c5! 6 ♔e2 (6 ♗g7 ♘d3+ and 7...♘b2) 6...♔b1 7 ♔d1 (7 ♗g7 ♘a4) 7...♘d3 8 ♔d2 ♘b2⊙−+.

Exercises

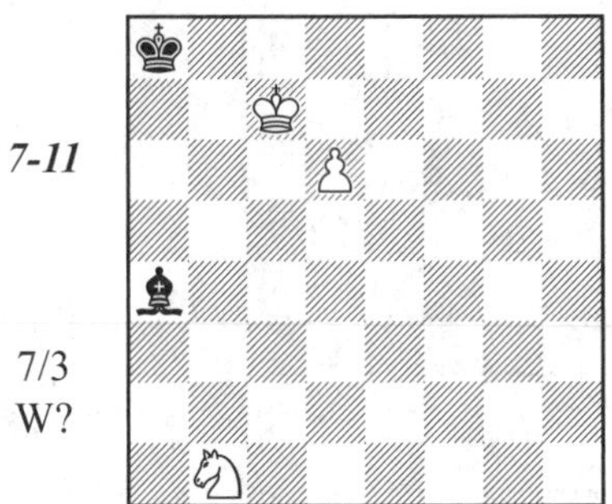

White to move - what result?

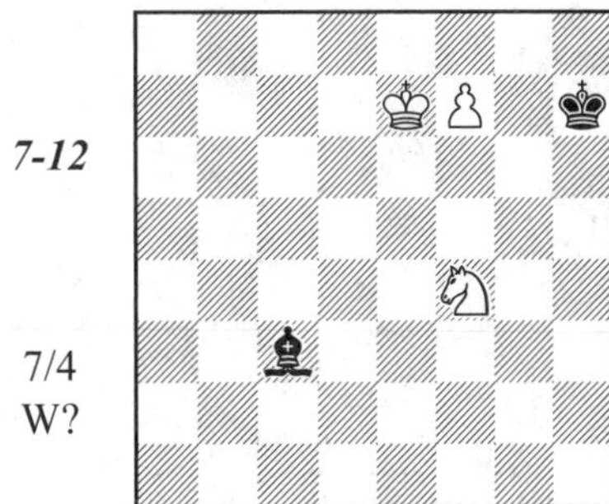

The Bishop is Superior to the Knight

Cutting the Knight Off

If the knight is on the edge of the board, the bishop can deprive it of moves.

7-13

W

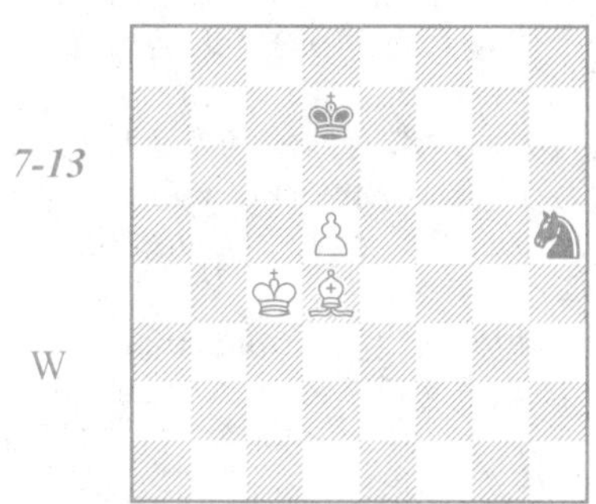

1 ♗e5! ♔e7 2 ♔c5 ♔d7 3 d6 (but not 3 ♔b6?? ♘f6!=) **3...♔e6 4 ♔c6 ♔×e5 5 d7+−**.

Sometimes it is not necessary to "arrest" the knight - it's enough to cut it off from the main theater of conflict (for example, from the passed pawn), as in the following example.

Goldberg - Tolush
USSR chsf, Moscow 1949

7-14

W?

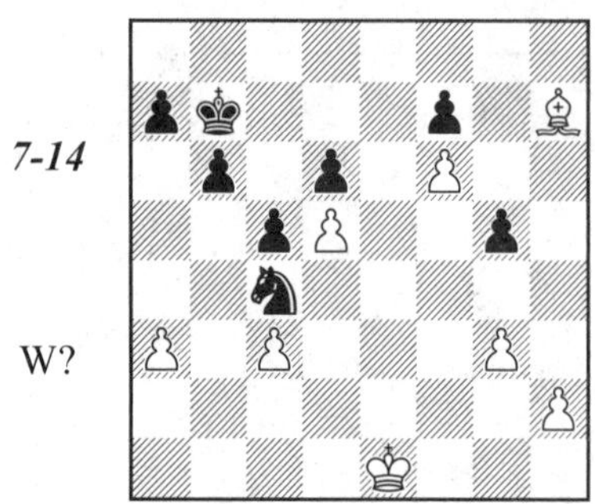

1 h4! gh 2 gh ♘e5 3 ♗f5!

The bishop deprives the knight of the important squares g4 and d7, which it would otherwise use for the fight against the h-pawn. It is true that the knight can immediately remove this pawn - but then it comes "under arrest."

3...♘f3+ 4 ♔f2 ♘×h4 5 ♗e4! ♔c7 6 ♔g3 ♘g6 7 ♗×g6 fg 8 f7 Black resigned

Tragicomedies

Bykova - Volpert
USSR 1951

7-15

B

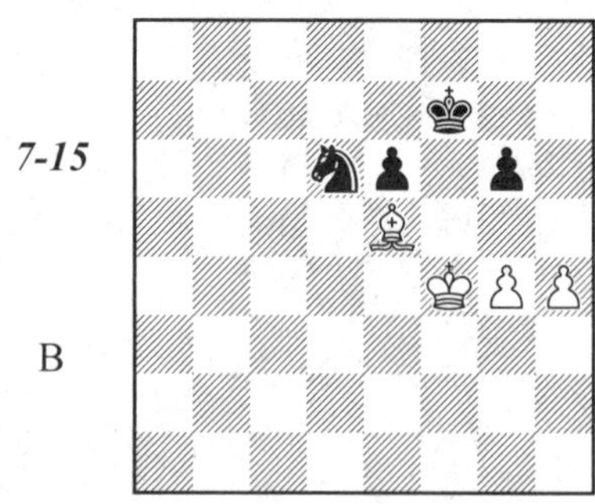

1...♘e8??

A mistake that's hard to explain. Almost any other retreat by the knight would have led to an uncomplicated draw. Now Black loses.

2 ♔g5 ♘g7 3 ♔h6

Black resigned, in view of 3...♘e8 4 g5⊙.

Exercises

7-16

7/5
W?

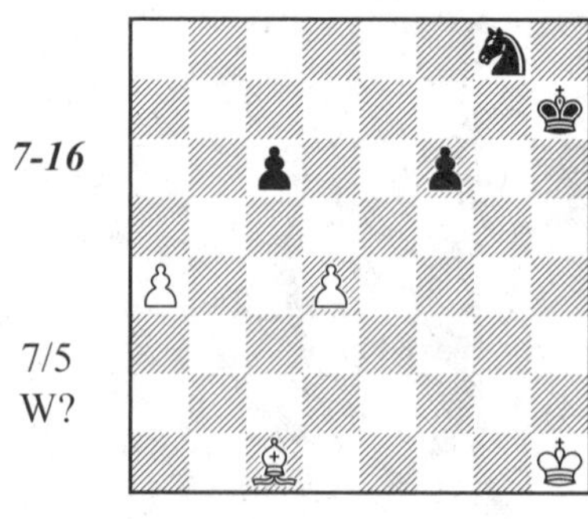

7-17

7/6
W?/Play

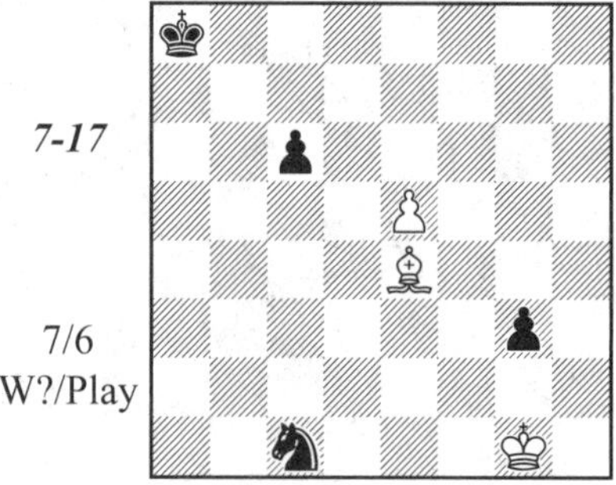

Fixing the Pawns

It is useful to fix the enemy pawns on squares where they may be attacked by the bishop. In this case either the king or the knight will be tied down to their defense.

Chiburdanidze - Muresan
Lucerne ol 1982

7-18

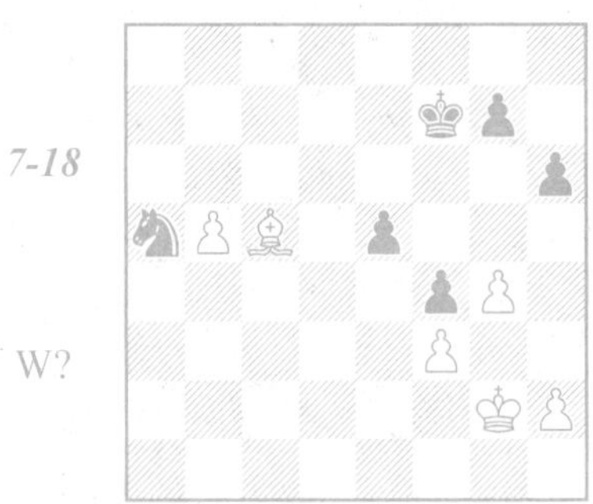

W?

In order to make progress, White must bring her king to the queenside - but this will be met by the black king coming to d5. For example: 1 ♔f2? g6! 2 ♔e2 ♔e6 3 ♔d3 ♔d5=. White also gets nothing from 2 b6 ♔e6 3 ♗f8 h5 4 gh gh 5 ♔g2 ♔d7! 6 ♔h3 ♘c4=.

One of the most important methods of converting one's advantage in endgames (and not just in endgames) is "the principle of two weaknesses." Sometimes it is impossible to win by working only on one part of the board. In such cases, the attacking side strives to create a second weakness in the enemy camp, or to exploit one which already exists. By attacking this second weakness, and then if necessary returning the attack to the first weakness, the attacker succeeds in breaking down and eventually overcoming the enemy's resistance.

1 h4!

An excellent positional move, stemming from the "principle of two weaknesses." The vulnerability of the h6-pawn prevents Black's king from heading towards the center; but how, then, is she to meet the advance of the enemy king to the queen's wing?

1...g6 2 h5! gh 3 gh

White's position is now won.

3...♔f6 4 b6 ♘b7 5 ♗f8 ♔g5 6 ♗g7 ♔×h5 7 ♗×e5

The h5-pawn is gone, but now the king must defend another vulnerable pawn - the one at f4.

7...♔g5 8 ♔f2

For now, White's king cannot penetrate the kingside: 8 ♔h3 ♘a5 9 ♗d6 ♘b7 10 ♗e7+ ♔h5.

8...♔f5 9 ♗g7 h5

9...♔g5 is met by 10 ♔e2, when the h-pawn must be advanced anyway. After h6-h5, White changes her plan, and decides the outcome on the kingside.

10 ♔g2! ♘c5 11 ♗f8 ♘b7 12 ♔h3 ♔g5 13 ♗e7+ ♔f5 14 ♔h4

Black resigned, since her king cannot simultaneously defend the pawns at h5 and f4. There can be no help from her knight, either - as before, it's tied to the queenside; meanwhile, throughout this endgame, White's bishop remained very active.

Miles - Dzhindzhikhashvili
Tilburg 1978

7-19

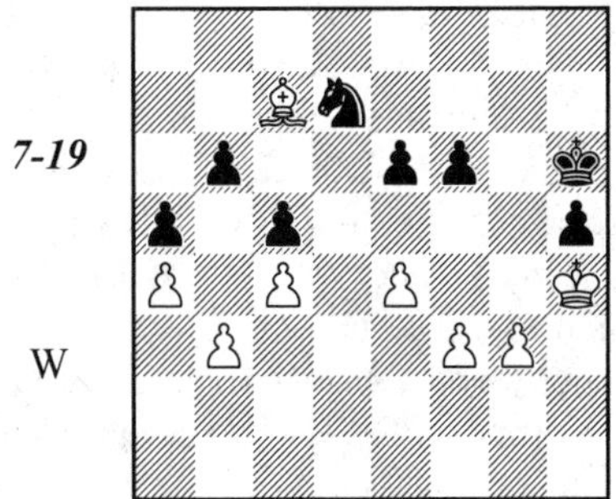

W

Whereas in the preceding example Black's king was forced to defend its pawns, here this role is played by the knight. In order to let his king break into the enemy camp, White uses the standard techniques of widening the beachead and zugzwang.

1 g4! hg 2 fg! ♔g6 3 ♔g3 ♔g5

On 3...f5 4 gf+ ef 5 ♔f4! decides.

4 ♔f3 ♔h6

Nor does 4...e5 help, in view of 5 ♔g3 ♔g6 6 ♔h4 ♔h6 7 ♗d8 ♔g6 8 g5! fg+ (8...f5 9 ef+ ♔×f5 10 ♔h5 e4 11 g6+−) 9 ♗×g5 ♘b8 10 ♗d8 ♘d7 11 ♔g4⊙+−.

5 ♔f4 ♔g6 6 e5! fe+ (6...f5 7 gf+ ef 8 e6) **7 ♗×e5 ♔f7 8 ♗c7 ♔f6 9 g5+ ♔f7 10 ♔g4 ♔g6 11 ♗d6**

Black resigned. He is in zugzwang, and will find himself in zugzwang over and over again, since his knight is tied to the defense of the b6-pawn, and cannot stir. For example: 11...e5 12 ♗c7⊙ e4 13 ♔f4 (13 ♗d8) 13...e3 14 ♔×e3 ♔×g5 15 ♔e4+−, or 11...♔f7 12 ♔h5 ♔g7 13

♗c7⊙ ♔h7 (13...e5 14 ♔g4+−) 14 g6+ ♔g7 15 ♔g5⊙+−.

Tragicomedies

Smyslov - Gurgenidze
USSR ch, Tbilisi 1966

7-20

W?

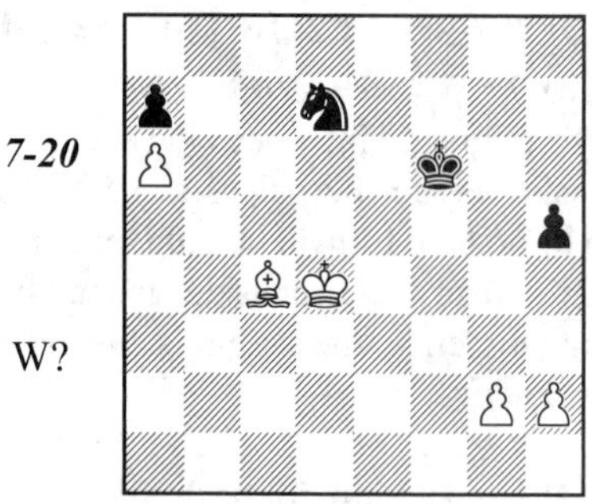

White wins, using exactly the same move (and the same technique) as in the Chiburdanidze - Muresan game: 1 h4! It is vital to fix the enemy pawn on the vulnerable h5-square, in order to tie one of Black's pieces to its defense, or in some lines to create a dangerous passed h-pawn.

In the game, White erred with **1 ♔d5?** After **1...h4!**, the position became drawn. If White sends his king after the a7-pawn, Black squeezes it into the corner with ...♔c7. And on g2-g3, Black exchanges pawns and easily blockades the passed g-pawn which results. Besides, he only needs to give up his knight for it, and then bring his king back to b8 (the elementary fortress already known to us) to secure the draw.

The continuation was: **2 ♗e2 ♘f8 3 ♔e4 ♔g5 4 ♔d5 ♔f6 5 ♗g4 ♘g6**, and the game ended in a draw.

The Passed Pawn

The presence of passed pawns on the board, as a rule, favors the side with the bishop. The bishop is a wide-ranging piece, able both to support its own pawns, while simultaneously dealing with the enemy's, whereas the knight generally succeeds in acting only upon a narrow segment of the board. If it succeeds, let's say, in blockading the passed pawn on one wing, it cannot successfully involve itself in the fray on the opposite wing.

A few of the endings we have examined have already illustrated the difficulties faced by the knight when battling against a passed pawn (Goldberg - Tolush, for instance, or Chiburdanidze - Muresan). Let's analyze some more examples of this theme.

Spassky - Fischer
Santa Monica 1966

7-21

B?

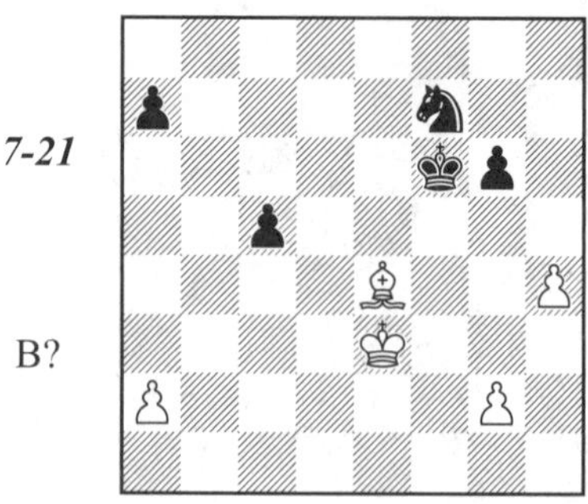

White would certainly love to play g2-g4 (for instance, in reply to 1...♘d6), tying one of the enemy pieces to the kingside. Then the king would move over to the queenside, and attack Black's pawns.

The most stubborn line was Gligoric's suggestion 1...♘h6! (and if 2 ♔f4, then 2...♘f7! 3 g4 g5+). Averbakh extends the line as follows: 2 ♔d3 ♘f5 3 ♔c4 ♘×h4 4 ♔×c5 ♔e5 5 ♗b7 ♔f4 6 ♔b5 ♔g3 7 ♔a6 ♘×g2 8 ♔×a7+− (the knight is, as usual, helpless against a rook's pawn).

But instead of the desperate king march to the g2-pawn, Zviagintsev suggested the more restrained plan of 5...♘f5, which offers Black realistic saving chances, in view of the small amount of remaining material. On 6 ♔b5 there follows 6...♔d6 7 ♔a6 ♔c5 8 ♔×a7 ♔b4= (after the king gets to a3, the knight will be given up for the g-pawn). Or 6 a4 ♘e3 7 ♔b5 ♔d6 8 a5 (8 ♔a6 ♔c5 △ 9...♔b4) 8...g5 9 ♗e4 g4 10 ♔a6 g3 11 ♔×a7 ♔c7 12 ♔a6 ♘c4 13 ♗f3 ♘e3 14 ♔b5 ♔b8 15 ♔c5 (15 ♔b6 ♘c4+) 15...♔a7 16 ♔d4 ♘×g2=.

Fischer's choice makes things considerably easier for White, since it gives him a passed pawn without even having to exchange pawns for it.

1...g5? 2 h5 ♘h6 3 ♔d3 ♔e5 4 ♗a8 ♔d6 5 ♔c4 g4 6 a4

Black's king can only defend one of the two queenside pawns. Seeing that the a7-pawn is doomed, Spassky does not hurry to attack it, preferring to strengthen his position maximally first.

6...♘g8 7 a5 ♘h6 8 ♗e4 g3 9 ♔b5 ♘g8 10 ♗b1 ♘h6 11 ♔a6 ♔c6 12 ♗a2 Black resigned.

The following sharp endgame features an interesting, though not wholly error-free, struggle.

Perelstein - Vepkhvishvili
Pushkin Hills 1977

7-22

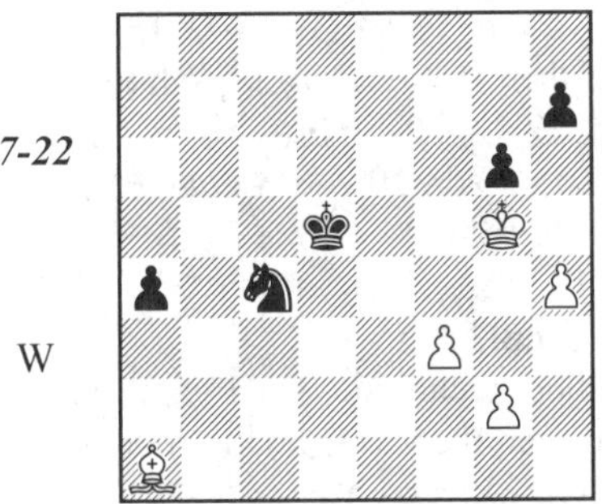

W

Who stands better? The black a-pawn could become very dangerous, while White will soon create a kingside passed pawn. In such sharp positions, the bishop is usually stronger than the knight, which is why Perelstein didn't go in for the drawing line 1 h5 gh 2 ♔×h5 ♘e3 3 g4 a3 4 ♔h6 ♘c2 5 ♔×h7! ♘×a1 6 g5 a2 7 g6=.

1 ♔h6 ♘e3 2 g4 a3?!

The accurate 2...♘g2! 3 h5 gh would have led to a draw. Black hopes for more, and does indeed achieve it - but only as a result of errors on the part of his opponent.

3 ♔×h7 ♘c2

Already pointless is 3...♘g2 4 h5 gh 5 gh.

7-23

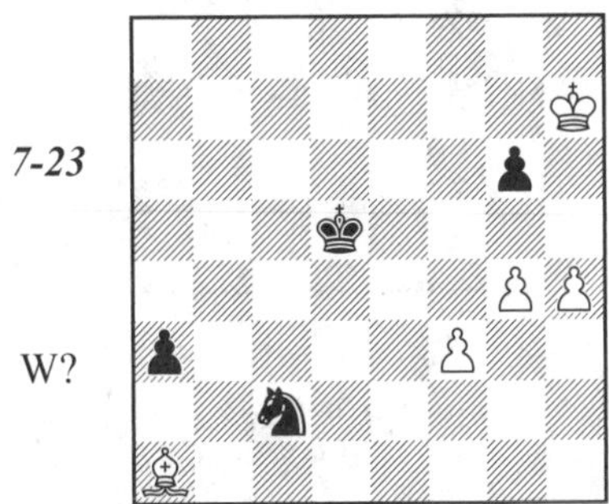

W?

The bishop can find no square on the long diagonal: 4 ♗f6? loses to the interference move 4...♘d4, and 4 ♗c3? is met by 4...♔c4. All that's left to hope for is his pawns.

The strongest move here was 4 g5!! After 4...♘×a1 5 h5 a2 6 hg ♘c2 7 g7 a1♕ 8 g8♕+ Black loses his knight. For example: 8...♔d6 (8...♔d4? 9 ♕g7+) 9 ♕g6+ ♔e7 10 ♕×c2 ♕h1+ 11 ♔g7 ♕×f3 12 ♕c7+ ♔e6 13 ♕b6+ ♔d7 14 ♕f6, with a winning queen endgame.

In Chapter 12, which is devoted to the theory of queen endgames, you will read that in such situations the only hope for salvation lies in the black king getting as close as possible to the corner square a1. Black should therefore play 8...♔c5! 9 ♕c8+ ♔b4 10 ♕×c2 ♕h1+ 11 ♔g7 ♕×f3. The computer assures us that the resulting position is drawn; however, to demonstrate this evaluation right at the board is quite difficult - as a rule, the defending side errs somewhere along the way, and loses.

4 h5? gh 5 g5?

White still draws after 5 gh! ♘×a1 6 h6.

5...♘e3!

Now it's Black who wins. On 6 g6 ♘f5 the knight will sacrifice itself for the g-pawn, and the bishop cannot stop both passed pawns ("pants").

6 ♔g6 h4 7 ♔f6 ♔d6! 8 g6 ♘d5+ 9 ♔f7 ♘e7 10 g7 ♘f5?!

10...h3 would have reached the goal a lot more simply.

11 g8♘! h3 12 ♘f6 h2

There was also a more elegant solution, based on the idea of a deflecting knight sacrifice: 12...♔c6! 13 ♘g4 (13 ♘e4 ♘d6+!) 13...♘h6+! 14 ♘×h6 h2−+.

13 ♘e4+ ♔d5 14 ♘f2 ♘d4

As a result of the inaccuracies committed, the knight must repeat his earlier task of attacking the bishop, and then returning to battle with the enemy passed pawns. He turns out to be just in time.

15 f4 ♘c2 16 f5 (there's nothing else) **16...♘×a1 17 ♔e7 ♘b3 18 f6 ♘d4**

White resigned, in view of 19 f7 ♘e6 (analysis by Dvoretsky).

Exercises

7-24

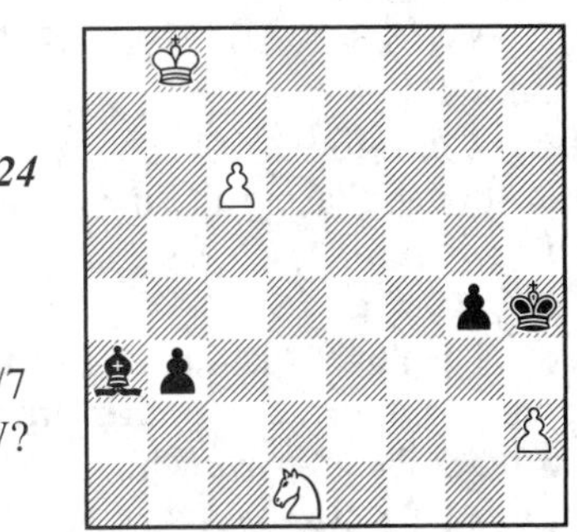

7/7
W?

Can White save himself?

An Open Position, A More Active King

The classic example of the exploitation of this type of advantage is the following endgame.

Stoltz - Kashdan
The Hague ol 1928

7-25

B

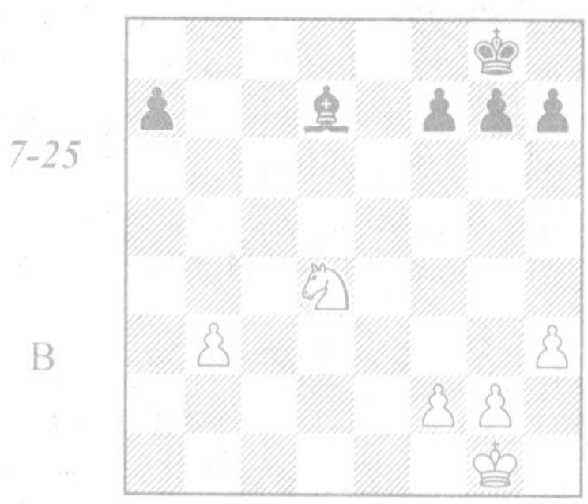

The position seems about equal, but it is not: Black has a significant advantage, in fact. First, because his king succeeds in occupying the d5-square, and will therefore stand better than its opposite number. And second, because the position is open, the bishop is stronger than the knight (although you would not say so, at first glance).

1...♔f8 2 ♔f1 ♔e7 3 ♔e2 ♔d6 4 ♔d3 ♔d5 5 h4 ♗c8!

After the bishop check at a6, the black king goes in the opposite direction to the one White's king retreats to.

6 ♘f3?!

6 f3 ♗a6+ 7 ♔e3 ♔c5 8 ♘c2 should have been preferred. Here's Averbakh's suggested continuation: 8...♗f1 9 g3 ♗a6 10 ♘d4 ♗b7 (10...♔b4 11 ♘c6+) 11 ♔d3 ♔b4 12 ♔c2 ♗d5 13 ♔b2 g6 14 ♔c2 a6 15 ♔b2, and it's still not clear how Black will break down his opponent's resistance.

6...♗a6+ 7 ♔c3

On 7 ♔e3 ♔c5 8 ♘g5 ♔b4 9 ♘xf7 ♔xb3, the a-pawn decides.

7...h6 8 ♘d4 g6 9 ♘c2?!

9 f3 is stronger, taking the important e4-square under control.

9...♔e4! 10 ♘e3 f5

Black has deployed his king to maximum effect. He intends to drive the knight from e3, and then to attack the g2-pawn with his bishop.

11 ♔d2 f4 12 ♘g4

Also hopeless is 12 ♘c2 ♗f1! 13 ♘e1 ♔f5 (△14...♔g4) 14 f3 g5 15 hg ♔xg5!, and the king reaches g3.

12...h5 13 ♘f6+ ♔f5 14 ♘d7?

Once again Stoltz fails to show defensive grit. As Müller and Lamprecht indicate, Black's task would have been considerably more difficult after 14 ♘h7! ♔g4 (14...♗f1 15 f3, and if 15...♗xg2, then 16 ♔e2) 15 ♘f8 ♔xh4 16 ♘xg6+ ♔g5 17 ♘e5 ♔f5 18 ♘f3 (the pawn endgame after 18 ♘d3 ♗xd3 19 ♔xd3 ♔g4 20 ♔e2 h4! 21 b4 a6 22 ♔f1 ♔f5 23 ♔e1 ♔e5! is lost) 18...♗b7 19 ♔e2.

14...♗c8!

Excellent technique. On 15 ♘c5 ♔g4 decides; however, the text is no improvement.

15 ♘f8 g5! 16 g3

Forced: after 16 hg ♔xg5 the knight is lost.

16...gh 17 gh ♔g4 18 ♘g6 ♗f5 19 ♘e7 ♗e6 20 b4 ♔xh4 21 ♔d3 ♔g4 22 ♔e4 h4 23 ♘c6 ♗f5+ 24 ♔d5 f3!

Of course not 24...h3? 25 ♘e5+ and 26 ♘f3.

25 b5 h3 26 ♘xa7 h2 27 b6 h1♕ 28 ♘c6 ♕b1 29 ♔c5 ♗e4 White resigned.

Karpov - A. Sokolov
Linares cmf(2) 1987

7-26

B?

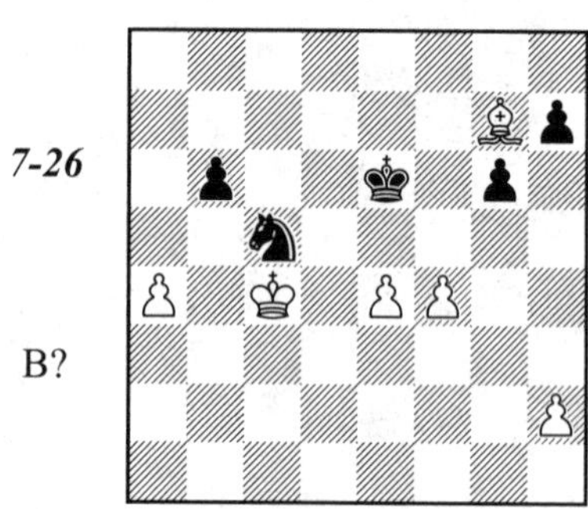

Which pawn should Black take? *In principle, when you have a knight against a bishop, the task is made easier, the narrower the battlefield: all the pawns should be on the same side.*

From this point of view, the logical move is 1...♘xa4! And in fact, this would have led to a draw: 2 ♗d4 ♔d6 3 ♔b5 (3 e5+ ♔e6 4 h4 h6 5 ♔b5 ♘c5 6 ♗xc5 bc 7 ♔xc5 g5=; 3 ♔b4 ♘c5 4 ♗xc5+ bc+ 5 ♔b5 g5=) 3...♘c5 4 ♗xc5+ bc (△5...g5) 5 h4 h6 6 ♔c4 ♔c6 7 e5 h5⊙=.

1...♘xe4? 2 ♔b5 ♘c5 3 ♗f8!

Sokolov probably counted on 3 ♗d4? ♘xa4! 4 ♔xa4 ♔f5 5 ♗e3 ♔g4 6 ♔b5 ♔h3=.

3...♘d7

Now 3...♘×a4 4 ♔×a4 ♔f5 5 ♗d6+− no longer helps.

4 ♗a3 ♔d5 5 ♗e7 ♔d4 6 ♗d8 Black resigned.

Tragicomedies

Krnic - Flear
Wijk aan Zee 1988

7-27

W

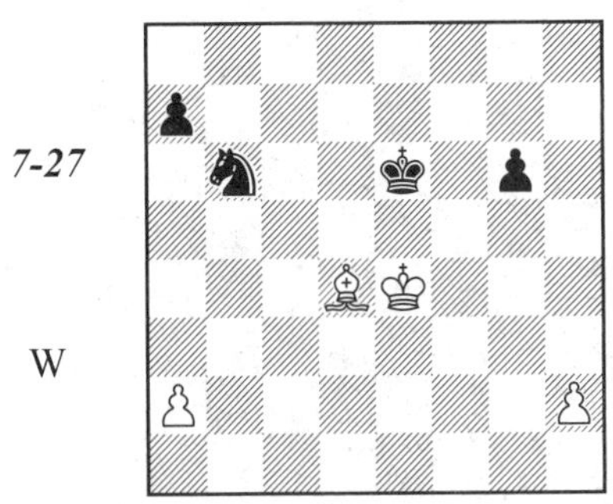

A draw was agreed here. Krnic probably just didn't realize that the bishop is completely dominating the knight, and therefore he had every reason to expect a win.

1 ♔f4 ♘c8 (1...♔f7 2 ♔e5 or 2 ♗×b6 ab 3 ♔e5 ♔e7 4 a4) **2 ♔g5 ♔f7 3 a4! a5!?**

White has a much simpler task after 3...♘b6 4 a5 or 3...a6 4 ♗c5 ♔g7 5 a5.

4 ♗c5 (cutting the knight off) **4...♔g7 5 h3!**

"Steinitz's Rule" in action! On 5 h4? ♔f7 6 ♔h6 ♔f6, it is White who falls into zugzwang.

5...♔f7 6 ♔h6 ♔f6 7 h4⊙ (White takes the opposition, in order to follow up with an outflanking) **7...♔f5** (7...♔f7 8 ♔h7 ♔f6 9 ♔g8+−) **8 ♔g7 ♔g4** (8...g5 9 h5) **9 ♔f6!**

On 9 ♔×g6? ♔×h4 the black king would get back to the queenside in time: 10 ♔f5 ♔g3 11 ♔e6 ♔f4 12 ♔d7 ♔e5 13 ♔×c8 ♔d5 14 ♗b6 ♔c4=.

9...♔×h4 10 ♔e6 ♔g4 11 ♔d7 ♔f5 12 ♔×c8 ♔e6 13 ♔c7 ♔d5 14 ♔b6+−

It is odd that Flear recommends 3 ♔h6 (instead of 3 a4). The GM even awards this move an exclamation mark, although in point of fact it deserves a question mark, and according to analysis by Zviagintsev and Dvoretsky, it probably lets slip the win.

3 ♔h6? a5! (Flear examines only the weaker 3...♘b6 and 3...a6) 4 ♗c5 (4 a4 ♘d6 5 ♔g5 ♘c4) 4...a4! 5 h3 (5 ♔h7 ♔f6 6 ♔g8 g5 is no better) 5...♔f6 6 h4⊙ ♔f5 7 ♔g7 ♔g4 8 ♔×g6.

In order to understand what follows, we must recall the conclusions we reached when studying Rauzer's positions with bishop and pawn vs. bishop (Diagrams 4-2 and 4-3). After 8 ♔f6 ♔×h4 9 ♔e6 ♔g4 10 ♔d7 ♔f5 11 ♔×c8 ♔e6 Black has no trouble drawing, with the white pawn on a3. Here, the pawn is on a2, which would give White a win (although a rather complicated one), if there weren't a black g-pawn on the board. That of course changes the evaluation.

8...♔×h4 9 ♔f5 ♔g3! 10 ♔e6 ♔f4 11 ♔d7 ♔e4 12 ♔×c8

7-28

B?

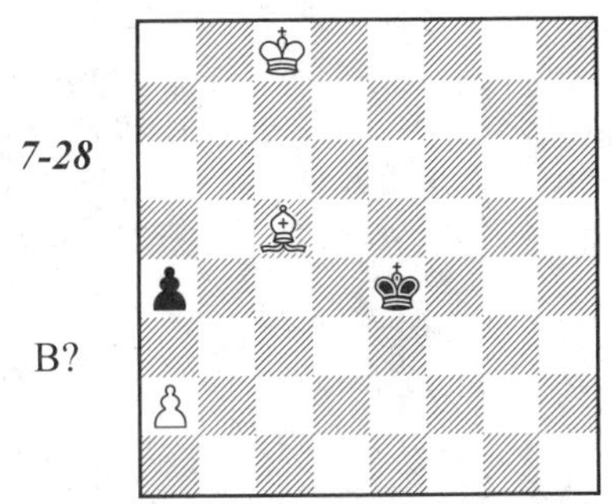

Doesn't White win now? Not necessarily - not if his opponent can force the move a2-a3 and then get back with his king.

12...♔d3! 13 ♔d7 ♔c2 (threatening 14...a3!=) 14 a3 ♔d3 15 ♔e6 ♔e4!

It turns out White can't prevent the black king from reaching the drawing zone. For example: on 16 ♗e7 Black can play either 16...♔f4 17 ♗f6 ♔g4! (17...♔e4? is a mistake, in view of 18 ♗e5! with a theoretically won position) 18 ♔e5 ♔h5 19 ♔f5 ♔h6 20 ♗e5 ♔h7!= (but not 20...♔h5? 21 ♗g7+−), or 16...♔d4 17 ♗d6 ♔c4! (17...♔e4? 18 ♗e5+− or 18 ♗h2+− would be a mistake).

Exercises

7-29

7/8
B?

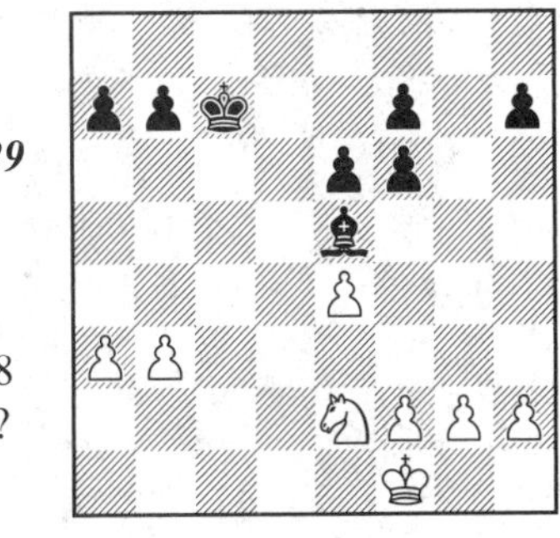

Defensive Methods with a Knight against a Bishop

Sometimes, an inferior position may be saved by tactical means - using ***knight forks***. But strategic methods are also often used. Let's enumerate the most important ones:

Blockading the passed pawns;

Fixing the enemy pawns on the same color squares as his bishop;

Erecting a barrier - the knight and pawns take control of a complex of important squares, preventing the incursion of the enemy king or at least making that incursion much more difficult;

Erecting a fortress.

These techniques are not usually employed singly, but in combination with each other. How this plays out, we shall see in the examples from this section.

Pirrot - Yusupov
Germany tt 1992

7-30

B

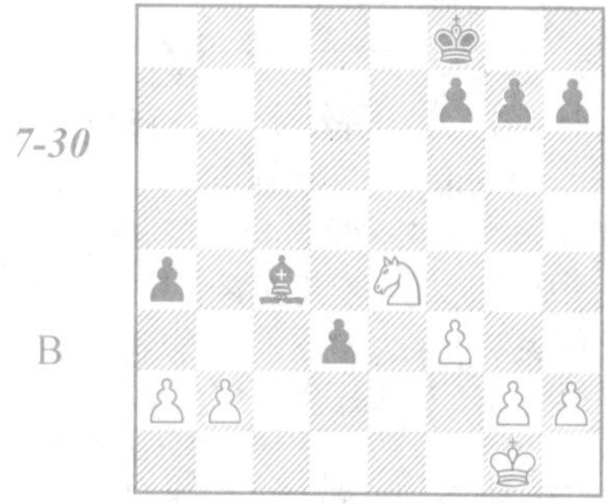

1...♗×a2 2 ♔f2 △♔e3 would lead to a roughly equal position. Yusupov finds the best practical chance.

1...f5! 2 ♘c3?

His opponent gets greedy: by maintaining the balance of material, he loses the game. 2 ♘d2! was necessary (blockading the passed pawn) 2...♗×a2 3 f4 (fixing the enemy pawn on the same color square as the bishop; on the other hand, 3 ♔f2 f4 4 ♘e4 ♔e7 5 ♔e1 or 5 g3 was good, too) 3...♔e7 4 ♔f2 ♗d5 6 g3 ♔d6 6 ♔e3 ♗e4 7 ♔d4, and there appears to be no way to break into the fortress White has constructed.

2...d2 (threatening 3...♗e2) **3 ♔f2 f4!**

White's position has become hopeless, since his king is cut off forever from the passed pawn.

4 b3 ab 5 ab ♗d3 6 g3 g5 7 h4 h6!

There is no need to calculate the variation 7...fg+ 8 ♔×g3 gh+ 9 ♔×h4 ♗e2, since the text provides a much simpler resolution.

8 hg hg 9 gf gf

White resigned, in view of 10 ♘d1 (10 ♔g2 ♗e2 11 ♔h3 ♗×f3−+) 10...♔e7 11 ♘b2 ♔d6 12 ♘d1 ♔c5 13 ♘b2 ♔b5 14 ♘d1 ♔b4−+.

Nebylitsyn - Galuzin
USSR 1969

7-31

B?

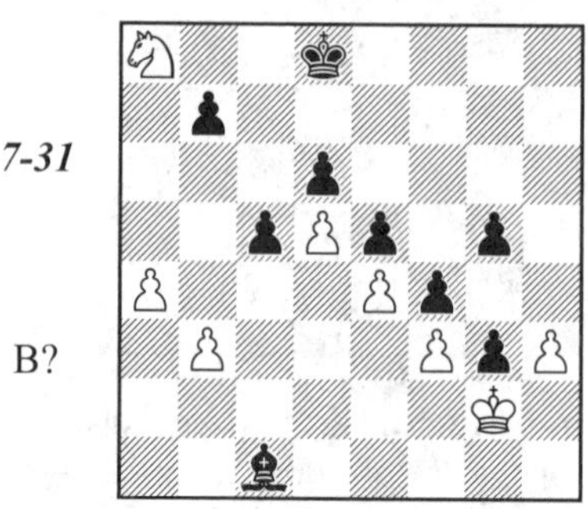

White's king is tied forever to the king's wing. The evaluation of this position hinges on whether the knight and pawns can erect an uncrossable barrier in the path of the enemy king.

1...c4?

A tempting, but incorrect pawn sacrifice. Black's goal is achieved by 1...♗d2! 2 ♘b6 ♗a5 3 ♘c4 ♗c7, when there appears to be nothing that can stop the transfer of the king to a6, followed by ...b7-b5. If 4 ♘a3, then 4...♔c8 5 ♘b5 ♗b8, followed by ...b7-b6 and ...♔b7-a6-a5.

2 bc ♗e3 3 a5 ♗d2

Or 3...♔c8 4 ♘b6+ ♔c7 5 ♘a8+ ♔b8 6 ♘b6 ♗d2 (6...♔a7 7 ♘c8+ ♔a6 8 ♘×d6; 6...♗c5 7 ♘d7+ ♔a7 8 ♘×c5 dc 9 ♔g1= ♔a6?? 10 d6+−) 7 a6, and we're back in the game continuation.

4 a6!!

After 4 ♘b6? ♗×a5 5 ♘a4 b6 (intending ...♔c7-b7-a6) 6 ♘b2 ♔c7 7 ♘d3 ♗d2! (it's important to prevent the maneuver ♘c1-b3) White loses.

4...ba (4...♔c8?? 5 a7 ♗e3 6 ♘b6+) **5 ♘b6 ♗e3 6 ♘a4 ♗d4 7 ♔f1 ♔e7**

The queenside barrier is erected, and the king can no longer penetrate here. Black therefore tries his last chance: marching his king to h4, in an attempt to place his opponent in zugzwang. True, White will then play the c4-c5 break; but then Black can sacrifice his bishop, and return his king to the queenside.

8 ♔g2 ♔f6 9 ♔f1 ♔g6 10 ♔g2 ♔h5 11 ♔f1 ♔h4 12 ♔g2 a5 13 c5! ♗×c5 14 ♘×c5 ♔h5

7-32

W

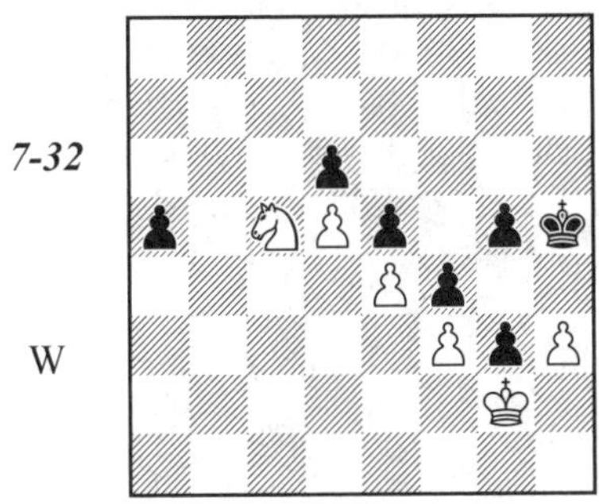

Here 15 ♘b7? a4 16 ♘×d6 a3–+ would be a mistake. White must set up a fresh barrier.

15 ♘a4 ♔g6 16 ♘c3 ♔g7 17 ♔f1 ♔f8 18 ♔g2 ♔e7 19 ♘b5! a4 20 ♔f1 ♔d8 21 ♔g2

Draw, since Black's king can advance no further.

Tragicomedies

Balashov - Smyslov
Tilburg 1977

7-33

B?

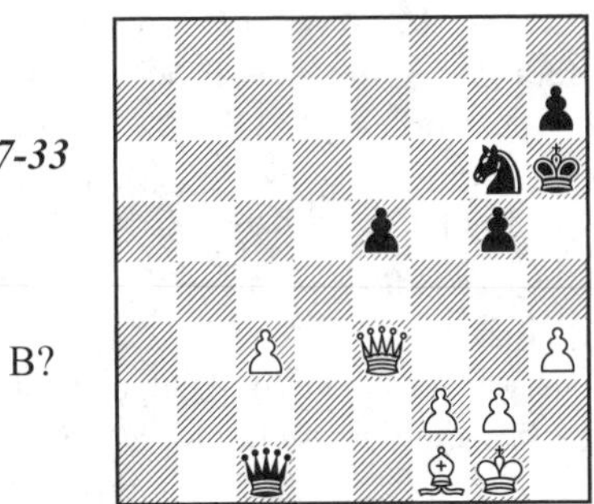

The game continuation was: **1...♕a1?? 2 g3** (△3 h4), and White won easily.

Black draws after 1...♕×e3! 2 fe ♘f8!. The knight moves inexorably to c5, from where it deprives the enemy king of the important squares d3 and e4 (barrier); after this, Black plays ...♔g7-f6 and ...h7-h6. 3 ♔f2 ♘d7 4 ♔f3 ♘c5 5 ♔g4 ♔g6 is not dangerous, since there can be no bishop check from d3. If White's king heads for the b-file, Black defends the knight with his king from d6.

Exercises

7-34

7/9
W?

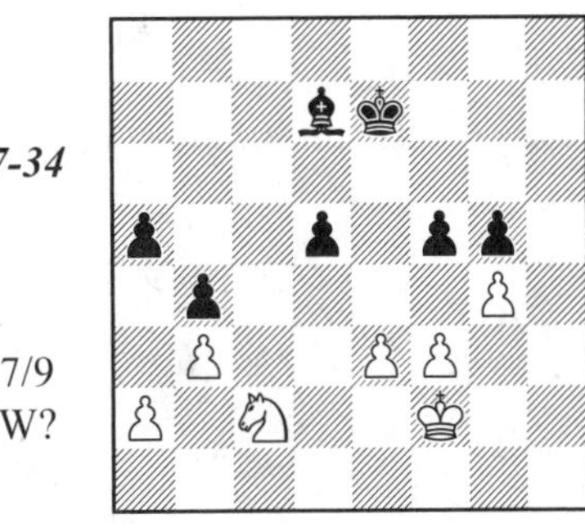

7-35

7/10
W?

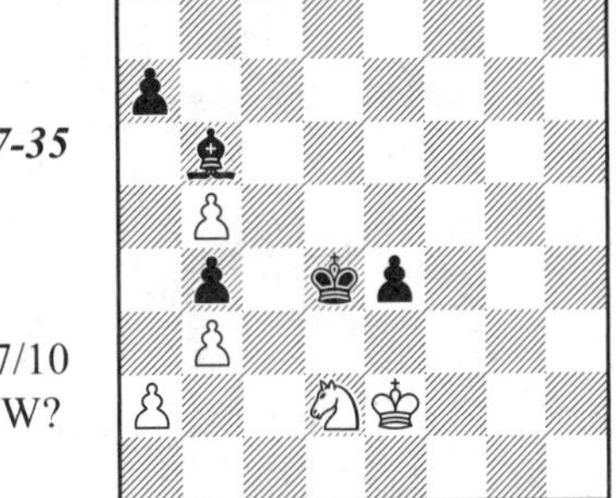

The Knight is Superior to the Bishop

Domination and Knight Forks

Nepomniaschy - Polovodin
Leningrad ch 1988

7-36

B?

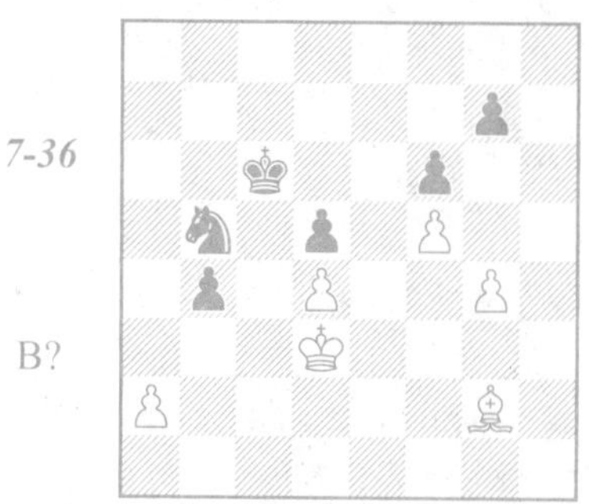

1...♘c3!

The key to the position is that on 2 a3 ♘e2!! decides: 3 ab (3 ♔×e2 ba) 3...♘f4+. Without this little combination, based upon a knight fork, there would be no win (with the bishop at f3, let's say, the position is drawn).

2 ♗f3 ♘×a2 3 ♗d1 b3!

Once again, Black has recourse to a fork, in order to advance his passed pawn (4 ♗×b3 ♘c1+ 5 ♔c3 ♘×b3 6 ♔×b3 ♔b5⊙ loses at once). On the other hand, 3...♔b5 4 ♗c2 ♘c1+ 5 ♔d2 b3 is strong, too.

4 ♔d2 b2 5 ♗c2 (5 ♔c2 ♘c3) **5...♘b4 6 ♗b1 ♔b6!**

An outstanding loss of tempo! The straightforward 6...♔b5? 7 ♔c3⊙ ♘c6 (7...♔a4 8 ♔×b2=) 8 ♗a2 ♘e7 9 ♔b3 leads to a draw.

7 ♔c3 ♔b5⊙ 8 ♔b3 (8 ♔×b2 ♔c4–+) **8...♘c6 9 ♔c3**

9 ♗d3+ ♔a5 10 ♔×b2 ♔b4–+ is no better.

9...♔a4 10 ♔×b2 (10 ♗a2 ♔a3) **10...♘b4!⊙** (but not 10...♘×d4? 11 ♗a2)

7-37

W

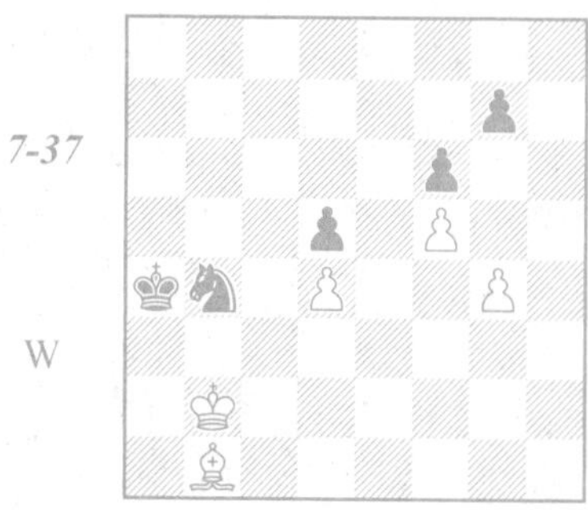

A picturesque domination of the knight over the bishop! Note that the knight takes away only three of the bishop's squares. Another is controlled by the d5-pawn (the pawns' placement on the squares of the same color as the opposing bishop is one of the means of restricting its mobility). But the chief blame for White's helplessness lies with his own kingside pawns, placed on squares the same color as his bishop, and turning it "bad."

11 ♔c3 ♔a3⊙ White resigned.

R. Réti, 1922

7-38

W?

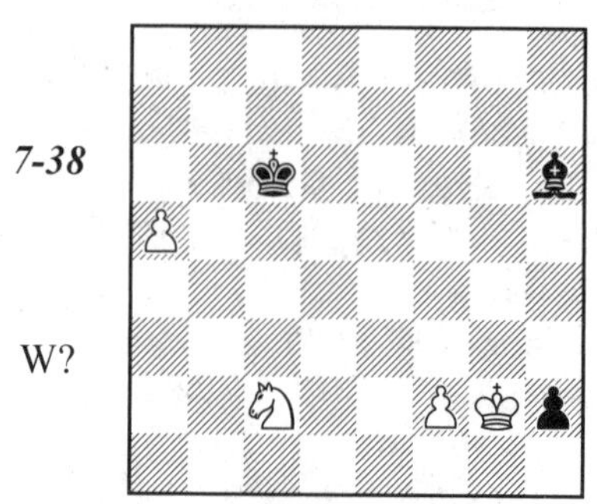

1 ♘d4+! ♔c5

On 1...♔b7 2 ♔×h2 ♔a6 3 ♘b3 ♗f4+ 4 ♔h3 ♔b5 5 ♔g4 ♗b8 6 f4 ♔b4 7 f5 (7 ♘d4? ♗×f4) 7...♔×b3 8 f6 ♔b4 9 f7 ♗d6 10 a6+– (pants) is decisive. In this line, Black needs just one tempo; therefore, with the king already at c5, this line would not work: 2 ♘b3+? ♔b5 3 ♔×h2 ♗f4+ 4 ♔h3 ♗b8 5 ♔g4 ♔b4=, or 2 ♔×h2? ♗f4+ 3 ♔h3 ♔×d4 4 a6 ♗b8=.

2 ♔h1!!⊙+–

There is not one square for the bishop where it would not be vulnerable to a knight fork.

Exercises

7-39

7/11
W?

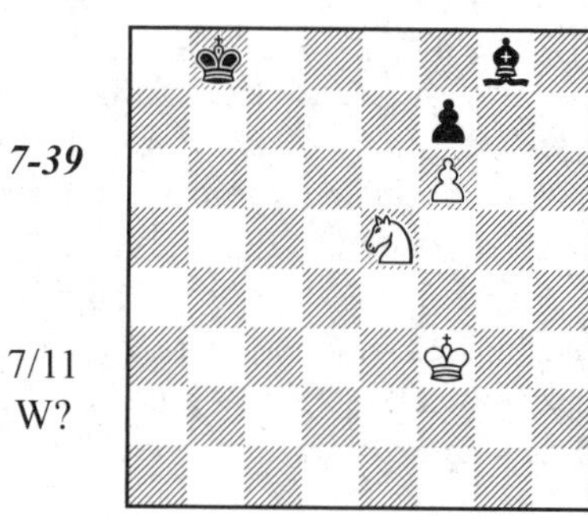

7-40

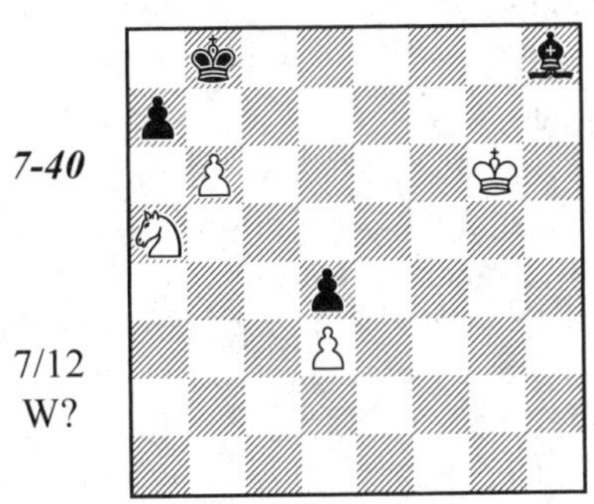

7/12
W?

Fixing the Pawns

We have already pointed out more than once how important it is to fix the enemy pawns on the same color squares as his bishop. Thus, we limit ourselves here to looking at two new examples.

Osnos - Bukhman
Leningrad ch tt 1968

7-41

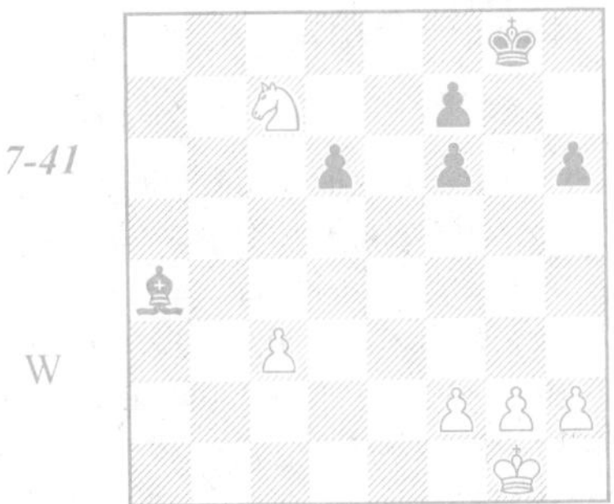

W

The advantage, of course, is White's, since all his opponent's pawns are isolated and weak. But this might not have been enough to win, had White not found the following maneuver, to force the d-pawn to advance onto a square the same color as his bishop.

1 ♘d5 ♔g7 2 ♘b6! ♗b3 3 ♘c8! d5 4 ♘e7 h5 5 h4!

One more pawn fixed on a light square.

5...♔f8 6 ♘f5 ♗c2 7 ♘e3 ♗b3 8 ♔h2 ♔e7 9 ♘f5+ ♔e6?? (a terrible blunder in a hopeless position) **10 ♘d4+** Black resigned.

Exercises

7-42

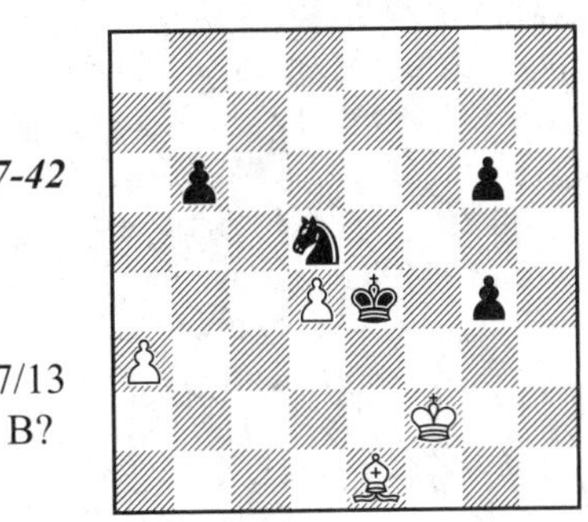

7/13
B?

Closed Position, Bad Bishop

In positions with pawn chains, the bishop has limited mobility, and therefore is sometimes weaker than the knight. The chief reason for a bishop being "bad" is that his own pawns are fixed on the same color squares as the bishop.

Zubarev - Alexandrov
Moscow 1915

7-43

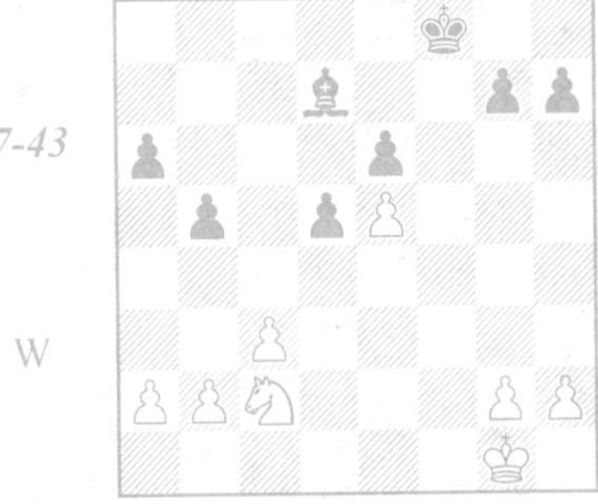

W

The exploitation of the knight's indisputable advantage over the bishop is uncomplicated, but quite instructive. First and foremost, ***the king must be made as active as possible,*** and there's an open road for him straight to c5.

1 ♔f2 ♔e7

On 1...♔f7 White neutralizes his opponent's activity on the kingside by erecting a ***barrier***: 2 ♔e2! ♔g6 3 ♘e3! ♔g5 4 g3!, after which the king continues its march to c5.

2 ♔e3 ♔d8 3 ♔d4 ♔c7 4 ♔c5 ♗c8

The next phase flows from the two-weaknesses principle. White cannot yet win on the queenside alone; therefore he sends the knight (via f4) to the kingside, to harry the enemy pawns. These in turn will have to be advanced, which will make them much weaker than they are in their initial positions.

5 ♘b4 ♗b7 6 g3

It's useful to deprive the opponent of tactical chances (such as ...d5-d4).

6...♗c8 7 ♘d3 ♗d7 8 ♘f4 (△9 ♘h5) **8...g6 9 ♘h3!** (△10 ♘g5) **9...h6 10 ♘f4 g5 11 ♘h5 ♗e8 12 ♘f6 ♗f7 13 ♘g4!**

One more black pawn must now be moved to the same color square as its bishop.

13...h5 14 ♘e3 ♗g6 (14...h4 15 gh gh 16 ♘g2; 14...g4 15 ♘g2 and 16 ♘f4) **15 h4!**

Fixing the pawns!

15...gh 16 gh (△♘g2-f4) **16...♗e4 17 ♘f1 ♗f3 18 ♘d2 ♗e2 19 ♘b3 ♗g4 20 ♘d4**⊙

The concluding phase of White's plan is to create a zugzwang position. For this the knight needs to be brought to f4, tying the bishop to the defense of two pawns at once.

20...♗h3 21 ♘e2 ♗f5 22 ♘f4 ♗g4 23 b4⊙

The end is achieved!

23...♔d7 24 ♔b6 ♗f3 25 ♔×a6 ♔c6 26 ♘×e6 Black resigned.

Karpov - Kasparov

Moscow wm (9) 1984/85

7-44

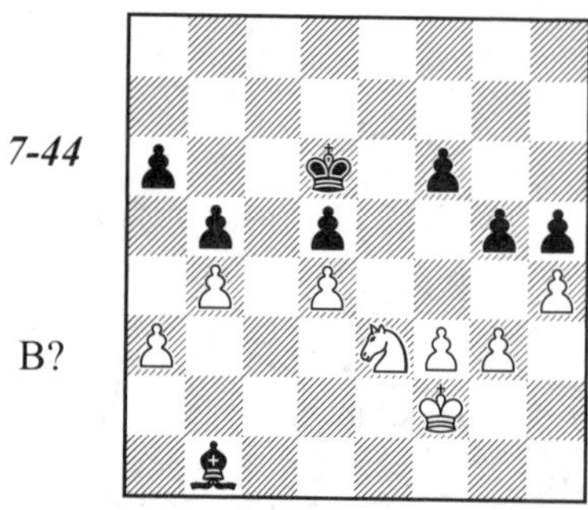

B?

White's task here is considerably more complicated. For the time being, the king has no route into the enemy camp; he must continue by "***widening the beachhead.***" The interfering kingside pawns can be removed in two ways: by g3-g4, or by exchanging on g5, followed by f3-f4.

The best defense was 1...♔e6!. On 2 hg fg 3 f4, Black can draw either by 3...gf 4 gf ♗g6, or by 3...g4!?. And after 2 g4 hg 3 hg, as John Nunn points out, Black must play 3...gf! (3...fg 4 ♘×g4, followed by ♔g3 and f3-f4, would be weaker) 4 ♔×f3 (4 gf ♗e4) 4...fg 5 ♔g4 ♔f6 6 ♘×d5+ ♔g6=. White keeps more practical chances by refraining from 3 hg in favor of 3 ♘×g4!? gh 4 ♔g2. And 2 ♔g2!? gh 3 g4! is also worth looking into.

1...gh?!

After home analysis, Kasparov decided to alter the pawn structure, judging (correctly) that after 2 gh ♗g6 White could no longer break through. Alas, neither he nor his trainers could foresee White's tremendous retort, securing his king a road into the enemy camp.

2 ♘g2!! hg+ (2...h3 3 ♘f4) **3 ♔×g3 ♔e6 4 ♘f4+ ♔f5 5 ♘×h5** (threatening ♘g7-e8-c7) **5...♔e6 6 ♘f4+ ♔d6 7 ♔g4 ♗c2 8 ♔h5 ♗d1 9 ♔g6**

7-45

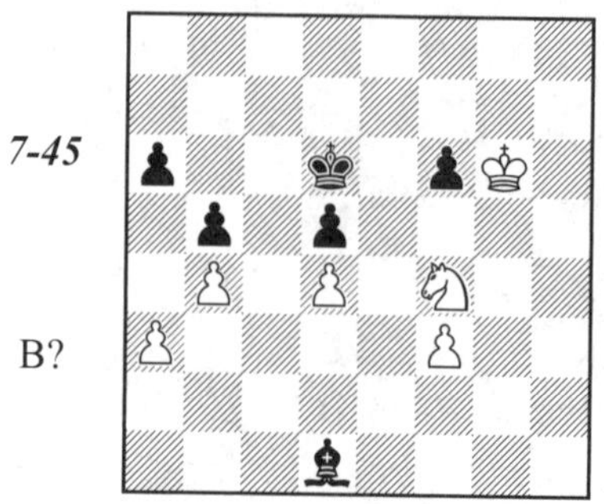

B?

9...♔e7!

9...♗×f3 10 ♔×f6 is absolutely hopeless. In such situations, we employ the ***steady driving off of the enemy king***: the knight goes to f5, and after the king's forced retreat (since the pawn endgame is lost), White's king goes to e5 or e7. Then the knight gives check again, etc.

10 ♘×d5+?

Unjustified greed – now Black gets the chance to activate his king, via the newly-opened d5-square.

10 ♘h5! ♗×f3 11 ♘×f6 was far stronger, for instance: 11...♔e6? 12 ♘e8 (△ 13 ♘c7+) 12...♔d7 (12...♗e4+ 13 ♔g5 ♔d7 14 ♘f6+ ♔e6 15 ♘×e4 de 16 ♔f4 ♔d5 17 ♔e3⊙ +–) 13 ♘g7 ♔e7 (otherwise 14 ♔f6) 14 ♔f5, and White wins.

The best defense would be: 11...♗e4+! 12 ♔g5 ♗d3!.

7-46

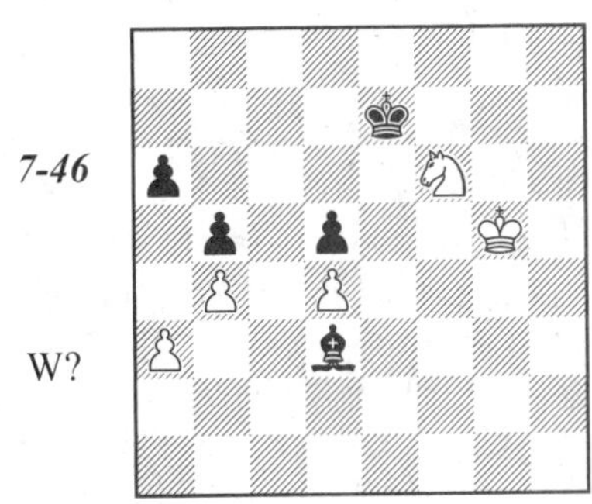

W?

White can't gain control of the f6- or e5-squares with his king. Capturing the pawn is also unconvincing: 13 ♘×d5+ ♔d6 14 ♘c3 (14 ♘e3 or 14 ♘f4 don't change anything) 14...♗f1! 15 ♔f4 ♗g2 16 ♔e3 (intending ♘e4-c5) 16...♗h3! 17 ♘e4+ ♔d5 18 ♘c5 ♗c8 19 ♔d3 ♗f5+ 20 ♔c3 ♗c8, and Black is apparently out of danger.

I thought that the variations I had found were sufficient to demonstrate the position was drawn. However, grandmaster Mihail Marin suggested an extremely dangerous plan: 13 ♘g4! with the idea of continuing ♘e5-c6-b8.

I attempted to hold the line by 13...♗f1! 14 ♘e5 ♗h3, and now 15 ♘c6+ ♔d6 16 ♘a5 (16 ♘b8?? ♗c8 and 17...♔c7) 16...♔e7! 17 ♘b3 ♔f7 18 ♘c5 ♗c8 is useless; while winning the d-pawn by 15 ♘g6+ ♔f7! 16 ♘f4 ♗c8 17 ♘×d5 ♔e6 would lead to the drawn position we already know. But Marin showed that White could play for zugzwang: 15 ♔g6! ♔e6!? 16 ♘c6 ♔d6 (16...♗f5+ 17 ♔g5 and 18 ♘b8) 17 ♘a5 ♔e7 18 ♘b3 ♗d7 19 ♘c5 ♗c8 20 ♔g7⊙ (but not 20 ♔g5 ♔f7) – Black loses the a6-pawn.

On the other hand, Black's resistance is not yet broken – he can lock the king in at g7 for a while by 20...♗f5 21 ♘×a6 ♗d3.

7-47

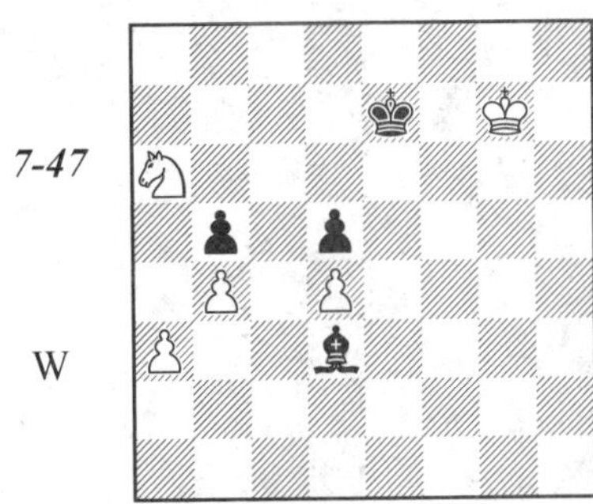

W

And White will not have an easy trip back: on ♔h6 there follows ...♔f6, and Black's king advances. White should continue 22 ♘b8 ♗c2 23 ♘c6+ ♔e6, when he has two ways to reach the goal:

a) 24 ♔f8 ♗g6 25 ♘a7 ♗d3 26 ♔e8 ♗e2 (26...♔f5 27 ♔d7 ♔e4 28 ♘c6+–) 27 ♘c6 ♔d6 28 ♘e7! (28 ♘e5 ♔e6 29 ♔d8 ♔f5 30 ♘c6 ♔e4 31 ♔c7 ♔d3! 32 ♔b6 ♔c4 would be weaker) 28...♔e6 29 ♔d8 ♔d6 (29...♗f1 30 ♘c6) 30 ♘f5+ ♔e6 31 ♘e3 ♔d6 32 ♔c8 ♔c6 33 ♔b8+–;

b) 24 ♘e5 ♔f5 (after the passive 24...♔e7 25 ♘g4, White brings the knight to e3, then returns the king unhindered to its own side, and begins preparations for a3-a4, bringing the knight to c3 at the right moment) 25 ♔f7 ♔e4 (25...♗d1 26 ♘c6! ♔e4 27 ♔e6) 26 ♘c6 ♗d1 27 ♔e6 (27 ♔e7? ♔d3 28 ♔d6 ♔c4 29 ♔e5 ♗f3 would be inexact) 27...♗h5 28 ♔d7! (but not 28 ♔d6? ♗e8 29 ♘e7 ♔×d4 30 ♘×d5 ♔c4=) 28...♗g6 (28...♗e2 29 ♔d6 and 30 ♔c5; 28...♔d3 29 a4!) 29 a4! ba 30 b5 a3 31 ♘b4+–.

10...♔e6

10...♔d6!? was more exact, leading, after 11 ♘c3 (or 11 ♘×f6 ♗×f3) 11...♗×f3 12 ♔×f6 ♗g2, to a position examined in the last note.

11 ♘c7+ ♔d7?

Now Black will be two pawns down. 11...♔d6 was stronger. If 12 ♘e8+, then 12...♔e7 (12...♔d5 13 f4 is inferior) 13 ♘×f6 ♗×f3 14 ♔f5 ♔d6 15 ♔f4 ♗g2 16 ♔e3 ♗h3, leading to roughly the same positions as after 10...♔d6. And on 12 ♘×a6 there follows 12...♗×f3 13 ♔×f6 ♔d5.

12 ♘×a6 ♗×f3 13 ♔×f6 ♔d6 14 ♔f5 ♔d5 15 ♔f4 ♗h1 16 ♔e3 ♔c4 17 ♘c5 ♗c6 18 ♘d3 ♗g2

18...♗e8!? 19 ♘e5+ ♔d5 was worth considering. Even with two extra pawns, the outcome is still far from clear - Black's king is too active. He must only be careful not to go after the a3-pawn (when White will lock him in by putting his own king at c3).

19 ♘e5+ ♔c3 (19...♔d5!?) **20 ♘g6 ♔c4 21 ♘e7**

7-48

B?

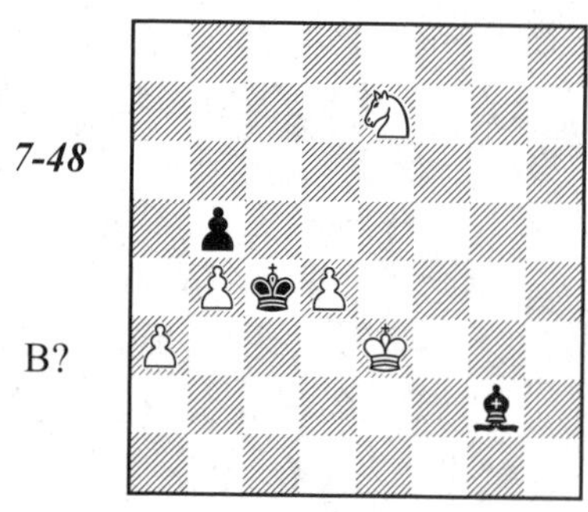

21...♗b7?

21...♔b3? would not have worked in view of 22 d5 ♔xa3 23 d6 ♗h3 24 ♘d5. However, it would be safer to keep the bishop in the lower half of the board: 21...♗h1! 22 ♘f5 (22 d5? ♗xd5=) 22...♔d5. Many analysts have diligently examined this position, but none have been able to find a win here. The move Black actually played is a decisive mistake.

22 ♘f5 ♗g2?

As Speelman and Tisdall indicated, neither 22...♔c3? 23 ♔f4! ♔b3 24 ♘e7 ♔xa3 25 d5, nor 22...♗c6? 23 ♔f4 ♔b3 24 ♔e5 ♔xa3 25 ♔d6 ♗e4 26 ♘g3 would save Black. He had to play 22...♔d5! 23 ♔d3 ♔e6!. For example: 24 ♘e3 (24 ♘g3 ♗g2 25 ♘e4 ♗f1+ 26 ♔e3 ♔d5 27 ♘c3+ ♔c4) 24...♗f3! (it's important to prevent White's knight from reaching c3).

7-49

W

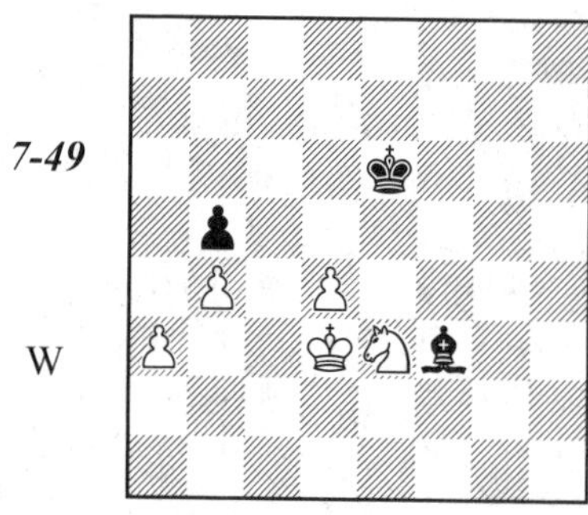

25 d5+ ♔e5! (but not 25...♗xd5? 26 ♔d4 △ 27 ♔c5) leads to nothing. On 25 ♔d2, intending to march the king into the enemy camp, Black responds, not with 25...♔f6? 26 ♘d1! and 27 ♘c3 (since Black no longer has 26...♔d5),but simply waits – when White's king reaches the 8th rank, the bishop will cut off its path to the queenside along the h3-c8 diagonal.

One interesting try is 25 ♔c3 ♔d6! (otherwise 26 ♔b3 followed by 27 a4 – Black can't reply 26...♗c6, because of 27 d5+!) 26 a4 (26 ♔b3 ♗c6 27 d5 ♗e8 28 ♔c3 ♔e5=) 26...ba 27 ♘c4+ ♔d5! (27...♔c7? 28 b5+–) 28 ♘b6+ (28 b5 ♗e2 29 b6 ♔c6 30 d5+ ♔b7 31 d6 ♔c6=) 28...♔c6 29 ♘xa4 ♔b5 (or 29...♗h5). Paradoxically, two extra pawns are insufficient to win here – White has no way to strengthen his position.

And nevertheless, Karsten Müller has found a subtle means of getting the knight to the key square c3. After 22...♔d5! 23 ♔d3 ♔e6!, White plays 24 ♘g7+! ♔d7 (24...♔d6 25 ♘e8+) 25 ♘h5. On 25...♔d6, there follows, not 26 ♘f4? ♗c8! and 27...♗f5+, but instead 26 ♘g3(f6)!, and then 27 ♘e4+ and 28 ♘c3. And on 25...♗g2 (hoping for 26 ♘g3? ♔e6! 27 ♘e4 ♗f1+ and 28...♔d5), then 26 ♘f4! ♗f1+ 27 ♔e4 ♔d6 28 ♔e3! (zugzwang) 28...♗c4 (28...♔c6 29 d5+ ♔d6 30 ♔d4 ♗c4 31 a4+–) 29 ♘e2+– (29...♔d5 30 ♘c3+, when the c4-square, which is needed by the king, is occupied by the bishop).

23 ♘d6+ ♔b3 24 ♘xb5 ♔a4 25 ♘d6
Black resigned.

Exercises

7-50

7/14
W?

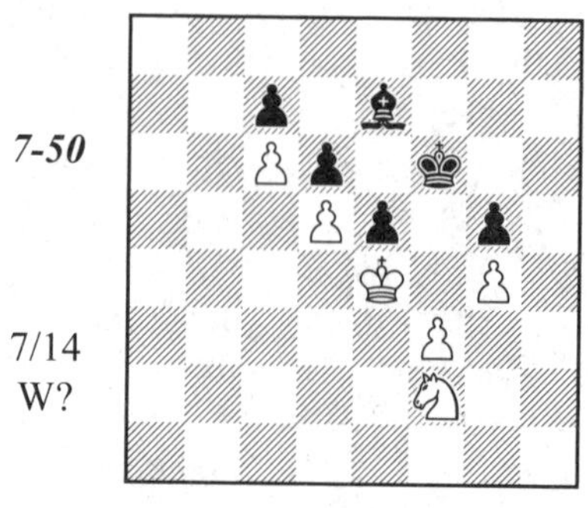

7-51

7/15
W?

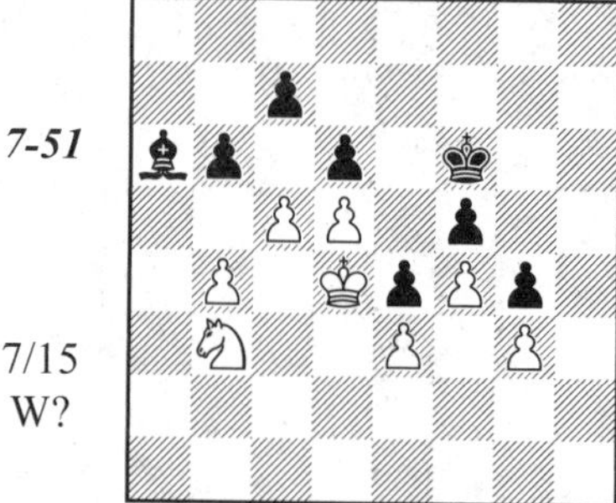

Chapter 8

ROOK VS. PAWNS

Practically all these endings are "rapid"; the outcome of the fight depends, as a rule, on a single tempo. We shall study typical techniques; mastering them does not free us from the necessity of deep and precise calculations, but makes this job much easier.

Rook vs. Pawn

"Moving Downstairs"

First let us look at the rarest case, when a pawn is stronger than a rook.

G. Barbier, F. Saavedra, 1895

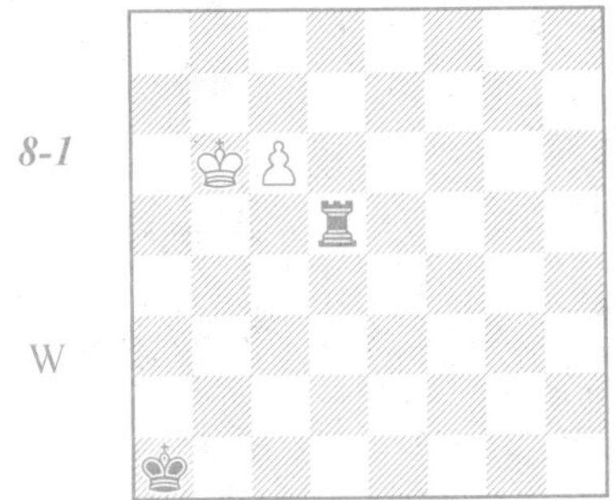

1 c7 ♖d6+ 2 ♔b5! (2 ♔c5? ♖d1) **2...♖d5+ 3 ♔b4 ♖d4+ 4 ♔b3 ♖d3+ 5 ♔c2**

This maneuver, which helps the king to avoid checks, is what we call "moving downstairs." However the fight is not over for the moment.

5...♖d4!

If 6 c8♕? then 6...♖c4+! 7 ♕×c4 stalemate.

6 c8♖!! (△ 7 ♖a8+) **6...♖a4 7 ♔b3!+–**

Cutting the King Off

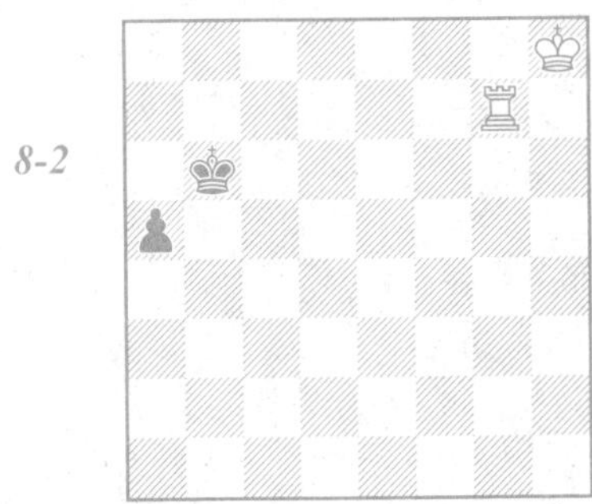

1 ♖g5!+–

When the black pawn reaches a3 it will be abolished by means of ♖g3 (the pawn may come even to a2 and then perish after ♖g1 followed by ♖a1).

With Black on move, after 1...♔b5(c5)! the position is drawn, because cutting the king off along the 4th rank brings nothing.

In the starting position, let us move the black king to c6 and the pawn to b5. The strongest move is still 1 ♖g5!, but Black can respond with 1...♔b6. However the king transfer to the a-file loses time, and its position is less favorable there than on the c-file (where it "gives a shoulder kick" to the rival king). After 2 ♔g7 ♔a5 3 ♔f6 White arrives in proper time to stop the pawn.

Pawn Promotion to a Knight

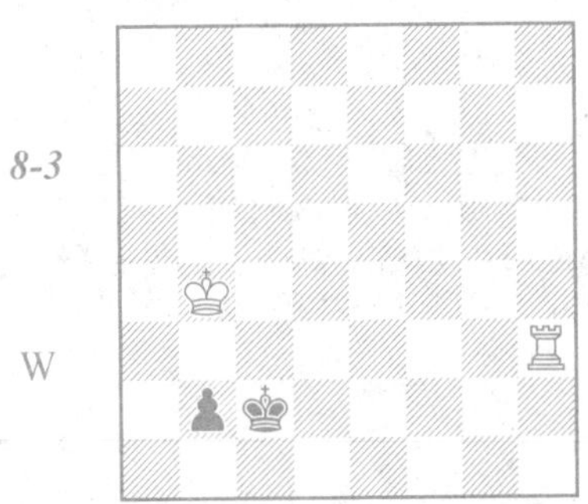

1 ♖h2+ ♔c1 2 ♔c3 b1♘+! 3 ♔d3 ♘a3 4 ♖a2 ♘b1! leads to a draw.

It is worth mentioning that the erroneous 4...♘b5? loses the knight. ***In rook-versus-knight endings, one should not separate the knight from the king.***

Black can also save himself by stalemate: 1...♔b1! 2 ♔b3 ♔a1! 3 ♖×b2. However, with a bishop or a central pawn his only drawing possibility is pawn-to-knight promotion.

If he has a rook pawn instead, this method does not work.

8-4

W

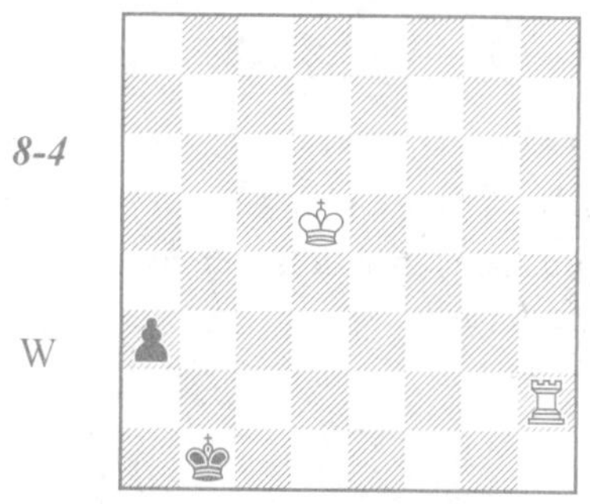

1 ♔c4 a2 2 ♔b3 a1♘+ 3 ♔c3⊙ +–

By the way, an additional pawn at b5 could not have helped Black.

8-5

W

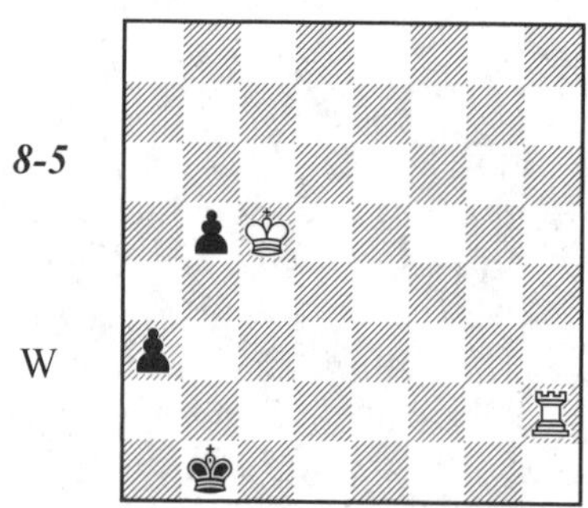

1 ♔b4 a2 2 ♔b3 a1♘+ 3 ♔c3 b4+ 4 ♔×b4 ♘c2+ 5 ♔c3 ♘e3 6 ♖h4! (another option is 6 ♔d3 ♘d5 7 ♖h4 ♔b2 8 ♖d4 and the knight, being separated from the king, will die soon) **6...♔a2** (6...♘d1+ 7 ♔d2 ♘b2 8 ♖b4 ♔a2 9 ♔c2 ♔a1 10 ♖b8; 6...♘d5+ 7 ♔b3 ♔c1 8 ♖c4+ ♔b1 9 ♖d4) **7 ♖a4+ ♔b1 8 ♖e4 ♘f5 9 ♖e5 ♘d6 10 ♔b3 ♔c1 11 ♖c5+ ♔b1 12 ♖d5+–.**

Stalemate

We have already seen a case of stalemate that has practical value (diagram 8-3). The following position is also worth keeping in mind.

8-6

B?

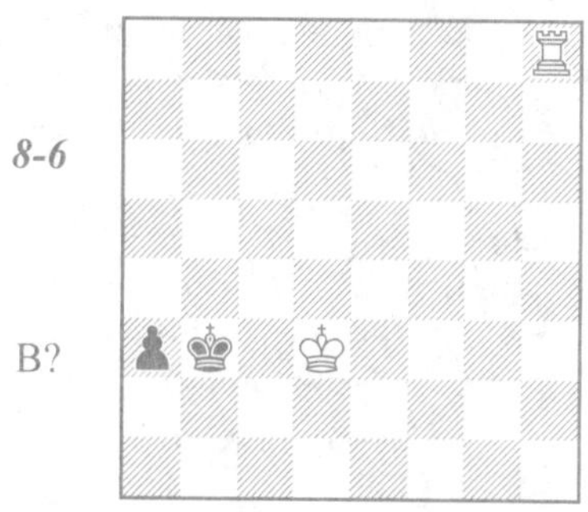

1...a2? 2 ♖b8+ ♔a3 3 ♔c2! a1♘+ 4 ♔c3 ♔a2 5 ♖b7⊙ is hopeless. Correct is **1...♔b2! 2 ♖b8+** (2 ♖h2+ ♔b3!, rather than 2...♔b1? 3 ♔c3) **2...♔c1! 3 ♖a8 ♔b2 4 ♔d2 a2 5 ♖b8+ ♔a1!**.

An Intermediate Check for a Gain of Tempo

Korchnoi - Kengis
Bern 1996

8-7

B

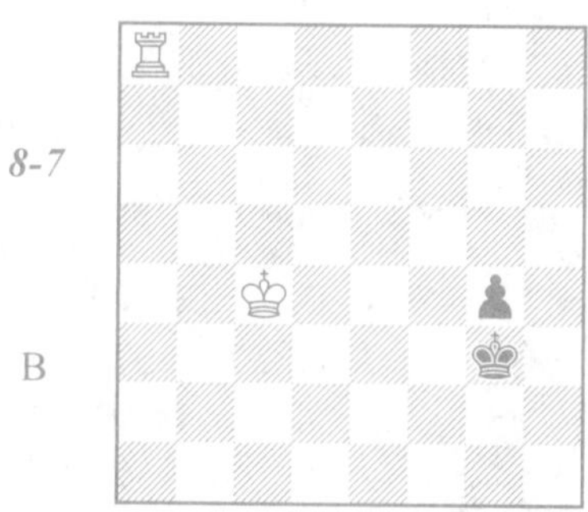

Kengis resigned in this position, depriving his opponent of the opportunity to demonstrate an exemplary winning solution:

1...♔f2 2 ♖f8+!

2 ♔d3? g3 3 ♖f8+ ♔e1! leads only to a draw.

2...♔e2 3 ♖g8! ♔f3

Because of the intermediate check, White succeeded in driving the opposite king back one square, from f2 to f3.

4 ♔d3 g3 5 ♖f8+ ♔g2 6 ♔e2+–.

Shouldering

8-8

W

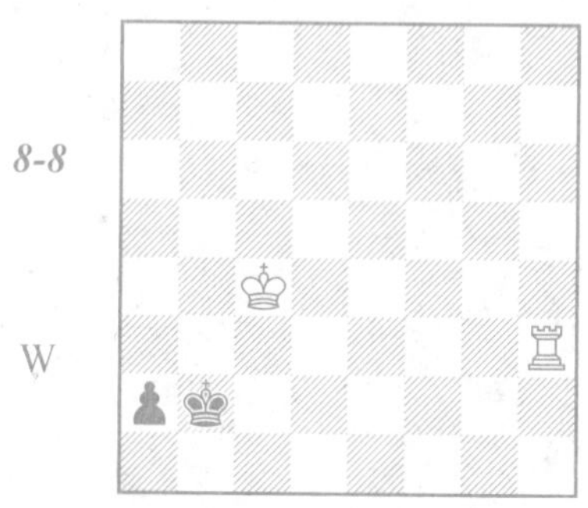

1 ♖h2+ ♔a3!

Black achieves a draw by not allowing the white king to approach the pawn. 1...♔b1? is erroneous in view of 2 ♔b3 a1♘+ 3 ♔c3.

Let us look at a slightly more complicated case in the following diagram.

I. Maizelis, 1950

8-9

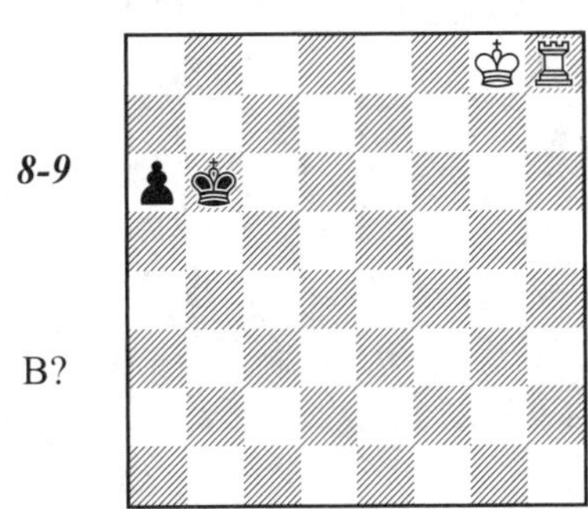

B?

1...a5? is bad because of 2 ♖h5! (cutting the king off). However 1...♔b5? 2 ♔f7 a5 3 ♔e6 a4 4 ♔d5 is no better.

Only **1...♔c5!** holds. Black does not allow the white king to approach his pawn.

Outflanking

Shouldering and outflanking ideas are distinctly represented in the following famous endgame study.

R. Réti, 1928

8-10

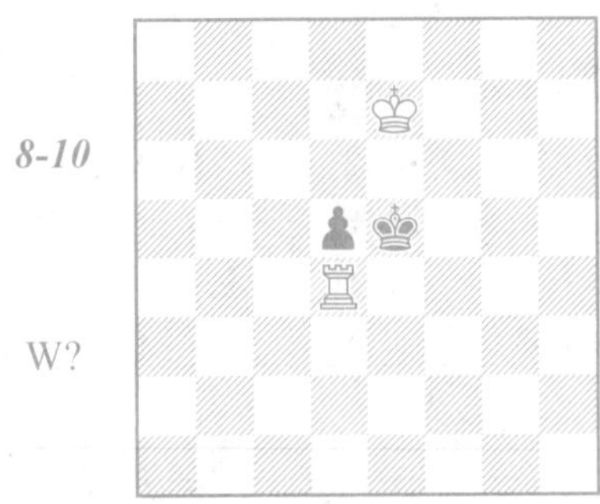

W?

1 ♖d2(d3)!! d4 2 ♖d1! ♔d5 3 ♔d7!

Black is in zugzwang: if 3...♔c4, then 4 ♔e6 and if 3...♔e4, 4 ♔c6.

1 ♖d1? is erroneous: 1...d4 2 ♔d7 (2 ♔f7 ♔e4 3 ♔e6 d3) 2...♔d5! (Black prevents an outflanking) 3 ♔c7 ♔c5! (3...♔c4? 4 ♔d6! d3 5 ♔e5), and it is White who has fallen into zugzwang.

Tragicomedies

Neumann – Steinitz
Baden-Baden 1870

8-11

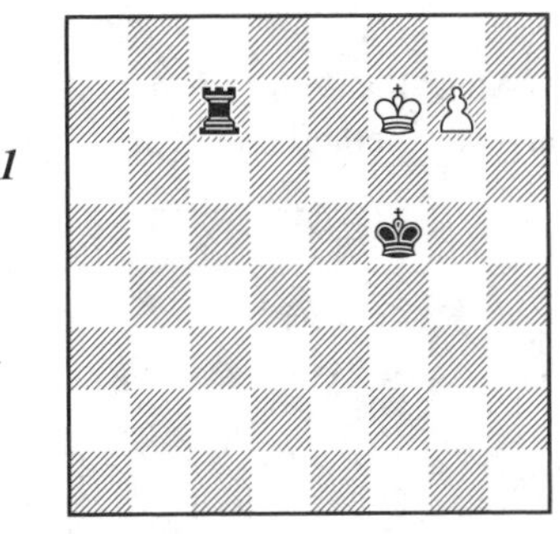

W

1 ♔f8

The simplest way is 1 ♔g8! ♔g6 2 ♔h8=.

1...♔f6 2 g8♘+! ♔e6 3 ♘h6 ♖h7 4 ♘g4??

As we already know, after 4 ♘g8! the game would have been drawn. Now White is lost.

4...♖h4

4...♖h3! could have won immediately.

5 ♘e3 (5 ♘f2 ♖f4+) **5...♖e4 6 ♘d1 ♖f4+ 7 ♔g7 ♖f3 8 ♔g6**

8 ♘b2 ♔d5 9 ♘a4 ♖b3 △ 10...♔d4 and 11...♖b4 makes no difference.

8...♔e5 9 ♔g5 ♔d4 10 ♔g4 ♖f1 11 ♘b2 ♖b1 12 ♘a4 ♖b4 White resigned.

Fries-Nielsen – Plachetka
Rimavska Sobota 1991

8-12

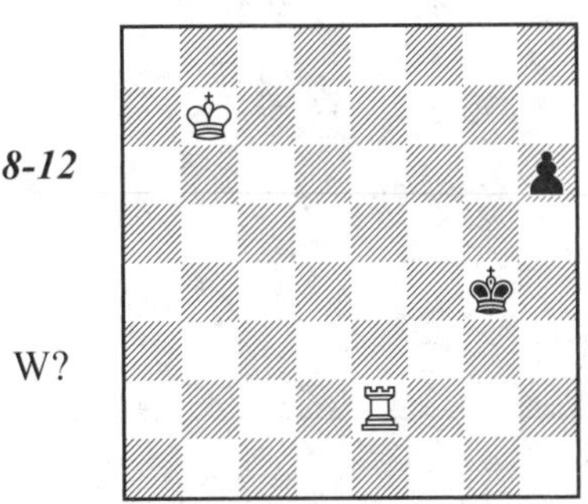

W?

The actual continuation was **1 ♔c6? h5= 2 ♔d5 h4 3 ♔e4 h3 4 ♔e3 ♔g3 5 ♖e1 h2 6 ♔e2 ♔g2 7 ♖h1 ♔×h1 8 ♔f1** Draw.

1 ♖e8? is no better: 1...h5 2 ♖g8+ ♔f3 3 ♖h8 ♔g4 4 ♔c6 h4 5 ♔d5 h3 6 ♔e4 ♔g3 7 ♔e3 ♔g2! (rather than 7...h2?? 8 ♖g8+ ♔h3 9 ♔f2! h1♘+ 10 ♔f3 ♔h2 11 ♖g7⊙) 8 ♖g8+ ♔f1!= or 8 ♔e2 h2 9 ♖g8+ ♔h1!=.

White should have gained a tempo by means of the intermediate check: 1 ♖g2+! ♔f4 (after

1...♔h3 2 ♖g8 h5 3 ♔c6 h4 4 ♔d5+− the black king, pressed to the edge of the board, is placed extremely badly) 2 ♖h2! ♔g5 3 ♔c6 h5 4 ♔d5 h4 5 ♔e4 ♔g4 6 ♖g2+ ♔h3 7 ♖g8+−.

Alekhine - Bogoljubow
Germany/The Netherlands wm (19) 1929

8-13

B?

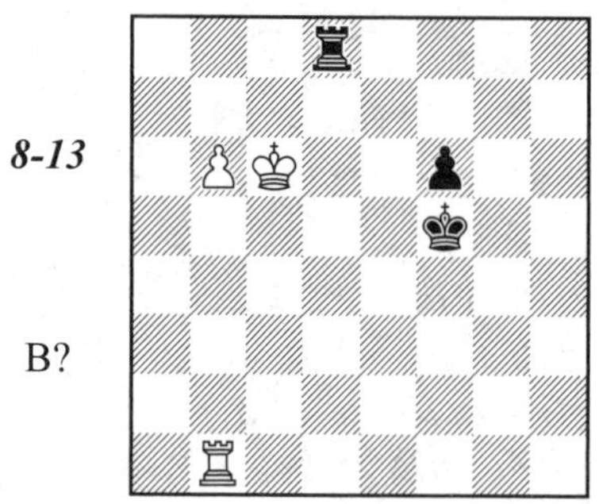

The world championship challenger played **1...♔g4??** and resigned after **2 b7 f5 3 b8♕ ♖×b8 4 ♖×b8 f4 5 ♔d5 f3 6 ♔e4 f2 7 ♖f8 ♔g3 8 ♔e3**

He should have applied the shouldering method: 1...♔e4!. It is easy to see that in this case the position would have been drawish: the black king prevents his opponent from getting to the black pawn in time.

Exercises

8-14

8-1
W?

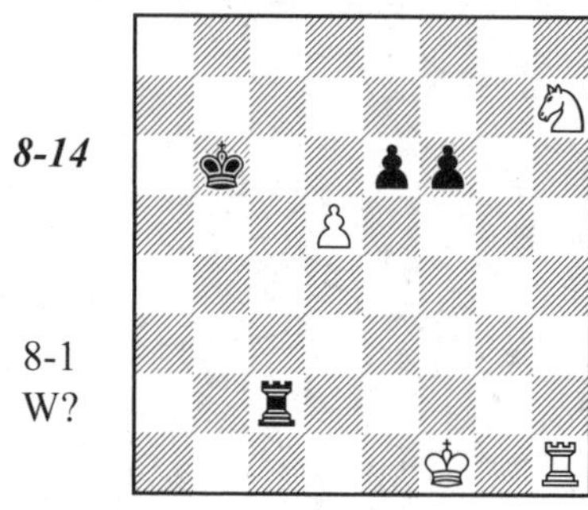

8-15

8-2
W?

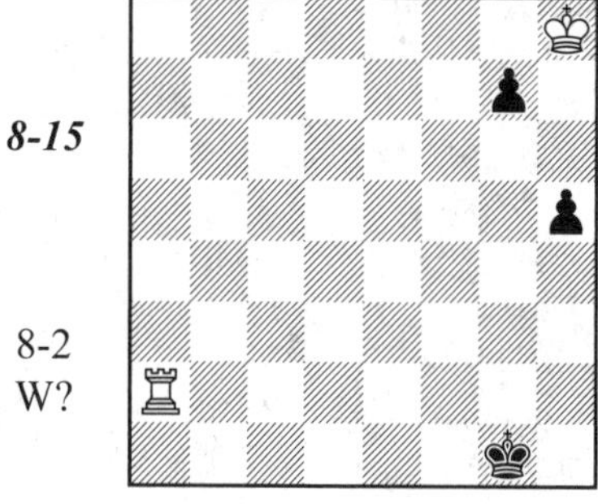

8-16

8-3
W?

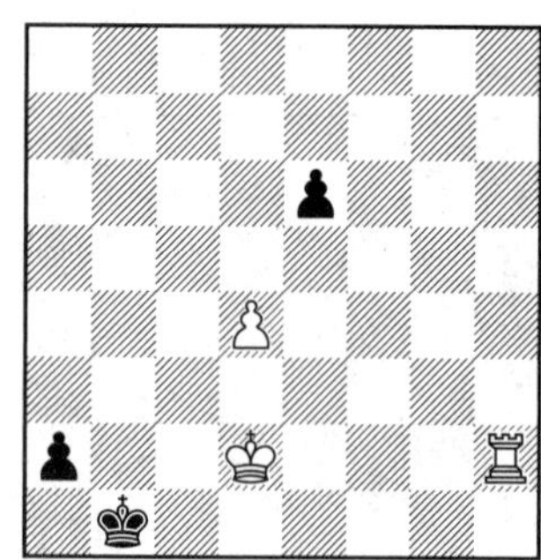

8-17

8-4
W?

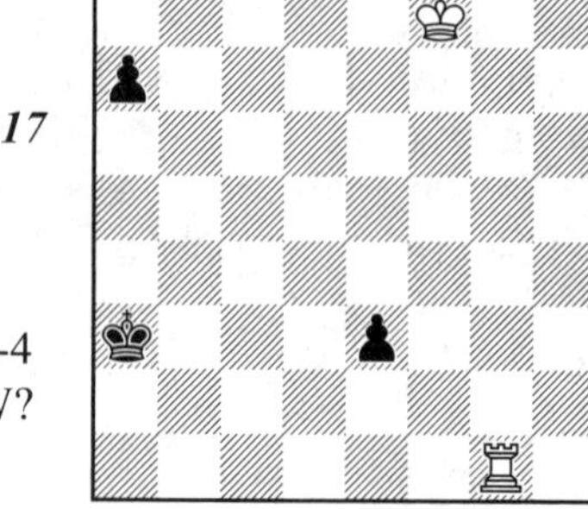

8-18

8-5
W?

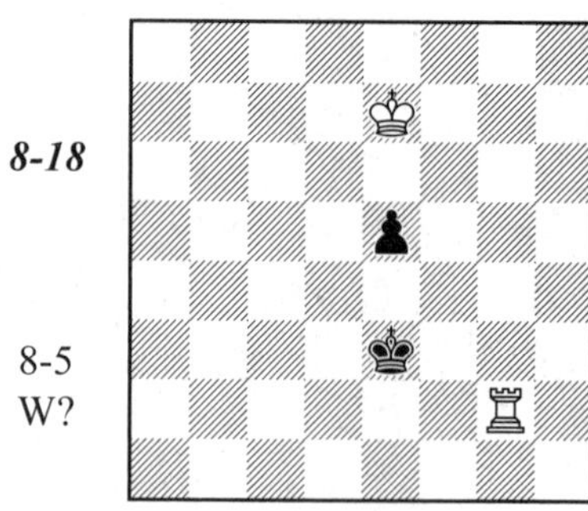

8-19

8-6
W?/Play

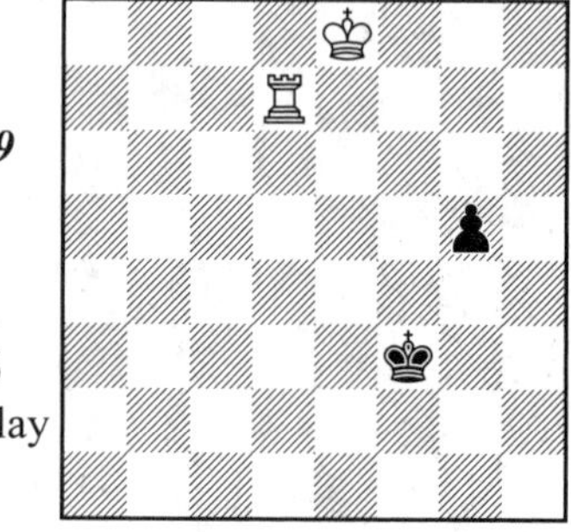

Rook vs. Connected Pawns

If two black pawns are placed on the 3rd rank, or one pawn has reached the 2nd rank while the other is on the 4th rank, a rook cannot stop them. Sometimes, however, White can save himself by creating ***checkmate threats***, when the black king is pressed to an edge of the board.

B. Horwitz, J. Kling, 1851

8-20

W

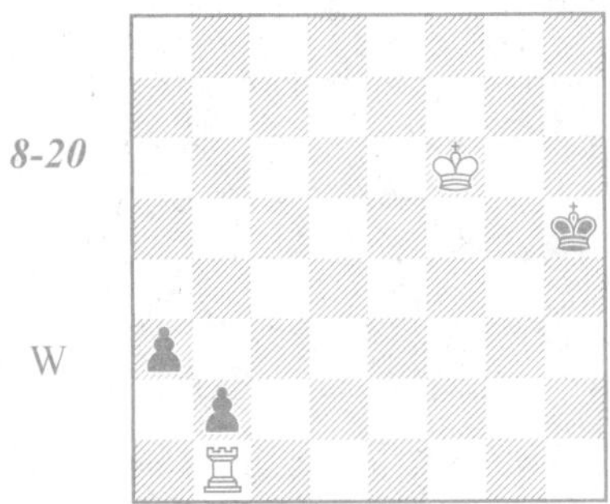

1 ♔f5 ♔h4 2 ♔f4 ♔h3 3 ♔f3 ♔h2 4 ♔e3! ♔g2

Or 4...♔g3 5 ♖g1+ ♔h4 6 ♔f4 ♔h3 7 ♔f3, and here 7...♔h2?? 8 ♖b1 even loses for Black in view of zugzwang.

5 ♔d3 ♔f3 6 ♔c3 a2 7 ♔×b2 (or 7 ♖f1+) with a draw.

The following simple example demonstrates several very important practical ideas.

Topalov – Beliavsky
Linares 1995

8-21

W?

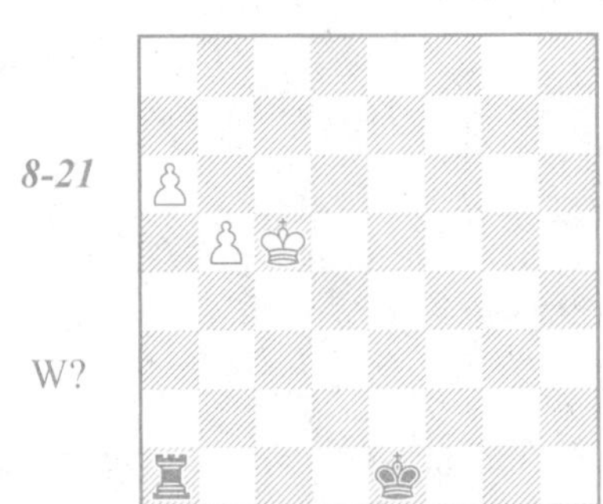

After 1 b6?, 1...♖×a6? 2 b7 ♖a5+ 3 ♔c4 etc., loses (moving downstairs). Black holds with the ***intermediate check prior to the capture of the pawn:*** 1...♖a5+!=.

1 ♔b6 ♔d2

If 2 a7? now, then 2...♔c3 3 ♔b7 ♔b4 4 b6 ♔b5=. Here we observe "***the tail-hook***" again; the techniques that we know from bishop versus pawn endings (diagram 4-29).

2 ♔a7!

Black resigned in view of 2...♔c3 3 b6 ♔c4 4 b7 ♖b1 5 b8♕ ♖×b8 6 ♔×b8.

We call this method "***a change of the leader***." Why does White push the less advanced b-pawn? First of all, because the rook, being placed on another file, does not prevent its march. In addition to it, the a-pawn that remains on the board after gaining the rook is more remote from the black king, so its "tail holding" will be more difficult.

In a battle against two connected passed pawns, ***the best position for the rook is behind the more advanced pawn.***

8-22

W?

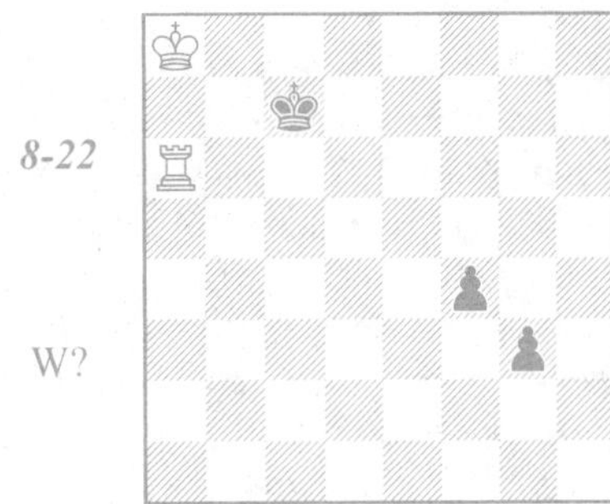

1 ♖g6! ♔d7 2 ♖g4! g2! 3 ♖×g2 ♔e6 4 ♖g5! and White wins because the black king is cut off from the pawn along the 5th rank.

Sozin demonstrated a similar position in 1931, with the only difference that the white king stood on a7. In that case, after 1 ♖g6! ♔d7 an alternative solution occurs: 2 ♔b6 ♔e7 3 ♔c5 ♔f7 4 ♖g4 ♔f6 5 ♔d4! (5 ♖×f4+? ♔g5 6 ♖f8 ♔g4 7 ♔d4 g2=) 5...♔f5 6 ♖g8+–.

This line does not work when the king is placed on a8: 1 ♖g6! ♔d7 2 ♔b7? ♔e7 3 ♔c6 ♔f7 4 ♖g4 ♔f6 5 ♔d5 ♔f5 6 ♖g8 f3! 7 ♔d4 (7 ♖×g3 ♔f4 8 ♖g8 f2=; 7 ♖f8+ ♔g4 8 ♔e4 f2 9 ♔e3 ♔h3=) 7...f2 8 ♔e3 f1♘+! with a draw.

It should be noticed that the rook should be placed in the rear of the more advanced pawn similarly, even when other forces conduct the fight.

Alekhine - Tartakower
Vienna 1922

8-23

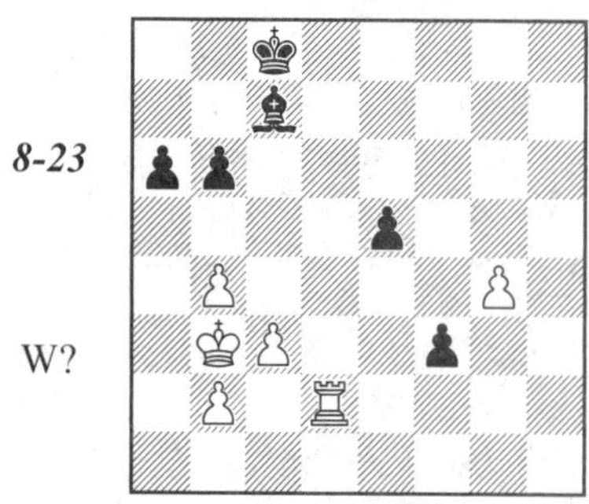

W?

Alekhine analyzes the natural continuations 1 ♔c2, 1 ♔c4, 1 g5, 1 ♖h2 and shows that all of them are good enough at best for a draw. But his beautiful concept wins:

1 ♖d5!!

"The variations springing from this rather unlikely move (it attacks one solidly defended pawn and allows the immediate advance of the other) are quite simple when we have descried the basic idea - *the black pawns are inoffensive*: 1) *When they occupy squares of the same color as their bishop*, for in that case White's king can hold them back without difficulty, by occupying the appropriate white squares, e.g. 1...f2 2 ♖d1 e4 3 ♔c2 ♗f4 4 ♖f1 followed by 5 ♔d1; and 2) *When the rook can be posted behind them, but without loss of time*, e.g. 1...e4 2 ♖f5 ♗g3 3 g5 e3 4 ♖xf3 e2 5 ♖e3" (Alekhine).

Tragicomedies

Arulaid – Gurgenidze
Lugansk tt 1956

8-24

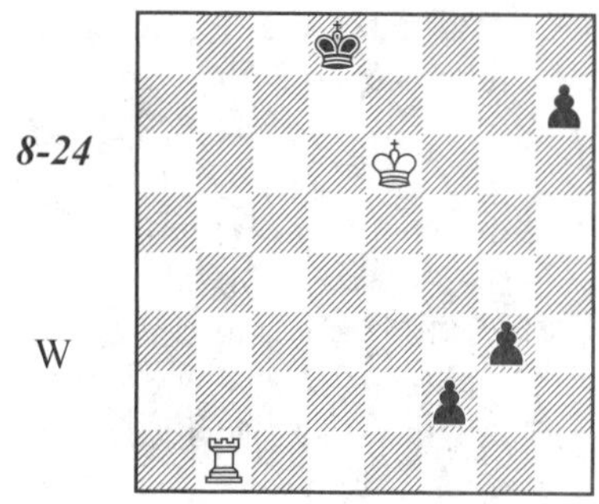

W

The game was adjourned and White resigned without resuming the play. However the adjourned position was drawish, White could have held it by means of checkmate threats:

1 ♔d6! ♔c8 (1...♔e8 2 ♔e6 ♔f8 3 ♔f6=) **2 ♖c1+ ♔b7 3 ♖b1+ ♔a6 4 ♔c6 ♔a5 5 ♔c5 ♔a4 6 ♔c4 ♔a3 7 ♔c3 ♔a2 8 ♖f1 h5 9 ♔d3=** △ 10 ♔e3; 10 ♖xf2.

Fridstein – Lutikov
USSR ch tt, Riga 1954

8-25

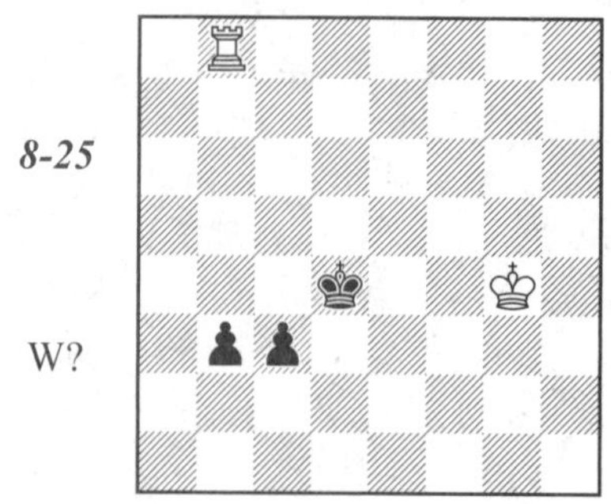

W?

Another case of a totally groundless capitulation. The intermediate check **1 ♖b4+!** led to a draw.

Maróczy – Tarrasch
San Sebastian 1911

8-26

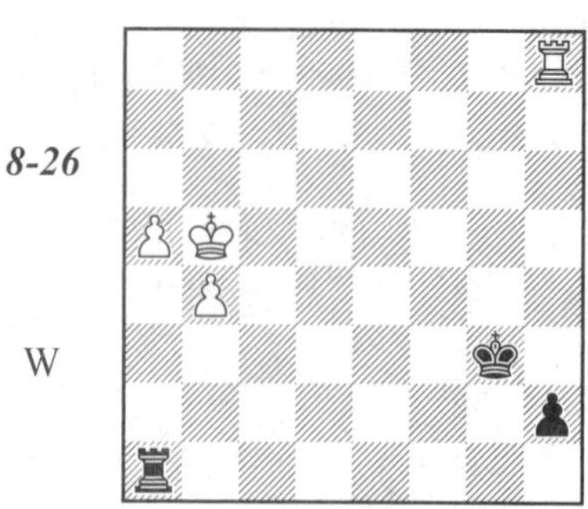

W

After 1 ♖xh2! ♔xh2, an immediate "change of the leader" wins: 2 ♔a6! ♔g3 3 b5 ♔f4 4 b6 ♔e5 5 b7 ♖b1 6 ♔a7 ♔d6 7 b8♕+ ♖xb8 8 ♔xb8+-. The move 2 a6? misses the win: 2...♔g3 3 ♔b6 ♔f4 4 b5 ♔e5 5 ♔a7 (5 a7 ♔d5 6 ♔b7 ♔c5=) 5...♔d6 6 b6 ♖b1! 7 ♔b7 (7 b7 ♔c7) 7...♔c5=.

White could also have played 1 ♔a6! ♖a4 (1...h1♕ 2 ♖xh1 ♖xh1 3 b5) 2 ♖xh2 ♖xb4 3 ♖h5 △ 4 ♖b5+-.

The actual continuation was **1 ♔c6?? ♖c1+ 2 ♔b6 ♖c4!** (△ 3...♖h4) **3 ♖xh2 ♖xb4+ 4 ♔c5 ♖a4 5 ♔b5 ♖xa5+** Draw.

Penrose – Perkins
Great Britain ch, Brighton 1972

8-27

B?

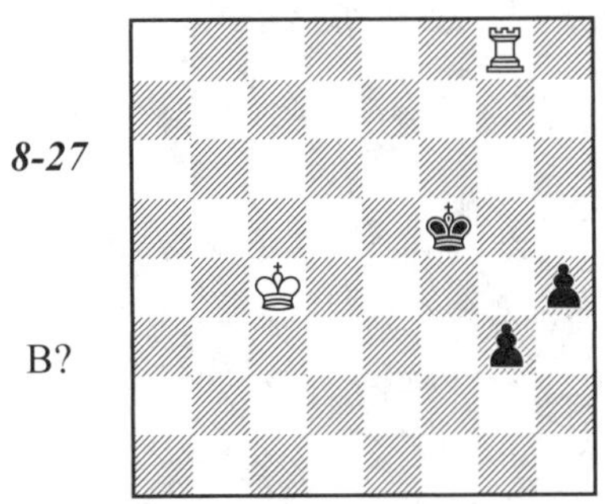

This position is evaluated as drawn in *Encyclopaedia of Chess Endings*. In fact Black can win it rather simply by means of shouldering followed by moving downstairs.

1...♔e4! 2 ♖g4+ (2 ♖g7 ♔f3−+) 2...♔f3 3 ♖×h4 g2 4 ♖h3+ ♔f4 5 ♖h4+ ♔f5 6 ♖h5+ ♔f6 7 ♖h6+ ♔g7−+.

The game continued **1...♔f4? 2 ♔d4 ♔f3** (2...h3 3 ♖f8+ ♔g4 4 ♔e4 h2 5 ♖g8+ ♔h3 6 ♔f4=) **3 ♖f8+ ♔g2 4 ♔e3 h3 5 ♖h8 ♔h2** (5...h2 6 ♔f4=) **6 ♖g8! g2 7 ♔f2 ♔h1 8 ♖g7 h2 9 ♖×g2** Draw.

A. Petrosian – Tseshkovsky
USSR ch (1), Minsk 1976

8-28

B?

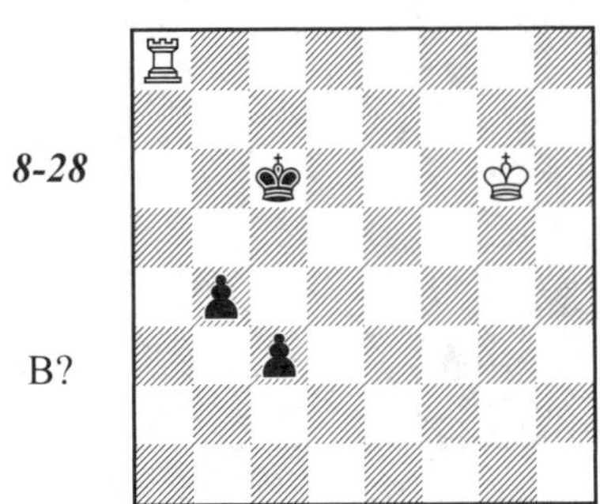

Black has an elementary win: 1...♔d7! (threatening with 2...c2 or 2...b3) 2 ♖a7+ ♔d6 3 ♖a6+ ♔d5, etc. He played less precisely:

1...♔d5?! 2 ♔f5

In this position, the game was adjourned. Later in a hotel room, Petrosian demonstrated the following continuation to his rival: 2...b3 (2...c2 3 ♖d8+ ♔c4 4 ♔e4!=) 3 ♖d8+ ♔c4 4 ♔e4, and showed him a volume of *Chess Endings* edited by Averbakh where the final position is evaluated as drawn in connection with the line 4...b2 5 ♖c8+ ♔b3 6 ♖b8+ ♔c2 7 ♔d4=.

The opponent's arguments and the authority of the book convinced Tseshkovsky, and he accepted the proposed draw.

It was however an unfounded decision! Black's play can be improved by means of 3...♔c5! (instead of 3...♔c4?) 4 ♖c8+ (4 ♔e4 b2 5 ♖c8+ ♔d6−+) 4...♔d4 5 ♖d8+ ♔e3 6 ♖b8 b2. Curiously enough, the resulting position is examined on the same page of the same book and, as Tarrasch proved in 1912, it is won!

7 ♔e5 ♔f3! (rather than 7...c2? 8 ♖b3+) 8 ♔f5 (8 ♖b3 ♔g4−+) 8...♔e2! 9 ♔e4 ♔d1 10 ♔d3 c2 11 ♖h8 c1♘+! and 12...b1♕.

Exercises

8-29

8-7
W?

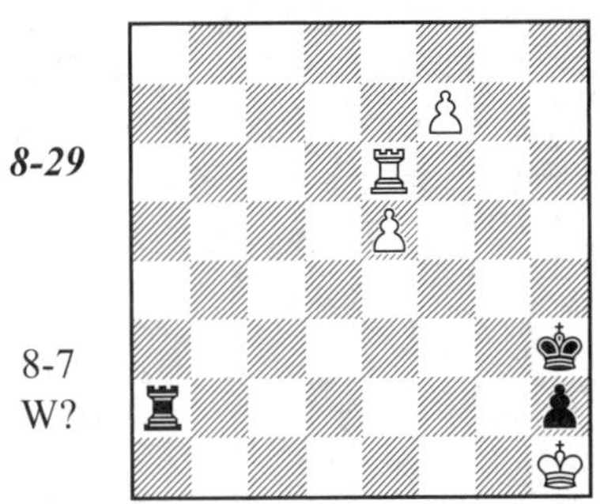

8-30

8-8
W?

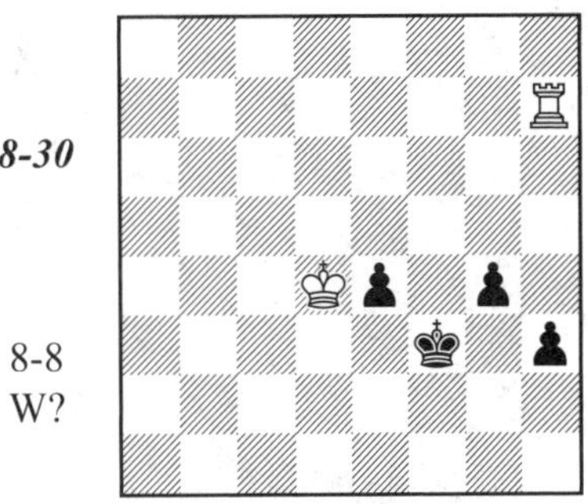

8-31

8-9
W?

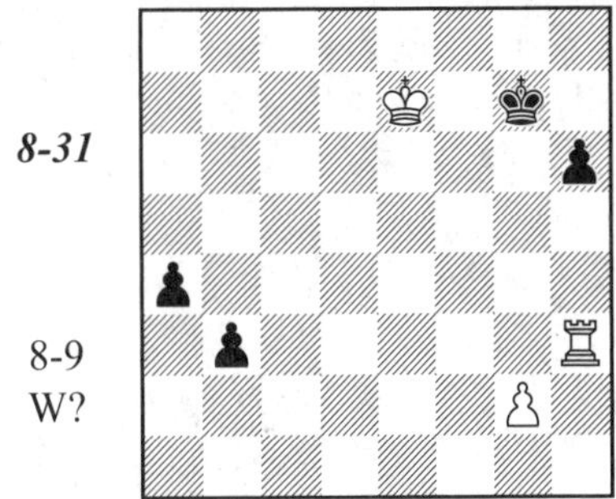

Rook vs. Separated Pawns

8-32

W

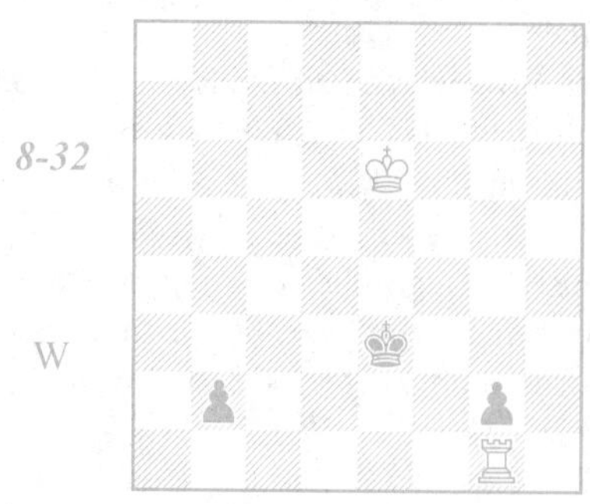

If four files separate the pawns, then the rook can stop them without help of its king.

1 ♖b1! (parrying the threat 1...♔f2) **1...♔d3** (△ 2...♔c2) **2 ♖g1!=**

Move the b2-pawn to c2. Now the position is lost (1 ♖c1 ♔d2–+).

8-33

B

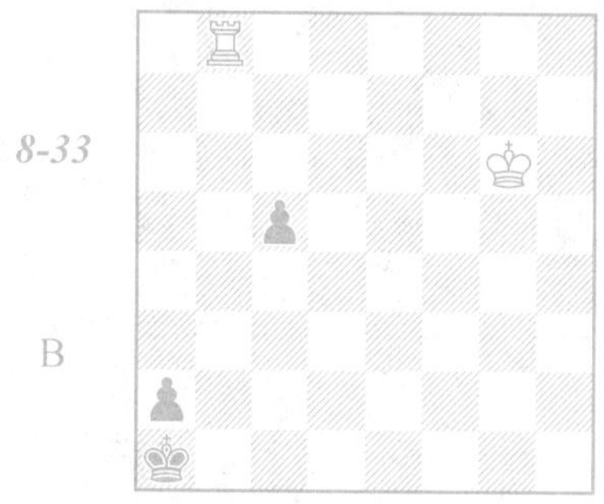

1...c4 2 ♔f5

2 ♖c8 c3!, and if 3 ♖×c3, then ...♔b2 and the a-pawn promotes.

2...c3 3 ♖c8

After 3 ♔e4 c2 4 ♖c8 ♔b2 5 ♖b8+ ♔c3 6 ♖c8+ both 6...♔d2 and 6...♔b4 win.

3...♔b2 4 ♖b8+ ♔c2(a3) 5 ♖a8 ♔b3 6 ♖b8+ ♔c4 7 ♖a8 c2–+.

This is perhaps all one should remember about this sort of position. Some additional ideas are shown to you in the exercises for this section.

Exercises

8-34

8-10
W?

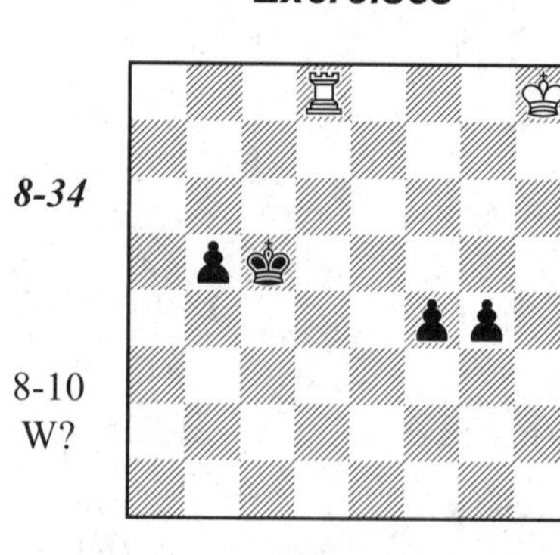

8-35

8-11
W?

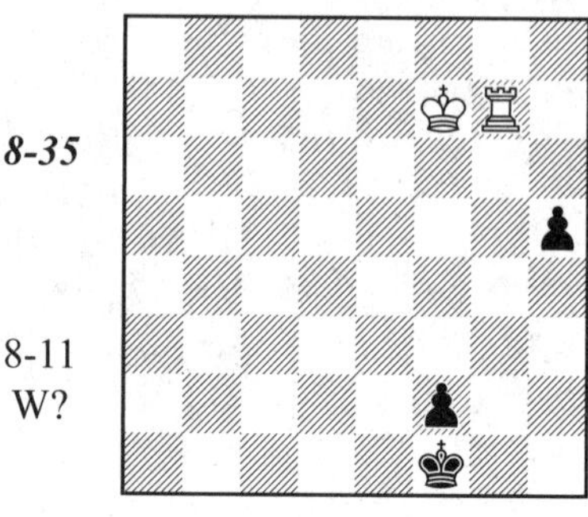

8-36

8-12
W?

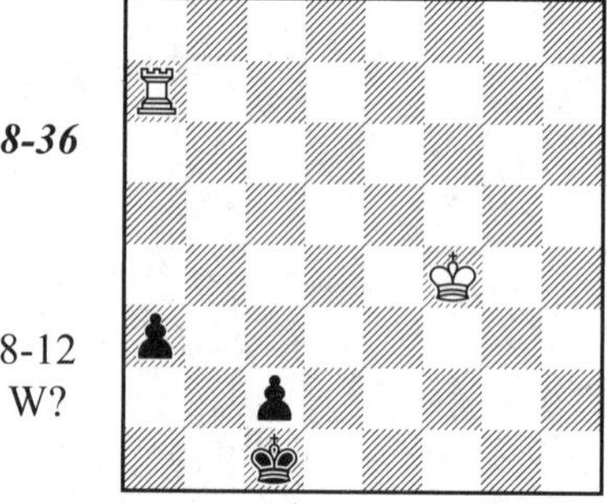

8-37

8-13
W?

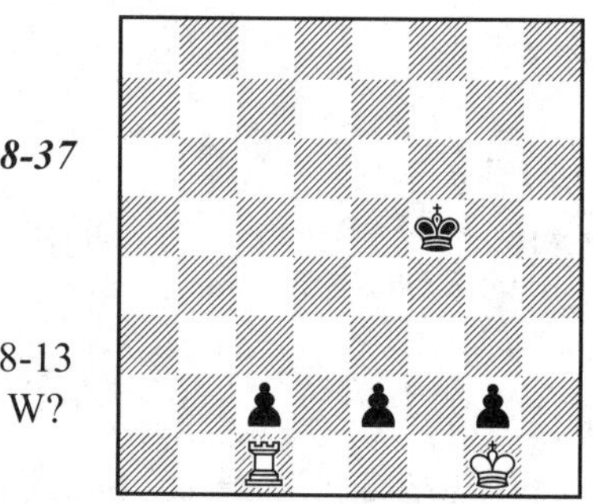

Chapter 9

ROOK ENDGAMES

Rook endings are perhaps the most important and most difficult kind of endgame. Most important, because they occur in practice much more often than other endings. Most difficult, because one must absorb and remember a much greater volume of knowledge than in endings with other material relationships.

The reason is that, in other endgames, situations with a minimum number of pawns on the board are either elementary or not very important. Therefore one needs only to remember a very limited number of precise positions; as it is highly improbable that one would meet them in practical play. So, mastering the basic ideas and methods is fully sufficient in those cases.

In rook endings, however, a sophisticated theory of positions with reduced material exists (for example, those with R+P against R), and these situations occur very often in practice. This means that we cannot omit studying a considerable number of precise positions.

Rook and Pawn vs. Rook

The Pawn on the 7th Rank

9-1

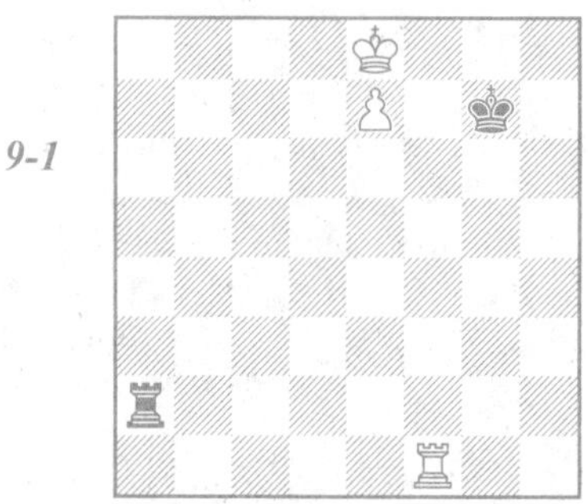

In chess literature, this situation is usually referred to as ***"The Lucena Position,"*** even though the Spaniard Lucena did not examine it in his book published in 1497. The first mention of an analogous position was in the book by Salvio (1634), which referred to Scipione of Genoa.

If White is on move he wins:

1 ♖g1+ ♔h7 2 ♖g4!

2 ♔f7 is premature in view of 2...♖f2+ 3 ♔e6 ♖e2+ 4 ♔f6 ♖f2+, and the king has only one way to take refuge from rook checks: by returning to e8. The rook move prepares an interference at e4. This method is called ***building a bridge***, or simply ***bridging***.

2...♖d2 (2...♖a8+ 3 ♔f7) **3 ♔f7 ♖f2+ 4 ♔e6 ♖e2+ 5 ♔f6 ♖f2+**

If 5...♖e1, then 6 ♖g5 △ 7 ♖e5.

6 ♔e5 ♖e2+ 7 ♖e4+−

It is worth mentioning that White has other winning options:

1 ♖g1+ ♔h7 2 ♖e1!+−.

1 ♖g1+ ♔h7 2 ♖d1!+− (the immediate 1 ♖d1 is also good) 2...♔g7 3 ♔d7 ♖a7+ 4 ♔e6 ♖a6+ 5 ♖d6 ♖a8 6 ♖d8+−.

Now let us see what happens if Black is on move.

1...♖a8+ 2 ♔d7 ♖a7+ 3 ♔d6 ♖a6+ 4 ♔c7 (4 ♔c5 ♖e6) **4...♖a7+** with a draw.

Let us shift all the pieces except for the black rook a single file to left. Then the side checks do not help anymore because the rook is not remote enough from the white pawn: 1...♖a8+ 2 ♔c7 ♖a7+ 3 ♔c8 ♖a8+ 4 ♔b7+−.

Hence we can conclude:

1) If the pawn is on the 7th rank, multiple winning methods exist. The most important ones are ***building a bridge*** for protection from checks along files and ***a rook maneuver for protection from side checks*** along ranks.

2) When the king of the weaker side is cut off from the pawn, the only defensive technique consists in ***side checks***.

3) A rook pursuit of the enemy king can only be successful when ***the rook and the pawn are separated at minimum by 3 lines***. As we shall see later, this rule does not only pertain to side checks.

4) A central or a bishop pawn divides the chessboard into two unequal parts: one is "long," another is "short." ***The correct positioning of forces for the weaker side is to keep the king on the short side, and the rook – on the long side***.

Tragicomedies

Sax – Tseshkovsky
Rovinj/Zagreb 1975

9-2

W?

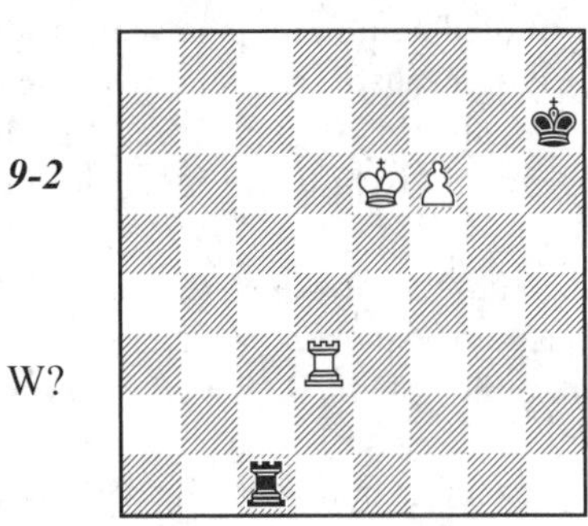

1 ♖h3+?

He should not move the rook away from the d-file where it was protecting the king from side checks. An easy win was 1 f7! ♖c8 (1...♔g7 2 ♖g3+; 1...♖e1+ 2 ♔f6 ♖f1+ 3 ♔e7 ♖e1+ 4 ♔f8 ♖a1 5 ♖h3+ ♔g6 6 ♔g8+–) 2 ♔e7 ♖c7+ 3 ♖d7+–.

1...♔g6 2 ♖g3+

Black resigned; as he failed to recognize that the position had become drawn: 2...♔h7 3 f7 ♖c8! (rather than 3...♖c6+? 4 ♔d7+–) 4 ♔e7 (4 ♖d3 ♔g7) 4...♖c7+ 5 ♔e8 ♖c8+ 6 ♔d7 ♖a8=.

Exercises

9-3

9/1
W?

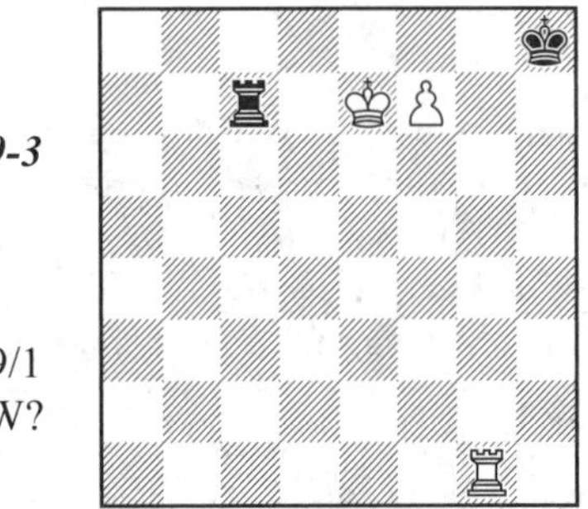

The Pawn on the 6th Rank

First let us examine the situation when the king of the weaker side is placed in front of the pawn.

9-4

W

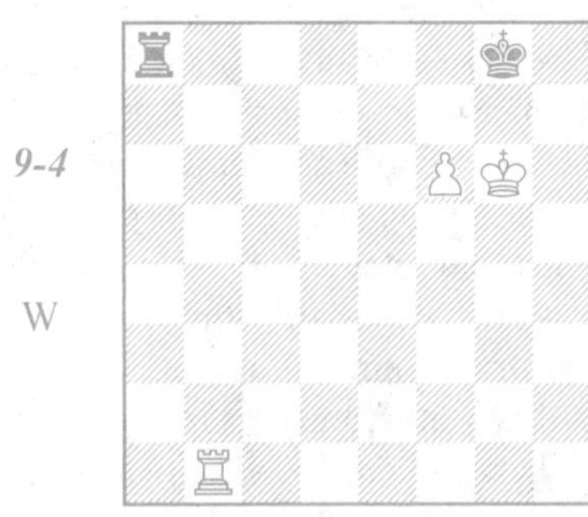

Black's rook must remain passive, staying on the 8th rank. White wins easily by bringing his rook to h7.

1 ♖b7 ♖c8 2 ♖g7+! (2 ♖h7 ♖c6) **2...♔f8 3 ♖h7 ♔g8 4 f7+**

It is worth mentioning that Black can hold the game when he is on move and his rook stands on a7: 1...♖g7+! 2 ♔f5 (2 fg stalemate) 2...♖g2. Also, White cannot win in the case when his king is placed on the other side of the pawn, at e6: 1 ♖b7 ♔f8 (there are other possibilities as well) 2 ♔f5 ♖a1!=.

9-5

W

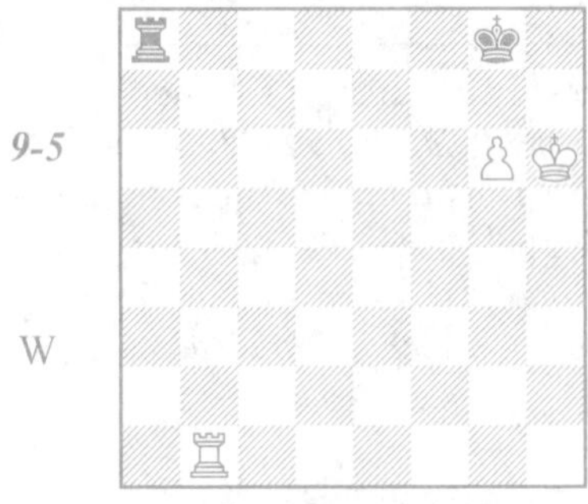

1 ♖b7 ♖c8 2 ♖g7+ ♔h8! (2...♔f8?? is erroneous in view of 3 ♔h7+–) **3 ♖h7+ ♔g8=**

Conclusion: passive defense holds against a knight pawn but loses against a bishop pawn or a central pawn.

When the stronger side has two knight pawns, then passive defense does not help.

9-6
$
W

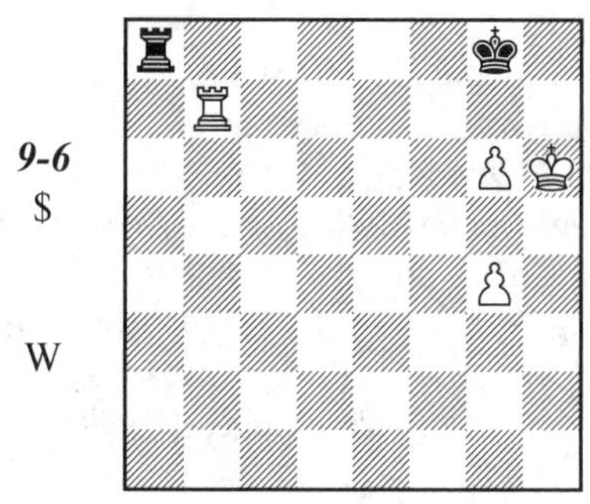

1 ♖b6! ♖f8 2 g5 (2 g7?? ♖f6+!) **2...♖a8 3 g7 ♖c8 4 ♖f6+–** △ 5 ♖f8+.

Now we come to positions with the king cut off from the enemy pawn.

9-7

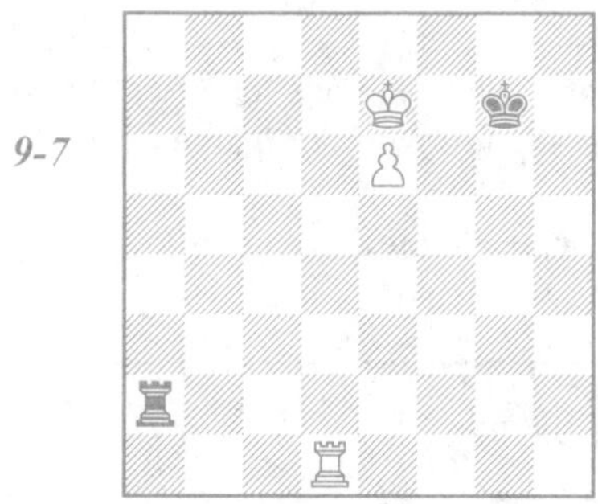

When on move, White wins. The simplest way begins with a check from g1, but 1 ♔e8 is also possible: we come to the position with the pawn on the 7th rank and the rook on the d-file delivering protection from side checks. For example, 1...♔f6 2 e7 ♖a8+ 3 ♖d8 ♖a7 4 ♖d6+ ♔g7, and now either 5 ♖d1!+– or 5 ♖e6!+– (but by no means 5 ♔d8?? ♖a8+ 6 ♔d7 ♔f7=).

With Black on move, the evaluation changes:

1...♖a7+□ 2 ♖d7

2 ♔e8 ♔f6 3 ♖e1 ♖e7+; 2 ♔d6 ♔f8.

2...♖a8!

The simplest defensive method: Black prevents the position with the pawn on the 7th rank. 2...♖a6?? would have been a grave error in view of 3 ♔e8+ ♔f6 4 e7, and if 4...♔e6, then 5 ♔f8!+–.

However any other rook retreat along the a-file, for example 2...♖a1, does not give up the draw because after 3 ♔e8+ (the only correct reply to 3 ♖d6!? is 3...♖a8!) 3...♔f6! 4 e7 ♔e6! 5 ♔f8 Black has 5...♖f1+!. Here he manages to hold only because of the fact that the white rook is misplaced at d7.

3 ♖d8

3 ♔d6+ is useless: 3...♔f6 (3...♔f8) 4 ♖f7+ ♔g6=.

The waiting attempt 3 ♖b7 can be met either with 3...♔g6 4 ♔d6 ♔f6 5 e7 ♔f7= or with 3...♖a1 4 ♔d7 ♖a8 5 e7 ♔f7= (but not 3...♔g8?? 4 ♔f6 ♖f8+ 5 ♖f7+–).

In case of 3 ♖d6!?, 3...♖a1? is bad because after 4 ♔e8 ♔f6 the pawn steps ahead with a check. 3...♖b8? loses to 4 ♖d8! ♖b7+ 5 ♔d6 ♖b6+ 6 ♔d7. The only correct reply is 3...♔g6!.

3...♖a7+ 4 ♔d6 ♖a6+ (4...♔f6?? 5 ♖f8+ ♔g7 6 e7) **5 ♔e5 ♖a5+! 6 ♖d5 ♖a8** (6...♖a7?? 7 ♖d7+; 6...♖a1!?) **7 ♖d7+** (7 e7 ♔f7 8 ♖d8 ♖a5+) **7...♔g6!=** (rather than 7...♔f8?? 8 ♔f6 because passive defense does not help against a central pawn).

The reason for the drawn final was the position of the black rook: it was placed on the long side. Let us shift all the pieces except for the black rook one file to the left. Now when the rook is on the short side, Black, as one can see easily, is lost.

Let us examine another position, not elementary but quite an important one.

9-8

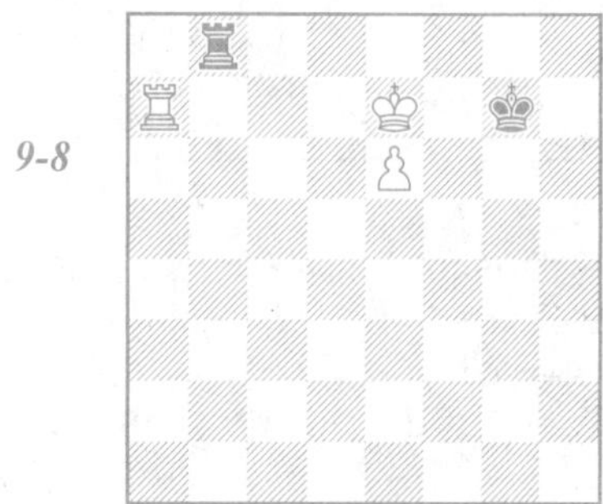

Only two files separate the black rook from the pawn, and this circumstance offers White winning chances. However a straightforward attempt 1 ♖a1? (△ 2 ♖g1+) misses the win: 1...♖b7+ 2 ♔d8 ♖b8+ 3 ♔c7 ♖b2 (△ 4...♔f8 or 4...♔f6) 4 ♖f1 ♖a2! 5 e7 ♖a7+ with a draw, because the rook managed to deliver long side checks in time.

For a win, White should yield the move to his opponent. As a matter of fact, 1...♖c8 loses to 2 ♖a1; in case of 1...♖b1, the white rook occupies the important square a8; 1...♔g8 2 ♔f6 ♖f8+3 ♖f7 is also bad. Only 1...♔g6 remains for Black but, as we shall see, this move also worsens his position.

1 ♔d6+!

But not 1 ♔d7? ♔f6⊙ 2 e7 ♔f7=.

1...♔f6 2 ♔d7⊙ ♔g7 (2...♖b1 3 e7; 2...♔g6 3 ♖a1) **3 ♔e7!⊙**

White has achieved his goal by means of triangulation.

3...♔g6

After 3...♖b1, 4 ♖a8! wins: 4...♖b7+ (4...♖b2 5 ♔e8 ♖h2 6 ♖a7+ ♔f6 7 e7 ♖h8+ 8 ♔d7) 5 ♔d6 ♖b6+ (5...♔f6 6 ♖f8+ ♔g7 7 e7) 6 ♔d7 ♖b7+ 7 ♔c6 ♖e7 8 ♔d6 ♖b7 9 e7.

4 ♖a1! ♖b7+ 5 ♔d8

5 ♔d6 is also good.

5...♖b8+

After 5...♔f6, White's winning method is instructive: 6 e7! ♖b8+ (6...♖×e7 7 ♖f1+) 7 ♔c7 ♖e8 8 ♔d6! ♖b8 9 ♖f1+ ♔g7 10 ♔c7 ♖a8 11 ♖a1!+–.

6 ♔c7 ♖b2

9-9

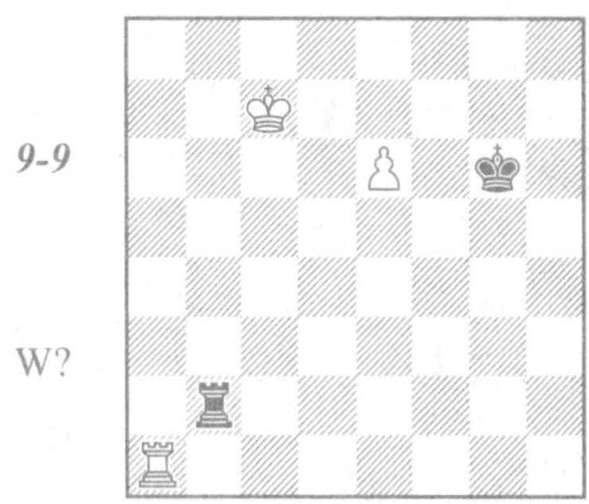

W?

7 ♖e1!

This is the point! With the king at g7, Black could have played 7...♔f8, while now the pawn cannot be stopped.

7...♖c2+ 8 ♔d7 ♖d2+ 9 ♔e8 ♖a2 10 e7+–.

Tragicomedies

Uhlmann – Gulko
Niksic 1978

9-10

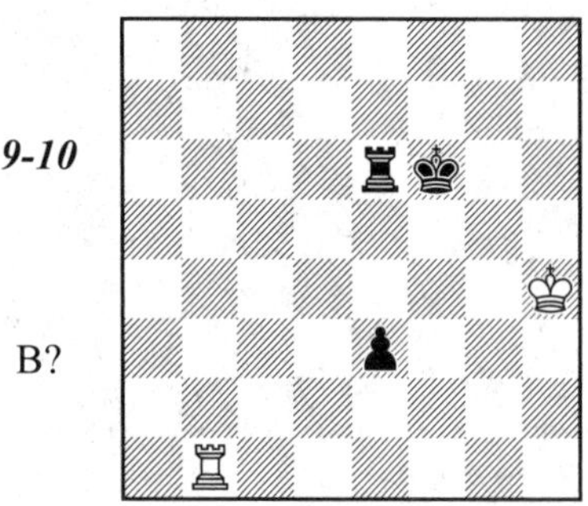

B?

1...♔f5??

After 1...e2! 2 ♖e1 ♖e3! 3 ♔g4 ♔e5 White would have had to resign.

2 ♔g3 ♔e4 3 ♔g2!

The only move. Both 3 ♖b4+? ♔d3 4 ♖b3+ ♔c2 and 3 ♖a1? ♖g6+ are erroneous.

3...♖g6+

After 3...♖f6 4 ♖a1! the white rook, occupying the long side, assures an easy draw.

4 ♔f1 ♔f3 5 ♖b3??

And again the position is lost (a passive defense against a central pawn). Necessary was 5 ♖b2! ♖a6 6 ♖f2+! (we saw this stalemate when discussing diagram 9-4).

5...♖a6 6 ♖b1 ♖h6 7 ♔g1 ♖g6+ White resigned.

One of the most famous "comedy of errors" occurred in the following endgame.

Capablanca – Menchik
Hastings 1929

9-11

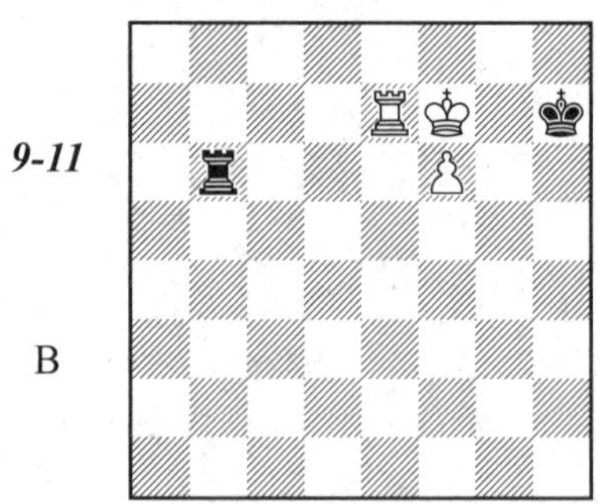

B

1...♖a6?? (1...♖b8=; 1...♖b1=) **2 ♖d7??**

Capablanca "amnesties" his lady rival. 2 ♔f8+ wins.

2...♖a8 3 ♖e7 ♖a6??

Black repeats the same error.

4 ♔f8+! ♔g6 5 f7 ♖a8+ (5...♔f6 6 ♔g8!) **6 ♖e8 ♖a7 7 ♖e6+ ♔h7 8 ♔e8??**

A single step away from reaching the goal, White misses again. Both 8 ♖e1 and 8 ♖f6 won.

8...♖a8+ 9 ♔e7 ♖a7+??

9...♔g7! led to a draw.

10 ♔f6 Black resigned.

Alburt – Dlugy
USA ch, Los Angeles 1991

9-12

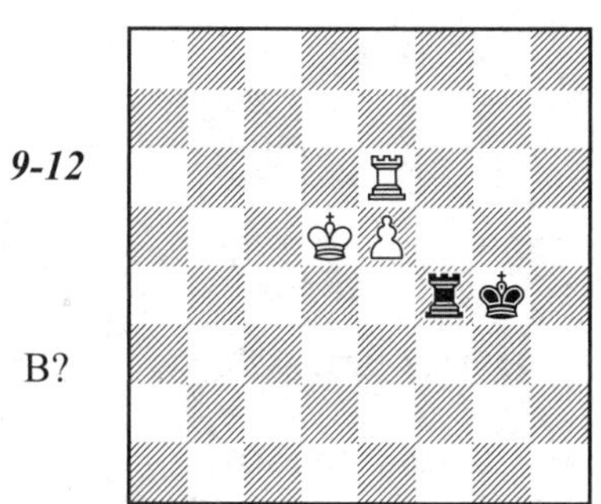

B?

1...♔g5?

Black could have had an easy draw after 1...♖a4!, occupying the long side with his rook.

2 ♖a6! ♖b4

The game was adjourned in this position. Grandmaster Dlugy, assisted during home analysis by two experienced colleagues, Wolff and Ivanov, failed to understand the essence of the position, and his first move after the resumption of play was a decisive error. What is even more striking is that Dlugy had the classic work by Levenfish and Smyslov on rook endings at his disposal. In that book, naturally, the position at diagram 9-8 is examined. Black had to avoid that position but, after a short while, it arose on the board anyway.

3 ♔e6

If 3 ♔d6 then 3...♔f5!= (3...♔g6?? 4.♔c5+).

3...♔g6??

After 3...♖b7 we have the above mentioned basic position but shifted one line down, and this circumstance could enable Black to hold. Both 3...♖b8 and 3...♖b1 were playable, too.

4 ♔e7+ ♔g7 5 ♖a7!+–

Black had obviously expected only 5 e6? ♖b7+ 6 ♔d8 ♖b8+ 7 ♔c7 ♖b1=.

5...♖b8

5...♖b6!? 6 e6 ♖b8 were more persistent; White had then to employ the triangular maneuver: 7 ♔d6+! ♔f6 8 ♔d7⊙ ♔g7 9 ♔e7!⊙.

6 e6⊙ ♔g6 7 ♖a1 ♖b7+ 8 ♔d6 ♖b6+ 9 ♔d7 ♖b7+ 10 ♔c6 ♖b8 11 ♔c7 ♖h8 (11...♖b2 12 ♖e1!) **12 e7** Black resigned.

Exercises

9-13

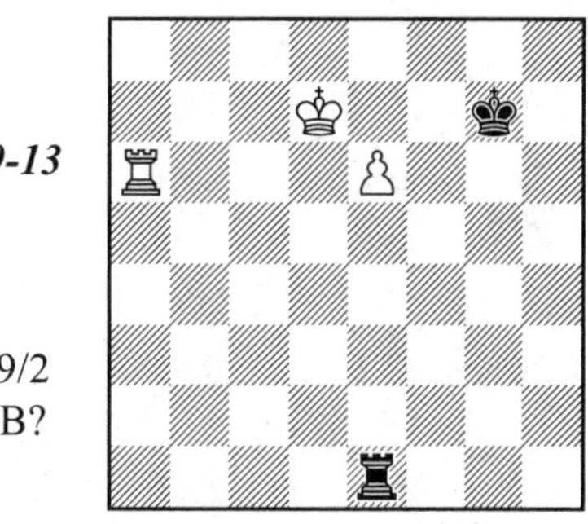

9/2
B?

9-14

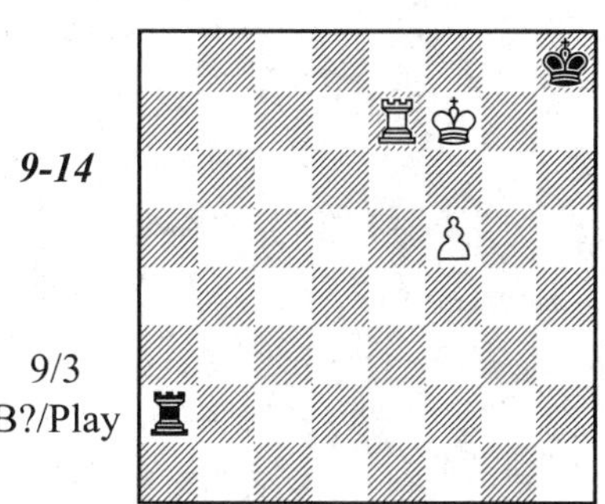

9/3
B?/Play

The Pawn on the 5th Rank

Philidor, 1777

9-15

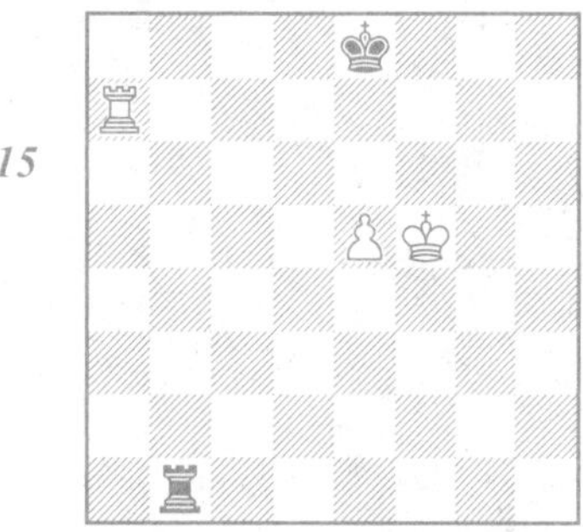

This is the so-called "***Philidor position***." The famous French chessplayer was the first to demonstrate, as early as the 18th century, the correct method of defense.

1...♖b6! (preventing a penetration of the white king to the 6th rank) **2 e6 ♖b1=**

If the pawn stood at e5 the white king would have had a ***refuge*** from vertical checks. But, as soon as the pawn has stepped forward, the refuge does not exist anymore.

If White is to move in the initial position, then, as Philidor thought, **1 ♔f6** wins, and his explanation was 1...♖f1+ 2 ♔e6 ♔f8 3 ♖a8+

♔g7 4 ♔e7 ♖b1 5 e6 (we know this position already: see diagram 9-8) 5...♖b7+ 6 ♔d6 ♖b6+ 7 ♔d7 ♖b7+ 8 ♔c6+−.

Later on, ***the second defensive method*** in the Philidor position was discovered: ***an attack from the rear*** that helps Black to hold as well. ***If the rook fails to occupy the 6th rank "à la Philidor," it must be placed in the rear of the white pawn.***

1...♖e1! 2 ♔e6 ♔f8! 3 ♖a8+ ♔g7

Now we can evaluate the position of the black rook. It prevents both 4 ♔e7 and 4 ♔d7. Plus, Black can meet 4 ♔d6 with 4...♔f7!, and White must retrace his steps: 5 ♖a7+ ♔e8 6 ♔e6 ♔f8! etc. If he tries 4 ♖e8, preparing 5 ♔d7, the black rook occupies the long side: 4...♖a1!=.

The move 2...♔f8! is undoubtedly correct (the king goes to the short side, leaving the long side for the rook), but 2...♔d8?! 3 ♖a8+ ♔c7 does not lose either.

9-16

W

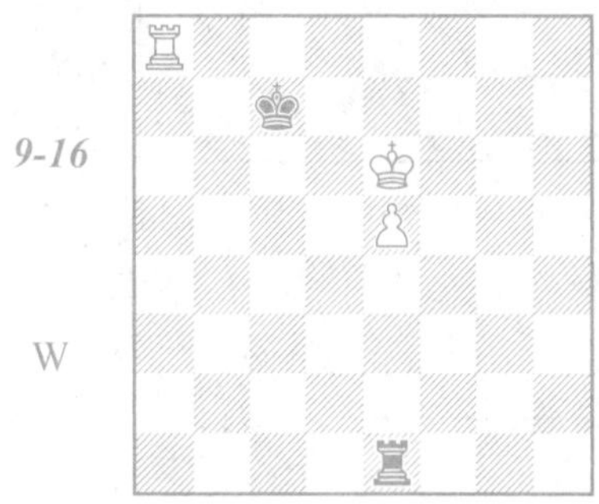

4 ♖e8 (4 ♔f6 ♔d7!) 4...♖h1! (rather than 4...♖e2? 5 ♔f7 ♖h2 6 ♖g8! ♖h7+ 7 ♖g7 ♖h8 8 ♔e7 ♔c6 9 e6 ♔c7 10 ♖g1+−) 5 ♖g8 ♖e1! 6 ♖g2 ♔d8=.

Obviously, such a defense with the king on the long side would have been impossible if the short side were even shorter (in case of an f- or g-pawn).

9-17

B

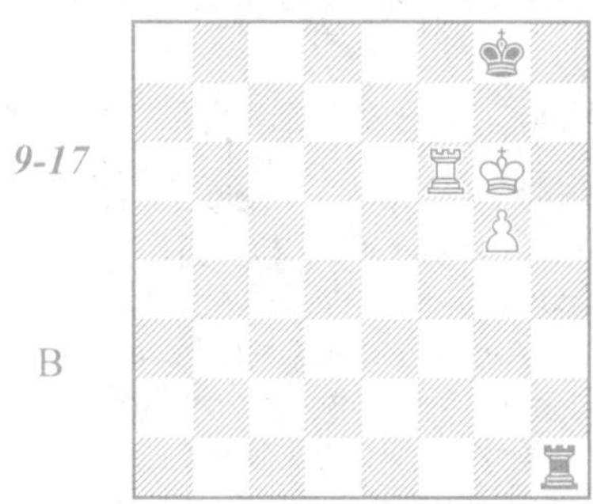

In this position, the attack from the rear does not work anymore: **1...♖g1? 2 ♖a6 ♔f8** (2...♖f1 3 ♖a8+ ♖f8 4 ♖×f8+ ♔×f8 5 ♔h7+−) **3 ♖a8+ ♔e7 4 ♖g8!** (White prepares 5 ♔h7!; the black rook will be unable to disturb the king from the side) **4...♖g2 5 ♔h7! ♔f7 6 g6+ ♔e7 7 ♖a8 ♖h2+ 8 ♔g8 ♖g2 9 g7+−**

But this position is also drawn. Black's rook comes in time for a passive defense along the 8th rank: 1...♖a1! 2 ♖b6 ♖a8=.

Tragicomedies

Lobron – Knaak
Baden Baden 1992

9-18

B?

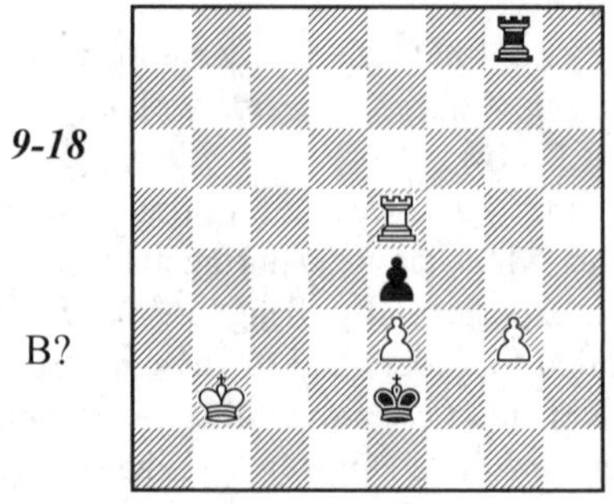

1...♔×e3? 2 ♔c2 ♖×g3 3 ♖e8 ♖g2+

Draw, according to the second defensive method in the Philidor position.

To avoid the theoretical draw, Black should have played 1...♔d3!. The white king is placed at the long side, and one cannot see how White can survive, for example 2 ♖d5+ ♔×e3 3 ♔c2 ♔e2!? (3...♖×g3 4 ♖e5!? ♔f4 5 ♖e8 ♖d3!−+, or 5 ♖d5 ♔f3 6 ♖e5 e3 7 ♔d3 ♔f2−+ is also playable) 4 ♖d2+ ♔f3 5 ♖d7, and now either 5...♖f8!? 6 ♔d1 ♔f2! 7 ♖d2+ ♔f1−+ or 5...♖×g3 6 ♖e7 e3 7 ♔d3 ♔f2−+ followed with ♖f3-f8.

Dreev – Beliavsky
USSR ch, Odessa 1989

9-19

W

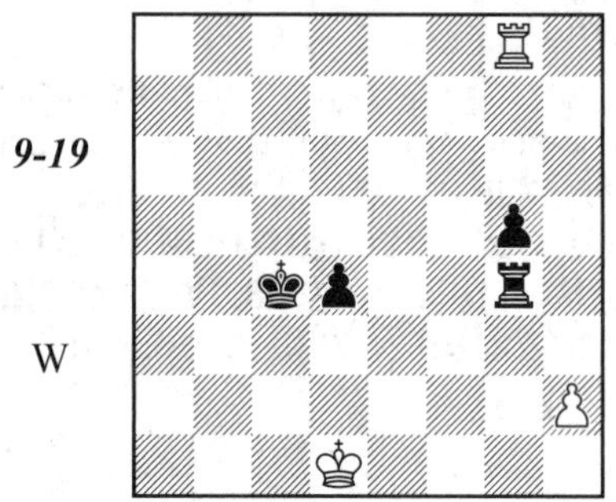

White is in a precarious situation: 1...♔d3 is threatened. Dreev tries his last chance.

1 h4! ♖×h4?? 2 ♖×g5 ♔c3 3 ♖d5!= ♖h1+ 4 ♔e2 ♖h2+ 5 ♔d1 ♔d3 6 ♔c1 ♖h1+ 7 ♔b2 ♖e1 8 ♖d8 ♖e4 9 ♔c1 ♔e2 10 ♔c2 Draw.

Black should have given a rook check and moved his pawn to g4. Later on, he could either trade kingside pawns, under more favorable circumstances than has actually happened, or move his king to the g-pawn. The eventual consequences of 1...♖g1+! were:

2 ♔d2 ♖g2+ 3 ♔e1 g4 4 ♔f1 (4 h5 ♔c3 5 h6 ♖h2 6 ♖h8 d3 7 ♖c8+ ♔d4 8 ♖d8+ ♔e3 9 ♖e8+ ♔f3−+) 4...♖h2 5 ♖×g4 ♔c3 6 ♔g1 ♖c2! 7 ♖g8 (7 h5 d3−+) 7...d3 8 ♖c8+ ♔b2−+;

2 ♔e2 d3+ 3 ♔d2 (3 ♔f2 d2) 3...♖g2+ 4 ♔d1 g4 5 h5 ♖h2 6 ♖c8+ (6 ♖×g4+ ♔c3−+) 6...♔d4 etc.

Larsen – Tal
Bled cmsf (9) 1965

9-20

W

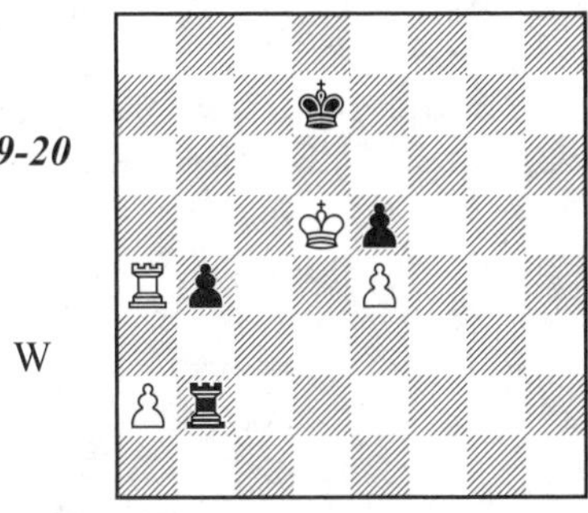

The queenside pawns will inevitably be traded, and the Philidor position will probably occur thereafter.

1 ♖a7+ ♔c8?

The black king goes the wrong way: he should have tried for the short side. After 1...♔e8! 2 ♔e6 ♔f8 3 ♖a8+ ♔g7 4 ♔×e5 b3 5 ab ♖×b3, the draw is obvious.

2 ♔×e5 b3? (as Müller indicates, after 2...♖h2 the position is still drawn) **3 ab ♖×b3 4 ♔d6 ♖d3+ 5 ♔e6?**

Larsen misses his chance to punish his opponent for a grave positional error and allows him to employ the second defensive method in the Philidor position. The winning continuation was 5 ♔e7! ♖h3 6 ♖a4 (△ ♖c4+; ♖d4) 6...♖h7+ 7 ♔e8 ♖h8+ 8 ♔f7+−.

5...♖h3 6 ♖a8+ (6 ♖a4 ♔d8!) **6...♔c7 7 ♖f8 ♖e3! 8 e5 ♖e1 9 ♖e8** (9 ♔f6 ♔d7!) **9...♖h1! 10 ♖a8 ♖e1!**

White played 18 more moves before he agreed to the peaceful outcome of the game; its result was vitally important for both rivals.

Exercises

9-21

9/4
B?

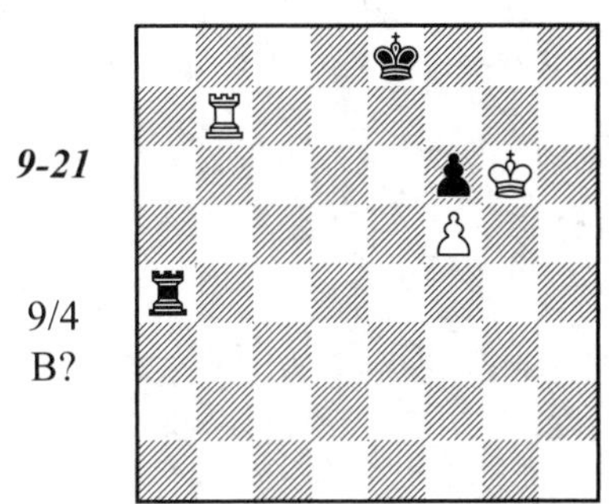

9-22

9/5
W?/Play

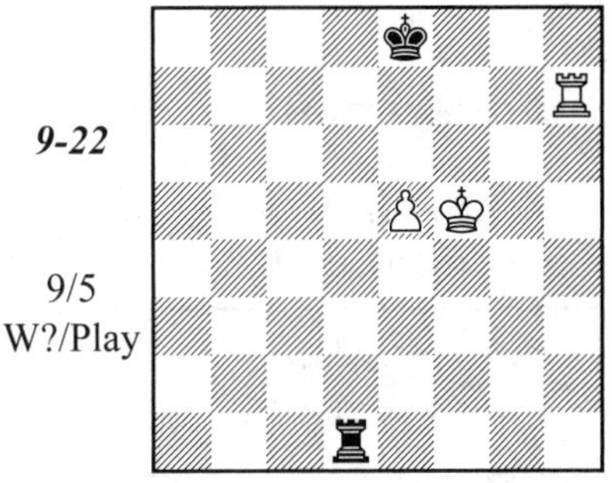

The Umbrella

Let us refresh our memory about the methods we have already seen, of sheltering the king from rook checks.

1) The king approaches the rook – an effective method when the rook is not too far away from the king and the pawn.

2) "Bridge" – the rook gives protection to the king.

3) "Refuge" – the king hides himself behind his own pawn.

It is a good time to show one more method. Sometimes an enemy pawn can serve as a sort of umbrella that protects the king from checks, as in the next diagram.

Velicka – Polak
Czech ch tt 1995

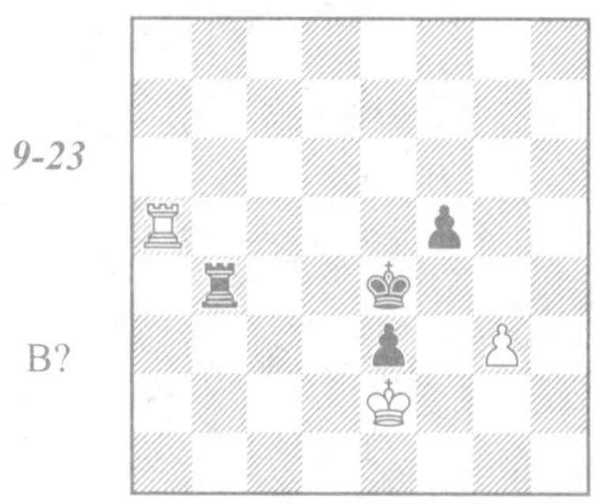
9-23
B?

1...f4! 2 gf ♖b2+ 3 ♔f1 ♔f3–+

White's own f4-pawn prevents him from saving himself with a check on f5.

4 ♖a1 ♖h2 5 ♔g1 ♖g2+ 6 ♔h1 ♖g8 7 ♔h2 e2 8 f5 ♔f2 9 ♔h3 ♖g5! White resigned.

Tragicomedies

A. Zaitsev – Hübner
Büsum 1969

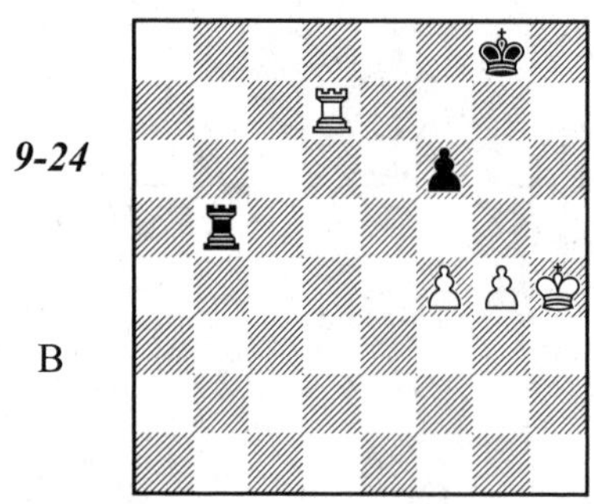
9-24
B

The game continued **1...♖b1?? 2 ♔h5 ♖g1** (otherwise 3 ♔g6) **3 g5 fg 4 f5! ♔f8 5 f6** Black resigned.

A draw could have been achieved with 1...♖b4 2 f5 ♖b1! 3 ♔h5 ♖g1!. The waiting tactic with 1...♖a5 was quite good, too: after 2 g5 (2 f5 ♖a1!) 2...fg+ 3 fg Black could defend the position either in the Philidor method (3...♖a6) or passively (3...♖a8).

The Pawn Hasn't Crossed the Mid-line

In this section, we shall learn one more defensive method, the one that is called "*the frontal attack*."

If, say, the white pawn stands on b5, it makes no sense for Black to keep his rook on b8 because it is too close to the pawn. However when the pawn has not crossed the middle line, such a rook position is justified, because the rook and the pawn are separated by no less than three rows, and therefore pursuing the king by the rook gives chances for a draw.

A. Chéron, 1923

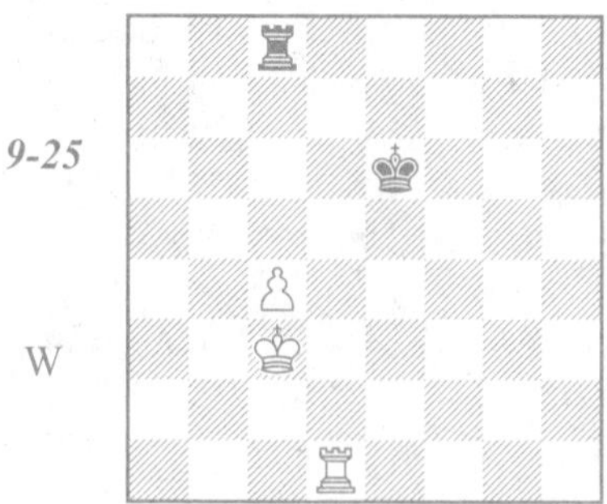
9-25
W

This is a typical case of an easy draw due to a frontal attack.

1 ♔b4 (△ 2 c5+–) **1...♖b8+ 2 ♔a5 ♖c8!**

2...♖a8+? is erroneous in view of 3 ♔b6+–.

3 ♔b5 ♖b8+ 4 ♔a6 ♖c8 5 ♖d4 ♔e5 6 ♖h4 ♔d6=

In the initial position, the rook is placed best at c8 where it prevents a pawn advance. However Black holds with a rook at h8, too. He meets 1 c5 with either 1...♔e7 2 ♔c4 ♖d8= or 1...♖h4 (cutting the king off the pawn) 2 c6 ♔e7 3 c7 ♖h8=. ***Horizontally cutting the king off from the pawn is a useful defensive method.***

Another important tip: ***in this sort of position, the black king should stay on the 5th or 6th rank.*** If he doesn't Black usually loses.

Kochiev – Smyslov
L'vov zt 1978

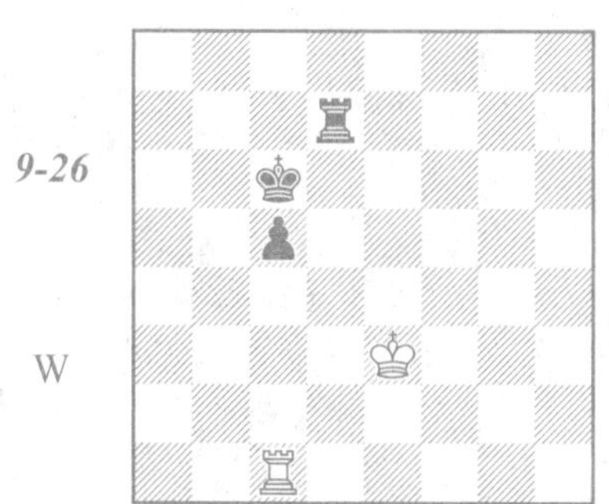
9-26
W

Both 1 ♔e4 and 1 ♖h1 might lead to a draw. However White carelessly moved the king away from a safe place.

1 ♔e2?? ♔b5 2 ♖b1+ ♔a4 3 ♖c1 ♔b4 4 ♖b1+ ♔a3! 5 ♖c1 ♖d5!

First of all, Smyslov has optimally activated his king (an ideal place for the king is 2 squares away from the pawn diagonally), and now he protects the pawn with the rook. Were the white king at e3, he could attack the rook immediately, while now White cannot do it in time.

6 ♔e3 ♔b2 7 ♖c4 (7 ♔e4 ♖d4+) **7...♔b3**

White resigned. The pawn crosses the middle of the board and, with the white king on the long side, the position is lost.

9-27

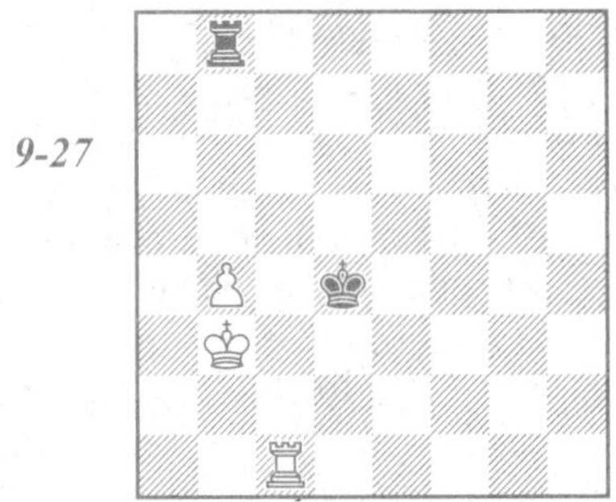

With Black on move, this is a draw: 1...♔d5! 2 ♖c4!? ♔d6! 3 ♔a4 ♔d5!.

White, if on move, wins.

1 ♖c6

1 ♖c5 △ 2 ♖h5, 3 b5 is no less strong.

1...♔d5 2 ♖a6 ♖b7 (or 2...♔d4) **3 ♔a4 ♔c4 4 ♖c6+ ♔d5 5 b5+−**

Conclusion: ***cutting off the king of the weaker side along a rank can often be more effective than the same procedure along a file.***

Now let us discuss situations with the black king being cut off from the pawn by more than one file.

A. Chéron, 1923

9-28

W

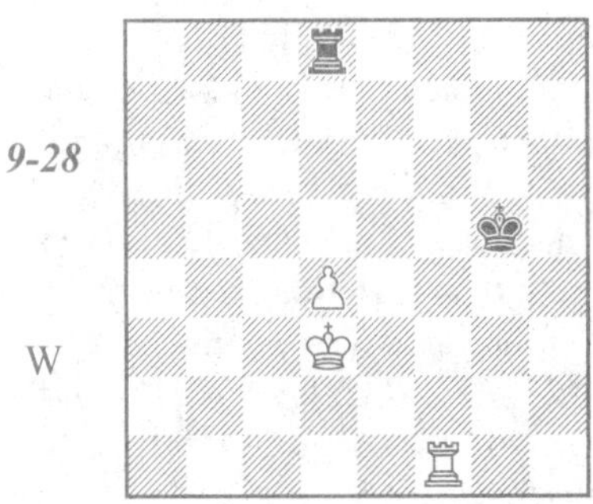

1 ♔c4 ♖c8+ 2 ♔b5 ♖d8 3 ♔c5 ♖c8+ 4 ♔b6! ♖d8

White has placed his king at its most active position. Now it is time to protect the pawn with the rook. Unlike the Kochiev vs. Smyslov endgame, he cannot do it horizontally. However the rook can be placed behind the pawn here, because the black king fails to help to his rook in time.

5 ♖d1! ♔f6 6 ♔c7 ♖d5 7 ♔c6 ♖a5

7...♖d8 8 d5 is also hopeless.

8 ♖e1!

It is important to cut off the king from the pawn again. Now Black loses in view of the unlucky distribution of his pieces: the king stands at the long side while the rook is at the short one. For example, 8...♖a6+ 9 ♔b5 ♖d6 10 ♔c5 ♖d8(a6) 11 d5 etc.

A. Chéron, 1926*

9-29

W?

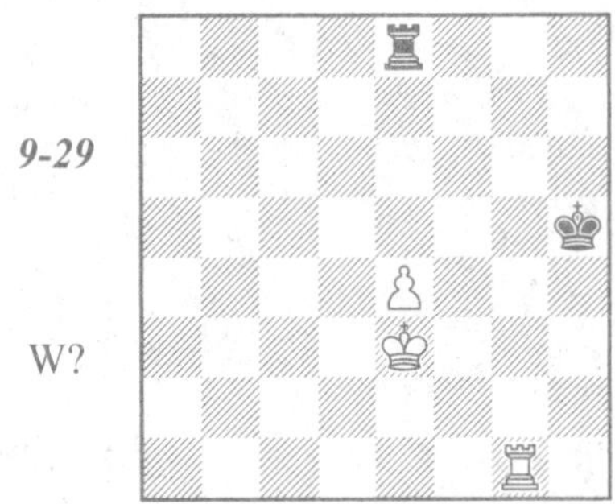

The method that was applied in the previous example does not work here. After 1 ♔d4 ♖d8+ 2 ♔c5 ♖e8 3 ♔d5 ♖d8+ 4 ♔c6 ♖e8 5 ♖e1? ♔g6 6 ♔d7 ♖a8 (or 6...♖e5 7 ♔d6 ♖a5) Black's rook occupies the long side with an obvious draw.

The winning idea is to create checkmate threats to the black king that is pressed to the edge of the board. His current position on h5 is optimally suited for defense. Therefore White, utilizing zugzwang, must drive it away from h5.

1 ♖g2! ♔h4! 2 ♖g7

2 e5? ♖×e5+ 3 ♔f4 is premature in view of 3...♔h3!=. 2 ♖g6 ♔h5 3 ♖d6? ♔g5 4 ♔d4 ♖a8= also brings nothing.

2...♔h5 3 ♖g1!⊙ ♔h6

Now 3...♔h4 loses to 4 e5! ♖×e5+ 5 ♔f4. The idea of cutting off the white king along the rank also does not help: 3...♖a8 4 e5 ♖a4 5 e6 ♔h6 (5...♖a6 6 ♔f4 ♖×e6 7 ♔f5+−) 6 e7 ♖a8 7 ♔f4 ♖e8 8 ♔f5 ♖×e7 9 ♔f6+−.

4 ♔d4 ♖d8+ 5 ♔c5 ♖e8 6 ♔d5 ♖d8+ 7 ♔e6! ♖e8+ 8 ♔f6! +–.

It is important to remember that ***in case of a knight pawn, cutting off the king by two files is not sufficient for a win.***

A. Chéron, 1923

9-30

W

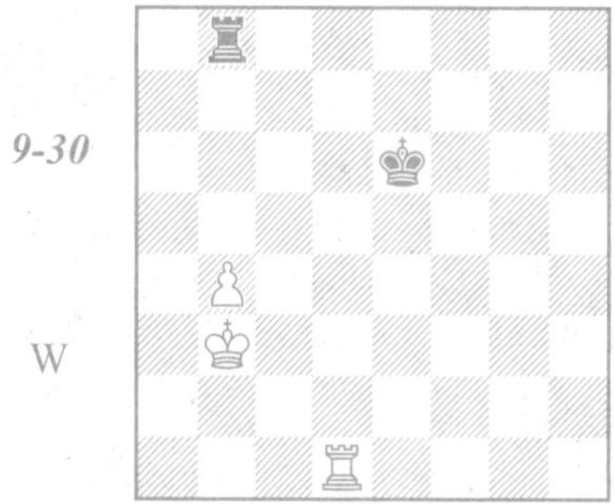

1 ♖d4

After 1 ♔a4 ♖a8+ 2 ♔b5 ♖b8+ 3 ♔a5 ♖a8+ 4 ♔b6 ♖b8+, the king can avoid checks only by returning to b3. The edge of the board is too close, and there is no comfortable square two steps away from the pawn diagonally.

1...♔e5! 2 ♔c3

If 2 ♖d7, 2...♔e6! 3 ♖a7 ♔d6 4 ♔a4 ♔c6= follows.

2...♖h8

Another method of defense deserves attention, too: 2...♖c8+ 3 ♖c4 (3 ♔d3 ♖b8) 3...♖b8 4 ♖c6 ♔d5 5 ♖a6 (a similar position with the king on b3 would have been winning) 5...♖c8+ 6 ♔b3 ♖c6! 7 ♖a7 ♖b6= (△ 8...♔c6).

3 ♖d7

3 b5 ♖b8! 4 ♖h4 ♔d6! 5 ♔b4 ♔c7=.

3...♔e6! =

It should be mentioned that 3...♖b8? loses to 4 ♔c4 ♔e6 5 ♖a7 (5 ♖d4+–) 5...♔d6 6 b5 ♖c8+ 7 ♔b4 ♖c7 8 b6. The continuation 3...♖c8+? occurred in Dolmatov vs. Sorm (Lugano 1986); White won after 4 ♔b3 ♔e6 5 ♖d4 ♔e5 6 ♖c4 ♖b8 7 ♖c6 ♔d5 8 ♖a6.

Until now, we have only considered positions with the pawn on 4th rank. The cases of a less advanced pawn are much more complicated, and they occur much less often, therefore we shall not investigate them. I wish only to mention that the distance between the pawn and the hostile rook is longer when the pawn stands on the 2nd or 3rd rank, and the defending resources are naturally more significant. Therefore, for example, if the pawn stands on the 3rd rank the king should be cut off by three files for a win (with only two files it is a draw if, of course, Black's king and rook are placed "in accordance with the rules").

It deserves to be mentioned that a frontal attack is particularly effective against a rook pawn. For example, with a pawn on a4 even cutting the king off by three files is not sufficient for a win.

Tragicomedies

We have seen a tragicomedy in a game by Kochiev, where his grave error had fatal consequences. A draw would have maintained excellent chances of his qualifying for the Interzonal tournament. After losing, he failed to qualify, and the whole career of this young talented grandmaster fell steeply down thereafter.

Many have erred in similar situations, even the greats of this world.

Tal – I. Zaitsev
USSR ch tt, Riga 1968

9-31

W?

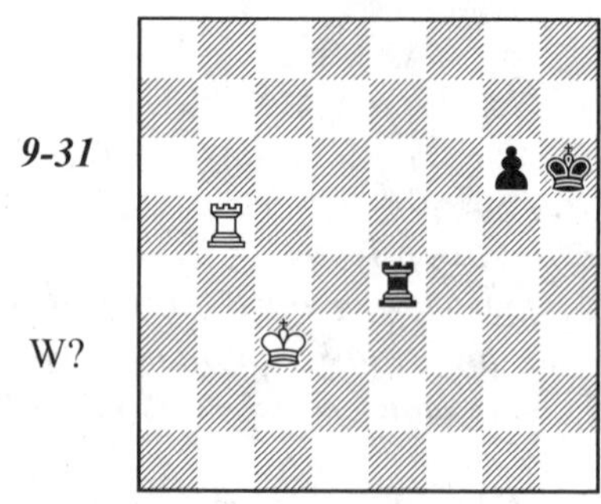

White should play ♔d3 and ♖b1, but which order of moves is correct?

A theoretical draw can be achieved after 1 ♖b1! g5 2 ♔d3 ♖e5 3 ♔d4 ♖e8 4 ♖g1 ♔g6 5 ♔d3 (see the previous diagram).

However **1 ♔d3?? ♖e1!** happened, the game was adjourned here, and White resigned without further play. In order to bring the rook to the 1st rank, White must attack the black rook with his king, but we know that a king is placed badly on the 2nd rank. Here are the eventual consequences if the game were continued:

2 ♔d2 ♖e6 3 ♖b1 g5 4 ♖g1 (4 ♔d3 g4 5 ♖b5 g3 6 ♔d2 g2 7 ♖b1 ♖g6 8 ♖g1 ♔h5 9 ♔e3 ♔h4–+) **4...♔h5!** (△ 5...g4)

It is useful to improve the king's position by bringing him from h6 to g6. A premature 4...♖e5? misses the win: 5 ♔d3 ♔h5 6 ♔d4 ♖e2 7 ♔d3 ♖h2 8 ♔e3=.

5 ♖h1+ ♔g6 6 ♖g1 (6 ♖e1 ♖×e1 7 ♔×e1 ♔h5 8 ♔f1 ♔h4! –+)

9-32
$

B

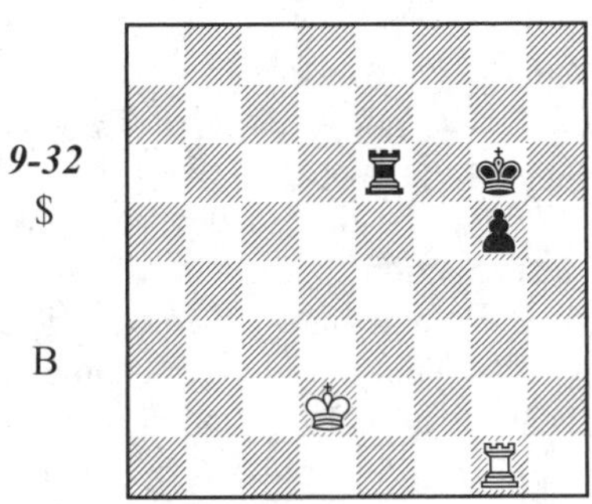

6...♖e5! 7 ♔d3 ♔f5! 8 ♔d4

After 8 ♖f1+ ♔g4 9 ♔d4 (9 ♖g1+ ♔f3 10 ♔d4 ♖a5 –+) both 9...♖a5 10 ♔e3 ♖a3+ 11 ♔e2 ♖a2+ 12 ♔e3 ♔h3 –+ and 9...♖e2 10 ♔d3 ♖h2 (10...♖g2) are strong.

8...♖e4+ 9 ♔d3 g4 10 ♖f1+

10 ♖g2 ♖f4 11 ♔e2 ♔g5 12 ♖f2 (12 ♖g1 ♔h4) 12...g3! leads to the same result.

10...♖f4 11 ♔e2

11 ♖g1 ♔g5 12 ♔e2 ♔h4.

11...g3! 12 ♖×f4+ ♔×f4 13 ♔e1 ♔e3! 14 ♔f1 ♔f3⊙ –+.

Exercises

9-33

9/6
W?

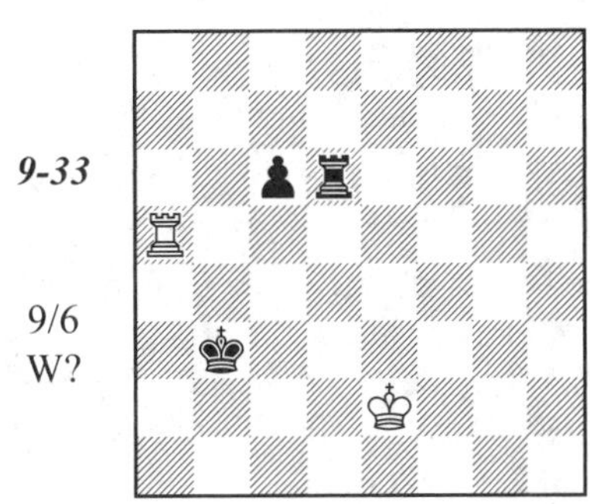

A Rook and a Rook Pawn vs. a Rook

The King is in Front of his Own Pawn

9-34

W

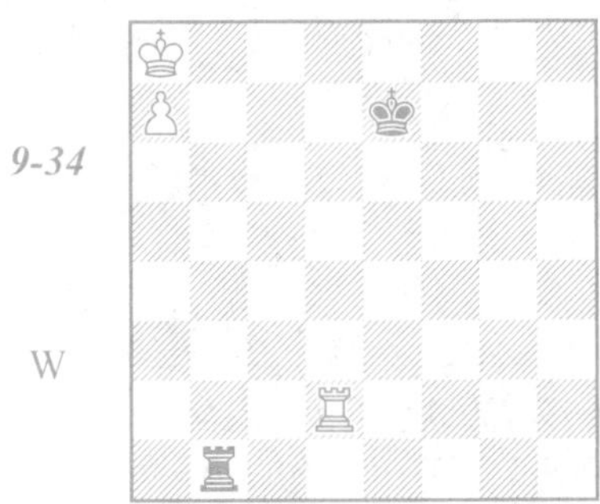

A draw is inevitable. The only possible attempt to free the king from custody is the transfer of the rook to b8, but then Black's king will stand in for the black rook on guard.

1 ♖h2 ♔d7 2 ♖h8 ♔c7 3 ♖b8 ♖c1 (or 3...♖h1 4 ♖b7+ ♔c8 5 ♖b2 ♖c1) **4 ♖b2 ♖c3**, and White cannot progress.

Let us move the black king and the white rook one file away, as in the next diagram.

9-35

W

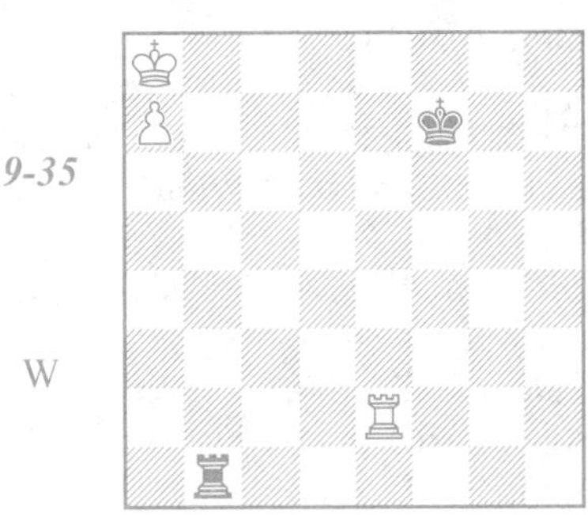

White wins, because the black king fails to reach c7 in time.

1 ♖h2 ♔e7 2 ♖h8 ♔d6

If 2...♔d7, then 3 ♖b8 ♖a1 4 ♔b7 ♖b1+ 5 ♔a6 ♖a1+ 6 ♔b6 ♖b1+ 7 ♔c5. With Black's king on d6, the square c5 is not available for escaping, so White must find another itinerary.

3 ♖b8 ♖a1 4 ♔b7 ♖b1+ 5 ♔c8 ♖c1+ 6 ♔d8 ♖h1 7 ♖b6+ ♔c5

Both 8 ♖e6? ♖a1 and 8 ♖a6? ♖h8+ 9 ♔d7 ♖h7+ 10 ♔e8 ♖h8+ 11 ♔f7 ♖a8 are useless now.

8 ♖c6+! ♔b5 (8...♔d5 9 ♖a6 ♖h8+ 10 ♔c7 ♖h7+ 11 ♔b6) **9 ♖c8 ♖h8+ 10 ♔c7 ♖h7+ 11 ♔b8+–.**

Tragicomedies

Vladimirov – Rashkovsky
USSR chsf, Chelyabinsk 1975

9-36

W?

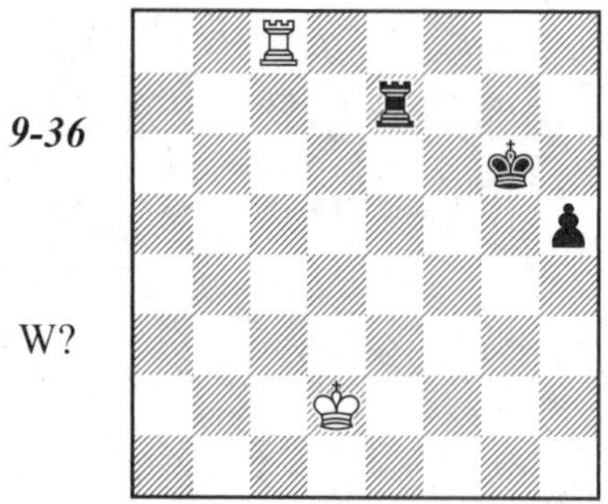

To achieve a draw, White should simply force Black's king to the h-file: 1 ♖g8+! ♚f5 2 ♖f8+ ♚g4 3 ♖g8+ ♚h3 4 ♖g5 h4 5 ♖g8=.

And 1 ♖c1! △ 2 ♖e1= is also good.

1 ♖c3? h4 2 ♖e3?

The decisive error! It was still not too late to return to the correct plan by playing 2 ♖c6+! ♚g5 3 ♖c8 h3 (or 3...♜h7 4 ♖g8+) 4 ♖h8 (4 ♖g8+) 4...♚g4 5 ♖g8+ ♚f3 6 ♖f8+ ♚g2 7 ♖g8+ ♚h1 8 ♖g6 h2 9 ♖g8=.

2...♜h7! 3 ♖e1 (3 ♖h3 ♚g5 4 ♔e2 ♚g4 is also bad) **3...h3 4 ♖h1 ♚g5 5 ♔e3 ♚h4 6 ♔f2 ♜f7+ 7 ♔g1** (7 ♔e2 ♜a7, planning 8...♜a2+ and 9...h2) **7...♜a7** White resigned.

If 8 ♖h2, then 8...♜a1+ (but, of course, not 8...♚g3?? 9 ♖g2+!) 9 ♔f2 ♚g4⊙ is decisive.

A similar position (like diagram 9-36, but with the white rook on d4 plus reversed wings and colors) occurred in Dvoiris vs. Kovalev, USSR ch(1), Simferopol 1988. Curiously enough, Kovalev lost precisely in the same way as Vladimirov: 1 ♖d3? h4 2 ♖e3?.

The Rook is in Front of the Pawn and the Pawn is on the 7th Rank

9-37

W

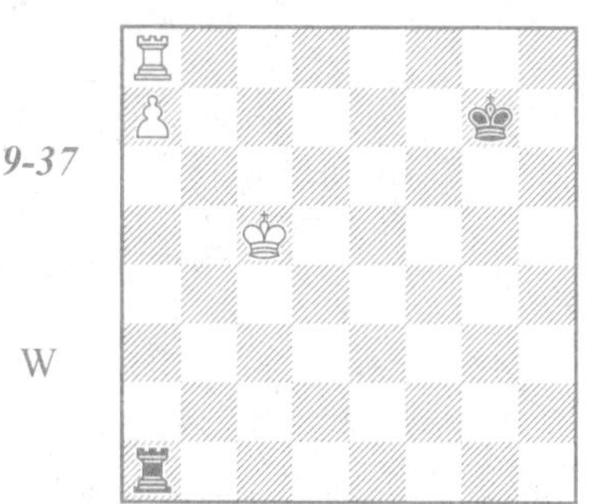

A standard defensive formation: Black's rook is behind the hostile pawn, while the king is placed on g7 or h7. White's rook is riveted to the pawn and cannot leave a8. If **1 ♔b6**, then **1...♜b1+**. The white king cannot escape from vertical checks. Black's rook drives the king away and returns to a1.

Other defensive systems occur much less frequently. The black king can hide in the "shadow" of his opponent, or (with the black rook on the 7th rank) in the "shadow" of his own rook. We just mention these ideas but do not study them here. Sometimes they are sufficient for a draw, and sometimes not. For example, if we move the black king from g7 to c3, the move 1 ♖c8! wins. A drawn position is one with the white king on c7 and the black king on c5.

Back to the last diagram, let's add a white pawn on h5. For the outcome, there will be no change: Black simply ignores its existence. The same is valid for a g5-pawn and even for 2 or 3 white pawns on the g-file.

However an f5-pawn wins.

9-38

W

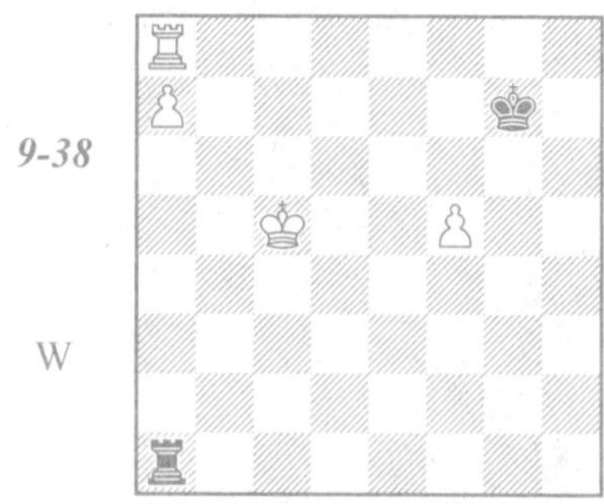

1 f6+ ♚f7 (1...♚×f6 2 ♖f8+; 1...♚h7 2 f7) **2 ♖h8,** and Black loses his rook.

Tragicomedies

Khaunin - Fridman
Leningrad 1962

9-39

B

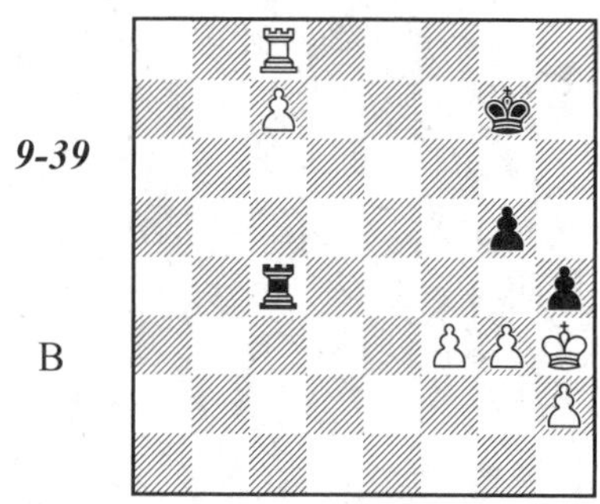

1...hg 2 hg? g4+! 3 fg. A draw is inevitable, as White has only g-pawns extra (no matter whether one or two).

The winning continuation was 2 ♔×g3! ♔h7 3 h4! gh+ 4 ♔h3 ♔g7 5 f4, and the f-pawn goes ahead with a decisive effect.

The Rook is in Front of the Pawn and the Pawn is on the 6th Rank

J. Vancura, 1924*

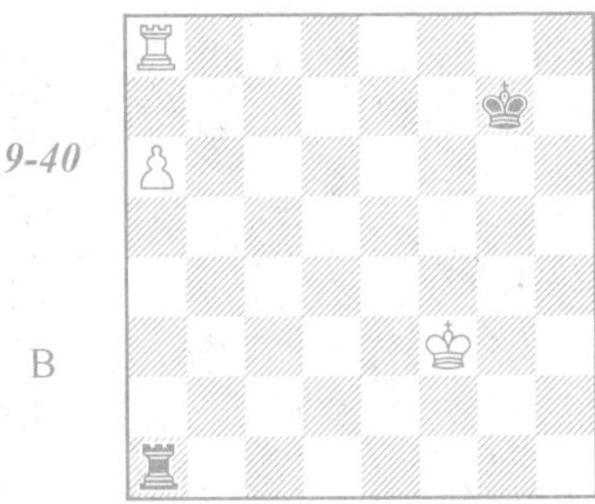

9-40

B

The main difference between this position and those discussed above, is the fact that here White's king has a refuge from vertical checks: the a7-square. The king hides there in order to free his rook from the job of protecting the pawn.

The black king, in contrast, fails to reach the queenside: 1...♔f7? 2 ♔e4 (2 a7? ♔g7 would have been premature) 2...♔e7 3 a7! ♔d7(f7) 4 ♖h8+–.

2...♖a5 (instead of 2...♔e7) is also hopeless: 3 ♔d4 ♔g7 4 ♔c4 ♔f7 5 ♔b4 ♖a1 6 ♔b5 ♖b1+ 7 ♔c6 ♖a1 8 ♔b7 ♖b1+ 9 ♔a7 ♔e7 10 ♖b8 ♖c1!? 11 ♔b7 (rather than 11 ♖b6? ♔d7) 11...♖b1+ 12 ♔a8 ♖a1 13 a7+–. Black's king fails to reach c7 in time (see diagram 9-35).

Because of this analysis, the diagrammed position had been considered winning for a long time. However a saving plan was finally discovered. This plan is based on the fact that the a6-pawn gives the king a refuge from vertical checks, but cannot hide him from side checks. Therefore Black should bring his rook to f6.

1...♖f1+! 2 ♔e4 ♖f6!. This is the so-called ***"Vancura position."*** Black follows the same "pawn in the crosshairs" method found in endings with bishops of opposite colors. The rook attacks the pawn in order to prevent the enemy's rook from leaving a8. What can White do? If a6-a7, Black always has ♖a6 (his king will obviously never leave the g7- and h7-squares). If White defends the pawn with his king, a series of checks follows, and then the rook returns to f6. For example, **3 ♔d5 ♖b6 4 ♔c5 ♖f6!** (the best place for the rook!) **5 ♔b5 ♖f5+!**, etc.

Now let us move the white king to f4.

P. Romanovsky, 1950

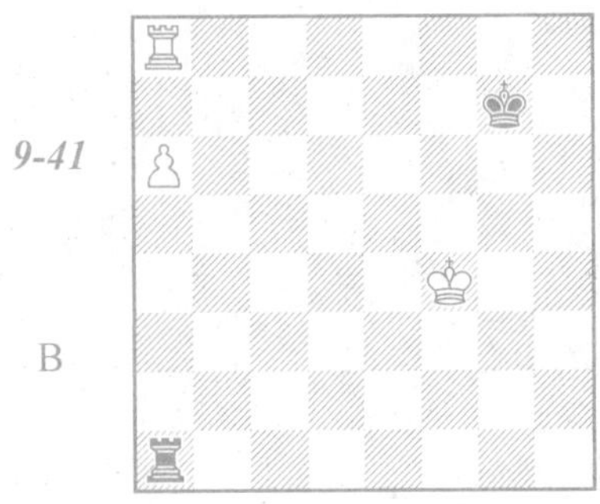

9-41

B

1...♖f1+? 2 ♔e5 ♖f6 is bad here on account of 3 ♖g8+!. However Black has no other defensive plan than the rook transfer to the 6th rank. Therefore **1...♖c1!**

If 2 ♔e5, then 2...♖c6= follows, achieving the Vancura position. White may use the opportunity for removing his rook from the corner.

2 ♖b8 ♖a1 3 ♖b6 (3 ♖b7+ ♔f6 4 a7 ♔e6 is weaker.)

When the rook stood on a8, the black king was riveted to the kingside; but now the time comes for a march to the pawn. But this should be done carefully: the premature 3...♔f7? 4 ♔e5 ♔e7 5 ♖b7+ ♔d8 6 a7 loses for Black.

3...♖a5! 4 ♔e4 ♔f7! 5 ♔d4

If 5 ♖h6, then 5...♔g7!, but not 5...♔e7? 6 a7 ♔d7 7 ♖h8!.

5...♔e7 6 ♔c4 ♔d7 7 ♔b4 ♖a1, and the draw is clear.

It is worth mentioning that 1...♖b1? (instead of 1...♖c1) would lose: 2 ♖a7+! ♔f6 (2...♔g6 3 ♖b7 ♖a1 4 ♖b6+ ♔f7 5 ♔e5+–) 3 ♔e4 ♖b6 4 ♖h7! ♔g6 5 a7 ♖a6 6 ♖b7+–.

However the first moves might have been transposed: 1...♖a5!? 2 ♔e4 ♖c5! (2...♖b5!) 3 ♖a7+ ♔g6 4 ♖b7 (4 ♔d4 ♖c6=) 4...♖a5=.

In many lines, the kings compete in a race to the queenside. If the white king stood closer to the pawn, then the black one would eventually arrive too late. This means that Black cannot delay the rook transfer to the 6th rank; this plan should be executed as soon as possible.

Tragicomedies

Vyzhmanavin – Lerner
USSR ch, L'vov 1984

9-42

B

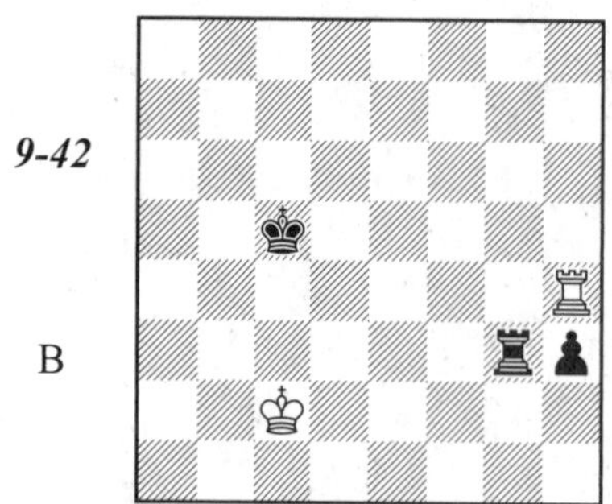

In this drawn position, Black uses his last available trap, and unexpectedly succeeds.

1...♖a3!? 2 ♔d2??

Correct was, of course, 2 ♔b2! ♖f3 3 ♔c2 ♔d5 4 ♔d2=.

2...h2! 3 ♔e2 ♖a1! White resigned.

Ivanchuk – Lautier
Horgen 1995

9-43

B

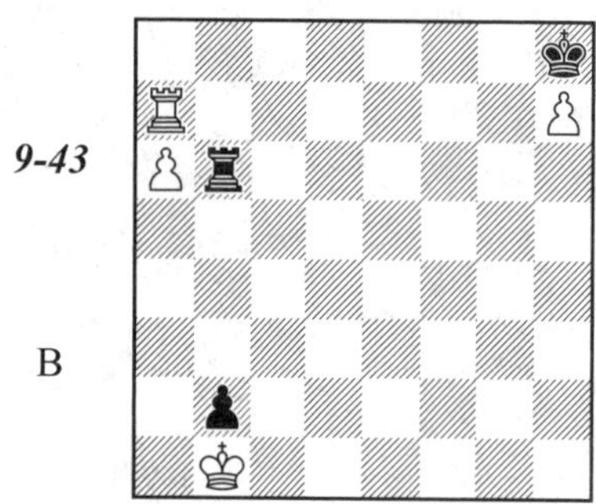

1...♖b4??

The Vancura position could be achieved through the elementary 1...♖f6! 2 ♖a8+ (after 2 ♔×b2 Black's rook would become "desperado" because his king is stalemated) 2...♔×h7 3 ♔×b2 ♔g7.

2 ♖c7 (2 ♖b7 is also good) **2...♖a4 3 ♖c8+??**

White makes his adversary a nice present: a vitally important tempo. 3 a7?? ♖×a7= was obviously erroneous, but the line 3 ♖c6! ♔×h7 4 ♔×b2 ♔g7 5 ♔b3 ♖a1 6 ♔b4 ♔f7 7 ♔c5(b5) ♔e7 8 ♔b6 ♔d7 9 ♔b7 led to a win.

3...♔×h7 4 ♖c6 ♖b4??

A present in return! After 4...♔g7! Black's king could have come to the queenside in time: 5 ♔×b2 ♔f7 6 ♔b3 ♖a1 7 ♔b4 ♔e7 8 ♔b5 ♔d7=.

5 a7 ♖a4 6 ♖c7+ ♔g6 7 ♔×b2 ♔f6 8 ♔b3 ♖a1 9 ♔b4 ♔e6 10 ♔b5 (10 ♔c5) **10...♔d6 11 ♖c6+** (11 ♖h7) **11...♔d5 12 ♖a6 ♖b1+ 13 ♔a5 ♔c5 14 ♖c6+! ♔×c6 15 a8♕+**, and White won.

Brodsky – Khmelnitsky
Kherson 1989

9-44

W?

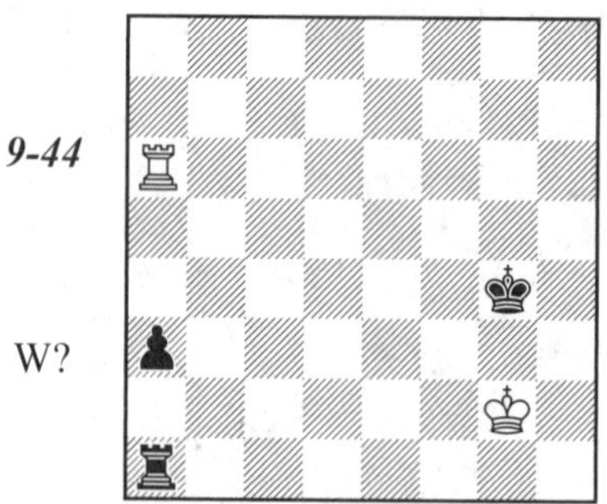

1 ♖a4+! ♔f5 2 ♖c4 ♖a2+ 3 ♔g3 ♖b2 4 ♖a4 would have led to a draw.

1 ♖g6+? ♔f4 (1...♔f5?? 2 ♖g3= is the Vancura position) **2 ♖a6**

White has no 2 ♖g3 on account of 2...♖g1+!. 2 ♖f6+ can be met by 2...♔e4!, while 2 ♖c6 - by 2...♖a2+!.

2...♔e4 3 ♖a4+ ♔e3?

An absurd move! If the king is going to move ahead, then why not to d3? But 3...♔d5 4 ♖f4 ♖a2+ 5 ♔g3 ♖b2 would have been a much simpler win.

9-45

$

W?

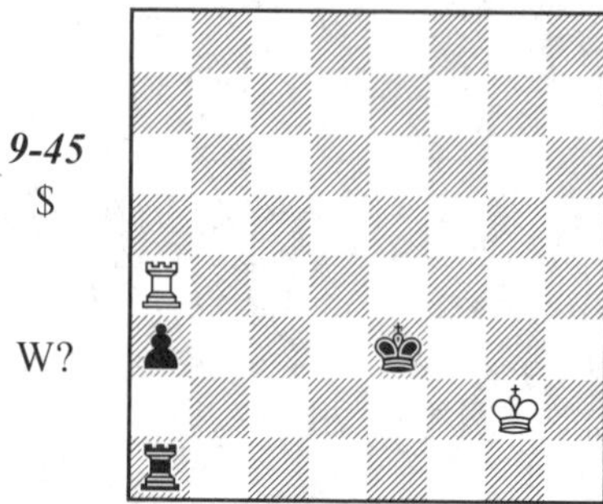

Now we have (with reversed wings and colors) the Romanovsky position (1950). Its solution is 4 ♖h4!! ♔d2 (4...♖a2+ 5 ♔g1! ♖f2 6 ♖a4 ♖a2 7 ♖h4=) 5 ♖h3! ♔c2 6 ♖f3! a2 7 ♖f2+! (7 ♖a3?? ♔b2) 7...♔d3 8 ♖f3+ ♔e4 9 ♖a3=.

4 ♖g4? (a decisive error) **4...♖a2+! 5 ♔h3**

After 5 ♔g1 ♔f3! 6 ♖a4 (6 ♖c4 ♖e2) Black has a pleasant choice between 6...♖a1+ 7 ♔h2 ♔e2 and 6...♔g3 7 ♔f1 ♖a1+ 8 ♔e2 a2 △ 9...♖h1.

5...♖f2! 6 ♖a4 a2 7 ♖a3+ ♔d4 8 ♔g3 ♖b2 9 ♔f4 ♖f2+

White resigned. The aim of the last check was probably to improve the rook position after 10 ♔g3, bringing it to c2 first, and to push the king thereafter. However the immediate 9...♔c4 10 ♔e4 ♔b4 11 ♖a8 ♔c3 −+ was sufficient for a win.

a- and h-Pawns

In the Vancura position, let us add a white pawn on the h-file. It is easy to see that the evaluation remains unchanged. The defensive method is precisely the same as before: the rook maintains the pawn in the crosshairs from the side and does not release the hostile rook from the corner.

9-46

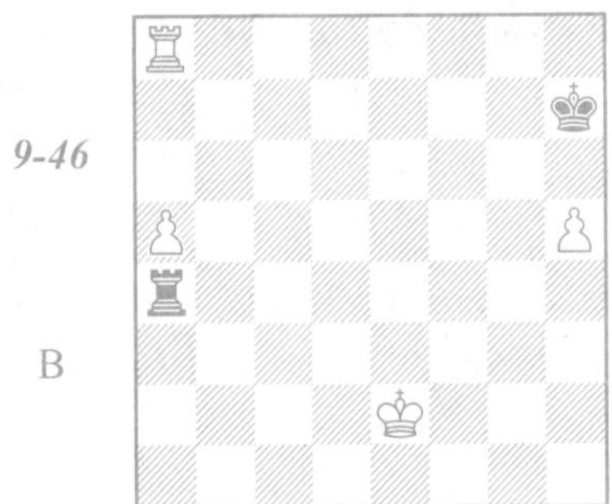

B

1...♖e4+! 2 ♔d3 ♖e5 3 ♔c4 ♖f5!

The best policy is to pay no attention to the h-pawn at all. 3...♖×h5? loses to 4 a6 ♖h6 5 ♔b5 ♖h5+ 6 ♔b6 ♖h6+ 7 ♔b7.

4 a6 (4 ♔b4 ♖f4+) **4...♖f6! 5 ♔b5 ♖f5+ 6 ♔c6 ♖f6+ 7 ♔d5 ♖b6** etc.

Tragicomedies

Suetin – F. Portisch
Belgrade 1977

9-47

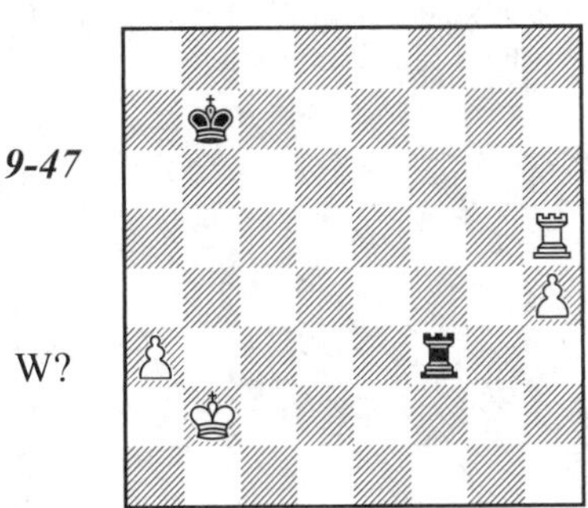

W?

White could move his rook to a more advantageous position: 1 ♖c5! (or 1 ♖b5+) 1...♔b6 2 ♖c3 ♖f2+ (2...♖f4 3 ♖h3) 3 ♔b3 (3 ♖c2!? △ 4 ♖h2) 3...♖h2 4 ♖c4 and 5 a4 with an easy win. However Suetin does not suspect any danger of a draw.

1 a4?? ♖f4! = 2 ♔b3 ♔a6! (the threat was 3 ♖b5+ followed by 4 h5 +−) **3 a5 ♖e4 4 ♔c3 ♖f4 5 ♔d3 ♖g4 6 ♔e3 ♖c4 7 ♔f3 ♖c3+**

The rook is placed best on the c-file. 7...♖b4? loses to 8 ♖h8 ♔a7 9 h5 ♖b5 10 h6 +−.

8 ♔e4 ♖c4+ 9 ♔d5 ♖g4 10 ♔e6 ♖c4 11 ♖h8 ♔b7 12 ♖h7+ ♔a6 Draw.

Szabó – Tukmakov
Buenos Aires 1970

9-48

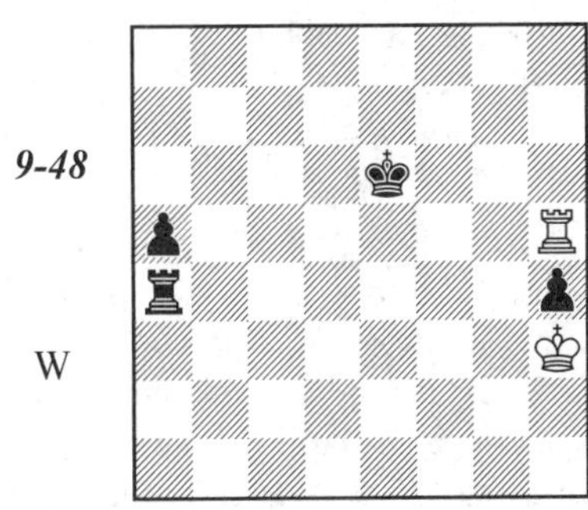

W

White may simply wait and maintain the a-pawn in the crosshairs. For example, 1 ♖b5 ♔d6 2 ♖f5 ♖a1 3 ♔h2! a4 4 ♖f4! a3 5 ♖f3! ♔c5 (5...a2 6 ♖a3) 6 ♖b3 ♔c4 7 ♖f3 ♔b4 8 ♖f4+! etc.

Szabó, an experienced grandmaster, did not know this defensive system.

1 ♔g2?! ♔d6 2 ♔f2?! ♖a2+ 3 ♔e1?

After 3 ♔g1! ♔c6 4 ♖f5! the position was still drawn.

3...♖a1+! 4 ♔e2

There is no salvation anymore: 4 ♔f2 a4 5 ♖×h4 a3 6 ♖h3 (6 ♖a4 ♔c5 −+) 6...a2 7 ♖a3 ♖h1, or 4 ♔d2 ♖h1! 5 ♖×a5 h3 6 ♖h5 h2 △ 7...♖a1 −+.

4...a4 5 ♖h6+ ♔e5 6 ♖h5+ ♔f6 7 ♔f2 a3 8 ♔g2 ♖c1 9 ♖a5 ♖c3 White resigned.

Twenty-three years later, precisely the same position occurred in Emms - Riemersma, Gausdal 1993. And again, White did not know the theory of this ending.

1 ♖h6+?! ♔d5 2 ♖h5+ ♔c4 3 ♖×h4+? (3 ♖f5! ♖a1 4 ♔h2 a4 5 ♖f4+ with a draw) **3...♔b3 4 ♖h5**

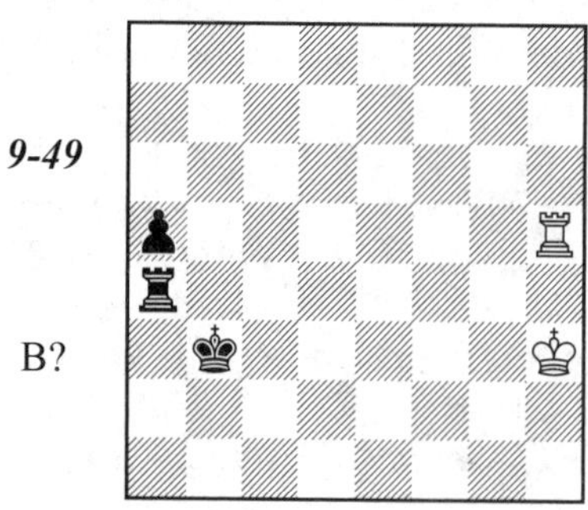

9-49

B?

4...♖a1?

White's rook is misplaced, and it is important to keep it on the h-file. Emms demonstrated that this could have been achieved by the subtle move 4...♖a3!, for example: 5 ♔h2 (5 ♖g5 ♔b4+ 6 ♔g2 ♖c3 7 ♖g8 a4 8 ♖b8+ ♔c4 9 ♔f2 a3 10 ♖a8 ♔b3 11 ♔e2 a2 12 ♔d2 ♖c4–+) 5...a4! 6 ♖h3+ ♔b2 7 ♖h4 ♖a2! 8 ♔h1 (8 ♖g4 ♔b3+ 9 ♔h3 ♖c2–+) 8...♖a1+ 9 ♔g2 a3 10 ♖h3 a2–+.

5 ♔g2?

An error in return. A draw was possible through 5 ♖g5! a4 6 ♖g3+ ♔b4 (6...♔c2 7 ♖g2+ ♔d3 8 ♖g4 a3 9 ♖g3+ ♔c2 10 ♔h2=) 7 ♖g4+ ♔b5 8 ♖g5+ ♔c6 9 ♖g6+! (the king should be driven as far away as possible; premature is 9 ♖g4? a3 10 ♔h2 ♖b1 11 ♖a4 ♖b3 12 ♔g2 ♔b5 13 ♖a8 ♔b4 14 ♔f2 ♔c3 15 ♔e2 ♔b2–+, or 10 ♔g2 ♔b5! 11 ♖g3 ♔b4 12 ♖g4+ ♔b3 13 ♖g3+ ♔b2–+) 9...♔d5 10 ♖g5+ ♔e6 11 ♔g2 ♖b1 (11...a3 12 ♖g3 △ ♖f3=) 12 ♖a5 ♖b4 13 ♔f2 ♔d6 14 ♔e2=.

5...a4–+ 6 ♔f2 (6 ♖h3+ ♔b2 7 ♖h4 a3–+) **6...a3 7 ♖b5+ ♔a2 8 ♔e2 ♖b1 9 ♖d5** (9 ♖a5 ♔b2 10 ♖b5+ ♔a1 11 ♖a5 a2–+) **9...♔b2 10 ♖d2+ ♔b3 11 ♖d3+ ♔a4 12 ♖d4+ ♖b4 13 ♖d8 a2 14 ♔d3 ♔b3** White resigned.

A Rook and Two Pawns vs. a Rook

As Tarrasch once said, ***"all rook endings are drawn."*** These endings are rife with drawish tendencies, and even as large a material advantage as two extra pawns is often not sufficient for a victory.

Doubled Pawns

If the king of the weaker side stands in front of the pawns, a draw can usually be easily achieved (except for those cases when the rook must stay on the back rank in view of mate threats). The applicable ideas here are familiar to us from the Philidor position (diagram 9-15).

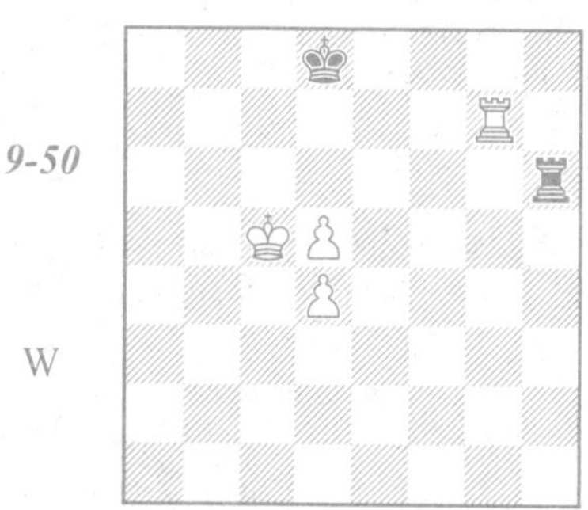

9-50

W

1 ♖b7 ♖g6 (1...♔c8!?) **2 ♖b6 ♖g4!**

Not the only move, but the safest. Black switches to the second defensive method in the Philidor position (if 3 ♔c6 then 3...♖×d4 4 ♖b8+ ♔e7=).

3 d6 ♖g1!

The rook prepares itself for giving rear checks because the white king has no refuge at d6 anymore.

4 ♔c6 ♖c1+ 5 ♔d5 ♖h1 6 ♖b8+ ♔d7 7 ♖b7+ ♔d8 8 d7 ♖h5+ (8...♔e7) **9 ♔c6 ♖h6+ 10 ♔c5 ♖h5+ 11 d5 ♖h6!=**

And again, Black returns to the defensive method suggested by Philidor.

Connected Pawns

Two extra connected pawns can be most easily exploited if the king supports them. However, sometimes they can advance for queening even when a rook alone supports them, as in the next diagram.

Szabó – Keres
Moscow 1956

9-51

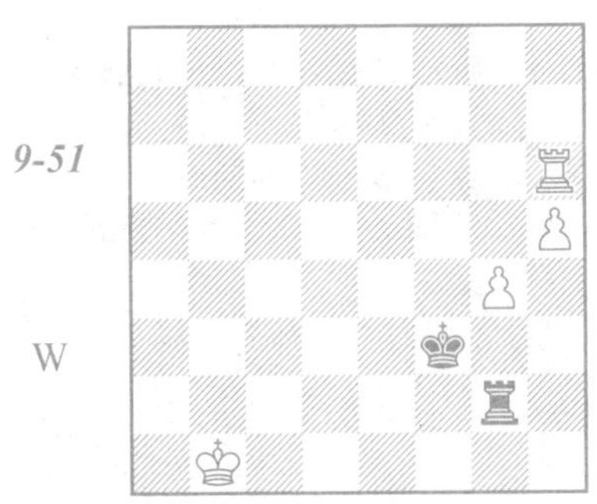

W

1 ♖g6

White is planning 2 h6, 3 g5, 4 ♖g7, 5 h7 etc. This simple plan cannot be prevented. Such pawns are sometimes called ***"self-propelled."***

1...♔e4 2 h6 ♖h2 3 g5 ♔d3 4 ♖g7 ♔c3 5 h7 (△ g6, ♖g8) **5...♔b3 6 ♖b7+** Black resigned.

The best chances for a successful defense exist when the king blocks the pawns. This is perhaps the most important drawn position:

J. Kling, B. Horwitz, 1851

9-52

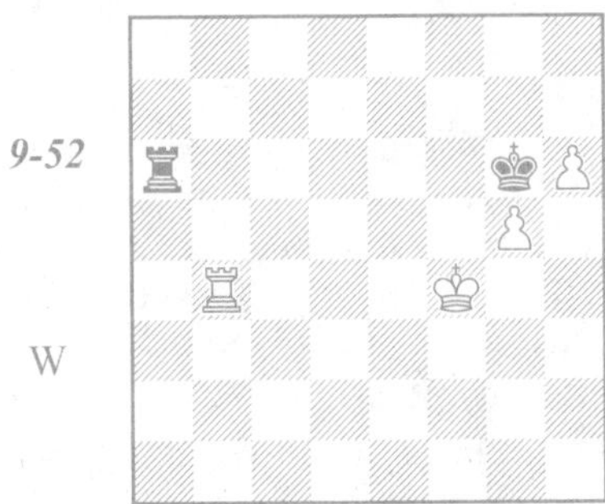

W

1 ♖d4 ♖b6 2 ♖d8! ♖b4+ 3 ♔e5 ♖b7!

The most precise: Black protects the 7th rank and threatens to take the g-pawn (he cannot of course do it immediately: 3...♔×g5?? 4 h7).

Erroneous is 3...♖g4? 4 ♖g8+ ♔h7 5 ♔f5!+– (rather than 5 ♖g7+?! ♔h8 6 ♔f5? ♖f4+! – a "desperado" rook). The *Encyclopaedia of Chess Endings* claims that 3...♖b5+ 4 ♖d5 ♖b7 5 ♔e6 also loses for Black. But I do not see how White can make any progress after 5...♖a7 6 ♖d7 ♖a6+ 7 ♖d6 (7 ♔e7 ♔×g5 8 h7 ♖a8 9 ♔f7 ♔h6=) 7...♖a7. 5...♖b6+ 6 ♔e7 ♖b7+ 7 ♖d7 ♖b5 (7...♖b8) 8 h7 ♖b8!= is also good.

4 ♖g8+ ♔h7 5 ♖e8 ♔g6

Black returns to the initial position of this ending. But he can now force a draw with 5...♖b5+ 6 ♔f6 ♖×g5!= (or 6...♖f5+!).

6 ♔f4 ♖b4+ 7 ♖e4 ♖b6=.

Let us look at a more complicated but quite useful situation that can occur in a practical game.

G. Kasparian, 1946

9-53

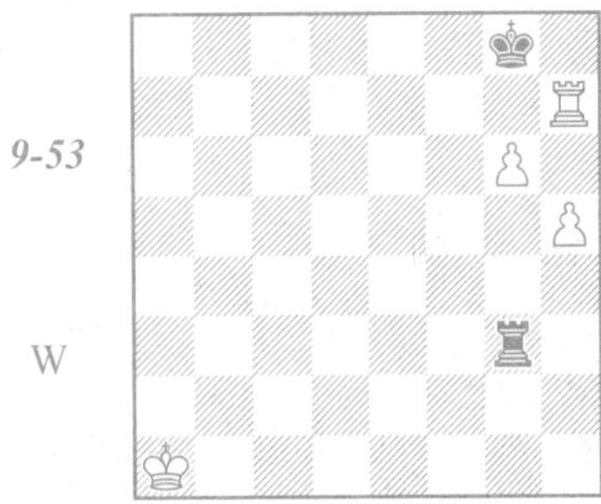

W

For the present, let us accept that White wins if he succeeds in transferring his rook to the 5th rank. This means that Black dare play neither 1...♔f8 2 ♖f7+ △ ...♖f5 nor 1...♖d3 2 ♖c7 ♖h3 (2...♖d5 3 h6) 3 ♖c5. Therefore his rook must stay on g3 and h3. But what can Black do when the white king comes to the kingside?

It turns out to be difficult for White. If his king comes to g2 when the black rook is on h3, then 1...♖a3 is playable, because 2 ♖b7 ♖a5! 3 h6 ♖g5+ loses a pawn; the same happens after 2 ♔h2 ♖b3 3 ♖a7 ♖b5!.

If White plays 2 ♔f2 the rook goes back to h3. By the way here, as in all similar positions, 3 h6 ♖h5 4 ♔f3 ♖g5 5 ♖g7+ ♔h8 6 ♔f4 ♖f5(g4)+! leads to nowhere.

However if, with the white king on f2 and the black rook on h3, Black is on move he comes to be in zugzwang. His rook must leave its comfortable position behind the pawns, and then the white rook has the opportunity to leave h7.

We have come to the conclusion that f2 and h3 are the squares of the reciprocal zugzwang. Obviously enough, another pair of such squares is e2 and g3. Furthermore, when the white king stands on any dark square of the 2nd rank the black rook must be on h3 while, when the king stands on a light square, the rook must be on g3!.

1 ♔a2!!

A paradoxical move that contradicts the standard approach ("first we move our king to the kingside, and only think thereafter"). It turns out that one should be thinking immediately because any other initial move misses the win.

After 1 ♔b2? ♖h3 2 ♔c2 ♖g3 3 ♔d2 ♖h3 4 ♔e2 ♖g3 5 ♔f2 ♖h3 White is in zugzwang: 6 ♔g2 ♖a3 7 ♖b7 ♖a5=.

If 1 ♖b7?, then 1...♖g5 2 ♖h7 ♖g2! 3 ♔b1 ♖h2 4 ♔c1 ♖g2 5 ♔d1 ♖h2 6 ♔e1 ♖g2 7 ♔f1 ♖h2 (the same zugzwang position, only by a rank lower) 8 ♔g1 ♖a2 9 ♖b7 ♖a5=.

In case of 1 ♔b1?, 1...♖g2? is erroneous: 2 ♔c1 ♖h2 3 ♔d1 ♖g2 4 ♔e1 ♖h2 5 ♔f1, and Black is in zugzwang: 5...♖a2 6 ♖b7+–. The correct method is 1...♖b3+!. The rook gives checks until the king steps on the 2nd rank, and then goes to a corresponding square. For example 2 ♔c2 ♖g3!, or 2 ♔c1 ♖c3+! 3 ♔d2 (3 ♔d1 ♖d3+!) 3...♖h3! 4 ♔e2 ♖g3 5 ♔f2 ♖h3⊙=.

1...♖h3 2 ♔b2 ♖g3 3 ♔c2 ♖h3 4 ♔d2 ♖g3 5 ♔e2 ♖h3 6 ♔f2⊙ ♖a3 7 ♖d7 ♖h3 8 ♖d5 ♔g7 9 ♔g2 ♖h4 10 ♔g3+–

It remains for us to prove that White wins if he succeeds in bringing his rook to the 5th rank. This fact is not quite obvious because Black blocks the pawns with his king. However his blockade is less efficient than in the Kling and Horwitz position.

1 ♔a2!! ♖d3 2 ♖b7! (but, of course, not 2 ♔b2? ♖h3!⊙=) **2...♖h3**

2...♖g3 can be met by 3 ♔b2 ♖g5 4 ♖h7 ♖g3 5 ♔c2, and it is Black who turns out to be in zugzwang again. This is the simplest way, but another, more universal way also exists: 3 ♖b3!? ♖g5 4 ♖h3 ♔g7 (otherwise the white king goes ahead) 5 h6+ ♔g8 6 g7! (rather than 6 h7+? ♔h8 7 ♖h6 ♖g1 and White's king will not have a refuge from rook checks from the rear) 5...♔h7 6 ♔b3, White activates his king and gradually wins (a similar position was analyzed by Kling and Horwitz as long ago as in 1851).

3 ♖b5 ♔g7 (3...♖g3 4 ♖b3) **4 ♖g5!**

Now Black has neither 4...♔h6 5 g7! nor 4...♖c3 5 h6+! ♔×h6 6 g7. But this position is winning for White even without this move (when the black king stands on h6).

4...♖h4

In case of 4...♔g8 5 ♔b2 ♖e3 White plays 6 ♔c2! ♖a3 7 ♔d2 ♖b3 8 ♔e2 ♖a3 9 ♔f2 ♖b3 10 ♖d5+–. A hasty 6 h6? ♖h3 7 h7+ ♔g7, on the contrary, leads to a theoretical draw.

5 ♔b3 ♖h1 6 ♔c4 ♖c1+ 7 ♔d5

The king must go ahead. Nothing can be achieved by 7 ♔d3 ♖h1 8 ♔e3 ♖h3+ 9 ♔f2 ♖h1 (rather than 9...♖h4? 10 ♔g2⊙+–) 10 ♔g2 ♖h4⊙, and the rook cannot be forced away from the h-file.

7...♖d1+ 8 ♔c6 ♖c1+ 9 ♔d6 ♖d1+ 10 ♖d5 ♖a1 11 ♔e7 ♖a6

White's task is less difficult in case of 11...♖e1+ 12 ♔d8! ♔g8 (12...♖a1 13 ♖d7+ ♔g8 14 ♔e7+–; 12...♔h6 13 ♖d7! ♔×h5 14 g7 ♖g1 15 ♔e8 ♔h6 16 ♔f8+–) 13 h6! (13 ♖f5!? ♖e6 14 ♔d7 ♖a6 15 ♖c5+–) 13...♖e6 (13...♖h1 14 ♔e7!; 13...♖g1 14 ♖d6) 14 h7+! (but not 14 ♖g5? ♖a6 15 ♔e7 ♖b6 16 h7+ ♔g7 17 ♖h5 ♖b7+ 18 ♔e6 ♖b6+ with a draw) 14...♔h8 15 ♖g5 ♔g7 16 ♖h5+–.

12 ♖d7

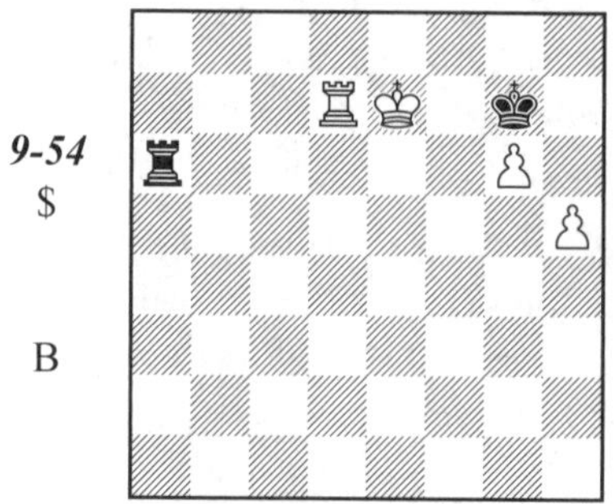

12...♖b6!?

12...♖a5 13 ♔e6+ ♔g8 14 h6+– is quite bad. After 12...♖c6, Kasparian gives 13 ♔d8+ ♔g8 14 ♖e7 ♔f8 (14...♖d6+ 15 ♔c7 ♖a6 16 ♔d7 ∆ 17 ♖e6) 15 ♔d7 ♖a6 16 ♖e6 ♖a7+ 17 ♔d6 ♖a6+ 18 ♔e5 ♖a5+ 19 ♔f6+–.

13 ♔d8+ ♔g8

13...♔f8 is met with 14 ♔c7! ♖a6 15 h6 (15 ♖d6) 15...♖×g6 16 ♖d8+ and 17 h7+–.

14 ♔c7! ♖a6 15 ♖d6 ∆ h6+–

In *Theory of Rook Endings* by Levenfish and Smyslov, in the very end of this line, another road to the win is suggested: 14 ♖e7 ♔f8 (14...♖d6+ 15 ♔c7 ♖a6 16 ♔d7 ♖b6 17 ♖e6+–) 15 ♖f7+ ♔g8 16 ♔e7 ♖a6 17 ♖f6 ♖a7+ 18 ♔e6 ♖a6+ 19 ♔f5 ♖a5+ 20 ♔g4 ♔g7 21 ♖f7+. But this recommendation is erroneous: instead of 18...♖a6+? Black plays 18...♔g7!, because after 19 ♖f7+? ♖×f7 20 gf ♔f8⊙ he holds a pawn ending despite being two pawns down.

This complicated analysis can hardly be (and certainly should not be) remembered in all its details. To know that the rook transfer to the 5th rank wins is quite enough, yet the proof of this fact turns out to be rather complicated.

Tragicomedies

Glek – Leitao
Wijk aan Zee 1999

9-55

B

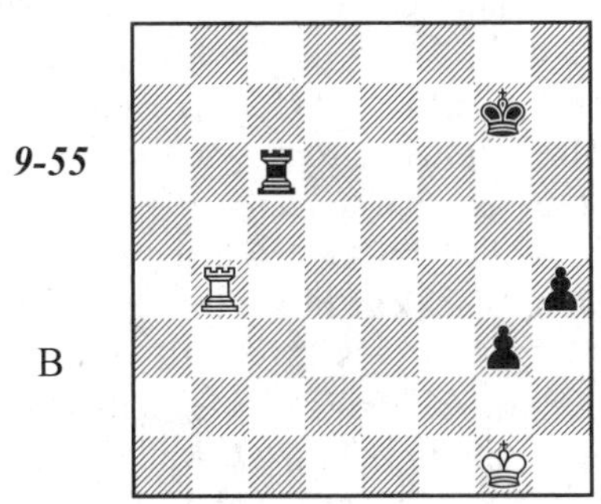

1...♖c1+?? 2 ♔g2 ♖c2+ 3 ♔g1 ♖h2 4 ♖b6

The Kasparian position – Black has no win.

4...♔f7 5 ♖h6 ♔e7 6 ♖g6 ♔f8 7 ♖f6+! ♔e8 8 ♖e6+! ♔d7 9 ♖h6! h3 10 ♖g6 Draw.

Black could have won by means of 1...h3! 2 ♖g4+ ♖g6 3 ♖h4 (3 ♖a4 g2) 3...h2+ 4 ♔g2 ♖h6 5 ♖g4+ ♔f6 6 ♖f4+ (6 ♔h1 ♖g6+–) 6...♔g5 7 ♖f1 ♔g4 8 ♖a1 h1♕+ 9 ♖×h1 ♖×h1 10 ♔×h1 ♔f3 (Glek).

Exercises

9-56

9/7
W?

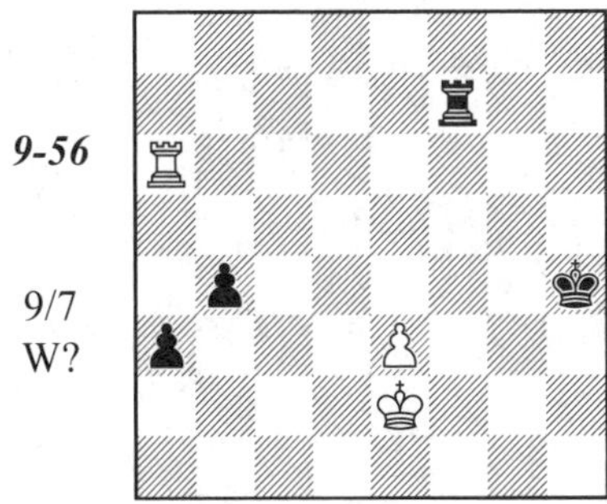

9-57

9/8
B?

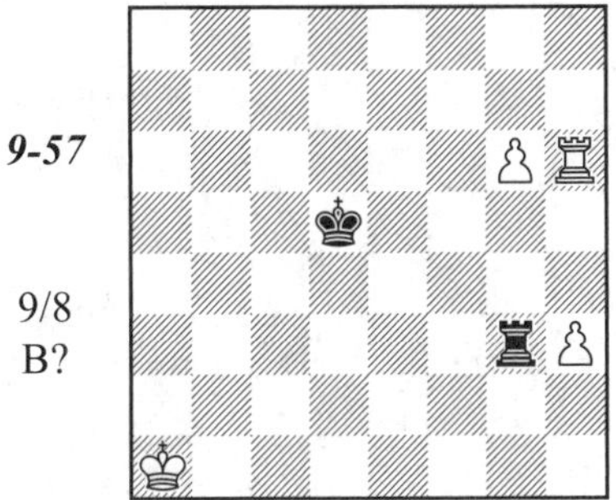

f- and h-Pawns

Endings with these pawns are mostly drawn. Their theory is rather complicated and that is why we will explain only the basic ideas here. The following example from practical play shows how one should defend these positions.

Gligoric - Smyslov
Moscow 1947

9-58

W

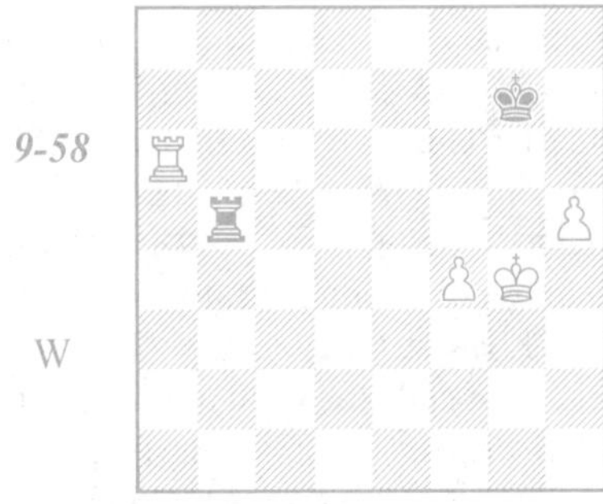

The black rook is excellently placed on the 5th rank: it prevents an advance of the hostile king. If 1 f5, then 1...♖b1, threatening a series of checks from the rear.

1 ♖g6+ ♔f7!

1...♔h7 was not losing, but Black would have had more problems than in the game.

2 ♖g5 ♖b1!

A typical retreat for this sort of situation: the rook maintains opportunities for checks from various directions, both from the side and rear.

3 ♖c5

In case of 3 h6, 3...♖g1+? is erroneous: 4 ♔f5 ♖h1 5 ♖g7+ ♔f8 6 ♔g6 ♖g1+ 7 ♔h7! ♖f1 8 ♖a7! (8 ♖g4 ♔f7) 8...♖×f4 9 ♔g6 ♖g4+ 10 ♔f6! ♖f4+ (10...♔g8 11 ♖g7+!) 11 ♔g5 ♖f1 12 ♖a8+ ♔f7 13 h7+–.

The waiting move 3...♖a1! helps, for example: 4 ♖h5 (4 ♔f5 ♖a5+; 4 h7 ♖g1+ 5 ♔f5 ♖h1) 4...♔g8 5 f5 ♔h7.

The following attempt is interesting: 4 ♖g7+ ♔f6 5 ♖c7!? ♔g6 (Black can also play 5...♖g1+ 6 ♔f3 ♖h1) 6 h7, (see next diagram).

9-59
$

B

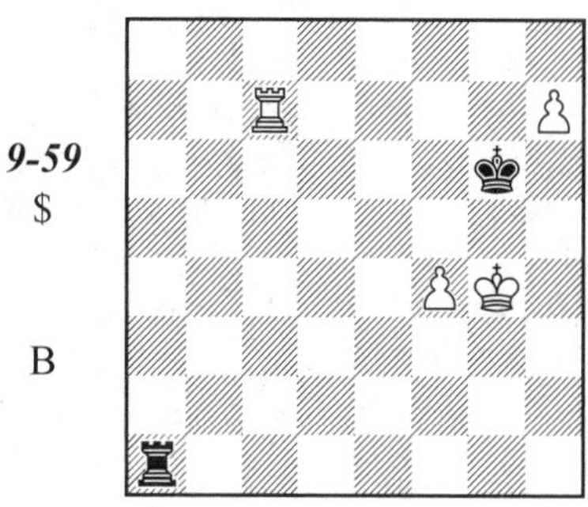

I once investigated the position that arises after 6...♖g1+? 7 ♔f3 ♖h1 8 ♔e4 ♖h5 together with grandmaster Gulko. The continuation 9 f5+? ♔f6 10 ♖c6+ ♔g7 11 ♔e5 ♔×h7 (11...♖h1!? is even simpler) 12 ♖c7+ ♔h6! 13 ♔f6 ♖h1 14 ♖c2 ♖h3!= does not promise White any success (see the ending below, Polugaevsky - Ree).

White should cede the right to move to his adversary, with the idea of forcing the black rook away from h5, and then advancing his king, when his rook stands precisely on c7. All this can be achieved in the following way: 9 ♖d7(e7) ♔f6 10 ♖a7 (10 ♖d8? ♖×h7 11 ♖d6+ ♔e7=) 10...♔g6 (10...♖h1? 11 ♖a8! ♖×h7 12 ♖a6+) 11 ♖c7!!⊙ ♖h1 (11...♔f6? 12 ♖c8!+–) 12 ♔e5 ♖e1+ 13 ♔d6 ♖d1+ (13...♖h1 14 ♖e7! △ 15 ♔d7) 14 ♔c6 ♖h1 (14...♖c1+ 15 ♔b7 or 15 ♔d7) 15 ♖e7! ♔f5 16 ♔d7 ♔×f4 17 ♔e8 ♔g5 18 ♔f8 ♔g6 19 ♔g8+–.

Later, I discovered the possibility of a more stubborn defense. Instead of 14...♖h1, Black should play 14...♖d8!?.

In order for White to win, he need only get his king back to the f-pawn, while keeping the Black rook tied to the 8th rank. But how is this to be accomplished? Black answers 15 ♔c5 with 15...♖a8!, after which 16 ♔d4 is useless: 16...♖a4+ 17 ♔e3 (17 ♔e5 ♖a5+ 18 ♔e4 ♖h5) 17...♖a3+ 18 ♔e4 ♖h3 (△ 19...♖h5) 19 ♔e5 ♖e3+ 20 ♔d5 ♖d3+ 21 ♔c6 ♖d8!, etc.

Before bringing the king back, it's important to bring the rook to d7 first. Then Black's rook maneuver to h3 (as in the variation we just examined) has no point – once again, White brings his king forward, and now the Black rook cannot get to d8. The most exact line is: 16 ♖a7! (not 16 ♖d7 at once: 16...♖a5+ 17 ♔d4?! ♖h5, and White must start all over again) 16...♖b8 17 ♖d7 ♔f6 (17...♖a8 18 ♔d4) 18 ♔d4 (threatening ♔e4-f3-g4) 18...♖a4+ 19 ♔e3 ♖a3+ 20 ♔e4 ♖h3 21 ♔d5 ♖d3+ 22 ♔c6 ♖c3+ 23 ♔b7 ♖h3 24 ♔c8+–.

Instead of 6...♖g1+? Black must play 6...♖h1! immediately. If White tries the waiting move 7 ♖b7, Black can wait too: 7...♖h2, with no fear of 8 ♖b5 ♔g7! 9 ♖g5+ ♔h8!. Another good line is 7...♖g1+ 8 ♔f3 ♖h1 9 ♔e4 ♖e1+, because when the white rook stands on b7 the king's route around it is too long: 10 ♔d5 ♖d1+ 11 ♔c6 ♖c1+! 12 ♔b6 ♖h1! with a draw.

If 7 ♔f3, Black can play either 7...♔f5! or 7...♔f6!? 8 ♔e4 ♖e1+ 9 ♔d5 ♖d1+ 10 ♔c6 ♖h1!. When the black king stands on f6, White has no important move 11 ♖e7, while after 11 ♖d7 (or 11 ♔b7) 11...♔f5 the black king abolishes the f4-pawn and returns to g6 in time.

3...♔f6 4 ♖c6+ ♔g7!

The main danger for Black is for his king to be forced to the back rank. This could have happened after 4...♔f7? 5 ♔g5 ♖g1+ 6 ♔f5 ♖h1 7 ♖c7+.

5 ♔g5 ♖g1+! 6 ♔f5 ♖a1 7 ♖c7+ (7 ♖g6+ ♔f7) **7...♔h6 8 ♖e7 ♖b1 9. ♖e8 ♔g7 10 ♖e5 ♖a1 11 ♖d5 ♖f1**

Not a bad move, but holding the rook in the corner was quite enough.

12 ♖d4 ♖a1 13 ♖d6 ♖a5+ 14 ♔g4 ♖a1

14...♖b5 is also playable: it leads back to the initial position.

15 ♖e6 ♖g1+ 16 ♔f5 ♖a1

9-60

W

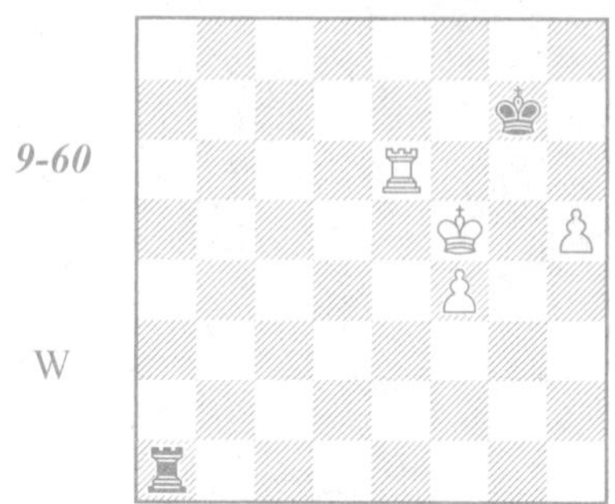

17 h6+ ♔h7! 18 ♖d6 ♖a2 19 ♔g5 ♖g2+ 20 ♔f6 ♔×h6! 21 ♔e7+ ♔h7 22 f5 ♖e2+ 23 ♖e6 ♖a2 24 f6 ♖a8!

We have discussed this sort of position in the section dedicated to the pawn on 6th rank. The black rook is placed on the long side, so a draw is inevitable.

25 ♔f7 ♚h6 26 ♖e1 ♜a7+ 27 ♖e7 ♜a8 28 ♖d7 ♚h7 29 ♖d1 ♜a7+ 30 ♔e6 ♜a6+ 31 ♖d6 ♜a8 32 ♖d4 ♚g8 33 ♖g4+ ♚f8 Draw.

In this example, Black kept his king on f7 until the danger of its being driven to the back rank arose. Thereafter the king went to g7 and later on – to h6, attacking the white pawn. But, strictly speaking, Kopaev's recommendation was to place the king in front of the more advanced pawn.

The best position for the rook is on a1; it is ideally suited for giving checks along files as well as ranks. However, if the pawns are not advanced too far, the rook stands quite well on the 5th rank, and sometimes on f1.

It goes without saying that not all positions with f- and h-pawns are drawn. The most important exception was already mentioned above: ***Black usually loses if his king is cut off on the back rank***.

Capablanca – Kostic
Havana m (1) 1919

9-61

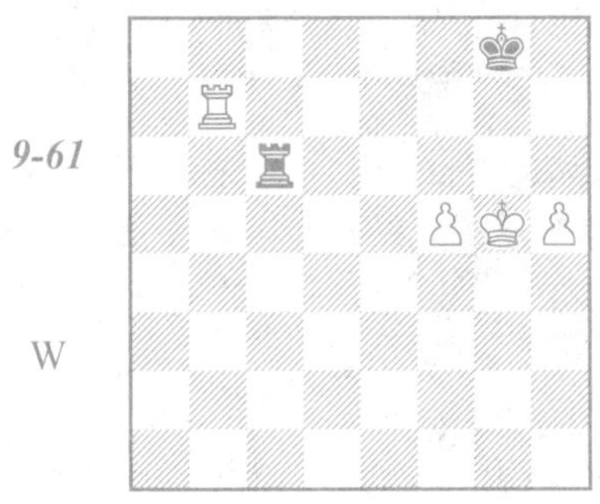

W

One does not need to keep the solution in mind because White has many winning ways to choose from.

1 f6

Kopaev suggests 1 ♖b8+ ♔h7 (1...♔f7 2 h6 △ 3 h7; 1...♔g7 2 f6+! ♖×f6 3 h6+) 2 f6 ♖c5+ (2...♖c7 3 ♖e8) 3 ♔g4 ♖c4+ 4 ♔f5 ♖c5+ 5 ♔e6 ♖c6+ 6 ♔e7 ♖c7+ 7 ♔f8 ♔h6 8 f7+–.

1...♜c1 2 ♖g7+

Belavenets's suggestion is also good: 2 h6 ♖g1+ 3 ♔f5 ♖f1+ 4 ♔e6. The king is striving for the 8th rank. If 4...♖e1+, then 5 ♔d6! (rather than 5 ♔d7? ♔f7 6 h7 ♖h1=).

2...♚f8?!

Loses at once, but 2...♔h8 could postpone the loss only for a little while: 3 ♔g6 ♖g1+ 4 ♔f7 ♖a1 5 ♖g8+ ♔h7 6 ♖e8 ♖a7+ 7 ♔f8. White's next move will be 8 f7 (the h5-pawn deprives the black king of the important g6-square).

3 h6

Black resigned; he cannot prevent h6-h7.

Tragicomedies

Polugaevsky – Ree
Amsterdam 1981

9-62

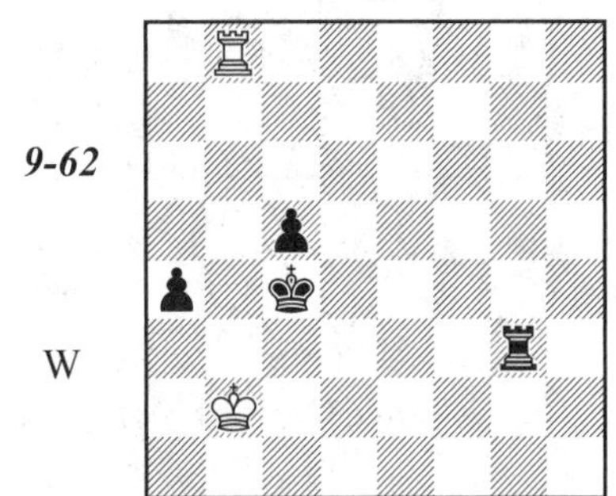

W

1 ♖a8?!

The simplest way is to keep the rook on h8, in order to profit by the side checks in case of emergency.

1...♜g2+ 2 ♔a3 ♚c3 3 ♖×a4

It was still not too late to bring the rook to the long side, for example 3 ♖h8!? c4 4 ♖h3+ ♔d2 5 ♔b4!=. However this capture does not lose, contrary to comments by Krnic in the *Chess Informant*.

3...c4 4 ♖a8 ♜g7 5 ♔a2??

This is the decisive error! Now the black king advances while the white rook remains chained to the a-file. He should have followed the waiting policy: 5 ♖a6! ♖d7 6 ♖a8 ♖d1 (6...♔c2 7 ♖h8!) 7 ♔a2 ♔c2 8 ♖h8 c3 9 ♖h2+ with a draw.

5...♚c2–+ 6 ♔a1 c3 7 ♔a2 ♜b7 8 ♖a6 ♜d7 9 ♖a8 ♚d2 White resigned.

Other Pairs of Disconnected Pawns

As a rule, two extra pawns are sufficient for a win. However exceptions occur now and then. They are caused either by the stronger side having badly placed pieces while the defender's pieces are active, or by inattention (when the stronger side anticipates a quick win too nonchalantly). This last case is illustrated by all the practical examples that follow.

Tragicomedies

Bernstein – Smyslov
Groningen 1946

9-63

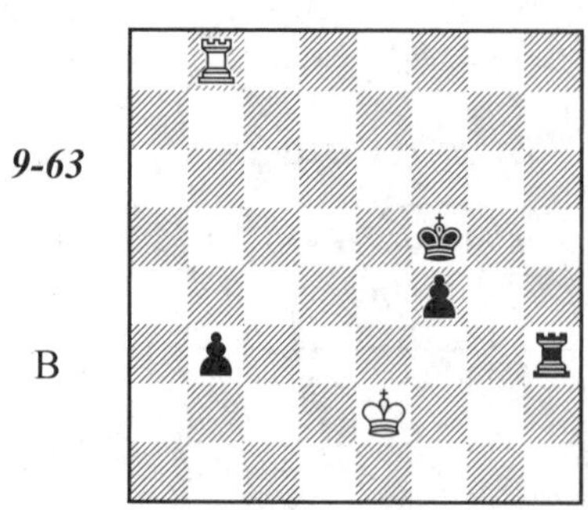

B

1...b2?? (both 1...♔e5 and 1...♔e4 won elementarily) **2 ♖×b2! ♔g4**

The planned 2...♖h2+ turned out to be ineffective because of the stalemate after 3 ♔f3 ♖×b2.

3 ♔f1

Draw. The Philidor position has arisen.

A similar story happened in the following endgame.

Gufeld – Bronstein
Kislovodsk 1968

9-64

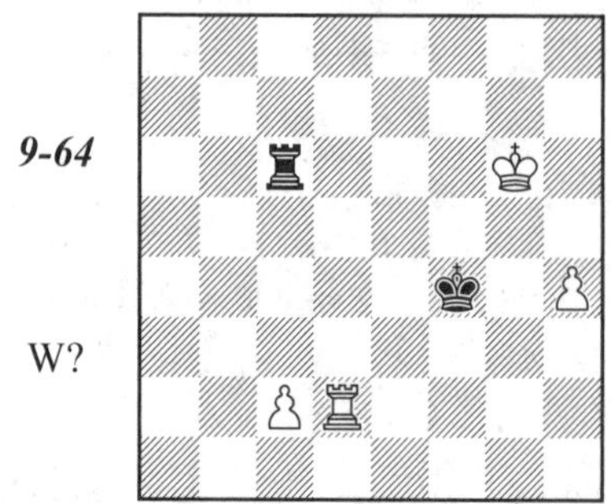

W?

With 1 ♔f7!, White maintains his two extra pawns: 1...♔g4 (1...♔e3 2 ♖h2) 2 ♖d4+ ♔f5 3 c4 ♖c7+ (3...♔e5 4 ♖d5+ ♔e4 5 ♖g5) 4 ♔e8! ♔e5 5 ♖g4 ♔f5 6 ♔d8! with an easy win.

1 ♔g7? ♔g4

Now 2 ♖d4+ ♔h5 3 c4 can be met by 3...♖×c4! 4 ♖×c4 – stalemate.

2 ♖h2 ♔g3! 3 ♖h1 ♖×c2 4 h5 ♖c7+ 5 ♔f6 ♖c6+ 6 ♔f7 ♖c7+ 7 ♔e6 ♖c6+ 8 ♔d5 ♖h6 9 ♔e4 ♔g2 10 ♖h4 ♔g3 11 ♖h1 ♔g2 Draw.

Kasparov – Short
London m (9) 1993

9-65

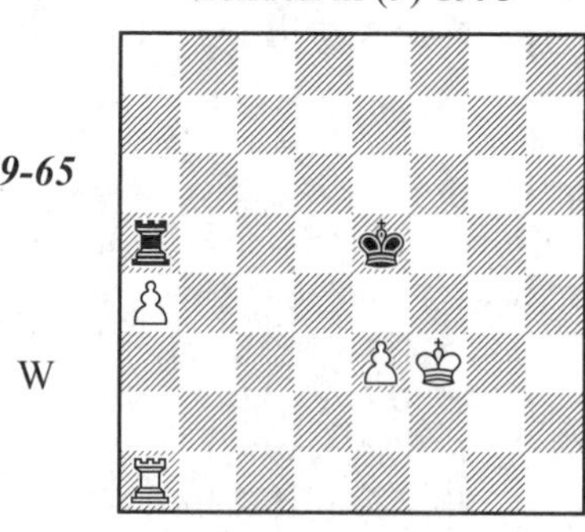

W

The rook that blocks a passed pawn cannot, as a rule, leave its post unpunished. Therefore it would have been wise to play for zugzwang: 1 ♖a2!? ♔f5 2 e4+ ♔e5 3 ♔e3, and now 3...♖a8 (3...♖c5 4 ♔d3) 4 a5 ♖h8 5 ♖a4 (or 5 ♖f2).

Another winning method was 1 ♔e2 (△ ♔d3-c4-b4) 1...♔e4 2 ♖f1! △ ♖f4+ (2 ♖h1 ♖h5! 3 ♖f1!).

1 e4?? ♔e6??

Both opponents are hypnotized by the above-mentioned rule. However this was a proper moment for neglecting it (there are no absolute rules in chess!) by playing 1...♖c5!. Black could then regain a pawn and block the a-pawn again in time, for example 2 a5 (2 ♖a3 ♖c4 3 a5 ♖×e4 4 a6 ♖f4+ △ ♖f8=) 2...♖c3+ 3 ♔g4 (3 ♔e2 ♔×e4 4 a6 ♖c8=) 3...♔×e4 4 a6 ♖c8 5 a7, and here the most precise defense is 5...♖g8+! 6 ♔h5 ♖a8, although 5...♖a8 6 ♖a5 ♔d4 7 ♔f5 ♔c4 8 ♔e6 ♔b4 9 ♖a1 ♔c5! is also sufficient for a draw (rather than 9...♔b5? 10 ♔d6 ♔b6 11 ♖b1+!), e.g. 10 ♔d7 ♔b6 11 ♖b1+ ♔c5! 12 ♖b7 ♖h8=.

2 ♔e3 ♔d6 3 ♔d4 ♔d7 4 ♔c4 ♔c6 5 ♔b4 ♖e5 6 ♖c1+ ♔b6 7 ♖c4 Black resigned.

Larsen – Torre
Leningrad izt 1973

9-66

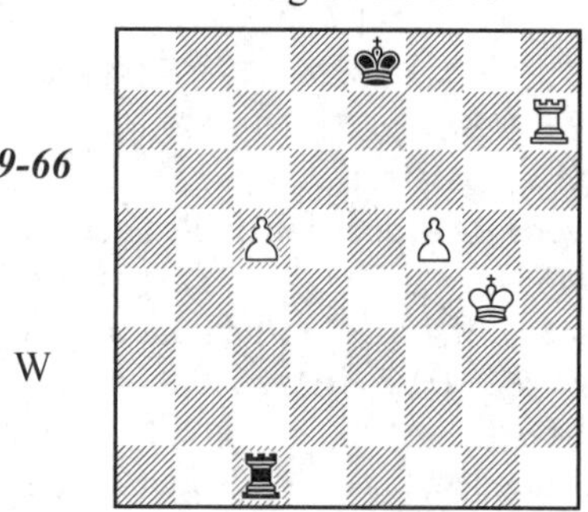

W

A natural method of exploiting two extra pawns is a transition to theoretically winning positions with one extra pawn.

This method could be applied here: 1 ♔g5! ♖×c5 2 ♔g6 △ ♖h8+. White has a simple win because the black king is on the long side.

1 ♖c7?! ♔d8 2 ♖c6 ♔d7 3 ♖d6+ ♔e7 4 f6+??

After 4 ♖e6+! ♔f7 5 c6 ♖f1 6 ♔g5 ♖f2 7 ♖d6 Black would have had no alternative to a resignation. 4 ♖d5+– was also good.

4...♔f7 5 c6 ♔g6! 6 ♔f3 ♖e1!=

9-67

W

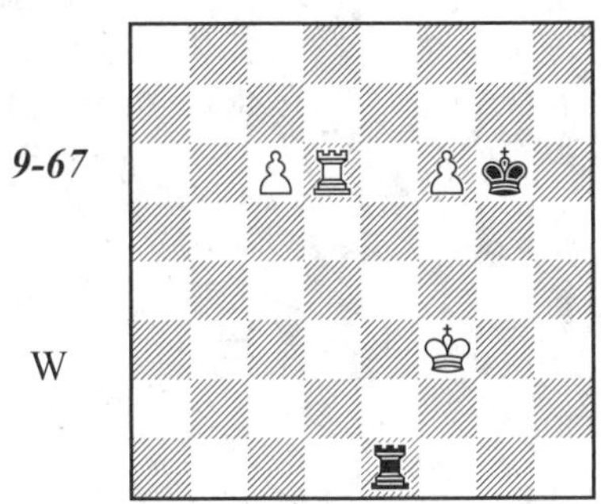

The rook cuts the hostile king off from both pawns. White cannot strengthen his position.

7 ♔f4 ♖e2 8 ♖d5 ♖c2

8...♔×f6? is erroneous: 9 ♖c5 ♖e8 10 ♖f5+! ♔g6 (10...♔e7 11 ♖e5+ ♔f7 12 ♖×e8 ♔×e8 13 ♔e5+–) 11 ♖e5! ♖c8 12 ♖e6+ ♔f7 13 ♔e5+–.

9 ♖d6 ♖e2 10 f7+ ♔×f7 11 ♔f5 ♔e7 12 ♖d7+ ♔e8 13 ♔f6 ♖e1 14 ♖d5 ♖c1 15 ♖d6 ♖f1+ 16 ♔e6 ♖e1+ 17 ♔d5 ♖d1+ 18 ♔c5 ♖×d6 19 ♔×d6 ♔d8 Draw.

Exercises

9-68

9/9
B?

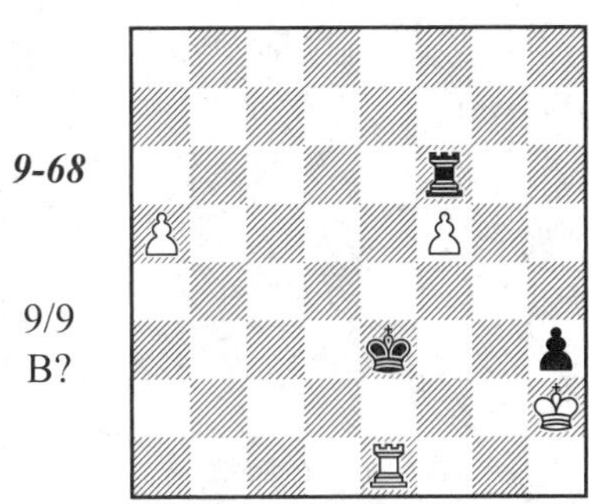

A Far Advanced Passed Pawn

Transition to a Rook vs. Pawns Endgame

It often happens that a passed pawn is so strong that the opponent must inevitably give a rook away for it. In such cases, one should know well and take into account the methods we have learned from studying rook versus pawns endgames.

Black's actions in the following endgame were based on two typical methods: shouldering and cutting off the king.

Yusupov - Tseshkovsky
Moscow tt 1981

9-69

B?

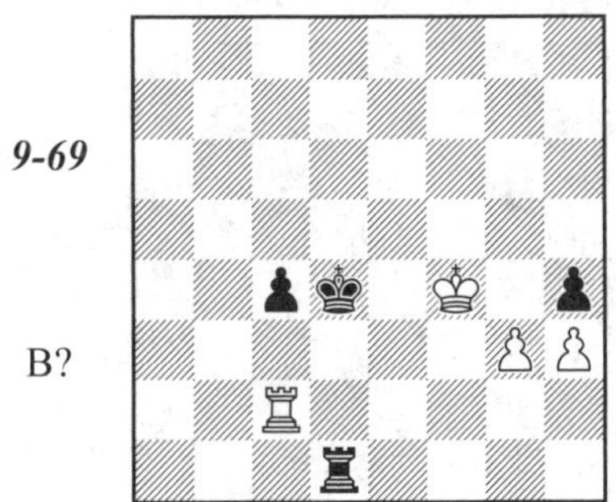

In case of the straightforward 1...hg? (1...♔d3? 2 ♖f2! or 2 ♖g2! has the same consequences) 2 ♔×g3 ♔d3 3 ♖a2 c3 4 h4 c2 5 ♖×c2 ♔×c2 White, of course, cannot play 6 h5?? ♖d4!, but 6 ♔g4? ♔d3 7 h5 ♔e4 8 ♔g5 ♔e5 9 ♔g6 ♔e6 10 h6 ♖g1+ also loses. It is shouldering that helps here: 6 ♔f4! ♔d3 7 h5 ♖h1 8 ♔g5 ♔e4 9 h6 ♔e5 10 ♔g6 ♔e6 11 ♔g7! (rather than 11 h7? ♖g1+ 12 ♔h6 ♔f7 13 h8♘+ ♔f6 14 ♔h7 ♖g2⊙ –+) 11...♔e7 (11...♖g1+ 12 ♔f8) 12 h7 ♖g1+ 13 ♔h8!=.

Deliberating over his next move, Tseshkovsky recognized White's defensive plan and found how to prevent its realization.

1...♖f1+!! 2 ♔g4 hg

Now, after 3 ♔×g3 ♔d3 4 ♖a2 c3 5 h4 c2 6 ♖×c2 ♔×c2, the white king cannot go to f4, and White loses.

3 ♖d2+ ♔e3 4 ♖g2

4 ♖c2 ♖f4+! 5 ♔×g3 ♖d4 6 h4 ♔d3 changes nothing.

4...♖f4+!

White could hold after 4...c3? 5 ♖×g3+ ♔d4 6 ♖g2 ♔d3 7 h4 (compared with the line 3 ♔×g3 ♔d3 he would have an extra tempo). Alas, Black wins easily by means of cutting the king off along the 4th rank.

5 ♔×g3 c3 6 h4 ♖c4 7 ♖c2 ♔d3 8 ♖c1 c2 9 h5 ♔d2 10 ♖h1 c1♕ 11 ♖×c1 ♔×c1! White resigned.

The most important method in sharp endings with a far-advanced passed pawn is ***interference*** ("building a bridge"). It occurs, together with other useful techniques, in the following example.

Balashov – Dvoretsky
USSR ch tt, Moscow 1967*

9-70

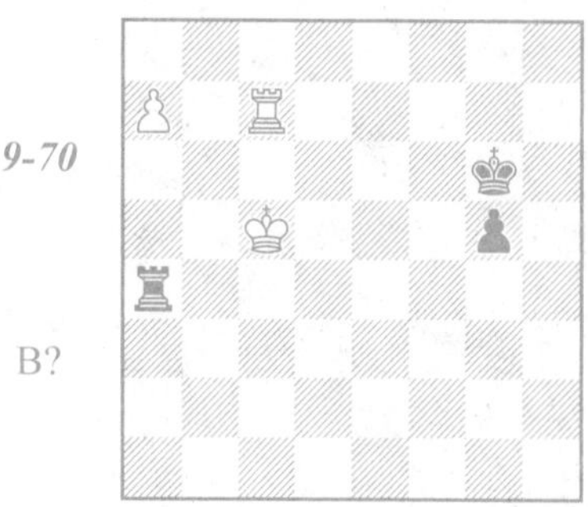

B?

The main threat is by no means ♔c5-b6-b7 – in that case the king will certainly be late when coming back to fight against the black pawn. White is planning 2 ♔b5! followed by the interference: ♖c6+ and ♖a6. If 1...♔f5?, then again 2 ♔b5! ♖a1 (2...♖×a7 3 ♖×a7 g4 4 ♔c4 ♔e4 5 ♖g7 ♔f3 6 ♔d3 g3 7 ♖f7+ and 8 ♔e2) 3 ♖c5+! ♔f4 4 ♖c4+ and 5 ♖a4, or 3...♔f6 4 ♖c6+ and 5 ♖a6.

Every tempo counts in such situations. Black holds by means of ***driving the king away by vertical checks***. The king should be driven as far as possible from the g-pawn.

1...♖a1! 2 ♔b6 ♖b1+! 3 ♔c6 ♖a1 4 ♔b7 ♖b1+ (the immediate 4...♔f5 is also sufficient for a draw) **5 ♔c8 ♖a1 6 ♔b8 ♔f5=**

Another method of preventing the threat of interference, 1...♔h5?, looks less attractive: the king on the h-file will be unable to render shouldering to his opponent. In reality, this move loses, and its eventual consequences are quite instructive:

2 ♔b6 (△ 3 ♖c8)

9-71

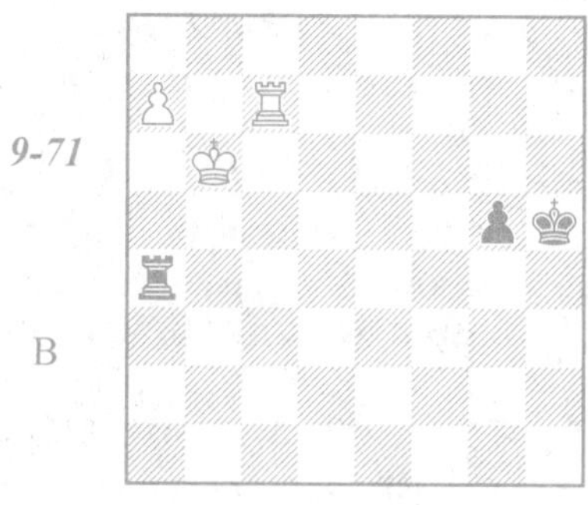

B

2...♖a1

2...g4 is very bad in view of 3 ♖c5+ and 4 ♖a5 (a bridge again). The same method decides in case of 2...♖b4+ 3 ♔a5 ♖b1 4 ♖c4!.

After 2...♔h4 White can apply another typical method: ***deflection*** of the rook, namely 3 ♖c4+ ♖×c4 4 a8♕. However after 4...♖f4 a theoretically drawn position arises (we will study this sort of ending later in the book). Therefore the interference method should be applied here, too: 3 ♔b5! ♖a1 4 ♖c4+ and 5 ♖a4.

3 ♖c8!

3 ♖c5? ♖×a7 is erroneous: the rook is placed badly on the 5th rank, and even more, it stands in the way of the white king.

3...♖×a7

Equivalent is 3...g4 (or 3...♔g4) 4 a8♕ ♖×a8 5 ♖×a8.

4 ♔×a7 ♔g4

Or 4...g4 5 ♔b6 g3 6 ♖g8! (6 ♔c5? ♔g4!=) 6...♔h4 7 ♔c5 ♔h3 8 ♔d4 g2 9 ♔e3 ♔h2 10 ♔f2+–.

5 ♔b6 ♔f3 6 ♖f8+!

A familiar method: zwischenschach for gaining a tempo.

6...♔e3 7 ♖g8! ♔f4 8 ♔c5 g4 9 ♔d4 ♔f3 10 ♔d3 g3 11 ♖f8+ ♔g2 12 ♔e2+–.

Tragicomedies

Peters – Browne
USA ch, South Bend 1981

9-72

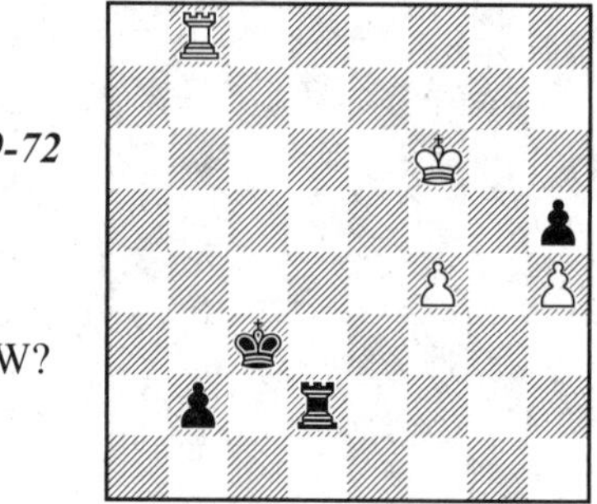

W?

Remembering the previous example, we can easily find the correct solution; it is based upon driving the king away by vertical checks: 1 ♖c8+! ♔d3 2 ♖b8 (2 ♖d8+) 2...♔c2 3 ♖c8+! ♔d1 4 ♖b8 ♔c1 5 f5 (5 ♔g6) 5...b1♕ 6 ♖xb1+ ♔xb1 7 ♔g6=.

1 f5?

White fails to tackle a relatively simple problem. The attempt to set another pawn in motion also loses: 1 ♔g6? ♖d1 2 ♖xb2 ♔xb2 3 ♔xh5 ♔c3 4 ♔g6 ♔d4 5 h5 ♔d5 6 f5 (6 h6 ♔e6) 6...♔d6 7 h6 (7 f6 ♔e6–+) 7...♔e7 8 h7 ♖g1+ 9 ♔h6 ♔f7 10 h8♘+ ♔f6 11 ♔h7 ♔xf5 12 ♘f7 ♔f6–+.

1...♖d1 2 ♖xb2 (the same is 2 ♔g6 b1♕ 3 ♖xb1 ♖xb1) **2...♔xb2**

In the 1 ♖c8+! line, the same position occurs, but with the king on b1: one square farther. This tempo turns out to be decisive.

3 ♔g6 ♔c3 4 ♔xh5 ♔d4 5 ♔g6 ♔e5 6 h5 ♖g1+ 7 ♔f7 ♔xf5 8 h6 ♖a1 9 h7 ♖a7+ 10 ♔g8 ♔g6 White resigned.

Tarrasch – Blümich
Breslau 1925

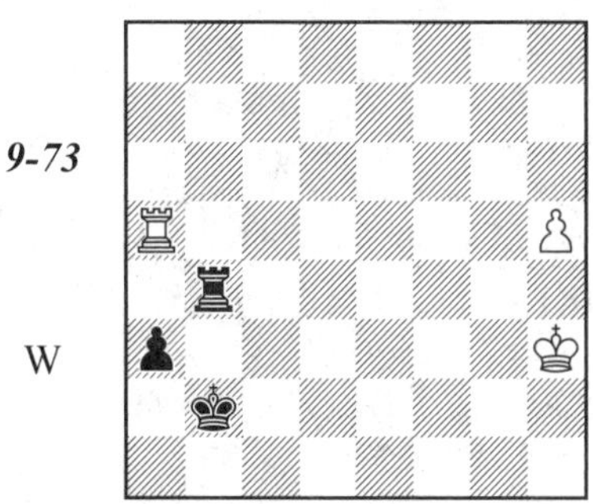

9-73

W

Tarrasch resigned! He saw that his king was cut off from his own pawn along the 4th rank, while the attempt to advance the pawn **1 h6** would have been met by **1...♖b6 2 ♖h5 a2 3 h7 ♖b8** (and, if 4 ♖a5, then 4...a1♕ 5 ♖xa1 ♔xa1 6 ♔g4 ♖h8–+).

The grandmaster had completely forgotten the possibility of deflecting the black rook from the 8th rank: **4 ♖b5+! ♖xb5 5 h8♕+**.

Exercises

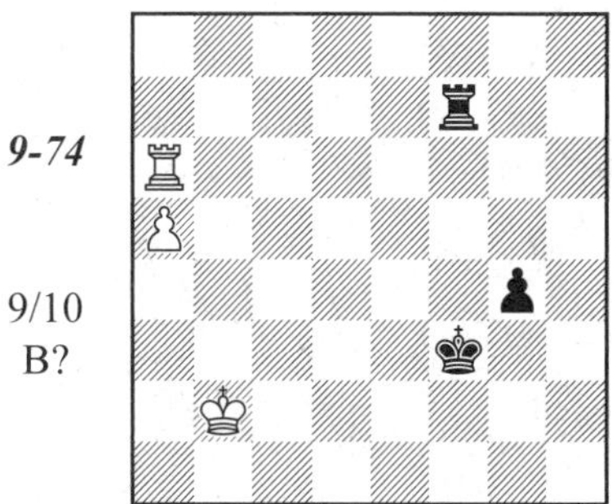

9-74

9/10
B?

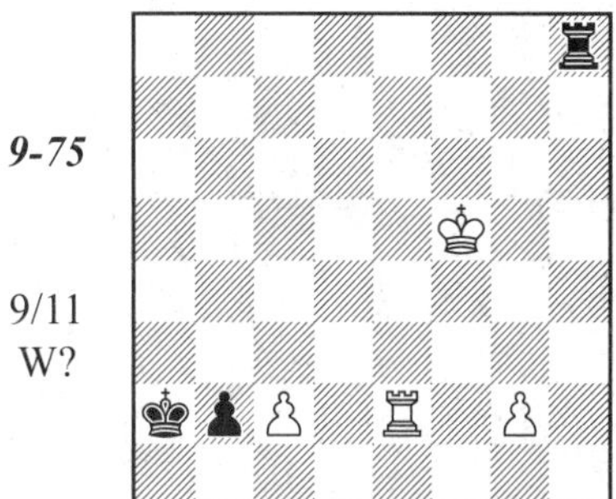

9-75

9/11
W?

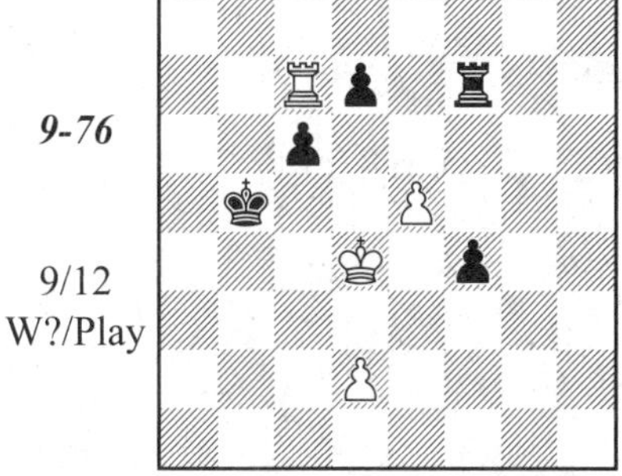

9-76

9/12
W?/Play

Lasker's Idea

Books on chess endings contain many interesting and instructive rook-and-pawn endings with a single pawn on each side. We have already studied some typical methods, that are characteristic for this material, in the previous section of this book. Now we shall discuss one more idea. The second world champion introduced it.

Em. Lasker, 1890

9-77

W?

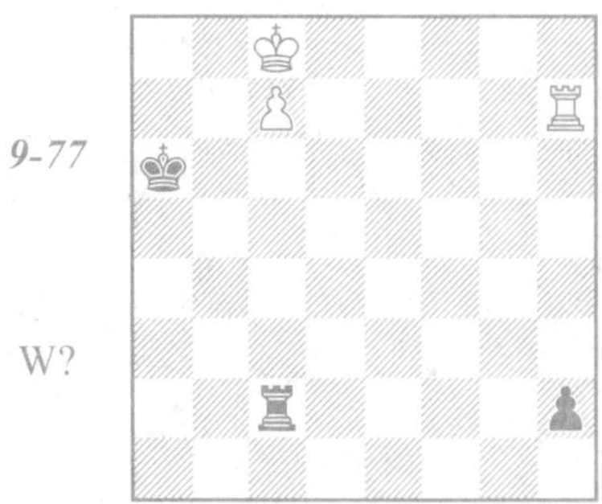

Were Black on move, he could hold the game by playing 1...♔a7! or 1...♖b2!. But it is White who is on move, and he sets into motion a mechanism that gradually drives the black king as far away as the 2nd rank.

1 ♔b8! ♖b2+ 2 ♔a8 ♖c2 3 ♖h6+ ♔a5 4 ♔b7 ♖b2+ 5 ♔a7 ♖c2 6 ♖h5+ ♔a4 7 ♔b7 ♖b2+ 8 ♔a6 ♖c2 9 ♖h4+ ♔a3 10 ♔b6 ♖b2+ 11 ♔a5! ♖c2 12 ♖h3+ ♔a2 13 ♖×h2+–.

A slightly more complicated version of the same idea is demonstrated in the following example.

P. Keres, 1947*

9-78
$

W

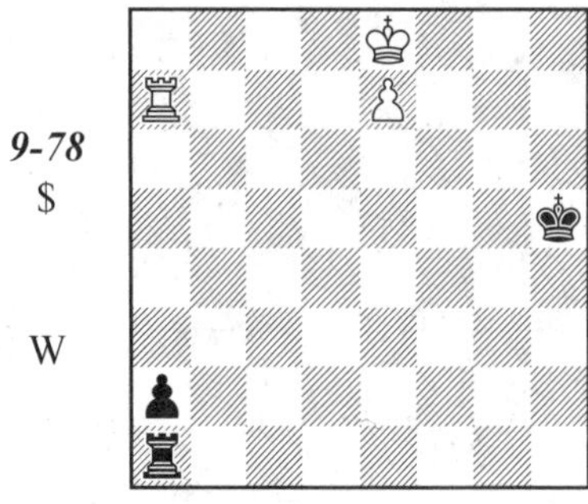

1 ♖a3 ♔h4!

Black prevents the rook transfer to the 2nd rank: 2 ♖h3+ and 3 ♖h2.

2 ♖a5!⊙

When the black king is placed on h4, 2 ♔f7? is senseless – after 2...♖f1+ 3 ♔g6 ♖g1+ 4 ♔h6 ♖e1 White's king has traveled too far away from the e7-pawn and cannot protect it. Therefore White waits: he realizes that Black's king is placed worse on whichever square other than h4.

It is worth mentioning that the diagrammed position occurred, with reversed colors, in the game I. Zaitsev - Dvoretsky, Moscow ch 1973. I did not know the endgame study by Keres and, having discovered the same idea, executed it in a slightly different way: 1 ♖a5+ ♔h4! 2 ♖a3!⊙. The game continued 2...♔g5 (in case of 2...♔g4 3 ♔f7, we transpose into the main line of the Keres' study) 3 ♖g3+ ♔f4 4 ♖g2 ♔f3 5 ♖h2 (Keres suggests 5 ♖b2 ♔e3 6 ♔d7 ♖d1+ 7 ♔c7 ♖c1+ 8 ♔b7 a1♕ 9 e8♕+) 5...♔e3 6 ♖b2⊙ ♔e4 7 ♖e2+ ♔d3 8 ♔d8 ♔×e2 9 e8♕+, and my opponent resigned after a few more moves.

2...♔g4 3 ♔f7! ♖f1+ 4 ♔g6 ♖e1 5 ♖a4+ ♔h3 6 ♔f6 ♖f1+ 7 ♔g5 ♖g1+ 8 ♔h5 ♖e1 9 ♖a3+ ♔g2 10 ♖×a2+

In the study by Lasker, this was the termination point; but here the fight goes on.

10...♔f3 11 ♖a7

9-79

B

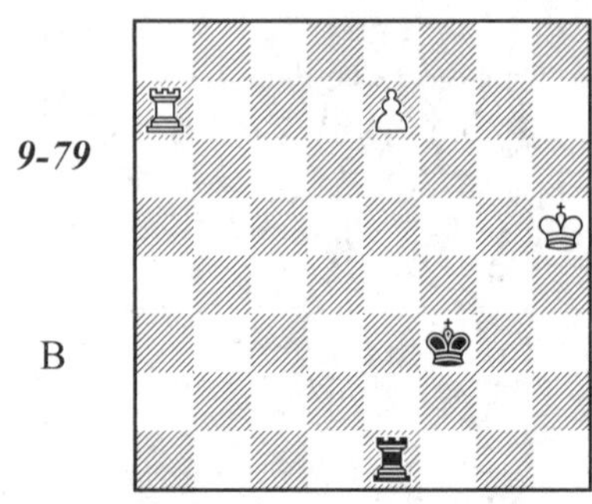

11...♖e6! 12 ♔g5 ♔e4 13 ♖b7(c7)!

13 ♖d7? is erroneous on account of 13...♔e5⊙=.

13...♔e5 (13...♔d5 14 ♔f5) **14 ♖d7**

Now it is Black who has fallen into zugzwang.

14...♔e4 15 ♖d1! ♔f3 16 ♖f1+ ♔e2 17 ♖f7 ♔e3 18 ♔f5+–.

Exercises

9-80

9/13
B?

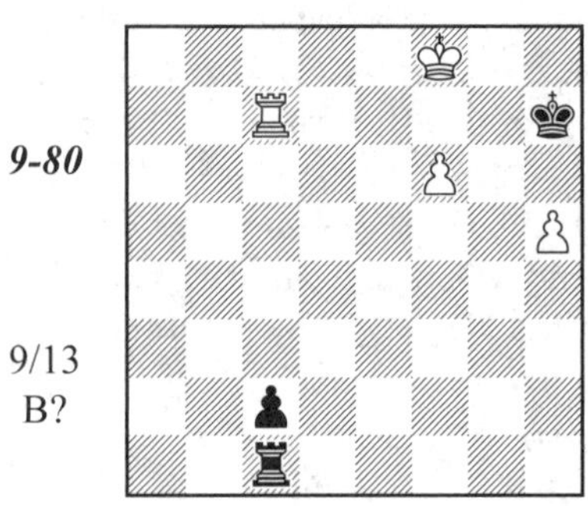

A Rook and Two Pawns vs. a Rook and Pawn

All Pawns are on the Same Wing

If all pawns are grouped on the same wing then a draw is the most probable outcome. Even when there is a passed pawn, defense is, as a rule, not too difficult.

Smyslov – Keres
USSR ch, Moscow 1949

9-81

W

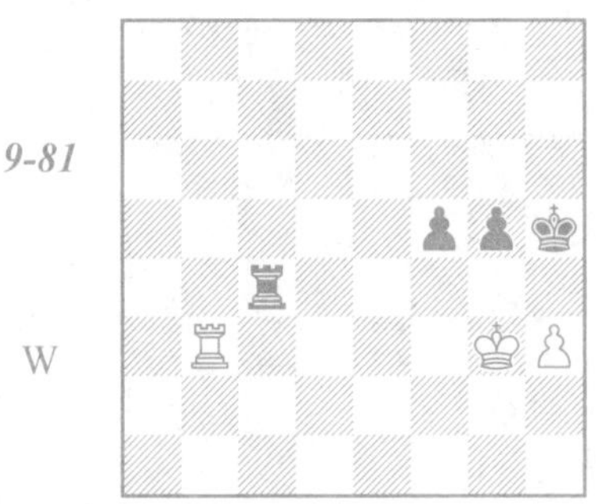

Black is planning 1...f4+ and 2...♔h4. A reliable method of preventing a king invasion is a rook check from h8.

1 ♖b8! f4+ 2 ♔g2 ♖c2+ 3 ♔f3!

3 ♔g1? loses to 3...♔h4 4 ♖b3 ♖e2 △ 5...♖e3.

3...♖c3+

There is no danger for White in 3...♖h2 4 ♖h8+ ♔g6 5 ♖g8+ ♔f6 6 ♖h8 ♔g7 7 ♖h5 ♔g6 8 ♖h8 ♔f6 9 ♔g4! (9 ♖h5? ♔f5 10 ♖h8 ♖×h3+!) 9...♖g2+ 10 ♔f3 ♖g3+ 11 ♔f2, and 11...♔g6 can be met, besides the waiting 12 ♔f1, even with 12 h4 g4 13 ♖g8+ (or 13 ♖f8 ♖f3+ 14 ♔g2).

4 ♔g2 ♖g3+ 5 ♔h2 ♖e3 6 ♔g2

6 ♖h8+ ♔g6 7 h4! g4 8 ♖g8+ ♔f5 (8...♔h5 9 ♖h8+) 9 ♖g5+ ♔e4 10 ♖×g4=.

6...♔g6 7 ♖f8!

The simplest solution: White cuts the enemy king off from the center of the board.

7...♖e2+ 8 ♔f3 ♖h2 9 ♖h8 ♔g7 10 ♖h5 ♔f6 11 ♖h8 ♖h1 12 ♔g2 ♖d1 13 ♖f8+ ♔g7 14 ♖f5 ♖d2+ 15 ♔f3 ♖d3+ 16 ♔g2 ♔g6 Draw.

Cutting the king off along the f-file is not obligatory (even more so because Black can overcome it). Instead of 7 ♖f8, 7 ♖a8 ♔f5 8 ♖a5+ ♖e5 9 ♖a8 is possible. The game Timman - Radulov, Wijk aan Zee 1974 (with reversed colors and wings) went 9...♖d5 10 ♖f8+ ♔e4 11 ♖e8+ ♔d3 12 ♔f3 ♔d2 13 ♔f2 ♔d1 14 ♖f8 ♖d2+ 15 ♔f1 ♖h2 16 ♖f5 ♔d2 17 ♖×g5 ♔e3 18 ♖a5 Draw.

If **9...♖e2+**, White should play 10 ♔f3 ♖e3+ (10...♖h2 11 ♖f8+! followed with ♖h8) 11 ♔g2=.

It is worth mentioning that here again, as on move 3, a retreat of the king to the back rank loses.

10 ♔g1? f3 11 ♖a4 ♖g2+! (11...♖e4? 12 ♖a2 ♔f4 13 ♔f2 ♖e2+ 14 ♖×e2 fe 15 h4!=) **12 ♔h1** (12 ♔f1 ♖h2 13 ♖a5+ ♔g6–+)

9-82

B?

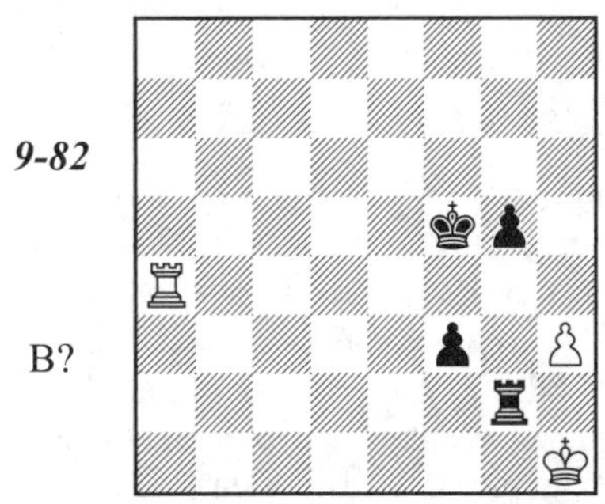

This position occurred in Schmidt - Plachetka, Decin 1976, with a single unimportant difference: the white rook stood on b4.

12...g4! 13 hg+ (13 ♖×g4 ♖×g4 14 hg+ ♔×g4–+) **13...♔g5!**

In case of 13...♖×g4? 14 ♖a2 ♔f4 15 ♔h2 ♖h4+ 16 ♔g1 ♔g3 White holds the endgame because of a stalemate: 17 ♖g2+!.

Now Black threatens 14...♖e2 followed by ...♔h4-g3. As we know, a passive defense with the rook on the 1st rank does not help against an f-pawn. As for checks from the rear, Black will use his g-pawn as an umbrella against them.

14 ♖a1 ♖e2!

In the game Plachetka choose an erroneous continuation 14...♔h4?, and White managed to hold the game by means of 15 ♖f1! ♖g3 (if 15...♔g3 16 ♖g1 ♔f2 17 ♖a1 ♖×g4, a stalemate saves White again: 18 ♖a2+ ♔g3 19 ♔g1 ♖b4 20 ♖g2+!) 16 g5! ♔×g5 17 ♖a1.

However a step by the king to the opposite direction would have led to a win: 14...♔f4! 15 g5 (15 ♖f1 ♖e2 16 g5 ♔g3 17 ♖g1+ ♔h3 18 ♖f1 f2, or 15 ♖g1 ♖e2) 15...♔g3 (16...♖h2+ 17 ♔g1 f2+ was threatened) 16 ♖g1 ♔f2 17 ♖a1 ♖g4! 18 ♖a2+ ♔g3 19 ♔g1 ♖b4 (the g-pawn is still on the board, so there is no stalemate possibility) 20 ♖a1 ♖b2 21 g6 ♖g2+ 22 ♔f1 ♖h2–+.

15 ♖g1 ♔h4 16 g5 ♔h3 (16...f2) **17 ♖a1 ♖h2+ 18 ♔g1 f2+ –+**.

Vaiser – Djuric
Szirak 1985

9-83

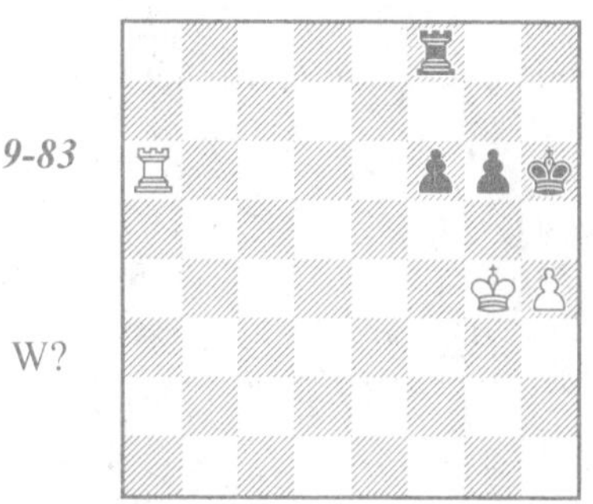

W?

In comparison with the previous ending, the black pawns are less advanced. This circumstance seems to be in White's favor, but actually he is faced with severe problems. His rook cannot reach h8, as with Smyslov's defensive method against a king penetration via the h-file.

For example: if 1 ♖b6? then 1...f5+ 2 ♔f4 ♖a8 3 ♖b7 ♖a4+ 4 ♔g3 ♖a3+ 5 ♔g2 (5 ♔f4 ♖h3) 5...♔h5 6 ♖h7+ ♔g4 7 ♖h6 ♖a6–+.

In Gliksman - Novak, Stary Smokovec 1976, the same position with reversed colors arose. The game continued 1 h5? g5! (1...gh+ leads to a drawn endgame with f- and h-pawns) 2 ♖b6 ♖f7 3 ♖a6 ♔g7 4 ♔f5 ♖b7 5 h6+ (5 ♖a5 ♔h6! 6 ♔×f6 ♖b1 7 ♔f5 ♔×h5) 5...♔×h6 6 ♖×f6+ ♔h5 7 ♔e5 ♖b3 8 ♖f1 ♔h4 9 ♖h1+ ♖h3 and Black won.

Vaiser discovered a new defensive method for this sort of ending, and thus a highly important one:

1 ♔h3!! f5 2 ♖a3!

Transposition is also possible: 1 ♖a3!? ♖b8 2 ♔h3! (not 2 ♖f3? f5+! 3 ♔h3 ♖b1! 4 ♖g3 ♖h1+ or 4 ♔h2 ♖b4) 2...♔h5 (2...♖b1 3 ♖a8! ♖b3+ 4 ♔g2 ♔h5 5 ♖h8+ ♔g4 6 ♖h6 ♖b2+ 7 ♔g1=) 3 ♖f3 ♖b6⊙ 4 ♖f1! (4 ♔g3? f5 △ 5...♖b4–+) 4...♖b3+ 5 ♔h2 f5 6 ♖g1=.

2...♖f7

2...♖b8 was more sensible, because here White, if he wished, could have played 3 ♖a8 transposing to the plan we already know.

3 ♖b3!? ♖e7 4 ♖g3! ♖e8 5 ♖g1 ♖e3+ 6 ♔h2

It becomes clear that the black king cannot go ahead when the white rook is placed on the g-file: 6...♔h5 7 ♖g5+.

6...♖d3 7 ♖g2 ♖d6

If 7...f4, then 8 ♖g4 (8 ♖f2 ♖d4 9 ♔h3 ♔h5 10 ♖d2!= is also good) 8...♖d2+ 9 ♔g1 (9.♔h3) 9...f3 10 ♖f4 ♖d3 11 ♖g4 △ ♔f2=.

8 ♔h3 ♖f6 9 ♖g5!

Draw in view of 9...f4 10 ♔g2 f3+ 11 ♔f2 ♖f4 12 ♖g3 ♔h5 13 ♖g5+!.

Tragicomedies

J. Polgar – Short
Monaco bl 1993

9-84

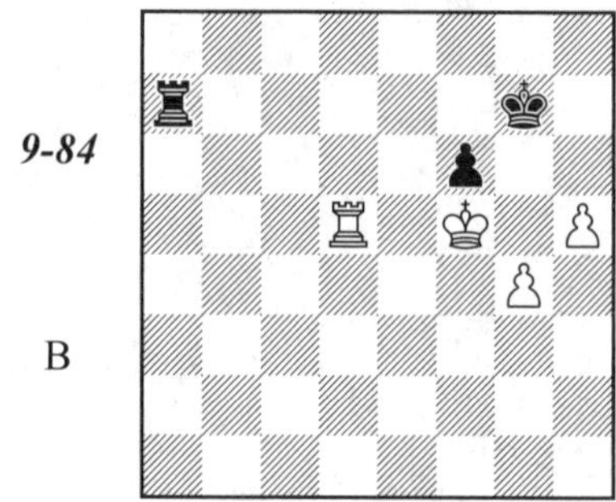

B

After the waiting move 1...♖b7 the position is still drawn: 2 ♔e6 ♖b4 (2...♖b1 is equivalent) 3 ♖d7+ ♔h6 4 ♔f5 ♖b5+ 5 ♔×f6 ♖b4! 6 g5+ (6 ♔f5 ♖f4+ or 6...♖×g4 leads to stalemate) 6...♔×h5 7 ♖h7+ ♔g4 8 g6 ♖b6+ 9 ♔f7 ♖b7+ 10 ♔g8 ♖b8+ 11 ♔g7 ♔g5= (Müller).

Short decided to at least prevent the king from invading at e6, but the remedy proved worse than the disease – his resourceful adversary found an elegant forced win.

1...♖e7?? 2 h6+! ♔f7 (2...♔×h6 3 ♔×f6+–) **3 g5!! fg 4 ♖d8! +–**.

Hebden – Wood
Hastings 1994/95

9-85

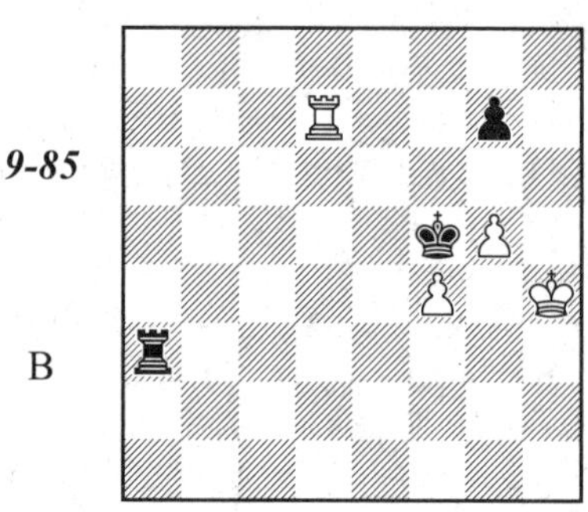

B

1...♔×f4??

A terrible error! The black king will be cut off along the f-file now, and the g7-pawn will be inevitably lost.

The simplest way to a draw was 1...♔g6 2 ♔g4 (2 f5+ ♔xf5 3 ♖xg7 ♖a1 4 ♖f7+ ♔g6=) 2...♖a4 3 ♖d6+ ♔f7.

Another way was 1...g6 2 ♖f7+ ♔e4 3 ♔g4 (3 ♖f6 ♖a1 4 ♔g3 ♖g1+ 5 ♔h2 ♖g4; 3 f5 gf 4 g6 f4 5 g7 ♖g3) 3...♖a1 4 ♖e7+ ♔d5 5 ♖g7 ♔e4! 6 ♖xg6 ♖g1+, and in case of 7 ♔h4?? ♔f3! White's king will be checkmated.

2 ♖f7+ ♔e5 3 ♔h5!+– ♖a6 4 ♖xg7 ♖a5 5 ♖e7+ ♔f5 6 ♖f7+ ♔e6 7 ♖f1 ♖a8 8 g6 ♖h8+ 9 ♔g5 ♔e7 10 ♖e1+ (10 g7) **10...♔f8 11 ♔f6 ♖h6** (11...♖h7!? 12 ♖e8+!) **12 ♖e2** Black resigned.

Chigorin – Tarrasch
Budapest 1896

9-86

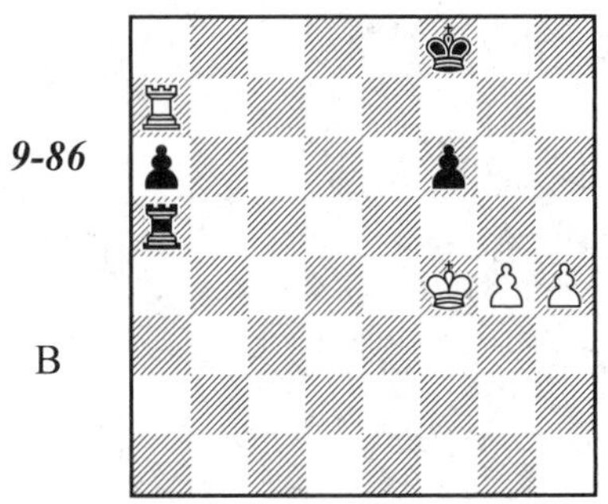

B

In the game, Black let the hostile king penetrate into his camp; this caused a rapid loss.

1...♖a1?? 2 ♔f5 ♖f1+ 3 ♔g6 ♖f4 4 g5! fg (4...♖xh4 5 ♖a8+ ♔e7 6 gf+) **5 hg ♖a4**

Both 5...♔g8 6 ♖a8+ ♖f8 7 ♖xf8+ ♔xf8 8 ♔h7 and 5...♖g4 6 ♖xa6 ♖g1 7 ♖a8+ ♔e7 8 ♖g8! are hopeless.

6 ♖a8+ ♔e7 7 ♔h6 a5 8 g6 ♖a1 9 g7 ♖h1+ 10 ♔g6 ♖g1+ 11 ♔h7 ♖h1+ 12 ♔g8 ♖a1 13 ♖a7+ ♔e8 14 ♖a6 ♖h1 (14...♔e7 15 ♔h7 ♖h1+ 16 ♖h6) **15 ♖xa5 ♖e1 16 ♖h5 ♖g1 17 ♖e5+ ♔d7 18 ♔h7** Black resigned.

The rook had to watch the 5th rank. The a6-pawn is not necessary for Black: its existence is not essential for a draw.

After 1...♔g8! 2 h5, the most solid defense was suggested by Fridstein: 2...♖b5!? 3 ♖xa6 ♔g7 4 ♖a7+ ♔g8 5 h6 ♖c5 6 ♖g7+ ♔f8! (6...♔h8? 7 ♖f7 ♖c6 8 ♔f5+–) 7 ♖g6 (7 ♔g3 ♖c1=) 7...♔f7 8 h7 ♖c8 9 ♖h6 ♔g7 (9...♖h8? 10 ♔f5 ♔g7 11 ♖h1 ♔f7 12 ♖a1+–) 10 ♖h1 ♖a8 and White cannot strengthen his position, because 11 ♔f5 is met by 11...♖a5+.

In the line 2...♔f8 3 h6 ♔g8 4 ♖g7+ ♔f8 5 ♖g6 ♔f7 6 h7 ♖a4+ 7 ♔g3 ♖a3+ 8 ♔h4 ♖a1 9 h8♘+ ♔f8 10 ♖xf6+ ♔g7 11 ♔g5 ♔xh8 (11...♖a5+? 12 ♖f5 ♖xf5+ 13 gf ♔xh8 14 ♔f6!+–) 12 ♔g6 White, according to the *Encyclopaedia of Chess Endings*, should win. However it is a mystery to me how he can do it after 12...♔g8 13 ♖b6 (13 g5 ♖b1 14 ♖xa6 ♖b8=) 13...♔f8 14 g5 a5.

Also playable is 2...♖g5 3 ♖xa6 ♔g7 4 ♖a7+ (4 h6+ ♔g6!=, but not 4...♔xh6? 5 ♖xf6+ ♖g6 6 ♔f5!+–) 4...♔g8 5 h6 ♖g6 6 h7+ ♔h8 7 ♖f7

9-87

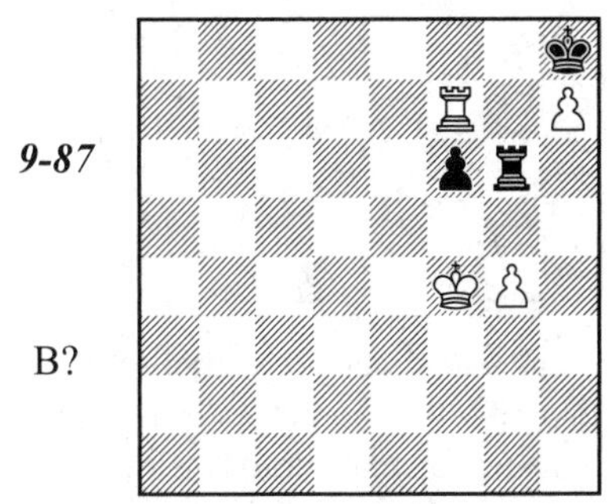

B?

Black should not cling to the f6-pawn. He achieves a draw by means of 7...♖g5! 8 ♖xf6 ♖a5 (8...♖g7 9 ♖h6 ♖a7=) 9 ♖h6 (9 ♖f7 ♖a4+ 10 ♔g5 ♖xg4+) 9...♖a4+ 10 ♔g5 ♖a5+ 11 ♔h4 ♖a7= or 11...♖a1=.

After 7...♖h6? 8 ♔f5! Black loses. The game Malisauskas - Sandler (USSR 1977) continued: 8...♖h4 (8...♖h5+ 9 ♔g6! ♖g5+ 10 ♔h6+–) 9 ♖d7 (9 ♖xf6? ♖xh7!=; 9 g5? fg 10 ♔g6 ♖f4=) 9...♖h6 10 ♖e7 (a simpler way is 10 ♖a7⊙ ♖h4 11 g5! fg 12 ♔g6+–) 10...♖h4 11 g5 ♖h5 12 ♔g6??

A gross error when just a step away from a win. 12 ♖e8+! ♔xh7 13 ♔xf6 was decisive.

12...♖xg5+ 13 ♔h6 ♖e5! 14 ♖f7 ♖e8 15 ♔g6 ♖d8 Draw.

Exercises

9-88

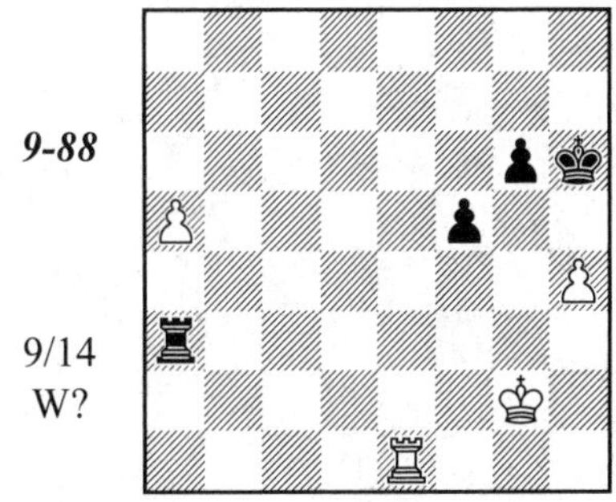

9/14
W?

Pawns on Opposite Wings

A common situation is when one side has two connected passed pawns while the adversary has a far-advanced pawn on the opposite wing. In these endgames, correct placement of one's pieces is highly important.

N. Grigoriev, 1936*

9-89

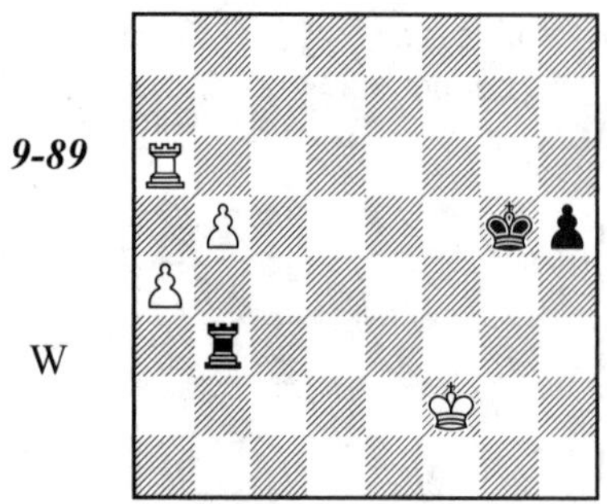

W

White has so-called self-propelled pawns. However, a lot of time is required for promotion, so Black manages to create counterplay in time.

1 b6 (△ 2 ♖a5+, 3 ♖b5)

1 ♖d6 ♖b2+ 2 ♔e3 h4 does not bring any success, either.

1...♔f4 2 a5 ♖b2+ 3 ♔e1 (3 ♔g1 ♔g3) **3...h4 4 ♖a7 h3 5 ♖h7 h2 6 ♖×h2**

6 ♔d1 is met by 6...♔g3! 7 ♔c1 ♖b5.

6...♖×h2 7 b7

A typical situation: the rook cannot stop the pawns, but Black nevertheless manages to hold by pursuing the hostile king, which is pressed to the edge of the board.

7...♔e3 8 ♔f1 (8 ♔d1 ♔d3 9 ♔c1 ♔c3 10 ♔b1?? ♖b2+) **8...♔f3 9 ♔e1=**

The careless 9 ♔g1?? even loses: 9...♖g2+! 10 ♔h1 (10 ♔f1 ♖b2) 10...♖b2 11 a6 ♔g3.

In this example, White's pieces were "engaged in a strange role reversal." As a rule, ***the king should support his own connected passed pawns while the rook's mission is to hinder the hostile pawn.***

The rook's placement is extremely important. ***If the rook of the stronger side is placed passively (in front of the enemy's pawn) a draw can be achieved simply by placing the king in front of the connected pair of pawns.***

Some time ago I was mighty impressed by a discovery that the ex-champion of the world produced during our joint analytical work.

V. Smyslov, 1976

9-90

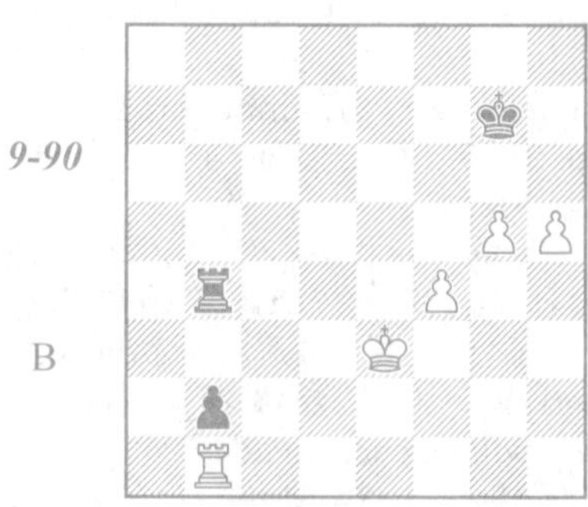

B

White has three finely placed connected passed pawns, but still the win is problematic.

1...♖b3+ 2 ♔d4 (2 ♔d2 ♖b4 3 f5 ♖b5= is no better.) **2...♖b4+ 3 ♔c3 ♖×f4 4 ♖×b2 ♖h4! 5 ♖b7+ ♔g8 6 ♖b8+** (6 h6 ♖g4) **6...♔g7!**

But not 6...♔f7(h7)? 7 g6+ coming to a winning Kasparian position (see diagram 9-53).

7 h6+ ♔g6 8 ♖g8+ ♔h7 9 ♖g7+ ♔h8 10 ♖e7 ♖g4 11 ♖e5 ♔h7 12 ♔d3 ♔g6=

Karsten Müller has showed that White still has a complicated path to victory. He suggested 2 ♔e4 ♖b4+ 3 ♔f5 ♖b5+ 4 ♔e6 (4 ♔g4 ♖b4 is useless) 4...♖b6+ 5 ♔d5 ♖b5+ 6 ♔c6 ♖b4 7 f5 ♖g4 8 h6+ ♔h7 9 ♖×b2 ♖×g5 10 ♖f2+–. If Black temporizes: 7...♖b8 8 h6+ ♔h7, then the most exact way is 9 ♔d5! (but not 9 ♔c5? ♖g8! 10 g6+ ♔×h6 11 ♖×b2 ♔g5 12 ♖f2 ♔f6=) 9...♖b4 10 ♔e5 (and now, thanks to zugzwang, Black must allow the king back into the lower half of the board) 10...♖b5+ 11 ♔f4 ♖b4+ 12 ♔g3 ♖b5 13 ♔g4 ♖b3 14 ♔h4⊙ +–.

I will note here, that with Black's pawn on the a-file, Müller's plan is not dangerous, so the position remains drawn.

Clearly, the problems with the realization of White's material advantage were obviously caused by the poor position of White's rook. Tarrasch's famous rule is perfectly to the point here: ***Place your rook behind the passed pawn, whether it's yours or your enemy's***. Thereby the rook can retain utmost activity.

Tarrasch's rule is valid for the overwhelming majority of rook-and-pawn endings but, as it goes without saying, not for absolutely all of them. Generally speaking, there is no rule in chess that has no exception.

An amateur followed Tarrasch's rule in a correspondence game and had to resign immediately after receiving his opponent's reply. He wrote an irritated letter to the grandmaster: "I relied upon your authority but lost because of you, with your stupid rule..."

Tarrasch published it in his chess column with the final position of that game, adding the following annotation: "Especially for this reader and a few similar to him (the majority, as I am sure, do not need it), I supplement my rule. You should always place your rook behind a pawn. Except for the cases when this is unfavorable!"

9-91

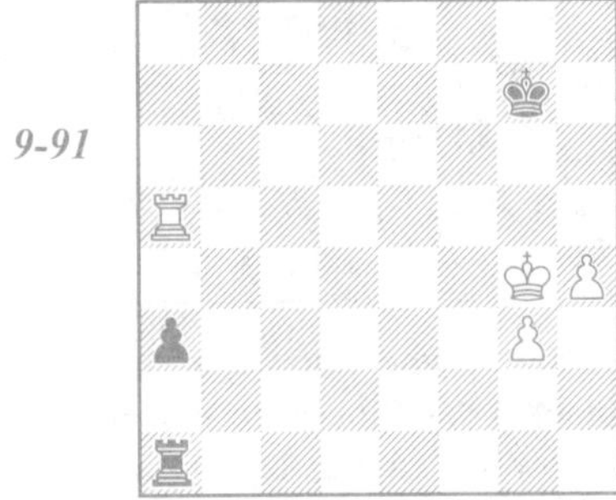

This is a very important type of position. The black king stands in front of connected passed pawns but the white rook is placed behind Black's passed pawn. In such cases, the chances of the defender are minimal. However, this position can be saved if Black is on move.

1...a2 2 h5 ♔h7 (but by no means 2...♔h6?? 3 ♖a7!⊙ +–) **3 ♔g5 ♖g1! 4 ♖a7+ ♔g8 5 ♖×a2 ♖×g3+**

The happy end resulted from the fact that one of the pawns had been standing on the 3rd rank. If White is on move he succeeds in advancing the pawn and wins without difficulty: 1 ♔g5 a2 2 g4 ♔f7 3 h5 ♔g7 4 ♖a7+ ♔f8 5 h6 ♔g8 6 ♔g6 – Black has no time for 6...♖g1 on account of the threatened checkmate.

If the pawn is on g2, White wins no matter who is on move. He simply advances his king and the h-pawn. The riposte ...♖g1 is useless because the white rook, capturing the a2-pawn, will protect the g2-pawn.

Finally, Black has no draw against the following White setup: pawns on h3-g4 and king on h4. After 1...a2 2 ♖a6 ♔h7 3 g5 ♔g7 3 ♔h5 ♖h1 4 ♖a7+ ♔f8(g8) 5 ♖×a2 ♖×h3+ 6 ♔g6 a winning endgame with a g-pawn arises.

In some cases, the weaker side holds when his rook protects his pawn from the side.

Tarrasch – Chigorin
St. Petersburg m (9) 1893

9-92
$

B?

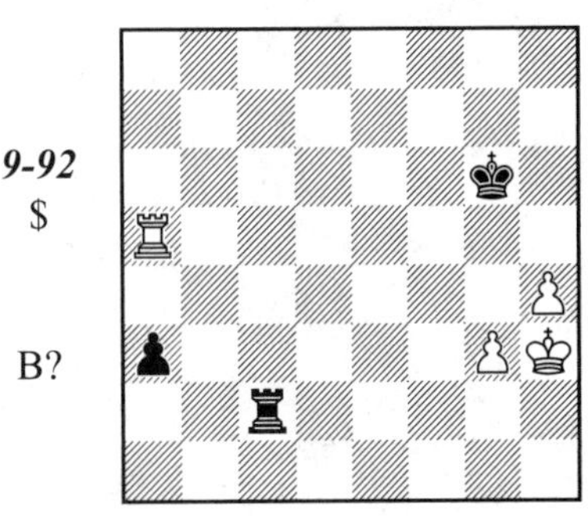

The game continued 1...♖a2? 2 ♔g4 ♖a1 3 ♖a6+ ♔f7 4 ♔g5 a2 5 g4! (of course, not 5 h5?? ♖g1=), and Black soon resigned.

We would like to mention another, much more complicated winning method: 2 g4 ♖a1 3 ♖a6+ ♔g7 4 h5 a2 5 ♔h2!!. Just so, in order to have, after 5...♔h7 6 g5 ♖b1 7 ♖a7+ ♔g8 8 ♖×a2 ♖b5, the protective move 9 ♖g2! +–.

As Maizelis proved, the diagrammed position is drawn (however against a luckier setup of White's pawns, at h3 and g4, Black has no chances).

1...a2! 2 h5+

If the pawn stepped ahead without giving a check (e.g. with the black king on f6), the move 2...♖c5! would have led to an immediate draw. Well, let us make use of this idea later, when the white pawns reach a higher rank.

2...♔f6 3 ♔h4! (3 g4 ♖c5! 4 ♖×a2 ♔g5=) **3...♖h2+ 4 ♔g4 ♖b2 5 ♖a6+ ♔g7 6 ♔g5 ♖b5+ 7 ♔h4 ♖b2 8 g4** (9 h6+ is threatened) **8...♔f7! 9 ♖a4**

9 h6 ♖b6! 10 ♖a7+ ♔g6= is nonsensical.

9...♔g7!

Rather than 9...♖c2? 10 h6 ♔g6 11 ♖a6+ ♔h7 12 ♔h5 +–.

10 ♖a7+ (10 ♖a6 ♔f7!) **10...♔f6! 11 g5+ ♔f5 12 h6 ♖h2+ 13 ♔g3 ♖h1 14 ♖×a2 ♔×g5=.**

Sometimes the weaker side employs another, more active defensive method: the king is advanced to support the passed pawn. As a consequence, this pawn will cost a whole rook for the stronger side, but in the meantime his own pawns, together with the king, will be advanced too far, and the endgame "two connected passed pawn against a rook" turns out to be winning.

Therefore this tactic has practical chances only against less advanced pawns and misplaced pieces of the stronger side. As, for example, in the following case:

Reshevsky – Alekhine
AVRO 1938

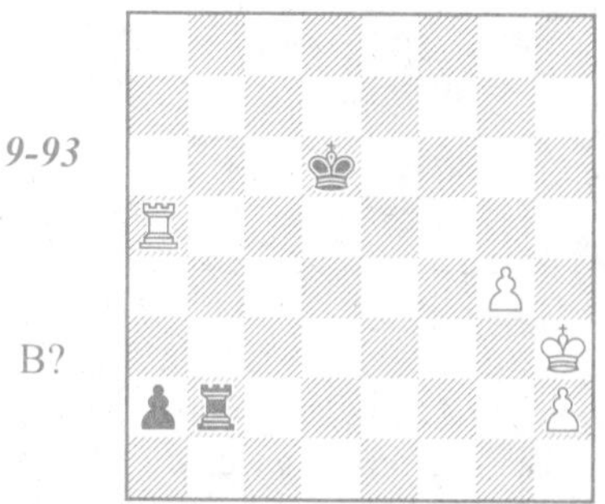
9-93
B?

It would have been an easy draw for Black with the white rook on a1: 1...♔e6 2 ♔g3 ♔f6. In our case, however, a passive defense is hopeless: 1...♔e6? 2 ♔g3 ♔f6 3 h3 ♔g6 (or 3...♖c2 4 ♔h4 ♖h2 5 ♖a6+ ♔e5 6 ♔g5! ♖xh3 7 ♖xa2 ♖h8 8 ♖e2+ ♔d6 9 ♔f6+–) 4 ♔h4 ♖h2 5 ♖a6+ ♔g7 6 g5 ♔h7 7 ♔g4 followed by h4, ♔h5 etc.

1...♔c6! 2 ♔g3

If 2 g5 then 2...♖b5! 3 ♖a6+ ♔b7 4 ♖xa2 ♖xg5 5 ♖c2 ♖g8=. The evaluation of the final position of this line is not quite obvious because we have not studied defense by frontal attack against a rook pawn. I think it is pertinent to say here that, with an h2-pawn, White has winning chances only when the black king is cut off on the a-file.

2...♔b6 3 ♖a8 ♔b5 4 h3

In case of 4 g5 both 4...♔b4 (△ ♖b3+) and the immediate 4...♖b3+ are good.

4...♔b4 5 ♔f4

The consequences of 5 ♔h4 are harder to calculate, but its result is still a draw: 5...♔b3 6 g5 (6 ♔g5 ♖b1 7 h4 a1♕ 8 ♖xa1 ♖xa1 9 h5 ♔c4 10 h6 ♔d5 11 ♔g6 ♔e5=) 6...♖b1 7 ♔h5 a1♕ 8 ♖xa1 ♖xa1 9 g6 ♔c4 10 g7 ♖g1 11 ♔h6 ♔d5 12 ♔h7 ♔e6 13 g8♕ ♖xg8 14 ♔xg8 ♔f5=.

5...♖c2!

As is presumed in endgames with a far-advanced passed pawn, Black speculates on the threat of interference, namely 6...♖c4+, 7...♖c5(c3)+ and 8...♖a5(a3).

6 ♖b8+ ♔c3 7 ♖a8 ♔b4! Draw.

Of course, there is no reason for Black to play 7...♔b2, but he seems not to be losing even after that move: 8 h4 a1♕ 9 ♖xa1 ♔xa1 10 h5 ♖h2 11 ♔g5 ♔b2 12 ♔h6 ♔c3 13 g5 ♔d4 14 g6 ♔e5 15 g7 ♖g2 16 ♔h7 ♔f6=.

Tragicomedies

Dreev – Ehlvest
USSR chsf, Tallinn 1986

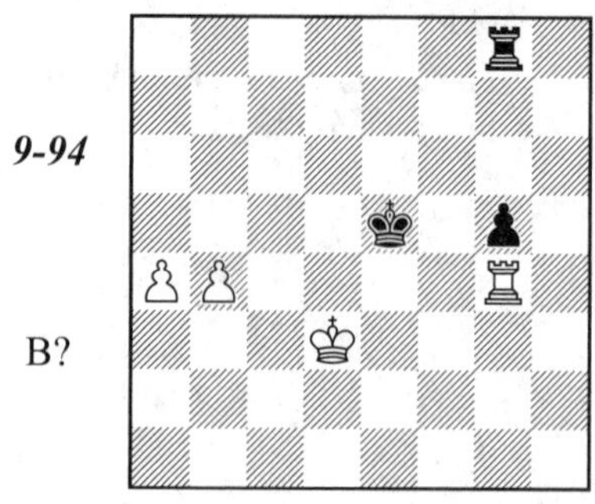
9-94
B?

As we know, when the white rook is passive the black king should be placed on the queenside. However after 1...♔d5?! 2 a5 △ ♔c3-b3-a4 Black is very probably lost. At the proper moment, the rook abandons the blockade square g4 in order to create threats to the king. Vulfson analyzed a similar endgame in detail in the book by Dvoretsky and Yusupov, *Technique for the Tournament Player*.

It is important to push the g-pawn at least a single step forward in order to reduce the active possibilities of the white rook.

1...♔f5 2 ♖g1 g4 3 ♔c4 g3?

But now the king fails to come back to the queenside in time. Black had to play 3...♔e6! 4 ♖g3 (in case of 4 ♔c5 he could resort to frontal checks: 4...♖c8+!?) 4...♔d6 5 b5 ♔c7 6 a5 ♔b7=.

3 ♔d5!+– (shouldering!) **3...♖d8+ 4 ♔c6 ♖c8+ 5 ♔b7 ♖g8 6 a5 ♖g7+ 7 ♔b6 ♔e5 8 a6 ♖g6+ 9 ♔c5** Black resigned.

Ostermeyer – Dueball
BRD ch, Mannheim 1975

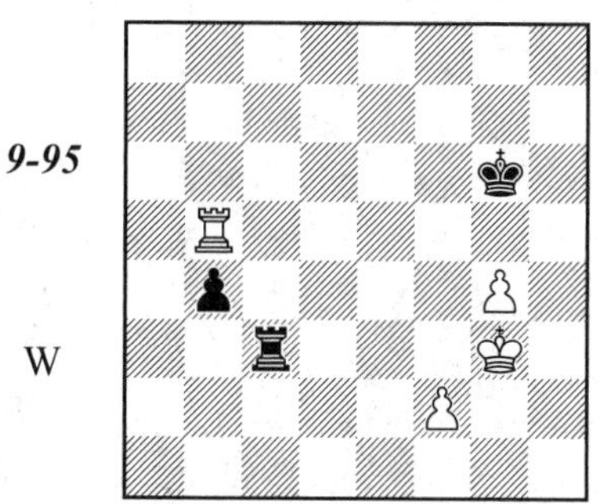
9-95
W

1 ♔g2?

An odd move: in endgames, the king should go forward, not backward. 1 f3 suggested itself, for example: 1...b3 (1...♖c4 2 f4 or 2 ♖b6+ △ 3 f4) 2 ♔f4 (△ ♖b6+) 2...♖c4+ (side checks are not efficient because the rook and the f3-pawn are only separated by two files) 3 ♔e3 ♖c3+ 4 ♔e4 ♔f6 (4...♖c4+ 5 ♔d3 ♖f4 6 ♔e3) 5 f4 ♖c4+ 6 ♔e3 ♖c3+ 7 ♔d4 ♖g3 8 ♖b6+ and 9 g5+−. White is playing in accordance with a principle that, by Nimzovitch's opinion, is a cornerstone of a correct endgame strategy: ***the collective advance!***

1...b3 2 f4??

A severe positional error: the king will be cut off from the pawns forever. It was still not too late for 2 f3! △ 3 ♔g3+−.

2...♔f6= 3 ♖b6+ ♔f7 4 g5 ♔g7 5 f5 ♖c5! 6 ♖b7+ ♔g8 7 ♖b8+

Draw. After 7...♔g7 8 f6+ Black can play either 8...♔f7 or 8...♔g6 9 ♖g8+ ♔f7 10 ♖g7+ ♔f8.

Exercises

9-96

9/15
B?

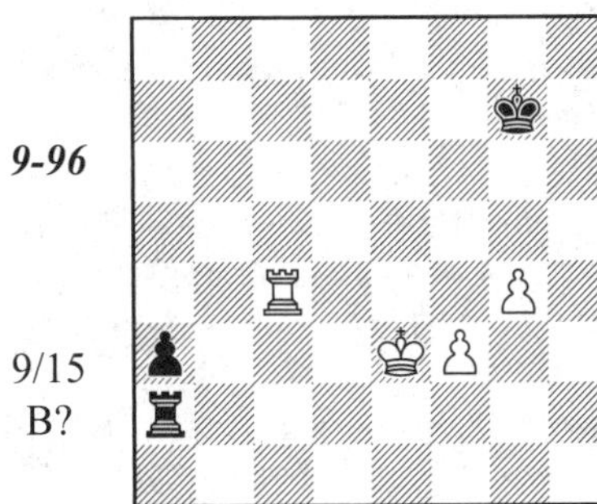

9-97

9/16
W?

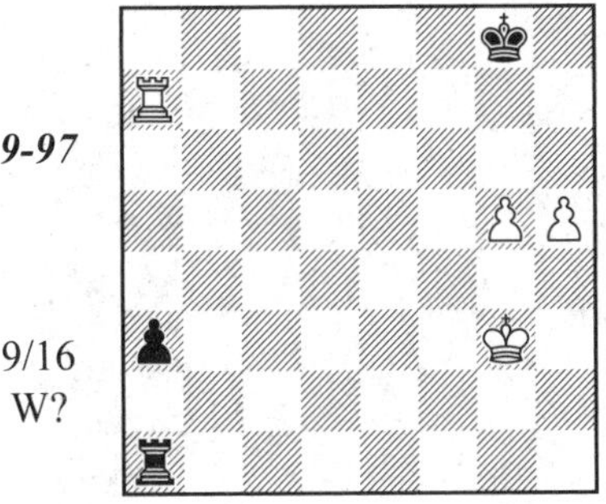

Disconnected Pawns, One of them is Passed

If one or two files separate pawns of the stronger side, the position is most often a draw. We shall analyze cases of more interest and practical value here: when the distance between pawns is great enough.

The defender must aspire for active counterplay. If his rook must merely defend his own pawn or protect the king from checks, his salvation is very problematic.

Miles – Webb
Birmingham 1975

9-98

W

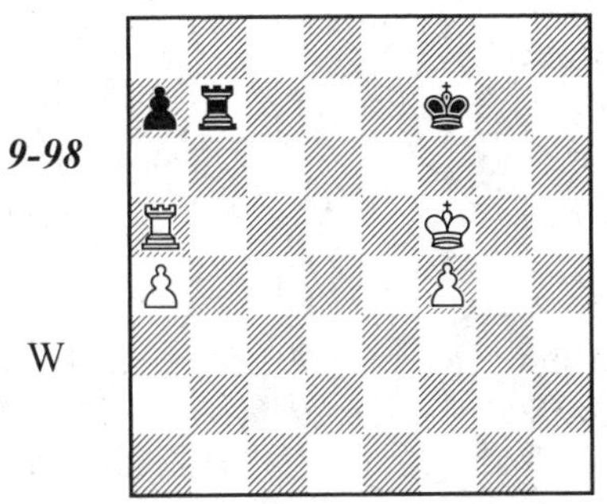

1 ♖a6 ♖c7 2 ♔g5 ♔g7 3 f5 ♖d7 4 a5 ♖c7 5 ♖d6!

White has improved his position to the maximum degree. Now he has in mind a typical plan for this sort of position, a usurpation of the 7th rank (a5-a6 and ♖d6-d8-b8-b7).

5...♔f8 6 ♖d8+ ♔e7 7 ♖h8 ♔d6 8 ♔g6 ♖c1 9 ♖a8

A wise technique: White combines the threat of advancing the f-pawn with an attack against the a-pawn.

9...♔e5 10 ♖e8+ ♔f4 (10...♔d6 11 ♖e6+ ♔d7 12 ♖a6+−) **11 f6 ♖g1+ 12 ♔f7 ♖a1 13 ♔g7 ♔f5 14 f7 ♖g1+ 15 ♔f8 ♔g6 16 ♖e6+** Black resigned.

I would like to draw your attention to the fact that if the queenside pawns were placed not on the same file, but on adjacent files (for example, the white pawn on the b-file), the black rook would have been less passive. It could then combine its defensive mission with a counterattacking one, and the drawing chances would have been considerably greater.

A typical method of bringing home a material advantage is the protection of all of one's pawns by the rook from the side.

Tsouros – Minev
Greece – Bulgaria m tt 1973

9-99

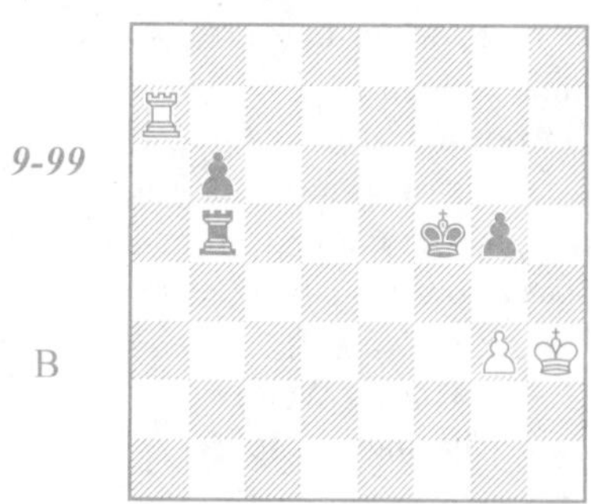

B

1...♖d5!–+

Black wants to play ...b6-b5; thereafter the king, being released from its troubles with the g5-pawn, will set off for the queenside. White is helpless against this simple plan. Other setups are much less efficient.

2 ♖f7+ (2 ♖e7 b5 3 ♖e8 ♖e5) **2...♔e4 3 ♖b7 b5 4 ♔g4 ♔d4 5 ♔f3**

5 ♔h5 ♔c4 6 g4 b4 7 ♖c7+ ♖c5 is equally hopeless.

5...♔c4 6 ♔e4 ♖c5 7 ♖d7 b4 8 ♖d1 b3 9 ♖b1 ♔c3 10 ♖c1+ ♔b4 11 ♖b1 ♖c4+ 12 ♔f5 g4 13 ♔g5 ♔c3 White resigned.

If the rook protects pawns from the side and the enemy king blocks the passed pawn, then the pieces of the stronger side attack the opponent's pawn on the other wing, while the passed pawn, if necessary, can be sacrificed.

An interesting example of this strategy follows in the next diagram. Studying it, we should refresh our memories about the theory of rook and pawn versus rook endgames, particularly the case of frontal attack.

Rigan – Yandemirov
Budapest 1993

9-100

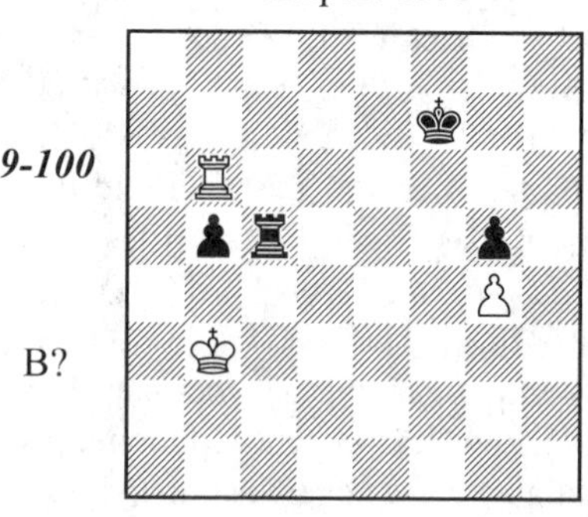

B?

According to the above-mentioned rule, Black must attack the g4-pawn. But how is he to do this? His king is cut off along the 6th rank while 1...♖c4? will be met by 2 ♖×b5 ♖×g4 3 ♔c3 ♔g6 4 ♔d3 ♖f4 5 ♖b1 (5 ♔e3=) 5...g4 (5...♔h5 6 ♔e3=) 6 ♔e3! (rather than 6 ♔e2? ♔g5 7 ♖f1 g3!) 6...♖f5 7 ♔e2! △ 8 ♖f1=.

1...♔g7!!

A superb waiting move that puts White in zugzwang. His rook is placed optimally and cannot abandon its place. In case of 2 ♔b4 ♖c4+ 3 ♔×b5 ♖×g4 4 ♔c5 ♖h4! (the only method of crossing the 6th rank with the king) 5 ♔d5 ♖h6 6 ♖b1 ♔g6 7 ♔e4 ♖h3!, the king is cut off along the rank, and this fact is decisive.

2 ♔b2 ♖c4 3 ♖×b5 ♔f6!

This is why the white king should have been thrown back! The rook is not hanging now, and Black manages to improve his king's position without letting White do the same. If 4 ♖f5+ ♔g6 5 ♖f1, then 5...♖×g4 6 ♔c3 ♖g2! 7 ♔d3 ♔h5 8 ♔e3 ♔g4–+.

4 ♔b3 ♖×g4 5 ♔c3 ♖e4 6 ♔d3 ♖e8

In a very similar position from the game Tal - I. Zaitsev (diagram 9-31), 6...♖e1!? 7 ♔d2 ♖e8 was played, but in our current case Black can even do without it.

7 ♔d2

7 ♖b1 is met by 7...g4! 8 ♖b5 (8 ♔d2 ♔g5! 9 ♖e1 ♖×e1 10 ♔×e1 ♔h4) 8...g3 9 ♔d2 ♖e4! 10 ♖b3 ♖g4 11 ♖b1 g2 12 ♖g1 ♔g5 13 ♔e2 ♔h4 14 ♔f2 ♔h3–+.

7...♔g6 (7...g4 is also good) **8 ♖b1 ♖e5!** (8...g4?? 9 ♖e1=) **9 ♖g1 ♔h5** (9...♔f5!?) White resigned.

As was said earlier, only an active defense gives the weaker side chances of salvation. We would like to emphasize two of the most important defensive methods:

1) King's attack against a pawn. Sometimes one succeeds in giving the rook up for a pawn, eating another pawn with the king and saving the game with a pawn against a rook.

2) Exchange of rooks. If the eventual pawn endgame is drawn, the weaker side drives away the hostile rook, from the rank where it is protecting both pawns, by means of the exchange threat.

These methods are often combined.

Marshall – Capablanca
New York m (9) 1909

9-101

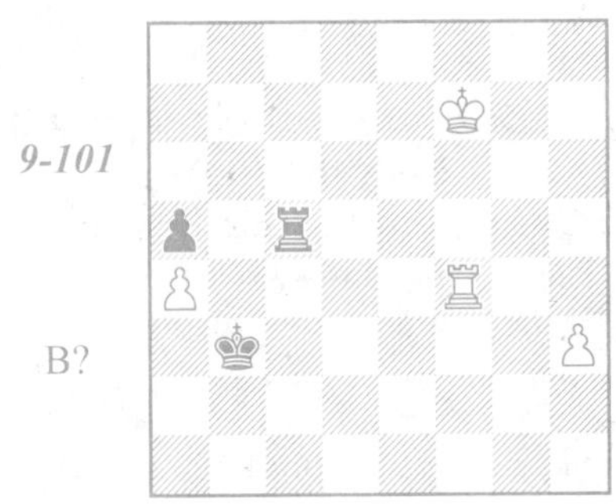

B?

1...♖c7+! 2 ♔g6 ♖b7 3 h4 ♖b4! 4 ♔g5

After 4 ♖×b4+ ab! 5 a5 ♔c4 6 a6 b3 7 a7 b2 8 a8♕ b1♕+ a drawn queen-and-pawn endgame arises.

4...♔×a4 5 h5 ♔a3!

But, of course, not 5...♔b5(b3)?? 6 ♖×b4+ ab 7 h6+–.

6 h6 ♖b8 7 h7 a4 8 ♖h4 ♖h8 9 ♔g6 ♔b3 10 ♔g7 ♖×h7+ 11 ♔×h7 a3 Draw.

The following example, as well as the exercises in this section, show how difficult precise calculation can be in this sort of position.

Taimanov – Averbakh
Leningrad 1947

9-102

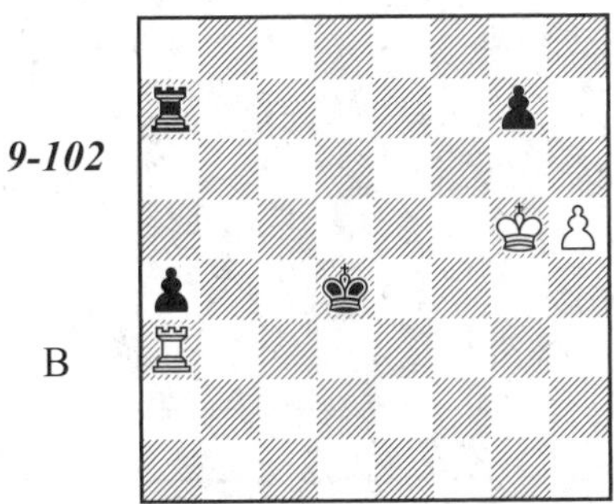

B

Deliberating over the natural continuation 1...♔c4! over the board, Black decided that he could get no more than a draw on account of 2 ♔g6 ♔b4 3 ♖g3 a3 4 ♖g2 a2 5 ♖×a2 ♖×a2 6 ♔×g7=.

Later on, Averbakh found an improvement: 4...♖c7! (instead of 4...a2?) 5 ♔h7 (5 ♖g4+ ♔b3 6 ♖g3+ ♔b2) 5...♖c5! 6 ♔g6 (6 ♖h2 ♖g5 7 ♖h4+ ♔b5) 6...♔b3 7 ♖g3+ ♔b2 8 ♖g2+ ♖c2 (this is why the zwischenzug 5...♖c5! was necessary – the king prevents a rook capture on g7) 9 ♖g1 ♖h2! (from here, the rook defends the g7-pawn indirectly and, at the same time, protects the king from checks along files and ranks) 10 ♖g5 a2 11 ♖b5+ ♔c1 12 ♖a5 ♖g2+ 13 ♔h7 ♔b1 14 ♖b5+ ♖b2 15 ♖a5 ♖b7–+.

The move 4 ♖g2 is not forced but 4 ♖g1 a2 5 ♖a1 ♔b3 6 ♖g1 is even worse. Curiously enough, Minev in the *Encyclopaedia of Chess Endings*, annotating a similar endgame from Marshall - Duras, San Sebastian 1912, evaluated this position as drawn, although 6...♖c7! is quite a simple win.

The rook is a long-range piece that is capable of driving the enemy king with checks far away from the decisive area. Therefore let us consider 4 ♖g4+!?.

The line 4...♔c3 5 ♖g3+ ♔d4? 6 ♖×a3! ♖×a3 7 ♔×g7 ♔e5 (7...♖g3+ 8 ♔f7 ♖h3 9 ♔g6 ♔e5 10 h6 ♔e6 11 ♔g7!=) 8 h6 ♔f5 (8...♖a7+ 9 ♔g6!) 9 h7 ♖a7+ 10 ♔h6!= leads to an immediate draw.

If 4...♔b5, then 5 ♖g5+! (5 ♖g2 ♖c7!) 5...♔c6 6 ♖g1 a2 7 ♖a1

9-103

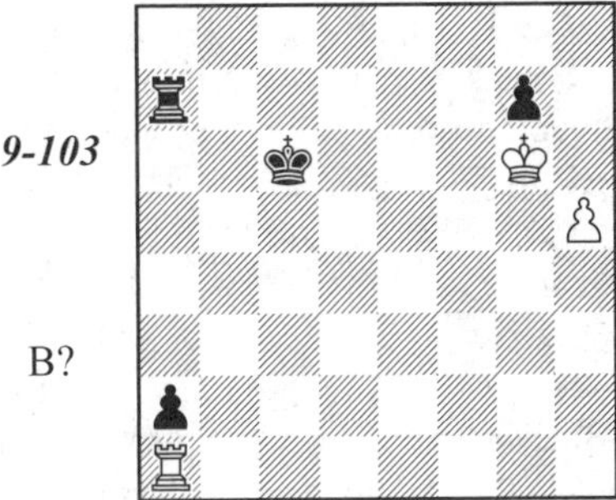

B?

What can Black undertake? In case of 7...♔c5 both 8 ♖c1+ ♔b4 9 ♖g1 ♖c7! and 8 ♖×a2 ♖×a2 9 ♔×g7 ♖g2+! (a familiar tool: zwischenschach for gaining a tempo) 10 ♔f6 (after 10 ♔h7 White will also be too late) 10...♖h2! 11 ♔g6 ♔d6 12 h6 ♔e7 13 h7 ♔f8 are bad. Summing up: a rook sacrifice for the a-pawn holds when the black king is on d4, c4, or b5, but not on c5 or c6.

Let us try the waiting move 8 ♔h7!. Now 8...♔c4 9 ♖×a2!= is useless; 8...g5+ 9 ♔g6 g4 10 h6 g3 11 h7 ♖×h7 12 ♔×h7 g2 is not dangerous for White either, because the black pawns are too far away from each other (look at diagram 8-33 again).

8...♔d5 is the strongest. After 9 ♔g6, Black does not play 9...♔e5 10 ♖e1+! (10 ♔h7? ♔f5) 10...♔d4 11 ♖a1! △ 12 ♖×a2 (the king is too late approaching the pawn). Instead, he has 9...♔d6!. This position could have been reached 2 moves earlier, if Black played 7...♔d6! (instead of 7...♔c5).

At first I did not see any danger for White here as well: 10 ♔h7! (10 ♖d1+? is bad because of 10...♔e7! 10 ♖a1 ♔f8 followed by ...♖a6+) 10...♔e5 11 ♔g6. However, grandmaster Müller finally discovered a winning continuation. Black suddenly sacrifices his g-pawn: 11...♖a6+!! 12 ♔×g7 ♔f5 13 ♔f7 (13 h6 ♖a7+) 13...♔g5 14 ♔e7 ♔×h5 and, as can easily be seen, his king comes to the queenside in time.

1...♖a6?!

An attempt to cut the king off from the g7-pawn does not work, although it does not spoil anything as well.

2 ♔f5 ♔c4 3 ♖g3!

This is the point! The line 3...a3 4 ♖×g7 a2 5 ♖g1 leads only to a draw.

3...♖f6+

Black should have played 3...♖a7! 4 ♔g6 ♔b4 (rather than 4...a3? 5 ♖×a3) 5 ♖g4+ ♔c5! (5...♔b5 6 ♖g3!) 6 ♖g5+ (6 ♖×a4 ♖×a4 7 ♔×g7 ♖g4+!) 6...♔c6(d6), transposing into situations that are already familiar to us. For example: 7 ♖g2 (7 ♖g1 a3) 7...a3 8 ♖a2 (8 ♖c2+ ♔b5 9 ♖g2 ♖c7!) 8...♔c5! 9 ♖a1 a2 10 ♔h7 ♔d5 11 ♔g6 ♔d6! etc. "à la Müller."

4 ♔e5?!

In spite of Averbakh's opinion, 4 ♔g5 gives no draw. Black should simply return with his rook to a6 (see the previous annotation).

Averbakh's line 4...♔b4 5 ♖g4+ ♔b3?! (5...♔b5! 6 ♖g3 ♖a6 7 ♔f5 ♖a7 8 ♔g6 ♔b4 9 ♖g4+ ♔c5! −+) 6 ♖g3+ ♔c2 7. ♖g2+ ♔c1 8 ♖g3 ♖a6? (8...♔b2! 9 ♖g2+ ♔b3 10 ♖g3+ ♔b4 11 ♖g4+ ♔b5 −+) 9 ♔f5 ♖a7 actually leads to a draw: 10 ♔g6 ♔b2, and now 11 ♔h7! a3 12 ♖×g7= rather than 11 ♖g2+? ♔b3 etc.

9-104

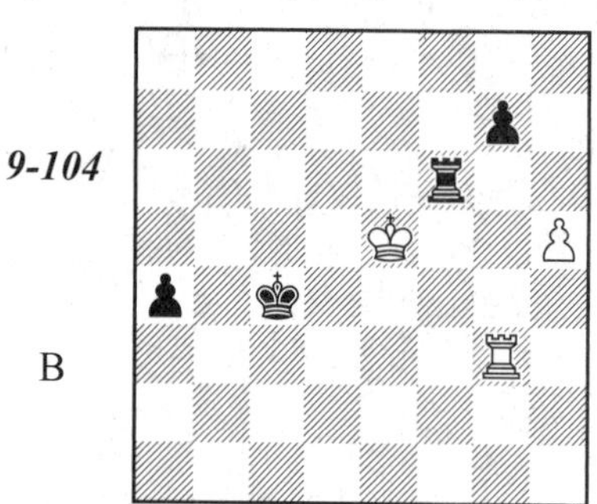

B

4...♖h6??

As is known, the one who wins errs next to last (White's decisive error is still to come). Black should have played 4...♖f7! 5 ♖g4+ ♔b5 6 ♖g3 ♖a7 7 ♔f5 a3 8 ♔g6 a2 9 ♖g1 ♔c4 etc.

5 ♖g4+ ♔b3 6 ♖g3+ ♔c2 7 ♖g2+ ♔d3 8 ♖g3+ ♔c4 9 ♖g4+ ♔b5 10 ♖×g7??

The elementary 10 ♔d4! led to an immediate draw. The capture is much weaker because Black maintains the possibility of interference with his rook along the 6th rank.

10...a3! 11 ♖a7 (11 ♖g1 ♖×h5+ 12 ♔d4 ♔b4 13 ♖b1+ ♔a4 14 ♔c3 a2 15 ♖g1 ♔a3 −+) **11...♖a6 12 ♖b7+**

12 ♖g7 a2 13 ♖g1 did not help: 13...♖h6! 14 ♖a1 (14 ♔d4 ♔b4) 14...♖×h5+ 15 ♔d4 ♖h2 16 ♔c3 ♔a4 −+.

12...♔a4 13 ♖g7 ♖a5+ 14 ♔f6 a2 15 ♖g4+ ♔b3 (15...♔b5?? 16 ♖g1=) **16 ♖g3+ ♔c4! 17 ♖g4+ ♔d3 18 ♖g3+ ♔e4 19 ♖g4+ ♔e3** (19...♔f3) **20 ♖g1 ♖×h5 21 ♖g3+ ♔d4 22 ♖a3 ♖h2 23 ♔f5 ♖f2+ 24 ♔g4 ♔c4**, and White resigned soon.

Exercises

In both cases, your task is to find whether Black can achieve a draw.

9-105

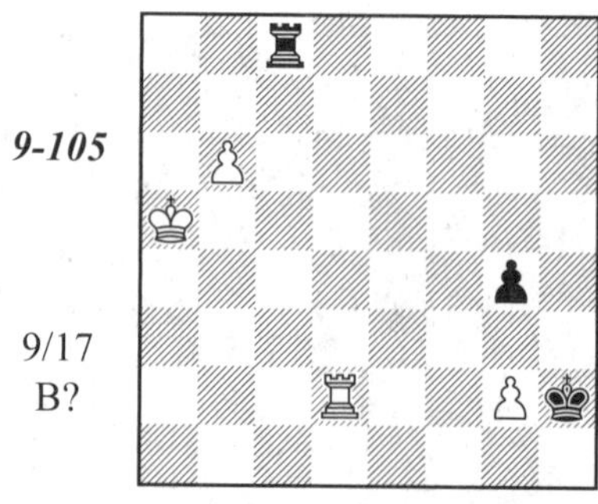

9/17
B?

9-106

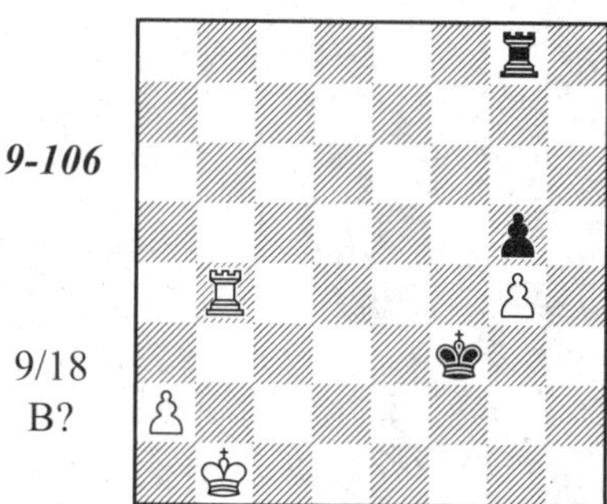

9/18
B?

Four Pawns vs. Three on the Same Wing

If all pawns are on the same wing, bringing the advantage home is frequently impossible (it is more precise to say, it should not be possible against correct defense). The fewer pawns, the easier the defense is.

Say, with 3 pawns against 2 or even with 4 against 3, in case of standard pawn structures, the task of the defender is not too difficult (once in a lightning tournament I managed to hold two such endings: against Tal and Vasiukov). As for the case of five pawns against four, the probability of losing is rather great.

Petrosian – Keres
USSR ch, Moscow 1951

9-107

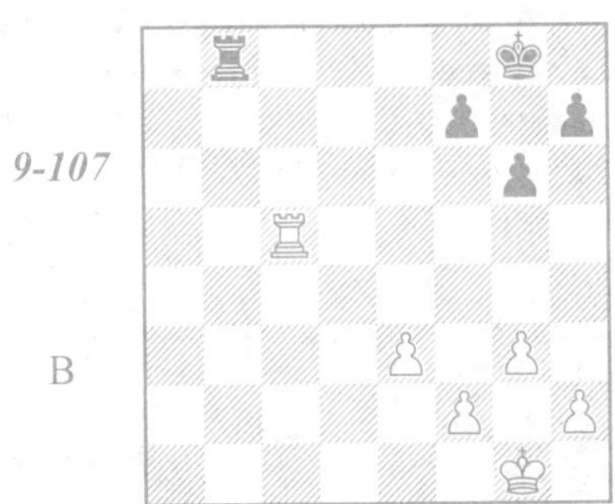

B

1...h5!

In this way Black makes his task of reaching a draw considerably easier. ***The defender should advance his h-pawn. The stronger side, whenever possible should prevent this by means of g3-g4!.***

The explanation consists in the fact that White's most logical plan is an advance of his e- and f-pawns in order to create a passed pawn. To accomplish this plan, he must sooner or later play g3-g4, allowing a pawn exchange on g4. But, as we know, ***pawn exchanges are usually favorable for the weaker side, and improve the drawing chances.*** Without ...h7-h5, the h-pawns would have stayed on the board.

In this game, Petrosian gradually carried out another plan: h2-h4 followed with f2-f3 and g3-g4, but also could not obtain victory.

2 ♖c2 ♔g7 3 ♔g2 ♖b5 4 ♔f3 ♔f6 5 h4 ♖f5+ 6 ♔g2 ♖a5 7 ♔h3 ♖a4 8 ♖d2 ♔e5 9 ♖b2 ♔f6 10 ♖b5 ♖a2 11 ♔g2 ♖a4 12 ♔f3 ♖a3 13 ♔f4 ♖a2 14 f3 ♖e2 15 e4 ♖e1 16 ♖b6+ ♔g7 17 ♖a6 ♖b1 18 ♖c6 ♖g1 19 ♖c2 ♔f6 20 ♖a2 ♔g7 21 ♖e2 ♔f6 22 ♖e3 ♔g7 23 e5 ♔f8 24 g4

If 24 ♔g5, the most simple is 24...♔g7, although 24...♖×g3+ 25 ♔f6 ♔g8 26 ♖d3 ♖h3 27 e6 fe 28 ♔×g6 ♖g3+ 29 ♔×h5 ♔g7= or 27 ♖d8+ ♔h7 28 ♔×f7 ♖×f3+ 29 ♔e7 g5 30 hg h4 31 e6 h3 32 ♖d2 ♔g6= is also playable.

24...hg 25 fg ♔g7 26 ♔g5 ♖f1 27 ♖e4 ♖f3 28 h5 (28 e6?? f6#) **28...gh 29 gh f6+ 30 ♔g4**

Or 30 ef+ ♖×f6 31 ♖e7+ ♖f7 32 h6+ ♔g8=.

30...♖f1 31 h6+

A little trap before the curtain falls. 31...♔×h6? loses to 32 e6 f5+ (if 32...♖g1+, then either 33 ♔f4 ♖g8 34 ♔f5 or 33 ♔f5 ♖f1+ 34 ♖f4 ♖×f4+ 35 ♔×f4 ♔g6 36 ♔e4) 33 ♔h3! fe 34 e7.

31...♔g6! Draw.

As can be seen, Black did not have serious troubles.

It should be mentioned that, when the white pawns had been set into motion, Keres used a typical strategic policy for this sort of position: ***attacking the pawns from the rear***.

What if Black could not play ...h7-h5 in time? We shall analyze two important endings that may serve as landmarks for both sides: the stronger side may pursue them while the weaker side should avoid these situations.

These endings are thoroughly analyzed in endgame handbooks. We skip some less important lines but bring respective conclusions.

Botvinnik – Najdorf
Moscow ol 1956

9-108

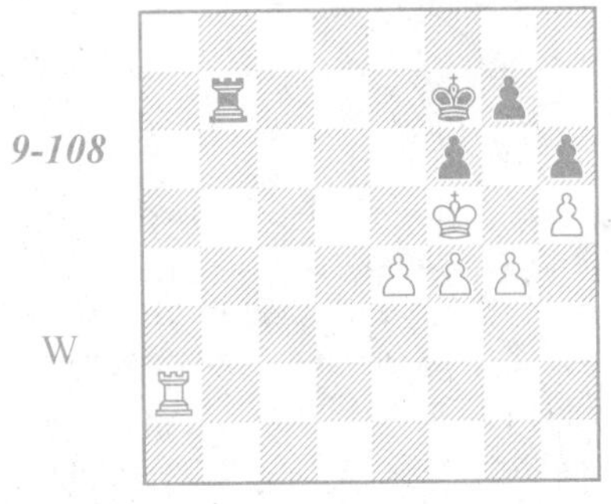

W

1 ♖a5 ♖c7 2 ♖d5 ♖a7 3 e5 fe 4 fe (5 ♖d7+! is threatened) **4...♔e7 5 e6 ♖a4!**

5...♖a6 6 ♖d7+ ♔f8 7 ♔g6! ♖×e6+ 8 ♔h7 is quite bad for Black.

6 g5!

6 ♖d7+ ♔f8 7 ♖f7+ ♔g8 8 g5 fails in view of 8...♖a5+! (8...hg? 9 ♔g6) 9 ♔e4 ♖a6=.

6...♖a7!

The best defense as suggested by Aronin. The rook may return because there is no danger of trading the rooks anymore: 7 ♖d7+? ♖×d7 8 ed ♔×d7 9 ♔g6 hg 10 ♔×g7 g4=.

The actual continuation was 6...hg?! 7 ♖d7+ ♔f8 8 ♖f7+ ♔g8 9 ♔g6 g4 10 h6! (the shortest way to a win) 10...gh 11 e7 ♖a8 12 ♖f6 (△ ♖d6-d8) Black resigned.

7 ♖e5!

A key move! White protects the pawn and prepares a king invasion.

An anticipatory pawn exchange is erroneous: 7 gh? gh 8 ♖b5 (△ ♖b6) 8...♖c7! 9 ♖b6 ♖c5+! 10 ♔g6 ♖e5! 11 ♔×h6 ♔f6! 12 ♖a6! ♖f5!.

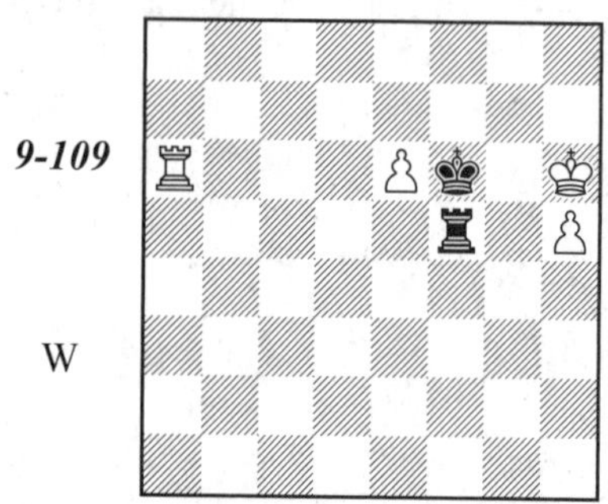

9-109

W

In this position, Black must play very precisely in order to achieve a draw, but theory says that this goal is within his reach.

7...hg

7...♔d6 8 gh gh 9 ♔f6; 7...♖a6 8 ♔g6 ♔f8 9 ♔h7 hg 10 e7+ ♔e8 11 ♔×g7 g4 12 h6+–.

8 ♔×g5 (8 ♔g6 ♔d6 9 ♖e1 g4 10 h6! gh 11 ♔f6 is also strong) **8...♖a1 9 ♔g6 ♖f1** (9...♖g1+ 10 ♖g5) **10 ♔×g7 ♖g1+ 11 ♔h6! ♖g2 12 ♖g5+–**.

In the next diagram, White's position is winning (the same evaluation is valid with the black pawn on h7 and the white pawn on g5). The winning plan is a rook transfer to the 8th rank followed by f4-f5-f6+. If the black rook aims at the e5-pawn, White defends it with the rook from e8.

Capablanca carried this plan through; however, as renowned rook endgame expert Kopaev

Capablanca – Yates

Hastings 1930/31

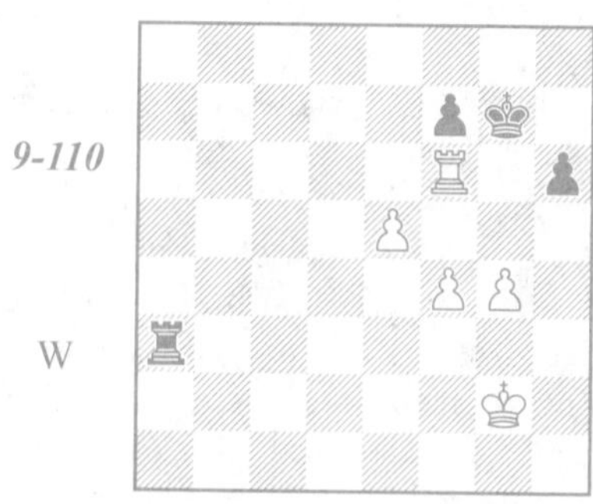

9-110

W

demonstrated, the opponents made a number of instructive errors on the way to the final outcome.

1 ♖b6?

White should have played 1 ♖d6! in order to use the rook to protect against checks from the side. The correct reply to the move actually played in the game was 1...♖a4! 2 ♔f3 (2 ♔g3 ♖a3+ 3 ♔h4 ♖a4 4 f5 ♖a5 5 e6 fe 6 fe ♔f6=) 2...♖a3+ 3 ♔e4 ♖a4+ 4 ♔f5 ♖c4 5 ♖b7 (△ 6 e6) 5...♔f8.

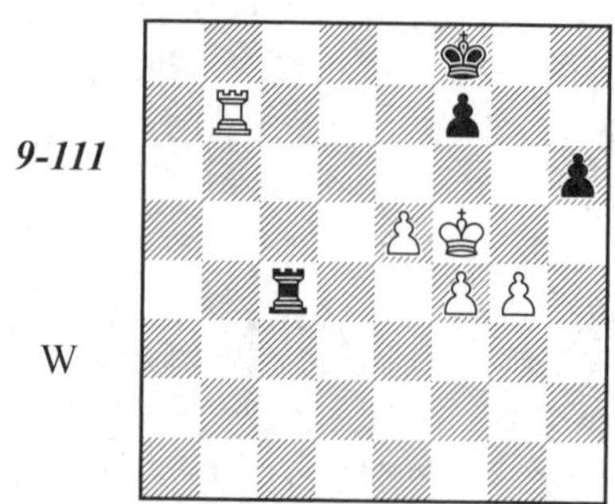

9-111

W

White missed the correct way: he has brought his king, not his pawn, to f5, so he cannot win anymore.

1...♖e3? 2 ♖b4

2 ♖b8 suggested itself, however after 2...♖e4 3 ♔f3 ♖e1 a straightforward 4 ♖e8? enables the salvation through 4...h5! 5 g5 (5 gh ♖f1+! 6 ♔e4 ♖e1+ 7 ♔f5 ♖h1) 5...♖f1+ 6 ♔e3 h4.

The most precise is 2 ♖b1! (temporarily denying the black rook the 1st rank). Black is in zugzwang. He must either worsen his king's position or move his rook off the e-file where it is best placed. In both cases, the invasion of the white rook gains in effectiveness. For example, 2...♖e4 (2...♖e2+ 3 ♔f3 ♖h2 4 f5 h5 5 ♖b7 hg+ 6 ♔g3 ♖h5 7 ♔×g4 ♖h1 8 e6+–) 3 ♔f3 ♖a4, and now time has come for the main plan: 4 ♖b8! ♖a3+ 5 ♔g2 ♖e3 6 ♖e8! ♖e2+ 7 ♔f3 ♖e1 8 f5 ♖f1+ 9 ♔e2 ♖f4 10 ♔e3 ♖×g4 11 f6+ ♔h7 12 e6+−.

2...♖c3 3 ♔f2? (3 ♖b8) **3...♖a3?**

Both adversaries missed the fact that after 3...h5! Black either trades a pair of pawns (4 gh ♖h3) or (in case of 4 g5 h4) obtains enough counterplay to save the game.

4 ♖b7?! (4 ♖b8!) **4...♔g8?!** (4...♖a2+!?) **5 ♖b8+! ♔g7 6 f5** (△ 7 f6+), and White won.

Korchnoi – Antoshin
USSR ch, Erevan 1954

9-112

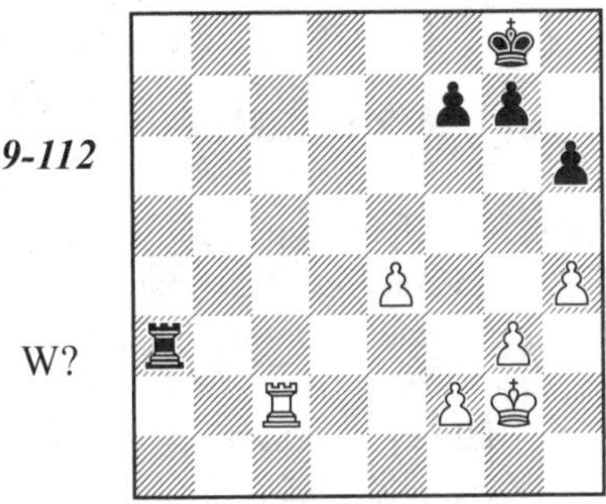

W?

1 h5!

Black, if he was on move, could have considerably simplified his task by placing his own pawn to h5. If 1 g4?!, then all the same 1...h5!.

1...♖a5!

As Korchnoi noted in his exceptionally deep and far-reaching comments to this endgame, it is useful for Black to force the advance g3-g4.

2 g4

2 ♖c8+ ♔h7 3 g4 is not dangerous yet because of 3...g5! 4 hg+ ♔×g6 (△ 5...h5) 5 f4 f6!.

9-113

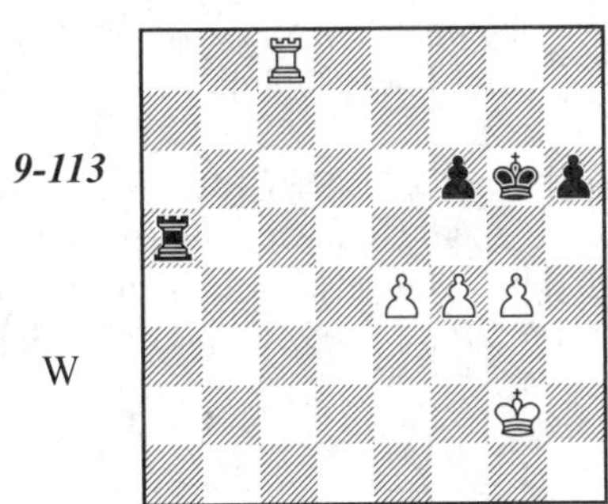

W

The last move is worth special attention. ***It is vitally important for Black to prevent the pressing advance e4-e5*** that leads to the setup from the Capablanca – Yates game. By the way, in that game the white pawn stood on e4 a few moves before the position of the diagram 9-110 arose, and Yates could have had an easy draw by means of ...f7-f6.

2...♖a7?

Antoshin had to keep in mind the danger of a check along the 8th rank: his king, when standing on h7, is too far removed from a passed e-pawn if White manages to create it. Therefore here, and later on too, he should have played f7-f6!. Black could then parry the threat of transposition into the winning position from the Botvinnik – Najdorf game by means of catching the white pawns from behind. A characteristic variation was demonstrated by Korchnoi: 2...f6! 3 ♖c8+ ♔f7 4 ♖c7+ ♔g8! 5 ♔f3 (5 f4 ♖a3 – White's king is cut off from his pawns) 5...♖a3+ 6 ♔f4 ♖a2 7 ♔f5 ♔h7! (this is why the black king drew back to g8) 8 f4 ♖f2!= as White fails to create the passed e-pawn.

It is time to explain why the move 1...♖a5 was given an exclamation mark. With a pawn on g3, this defensive plan does not work: the f4-pawn is protected, so White can play ♔e6, while Black can hardly prevent the penetration of the white king to f5 (via g4) at an earlier stage.

3 ♖c6?

After 3 ♖c8+! ♔h7 4 e5! (△ ♔g3, f4, ♖e8+−) Black would have been faced with problems one can hardly tackle over the board.

9-114

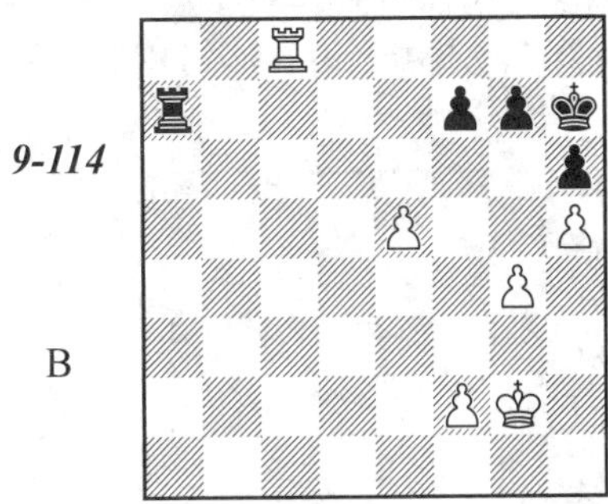

B

As Korchnoi showed, almost all defensive methods are doomed to lose: White either creates a dangerous passed e-pawn or transposes to positions from the game Capablanca – Yates. For example, 4...g5? 5 hg+ ♔×g6 6 f4+−, or 4...♖a4?! 5 ♔g3 ♖e4 6 ♖e8 g5 (6...♖a4 7 ♖f8 ♖a7 8 f4+−; 6...f6 7 e6 g5 8 hg+ ♔×g6 9 f3 ♖e1 10 ♔f2 ♖e5 11 f4+−) 7 hg+ ♔×g6 8 f3!+− (8 f4? is not precise, Black holds after 8...h5!). Of course, only basic results are shown here, as a detailed explanation would have been rather complicated and too vast.

4...♖e7! (the only defense) 5 f4 f6! 6 ♖c5 fe 7 fe, and now Black must prevent the white king's march to the center, that would transpose to the Botvinnik-Najdorf ending, by 7...♖f7!. Here Korchnoi gives 8 ♔g3 g6!= and 8 e6 ♖e7 9 ♖c6 g6 10 ♖d6 (△ 11 ♖d7) 10...♖e8 11 ♔f3 gh 12 gh ♔g7 13 ♔e4 ♔f6 14 ♔d5 ♖e7=.

The prophylactic move 8 ♖d5! is more dangerous for Black. He cannot play 8...g6? on account of 9 e6 ♖f8 (9...♖e7 10 ♖d7) 10 ♖d7+ ♔g8 11 e7 ♖e8 12 ♖d8 ♔f7 13 ♖×e8 ♔×e8 14 g5!+–, and 8...g5? 9 e6 ♖f8 10 e7 ♖e8 11 ♖e5 ♔g7 12 ♖e6+– is also bad. Therefore he must wait: 8...♖f8 9 ♔g3 ♖f1, and if 10 ♖d3, then 10...g5!. But I doubt whether Black can hold this endgame after 10 ♖d7!⊙ ♖f8 (the same reply follows to 10...♔g8) 11 ♖d3 g5 12 ♖f3 ♖e8 13 ♖f5 followed by 14 ♔f3.

3...♜a3? (3...f6!=) **4 f3?**

4 ♖c8+! ♔h7 5 e5! was winning.

4...♜a5!? (4...f6!)

Now White can gradually strengthen his position by means of ♖c8-d8, ♔g3-f4 or f3-f4, but, as his pawn cannot come to e5, the game will be drawn if Black defends precisely.

Korchnoi decided to force the events and was successful, but only due to a new mistake by Black.

5 ♜c8+ ♚h7 6 f4?! (△ 7 e5+–) **6...♜a2+ 7 ♚f3 ♜a3+ 8 ♚f2 ♜a2+ 9 ♚e3 ♜a3+ 10 ♚d4**

9-115

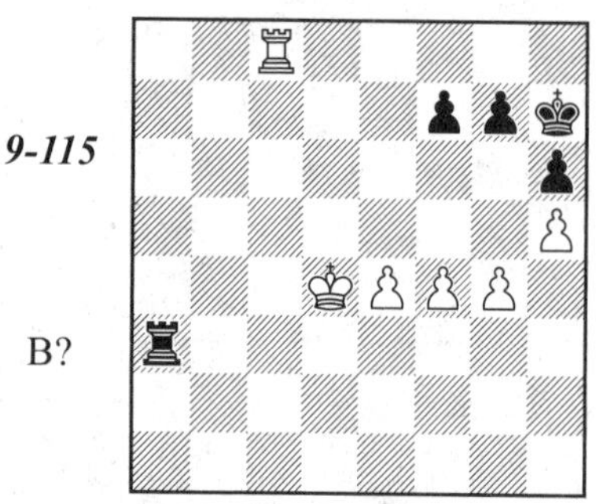

B?

Black can hold the game rather simply: 10...♖f3! 11 ♔e5 (11 f5 f6=) 11...f6+ 12 ♔f5 ♖f1, achieving the position from the note to Black's move 2.

10...♜g3?

He chases after material gain but lets White create a passed pawn that will cost him a rook.

11 ♜f8! f6 12 e5! ♜×g4

12...fe+ 13 fe ♖×g4+ 14 ♔d5 ♖g1 15 e6 ♖d1+ 16 ♔c6 ♖e1 17 ♔d7 ♖d1+ 18 ♔e8+– is no better.

13 e6 ♜×f4+ 14 ♚d5 ♜f5+ 15 ♚d6 ♜×h5 16 e7 ♜e5 17 e8♛ ♜×e8 18 ♜×e8

The fight is almost over. When the white king comes back to his home side of the board, the rook will be stronger than 3 pawns.

18...♚g6 19 ♚d5 ♚f5!? 20 ♜e1

20 ♔d4 ♔f4 21 ♔d3 ♔f3 22 ♖g8 g5 23 ♖f8+– is also strong.

20...h5 21 ♜f1+ ♚g4 22 ♚e4 g5 23 ♜×f6 h4 24 ♚e3 ♚g3 25 ♚e2 g4 26 ♚f1 ♚h2 27 ♜f4 h3 28 ♜×g4 ♚h1 29 ♚f2 h2 30 ♚g3 ♚g1 31 ♚h3+ Black resigned.

Tragicomedies

The two last endings fully fit this category, but I would like to add some new examples, the last of which has some theoretical value.

Bellón – Chekhov
Barcelona 1984

9-116

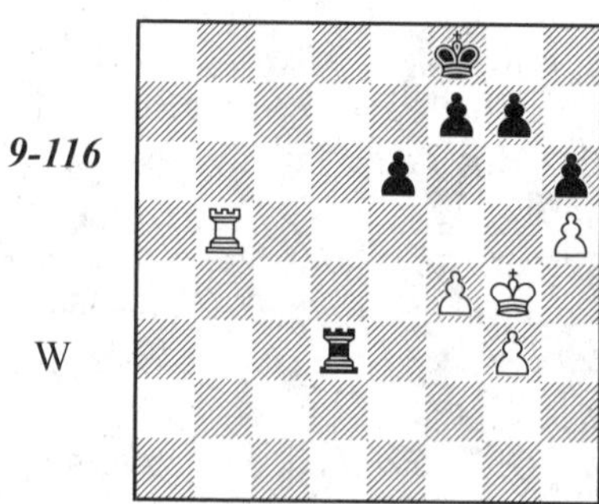

W

The waiting policy (1 ♖a5 or 1 ♖b7) gave a rather easy draw, but Bellón decided to chase after the g7-pawn.

1 ♜b8+ ♚e7 2 ♜g8?? ♜d8!

White resigned. The pawn endgame is quite hopeless for him, while after 3 ♖×g7 his rook is lost: 3...♔f8 4 ♖h7 ♔g8 5 ♖×h6 ♔g7 6 ♔g5 ♖d5+.

Norri – Svidler
Erevan ol 1996

9-117

W

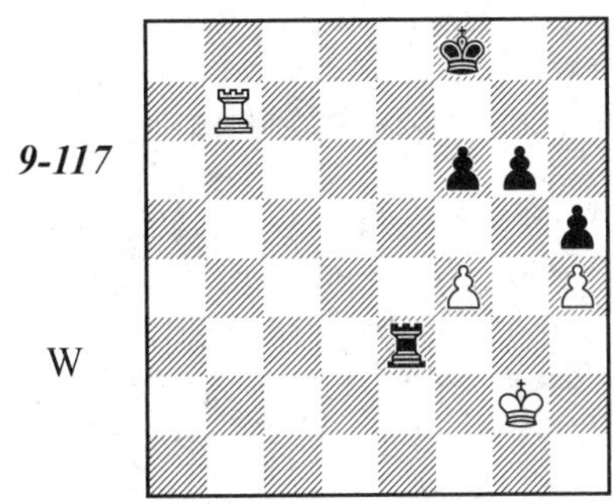

Here again White did not have enough patience and made an analogous error.

1 f5? (1 ♖a7=) **1...gf 2 ♖h7 ♔g8 3 ♖×h5??**

3 ♖a7 could still hold the game.

3...♖e5 4 ♔f3 f4! White resigned.

Piket – Kasparov
An Internet Tournament, 2000

9-118
$

B

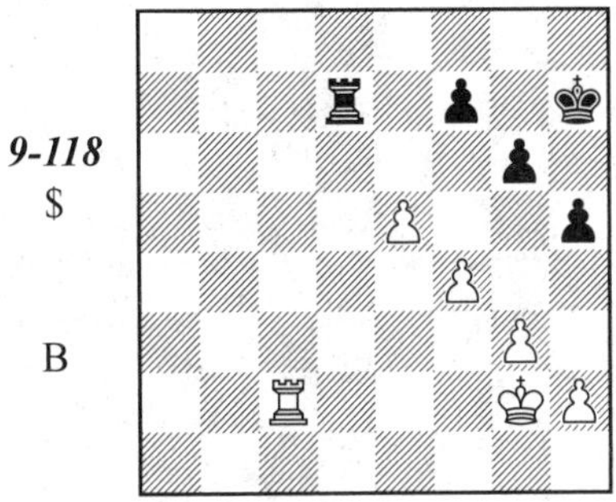

White succeeded in bringing his pawn to e5 (generally speaking, it would have been favorable for Black if he prevented this by playing ...f7-f6 at an earlier stage). On the other hand, ...h6-h5 is already played, so reaching a draw should not be a very difficult problem.

Kasparov had to decide how to behave in case of the white king's march to g5 via h3 and h4. The simplest method was to play ...♔h6 at a proper moment. For example 1...♔g7 2 ♔h3 ♖a7 3 ♔h4 ♔h6!, and one cannot see how White could make any progress.

Moreover, a king invasion to g5 is not too dangerous. Even with the white rook on the 7th rank Black can survive. Averbakh analyzes 3...♖a6 (instead of 3...♔h6) 4 ♖c7 ♖b6 5 ♖e7 ♖a6 6 ♔g5 (6 e6 ♔f6! 7 ♖×f7+ ♔×e6=) 6...♖a5! (as Bologan says, even 6...♖b6!? 7 e6 ♖b5+! or 7 f5 gf does not lose) 7 f5 gf 8 e6 (8 ♔×h5 ♔f8 △ 9...♖×e5) 8...f4+! 9 ♔×f4 ♔f6 10 ♖×f7+ ♔×e6=.

1...♖d3?!

In many similar situations, to place the rook behind the e-pawn makes some sense; particularly, such a maneuver is not bad when h-pawns are absent. But here this transfer is erroneous. Its slightly modified version does not work, either: 1...♖d4?! 2 ♔h3 ♖e4? (in case of 2...g5? White does not play 3 fg ♔g6, he has 3 ♖c7! instead) 3 ♖c7! (3 ♔h4 ♔h6 △ 4...g5+) 3...♔g7 4 ♔h4 ♖e2 5 ♔g5!, and we come to situations that have actually occurred in the game.

2 ♔h3 ♖e3?

2...♖d7 3 ♔h4 ♔h6= was necessary.

3 ♔h4?!

Playing 3 ♖c7! ♔g7 4 ♔h4, Piket could have chained the hostile rook to the e-file and, as we shall see, this was a winning method.

3...♔g7?

He should have tried 3...♔h6! 4 ♖c7 ♖e2!. If 5 ♔h3, then 5...♔g7 (5...g5!? is also playable) 6 ♖b7 g5! 7 fg ♔g6. The line 5 g4 hg 6 ♖×f7 ♖×h2+ 7 ♔×g4 is more dangerous for Black, but after 7...♖e2 he seems to be surviving.

4 ♔g5?

An erroneous order of moves, again 4 ♖c7! ♖e2 5 ♔g5 is correct. Now Black could return to Averbakh's plan: 4...♖a3! 5 ♖c7 ♖a5=. However Piket could hardly expect that his opponent would suddenly change his mind and move the rook back.

4...♖e1? 5 ♖c7 ♖e2 6 ♖e7! ♖a2 7 f5! gf 8 e6 h4 9 ♖×f7+ ♔g8 10 ♔f6 Black resigned.

Let us look at 6...♖e4 (instead of 6...♖a2).

9-119
$

W

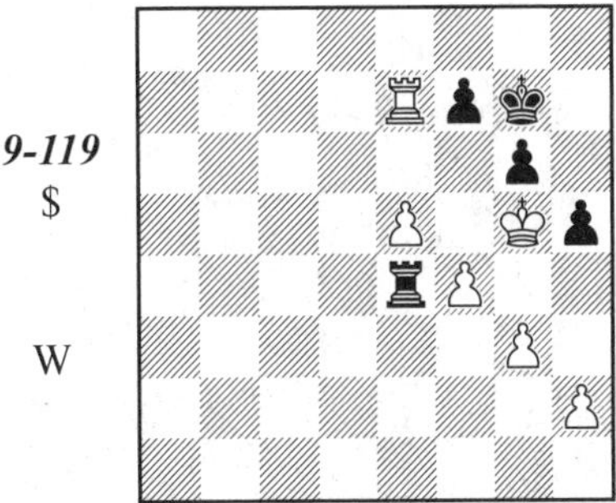

This position occurred in the following games: Stean – Hartston (Great Britain ch, Brighton 1972), Ionov – Karasev (Leningrad 1983) and Matveeva – Rappoport (Baku 1983). In all these games, White found a forced win.

7 e6! ♖×e6 8 ♖×e6 fe 9 h3 ♔f7 10 ♔h6 ♔f6 11 g4 h4 (11...hg 12 hg⊙ +–) **12 g5+** (12 ♔h7? g5) **12...♔f5 13 ♔g7 ♔×f4 14 ♔×g6 e5 15 ♔f6! e4 16 g6 e3 17 g7 e2 18 g8♕ e1♕ 19 ♕g4+ ♔e3 20 ♕e6+ ♔f2 21 ♕×e1+ ♔×e1 22 ♔g5+–**

Finally, instead of 5...♖e2 Black could have played 5...♖e4!? at once. The point is to meet 6 ♖e7 with 6...♖a4!, and 7 f5, as was played by Piket, is not possible anymore, while if 7 e6, then 7...♖a5+ 8 ♔h4 ♔f6 9 ♖×f7+ ♔×e6=.

White must wait: 6 ♖b7!⊙ ♖a4 (6...♖e2 7 ♖e7! transposes to the actual course of the game), and here Bologan has discovered a brilliant solution: a double pawn sacrifice 7 g4!! hg (7...♖e4 8 gh gh 9 h4 is hopeless) 8 f5! gf 9 e6+–.

A gain of another pawn is much weaker: 7 e6 ♖a5+ 8 ♔h4 ♔f6 9 ef ♔g7 10 ♖e7 ♔f8! 11 ♖e5 ♖a2, or 10 h3 ♔f8 11 g4 hg 12 hg ♖c5 13 f5 ♖c6! (rather than 13...gf? 14 g5+-). It looks like Black holds in both these lines.

Balance on One Wing and an Extra Pawn on Another

Situations with an extra remote passed pawn occur now and then, therefore it is very important to learn their correct evaluation and handling. ***The decisive factor in this sort of endgame is the position of the rook of the stronger side. In majority of cases the rook is placed best "à la Tarrasch," behind its own passed pawn; sometimes its sideways position is preferable.***

Quite often, however, we lack free choice, so the rook mostly stands in front of the pawn in practical games. Therefore we shall pay more attention to these cases.

The Rook Behind its Own Pawn

Botvinnik – Boleslavsky
Leningrad/Moscow 1941

9-120

W?

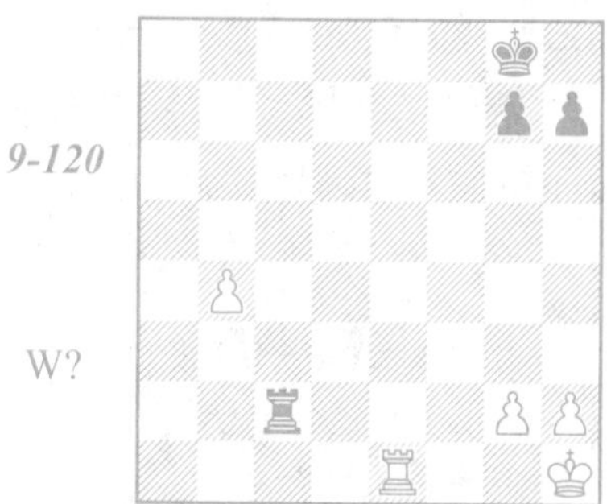

1 ♖b1!

The rook has occupied its correct position behind the pawn. After 1 h3? ♖b2! 2 ♖e4 Black could have achieved a draw.

1...♔f7?

The passed pawn should be blocked as soon as possible. Black had to play 1...♖c6! 2 b5 ♖b6. I do not think this was enough for a draw but, anyway, his opponent would have then been faced with more complicated problems. After a king's march to the queenside Black removes his rook from b6 either for protecting his own pawns or for attacking the hostile ones.

2 b5 ♔e6 3 b6 ♖c8 4 h3

4 b7? ♖b8 is erroneous because it allows Black to eliminate the b-pawn and thereafter to bring his king back to the kingside in time. For example, 5 ♔g1 ♔d6 6 ♔f2 ♔c6 7 ♔e3 ♖×b7 8 ♖×b7 ♔×b7 9 ♔e4 ♔c6 10 ♔e5 ♔d7=.

4...♖b8 5 ♔h2 ♔d5

If the black king stays with his pawns, his adversary heads to the b-pawn. Black cannot prevent this by means of the opposition because White can make a waiting rook move; Black will then be obliged to give way to the white king because his rook has no waiting moves. This clearly demonstrates the difference between the rook positions.

6 ♔g3 ♔c6 7 ♔g4 ♔b7

A capture on b6 is impossible now; therefore ***Black blocks the pawn with his king, releasing the rook from this duty.*** A standard and often quite useful method; but alas, it does not bring any relief to Black in this particular case.

8 ♖e1!

Excellently played! While the rook was pinning the black rook down it was superbly placed on b1, but now it will be more active when placed sideways. In case of 8...♔×b6 9 ♖b1+ Black loses the pawn endgame.

8...♖g8 9 ♖e6 ♔a6 10 ♔g5 ♔b7 11 h4

The rest is simple. White attacks on the kingside, having an extra piece there.

11...♔a6 12 h5 ♔b7 13 g4 ♔a6 14 ♔h4 ♔b7 15 h6 gh 16 ♖×h6 ♖g7 17 ♔h5

(△ g5, ♖e6, ♔h6+–) **17...♔a6 18 ♖c6 ♖e7 19 ♖c7 ♖e5+ 20 g5 ♔×b6 21 ♖×h7 ♔c6 22 ♔h6 ♔d6 23 g6 ♖e1 24 ♖f7 ♔e6 25 ♖f2 ♖a1 26 g7 ♖h1+ 27 ♔g6 ♖g1+ 28 ♔h7 ♖h1+ 29 ♔g8 ♔e7 30 ♖e2+ ♔d7 31 ♖e4** ("bridging") **31...♖h2 32 ♔f7** Black resigned.

Botvinnik – Borisenko
USSR ch, Moscow 1955

9-121

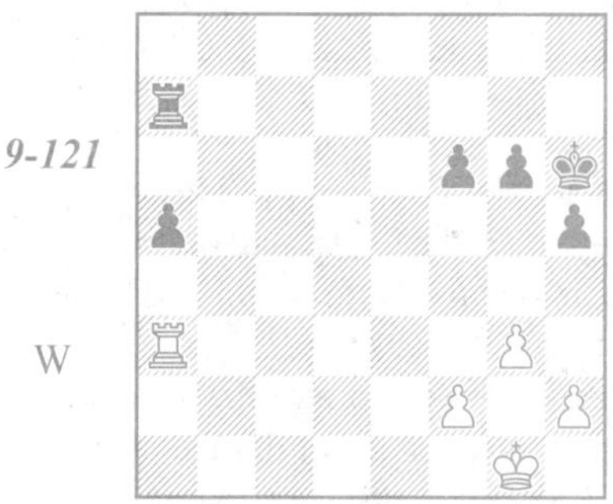

W

1 ♖a4!

Botvinnik blocks the pawn immediately. If he allowed ...a5-a4 he would have had no chances at all. Alekhine won a similar ending from Capablanca in the last, 34th, game of their match for the World Championship in 1927: it can be found in almost every book on endgames.

1...♔g5?

An instructive error. The king heads for the queenside, but a safer road was via g7. Why? The point is that ***the best chance for a successful defense in this sort of position is counterplay on the kingside: creation of a passed pawn or weakening the opponent's position.*** The position of the king in front of the pawns contributes, as we shall see, to the adversary's counterplay.

After 1...♔g7! White is not getting on:

2 f3 ♔f7 3 g4 h4–+

2 ♔g2 ♔f7 3 ♔f3 ♔e6 4 h4 (4 g4 h4 5 g5 fg 6 ♔g4 ♔f6 7 h3 ♖a8–+) 4...f5 5 ♔f4 ♔d5 6 ♔g5 ♖a6 7 f3 ♔c5 8 g4 fg 9 fg hg 10 ♔×g4 ♔b5 11 ♖a1 a4–+ (Levenfish, Smyslov)

2 h4 ♔f7 3 ♔f1 ♔e6 4 ♔e2 ♔d6 5 ♔d3 (5 g4 hg 6 ♖×g4 a4 7 ♖×g6 a3 8 ♖g1 a2 9 ♖a1 ♔e5 10 ♔f3 ♖a4–+) 5...f5! (5...♔c6? is erroneous in view of 6 g4 ♖d7+ 7 ♔c3 ♖d5 8 ♖f4 f5 9 gh gh 10 ♔c4=) 6 f3 ♔c5 7 g4 ♔b5 8 ♖d4 a4 9 ♔c2 a3 10 ♔b1 ♖a4! 11 ♖d6 hg 12 ♖×g6 gf–+ (Kopaev).

2 f3! ♔f5

After 2...f5!? 3 ♔f2 ♔f6 4 h4 ♔e5 5 ♔e3 ♔d5 6 g4! the outcome is also unclear.

3 g4+! hg?

The exchange of pawns makes White's task easier. As was revealed in later analyses, after 3...♔e6! Black would still have had winning chances.

4 fg+ ♔e5

In case of 4...♔g5!? White simply waits: 5 ♔g2 ♔h4 6 ♔g1 ♔h3 7 ♔h1 ♖e7 (7...f5 8 gf gf 9 ♔g1 f4 10 ♔f2=) 8 ♖a3+ ♔×g4 9 ♖×a5. Kopaev, as well as Levenfish and Smyslov, evaluate this position as drawn although after 9...♔f3! this is far from obvious. Instead of 6 ♔g1, Botvinnik recommended 6 h3!?; and Marin proved that it is indeed enough for a draw: 6...g5 7 ♔h2 ♖b7 8 ♖×a5 ♖b2+ 9 ♔g1 ♔×h3 10 ♖a6 ♔×g4 11 ♖×f6 ♔g3 12 ♖f1!=.

5 h4 ♔d5 6 h5 gh 7 gh

The goal is reached; White has created a passed pawn. Black cannot win anymore, for example 7...♔c5 8 h6 ♔b5 9 ♖h4 ♖h7 10 ♖h5+ ♔b4 11 ♖h4+ ♔b3 12 ♖h3+ ♔b2 13 ♖h4=.

7...♔e6 8 h6 ♔f7 9 ♖g4! ♔f8 10 ♖f4 ♖a6 11 ♖g4 ♖a7 12 ♖f4 ♔g8 13 ♖×f6 a4 14 ♖f2 ♔h7 15 ♖a2 ♔×h6 16 ♔f2 ♔g5 17 ♔e3 Draw.

Tragicomedies

Dvoretsky – Kupreichik
USSR ch(1), Minsk 1976

9-122

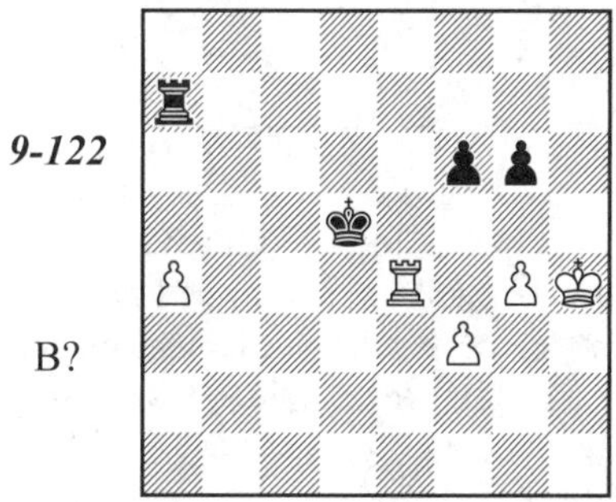

B?

The diagrammed position arose in an adjourned game a few moves after resumption of play, so both the adversaries had reached it in their home analyses.

I only expected a logical maneuver that placed the rook behind the passed pawn: 1...♖h7+! 2 ♔g3 ♖h1. In that case, after 3 ♔f4 ♖a1? 4 g5! fg+ 5 ♔×g5 ♖a3 6 ♖f4 Black was lost, but 3...♖f1!, preparing ...g6-g5+, destroyed White's plan.

1...♖b7?!

A peculiar move: my rook can occupy a position behind the pawn now, and so even in two ways: 2 ♖e3 △ 3 ♖a3 and 2 a5 △ 3 ♖a4.

The second way is apparently more attractive: in principle, it is favorable to push the pawn farther. So I stepped into it, failing to discover a cleverly prepared trap. The correct continuation was 2 ♖e3! ♖a7 3 ♖a3 ♖a5! 4 ♔g3 and Black's position is still very difficult, very probably lost.

2 a5? ♖b3! 3 ♖a4 ♖×f3 4 a6

It seems so that the pawn can only be stopped by means of 4...g5+ 5 ♔h5 ♖h3+ 6 ♔g6 ♖h8 7 a7 ♖a8, and this is surely hopeless for Black.

4...♔e6!!

It comes to light that after 5 a7? g5+ 6 ♔h5 ♔f7 White will be checkmated.

5 g5 fg+ 6 ♔×g5 ♖f8 Draw.

Em. Lasker – Levenfish
Moscow 1925

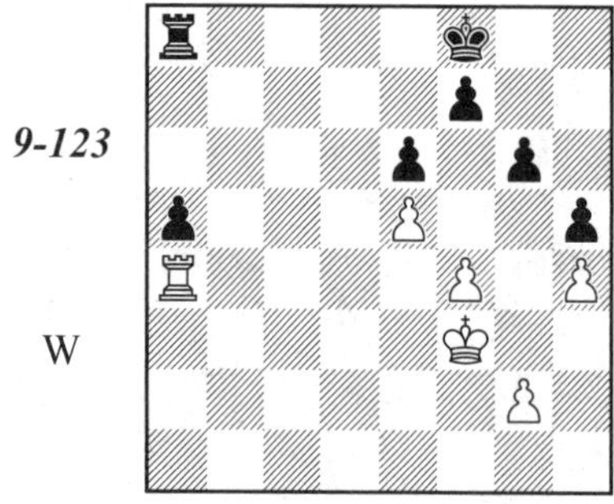

9-123

W

1 g4

Lasker aspires for counterplay on the kingside. An alternative method was 1 ♔e4 ♔e7 2 ♔d4, trying to prevent the black king from joining his pawn. However 2...♖d8+! was strong then.

1...hg+?

Levenfish lets the white king go ahead for no reason whatsoever. An easy win was 1...♔e7 2 gh gh, for example: 3 ♔e4 ♔d7 4 f5 ♔c6 5 f6 ♔b5 6 ♖a1 a4 7 ♔f4 ♖g8–+, or 3 f5 ef 4 ♔f4 ♔e6 5 ♔g5 ♔×e5 6 ♔×h5 ♔f6! with an inevitable mate.

2 ♔×g4 ♔e7 3 ♔g5 ♖a7⊙ 4 ♔h6 ♔d7 5 ♔g7 ♔c6

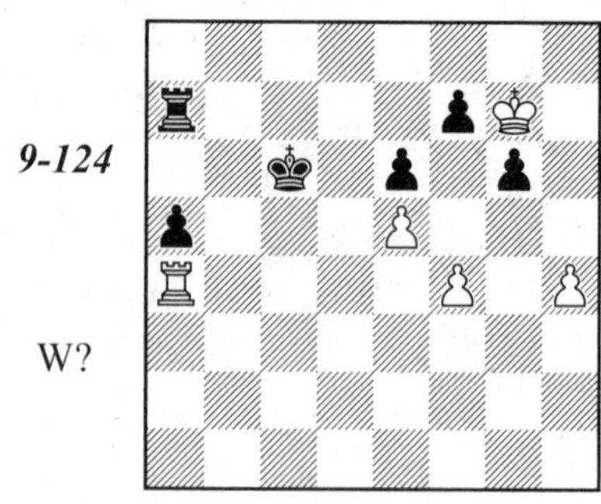

9-124

W?

6 ♔f6?

A decisive loss of a tempo! Lasker saw the correct way but, as he explained after the game, he wanted instinctively to avoid a discovered check along the 7th rank.

He should have performed the breakthrough that gave him a passed pawn immediately: 6 f5! ef (6...gf 7 h5) 7 e6 fe+ 8 ♔×g6. After 8...♔b5 9 ♖a1 f4 10 h5, both 10...f3 11 ♖f1 a4 12 ♖×f3 a3 13 ♖f1 a2 14 ♖a1 ♔c4 15 h6 ♔b3 16 h7 ♖a8 17 ♖e1! e5 (17...♔b2 18 ♖e2+) 18 ♔g7 e4 19 h8♕ ♖×h8 20 ♔×h8 (the black pawn cannot reach e2, so there is no win) and 10...e5 11 ♖e1! ♔c4 (11...a4 12 ♖×e5+ ♔c6 13 ♖e4 a3 14 ♖×f4 a2 15 ♖f1=) 12 ♖×e5 ♔d3 13 h6 f3 14 h7 ♖×h7 (14...♖a8 15 ♖×a5) 15 ♔×h7 f2 16 ♖f5 ♔e3 17 ♖f8 (or 17 ♖e5+ ♔f4 18 ♖e8) 17...a4 18 ♖e8+ ♔f3 19 ♖f8+ ♔g2 20 ♖g8+ ♔h3 21 ♖f8= lead to a draw.

6...♔b5 7 ♖a1 a4 8 f5 ef 9 e6 fe 10 ♔×g6 f4! 11 h5 f3! 12 h6 (12 ♖f1 a3–+) **12...e5! 13 ♖e1**

Neither 13 h7 ♖×h7 (13...♖a8) 14 ♔×h7 e4 15 ♖f1 a3 16 ♔g6 a2 17 ♔f5 e3 18 ♔e4 e2–+ nor 13 ♔f5 ♖h7 14 ♖h1 f2 15 ♔×e5 ♖×h6–+ can help White.

13...a3 14 ♖×e5+ ♔c4 15 ♖e1 a2 16 h7 ♖a8!

The pawns are separated by 4 files; therefore 16...♖×h7? 17 ♔×h7 f2 18 ♖f1 ♔d3 19 ♖a1! ♔c3 20 ♖f1! enabled White to reach a draw.

17 ♔g7 f2 18 ♖f1 (18 ♖a1 ♔b3) **18...a1♕+ 19 ♖×a1 ♖×a1 20 h8♕ ♖g1+** White resigned.

Exercises

9-125

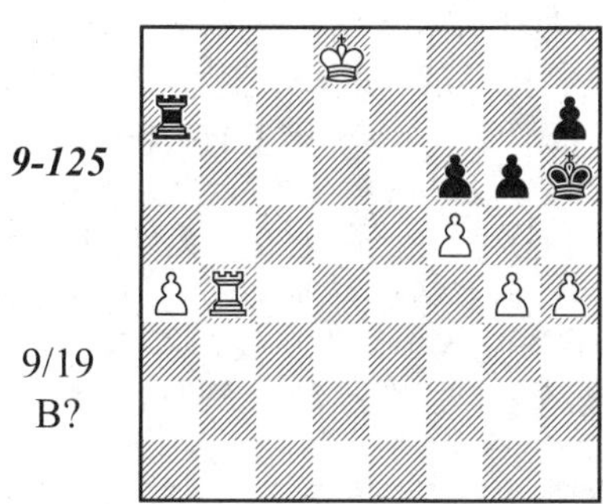

9/19
B?

9-126

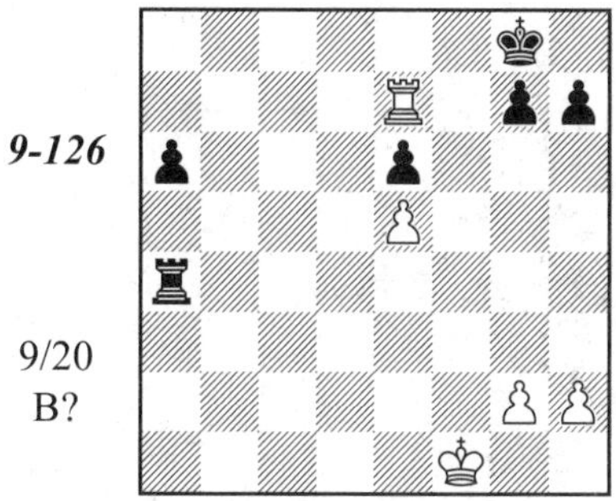

9/20
B?

What is the outcome with correct play?

The Rook in Front of the Pawn, with the Pawn on the 7th Rank

We have seen a section with an identical title in the theory of "a rook and a rook pawn versus a rook" endgames. The ideas from that section will be useful for our current considerations.

A pawn advance to the 7th rank absolutely chains the opponent's forces. However, if there are no vulnerable points in his camp, the game is still drawn because a king march to the pawn is useless: no refuge from rook checks from behind is provided.

Pushing the pawn to the 7th rank makes sense, and offers winning chances, when one of the following three plans is possible:

Plan 1

It is sometimes possible to sacrifice the passed pawn, in order to exchange rooks by means of a 7th-rank check, transposing into a won pawn endgame.

Benko – Gereben
Budapest 1951

9-127

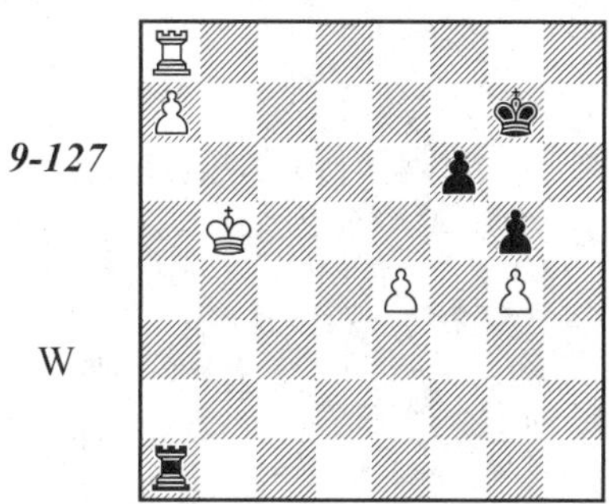

W

If the pawn stood on a6, then after 1 ♔b6 the king could escape the checks at a7. But here, the king has no shelter, so White's only hope lies in the exchange of rooks.

1 ♔b6 ♖b1+ 2 ♔c6 ♖c1+ 3 ♔d6 ♖a1?

The key question in a pawn endgame will be: Who controls the opposition? After this mistake, it turns out to be White. Black had to continue 3...♖d1+! 4 ♔e6 ♖a1 5 ♖d8 (5 ♖e8 ♖a6+! 6 ♔f5 ♖xa7=) 5...♖xa7 6 ♖d7+ ♖xd7 7 ♔xd7 ♔h7!=. Note that Black must have the distant opposition, not the close: 7...♔f7? 8 ♔d6+–. We examined very nearly the same situation in the pawn endings chapter (Neishtadt's study, diagram 1-8).

4 ♖c8! (of course not 4 ♖e8? ♖a6+!) **4...♖a6+ 5 ♖c6 ♖xa7 6 ♖c7+ ♖xc7 7 ♔xc7**

Now White has the distant opposition! There followed: **7...♔h7 8 ♔d7! ♔g6 9 ♔e6 ♔g7 10 ♔e7 ♔g6 11 ♔f8** Black resigned.

Plan 2

Sometimes the passed pawn can be exchanged for some of the enemy pawns, leading to a winning endgame with the pawns all on the same side.

The following endgame is very important: we shall find ourselves referring to it again and again.

Unzicker – Lundin
Amsterdam ol 1954

9-128

W?

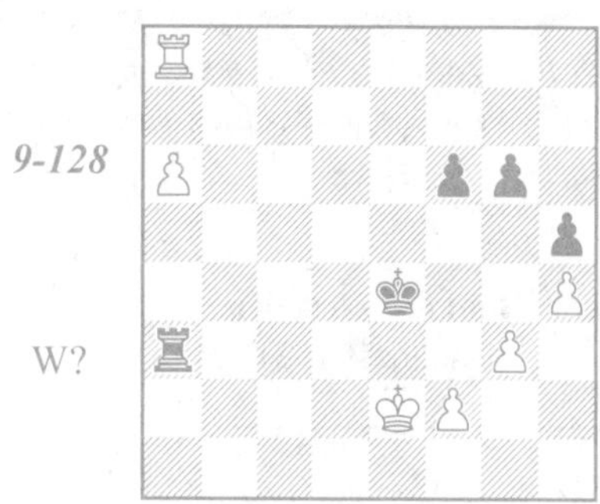

1 f3+! (1 a7 ♖a2+ △ 2...♔f3) **1...♔f5 2 a7! ♖a2+**

2...♖a6 changes nothing: 3 ♔d3 ♖d6+ 4 ♔c4 ♖d7 5 ♔c5 ♖e7 6 ♔d6! ♖e6+ (6...♖b7 7 ♖b8! ♖×a7 8 ♖b5#) 7 ♔d7 ♖a6 8 ♔e7.

3 ♔d3 ♖a1 4 ♔d4

Observe the following tactical trick: 4 g4+ hg 5 fg+ ♔×g4 6 h5!. However in this particular position it fails because 4 g4+? can be met with 4...♔f4!.

4...♖a5 5 ♔c4 ♖a3 6 ♔c5

When Black's pawn stands on f7, his king can return to f6 or g7 with an absolutely drawn position. Here, however, White has a clear plan: a king transfer to h6 followed by an exchange of the a7-pawn for Black's kingside pawns. Black has nothing to oppose this plan.

In case of 6...♖×f3 7 ♖f8 ♖a3 8 a8♕ ♖×a8 9 ♖×a8 ♔g4, the simplest solution is 10 ♖a3 g5 11 hg fg 12 ♔d4 h4 13 gh gh 14 ♔e3 ♔g3 15 ♖a8.

6...♖a1 7 ♔d6 ♖a3?! (7...♖a6+) **8 ♔e7?!**

White follows his plan, missing an immediate winning opportunity: 8 ♖c8! △ 9 ♖c5#.

8...♖a6

8...♖a2 is slightly more clever; the point is 9 ♔f7?! ♖a6! 10 ♔g7 g5 11 hg ♔×g5 12 ♔f7 ♔f5 13 g4+ hg 14 fg+ ♔f4, with an important circumstance: the f6-pawn is protected by the rook. The squares a6 and f7 are corresponding; White should come round the mined field, the simplest way is 9 ♔f8! ♖a6 10 ♔f7!⊙ ♖a3 11 ♔g7, and 11...g5 is absolutely hopeless here.

9 ♔f7 ♖a3 10 ♔g7 ♖a1 11 ♔h6! ♖a6 12 ♖b8 ♖×a7 13 ♖b5+ ♔e6 14 ♔×g6 ♖a8 15 ♔×h5 ♖g8 16 g4 ♖h8+ 17 ♔g6 Black resigned.

Plan 3

The most important method of playing for the win with the pawn on the 7th rank is to try to win the rook for the passed pawn. For this to work, the enemy king must be decoyed into the path of a rook check (as, for instance, we tried to do in the Unzicker - Lundin endgame, in the 4.g4+? variation). ***Most often, the stronger side will try to create a kingside passed pawn, which will knock the king out of his safe square g7. An important point to remember is that this end can be achieved by advancing a bishop pawn, but a knight's or rook's pawn is generally useless.***

9-129

W

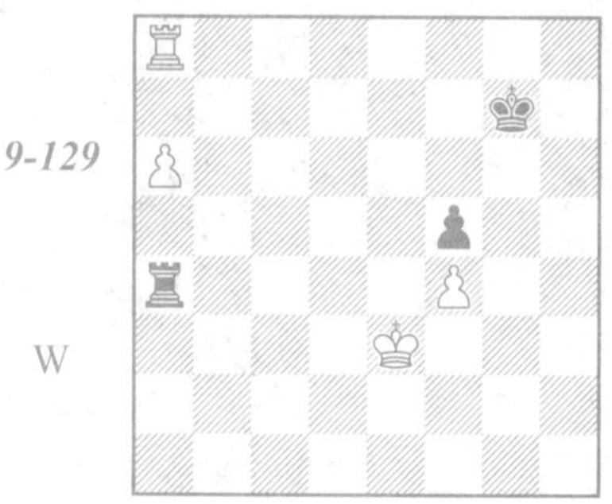

1 a7!

This renders the f4-pawn untouchable; now the king goes after the Black pawn, which must fall, because of zugzwang.

1...♔h7 2 ♔d3 ♔g7 3 ♔c3 ♔h7 4 ♔b3 ♖a1 5 ♔b4 ♔g7 6 ♔c5 ♖a6 7 ♔d5 ♖a1 8 ♔e5! ♖a5+ 9 ♔e6⊙ ♔h7 10 ♔f6⊙ +–

It should be noted that the inexact 8 ♔e6?! ♖a5 leaves White, not Black, in zugzwang (9 ♖d8?? ♖×a7 10 ♖d7+ leads to a drawn pawn endgame). But he can easily give his opponent the move by playing 9 ♔d6 ♔h7, and now either 10 ♔e7 ♔g7 (10...♖a6 11 ♔f7⊙) 11 ♔e6, or 10 ♔c6 (threatening 11 ♔b6) 10...♖a1 11 ♔d5 ♖a5+ 12 ♔d6! ♔g7 13 ♔e6⊙ +–.

Rovner – Shchipunov
Kiev 1938 (sides reversed)

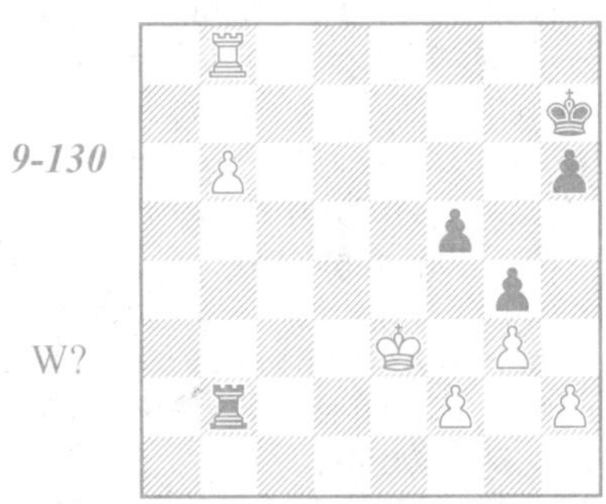

9-130

W?

1 b7?

As we have just seen Black inevitably loses his f-pawn. But, in contrast to the previous example, White fails to get a passed f-pawn. The winning way was 1 ♔d4! ♖×f2 2 ♖c8 ♖b2 3 ♖c7+ ♔g6 4 b7 etc.

1...♔g7 2 ♔d4 ♖b5 3 ♔c4 ♖b2 4 ♔d5 ♖d2+! 5 ♔e5 ♖e2+ 6 ♔×f5 ♖×f2+ 7 ♔×g4 ♖b2

Even two extra pawns cannot bring the advantage home. The game was drawn.

A slightly more complicated example of the same theme.

R. Kholmov, 1983

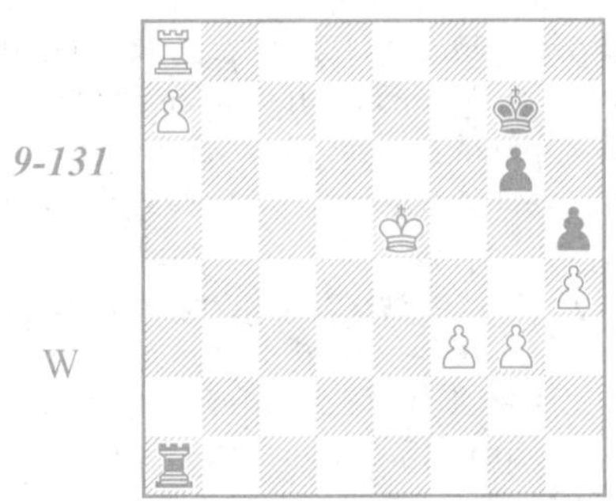

9-131

W

Here again, two extra pawns are not sufficient for a win. Black can easily prevent creation of a passed f-pawn.

1 ♔f4

The threat is 2 g4 ♖a4+ (2...hg 3 ♔×g4 △ h4-h5+-) 4 ♔g3 hg 5 f4!, followed by h4-h5. The immediate 1 g4 hg 2 fg leads to an obvious draw. Black need only remember to harass his opponent with checks from the rear when the white king comes to the 6th rank, otherwise a winning pawn endgame can arise.

1...♖a4+! 2 ♔e3 ♖a3+ 3 ♔f2 ♖a2+ 4 ♔g1 ♖a1+! (the simplest, although 4...♖a3 5 g4 hg 6 f4! ♔h7! also holds) **5 ♔g2 ♖a2+ 6 ♔h3 ♖a3**

6...♖a4 7 f4 ♖a3 is also good.

7 f4 ♖a2 8 g4 ♖a3+

The king can only escape from the checks by approaching the rook, but this is too dangerous: Black takes on g4 and his g-pawn rushes to the promotion square.

Let us examine two considerably more complex and eventful examples.

M. Dvoretsky, 2003

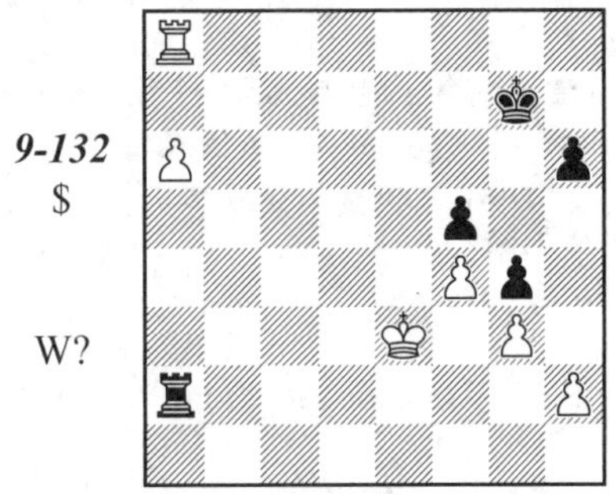

9-132

$

W?

1 a7!

White's plan is clear: his king will go after the f5-pawn. If the Black h-pawn were at h5, White would win without the slightest difficulty - just as he does in diagram 9-129. However, with the pawn at h6 instead, Black has counterchances involving the attempt to zip the king up in the stalemate haven at h5. With this configuration, this stalemate defense is well known from pawn endgames; it does not appear to have been employed before in a rook endgame.

After 1 ♔d4? ♖×h2 2 ♔e5 Black saves himself by playing for stalemate: 2...♔g6! 3 a7 ♖a2 4 ♖g8+ ♔h5 5 a8♕ ♖a5(e2)+ - the rook has become a desperado, or 3 ♖g8+ ♔h5 4 ♖f8 ♖e2+! 5 ♔×f5 (5 ♔d6 ♖a2=) 5...♖e8!=.

1...♖a4 2 ♔d3 ♔h7 3 ♔c3

9-133

B

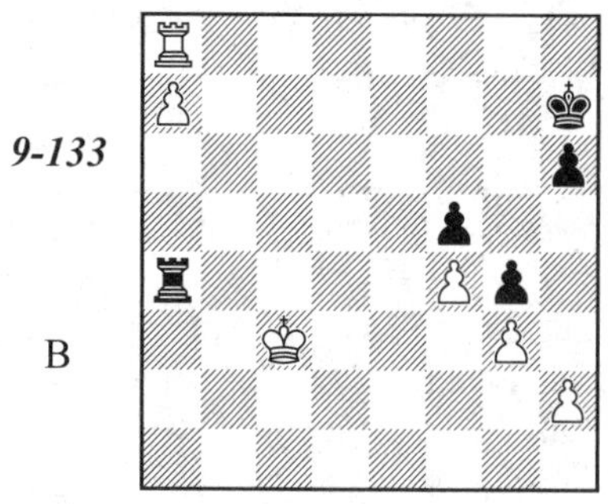

3...♔g7

A clever attempt 3...♔g6!?, suggested by Gansäuer, is refuted by means of 4 h3!! gh (4...♔h5 5 hg+ ♔×g4 6 ♖g8+ ♔h5 7 g4+!) 5 ♖g8+ ♔h5 6 a8♕ ♖×a8 7 ♖×a8 ♔g4 8 ♔d4 h2 9 ♖a1 ♔×g3 10 ♔e5+−. Note that White wins only because his king can get to e5 in time. If White's king had been cut off on the 2nd rank in the starting position, then as soon as it gets to c2 (or even d2), Black plays ...♔g6!, and the move h2-h3 no longer works.

But what would happen if Black's king could reach h5? We shall see about this in the next annotation.

4 ♔b3 ♖a6 5 ♔c4!

5 ♔b4? is erroneous because of 5...♔g6! as the move 6 h3 no longer works since the white king is too far away from the f5-pawn. Interesting lines arise after 6 ♔c5 ♔h5! 7 ♔d5 ♖a2 8 ♔e5.

9-134

B?

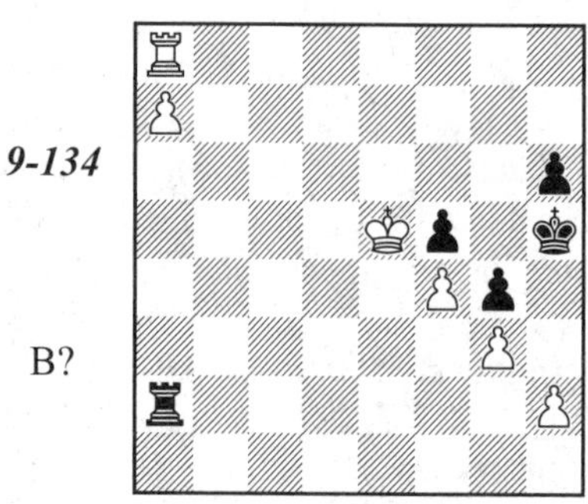

The obvious 8...♖a5+? 9 ♔e6 ♖a6+ (9...♔g6 10 h3!!) 10 ♔×f5 ♖×a7 would lose to 11 h3!! ♖f7+ (checkmate was threatened) 12 ♔e6 ♖b7 13 hg+ (13 ♖a5+ ♔g6 14 hg ♖b3 is less convincing) 13...♔×g4 14 ♖g8+ ♔h5 15 g4+ ♔h4 16 f5.

8...♖e2+! 9 ♔×f5 ♖e7!! (but not 9...♖e8? 10 h3!!+−) is much stronger. It's reciprocal zugzwang! If 10 ♔f6? Black can already sacrifice his rook: 10...♖e8!=. So White must give up his a-pawn: 10 ♖d8 ♖×a7, but here I don't see a clear way to win. For example: 11 ♔e6 ♔g6 12 f5+? ♔g5 13 ♖g8+ ♔h5= or 11 ♖d5 ♖a6.

5...♖a5 6 ♔b4 ♖a1 7 ♔c5 ♖a6 8 ♔d5 ♖a1 9 ♔e5 ♖a5+ 10 ♔e6⊙ ♔g6!?

On 10...♔h7 the simplest reply is 11 ♔f6⊙. Also possible is 11 ♖d8 ♖×a7 12 ♔×f5, obtaining a won ending with all the pawns on the same side – though not, of course, 12 ♖d7+? ♖×d7 13 ♔×d7 ♔g6 14 ♔e6 ♔h5!=.

11 h3!! ♖a6+ 12 ♔e7 gh 13 ♖g8+ ♔h5 14 a8♕ ♖×a8 15 ♖×a8 ♔g4 16 ♔f6+−.

Zurakhov – Vaisman
USSR 1966

9-135

W

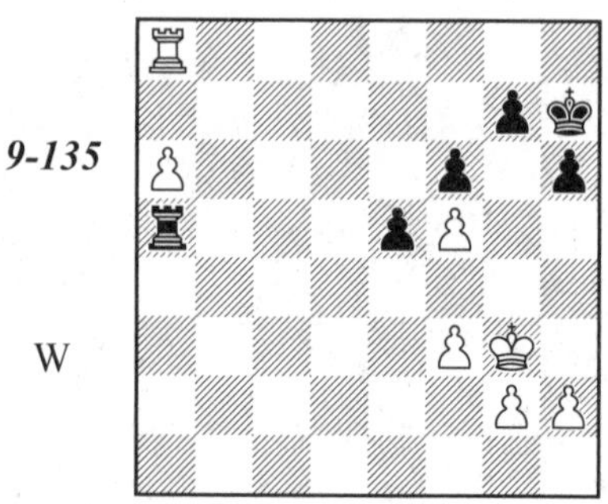

1 a7?!

Leaving the pawn on a6 made more sense. White could have played h2-h4-h5 and ♖a7, after which his king goes to the queenside at the cost of the g-pawn (or the f3-pawn if he could not avoid g2-g4). A win was rather easy because the black king was forever locked on h7.

With his actual move, White plans h2-h4 and g2-g4-g5. After a forced double capture on g5, he wants to take the g5 and e5 pawns with his king and to play f5-f6 thereafter.

1...♖a2

If 1...♖a3!? (△ 2...e4!=) then both 2 ♔g4 and 2 ♔f2 are good: Black only postpones an advance of the white kingside pawns for a while but cannot prevent it.

2 h4 ♖a3

2...h5? loses immediately: after 3 ♔h3 Black has no defense against g2-g4-g5-g6+.

3 ♔h2

This is correct: White's task is simpler when the king hides behind the pawns. 3 ♔g4 ♖a4+ 4 ♔h5 is also playable, but then White has to show more attention and accuracy. Black responded with 4...♖a5!? and in case of the indecisive 5 g3? saves the game by means of 5...e4! 6 fe g6+ 7 ♔g4 gf+ (rather than 7...h5+? 8 ♔f4 gf 9 ♖f8! ♖×a7 10 ♔×f5 ♖g7 11 ♖×f6 ♖×g3 12 e5) 8 ef ♔g7 9 ♔f4 h5=.

After 5 g4!, however, both 5...g6+? 6 fg+ ♔g7 7 g5 hg 8 hg fg (8...e4 9 ♖e8!) 9 ♔g4!⊙ +– and 5...e4? 6 g5 (6 fe?? g6#) 6...hg 7 hg g6+ 8 fg+ ♔g7 9 ♖e8! +– (or 9 f4!? f5 10 ♖e8 ♖×a7 11 ♖e5+–) fail. Black has to play 5...♖a1 6 g5 hg 7 hg fg, transposing to the game continuation.

3...♖a2 4 ♔h3 ♖a3 5 g3⊙ ♖a2 6 g4 ♖a3 7 ♔g2 ♖a2+ 8 ♔g3 ♖a4 9 g5 hg 10 hg fg 11 ♔h3 ♖h4+ 12 ♔g2 ♖a4 13 ♔g3⊙ ♖a1 14 ♔g4 ♖g1+ 15 ♔h5 ♖a1 16 ♔×g5 ♖a6 17 ♔g4 ♖a3 18 ♔h4⊙ ♖a4+ 19 ♔h3 ♖a2 20 ♔g3⊙ ♖a5 21 ♔f2 ♖a3 22 ♔e2 ♖a5 23 ♔d3 ♖a4 24 ♔c3 ♖a1 25 ♔b4 ♖a2 26 ♔c5 ♖a1 27 ♔d6 ♖a5 28 ♔e6 ♖a1 29 ♔×e5 ♖a6 30 f4 ♖a5+ 31 ♔e6

9-136

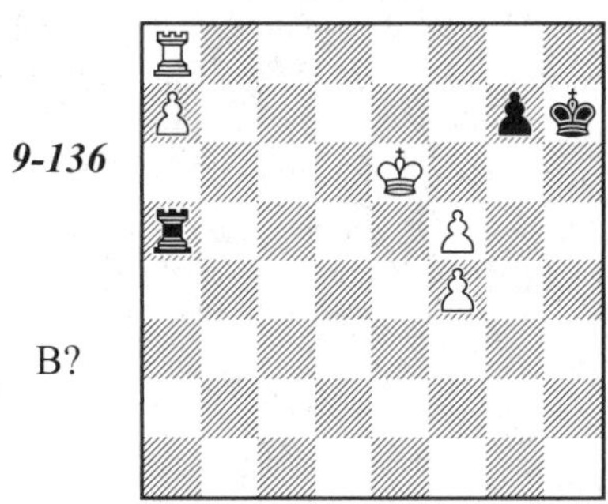

B?

31...♖a1!

31...♖a6+? loses to 32 ♔e7!⊙ ♖a4 33 f6! gf 34 ♔f7!⊙ ♖a6 (34...f5 35 ♔e6 ♖a5 36 ♔f6⊙ +–) 35 f5⊙. The same zugzwang position (with Black on move) arises after 31...♖a4? 32 ♔f7! ♖a6 33 ♔e7.

Now 32 f6 does not bring an easy win in view of 32...♖a6+ 33 ♔e7 (33 ♔f7 ♖×f6+) 33...gf 34 ♔f7 (34 f5 ♔g7) 34...♖a4! 35 f5 ♖a6⊙.

32 ♔e7 ♖a6!

Only this prevents the menacing advance f5-f6. 32...♖a4? 33 f6 gf 34 ♔f7⊙ is an error. We may come to the conclusion that the squares f7-a4 and e7-a6 are corresponding: this is a case of reciprocal zugzwang. And if Black defends himself correctly he does not fall into the zugzwang.

33 ♔f7 ♖a4!

On 33...♖f6+? White could have passed the move to the adversary by means of triangulation: 34 ♔e8! ♖a6 35 ♔e7⊙ +–.

34 ♔f8 (34 f6 gf 35 f5 ♖a6⊙) **34...♖a5** (34...♖a6? 35 ♔e7⊙ +–) **35 f6** (he has nothing else) **35...gf 36 f5 ♖a1** (36...♖a6? 37 ♔f7!⊙ +–)

9-137

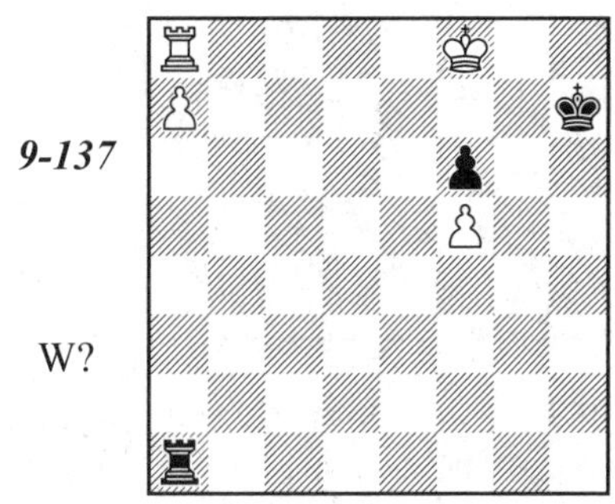

W?

37 ♖e8?

This natural move (White intends a transition to a winning pawn endgame) is wrong. Black has a defense based upon stalemate! Dolmatov suggested the correct procedure:

37 ♔f7! (it is important to drive the rook to a6) 37...♖a6 38 ♔e7! (by the way, after the immediate 37 ♔e7? ♔g7 there is no win anymore) 38...♔g7 (White could of course have had this position earlier) 39 ♔d8! (39 ♔e8?! ♔g8!) 39...♖a1 (both 39...♔g8 40 ♔c7+ ♔g7 41 ♔b7 and 39...♔h6 40 ♔c7 ♔g5 41 ♖g8+ ♔×f5 42 a8♕ ♖×a8 43 ♖×a8 are hopeless) 40 ♖c8! ♖×a7 41 ♖c7+ ♖×c7 42 ♔×c7 ♔h6 43 ♔d7 ♔h5 44 ♔e7! ♔g5 45 ♔e6⊙ +–.

37...♖×a7 38 ♖e7+ ♔h8! 39 ♔f7

White cannot take the rook because of stalemate. Hence he goes for the f6-pawn.

39...♖a6 (39...♖a1 is also good) **40 ♔g6 ♖a8 41 ♔×f6 ♔g8??**

A serious mistake when the goal was within reach. The draw could be achieved by means of 41...♖a6+ (41...♖a1) 42 ♖e6 (42 ♔f7 ♔h7 43 f6 ♖a8, or 43...♖a1, but not 43...♖b6??) 42...♖a1! 43 ♔g6 ♖g1+ 44 ♔f7 ♔h7 (44...♖g7+) 45 f6 ♖g7+! 46 ♔e8 (46 fg - stalemate) 46...♖g8+, and the rook returns to the long side.

42 ♔g6 Black resigned.

Tragicomedies

Pähtz – Kosteniuk
Mainz m (5) 2002

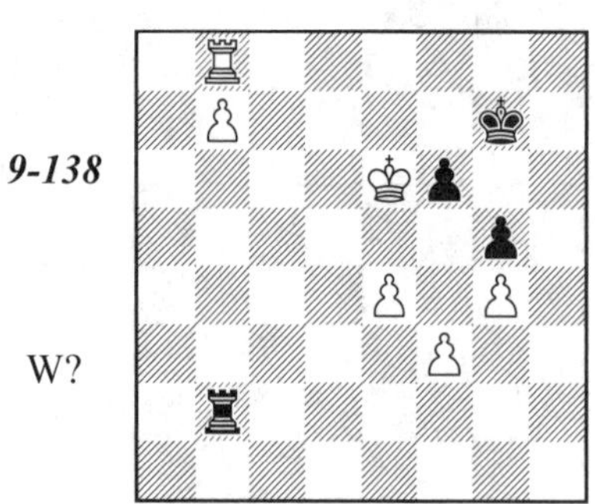

9-138

W?

The main distinction between this position and the very similar endgame Benko – Gereben (diagram 9-127) – is that here White has a pawn at f3, thanks to which every possible pawn endgame is won. An elementary path to victory lay in 1 ♖d8! ♖b6+ 2 ♖d6 ♖×b7 3 ♖d7+ ♖×d7 4 ♔×d7.

1 ♖e8?? ♖b6+! 2 ♔f5 ♖×b7

The position has now become drawn – but the adventures have not ended yet.

3 e5 fe 4 ♖×e5 ♖f7+ 5 ♔×g5 ♖×f3 6 ♖e7+ ♔f8 7 ♖a7

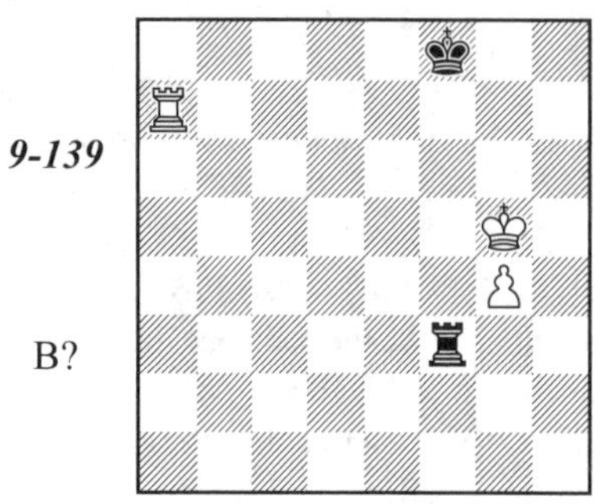

9-139

B?

7...♖c3??

7...♔g8! 8 ♔g6 ♖f8= was necessary – as we know, against a knight pawn, passive defense by the rook on the 8th rank guarantees a draw.

8 ♔h5?? After 8 ♔g6! White must reach the "Lucena Position," for example: 8...♖c6+ 9 ♔h7 ♖c5 10 ♖g7.

8...♔g8 9 ♖d7 ♖c6 And now we have reached "Philidor's Position." The game was eventually drawn.

Ljubojevic – Gligoric
Belgrade m (9) 1979

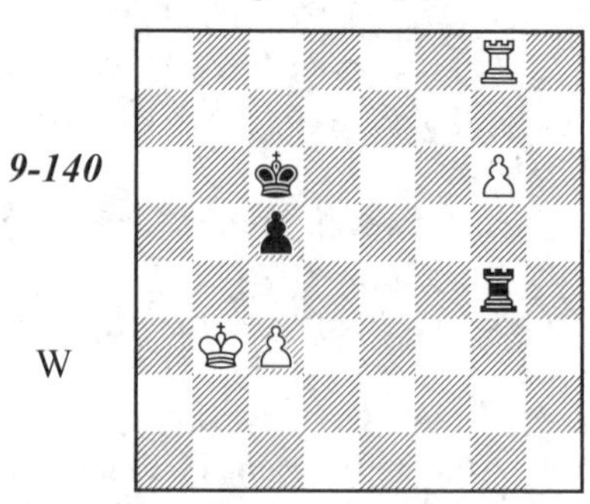

9-140

W

1 g7 ♔b7??

1...c4+! 2 ♔b4 ♔b7 3 ♔b5 ♔a7 led to a draw. White's king cannot stop both the rook and the king at the same time: after 4 ♔c6 the rook is released from the burden of protecting the pawn.

2 c4! ♖g2 3 ♔c3

Black resigned. The white king goes through the center to the c5-pawn and gains it by means of a zugzwang.

Milic and Bozic annotated this endgame for the *Chess Informant, Vol. 27.* In their opinion, White could have won it after 1 c4 ♖g3+ 2 ♔c2. But they are obviously wrong: 2...♔d6 3 g7 ♔e6(e7) leads to a drawn pawn endgame, while after 2 ♔a4 ♔b6 3 g7 ♔b7 4 ♔b5 ♖g5 5 ♔a4 ♖g3! White's king cannot break loose.

Y. Averbakh

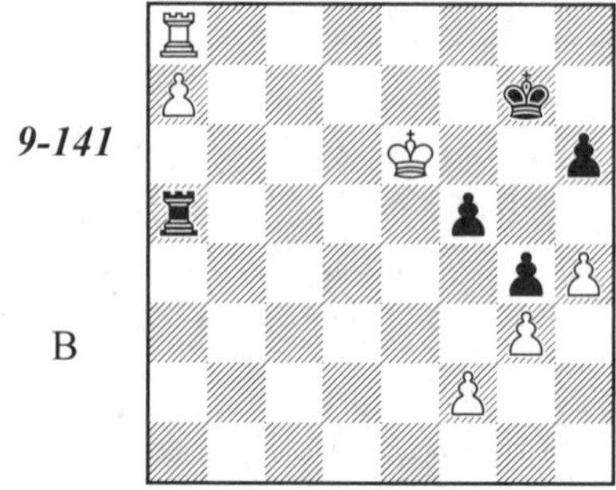

9-141

B

This example is taken from Averbakh's endgame handbook. It's amusing not only in itself, but also because of several grave errors committed by this famous connoisseur of endgame theory. Averbakh believes the position is drawn on account of 1...♖a2 2 ♔×f5 ♖×f2+ 3 ♔×g4 ♖a2=. Black applied this defensive method in a similar situation in Rovner – Shchipunov (diagram 9-130). But there, first of all, White's king was less active and he was unable to force the exchange of rooks; and secondly, White's pawn was at h2, which means the pawn endgame would still have been a draw. But here, with the pawn at h4, the pawn endgame is won!

2 ♖e8! (instead of 2 ♔xf5?) 2...♖xa7 (2...♖a6+ 3 ♔xf5 ♖xa7 4 ♔xg4) 3 ♖e7+ ♖xe7+ 4 ♔xe7 ♔g6 5 ♔e6 ♔h5 (Black's last hope is a chance for a stalemate) 6 ♔f6!⊙ f4 7 gf ♔xh4 8 ♔g6+– (or 8 f5+–).

Another try is **1...h5!?**. Levenfish and Smyslov analyze this in their book on rook-and-pawn endings. They convincingly prove that the outcome depends on whose turn in is to move.

Black, if on move, achieves a draw as follows: 2...♖a6+! 3 ♔xf5 ♖a5+ 4 ♔f4 ♖a4+, or 3 ♔e5 ♖a2! (3...♖a3? is wrong in view of 4 ♔f4 ♖a5 5 ♖b8 ♖xa7 6 ♔g5, but 3...♖a4!= is also playable) 4 ♔f4 ♖xf2+ 5 ♔g5 ♖a2 6 ♔xh5 f4!=.

If White is on move, he wins by 2 ♖e8! ♖a6+ (2...♖xa7 3 ♖e7+) 3 ♔xf5 ♖xa7 4 ♖e5! (Averbakh only examines 4 ♔g5? ♖a5+ 5 ♔f4 ♖a2=) 4...♔h6 (otherwise 5 ♔g5) 5 ♖e6+ ♔g7 6 ♖g6+ ♔h7 7 ♖f6! (△ 8 ♔g5) 7...♖a5+ (7...♖g7 8 ♖f8⊙) 8 ♔f4 ♖a2 (8...♔g7 9 ♖f5) 9 ♔g5 ♖a5+ 10 ♖f5+–.

Averbakh's evaluations are the opposite: he suggests passing the move to the adversary. Therefore almost all his analysis is erroneous!

2 ♔d6? (! Averbakh) **2...♔h7?** (2...♖a6+!) **3 ♔e7?** (3 ♔c6! ♖a2 4 ♖d8! ♖xa7 5 ♖d7+ ♖xd7 6 ♔xd7 and 3 ♔e6! ♔g7 4 ♖e8! or 3...♖a6+ 4 ♔e5! ♔g7 5 ♔f4! are winning) **3...♔g7 4 ♔e6 ♖a2?** (4...♖a6+!) **5 ♔xf5?** (5 ♖e8!+–) **5...♖a5+** (5...♖xf2+? 6 ♔g5 ♖a2 7 ♔xh5 ♖a4 8 ♖e8 ♖xa7 9 ♔xg4) **6 ♔f4 ♔h7??** (6...♖a4+ is a draw) **7 ♖f8! ♖xa7 8 ♔g5 ♖a5+ 9 ♖f5+–**.

Exercises

These two exercises are not complicated; in fact, they could have been included in the previous "tragicomedies."

9-142

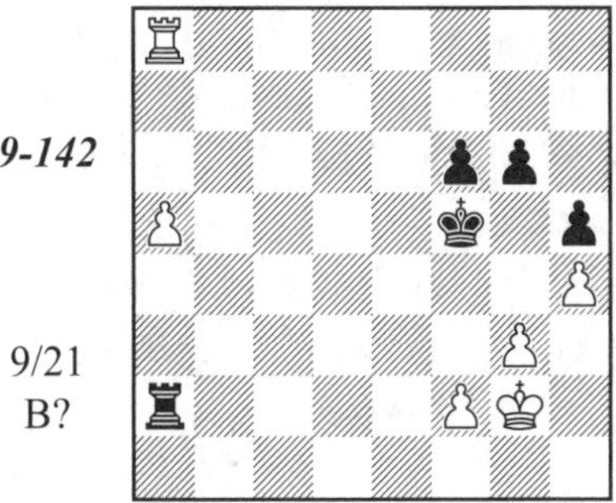

9/21
B?

9-143

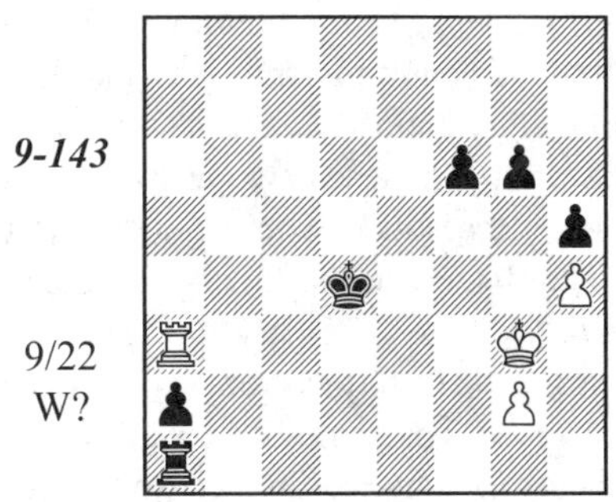

9/22
W?

The Rook in Front of the Pawn, with the Pawn on the 6th Rank

If a pawn advance to a7 makes no sense, White leaves the pawn on a6 and brings his king to the queenside where it has a refuge against vertical checks. But it is a long way to go, leaving the black rook enough time to capture one or two pawns, before it must be sacrificed for the a-pawn. This leads to a sharp "Rook vs. Pawns" endgame, the outcome of which will depend on whether White's king can get back to the kingside in time.

For many years, it was believed that with correct defense, the draw was an easy matter, something Black could achieve with a couple of tempi to spare. This point of view was espoused in, among other places, the German editions of this Manual.

But in the latter half of 2003, the theory of this portion of the endgame underwent some revolutionary changes. Black's position, it turned out, was far more dangerous than it had seemed.

Johannes Steckner, a Swiss player, while checking the analysis of one of the basic positions which had been considered drawn, found a tremendous improvement for White, leading to a win for him. And his discovery led, in turn, to new researches that were conducted by Steckner, grandmasters Karsten Müller and Rustem Dautov, and myself; along with other endgame aficionados that came upon our researches in the chess press.

Here I shall present only the most important analyses. For those who seek more detailed information, I would recommend visiting www.chesscafe.com and looking for my articles entitled, *Theoretical Discoveries*, as well as various articles authored by Karsten Müller.

Nevertheless, even in edited form, the material I offer for your consideration is so large and complex, that it clearly exceeds the boundaries I tried to maintain when I wrote this Manual. The excuse I offer is its newness and enormous practical significance to the theory of this sort of endgame.

Nothing could be further from my mind than to label the analysis presented below as the "last word of theory" - long, complicated variations rarely turn out error-free. But in any case, they go a long way to correct and develop the pre-existing conclusions, and may in turn serve as a starting point for additional theoretical researches.

V. Kantorovich, 1988
J. Steckner, 2003

9-144

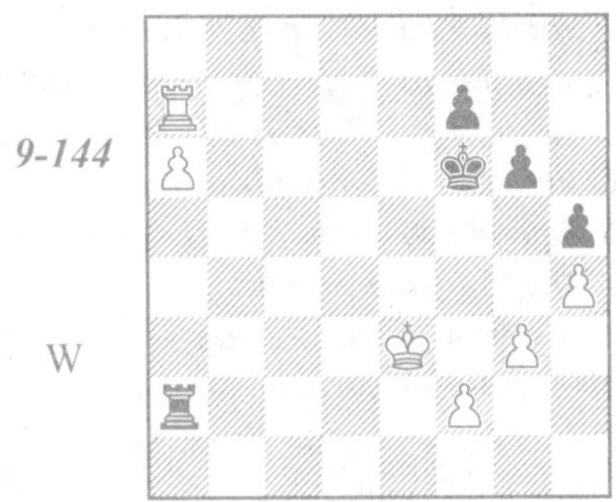

W

In 1989, Vadim Kantorovich, of Moscow, published an interesting article titled, *The Outside Passed Pawn*. The article opened with the diagrammed position. The main conclusion of the analysis was: Black draws with two tempi to spare.

But in fact, he's lost!

1 Kd4!

The pawn must be sacrificed ***precisely*** with the rook on a7! 1 Ra8? Kf5 would be much weaker. Please note that ***Black's pieces are optimally placed: the rook holds the f-pawn in the crosshairs, while the king occupies the most active available square***.

Black would have an easy draw after 2 Kd4 R×f2 3 Rf8 Ra2 4 R×f7+ Kg4= or 2 f3 Ra3+ 3 Kd4 R×f3 4 Rf8 Ra3 5 R×f7+ Kg4 6 Rf6 K×g3 7 R×g6+ K×h4 8 Kc5 Kh3 9 Kb6 h4= (both lines by Kopaev).

On 2 Ra7!? retreating the king by 2...Kf6? or 2...Ke6? loses, as will become clear later on. A more logical approach is to begin counterplay immediately by 2...f6!? (2...Kg4 3 R×f7 R×a6 doesn't lose, either). After 3 Kf3 g5! 4 hg fg 5 Ra8 g4+ 6 Ke3 Kg6 the king gets back to g7, so White plays 3 Ra8 instead, threatening to obtain a winning position with the pawn on the 7th, known to us from the Unzicker - Lundin game (diagram 9-128), by 4 f3 Ra3+ 5 Ke2 Ra2+ 6 Kd1 Ra3 7 a7. But Black draws by playing 3...Kg4 4 a7 f5!? (4...Ra3+ 5 Ke4 f5+ 6 Ke5 Kf3= is good too) 5 Rg8 f4+! 6 gf Ra3+ 7 Ke4 (7 Ke2 R×a7 8 R×g6+ K×f4=) 7...Ra4+ 8 Ke5 Ra5+ 9 Ke6 Ra6+ 10 Kf7 R×a7+ 11 K×g6 Ra6+ 12 Kf7+ K×f4= (analysis by Dvoretsky).

1...R×f2 2 Rc7! Ra2 3 a7

On 3 Rc6+? Kf5 4 Kc5 Kg4 5 Kb5 K×g3 6 Rc4 f6! 7 Ra4 Rb2+ 8 Kc6 Rb8 9 a7 Ra8 (Kantorovich), Black does indeed obtain a draw with two tempi to spare.

3...Kf5

Kantorovich's analysis continued 4 R×f7+ Kg4 5 Kc5 K×g3 6 Kb5! Rb2+! 7 Kc6 Ra2 8 Kb7 K×h4 9 Rf6 R×a7+ – here too, the draw is completely obvious.

It was Steckner who offered the powerful improvement: **4 Kc4!!**.

9-145

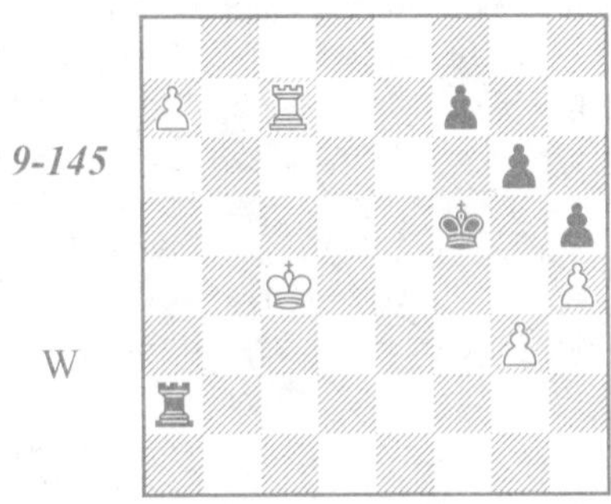

W

His idea becomes clear in the variation **4...Kg4 5 Kb3! Ra6 6 Rc4+ K×g3 7 Ra4**.

Now White forces the sacrifice of Black's rook without wasting time on the king's long march to a7, and wins move-on-move ("Chess is the tragedy of a single tempo!").

7...R×a7 8 R×a7

9-146

B

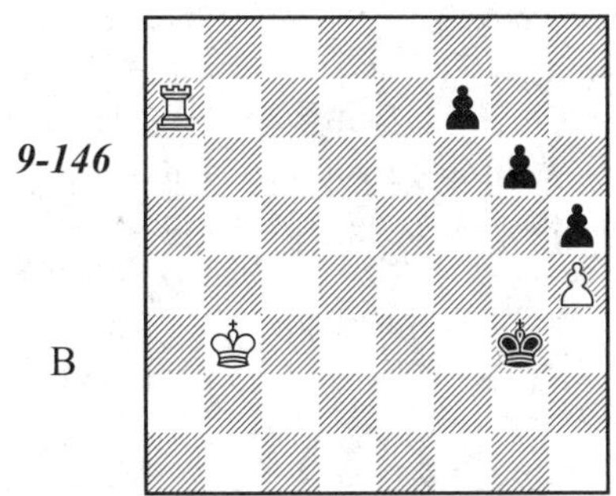

8...♔×h4 9 ♔c3 (there's no time to take the pawn: 9 ♖×f7? ♔g3=) **9...♔g3**

9...f5 10 ♔d3 g5 doesn't help: the rook can deal with all three pawns.

10 ♔d2 h4 (10...g5 11 ♖×f7+–) **11 ♔e2 ♔g2** (11...h3 12 ♔f1) **12 ♖×f7 h3 13 ♖f2+! ♔g3 14 ♖f6+–**

Let's try a different defense, such as 4...♖a1, getting the rook away from the tempo-gaining ♔b3. After 5 ♔b5 however, the only way to forestall the threat of closing off the a-file is by a series of checks, which drive the white king forward: 5...♖b1+ 6 ♔c6 ♖a1 7 ♔b7 ♖b1+ 8 ♔c8 ♖a1 9 ♖×f7+ ♔g4.

9-147

W?

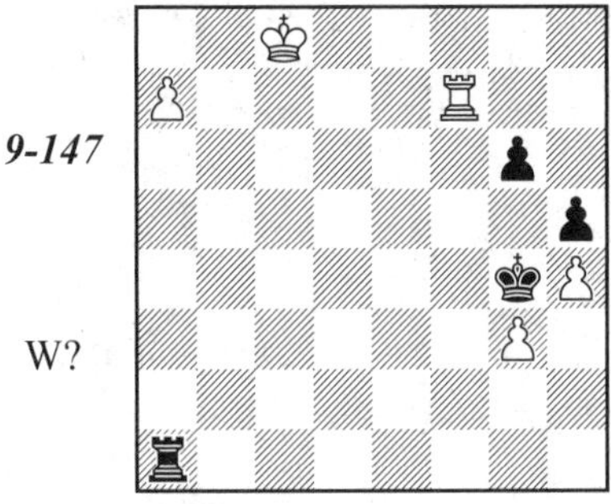

Here 10 ♔b7 ♖b1+ is useless; and 10 ♔b8? ♔×g3 11 ♖f6 ♔×h4 12 ♖×g6 ♔h3 13 ♔b7 ♖×a7+ is only a draw. White gains the tempo he needs by 10 ♖g7! ♔×g3 11 ♖×g6+ ♔×h4 12 ♔b7 ♖×a7+ (13 ♖a6 was threatened) 13 ♔×a7 ♔h3 14 ♔b6 h4 15 ♔c5 ♔h2 16 ♔d4 h3 17 ♔e3 ♔h1 18 ♔f3+–.

The only thing left to try is 4...f6. White can't respond with 5 ♔b4? ♔g4 6 ♔b3 ♖a6 7 ♖c4+ ♔×g3 8 ♖a4 ♖×a7 – by comparison with the line 4...♔g4, Black has gained the useful move ...f7-f6, which alters the assessment of the position (9 ♖×a7 g5=). Now comes a series of forced moves: 5 ♔b5 ♖b2+ 6 ♔c6 ♖a2 7 ♔b7 ♖b2+ 8 ♔c8 ♖a2.

Alas, White wins here too, with 9 ♖g7!.

9-148

B

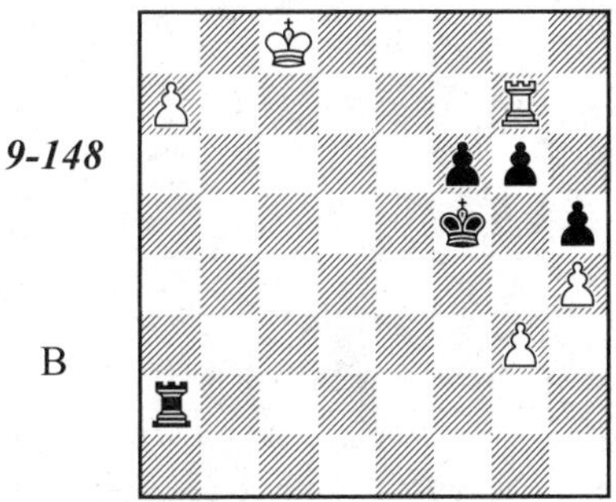

a) 9...g5 10 ♔b8 ♔g4 11 a8♕ (but not 11 hg? fg 12 a8♕ ♖×a8+ 13 ♔×a8 h4 14 gh ♔×h4 15 ♔b7 g4 16 ♔c6 ♔g3! 17 ♔d5 ♔f3=) 11...♖×a8+ 12 ♔×a8 ♔×g3 13 hg fg 14 ♖×g5+ ♔h4 15 ♖g8 ♔h3 16 ♔b7, and the king gets back to f3 in time.

b) 9...♔g4 10 ♖×g6+ ♔h3 11 ♖g7 ♖a3 12 ♔b8 ♖b3+ 13 ♖b7 ♖×g3 14 ♔c7!? (14 ♖b4 is also strong) 14...♖a3 (14...♖g8 15 ♖b8 ♖g7+ 16 ♔b6 ♖×a7 17 ♔×a7+–) 15 ♖b3+! ♖×b3 16 a8♕.

At the start of this section, I presented a formula in the most general terms for how play might develop in this kind of ending. Now we can more precisely restate White's most dangerous plan. ***The pawn advances to a6; the rook stands on a7, and at the first opportunity will move aside to c7, clearing the path of the pawn. White's king selects a path to advance which will allow him to execute the interference idea as quickly as possible – that is, moving the rook with tempo to the a-file.***

Let's return to the starting position for this endgame – diagram 9-144 – and ask ourselves this question: can Black save himself if he is on the move? And the draw turns out to be no simple thing to achieve in this case, either.

I. I began my testing with the obvious move **1...♔e5**, and quickly found the line **2 ♔d3! ♖×f2 3 ♖e7+!** (the immediate 3 ♖c7 also deserves study) **3...♔f6 4 a7 ♖a2 5 ♖c7 ♔f5 6 ♔c4!**, leading to the position in diagram 9-145, in which Steckner demonstrated the win for White.

But what if Black chooses 4...♔×e7 5 a8♕ ♖f5, hoping to set up a rook-vs.-queen fortress?

9-149

W

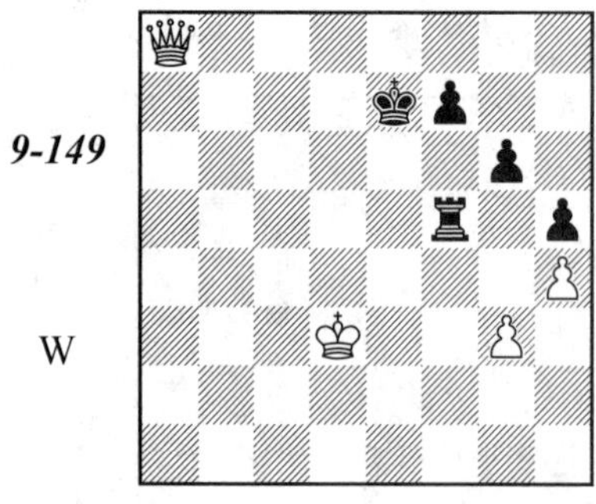

Look in Chapter 13 – there you will find a similar position that occurred in the game Dorfman - Beliavsky (diagram 13-33) and which shows that Black (or in that game – White) was quite correct to expect a draw, except that his king had to be on g7. With the king stuck in the center, however, he loses.

In the variation we have just examined: 1...♔e5 2 ♔d3 ♖×f2 3 ♖e7+, Black could keep his king in the center: 3...♔d5 (or 3...♔d6) 4 a7 ♖a2. White continues 5 ♖×f7 (and with the king on d5, perhaps, 5 ♔c3!?) and wins by attacking the kingside pawns at the appropriate moment with his rook. Let's examine a characteristic and quite important variation. Steckner uncovered it, while I have added a few explanations and touched some things up.

1...♔e5 2 ♔d3 ♔d5 (instead of 2...♖×f2) **3 ♔c3 ♖×f2 4 ♖c7 ♖a2 5 a7 f6 6 ♔b4 ♔d6**

9-150

W?

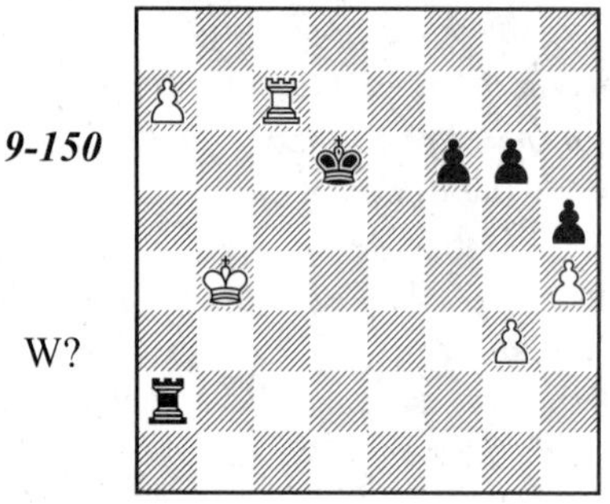

a) White only gets a draw after 7 ♖f7 ♔e6 8 ♖g7? (8 ♖c7) 8...♔f5 9 ♔b5 g5 (Black could transpose the last two moves) 10 ♔b6 ♔g4. Now 11 hg fg 12 ♔b7 h4 (12...♖b2+!?) 13 gh ♔×h4 14 ♖g6 ♖×a7+ 15 ♔×a7 g4 16 ♔b6 ♔g3! 17 ♔c5 ♔f3= is harmless. If 11 ♔b7, the immediate capture on g3 loses – first, Black must drive back the White king: 11...♖b2+! 12 ♔c8 ♖a2 13 ♔b8; only now can he play 13...♔×g3 14 hg fg 15 ♖×g5+ ♔h4=. The most dangerous try is: 11 ♖g8!?, after which 11...♔×g3?? is bad: 12 hg fg 13 ♖×g5+ and 14 ♖a5, while 11...♖b2+? 12 ♔c5 ♖a2 13 a8♕ ♖×a8 14 ♖×a8 ♔×g3 15 ♔d4! ♔×h4 16 ♔e3(e4) leads to a position in which the rook more than likely wins against the three pawns. Black can secure the draw by means of the waiting move 11...♖a1!, for example, 12 ♔b7 ♖b1+ 13 ♔c6 ♖a1 14 a8♕ ♖×a8 15 ♖×a8 ♔×g3 16 ♔d5 gh=.

b) The strongest line is **7 ♖g7! ♔c6** (after 7...♔e6 Black has a tempo less in comparison with the previous variation, and loses after 8 ♔b5 ♔f5 9 ♔b6 g5 10 ♔b7) **8 ♖f7!** (but not 8 ♖×g6? ♖×a7 9 ♖×f6+ ♔d5 10 ♖f5+ ♔e4 11 ♖×h5 ♖g7=) **8...f5 9 ♖g7 ♔b6 10 ♔c4**, when White must win.

II. 1...♔e6 2 ♔d4! f6 (we already know the consequences of 2...♖×f2 3 ♖c7 ♖a2 4 a7+–).

Steckner demonstrated the win for White after 3 ♔c5 ♔f5 4 f3! ♖a3 5 ♔b4 ♖×f3.

9-151

W

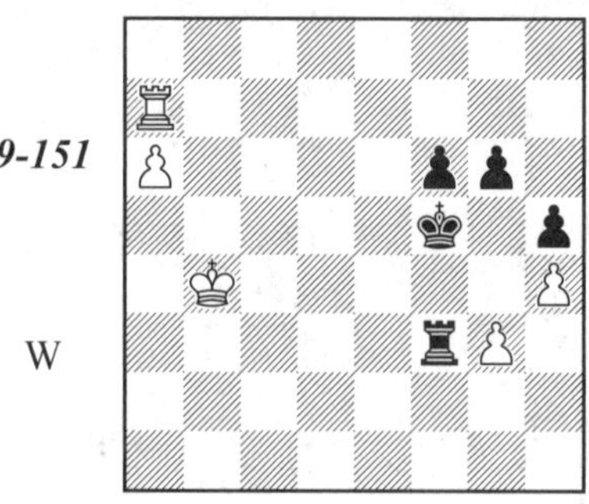

This is a good time to draw your attention to a problem that must often be resolved: which is the best square for the rook – b7 or c7 (or, with the rook on a8 – b8 or c8)? Sometimes, the choice is made on purely tactical considerations: for example, with the king at c5 and the rook at a8, the move ♖c8 would be impossible because of ...♖c2+. And if, with the rook at a7, Black's rook were to occupy the 8th rank, then it would make sense to continue ♖b7 and a6-a7, creating the threat of ♖b8. But, ***it seems to me that it most often makes sense to retreat the rook to the c-file.*** In that case White's king on the b-file will not hinder the rook's mobility; and the threat of checks from the side by White's rook followed by the a-file interference becomes more realistic.

Naturally, I cannot prove my assertion; I can only provide illustrations.

Let's return to the last diagram. On 6 ♖b7? Black, as noted by Mileto, saves himself by 6...♖f1! 7 a7 (7 ♖b5+ ♔g4 8 a7 ♖b1+ 9 ♔c5 ♖a1 10 ♔b6 ♖×a7) 7...♖b1+! 8 ♔c5 ♖a1 9 ♖g7 g5 10 ♔b6 ♔g4 – we have already examined this drawn position (see variation "a" under diagram 9-150).

But if he plays 6 ♖c7!, White wins: 6...♖f1 7 ♖c4! ♖a1 8 ♔b5 g5 9 ♖a4 ♖b1+ 10 ♔a5 ♖b8 11 a7 ♖e8 12 ♔b6 gh 13 gh. No better is 6...♖e3 7 ♖c4 ♖e7 (7...g5 8 a7 ♖e8 9 ♔b5; 7...♖e8 8 ♔b5) 8 ♔b5 g5 9 ♖a4 gh 10 gh ♖a7 11 ♔b6+–.

On the other hand, after 1...♔e6 2 ♔d4 f6 White can win much more simply by continuing **3 ♖a8! ♔f5** (3...♔f7 4 ♔c5 is hopeless) **4 f3** and 5 a7, transposing into the ending of the game Unzicker – Lundin, where White wins by marching his king to h6.

III. 1...g5!? The "un-theoretical" advance of the g-pawn is, as a matter of fact, the strongest plan in these positions. Here, kingside counterplay is created a little faster than by maneuvering the king.

2 ♔d4!

After 2 hg+ ♔×g5 3 ♖×f7 ♖×a6, the draw is achieved with no great effort.

2...gh 3 gh

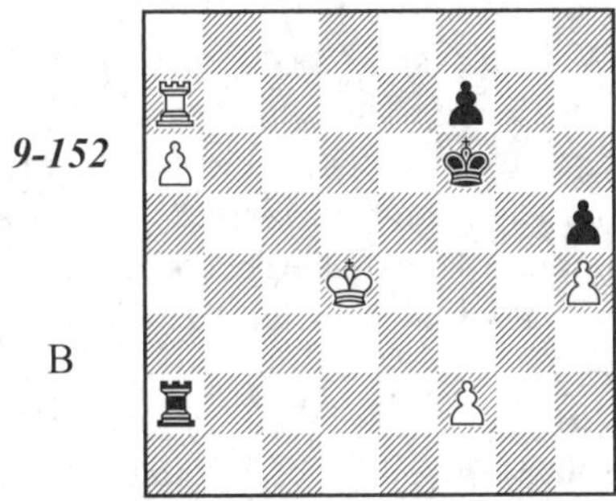

9-152

B

Black would be ill-advised to take either pawn:

3...♖×f2? 4 ♖c7 ♖a2 5 a7 ♔f5 6 ♔c5 (but not 6 ♖×f7+? ♔g4=) 6...♔g4 7 ♔b5 (7 ♔b4!? f5 8 ♔b3) 7...♖b2+ 8 ♔c4 ♖a2 9 ♔b3+–;

3...♖a4+? 4 ♔c5 ♖×h4 5 ♖b7 ♖a4 6 a7 ♔g5 (6...h4 7 ♔b5 ♖a1 8 ♖b6+ △ 9 ♖a6+–; 6...♖a1 7 ♔b6+–) 7 ♖b5!+–.

Steckner examined 3...♖a5?! – a move which, though sufficient to draw, is not the strongest, and therefore can be ignored. But the finesses found while analyzing the long forcing variations involved are so interesting and instructive, that I find myself unable to resist the temptation to show them to you endgame "gourmands."

4 ♔c4 ♔e5 5 ♔b4 ♖a2

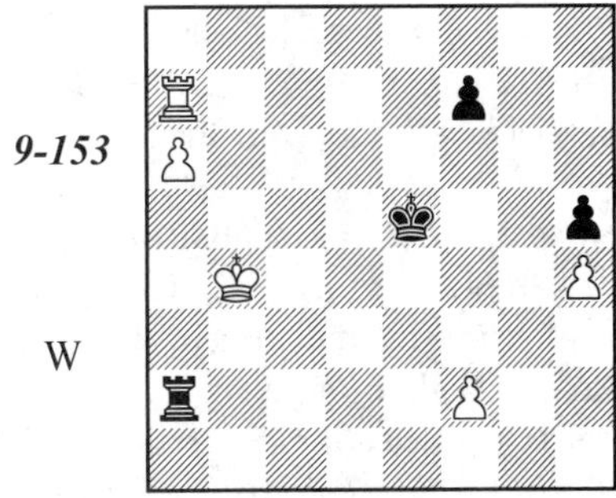

9-153

W

White must choose between two tempting continuations.

A) 6 ♔b5 ♖b2+ 7 ♔c6 ♖c2+ 8 ♔b6 ♖b2+ 9 ♔c7 ♖a2 10 ♖a8 (10 ♔b8 f5 11 ♖e7+ ♔f6 is weaker) 10...♔f4 11 ♔b7 ♖b2+ 12 ♔a7 f5!

As we shall soon see, 12...♖×f2? loses to 13 ♖g8!. The move 12...♔g4!? leads, after 13 ♖b8 ♖×f2 14 ♖b4+ ♔g3 15 ♔b6! (14 ♔b7 ♖a2 15 a7 f5=) 15...♖a2 16 ♖b5! ♔×h4 17 ♖a5 ♖b2+ 18 ♔c7, to the position in diagram 9-157 (from variation "B"), which we will be studying later.

13 ♖g8! (13 ♖b8 ♖×f2=)

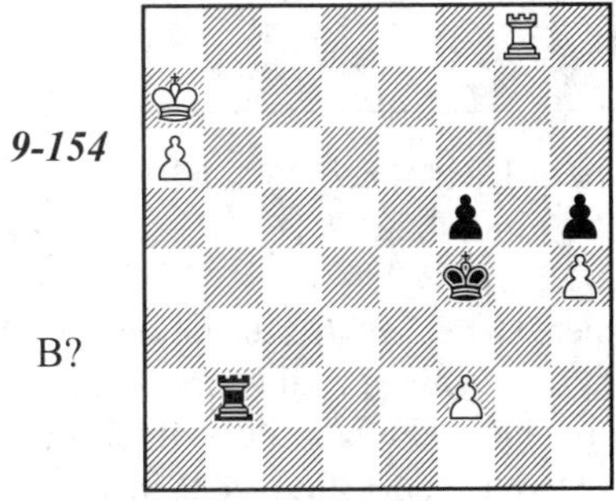

9-154

B?

Black gets a safe draw with 13...♔f3! 14 ♖g5 f4 15 ♖×h5 ♔×f2 or 14 ♖b8 ♖×f2 15 ♖b5 ♖e2! (but not 15...♔g4? 16 ♔b6 ♖a2 17 ♖a5 ♖b2+ 18 ♔c7+–) 16 ♖×f5+ (16 ♔b6 ♖e6+) 16...♔g4= (Steckner)

The direct 13...♖×f2? is much weaker, in view of 14 ♔a8!. For example: 14...♖b2 15 a7 ♔e3 16 ♖b8 ♖a2 17 ♖e8+! (the standard "in-between check to win a tempo") 17...♔d3 18 ♖f8! ♔e4 19 ♔b7 f4 20 a8♕, and the white king gets back in time (with the king on e3, he would not have). Or 17...♔f3 18 ♔b7 ♔g3 19 a8♕ ♖×a8 20 ♖×a8 ♔×h4 (20...f4 21 ♔c6 f3 21 ♔d5 f2 22 ♖f8 ♔g2 23 ♔e4+–) 21 ♔c6 ♔g3 22 ♔d5 (here, the in-between check would be inappropriate, driving the king to where it supports the f-pawn) 22...h4 23 ♔d4! f4 (23...h3 24 ♔e3+–) 24 ♔d3! h3 25 ♔e2 h2 26 ♖g8+ ♔h4!? 27 ♖g7! (a waiting move that places Black in zugzwang) 27...♔h3 28 ♔f2 h1♘+ 29 ♔f3 ♔h2 (with the king on h4, Black saves himself by ...♘g3) 30 ♔×f4+–.

I tried to hold Black's position (after 13...♖×f2? 14 ♔a8!) by 14...♔e5!?, with the unusual idea of bringing the king over to the queenside to deal with the a-pawn.

The idea is justified after 15 a7? (or 15 ♖d8? ♖f4 16 a7 ♖×h4=) 15...♔d6! 16 ♖g7 (16 ♔b7 ♖b2+ 17 ♔a6 ♖a2+; 16 ♖g5 ♔c7 17 ♖×h5 ♖e2 18 ♖g7+ ♔b6=) 16...♖b2! 17 ♖b7 ♖g2(e2)=. Therefore, White would continue 15 ♖h8! ♔d6 16 ♖×h5 ♔c7 (analysis shows that 16...♖h2 17 ♔a7! doesn't help either).

9-155

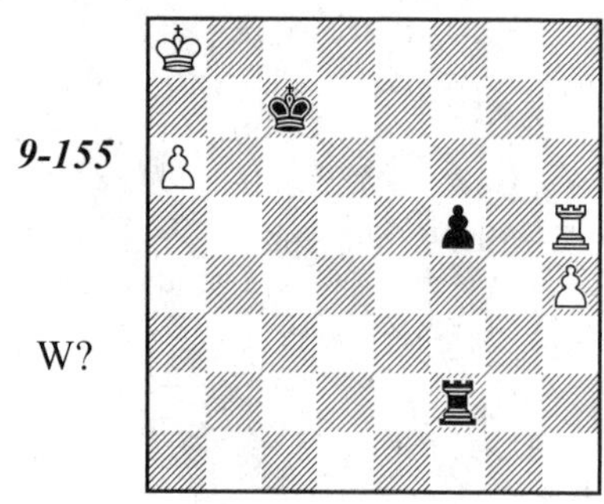

W?

And here I examined 17 ♖h7+ ♔b6 18 ♖h6+ ♔c7 19 h5 f4! 20 ♔a7!? ♖d2 (20...♖e2) 21 ♖f6 ♖d7! 22 h6 f3=.

Steckner established that the immediate 17 ♔a7! would save White a vital tempo, sufficient to win. I give his main variation (which I also would have seen, had I analyzed, instead of 19...f4!, the inaccurate 19...♖h2? 20 ♔a7!): 17...♖h2 (17...f4 18 ♖f5! ♔d6 19 ♔b7) 18 ♖h7+ ♔c6 19 h5 f4!? (19...♖d2 20 ♖h6+ ♔c7 21 ♖f6 ♖d7 22.♖b6+–) 20 ♔b8! ♖e2 21 ♖h6+ ♔c5 (21...♔b5 22 ♖f6!) 22 a7! ♖b2+ 23 ♔c8 ♖a2 24 ♖h7 f3 25 ♖c7+ ♔d5 26 h6 f2 27 h7 f1♕ 28 h8♕ ♕a6+ 29 ♔b8 ♕b6+ 30 ♖b7 ♕d6+ 31 ♔a8+–.

And now, we return to the position in diagram 9-153.

B) 6 f4+!? ♔e6! (6...♔×f4? 7 ♖×f7+ ♔g4 8 a7 ♔×h4 9 ♖c7! or 9 ♖d7!; 6...♔e4? 7 ♖e7+) 7 ♔b5 ♖b2+ 8 ♔c6 ♖c2+ 9 ♔b6 ♖b2+ 10 ♔c7 ♖a2 11 ♖a8 ♔f5 12 ♔b7 ♖b2+ 13 ♔a7 ♔×f4 14 ♖b8 ♖a2 (14...♖e2? 15 ♖g8! f5 16 ♔a8+– we already examined this position in variation "A.") 15 ♖b5 (in this situation, neither 15 ♔b7 ♔g3, nor 15 ♖g8 f5 wins).

9-156

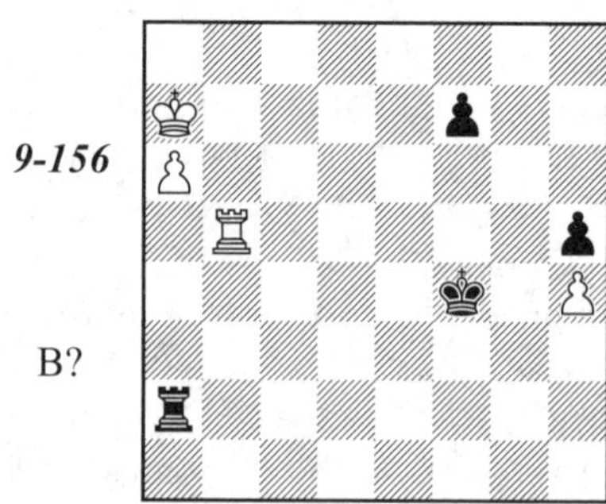

B?

Steckner went on to examine 15...f5 16 ♔b6 ♔g4 17 ♖a5! (but not 17 a7? ♖×a7 18 ♔×a7 ♔×h4=) 17...♖b2+ 18 ♔c7, and after winning the rook for the a-pawn (18...♖e2 19 a7 ♖e8 20 a8♕ ♖×a8 21 ♖×a8), White's king gets back to the kingside in time.

As Vulfson quite rightly observed, it is more logical to try 15...♔g4!. After the h4-pawn is captured, Black may try advancing either the f- or the h-pawn; in the latter case, ...f7-f5 is just a lost tempo.

Here 16 ♖b4+ ♔g3 17 ♔b7 f5= is no use; therefore, White plays 16 ♔b6, preparing the interference by 17 ♖a5. The following complications can serve as an excellent test-polygon for training in the calculation of complex variations. Here's a sample task: evaluate the consequences of the immediate rook sacrifice 16...♖×a6+ 17 ♔×a6 ♔×h4.

Analysis shows that White can refute his opponent's idea by a series of accurate moves: 18 ♖b8! (just so!) 18...♔g3 19 ♖g8+ (or 19 ♔b5 h4 20 ♖g8+!) 19...♔f3 20 ♔b5! (but not the 20 ♖h8? White usually plays in such situations, in view of 20...f5=) 20...h4 21 ♖h8! (but here this move is necessary) 21...f5 (21...♔g3 22 ♔c4 h3 23 ♔d3 h2 24 ♔e2+–) 22 ♔c4 ♔e3 23 ♖e8+!, and wins.

Thus, Black must continue 16...♔×h4! 17 ♖a5 ♖b2+! (but not 17...♖e2? 18 a7 ♖e8 19 a8♕ ♖×a8 20 ♖×a8+–) 18 ♔c7.

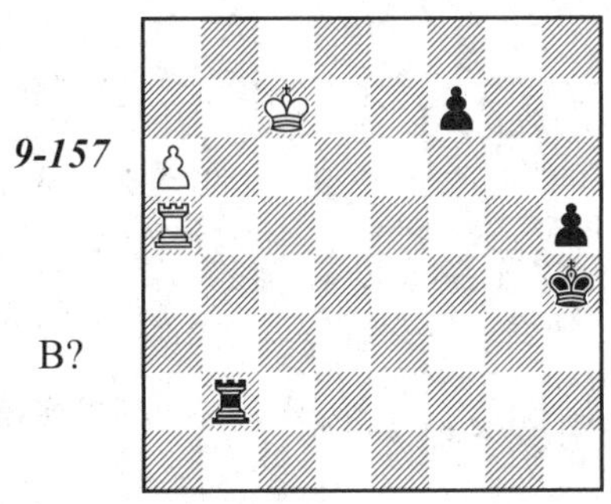

9-157

B?

And now, another task: how exactly should Black sacrifice the rook for the pawn?

The line 18...♖g2? 19 a7? ♖g8 20 a8♕ ♖×a8 21 ♖×a8 ♔g3 22 ♖g8+ ♔f3 23 ♖h8 f5 leads to a draw; however, as Steckner points out, White's play can be strengthened by 19 ♖a1!, preventing the rook from returning to g8. After 19...♔h3 (19...♖g8 20 ♖h1+) 20 a7 ♖g8 21 ♖h1+! ♔g2 22 ♖×h5, White wins.

At first, it appeared to me that even the in-between check 18...♖c2+! would not save Black, since in the line 19 ♔d7 (19 ♔d8 ♖g2 and 20...♖g8+ is useless) 19...♖g2 20 a7 (here 20 ♖a1? is much less effective: 20...♔h3 21 a7 ♖g8 22 ♖h1+ ♔g2 23 ♖×h5 ♖a8 24 ♖a5 f5=) 20...♖g8 21 a8♕ ♖×a8 22 ♖×a8 the position is lost: 22...♔g3 23 ♖g8+! ♔f3 24 ♖h8! f5 (24...♔g4 25 ♔d6 is also bad) 25 ♔e6 (with the king on c7, this move would not be possible, hence there would be no win; this is why I was unwilling to give the rook check on move 18) 25...♔e4 (25...f4 26 ♔f5+–) 26 ♔f6 (the decisive outflanking) 26...f4 27 ♔g5 f3 28 ♔h4+–.

But then a solution to the position was found: on 19 ♔d7, Black has to answer, not 19...♖g2?, but 19...♖b2!!. The point is that after 20 a7 (I see nothing better) 20...♖b7+ 21 ♔d6 ♖×a7 22 ♖×a7 ♔g3, White's rook would stand on the 7th rank, not on the 8th, where the f7-pawn prevents him from giving the important check on the g-file. This tiny difference proves decisive: Black is saved.

Along with 18...♖c2+!, Black also has a draw with 18...♖e2! 19 ♔d7 ♖b2!! or 19 a7 ♖e7+ 20 ♔b6 ♖×a7. But after 18...♖g2? 19 ♖a1! he can no longer have recourse to the same defensive idea: on 19...♖e2 there follows, not 20 a7? ♖e8=, and not 20 ♔d7?! ♖b2!, but 20 ♔d8!! ♖g2 (the move ♖b2 is no longer available) 21 ♔e7! and wins, since, as before, the rook cannot reach the g8-square.

Having gotten through this hugely complex analysis, we return once again to diagram 9-152, in order to reject the move 3...♖a5?! in favor of Anand and Dautov's suggestion **3...♔e6! 4 ♔c4 ♔e5**. The point is that, with the rook on a5, White wins a tempo by 5 ♔b4, and after 5...♖a2 6 f4+!?, the pawn capture 6...♔×f4? would lead to an immediate loss. But with the rook at a2, the king cannot reach it, and in the variation 5 f4+ ♔×f4! 6 ♖×f7+ ♔g4 7 a7 ♔×h4 8 ♔b4 ♔g3(g4) the draw becomes inevitable.

A more dangerous try is **5 ♖a8 ♔f4 6 ♔b6 ♖b2+ 7 ♔a7**. But we have already examined a similar situation in Variation "A", after diagram 9-153, and we already know the defensive recipe: don't be in a hurry to take the f2-pawn with your rook. Black secures the draw by **7...f5! 8 ♖g8! ♔f3! 9 ♖b8 ♖×f2 10 ♖b5 ♖e2!** (Steckner)

IV. Grandmaster Dautov demonstrated the surest drawing line. It turns out that, before playing ...g6-g5, Black will find it useful to restrict the activity of White's king.

1...♖a4! 2 ♔d3

2 f4 ♔e6! 3 ♔d3 f6 4 ♔c3 ♔f5 5 ♔b3 ♖a1 6 ♔b4 ♔g4= is not dangerous. On 2 ♖a8 the simplest reply is 2...♔f5! 3 ♔d3 (3 f3 ♖a3+) 3...♔g4 4 ♖f8 ♖×a6 5 ♖×f7 ♔h3= (Steckner). And 2...g5 3 hg+ ♔×g5 4 f3 (4 a7 ♔f6=) 4...♔f5 5 ♔d3 ♖a3+! 6 ♔c4 ♖×f3 will not lose either.

2...g5!

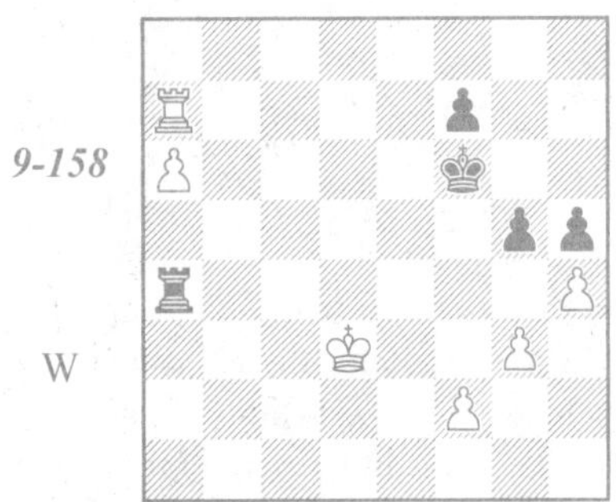

9-158

W

If White allows 3...gh, then the rook will take the h4-pawn, while White's king will be less active than after the immediate 1...g5!? 2 ♔d4! – this is in fact the point to cutting off the white king on the 4th rank. For example: 3 ♔c3 gh 4 gh ♖×h4 5 ♖b7 (5 ♔b3 ♖h1) 5...♖a4 6 a7 h4=.

And exchanging pawns on g5 allows Black to begin his kingside counterplay immediately.

3 hg+ ♔×g5 4 ♔c3 ♔g4 5 ♔b3 ♖a1 6 ♔b4 ♖a2

6...f5 7 ♖g7+ ♔f3 8 a7 ♔×f2 is also possible.

7 ♔b5 (7 ♖×f7 ♖×a6=) **7...♖×f2 8 ♖a8** (8 ♖b7 ♔×g3 9 a7 ♖a2) **8...♖b2+**

Just not 8...♔×g3? 9 ♖g8+ ♔f3 10 a7 ♖a2 11 a8♕+ ♖×a8 12 ♖×a8 h4 13 ♖h8! ♔g3 14 ♔c4+−.

9 ♔c4 ♖a2 10 ♖g8+ ♔f3 11 ♔b5 ♖b2+ 12 ♔c6 ♖a2 13 ♔b7 ♖b2+ 14 ♔a8 f5 (or 14...♖b6 15 a7 f5 16 ♖g5 ♖b5 17 ♖g7 f4=) **15 ♖g5 f4 16 gf h4 17 f5 ♔f4 18 ♖h5 ♔g4 19 ♖h8 ♔×f5 20 ♖×h4 ♔e6**, with a well-known theoretical draw – if White's rook tries to get to b8 to release the king from its prison, Black's king can get back to c7.

Our analysis of the Kantoroich/Steckner position acquaints us with the most important contemporary ideas for playing this endgame with the standard pawn structure f7-g6-h5 versus f2-g3-h4.

Now we proceed to an endgame with a different structure.

G. Levenfish, V. Smyslov, 1957

9-159

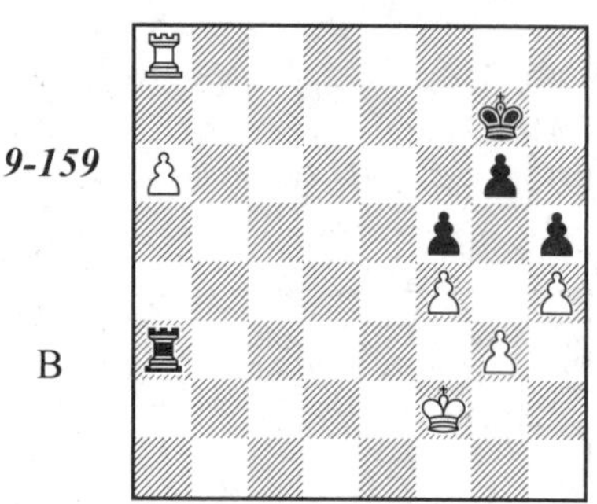

B

Here Black is faced with quite unpleasant problems: even after gaining the g3-pawn he cannot activate his king, and creating a passed pawn is difficult, too. In addition, each initial move harms his position in some way, so he has to choose the least of the evils.

An attempt to force the matters loses 1...♖a2+? 2 ♔e3 ♖a3+ 3 ♔d4 ♖×g3 4 ♖c8 ♖a3 5 ♖c7+ ♔f6 6 a7 ♔e6 7 ♔c5 ♖a1 8 ♔b6 ♖b1+ (8...♔d5 9 ♖c5+ ♔e4 10 ♖a5) 9 ♔c6 ♖a1 10 ♔b7 ♔d5 11 a8♕ ♖×a8 12 ♔×a8 ♔e4 13 ♖g7 ♔×f4 14 ♖×g6 ♔e3 15 ♖g5. Obviously, the king should be cut off along the 3rd rank.

1...♔h7?! is also dubious, as after 2 ♖a7+! ♔h6 3 ♔e2 ♖×g3 4 ♖b7 ♖a3 5 a7 the black king is poorly placed on h6.

But Black nevertheless manages to hold by a correct defense.

1...♔f7! 2 ♔e2 (2 a7? ♔g7=) **2...♔g7!**

He has to lose a tempo, because 2...♖×g3?? 3 a7 ♖a3 4 ♖h8 is bad.

3 ♔d2 ♖×g3 4 ♖b8 ♖a3 5 ♖b7+ ♔f6 6 ♖b6+

On 6 a7 the black king breaks loose: 6...♔e6 7 ♔c2 ♔d5, and if 8 ♔b2 ♖a6 9 ♔b3 then 9...♔c5!, bringing the white king back.

6...♔g7 7 ♔c2

9-160

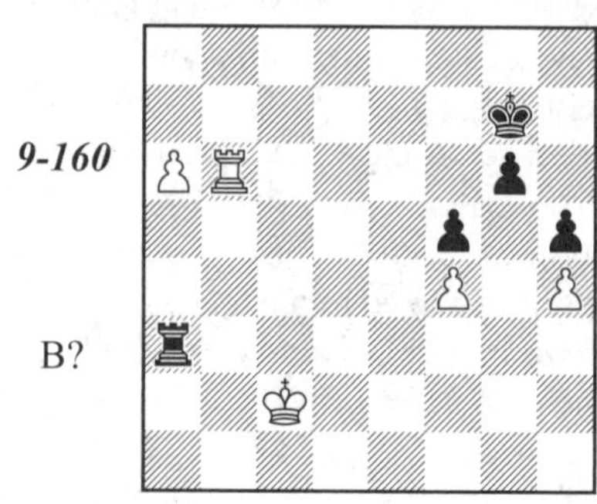

B?

7...g5!

A pawn sacrifice for creating a passed pawn, Black's only resource, but a sufficient one.

8 fg f4 9 ♔d2 f3 10 ♖b7+ ♔g6 11 a7 ♖a2+ 12 ♔e1 ♔f5 13 ♖f7+ (13 ♖g7 ♖e2+ 14 ♔f1 ♖a2=) **13...♔g6 14 ♖×f3 ♖×a7=**

If 15 ♖f6+ ♔g7 16 ♖h6 then 16...♖a4 17 ♖×h5 ♖a6!, forever imprisoning the white rook, is the simplest.

Tragicomedies

Let us now look at a few examples from current practice, and make use of our knowledge of theory to determine why strong grandmasters should suffer misfortune in drawn positions. We shall also learn some new ideas, which will enrich our theoretical understanding; in order to do this, however, we shall have to dive again and again into analytical debris.

Svidler – Akopian
European Cup, Kallithea 2002

9-161

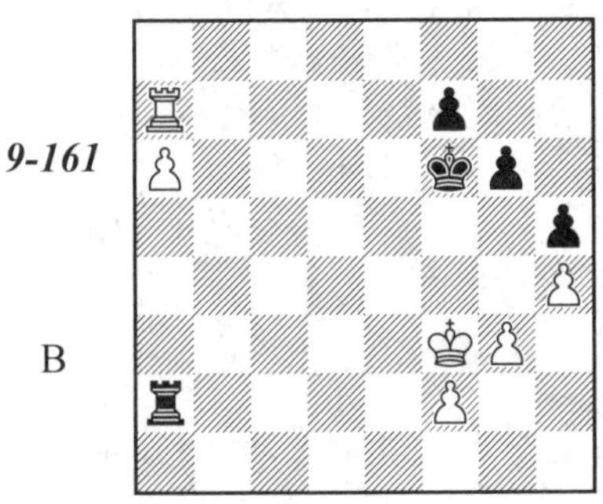

B

This is the Kantorovich/Steckner position, with the white king slightly less well-placed. In some lines, obviously, Black will have an extra tempo, which enlarges the sphere of drawing possibilities at his disposal.

1...♔e5

With the king at e3 this move would have lost; here, I believe it's not bad. He might also have played in "Dautov style:" 1...♖a4!? 2 ♔e3 g5, for example: 3 hg+ ♔×g5 4 ♖a8 ♔g4 5 a7 ♖a3+ 6 ♔e4 ♖a4+ 7 ♔e5(d5) ♔f3=. The immediate 1...g5 would not have been any worse (the only move that could have been dangerous in reply would have been 2 ♔d4! – even though this would not have been fatal, either – but White can't play that here.)

2 ♔e3 ♖a3+

In *Informant #85*, Svidler recommends 2...f6 3 ♔d3 ♖×f2 4 ♖b7 ♖a2 5 a7 ♔f5 6 ♔c4 ♔g4 7 ♔b3 ♖a6 8 ♖b4+ ♔×g3 9 ♖a4 ♖×a7=. Our attentive readers may possibly recall the analysis of the Kantorovich/Steckner position (with White to move): in the line 4 ♔c4!! f6 5 ♔b4? ♔g4 6 ♔b3 we reached precisely the same position, and concluded that it would be won with Black's pawn at f7, but with the pawn at f6, it was drawn.

Neverthelss, 2...f6? is still a bad move, in view of 3 ♖a8! ♖a3+ 4 ♔e2, when Black will have a hard time avoiding transposition to the won position from the Unzicker – Lundin game (after f2-f3 and a6-a7) without substantial losses.

3 ♔d2

9-162

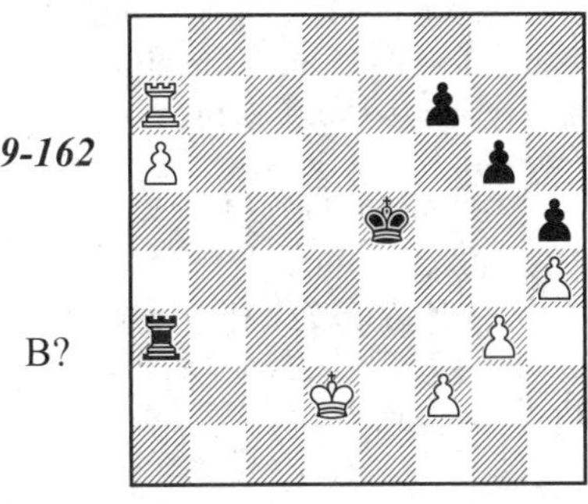

B?

3...♖a2+?

The fatal error! In this situation, the proper defensive plan involves the advance of the f-pawn. Here are a few sample variations: 3...f5! 4 ♔c2 (4 f3 f4 5 g4 hg 6 fg ♖a2+ and 7...f3=; 4 ♖a8 ♔e4 5 ♖e8+ ♔d5!=) 4...f4 (but not 4...♔e4? in view of 5 ♖e7+!, when the king cannot enter f3 because of 6 ♖e3+) 5 ♔b2 ♖a5 6 ♔b3 (6 ♖a8 fg 7 fg ♔f5 and 8...♔g4=) 6...fg 7 fg ♔f5 8 ♔b4 (8 ♖f7+ ♔e6!=, but not 8...♔g4? 9 ♖f4+ ♔×g3 10 ♖a4 ♖b5+ 11 ♔c4 ♖b8 12 a7 ♖a8 13 ♔d5+–) 8...♖a1 9 ♔b5 ♔g4 or 9...♖b1+, and draws (analysis by Dvoretsky).

Steckner noted that if White had played 3 ♔e2, the above-cited plan would not work: 3...f5? 4 ♖a8! ♔e4 5 f3+ ♔d5 6 a7+–. And 3...f6? is also a mistake: 4 ♖a8!; while after 3...♖a2+? 4 ♔d3 ♖×f2 White wins as in the main line of his analysis of diagram 9-144 (5 ♖e7+ ♔f6 6 a7 ♖a2 7 ♖c7 ♔f5 8 ♔c4!). The draw is reached by 3...♔e6! 4 ♔d2 f6 5 ♔c2 (here 5 ♖a8 ♔f5, is useless: White does not have f2-f3, and if he can't play that, the black king gets to g4) 5...♔f5 6 ♔b2 ♖a5 7 f3 (7 ♔b3 ♔g4) 7...g5 8 ♔b3 gh 9 gh ♔f4 10 ♔b4 ♖a1 11 ♔b5 ♖b1+, etc.

4 ♔c3

On 4 ♔d3 we have the winning position mentioned above (diagram 9-144). But of course, moving the king to c3 is more natural.

4...♖×f2 5 ♖b7

The rook could have gone to c7 also. But here, the rook check, which we recommended with the white king on d3, is bad: 5 ♖e7?!+ ♔d6! (5...♔f6 6 ♖c7+–) 6 a7 ♖f3+! (here's the problem: in that line, this check would not exist, as the king would be attacking the rook) 7 ♔b4 (or anyplace else) 7...♔×e7 8 a8♕ ♖×g3. Since the rook is not lost, Black keeps saving chances.

5...♖a2 6 a7 ♔f6

6...f6 was more stubborn. After 7 ♔b4 ♔d6

(both 7...♖b2+ 8 ♔c5 ♖×b7 9 a8♕, and 7...♔f5 8 ♖b5+ are hopeless) we reach the situation we know from diagram 9-150. Let me remind you of the fine win found by Steckner: 8 ♖g7! ♔c6 (8...♔e6 9 ♔b5 ♔f5 10 ♔b6 g5 11 ♔b7+-) 9 ♖f7! f5 10 ♖g7 ♔b6 11 ♔c4.

7 ♔c4 ♖a1 8 ♔b5 ♖b1+ 9 ♔c6 ♖c1+ 10 ♔b6 ♖b1+ 11 ♔c7 ♖a1 12 ♔b8 ♔f5 13 ♖b4 Black resigned.

Lerner – Dorfman

USSR ch(1), Tashkent 1980

9-163

B?

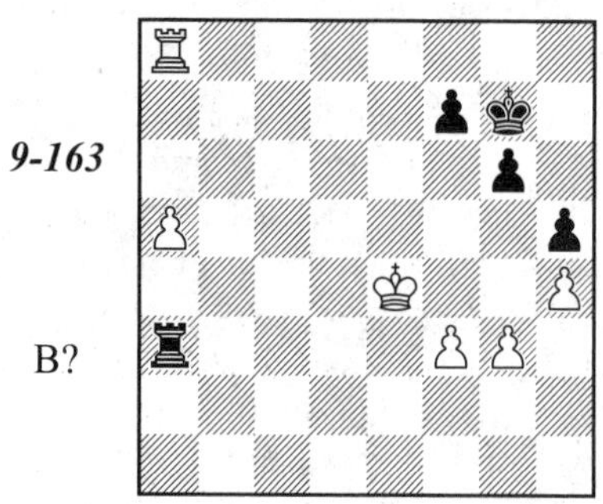

1...♖a4+?

The rook was placed ideally (targeting the white pawns), but the king could and should have been activated. After 1...♔f6! 2 a6 ♔e6 3 ♔d4 ♔f5! Black is saved. For example: 4 ♔c4 ♖×f3 5 ♖d8 (5 ♔b4 ♖f1 6 ♖c8 ♖b1+) 5...♖a3 6 ♔b5 ♔g4 7 ♖d4+ ♔×g3 8 ♖a4 ♖b3+ 9 ♔c6 ♖b8 10 a7 ♖a8 11 ♔b7 ♖×a7+ (11...♖e8) 12 ♔×a7 f6 13 ♔b6 g5=.

2 ♖a6+ ♔g7 3 ♔d5 ♖×f3 4 ♖b6 ♖×g3 5 a6 was also insufficient to win. The same position later arose in the game, but with White to move. Had he played 6 ♔c6, Lerner would have won; with a tempo less here, he could not have hoped for victory.

2 ♔d5 ♖a3 3 a6 ♖×f3?!

Now Black's king remains cut off on the 6th rank. 3...♔f6 suggests itself, for example, 4 ♔c6 ♖×f3 5 ♖b8 ♖a3 6 ♖b6 ♔f5 7 ♔b7 ♔g4 8 a7 ♖×a7+ 9 ♔×a7 ♔×g3 10 ♖b4 f6 and 11...g5=.

Nonetheless, we cannot rate this last move as the decisive error (that was committed earlier). White has a winning plan at his disposal here, suggested by Vladimir Vulfson, beginning with the move 4 ♔c5!.

9-164

B

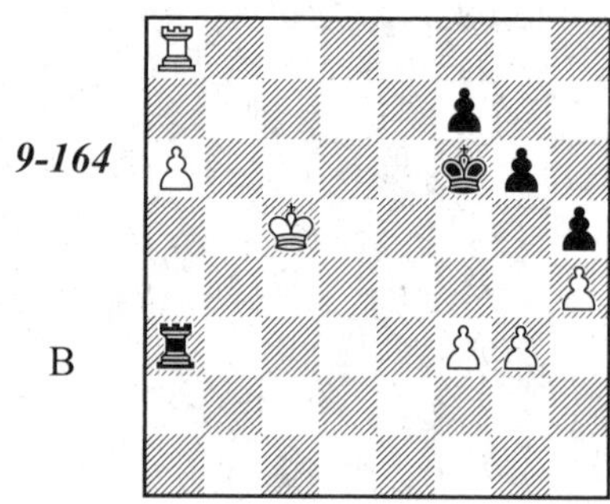

After 4...♖×f3 5 ♖d8! ♖a3 6 ♔b5 (intending 7 ♖d4) 6...♔e5 7 ♖d7 f6 8 a7 I don't see what Black can do against the threat of 9 ♖c7 followed by the interference maneuver: 10 ♖c5+, 11 ♖c4(c6)+ △ 12 ♖a4(a6).

I also looked at the attempt to refrain from the immediate pawn capture in favor of 4...♔f5. It succeeds after 5 ♖a7? f6 6 ♔b4 ♖×f3 7 ♖b7 ♖f1 8 ♖b5+ (8 a7 ♖b1+ 9 ♔c5 ♖a1 10 ♖g7 g5 11 ♔b6 ♔g4=) 8...♔g4 9 ♖a5 ♖b1+ 10 ♔c5 ♖b8 11 a7 ♖a8 12 ♖a3 g5=.

But White wins by continuing 5 ♔b4! ♖a1 6 ♔b5 ♖b1+ 7 ♔c6. If 7...♖c1+, then he shouldn't play 8 ♔b7? ♖b1+ 9 ♔a7 ♖b3 10 ♖b8 ♖×f3, but 8 ♔d7! ♖a1 9 ♔e7+-. On 7...♖a1, 8 ♖a7! is decisive (not 8 ♔d7? ♖a3) 8...f6 (8...♔f6 9 ♔d7! followed by 10 ♔e8+-; 8...♔e6 9 ♔b6 ♖b1+ 10 ♔c7 ♖a1 11 ♔d8+-) 11 ♖a8 △ 12 a7, transposing into our well-known winning position from the Unzicker – Lundin game (diagram 9-128).

The move 4 ♔c6!? (instead of 4 ♔c5!) is also possible, although it's less accurate. On 4...♖×f3 the same answer decides: 5 ♖d8! ♖a3 6 ♔b5, but after 4...♔f5!? the white king won't get to b4.

Analysis shows that the line 5 ♔b5 ♖×f3 6 ♖c8 ♖b3+ 7 ♔a4 ♖b1 8 ♖c3 ♖b8 9 ♔a5 ♔g4! (9...♖a8? 10 ♖c4!) 10 a7 ♖a8? 11 ♔b6 f6 12 ♔b7 leads to a win for White, but that 10...♖e8! 11 ♔b6 f6 12 ♔b7 g5 13 ♖c8 ♖e7+ leads to a draw.

Steckner found a way to strengthen White's play: 6 ♖f8! (instead of 6 ♖c8?). For example: 6...♔g4 (6...♖a3 7 ♖×f7+ ♔g4 8 ♖f4+ ♔×g3 9 ♖a4+-; 6...♖b3+ 7 ♔a4 ♖b1 8 ♖×f7+ ♔g4 9 ♖f4+ ♔×g3 10 ♖b4+-) 7 a7 ♖a3 8 a8♕ ♖×a8 9 ♖×a8 ♔×g3 10 ♖a4 f6 11 ♔c4! ♔×h4 12 ♔d3+, when the rook gradually overcomes the three pawns.

4 ♖b8 ♖a3 5 ♖b6 ♖×g3 6 ♔c6 ♖a3 7 ♔b7 g5

Or 7...f6 8 a7 ♖×a7+ 9 ♔×a7 g5 10 ♖b4!? ♔g6 11 ♔b6 ♔f5 (11...gh 12 ♖×h4 ♔g5 13 ♖h1 h4 14 ♔c5 ♔g4 15 ♔d4 h3 16 ♔e3 ♔g3 17 ♖g1+ – Anikaev) 12 ♔c5 g4 13 ♔d4 (13 ♖b1 g3 14 ♖f1+ ♔g4 15 ♖×f6 ♔×h4 16 ♔d4 ♔h3 17 ♔e3+-) 13...♔f4 14 ♔d3+.

8 hg h4 9 a7 h3 10 a8♕ (10 ♖a6? h2) **10...♖×a8 11 ♔×a8 h2 12 ♖h6 f6 13 ♖×h2 fg**

9-165

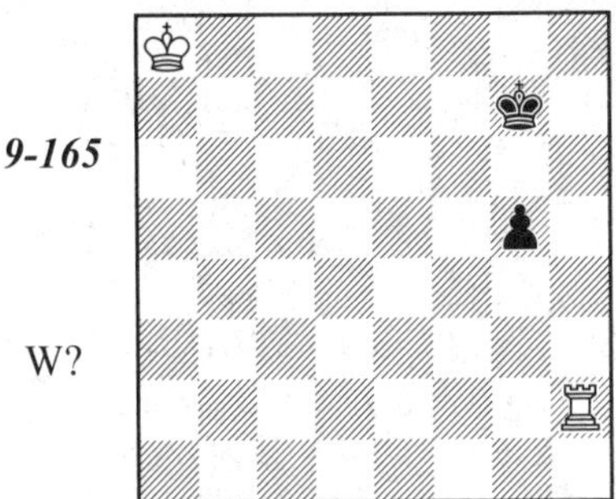

W?

14 ♖f2!!

Excellent! The rook prevents the shouldering maneuver that was possible after 14 ♔b7? ♔f6 15 ♔c6 ♔e5!=. For the sake of restricting the enemy king, White does not begrudge a vital tempo.

14...♔g6 15 ♔b7 g4 16 ♔c6 ♔g5 17 ♔d5 g3 18 ♖f8! ♔g4 19 ♔e4 Black resigned.

Akopian – Kir. Georgiev
Las Vegas wch 1999

9-166

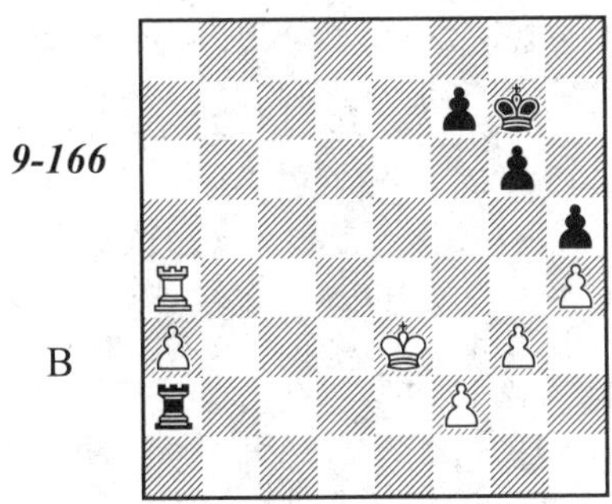

B

1...♖a1?!

As in the previous example, Black does not care about the activation of his king. Perhaps Georgiev rejected 1...♔f6! in view of 2 ♖f4+ ♔e6 3 a4, but he could play 3...f6! then, followed by ...g6-g5, driving the rook back from its comfortable position on f4 where it has been protecting all the white pawns.

2 ♖a6! ♖a2 3 a4 ♖a3+?

The same pernicious strategy that was fatal for Dorfman. In our current case, the a-pawn is still two steps away from a6 but White does not need extra time for bringing his rook from the 8th rank to the 6th.

Black should have performed the useful pawn advance 3...f6! followed by 4...g5; then a draw could have been achieved relatively easily.

4 ♔d4 f6?!

In this case, the "?!" symbol expresses my perplexity. Black's operations are devoid of logic. He comes to the aforementioned plan after all, but why has he driven the white king nearer to the queenside and why has he released the pressure from the f2-pawn? The rook check could have been logically combined with 4...♖f3 or 4...♖a2.

The position after 4...♖a2 5 a5 arose (with reversed colors) in the game Krakops – Dautov, Batumi ech tt 1999.

9-167

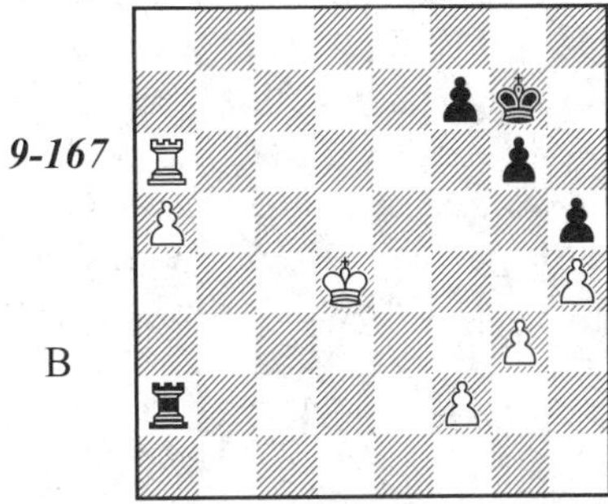

B

Krakops refused to capture the pawn, but after 5...f6 6 f4! ♖a3 7 ♖a7+ ♔h6 8 a6 g5 9 f5! his position turned out to be lost. The remainder of the game was 9...gh (9...♖×g3 10 ♖a8 ♖a3 11 a7 ♔g7 12 hg fg 13 f6+ ♔f7 14 ♖h8) 10 gh ♖a4+ 11 ♔c5 ♖×h4 (in case of 11...♖c4+ 12 ♔d6 the king escapes easily from attacks of the desperado rook) 12 ♖a8 ♖a4 13 a7 ♔g5 (13...♔g7 14 ♔b6 ♖b4+ 15 ♔a5) 14 ♖g8+ ♔×f5 15 a8♕ ♖×a8 16 ♖×a8 h4 17 ♔d4 ♔f4 18 ♖h8 ♔g3 19 ♔e3 f5 20 ♖g8+ ♔h2, and Black resigned.

Let us analyze the critical continuation 5...♖×f2 6 ♖c6!

In the summer of 2002, Artur Yusupov was conducting a class with some young German players. When he demonstrated this game, one of his students, David Baramidze, suggested an interesting counterplan: 6...f5!?.

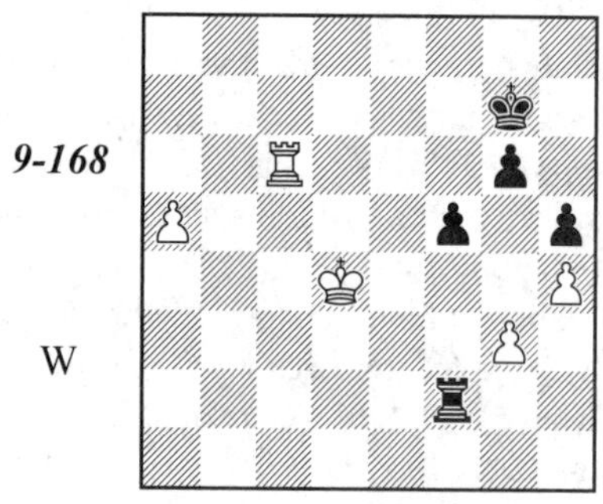

Black hurries to force matters on the kingside. 7 ♔e5 ♖f3 or 7 ♔c5 f4 8 gf ♖×f4 followed by 9...♖×h4 wouldn't be dangerous for Black, who has time to give up his rook for the passed pawn, with a draw.

Therefore White plays 7 a6 f4 8 a7 ♖a2 9 ♖c7+ ♔f6 10 gf ♔f5 11 ♔c5. On 11...♔×f4 12 ♔b5, Black can only prevent interference along the a-file with 12...♔g3 13 ♖c3+ ♔h2, but then a deflection decides: 14 ♖c2+! ♖×c2 15 a8♕, and the position that arises after 15...♖g2 is lost.

11...♔g4 12 ♔b5! ♖b2+ (12...♔×h4 13 f5!) is apparently stronger, after 13 ♔c6 ♖a2 14 ♔b7 ♖b2+ (14...♔×h4) 15 ♔c8 ♖a2 16 ♔b8 ♔×h4 Black holds. However, as Müller shows, White manages to arrange an interference here as well: 13 ♔c4! ♖a2 14 f5! ♔×f5 (14...gf 15 ♔b3 ♖a6 16 ♖c4+ f4 17 ♖a4+–) 15 ♔b4 ♔g4 (15...♔f6 16 ♔b5+–) 16 ♖c4+ ♔g3 17 ♖c3+ ♔×h4 18 ♖a3+–.

The main line is definitely 6...♖g2:

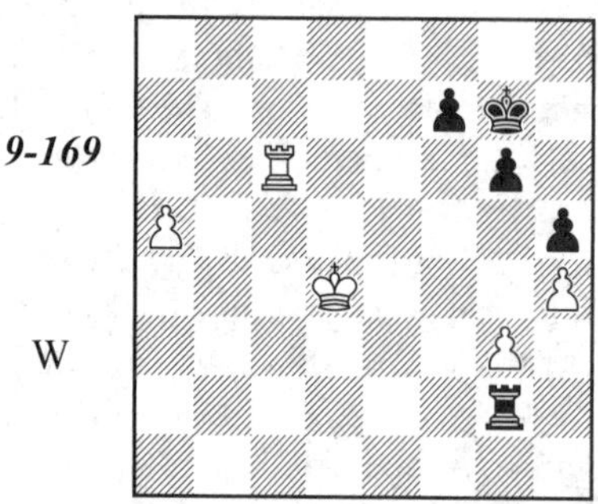

After 7 a6 ♖×g3 8 ♔c5 Black's mission of achieving a draw is still very far from simple. For example, 8...f6 9 a7 ♖a3 10 ♔b6 g5 11 ♖c8! ♖×a7 12 ♔×a7 ♔g6 13 ♔b6 ♔f5 14 ♔c5 gh 15 ♔d4 ♔f4 16 ♖c3! (16 ♔d3? h3 17 ♔e2 h2 18 ♖c1 ♔g3=; 16 ♖h8? h3 17 ♖×h5 ♔g3=) 16...f5 17 ♖a3⊙ ♔g4 18 ♔e3 ♔g3 19 ♔e2+ ♔g2 20 ♖a8+–.

I suppose that Black still can save the game by playing either 8...g5! or 8...♖a3 9 ♔b6 g5! with the following eventual consequences:

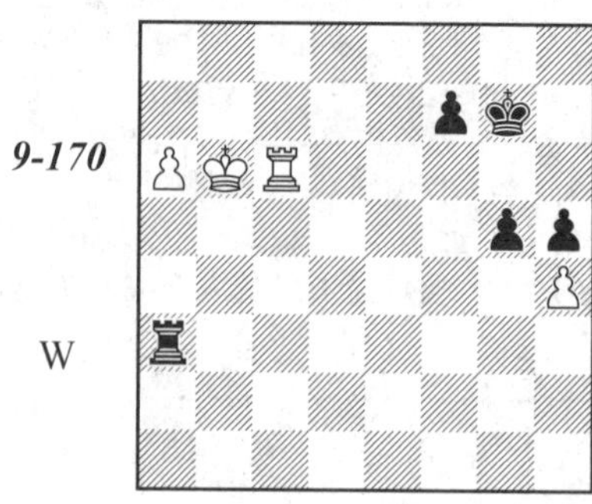

a) 10 ♖c5 gh 11 ♖×h5 (11 a7 ♖×a7 12 ♔×a7 ♔g6 13 ♔b6 h3) 11...h3 12 a7 ♖a1! 13 ♖×h3 (13 ♖a5 ♖b1+ 14 ♔c7 h2 15 a8♕ h1♕) 13...♖b1+ 14 ♔c7 ♖c1+ 15 ♔b7 ♖b1+ 16 ♔a8 f5 17 ♖c3 ♔f6 18 ♖c8 ♔e5 19 ♖b8 ♖a1=

b) 10 hg h4 11 a7 h3 12 ♖c3! (12 ♖h6 ♖b3+ 13 ♔c7 ♖c3+ 14 ♔b7 ♖b3+ 15 ♖b6 h2) 12...♖×c3! (both 12...♖a1 13 ♖×h3 ♖b1+ 14 ♔c7 ♖a1 15 ♔b7 ♖b1+ 16 ♔a8 ♔g6 17 ♖h8 ♔×g5 18 ♖b8 ♖a1 19 ♔b7 f5 20 a8♕ ♖×a8 21 ♖×a8 f4 22 ♔c6 and 12...h2 13 ♖×a3 h1♕ 14 a8♕ are losing; in the last line, the white king finds asylum on the kingside, on h2) 13 a8♕ ♖g3=. White can eliminate the h-pawn only at the cost of his g5-pawn; thereafter the black rook will be placed on g6 with an easy draw (see Chapter 13).

For some time I believed that these complex variations showed that the position was drawn after the capture of the f2-pawn. Grandmaster Dautov overturned my assessment, and by somewhat paradoxical means. Who would think that, in the position from diagram 9-169, White shouldn't play the absolutely natural move 7 a6?!, and instead pull his rook back from the 6th rank to the 5th!

7 ♖c3!! ♖a2 8 ♖c5 ♖a3 (8...♔f6 9 ♔c4 ♔e6 10 ♔b5 ♔d6 11 ♔b6 △ 12 ♖b5 is no help, nor is 8...f6 9 ♔c4 g5 10 hg fg 11 ♖×g5+ ♔h6 12 ♖c5 ♖a3 13 ♔b5+– the assessment of this position might not be obvious to the reader; therefore I suggest you try to verify it independently) 9 ♔c4 ♖×g3 10 a6 ♖a3 11 ♔b5

At first, Dautov examined only 11...f6 12 ♔b6 ♔h6 13 ♖a5 ♖b3+ 14 ♔c7 ♖c3+ 15 ♔d7 ♖d3+ 16 ♔e7 ♖e3+ 17 ♔f7+–. But the move 11...f5! gives White far more complex problems.

9-171

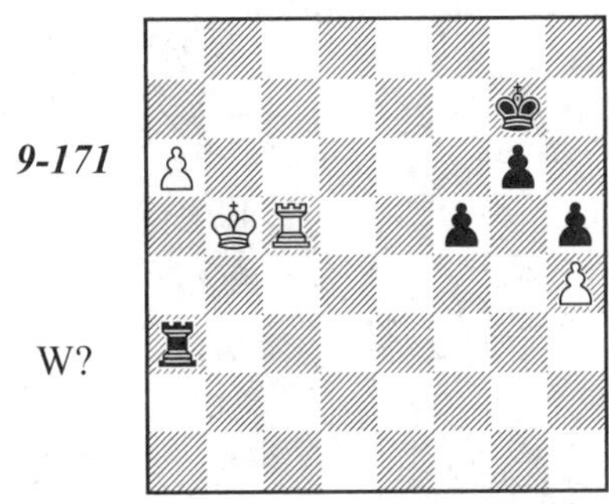

W?

Nothing comes of 12 ♔b6? f4 13 a7 f3 14 ♖c7+ ♔h6 15 ♖c3 ♖a1 16 ♖×f3 ♖b1+ 17 ♔c7 ♖c1+ 18 ♔b7 ♖b1+ 19 ♔a8 g5 20 ♖f6+ ♔g7 21 hg h4 22 ♖h6 ♖b4=. In case of 12 ♖c4?! g5 13 ♖a4 ♖b3+ 14 ♔c6 Black does not play 14...♖b8? 15 a7 ♖a8 16 ♔b7+–; he has 14...♖c3+! (driving the king away from the b7-square) 15 ♔d7 ♖d3+ 16 ♔e6 ♖d8 17 a7 ♖a8 18 ♔×f5 gh=.

Dautov found a clever in-between check: 12 ♖c7+!! ♔h6, and only now 13 ♖c4 g5 14 ♖a4 ♖b3+ 15 ♔c6. Here 15...♖c3+ 16 ♔d7 is useless because the king finds asylum from the checks on f7. If 15...♖b8 16 a7 ♖a8, the move 17 ♔b7?, which would win with Black's king at g7, now leads to a draw: 17...♖×a7+ and 18...gh. But 17 ♖a6! ♖×a7 (17...gh 18 ♔b7+) 18 hg+ (or 18 ♖×a7 gh 19 ♔d5+–) 18...♔×g5 19 ♖×a7 h4 20 ♔d5 ♔f4 21 ♔d4 h3 22 ♖h7 ♔g3 23 ♔e3+– is decisive.

This extremely complicated analysis brings us to conclude that the attack on the f2-pawn does not save Black.

5 ♖a7+ ♔h6 6 a5 g5

6...♖f3 7 a6 ♖×f2 8 ♖c7 ♖a2 9 a7 g5 10 ♔c5 is hopeless.

7 ♔c5 gh 8 gh

9-172

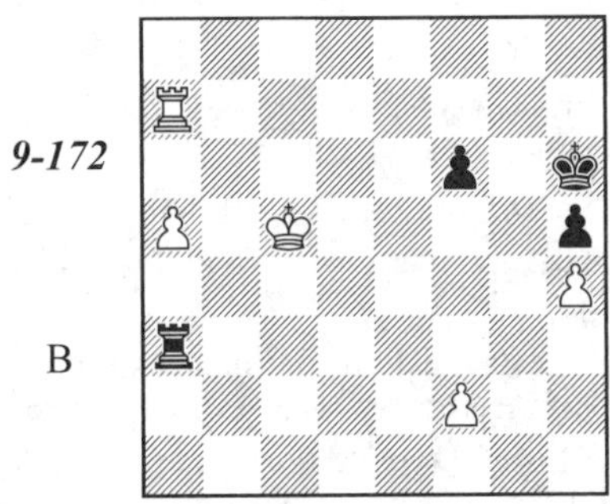

B

8...♖a4?

Another completely illogical move as it makes sense only in connection with a capture on h4, but Black cannot take this pawn. Both 8...♔g6 and 8...♖a2 would have been better. On the other hand, even with the tempo saved, Black probably still couldn't have saved the game. I shall present (with some emendations) the main variation offered by Steckner.

8...♔g6 9 a6 ♖a2 (9...♔f5 10 ♔b5 followed by ♖c7) 10 ♖a8 ♔f5 11 ♔b6 ♖b2+ 12 ♔a7 ♖×f2 13 ♖b8 ♔g4 (13...♖f4 14 ♖b5+ ♔g4 15 ♔b6+–; 13...♖e2 14 ♖b4 ♖e7+ 15 ♔b6 ♖e6+ 16 ♔a5 ♖e7 17 ♖b7 ♖e8 18 a7 ♖a8 19 ♔a6+–) 14 ♖b4+ ♔g3 15 ♔b6 ♖a2

9-173

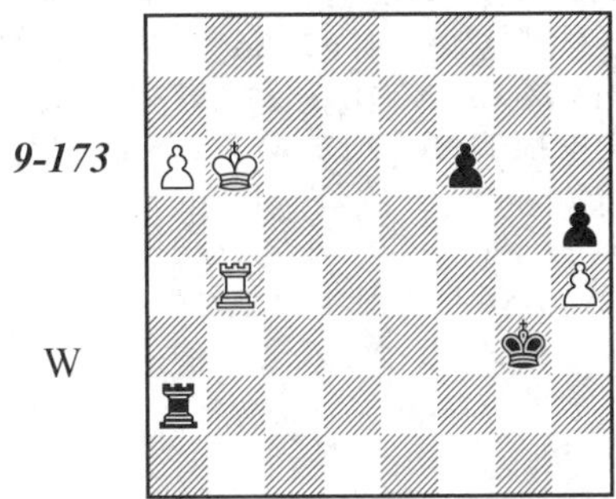

W

16 ♔b5! (the hasty 16 a7? f5 would let slip the win) 16...f5 17 ♖a4 ♖b2+ 18 ♔c6 ♖b8 19 a7 ♖a8 20 ♔b7 ♖×a7+ 21 ♖×a7! (21 ♔×a7? f4 22 ♔b6 ♔×h4=) 21...♔×h4 (21...f4 22 ♔c6 f3 23 ♔d5+–) 22 ♔c6 ♔g3 23 ♔d5 h4 24 ♔d4! f4 (24...h3 25 ♔e3 ♔g2 26 ♔e2 h2 27 ♖g7+, Black's own pawn at f5 is fatal: if it were no longer on the board, he could save himself by 27...♔h1!) 25 ♔d3! h3 26 ♔e2 h2 27 ♖g7+ ♔h4 28 ♖g8!⊙ ♔h3 29 ♔f2 h1♘+ 30 ♔f3 ♔h2 31 ♔×f4, and the knight is lost. The concluding moves might look familiar – indeed, as part of the analysis of the position in diagram 9-154 one of the variations (after 13...♖×f2?) ended exactly thus.

By the way, while we're speaking of that analysis, we may conclude that 12...♔f4 (instead of 12...♖×f2) 13 ♖b8 ♖×f2 would not have saved Black either. The position would have been drawn with Black's pawn at f5; but here it's at f6, and the tempo Black is missing changes the assessment.

Besides 16 ♔b5!, White also wins after 16 ♖b5! ♔×h4 17 ♖a5 ♖b2+ 18 ♔c7. This leads to almost exactly the same position as in diagram 9-157, the only difference being the position of the black f-pawn. With the pawn on f7 the move

18...♖g2 is refuted by 19 ♖a1!, and here it's refuted the same way (19...♖g7+ 20 ♔b6 doesn't help Black). But now the idea 19...♖c2+ 20 ♔d7 ♖b2, which saved Black in that position, is useless with the pawn on f6: 21 a7 ♖b7+ 22 ♔e6 ♖×a7 23 ♖×a7, and the rook can give check at the proper time from the g7-square.

9 a6 ♖a2

Black loses at once after 9...♖×h4 10 ♖a8 ♖a4 11 a7 ♔g7 12 ♔b6 ♖b4+ 13 ♔a5+–.

10 ♖a8 ♔g6 11 ♔b6 ♖b2+ 12 ♔a7 ♖×f2 13 ♖b8 ♖f4 14 ♖b5 ♖×h4 15 ♔b6 ♖e4 16 a7 ♖e8 17 ♖a5 h4 18 a8♕ ♖×a8 19 ♖×a8 ♔g5 20 ♔c5 h3 21 ♖h8 ♔g4 22 ♔d4 ♔g3 23 ♔e3 ♔g2 24 ♔e2 h2 25 ♖g8+ ♔h3 26 ♔f2 h1♘+ 27 ♔f3 ♔h2 28 ♖g2+ ♔h3 29 ♖g6 ♔h2 30 ♖×f6 ♔g1 31 ♖g6+ Black resigned.

The two last examples prompt us to make the following useful conclusions:

Quick activation of the king is a high priority for the weaker side.

In a standard pawn structure, posting the rook on a6, with the idea of confining the black king to g7, is no less dangerous in a practical sense than a pawn advance to a6.

The defender has a good counter-plan at his disposal: ...f7-f6 followed with ...g6-g5.

A Knight Pawn

If a passed pawn stands on the b-file, a king saves a tempo when heading towards it – and another tempo when returning after winning a rook for the pawn. Therefore the stronger side is almost always successful in practical endings. But a detailed postmortem analysis usually shows that the defense could have been improved and the defender's claims of a missed draw have not been groundless.

Hollis – Flórián
ol cr 1972

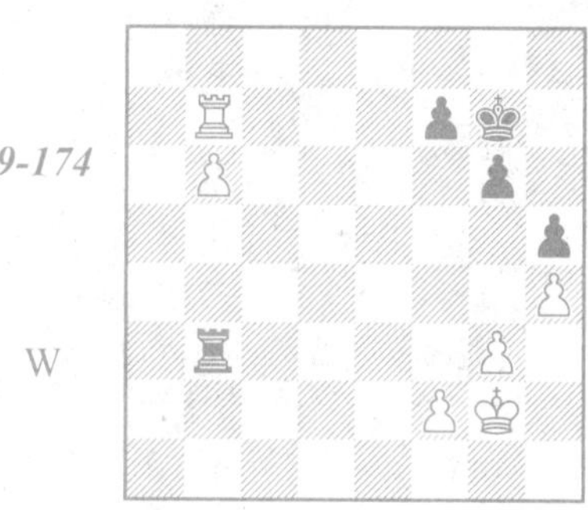

9-174
W

Hollis pretended in his comments that his win had been a natural phenomenon. Later on, Averbakh demonstrated how Black could survive. A Moscow player, Kantorovich, has made a precious contribution to our understanding of this sort of ending; he suggested a new, purely positional defensive method.

1 ♔f1 ♖b2 2 ♔e1 ♔f6 3 f3 ♖b3 4 ♔d2 ♖×f3 5 ♔c2

The threat is 6 ♖×f7+ ♔×f7 7 b7. A weaker option is 5 ♖c7 ♖b3 6 b7 ♔f5 7 ♔c2 ♖b6 8 ♖×f7+ (8 ♔c3 f6! 9 ♖c5+ ♔e6=) 8...♔g4 9 ♖d7, and here 9...♔h3!= (Dvoretsky) rather than 9...♔×g3? 10 ♖d3+ ♔×h4 11 ♖b3+– (Kantorovich).

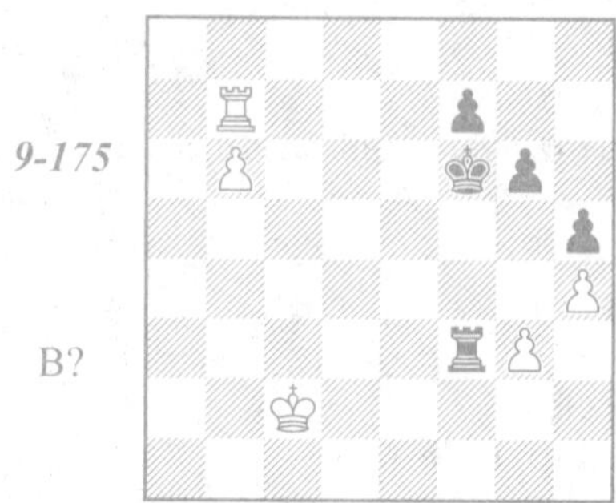

9-175
B?

5...♖e3!

The only way to survive. After bringing the rook to the 8th rank Black will not be afraid of an interference along the b-file, and his king can advance. All other defensive plans are inadequate.

The game in question continued as follows: 5...♖f5? 6 ♖c7 ♖b5 7 b7 ♔e6 8 ♔c3 f6 9 ♔c4 ♖b1 10 ♔c5 ♔f5 11 ♖d7! ♖c1+ (11...♔g4 12 ♖d4+ and 13 ♖b4+–) 12 ♔d6 ♖b1 13 ♔c7 ♖c1+ 14 ♔d8 ♖b1 15 ♔c8 ♔g4 16 ♖d6 g5 17 ♖×f6 gh 18 gh ♔×h4 19 ♖g6! ♔h3 20 ♔c7.

Black resigned in view of 20...♖×b7+ (20...h4 21 ♖b6) 21 ♔×b7 h4 22 ♔c6 ♔h2 23 ♔d5 h3 24 ♔e4 ♔h1 25 ♔f3+–.

The radical line that starts with 5...♖×g3 does not help. The idea behind it is 6 ♖×f7+? ♔×f7 7 b7 ♖g2+ 8 ♔c3 ♖g3+ 9 ♔c4 ♖g4+ 10 ♔c5 ♖f4! (10...♖×h4 11 b8♕ ♖e4 also deserves attention) 11 b8♕ ♖f5+ 12 ♔d6 ♔g7!, and White cannot breach the black fortress (Averbakh).

The move 6 ♖c7!, suggested by Hollis and analyzed by Averbakh, is much stronger than the rook sacrifice. For example, 6...♖g2+ (6...♖g4 7 ♔b3) 7 ♔b3 ♖g1 8 ♔b2 ♖g2+ 9 ♖c2 ♖g4 10 ♖c3 ♖×h4 (10...♖g2+ 11 ♔a3 ♖g1 12 b7+–; 10...♖b4+ 11 ♖b3+–) 11 ♔a3! ♖e4 12 b7 ♖e8 13 ♖c8 ♖e3+ 14 ♔b2 ♖e2+ 15 ♔c3 ♖e3+ 16 ♔d2 ♖b3 17 b8♕ ♖×b8 18 ♖×b8 ♔g5 19 ♔e3 ♔g4 20 ♔f2+–.

Trying for an intermediary series of checks prior to the pawn capture - 5...♖f2+? 6 ♔b3 ♖f3+ - could have been justified in case of 7 ♔a4 ♖×g3 8 ♖c7 ♖g1 9 ♖c5(c4) ♖b1!; however it is refuted by 7 ♔c4! ♖×g3 8 ♖c7 ♖g1 9 ♖c5!+– (Yusupov, Dvoretsky).

6 ♖c7 ♖e8 7 b7 (7 ♖c3 ♖b8 8 ♖b3 ♔e6=) **7...♖b8 8 ♔d3 ♔f5! 9 ♖×f7+**

Or 9 ♔e3 ♔g4 10 ♔f2 f6 11 ♖c4+ ♔f5! 12 ♖b4 g5 13 ♔f3 ♔e5 14 ♖b5+ ♔d6 15 ♔e4 (15 hg fg 16 ♖×g5 ♖×b7 17 ♖×h5 ♔e6=) 15...♔c6 16 ♖b1 gh 17.gh ♖×b7 18 ♖×b7 ♔×b7 19 ♔f5 ♔c7=.

9...♔g4 10 ♖f4+ ♔×g3 11 ♖b4 g5! 12 hg h4 13 g6 h3 14 g7 h2 15 ♖b1 ♔g2= (analysis by Averbakh).

We come to the most interesting point. The fact that the b-pawn is nearer to the kingside in comparison with a rook pawn has its sunny side for Black. He can abandon the idea of a race and apply another, somewhat surprising strategy: building a fortress! His king succeeds in two matters simultaneously: protection of the f7-pawn and prevention of an invasion by his counterpart.

4...♔e6!! (instead of 4...♖×f3) **5 ♔c2 ♖b5 6 ♔c3 ♖b1**

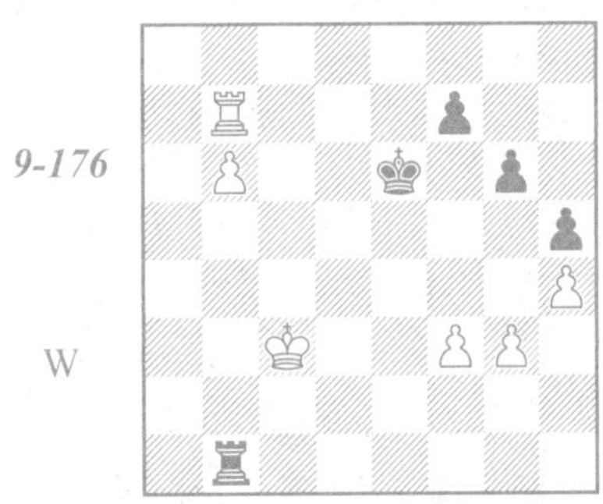

9-176

W

7 ♔c4 is met by 7...♖c1+ 8 ♔b5 ♖b1+ 9 ♔c6 ♖c1+, and the king must go back. If 7 ♖b8 (freeing the b7-square but releasing the f7-pawn from an attack), then either 7...♔d6 8 ♔c4 ♖b2! (Kantorovich's recommendation: the white king has no paths of invasion) 9 ♖b7 ♔e6, or 7...♔d5!?, without fear of 8 b7 ♔c6 9 ♖c8+ ♔×b7 10 ♖f8 ♖g1 11 ♖×f7+ ♔c8.

Kantorovich did not provide any analysis for his remarkable defensive method; in fact, he was not even sure that his plan was sufficient for a draw. Yes, of course, the fight is far from over; White has various attempts such as king maneuvers or pawn advances (g3-g4, f3-f4-f5). I investigated these possibilities and came to the conclusion that Black can survive if he plays precisely.

A) **7 g4** (if 7 ♖b8 ♔d6 8 ♔c4 ♖b2 9 g4 then 9...hg 10 fg ♔c6!) **7...hg 8 fg f5! 9 h5** (9 g5 f4 10 ♖b8 ♔f5 11 b7 ♔g4 12 h5 f3=) **9...gh** (9...fg? 10 hg g3 11 g7 ♖c1+ 12 ♔d2 ♖c8 13 ♔e2+–) **10 gh**

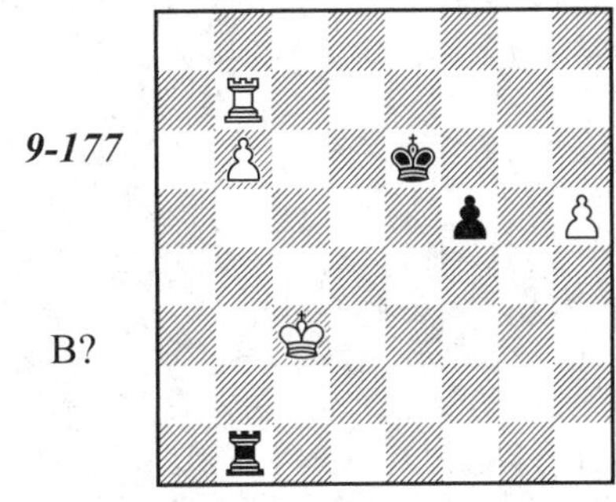

9-177

B?

10...f4!

10...♔f6? 11 h6 and 10...♔d6? 11 ♖g7 are obviously bad. 10...♖h1? is met with 11 ♖c7!! (rather than 11 ♖h7? ♖b1! 12 b7 ♔f6=) 11...♔d6 12 ♖h7 ♖b1 13 b7 ♔e5 14 h6 ♔f6 15 ♖d7+–.

11 ♔d3 ♖h1! 12 ♖h7 (12 ♖c7 ♖×h5 13 b7 ♖b5) **12...♖b1 13 b7** (13 ♔e4 ♖b4+ 14

♔f3 ♔f5) **13...♔f6!** (13...♔f5? 14 ♖g7) **14 ♔e4 ♖b4+ 15 ♔f3 ♔g5=**

B) **7 ♖b8 ♔d6** (7...♔d5!?) **8 ♔c4 ♖b2! 9 f4!? ♖b1 10 f5 gf** (otherwise 11 fg fg 12 ♖g8) **11 ♖h8 f6! 12 ♖h6! ♔e6!**

9-178

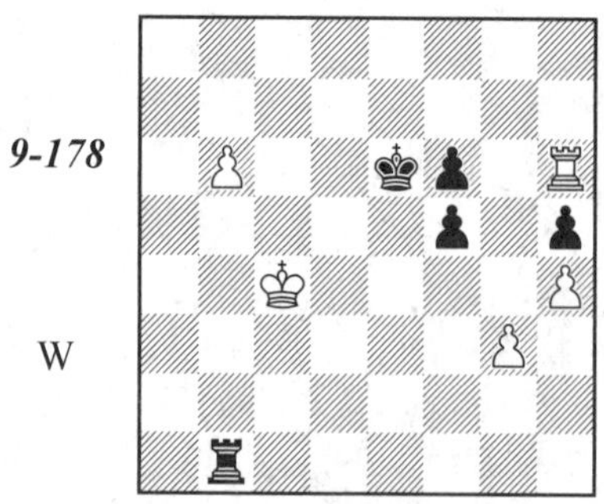

W

An important move! The natural looking 12...♔e5? loses to 13 ♔c5 ♖b3 14 ♖g6 f4 15 gf+ ♔×f4 16 ♔c6.

13 ♔c5 ♖c1+!

Prior to attacking the g3-pawn, it is useful to drive the king to b7 where it blocks his own pawn. By the way, if the black king stands on e5 his adversary can find a better refuge on b8.

14 ♔b5 ♖b1+ 15 ♔c6 ♖c1+ 16 ♔b7 ♖c3

Now the main advantage of the king's position on e6 is evident: White cannot defend the g-pawn with his rook (17 ♖g6 ♔f7!).

17 ♖×h5 ♖×g3 18 ♔c7!? ♖c3+ (18...♖g7+ 19 ♔c6) **19 ♔b8 ♖b3!?** (19...f4 20 ♖b5 f3) **20 b7 ♖b1! 21 ♖h8**

After 21 ♖h7 f4 22 ♖c7 Black can choose from 22...♔f5 23 ♔c8 ♔g4 24 ♖c4 f5 25 b8♕ ♖×b8+ 26 ♔×b8 ♔×h4 27 ♖×f4+ ♔g5 28 ♖f1 f4 29 ♔c7 ♔f5! 30 ♔d6 ♔e4= and 22...f3 23 ♖c2 ♔f5 24 ♔c7 (24 h5 ♔g5 25 ♖h2 ♔h6=) 24...♔g4 25 ♖c4+ ♔g3!=.

21...f4 22 ♖e8+ (22 ♔c7 ♖c1+ 23 ♔b6 ♖b1+ 24 ♔c6 ♖c1+ and the king cannot escape from the corner) **22...♔f5 23 ♔c7 ♔g4!** (23...f3? is a mistake: 24 b8♕ ♖×b8 25 ♖×b8 ♔g4 26 ♖b4+) **24 ♖e4** (24 b8♕ ♖×b8 25 ♖×b8 ♔×h4=) **24...f5 25 ♖c4 ♔×h4 26 ♖×f4+ ♔g5 27 ♖f1 ♖b2 28 b8♕ ♖×b8 29 ♔×b8 f4 30 ♔c7 ♔f5! 31 ♔d6 ♔e4=**

C) **7 ♔c4 ♖c1+ 8 ♔b3 ♖b1+ 9 ♔a2!?** White plans ♖b8 followed by a king advance. He could not break through to the pawn along the c-file, but the a-file lies open.

In case of 9 ♔a3 Black parries the threat by 9...♔d5! (both 9...♖b5? 10 ♔a4 ♖b1 11 ♖b8! ♔d6 12 ♔a5 and 9...♖a1+ 10 ♔b2 ♖a5 11 ♔b3 ♖a1 12 ♖b8! ♔d6 13 ♔b4 ♔c6 14 ♖f8 ♔×b6 15 ♖×f7 are bad). White responds with 10 ♔a4! (10 ♖b8 ♔c6 11 ♖c8+ ♔d6 or 11 ♖f8 ♖×b6 12 ♖×f7 ♔d5=) 10...♖a1+ 11 ♔b3 ♖b1+ 12 ♔c2 ♖b5 13 ♖×f7 ♖×b6 14 ♖e7!.

9-179

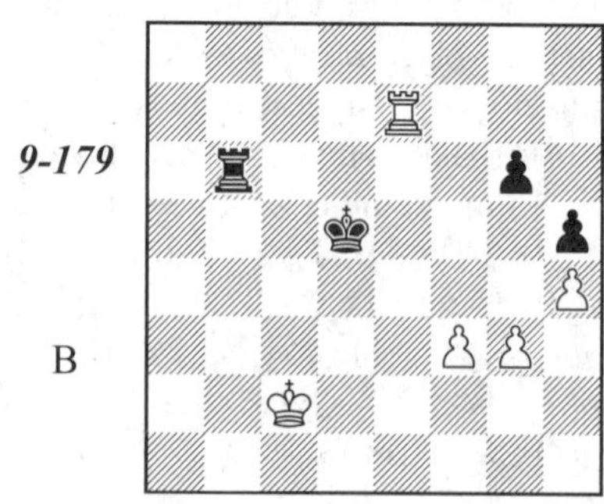

B

With the king cut off from the pawns, Black experiences difficulties. An immediate transition to a pawn endgame loses 14...♖e6? 15 ♖×e6 ♔×e6 16 ♔d3 ♔d5 17 ♔e3 ♔e5 18 g4! hg 19 fg ♔f6 20 ♔d4!.

14...♖f6! is met with 15 ♖e3! (after 15 f4 Black may trade rooks: 15...♖e6). But still, objectively speaking, the position is drawn. For example, not a bad idea is 15...♖a6!? 16 ♔d3 ♖a2 17 ♖e4!? (17 f4 ♔d6) 17...♖g2 18 ♔e3 ♖×g3 19 ♔f2 ♖g4! 20 ♖×g4 hg 21 fg ♔e4 22 ♔g3 ♔e5 23 ♔f3 ♔f6!= (we have seen such a finale in Yusupov – Ljubojevic, diagram 1-13).

Black can also play 15...♖f5 16 f4 (16 ♔d3 g5 17 hg ♖×g5 18 f4 ♖g4 △ 19...h4=) 16...♔d6 (if 16...♖f6 then 17 ♔d3, and 17...♖e6 is bad on account of 18 ♖×e6 ♔×e6 19 ♔e4 ♔f6 20 f5! gf+ 21 ♔f4+–) 17 ♔d3 ♖a5 18 ♔e2 (18 ♔e4 ♔e6=) 18...♔d7 (Black cannot do without this move: the rook will be obliged to defend the g-pawn along the 6th rank) 19 ♔f3 ♖a1!? (preventing g3-g4) 20 ♖e5 ♖a3+ 21 ♔g2 ♖a2+ 22 ♔h3 ♖a6 23 f5 gf 24 ♖×f5 ♖h6 25 ♔g2 ♔e6 26 ♖g5 ♔f7=.

9...♖b5 10 ♔a3 ♖b1

A quicker draw can be achieved in a pawn endgame with pawn less: 10...♔d5 11 ♔a4 ♔c5!? 12 ♖c7+ ♔×b6 13 ♖×f7 ♖f5! 14 ♖×f5 gf 15 ♔b4 ♔c6 16 ♔c4 ♔d6 17 ♔d4 ♔e6= (a reciprocal zugzwang!).

11 ♖b8! ♔d6 12 ♔a4 ♔c6 13 ♖c8+! ♔b7! (13...♔×b6?? 14 ♖b8+; 13...♔d6? 14 ♔a5) **14 ♖c7+ ♔×b6 15 ♖×f7 ♔c5 16 ♖f6**

9-180

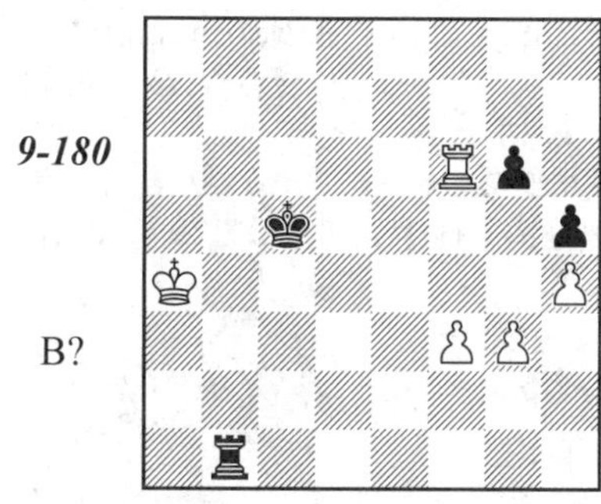

B?

How should Black proceed? 16...♖f1? 17 f4 △ ♖×g6 is hopeless, while 16...♖a1+? 17 ♔b3 ♖f1 18 ♔c3! ♔d5 19 ♔d3 ♔e5 20 ♔e2! ♔×f6 21 ♔×f1 leads to a lost pawn endgame.

16...g5!! (Suggested by Zviagintsev) **17 hg** (17 ♖f5+ ♔c4; 17 ♖h6 ♔c4) **17...♖g1 18 f4 ♖×g3 19 g6 h4 20 f5 h3 21 ♖f8 ♔d5=**

I would like to add that even with the white pawn on f2 (instead of f3) it is still a draw: 16...♖b4+ 17 ♔a3 ♖g4 18 ♔b2! ♔d4! (18...♔d5? loses to 19 ♖a6! ♔e5 20 f4+ ♔f5 21 ♖a3, the same is 19...♔e4 20 ♖a3 ♔f5 21 f4 – because of the tragicomical rook position on f4) 19 ♔c2 (19 ♖a6 ♔d3! 20 ♖a3+ ♔e2 21 f4 ♔f2; 19 ♖e6 g5 or 19...♖e4) 19...♔e5 20 ♖a6 ♔f5=.

As can be seen, this endgame is extremely complicated. One can hardly remember all its intricacies, but after all, one should not. Understanding the basic ideas is enough.

Portisch – Petrosian

Palma de Mallorca cmqf (12) 1974

9-181

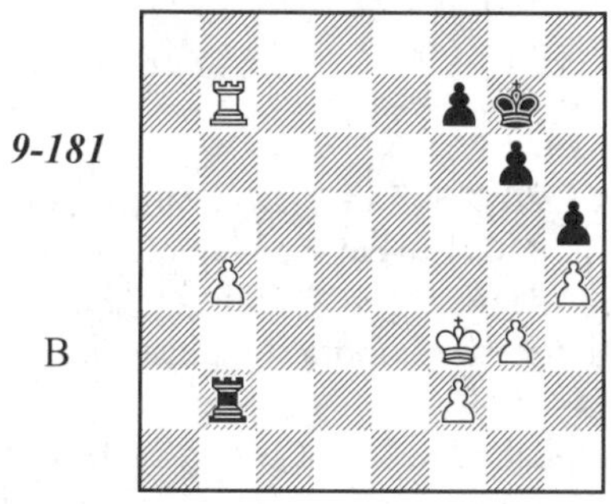

B

1...♔h6

Petrosian prepares ...f7-f6 and ...g6-g5. The positional defense method (à la Kantorovich), starting with 1...♔f6 was not yet discovered and still is not widely known.

2 ♔e3?!

Portisch suggested a more energetic approach: 2 b5! f6 3 b6 g5 4 ♖b8 gh 5 gh ♔g6 6 ♔e4+–. However his line is not convincing. White could have played ♔e4! a few moves earlier; on the other hand, Black could easily prevent this by means of ...♖b4!. To evaluate the resulting positions properly, a detailed analysis is required.

2...f6 3 ♖b6 ♔g7 4 ♖b7+ ♔h6 5 ♖b8?!

Another delay; Black can save the game now. Kantorovich suggests that the winning line is 5 b5 g5 6 ♔d4 gh 7 gh ♔g6 (7...♖b4+ 8 ♔c5 ♖×h4 9 ♖a7 ♖h1 10 ♖a4 h4 11 b6 h3 12 b7 ♖b1 13 ♖b4 ♖c1+ 14 ♔b6+–) 8 b6 ♖×f2 9 ♖a7 ♖b2 10 ♔c5 ♖c2+ 11 ♔d6 ♖b2 12 ♔c6 ♔f5 13 ♖a4+–. But Black improves his play by 8...♔f5! (instead of 8...♖×f2), so the result becomes questionable.

5...g5 6 b5 gh 7 gh ♔g6 8 b6 ♔f5 9 ♔d4

9 b7 does not win in view of 9...♖b4! 10 ♔d3 ♔f4 11 ♔c3 ♖b1 12 ♔d4 ♔f3 13 ♔d5 ♔×f2 14 ♔e6 ♖b6+ 15 ♔f5 ♔f3 16 ♔g6 ♔g4= (Kantorovich).

9-182

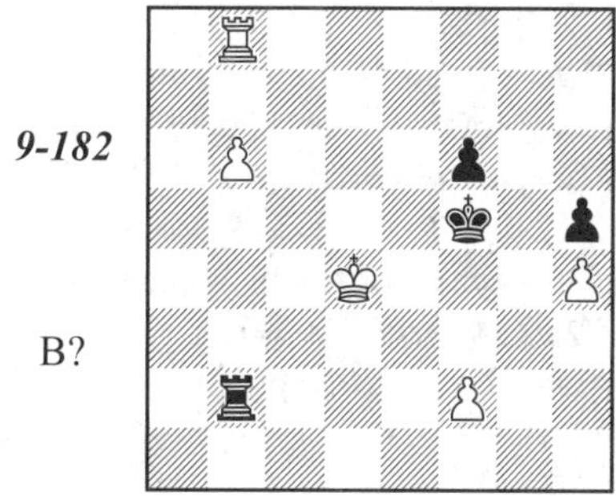

B?

9...♖×f2?

A draw could be achieved rather simply: 9...♔g4! 10 ♖g8+ ♔×h4 11 ♔c5 ♖c2+! (a standard method: the king is driven back with checks so that it is forced to stand in front of the pawn) 12 ♔d6 ♖b2 13 ♔c7 ♖c2+ 14 ♔b8 ♖×f2 15 b7 ♖b2 16 ♔c7 f5= (Averbakh).

10 ♖a8 ♖b2 11 ♔c5 (△ 12 ♖a4+–) **11...♖c2+** (11...♔g4 12 ♖a4+ ♔g3 13 ♖b4 ♖c2+ 14 ♔d6 ♖c8 15 ♔e6 is hopeless) **12 ♔d4 ♖b2 13 ♖a5+**

9-183

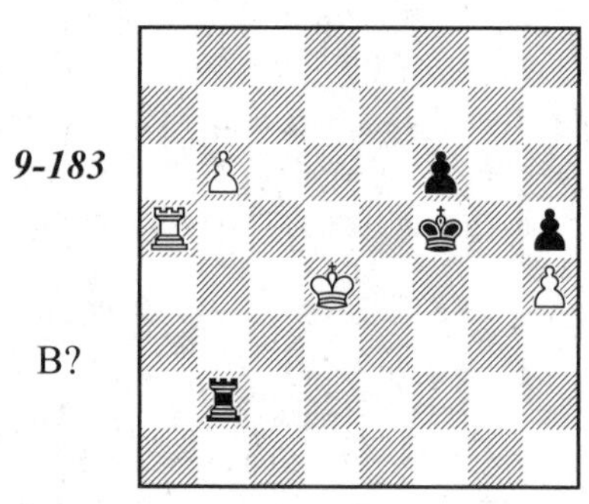

B?

Should the king go forward or backwards? Of course, 13...♔g4 suggests itself (and works after 14 ♔c5 ♔×h4=). However White has the strong reply 14 ♖a4! with the threat 15 ♔c3+. Let us look further: 14...♔g3 15 ♔c5 f5 16 ♖b4 ♖c2+ 17 ♔d6 ♖c8 18 b7 ♖b8 19 ♔c7 ♖h8 20 b8♕ ♖×b8 21 ♖×b8 ♔×h4 (21...f4 22 ♔d6 f3 23 ♔e5 f2 24 ♖f8 ♔×h4 25 ♔e4+−) 22 ♔d6 ♔g4 (22...♔g3 23 ♔e5 f4 24 ♔e4+− or 23...h4 24 ♔×f5 h3 25 ♖b3+ ♔g2 26 ♔g4 h2 27 ♖b2+ ♔g1 28 ♔g3+−) 23 ♔e5 h4 24 ♔d4! (24 ♖b4+ f4!) 24...h3 (24...f4 25 ♔d3 ♔f3 26 ♖h8! or 25 ♔e4 ♔g3 26 ♖g8+) 25 ♔e3 h2 26 ♖g8+ ♔h3 27 ♔f2 h1♘+ 28 ♔f3+−.

Yet Black can survive even after 14 ♖a4, as I. Zaitsev has shown! He discovered 14...♔h3!! (instead of 14...♔g3?) 15 ♔c5 f5 16 ♖b4 ♖×b4! 17 ♔×b4 f4 18 b7 f3 19 b8♕ f2=: a queen does not win against a bishop pawn!

13...♔e6 14 ♔c5 ♖c2+?

An error that leads to a rapid loss. He should have played 14...♔d7!

9-184

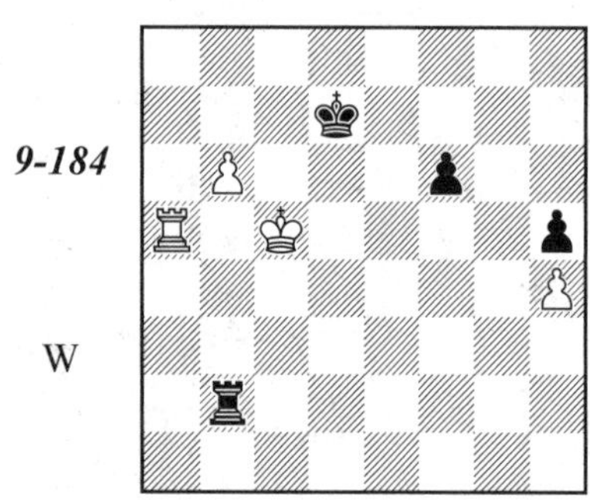

W

Neither 15 ♖a7+ ♔c8 16 ♖h7 ♖c2+ 17 ♔d5 ♖b2 nor 17 ♔d6 ♖c4! 18 ♖×h5 ♔b7 19 ♖h8 f5 is dangerous.

At first I thought that White would win by continuing 15 ♖a8! f5 16 ♖h8 (16 ♖f8 ♔e6!) 16...f4 17 ♖×h5 f3 18 ♖f5 f2 (18...♖h2 19 ♖f8!) 19 ♖f8 (19 h5 ♖e2!? △ 20...♖e5+) 19...♔e7 20 ♖f3 ♔d7 21 h5+−. But Black can improve his defense by 19...♖c2+! 20 ♔b5 ♖b2+ 21 ♔a6 ♔c6! 22 ♖f6+ ♔c5=.

15 ♔b5 ♔d6 16 ♔a6 ♔c6 17 ♖a1 ♖c4 18 b7 ♖b4 19 ♖c1+ ♔d7 20 ♖c8 Black resigned.

The Rook at the Side of the Pawn

As we have already seen, ***putting the rook to one side of the passed pawn makes sense if the pawn is far advanced, and also when it's blockaded by the king.*** Here we shall be discussing one more case: ***the rook should go to the side of the pawn, when it is simultaneously defending the pawns on the other wing.***

I. Rabinovich – Ragozin
USSR ch, Tbilisi 1937

9-185

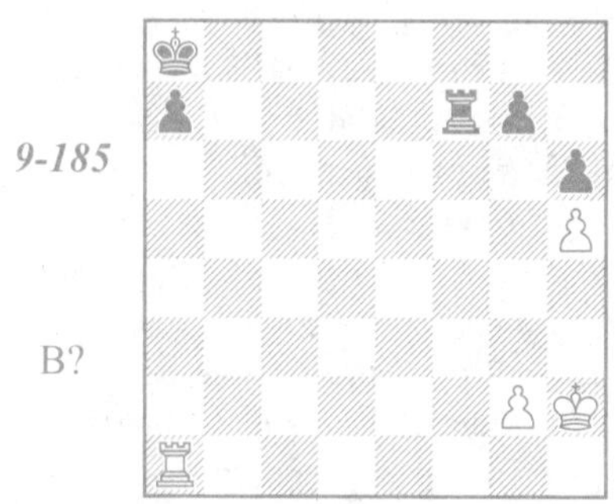

B?

1...♖f5! 2 g4 ♖g5 3 ♔g3 a5−+

After this maneuver, the king goes to the passed pawn in order to support its advance to the promotion square. The adversary lacks counterplay because the rook securely protects all the pawns.

4 ♔f3 ♔a7 5 ♖a4 ♔b6 6 ♔e3 ♖d5!

It is important to cut the king off from the queenside. After 6...♔b5?! 7 ♖d4 a4 8 ♔d3 winning would have been more complicated.

7 ♖f4

If 7 ♔e4, then 7...♖b5! (△ 8...♖b4+) 8 ♖a1 ♖g5 (driving the king back) 9 ♔f4 ♔b5. Defense by frontal attack is useless here.

7...♖d7 (△ 8...♔b5) **8 ♖f5 a4 9 g5 hg 10 ♖×g5 a3 11 ♔e4 a2 12 ♖g1 ♔b5 13 ♖a1 ♖a7 14 ♔d3**

On 14 ♔f5, the simplest reply is 14...♖a6!, but 14...♔b4 15 ♔g6 ♔b3 16 ♖g1 ♖c7! is also strong enough (as in Taimanov – Averbakh, diagram 9-102).

14...♔b4 15 ♔c2 ♔a3 16 ♖g1 ♖c7+ 17 ♔d3 ♔b2 White resigned.

It's almost always sensible to go to the defense from the side, when the passed pawn has not advanced further than the 2nd or 3rd ranks - because in that case, the rook is usually protecting its other pawns, as well.

This sort of position occurs quite often in practical play but still does not have any definite evaluation.

Karpov – Knaak
Baden-Baden 1992

9-186

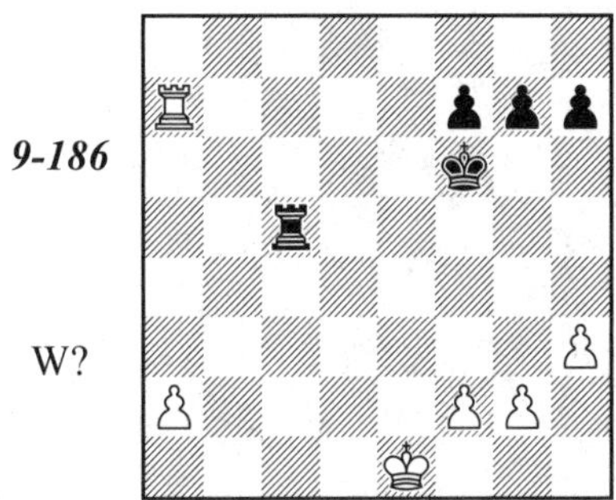

W?

1 ♖a3!

After 1 ♔d2? ♖d5+ the king can hardly escape from the rook checks because it must watch the 2nd rank, while 1 a4? ♖c2 leads to a standard situation with the black rook behind the passed pawn. Karpov brings his rook to the 3rd or 2nd rank where it will protect everything.

1...g5?

An unfavorable setup, particularly in combination with Black's next move (the king should have been kept in the center, to fight against the passed pawn if necessary). A cleverer idea was 1...h5!?, planning an eventual ...h5-h4 and ...♖g5. Another natural continuation was 1...♖c2!? 2 ♖f3+ ♔e6. If White tries 3 a3?!, then 3...♖a2 4 ♔d1 f5 5 ♔c1 g5 6 ♔b1 ♖d2 and White, with his king cut off, can hardly expect success. A stronger alternative is 3 ♖e3+ ♔d6 4 ♖e2 ♖c3 5 ♔d2 ♖a3 6 ♔c1. I dare not judge whether White's advantage is sufficient for a win here.

2 ♔d2 ♔g6 3 ♖c3 ♖a5 4 a3 h5 5 ♔c2 ♖a8 6 ♔b3 ♖b8+ 7 ♔a2 ♖a8

7...♖d8!? 8 ♖c2 ♖d3 deserved attention. But if Black enters this way then 5...♖a8 was senseless (5...h4!? 6 ♔b3 ♖b5+ 7 ♔a2 ♖d5).

8 ♖c4 f5 (8...♖e8 9 ♖b4 ♖e2+ 10 ♖b2 ♖e4 11 ♔b3+–) **9 a4 ♔f6 10 ♔a3 ♔e5 11 ♖c5+ ♔e4** (11...♔f4!?) **12 a5 h4 13 ♔a4 ♔f4 14 ♖c4+**

14 ♔b5 is also strong. Ftacnik criticizes it on account of 14...♖b8+ 15 ♔c6 ♖b2 16 a6 ♖×f2 17 ♖a5 ♖c2+ 18 ♔b6 ♖c8 19 ♔b7 ♖h8 20 a7 ♔g3, but if White, instead of 16 a6?, includes the zwischenschach 16 ♖c4+!, Black gets no counterplay.

14...♔e5 15 ♖b4 ♔d5 16 ♖b5+ ♔e4 17 ♖b6 ♔f4 18 a6 g4 19 ♔a5 g3 (19...gh 20 ♖b4+! ♔e5 21 gh+–) **20 ♖b4+ ♔e5 21 f3 f4 22 ♖e4+ ♔f5 23 ♖e2 ♔f6 24 ♔b6** Black resigned.

Tragicomedies

Averbakh – Euwe
Switzerland ct 1953

9-187

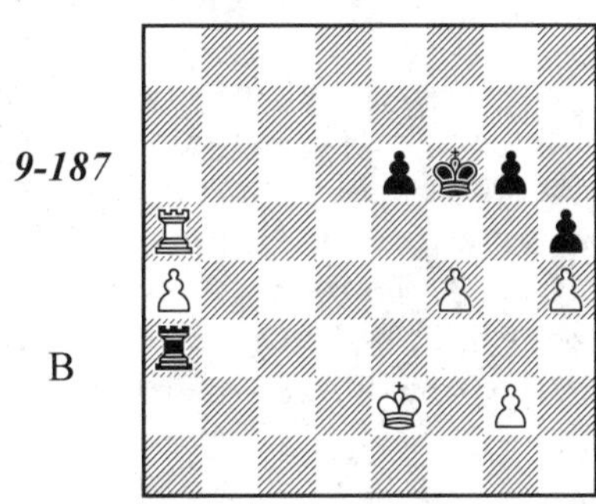

B

1...♖g3??

A grave mistake as Euwe allows his opponent to bring his rook to g5 with tempo. White's rook will safely protect all his pawns there (after g2-g3 and a4-a5). After 1...♖a2+! a draw was absolutely obvious.

2 ♖g5! ♖a3 3 a5 ♔f7

Sometimes in similar situations one succeeds in preventing the king's approach to the passed pawn by cutting the king off along a file: say, 3...♖c3 4 ♔d2 ♖c4 5 g3 ♖c6. This method does not work in our case: White plays 6 ♔d3 ♖c1 7 ♔d4 ♖c2 8 ♖c5 ♖g2 9 a6 ♖a2 (9...♖×g3 10 ♖a5) 10 ♖c6 ♔f5 11 ♔c5, obviously outrunning his opponent.

4 ♔d2 ♔e7 5 ♔c2 ♔d7 6 ♔b2 ♖a4 7 g3 ♔c6 8 ♔b3 ♖a1

The simple 9 ♖×g6 is strong enough for a win, but Averbakh finds a more accurate solution: a triangular maneuver with his king, putting Black in zugzwang.

9 ♔b4 ♖b1+ 10 ♔c4 ♖a1 11 ♔b3!⊙ Black resigned.

Every king's move opens the road to the white king, while 11...♖b1+ is met with 12 ♔a2 ♖b4 (12...♖b5 13 ♖×b5 ♔×b5 14 ♔b3 ♔×a5 15 ♔c4+–) 13 ♔a3, and Black's g-pawn will be captured without losing the passed pawn.

Leko – Anand
Linares 2003

9-188

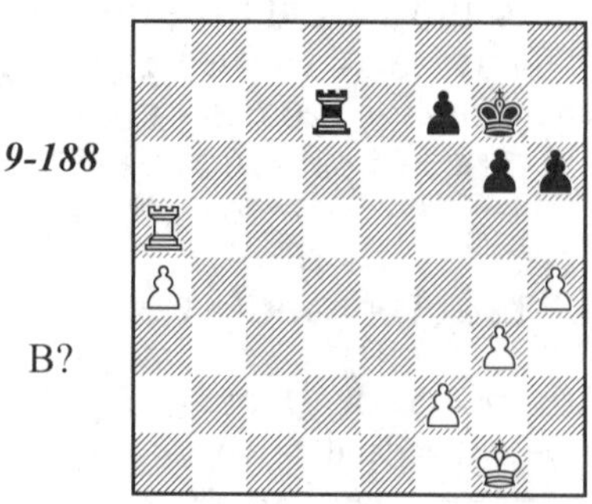

B?

Viswanathan Anand undoubtedly knew that such endgames are, as a rule, drawn. So it's hard to understand why he decided not to set up the standard pawn structure with 1...h5!. After 2 ♔g2 ♖d3! and 3...♖a3, the rook gets behind the passed pawn, while also restricting the enemy king, and Black would draw without any particular difficulty.

There was no need to fear 2 ♖c5 and 3 a5 (or 3 ♖c4). He would have a reason to concern himself with the flank defense of the pawn if the a-pawn had already reached the 6th or 7th rank.

1...♖d1+?! 2 ♔g2 ♖a1?

"When the engineer starts looking for new paths, the train goes off the rails." It was still not too late to play 2...h5, even though at this point it would be a little weaker than on the previous move, since White's king can now reach f3.

3 g4!

Of course! With this structure, Black has a much harder time getting counterplay on the kingside. Additionally, this relatively new situation means that the standard recipes are no longer any good. Black must now create a brand-new defensive method, without knowing if his choice of plan will offer him realistic saving chances or not.

As an example, the international master Julen Arizmendi suggested that Black play 3...h5!? 4 g5! ♖a3 here, and presented a tremendously complex analysis, showing that Black draws with exact play. However, at the very end of his main variation, Steckner found an improvement for White, which wins. (You can read all the details in Karsten Müller's January 2004 article at chesscafe.com.)

3...♔f6 4 ♔g3

Grandmaster Mihail Marin, in his book, *Secrets of Chess Defence*, opined that 4 g5+ would have been an easy win. But, if there is in fact a win there, it would not be simple at all. Here are a few variations based on some later material published by Marin and my own analyses.

The first moves are obvious: 4...hg 5 hg+ ♔e6.

9-189

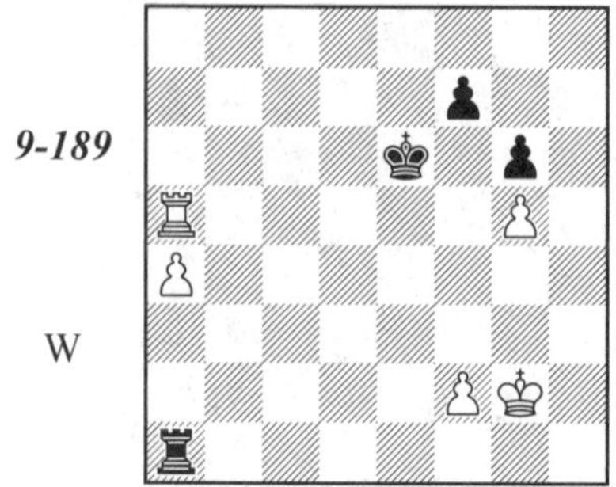

W

The premature 6 f4? would allow Black to restrict the mobility of the enemy king: 6...♖a3! 7 ♔f2 f5!? (7...♔d6 is also possible) 8 ♔e2 ♔d6 9 ♔d2 ♔c6 (threatening 10...♔b6) 10 ♖a6+ ♔d5 11 ♔c2 ♔e4 12 ♔b2 ♖d3 13 ♖×g6 ♔×f4 14 a5 ♔g4, with an easy draw.

It would be more logical to play 6 ♔g3 ♖a2 7 f3 ♖a1 8 ♔f4. Black continues 8...♔d6, and if 9 ♖a7, then 9...♔e6 10 a5 (10 ♔e4 ♖e1+ 11 ♔d4 ♖d1+ 12 ♔c4 ♖c1+ 13 ♔b5 ♖b1+ 14 ♔a6 ♖f1) 10...♖a4+ 11 ♔e3 ♔f5 12 ♖×f7+ ♔×g5 13 ♖a7 ♔h4 14 a6 ♔g3 15 ♖a8 ♖a3+ (nor does 15...g5 16 a7 ♔g2 lose) 16 ♔e4 ♖a4+ 17 ♔e5 ♔×f3 18 ♔f6 ♔g4 19 ♔×g6 ♖a1 20 ♔f6 ♔f4 21 ♔e6 ♔e4 22 ♔d6 ♔d4 23 ♔c6 (23 a7 ♖a6+! 24 ♔c7 ♔c5 25 ♔b7 ♖b6+, but not 23...♖a2? 24 ♔c6 ♔c4 25 ♖c8!+–) 23...♖c1+! 24 ♔b7 ♖b1+ 25 ♔a7 ♔c5 26 ♖b8 ♖h1=.

9 ♔e4 ♖e1+ 10 ♔d4 is stronger. On 10...♖f1 White replies 11 ♖a6+ ♔e7 12 ♔e4 – with the king cut off on the 6th rank, Marin demonstrated a win for White. It's worth noting that if Black waits, White will play f3-f4, ♖a8, pawn to a7, and then the kingside breakthrough with f4-f5!, and if the pawn is taken, g5-g6! decides.

After 10...♖d1+ 11 ♔c3! Marin examined 11...♖c1+ 12 ♔b2 ♖c4 13 ♔b3 ♖f4 14 ♖a6+ ♔c5 15 ♖f6 (getting the rook to f6, where it can defend all the pawns, is White's main strategic idea in this line) 15...♖b4+ 16 ♔a3 ♖b7 17 f4! (Black is in zugzwang) 17...♖e7 (17...♔c4 18 ♖c6+ ♔d5 19 ♖c2) 18 ♔b3 ♖a7 19 f5! gf 20 ♖×f5+, and Black is in deep trouble.

I found a different defensive method – having the black rook attack various White pawns: 11...♖f1! 12 ♖a6+ ♔c5 13 ♖f6 (looks decisive – and it would be if White's pawn were already on a5) 13...♖a1 (13...♖g1 14 f4 ♖g3+ amounts to the same thing) 14 ♔b3 ♖b1+ 15 ♔a2 ♖g1! 16 f4 ♖g2+ (on 16...♔b4? White wins by force: 17 ♖×f7 ♔×a4 18 ♖f6 ♖g4 19 ♔b2 ♔b4 20 ♔c2 ♔c4 21 ♔d2 ♔d4 22 ♔e2 ♔e4 23 ♔f2 ♖×f4+ 24 ♔g3) 17 ♔b1!! (the most exact – 17 ♔b3 ♖g3+ 18 ♔c2 ♖a3 or 18 ♔b2 ♖g2+ 19 ♔c3 ♖g3+ 20 ♔d2 ♖a3 would be weaker) 17...♖g1+ 18 ♔c2 ♖g2+ 19 ♔d3 ♖a2 20 ♖a6 (neither 20 ♖×f7 ♖×a4 21 ♔e3 ♔d5 22 ♖f6 ♖a3+ 23 ♔f2 ♔e4, nor 22 ♔f3 ♖a3+ 23 ♔g4 ♖a6 wins for White) 20...♖f2 (20...♖a1 21 ♖a7 ♔d5 22 ♔c3 is less accurate) 21 ♔e3 ♖a2, and the outcome remains unclear.

We could continue analyzing this variation, but it's time for us to return to our game.

9-190

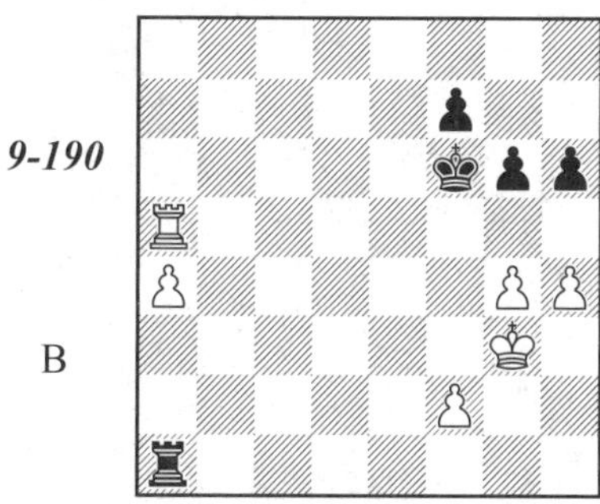

B

It might make sense to wait here: 4...♖a2. The incautious response 5 f3? would have led to a draw in view of 5...g5! 6 ♖f5+ ♔g6 7 h5+ ♔g7 8 a5 ♔g8. This pawn configuration would be ideal for White: his rook defends everything, leaving only the task of bringing his king over to the a-pawn. Unfortunately, the king is locked forever onto the kingside.

Leko had intended to continue with 5 ♔f3 ♔e6 6 ♔e3, followed by f2-f3 and ♔e4. But it's not clear whether White has a win after Steckner's suggestion of 5...g5!?:

6 hg+ hg 7 ♖f5+ ♔g6 8 a5 ♖a4, and the white king cannot get his queenside voyage underway;

6 h5 ♔e6 7 ♔e3 f6 8 f3 f5!? (8...♖a1 9 ♔e4 ♖e1+ 10 ♔d4 looks weaker) 9 gf+ ♔f6 10 ♔e4 ♖e2+ 11 ♔d4 ♖h2 with counterplay (Dvoretsky);

6 ♖f5+ ♔g7 7 a5 (7 hg ♖a3+! 8 ♔g2 ♖×a4 9 gh+ ♔×h6=) 7...gh 8 ♔g2 ♖a3 9 f3 ♖a1, and this position appears to be drawn.

4...♖c1?!

Anand changes his defensive plan – now he intends to put his rook on the 4th rank, attacking the enemy pawns while restricting the activity of his rook and king. So Leko immediately takes his rook off the a-file, changing to the sidelong defense of his passed pawn.

5 ♖b5 g5?! 6 ♖f5+ ♔g6 7 h5+ ♔g7 8 a5

9-191

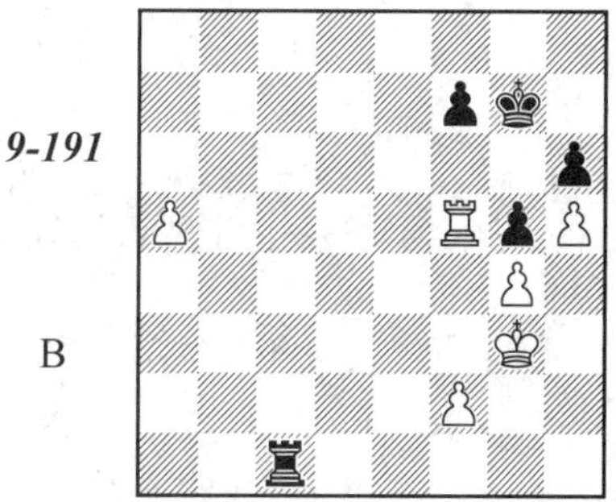

B

8...♖a1?!

An inconsistent move, allowing White to set up the ideal configuration, where the rook securely defends all the pawns, while the king gets ready to set out for the queenside.

8...♖c4 looks more logical. In reply, Leko recommended the pawn sacrifice 9 ♔f3 ♖a4 10 ♔e3 ♖×g4 11 ♔d3 f6 12 ♔c3, while Marin suggested 10 ♖d5 (instead of 10 ♔e3) 10...♔f6 11 ♔e3 ♔e6 (11...♖×g4? is bad, in view of 12 ♖d4 and 13 ♖a4) 12 ♖b5 ♖×g4 13 ♖b6+ and 14 ♖×h6. Some analysts – myself included – studied the resulting complications; but the final verdict appears to be indefinable. However, this has no bearing on the overall assessment of the position.

The problem is that White isn't obliged to give up the pawn. The strongest continuation is 9 f3 ♖c2 10 f4! (otherwise 10...♖a2, when the king will never get out of g3; alternatively the pawn could also have advanced to f4 on the preceding move) 10...♖c3+! 11 ♔f2 gf (as Arizmendi showed, 11...f6 12 ♖b5 ♖a3 loses to 13 f5!) 12 ♖xf4 ♖a3 13 ♖f5 f6 14 ♖b5 ♔f7:

9-192

W?

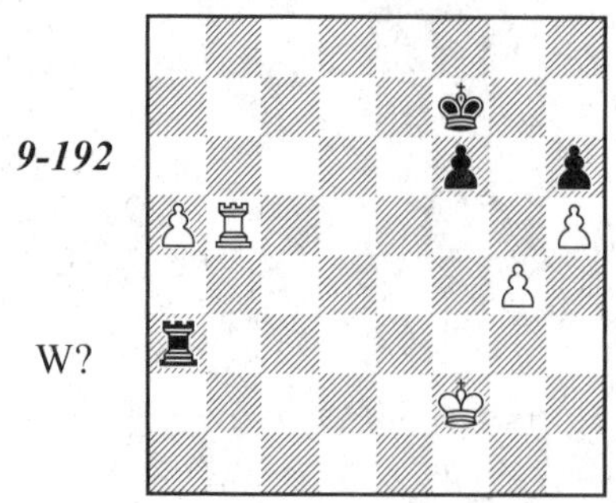

Leko continued the variation as follows: 15 ♖b7+ ♔e6 16 ♖b6+ ♔e5 17 a6 ♔f4! 18 ♖xf6+ ♔xg4 19 ♖xh6 ♔g5 20 ♖b6 ♔xh5 21 ♔e2 ♔g5 22 ♔d2 ♔f5 23 ♔c2 ♔e5 24 ♔b2 ♖a5 25 ♖h6 (25 ♔b3 ♔d5 26 ♔b4 ♖a1 27 ♖h6 ♖b1+ 28 ♔a5 ♔c5=) 25...♔d4 26 ♖h4+ (26 ♔b3 ♖a1=) 26...♔d3 27 ♖h3+ ♔c4 28 ♖a3 ♖b5+ 29 ♔c2 ♖b8=.

Arizmendi established that if White plays 15 ♔e2! (instead of 15 ♖b7+?), he can win a vital tempo over Leko's variation. For example: 15...♔e6 (on 15...♖a4 both 16 ♔f3 and 16 ♔d3 ♖xg4 17 a6 are strong) 16 ♖b6+ ♔e5 17 a6 ♔f4 (17...♖a4 18 ♔d3 ♖d4+ 19 ♔c3 ♖xg4 20 ♖b5+ ♔e6 21 ♖a5 ♖g8 22 a7 ♖a8 23♔d4+-) 18 ♖xf6+ ♔xg4 19 ♖xh6 ♔g5 20 ♖b6 ♔xh5 21 ♔d2 ♔g5 22 ♔c2 ♔f5 23 ♔b2 ♖a5 24 ♔b3 ♔e5 25 ♔b4 ♖a1 26 ♔c5+-.

We may conclude that there is no longer any saving Black.

9 ♔g2! (of course not 9 f3?? ♖a2=) **9...♖e1**

Yet another change of defensive plans – Black tries to restrict the white king by cutting him off on the e-file. In this situation, such a method is equally as hopeless as the waiting game with: 9...♖a4 10 f3 ♖a2+ 11 ♔f1 ♔f8 12 ♔e1 ♔e7 13 ♔d1 ♔e6 14 ♔c1, etc.

10 f3 ♖e6 11 ♔f2 ♔f8 12 ♖b5 ♔g7

On 12...♔e7, 13 ♖b7+ and 14 ♖b6 decides. Here Leko could have brought his rook around behind the passed pawn by 13 ♖b3 ♖a6 14 ♖a3, with an easy win. But he preferred to maneuver a bit first, hoping Black would worsen his king's position.

13 ♖f5 ♔f8 14 ♖c5 ♔g7 15 ♖b5 ♔f8 16 ♖b6 ♖e5 17 a6 ♔g7 18 a7 ♖a5 19 ♖b7 ♖a3 20 ♔e2 ♔f6 21 ♔d2 ♔e6 22 ♔c2 f6 23 ♔b2 ♖a4 24 ♔b3 ♖a1 25 ♔b4 ♔d6 26 ♖h7 ♔e5 27 ♔b5 ♖a2 28 ♔b6 ♔d5, and Black resigned.

Exercises

9-193

9/23

W?

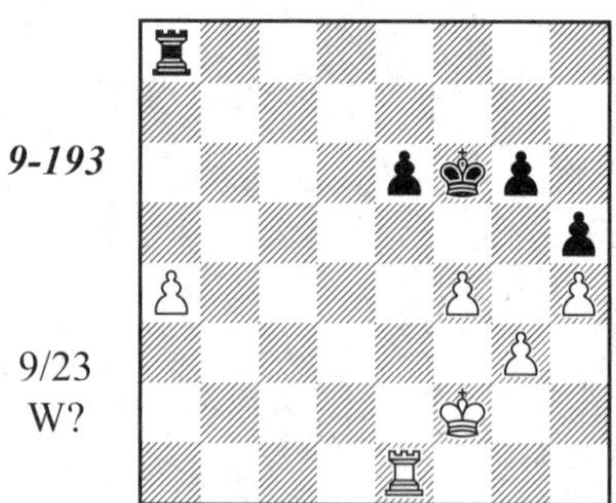

Common Observations about Endgames with Many Pawns

The Rook's Activity

The rook's activity is the main principle for evaluation and practical play in rook-and-pawn endgames. It can take various forms: attacking the enemy's pawns, supporting its own passed pawns, cutting the opponent's king off, or pursuing the king.

It also happens that the rook must sometimes behave passively, its functions being limited purely to defense. But in these cases ***one should relentlessly seek for opportunities to activate the rook, even at cost of pawn sacrifices or deteriorated king's position.***

The following classic ending illustrates this principle excellently.

Flohr – Vidmar
Nottingham 1936

9-194

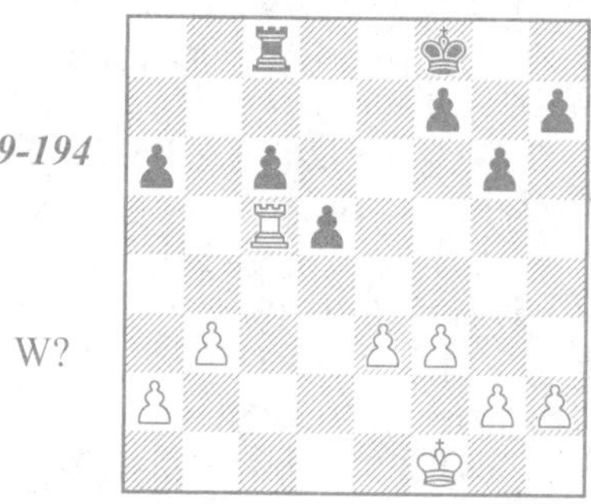

W?

White has an obvious positional advantage, but as for a win, it is surely a long way off. The outcome of the game depends on the endgame artistry of the players.

1 ♔e2!

First of all, to centralize the king. In case of 1 ♖a5? Black sacrifices a pawn to activate his rook: 1...c5! 2 ♖×a6 c4 with excellent chances for a draw. 1 b4? is also not precise: 1...♔e7 2 ♔e2 ♔d6 3 ♔d3 ♖b8!? (3...♔c7) 4 a3 ♖b5.

1...♔e7 2 ♔d3 ♔d6 3 ♖a5!

Rather than 3 ♔d4? in view of 3...♖b8 4 ♖a5 c5+! 5 ♔d3 ♖b6.

3...♖a8 4 ♔d4

Black must reckon with e3-e4 now.

4...f5!? 5 b4

Flohr strengthens his control over weak squares on the queenside. Black is faced with a problem: which defensive plan to choose.

9-195

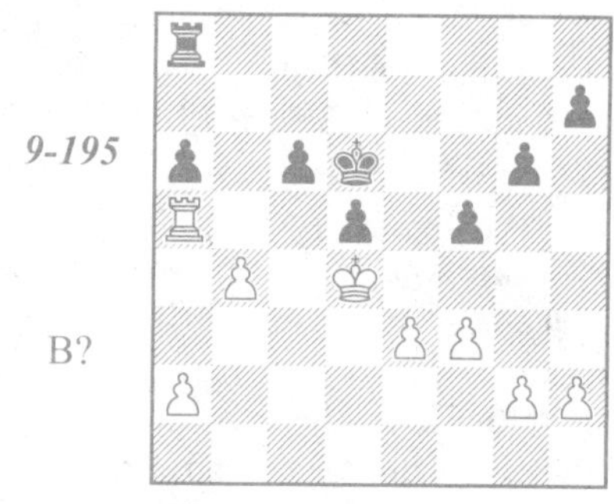

B?

5...♖b8?

Too passive: the rook will be forced back to the unenviable role of bodyguard to the a-pawn as early as the next move.

He should have protected the pawn with the king: 5...♔c7! (△ ...♔b6). Oh yes, the king would have gone away from the center, the white king – in contrast – would have had an open road for invasion, but the rook could enjoy freedom. And, as we have said, the rook's activity in rook-and-pawn endings is paramount!

White would very probably have played 6 ♔c5 ♔b7 7 ♔d6 ♖e8 8 ♖a3 (△ ♖c3). Now Black should pave the way to the 2nd rank for his rook.

A) 8...f4? is entirely bad in view of 9 ef ♖e2 10 g4 with f4-f5+– to follow. Black cannot fight against the passed f-pawn because another pawn, on f3, is blocking the file from rook attacks.

B) Levenfish and Smyslov suggest 8...d4!? 9 ed ♖e2 10 ♖c3 ♖×g2 (10...♖d2 11 ♖c4) 11 ♖×c6 ♖×h2 12 a4 g5 (△ ...g4; ...♖h6+). However White maintains the advantage by placing the rook behind the g-pawn: 13 ♖c7+! ♔b6 14 ♖g7!, because his own passed pawn is quite dangerous.

Such an alternative (with consequences that can hardly be calculated and evaluated over the board) is practically still better than the passive defense with the rook on a8. Moreover, it can be improved: a third way exists, although endgame treatises do not mention it.

C) 8...g5! 9 g3

After 9 ♖c3 f4 10 ef gf Black maintains enough counterplay, for example 11 ♖×c6 ♖d8+ 12 ♔c5 d4 13 ♖e6 d3 14 ♖e1 ♖g8=.

9...g4!

Again, 9...d4?! 10 ed ♖e2 is dubious here in view of 11 ♖a5! (11 ♖c3 ♖×h2 and the c6-

pawn is inviolable) 11...h6! 12 a4! (12 ♖×f5 ♖×a2 13 ♖f7+ ♔b6 14 ♖c7 ♖×h2 15 ♖×c6+ ♔b5) 12...♖b2 13 ♖×f5 ♖×b4 14 ♔c5 ♖×a4 15 ♖f7+ and Black's position is difficult.

10 f4 (10 fg fg 11 ♖c3 ♖f8=) 10...♖e4 11 ♖c3 ♖c4∞.

6 a3 ♖a8

The b6-square is perhaps even a worse place for the rook than a8.

7 e4!

White has achieved the maximum on the queenside and cannot improve his position in this sector anymore (7 a4? ♖b8). Therefore he applies a standard method: widening the beachhead! After the exchange of the central pawns the white king attacks the kingside while the rook gets full control over the 5th rank.

7...fe 8 fe de 9 ♔×e4

9-196

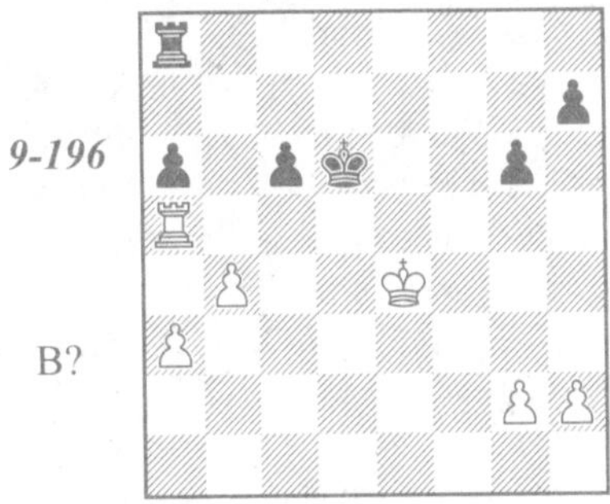

B?

9...♖a7?

Black follows the same fatal policy of passively marking time. He still should have done what we have said: to release the rook from its mission (guarding the a-pawn) by bringing the king to b6: 9...♔c7!. Now 10 ♔f4? gives nothing in view of 10...♖f8+! 11 ♔g3 ♔b6=. Levenfish and Smyslov give the following line: 10 ♖e5!? ♔b6 11 ♖e7 a5! 12 ♖×h7 ab 13 ab ♖a4 14 ♖g7 ♖×b4+ 15 ♔f3 ♖h4! 16 h3 ♖h6 (this is only a short-term passivity: the rook heads for the 8th rank, to take a position behind the passed pawn) 17 ♔g4 c5 18 ♔g5 ♖h8 19 ♖×g6+ ♔b5 20 ♖g7 c4 △ ...♖c8⇄.

I think that White should not force events. The restraining method 10 h4!? ♔b6 11 g4 (11 ♔f4!?) 11...♖f8 12 h5 maintains an indisputable advantage; the question is solely whether it is sufficient for a win.

10 ♔f4 h6

Otherwise the king passes to h6 with a decisive effect: 10...♖a8 11 ♔g5 ♖a7 12 ♔h6 ♔e6 13 g4 △ h4-h5+−.

11 h4 ♔e6 12 ♔g4 ♖a8 13 h5! g5 (13...gh+ 14 ♔×h5 ♖g8 15 g4+−) **14 g3!**

White has created and fixed a new weakness in Black's camp: the h6-pawn. Prior to returning his king to the center, he takes control over the f4-square. 14 ♔f3 is less accurate in view of 14...♖f8+ 15 ♔e4 ♖f4+.

14...♖a7 15 ♔f3! ♖a8 16 ♔e4 ♖a7 17 ♔d4 ♔d6 18 ♔e4 ♔e6 19 ♖e5+! ♔d6

If 19...♔f6, then 20 ♖c5 ♖c7 21 ♖a5 ♖a7 22 ♔d4 ♔e6 23 ♔c5+−.

20 ♖e8 c5

The pawn endgame after 20...♖e7+ 21 ♖×e7 ♔×e7 22 ♔e5 is absolutely hopeless.

21 ♖d8+!

Perfect endgame technique. Flohr had calculated the following line: 21...♔c7 22 ♖h8 cb 23 ♖h7+ (23 ab, of course, also wins) 23...♔b8 24 ♖×a7 ♔×a7 25 ab ♔b6 26 ♔f5 ♔b5 27 ♔g6 ♔×b4 28 ♔×h6 a5 29 ♔×g5 a4 30 h6+−. Other king retreats lose the c5-pawn.

21...♔c6 22 ♖c8+ ♔b6 23 ♖×c5 ♖h7

The rook has changed its parking space, but the new one is as unattractive as the previous.

24 ♖e5 ♔c6 25 ♖e6+ ♔b5 26 ♔f5 ♖f7+ 27 ♖f6 Black resigned.

Tragicomedies

Ilivitsky – Taimanov
USSR ch, Moscow 1955

9-197

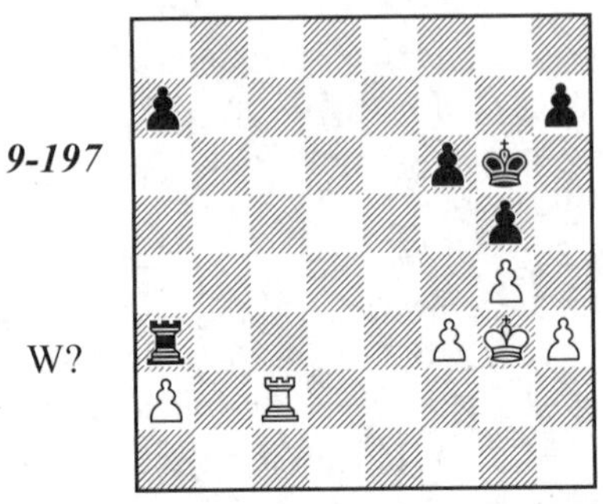

W?

Material is balanced, but Black stands better because his rook is more active. At this moment, both sides would like to improve the structure on the kingside by means of an h-pawn advance, but Black is ready to do it while White is not (because he then loses his f-pawn).

With the pawn sacrifice 1 ♖c6! ♖×a2 (1...h5 2 gh+ ♔×h5 3 ♖×f6) 2 h4 gh+ 3 ♔×h4, White could solve two problems at once: he activates his rook and improves the kingside situation. Then the draw is an easy matter.

1 ♖h2? h5! 2 ♖c2

If 2 gh+ ♔xh5 (△ ...f6-f5-f4+) 3 h4, then 3...g4. 2 h4 could have been a logical continuation but, as Levenfish demonstrated, Black maintains a considerable advantage after 2...hg 3 ♔xg4 (3 hg f5 4 ♖f2 ♔xg5 −+) 3...f5+! (3...♖a4+? 4 ♔g3 gh+ 5 ♖xh4 ♖xa2 leads to a drawn position) 4 ♔g3 g4 5 ♖f2 ♔h5 6 ♖f1 (6 ♔f4 ♖a4+ 7 ♔xf5 g3 −+) 6...♖a4! (△ f4+) 7 fg+ ♖xg4+ 8 ♔f3 ♔xh4! (8...♖xh4 is less accurate: White plays 9 ♖g1, and the pawn endgame after 9...♖g4? is drawn) 9 ♖c1 ♔g5 10 a3 ♖a4 11 ♖c3 a5. Do you recall that we have seen a very similar position in Miles – Webb (diagram 9-98)?

2...h4+

This pawn is very strong: it presses on the white king and fixes the weakness at h3. White's defensive mission is quite hard. In the remainder of the game, however, Taimanov was not precise enough, but his opponent missed his chance to save the game.

3 ♔f2 a6 (an inconceivable move) **4 ♖b2 ♖c3?**

The rook should have stayed on a3 until Black moved the a-pawn well ahead and instead improved his king's position. White would probably still expect a draw after placing his rook on e2 in order to prevent the black king's appearance in the center.

5 ♔g2 a5? (correct was 5...♖a3 followed by ...♔f7)

9-198

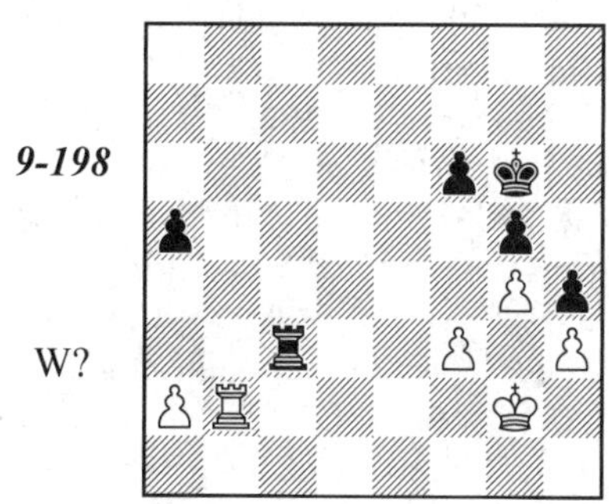

W?

6 ♖f2?

The same passive policy (by the way, the game was annotated by many yet no one revealed the errors that were committed by the players at this stage). Again, White should have taken the opportunity to activate his rook: 6 ♖b7! ♖c2+ 7 ♔g1 ♖xa2 8 ♖a7.

Grandmaster Krogius evaluates the resulting position as lost for White "because of the bad position of White's pawns, and especially that of his king – cut off on the first rank." But what about Black's king? He will stay offside forever, because ...f6-f5 can be always met with ♖a6+ followed by gf. White's rook stays on a7, the king calmly waits on g1-h1; Black pushes his pawn ahead, it comes to a3, what then?

6...♖a3

6...♖c4 was more accurate because White could play 7 f4!? gf 8 ♖xf4 now, this pawn sacrifice deserved earnest attention.

7 ♔f1 ♔f7?!

Black probably rejected 7...f5 because of 8 f4!. A good idea could be 7...♖a4!?, preventing the opponent's activity on the kingside, although White could then cut off the black king by means of 8 ♔g2 ♔f7 9 ♖e2.

8 f4! gf 9 ♖xf4 (△ 10 g5) **9...♔g6 10 ♖f2?**

White made this passive move and resigned, realizing that his position is absolutely hopeless after 10...♖xh3. Meanwhile he could probably hold after 10 ♖f5! He has no time for capturing the h-pawn: 10...♖xa2 11 ♖h5? a4 12 ♖xh4 a3 13 ♖h8 ♖b2 −+; 12 ♖a5 ♔f7! 13 ♖a6 a3 is also hopeless. But he can employ the Vancura idea (see diagram 9-40): 11 ♔g1! a4 12 ♖f4!. Even if Black's king manages to leave the kingside by means of zugzwang: 12...♖a3 13 ♔h2 (13 ♔f2! ♔g7 14 ♔f1!= is even simpler) 13...♔g7!⊙ (13...♔f7 14 g5) 14 ♖b4 (14 ♔g2? ♖g3+ and 15...a3) 14...♔f7 15 ♖e4 ♔f8!⊙ 16 ♖f4 ♔e7, no more progress can be made: the king has no refuge from checks from the side near the passed pawn, therefore the rook cannot abandon the a-file.

Exercises

9-199

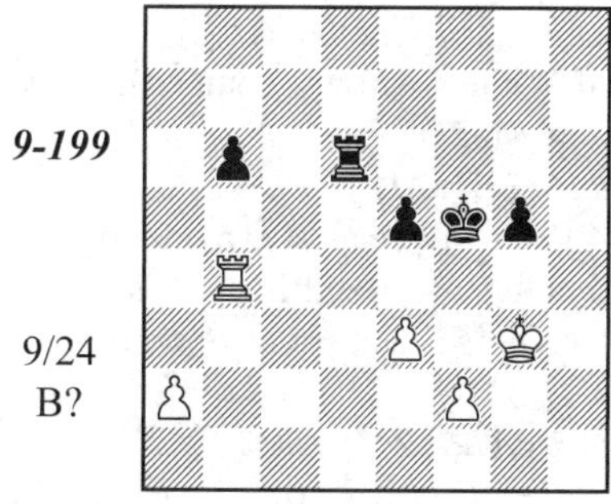

9/24
B?

9-200

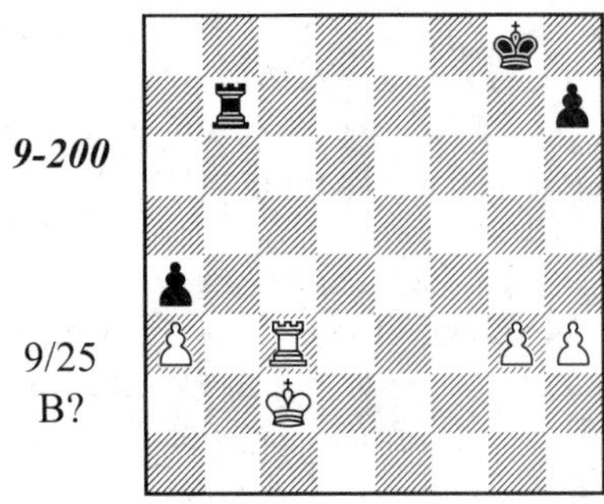

9/25
B?

The King's Activity

The importance of an active king position does not require detailed explanations. A few practical examples are enough.

Flear – Legky
Le Touquet 1991

9-201

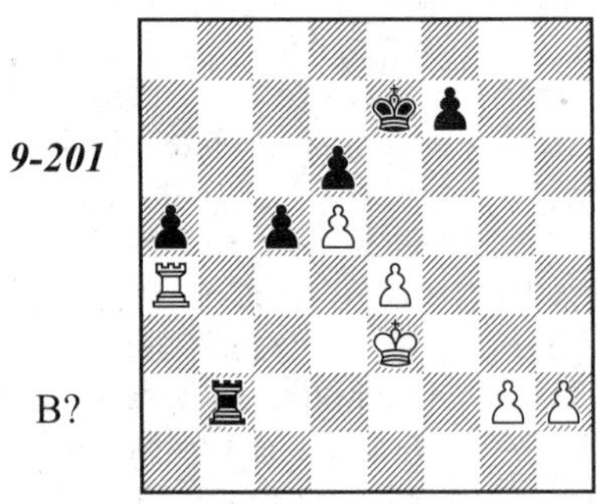

B?

1...♔f6!

King activity is more important than material gain! 1...♖b5? 2 ♔f4 ♔f6 3 g4 is too passive, 1...♖×g2? 2 ♖×a5 ♖×h2 3 ♖a7+ ♔f6 4 ♖d7 ♔e5 5 ♖e7+ leads to an immediate draw.

2 ♖×a5

As Legky wrote, White could deny the king access to e5 by 2 ♔f4!! ♖f2+ 3 ♔e3! (3 ♔g3? ♖f1! △ 4...♔e5) 3...♖×g2 4 ♖×a5, and after 4...♔e5 4 ♖a7 Black, in contrast to the game continuation, has no check along the 3rd rank. If 4...♖×h2 then 5 ♖a7 ♖h6 6 ♖d7 ♔g7 7 e5!? de 8 ♔e4, and White's activity compensates him for the two missing pawns.

2...♔e5! 3 ♖a7?!

Oleg Chebotarev suggested a safer defense: 3 ♖a4!. As before, 3...♖×g2 is useless because of 4 ♖a7, while if Black tries the temporizing 3...f6, then 4 g3.

3...♖b3+ 4 ♔f2 ♔×e4 5 ♖×f7

5 h4 loses to 5...♖b2+ 6 ♔g3 c4 7 h5 c3 8 ♖c7 ♔d3! 9 h6 c2 10 h7 ♖b8. However 5 g4!? f6 6 ♖f7 deserved attention, as after 6...♖b2+ 7 ♔g3 the king does not stand in the way of his pawn.

5...♖b2+ 6 ♔g3 c4!

There is no sense in capturing the d5-pawn; the rapid advance of his own passed pawn is more important.

7 ♖c7

9-202

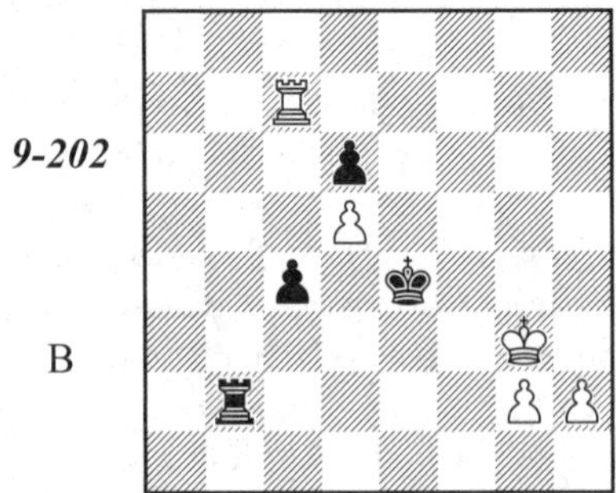

B

7...♔d3?! 8 h4?

The decisive error. 8 ♖c6! was necessary. Legky continues the line with 8...c3 9 ♖×d6 ♖b5! 10 ♖c6 ♖×d5 11 h4 c2 12 ♔h3 ♖d4 13 ♖×c2 ♔×c2∓. As a matter of fact, the final position is won because of the poor position of the white king. However, Flear could achieve a draw by sending his king ahead: 12 ♖×c2! ♔×c2 13 ♔f4 (or 13 ♔g4 ♔d3 14 h5 ♔e4 15 h6) 13...♔d3 13 g4.

Black should have played 7...♔d4!! on his previous move, in order to protect indirectly his d6-pawn (8 ♖c6? c3 9 ♖×d6 c2 10 ♖c6 ♖b3+ and 11...♖c3). After 8 h4 c3 9 h5 ♔d3! (9...c2? is not precise, White saves himself by an immediate activation of his king: 10 ♔f4! ♔d3 11 ♔f5) 10 h6 (10 ♔f4 ♖×g2 11 ♔f5 ♖e2! 12 h6 c2 13 h7 ♖h2 14 ♔g6 ♔d2–+) 10...c2 11 ♔f4 ♖b1 12 g4 (12 h7 ♖h1 13 g4 ♖×h7) 12...c1♕ 13 ♖×c1 ♖×c1 14 ♔f5 ♔d4 15 g5 ♖h1! 16 ♔g6 (16 ♔e6 ♔c5–+) 16...♔e5!–+, and the black king arrives just in time!

But Müller indicated that White could hold this endgame by means of 9 ♔f3!! (instead of 9 h5) 9...c2 (9...♔d3 10 g4 c2 11 g5=) 10 ♔f4! ♔d3 11 ♔f5, for example: 11...♖b5 12 ♖×c2 ♔×c2 13 ♔e6 ♔d3 14 g4 ♔e4 15 g5 ♖×d5 16 g6 ♖e5+ 17 ♔f6 ♖f5+ 18 ♔e6=.

Is this not a bizarre endgame? In a sharp position, White twice had a good reason for granting a tempo to his opponent (2 ♔f4!! and 9 ♔f3!!), while Black's best try also involved a loss of a tempo (7...♔d4!!).

8...c3–+ 9 h5 c2 10 h6 ♖b1 11 ♔f4 (11 h7 ♖h1 12 ♔g4 ♖×h7–+) **11...c1♕+ 12 ♖×c1 ♖×c1 13 g4 ♖f1+ 14 ♔g5 ♔e4 15 ♔g6 ♖g1** White resigned.

Tragicomedies

Bogatyrchuk – Mazel
USSR ch, Moscow 1931

9-203

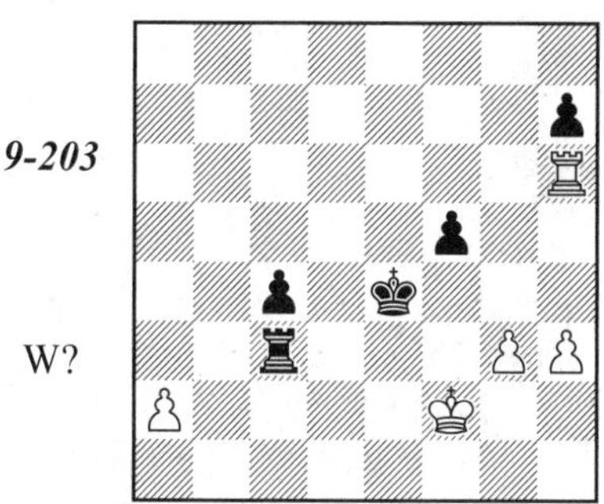

W?

1 ♖×h7?

A grave positional error that allows the white king to be driven to the back rank. After 1 ♖h4+! ♔d3 2 ♖×h7 the game would be drawn (2...♖c2+ can be met with 3 ♔f3).

1...♖c2+ 2 ♔e1 ♖×a2 3 ♖e7+ ♔d3 4 ♖d7+ ♔c2 5 ♖d5? (5 ♔e2!) **5...c3 6 ♖×f5 ♔b1! 7 ♖f1 ♖h2** White resigned.

Exercises

9-204

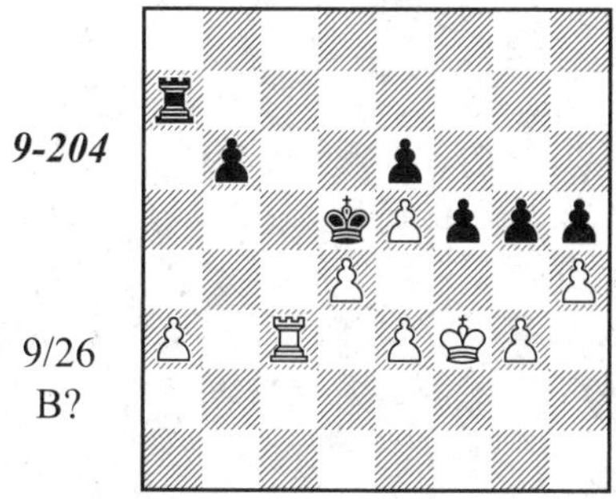

9/26
B?

9-205

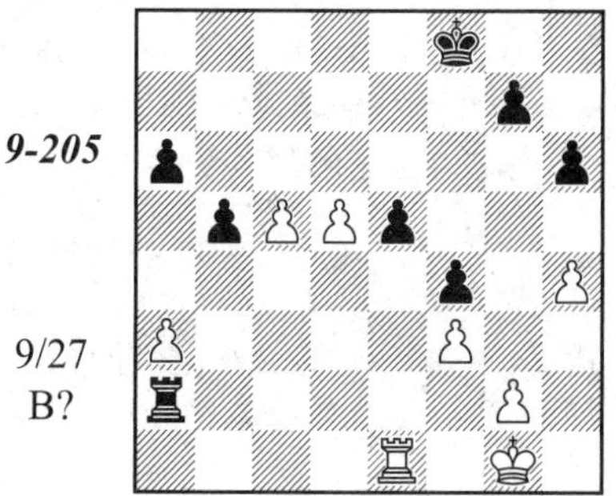

9/27
B?

King on the Edge

A king on the edge of the board is unfavorably placed and not only because the king is far away from the focal point of events. Quite often the opponent creates checkmate threats by sending his own king to attack. This strategy can enable him to bring home an advantage or save a difficult position.

Capablanca – Tartakower
New York 1924

9-206

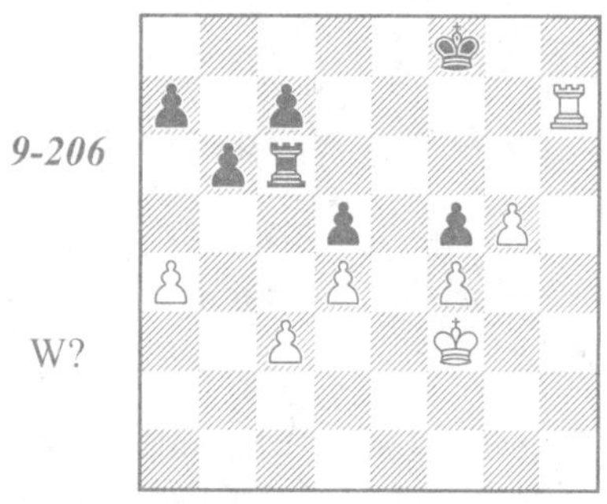

W?

1 ♔g3!

White can exploit the poor position of the black king only by implementing Nimzovitch's principle of the collective advance. The white king must take part in the attack, and one should not grudge a few pawns for this purpose. An unclear position arises after the primitive 1 ♖d7? ♖×c3+ 2 ♔e2 ♖a3 3 ♖×d5 ♖×a4 4 ♖×f5+ ♔g7.

1...♖×c3+ 2 ♔h4 ♖f3?

Simplifies White's task. Nor is 2...♖c1 any better: 3 ♔h5! c5 (3...♖h1+ 4 ♔g6) 4 ♖d7! cd (4...c4 5 ♔g6) 5 ♖×d5 ♖d1 6 ♔g6 d3 7 ♔f6 ♔e8 8 g6 (Fine).

Goldin suggested the toughest defense, which is 2...a6! There has been a lively analytical discussion on this subject in Russian chess magazines.

White can't show the win on 3 ♖d7?! ♖f3 4 g6 ♖×f4+ 5 ♔g5 ♖e4 or 3 g6?! b5 4 ab ab 5 ♔g5 b4 6 ♖f7+! ♔g8! Nor could a win be found after 3 ♔h5 b5 4 a5 ♖c6 5 g6 b4 6 ♔h6 b3 7 ♖h8+ ♔e7 8 ♖b8 ♖c2!, or 4 ab ab 5 ♔g6 ♔g8! (△ ...♖c6+) 6 ♖h1 b4 7 ♔×f5 ♔g7!

I. Zaitsev found the key to this position: 3 ♔h5! b5 4 ♔g6!! ♔g8 (nor does 4...ba 5 ♔×f5 a3 6 ♖h6 save him) 5 ♖g7+! ♔f8 6 ♖f7+ ♔g8 7 ♖f6!, with the unstoppable threat of 8 ♖×a6. Had White exchanged pawns earlier on b5, his opponent could have parried the threat by 8...b4 9 ♖a6 ♖a3! 10 ♖c6 ♖c3=.

3 g6! ♖×f4+ 4 ♔g5 ♖e4 (4...♖×d4 5 ♔f6 is also hopeless) **5 ♔f6!** (the f5-pawn is useful for the time being – it serves as an umbrella) **5...♔g8 6 ♖g7+!**

Good endgame technique: prior to capturing the pawn, it is useful to worsen the position of the black king just a little.

6...♔h8 7 ♖×c7 ♖e8 8 ♔×f5!

It is time to kill the f5-pawn, otherwise it could move ahead (8 ♔f7 ♖d8 △ ...f4⇄). As we know, a knight pawn, unlike a bishop pawn, cannot be promoted against a passive defense with a rook on the back rank.

8...♖e4 9 ♔f6 ♖f4+ 10 ♔e5 ♖g4 11 g7+!

This is where the zwischenschach on move six tells: White brings his pawn under the protection of the rook with a tempo (11...♖×g7 12 ♖×g7 ♔×g7 13 ♔×d5+–).

11...♔g8 12 ♖×a7 ♖g1 13 ♔×d5 ♖c1 14 ♔d6 ♖c2 15 d5 ♖c1 16 ♖c7 ♖a1 17 ♔c6 ♖×a4 18 d6 Black resigned.

Lilienthal – Smyslov
Leningrad/Moscow 1941

9-207

B

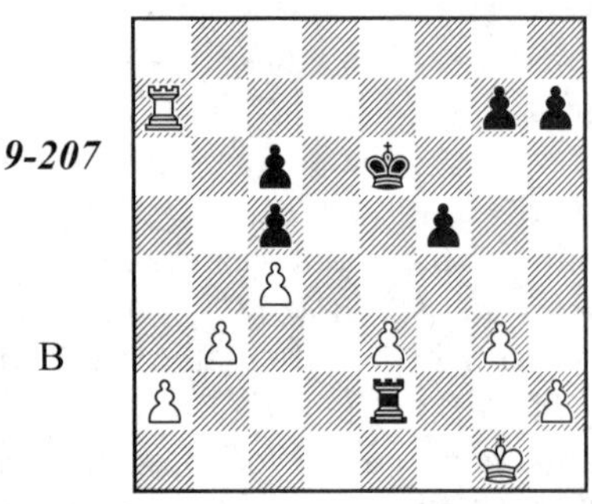

Almost all Black's pawns are vulnerable but Smyslov easily compensates himself for the missing material by means of an attack against the white king.

1...g5! 2 ♖×h7 ♖×a2 3 ♖h6+ ♔e5 4 ♖×c6 ♔e4 5 ♖×c5 f4! (prepares an umbrella against checks along the f-file) **6 ef ♔f3 7 h3 ♖a1+** Draw.

White has four (!) extra pawns in the final position.

Exercises

9-208

9/28
W?

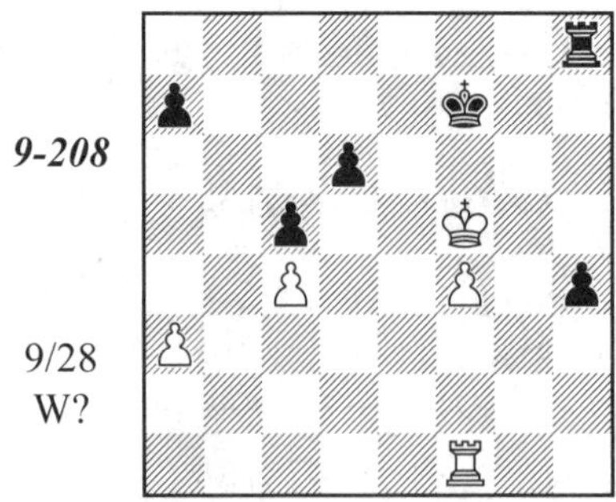

Cutting the King Off

An important technique in rook-and-pawn endings is cutting the hostile king off from strategically important areas. From his own pawns that need protection, from our pawns that he could attack, from our passed pawn that could otherwise be stopped by him, or from his passed pawn that could be assisted by the king.

Janetschek – U. Geller
Skopje ol 1972

9-209

W?

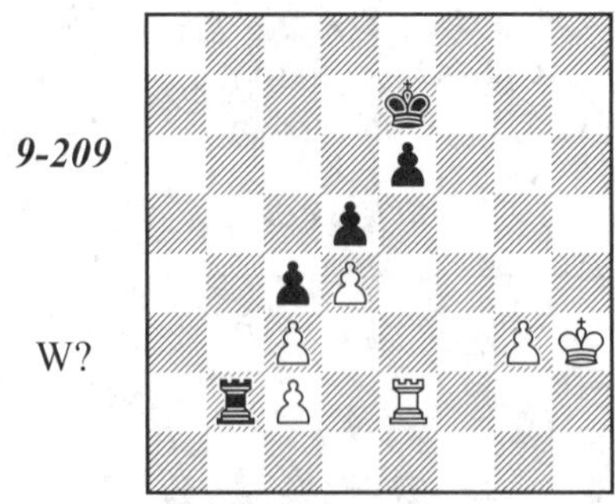

1 ♖f2!

Cutting the king off from the passed pawn, White considerably aggravates the threat of its advance.

1...♖a2?

Black wants to snap up one of White's queenside pawns but ignores his fundamental problem. Only a defense by frontal checks could give him chances for salvation: 1...♖b8! 2 g4 ♖h8+ 3 ♔g3 ♖g8. To achieve progress, White should have played ♖h2, but then the black king comes to the f-file. Only then the rook might go ahead against White's pawns.

2 g4 ♖a3 3 ♔h4 ♖×c3 4 g5 ♖e3 5 g6 ♖e1 6 ♖f7+ ♔d6 7 g7 ♖g1 8 ♔h5 Black resigned.

Savon – Zheliandinov
Riga 1964

9-210

B?

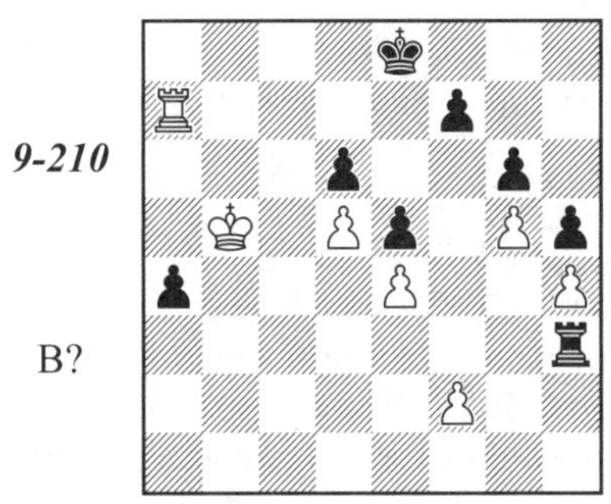

The actual continuation was 1...♖×h4? 2 ♔c6 ♖×e4 3 ♔×d6 ♔f8 4 ♖a8+ ♔g7 5 ♔e7+– (the d-pawn will cost Black a rook) 5...♖d4 6 d6 e4 (6...h4 7 d7 h3 8 d8♕ ♖×d8 9 ♖×d8 h2 10 ♖d1 a3 11 ♖h1 a2 12 f3⊙ ♔g8 13 ♔f6+–) 7 d7 e3 8 fe ♖e4+ 9 ♔d6 ♖×e3 10 d8♕ ♖d3+ 11 ♔e5 Black resigned.

Black should have cut the king off from the d6-pawn.

1...♖c3! 2 ♖×a4 ♖c5+

The pawn endgame that arises after 2...♔d7 3 ♖a7+ ♖c7? (3...♔e8!) 4 ♖×c7+ ♔×c7 5 ♔a6 is lost. This evaluation is not quite obvious because Black has a chance for a pawn breakthrough: ...f7-f6 and, after g5×f6, ...g6-g5. However, White wins the race that happens thereafter (doubters may check this fact for themselves).

But there is no sense in calculating sharp lines because we have a fortress after this check. The white king cannot cross the c-file.

3 ♔b6 ♖c1 4 ♖a8+ ♔d7 5 ♖a7+ ♔e8 6 ♖c7 ♖a1! 7 ♔c6 ♖a6+ 8 ♔b7 ♖a1=.

Tragicomedies

Timoshchenko – K. Grigorian
USSR ch(1), Frunze 1979

9-211

B

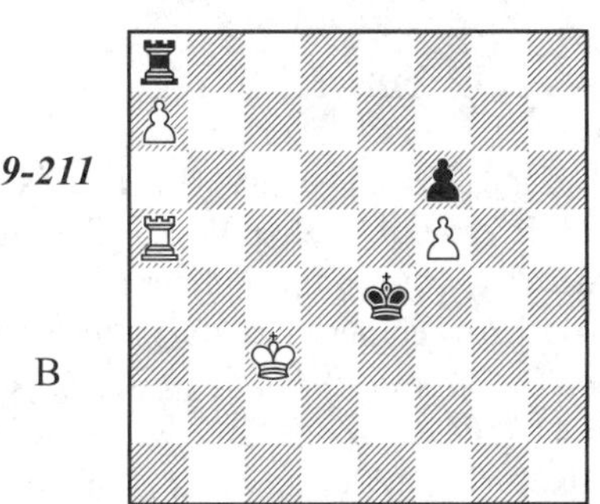

One single move was actually made in the game:

1...♔e3? 2 ♖a4!

Black resigned. Now when his king is cut off from the f5-pawn, he will be inevitably put into zugzwang: 2...♔f3 3 ♔d3 ♔g3 4 ♔e3⊙ ♖e8+ (4...♔h3 5 ♔f3⊙) 5 ♔d4 ♖a8 6 ♔c5+–.

The best defense is 1...♔f4 2 ♔d4 ♔g4. In *Chess Informant*, Timoshchenko evaluated the position that arises as drawn, despite the extreme passivity of the black rook. 3 ♔e4 is met with 3...♖e8+!, and White does not have 4 ♔d5?? in view of 4...♖e5+, while an attempt to cross the 5th rank with the king loses the f5-pawn: 3 ♔d5 ♔×f5 4 ♔c6+ ♔e4 5 ♔b7 ♖×a7+ 6 ♖×a7 f5=.

However one can easily improve this line for White. After the capture on f5, it is enough to win if the black king is temporarily cut off from the approach to the lower half of the board: 4 ♖a4! (instead of 4 ♔c6+?) 4...♔g5 5 ♔c6 f5 6 ♔b7 ♖e8 7 a8♕ ♖×a8 8 ♖×a8+–.

Exercises

9-212

9/29
B?

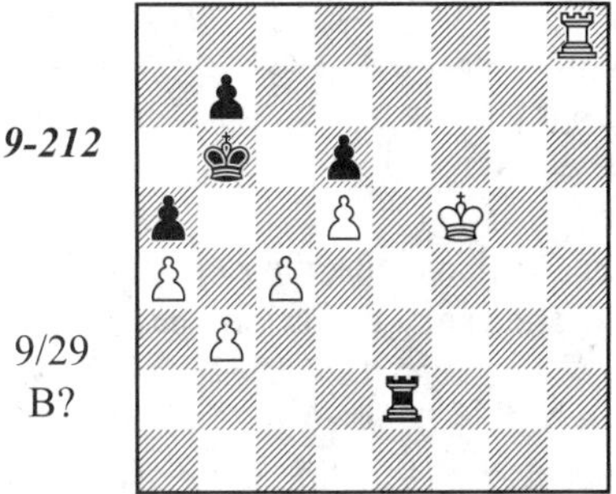

Akiba Rubinstein's Masterpiece

As Tartakower wrote, "Rubinstein is a rook ending of a chess game that was started by God a thousand years ago." I want to conclude the chapter on rook-and-pawn endings with an example from the creative work of the outstanding Polish grandmaster. It is rumored that after the game finished (a final stage of which we shall study) Rubinstein's respected opponent, grandmaster Spielmann, shouted: "Akiba, if you lived in the Middle Ages you would have been burned at the stake: what you do in rook endgames can only be called witchcraft!"

Spielmann – Rubinstein
St. Petersburg 1909

9-213

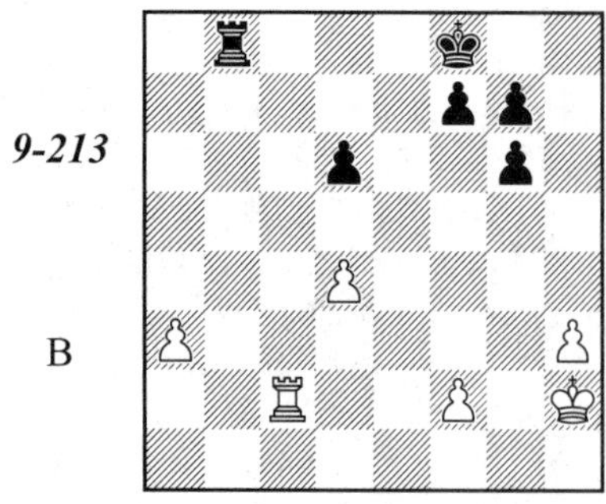

B

A positional disadvantage that occurs often is an abundance of "pawn islands." White has four islands against Black's two; this means that White has more vulnerable pawns that cannot protect each other. Therefore his position is inferior.

1...♖a8!

The first stage of Black's plan is to attack White's pawns so that the white rook will be chained to their protection. Chasing after material gain with 1...♖b3? would have been a grave error, because after 2 ♖a2 ♖d3 3 a4 ♖×d4 4 a5 ♖c4 5 a6 the white rook is actively placed behind a passed pawn while the black rook must stand passively on a8.

2 ♖c3

Spielmann thinks that the rook stands even worse on a2 and explains this judgment with the line 2 ♖a2 ♖a4 3 ♔g3 ♔e7 (3...♖×d4? 4 a4∞) 4 ♔f3 ♔e6 5 ♔e4 d5+ 6 ♔e3 ♔f5. However, the final position of this line is far from clear. And secondly, instead of 6 ♔e3 White can play 6 ♔d3!? ♔f5 (6...♔d6 7 ♔c3 ♔c6 8 ♔d3 ♔b5 9 ♖b2+) 7 ♔c3 ♔e4 8 ♖e2+. As we can see, the rook behind the pawn has some hidden potency although it is currently passive. It chains the black rook; for as soon as the black rook leaves a4 the white rook supports the advance of the a-pawn.

Levenfish and Smyslov also analyze 5...g5!? (instead of 5...d5+). This continuation is more dangerous, but their line shows that White maintains sufficient defensive resources: 6 ♖a1 f6 7 ♖a2 f5+ 8 ♔d3 ♔d5 9 ♔c3 ♖c4+ 10 ♔b3 ♖×d4 11 a4 ♖d3+ (11...♔c6 12 a5 ♔b7 13 a6+ ♔a7 14 ♖a5 ♖f4 15 ♖d5 ♖×f2 16 ♖×d6 ♖f3+ 17 ♔c4 ♖×h3 18 ♖g6 g4 19 ♔b5 ♖b3+ 20 ♔a5=) 12 ♔b4 ♖×h3 13 a5 ♖h8 14 a6 ♔e4 15 a7 ♖a8 16 ♔b5 ♔f3 17 ♔b6=.

However the position of the rook on the 3rd rank has its own virtues, but Spielmann fails to exploit them.

2...♖a4 3 ♖d3 ♔e7

The second stage: the king goes to the center.

4 ♔g3

4 d5 is met with 4...g5! (4...♔f6 5 ♖f3+) 5 ♔g2 ♔f6 6 ♖f3+ ♔g6 (△ ♖d4) 7 ♖d3 f6! △ ...♔f5.

4...♔e6 5 ♔f3?

In my opinion this is an obvious positional error that was somehow left unnoticed by the annotators. Letting the black king pass to d5, White condemns himself to a passive defense that, as we know, forebodes gloom in rook-and-pawn endings. He could get excellent chances for a draw by playing 5 ♖e3+! ♔d7 (5...♔d5 6 ♖e7), and now either 6 ♖f3!? f6 7 d5 ♖d4 8 ♖b3 or 6 ♖d3 ♔c6 7 ♖c3+! ♔d5 8 ♖c7 ♖×a3+ 9 ♔g2 ♔e6 10 d5+ ♔f6 11 ♖d7 ♖a6 12 h4.

5...♔d5 6 ♔e2?!

Another inaccuracy. A good idea was to restrain Black's pawns on the kingside by means of 6 h4!. It's worth mentioning that here, as well as later on, White is not afraid of 6...♖×d4, because he has a distant passed pawn in the ensuing pawn endgame after 7 ♔e3.

6...g5!

The third stage of the plan: it is important to improve the pawn structure on the kingside.

7 ♖b3

9-214

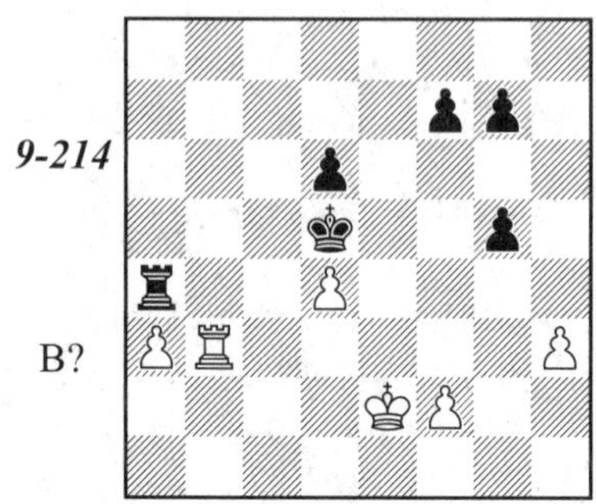

B?

7...f6!

7...♖×d4? can be met either with 8 ♖b5+ or with 8 ♖d3. In case of 7...♔×d4!? 8 ♖b7 White has considerably reduced the number of pawns. Although Kasparov claims the ending after 8...f6! (8...♖×a3? 9 ♖×f7 ♖×h3 10♖×g7∓) 9 ♖×g7 ♖×a3 10 h4! gh 11 ♖g4+ ♔c3 12 ♖×h4 ♖a2+ to be won for Black, it is not clear whether his judgment is correct. In addition, Black should take

8 ♖g3!? (Δ ♖g4+) 8...♖a5 9 a4 into account.

Rubinstein's move is safer. 8 ♖b7 can be met with 8...♖×a3 9 ♖×g7 ♖×h3 (9...♔×d4 brings us to the above-mentioned line) 10 ♖g6 (10 ♖f7 ♔e6! 11 ♖f8 f5 12 ♖e8+ ♔d5 13 ♖f8 ♔e4 Δ ...g4, ...♖f3−+) 10...♔e6 11 ♖g8 ♖h4 12 ♔e3 ♔d5. This position, as Kasparov has proven, is winning, and here I agree with him. One who fights for a win should avoid pawn exchanges; in this line, an extra pawn pair remains on the board compared with the 7...♔×d4 line.

8 ♔e3 ♔c4 9 ♖d3

9 ♖b7 ♖×a3+ 10 ♔e4 d5+ 11 ♔f5 ♖×h3 12 ♖×g7 ♖f3+ is hopeless.

9...d5

Black has improved his pawn structure and optimally placed his king. Now it is time for the rook. It has completed its mission on a4 and may find a new application for its talents.

10 ♔d2 ♖a8 11 ♔c2

11 ♔e2? ♖b8 12 ♔d2 ♖b2+ 13 ♔e3 ♖×f2−+ (or 13...♖a2⊙).

11...♖a7! 12 ♔d2 ♖e7⊙ 13 ♖c3+!

The last chance to display activity. A continued passive policy would have led to an inglorious demise: 13 ♔c2 ♖e2+ 14 ♖d2 ♖×d2+ 15 ♔×d2 ♔b3!−+, or 13 ♖e3 ♖×e3! (13...♖b7!) 14 fe (14 ♔×e3 ♔b3) 14...f5! 15 ♔c2 g6⊙ 16 ♔d2 (16 ♔b2 g4) 16...♔b3−+.

13...♔×d4 14 a4! ♖a7 15 ♖a3 ♖a5!

The pawn must be stopped as soon as possible. Black intends to approach it with his king: either simply for winning it or for blocking it and releasing the rook from its passive position.

16 ♖a1 ♔c4

9-215

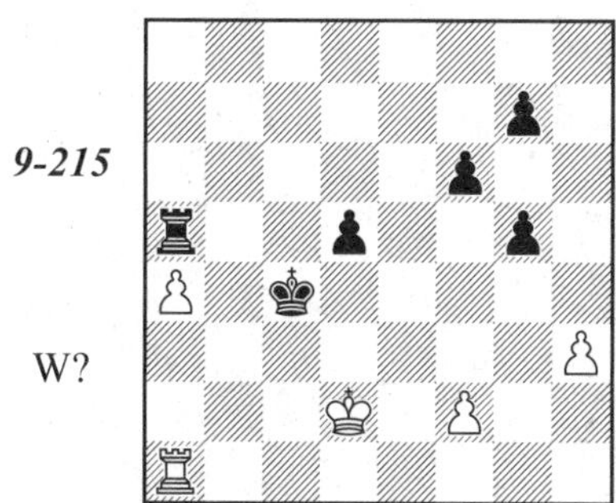

W?

17 ♔e3?!

White should have tried 17 ♖c1+! ♔b4 18 ♖b1+! ♔×a4 19 ♔d3 (19 ♖b7!?). The position of the black king on the edge could give some practical chances. For example, after 19...♖b5? 20 ♖a1+ ♔b4 21 ♔d4 it would be Black's turn to seek a draw.

Levenfish and Smyslov analyzed 19...♖c5! 20 ♔d4 (20 ♖b7? ♖c4 21 ♖×g7 ♔b5) 20...♖c2 21 ♖b7 ♖×f2 22 ♖×g7 and concluded that White maintains chances for a draw. Kasparov extended this line in the *Encyclopedia of Chess Endings* with 22...♖d2+! 23 ♔c5 ♔b3 24 ♖g6 ♔c3 25 ♖×f6 d4 and evaluated the final position as winning.

9-216

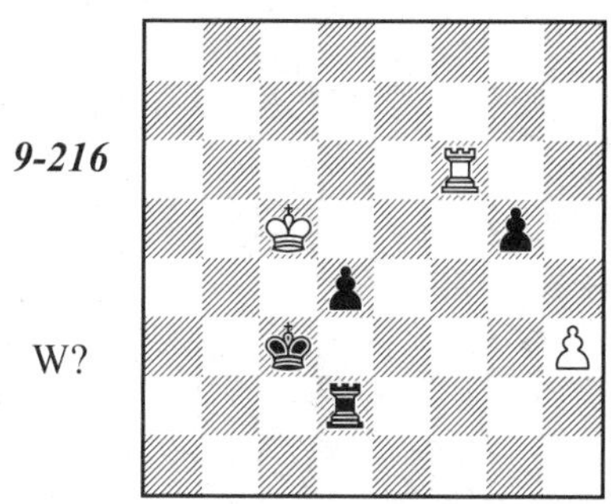

W?

I think he is incorrect here: White saves himself with 26 ♖a6! d3 27 ♖a3+ ♔b2 28 ♔b4 ♖d1 29 ♖b3+ (29 ♖c3!) 29...♔c2 30 ♔c4 d2 31 ♖c3+ ♔b2 32 ♖b3+ ♔a2 33 ♔c3=, or 26...♔d3 27 ♔d5 ♔e3 28 ♖e6+ ♔f4 29 ♖f6+ ♔g3 30 ♖g6=. It seems that, in spite of previous errors, Spielmann's position remained tenable.

17...d4+ 18 ♔d2 ♖f5!

Black's precise 15th move tells: the rook may leave the blockade position. If 19 a5 then 19...♖×f2+ 20 ♔e1 ♖b2! (rather than 20...♖h2? 21 ♖a4+ ♔b5 22 a6!) 21 a6 ♖b8 22 a7 ♖a8 23 ♔d2 ♔c5 24 ♔d3 ♔b6 25 ♔×d4 ♖×a7−+ (Spielmann). However 25 ♖b1+! ♔×a7 26 ♔×d4 (Müller) is more stubborn, and Black's win is still not a simple matter.

19 ♔e1 ♔b4!

A typical reassignment of pieces: the king will block the passed pawn while the rook will attack White's weak pawns.

20 ♔e2 ♔a5 21 ♖a3

After 21 ♖b1 ♔×a4 22 ♖b7 Kasparov suggests 22...d3+ 23 ♔×d3 ♖×f2 24 ♖×g7 ♖f3+ 25 ♔e4 ♖×h3−+. This line is erroneous: White holds by means of 25 ♔c4! ♔a3 (25...♖f4+ 26 ♔d5 ♔b3 27 ♔e6) 26 ♖g6 ♔b2 27 ♔d5 ♔c3 28 ♔e6. However 22...g6!−+ is much stronger.

21...♖f4 22 ♖a2

22 ♔f1 ♖h4 23 ♔g2 ♔b4! 24 ♖a1 d3 25 a5 d2 26 a6 ♖h8 27 a7 (27 ♔f1 ♔c3) 27...♖a8 28 ♔f3 ♖×a7 –+ (Spielmann).

22...♖h4 23 ♔d3 (23 ♖a3 ♔b4) **23...♖×h3+ 24 ♔×d4 ♖h4+ 25 ♔d3**

25 ♔e3 ♖×a4 26 ♖d2 ♔b6!, and if 27 ♖d7 then 27...♖a7.

25...♖×a4 26 ♖e2 (△ 27 ♖e7) **26...♖f4!**

26...♔b6? is wrong: 27 ♖e6+! and 28 ♖e7.

27 ♔e3 ♔b6 28 ♖c2 ♔b7!

Accurate to the last! Black prevents the maneuver ♖c8-g8 and prepares to cross the c-file with his king after ...♖a4-a6-c6.

29 ♖c1 ♖a4 30 ♖h1 ♔c6 31 ♖h7 ♖a7 32 ♔e4 ♔d6 33 ♔f5 g6+! 34 ♔×g6 ♖×h7 35 ♔×h7 ♔e5 36 ♔g6 g4 White resigned.

Chapter 10

ROOK VS. KNIGHT

The Knight Alone

In the chapter, "Rook vs. Pawns" (the portion devoted to "Promoting the Pawn to a Knight"), we were introduced to the most important knight-vs.-rook positions for the practical player. Let's revisit the basic conclusions:

Usually, a knight draws easily against a rook. But there are exceptions:

When the knight becomes separated from the king, then it can sometimes be trapped;

When the knight is in the corner, it will be lost through zugzwang.

We should also note that the knight stands poorly at g7 (or b7).

Al'Adli
IX Century

10-1
$

W

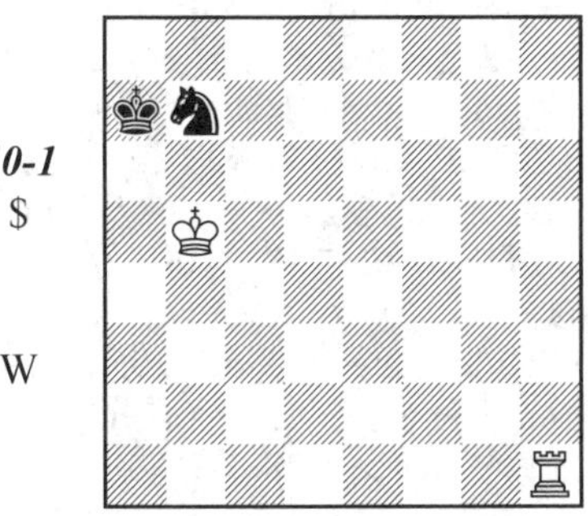

Several such endings were discovered in Arab manuscripts from the Middle Ages. At that time, the game was *shatranj*, a game which differed markedly from contemporary chess, although the kings, rooks and knights in fact moved the same as they do today.

White can win in several different ways.

1 ♖d1! (Averbakh says this is the simplest) **1...♔b8 2 ♔a6! ♘c5+**

No better is 2...♔c8 3 ♖c1+ ♔b8 4 ♖b1 ♔a8 5 ♔b6 ♘d6 (5...♔b8 6 ♔c6 ♔a8 7 ♔c7) 6 ♖d1+-.

3 ♔b6 ♘a4+ (3...♘b7 4 ♖d7 ♔a8 5 ♖h7) **4 ♔c6 ♘c3 5 ♖e1**, and the knight is soon lost.

There are times when a lone knight can hold even against rook and pawn - and not just in those cases where the pawn may be attacked and captured. It can be enough just to prevent the enemy king from reaching its pawn.

Em. Lasker - Ed. Lasker
New York 1924

10-2
$

W

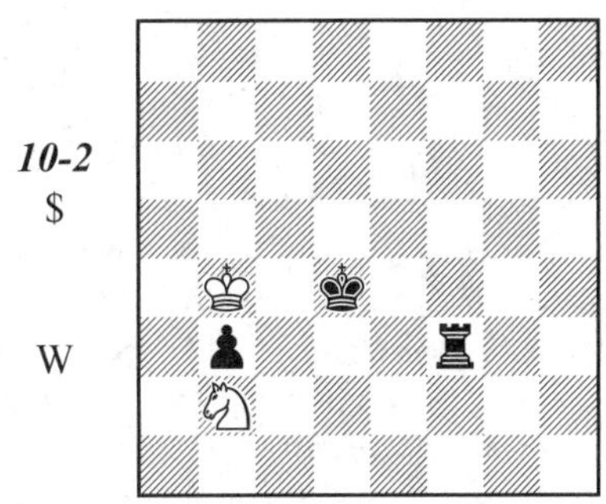

1 ♘a4 ♖e3 2 ♘b2 ♔e4 3 ♘a4 ♔f3

Black can only improve his position if he can get his king over to the pawn. And the only way to get there is by bringing it around the rook. White must take measures against ...♔e2-d2-c2-+.

4 ♔a3!

Averbakh believes White can also play 4 ♘b2 ♔e2 5 ♘c4 (5 ♔a3 ♔d2! 6 ♘c4+ ♔c1-+) 5...♖g3 6 ♔a3, followed by 7 ♔b2. However, Black in fact wins here with 6...♖c3! 7 ♘a5 (7 ♘d6 ♔d3 8 ♔b2 ♖c6!; 7 ♘e5 ♔e3 8 ♔b2 ♔d4) 7...♔d3! 8 ♔b2 ♖c5! 9 ♘xb3 ♖b5 10 ♔a2 ♔c3.

4...♔e4

If 4...♔e2, then 5 ♘c5 ♔d2 6 ♔b2!, and the pawn goes.

5 ♔b4

Of course not 5 ♘c5?? ♔d4 6 ♘xb3 ♔c4-+.

5...♔d4 6 ♘b2 ♖h3 7 ♘a4 ♔d3 8 ♔xb3 ♔d4+ Drawn.

Exercises

10-3

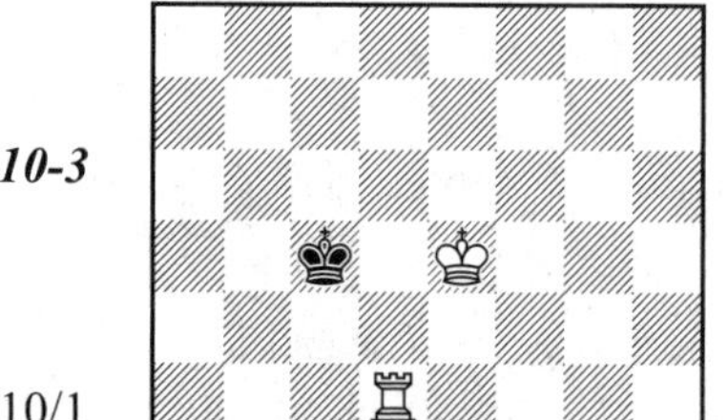

10/1
W?

10-4

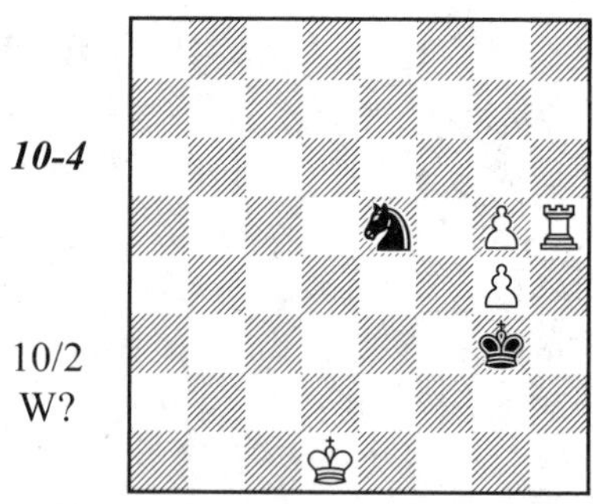

10/2
W?

Rook and Pawn vs. Knight and Pawn

Now let's look at the situation where the pawns are on the same or adjacent files (that is, when neither pawn is passed). In order to win, it will be necessary for the stronger side to attack the pawn with his king - which the weaker side may sometimes be able to prevent by a proper piece placement. ***The best position for the knight is one from which it controls the invasion square, while simultaneously attacking the enemy pawn.***

de Firmian - Alburt
USA ch 1983

10-5

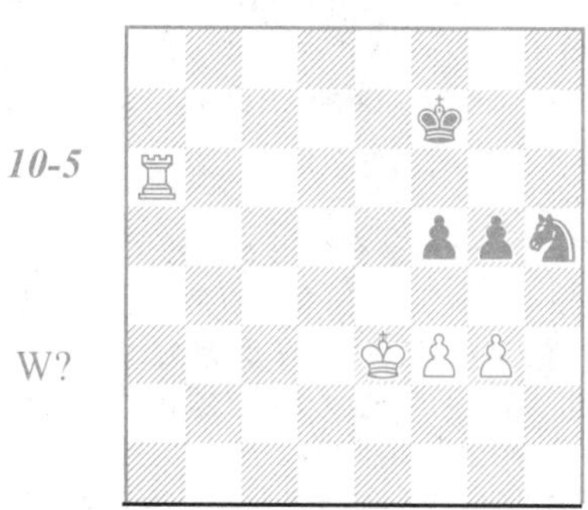

W?

1 g4? fg 2 fg ♘f6 leads to the ideal defensive setup for Black, wherein the knight guards important squares, while simultaneously attacking the g4-pawn - an effortless draw.

There are two things to keep in mind in situations of this type. The first is, that if the whole position were moved one rank higher, White would win by sacrificing the exchange. And secondly, White would prefer the pawns not to be blocking one another - that is, it would be better to have his pawn on g2, than g4, because then he would not have to defend it.

1 f4! gf+

No better is 1...g4 2 ♔d4! ♘×g3 3 ♔e5+-.

2 gf

Black could draw, if his knight were at e6 or g6. From h5, although the knight would be attacking the pawn, it would not control the invasion squares d4 or e5.

2...♔g7 3 ♖b6

The immediate 3 ♖a1 ♔f6 (intending ...♘g7-e6) 4 ♖h1 ♘g7 5 ♖h6+, followed by 6 ♔d4+- was also possible.

3...♔h7

After 3...♔f7 4 ♖h6 ♘f6 5 ♔d4 ♘g4 6 ♖a6 ♔e7 7 ♔d5 ♔f7, we reach a position examined in 1941 by Reuben Fine. His analysis: 8 ♔d6 ♔f6 9 ♖a8 ♔f7 10 ♖d8⊙ ♔f6 11 ♖f8+ ♔g6 12 ♔e6 ♘e3 (12...♘h6 13 ♖f6+ ♔g7 14 ♖×h6) 13 ♖f7⊙ ♘c2 14 ♖f6+ ♔g7 15 ♔×f5+-.

4 ♖b1

As Müller indicates, the immediate 4 ♔d4!? also wins: 4...♘×f4 5 ♔e5 ♘g6+ (after 5...♘h5+ 6 ♔×f5 ♘g7+ we come to the Al'Adli position: see diagram 10-1) 6 ♔f6!. For example: 6...f4 7 ♖b1 ♘f8 8 ♖d1!⊙ (rather than the hasty 8 ♖h1+ ♔g8 9 ♖g1+ ♔h7 10 ♔f7? in view of 10...♔h6! 11 ♔×f8 ♔h5=) 8...f3 (8...♔g8 9 ♖d8), and only now 9 ♖h1+ ♔g8 10 ♖g1+ ♔h7 11 ♔f7+-.

4...♔g6 5 ♖h1 ♘f6

The same reply wins after 5...♘g7 or 5...♔h6.

6 ♔d4 ♘d7 7 ♔d5 ♘f6+ 8 ♔e5 (8 ♔e6!) **8...♘d7+ 9 ♔e6 ♘f8+?!** (9...♘c5+) **10 ♔e7** Black resigned.

In the next diagram, the knight at e4 prevents the king's invasion of the kingside; but it will be vulnerable to attack by ...♔e6-e5. In this case, its place is on h5. In his detailed study of these kinds of positions, Averbakh showed that White can get a draw.

Larsen - Tal
Bled, cmsf (7) 1965

10-6

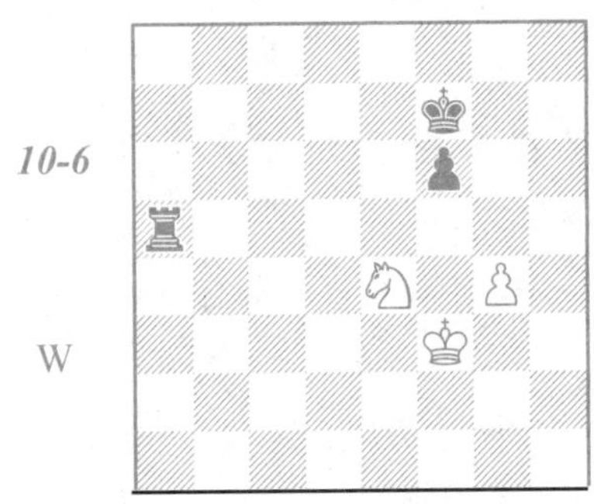

W

1 ♘g3 ♔e6 (1...♔g6 2 ♘e4!) **2 ♔f4 ♖a4+ 3 ♔f3 ♔e5 4 ♘h5! ♖a8!? 5 ♔e3!=**

Let's look at the possibilities after 5 ♔g3?!.

White holds the draw after 5...♖a3+ by retreating his king to the 2nd rank (6 ♔h4? would be a mistake: 6...♖b3⊙ 7 ♘g3 ♖b8 8 ♘h5 ♖h8 9 ♔g3 f5 10 ♔f3 f4-+).

Black therefore continues 5...♖h8 6 ♘f4 ♔e4 (after 5 ♔e3! the king could not occupy the e4-square).

10-7

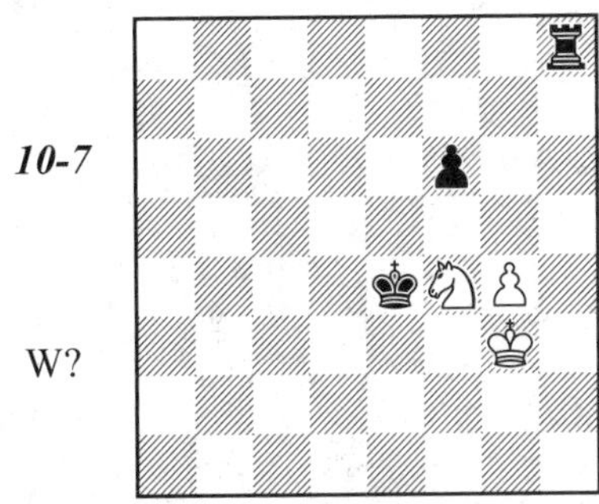

W?

Tal subjected the position after 7 ♘h3 to exhaustive analysis, and found a subtle winning method.

7...♖g8? is insufficient after 8 ♘f2+ ♔e3 9 ♘d1+ ♔d2 (9...♔e2 10 ♘c3+ ♔d3 11 ♘d5 f5 12 ♘e7! ♖×g4+ 13 ♔f3=) 10 ♘f2 ♔e2 11 ♘e4 f5 12 ♘f6 ♖g6 13 ♔f4! ♖×f6 14 gf ♖f8 15 ♔e4! (shouldering, preventing the outflanking by the king) 15...♔f2 16 ♔f4!=.

Black must get his king to e3 first, but more importantly, he must get his rook from the 8th to the 7th rank; only then can he attack the g4-pawn.

7...♖c8! 8 ♘f2+ ♔e3 9 ♘h3 (9 ♘d1+ ♔e2, and he cannot check from c3 now; 9 g5 f5 10 ♘d1+ ♔e4 11 ♘f2+ ♔d5 12 ♔f4 ♔e6 13 ♘d3 ♖c4+ 14 ♔f3 ♖g4-+) 9...♖c4 10 ♘f2 ♖c7! 11 ♘h3 ♖g7 12 ♘f2 f5 13 ♘d1+ ♔e2 14 ♘f2 f4+ 15 ♔×f4 ♔×f2 16 g5 ♖g8!⊙ (the decisive handoff of the right to move to the opponent) 17 ♔g4 ♔g2! (zugzwang, again) 18 ♔f5 ♔h3-+, or 18 ♔h5 ♔f3-+. As you can see, Black's basic idea is the same as the one in the Réti study of Diagram 8-10.

Tal thought 7 ♘h5! impossible, because of the reply 7...f5. However, White saves himself then by 8 ♘f6+ ♔e5 9 ♘d7+ ♔e6 (9...♔d6 10 ♘b6! ♖g8 11 ♘c4+) 10 ♘c5+ ♔d5 11 ♘d3 ♖g8 12 ♘f2=.

Let's return to the game, where Tal, despite lengthy maneuvering, was unable to refute Averbakh's evaluation.

5...♖b8 6 ♔f3 ♖e8 7 ♘f4 ♔d4 8 ♘h5 ♖e1 9 ♔f2 ♖e4 10 ♔f3 ♔e5 11 ♔g3 ♖e3+ 12 ♔f2 ♖b3 13 ♔g2 ♖b7 14 ♔f3 ♖b8 15 ♔e3 ♖g8 16 ♔f3 ♖h8 17 ♘g3 ♖h7 18 ♔e3 ♖h8 19 ♔f3 ♖h2 20 ♔e3 ♖b2 21 ♘h5 ♖b3+ 22 ♔f2 ♖d3 23 ♔g2

10-8

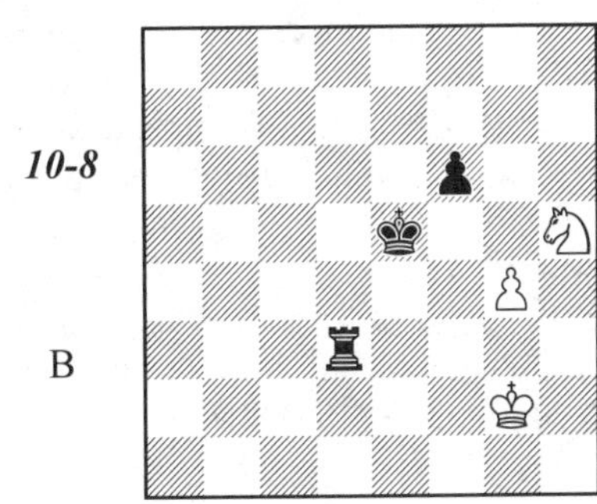

B

23...♔e4 24 ♘×f6+ ♔f4 25 ♔f2

After 25 g5??, Black wins either by 25...♖g3+ △ 26...♖×g5; or by 25...♔×g5 26 ♘e4+ ♔f4 27 ♘f2 ♖d2⊙. And 25 ♔h2? is a mistake, owing to 25...♖d6 26 g5 ♖d8!-+.

25...♖d2+ 26 ♔e1 ♖d6 27 g5

If it weren't for the g-pawn, the knight, cut off from its king, would be lost.

27...♔f3 28 ♘h7 (forced) **28...♔e3 29 ♘f6 ♔f3 30 ♘h7 ♖d5**

Or 30...♖g6 31 ♔d2 ♖g7 32 ♘f6 (32 ♘f8) 32...♖×g5 33 ♔c3=.

31 g6 ♖d7 32 ♘g5+ ♔e3 33 ♘e6 ♖d2 34 ♘f4 ♖h2 35 ♘d5+ ♔f3 36 ♔d1 ♖g2 37 g7 Drawn

In the next diagram we have the same position as in the previous example, except that it has been shifted slightly. As Averbakh and Bronstein's joint analysis showed, this tiny difference changes the evaluation of the position.

Taimanov - Bronstein
USSR chsf, Leningrad 1946

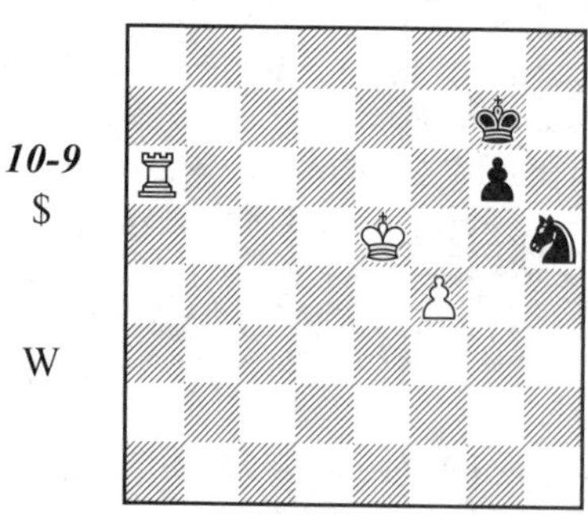

1 ♖a7+ ♔f8

We already know the refutation of 1...♔h6: 2 ♖b7⊙ ♘g3 3 ♖b3 ♘h5 4 ♖h3 ♔g7 5 f5 ♔f7 6 f6+-.

Taimanov was unable to find the winning line: after 2 f5? gf, the game ended in a draw.

White needs to sacrifice the f4-pawn, not trade it. However, the immediate 2 ♔e6? ♘×f4+ 3 ♔f6 would not work: 3...♘d5+ 4 ♔×g6 ♘e7+ (4...♔e8) 5 ♔f6 ♘g8+ 6 ♔e6 (the drawing position we saw several times in the "Rook vs. Pawns" chapter) 6...♘h6 7 ♖h7 ♘g8!= (but not 7...♘g4??+-).

2 ♖d7! ♔g8 (2...♔e8 3 ♖h7 ♔f8 4 f5+-) **3 ♔e6! ♘×f4+**

3...♔f8 doesn't help: 4 ♖f7+ ♔g8 (4...♔e8 5 ♖f6! ♔d8 6 ♔f7 or 6 ♔e5) 5 ♔e7 ♔h8 6 ♔f8 ♘g3 7 ♖g7 ♘h5 8 ♖×g6+-.

4 ♔f6 ♘h5+

Also hopeless are 4...g5 5 ♔×g5, and 4...♔h8 5 ♖d4! g5 6 ♖d7 g4 (6...♔g8 7 ♔×g5) 7 ♖d4 ♘g2 8 ♖×g4 ♘e3 9 ♖e4 ♘d5+ 10 ♔f7.

5 ♔×g6 ♘f4+ 6 ♔g5 ♘e6+ 7 ♔f6 ♘f4 (7...♘f8 8 ♖d8⊙) **8 ♖d4 ♘e2**

Now that the knight has been cut off, the rest is simple.

9 ♖g4+ ♔f8 10 ♖c4 ♔g8 11 ♔g6 (11 ♔e5) **11...♔f8 12 ♔g5 ♘g3 13 ♔g4 ♘e2 14 ♔f3 ♘g1+ 15 ♔g2 ♘e2 16 ♔f2+-.**

When Artur Yusupov showed me this ending he had just played, in the following diagram, I said right at the start that White should place his knight on h3, and his pawn at g4. Why? From h3, the knight not only hinders the approach of the black king, but is also prepared to hit the h7-pawn with ♘g5. If Black advances that pawn to h6, then he will have to consider White's possible g4-g5.

Sturua - Yusupov
Baku jr 1979

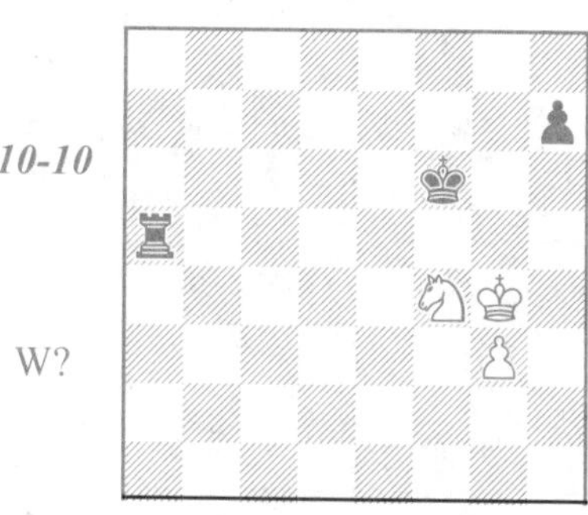

After further detailed analysis, Yusupov showed that in fact, White can draw by retreating the knight, while the game continuation ought to have lost.

Thus: 1 ♘h3! (intending ♔h4, g4) 1...♖a4+ (1...♔e5 2 ♘g5 or 2 ♔g5) 2 ♔h5 ♖a3.

2...♔f5 3 ♘g5 ♖a1 4 g4+ ♔f6! is another try. Now 5 ♘×h7+?? ♔g7 6 ♘g5 ♖h1+, or 5 ♘f3?? ♖h1+ 6 ♘h4 h6⊙ is bad; but 5 ♘h3! ♖h1 6 ♔h4 is sufficient.

3 ♔h4 ♔e5 4 g4 ♖a1 (4...h6 5 ♘f2!, but not 5 g5? h5! 6 ♘g1 ♔f5!) 5 ♔g3 h6 (5...♖h1 6 ♔g2) 6 ♔h4 ♖h1 (6...♔e4 7 g5) 7 ♔g3 ♔d4 8 g5=.

1 ♘h5+? ♔e5 2 ♔g5 ♖a6 3 ♘f4 ♔e4 4 ♔g4

4 ♘h3!? was also worth a look here. On 4...♔f3? White saves himself with 5 ♔h5! h6 (5...♔×g3 6 ♘g5=) 6 g4 ♔g3 7 g5=.

But Black wins with 4...♖g6+! 5 ♔h4 ♔f5! (5...♔f3? 6 ♘g5+ ♔g2 7 ♔h5 ♖g7 8 ♔h6=) 6 ♘f4 ♖h6+! 7 ♘h5 ♖a6 (7...♔e4!?) 8 g4+ (8 ♘f4 ♖a2! 9 ♘h3 ♖g2! 10 ♘f4 ♖h2+ 11 ♘h3 h5!, winning by zugzwang; or 9 ♔h3 ♔e4 10 ♔g4 ♖a5, reaching the same position that occurs later in the game) 8...♔e4 9 ♔g3 (9 ♔g5 ♔f3 10 ♘f6 ♖×f6-+; 9 g5 ♔f3 10 ♘f6 ♖a1-+) 9...♖a3+ 10 ♔f2 (10 ♔h4 ♔f3 11 ♘f6 ♖a6!) 10...h6 11 ♔g2 ♖b3 12 ♔f2 ♖f3+ 13 ♔g1!? ♔d3! 14 ♔h2 ♔e2 15 ♔g2 ♔e3⊙ 16 ♘g3 (16 ♔h2 ♔f2-+) 16...♔f4 (16...♖f2+) 17 ♘f5 ♔×g4 18 ♘×h6+ ♔f4 19 ♘f5 ♖d3!-+.

4...♖a5 5 ♘e6

5 ♘h3 h6! 6 ♔h4 ♔f3 7 ♘g1+ (7 g4 ♖a4 8 ♘g1+ ♔f2 9 ♘h3+ ♔g2, and wins by zugzwang) 7...♔g2 8 ♘h3 (8 ♘e2 ♖e5! 9 ♘f4+ ♔f3 10 ♘h3 ♖e1-+) 8...♖a1 9 ♘f4+ (9 ♔g4 h5+! 10 ♔h4 ♖h1-+) 9...♔f3 10 ♔h5 ♔×g3-+.

5...h6 6 ♔h4

6 ♘f4 ♖g5+ 7 ♔h4 ♔f3 8 ♘h5 ♖g4+ 9 ♔h3 ♖a4 10 ♘f4 ♖a1 11 ♔h2 ♔g4-+.

6...♖e5 7 ♘d8

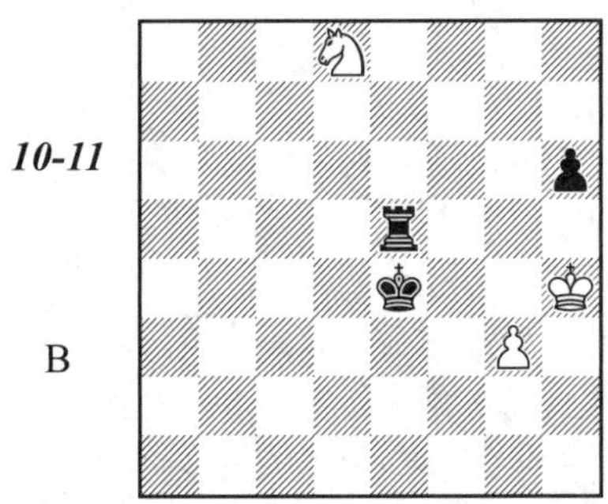

7 ♘f4 ♔f3 8 ♘h3 ♖e1-+; 7 ♘f8 ♖d5-+.

Black has achieved a great deal in driving the knight away from the pawn. Here, he could win by 7...♖e7!? (threatening 8...♔d5 and 9...♖d7) 8 ♔h5! ♔f5 (9...♔d5? 9 ♔g6) 9 g4+ (9 ♘c6 ♖e4 10 ♘d8 ♖e1 11 ♔×h6 ♔f6 12 ♔h5 ♖c1!, etc.) 9...♔f6! 10 ♔×h6 (10 ♘c6 ♖e4!) 10...♖g7 11 ♘e6 ♖g8 12 ♔h7 ♖×g4 13 ♘f8 ♔f7. On the other hand, the move played is no worse.

7...♔f5!? 8 ♘c6

8 ♘f7 is met by 8...♖d5! (but not 8...♖e1? 9 g4+! ♔f6 10 ♘d6) 9 ♘×h6+ (9 ♔h5 ♔f6+) 9...♔g6 10 ♘g8 (10 ♘g4 ♖h5#) 10...♖d7-+.

8...♖e4+! 9 ♔h5 ♔e6

9...♔f6 was simpler: 10 ♔×h6 ♖c4 11 ♘b8 (11 ♘a5 ♖g4 or 11...♖c1 12 ♔h7 ♖c5) 11...♔e6, intending 12...♔d6, and the knight is caught.

10 ♔×h6

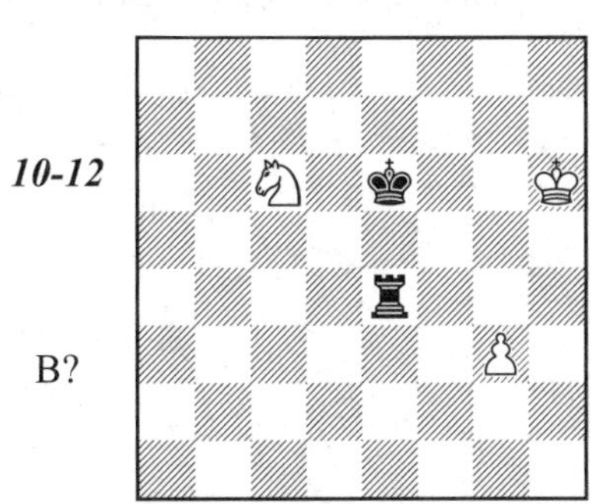

10...♔d7?!

Black had the time to take the g3-pawn: 10...♖g4! 11 ♔h5 (11 ♘d8+ ♔f6) 11...♖×g3 (11...♖c4!? keeps the knight out of a5) 12 ♘d4+ ♔e5 13 ♔h4 (13 ♘e2 ♖g2) 13...♖e3-+.

Yusupov believed that it was here he let slip the win; however, that came later.

11 ♘a5! ♖b4!

11...♖g4? 12 ♘b3! ♔e6 (12...♖×g3 13 ♘d4; 12...♔d6 13 ♘d2) 13 ♘d2! ♖×g3 14 ♘e4 and 15 ♘g5+.

12 ♔g7! ♔c7?

Here's the fatal error! 12...♔d6? would not have won, either, in view of 13 ♔f7! (13 ♔f6? ♔d5! 14 g4 ♖×g4 15 ♘b7 ♖g8!-+) 13...♔d5 14 g4 ♖×g4 15 ♘b7 ♔c6 16 ♘d8+ ♔d7 17 ♘e6=. The only right way was 12...♔e6!! 13 ♘c6 ♖c4, for example: 14 ♘a5 ♖c5 15 ♘b3 ♖c3 16 ♘d4+ ♔e5 17 ♘e2 ♖e3-+, or 14 ♘d8+ ♔e7 15 ♘b7 ♖g4+ 16 ♔h6 ♖×g3 17 ♘c5 ♖e3!-+.

13 ♔f6! ♔d6

13...♔b6 14 g4! ♖×g4 15 ♘b3 ♖b4 (15...♔b5 16 ♔f5) 16 ♘c1!=.

14 g4 (14 ♔f7 ♔d5 15 g4=) **14...♖×g4 15 ♘b7+ ♔d5 16 ♘d8 ♖f4+ 17 ♔g6 ♖f1 18 ♘f7 ♔e6 19 ♘g5+ ♔e7 20 ♘e4 ♖f4** Drawn.

Tragicomedies

Suba - Chiburdanidze
Dortmund 1983

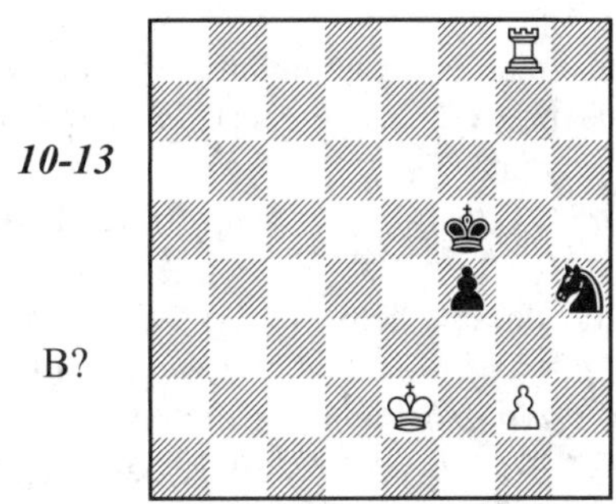

It's a draw after 1...♘g6! 2 ♔d3 ♘e5+ 3 ♔d4 f3!? (3...♘g6 is also possible) 4 ♖f8+ ♔g4 5 ♔×e5 fg 6 ♔e4 ♔g3.

But in the game, Black played **1...♔e4?? 2 g3!+- ♘f3 3 ♖g4 ♘d4+ 4 ♔f2 ♘e6 5 gf ♘d4 6 f5+**, and Black resigned.

Exercises

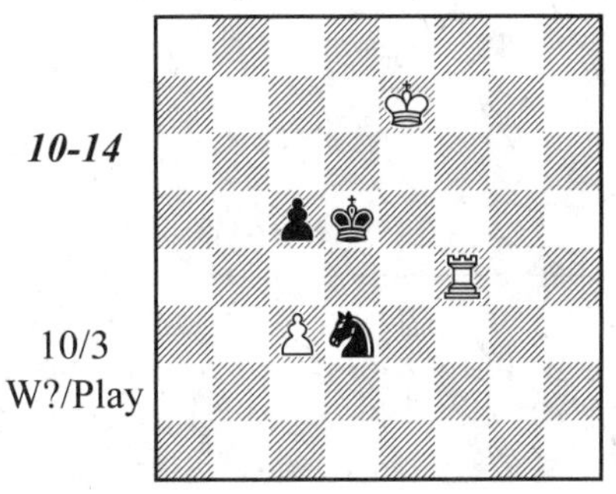

Multi-Pawn Endgames

Pawns on One Side of the Board

When there are three pawns against three, or even two pawns against two pawns, all on the same side of the board, the rook will, in the overwhelming majority of cases, win against the knight. But if the weaker side has an extra pawn, then he has real chances to draw.

Fridstein - Klaman
USSR ch tt, Riga 1954

10-15

W

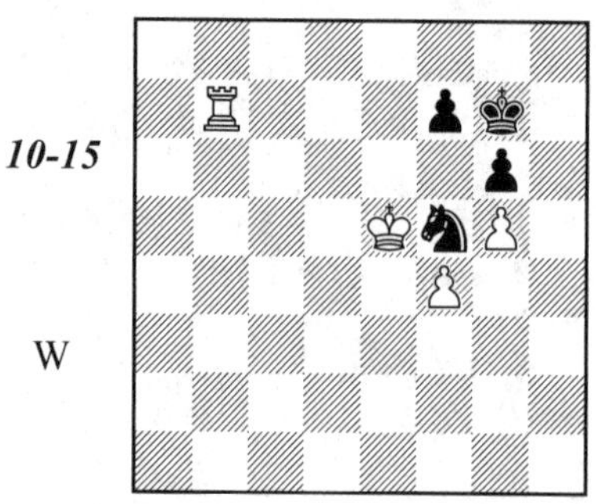

White's plan is a routine and simple one: attack the f7-pawn. The king gets to e8, and then forces its way into f6.

1 ♖b8⊙♘g3 (1...♔h7 2 ♔f6) **2 ♔d6 ♘f5+**

2...♘h5 doesn't help: 3 ♖b4 ♔f8 4 ♔d7 wins by zugzwang. Note that ***zugzwang is used again and again to bring home the advantage.***

3 ♔d7 ♔h7 4 ♔e8 ♔g8 5 ♖d8! ♔g7 6 ♖d7 ♔g8 7 ♖c7⊙ ♘g7+ 8 ♔e7 ♘f5+ 9 ♔f6 ♘d6 10 ♖c6 ♘e4+ 11 ♔e7 ♔g7 12 ♖f6! Black resigned.

Vidmar - Alekhine
San Remo 1930

10-16

W

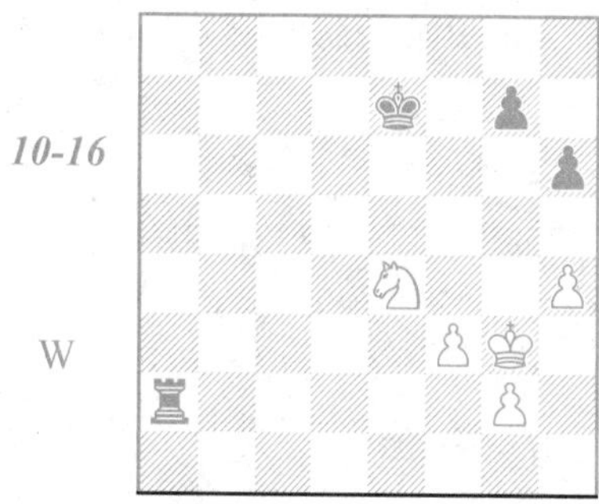

Alekhine considered the position won, based on the outcome of the game. Afterwards, however, safe defensive methods were discovered.

One of these was proposed by Leykin in 1940. He held that White would do well to place his pawn at g4. Afterwards, his knight could combine threats against the enemy pawns with control over the access routes into his camp (the same strategy we saw in the preceding section). The best move: 1 ♔h3! (intending 2 g4).

A) 1...♖a3 2 ♔g4 ♔e6 3 ♔f4 ♔d5 (3...g6 4 g4) 4 h5 ♔d4 5 ♘d6 ♔d3 6 ♘f5 ♖a4+ 7 ♔g3 ♖a5 8 ♔f4 ♖a7 9 g4 ♔e2 10 ♔g3= (10...♖a3 is met by 11 ♘d4+, or even by 11 ♘h4). In the final position of this variation, the knight would be just as favorably posted, were it to stand anywhere covering the f4-square - on e6 or g2, for instance.

B) 1...♔e6 2 g4! ♔e5 3 ♔g3 g6 (3...♔d4 4 h5! ♔e3 5 ♘d6=) 4 ♘f2 ♖a3 (4...♔d4 5 ♘h3 ♔e3 6 ♘f4, and the knight occupies its ideal square - f4) 5 ♘h3 ♖a4. Here, 6 ♘f2? ♔d4 7 ♘h3 ♔e3 is bad, but White has 6 ♔f2!, without fear of 6...h5 (6...♔d4 7 ♘f4) in view of 7 gh! ♖×h4 8 hg!=.

1 ♘f2?! ♔e6 2 ♘d3 ♔f5 3 ♘f4 ♖a4 4 ♘d3 ♖c4 5 ♘f2 ♖c6 6 ♘h3 ♔e5 7 h5

Alekhine considered this a bad move, since the h5-pawn, unsupported by its neighboring g-pawn, now comes under attack by the black rook. However, as we shall see, the draw is not lost yet.

Still, 7 ♘f4 ♖c2 8 ♘h3 ♖d2 9 ♘f4 ♖a2 10 ♘h3 ♔d4 11 ♘f4 ♔e3 is safer.

10-17

W

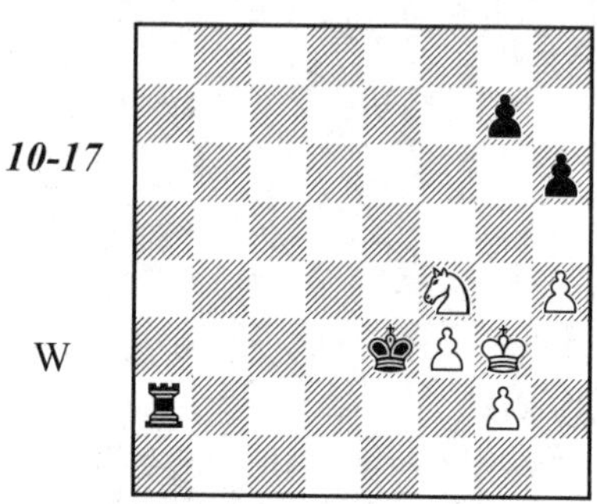

Here, Alekhine continued: 12 ♘e6 ♖a7 13 ♘f4 ♖a6! 14 ♘h3 ♔e2 15 ♘f4+ ♔f1, rightly considering this position won. In fact, 16 ♘h3 fails to 16...♖g6+, and 16 h5 is met by 16...♖a5 17 ♔h2 ♔f2 18 ♔h3 ♖g5 19 ♔h4 ♔e3-+.

But the defense can be strengthened. If we leave the king at h2 and the knight at e4, the incursion of the black king is not dangerous: it will be driven off the f1- and f2-squares by checks at g3 and e4. This plan was successfully employed in the game Kuzmin - Miles (Bath, ech tt 1973), in which the same position arose, but with the black rook at a4.

12 ♘h5 ♖a6 13 ♔h2! ♔f2 14 ♘g3 ♖e6 (14...♖g6 15 ♘e4+ ♔f1 16 ♘g3+ ♔f2 17 ♘e4+ ♔e3 18 ♘g3=) 15 ♘e4+ ♔e3 16 ♔g3 ♖g6+ 17 ♔h2 ♔f4 18 ♘f2 ♖d6 19 ♘e4 ♖d5 20 ♘g3 ♖a5 21 ♔h3 g6 22 ♘e2+ ♔e3 23 ♘g3 ♔f4 24 ♘e2+ ♔e3 Drawn.

By the way, even after 12 ♘e6 ♖a7, it's not yet too late to play 13 ♘c5!, or 13 ♔h2! intending ♘c5-e4=.

7...♖c2! 8 ♘f4

8 ♘f2 ♔d4 9 ♘e4 ♔e3 10 ♘d6 (10 ♔h3 ♔f4-+) 10...♖c5 11 ♔h4 ♖g5-+.

8...♖d2

10-18

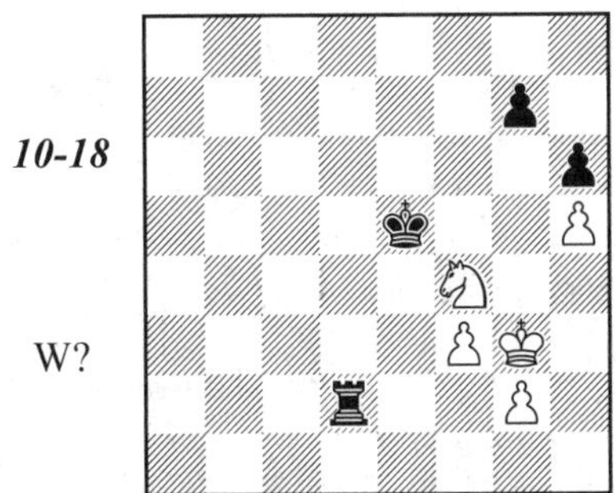

W?

9 ♘h3?

Here's the fatal error. As Miles pointed out, it was not yet too late to transpose into one of the drawn Leykin positions, with the pawn on g4, by playing 9 ♘g6+! ♔d4 (9...♔f5 10 ♔h3! intending g4+, ♔g3, ♘f4=) 10 ♘h4 ♖a2 (10...♔e3 11 ♘f5+) 11 ♔f4! ♔d3 12 g4 ♔e2 13 ♔g3=.

9...♔d4 10 ♘f4 ♔e3 11 ♘e6

Also hopeless are 11 ♘h3 ♖a2 12 ♘f4 ♖a5 13 ♘e6 ♖e5, and 11 ♔g4 ♖d4 12 g3 ♖a4 13 ♔f5 ♔xf3 (but not Fine's suggestion 13...♖a5+? 14 ♔g6 ♖g5+, in view of 15 ♔h7! ♔xf3 16 ♘e6 ♖xh5 17 ♘xg7, with a drawn position).

11...♖d5! 12 f4

12 ♔h4 ♖e5! 13 ♘xg7 ♖g5 14 ♘e6 ♖xg2-+ (Alekhine).

12...♖f5! 13 ♔g4 ♖f6! (13...♔e4? 14 g3) **14 f5** (14 ♘xg7 ♖xf4+)

(See diagram top of next column)

14...♖f7?!

A bit of dawdling - which doesn't spoil anything. The strongest continuation was 14...♔e4! 15 ♘xg7 (15 ♘c5+ ♔d5 16 ♘d3 ♔d4

10-19

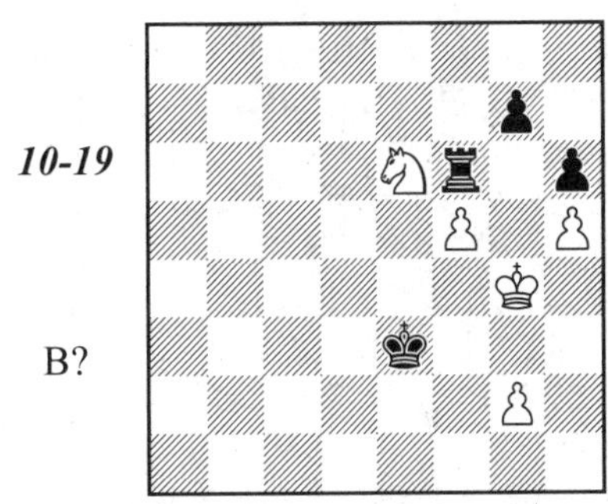

B?

17 ♘f4 ♔e4) 15...♖f7 16 ♘e6 (16 ♘e8 ♔e5! 17 f6 ♖f8 18 ♘c7 ♖xf6-+) 16...♖xf5, and White's in a bad way. For example:

17 g3 ♖e5 18 ♘d8 (18 ♘f4 ♖g5+ 19 ♔h4 ♔f3-+) 18...♖g5+ 19 ♔h4 ♔f3 20 ♘f7 ♖g4+ 21 ♔h3 ♖xg3+ 22 ♔h4 ♔f4! 23 ♘xh6 ♖g7! 24 ♔h3 ♖h7-+;

17 ♔h4 ♔e5 18 ♘c5 ♖f4+ 19 ♔h3 ♖d4 20 g3 ♔d6! 21 ♘b3 (21 ♘a6 ♖a4) 21...♖d1 22 ♔h4 ♔d5 23 g4 ♖d3 24 g5 (24 ♘c1 ♖e3 25 g5 ♖e4+) 24...♖xb3 25 gh ♔e6 26 h7 ♖b8 27 ♔g5 ♔f7-+ (analysis by Fine).

15 g3?!

After 15 ♘d8!, Alekhine would have had to return to the above-cited variation 15...♖f6 16 ♘e6 ♔e4!.

15...♔e4 16 ♘c5+ ♔d4! 17 ♘b3+ ♔e5 White resigned.

Tragicomedies

Romanishin - Rodriguez
Moscow 1985

10-20

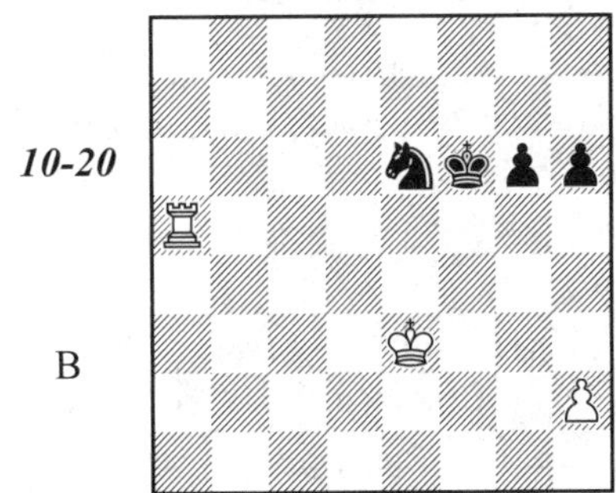

B

1...h5

1...♘g7, intending 2...♘f5, was simpler; but the text doesn't spoil anything.

2 ♔e4 ♘g5+ 3 ♔f4 ♘e6+ 4 ♔e3

White triangulates with his king, in order to give the move back to his opponent.

4...♘g5 5 h4

5 ♔f4 ♘e6+ 6 ♔e4 ♘g5+ 7 ♔d5 ♘f3.

5...♘e6?

An unfortunate retreat. The draw was available with 5...♘f7! (intending 6...g5) 6 ♔f4 ♔g7 (as Rodriguez and Vera noted, 6...♘h6 was also possible, for instance: 7 ♖a6+ ♔g7 8 ♔e5 ♘g4+ 9 ♔e6 g5=) 7 ♖a6 ♔h7 8 ♖a7 ♔g7 9 ♔e4 ♔f6 10 ♖a6+ ♔g7 11 ♔d5 g5 (11...♘h6? 12 ♔e6 ♘f5 13 ♖a4) 12 ♔e6 gh (12...♘d8+; 12...♔g6 13 ♔e7+ ♔g7) 13 ♖a7 ♔g6 14 ♖×f7 ♔g5 15 ♔e5 h3=.

6 ♔e4 g5 7 ♖f5+! ♔g6 8 ♔e5 gh 9 ♔×e6 h3 10 ♔e5 h2 11 ♖f1 ♔g5 12 ♖h1 ♔g4 13 ♖×h2 h4 14 ♖g2+! ♔f3 15 ♖a2

Black resigned, in view of 15...h3 (15...♔g4 16 ♖a4+! ♔g3 17 ♔f5) 16 ♔f5 ♔g3 17 ♖a3+ ♔g2 (17...♔h4 18 ♔f4 h2 19 ♖a1 ♔h3 20 ♔f3) 18 ♔g4 h2 19 ♖a2+ ♔g1 20 ♔g3 h1♘+ 21 ♔f3+-.

Exercises

10-21

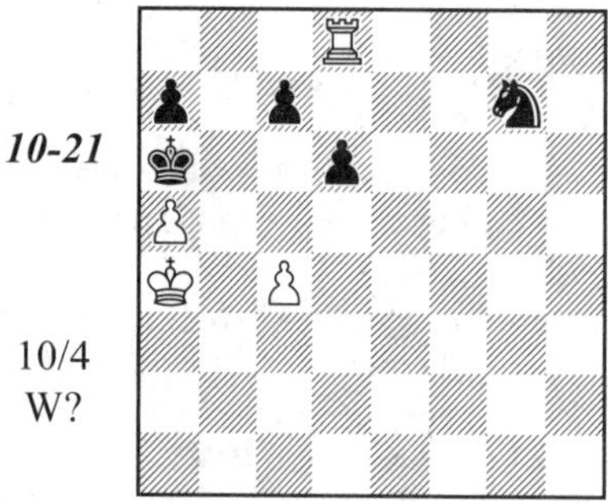

10/4
W?

Pawns on Both Sides

The rook is a much more mobile piece than the knight. When the battle takes place on both sides of the board, especially when there are passed pawns involved, the rook is usually stronger.

Matanovic - Larsen
Portoroz izt 1958

10-22

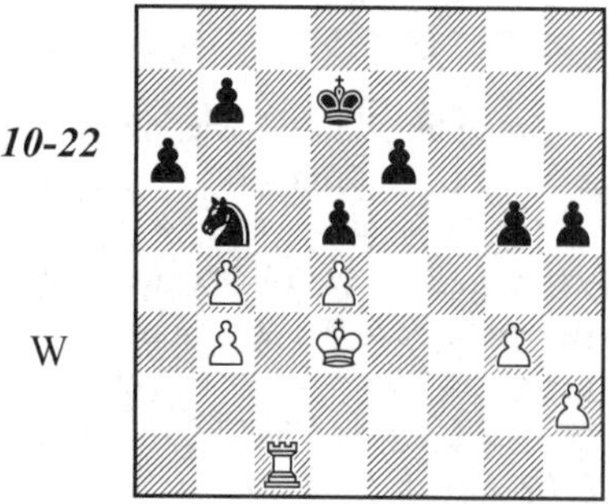

W

Black's position looks solid. His king can defend the invasion squares on both open files, "c" and "f." But White shatters his defenses by alternating threats to various parts of the board.

1 ♖e1 (threatening 2 ♖e5) **1...♘d6 2 b5!**

White gets nothing from 2 ♖e5 ♘f5 3 h3 g4! But now, after 2...♘×b5, White will play 3 ♖e5+- while taking the b-pawn opens up the a-file.

2...ab 3 ♖a1 h4

If 3...b4 4 ♖a8 ♘c8, then 5 ♔e3 ♔c7 6 h4! gh 7 gh (threatening ♔f4) . On 7...♘d6, the most precise way is 8 ♖f8! ♔d7 (8...♘f5+ 9 ♖×f5!) 9 ♔f4 ♔e7 10 ♖h8 ♘f5 11 ♔e5 ♘×h4 12 ♖h7+ ♔d8 13 ♔×e6+-. 7...♘e7! is better for Black - from here, the knight is ready to go not just to f5, but also to c6. This would force White into the sharp line 8 ♔f4 ♘c6 (8...♘f5 9 ♔e5) 9 ♖h8 ♘×d4 10 ♖×h5 ♘×b3 11 ♖g5. Observe the concluding position. White has only one pawn, against four of Black's; nevertheless, it is White who holds the advantage. The rook slings itself instantly from wing to wing, and can stop the enemy passed pawn in one move. The knight, on the other hand, is a short-stepping piece; even if it can get to the kingside, then it leaves the b-pawn undefended.

4 gh gh 5 ♖a8 b4 6 ♖a4?!

Unnecessary dawdling - the pawn can't be taken anyway. 6 ♖f8! was right.

6...♔c7 7 ♔e2 (7 ♖×b4?? b5-+) **7...♔c6 8 ♖a8 ♘f5 9 ♔d3 ♔d7 10 ♖b8 ♔c7 11 ♖f8! ♔d6 12 ♖f7 b6 13 h3⊙ ♘h6**

13...♔c6 14 ♖×f5! ef 15 ♔e3 ♔d6 16 ♔f4 ♔e6 16 ♔g5+-.

14 ♖f4! ♘f5 15 ♔e2

After the rook protects the d4-pawn, the king can advance, creating the unstoppable threat of sacrificing the exchange.

15...♔e7 16 ♔f3 ♔f7 17 ♔g4 ♔g6 18 ♖×f5! ef+ 19 ♔×h4

The outside passed h-pawn decides the game.

19...b5 20 ♔g3 ♔g5 21 h4+ ♔h5 22 ♔f4 ♔×h4 23 ♔×f5 ♔g3 24 ♔e5 ♔f3 25 ♔×d5 ♔e3 26 ♔c5 ♔d3 27 ♔×b4 Black resigned

Tragicomedies

Minev - White
Vancouver 1985

10-23

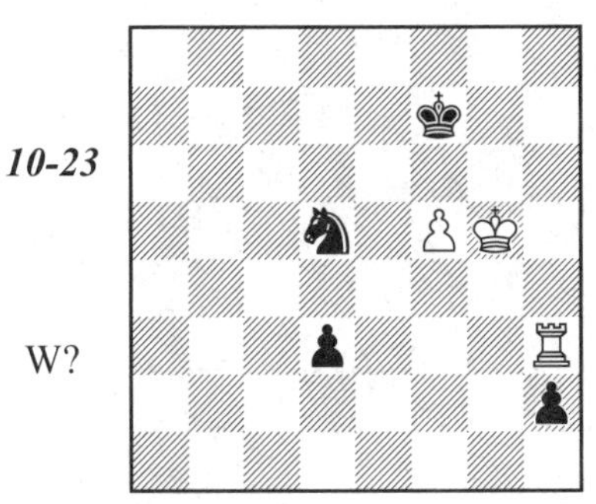

W?

1 ♖×h2??

Not very precise! A zwischenschach would have cleared a square on the 6th rank for White's king, thus: 1 ♖h7+! ♚e8 2 ♖×h2 ♘c3 3 f6+-.

1...♘c3 (threatening 2...d2) **2 ♖h7+?**

White could still have won by means of 2 ♔f4! ♘e2+ 3 ♔e5 d2 4 ♖h7+ ♚e8 5 ♖h1 ♘c3 6 ♔e6 (Müller).

2...♚f8??

An answering mistake. Black draws by 2...♚e8! 3 ♔f6 (3 ♔g6 d2 4 ♖h8+ ♚d7 5 ♖h1 d1♕ 6 ♖×d1 ♘×d1 6 f6 ♘e3 7 f7 ♚e7 8 ♔g7 ♘f5+) 3...♘e4+! (3...d2? 4 ♔e6+-) 4 ♔g7 d2 5 ♖h1 ♘g3=.

3 ♔g6+-

Black hasn't time for 3...d2, since 4 f6 creates the threat of mate.

When the Knight is Stronger than the Rook

The knight is no weaker, and sometimes even stronger, than the rook, when the board is strewn with pawn chains and the rook has nowhere to break into the enemy camp.

Another possibility: sometimes, the rook has a hard time dealing with a far-advanced enemy passed pawn, supported by the knight. In such situations, the knight's tactical abilities come to the fore: it can create forks, win tempi by checking the enemy king, or cut the rook off from the pawn.

Sternberg - Pawelczak
Berlin 1964

10-24

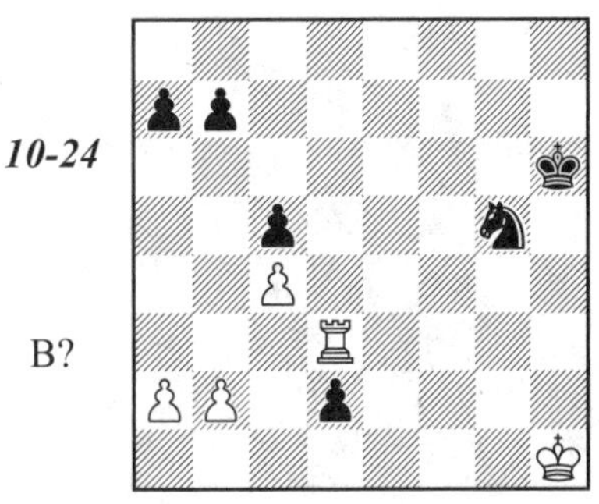

B?

1...♘f3! (threatening ♚g5-f4-e4)

White resigned, owing to his utter helplessness. He cannot play 2 ♔g2, because of the fork 2...♘e1+; after 2 ♖d6+ ♚g5, Black threatens the interference 3...♘d4. And on 2 b4, simply 2...b6! (but not 2...cb? 3 ♖d5 intending 4 ♔g2) 3 bc bc -+.

H. Mattison, 1913

10-25

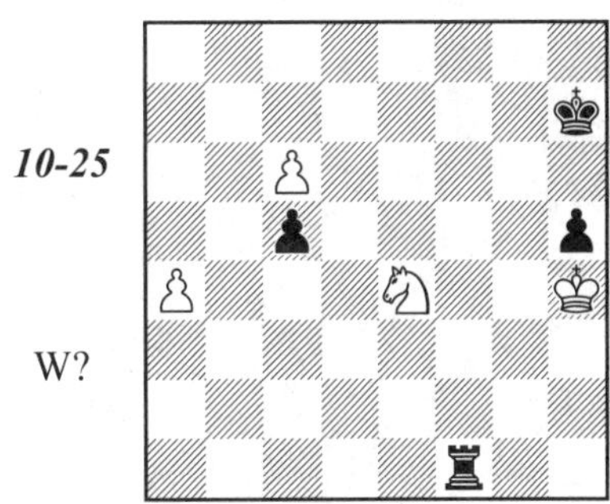

W?

1 c7? ♖f8 2 ♘d6 fails against 2...c4.

1 ♘g5+! ♚g6(g8)

1...♚g7 2 c7 ♖f8 3 ♘e6+ is completely bad. If 1...♚h6(h8), then 2 c7 ♖f8 3 ♘f7+ and 4 ♘d8.

2 ♘e6 ♖a1

The a-file is the only way for the rook to reach the 8th rank.

3 c7

White only gets a draw from 3 ♘f4+? ♚f5 4 c7 ♚×f4! 5 ♔h3 ♚f3 6 ♔h2 ♖a2+ 7 ♔h3 ♖a1.

3...♖×a4+ 4 ♘d4!! ♖a8

Either 5...♖×d4+ or 5...cd lets the pawn queen. Black's hope of creating a fortress with the rook on g4 is illusory: theory holds that such positions are won without difficulty.

5 ♘c6

Threatening the interference 6 ♘b8, and 5...♖e8 fails against 6 ♘d8.

5...♖c8 6 ♘e7+ (a fork), followed by 7 ♘×c8+-.

Exercises

10-26

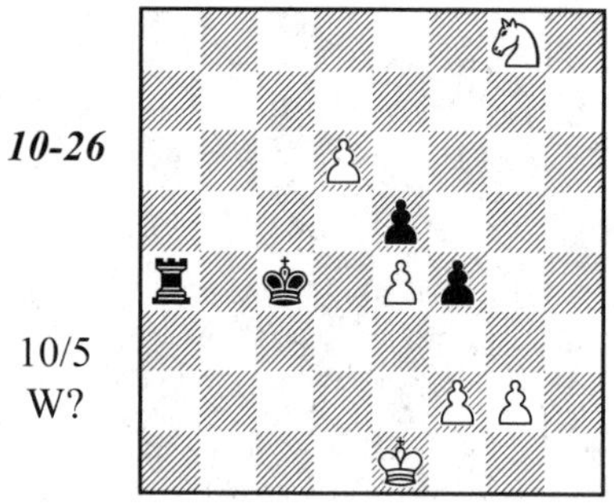

10/5
W?

10-27

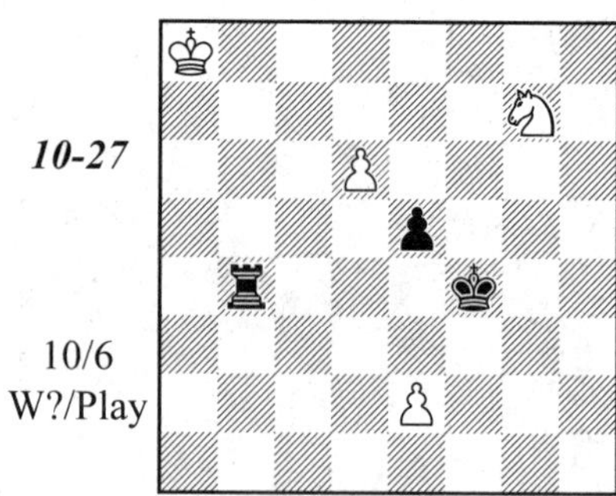

10/6
W?/Play

Chapter 11

ROOK vs. BISHOP

This chapter is dedicated solely to static situations, with all pawns on the same wing, where the weaker side tries, successfully or not, to build a fortress.

In rook versus knight duels, precise positions that need to be remembered are rare. However, the case in question is characterized by frequent motifs of "elementary fortresses" that should be included in our endgame arsenal.

The Lone Bishop

A Dangerous Corner

If there are no pawns on the board, a bishop can usually achieve an easy draw. Even squeezing the king to the edge of the board is not dangerous for the defender provided that ***the king is driven to the safe corner (opposite to the bishop's color; the dangerous corner, on the contrary, is that of the bishop's color).***

When the king is imprisoned in the dangerous corner, the endgame is lost.

B. Horwitz, J. Kling, 1851*

11-1

W

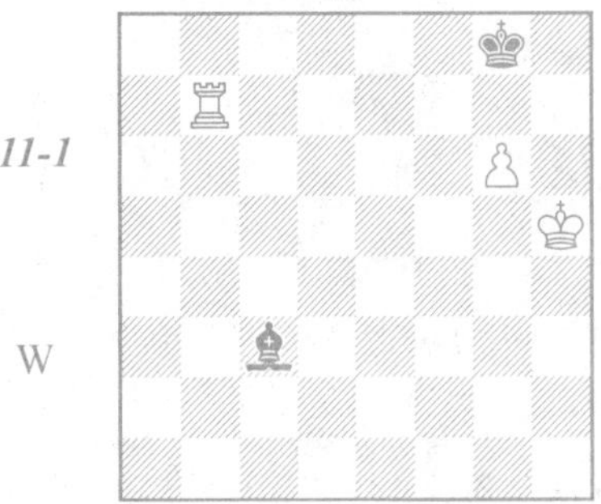

The g6-pawn is by no means a precious fighting unit for White: if it stood on g5 its value would have been much greater, here it only robs its own king of the important square g6. White should get rid of it.

1 g7! ♔h7

The capture 1...♗×g7 leads to an even more rapid final: 2 ♔g6 ♗e5 3 ♖e7 ♗d6 4 ♖e8+ ♗f8 5 ♖d8⊙. But when similar events occur in the safe corner (♔h8, ♗g8), the final position is a stalemate rather than a zugzwang!

2 ♖f7!

It is important to prevent the king's flight from the dangerous corner.

2...♗d4 3 g8♕+ ♔×g8 4 ♔g6

If there were no rook on f7, Black could hold by means of 4...♔f8. Now White intends 5 ♖d7 threatening both 6 ♖×d4 and 6 ♖d8+.

4...♗g1!?

The only defensive chance: the bishop hides in the "shadow" of the white king. Unfortunately, the shadow is too short.

5 ♖f1 ♗h2 6 ♖f2

6 ♖h1 ♗g3 7 ♖h3 ♗f4 8 ♖a3 ♔f8 9 ♖f3 is also good.

6...♗g3 7 ♖g2! ♗d6 (7...♗h4 8 ♔h5+; 7...♗e5 8 ♖e2) **8 ♖d2 ♗e7 9 ♖c2+−.**

Exercises

11-2

11/1
W?

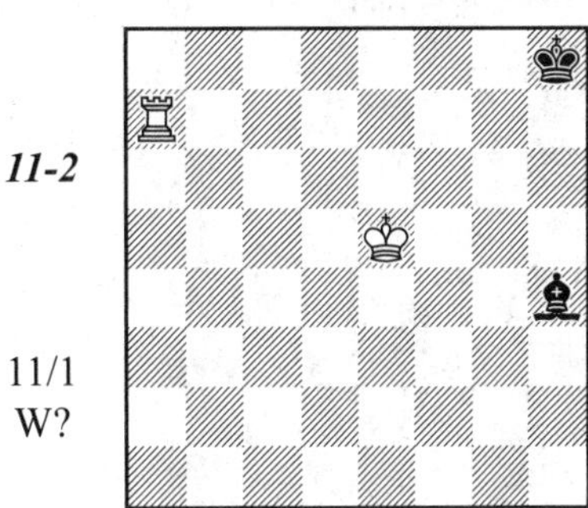

A Safe Corner

E. Lequesne, J. Berger*

11-3

B

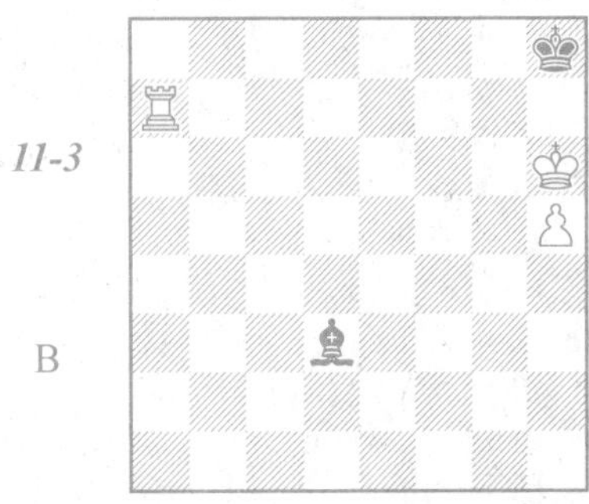

Without the h5-pawn, both 1...♔g8 and 1...♗c4 2 ♖a8+ ♗g8 lead to a draw.

If the pawn stands on h6 and the white king on g5 (Cozio, 1766), the draw is also quite elementary. All that is needed is for the black bishop to keep the b1-h7 diagonal under control.

The diagrammed position is more complicated as some accuracy is required. As Lequesne has shown, playing for a stalemate with 1...♗c4? can be refuted because the bishop loses control over the important diagonal b1-h7:

2 ♖a8+ ♗g8 3 ♔g5 ♔g7 4 ♖a7+ (or 4 h6+ ♔h8 5 ♖d8 ♔h7 6 ♖d7+ ♔h8 7 ♔g6) 4...♔h8 5 ♔g6 ♗d5 6 ♖h7+! ♔g8 7 ♖e7! ♔h8 (7...♔f8 8 ♔f6 ♗c4 9 h6 ♔g8 10 h7+ ♔h8 11 ♔g6) 8 h6 ♗a2 9 h7 ♗b1+ 10 ♔h6+–.

Berger suggested the correct defense method: the black king should temporarily leave the corner.

1...♔g8! 2 ♖g7+ ♔f8! 3 ♖g4 ♗c2 4 ♖c4 (4 ♔g5 ♔g7) **4...♗b1 5 ♖f4+ ♔g8=.**

Hence ***when the black king is placed in the safe corner, a pawn on h6 or h5 does not bring a win. A position is winning only when the pawn has not crossed the middle line.***

B. Guretzky-Cornitz, 1863*

11-4

W

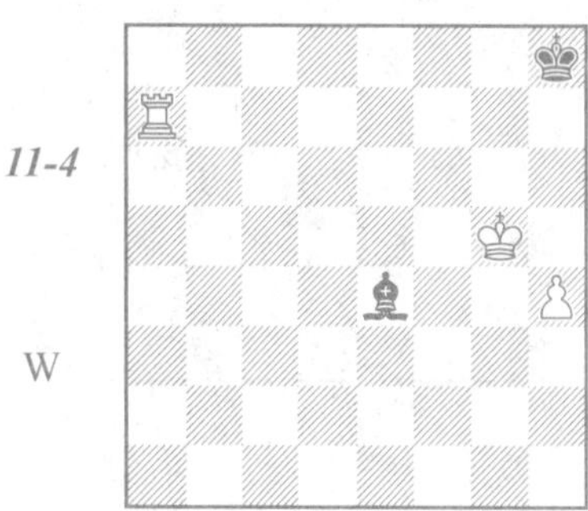

1 ♔h6 ♔g8

The winning technique after 1...♗d5 is already familiar to us: 2 ♖d7 ♗e6 3 ♖d8+ ♗g8 4 ♔g5 ♔g7 5 ♖d7+ ♔h8 6 ♔g6 ♗b3 7 ♖h7+! ♔g8 8 ♖c7! ♔h8 (8...♔f8 9 ♖g7) 9 h5 ♗d5 10 ♖h7+! ♔g8 11 ♖e7! etc.

2 ♖g7+ ♔f8 (2...♔h8 3 ♖e7!)

White's forthcoming strategy can be described as follows: he creates the threat of the king retreat via h5 to g4 while his rook stands on g5 (this is why he should not advance the pawn to h5). If he succeeds then the black king will be cut off from the pawn. If the black bishop tries to prevent this, it will lose control over the b1-h7 diagonal and White wins à la Lequesne. And, if the black king comes to f6 then a check along the f-file can push him away from the pawn even farther.

The following lines illustrate how this plan can be carried out.

3 ♖g5 ♔f7 4 ♖g3 (4 ♔h5 ♗f3+) **4...♗c2 5 ♔h5 ♔f6**

5...♗d1+ (or 5...♗a4) 6 ♔g5 ♔g7 (6...♗c2 7 ♔f4) 7 ♖c3!+–; 5...♗b1 6 ♖g5! (△ 7 ♔g4) 6...♔f6 7 ♔g4 ♗g6 8 h5 ♗h7 9 h6 ♗g6 10 ♔f4 ♗h7 11 ♖g7 ♗d3 12 ♖a7 △ 13 h7+–.

6 ♖g5 (△ ♔g4) **6...♗d1+** (6...♗f5 7 ♔h6 ♗c2 8 ♖g2! △ ♖f2+) **7 ♔h6 ♔f7** (7...♗f3 8 ♖g1 △ ♖f1) **8 ♖g7+ ♔f6** (8...♔f8 9 ♔g6 △ ♔f6) **9 ♖g1 ♗e2 10 ♖g2 ♗d3 11 ♖f2+.**

N. Gusev – Zhukhovitsky
Alma Ata 1958

11-5

W?

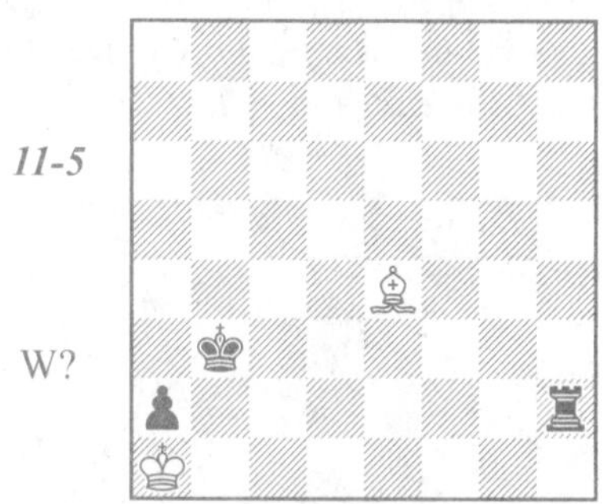

If the rook stands on some other file (say, on f2 or d2) the position is totally hopeless. But here White can save himself by means of **1 ♗d5+! ♔a3 2 ♗g2!⊙ ♖h5 3 ♗d5!** (△ ♗×a2) **3...♖h2 4 ♗g2!.**

However the game continued 1 ♗g2?? ♔a3. Now it was White who was put into zugzwang; after 2 ♗f1 ♖c2 he had to resign.

Tragicomedies

Euwe – Hromádka
Pistyan 1922

11-6

B

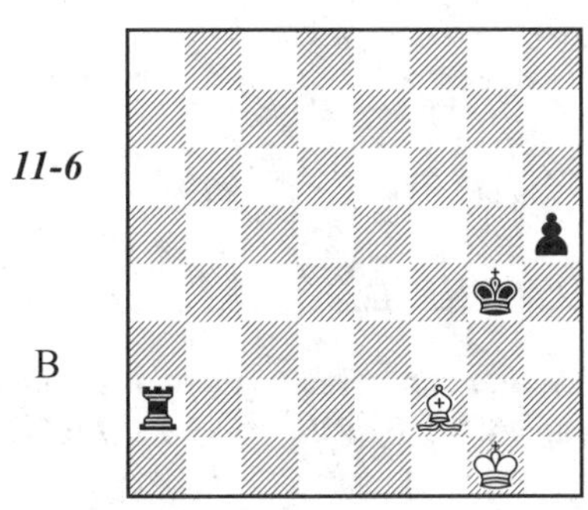

1...h4??

Black could have won quite easily: 1...♔h3! 2 ♗d4 ♖g2+ 3 ♔f1 (3 ♔h1 ♖d2 etc.) 3...♔g3! 4 ♗e5+ ♔f3 5 ♗f6 ♖g4.

2 ♗d4 ♔h3?

Now the bishop comes to the h2-b8 diagonal, and the position becomes drawn. A win, although rather complicated, was still possible: 2...♖e2! 3 ♗a7 ♖e8 (3...♖b2) 4 ♗b6 ♖e7 5 ♗c5 ♖d7. The rook gradually deprives the bishop of important squares prior to decisive action on the kingside.

3 ♗e5 ♖g2+ 4 ♔f1! Draw.

Hedge - Palatnik
Calcutta 1988

11-7

B

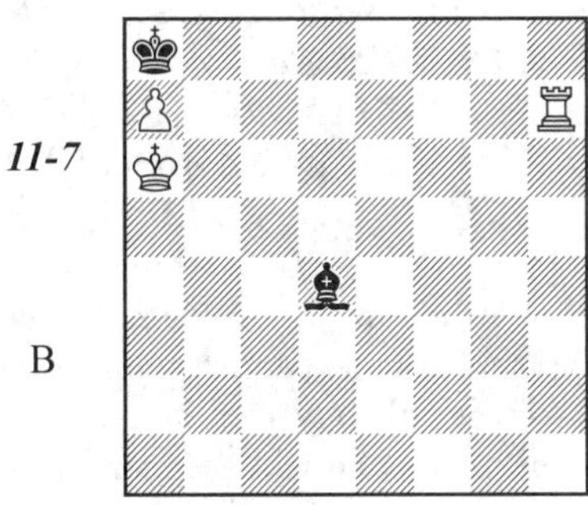

Grandmaster Palatnik resigned in this well-known theoretically drawn position (1...♗g7! 2 ♖h4 ♗d4!=).

Exercises

11-8

11/2
W?

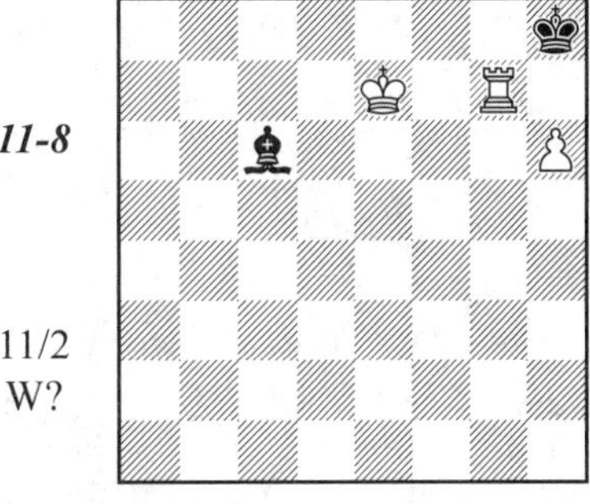

11-9

11/3
W?

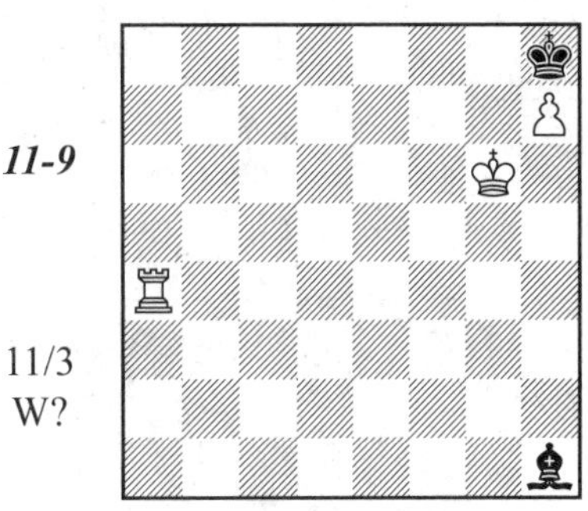

A Bishop Pawn

Szabó – Botvinnik
Budapest 1952

11-10

W

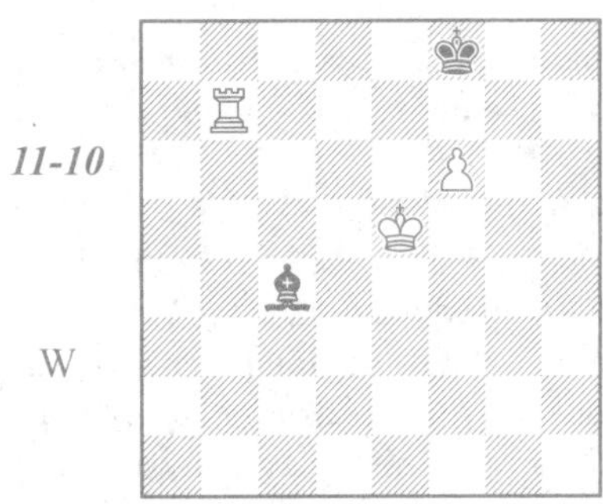

In the middle of the 18th century Ercole del Rio proved that this position is drawn. Two centuries later, Botvinnik followed his analysis and saved a difficult endgame against Szabó.

When the pawn is still on f5, White has no problem, but here the pawn occupies the important square f6. If 1 f7 (hoping for 1...♗×f7? 2 ♔f6+–), then 1...♔g7!=. All attempts to prepare an invasion by the king to g6 or e6 can be parried by Black if he defends correctly.

1 ♖b4 ♗a2 2 ♔f5 ♗d5□

2...♔f7? 3 ♖b7+ ♔f8 4 ♔g6+–.

3 ♔g6 ♗f7+ 4 ♔g5 ♗d5 5 ♖h4 ♗b3 6 ♖h8+ ♔f7 7 ♖h7+ ♔f8 8 f7 ♔e7! 9 ♔g6 ♗c4!

But, of course, not 9...♗c2+?? 10 ♔g7+–.

10 ♖g7 ♗b3 11 f8♕+ ♔×f8 12 ♔f6 ♔e8 13 ♖e7+ ♔d8 Draw.

We should add that, if all the pieces are shifted down by a rank, a similar defense does not work. As Centurini proved in 1865, White wins, although it can take some effort. All similar situations are lost also against a central or a knight pawn, so the del Rio position is the only successful elementary fortress of this kind.

Dolmatov – Georgadze
Erevan zt 1982

11-11

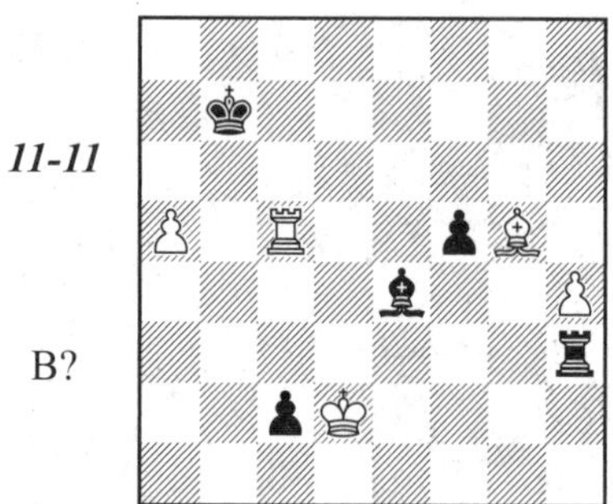

B?

Dolmatov knew the del Rio position and built his defense upon it. The game continued: 1...♖f3 2 ♔e2 f4?! 3 ♖×c2! ♖e3+ 4 ♔d2 ♗×c2 5 ♔×c2 ♖e4 6 ♔d3 f3 7 ♗e3 ♖×h4 8 ♗f2 ♖f4 9 ♔e3 ♖f7 10 ♗g3 ♔a6 11 ♔f2 ♔×a5 12 ♗e5, and White achieved a draw.

Georgadze did not exploit his chances fully. It is obvious that Black has no other plan than ...♖f3 and ...f5-f4, only he had to carry it out after first bringing his king to a6.

1...♔a7! 2 ♔e2 ♔a6⊙ 3 ♔d2□ (3 ♔f2? f4; 3 ♔e1? ♖h2) **3...♖f3 4 ♔e2 f4 5 ♖×c2! ♖e3+ 6 ♔d2 ♗×c2 7 ♔×c2 ♖e2+! 8 ♔d1!** (8 ♔d3? f3–+) **8...f3 9 ♗f4□** (9 h5? ♖e4!; 9 ♗d8? ♖e3!; 9 ♗d2? ♖e8 10 ♗e1 ♖d8+) **9...♔×a5 10 h5 ♔b5 11 h6 ♔c4 12 h7 ♖e8**

11-12

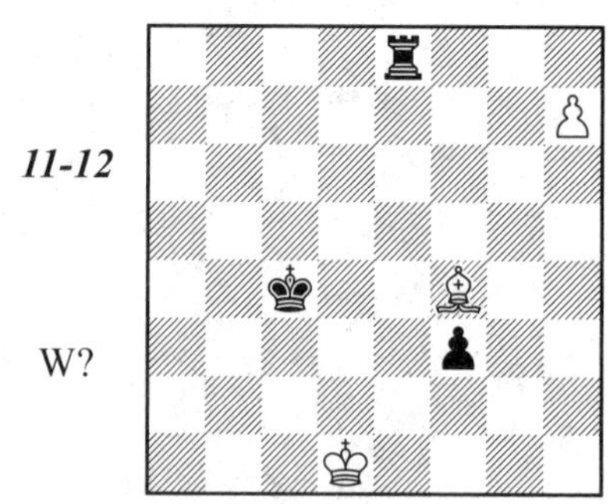

W?

Now White can come to the del Rio position by means of **13 ♗e3!! ♔d3 14 ♗b6 ♖h8 15 ♔e1=**

Another tempting option, **13 h8♕? ♖×h8 14 ♔e1** is refuted in an instructive way. A look into eventual lines will help in understanding dangers that await the weaker side if the bishop is placed badly.

14...♔d3 15 ♔f2 ♔e4 16 ♗c7 (16 ♗d6 ♖c8! △ 17...♖c2+ 18 ♔f1 ♔e3) **16...♖h6!**

Black does not let the bishop to come to the a7-g1 diagonal.

17 ♗b8 ♖a6! 18 ♗c7 ♖a2+ 19 ♔f1 ♖a1+! 20 ♔f2 ♖a6!

Zugzwang! Both 21 ♔f1 ♔e3 and 21 ♗b8(g3) ♖a2+ 22 ♔f1 ♔e3 are very bad, so the bishop must leave the b8-g3 diagonal.

21 ♗d8 ♖c6 22 ♗e7

If 22 ♗a5 then 22...♖c2+ 23 ♔f1 ♔f4 (△ 24...♔g3) 24 ♗b4 f2 25 ♔g2 ♔e3–+, while on 22 ♗g5 Black wins by means of 22...♖c5! 23 ♗h6 ♖c2+ 24 ♔f1 f2! 25 ♔g2 ♖c6!.

22...♖c2+ 23 ♔f1 f2 24 ♔g2 ♔e3 25 ♗h4 (there is no check from c5) **25...♖b2⊙ 26 ♗g3 f1♕+! 27 ♔×f1 ♔f3–+** (Dvoretsky).

This sort of ***a rook's domination over a bishop*** is typical for many endings with an extra exchange. We have already seen it in some examples and exercises and will see more of it in the future.

Tragicomedies

Levitina – Gaprindashvili
Tshaltubo ct 1988

11-13

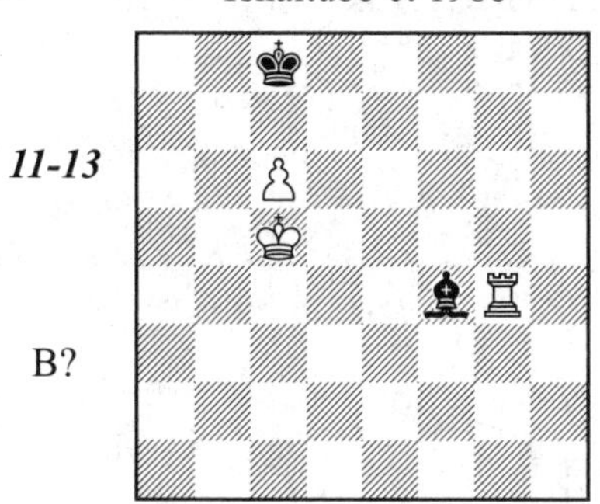

B?

1...♗h2?? (1...♗e5=) **2 ♖g8+ ♔c7 3 ♖g7+**

Black resigned in view of 3...♔c8 4 ♔b6+–.

Exercises

11-14

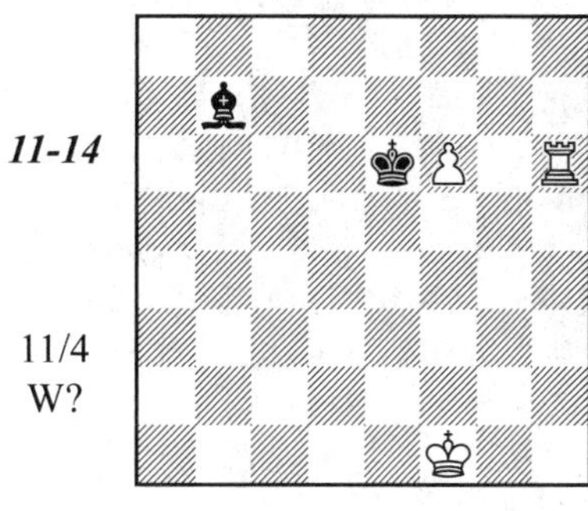

11/4
W?

Rook and Pawn vs. Bishop and Pawn

The Pawns are on the Same File or on Adjacent Files

One should not protect the pawn by placing it on a square of the bishop's color. Almost all these positions are lost. The adversary advances along squares of the opposite color, drives the king away from the pawn, and finally wins by means of an exchange sacrifice.

I confine myself to a single illustration of the above-mentioned technique.

Rohácek – Stoltz
Munich 1942

11-15

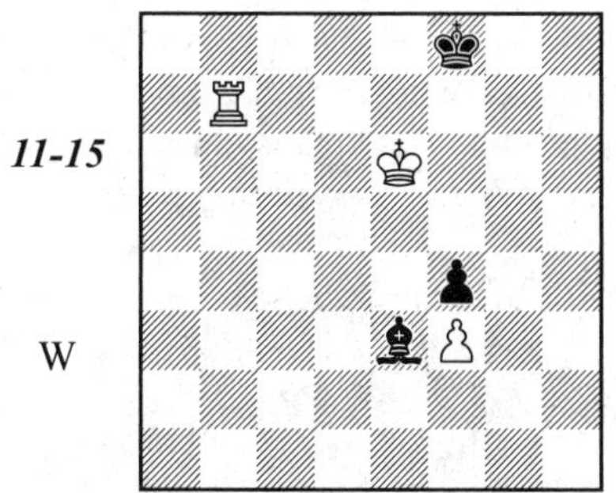

W

1 ♖f7+ ♔e8 2 ♖f5! ♗d2 3 ♔f6

3 ♖c5 ♔f8 4 ♔f6 ♔e8 5 ♖e5+ ♔f8 6 ♖d5 ♗c3+ 7 ♔f5+– is no worse.

3...♔f8

3...♗c3+ 4 ♔g6 ♗d2 5 ♔g7 ♗c3+ 6 ♔g8! ♗d2 7 ♖e5+.

4 ♖c5 (4 ♖d5) **4...♔g8 5 ♖c8+ ♔h7 6 ♔f7** Black resigned.

White plays ♖g8-g4, approaches the pawn with his king and takes it with his rook.

Chances of salvation can result from either ***an active defense*** (an attack against the hostile pawn by the bishop or the king). Or ***building a barrier*** that prevents an invasion of the hostile king (squares of one color are controlled by the bishop, squares of the other color – by the pawn).

Rubinstein – Tartakower
Vienna 1922

11-16

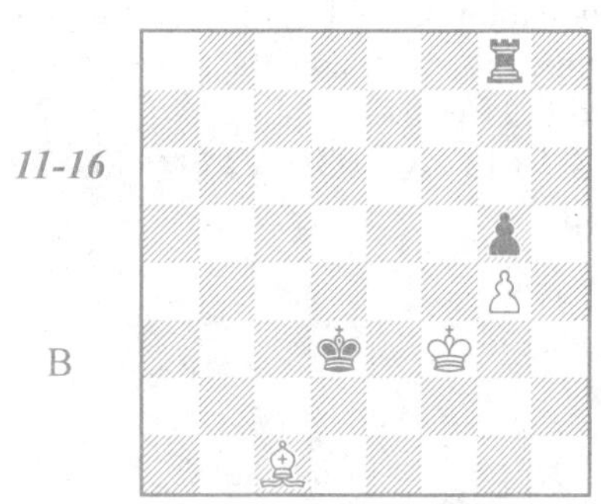

B

Black must protect his pawn with the king, bring the rook to the 5th rank, and finally move his king ahead again by going around the rook. This plan has no alternatives, but is not sufficient for a win.

1...♔d4 2 ♗d2 ♔e5 3 ♗e3 ♔f6 4 ♗d4+ ♔g6 5 ♗e3

White is still keeping the pawn in the crosshairs. Another equally good defensive method consists in building a barrier: 5 ♗e5 ♖c8 6 ♗g3=.

5...♖b8 6 ♗d2 ♖b5 7 ♔e4 ♔f6 8 ♗c3+ ♔e6 9 ♗d2 ♔d6 (9...♖e5+ 10 ♔f3 ♔d5 11 ♗c3 ♖e6 12 ♗d2=) **10 ♗e3 ♔c6 11 ♗d2 ♔b6 12 ♗e3+ ♔a5 13 ♗d2+ ♔a4 14 ♗e3**

The bishop sacrifice on g5 is already in the air, but it does not work right now: 14 ♗×g5? ♖×g5 15 ♔f4 ♖g8 16 g5 ♔b5 17 ♔f5 ♔c6 18 g6 ♔d7 19 ♔f6 ♖f8+.

14...♔b3 15. ♗c1 ♔c2 16 ♗×g5! (It is time!) **16...♖×g5 17 ♔f4 ♖g8 18 g5 ♔d3 19 ♔f5 ♔d4 20 g6 ♔d5 21 ♔f6** Draw.

Chistiakov – Dvoretsky
Moscow ch 1966

11-17

B?

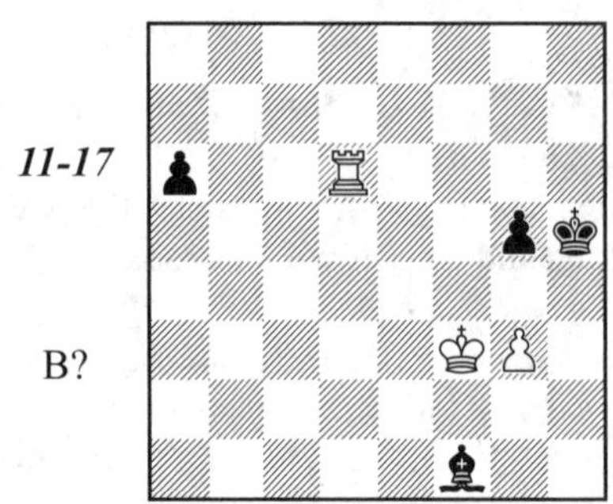

1...♗h3!

1...g4+? 2 ♔f4 ♗e2 3 ♔f5 is hopeless.

2 ♖×a6 ♗d7 3 ♖d6 ♗g4+ 4 ♔e3 ♗c8 5 ♖d8 ♗e6 6 ♖d4 ♗c8

The only winning attempt is a transfer of the king to f6 followed with ♖d5. Black responds with a counter-attack against the g3-pawn.

7 ♔d3 ♗f5+ 8 ♔c4 ♗e6+ 9 ♔c5 ♗c8 10 ♔d6 ♗f5 11 ♖c4 ♗h3 12 ♔e5 ♗d7 13 ♔f6 ♗h3

11-18

$

W

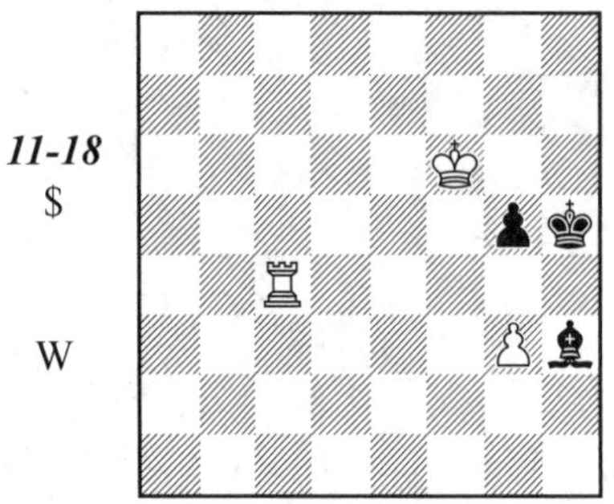

14 ♖c5

After 14 ♖d4 ♗c8 15 ♖d5 a position from the game Romanovsky – I. Rabinovich arises (from Leningrad 1924, with reversed colors). Romanovsky drew the game after 15...♔g4! 16 ♖×g5+ ♔f3 17 ♖c5 ♗h3! (17...♗b7? is erroneous in view of 18 ♖c3+! ♔g4 19 ♖c7 △ ♖g7+) 18 ♖c3+ ♔g4 followed with ...♗g2-f3.

14...♔g4! 15 ♖×g5+ ♔f3 16 ♔e5 ♗g4 17 ♔d4 ♔×g3 (17...♗h3! is perhaps simpler) **18 ♔e3 ♔h3**

It would have been nice to stay farther from the dangerous corner (h1) but 18...♔h4? loses to 19 ♔f4+–.

19 ♔f4 ♗d7??

A grave blunder in a drawn position. Black should have kept the f3-square under control: 19...♗d1 or 19...♗e2.

20 ♖g3+ ♔h2 21 ♔f3+–

The black king stays locked in the dangerous corner.

21...♗a4 22.♖g2+ ♔h3 23 ♖g3+ ♔h2 24 ♔f2 ♗c2 25 ♖c3 ♗d1 26 ♖c1 ♗b3 27 ♖c6 Black resigned.

G. Barcza, 1967

11-19

$

W?

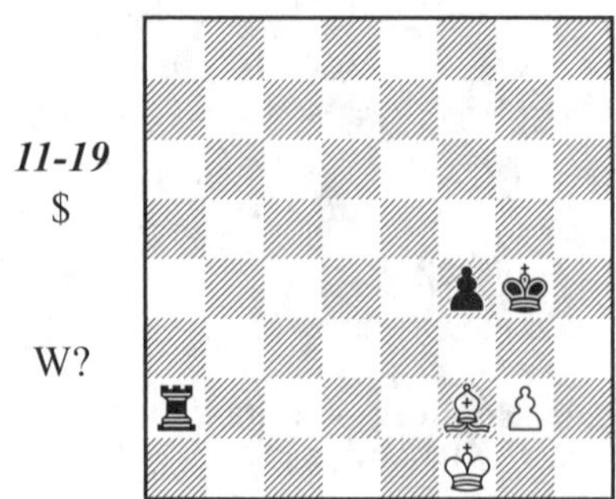

White's position looks perilous but he still holds, as Black cannot breach the barrier. Two factors help White: his king is close to the safe corner h1, and Black has a bishop pawn.

1 ♔e1!

Both 1 ♗e1? f3! 2 g3 ♖a1 3 ♔f2 ♖×e1 4 ♔×e1 ♔×g3 and 1 ♔g1? ♖a1+ 2 ♔h2 ♖c1⊙ 3 ♗d4 ♖c2 (△ f3) 4 ♔g1 ♔g3 or 3 ♗g1 ♖c2 4 ♔h1 ♖e2⊙ 5 ♗h2 ♖e8 6 ♗g1 (6 ♔g1 ♖e1+) 6...♖h8+ 7 ♗h2 ♔f5 8 ♔g1 ♔e4 9 ♔h1 ♔e3 10 ♔g1 ♖h7⊙ 11 ♔h1 ♔f2 are bad.

By the way, Averbakh has proven that even when all the kingside pieces are moved one file to the left the position remains drawn. In such a case, the defensive plan must be changed: the king should go in the opposite direction in order to hide itself behind the pawn. There is no zugzwang anymore because the h5-square is available to the bishop, which is now on e2.

1...♖a1+

1...♖b2 2 ♔f1 f3 leads to nowhere in view of 3 ♔g1! ♖b1+ 4 ♔h2=.

2 ♔e2 ♖c1

2...♖h1 3 ♗e1! ♖h2 4 ♔f1 f3 5 gf+ ♔×f3 6 ♔g1 ♖g2+ 7 ♔h1!=.

3 ♔d2! (3 ♗e1? ♖c2+ 4 ♔f1 f3–+)

3...♖h1 4 ♔e2 ♖h2 5 ♔f1 f3

It seems like the defense is broken, but White saves the game by means of a pawn sacrifice that leads to the del Rio position.

6 ♔g1! ♖×g2+ 7 ♔f1=.

N. Elkies, 1993

11-20

W

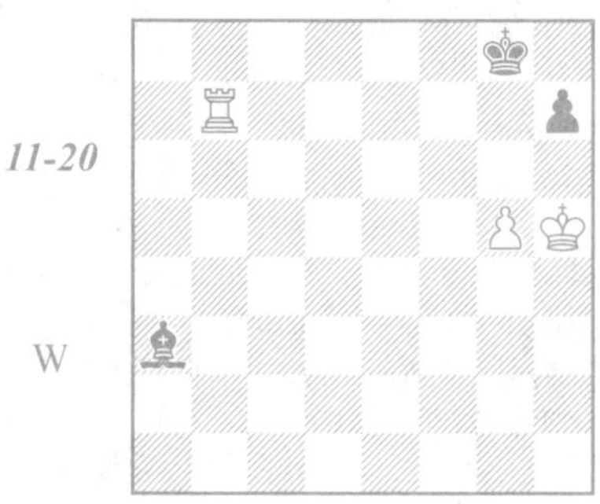

Keres evaluated the diagrammed position as drawn, and numerous authors reproduced this judgment. Yet Elkies, an Israeli endgame study composer, discovered a subtle winning method many years later.

Its idea can be briefly described as follows: the king retreats to g4, the rook goes to b5 or d5, denying the bishop important squares. Thereafter, depending on the bishop's position, the white king breaks through to f6 or h6, while if the bishop is on f8 or g7, the advance g5-g6 is very strong.

1 ♖b3!

1 ♔g4?! is inaccurate: 1...♗c1! 2 ♔f5 ♗d2 (2...h6? 3 ♔g6!) 3 ♖b2 (3 ♖b3 ♔g7) 3...♗e3 4 ♖b3 ♗d4.

1...♗d6

1...♗f8 loses rapidly: 2 ♖b8 ♔g7 3 ♖b7+ ♔g8 4 g6. If 1...♗c5 2 ♔g4 ♗d6, then 3 ♖b5 ♗c7 4 ♖d5! and the king is ready for a march.

2 ♔g4 ♗f8!

2...♗c5 is met with 3 ♖b5!, and the bishop cannot prevent an invasion by the king. For example, 3...♗d4 4 ♔h5 (△ ♖b8+, ♖b7+, ♔h6) 4...♗g7 5 g6 h6 6 ♖b8+ ♗f8 7 ♖×f8+ ♔×f8 8 ♔×h6, or 3...♗a3 4 ♔f5 (△ 5 ♔f6), or 3...♗d6 4 ♔f5 ♗c7 5 ♖d5! ♗b6 (5...♗g3 6 ♔f6) 6 ♔f6 ♗c7 7 ♖d7 ♗a5 8 ♖g7+! ♔h8 9 ♔f7, or 3...♗f8 4 ♔f5 h6 (4...♗g7 5 g6! h6 6 ♖b8+ ♗f8 7 ♔f6; 4...♗e7 5 ♖b8+ ♔f7 6 ♖b7 and there is no defense against ♔g4-h5-h6) 5 g6 (5 gh ♔h7 6 ♖b6 ♗×h6 7 ♖b7+ is also good) 5...♗e7 (5...♗d6 6 ♔f6) 6 ♖b8+ ♔g7 7 ♖b7+–.

3 ♔f5!

White has no time for his plan of 3 ♖b5?, because after 3...h6! 4 g6 ♗d6 he can't prevent Black from transfering the bishop to the c1-h6 diagonal: 5 ♔f5 ♗g3! 6 ♖a5 ♗h4 7 ♖a8+ ♔g7 8 ♖a7+ ♔g8 9 g7 ♔h7 10 ♔e6 (nor does 10 ♖f7 ♗g5 11 g8♕+ ♔×g8 12 ♔g6 ♗d2 13 ♖d7 ♗g5 acheive anything) 10...♔g8=.

3...♗c5 4 ♖d3! ♗b4

If 4...♗e7 then 5 ♖c3! ♗b4 6 ♖c8+ ♔f7 7 ♖c7+ ♗e7 (7...♔g8 8 ♔f6) 8 ♔g4 and ♔h5-h6 is irresistible.

5 ♔f6 ♗a5 6 ♖b3 ♗d8+ (6...♗c7 7 ♖b5 ♗d8+ 8 ♔e6! ♔g7 9 ♔d7) **7 ♔f5 ♗a5** (7...♗c7 8 ♖b5) **8 ♔g4 ♗c7 9 ♖b5! ♗d6 10 ♔f5 ♗c7 11 ♖d5+–.**

Exercises

11-21

11/5
B?

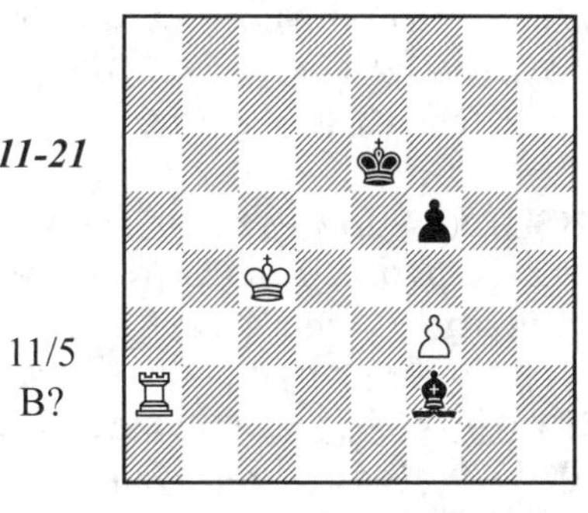

11-22

11/6
B?

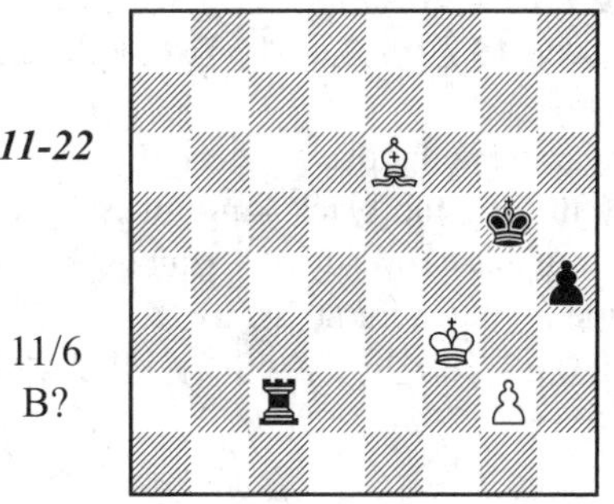

Rook Pawns

Positions with rook pawns are quite difficult, even top grandmasters cannot avoid errors when playing them. Nevertheless knowledge of their basic ideas makes certain practical sense.

J. Enevoldsen, 1949*

11-23

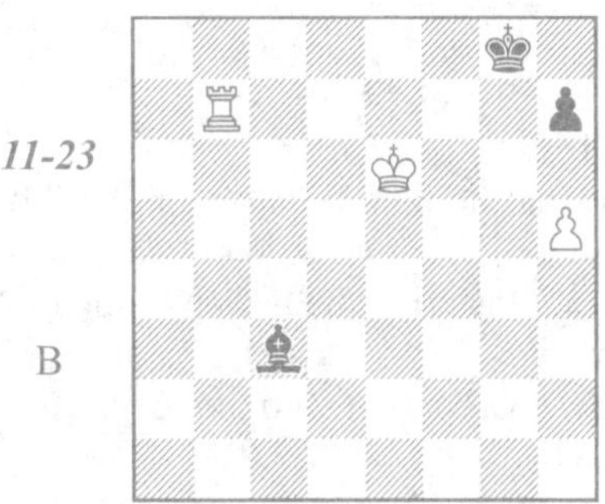

B

This is perhaps the most favorable situation for the stronger side. The pawn has crossed the middle line and the black king is in the dangerous corner. White forces ...h7-h6, then drives the black king farther away and cuts him off along a file; finally White comes back to the pawn with his king and sacrifices his rook for the bishop.

1...h6

If 1...♗d2 then 2 ♔f5 ♗e3 3 ♖c7!⊙, and Black cannot do without h7-h6, because all other moves – 3...♗h6(d2) 4 ♔f6; 3...♗d4 4 h6; 3...♗b6 4 ♖c6 (or 4 ♖c8+) and 5 h6 – are even worse.

2 ♔f5 ♗d2 3 ♔g6 ♔f8 4 ♖f7+ ♔e8

If Black keeps his king in the corner he is set into zugzwang very soon: 4...♔g8 5 ♖f3 ♗g5 6 ♖f2⊙ ♗e3 7 ♖e2+–.

5 ♖f2 ♗g5 6 ♔g7 ♔e7 7 ♖e2+ ♔d7 8 ♔f7 ♔d6 9 ♖e4! (a zugzwang again) **9...♗c1 10 ♖e6+ ♔d5 11 ♔f6 ♗d2 12 ♔f5 ♗g5 13 ♖g6** (△ 14 ♖×g5) **13...♗d2 14 ♖g2 ♗e3 15 ♖g3 ♗c1 16 ♖d3+ ♔c4 17 ♖d7**

Endgame handbooks suggest 17 ♔e4 followed by driving the black king away by one more file, but this is already superfluous: he may go after the h6-pawn immediately.

17...♗g5 18 ♔g6 ♔c5 19 ♖h7 ♔d6 20 ♖×h6+–.

Salwe – Rubinstein
Prague 1908

11-24

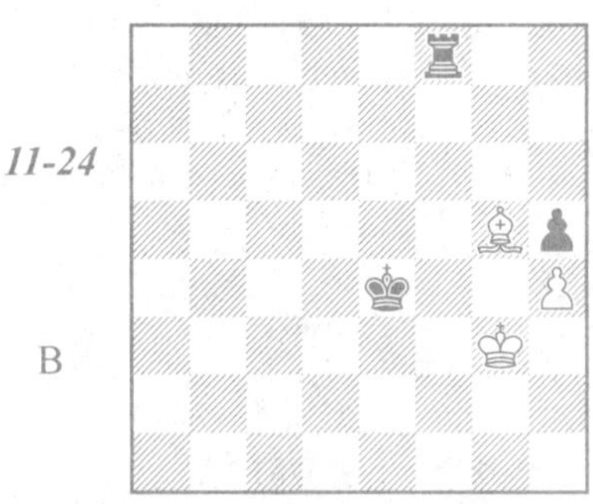

B

Rubinstein carried out the same plan of driving the king off from the pawn that we have seen in the previous example, and was successful with it. However it was later proven that White could have held the position with a precise defense.

Maizelis found the answer to this endgame puzzle in 1963. It turned out that White should not drive the black king away from the corner. On the contrary, the king should be locked in the corner, with idea of putting Black in zugzwang. Let us study the analysis by Maizelis.

1...♔d3! 2 ♗f4 ♔e2 3 ♗g5 ♖f3+ 4 ♔g2 ♖a3 5 ♗e7 ♖a4 6 ♗d8 ♖g4+ 7 ♔h3 ♔f3 8 ♗c7 ♖g1 9 ♗h2

If 9 ♔h2 then 9...♖f1 10 ♗d8 ♔g4 11 ♔g2 ♖f5 12 ♗g5 ♖f8!⊙ 13 ♗e7 ♖e8 14 ♗g5 ♖e2+ 15 ♔f1 ♔f3 16 ♔g1 ♔g3! 17 ♔f1 ♖e8!⊙ –+.

11-25

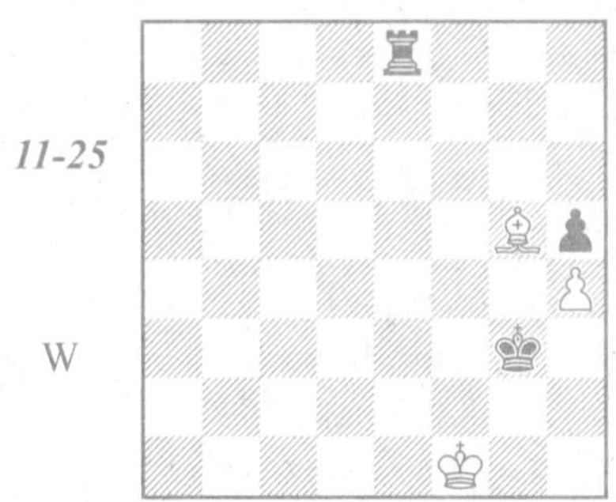

W

This is the decisive zugzwang – Black's goal in all the lines. White cannot maintain the h4-pawn. The resulting position is lost for him in spite of the safe corner, because the black pawn has not crossed the middle line.

9...♖f1 10 ♗g3 ♖h1+ 11 ♗h2 ♔e4! 12 ♔g2 ♖d1! 13 ♗c7

The same is 13 ♗g1 ♔f4! 14 ♗c5 ♔g4 15 ♗e7 ♖e1 16 ♗g5 ♖e2+ 17 ♔f1 ♔f3 18 ♔g1 ♔g3 19 ♔f1 ♖e8!⊙ –+; 13 ♗g3 ♔f5 14 ♔f3

♖d3+ 15 ♔g2 ♔g4 16 ♗e1 ♖b3 17 ♗f2 ♖b2 18 ♔f1 ♔f3 is also hopeless.

13...♖d7! 14 ♗a5 (14 ♗b8 ♔f5 15 ♔f3 ♖d3+ 16 ♔g2 ♔g4) **14...♔f4 15 ♗c3 ♔g4 16 ♗f6 ♖f7 17 ♗d8 ♖f5 18 ♗g5 ♖f8!⊙ 19 ♗e7 ♖e8 20 ♗g5 ♖e2+ 21 ♔f1 ♔f3 22 ♔g1 ♔g3 23 ♔f1 ♖e8!⊙ −+**

Now let us look at what actually happened in the game.

1...♖f7 2 ♗h6 ♖f3+ 3 ♔g2 ♖d3? (3...♖f7! △ ♔d3−+) **4 ♗g5?** (4 ♔f2!) **♔f5?**

He had to move the rook back: 4...♖f3!. Now the white king breaks loose and the position becomes drawn.

5 ♔f2 ♔g4 6 ♔e2! ♖f3 7 ♗h6 ♔g3 8 ♗g5 ♖f8 9 ♔e3 ♖e8+ 10 ♔d3 ♔f3 11 ♔d4 ♖e6

11...♖e4+ 12 ♔d3 ♖g4 13 ♔d2 ♔g3 14 ♔e1; White defended himself against the exchange sacrifice in time.

11-26

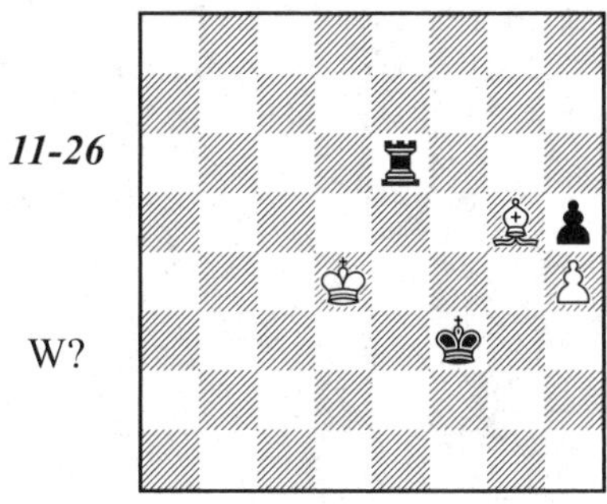

W?

12 ♔d5?

The decisive error! As Baranov proved in 1954, White should not be afraid of driving his king away by one more file, therefore he had to play 12 ♔d3! ♖d6+ 13 ♔c3. Further driving-away actions will not succeed if White only avoids placing the kings on the same file. After 13...♖d7, both 14 ♔c2 and 14 ♔c4 are possible.

Upon 14 ♔c2 there follows 14...♔e2 15 ♔c3 ♖d3+ 16 ♔c4! (rather than 16 ♔c2? ♖g3 17 ♔b2 ♔d1!). And if 14 ♔c4 then 14...♔e4 (14...♔g3 15 ♔c3 ♖d1 16 ♗f6 ♖h1 17 ♔d2 ♖×h4 18 ♗×h4+ ♔×h4 19 ♔e2 ♔g3 20 ♔f1=) 15 ♔c3 ♖d3+ and now 16 ♔c2!=, rather than 16 ♔c4? ♖g3 17 ♗f6 (17 ♔b4 ♖×g5! 18 hg ♔f5) 17...♖g6 18 ♗e7 ♖c6+).

12...♖e4 13 ♗f6 ♔f4 14 ♗d8 ♔f5 15 ♗g5 ♖g4 (△ ...♖×g5) **16 ♗e7 ♖g7 17 ♗f8 ♖d7+ 18 ♔c6** (18 ♔c4 ♔g4) **18...♖d4** (a simpler way was 18...♖f7! followed by 19...♔g4) **19 ♗e7 ♔e6** (19...♔g4 20 ♔c5 ♖d3 21 ♔c4 ♖h3 22 ♔d4 ♖×h4 23 ♔e3 ♖h2) **20 ♔c5 ♖d5+ 21 ♔c4 ♖f5! 22 ♗d8 ♔d7! 23 ♗b6** (23 ♗g5 ♖×g5) **23...♖f4+ 24 ♔d3 ♖×h4**

The outcome seems to be clear after the loss of the pawn, but both sides err in the remainder of the game.

25 ♔e2 ♔e6 26 ♔f3 ♖g4 27 ♗f2 ♔f5 28 ♗g3 h4 29 ♗h2 ♖b4??

Correct was 29...h3 △ ...♖g2+−.

30 ♔g2 ♔g4 31 ♗e5 ♖a4 32 ♗d6 ♖a2+ 33 ♔h1 ♔h3 34 ♗c5??

As we know, 34 ♔g1! ♖g2+ 35 ♔f1 would have led to a draw.

34...♖a1+ 35 ♗g1 ♔g4 36 ♔h2 ♖a2+ 37 ♔h1 ♔g3 38 ♗c5 ♖h2+ 39 ♔g1 ♖d2! 40 ♔h1 h3 White resigned.

Kasparov – Yusupov
Linares 1993

11-27

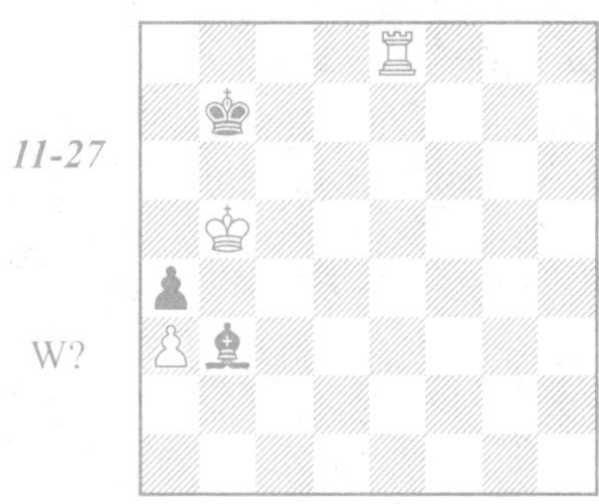

W?

The logic of the previous example can be applied here: the correct plan is to play for zugzwang rather than driving the king off.

1 ♖d8! ♔c7 2 ♖d4⊙ ♔b7 3 ♖d7+ ♔c8 4 ♔c6 ♗c2 5 ♖d4 ♗b3 (5...♔b8 6 ♔b6+−) **6 ♔b6⊙ +−**

Kasparov did not find this plan, and the game ended in a draw.

1 ♖e7+? ♔c8 2 ♔c6 ♔d8! 3 ♖d7+ ♔e8 4 ♔c7 ♗c2 5 ♖d2 ♗b3 6 ♖e2+ ♔f7 7 ♔d6 ♗c4 8 ♖e7+ ♔f8 9 ♖e4 ♗b3 10 ♔d7 ♔f7 11 ♖f4+ ♔g6!

It is important to come nearer to the rook as 11...♔g7? loses to 12 ♔c6 ♔g6 13 ♔b5 ♔g5 14 ♖×a4.

12 ♔d6 ♔g5 13 ♔e5 ♔g6 14 ♖f3 ♔g7 15 ♖f6 ♗c4 16 ♔f5 ♗b3 17 ♔g5 ♗c2 Draw.

For the sake of completeness, we might have added an analysis of the position with the black pawn on a3 and the bishop on b2, as in

Timman – Velimirovic, Rio de Janeiro izt 1979; it was proven that White should win. However the probability of its occurrence in a practical game is rather low, while the proof itself is quite complicated, so we have decided to omit it.

Tragicomedies

Bellón – Tatai
Rome 1977

11-28
$

B?

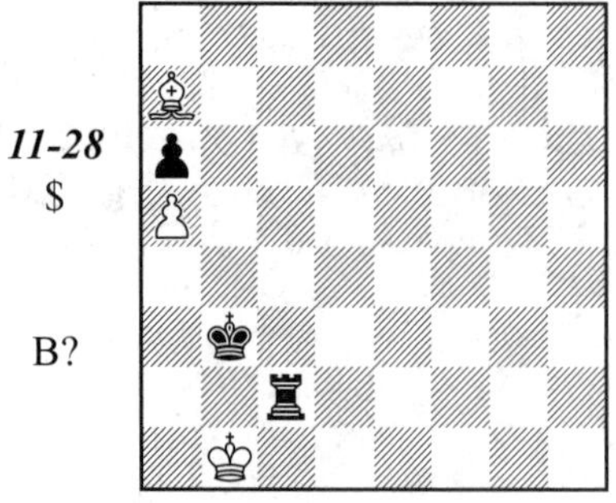

Recalling the Kasparov – Yusupov endgame, we can find the solution easily: 1...♖c6! (or 1...♖c7!) 2 ♗b6 (2 ♗b8 ♖c5; 2 ♗e3 ♖e6 3 ♗d2 ♖f6) 2...♖d6 3 ♔c1 ♖d5!⊙ –+.

1...♖h2?

Curiously enough, Milic awarded this move, which gave the win away, an exclamation mark.

2 ♔c1 ♔c3 3 ♔d1 ♖d2+ 4 ♔e1 ♔d3 5 ♗b6 ♖h2 6 ♗d8 ♖h1+ 7 ♔f2 ♖h8 8 ♗b6 ♖e8 9 ♔f1 ♔d2 10 ♗c5?

A mistake in return, unnoticed by both *Chess Informant* and *Encyclopaedia of Chess Endings*. The correct defensive method, as demonstrated by Yusupov against Kasparov, was 10 ♔g2(f2)! ♖f8 11 ♔g3 ♔c3 12 ♔g4 ♔b4 13 ♔g5! (it is important not to let the rook to f5) 13...♖f1 14 ♔g4 ♖a1 15 ♔f3 ♖×a5 16 ♗×a5+ ♔×a5 17 ♔e2=.

10...♖e5! 11 ♗b4+

Or 11 ♗b6 ♖f5+! 12 ♔g2 ♔c3 13 ♔g3 ♔b4 14 ♔g4 ♖×a5 –+.

11...♔d3 12 ♔f2 ♖b5 13 ♗e1 ♖f5+ 14 ♔g3 ♔e2 15 ♔g4 (15 ♗b4 ♖b5 16 ♗c3 ♖b3) **15...♖c5!** White resigned.

Two Pawns vs. Two on the Same Wing

First the most important position that everybody should know.

11-29

W

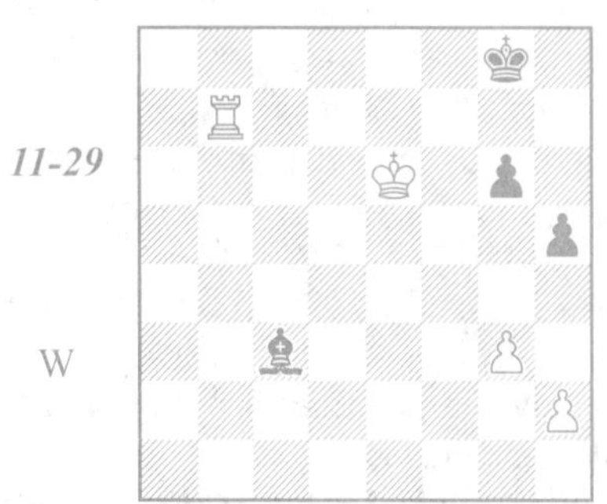

This is an elementary fortress; White cannot breach the barrier. If the king returns to f4, Black takes g5 under control by means of ♗f6. An advance of pawns brings no change.

Why is this position so important? It is rather simple but delivers plenty of useful information. For example, it tells us what to do when the black pawn stands on h7: then h7-h5! is essential, while White, when he is on move, should prevent this advance by means of g3-g4!. Moreover, the evaluation of the diagrammed position extends automatically to a number of related situations that occur after a pawn exchange on g4, when Black remains with a g6-pawn against White's g- or h-pawn. The position with the white pawns g5 and h4 against Black's g6- and h5-pawns is also drawn.

The only possible attempt to set problems for Black, a rook transfer to the g-file after an exchange of pawns (g3 against h5), can be parried by correct defense.

1 h4!? ♗a1! 2 ♖b4 ♔g7! 3 g4 hg 4 ♖×g4 ♔h6 5 ♖g5 (5 ♔f7 ♔h5) **5...♗d4 6 ♔f7 ♗f2 7 ♖×g6+ ♔h5=**

In case of 1...♗d4? White plays 2 ♖b4 with tempo, and this fact turns out to be decisive. After 2...♗c3 3 ♖c4 ♗b2 (4...♗e1 5 ♔f6 ♔h7 6 ♖c6! ♗×g3 7 ♔g5+–) 4 g4 hg 5 ♖×g4 ♔h7 (5...♔g7 6 h5) 6 ♔f7 ♔h6 7 ♖×g6+ ♔h5 8 ♖g2! ♗c3 9 ♖h2 ♗d4 (9...♗e1 10 ♔f6 ♗×h4+ 11 ♔f5⊙) 10 ♔e6 ♗g1 11 ♖h1 ♗f2 12 ♔f5 we come to a theoretical position that is won for White, although the proof is very complicated: the main line lasts some twenty moves!

Let us check another method of exploiting the same idea: a frontal rook attack against the g6-pawn.

1 ♔d5 ♗f6 2 ♔e4 ♗c3 3 ♔f4 ♗f6

4 g4!? hg 5 ♔×g4 ♗e5 6 h3 ♗f6 7 ♔f4 ♔f8 8 ♔e4 ♔g8 9 ♔d5 ♗a1 10 ♔e6 ♗c3 11 ♖c7 ♗b2 12 h4 ♗d4 13 ♖c4

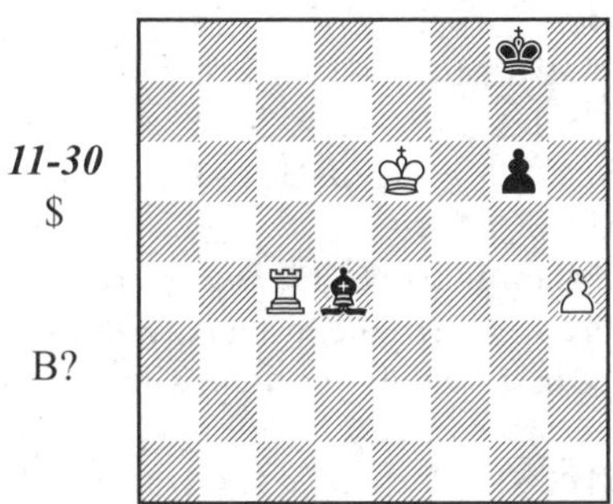

11-30
$
B?

A key moment, this position (with reversed colors) happened in a grandmaster duel at the New York tournament, 1987. Ftacnik played against Murey as follows: 13...♗b2? 14 ♖g4 ♔h7 15 ♔f7, and White won (see the line 1 h4 ♗d4?). 13...♗f2? 14 ♔f6 ♔h7 15 ♖g4 ♔h6 16 ♖×g6+ ♔h5 17 ♖g2+– is no better.

Black should have played **13...♗e3! 14 ♔f6** (14 ♖e4 ♗d2 15 ♖e2 ♗c3) **14...♔h7 15 ♖g4 ♔h6 16 ♖×g6+ ♔h5 17 ♖g3 ♗b6!! 18 ♖h3 ♔g4! 19 ♖h1 ♗d8+** with a draw.

Khalifman – Leko
Budapest m (3), 2000

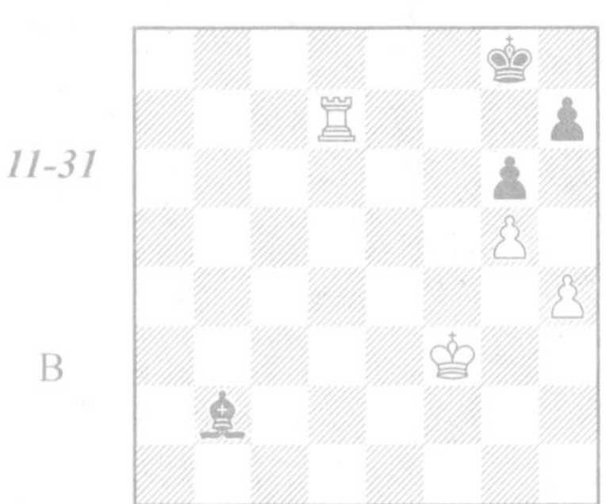

11-31
B

This pawn structure has occurred many times in practice and, up to the present day, was always evaluated as drawn. In fact, White wins by means of h4-h5, transposing to the Elkies position (diagram 11-20), although everything is not so simple – there are many subtle points in this ending.

1...♗g7!

Leko is trying to oppose White's plan. If 2 ♔g4? then 2...h5+! 3 ♔f4 ♗b2 or 3 gh ♗×h6 with an obvious draw.

1...♗c1, with the same idea, is worse on account of 2 ♖d1 ♗b2 2 ♖d8+ ♔g7 3 ♖d7+ ♔g8 4 ♔g4.

2 ♔f4

This is not a bad move, however the most direct way to a victory starts with 2 ♖d8+!? ♔f7 3 ♖b8.

A) 3...h5 4 ♖b7+ ♔g8 5 ♖×g7+! ♔×g7 6 ♔e4 ♔f7 7 ♔d5+–;

B) 3...h6 4 ♖b7+ ♔g8 5 ♔e4 (5 ♖×g7+? ♔×g7 6 ♔e4 is premature in view of 6...♔f7 7 ♔d5 ♔e7! 8 gh ♔f7= or 8 ♔e5 h5=) 5...hg 6 ♖×g7+! ♔×g7 7 hg ♔f7 8 ♔d5+–;

C) 3...♗c3 4 ♖b7+ ♔g8 5 ♔g4 △ 6 h5+–;

D) 3...♔e7 4 h5! gh 5 ♖b6 ♔f7 6 ♔g3 △ ♔h4×h5+–;

E) 3...♗f8 4 ♖b7+ (4 h5? gh 5 ♖b6 fails on account of 5...♔g8! 6 ♔g3 h6! 7 gh ♔h7 8 ♔h4 ♗×h6 9 ♔×h5 ♗d2=) 4...♔g8 5 ♔g4! (△ 6 h5+–) 5...h5+ 6 ♔f3! (rather than 6 ♔f4? ♗d6+ 7 ♔e4 ♗g3). Black could have held this position if he was able to bring the bishop to the a1-h8 diagonal, but all the roads to it are cut off: 6...♗g7 7 ♖×g7+!; 6...♗d6 7 ♖b6; 6...♗a3 7 ♔e4 △ ♔e5-f6; 6...♗c5 7 ♔e4 ♗f2 8 ♔e5 ♗×h4 9 ♔f6+–.

2...♗f8

If 2...♔f8 then 3 ♖d8+! ♔f7 4 ♖b8.

2...♗b2 is met by 3 ♔g4. Now 3...♗g7? only accelerates the loss: 4 h5 gh+ 5 ♔×h5 ♔f8 (5...♗c3 6 ♔h6; 5...♗f8 6 g6) 6 ♖b7⊙ ♔g8 7 g6. In case of 3...♗c3 White can play 4 h5 right away, but let us look at a somewhat abstract move 4 ♖c7 that leads to a position from Wolff – Browne, USA ch, Durango 1992.

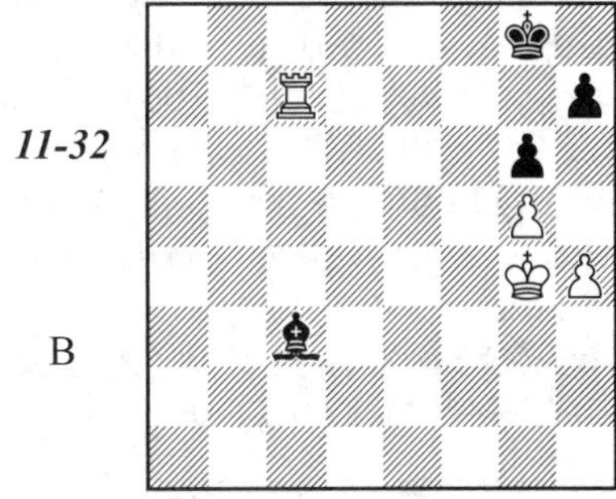

11-32
B

Where should the bishop go? We know from the previous note that 4...♗g7? 5 h5 is bad; 4...♗d4? 5 h5 gh+ 6 ♔×h5 (△ 7 ♔h6) is no better, because the bishop fails to enter the a3-f8 diagonal. The toughest resistance can be rendered by 4...♗b2 5 h5 gh+ 6 ♔×h5 ♗a3, and White has to demonstrate a truly complicated winning procedure that, by the way, had not yet been discovered when the game was played.

Browne played 4...♗e5?, and Wolff managed to carry out h4-h5 in a more favorable situation, avoiding the Elkies position. The main motif is making the access of the bishop to the a3-f8 diagonal most difficult.

5 ♖c6! ♗b2 6 ♖a6 ♗c3 (6...♗d4 7 ♖a5 ♗c3 8 ♖a4 does not change anything) 7 ♖a4! ♗e5 (7...♗g7 8 ♖a8+ ♔f7 9 ♖a7+ ♔g8 10 h5) 8 h5! gh+

In the game, Black allowed h5-h6 and, of course, lost rapidly: 8...♗c3 9 h6 ♔f7 10 ♖c4 ♗e5 11 ♔f3 ♗d6 12 ♖c8 ♔e6 13 ♖h8 ♔f5 14 ♖×h7 ♔×g5 15 ♖d7 Black resigned.

9 ♔×h5 ♗d6

The bishop has finally managed to reach the key diagonal but it stands badly on d6. White carries g5-g6 out while the black king's refuge from the dangerous corner fails.

10 ♖a8+ ♔g7 11 ♖a7+ ♔g8 12 g6 hg+ 13 ♔×g6 ♔f8 14 ♔f6 (here the bad placement of the bishop tells: after 14...♔e8 White plays 15 ♔e6 with a tempo) 14...♔g8 15 ♖g7+ ♔h8 (15...♔f8 16 ♖d7) 10 ♔g6+-.

3 h5?

White advances the pawn at the most inappropriate moment. The simplest solution was 3 ♖a7!? ♗g7 4 ♖b7! ♗f8 5 ♔g4 h5+ 6 ♔f3 +- (see the E line, the annotation to White's move 2. As Shipov noted the immediate 3 ♔g4 also wins, but after 3...h5+ White should play 4 ♔f3! ♗b4 (4...♗g7 5 ♖×g7+; 4...♗a3 5 ♖b7 ♗d6 6 ♖b6) 5 ♖c7! (preventing 5...♗c3) 5...♗e1 6 ♖c4 ♔f7 7 ♔e3 △ ♔d3, ♖e4, ♔c4-d5+- rather than 4 ♔f4? ♗a3 (△ 5...♗b2=) 5 ♖b7 ♗d6+ 6 ♔e4 ♗g3 7 ♖b3 ♗×h4 8 ♔f4 ♔f7 9 ♖b7+ ♔g8=.

3...gh 4 ♔g3 h6! 5 g6 ♗a3 6 ♔h4 ♗c1

As we know from the Elkies's analysis, this position is drawn.

7 ♔×h5 ♗g5 8 ♔g4 ♗c1 9 ♔f5 ♗g5 10 ♔e6 (10 g7 ♔h7 11 ♔e6 ♔g8)

11-33
$
B

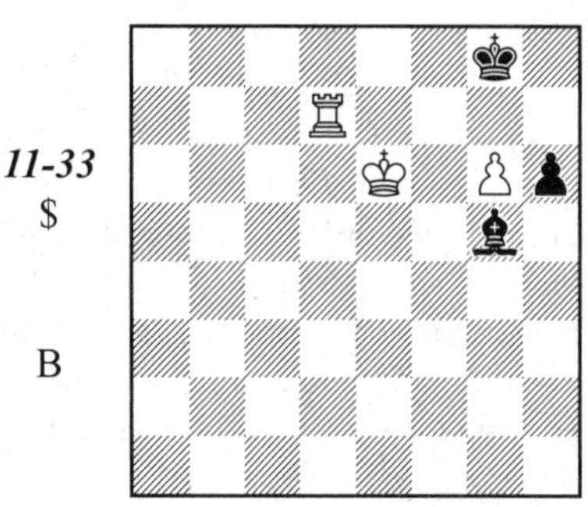

10...♗h4?!

10...♗e3 is simpler; if 11 ♖h7 ♗d2 12 g7 then 12...♗c3 or 12...♗g5.

11 ♖h7 ♗g5 12 g7!? h5□

A study-like salvation! All other moves lose: 12...♔×h7? 13 ♔f7; 12...♗d8? 13 ♖h8+; 12...♗h4? 13 ♖×h6; 12...♗e3? 13 ♔f6.

13 ♖×h5 ♗f6!

The bishop is taboo in view of the stalemate. The g7-pawn will be lost, and White cannot reach the basic winning position with the king in the dangerous corner.

14 ♖h3 ♗×g7 15 ♔e7 ♗b2 16 ♖b3 ♗d4 17 ♖d3 ♗b2 18 ♖g3+ ♔h7 19 ♔e6 ♔h6 20 ♔f5 ♔h7 21 ♖g6 ♗c3 22 ♔g5 ♗b2 23 ♔h5 ♗c3 24 ♖g2 ♗d4 25 ♖d2 ♗c3 26 ♖c2 ♗a1 27 ♖c7+ ♔g8 28 ♖d7 Draw.

Even if White succeeds in preventing such a fortress as that of diagram 11-29, by playing g2-g4 at the proper moment, Black still can hold if he builds another elementary fortress.

Olafsson – Larsen
Las Palmas 1974

11-34
B

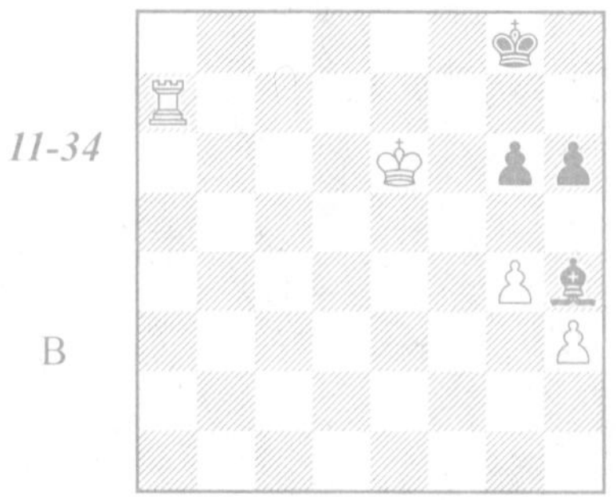

This barrier is also not to be breached.

1...♗g5 2 ♖a5 ♗h4 (but surely not 2...♔g7? 2 ♖×g5 hg 3 ♔e7+-) **3 ♖a1 ♗g5 4 ♖a4** (4 ♖h1 ♗h4!) **4...♔g7 5 ♖a7+ ♔g8 6 ♖f7 ♔h8 7 ♔e5** (7 ♖f6 ♔g7) **7...♔g8**, and the game ended in a draw.

Would the evaluation of the position be changed with the white pawn at h2 instead of h3? In such cases, White has the following way to play for a win: the king comes to h3 and drives the bishop away from h4, then ♔g3 and h2-h4-h5 follow. I have seen analysis of this situation only in a two-volume endgame treatise by Villeneuve (in French, 1984).

11-35
$
W

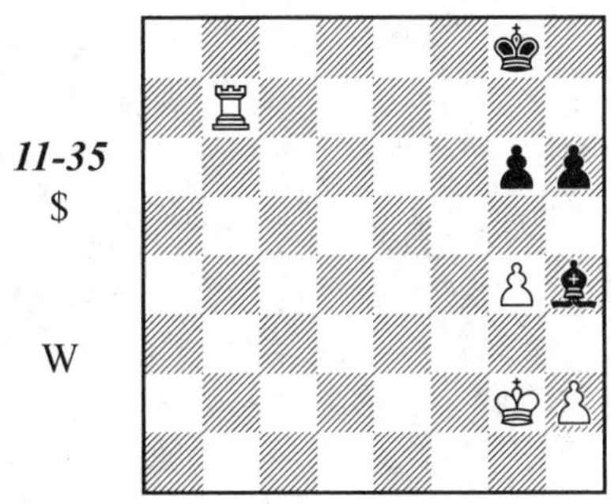

1 ♔h3 ♗f2 (1...♗f6!?) **2 ♖b2 ♗d4 3 ♖e2 ♗f6** (or 3...♔g7 4 ♔g3 ♗f6!) **4 ♔g3 ♔g7 5 h4** (5 ♖e6 ♔f7 6 ♖a6 ♗e5+) **5...h5! 6 gh** (6 g5 ♗c3, transposing to the main fortress as in the diagram 11-29) **6...gh**

It seems that Black achieves a draw. For example: 7 ♖e4 ♔g6 8 ♔f3 ♔f5 9 ♖f4+ ♔e5 10 ♔e3 ♗d8 etc.

Tragicomedies

Smyslov – Chiburdanidze
Monaco 1994

11-36
B

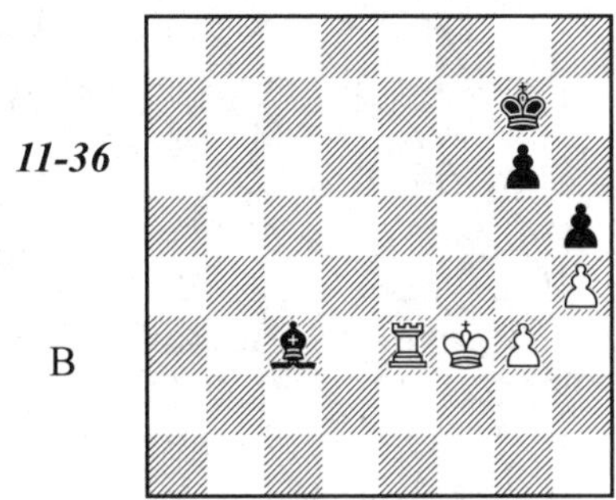

1...♗d2?

Chiburdanidze obviously did not know the basic drawn position, otherwise she would have kept the bishop on the main diagonal: 1...♗f6=.

2 ♖d3 ♗e1?

2...♗c1! (△ 3...♗b2) 3 ♖b3 g5 would have held out longer; but as Karsten Müller indicated, White would still win by continuing 4 ♖b1 ♗d2 5 ♖b7+ ♔g6 6 ♖b6+ ♔g7 7 ♔e2 ♗a5 8 ♖b5 ♗d8 9 ♖d5 ♗f6 10 hg, etc.

3 ♔f4+– ♔f6 4 ♖d6+ ♔f7 5 ♔g5 ♗×g3 6 ♖f6+ ♔e7 7 ♖×g6 ♗e1 8 ♔×h5 ♔f7 9 ♖g2 ♔f6 10 ♖e2 ♗g3 11 ♖e4 Black resigned.

Exercises

11-37
11/7
W?

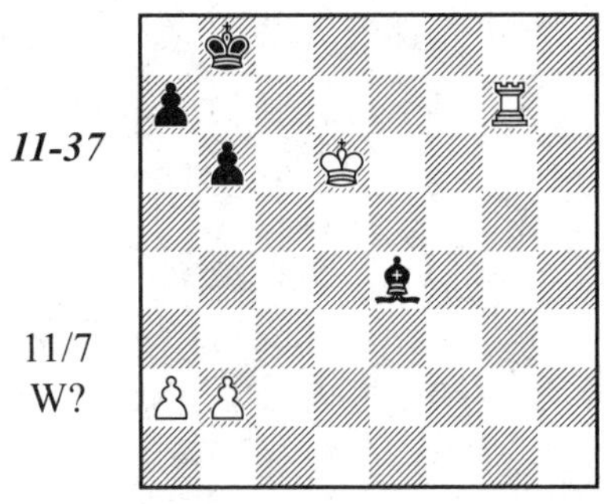

11-38
11/8
W?

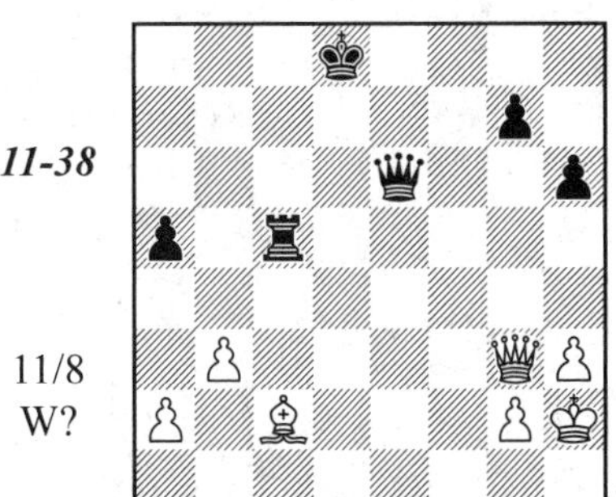

Three Pawns vs. Three on the Same Wing

With three pawns on each side a fortress, as a rule, cannot be built. Salvation is possible only in exceptional cases: when the pawn structure of the stronger side has flaws.

Radev – Pribyl
Tbilisi 1971

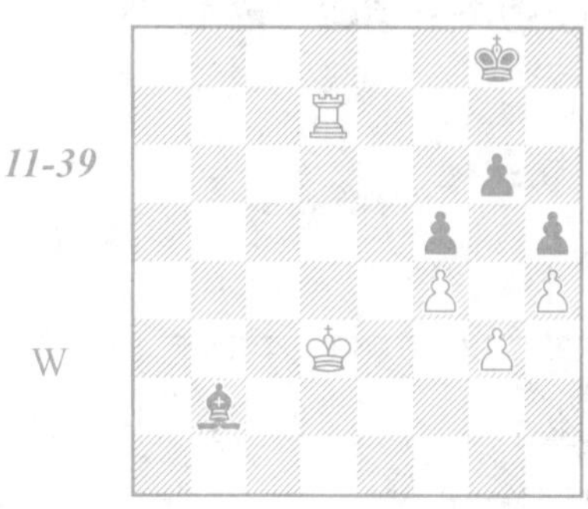

11-39

W

This situation resembles diagram 11-29, only the f-pawns are added. It again seems as if White cannot overcome the barrier, but in actuality, he can by means of a spectacular pawn breakthrough.

Two years later, a similar endgame occurred in a game Kholmov – Tseshkovsky, USSR chsf 1973. Grandmaster Kholmov wrote a detailed analysis, which was published in a periodical, and I reproduce it here in a slightly abridged and corrected form.

1 ♔c4 ♔f8 2 ♔d5 ♔g8 3 ♔e6 ♗c3 4 ♖d3! ♗b2 5 g4!!+–

The game continued:

5...hg?! 6 h5 ♔g7

Or 6...gh 7 ♔xf5 ♔g7 (7...♗c1 8 ♔g6 ♔f8 9 f5) 8 ♖d7+ ♔h6 (8...♔g8 9 ♔g6; 8...♔f8 9 ♖h7) 9 ♖d6+ ♔h7 (9...♔g7 10 ♖g6+ ♔h7 11 ♔g5 ♗c1 12 ♖h6+ ♔g7 13 ♖xh5 g3 14 ♖h3) 10 ♔g5 ♗c1 11 ♖d7+ ♔g8 12 ♔g6 ♔f8 13 f5 g3 14 f6+–.

7 hg ♔xg6 8 ♖d5 ♗c1

Black still follows the path of least resistance. However a rapid climax also occurs after 8...♔h5: 9 ♔xf5 ♔h4 (9...g3 10 ♖d1) 10 ♖d6! ♗c1 (10...♔h3 11 ♖h6+ ♔g3 12 ♖g6) 11 ♖g6+–.

9 ♖xf5 ♗xf4 (9...♔h6 10 ♔e5 △ 11 ♖g5) 10 ♖xf4 ♔g5 11 ♔e5 g3 12 ♔e4 g2 13 ♖f8 ♔h4 14 ♖g8 Black resigned.

A tougher method is **5...fg!? 6 f5 gf 7 ♔xf5** (△ 8 ♔g6) **7...♔f7 8 ♔g5**

An alternative is 8 ♖d7+, for example 8...♔e8 9 ♖h7 g3 10 ♖xh5 ♗c1 11 ♔f6! (rather than 11 ♖h7?, in view of the pretty response 11...♗g5!!=) 11...♔d7 (11...g2 12 ♖h8+ ♔d7 13 ♖g8; 11...♗b2+? 12 ♔e6) 12 ♖d5+ ♔e8 (12...♔c6 13 ♖d8 △ 14 ♖g8) 13 ♖e5+ ♔d7 (13...♔f8 14 ♖c5 ♗b2+ 15 ♔g6) 14 ♖e4 and 15 ♖g4+–.

Black can also try 8...♔f8!?.

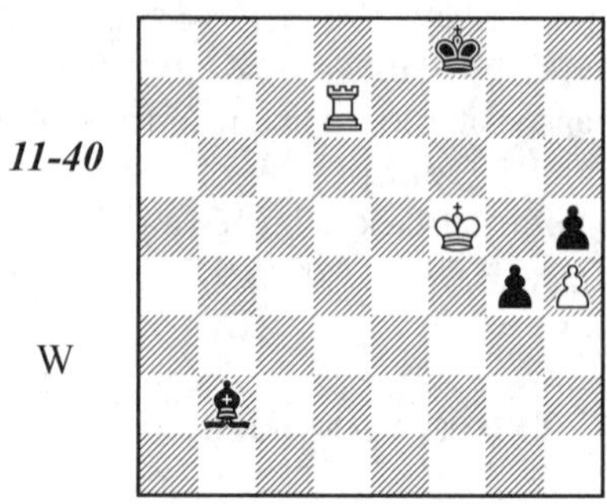

11-40

W

Now Nunn's idea was 9 ♖h7? g3 10 ♖xh5 ♗c1 11 ♔f6 ♔g8 (11...♗b2+? 12 ♔g6 ♗c1 13 ♖f5+ and 14 ♖f3) 12 ♖c5 ♗e3 13 ♖c7 ♗d4+ (here Black already can improve Nunn's analysis with 13...♗b6! 14 ♖g7+ ♔f8 15 ♖xg3 ♗d8+ and 16...♗xh4=, or 14 ♖c2 ♔h7! followed with ...♗f2=) 14 ♔g6 ♔f8 15 ♖c2 ♔e7 (15...♗f2 16 ♖e2!+–) 16 ♖e2+ ♔d6 17 ♖g2 ♗f2 18 h5, but it does not work because the final position is drawn: 18...♔e5! 19 h6 ♔f4 20 h7 ♗d4=.

White should play 9 ♔g6! g3 10 ♖d5 (10 ♖f7+!?) 10...♗c1 11 ♖d8+!

An important intermediate check that prevents the bishop from accessing e3 in the future. Kholmov analyzed solely 11 ♖d3, but after 11...♗f4 White has neither 12 ♖f3? g2 13 ♖xf4+ ♔g8= nor 12 ♖d1? ♗e3= (however 12 ♖d8+ ♔e7 13 ♖d1 is still playable).

11...♔e7 12 ♖d1 ♗a3 (12...♗e3?? 13 ♖e1; 12...♗f4!?) 13 ♖g1 (13 ♔xh5? ♗c5=) 13...♗d6 14 ♔xh5 ♔f6 15 ♔g4+–. This position can be achieved much more rapidly after 8 ♔g5, and we now return to this move.

8...♗e5 9 ♔xh5 g3 10 ♖d2 ♔f6 11 ♔g4 ♔g6 12 ♖e2 ♗b8 13 h5+ ♔h6 14 ♖e6+ ♔h7 15 ♖g6 ♗c7 16 ♔f5 ♗b8

Kholmov proceeds with 17 h6 and demonstrates a win after 10 more moves. But **17 ♖b6!** wins immediately.

If the pawns are still not in contact (for example, Black's pawns f7, g6, and h5; White's pawns on their initial squares), the winning procedure is easier. If Black has a white-squared bishop that protects the f7-pawn, White comes with his king to e7, places the rook on f6, and advances the pawns (h2-h3, g2-g4, f2-f4-f5).

In the case of a dark-squared bishop, the white king goes to e8 and attacks the f7-pawn in order to force its advance. After ...f7-f5, White can build the position that we have just seen; but a simpler way is to come back to e6 with the king, to bring all the pawns to the 3rd rank and the rook to g2, and finally to carry out the advance g3-g4.

Tragicomedies

Balashov – Shirov
USSR ch(1), Klaipeda 1988

11-41

B?

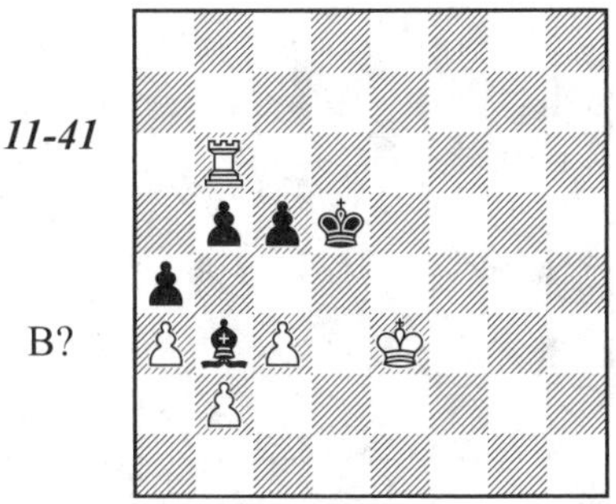

This is the rare case when the defender can hope for salvation because of the counterattacking possibility: ...♔d5-c4-b3. However he should not carry out this counterattack prematurely.

The game continued **1...♔c4? 2 ♔d2**, and Black resigned in view of 2...♗a2 3 ♔c1 ♗b3 4 ♖d6⊙ ♗a2 5 ♔c2 ♗b3+ 6 ♔b1 with a decisive zugzwang. (6...b4 7 ab cb 8 ♖d4+).

The correct defense was: 1...♗c4!, for example: 2 ♖b8 ♔e5 3 ♖e8+ ♔d5 4 ♔f4 ♗d3! 5 ♖d8+ ♔c4 6 ♔e5 ♗c2! 7 ♔d6 b4! 8 cb cb with a probable draw after 9 ab ♔×b4 or 9 ♖b8 ba.

Stefan Sievers has established that the position is still won. The correct plan begins with the move 2 ♖f6!, taking away the f1-square from the bishop, and preparing to cut off the king on the rank. Once again, counterplay on the light-squares fails because of the bishop's unfortunate position: 2...♗a2 3 ♖f1 ♔c4 4 ♔d2 ♔d5 (on 4...♔b3 5 ♔c1 ♔c4 6 ♖d1, we soon arrive at our familiar zugzwang) 5 ♖f5+ ♔c4 6 ♔c2 ♗b3+ 7 ♔c1 ♗a2 8 b4! +–. And if 2...♔e5, then 3 ♖g6 ♗a2 4 ♖g5+ ♔d6 5 ♔f4 ♗b1 6 ♖h5 ♗d3 7 ♔g5 ♔d5 8 ♖h4 ♔e5 9 ♔h6, and Black has no way to prevent the enemy king from coming in behind him.

Chapter 12

QUEEN ENDGAMES

Queen and Pawn vs. Queen

If the defender's king stands in front of the pawn, the draw is usually an easy matter.

Botvinnik – Tal
Moscow wm (12) 1960

12-1

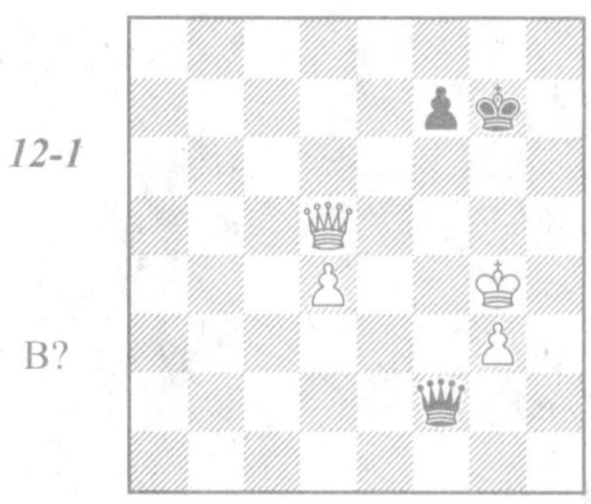

B?

1...f5+! 2 ♔g5

After 2 ♕×f5 ♕×d4+ Black's defense is even simpler because his king is already standing in front of the pawn and almost every instance of a queen exchange is acceptable for him.

2...♕×g3+ 3 ♔×f5 ♕g6+ 4 ♔f4 ♕f6+ 5 ♔e3 ♔f8! 6 ♔d3

If Tal played 6...♔e7 here, there would have been no doubt about a draw. What he did instead made his task more complicated.

6...♕f1+ 7 ♔e4 ♕g2+?! (7...♔e7!=) **8 ♔e5 ♕g5+ 9 ♔e6 ♕e7+ 10 ♔f5**

If 10...♕f7(h7)+ then 11 ♔e5. After 11...♕h5+? (11...♕e7+ is better) 12 ♔d6 Black cannot trade queens, the checks will soon expire, and his king will be forced to the g-file, farther from the pawn.

10...♕c7!

"However strange it may seem, Black evidently has secured the draw only with this move... Now White's pieces are ideally placed; any move will just worsen his position." (Tal).

11 ♕a8+ ♔e7 12 ♕e4+ ♔d8 13 ♕h4+ ♔c8 14 ♕h8+ ♔b7 15 ♕e5 ♕f7+ 16 ♔e4 ♕g6+ 17 ♕f5 ♕d6! 18 ♕f7+ ♔c8 19 ♕f5+ ♔d8 20 ♕a5+ ♔e8 21 d5 ♔e7 22 ♕a7+ ♔d8 23 ♕a8+ ♔d7 24 ♔f5 ♔e7 Draw.

Now we come to those exceptionally complicated cases when the king of the weaker side is placed far away from the pawn. Computers have proved that a win, when it exists, can often be achieved (when both sides play correctly) only after more than 50 moves! Practical players should not delve too deeply into this jungle, for these endings occur quite seldom. We shall confine ourselves to basic theoretical statements and the most important practical methods.

Botvinnik was the first to find the correct method for the stronger side, during an analysis of the following adjourned game:

Botvinnik - Minev
Amsterdam ol 1954

12-2

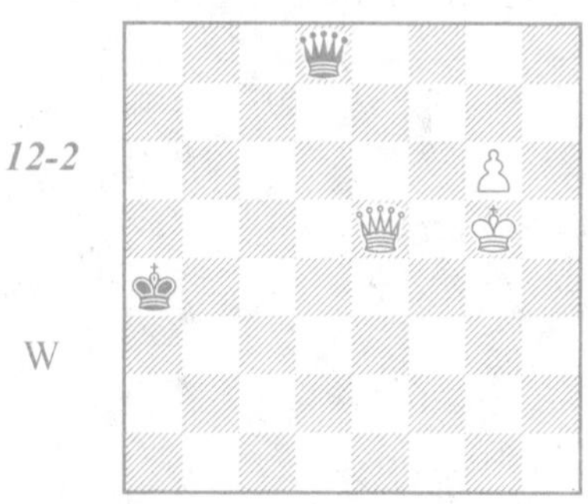

W

1 ♕f6

1 ♔h6? ♕h4+ 2 ♔g7 is much weaker, as Botvinnik played in an identical position against Ravinsky eight years earlier. ***One should not place his king in front of his pawn.***

According to computer analysis, 1 ♔f5! is more precise; if 1...♕c8+ (this position already occurred on a previous move) then 2 ♔f4! ♕c1+ 3 ♕e3 ♕c7+ 4 ♔g4 ♕d7+ 5 ♔h4 ♕d8+ 6 ♔g3 (there are no checks anymore, 6...♕d6+ loses to 7 ♕f4+), or 5...♕g7 6 ♔g5 etc. (this "etc.," by the way, lasts more than 20 moves at least).

1...♕d5+ 2 ♕f5 ♕d8+ 3 ♔h5

The stronger side should place the king on the same file or rank where the defender's king is standing, or an adjacent file or rank (this rule is also valid when more pawns are present on the board).

This tactic often enables counter-checks when the queen provides protection from a defender's check by interference. For example, now Black cannot play 3...♕d1+ in view of 4 ♕g4+. Or 3...♕h8+ 4 ♔g4, and Black cannot play 4...♕d4+ because of 5 ♕f4 as 4...♕g7 loses to 5 ♕f7! ♕c3 6 g7!.

3...♕e8 4 ♕f4+?

An error that was left unnoticed by Botvinnik. The computer analysis shows that the correct winning process is 4 ♔g4! ♕e2+ 5 ♔f4 ♕d2+ 6 ♔e5 ♕b2+ 7 ♔d6 ♕b8+ 8 ♔e7 ♕b4+ 9 ♔f7 ♕b7+ 10 ♔f6 ♕b6+ 11 ♕e6 (this is only an introduction: a lot of precise moves are still required for achieving success).

But why is the move actually played wrong? Because, ***when dealing with a knight or rook pawn, the defender's king is best placed near the corner that is diametrically opposite to the pawn promotion square. In this case, when the stronger side defends his king from checks with a queen interference, a counter-check is less probable.***

Black could have played 4...♔a3! here and theory says that it is a draw, although it is a long way from a theoretical evaluation to a half-point in the tournament table, because these positions are very difficult to defend.

We should add that ***the indicated drawing zone does not exist in case of a bishop or central pawn***. One can only expect that the opponent's play will not be precise (although defender's errors are more probable in these situations) or... that the king manages to reach the area in front of the pawn like in the Botvinnik - Tal endgame.

By the way, ***the drawing zone, near the pawn, is considerably larger in case of a rook pawn, compared with other pawns, because the defender can go for a queen exchange much more often***.

Having arrived at general considerations about various pawn cases, I add two more remarks:

1) The farther the pawn is advanced, the less the defender's chance for a draw;

2) The closer the pawn is to the edge of the board; the greater the drawing chances. With central and bishop pawns, practically all positions with a remote king are lost. With a knight pawn, winning positions occur very often. With a rook pawn, a draw can be reached in a majority of positions, although the defense is not simple.

4...♔a5?

The wrong way! But this choice was not made purely by chance. The above-mentioned game Botvinnik - Ravinsky was thoroughly annotated by Keres, and the Estonian grandmaster erroneously suggested keeping the king on a5 and a4.

5 ♕d2+ ♔a4 6 ♕d4+ ♔a5 7 ♔g5

Take notice of White's last moves. ***The queen is placed best on the central squares (this is usually valid for the defender's queen as well). The closer the queen is to the edge of the board, the winning process is more difficult and the probability of a perpetual check is higher.***

By the way, now we can easily explain why Botvinnik's 1 ♕f6 was less accurate than 1 ♔f5!. His queen should not leave the center unless it's an emergency.

7...♕e7+ 8 ♔f5! ♕f8+ 9 ♔e4 ♕h6 10 ♕e5+ ♔a4 11 g7

Finally the pawn succeeds in moving forward, and the climax is near. The finish is also very instructive: White approaches the black king with his monarch in order to create a situation when every check can be met with a countercheck. This method (***king-to-king***) is characteristic for queen-and-pawn endings.

11...♕h1+ 12 ♔d4 ♕d1+ 13 ♔c5 ♕c1+ 14 ♔d6 (14 ♔d5?! ♕c8) **14...♕d2+** (14...♕h6+ 15 ♔d5!) **15 ♔e6 ♕a2+ 16 ♕d5 ♕e2+ 17 ♔d6 ♕h2+ 18 ♔c5!**

12-3

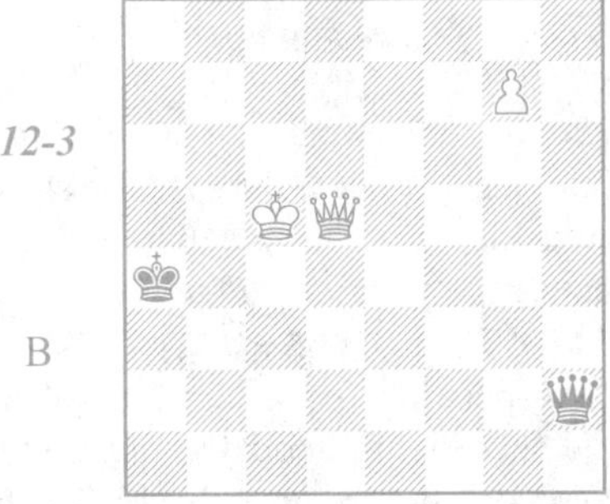

B

Black resigned.

Tragicomedies

Shamkovich – Wirthensohn
Biel 1980

12-4

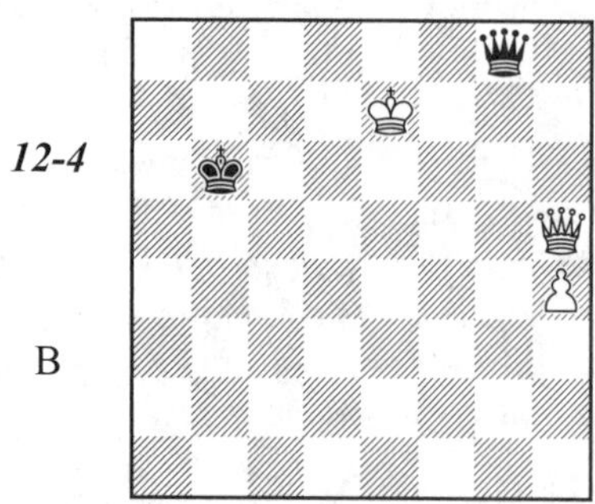

B

We shall not go deeply into the intricate lines; instead, we merely want to match the computer evaluations of the actual moves with the general considerations that are already known to us from the annotations to the previous example. Because of the rook pawn, Black can hope for a successful defense. And, as a matter of fact, the position was still drawn after 1...♕g3 or 1...♕c4.

1...♕g7+?

This move would have made sense if the series of checks could continue. However, the white king is superbly placed on the rank adjacent to his adversary's, and even one single check will not be possible after White's reply. Hence Black's move is bad. It allows White to rescue his queen from boredom with tempo.

2 ♕f7!+– ♕g3 (2...♕e5+? 3 ♕e6+) **3 ♕f6+ ♔c7 4 ♕g5?**

Shamkovich only worsens the position of his queen, moving it closer to the edge. He should have pushed his pawn in order to obtain a position that can be won in ... 69 moves (!).

4...♕a3+ 5 ♔f7 ♕b3+ 6 ♔g7 ♕c3+?

A drawn position (not a draw as such – Black would have spent a good deal of sweat for it) could be maintained after a check from b2. Detailed analysis is not required to see that the black king will get in the queen's way in some lines now.

7 ♕f6 ♕g3+ 8 ♔h7?

But this is not merely an error; this is neglect of principles. As we have stated, the king should not seek exile in front of the pawn. Both 8 ♕g5 and 8 ♔f7 are winning, but 8 ♔f8! is the most precise.

8...♕h3 9 ♕g5 ♔b6?

This counter-error is also very instructive. As we know, there is a drawing zone near a rook pawn, and this zone is rather spacious (its precise borders depend on the placement of the pieces, and most important on how far advanced the pawn is; we shall not give precise definitions here). The king was already standing in the zone, therefore many queen moves were not losing, but the most logical decision was to go towards the pawn: 9...♔d7(d6)!=.

10 h5 ♕d7+

12-5

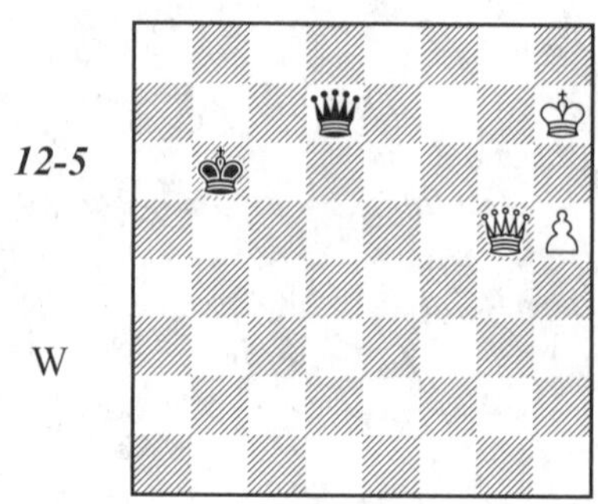

W

11 ♕g7?

White worsens his queen's position. All king moves were winning.

11...♕h3?

The black queen had to guard the central squares. 11...♕d5! was good enough for a draw.

12 ♕e5!+–

The white queen has finally arrived in the center, Black's king is out of the drawing zone – White's position is winning!

12...♕d7+ 13 ♔g6 ♕d3+ 14 ♕f5 ♕g3+ 15 ♔f7 ♕c7+ 16 ♔g8 ♕b8+ 17 ♔g7 ♕c7+ 18 ♕f7 ♕h2 19 h6 ♔a5 20 h7 ♕e5+ 21 ♕f6 ♕g3+ 22 ♔h6!

Black resigned in view of 22...♕h2+ 23 ♔g6! and the checks expire because of the correct position of the white king (on a rank adjacent to his black counterpart).

Winning Tactical Tricks

The queen is the strongest piece; therefore ***play for checkmate*** occurs in queen endgames more often than in other kinds of endings. Among other techniques, ***gaining a queen*** (usually by means of a skewer check) and ***exchange of queens*** should be mentioned.

These three tools can all be seen in the next example.

K. Eucken, 1947*

12-6

W?

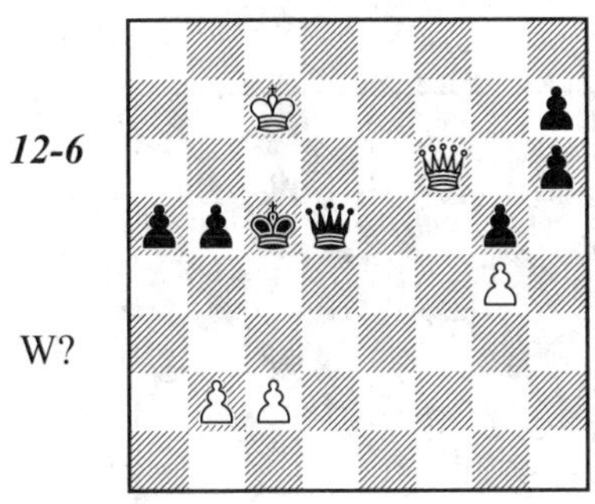

1 c4!!

Every capture of the pawn leads to a mate in one. After 1...♕d3 White forces an exchange of the queens by means of 2 ♕c6+ ♔d4 3 ♕d5+ ♔e3 4 ♕×d3+ ♔×d3 5 cb; 1...♕e4 has the same consequences after 2 ♕f5+! ♕×f5 3 gf+−. Finally, every other retreat of the queen leads to its loss, for example:

1...♕a8 2 ♕e5+ ♔×c4 3 ♕c3+ ♔d5 4 ♕f3+;

1...♕h1 2 ♕e5+ ♔×c4 3 ♕c3+ ♔d5 4 ♕c6+;

1...♕g8 2 ♕e5+ ♔×c4 3 ♕c3+ ♔d5 4 ♕b3+.

Tragicomedies

Batuev – Simagin
Riga 1954

12-7

B

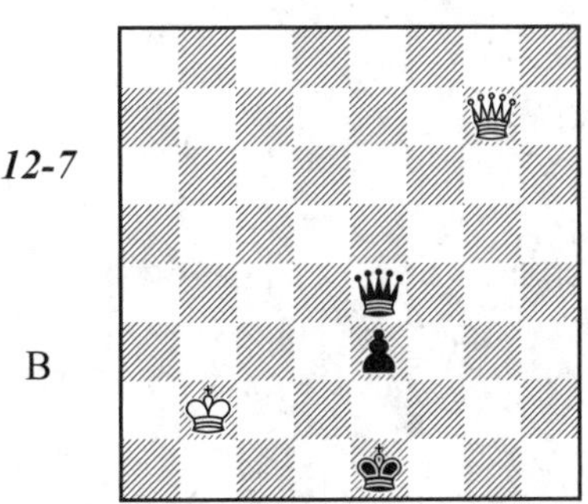

As we know, a defense against a central pawn is practically always a hopeless matter. The simplest winning process here is 1...♕b4+ 2 ♔c2 ♕c4+ 3 ♔b2 ♔d2 (king-to-king!). But miracles happen from time to time.

1...e2?? 2 ♕g1+ ♔d2 3 ♕c1+ ♔d3 4 ♕c3#.

A year later, Simagin got a gift in return.

Borisenko – Simagin
USSR ch, Moscow 1955

12-8

W

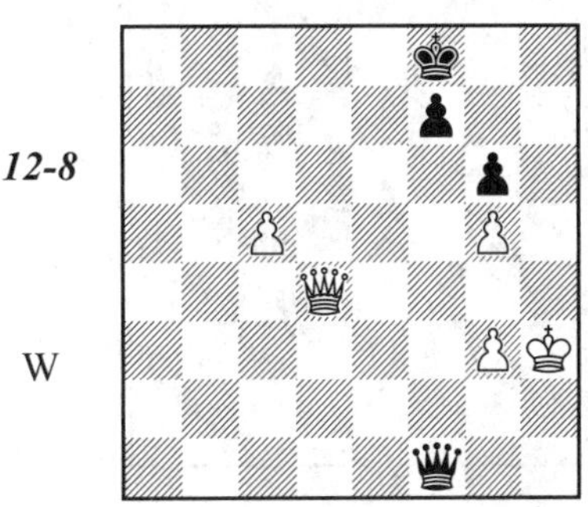

Contrary to the previous example, the extra pawn cannot be exploited here. If 1 ♔h4, 1...♕e2! is strong, while 1 ♔h2 is met with 1...♕e2+ 2 ♔g1 ♕e1+ 3 ♔g2 ♕e2+ 4 ♕f2 ♕d3(c4)!=.

Winning chances can only be obtained by a king march to the passed pawn, so Borisenko pushed his king ahead.

1 ♔g4??

White had only expected 1...♕e2+ 2 ♔f4 or 1...♕f5+ 2 ♔h4, and 2...♕f3 fails to 3 ♕d8+ ♔g7 4 ♕f6+!.

1...f5+!

White resigned because he cannot avoid a checkmate: 2 ♔h4 ♕h1# or 2 gf ♕f5+ 3 ♔h4 ♕h5#.

Exercises

12-9

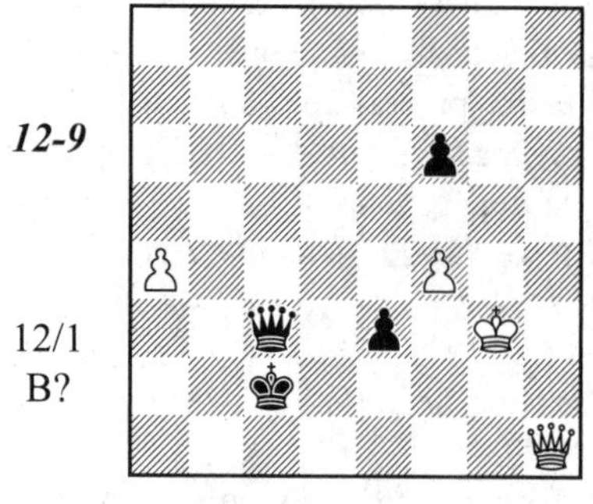

12/1
B?

12-12

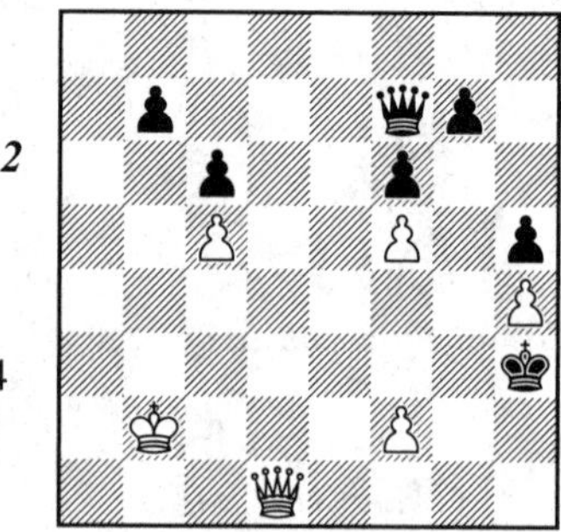

12/4
W?

12-10

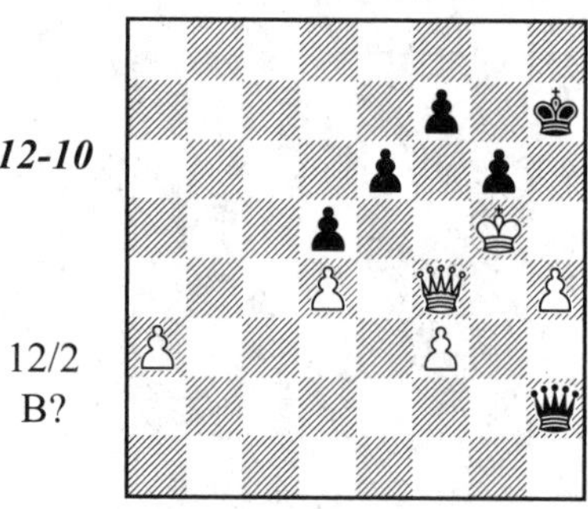

12/2
B?

12-13

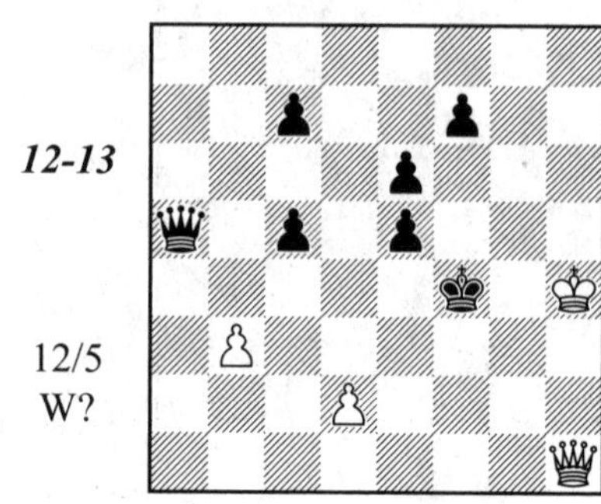

12/5
W?

12-11

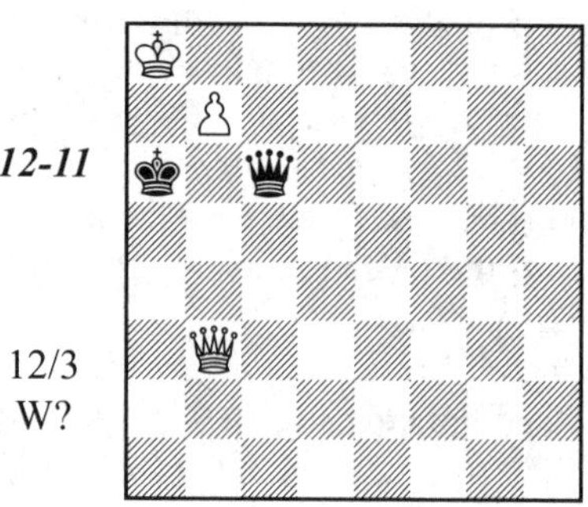

12/3
W?

Defensive Tactics

The main tactical tools that can save a difficult queen-and-pawn endgame are *stalemate* and *perpetual check*.

Y. Averbakh, 1962

12-14
$
W

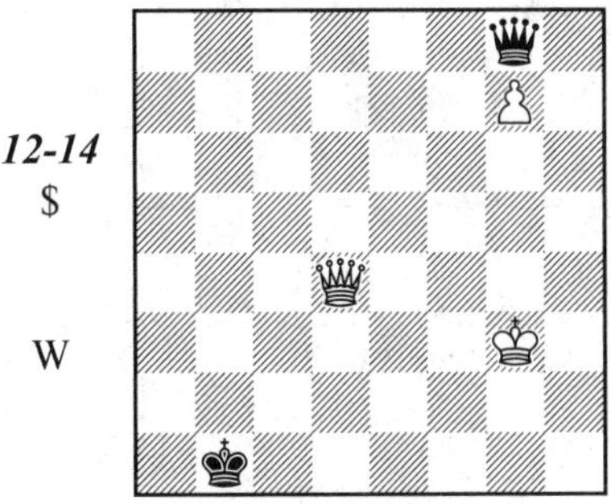

A straightforward implementation of the king-to-king process does not bring any success here.

1 ♔f2? ♕f7+ 2 ♔e1 ♕e6+ 3 ♔d1 ♕b3+ 4 ♔d2 ♕a2+! 5 ♔e3 (the checks seem to be exhausted) **5...♕b3+! 6 ♕d3+? ♔a1!=**

The queen cannot be captured because of stalemate, while a king's retreat loses the pawn: 7 ♔d4 ♕b4+! 8 ♕c4 (8 ♔d5 ♕b7+; 8 ♔e5 ♕e7+) 8...♕d2+ 9 ♔c5 ♕g5+.

Both 1 ♕e4+ and 1 ♕g4 win, but the simplest winning procedure is moving the king downstairs to g1 (where the black queen cannot reach him) followed by a queen transfer to f8.

1 ♕g1+! ♔a2 2 ♕g2+ ♔a1 (2...♔a3 is the same) 3 ♔h2! ♕b8+ (3...♕h7+ 4 ♕g1) 4 ♔h1 ♕g8 5 ♕g1! ♔b1 6 ♕f1+ ♔b2 7 ♕f8+–.

J. Speelman

12-15
B

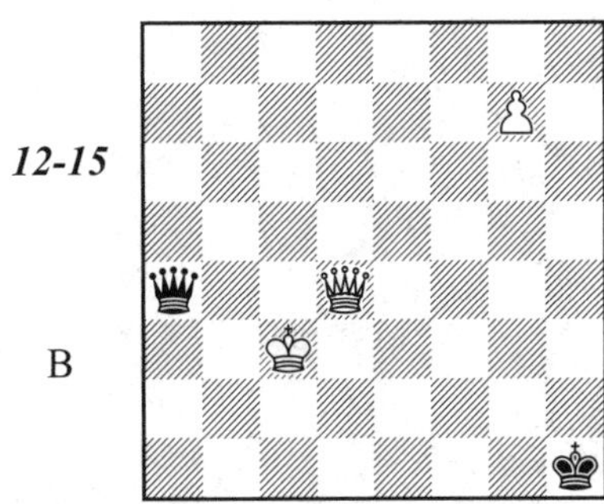

This is a standard configuration of a perpetual check, when the king cannot abandon its queen.

1...♕a1+! 2 ♔d3 ♕d1+ 3 ♔e3 ♕g1+! 4 ♔e4 ♕g4+ 5 ♔d5 ♕d7+ 6 ♔c5 ♕a7+ 7 ♔c4 ♕a4+ 8 ♔c3 ♕a1+, etc.

The following example demonstrates an interesting maneuver of the white king. After the threat of a perpetual check had been eliminated, White exploited his advantage in an instructive way.

Tukmakov – Agzamov
Erevan zt 1982

12-16
W?

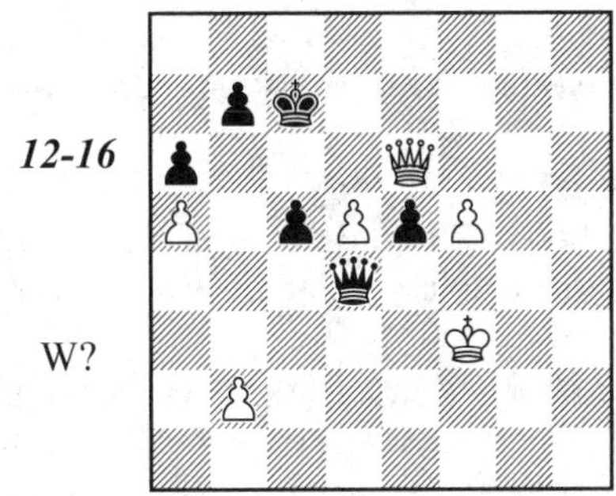

1 ♔g3!

The premature advance 1 f6? leads to a draw: 1...♕f4+ 2 ♔g2 ♕g5+ 3 ♔h3 ♕h5+. Therefore Tukmakov brings his king to h3 first, and only thereafter he intends to push the f-pawn. For example, 1...c4!? 2 ♔h3! (2 f6? is still wrong; 2 ♕b6+? also does not win in view of 2...♕×b6 3 ab+ ♔d7! 4 f6 a5 5 ♔g4 e4!=) 2...♕×b2 3 f6! ±.

1...♕f4+ 2 ♔h3 c4

While the white queen protects the h6-square, Black has no perpetual check.

3 ♕e7+ ♔c8

3...♔b8 4 ♕f8+ ♔a7 was more tenacious, although after 5 d6! e4 6 d7 or 5...♕g5 6 ♕f7 Black's situation still would have been difficult.

4 ♕f8+ ♔d7 5 f6+– ♕f3+ 6 ♔h4 ♕f4+ 7 ♔h5 ♕f3+ 8 ♔g6 ♕e4+ 9 ♔g7 ♕g2+ 10 ♔h7 ♕e4+ 11 ♔g8

The king, as usual, has found an exile from the checks on an adjacent rank to his adversary.

11...♕×d5+ 12 f7 ♔c6

12...♕e6 13 ♕g7 e4 14 ♔h8+–.

13 ♕c8+ ♔b5 14 ♔g7 ♕g2+ 15 ♔f6 ♕f3+ 16 ♔e7 Black resigned.

Tragicomedies

Chigorin – Schlechter
Ostende 1905

12-17

B

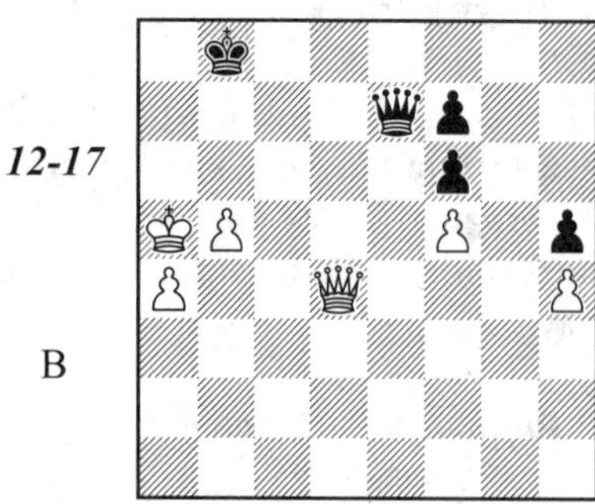

1...♕c7+!

The last trap in this totally hopeless position.

2 ♕b6+??

After 2 b6 or 2 ♔b4 Black would have had only one option – to capitulate.

2...♔a8!

Draw. If White takes the queen Black is stalemated, otherwise a sort of perpetual check happens: 3 ♔a6 ♕c8+ 4 ♔a5 ♕c7!.

Alekhine – Maróczy
New York 1924

12-18

W

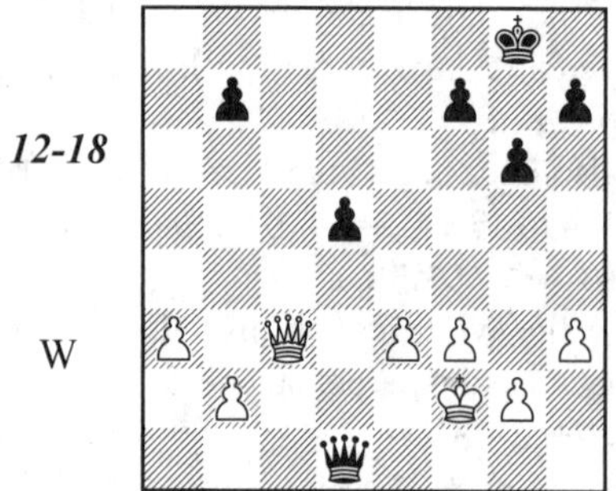

White's extra pawn must bring him a relatively easy win. Alekhine recommends 1 ♕d4! ♕c2+ 2 ♔g3 (△ 3 ♕×d5 ♕×b2 4 ♕d8+ ♔g7 5 ♕d4+) 2...♕c6 3 a4. 1 ♔g3!, planning 2 ♔h2, was also strong.

However, White greedily went after the b7-pawn.

1 ♕c8+?! ♔g7 2 ♕×b7?? (it was not too late to retreat: 2 ♕c3+) **2...♕d2+ 3 ♔g3 d4! 4 ed ♕g5+**

Draw. The king cannot escape from the checks.

Exercises

12-19

12/6
W?

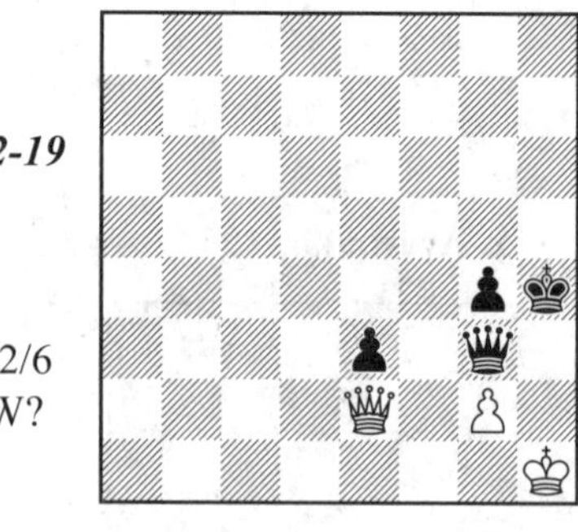

12-20

12/7
B?

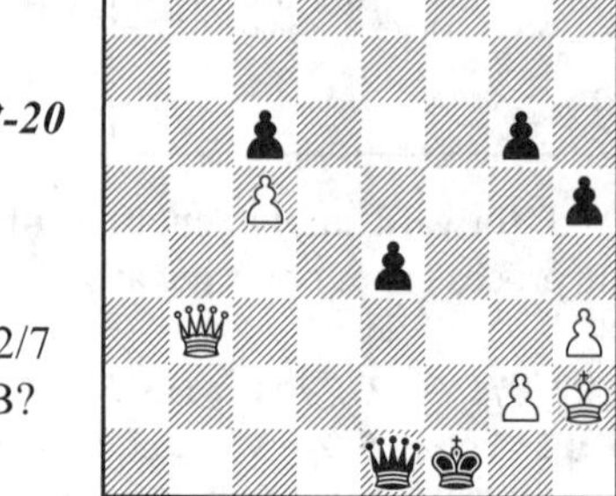

Pawns on the Same Wing

With a normal pawn structure, endgames of "one pawn versus two," "two pawns versus three," and "three pawns against four" on the same wing are drawn.

Larsen – Keres
San Antonio 1972

12-21

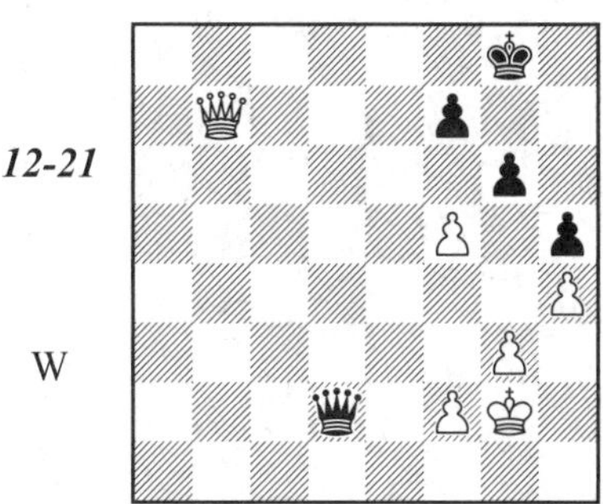

W

1 f6

An alternative was 1 fg fg 2 ♕e4±. The basic defensive principle is simple: Black should prevent an invasion by the white king.

The move actually played also does not promise any winning chances. Even with the f5-pawn moved to the e-file, there would have been no win.

1...♕d8 2 ♕c6 ♔h7 3 ♕c3 ♕d5+ 4 f3 ♕a2+ 5 ♔h3 ♕b1 6 ♔g2 ♕a2+ 7 ♔f1 ♕a6+ 8 ♔e1 ♕e6+ 9 ♔f2 ♕a2+ 10 ♔g1 ♕b1+ 11 ♔g2 ♕a2+ 12 ♔h3 ♕b1 13 g4 ♕h1+ 14 ♔g3 ♕g1+ 15 ♔f4??

White should have accepted a drawish outcome: 15 ♔h3. The attempt to play for a win turns out to be playing for a loss.

15...♕h2+ 16 ♔g5?!

After 16 ♔e4 ♕×h4 White's position is difficult but it is better than the game continuation.

16...♕g3!

There is no satisfactory defense from 17...hg.

17 ♕e3 hg 18 ♕f4 ♕×f3 19 ♕×g4 ♕e3+ 20 ♕f4 ♕e2 21 ♕g3 ♕b5+ 22 ♔f4 ♕f5+ 23 ♔e3 ♕×f6−+

12-22

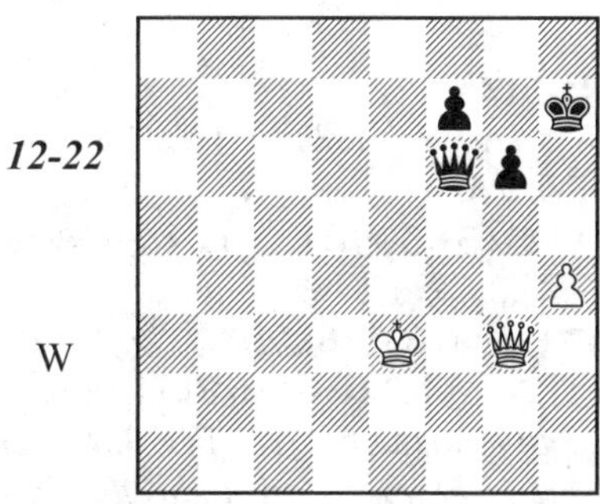

W

In this case, two pawns win against one. Firstly, because one of them is passed; secondly, because the white king is cut off from the kingside and the h4-pawn is therefore vulnerable.

24 ♕g5 ♕f1 25 ♕g4 (25 ♕d8 ♔g7 △ ♕f6) **25...♕e1+** (the king is driven away even more) **26 ♔d3 ♕e6 27 ♕f4 ♔g7 28 ♕d4+ f6 29 ♕b4** (29 ♕f4 ♕e5 30 ♕g4 ♔h6) **29...♕f5+ 30 ♔e2**

If 30 ♔e3, Black wins by means of 30...♔h6 31 ♕f8+ ♔h5 32 ♕h8+ ♔g4 33 ♕h6 ♕f3+!, forcing a queen exchange.

30...♔h6 31 ♔e1

After 31 ♕f8+ ♔h5 32 ♕h8+ ♔g4 33 ♕h6 the check from f3 is weaker because of 34 ♔e1, but Black has 33...♕h5!, and every queen retreat will be met with ...♔×h4 resulting in a discovered check. Quicker success can be achieved by means of 33...♕c2+! and 34...♔f3: a mating attack.

31...♔h5 32 ♕c4 ♕g4 33 ♕c5+ ♔×h4 34 ♕e7 ♕f5 35 ♕b4+ ♔h5 36 ♕c4 g5 37 ♕f7+ ♔h4 38 ♕f8 ♔g3 39 ♕a3+ ♕f3 40 ♕d6+ ♔g2 41 ♕d2+ ♔h3 42 ♕d7+ f5 43 ♕g7 g4 44 ♕h8+ ♔g3 45 ♕e5+ f4 46 ♕b8 ♕e3+ 47 ♔d1 ♔g2 White resigned.

Averbakh – Suetin
USSR ch, Kiev 1954

12-23

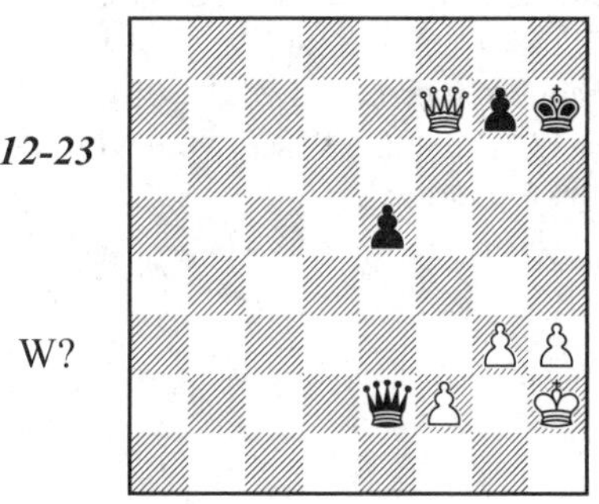

W?

White's plan is a king attack and it must be successful because Black's pawn structure is destroyed.

1 g4! ♕d2

1...e4 2 ♔g3 e3? fails to 3 ♕h5+ ♔g8 4 ♕e8+ ♔h7 5 ♕×e3.

2 ♔g3 ♕c3+ 3 ♔h4 ♕d4 4 ♕f5+ g6

Or 4...♔g8 5 ♔h5! and g4-g5-g6.

5 ♕f7+ ♔h6 6 ♕f6 ♔h7 7 ♔g5 ♕d2+ 8 f4! ef 9 ♕f7+ ♔h8 10 ♔h6 Black resigned.

Please pay attention to the fact that White exploits Black's pawns as ***an umbrella*** giving protection from queen checks. We learned this technique when studying rook-and-pawn endings; it is no less important for queen endgames, too.

Tragicomedies

Shcherbakov – Arlazarov
USSR 1972

12-24

W?

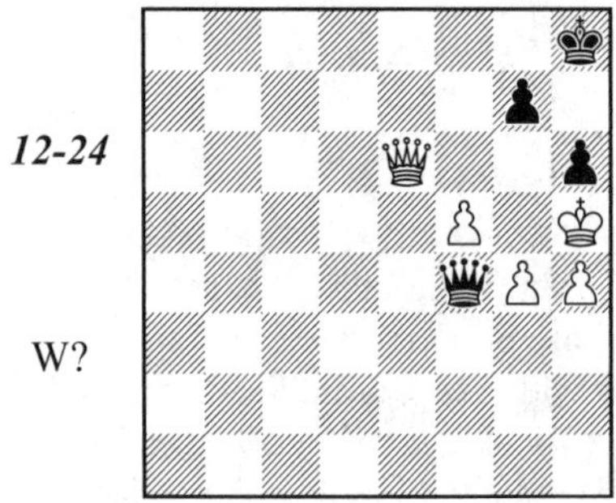

1 f6!

The game Mackenzie – Sergeant (Edinburgh 1920), where the same position occurred, continued 1 ♔g6? ♕×g4+ 2 ♔f7 ♕h5+?? (2...♔h7!=) 3 ♔f8, and Black resigned because of an inevitable mate.

1...♔h7!? (1...gf 2 ♔g6) **2 fg??**

White overlooks a queen sacrifice that forces a stalemate. Both 2 ♕f5+! ♕×f5+ 3 gf gf 4 ♔g4 ♔g7 5 ♔f4 ♔f7 6 ♔e4 ♔e7 7 ♔d5 ♔d7 8 h5⊙ and a more spectacular 2 f7! ♕e5+! 3 g5! (3 ♕×e5?? g6#) 3...♕×e6 4 f8♘+! were winning.

2...♕f7+! Draw.

A Passed Pawn

A passed pawn supported by a queen is a powerful instrument. To stop it, the combined efforts of a king and a queen are required; a queen alone cannot manage against it.

When the passed pawn is well advanced it can outweigh an opponent's huge material advantage on another wing.

Averbakh – Zurakhov
Minsk 1952

12-25

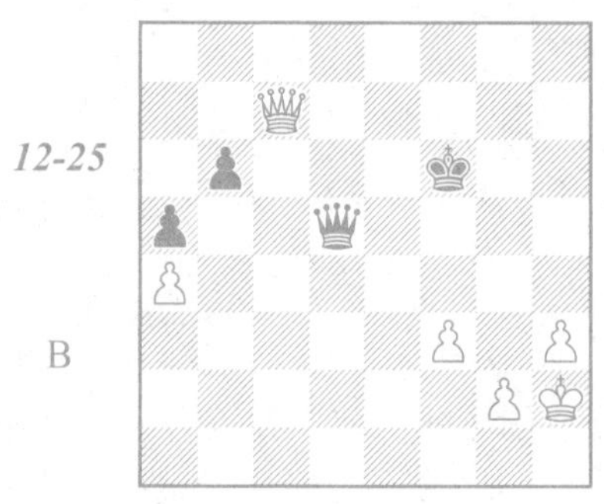

B

1...b5! 2 ab (2 ♕×a5? ♕e5+) **2...♕×b5**

2...♕e5+? 3 ♕×e5+ ♔×e5 fails because of 4 h4! a4 5 h5 a3 6 h6 ♔f6 7 b6+–.

3 ♕d6+ ♔f7 (3...♔g7!?) **4 h4**

If the a-pawn were a little bit more advanced, the peaceful outcome would not be in doubt: White would have had to submit to perpetual check. But, under current conditions, he still has winning chances.

The point is that, if the black king stands in the way of the white pawns, their advance (and, eventually, a king intervention) can create mating threats. On the other hand, if Black holds his king aside then the h-pawn can balance Black's passed pawn, while their exchange still leaves White his two extra pawns.

Only a detailed analysis can tell us who comes first in implementing his plans. In Averbakh's opinion, only 4...♕b4! 5 ♕d5+ ♔g7 6 ♕e5+ ♔h7 7 f4 a4 8 h5 a3 9 ♕f5+ ♔g7 10 ♕g6+ ♔h8 11 ♕f6+ ♔g8! was good enough for a draw, while the natural-looking move from the game was erroneous.

4...a4? 5 ♕f4+ ♔e6

According to Averbakh, 5...♔g6 also did not help.

6 ♕g4+ ♔d6?!

White's task was much more complicated after 6...♔f6 7 h5 ♕e5+! 8 f4 ♕f5, although he was still on the winning path.

7 ♕g6+ ♔c7 8 h5 ♕e5+ 9 ♔h3

Black resigned in view of 9...a3 10 h6 a2 11 ♕g7+ ♕×g7 12 hg a1♕ 13 g8♕+–.

Euwe – Reshevsky
Nottingham 1936

12-26

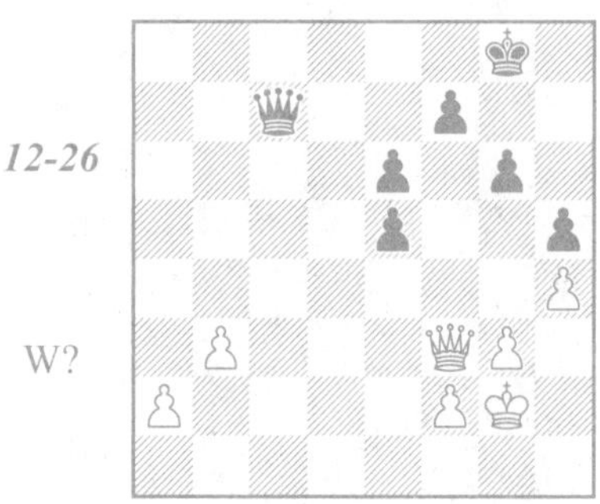

W?

In this sort of position, White's standard plan is to place his queen on a8 and then to push the a-pawn to the promotion square. The queen not only supports the pawn advance; it also protects the king from checks along the main diagonal. The only constructive idea for the weaker side is to achieve a perpetual check; for this purpose, he must destroy the position of the white king.

1 ♕a8+!

1 b4? ♕c4 2 a3 e4∞ is not good; 1 a4 ♕a5 is also erroneous.

1...♔g7 2 a4 ♕b6?

Alekhine indicated that 2...♕c3! was much more tenacious. 3 a5 could be met with 3...e4 4 ♕×e4 ♕×a5, eliminating White's most dangerous pawn. If 3 ♕b7 then 3...e4 4 ♕×e4 ♕×b3 5 ♕a8 e5, and the outcome is still unclear because White must always take ...e5-e4 into account.

3 a5!+– ♕×b3 4 a6 ♕a3

After 4...♕a2 5 a7 e4 6 ♕b7 e3 7 a8♕ ♕×f2+ 8 ♔h3 Black has no perpetual check.

5 a7 e4 6 ♕b8 ♕f3+ 7 ♔g1 ♕d1+

7...e3 8 a8♕ ♕×f2+ 9 ♔h1+–.

8 ♔h2 ♕e2 9 ♕e5+

Black resigned (9...♔h7 10 ♕f4).

The following endgame was annotated superficially in endgame treatises, therefore the opponents' actions were not evaluated correctly.

Maróczy – Bogoljubow
Dresden 1936

12-27

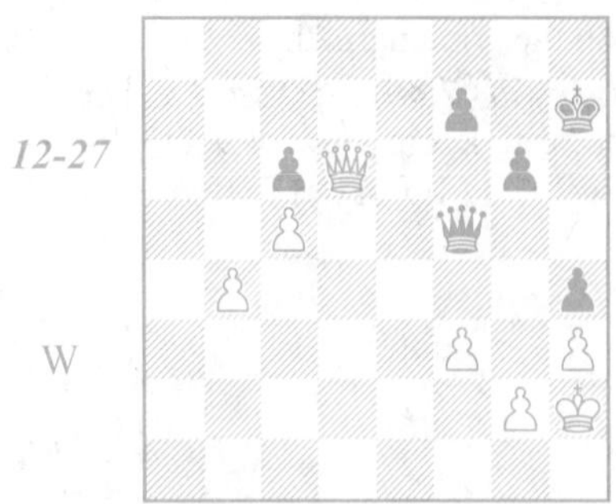

W

1 b5! cb 2 c6

The same strategy that we have seen in the previous example, but there is a cardinal difference between these two endings: White's queen will be obliged to abandon the h2-b8 diagonal in order to take control over the promotion square, giving Black opportunities for checks. The question is whether these will be perpetual checks.

2...♕c2?!

As will be seen, it was good for Black to get rid of his b-pawn: 2...b4! 3 ♕×b4 ♕e5+ 4 f4 ♕c7. I am not sure that this position can be won.

3 ♕d5?

"3 c7 at once was simpler," - comments Averbakh. No, it was not, in view of the reply 3...♕c3! (we shall study its consequences later). The precise order of moves is 3 ♕d7! (the f7-pawn is attacked) 3...♕c4 4 c7, coming directly to a position that will occur later on in the game.

3...♔h6

Black does not allow a capture on f7 with a check. 3...♔g7?, with the same purpose, is weaker in view of 4 ♕d4+!.

4 ♕d6!?

Maroczy, this recognized expert in queen endings, leaves the b5-pawn alive, hoping that it will eventually serve his king as an "umbrella."

4...♕c4?

4...♔h7? 5 ♕d7! ♕c4 6 c7 led to a transposition of moves; if 4...♔g7? then the same check 5 ♕d4+! is again very strong. Finally, 4...b4? is quite bad because of 5 c7 with the threats 6 ♕f8+ and 6 ♕d7.

The best defense is 4...♕c3!. The queen must seek to check from e5 rather than f4. White has a choice: 5 c7 or 6 ♕f8+.

A) 5 ♕f8+ ♔h5 6 ♕×f7 ♕×c6 7 f4 ♔h6 8 ♕e7 ♕c4 9 ♕×h4+ ♔g7 10 ♕e7+ ♔g8. This position is similar to that from the Averbakh – Zurakhov game but the g6-pawn is present here; it gives the king protection, and therefore a draw is evident.

B) 5 c7 ♔h7 (5...♔g7!?). We have reached the position that could have arisen after 3 c7?!.

12-28

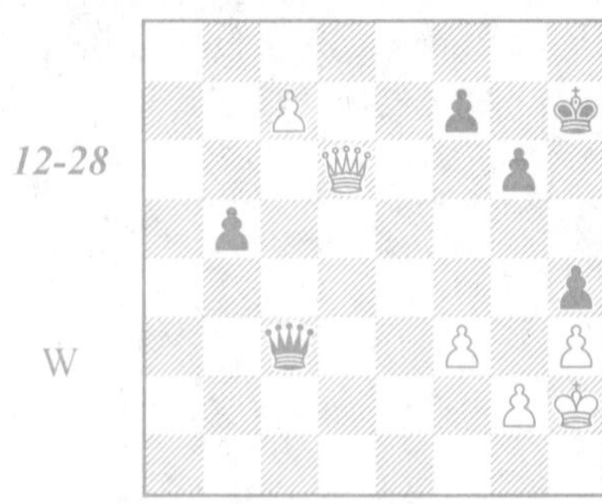

W

Let us check the most committal line: 6 ♕d7 ♕e5+ 7 f4 (otherwise White cannot escape from checks) 7...♕×f4+ 8 ♔g1. The absence of the f3-pawn allows Black to achieve a perpetual check: 8...♕e3+ 9 ♔f1 ♕f4+ 10 ♔e2 ♕e4+ 11 ♔d2 ♕f4+! (9...♕×g2+? 10 ♔c3 b4+ 11 ♔b3!, and the checks will expire soon) 10 ♔d3 ♕f1+ 11 ♔e4 (11 ♔d4?? ♕d1+; 11 ♔c3 ♕c4+) 11...♕×g2+ 12 ♔e5 ♕b2+ 13 ♔d5 (13 ♕d4?! ♕h2+! 14 ♕f4 f6+ 15 ♔e4, and now, say, 15...♕g2+ 16 ♔d4 ♕c6) 13...♕a2+! 14 ♔c5 (14 ♔c6 ♕a6+) 14...♕a7+! 15 ♔d6 ♕a3+! and the king cannot escape from the pursuit.

Notice Black's defensive method, particularly the last moves of this line. ***In queen-and-pawn endgames, diagonal checks are often the most effective***.

What else can White do? One can easily see that 6 ♕d8 is not an improvement of White's play: the black queen gets the e6-square for checks. He can try 6 ♕e7 ♔g7□ 7 f4 ♕c4 (7...♕g3+?? 8 ♔g1+−) 8 ♕e5+ ♔h7 9 f5, but after 9...g5 or 9...b4 8 fg+ ♔×g6 White is faced with the same problems. No win can be seen! (Analysis by Dvoretsky)

Now let us see the remainder of the game:

5 c7 ♔h7 6 ♕d7! ♕f4+ 7 ♔g1 ♕c1+ 8 ♔f2 ♕c5+ 9 ♔e2 ♕c2+ 10 ♔e3 ♕c5+ 11 ♔e4 Black resigned.

In case of 11...♕c2+ (with the idea of 12 ♔d5 ♕a2+) White proceeds with 12 ♔e5 ♕c3+ (12...♕b2+ 13 ♕d4!) 13 ♔d5 ♕c4+ 14 ♔d6 ♕b4+ 15 ♔c6 ♕c3+ 16 ♔b7. His plan to use the b5-pawn as an umbrella was successful.

Alekhine – Reshevsky
Amsterdam 1938

12-29

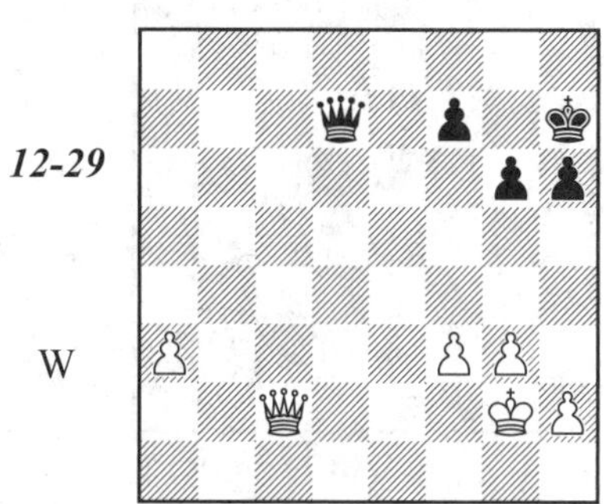

W

1 ♕a2 ♔g8 2 a4 ♕c6 3 a5 ♕a6

White could have had chances for success with his pawn on f2, although the winning process would have required much effort. In the actual position, his king is too exposed and a win is therefore beyond his reach.

4 g4 g5 5 ♔f2 ♕d6 6 ♔f1 ♕a6+ 7 ♔g2 ♔g7 8 ♕b2+ ♔g8 9 ♕b8+ ♔g7 10 ♕e5+ ♔g8 11 ♔f2 ♕a7+ 12 ♔e2 ♕a6+ 13 ♔d2 ♕c4!

Reshevsky prevents the white king from drawing near the pawn.

14 ♕f5 ♕d4+ 15 ♔e2 ♕b2+ 16 ♔d3 ♕b3+ 17 ♔e2 ♕b2+ Draw.

Prandstetter – Gheorghiu
Warsaw zt 1979

12-30

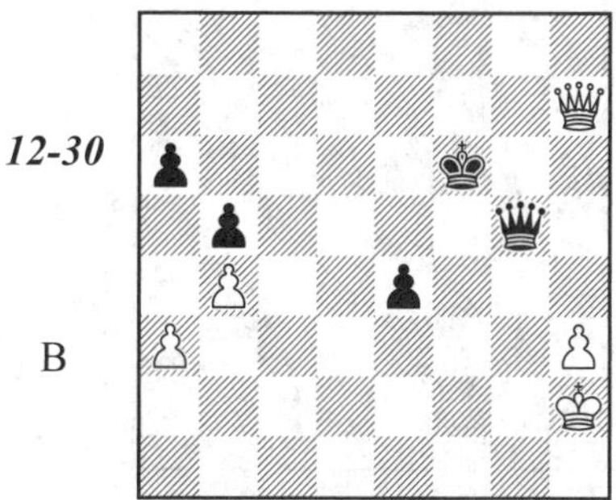

B

Black obviously stands better because his passed pawn is far more advanced than White's. But can he exploit this advantage? Black could achieve success by means of a king invasion to support his pawn, but this is not easy to do. Let us study a few of possible attempts.

1...e3?! is harmless in view of 2 ♕e4!=.

After 1...♕d2+ 2 ♔g3 e3 Black threatens a further pawn advance as well as 3...♔e5. However, White has 3 ♕h4+! (control over the f2-square is vital) 3...♔e5 4 ♔f3!=.

The immediate activation of the king – 1...♔e5!? – looks tempting; the pawn endgame that arises after 2 ♕c7+? ♔d4 3 ♕c5+ ♕×c5 4 bc will soon become a queen-and-pawn again, and thus a winning one for Black: 4...♔×c5! (4...e3? 5 ♔g2=) 5 h4 (5 ♔g2 ♔d4 6 ♔f2? ♔d3 7 ♔e1 a5–+) 5...♔d4! 6 h5 e3 (6...♔e5? 7 ♔g3 a5 8 h6 ♔f6 9 ♔f4 b4 10 ab a4 11 b5=) 7 ♔g2 (7 h6 e2 8 h7 e1♕ 9 h8♕+ ♕e5+) 7...♔d3 8 h6 e2 9 h7 e1♕ 10 h8♕ ♕d2+ and 11...♔c2–+.

Another diagonal check helps White out: 2 ♕h8+! ♔d5 (after 2...♔f4 3 ♕f8+ ♔e3 4 ♕c5+ the pawn endgame is drawn already) 3 ♕c3!, and the king fails to break through.

1...♕f4+ 2 ♔g1 ♕g3+ 3 ♔f1 ♕f3+ 4 ♔e1=

The white king has managed to stand in front of the black pawn, so it is a simple draw. What happens now resembles the Larsen - Keres ending: Black, in search of winning chances, forgets all caution and allows an exchange of queens when it is already winning for White.

4...♔e5 5 ♕c7+ ♔d4?? 6 ♕c5+ ♔d3 7 ♕d5+ ♔c3 8 ♕d2+ ♔b3 9 ♕d1+! ♔×a3 10 ♕×f3+ ef 11 h4 Black resigned.

Tragicomedies

Karpov – Agdestein
Gjovik m (1) 1991

12-31

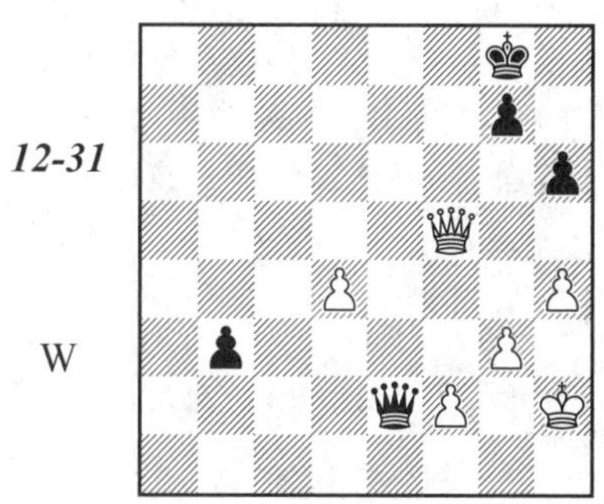

W

White should have accepted that there is no win, playing either 1 ♕c8+ or 1 ♕d5+ ♔h8 2 ♕×b3 ♕×f2+ 3 ♔h3 ♕×d4.

1 d5??

Karpov expected only 1...b2? 2 d6 ♕d1 (2...b1♕ 3 ♕×b1 ♕×f2+ 4 ♔h3) 3 d7 b1♕ 4 ♕×b1 ♕×d7 and wished to torment his opponent some more in a drawn endgame, a delusion that was very unpleasant.

1...♕c2!−+

By taking control over the b1-h7 diagonal Black assures both the safety of his king and the promotion of his pawn.

2 ♕f3 b2 3 d6 b1♕ 4.d7 ♕bd1 5 ♕a8+ ♔h7 White resigned.

Exercises

12-32

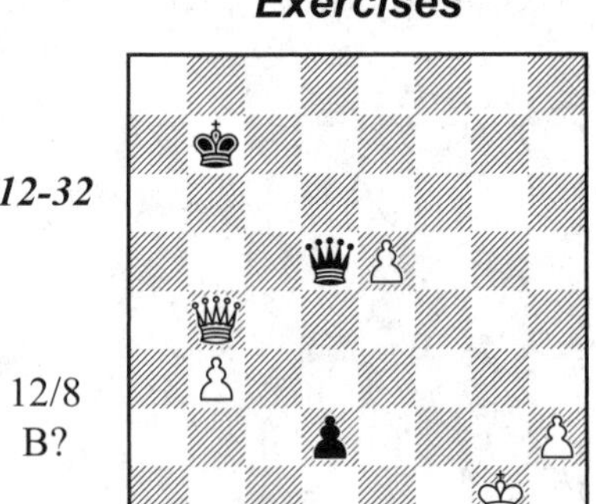

12/8
B?

An Active Queen

The queen is a very mobile piece that can rapidly reach any part of the board. Therefore a more active position of the queen (compared with the opponent's queen) is usually only a temporary advantage, which should be exploited immediately. But this advantage can be lasting, too: it is so when the enemy's queen is chained to his own weak pawns.

This advantage is particularly tangible when the opponent's king is exposed. The stronger side's resources are dramatically rich in such cases: from a queen transfer (with checks) to a more favorable position or a double attack to a queen exchange and even a mating attack.

Marshall – Maróczy
Ostende 1905

12-33

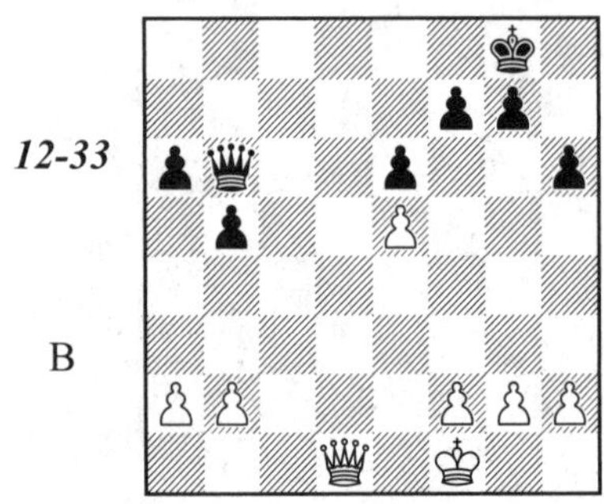

B

1...♕c5

The e5-pawn is White's main weakness. If it were standing on e3 the position would have been even.

2 ♕d8+ (2 f4? ♕c4+) **2...♔h7 3 ♕d3+ g6 4 ♕c3 ♕d5! 5 a3**

5 b3 is no better. Villeneuve gives the following line: 5...♕d1+ 6 ♕e1 ♕d3+ 7 ♔g1 ♕c2 8 ♕a1 b4! 9 f4 (9 ♔f1 g5) 9...♕c3 10 ♕f1 ♕d4+ 11 ♔h1 ♕b2−+.

5...♕d1+! 6 ♕e1 ♕d3+ 7 ♔g1 ♕c2 8 ♕a1

By means of threats to one or another pawn, and sometimes to a king, Black has precisely driven the white queen away to a corner. The pawn sacrifice 8 b4 ♕b2 9 h4, suggested by Panchenko, brings White no relief: 9...♕×a3 (9...h5 10 ♕e3 is weaker) 10 h5 (10 ♕e4 ♕c1+ 11 ♔h2 ♕c4−+) 10...♕d3 (after 10...gh 11 ♕e4+ ♔g7 12 ♕f4 ♕d3 13 ♕f6+ ♔g8 14 ♕×h6 White obtains a counterplay) 11 hg+ ♔×g6−+.

8...a5! 9 g3

9 b4 ab 10 ab ♕e4 is hopeless.

12-34

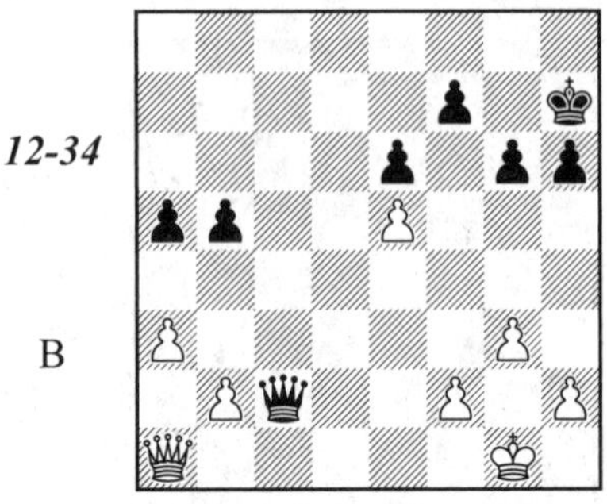

B

9...a4

Maróczy fixes the queenside pawns while the white queen is still occupying a miserable position. 9...g5?! would have been less precise in view of 10 b4 ab 11 ab ♕e4 12 ♕c3 ♔g6 13 h3 h5 14 ♕c5 and almost all Black's advantage is melted away.

10 f4 ♔g8!

A zugzwang! If 11 ♔h1 then 11...♕f2 and ...h6-h5-h4.

11 h3 h5 12 h4 ♔g7 (a zugzwang again) **13 ♔h1**

13 ♔f1 loses right away to 13...♕h2. If 13 ♕a2 then 13...♕d1+ 14 ♔f2 ♔f8 and the white queen is arrested.

13...♕f2! 14 ♕g1 ♕×b2 15 ♕c5

White lunges in a desperate counterattack but his hopes for a perpetual check do not come true.

15...b4! 16 f5!?

After 16 ♕e7 ba?! 17 ♕f6+ ♔g8 18 ♕d8+ ♔h7 19 ♕e7 ♕b1+ 20 ♔h2 ♕f5 21 ♕×a3 White still could have had some hopes. However, Black plays 16...b3! 17 ♕f6+ ♔g8 18 ♕d8+ ♔h7 19 ♕e7 ♕b1+ 20 ♔h2 ♕f5 21 ♕b7 ♔g7 with an easy win.

16...ef 17 e6 ba 18 ef

18 e7 a2 19 e8♘+ ♔g8(h7) makes no sense.

18...♔×f7

The black king easily escapes from the checks in White's territory.

19 ♕c7+ ♔e6 20 ♕c6+ ♔e5 21 ♕×a4 a2 22 ♕e8+ ♔d5 23 ♕d7+ ♔e4 24 ♕c6+ ♔e3 25 ♕c5+ ♕d4 26 ♕a3+ ♕d3 White resigned.

Exercises

12-35

12/9
W?

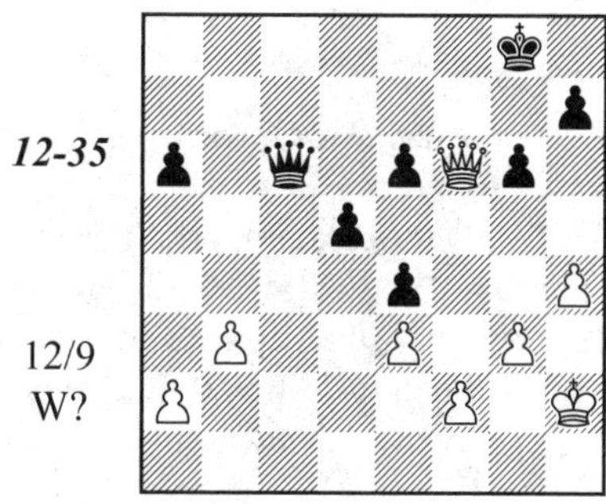

12-36

12/10
W?/Play

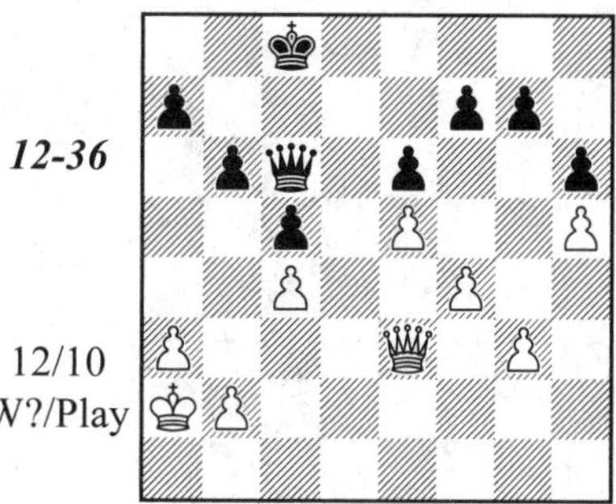

Chapter 13

QUEEN VS. ROOK

The side that has a rook tries, except for very rare cases, to build a fortress.

We shall study the most important theoretical positions here, both drawn and winning. Sometimes one must play dozens of precise moves in a row in order to destroy the opponent's line of defense. However, the winning plans that we should know are mostly standard, even when they are quite complicated tactically.

Master Khenkin has greatly contributed to the theory of this sort of endgame; he wrote the corresponding section for Averbakh's endgame treatise and, for this purpose, analyzed a huge number of new positions.

A Solitary Rook

A queen wins against a solitary rook. The cases when a king cannot escape from checks in view of a stalemate or a loss of a queen are exceptions.

D. Ponziani, 1782

13-1
$
B

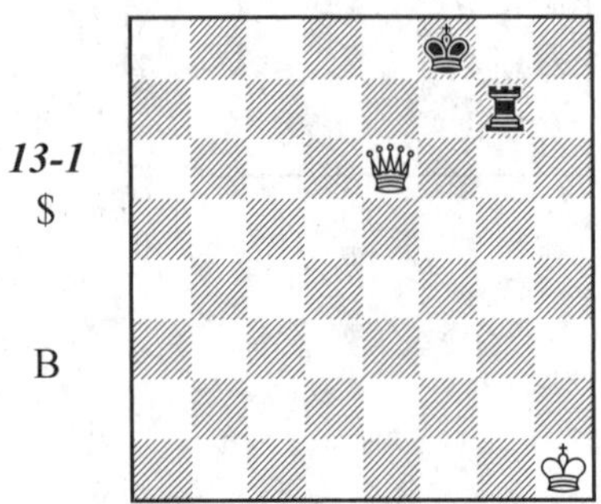

1...♖h7+ 2 ♔g2 ♖g7+ 3 ♔f3 ♖f7+ 4 ♔g4 (4 ♔e4 ♖e7) **4...♖g7+ 5 ♔f5 ♖f7+ 6 ♔g6 ♖g7+ 7 ♔h6** (7 ♔f6 ♖g6+!) **7...♖h7+!.**

A standard winning method is shown in the following classical endgame.

Philidor, 1777

13-2
W

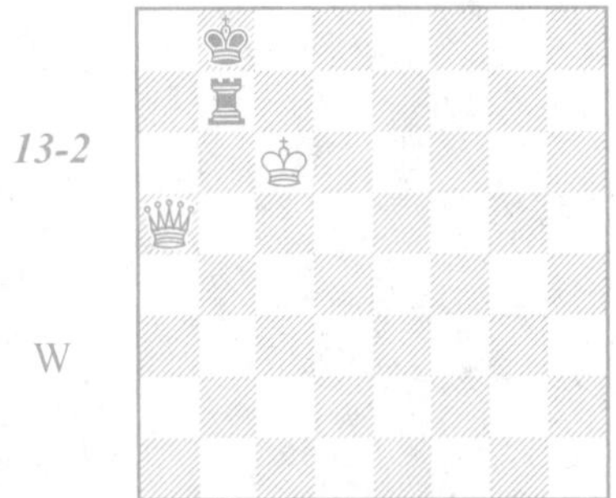

White's pieces are ideally placed. Now he should cede the necessity to move to his opponent by means of a triangular maneuver by the queen.

1 ♕e5+ ♔a7(a8) 2 ♕a1+ ♔b8 3 ♕a5!

Zugzwang! The rook must abandon the black king. As a result, it inevitably becomes a victim of a double attack.

3...♖b1 (3...♖h7 4 ♕e5+ ♔a8 5 ♕a1+ ♔b8 6 ♕b1+) **4 ♕d8+ ♔a7 5 ♕d4+ ♔a8 6 ♕h8+ ♔a7 7 ♕h7+** and 8 ♕×b1.

The methods in this elementary example (***zugzwang, triangulation as a tool for passing the obligation to move, and double attack***) are standard for almost all queen-versus-rook endings, with or without pawns.

If the defender's king is standing in the center, the stronger side gradually drives him to an edge of the board to create mating threats. However this mission is not elementary, since the rook may sometimes be placed far away from the king without fear of being lost immediately.

Under time controls that are characteristic for modern chess, queen-versus-rook endings usually occur when the both sides are suffering from time shortage. For example, grandmaster Svidler, playing against Gelfand at the World championship-2001 in Moscow, had a few minutes (plus an additional 10 seconds after every move) and failed to outplay his opponent over 50 moves; thereafter the arbiters duly declared a draw.

In order to avoid such an unpleasant occurrence, one can practice with a computer program that is designed for this sort of endgame; it defends against the queen in a most tenacious way.

The study of the following position is based upon computer-generated lines that indicate the best moves for both sides (of course, these are not the only moves one can play). Naturally, there is no sense in remembering these lines by heart; typical ideas behind the moves are much more important.

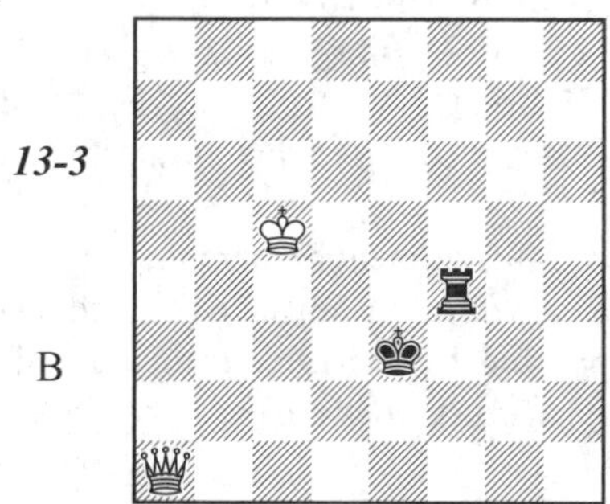
13-3
B

1...♖f8!? 2 ♕d4+ ♔e2 3 ♕g4+ ♔e3 4 ♕e6+ ♔f3 5 ♔d4 ♖d8+ 6 ♔c3 ♖f8 7 ♕c6+

If White had played this two moves earlier, Black could have replied with 5...♔e3. Now, 7...♔e3? is impossible in view of the double attack ...♕c5+.

7...♔g4 8 ♕g6+ ♔f3 9 ♕h5+!

An excellent square for the queen. Black's king is forced to the g-file: after 9...♔e3?, 9...♔f4? or 9...♔f2? the rook is lost immediately, 9...♔e4? is also bad in view of 10 ♕e2+ ♔d5 11 ♕c4+. In addition, the queen takes control over the important squares e8 and f3, thereby helping the king to come closer to its counterpart.

9...♔g3 10 ♔d3 ♖f3+ (10...♖d8+ 11 ♔e3 ♖e8+? is impossible...) **11 ♔e4 ♖f4+ 12 ♔e3** (and 12...♖f3+? is impossible, too) **12...♖g4**

Another possibility is 12...♖a4. White cannot gain the rook by force. He must drive the black king away to an edge, place his queen optimally and then move his king closer to its counterpart. The main line is 13 ♕e5+ ♔h3 14 ♕e6+ ♔h4 15 ♕e7+ ♔g3 16 ♕d6+! ♔h4 17 ♔f3! (the queen from d6 prevents a rook check from a3) 17...♔h5 (the rook is finally unable to escape from a double attack now) 18 ♕d5+ ♔h4 19 ♕d8+ ♔h5 20 ♕e8+.

13 ♕e5+ ♔g2 14 ♔e2⊙ ♖g3 15 ♕h5! ♔g1 16 ♕d5⊙

Quiet moves that limit the mobility of enemy pieces or create a zugzwang situation are often much more effective than checks.

16...♖g6

In case of 16...♖g2+ 17 ♔f3 ♔h2 18 ♕h5+ ♔g1 19 ♕h4⊙ we come to the Philidor position that is already familiar to us. The main line brings us the same result.

17 ♕d4+ ♔h2 18 ♕f4+ ♔g1 19 ♔f3 ♖g2 20 ♕h4⊙ +–

Now we return to an earlier moment and study 4...♔f2 (instead of 4...♔f3) 5 ♔d4 ♖f4+. With Black's king on f3, White could have played 6 ♔d3, while now this is weaker in view of 6...♖f3+ 7 ♔d2 ♔g3. The computer suggests 6 ♔e5! ♖f3 7 ♕a2+ ♔e3 8 ♕c2 (zugzwang) 8...♖g3 9 ♕c3+ ♔f2 10 ♕d2+ ♔f3 11 ♔f5 (the same zugzwang again, but this time closer to the edge) 11...♖g2 12 ♕d3+ ♔f2 13 ♔f4.

If Black plays 13...♔g1 now, then 14 ♕d4+ ♔h2 15 ♔f3 ♖g3+ 16 ♔f2 ♖g2+ 17 ♔f1+–. Examine the final position closely: the rook cannot proceed with checks because the queen is controlling the g1-square. ***This is the method the stronger side uses for approaching with the king: first the queen takes control of one of the adjacent squares.***

13...♔e1 14 ♕c4 ♔f2 15 ♕c6!

The natural looking 15 ♕e4 leads to a reciprocal zugzwang position after 15...♔f1 16 ♔f3 ♖f2+ 17 ♔g3 ♖d2!; this position should be reached with the adversary on move. If 15...♔f1 now, 16 ♔f3 ♖f2+ 17 ♔g3 ♖d2 18 ♕e4!⊙ +– is decisive.

15...♖h2 16 ♕f3+ ♔g1 17 ♕d5! (but, of course, not 17 ♔g3?? ♖h3+!) 17...♔f2 18 ♕d4+ ♔g2 19 ♔g4⊙ ♔f1 20 ♔g3 ♖g2+ 21 ♔f3+– (the queen guards the f2-square).

Exercises

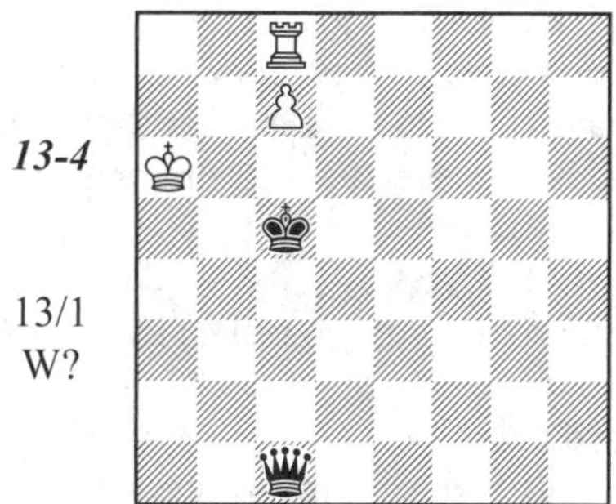
13-4
13/1
W?

Queen vs. Rook and Pawn

The Rook Behind the Pawn

The further the pawn is advanced the greater are the chances for a draw. For instance, Black wins in all cases when his king blocks a white pawn that has not crossed the middle line. Almost all positions with the pawn on the 5th rank are won. However if the pawn has reached 6th or 7th rank, a draw is quite probable.

N. Grigoriev, 1933

13-5
$

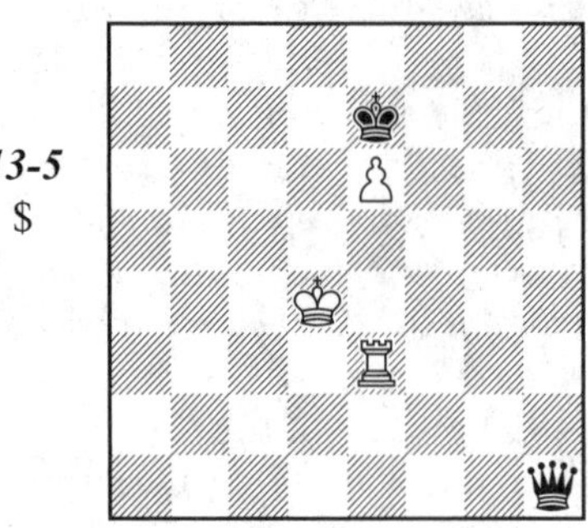

It is good for White to keep his king on the lower ranks. He would have had no problems if his king were standing on e2; then Black could not create a zugzwang.

With White on move, a draw can be achieved by means of **1 ♔d3! ♕d1+ 2 ♔c3!⊙.**

An important position of reciprocal zugzwang. After 2...♔f8 (2...♕d5 3 ♔c2 is useless) 3 e7+ ♔e8 4 ♖e4 ♕f3+ 5 ♔d4 ♕b3 6 ♖e3 ♕c2 7 ♖e4 White is out of danger.

However with Black on move, the evaluation differs. He manages to press White's pieces out, by means of zugzwang, closer to the pawn, which means closer to the black king. The king then joins the queen at an appropriate moment with decisive effect.

1...♕b1! 2 ♔c3

2 ♔d5 ♕a2+ 3 ♔e5 ♕b2+ 4 ♔f4 ♕f2+ loses even faster.

2...♕d1!⊙

The familiar zugzwang position has arisen, but this time with White on move.

3 ♖e4 (3 ♔c4 ♕c2+ 4 ♔d4 ♕d2+) **3...♕f3+ 4 ♔d4 ♕b3⊙ 5 ♔e5**

If 5 ♖e3 then 5...♕c2! 6 ♖e4 ♔d6! 7 ♔e3 (7 e7 ♕d2+ 8 ♔c4 ♕d5+) 7...♔d5! −+. After the king move, a similar finale happens on the other wing.

5...♕b2+ 6 ♔f4 (6 ♔d5 ♕c3!⊙ 7 ♖e5 ♕d3+ 8 ♔c5 ♕d6+) **6...♕f2+ 7 ♔g4** (7 ♔e5 ♕f6+ 8 ♔d5 ♕c3!⊙) **7...♕g2+ 8 ♔f4 ♔f6! 9 ♔e3** (9 e7 ♕f2+ 10 ♔g4 ♕f5+) **9...♔f5! −+**.

I would like to mention here that in multi-pawn endings with a far-advanced passed pawn being supported by the rook from behind, a queen, when it must block the pawn, can be even weaker than a rook.

Bron – Ordel
Kharkov 1936

13-6
W

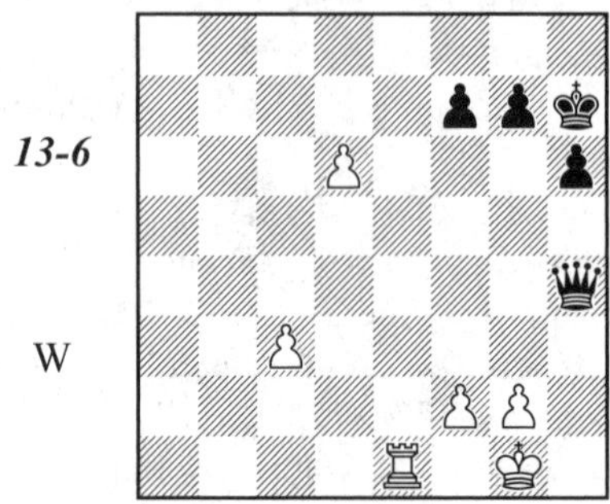

1 d7 ♕d8 2 ♖d1 ♔g8 3 c4 ♔f8 4 c5 ♔e7 5 c6 f5?

Black could probably save the game after 5...♕a5! (△ 6...♔d8). The transition to the pawn endgame via 6 d8♕+ is unfavorable for White, the rook has no e1-square, while 6 ♖d3 is met by 6...♕e1+ 7 ♔h2 ♕e5+ 8 g3 ♔d8 9 ♖e3 ♕h5+ 10 ♔g1 ♕d1+ with a perpetual check.

6 ♖e1+ ♔f7 7 ♖c1! ♕c7 8 g3!

8 ♔f1! is equivalent. 8 ♖d1? ♔e7 9 ♖e1+ ♔f7 10 ♖e8 (10 g3 ♕d6!) is premature in view of 10...♕f4! 11 d8♕ (11 ♖e1 ♕d2; 11 g3 ♕c1+ 12 ♔h2 ♕f1) 11...♕c1+ 12 ♖e1 (12 ♔h2 ♕f4+) 12...♕×e1+ 13 ♔h2 ♕×f2 and White cannot escape from checks (Dvoretsky).

8...f4 9 ♖d1 ♔e7 (9...♕d8 10 c7) **10 ♖e1+ ♔f7 11 ♖e8 ♕×c6 12 d8♘+!** Black resigned.

Now we come to the most important class of positions: the king protects the pawn while the rook tries to keep hostile pieces away from it.

The Pawn on the 7th Rank

Philidor, 1777

13-7

W

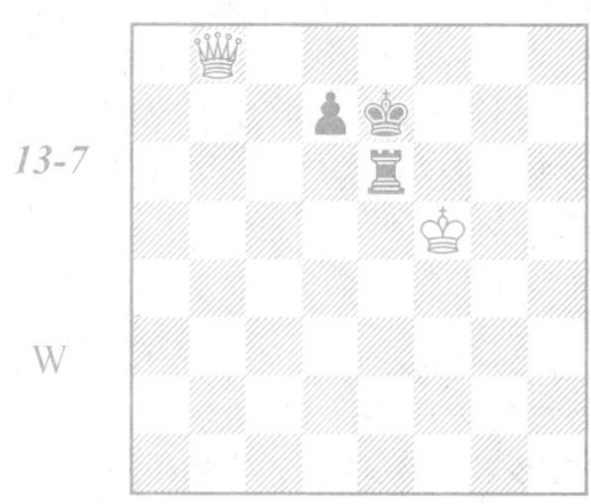

1 ♕h8 ♖c6=

Black holds his king on the 7th and 8th ranks, preventing the white queen from entering the important d8-square. The rook has two protected squares at its disposal (e6 and c6); therefore a zugzwang cannot be created.

V. Khenkin, 1981*

13-8

$

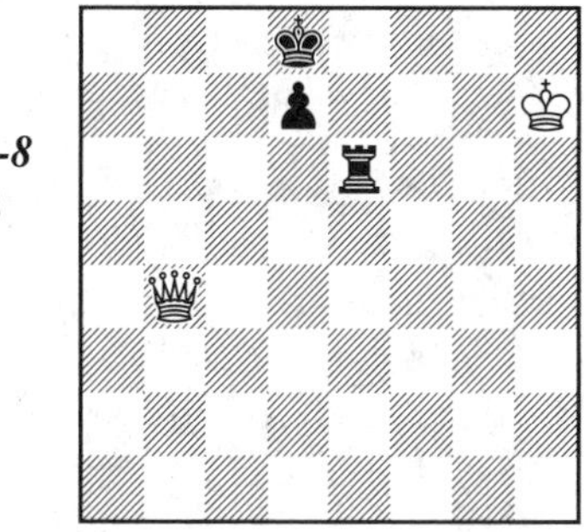

If the white king has crossed the 6th rank, Black's position is not foolproof anymore. For example, this case depends on who is on move.

Black on move achieves a draw after 1...♔c7(c8)!. ***He should keep a distance between the kings in order to avoid mate threats.***

White on move wins.

1 ♕b8+! ♔e7 2 ♔g7 (△ 3 ♕f8#) **2...♖c6** (2...♖d6 3 ♕b4) **3 ♕f8+ ♔e6 4 ♕f6+** 4 ♕b4!⊙ ♔d5 5 ♔f7 ♖e6 6 ♕b7+ ♔d6 7 ♕b6+ ♔d5 8 ♕c7 is also good (Dvoretsky).

4...♔d5 5 ♕d8 ♔d6 6 ♔f7

The queen has occupied the important d8-square, and now the king can attack the pawn. His opponent, forced to stand in front of the pawn, only hinders his own rook.

6...♖c5 7 ♕b6+ ♖c6 8 ♕b8+ ♔d5 9 ♔e7+–.

V. Khenkin, 1981

13-9

$

B

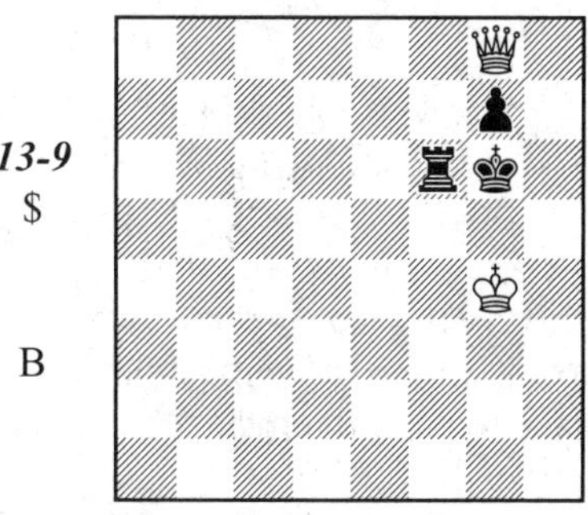

The closer the pawn is to the edge the greater the defensive resources are. This sort of position (with the king in front of the pawn) is lost when the pawn is central. With a bishop pawn, the outcome depends on specifics of piece placement. Here (the knight pawn) Black holds a draw easily; the same is valid against the white king on e5, but not if the king gets to e7.

Khenkin analyzed 1...♖f1 (but of course not 1...♔h6?? 2 ♕h8+ ♔g6 3 ♕h5#) 2 ♕d5 ♖g1+ 3 ♔h3 (3 ♔f3 ♖f1+ 4 ♔g3 ♖f6=) 3...♔h7 4 ♔h4 ♔h8 5 ♔h5 ♔h7 6 ♕e4+ ♔h8, and White cannot make any progress. If his queen abandons the a8-h1 diagonal Black transposes into the drawn Philidor position after ...♖h1-h6.

However White wins if he, instead of 2 ♕d5?, plays 2 ♕e8+! ♔h7 (2...♖f7 3 ♔h4 ♔f6 4 ♔h5) 3 ♕h5+ ♔g8 4 ♕d5+ ♔f8 (4...♔h8 5 ♕d8+ ♔h7 6 ♕d3+) 5 ♕c5+ ♔g8 6 ♕c4+ ♖f7 7 ♔g5.

To avoid the double attack, Black should place his rook on a dark square. 1...♖f2! 2 ♕d5 ♔h7 is an easy draw; 1...♖d6! and 1...♖b6! are also good.

With the rook pawn on the 7th rank, Black is lost because the rook has only one protected square at its disposal.

J. Berger, 1921*

13-10

W

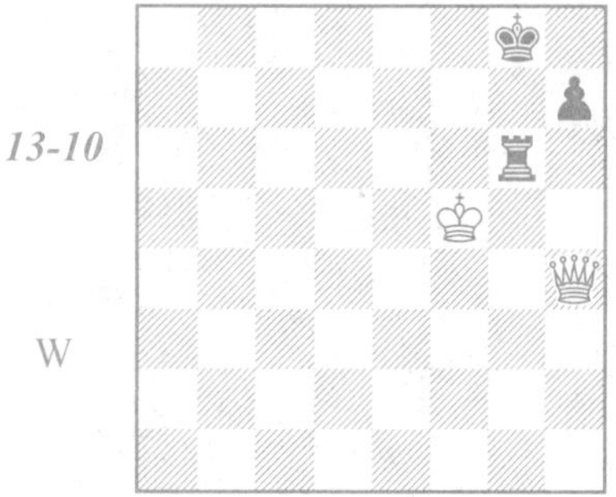

1 ♕e7

Black is in zugzwang! Any move drastically worsens his position.

1...♖g2 2 ♕d8+ ♔g7 3 ♕d4+ ♔h6 4 ♕e3+ ♔g7 5 ♕c3+! ♔g8 6 ♕c8+ ♔g7 7 ♕b7+;

1...♖g1 2 ♕d8+ ♔f7 3 ♕c7+ ♔g8 4 ♕b8+ ♔g7 5 ♕a7+;

1...♔h8 2 ♕f8+ ♖g8 3 ♕f6+ ♖g7 4 ♔e6! (4 ♕e5? h6!= is erroneous: you can find the situation with the rook pawn on the 6th rank in the next section) 4...h5 5 ♕h6+;

1...♖h6 2 ♔g5 ♖g6+ 3 ♔h5 ♔h8 (3...♖a6 4 ♕d8+ ♔g7 5 ♕c7+) 4 ♕f8+ ♖g8 5 ♕f6+ ♖g7 6 ♔h6+–.

1...♖a6 2 ♕d8+ ♔g7 3 ♕d7+ ♔h6 4 ♕b7 ♖d6 (4...♖a3 5 ♕c6+ ♔g7 6 ♕d7+) **5 ♕e7 ♖g6**

A reciprocal zugzwang. White, with the help of the triangular queen maneuver, gives his opponent the move.

I would like to make a comment here: White could have obtained this position with Black to move by playing 4 ♕c7!⊙ ♖g6 5 ♕e7! at once.

6 ♕f8+ ♔h5 7 ♕f7 ♔h6 8 ♕e7!⊙ ♖g2 9 ♕e3+ ♔g7 10 ♕c3+ ♔f7 11 ♕c7+ ♔g8 12 ♕b8+ ♔g7 13 ♕b7+.

The Pawn on the 6th Rank

Our survey starts with a rook pawn. If it stands on its initial position then, as we already know, the stronger side wins. With the black pawn on the 6th rank, the position is drawn.

B. Guretzky-Cornitz, 1864

13-11

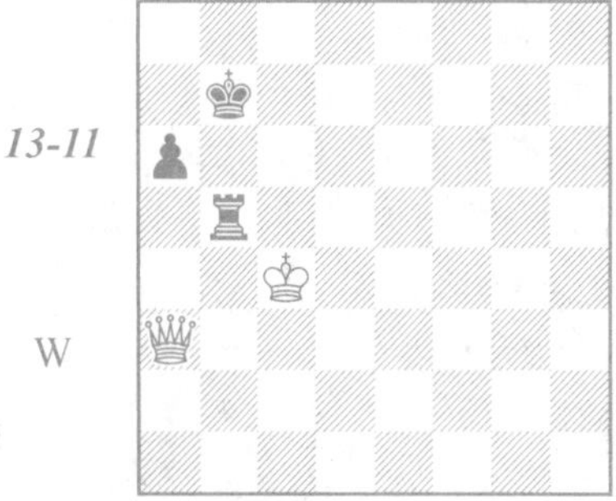

W

The rook has only one protected square (b5), therefore the white king breaks through using a zugzwang technique. However White's achievements end with that: he can neither force a gain of the rook nor smoke the king out from the corner.

1 ♕e7+ ♔b8 2 ♕e8+ ♔b7 3 ♕d8 ♔a7 4 ♕c8 ♖b7!

Black should by no means abandon the corner. 4...♔b6? loses after 5 ♕b8+ ♔c6 (5...♔a5 6 ♕d8+ ♔a4 7 ♕d2 ♔a3 8 ♕d6+) 6 ♕a7 ♖b6 (6...♖a5 7 ♔b4 ♖b5+ 8 ♔a4 ♖b6 9 ♔a5) 7 ♔d4 ♔b5 (7...♖b4+ 8 ♔c3 ♖b6 9 ♔c4⊙) 8 ♕d7+ ♔b4 9 ♕c7 ♖h6 10 ♕e7+ ♔a4 11 ♕e8+ ♔a5 12 ♔c5.

5 ♕c5+

This is stronger than 5 ♔c5 ♖b5+ 6 ♔c6 ♖b6+ 7 ♔c7 ♖b5 8 ♕g4 ♖b7+ 9 ♔c6 ♖b6+.

5...♔a8 6 ♕d6 ♔a7 7 ♕d4+ ♔a8 8 ♔c5 ♔a7 9 ♔c6+ ♔a8

13-12

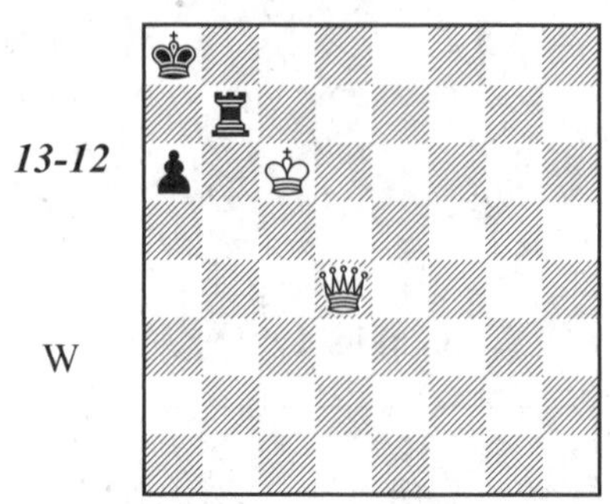

W

10 ♕d8+ ♖b8 11 ♕a5 ♔a7 12 ♕c7+ ♔a8 13 ♕f4 ♖b7!=

This precise defensive move prevents occupation of the important c7- and c8-squares by the white king. 13...♖b5? is erroneous in view of 14 ♔c7! ♔a7 (14...♖b7+ 15 ♔c8 ♖b5 16 ♕c7) 15 ♕d6 ♖b8 16 ♕c5+ ♔a8 17 ♕c6+ ♔a7 18 ♕d6! (a decisive zugzwang) 18...♖b7+ 19 ♔c8 ♖b5 20 ♕d7+ ♔a8 21 ♕c7⊙ ♖b1 22 ♕c6+ ♔a7 23 ♕c5+ ♔a8 24 ♕d5+ ♔a7 25 ♕d4+ ♔a8 26 ♕e4+.

We should add that, if we shift the starting position one or two ranks lower, Black loses. Too many squares demand protection behind the pawn in this case, and the pieces cannot successfully tackle this problem.

As Khenkin stated, White wins against the pawn on a6, too, if his king is standing on the a-file. He prepares ♔a5 by means of resolute queen actions, pressing the black king away from the 7th rank and the rook – away from b5.

If the black pawn is a central or a bishop pawn and stands on the 5th or 6th rank, Black is lost.

Philidor, 1777

13-13

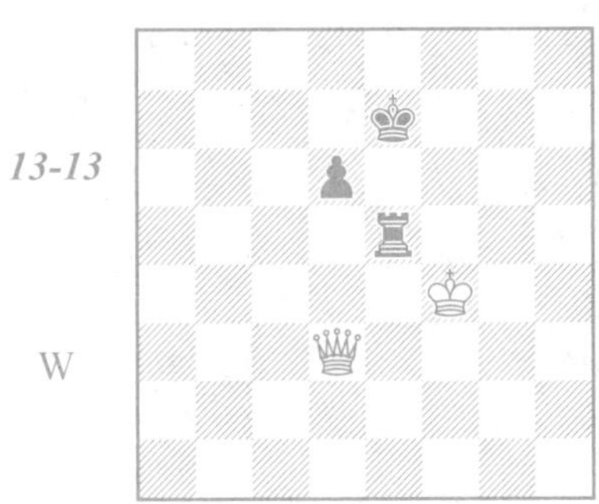

W

White's plan consists of the following stages:

1) To occupy squares behind the pawn, with the help of zugzwang, and drive the black king out to d5 where he will obstruct his own rook.

2) To cross the 5th rank with his king.

3) To break through with the king to the e-file and the pawn.

1 ♕h7+ ♔d8

Both 1...♔f8? 2 ♕d7 and 1...♔e8? 2 ♕c7 are hopeless. In case of 1...♔e6?! 2 ♕c7 ♖c5 3 ♕d8 White's mission becomes easier than after the text move.

2 ♕f7!⊙ ♔c8

This is better than 2...♖e7? 3 ♕g8+ ♔d7 4 ♔f5; 2...♖c5?! 3 ♕e6 ♔c7 4 ♕e7+ ♔c6 5 ♕d8 ♖e5 6 ♕c8+ ♔d5 7 ♕a8+ ♔e6 8 ♕e8+ ♔d5 9 ♕c8! transposes into the main line.

3 ♕a7 ♔d8 (3...♖c5? 4 ♕e7) **4 ♕b8+ ♔d7 5 ♕b7+ ♔d8 6 ♕c6! ♔e7 7 ♕c7+ ♔e6 8 ♕d8 ♔d5** (the same is 8...♖f5+ 9 ♔g4 ♖e5 10 ♕e8+ ♔d5 11 ♕c8) **9 ♕c8!?** (Chéron recommended 9 ♕d7!?)

13-14

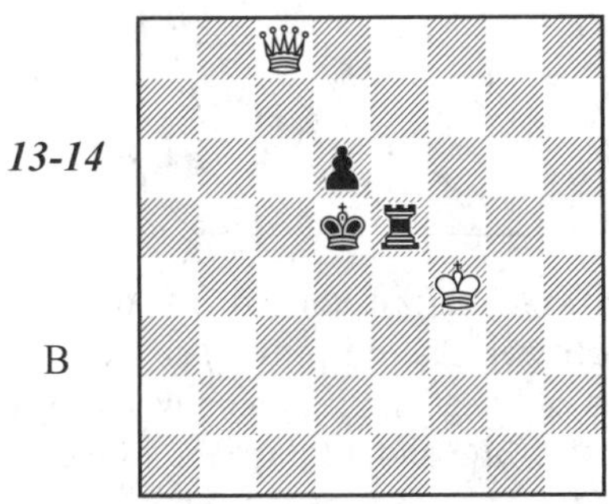

B

The first stage ends successfully. Black is in zugzwang and he is forced to give way to the white king because 9...♖h5? loses immediately: 10 ♕a8+ ♔d4 11 ♕a4+. If 9...♔d4 then 10 ♕c6 ♖d5 and, according to Salvioli, 11 ♔f3! ♔e5 (11...♖f5+ 12 ♔g4 ♖d5 13 ♔f4⊙) 12 ♔e3 ♖c5□ 13 ♕e8+ ♔f6 (13...♔f5 14 ♕f7+ ♔e5 15 ♕e7+) 14 ♕d7 ♖d5 15 ♔e4+−.

9...♖e4+ 10 ♔f5 ♖e5+ 11 ♔f6

The second stage is also fulfilled.

11...♖e4

Both 11...♖e1 12 ♕b7+ ♔c5 13 ♕c7+ ♔d5 14 ♕a5+ and 11...♖e2 12 ♕a8+ ♔d4 13 ♕a4+ ♔c5 14 ♕a3+ lose rapidly.

12 ♕c3!

A neat method that stems from Guretzky-Cornitz (1864). Philidor analyzed a slightly slower process: 12 ♕f5+ ♖e5 13 ♕d3+ ♔c5 14 ♕d2!, while computer prefers 12 ♕b7+ ♔d4 13 ♕c6 d5 14 ♕b6+ ♔d3 (14...♔c4 15 ♔f5⊙) 15 ♕c5 d4 16 ♕a3+ ♔e2 (16...♔c4 17 ♕c1+; 16...♔c2 17 ♕b4) 17 ♕b2+ ♔e3 18 ♕c1+ ♔e2 19 ♕c2+ ♔e3 20 ♔f5 ♖f4+ 21 ♔e5 d3 22 ♕c5+ ♔f3 23 ♕c6+ ♔e3 24 ♕h6.

12...♖e6+ (12...♖e5 13 ♔f7!⊙) **13 ♔f7 ♖e5 14 ♔f8!**

13-15

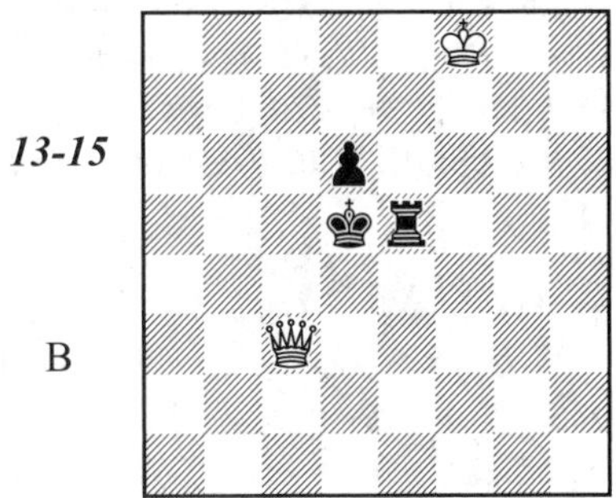

B

Zugzwang again. Black must let the white king cross the e-file.

14...♖e4

14...♔e4 15 ♕c4+ ♔f5 16 ♕d3+ ♔e6 17 ♔e8+−, or 14...♖e6 15 ♕b3+ ♔e5 16 ♔f7 ♖f6+ 17 ♔e7+−.

15 ♕d3+ ♖d4

Or 15...♔e5 16 ♔e7 d5 17 ♕g3+ ♖f4 (17...♔d4+ 18 ♔d6 ♔c4 19 ♕g2 ♖d4 20 ♕c2+; 17...♔f5+ 18 ♔d6 d4 19 ♕d3 ♔f4 20 ♔d5) 18 ♕e3+ ♖e4 19 ♕g5+ ♔d4+ 20 ♔d6.

16 ♕f5+ ♔c4 17 ♕c2+ ♔d5 18 ♔e7 ♔e5 19 ♔d7 ♖d5 20 ♕e2+ ♔f4 21 ♔c6 ♖d4 22 ♔b5 ♔f5 23 ♕e3 ♖e4 24 ♕d3 ♔e5 25 ♔c6 ♖d4 26 ♕e3+ ♖e4 27 ♕g5+ ♔e6 28 ♕g6+ ♔e5 29 ♕×d6+.

The identical plan brings success against a black pawn on d5. With the pawn on d4, Black also loses.

If the pawn stands on c6 or c5, White wins too, although his task is even more complicated.

Tragicomedies

Penrose – Hartston
England ch, Coventry 1970

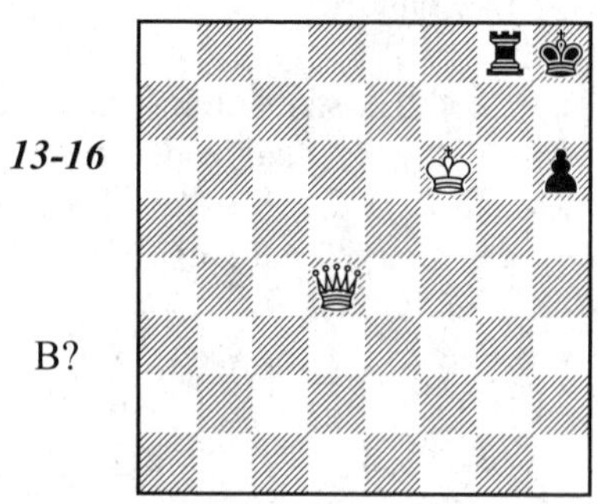

13-16

B?

1...♔h7??

Black should not let the white king settle on the f7- and f8-squares. 1...♖g7! led to a draw.

2 ♔f7+– ♖g5 3 ♕f6 ♖g8 4 ♕e6⊙ ♖g5 5 ♔f8 h5 6 ♕f7+ ♔h6 7 ♕f6+ ♖g6 8 ♕f4+ ♔h7 9 ♕e5! ♔h6 10 ♔f7 h4 11 ♕e4 Black resigned.

A Knight Pawn on the 5th or 6th Rank

A draw still can be achieved when the knight pawn has left the 7th rank. If it is standing on the 6th rank, Black should keep his king behind it; if the pawn has reached the 4th or 5th rank; the king may be placed in front of it as well.

B. Guretzky-Cornitz, 1864

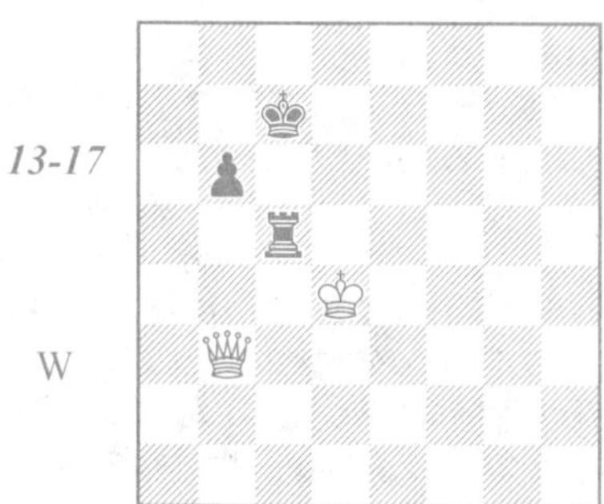

13-17

W

1 ♕f7+ ♔b8! 2 ♕e6 ♔b7 3 ♕d7+ ♔b8 4 ♔e4 ♔a8 5 ♕a4+ ♔b7 6 ♔d4 ♖c7! Black lets the white king go ahead in order to keep his own king behind the pawn.

7 ♔d5 ♖c5+ 8 ♔d6 ♖c7

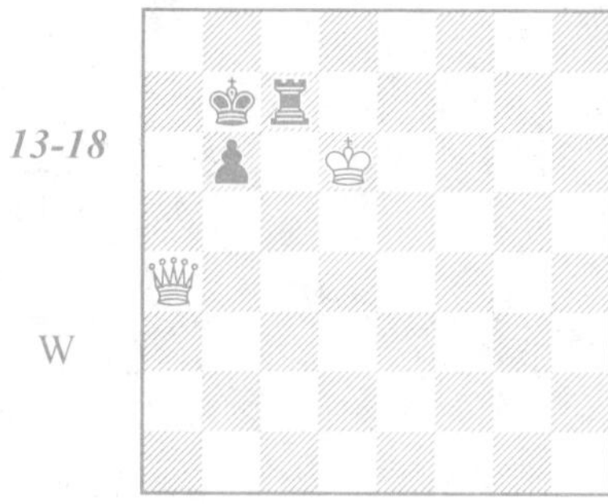

13-18

W

The main difference in this position from those with a bishop pawn, or a central pawn, is the impossibility of queen attacks against the king from the left. The defensive method is similar to that with the a6-pawn (diagram 13-12).

And, as Khenkin noted, even with the white king on d8 (while the queen is standing on e6 and the rook on c5) there is no win: unlike the case of a rook pawn (won for White), Black holds here thanks to the waiting move ♔a7.

9 ♕b5 ♖c5 10 ♕d7+ ♔b8 11 ♕g4 ♖c7 12 ♕e2 (△ 13 ♕a6) **12...♔b7!=**.

Now let us investigate 6...♖a5? (instead of the correct continuation 6...♖c7!) 7 ♕d7+ ♔b8 8 ♕c6 ♔a7 9 ♕c7+ ♔a6 10 ♕b8 ♖c5 11 ♕a8+ ♔b5.

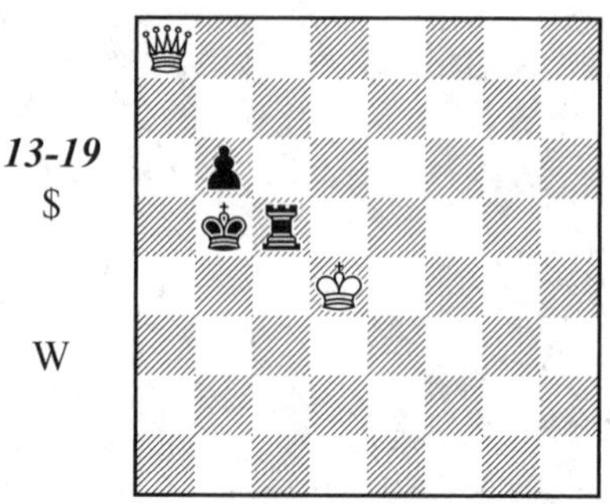

13-19
$

W

Guretzky-Cornitz evaluated this position as drawn. However Chéron proved in 1950 that White wins, although in a very complicated way. (First of all White should pass the move, for example 12 ♕b7! ♔a5 13 ♕a7+ ♔b5 14 ♕a8!). Let us accept this as fact and anyone who wants to know more may look into endgame handbooks.

B. Guretzky-Cornitz, 1864

13-20

B

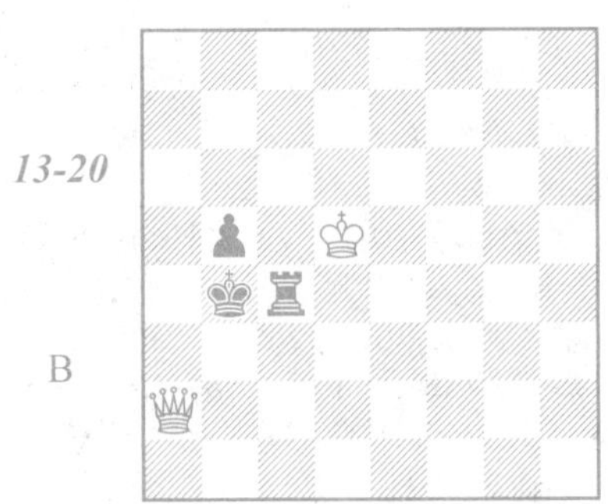

Another important case of a draw. If shifted down or with the black king on b6, it remains drawn.

1...♖c5+ 2 ♔d6 ♖c8!

The rook is safe here, in distinction to similar situations with a central pawn.

3 ♔d7 ♖c4 4 ♔d8 ♖c5 5 ♕b2+ ♔a4! (but not 5....♔c4? 6 ♔d7+–) **6 ♔d7 ♖c4=** (or 6...b4=).

Piket – McShane
Germany tt 1997

13-21

W?

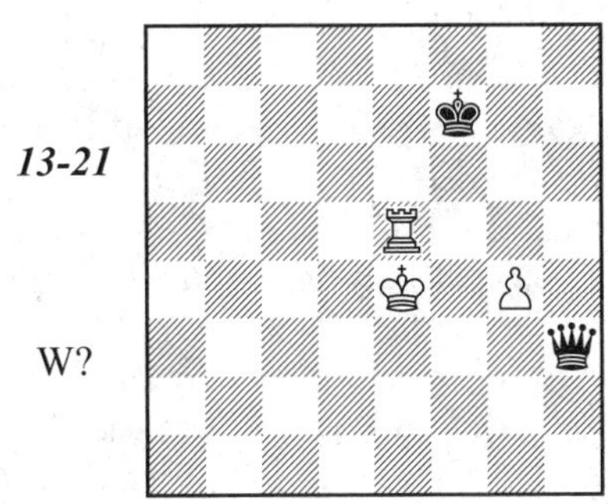

1 ♖f5+!

Surely not 1 ♔f4? ♕h2+ 2 ♔f5 ♕f2+ 3 ♔e4 ♔g6, and as White's king is cut off from the pawn, he loses.

1...♔g6 2 ♔f4 ♕h2+

If 2...♕g2 then 3 ♖g5+! ♔f6 4 ♖f5+ ♔e6 5 ♔g5= (see diagram 13-20).

3 ♔f3 ♕g1 4 ♖h5! ♕f1+ 5 ♔g3 ♕e2 6 ♖f5 ♕e4 7 ♔h3 ♕e1 8 ♔g2 ♕e3 9 ♔h2 ♕e4 10 ♔g3 ♕×f5 Draw.

Exercises

13-22

13/2
W?

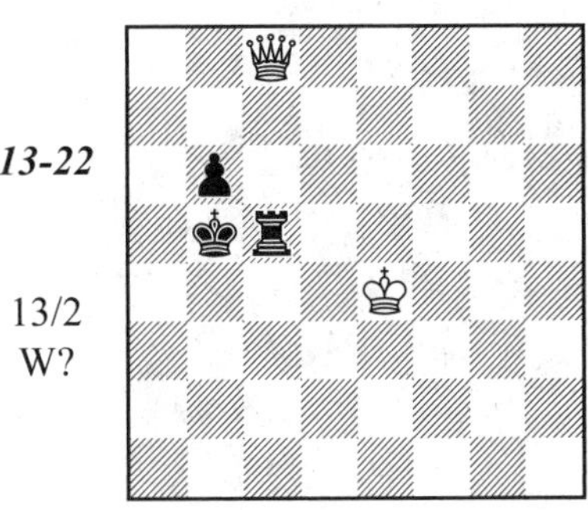

Queen and Pawn vs. Rook and Pawn

Passed Pawns

If the pawns are passed, a queen usually wins with ease, but a single important exception exists.

N. Grigoriev, 1917

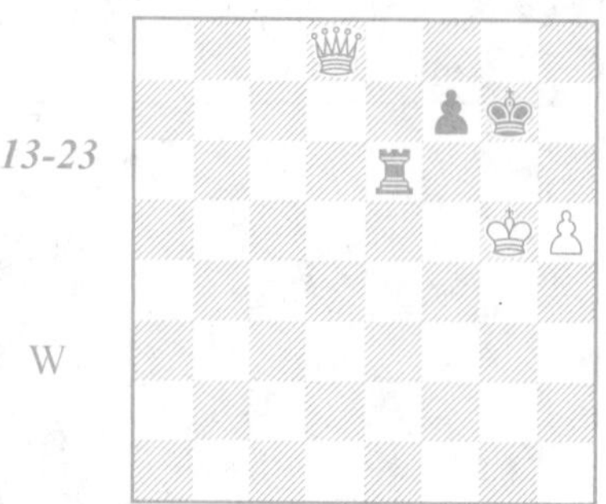
13-23
W

Grigoriev did an analysis of the diagrammed position, but it was only discovered among his archives in 1954. Independently, Kasparian published an analysis in 1948. He did not know Grigoriev's conclusions and managed to discover the truth independently when he checked one of his endgame studies for correctness.

The rook has two safe squares, a6 and h6; therefore White cannot create a zugzwang position. The defense is rather simple: Black should not give the f8-square to the white queen and should not permit h5-h6.

1 ♕d4+ ♔h7 2 ♕c3 ♖h6 3 ♕b4 (threatening 4 ♕f8) **3...♔g7! 4 ♕b3 ♖e6 5 ♕h3 ♖h6!** (preventing 6 h6+) **6 ♕h1 ♔h7!=**

In case of 5...♖c6? White wins by means of 6 h6+! ♔h7 7 ♕f5+ ♖g6+ 8 ♔h5 ♔h8.

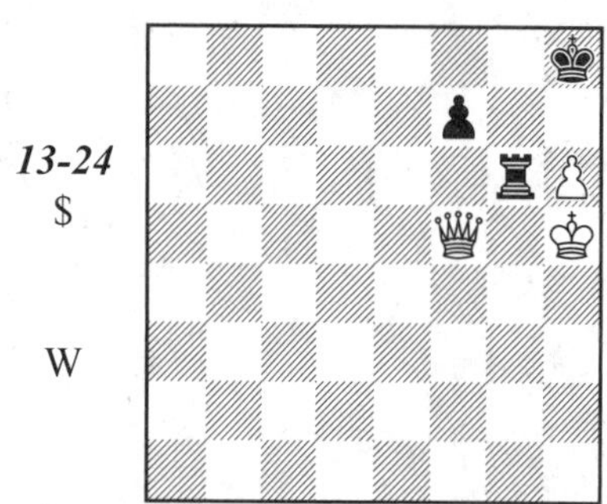
13-24
$
W

The f7-pawn is obviously invulnerable: 9 ♕×f7?? ♖g5+ (or 9...♖×h6+), and the rook becomes a desperado. However White wins rapidly by means of 9 ♕c8+! ♖g8 (9...♔h7 10 ♕f8) 10 ♕c3+ ♔h7 11 ♕f6+−.

In the game Andric - Rogulj, where this position occurred (with reversed colors and wings), White played 9 h7?. His opponent resigned right away, although he could make White's task truly difficult by playing 9...♖e6! (rather than 9...♖g7? 10 ♕c8+ ♔×h7 11 ♕f8⊙ or 9...♔g7? 10 ♕×f7+! ♔×f7 11 h8♕) 10 ♔g5 (10 ♕×f7? ♖h6+ 11 ♔g5 ♖g6+! 12 ♔f5 ♖g5+) 10...♖d6.

If White chooses 11 ♕c8+? ♔×h7 12 ♕f8 ♖g6+ 13 ♔f5, Black manages to hold after 13...♖f6+! 14 ♔g5 (or 14 ♔e5 ♖e6+ 15 ♔d5 ♖f6=) 14...♖g6+ 15 ♔h5 ♖f6! 16 ♕e7 ♖h6+ 17 ♔g5 ♖g6+ 18 ♔f5 ♔g7=.

The winning continuation is 11 ♔f4! ♖e6 12 ♔f3⊙ (12 ♕×f7? ♖e4+) 12...♖g6 13 ♔e4 ♖g7 (13...♖e6+ 14 ♔d4 ♖g6 15 ♔d5 ♖e6 16 ♕×f7+−), and only now 14 ♕c8+ ♔×h7 15 ♕f8 ♔g6 (15...♖g4+ 16 ♔f5 ♖g7 17 ♕e8!⊙) 16 ♔e5 ♖h7 17 ♕g8+ ♖g7 18 ♕h8⊙.

Back to the diagram 13-23, we should add that the ***evaluation of this position would be changed if the white king were standing on the 7th or the 8th rank***. For example, if the king is on d7 then 1 ♕g5+ ♔h7 2 h6 wins.

A draw cannot be reached also if all the pieces are shifted to the left or downwards.

As Grigoriev proved, Black loses if he has an additional pawn on h6. The reason is obvious: the pawn deprives the rook of the second protected square.

Tragicomedies

Averbakh – Bondarevsky
USSR ch, Moscow 1948

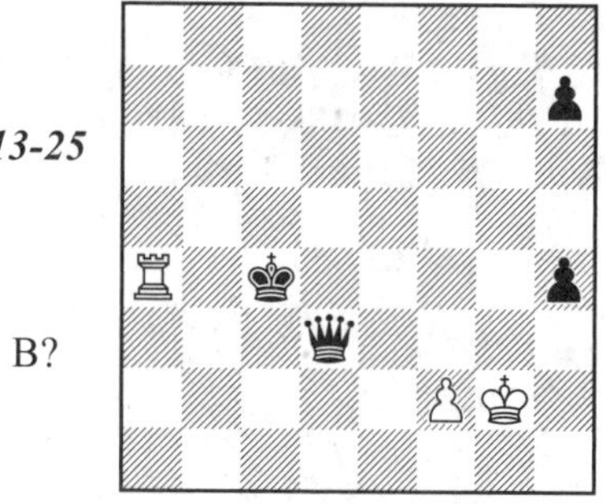
13-25
B?

Averbakh, in contrast to his opponent, knew Kasparian's freshly published analysis; this fact enabled him to hold this hopeless position.

1...♔d5?

1...♔b3! 2 ♖×h4 ♔c2 was an easy win.

2 ♖×h4 ♔e6?

As Abramov demonstrated, Black could avoid Grigoriev's drawn position by playing 2...♕g6+! 3 ♔h2 ♕f5 4 ♔g3 ♕e5+ 5 ♔f3 (5 ♔g2 ♕g5+ 6 ♔h3 ♕g1 –+; 5 ♖f4 h5 6 ♔f3 ♕g5 –+) 5...♕g5 6 ♖h3 ♔d4 7 ♖g3 ♕d5+ 8 ♔g4 ♕h1 –+.

3 ♖h3! =

A draw has become inevitable.

3...♕e4+ 4 ♔h2 ♔f6 5 ♖e3 ♕d5 6 ♖g3 h5 7 ♖e3 ♔g5 8 ♖g3+ ♔f4 9 ♖e3 h4 10 ♖h3 ♕b7 11 ♖e3 ♔g4 12 ♖h3 ♕b1 13 ♔g2! ♕h7 14 ♔h2! ♕c7+ 15 ♔g2 ♕c2 16 ♖e3 Draw.

Timman – Nunn
Wijk aan Zee 1982

13-26

W?

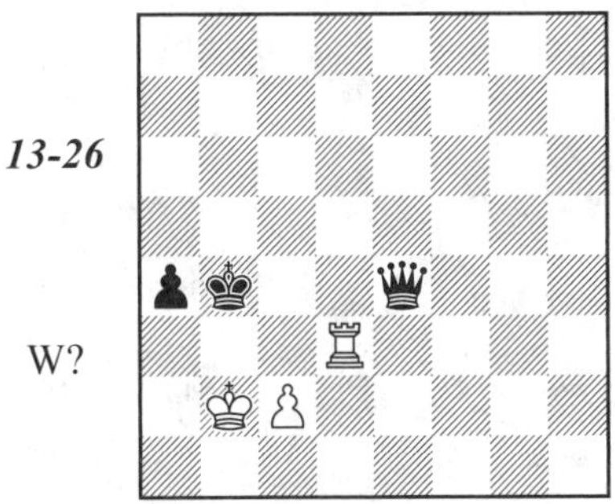

1 ♔a2?? (1 ♖a3! ♕e5+ 2 ♔a2 led to a draw) **1...a3!**

The pawn has crept in at a3, and White's position is lost now. He resigned in view of rather simple variations: 2 ♔b1 ♕e1+ 3 ♔a2 ♕c1 4 ♖b3+ ♔a4 and 2 ♖b3+ ♔c4 3 ♔×a3 ♕×c2.

Pawns on Adjacent Files

Almost all positions with the pawns on the same files are lost. Positions with the pawns on adjacent files, however, are sometimes tenable, but only if the weaker side's pawn stands on the initial square.

In the next diagram, if Black is on move he holds by means of transferring his king to g7.

F. Dedrle, 1925*

13-27

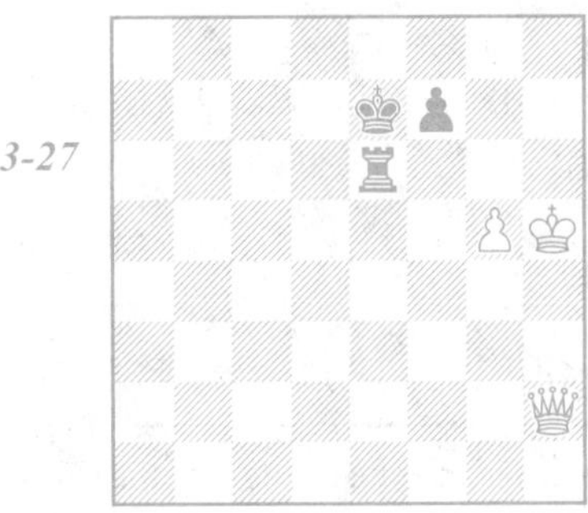

1...♔f8! 2 ♔g4 ♔g7 3 ♔f5 ♖g6 4 ♕b2+ ♔h7

White cannot do anything as 5 ♕f6 leads to a drawn pawn endgame.

If White is on move in the initial position, he wins by preparing a sacrifice of his queen for the rook.

1 ♕b8! ♖g6 2 ♕b4+ ♔e8 3 ♕e4+ ♖e6 (3...♔f8 4 ♕×g6!) **4 ♕×e6+! fe 5 ♔h6+–**

From this example, the following conclusions can be drawn:

1) An important technique of exploiting an advantage can be a queen sacrifice that results in a winning pawn endgame.

2) The weaker side should keep his king in front of the opponent's pawn; this can often (but by no means always!) neutralize the threat of the queen sacrifice. If the pawn stands on e5 (instead of g5) the king should stay on e7.

3) With the white king on the 7th rank, Black's position is most often lost.

One should not accept these rules absolutely, exceptions sometimes happen.

13-28

$

W

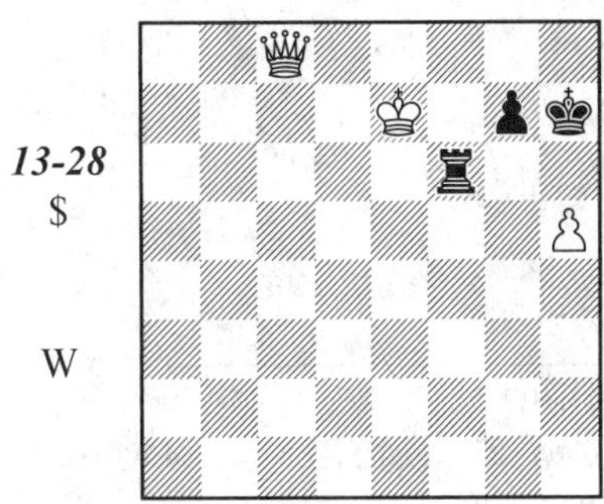

1 ♕c2+ ♔g8 = (rather than 1...♔h6?? 2 ♕e4⊙ +–). Although the white king reached the 7th rank there is still no win. The reason is that any pawn endgame with a rook pawn is drawn.

13-29
$
B

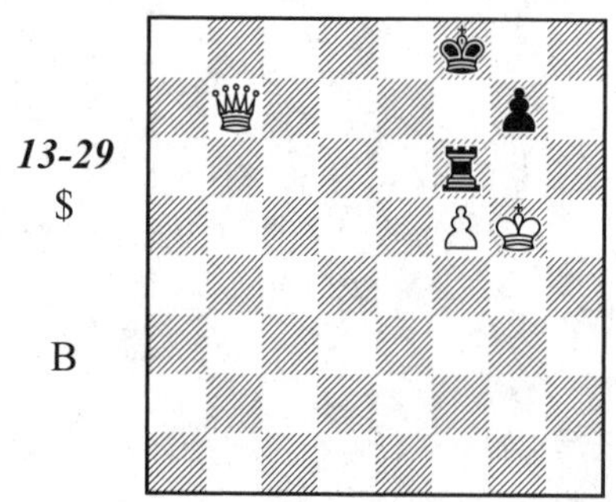

Black loses in spite of the fact that his king occupies a “regular” position in front of the pawn.

1...♖h6 2 ♕d7

Zugzwang. If 2...♖f6 then 3 ♕d8+ ♔f7 4 ♕×f6+ gf+ 5 ♔h6 is decisive. **2...♔g8 3 ♕e8+ ♔h7** does not help. The king has abandoned the position in front of the pawn, and a queen sacrifice cannot be avoided anymore: **4 ♔f4 ♖f6 5 ♔e5 ♖h6 6 ♕e6!+–**

Now let us move the entire position after 2 ♕d7 to the left by one file (Black’s pawn on f7, rook on g6 etc.) There is no zugzwang anymore because Black has a waiting move 2...♖h6!; therefore White cannot win.

Tragicomedies

Sämisch – Prins
Hastings 1938/39

13-30
W

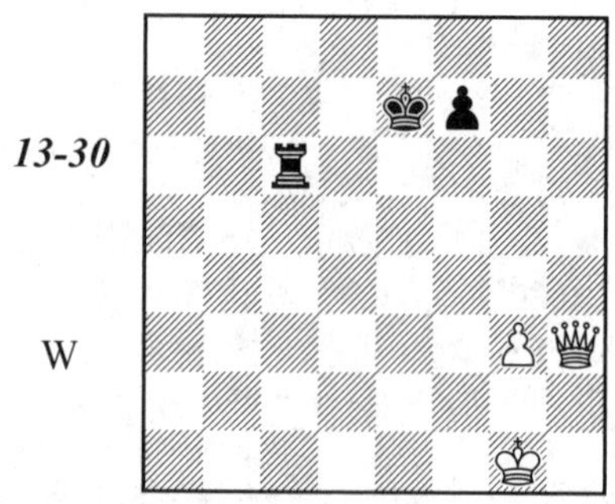

Sämisch agreed to a draw without any knowledge that he had a winning position. He had only not to let the black king to come to g7. Here is Keres’ analysis:

1 ♕h4+ ♔f8 2 ♕h8+! ♔e7 3 ♔f2 ♖g6 4 ♔f3 ♖e6 5 ♔g4 ♖g6+ 6 ♔h5 ♖e6 7 g4 ♖g6 8 g5 ♖e6 9 ♕b8 (Dedrle’s position) 9...♖g6 10 ♕b4+ ♔e8 11 ♕e4+ followed by a queen sacrifice.

A Fortress with Multiple Pawns

From the multitude of theoretically known positions where a rook opposes a queen more or less successfully, we select several of the most important and characteristic cases.

V. Khenkin, 1962

13-31
$
B

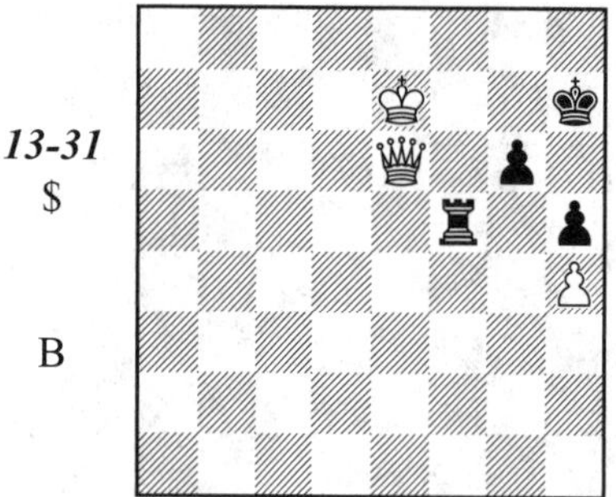

1...♔h8!?

Both 1...♔g7 and 1...♖f1 are not worse that this, by any means.

2 ♕×g6 ♖f7+ (2...♖e5+) **3 ♔e6 ♖e7+**, with a draw by a stalemate or a perpetual check.

With a shift up, the position is still drawn. But when shifted down, it is lost: White wins by means of a queen attack along the last rank.

V. Khenkin, 1966

13-32
W

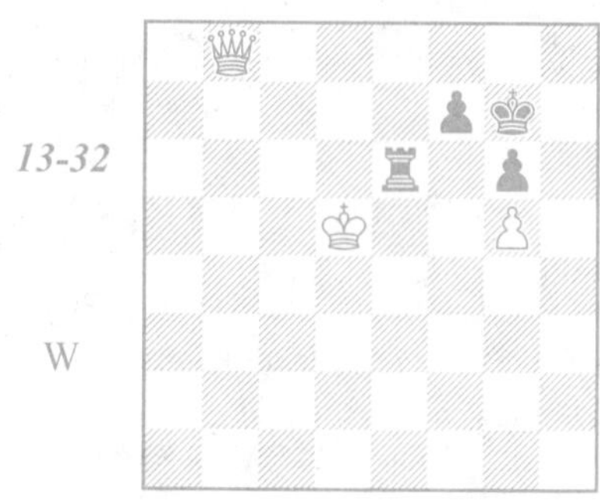

As we know, a similar position, without the g6-pawn, is drawn. But here, when this pawn deprives the rook of the second protected square, White wins: he gradually approaches the black pawn with his king using the zugzwang technique.

It is worth mentioning that White is helpless in making any progress if his king is cut off in the right corner, be it in the diagrammed position or in many similar situations.

1 ♕c7!⊙ ♖e3

Other moves are no better:

1...♖a6 2 ♕c3+ ♔h7 3 ♕c4! ♖e6 (3...♖a5+

4 ♔d6 ♖×g5 5 ♕×f7+ ♔h6 6 ♕f4 ♔h5 7 ♕h2+ ♔g4 8 ♕h6+–; 3...♖b6 4 ♕c7 ♖b5+ 5 ♔d6 ♖f5 6 ♔e7+–) 4 ♕c8 (threatening 5 ♕×e6) 4...♖e1 5 ♕f8 ♖f1 6 ♔d6 with 7 ♔e7 and 8 ♕×f7+ to follow;

1...♔f8 2 ♕c8+ ♔e7 3 ♕b8!⊙ ♔d7 4 ♕f8 ♖e7 5 ♕g8 ♔c7 6 ♕a8 ♖d7+ (6...♔d7 7 ♕f8⊙) 7 ♔e5+–.

2 ♕c2! ♔g8

If 2...♖a3 or 2...♖g3, 3 ♕b2+ decides immediately; if 2...♖e6 then 3 ♕c3+ ♔g8 (3...♔h7 4 ♕h3+; 3...♔f8 4 ♕c8+ ♔e7 5 ♕b8!⊙) 4 ♕c8+ and 5 ♕×e6.

3 ♔d6 ♖e6+ 4 ♔d7 ♖e3 (4...♔g7 5 ♕c4!+–) **5 ♕c4!**

The rook must leave the e-file because 5...♖e1 6 ♕c8+ is bad.

5...♖a3 6 ♕e4 ♔g7 7 ♕e5+

This decides a bit more rapidly than Khenkin's suggestion 7 ♔e7 ♖a7+ 8 ♔e8.

7...♔g8 8 ♕b8+ ♔h7 (8...♔g7 9 ♕b2+) **9 ♔e7+–.**

Dorfman – Beliavsky
Lvov zt 1978

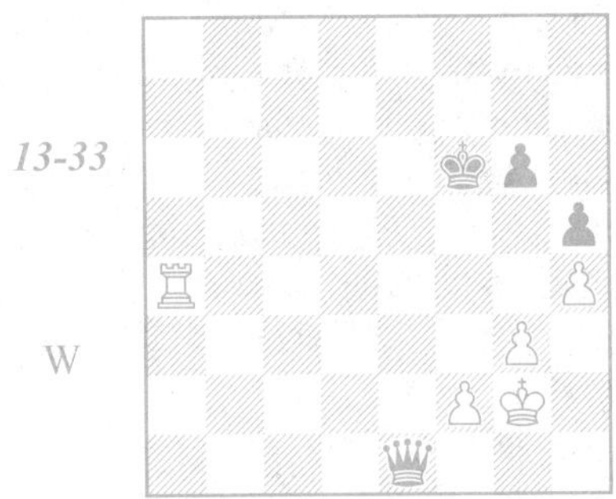

13-33
W

Khenkin supplied a detailed analysis for this ending.

Where does the rook belong, on e3 or f4? It turns out that both squares are good when the black king is on d5; but the rook should stand on f4 (to protect g4) while the black king remains on the kingside.

A draw could be reached by means of 1 ♖f4+! ♔e5 2 ♖f8 (2 ♖a4 is also good) 2...♕e4+ 3 ♔g1 ♕c6 4 ♖f4 ♕c1+ 5 ♔g2 ♕d1.

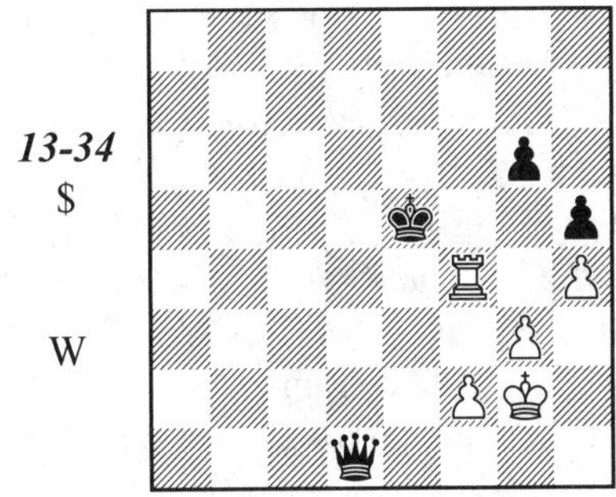

13-34
$
W

If the rook remains on the 4th rank – 6 ♖b4 – then after 6...♔d5 7 ♖f4 ♔c5, as theory says, 8 ♖e4? loses to 8...♕d5 9 ♔f3 ♔c6! 10 ♔e3 (10 ♔f4 ♕d3! 11 ♖e8 ♔c7! 12 ♖e7+ ♔d8 13 ♖e4 ♔d7⊙) 10...♕d1!. Therefore White should play 8 ♖f8!, giving way to the black king and planning a rook transfer to e3.

This maneuver can be started immediately, too – 6 ♖f8!? ♕d5+ 7 ♔g1 ♔e4 8 ♖e8+ ♔f3 9 ♖f8+! ♔e2 (9...♔g4?! 10 ♔h2 ♕d2 11 ♔g2! g5□ 12 hg ♔×g5 13 ♖f4= followed with ♖h4-f4-h4) 10 ♖e8+ ♔d2 11 ♖e3!=. Black cannot make any progress.

In the actual game, Dorfman undertook a premature transfer to e3.

1 ♖a3? ♕e4+ 2 ♔h2 ♔f5 3 ♖e3?!

White loses rapidly after 3 ♔g1 ♕b1+ 4 ♔g2 ♕b7+ 5 ♔h2 ♔g4! (of course, not 5...♕b2? 6 ♖f3+ ♔e4 7 ♖e3+ ♔d4 8 ♔g2=) 6 ♖a4+ ♔f3 7 ♖f4+ ♔e2.

However after 3 ♖a7! the winning process would have been very complicated. In case of even the slightest inaccuracy White could have reached one of the drawn positions that have been mentioned above (with the rook on f4 or e3).

3...♕c6 (3...♔g4? 4 ♖f7!=) 4 ♖f7+ (4 ♖e7 ♕f6! △ 5...♔g4–+) 4...♔e4 5 ♔g1! ♕d6! (5...♔d3? 6 ♖e7! △ ♖e3=) 6 ♔g2 (6 ♖f4+ ♕×f4; 6 ♔h2 ♔d3) 6...♕d5! (6...♔d3? 7 ♖f3+ and 8 ♖e3=; 6...♕e6? 7 ♖f4+) 7 ♖f8 ♔d3+ 8 ♔g1 ♕c6! 9 ♖f7! (10 ♖e7= is threatened) 9...♕e4!

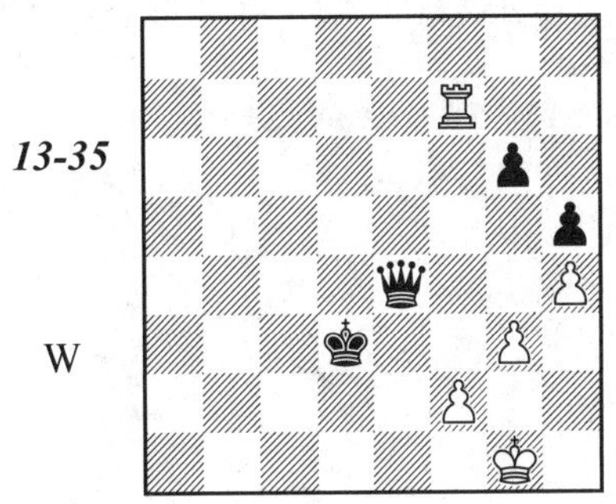

13-35
W

10 ♖f4 ♕e2 11 ♔g2 (11 ♖f8 ♕e1+ 12 ♔h2 ♕e4! 13 ♖f4 ♕c6 14 ♔g1 ♔e2 −+) 11...♔d2 12 ♖a4 ♕e6! 13 ♖b4 (13 ♖a3 ♕c6+ 14 ♔h2 ♔e2) 13...♕d5+ 14 ♔g1 ♔e2 15 ♖b2+ ♔f3 −+;

10 ♖a7 ♕b4! (△ 11...♔e2) 11 ♖a6(a8) ♕b1+ 12 ♔h2 (12 ♔g2 ♕b7+) 12...♔e2 −+, or 11 ♔g2 ♕c5! 12 ♖a6 ♕d5+ 13 ♔g1 ♔e2 14 ♖×g6 ♕d1+ 15 ♔h2 ♔f1! (rather than 15...♔×f2? 16 ♖f6+ ♔e3 17 ♖f4, arriving to the drawn position from diagram 13-31) 16 ♖b6 (16 ♖a6 ♕d4) 16...♕c2 17 ♖f6 ♕e4 −+.

In the last line, Khenkin does not investigate the most stubborn defense: 11 ♔f1!, preventing the king invasion to e2. Black responds with 11...♕d6!, planning to bring his king to g4. For example, 12 ♖a1 (12 ♔g2 ♕c5!; 12 ♖a2 ♕c6!) 12...♕c6! 13 ♖a3+ (13 ♖d1+ ♔e4 14 ♔g2 ♔f5+) 13...♔e4 14 ♖e3+ ♔f5 15 ♔g1 ♔g4 etc.

3...♕d5 4 ♔g1 (4 ♖e7 ♔g4; 4 ♖e8 ♕f7!) **4...♔g4** (threatening 5...♔h3) **5 ♔h2 ♕c6! 6 ♖a3** (6 ♖b3 ♕c2) **6...♕c1! 7 ♖e3 ♕f1 8 ♖e4+ ♔f3 9 ♖f4+ ♔e2 10 ♖e4+ ♔d3 11 ♖f4 ♕b1 12 ♔g2 ♔e2**

13-36

W

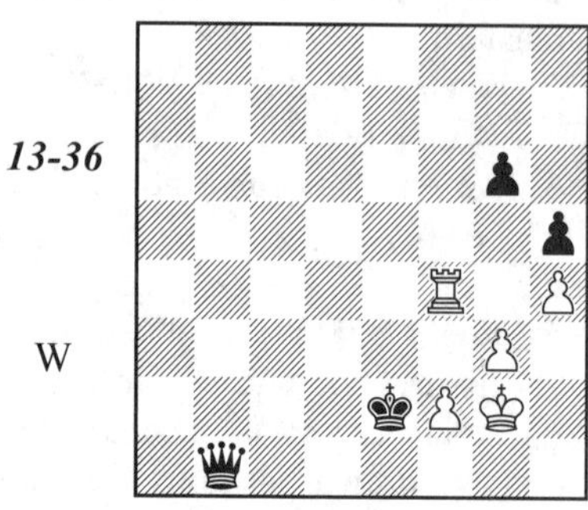

13 ♖f6?

This leads to an immediate collapse. However the best choice 13 ♖f8 was good enough only for postponing the deadly end for a while: 13...♕b7+ 14 ♔g1 ♕c6! 15 ♖f4 ♕a8!⊙ (the rook is forced to occupy a light square) 16 ♖f7 ♕a1+ 17 ♔g2 ♕f1+ 18 ♔h2 ♕d1! 19 ♖f4 (19 ♔g2 ♕d5+) 19...♔f1 −+.

13...♕f1+ 14 ♔h2 ♕a1!

White resigned in view of the inevitable 15...♔f1.

To fully understand the following endgame, we should refresh our memories with the evaluations of several already known positions.

V. Khenkin, 1966

13-37

$

W?

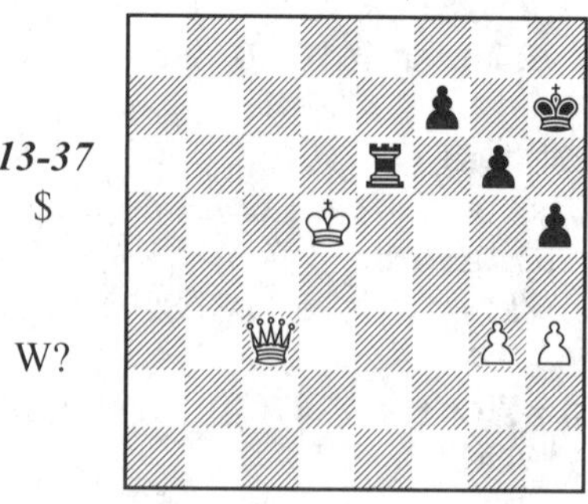

As we know from the previous example, it would have been an easy draw if the white pawn stood on h4. Here, on the contrary, White has a clear plan: to push his pawn to g5, obtaining Khenkin's winning position from the diagram 13-32.

However the immediate 1 g4? hg 2 hg meets a strong response 2...g5!=. When White gains the g5-pawn, the drawn position of Dedrle arises (diagram 13-27).

When analyzing it, we have mentioned that White wins if his king is on the 7th rank. From this, we come to the correct plan: first White should cross the 5th rank with his king and only thereafter may he push the g-pawn.

1 ♔c5! ♔g8 2 ♕d4 ♔h7 3 ♕d8 ♔g7 4 ♔b5⊙ ♖e1

Nothing else helps, viz.:

4...♔h7 5 ♕f8 +−;

4...♖f6 5 ♕d4 g5 6 ♕d8! ♖g6 7 ♔c5 h4 (7...g4 8 h4 +−) 8 g4! +−;

4...♖e4 5 ♔c6 ♖c4+ 6 ♔d5 ♖c3 7 ♕b8 ♖d3+ 8 ♔e4 ♖d1 9 ♕b2+ ♔g8 10 ♕c3 ♖d6 11 ♔e5 ♖e6+ 12 ♔f4 ♔h7 13 ♔g5 +−.

5 ♕d4+ ♔g8 6 ♔c6 ♖e6+

6...♖h1 7 ♔d7! ♖×h3 8 ♔e7 ♖×g3 9 ♕f4 ♖a3 10 ♕×f7+ ♔h8 11 ♕×g6 is hopeless.

7 ♔d7 ♖e1 8 g4! hg 9 hg

After 9...g5 10 ♕d2 ♖e6 11 ♕×g5+ or 9...♖e6 10 g5! we come to one of the aforementioned positions.

In the last diagram, move the h5-pawn to h6. The evaluation is changed.

13-38
$

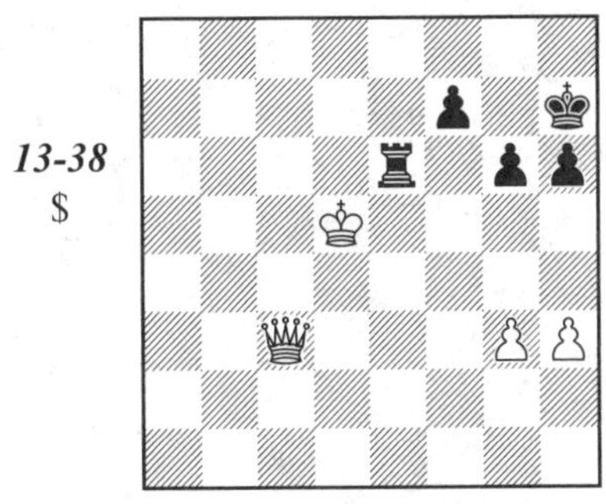

Black, if on move, plays **1...g5**, getting another protected square for the rook (g6). After **2 h4 gh 3 gh** he comes to the drawn position of Grigoriev (diagram 13-23) by means of the pawn sacrifice **3...h5!**. He must sacrifice; otherwise White advances his pawn to h5 and wins.

If White is on move he can prevent ...g6-g5 solely by playing 1 h4, but then 1...h5!= follows.

M. Botvinnik, 1952

13-39
$

W

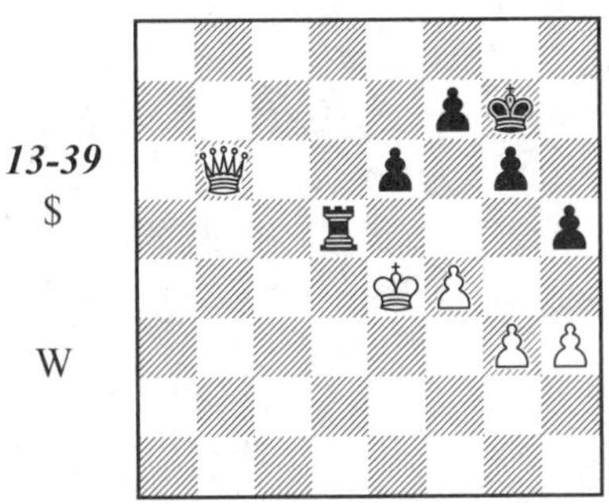

Botvinnik investigated this position (with reversed colors) when he analyzed his adjourned game versus Troianescu (1952). He proved that the inevitable queen sacrifice on d5 leads to a winning pawn endgame.

1 g4 hg 2 hg ♔g8 3 ♕c7 ♔g7 4 ♕c6 ♔f8

Otherwise the white king breaks through:

4...♖d8 5 ♕c3+ ♔g8 6 ♔e5 ♔g7 7 f5! ef 8 gf ♖e8+ (8...gf 9 ♕g3+ ♔f8 10 ♔f6) 9 ♔f4+ ♔g8 10 fg fg 11 ♔g5 ♖e6 12 ♕c7 ♔f8 13 ♕d7+– (Khenkin). 8...f6+!? 9 ♔f4 ♖d5 is more tenacious; it leads to a theoretical position with a bishop pawn on the 6th rank that is winning for White, although not easily.

4...♖d1 5 ♕c3+ ♔g8 6 ♔e5 ♔g7 (6...♖f1 7 ♕c4 ♖g1 8 ♔f6 ♖×g4 9 ♕c7) 7 f5! ef 8 gf ♖f1 (8...gf 9 ♕g3+ ♔f8 10 ♔f6) 9 fg fg 10 ♔e6+ ♔g8. This line is given a strange verdict in endgame books: 11 ♕d3 ♖g1 12 ♔f6+–. However after 11...♖f5! we come to a known drawn position. Therefore, instead of 11 ♕d3?, White should play 11 ♕h3!, threatening to invade h6.

5 ♕a8+!

Prior to the queen sacrifice White should drive the black king back. He cannot go to the center: 5...♔e7 6 ♕a3+ ♔e8 7 ♕b4⊙ +–.

5...♔g7 6 ♕×d5! ed+ (6...f5+ 7 ♔e5 ed 8 g5+–) **7 ♔×d5**

13-40

B

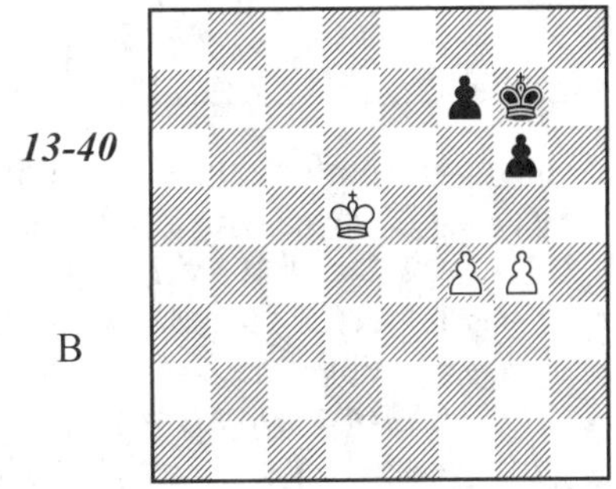

7...♔f8

7...♔h6 8 ♔e5 ♔g7 9 ♔d6 ♔h8!? makes no difference: 10 ♔d7 ♔h7 11 ♔d8! (11 ♔e7? ♔g8!) 11...♔g7 (11...♔h8 12 f5) 12 ♔e8! (an opposition is required when the pawn stands on f5, but not in this case) 12...♔g8 13 ♔e7 ♔g7 14 f5 g5 15 ♔e8+–.

8 ♔d6 ♔e8 9 f5! g5 10 ♔c7 ♔e7 11 ♔c8! ♔d6 12 ♔d8 ♔e5 13 ♔e7 f6 14 ♔f7+–.

Tragicomedies

Ambroz – Ciocaltea
Baile Herculane zt 1982

13-41

W?

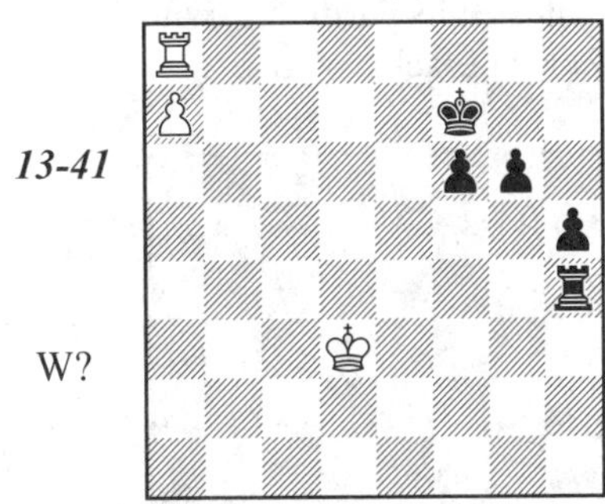

After 1 ♖b8 ♖a4 2 a8♕ ♖×a8 3 ♖×a8 the rook could easily get the upper hand against the three pawns.

1 ♖f8+?? ♔×f8 2 a8♕+ ♔e7 3 ♕b7+

Draw. Black should just bring his rook to g4, f5 or e5.

Martín González – Pétursson
Biel izt 1985

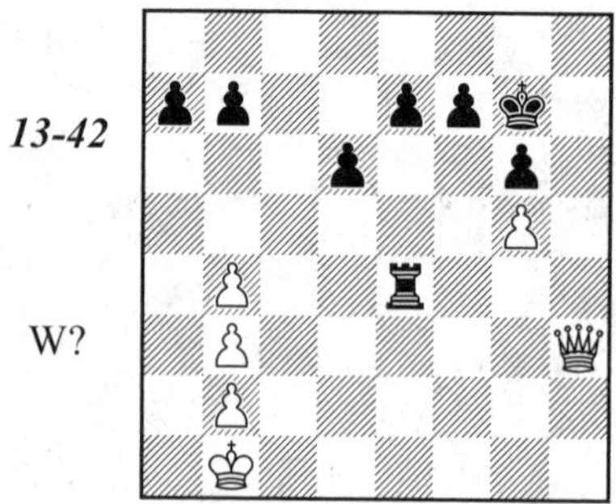
13-42
W?

White could win comfortably after 1 b5!, attacking the queenside pawns with his queen.

1 ♕f3?? ♖e1+! 2 ♔c2 b5! 3 ♕b7 ♖e5 =

The rook has protected all the important pawns, and an indestructible fortress is created.

4 ♕×a7 ♔f8 5 ♕b8+ ♔g7 6 ♕c7 ♔f8 7 ♕d8+ ♔g7 8 ♕e8 ♖×g5 9 ♕×e7 ♖f5 10 ♕×d6 ♔g8 11 ♔d3 Draw.

Exercises

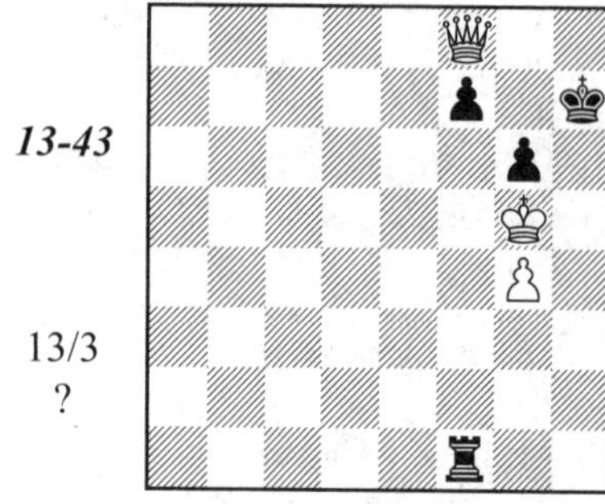
13-43
13/3
?

Evaluate this position 1) with White on move, 2) with Black on move.

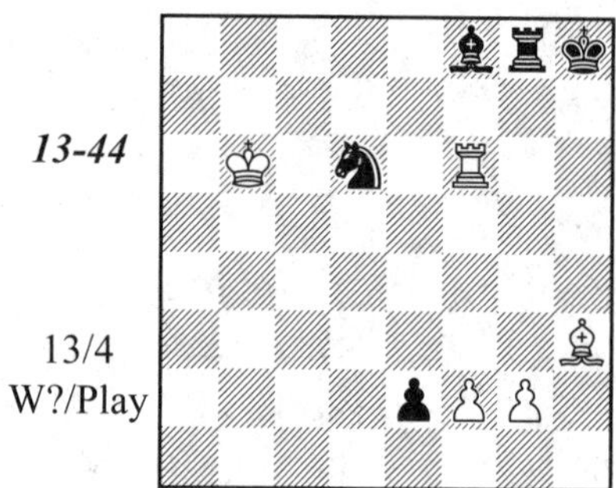
13-44
13/4
W?/Play

Chapter 14

OTHER MATERIAL RELATIONS

In this chapter we shall discuss various types of endgames with non-standard material. We will be brief because their consequent theory is not yet fully developed. Often one can find a variety (rich or poor) of endgame studies and examples from practical play that are not systematized nor coordinated well enough. And even when the theory of a certain type of ending is developed, there is no sense in going deeply into it because the analyses are mostly complicated and perplexing, while the probability of their practical use is utterly unlikely.

Two Extra Pieces

Checkmating with Bishop and Knight

I was unsure whether this subject should be included in the book, because the mating technique with a bishop and a knight against a lone king is explained in every tutorial for beginners. However, my experience as a chess trainer finally put and end to these doubts because I have seen how many chessplayers, including very strong ones, either missed learning this technique at an appropriate time or had already forgotten it.

Therefore they risk presenting their opponents with a half-point (and this has happened more than once), particularly under modern time controls when checkmating must often be performed in severe time trouble.

A king can be checkmated only in a corner of the bishop's color. The plan for the stronger side is obvious: first the enemy king is driven to an edge (this stage is simple but the king naturally aims to reach a safe corner). Thereafter the king is forced to a "proper" corner where mate is possible.

14-1

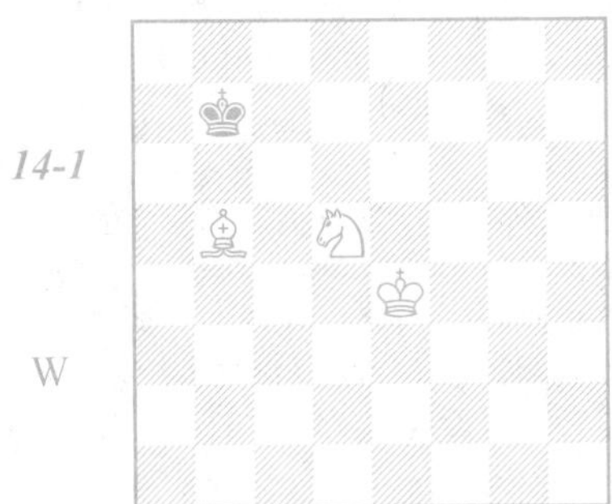

W

This is the type of position that the stronger side aims for. Notice that White's pieces have built ***a barrier*** that holds the black king in the corner. What remains is only to drive the king into the corner.

1 ♔e5 ♔c8 2 ♔e6 ♔d8 3 ♔d6⊙ ♔c8 4 ♔e7 ♔b7 5 ♔d7 ♔b8 6 ♗a6! ♔a7 7 ♗c8 ♔b8 8 ♔d8 ♔a7 9 ♔c7 ♔a8 10 ♘e7 ♔a7 11 ♘c6+ ♔a8 12 ♗b7#.

And this is how the king is driven to the "proper" corner.

14-2

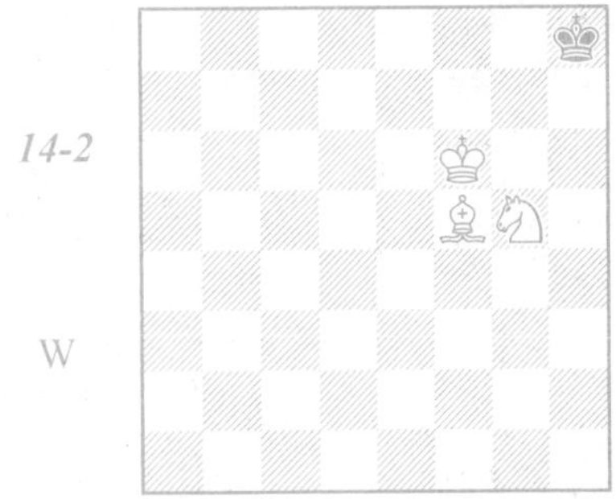

W

1 ♘f7+ ♔g8 2 ♗e4 ♔f8 3 ♗h7 ♔e8 4 ♘e5 ♔d8

4...♔f8 makes White's task easier: 5 ♘d7+ ♔e8 6 ♔e6 ♔d8 7 ♔d6 ♔e8 8 ♗g6+ ♔d8 9 ♘c5 ♔c8 10 ♗e8 ♔d8 11 ♗b5 ♔c8 12 ♗d7+ ♔b8 13 ♔c6 etc.

5 ♔e6 ♔c7

The king has broken loose from the edge of the board, but only for a while. White, with two accurate moves, creates a barrier, and locks the king in the corner.

6 ♘d7! ♔c6 7 ♗d3! ♔c7 8 ♗b5 ♔b7 (8...♔d8 9 ♘f6 ♔c7 10 ♘d5+) **9 ♔d6 ♔c8 10 ♘f6** (10 ♘c5!? ♔d8 11 ♘b7+ ♔c8 12 ♔c6) **10...♔d8 11 ♘d5**, and we have come to the position of the previous diagram.

Checkmating with Two Knights

Driving the king to an edge of the board is an easy task. Alas, you can only stalemate it thereafter, not checkmate, but three knights will win against a single knight.

However ***if the defender has a pawn, and this pawn is not too advanced, and it is blocked with one of the knights, an eventual win is quite possible***, although the winning process is very difficult; it may require dozens of precise moves.

As Russian study composer, Troitsky, proved in the beginning of the 20th century, a knight together with a king can drive the solitary king either to a corner or towards the "spare" knight (the one that is blocking the pawn). Thereafter, the spare knight joins the hunt, and a checkmate is delivered with its help.

From the next diagram play begins: **1 ♘f2! ♔g8 2 ♔e7 ♔h7** (2...♔h8? 3 ♔f7 ♔h7 4 ♘e4 f2 5 ♘f6+ ♔h8 6 ♘h4 f1♕ 7 ♘g6#) **3 ♔f7 ♔h8 4 ♔g6! ♔g8 5 ♘g7!**

Troitsky's standard maneuver that enables

A. Troitsky

14-3

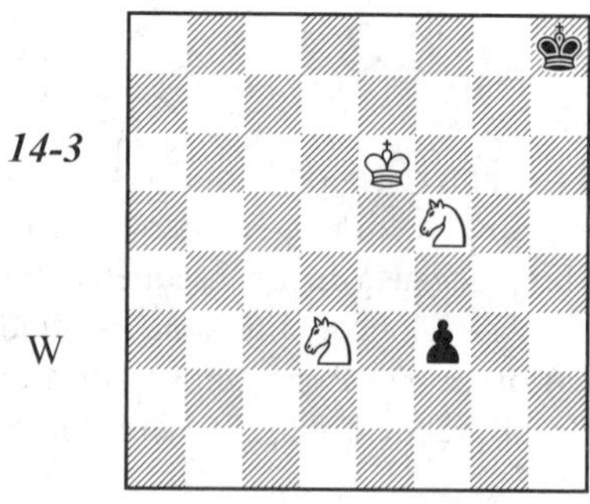

W

the knight's transfer to e6, where this piece will be more dangerous for the black king.

5...♔f8 6 ♔f6 ♔g8 7 ♘e6! ♔h7 8 ♔g5! ♔g8 (8...♔h8 9 ♔g6 ♔g8 10 ♘g4 f2 11 ♘f6+ ♔h8 12 ♘g5 f1♕ 13 ♘f7#) **9 ♔g6 ♔h8 11 ♔f7! ♔h7 12 ♘g4! f2 13 ♘f8+ ♔h8 14 ♘f6 f1♕ 15 ♘g6#**

The pawn was very far advanced; therefore, White managed to deliver checkmate because the black monarch was already locked in a corner close to f2-knight. If the king had more freedom it would run to a8, and White's knight cannot reach that corner in time.

Rook and Knight vs. Rook

A draw with a rook against a rook and a knight is not a hard procedure. Even when your king is pressed to the edge of the board you can usually slip away from mating threats (sometimes with the help of a stalemate).

The following endgame is taken from a practical play; it illustrates various defensive resources (alas, not exploited by White) and the dangers that can punish the careless defender.

J. Polgar – Kasparov
Dos Hermanas 1996

14-4

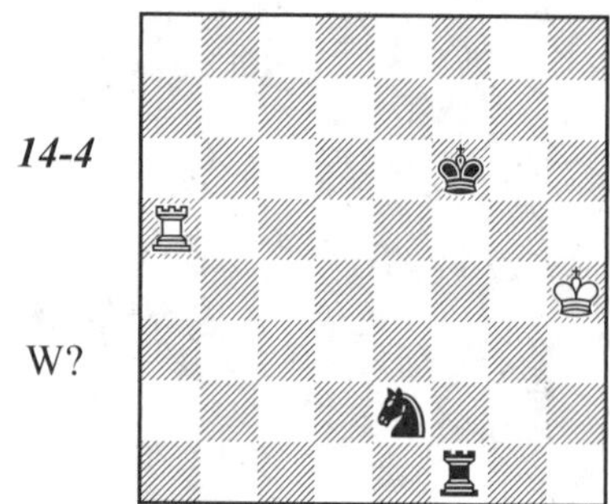

W?

1 ♖a8?

Why does Polgar not flee from the edge with her king? 1 ♔g4! ♖f4+ 2 ♔h3 △ 3 ♔g2= suggests itself.

1...♖g1! 2 ♖f8+ ♔e5 3 ♖e8+ ♔f4

The knight is taboo in view of checkmate.

4 ♖f8+ ♔e4 5 ♖e8+ ♔f3 6 ♔h5

She could try playing for a stalemate: 6 ♖f8+!? ♘f4 7 ♖g8!. For example, 7...♖h1+ 8 ♔g5 ♖g1+ 9 ♔h4! ♘g6+ 10 ♔h5 ♔f4! (the only method of holding the white king on the edge) 11 ♖g7 ♔f5 12 ♖f7+, pushing the black king somewhat away and thereby reducing the danger of a mating attack.

6...♘g3+ 7 ♔h6?!

A better possibility was 7 ♔g6! ♘e4+ 8 ♔h6 (unfortunately, other squares are not available in view of knight forks). From e4, the knight cannot protect the king from the inevitable 9 ♖f8+.

7...♘f5+ 8 ♔h7 ♔f4 9 ♖b8 ♖g7+ 10 ♔h8 ♖d7 11 ♖e8

The king in the corner is in real danger. A line suggested by Nunn can illustrate it: 11 ♖f8 ♔g5 12 ♖a8 ♔g6 13 ♖g8+ ♔h6 14 ♖g1 ♖d8+ 15 ♖g8 ♖d3 (15...♖d2 is less precise in view of 16 ♖g2!) 16 ♖g1 ♖f3 17 ♖g4 ♘e7 18 ♖h4+ ♔g6

19 ♖h6+ ♔f7 20 ♖h7+ ♔f8 21 ♖h1 ♘g8 22 ♔h7 ♔f7 23 ♔h8 ♘f6 −+. Notice how the final construction looks: with the knight on f6, White cannot avoid checkmate while a rook sacrifice for the sake of a stalemate cannot be arranged.

11...♔g5 12 ♖e6 ♘d4 13 ♖e1 ♔f6 14 ♖d1?! (14 ♖f1+ ♘f5 15 ♔g8) **14...♖d5! 15 ♖a1??**

The decisive error! 15 ♖f1+! ♘f5 16 ♖f2 (16 ♔g8) 16...♖d4 17 ♔g8!= was still good enough for a draw.

15...♘e6! −+ 16 ♖a6 ♔f7 17 ♖a7+ ♔g6 18 ♖a8 ♖d7

Here and later on, Kasparov fails to find a proper grouping for his pieces (similar to that from the notes to the 11th move): 18...♖d6! 19 ♔g8 ♘g5 20 ♔f8 ♖e6 21 ♔g8 ♘h7 22 ♖b8 ♖e7 followed by 23...♘f6+. However his position remains winning, as the black king cannot escape from the corner.

19 ♖b8 ♖c7 20 ♔g8 ♖c5 21 ♖a8 ♖b5 22 ♔h8 ♖b7 (22...♖b6) **23 ♖c8 ♘c7?!**

23...♖b6! −+ △ ...♘g5, ...♖e6, ...♘h7-f6.

24 ♖g8+ ♔h6 25 ♖g1?

This error makes Black's task easier. 25 ♖f8!? would have been more tenacious. White sets a trap (25...♘d5? 26 ♖f6+!) and waits as to whether Black finds the winning plan.

25...♖b8+ 26 ♖g8 ♘e8

White resigned on account of 27 ♖f8 ♔g6 28 ♖g8+ ♔f7 −+.

Tragicomedies

Yudovich (jr.) – Bebchuk
Moscow ch 1964

14-5

B

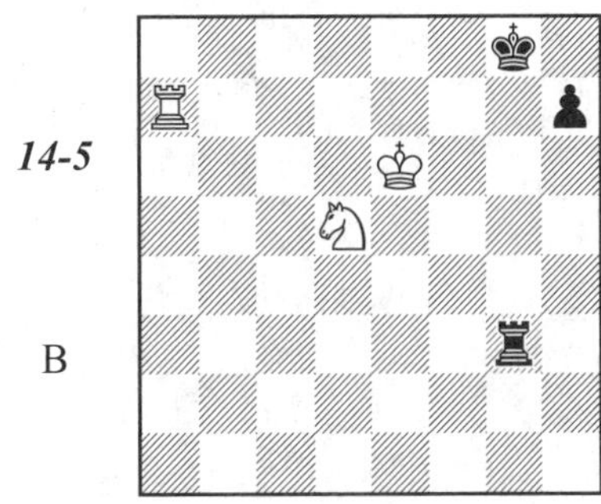

Black resigned without reason, for he could easily parry any mating threats: **1...♔f8! 2 ♖f7+** (2 ♘f6 ♖e3+) **2...♔e8 3 ♖×h7 ♖g6+ 4 ♘f6+ ♔d8=**.

Rook and Bishop vs. Rook

Without Pawns

An illustration of the dangers fatal to the defender, when his king is pressed to the edge of the board, is the following position that was known as early as the 18th century.

Philidor, 1749

14-6
$

W

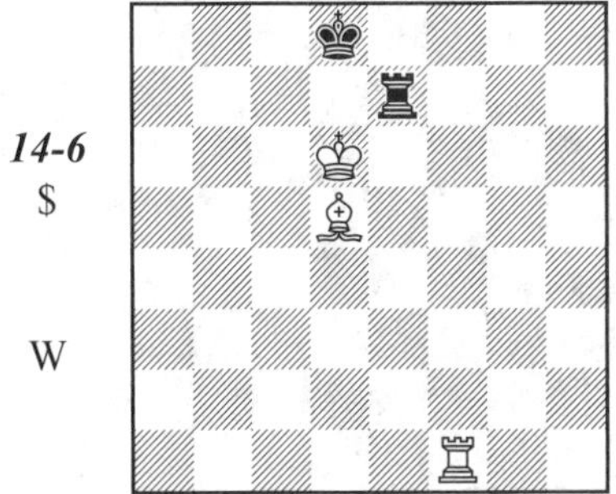

1 ♖f8+! ♖e8 2 ♖f7 (△ 3 ♖a7) **2...♖e2!**

2...♔c8 loses rapidly: 3 ♖a7 ♖d8+ 4 ♔c6 ♔b8 5 ♖b7+ ♔a8 6 ♖b1 ♔a7 7 ♔c7.

3 ♖h7!⊙

An important waiting move. The black rook must leave the 2nd rank where it stands best. The following line proves that the 3rd rank is the worst for the rook: 3...♖e3 4 ♖d7+ ♔e8 (4...♔c8 5 ♖a7) 5 ♖a7 ♔f8 6 ♖f7+ ♔e8 7 ♖f4 (8 ♗c6+ is threatened) 7...♔d8 (7...♖d3 8 ♖g4) 8 ♗e4! (the point – Black has no check along the d-file) 8...♔e8 9 ♗c6+.

3...♖e1 4 ♖b7

These alternate threats from both wings are typical for this sort of position. If 4...♔c8, 5 ♖b2 ♖d1 6 ♖h2 ♔b8 7 ♖a2 is decisive.

4...♖c1 5 ♗b3!

The key move! If the black rook was standing on the 2nd rank, a check from d2 could follow, while now Black must place his rook on the unfavorable 3rd rank.

5...♖c3

If 5...♔c8 then 6 ♖b4 ♔d8 7 ♖h4 ♖e1 (7...♔c8 8 ♗d5) 8 ♗a4 (there is no saving check along the d-file again) 8...♔c8 9 ♗c6 ♖d1+ 10 ♗d5 ♔b8 11 ♖a4+−.

6 ♗e6 ♖d3+ 7 ♗d5 ♖c3 8 ♖d7+ ♔c8 (8...♔e8 9 ♖g7) **9 ♖h7 ♔b8 10 ♖b7+ ♔c8 11 ♖b4 ♔d8 12 ♗c4! ♔c8 13 ♗e6+** and mate in two.

Not all positions with the king on the edge are, of course, lost. But the line between a draw and a loss is quite narrow; it can be easily crossed.

In a practical game one can usually avoid danger by means of orientation at the "Cochrane position" or by using "a defense along the 7th rank."

Both these techniques can be seen from the following instructive example.

Timman – Lutz
Wijk aan Zee 1995

14-7

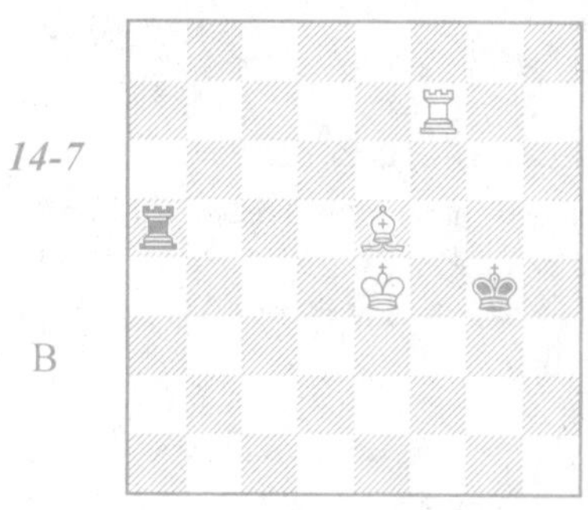

B

1...♖a4+ 2 ♗d4 ♔g5 3 ♖g7+ ♔h4 (rather than 3...♔h5? 4 ♔f5)

This is called the Cochrane position – the safest defensive method when the king is already pressed to the edge. The rook pins the bishop and does not allow the hostile king to come closer. If 4 ♖d7 (△ 5 ♔f4) then 4...♔g4. In case of the waiting attempt 4 ♖g8, Black follows the same policy with 4...♖b4.

4 ♔e5 ♔h3!

The king escapes from a bishop check in advance, and moves in the opposite direction from the white king. If White played 4 ♔e3, the reply would have been 4...♔h5!.

5 ♖g1 ♖b4 6 ♗e3 ♖g4!

This is the point! In order to bring his king closer, White had to move his bishop away, and Black takes advantage of this circumstance immediately. By offering the rook exchange, he releases his king from the edge.

7 ♖a1 ♔g2 8 ♗f4 ♖g8 9 ♖a2+ ♔f3 10 ♖a3+ ♔e2 11 ♔e4 ♖e8+ 12 ♗e5 ♖e7 13 ♖a2+ ♔e1!

14-8

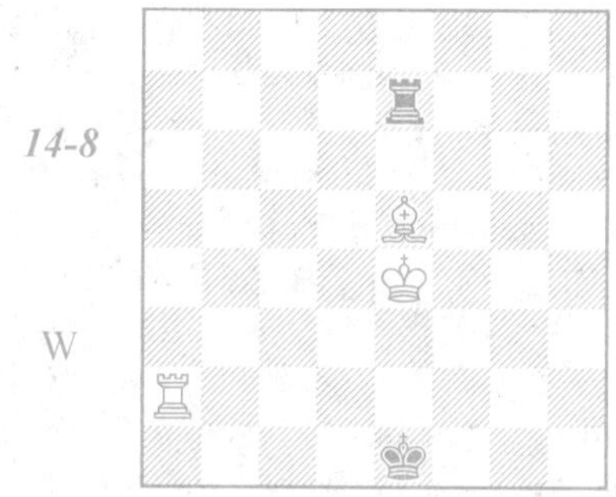

W

The Cochrane position has arisen again only rotated by 90 degrees.

14 ♔d4 ♔f1! 15 ♗f4 ♖e2! 16 ♖a8 ♖e7 17 ♔d3 ♔g2 18 ♖f8 ♖e6 19 ♖f7 ♖e8 20 ♗e3 ♖a8 21 ♗c5 ♖a4 22 ♔e3 ♖g4

Black changes his defensive setup. After 22...♔g3!? 23 ♖g7+ ♔h4 24 ♗d4 ♔h5!, he could reach the Cochrane position for the third time.

23 ♗d6 ♖g6 24 ♖f2+ ♔h3 25 ♗e5 ♔g4 26 ♔e4 ♔h5 27 ♗f6 ♔g4

14-9

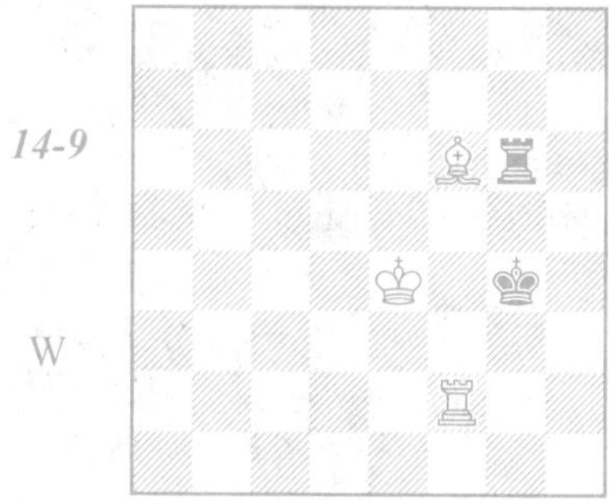

W

We are observing "the defense along the 7th rank" that prevents pressing the king to the edge of the board. The rook is placed two squares away from the king, so that after 28 ♖g2+ ♔h5 White has no time for 29 ♔f5. It may seem that the waiting move 28 ♖f1 puts Black in zugzwang, but here a stalemate bails him out 28...♔h5 29 ♔f5 ♖g5+! (this is why this technique works only on the 7th rank or the knight file). The rook cannot be captured, while after 30 ♔e6 ♖g2 31 ♖f4 ♔g6 32 ♖h4 ♖e2+ 33 ♗e5 ♖g2 34 ♖h8 ♖g4 the defense along the 7th rank is recreated.

28 ♖f4+ ♔g3 29 ♔e3 ♔h3 (29...♖g8) **30 ♖f5 ♖g3+** (30...♔g4) **31 ♔f2 ♖g2+ 32 ♔f1 ♖c2**

A retreat of the rook to g6, preparing 33...♔g4 or 33...♔g3 was simpler.

33 ♖g5 ♖c4 34 ♗e5 ♔h4 35 ♖g8 ♖e4 (35...♖g4!) **36 ♗g3+ ♔h5 37 ♔f2 ♖a4?!**

After 37...♖g4! Timman would have probably offered a draw because the black king leaves the edge.

38 ♔f3 ♔h6 39 ♗e5 ♖b4 40 ♗f4+ ♔h7 41 ♖g5 ♖a4 42 ♔g4 ♖b4 43 ♔f5

14-10

B

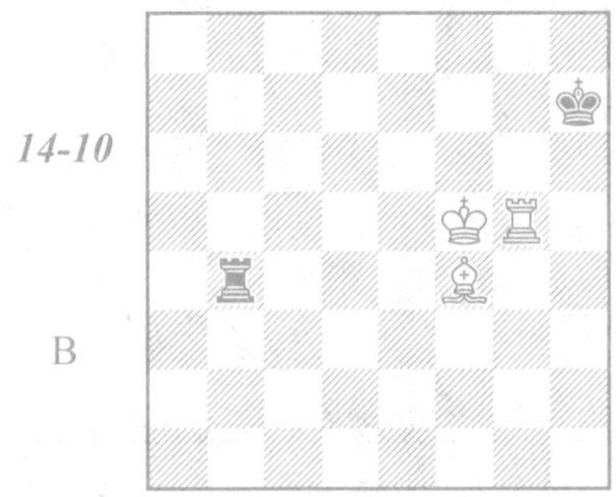

After a few nonchalant moves Black's position has become suspect. However, as Lutz pointed out, a draw could be still reached by means of 43...♖b1 44 ♗e5 ♖f1+ or 43...♖b6 44 ♗e5 ♖g6! 45 ♖h5+ ♖h6 46 ♖g5 ♖g6!=.

43...♖b5+?

A decisive threat that caused... an immediate draw agreement! The point is that the last pawn had been captured 53 moves ago, and "the rule of 50 moves" was duly applied.

After 44 ♗e5 ♖b6 (44...♖a5 45 ♖h5+ ♔g8 46 ♔g6; 44...♖b7 45 ♖h5+ ♔g8 46 ♖h8+ ♔f7 47 ♖h7+; 44...♔h6 45 ♖g8 ♖b7 46 ♖g1) 45 ♖g7+ ♔h6 46 ♖g8 ♔h5 the Philidor position, rotated by 90 degrees, could have arisen. The winning procedure is already known: 47 ♖g2 ♖b4 48 ♖g1! (a zugzwang, the rook is forced away from the b-file) etc.

With Pawns

Let us analyze a case with an extra bishop that has occurred a number of times in tournament practice.

Suba – D. Gurevich
Eksjo 1982

14-11
$

W

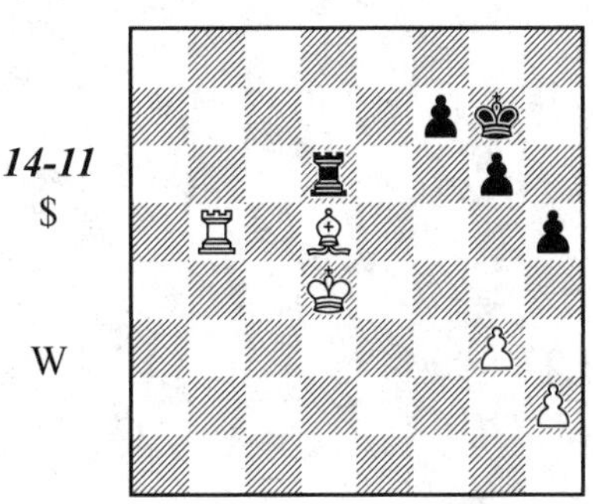

White must be accurate in view of the reduced material on the board. By the way, we should emphasize that he may exchange rooks, although his bishop and the h8-square are of different colors.

It is obvious that he should attack the f7-pawn, but from which direction – along the file or along the rank?

The game continued 1 ♖b3 ♖a6 2 ♖f3 ♖a7 3 ♖f2 ♖d7 4 ♔c5 ♖a7 5 ♔c6 f5 (against 5...♖e7, White had probably planned 6 ♔d6 ♖a7 7 ♖a2, forcing the exchange of rooks) 6 ♔d6 ♔f6 7 ♖e2. The forced advance of the f-pawn had weakened Black's position, and White gradually exploited his advantage.

As Suba stated, an occupation of the 7th rank could be an even more convincing winning method.

1 ♖b7 ♖f6 2 h3 ♖f1 3 ♔e4 ♖f6 4 g4 hg 5 hg ♖f1

If 5...g5!?, Ch. Lutz suggests 6 ♔e5 ♖f4 7 ♗e6 ♖f6 8 ♗f5 ♖a6 9 ♖b5! ♖c6 (9...♖a4 10 ♗e4 ♖c4 11 ♔f5 ♖d4 12 ♗b1; 9...♔h6 10 ♖c5 △ 11 ♗e4; 9...♖f6 10 ♖c5 ♖b6 11 ♗e4 △ 12 ♖c6) 10 ♗e4 ♖f6 11 ♔d4 ♔h6 12 ♖f5 ♖d6+ 13 ♗d5 ♔g6 14 ♔c5 ♖d7 15 ♔c6 ♖e7 16 ♗b3 ♖a7 17 ♗c4 ♖e7 18 ♗d5 ♖a7 19 ♔d6⊙ ♖a6+ 20 ♔d7 ♖a7+ 21 ♔d8⊙ f6 (White has finally forced this weakening) 22 ♗e4+– etc.

6 ♗c4 ♖f6 7 g5 ♖f5 8 ♖×f7+! ♖×f7 9 ♗×f7 ♔×f7 10 ♔d5+–.

Tragicomedies

Gufeld – Rahman
Calcutta 1994

14-12

W

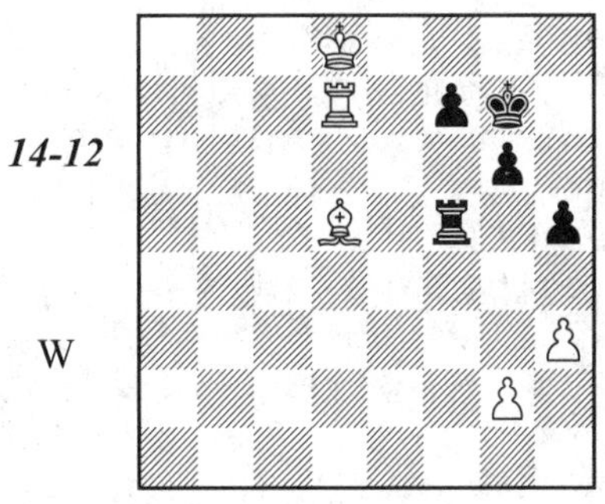

1 g4?

Curiously enough, precisely this position (with reversed colors) happened in Gufeld's earlier game versus Honfi (Kislovodsk 1968). In that game Gufeld found the correct idea, he realized that the advance g2-g4 is premature and chose another plan – a rook transfer to the f-file.

That game continued 1 ♔e7 ♖e5+ 2 ♔d6 ♖f5 3 ♖a7 ♖f6+ 4 ♔c5 ♖f2 5 ♖a2 (5 ♖a3 ♔h6 6 ♖f3? ♖×g2) 5...♖f1 6 ♖a3 ♖e1 (6...♔h6 7 ♖f3 ♖×f3 8 ♗×f3 ♔g5 9 ♗d5 f5 10 ♗f7 ♔f4 11 ♗×g6 ♔g3 12 ♗×f5 ♔×g2 13 ♔d5 ♔g3 14 ♔e5 ♔h4 15 ♔f6+–) 7 ♔d6 ♖e2 8 ♖f3 and Black, like in the Suba - Gurevich endgame, had to push his f-pawn; gradually, this fact caused his loss. After 25 years, Gufeld forgot his conclusions drawn during that earlier game; he pushed his g-pawn prematurely and missed a win.

The plan with g2-g4 is nevertheless good, only White should bring his king back beforehand. For example: 3 ♖c7 (instead of 3 ♖a7) 3...♖f6+ 4 ♔e5 ♖f5+ 5 ♔e4 ♖f2 6 ♔e3 ♖f5 7 ♗c4! (from here the bishop denies the important f1-square to the black rook) 7...♔f8 (7...♖e5+ 8 ♔d4 ♖f5 9 ♔e4 ♖f2 10 g4) 8 g4 hg 9 hg ♖f6 (9...♖e5+ does not help, either: 10 ♔d4 ♖e7 11 ♖×e7 ♔×e7 12 ♔e5 f6+ 13 ♔d5 ♔f7 14 ♔d6+ and 15 ♔e6) 10 ♔e4 (the threat is 11 g5 and 12 ♖×f7+) 10...g5 11 ♔e5 ♖f4 12 ♗d3! ♖×g4 13 ♔f6+– (the final part of this line is suggested by Yanvarev).

In Gufeld's opinion, the move 1 g3?! wins even more rapidly due to a zugzwang: if 1...♖f2 then 2 ♔e8 ♖e2+ 3 ♖e7+–. Other alternatives do not help 1...♔f8 2 g4 hg 3 hg ♖f4 4 g5 ♖f5 5 ♖×f7+ ♖×f7 6 ♗×f7, or 1...♔g8 2 g4 hg 3 hg ♖f4 4 ♖×f7! ♖×f7 5 ♔e8+–. However he did not take into consideration the strongest reply, 1...♖g5!, which makes White's task considerably more difficult: 2 ♖×f7+ ♔h6 3 ♗e6 ♖×g3 4 ♔e7 (4 h4 ♖d3+ 5 ♔e7 ♖d4=) 4...♔g5.

1...hg 2 hg ♖f4 3 g5

It seems that a general exchange on f7 is inevitable. In reality, Black has two possibilities to avoid it:

3...♖g4!=

White's last pawn must die. Another good method was 3...♖f5 4 ♖×f7+ ♔h8! 5 ♖×f5 gf 6 ♔e7 ♔g7 7 ♗f7 f4 8 ♗h5 f3=.

In the case of the next diagram, the characteristic difference (in comparison with those we have seen previously) is the position of the black h-pawn – here it is far less favorable. Firstly, Black does not have the familiar plan with g6-g5-g4 followed with a transition to a pawn endgame. Secondly, in case of an exchange of rooks White will be able to exchange a pair of pawns without problems, and Black's remaining h-pawn will be quite useless against the king in the safe corner h1.

Mark Tseitlin – Finkel
Beersheba 1996

14-13

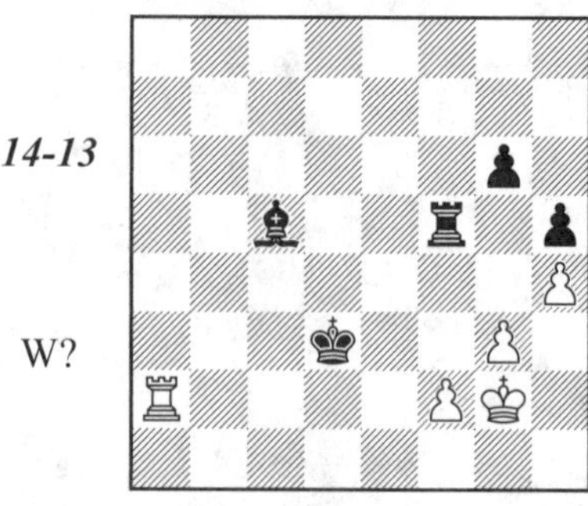

W?

White could achieve a draw by playing 1 ♔g1!, for example 1...♗d4 2 ♔g2 ♖f6 3 ♔g1 ♖b6 4 ♔g2 ♖b2 5 ♖×b2 ♗×b2 6 g4 hg 7 ♔g3 ♗c1 8 ♔×g4 ♗h6 9 f4 and 10 h5= (Ch. Lutz).

1 ♔f1?? ♗×f2!–+

All of a sudden, it becomes obvious that 2 ♖×f2 is bad in view of 2...♔e3 3 ♖×f5 gf 4 ♔g2 ♔e2⊙.

2 ♔g2 ♗b6 3 ♖b2 ♗d4 4 ♖a2 ♔e4 5 ♖e2+ ♗e3 6 ♖a2 ♖d5 7 ♖a4+ ♔f5 8 ♔f3 ♗d4 9 ♖a3 ♗e5 White resigned.

An Extra Bishop or Knight with Queens or Minor Pieces

Let us first discuss positions without pawns.

A bishop and a knight can win only in exceptional cases against a knight, and all the more so against a bishop.

But two bishops can practically always cope with a knight.

14-14

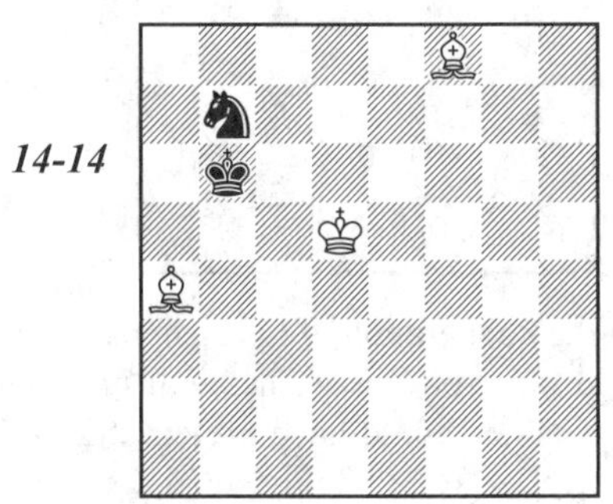

Kling and Horwitz (1851) thought that this position is drawn. As a matter of fact, the knight is quite favorably placed on b7 for defensive purposes. Only in 1983 did computer analysis show that this defensive set up could be destroyed without permitting its restoration in another corner. If both sides play this endgame perfectly, the winning process lasts more than 50 moves; it is too complicated to reproduce it here.

A queen and a minor piece cannot, generally speaking, win against a queen. But exceptions are not so rare with this material: an attack against the king can lead to mate or to a win of the queen.

From the wide variety of positions with pawns, I would like to distinguish those with bishops of opposite colors. It turns out that the drawish tendencies typical in 'pure' cases of such bishops (i.e., with balanced material), are valid here too, helping the weaker side to survive even when a piece down. Two examples of this sort follow.

A. Sokolov – Yusupov
Riga cmf (7) 1986*

14-15
$
W

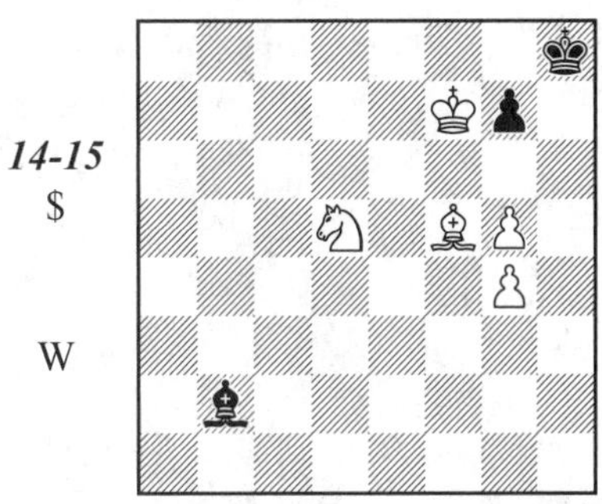

White has no win despite his extra piece and pawn. The black king cannot be driven away from the corner (♘g6+ will be met with ...♔h7; and ♘f7+ with ...♔g8). The attempt to bring the bishop to g8 for creating a mating net is easily parried.

1 ♘f6 ♗c1! (1...♗d4? 2 ♗h7) **2 ♘h5** (2 ♗h7 gf 3 g6 ♗h6=) **2...♗b2 3 ♘f4** (threatening 4 ♘g6+ ♔h7 5 ♘f8+ ♔h8 6 ♗h7) **3...♗a3!** etc.

Yachmennik – Belov
Smolensk 1989

14-16
$
B

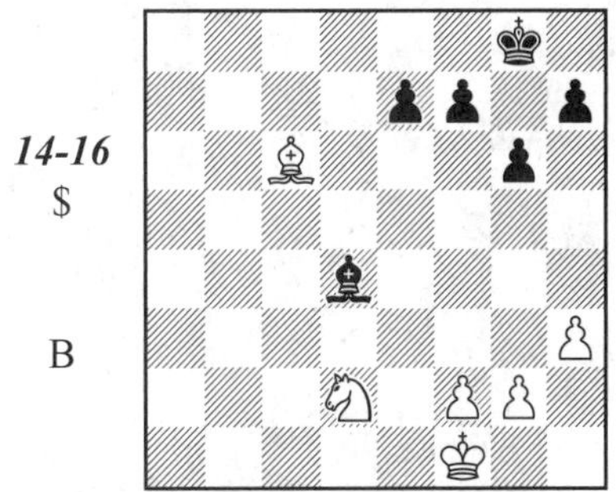

1...h5 2 ♔e2 ♔g7 3 f3 e6

To achieve success, White must attack the f7-pawn with two pieces, but this is very difficult to do against a precise defense. All his attempts were in vain; the game ended in a draw.

Rook vs. Two Minor Pieces

In the middlegame two minor pieces are usually much stronger than a rook. In an endgame this advantage is much less substantial, sometimes a rook can even gain the upper hand. The reason is that pawn chains in a middlegame restrict the rook's mobility. In an endgame, on the contrary, the rook enjoys full mobility.

A rook is especially dangerous when it attacks pawns (usually placed along the 7th rank) that cannot be protected by the king and cannot be defended comfortably with the pieces; another case of a dangerous rook is when it supports a distant passed pawn.

Beliavsky – Dolmatov
USSR ch, Minsk 1979

14-17

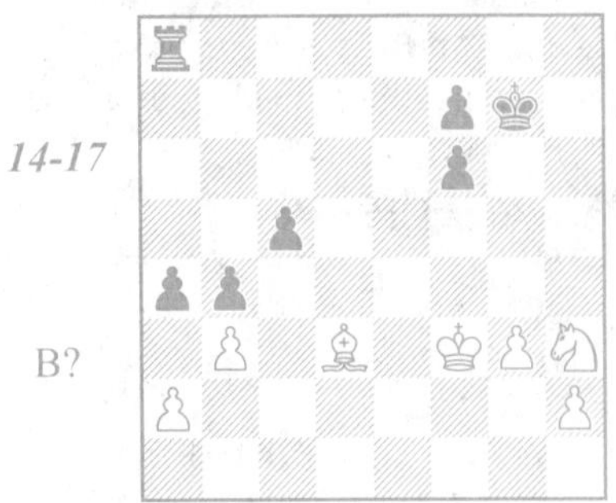

B?

After the natural-looking 1...♖h8 2 ♘f2! ab (2...♖×h2 3 ba) 3 ab ♖×h2 4 ♘e4 the position remained static; it is usually favorable for the side with two pieces. White would then have had excellent winning chances.

Dolmatov found an amazing resource.

1...c4!! 2 ♗×c4 (if 2 bc then 2...♖b8!?) **2...♖c8!**

The threat 3...♖×c4! 4 bc b3 5 ab a3 forces White to drive his bishop away from c4.

3 ♗d3 a3!

White must now beware both 4...♖c1 △ 5...♖a1 and 4...♖c3 △ 5...♖×b3. Black has seized the initiative.

The rook, in the next diagram, fighting inside the hostile camp, is again stronger than two minor pieces.

Miles – Kindermann
Bath 1983

14-18

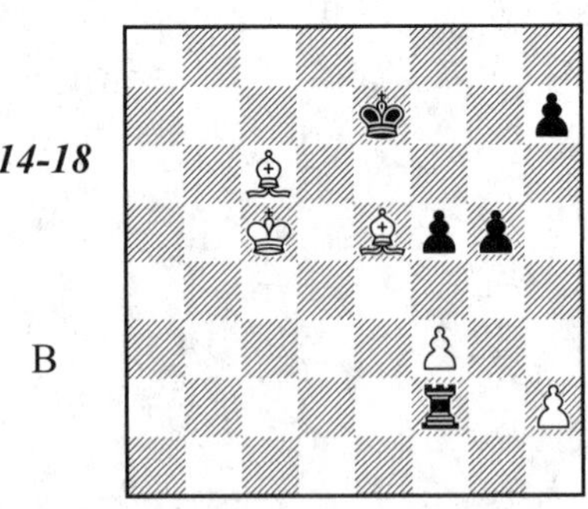

B

1...♔e6

Black rejected the immediate 1...f4!?, probably in view of 2 ♔d4!? ♖×h2 3 ♔e4 △ 4 ♔f5.

2 ♗c3?!

Miles gives the h2-pawn away, pinning his hopes on the cooperation of his bishops and his centralized king, but his wishes will not come true. Perhaps he should have preferred 2 ♗c7. Then neither 2...♖c2+?! 3 ♔b6 h6 4 ♗e8!? f4 5 h3 ♖h2 6 ♗h5 nor 3...f4 4 ♗d8! h6 5 h3 ♖h2 6 ♔c7 is precise. The immediate 2...f4! is stronger. Now 3 h4? loses to 3...♖c2+ 4 ♔b5 gh 5 ♗×f4 h3, while 3 h3 is met by 3...♖h2. If 3 ♗d8! then 3...h6!, and the natural 4 h4 is refuted by means of 4...♖d2! 5 ♗c7 gh and Black gains a bishop for the h-pawn. What remains is 4 h3 ♖h2 5 ♗b7 ♔d7 6 ♗f6 ♖×h3 7 ♔d4∓ (Dvoretsky).

2...♖×h2 3 ♗d5+ ♔e7 4 ♔d4 ♔f6 5 ♔e3+ ♔g6 6 ♗e1 f4+ 7 ♔d4 h5 8 ♔e5 h4 9 ♗e4+ ♔f7?!

As Kindermann indicated, an easy win could been achieved with 9...♔h6 10 ♔f6 (10 ♔f5 ♖g2 11 ♗b4 h3 12 ♔f6 ♔h5 13 ♗g6+ ♔h4 14 ♗e1+ ♖g3) 10...h3 11 ♗b4 ♖e2 12 ♗g6 ♖e6+! 13 ♔×e6 ♔×g6. Now White finds a clever method for a tough resistance.

14-19

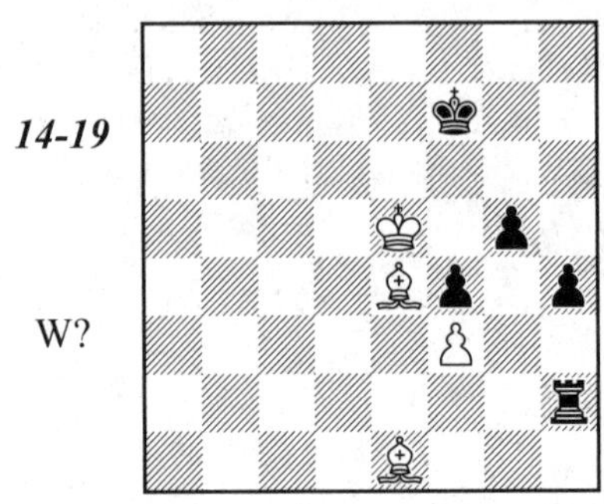

W?

10 ♗×h4! gh

10...♖×h4? 11 ♔f5 ♖h6 12 ♔×g5 ♖f6 13 ♗f5=.

11 ♔×f4 ♖g2 12 ♗f5 ♔f6 13 ♗h3 ♖g1 14 ♗g4

There were opinions that this position is drawish, however, Dolmatov suggested an uncomplicated plan that could still bring Black victory. With 14...♖g3! he chained the white king to the f4-square (if the king retreats then h4-h3 wins at once). Thereafter the black king marches into the hostile camp: ...♔e7-d6-d5-d4 etc.

14...♖b1?! 15 ♗h3 ♖b4+?

It was not too late for a rook retreat to g1.

16 ♔e3 ♔e5 17 ♗g4 ♖b3+ 18 ♔f2 ♔f4 19 ♔g2 ♖b2+ 20 ♔h3 ♔g5 (20...♖f2 21 ♗h5) **21 ♗c8**, and the game soon ended in a draw.

Alexandria – Chiburdanidze
Borzhomi/Tbilisi wm (4), 1981

14-20

B

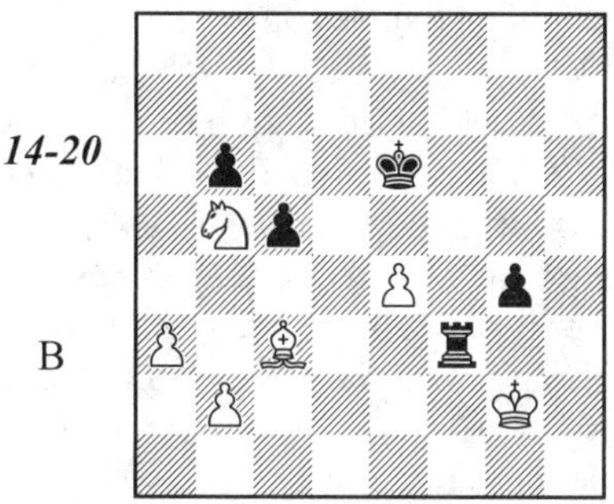

The game was adjourned in this position. The minor pieces are stronger than the rook here, but, as the analysis has showed, White's advantage is not sufficient for a win against a precise defense.

1...♔d7!

An excellent maneuver that emphasizes the unlucky position of the white knight. Black will use the time that must be wasted on bringing it into play to arrange counterplay on the queenside by means of ...b6-b5. Black's main goal is to exchange as many pawns as possible.

An immediate attack against the e-pawn was much weaker. After 1...♖f4? 2 e5 ♔d7 3 ♔g3 ♖a4 4 ♘d6 ♔e6 5 ♔h4 Black loses because of zugzwang: 5...♔d5 6 ♘c8! ♔c6 7 ♘e7+ ♔d7 8 ♘d5 ♔c6 9 ♘f6 b5 10 ♔g3! b4 11 e6!, or 5...♖f4 6 ♘e8! ♔f5 7 ♘g7+ ♔g6 8 e6 ♖e4 9 a4! c4 10 ♗d4! ♔h7 11 ♗f6 ♔g6 12 e7.

If Black plays 1...♖e3? then 2 e5? ♔d5 3 ♘c7+ ♔c6 4 ♘e8 b5 transposes to the actual course of the game, but White has a better choice: 2 ♘c7+! ♔d6 (2...♔d7? 3 ♘d5 ♖×e4 4 ♘f6+) 3 ♘e8+ (3 ♘d5? ♖×e4 4 ♘×b6 ♔c6) 3...♔e7 (3...♔e6 4 ♘g7+ ♔d7 5 e5!+–) 4 ♘f6 ♔e6 5 ♘d5! (5 e5 ♔f5) 5...♖×e4 6 ♘×b6 ♔d6 7 a4 ♔c6 8 a5 with excellent winning chances.

2 e5 ♔c6 3 ♘d6 b5! 4 ♔g1!

A clever trap. The natural looking 4...♖f4? (△ 5...b4) will be refuted by 5 e6!! ♔×d6 6 ♗e5+!.

4...♖g3+ 5 ♔f2 ♖d3! 6 ♔g2 (6 ♘e4 b4! 7 ab cb 8 ♗×b4 ♖d4) **6...♖f3** (rather than 6...♖e3? 7 ♘f5) **7 ♘e8 ♖e3 8 ♘f6**

14-21

B?

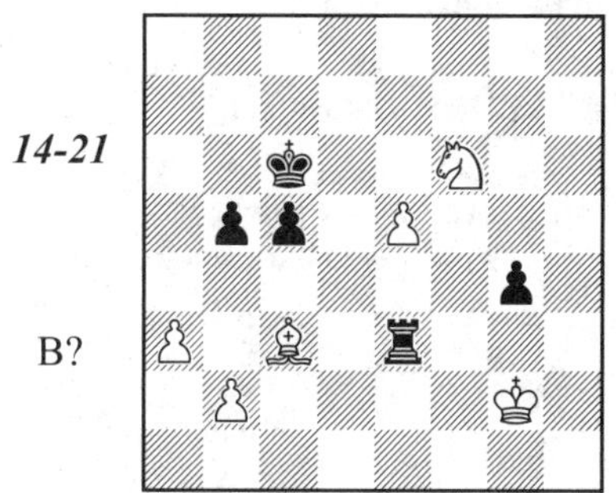

8...b4! 9 ab cb 10 ♗d4!?

After 10 ♗×b4 ♖×e5 11 ♗c3 ♖f5!? (11...♖c5!?) 12 ♘×g4 ♔b5 White had no time to preserve his last remaining pawn in safety.

10...♖e1!

A final point. 10...♖d3? would have been erroneous in view of 11 e6! ♔d6 12 ♘e4+! ♔×e6 (12...♔e7 13 ♗f6+) 13 ♘c5+ ♔d5 14 ♘×d3 ♔×d4, and now White employs the familiar technique of protecting the pawn with the knight: 15 ♘c1! ♔e3 16 ♘b3! ♔d3 17 ♘a5 b3 18 ♔g3 ♔c2 19 ♘c4 ♔d3 20 ♘a3+–.

11 ♔g3 ♖d1 12 ♗e3 ♖b1 13 ♗d4 ♖d1 14 ♗e3 Draw.

If both sides have three pawns placed on the same wing, the defender may hope for a draw (only if, of course, his pawn structure is devoid of grave flaws).

Capablanca – Lasker
St. Petersburg 1914

14-22

B

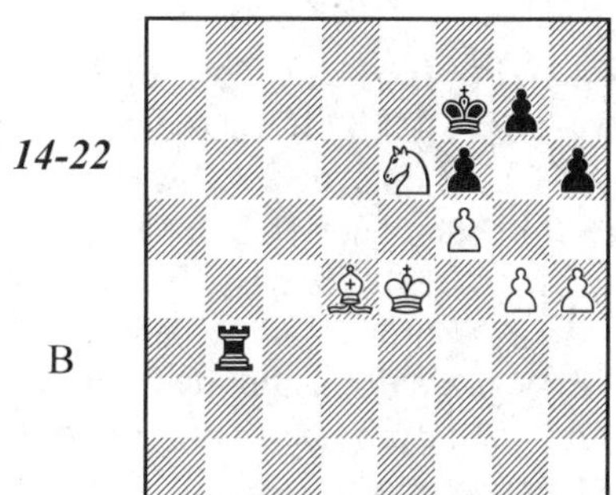

1...♖b4 2 ♔d5 ♖b1 3 g5 (White has no better plan to follow) **3...hg 4 hg fg 5 ♘×g5+ ♔g8 6 ♘e6 ♖d1! 7 ♔e4** (7 ♘×g7 ♖×d4+) **7...♔f7 8 ♘g5+**

8 ♗×g7 could be met with 8...♖e1+ 9 ♔d5 ♖f1=.

8...♔g8 9 ♔e5 ♖e1+

Capablanca made 20 more moves trying to win, but finally agreed to a draw.

Tragicomedies

Timman – Karpov
Bugojno 1980

14-23

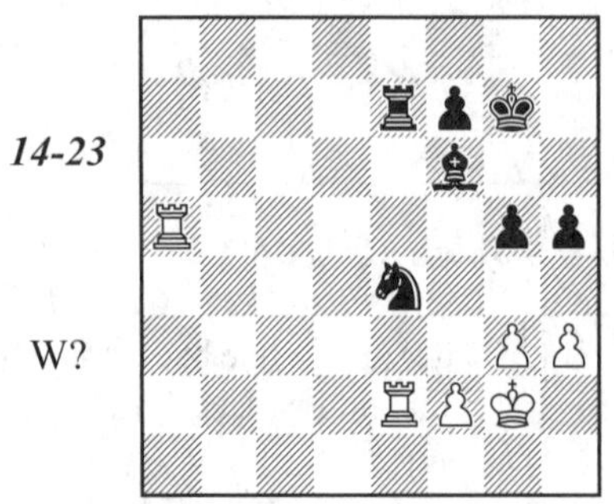

W?

One pair of rooks will certainly be exchanged, but how can White do it favorably?

1 f3?

A grave positional error based on a tactical oversight. Timman planned to exchange pawns after 1...♘d6 2 ♖×e7 ♗×e7 3 h4! gh 4 ♖e5! (but not 4 ♖×h5? immediately in view of 4...f5!, and if 5 gh then 5...♗f6 △ 6...♔g6+–) 4...♔f6 (4...♗d8 5 ♖d5!) 5 ♖×h5=, but underestimated Black's strong reply.

1...♘c5! 2 ♖×e7 ♗×e7 3 ♖a7

After 3 f4 gf 4 gf f5 (△ ...♔f6, ...♗d6, ...♘e6) the f4-pawn is lost.

3...♗d6

The erroneous advance of the f-pawn has weakened the dark squares, and White's position is hopeless now.

4 ♖a8 h4 5 gh gh 6 ♔f2 ♘e6 7 ♖a1 ♗g3+ 8 ♔e3 ♘f4 9 ♖h1 ♔f6 10 ♔e4 ♔e6 11 ♔d4 ♔f5 12 ♔c3 ♘e6 13 ♔d3 ♔f4 14 ♔e2 ♘g5 (of course, not 14...♘d4+ 15 ♔d3 ♘×f3?? 16 ♖f1 △ ♔e2) White resigned.

Let us try to improve White's defense. The attempt to force pawn exchanges by means of 1 h4? gh 2 ♖×h5 should be rejected at once in view of the counterstroke 2...♘×g3! 3 ♖×e7 ♘×h5–+.

The choice should be made between 1 ♖a4 and 1 ♔f3.

Timman recommends 1 ♖a4!?, and if 1...♘d6 then 2 ♖×e7 ♗×e7 3 f4! (3...g4 is met by 4 hg hg 5 f5). 1...♘c5! is better: 2 ♖×e7 ♗×e7 (2...♘×a4 3 ♖c7 ♘c3 4 ♔f3) 3 ♖c4 (3 ♖a7 ♗d6) 3...♔g6. This position is certainly better for White than that from the actual game, but still not fully safe. Timman demonstrates that the following disposition of Black's forces can be successful against White's passive defense: the pawn goes to f6, bishop to e5, knight to f5, and thereafter ...h5-h4 follows. It is not clear whether White can prevent this setup by active measures.

Timman condemns 1 ♔f3!? because of 1...g4+! 2 hg ♘g5+. But in fact, the outcome here would be anything but clear.

First, let's look at 3 ♖×g5+ ♗×g5 4 gh ♔h6?! 5 ♖a2! ♔×h5. Can Black convert his extra bishop to a win? We looked at a similar situation with Black's pawn on the g-file – there, Black retained real winning chances – among other things, there is the idea of pushing the pawn to g4, followed by the exchange of all the pieces at f2. With an f-pawn instead, Black has fewer resources, so the position looks drawn.

However, as pointed out by Karsten Müller, the immediate exchange of rooks would lead to victory: 4...♖×e2! 5 ♔×e2, and now not 5...♔h6? 6 f4 △ 7 g4=, but 5...♗c1! followed by 6...♔h6. The attempt to avoid the exchange of rooks by 4 ♖a2 (instead of 4 gh) would allow Black, by means of 4...h4!, to execute the exchange of pawns in a more favorable way. White's setup grows flimsier, and probably won't last.

But now, let us offer an improvement for the defense: 2 ♔g2! gh+ 3 ♔h2!. Here's an approximate line: 3...h4 4 gh (4 g4? ♘g5! 5 ♖×e7 ♗×e7 6 f4 ♘e6–+) 4...♗×h4 5 ♖aa2! (5 ♖f5? is bad: 5...♗f6 6 f3 ♘g5 7 ♖×e7 ♗×e7 8 f4 ♘e6 9 ♔×h3 ♔g6 10 ♔g4 ♗d6–+) 5...♗×f2 (otherwise ♔×h3) 6 ♖×f2 ♘×f2 7 ♖×f2, with a drawn rook-plus f- and h-pawns endgame.

Exercises

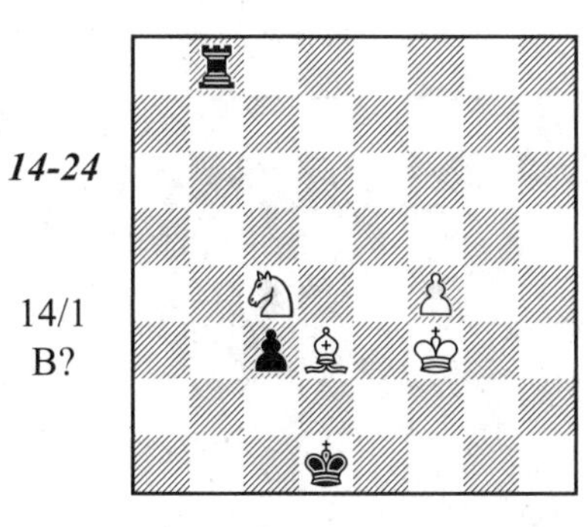

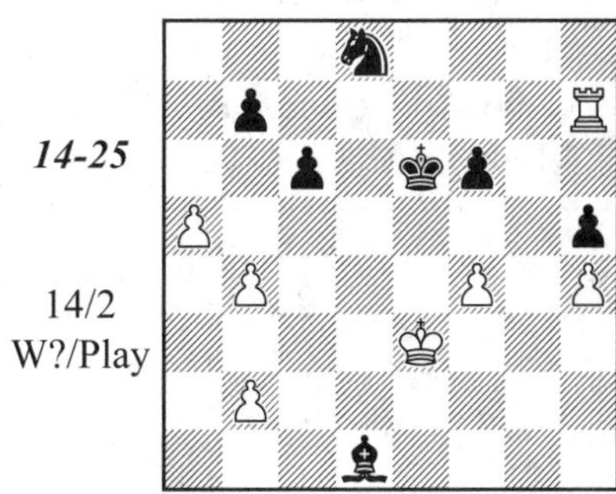

Queen vs. Various Pieces

A rook and a bishop or a rook and a knight (without pawns) draw easily against a queen if, of course, they are not so disunited that the opponent can rapidly gain one of pieces.

Two knights can resist the queen successfully. They are best placed on squares adjacent to the king.

Two bishops, curiously enough, are almost never able to draw against a queen, although the winning process is often complicated and requires many dozens of moves.

The only drawing position was discovered as early as the 18th century.

G. Lolli, 1763

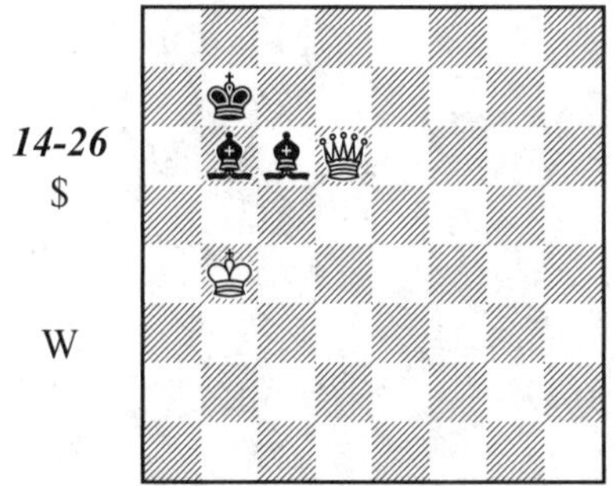

1 ♕e7+ ♔c8 2 ♕e6+

In case of 2 ♕d6 ♔b7 3 ♔c4 Black should play 3...♗a7! 4 ♕e7+ ♔b8 (with the idea 5...♗b6=) or even 4...♔b6=, as 3...♗c7? loses to 4 ♕e7 ♔b6 5 ♕b4+ ♔a6 6 ♔c5.

2...♔b7 3 ♕d6 ♗a7

3...♗c7 4 ♕e7 ♔b6 is also playable, White has no 5 ♕b4+.

4 ♕e7+ ♔b6! (rather than 4...♔b8? 5 ♔a5+–) **5 ♕d8+ ♔b7 6 ♔a5 ♗c5!**

White is in zugzwang, every possible move allows the black bishop to return to b6.

If White brings his king to e7, the bishop occupies the c7-square, with the same position. This defensive method saves Black only when his king is on b7 (or symmetrically on g7, b2, and g2).

A bishop and a knight usually lose, but some very rare exceptions exist; one of them should be remembered.

In the next diagram, Black's pieces protect his king from all of White's attempts to approach; this set up cannot be destroyed.

M. Karstedt, 1903

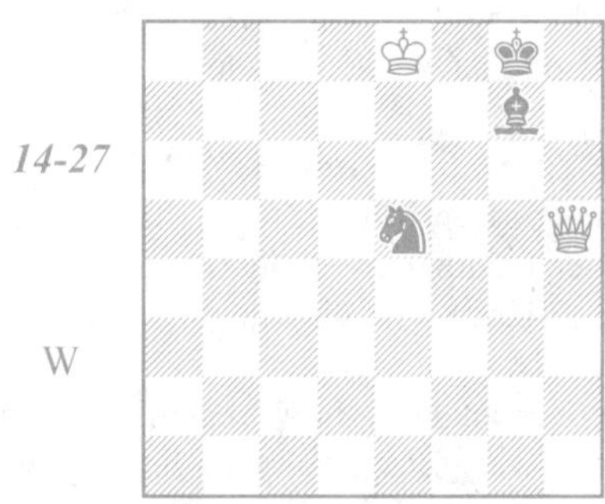

1 ♔e7 ♗h8 2 ♔e6 ♗g7 3 ♔f5 ♗h8 4 ♔g5 ♗g7 5 ♕e8+ ♔h7 6 ♔h5 ♗h8 7 ♕e7+ ♗g7=.

In practical situations (with pawns on the board) one can often save a difficult position by means of a queen sacrifice or by letting an enemy pawn queen for the sake of building a fortress.

Let us come back to the position where we have made a break when analyzing the Beliavsky

– Dolmatov endgame (in the section "Rook versus two minor pieces").

Beliavsky – Dolmatov
USSR ch, Minsk 1979

14-28

W?

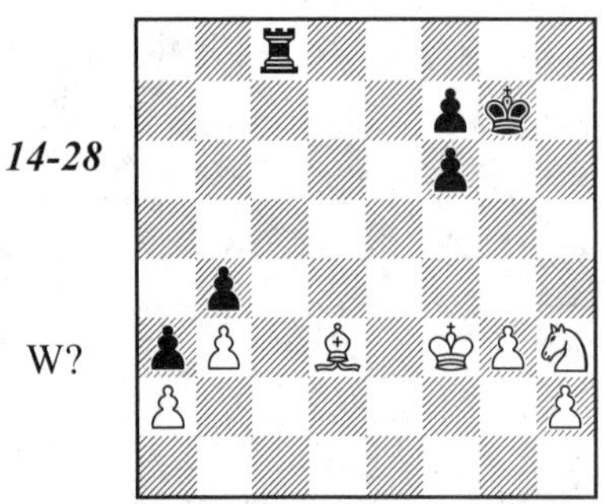

White stands worse and has to fight for a draw. The most reliable method is:

1 ♘f2! ♖c1

1...♖c3 is weaker because after 2 ♔e3 the sacrifice 2...♖×b3? fails to 3 ♘d1! ♖b2 4 ♘×b2 b3 5 ♗b1!+–. If 2...♖c1 then 3 ♔d2 ♖a1 4 ♗c2 ♖×a2 5 ♘d3=.

2 h4!! (the pawn should leave the 2nd rank) **2...♖a1**

2...f5 is useless: 3 ♗×f5 ♖a1 (3...♖c3+ 4 ♔f4 ♖×b3 5 ♘d1!) 4 ♘d3 ♖×a2 5 ♘×b4 ♖b2 6 ♗c2=.

3 ♗c4 ♖×a2 4 ♘d3 ♖f2+

Or 4...♖d2 5 ♘×b4 a2 6 ♘×a2 with a draw. The idea behind h2-h4 is clear now – the endgame would have been hopeless without the h-pawn.

5 ♔×f2 a2 6 ♘×b4 a1♕ 7 ♘d3 with the following setup in mind: ♘f4, ♗d5, ♔g2, and Black can neither create mating threats nor attack the g3-pawn with his king and his queen simultaneously.

Moreover, analysis shows that this position is drawn even when Black maintains his b4-pawn, as could happen in the line 1 ♘f4?! ♖c3! (1...♖c1? 2 ♘d5) 2 h4! ♖×b3 3 ab a2 4 ♗c4 a1♕ 5 ♔g2.

Beliavsky, despite long consideration, failed to find the idea of a fortress with two minor pieces; he played 1 ♔e3?! ♖c1 (1...♖c3 2 ♘f2! ♖×b3? 3 ♘d1!+–) 2 ♘f4 ♖a1 3 ♘d5 ♖×a2 4 ♘×b4 ♖×h2∓.

Readers may learn how Dolmatov managed to win this captivating endgame in brilliant fashion from my book *School of Chess Excellence 1 – Endgame Analysis*, in the chapter "The Strongest Piece is the Rook!."

Sveshnikov – Psakhis
Erevan zt 1982

14-29

W?

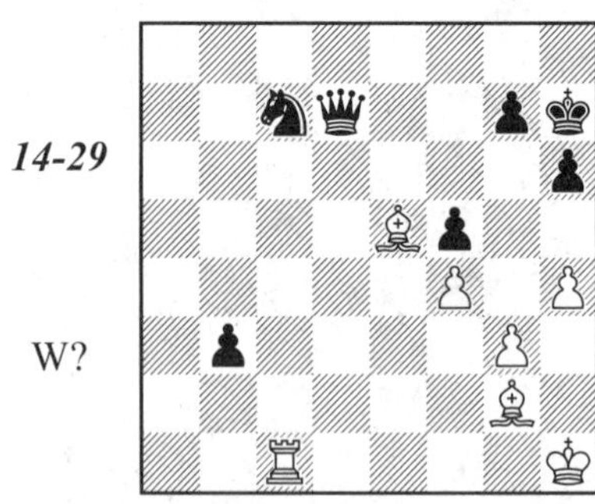

1 ♖×c7! ♕×c7 2 ♗×c7 b2 3 ♔h2 b1♕ 4 ♗e5

The queen enjoys unlimited freedom of action but cannot destroy the enemy defense without the king's support. Yet the king cannot break through as the bishops keep two adjacent diagonals, h1-a8 and e5-b8, under control. Hence the way to the queenside is closed. If the king comes to h5, White denies access to g4 by playing ♔h3.

In case of g7-g5, the simplest reaction is a double exchange on g5: the dark-squared bishop will safely protect White's remaining pawn from f4. But White may also trade only the h-pawns and allow Black's ...g5-g4.

4...♕d3 5 ♗b8 ♕e3 6 ♗c7 ♕e2 7 ♗e5 ♕h5 8 ♔g1 ♔g6 9 ♗c7 ♕e2 10 ♔h2

14-30

B

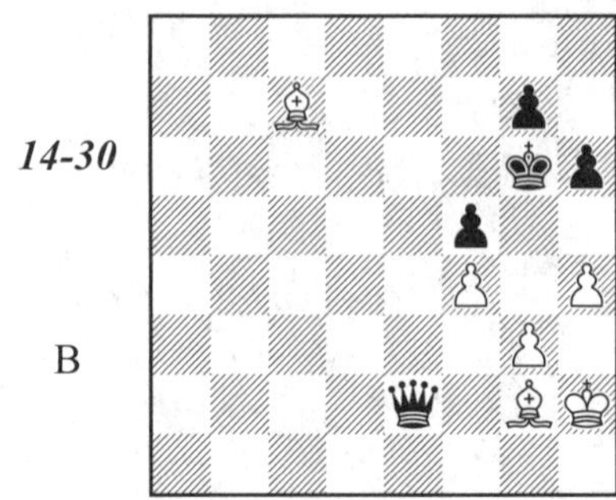

10...♔h7

Black prepares ...g7-g5. Another plan offered better practical chances: to force ♔h3, to occupy g1 with the queen, to bring the king back into the center, and finally to push the g-pawn to g5 in order to exploit the unsafe position of the white king. For example, 10...♕e1 11 ♗e5 ♕f2 12 ♗c7 ♔h5 13 ♔h3□ ♕g1! 14 ♗e5 ♔g6 15 ♗d5 ♔h7 16 ♗b8 g6 17 ♗g2 (17 ♗e5 g5 18 hg hg 19 fg ♕c5) 17...♔g7 18 ♗e5+ ♔f7 19 ♗d5+ ♔e7 20 ♗g2 ♔e6 21 ♗b8 (21 ♗c7 g5! 22 hg hg

23 fg ♕a7! –+) 21...g5! 22 hg hg 23 fg ♕d4 –+ (or 23...♕a1 –+).

The simplest way to parry this plan is 12 ♗c3! (instead of 12 ♗c7). In that case, 12...♔h5 13 ♔h3 ♕g1 was useless in view of 14 ♗×g7.

11 ♗b8 ♔g8 12 ♗c7 ♔f7 13 ♗b8 ♔e7 14 ♗c7 ♔d7 15 ♗e5 g5 16 hg hg 17 ♗b8 ♔c8 18 ♗e5 ♕e3 19 ♗h1 ♔d7 20 ♗g2 g4 21 ♗h1 ♕e2+ 22 ♗g2 ♕e3 23 ♗b8 ♕b6 24 ♗e5 ♔e7 25 ♔h1 ♕h6+ 26 ♔g1 ♔d7 27 ♗d4 Draw.

Bronstein – Keres
Amsterdam ct 1956

14-31

W?

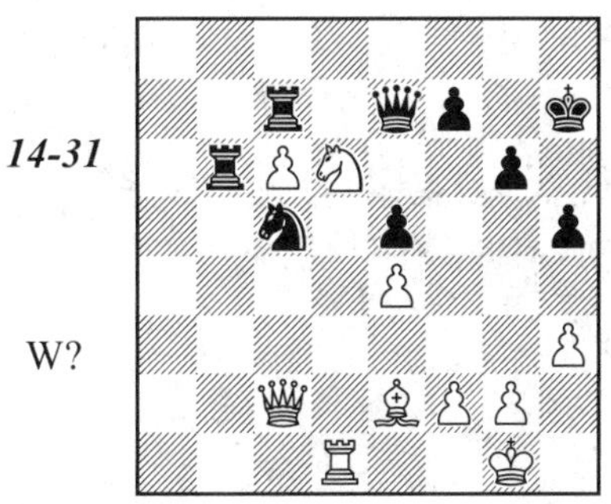

White lost this position rapidly:

1 ♗b5? ♘e6 2 ♗a4?!

2 ♕c4 ♘d4 3 ♖×d4! (3 ♕d5 ♘×b5 4 ♘×b5 ♖c×c6 –+) 3...ed 4 ♕×d4 would have been more tenacious, but the game could hardly be held anyway.

2...♘d4 3 ♕c5 ♖b×c6! 4 ♗×c6 ♖×c6 White resigned.

White missed a rather simple combination that would have led to a drawn position with a rook and a bishop against a queen:

1 ♕×c5!! ♖c×c6 2 ♕×b6! ♖×b6 3 ♘c8 ♕c5 4 ♘×b6 ♕×b6∓.

Tragicomedies

Fichtl – Blatný
Bratislava 1956

14-32

W

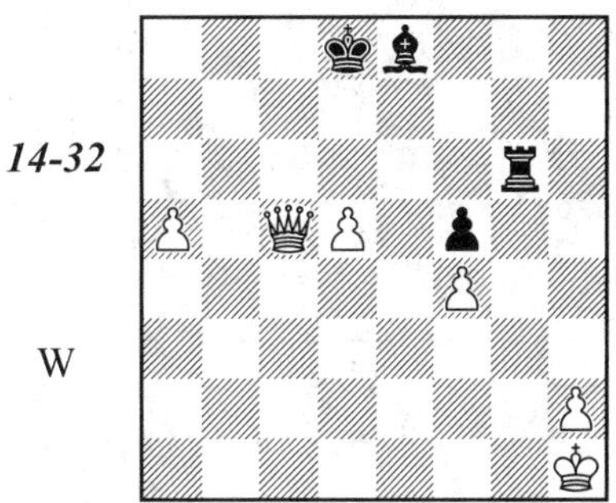

White, in this completely winning position, lost his vigilance for a moment.

1 d6?? ♗c6+! 2 ♕×c6 ♖g1+ 3 ♔×g1 Stalemate.

Zagoriansky – Tolush
Moscow tt 1945

14-33

B?

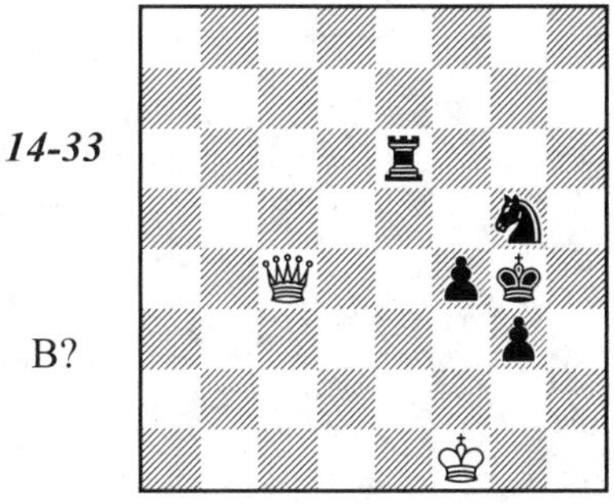

Black has an obvious advantage. He can win, for example, by means of 1...♖e8! 2 ♕a4 (2 ♕d4 ♖e1+!; 2 ♕b4 ♘f3; 2 ♕b5 f3! 3 ♕×e8 g2+ 4 ♔f2 ♘h3+; 2 ♔g2 ♖e2+! 3 ♕×e2+ f3+) 2...♖e4 3 ♕d7+ ♔h4, and the menace 4...f3 cannot be parried. However Tolush decided to produce a "brilliant" win.

1...♔h3? 2 ♕×f4 g2+ 3 ♔f2 (3 ♔g1? ♖e1+) **3...♖f6**

Black had only expected 4 ♕×f6? ♘e4+.

4 ♔g1! ♖×f4 Stalemate.

Exercises

14-34

14/3
W?

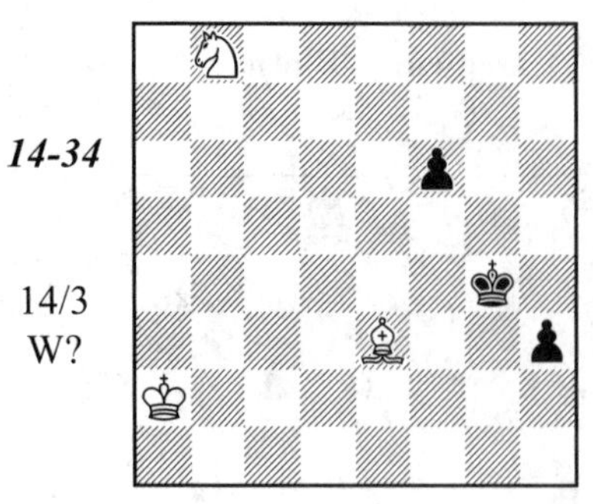

14-35

14/4
W?

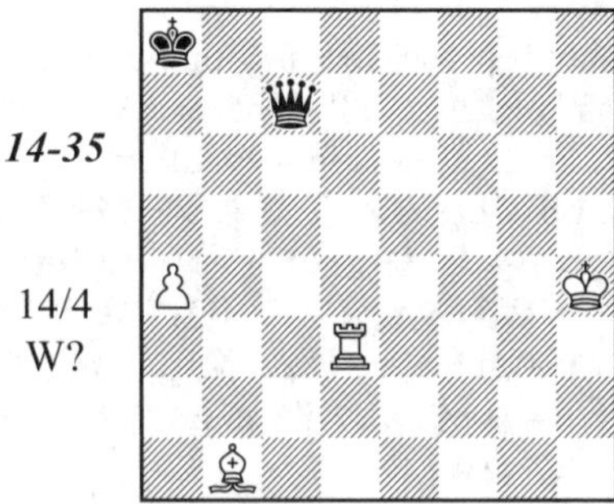

Queen vs. Two Rooks

Rooks are powerful when they act together. ***A standard method is doubling the rooks to gain, or at least stop, an enemy's pawn.*** Rooks can also create mating threats, particularly when the opponent's king is cut off at an edge.

Chernin – Marjanovic
Subotica izt 1987

14-36

W

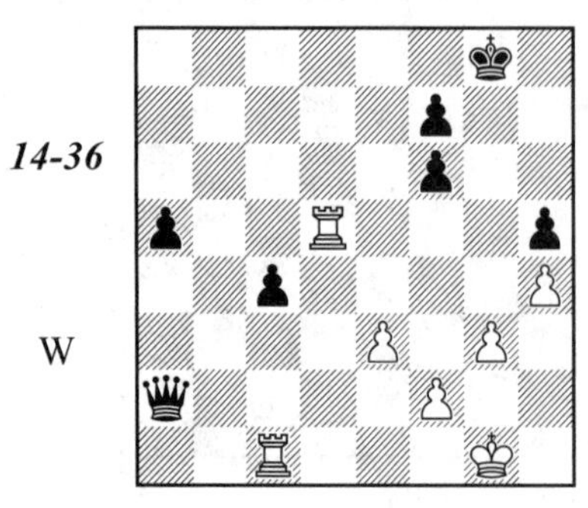

It was the last round of the Interzonal tournament; grandmaster Chernin followed my recommendation and employed a sharp line of the Queen's Gambit that led to the diagrammed position if Black, as was the case, made a slight inaccuracy. I evaluated this position as winning for White when it was reached in analysis. Black's pawns are isolated and weak; White consequently eliminates them by doubling the rooks and switches to a kingside attack thereafter.

1 ♖c5!

In case of 1 ♖×h5? ♕d2!, the separation of the rooks tells: 2 ♖×c4?? ♕d1+.

1...a4 2 ♖1×c4 ♔g7 3 ♖b4

Chernin hastens to double the rooks against the a-pawn. The sharper continuation 3 ♖f4!? merited attention. The advance 3...a3 is still not favorable for Black, as on the previous move: 4 ♖a5 ♕b1+ 5 ♔g2 (△ 6 ♖fa4) 5...♕b7+ 6 e4 ♕b4 7 ♖a6 △ ♖f3. After 3...♕b1+ 4 ♔h2, 4...♕b2 is useless in view of 5 ♖a5 a3 6 ♔g2+−. If 4...♕b6 instead, then 5 ♖×h5! ♕a6 6 ♖g4+ ♔f8 7 ♖h8+ ♔e7 8 ♖e4+ ♔d7.

14-37

W

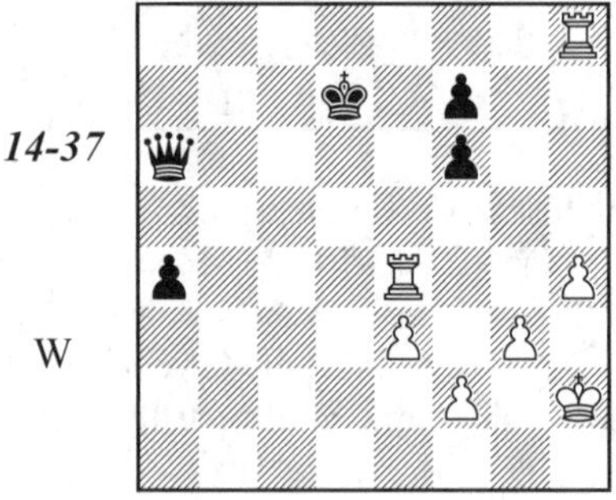

Now White can bring his rook back to the defense: 9 ♖d4+ ♔e7 10 ♖d2 a3 11 ♖a2. The attack against the king is however even stronger: 9 ♖f8! a3 (9...♔d6 10 ♖×f7+−) 10 ♖×f7+ ♔d8 11 ♖b4 ♔c8 (11...♕d6 12 ♖a4) 12 ♖g4 with an inevitable mate or win of the queen. A rather standard attack with two rooks!

3...♕a3 (3...a3 4 ♖a5+−) **4 ♖cc4 ♕a1+ 5 ♔g2 a3 6 ♖c5 ♕d1 7 ♖a5 ♕d6 8 ♖c4!?**

Chernin is not satisfied with the position after 8 ♖ba4 ♕c6+ 9 e4 f5 10 ♖×a3 fe, so he tries to get more.

8...♕d7!

8...f5 is quite bad: 9 ♖c3 a2 10 ♖ca3.

9 e4

14-38

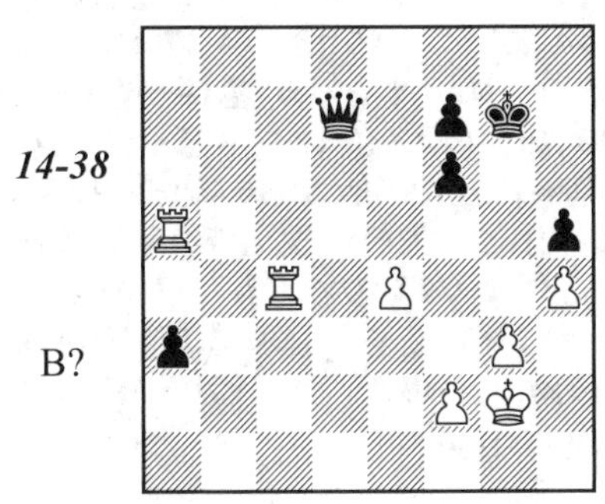

B?

9...♕d3?!

Black could have made it harder for his opponent by playing 9...f5! 10 ♖×a3 (10 ♖×f5 ♕a7; 10 ef ♕b7+) 10...fe. Here is a possible continuation: 11 ♖c5 ♕b7! (11...f5? 12 ♖aa5 ♕b7 13 ♖×f5 e3+ 14 ♖f3; 11...♕d6? 12 ♖g5+) 12 ♖e3 ♔g6 13 ♖g5+ ♔h6 14 ♖e5, and now neither 14...f6? 15 ♖e6 ♔g6 16 ♖3×e4 nor 14...♔g6? 15 ♖3×e4 f5 16 ♖e6+ ♔f7 17 ♖e7+ but 14...♕a8!, and Black is still in business.

10 ♖ca4 ♕c2 11 ♖×a3 ♕×e4+ 12 ♖f3

This is the position Chernin aimed for from the very beginning. The win is an elementary matter because of Black's pawn weaknesses. However even with a regular pawn structure (the pawn f6 is moved to g6), as happened in Gurgenidze – Averbakh (USSR ch, Baku 1961), White won by means of a double rook attack against the f7-pawn.

12...♔g6 13 ♖a6 ♕d4 14 ♖f4

The immediate 14 ♖a×f6+ was also playable, but this delay of the capture does no harm to White.

14...♕d5+ 15 ♔h2 ♕d8 16 ♖c6 ♕e7 17 ♖a6

Another way was 17 g4!? hg 18 ♔g3 (planning 19 ♖c×f6+) 18...♕a3+ (18...♔h5 19 ♖f5+) 19 ♔×g4+–.

17...♕d8 18 ♖a×f6+ ♕×f6 19 ♖×f6+ ♔×f6 20 ♔h3 ♔f5 21 f3 f6 22 ♔g2!

22 g4+? hg+ 23 fg+ ♔f4⊙= was premature.

22...♔g6

Or 22...♔e5 23 g4 hg 24 fg ♔f4 25 ♔h3⊙+–.

23 g4 Black resigned.

The queen has the upper hand when the rooks are disconnected or doomed to passivity because of the need to stop an opponent's passed pawns or to defend their own pawns.

Evans – Rossolimo
USA ch, New York 1965/66

14-39

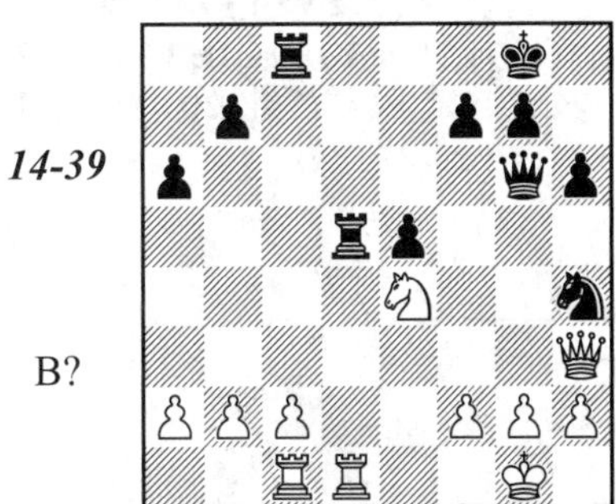

B?

I do not want to deny my readers the pleasure of enjoying the nice combination that resulted in the balance of material being discussed here.

1...♖×c2!! 2 ♕×h4 ♖d4!

Rather than 2...♖×c1? 3 ♖×c1 ♖d4, in view of 4 f3! f5 5 ♕g3!.

3 ♕d8+!

3 f3?? fails now to 3...♕×g2#.

3...♖×d8 4 ♖×d8+ ♔h7 5 ♖×c2 ♕×e4 6 ♖c1 ♕e2!

14-40

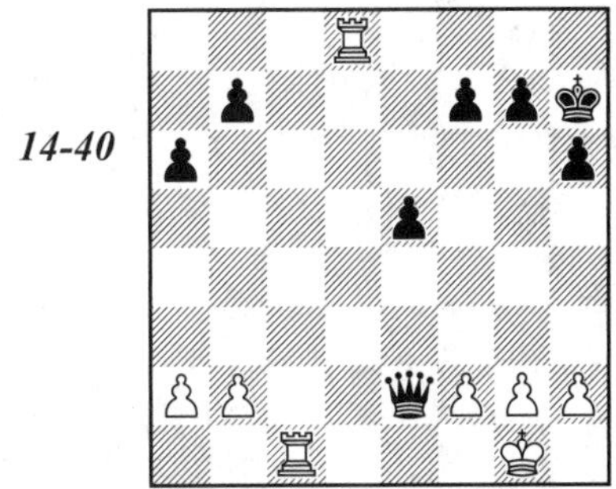

7 ♖b1

Evans did not want to give the pawn away and chose a passive continuation. Now it's possible to double his rooks only on the first rank. In the remainder of the game, Rossolimo cleverly combines strengthening his own position with prophylactic measures against an activation of White's rooks and his win is fully deserved.

I grant my readers the possibility of improving White's defense (I failed to do so) and to decide whether White should have tried for active counterplay instead: 6 g3!? ♕×b2 7 ♖c7 b5 (7...♕×a2 8 ♖×b7) 8 ♖×f7 ♕×a2 9 ♖dd7 ♕a1+ 10 ♔g2 e4 11 ♖b7 (or 11h4!?) and sometimes even an attack on the 8th rank is possible in combination with the move h4-h5.

7...f5! 8 ♖dd1 e4 9 ♖e1 ♕c4 10 a3 ♕a2! 11 g3 ♔g6 12 ♔g2 ♕b3 13 ♔g1 ♕a2 14 ♔g2 ♔f6 15 f3 ♔e5 16 fe fe 17 h4 ♕b3 18 ♔h3 ♕c2 19 ♖ec1 ♕f2 20 ♖f1 ♕b6 21 ♔g2 g6 22 ♖f8 ♕b5! 23 ♖f2 e3 24 ♖e1 ♔e4 25 a4 ♕c5 26 ♔h3 b5! 27 ab ab 28 ♖f6 ♕e5 29 ♖f8 ♕e7 30 ♖f4+ ♔d3 31 ♖f3 ♔d2 32 ♖f×e3 ♕×e3 33 ♖×e3 ♔×e3 34 ♔g4 ♔e4 35 b4 ♔e5! 36 ♔f3 ♔d5 37 ♔f4 ♔c4 38 g4 ♔×b4 39 g5 h5 40 ♔e5 ♔c5 41 ♔f6 b4 42 ♔×g6 b3 43 ♔h6 b2 44 g6 b1=♕ 45 g7 ♕b3 46 ♔h7 ♔d6 47 g8=♕ ♕×g8+ 48 ♔×g8 ♔e5 49 ♔f7 ♔f5! White resigned.

Exercises

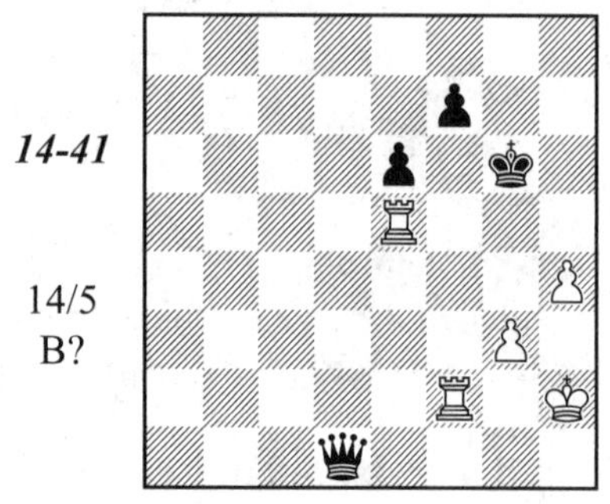

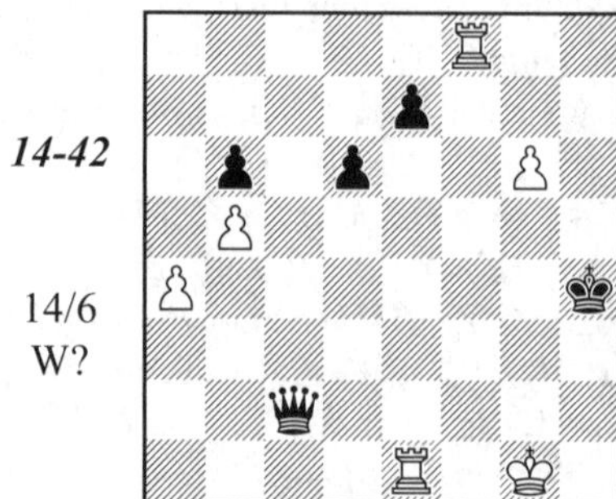

Chapter 15

GENERAL ENDGAME IDEAS

Along with the many techniques that apply to specific material relationships, this book also deals with more general principles and methods of playing the endgame which are used in a wide variety of circumstances. In this chapter we will reiterate the most important endgame ideas, and refine our impressions of them here and there.

Emanuel Lasker wrote in *Common Sense in Chess* that the main characteristic of the endgame is that "the king now becomes a powerful weapon of offense and aggression." In combination with this, two new factors enter into the endgame: "the facility to lead your passed pawns to queen" and the "principle of exhaustion" - or zugzwang, as it is called. We shall begin by examining these three defining characteristics of the endgame.

Having studied the preceding chapters, I hope you are now convinced that skillful endgame play doesn't merely consist of automatically following some prescribed formula of dry and dull rules. In endgames, just as in other stages of the struggle, complex variations must be calculated and beautiful hidden combinations must be discovered. Theory only aids our search for the proper solution. Some of the practical endgames and studies that we have examined are by no means aesthetically inferior to the finest creative examples from the opening and middlegame.

Here I would like to acquaint the readers with some new and spectacular examples that were not included earlier. Thus, this chapter is devoted not only to endgame strategy, but also to endgame tactics, especially in the exercises at the end of each section.

King's Activity

"In the middlegame the king is a mere 'super', in the endgame on the other hand – one of the 'principals'," – Nimzovitch wrote in *My System*. **Make use of every available moment to improve your king's placement, – its active position is often decisive for the outcome of the fight.**

Tondivar – Lutz
Leeuwarden 1994

15-1

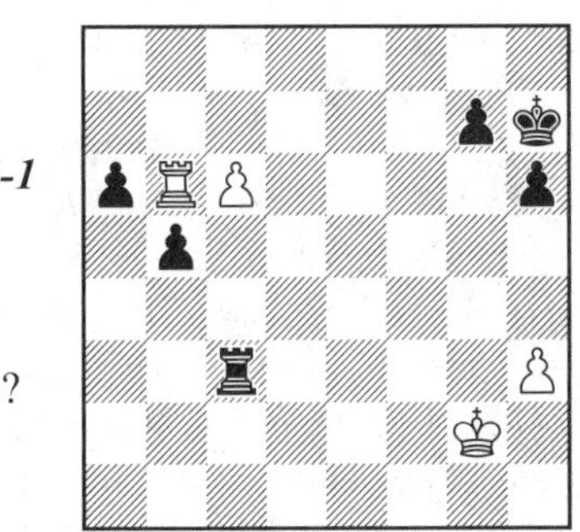

B?

1...b4? 2 ♖×a6 b3 3 ♖b6 followed with 4 c7 results in a draw, while 1...♖a3 can be met, say, with 2 ♖b8, and the black rook must go back to c3.

Black can win only through a king advance!

1...♔g6! 2 ♖×a6 ♔h5 3 ♖b6

3 ♖a7 fails after 3...♖×c6 4 ♖×g7 ♖g6+.

3...♔h4 4 ♖×b5 ♖c2+ 5 ♔g1 ♔×h3 (rather than 5...♖×c6? 6 ♖b3=) **6 ♖b7**

6 ♖b3+ ♔h4 7 ♖b4+ ♔h5 8 ♖b6 does not help in view of 8...g5 9 ♔f1 g4 followed with ...♔g5, ...h5, ...♔h4.

6...g5 7 c7 g4 8 ♖b6 h5 White resigned.

A king's advance is mostly directed to the center of the board, from where both wings are equally accessible. However this should not become a strict rule to follow blindly: in principle, a king's place is wherever the position requires.

Taimanov – Ree
Wijk aan Zee 1981

15-2

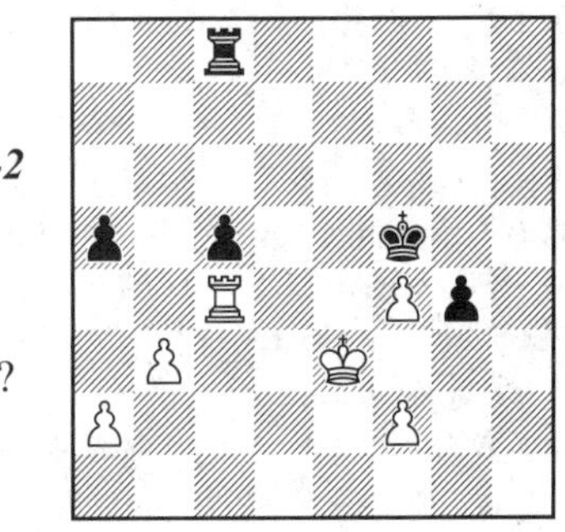

W?

White has an extra pawn and his rook is more active than Black's, but how does he bring the advantage home? The straightforward 1 ♖e4?! ♔f6! 2 ♖e5? lets Black create enough counterplay to save the game after 2...a4! 3 ♔d3 ab 4 ab ♖b8 (4...♖d8+) 5 ♔c3 ♖b4.

The winning plan involves the king march to g3 in order to attack the g4-pawn, no matter how far the king moves from the center.

1 ♔e2! ♖c7 2 ♔f1 ♖d7

Otherwise ♔g2-g3 followed with either ♖c3-e3-e5+ or a2-a3 and b3-b4.

3 ♖×c5+ ♔×f4 4 ♔g2 ♖d2 5 ♖×a5 ♖c2 (5...g3 6 ♖a4+) **6 ♖a4+ ♔g5 7 ♖c4 ♖×a2 8 ♔g3** Black resigned.

Sometimes the route for a king's march should be prepared by means of pawn exchanges. This technique is called ***"widening the beachhead."***

A. Yusupov, 1995

15-3

W?

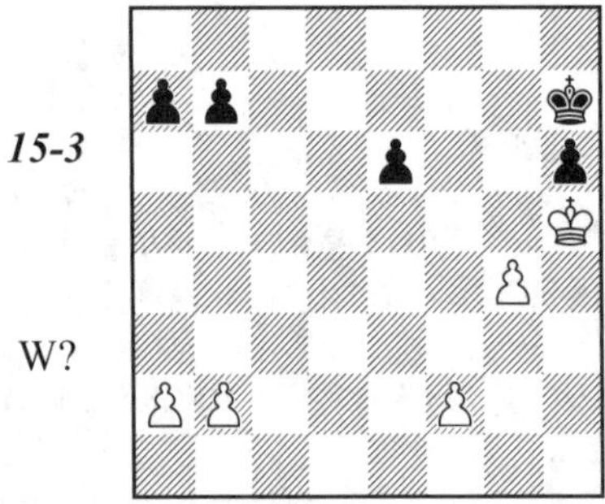

White has two active possibilities:

a) to create a distant passed pawn by means of f2-f4, g4-g5, and f4×g5;

b) widening the beachhead: the move g4-g5 is made when the f-pawn is still on f2, then the king goes to the e-pawn and, eventually, to the queenside.

However, both these plans fail if started immediately:

1 f4? ♔g7 2 g5 hg 3 fg e5 4 ♔h4 ♔g6 5 ♔g4 e4 6 ♔f4 e3 7 ♔×e3 ♔×g5 8 ♔e4 ♔f6 9 ♔d5 ♔e7=

1 g5? hg 2 ♔×g5 ♔g7 3 ♔f4 ♔f6 4 ♔e4 e5 5 ♔d5 ♔f5 6 b4 (if 6 f3, both 6...♔f6 and 6...♔f4 7 ♔e6 ♔×f3 8 ♔×e5 ♔e3 9 ♔d6 ♔d3= are good) 6...b5 7 ♔c5 a6 8 ♔d5 e4 9 a3 ♔f4 10 ♔e6 ♔g4! 11 ♔e5 ♔f3= (12 ♔f5? e3).

Before White clarifies the situation on the kingside he should strengthen his position on the queenside to the utmost by means of a pawn advance.

1 b4! ♔g7

Black has to wait. If 1...b5?, the plan with the distant passed pawn decides: 2 f4! ♔g7 3 g5 hg 4 fg e5 5 ♔h4! ♔f7 6 ♔g3! (the king detours around the mined field g4) 6...♔g6 7 ♔g4⊙ e4 8 ♔f4 e3 9 ♔×e3 ♔×g5 10 ♔d4 and Black's queenside pawns die as a consequence of the weakening advance ...b7-b5.

2 b5 ♔h7 3 a4 ♔g7 4 a5 ♔h7 5 b6 ab 6 ab ♔g7

From the point of view of the first plan, the situation is not changed. But the widening of the beachhead has become much more effective than in the initial position.

7 g5! hg 8 ♔×g5 ♔f7 9 ♔f4 ♔f6 10 ♔e4 ♔f7

10...e5 is impossible here in view of 11 ♔d5 ♔f5 12 ♔d6 ♔f4 13 ♔c7 ♔f3 14 ♔×b7 ♔×f2 15 ♔c6 e4 16 b7 with the winning endgame (a queen versus a central pawn).

11 ♔e5 ♔e7 12 f3! (White should preserve his second spare tempo for the future) **12...♔d7 13 ♔f6 ♔d6**

13...♔c6 14 ♔×e6 ♔×b6 15 f4 transposes into the main line.

14 f4 ♔d7 15 ♔f7 ♔d6 16 ♔e8! (a routine technique: the opposition is utilized by means of an outflanking) **16...♔c6 17 ♔e7 ♔×b6** (17...♔d5 18 ♔d7) **18 ♔×e6 ♔c7 19 f5 ♔d8 20 ♔f7! b5 21 f6 b4 22 ♔g7 b3 23 f7 b2 24 f8♕+**

Grandmaster Bologan has suggested his own method that leads to a more rapid win:

1 a3!? ♔g7 2 a4 ♔h7 3 ♔h4!? ♔g6 4 ♔g3 (planning 5 ♔f4) 4...e5 (4...h5 5 gh+ ♔×h5 6 ♔f4 ♔g6 7 ♔e5 ♔f7 8 ♔d6+–; 4...♔g5 5 f4+ ♔f6 6 ♔f3, and if 6...e5 then 7 f5+–) 5 ♔h4! a5 (5...e4 6 b4⊙ or 6 ♔g3 ♔g5 7 b4⊙ - this is why White wanted to have the pawn on a4) 6 f3⊙ ♔f6 7 ♔h5 ♔g7 8 g5+–. The widening of the beachhead was particularly effective here because the e-pawn was gained immediately.

In the chapter about pawn endgames we have seen "strategic double strokes" – maneuvers aimed at two goals simultaneously. The proverb about chasing after two birds is not valid on the chessboard.

Böhm – Timman
Amsterdam 1977

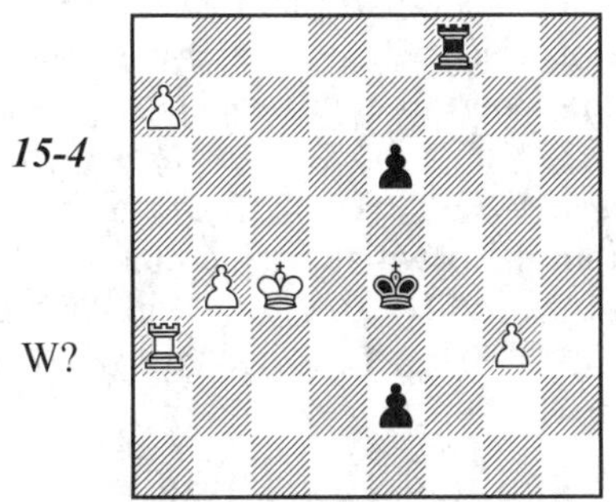

15-4

W?

1 ♖a1? ♖a8 2 ♖e1 ♔e3 followed by 3...♖×a7 is quite hopeless for White.

1 ♖a6!! e5 2 ♖a1 ♖a8 3 ♖e1 ♔f3 4 ♔d5!

This is the reason for 1 ♖a6!. The white king has enough time to eliminate the e5-pawn (if 4...e4 then 5 ♖×e2).

4...♖×a7 5 ♔×e5

The white king is looking at both wings. The black rook can attack any one of the pawns but then the king will support the remaining pawn.

5...♖b7 6 g4! ♔×g4 7 ♔e4 (7 ♖×e2 ♖e7+ 8 ♔d6 ♖×e2 9 b5= is also possible) **7...♖e7+ 8 ♔d5** Draw.

The most characteristic case of "chasing after two birds" is ***Réti's idea***: the king overtakes the hostile passed pawn after initially being out of its square. The necessary tempi are gained by counter-threats (supporting one's own passed pawn or attacking enemy's pieces).

M. Zinar, 1982

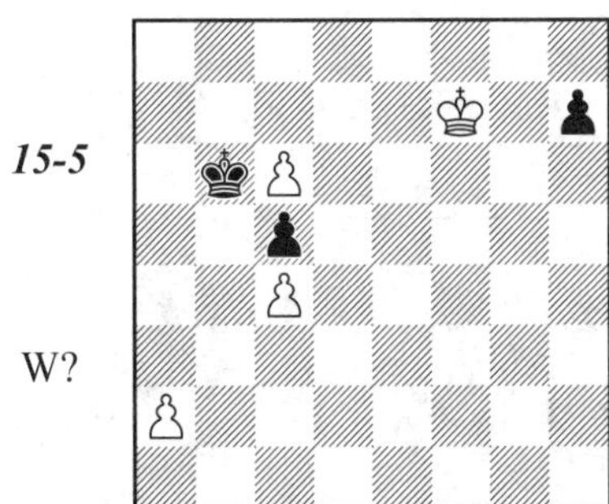

15-5

W?

The trivial continuation 1 ♔f6? ♔×c6 2 ♔g5 ♔b6 3 ♔h6 ♔a5 4 ♔×h7 ♔b4 5 ♔g6 ♔×c4 6 ♔f5 loses. The simplest is 6...♔c3 7 ♔e4 c4 8 a4 ♔b4–+ here, but 6...♔d5 7 ♔f4 (7 a4 c4 8 a5 c3 9 a6 ♔c6) 7...♔d4! ("shouldering") is also strong: 8 ♔f3 (after 8 a4 c4 9 a5 c3 Black promotes with a check) 8...♔d3! 9 ♔f2 (9 a4 c4 10 a5 c3 11 a6 c2 12 a7 c1♕ 13 a8♕ ♕h1+) 9...c4 10 ♔e1 ♔c2! 11 a4 c3 12 a5 ♔b2 13 a6 c2 14 a7 c1♕+.

1 ♔g7!! h5 2 ♔f6! h4 3 ♔e5!

Réti's maneuver! If 3...h3 then 4 ♔d6 h2 5 c7=.

3...♔×c6 4 ♔f4 ♔b6 5 ♔g4 ♔a5 6 ♔×h4

White has neither gained nor lost a tempo compared with the 1 ♔f6? line, but the black pawn, because of its provoked advance, was captured on h4 rather than h7. From there the white king has an easier way back to defense.

6...♔b4 7 ♔g3! ♔×c4 8 ♔f2!

8 ♔f3(f4)? is erroneous because of the shouldering 8...♔d3!, similar to the 1 ♔f6? line.

8...♔c3!? 9 ♔e2!

The only move! 9 a4? is premature in view of 9...♔b4, while after 9 ♔e3(e1)? c4 the c-pawn promotes with a check.

9...c4 10 a4=.

It is obvious that correct endgame strategy involves not only an activation of one's own king, but preventing the activation of the hostile king as well. We have already seen one of standard techniques - ***shouldering*** - in the previous example. Another instructive case follows:

Velea – Vidoniak
Romania 1992

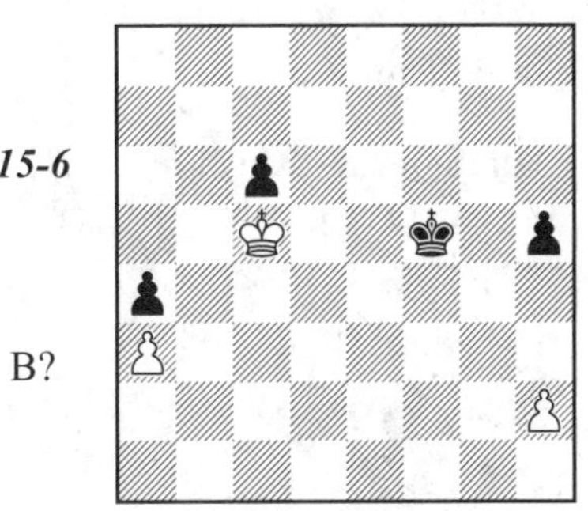

15-6

B?

1...♔g4? leads only to a draw: 2 ♔b4! ♔h3 3 ♔×a4 ♔×h2 4 ♔b3! h4 5 a4 h3 6 a5 ♔g3 7 a6=. Black's own pawn on c6 turned out to be an obstacle.

1...♔e4!

A move with a double purpose! Generally, the king intends to go to the queenside, but after 2 ♔×c6 the direction will be changed: 2...♔f3! 3 ♔b5 (3 ♔d5 h4 4 ♔d4 ♔g2 5 ♔e3 ♔×h2 6 ♔f3 ♔h3–+ – Black wins because his a-pawn has already entered the hostile half of the board) 3...h4 4 ♔×a4 ♔g2 5 ♔b3 ♔×h2 6 a4 ♔g3 7 a5 h3, and White fails to queen his pawn because the c6-pawn does not exist anymore.

As Bologan has shown, 1...h4! also wins: 2 ♔b4 ♔e4 (2...c5+) 3 ♔×a4 c5 4 ♔b5 ♔d4 5 a4 c4 6 a5 c3 7 a6 c2 8 a7 c1♕, and after 9 a8♕ almost every check forces a queen exchange. Or 4 ♔b3 ♔d3 5 ♔b2 (the defensive technique that we call pendulum does not help here) 5...c4 6 ♔c1 ♔c3–+ (the same situation as in the 2 ♔×c6 ♔f3 3 ♔d5 line but with reversed wings).

2 h4!? ♔d3 3 ♔b4

3 ♔×c6 ♔c4!–+ (shouldering), rather than 3...♔c3? 4 ♔d5 ♔b3 5 ♔d4 ♔×a3 6 ♔c3=.

3...♔d4 4 ♔×a4 ♔c4

Shouldering again, the white king is being squeezed to the edge of the board. 4...c5? is erroneous in view of 5 ♔b3 ♔d3 6 ♔b2 ♔d2 (6...c4 7 ♔c1 ♔c3 8 a4 ♔b4 9 ♔c2=) 7 ♔b3= (a pendulum).

5 ♔a5 c5 6 ♔b6 ♔d4 7 a4 c4 8 a5 c3 9 a6 c2 10 a7 c1♕ 11 a8♕ ♕c5+

White resigned. After the inevitable queen exchange, his king is too far away from the kingside.

A king can be kept out of strategically important areas not only by the hostile king but by other pieces as well. A rook can ***cut the king off***, while other pieces can ***create a barrier*** (usually together with pawns).

Ljubojevic – Xie Jun
Novi Sad ol 1990

15-7

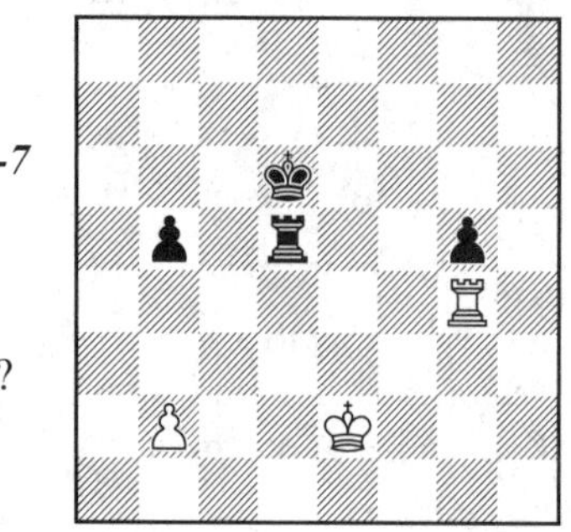

B?

1...♖f5!–+

The most precise, as the white king will be unable to help his rook in its fight against the passed pawn, which will soon march unstoppably ahead with support from its own king.

2 ♔e3 ♔e5 3 b3 ♔f6 4 ♔e4 ♔g6 5 ♖g1 ♖f4+ 6 ♔e5 ♖b4 7 ♖g3 g4 (the king is cut off from the pawn along the rank now) **8 ♔d5 ♖f4 9 ♔c5 b4 10 ♔b5 ♔g5 11 ♖g1 ♔h4 12 ♖h1+ ♔g3 13 ♔c5 ♔g2** White resigned.

A. & K. Sarychev, 1930

15-8

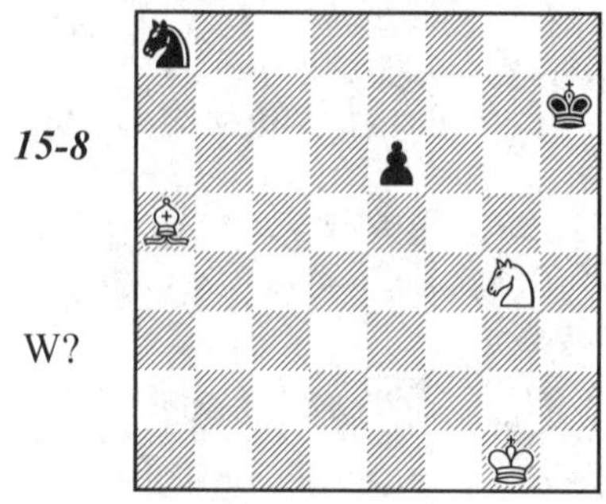

W?

The a8-knight is under arrest, but the black king hopes to release it, for example after 1 ♔f2? ♔g6 2 ♔e3 ♔f5 3 ♘f2 ♔e5 4 ♔d3 ♔d6 and 5...♘c7=.

1 ♘e5! ♔g7 (△ 2...♔f6) **2 ♗d8!**

White has built a barrier. The black king can still overcome it, but only at a cost of time and this loss of time turns out to be decisive.

2...♔f8 3 ♔f2 ♔e8 4 ♗a5 ♔e7 5 ♔e3 ♔d6 6 ♔d4⊙ ♘c7 (6...♔e7 7 ♔c5+–) **7 ♗b4#.**

Another technique of immobilization is ***pawns in the crosshairs***: the king is impelled to defend his own pawns.

Tukmakov – Veingold
USSR 1979

15-9

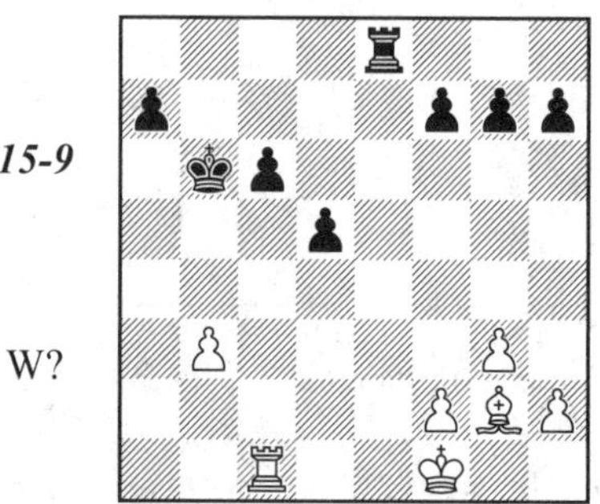

W?

Black has only two pawns for a bishop, but for White to capitalize on his advantage is by no means simple. How should he proceed? His king is out of play; therefore 1 ♖e1 looks quite natural, but after 1...♖×e1+ 2 ♔×e1 ♔c5 3 ♔d2 ♔d4 followed by ...a7-a5 and ...c6-c5 Black's king is active. The corner square h8 is of the "wrong" color and this fact will be important in case of massive pawn exchanges.

Susan Polgar suggested a promising plan: 1 b4!? followed by ♖a1 (or ♖c5-a5), ♗f3-e2, ♖a6+ and b4-b5. Tukmakov has found another plan: he still exchanged the rooks but in a more favorable way.

1 ♗h3! (2 ♗d7 is threatened) **1...♖e7**

The advance 1...c5?! just weakens Black's position, offering new possibilities to the white bishop: 2 ♗g2 d4 (2...♖e5 3 f4; 2...♖d8 3 ♔e2) 3 ♗d5+−.

2 ♖e1! ♖×e1+

A tougher resistance was possible after 2...♖b7 3 ♔e2 ♔c5(c7); White probably should have then played the sharp 4 ♖a1 or 4 ♔d2.

3 ♔×e1 ♔c5 4 ♗d7!+−

This is the point! By keeping the c-pawn in the crosshairs White has prevented the activation of the black king. The rest is a rather simple process.

4...a5 5 ♔d2 ♔d6 6 ♗e8 f6 7 h4 c5 8 ♗f7 ♔e5 9 ♔e3 h6 10 f4+ ♔d6 11 h5 c4 (otherwise the white king goes to the a5-pawn) **12 bc a4 13 ♔d4 dc 14 ♔×c4** Black resigned.

Tragicomedies

Bronstein – Bareev
Rome 1990

15-10

W?

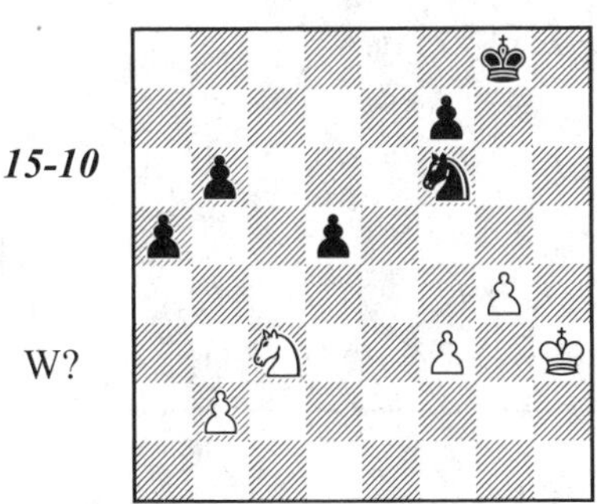

White could easily equalize by activating his king, in spite of his pawn minus: 1 ♔g3! d4 (1...♔g7 2 ♔f4 △ ♔e5) 2 ♘b5 d3 3 ♔f2=.

Bronstein is an outstanding grandmaster, but his Achilles' heel was always his endgame technique. For example, when he drew the World championship match against Botvinnik in 1951 (12:12), he lost 5 games – three of them from absolutely drawn endgames.

Here he also commits an elementary technical error, forgetting to centralize his king at the proper moment.

1 g5? d4! 2 ♘b5 (2 gf dc 3 bc a4) **2...d3! 3 ♔g3**

After 3 gf d2 4 ♘c3 b5! 5 ♔g3 b4 6 ♘d1 a4 7 ♔f2 a3 the a-pawn promotes.

3...d2

White resigned. The finish could be 4 ♘c3 ♘d5! 5 ♘d1 ♔g7 6 f4 (6 ♔f2 ♔g6 7 ♔e2 ♔×g5 8 ♔×d2 ♔f4, and Black has an extra pawn and the much more active king) 6...b5 7 ♔f3 b4 8 ♔e2 (8 f5 a4) 8...♘×f4+ 9 ♔×d2 ♔g6−+.

Svidler – Anand
Dos Hermanas 1999

15-11

W?

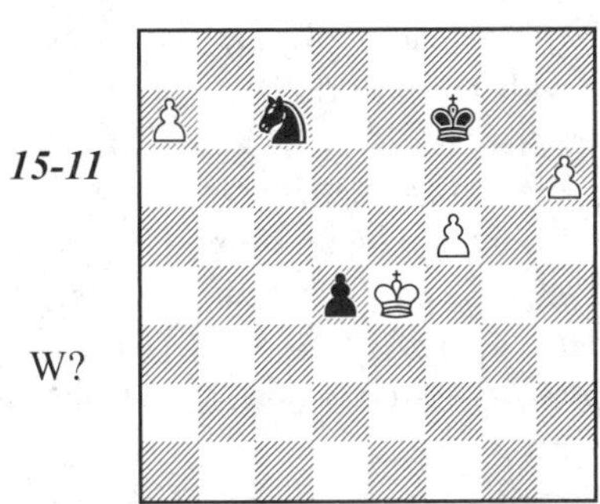

In this position a draw was agreed. Meanwhile White had a forced win:

1 ♔×d4! ♘b5+ 2 ♔c5 ♘×a7 3 ♔b6!

Chasing after two birds! By pursuing the knight, White wants to bring the king closer to his pawns.

3...♘c8+ 4 ♔c7 ♘a7

If 4...♘e7 then 5 h7 ♔g7 6 f6+!.

5 ♔d7! ♘b5

Or 5...♔f6 6 h7 ♔g7 7 f6+ ♔×h7 8 f7 ♔g7 9 ♔e8!+−.

6 h7 ♔g7 7 f6+ ♔×h7 8 f7 ♔g7 9 ♔e7!+−.

Ricardi – Valerga
San Martin 1995

15-12

B?

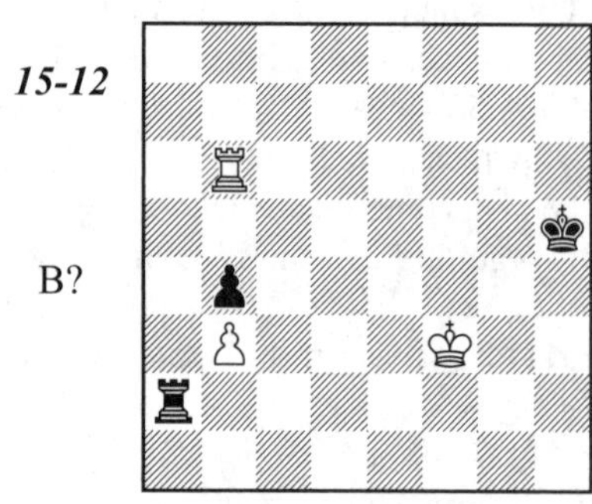

1...♔g5??

Apparently logical – the king goes to the queenside. However, in this case restricting the hostile king was much more important. This could be achieved by 1...♖h2! 2 ♖×b4 (2 ♔e4 ♖h3! and White cannot take the pawn) 2...♖h3+ 3 ♔e2 ♔g5 (only now, when the white king is cut off along the 3rd rank, has the time come to bring the king closer) 4 ♔d2 ♔f5 5 ♔c2 ♔e5 6 ♖c4 ♖h8 (in order to apply the frontal attack technique) with an easy draw.

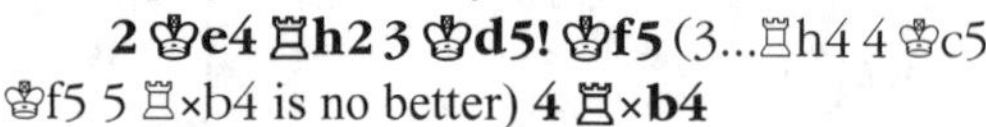

2 ♔e4 ♖h2 3 ♔d5! ♔f5 (3...♖h4 4 ♔c5 ♔f5 5 ♖×b4 is no better) **4 ♖×b4**

White's king is comfortably placed in the center and prevents his opponent coming closer.

4...♖h3 (4...♖h8 5 ♖b6+–) **5 ♖b7 ♖d3+ 6 ♔c4 ♖d8 7 b4 ♔e6 8 ♔c5 ♖c8+ 9 ♔b6** Black resigned.

Exercises

15-13

15-1
W?

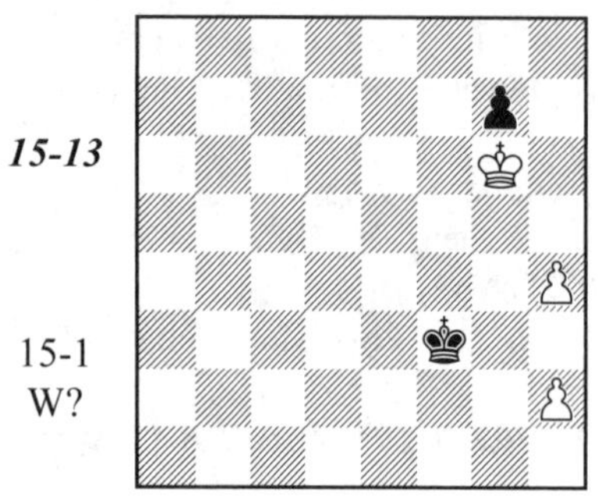

15-14

15-2
W?

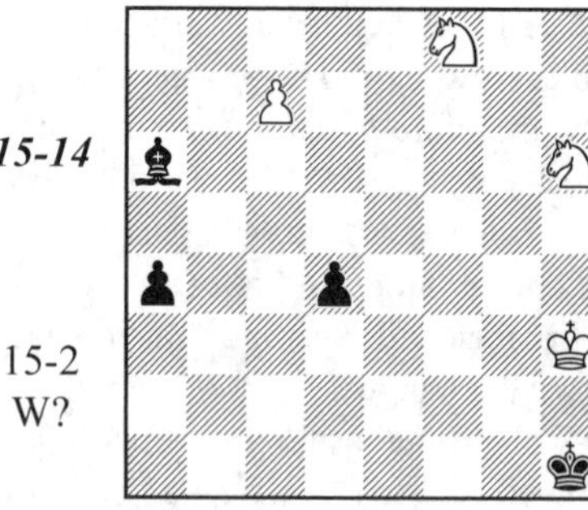

15-15

15-3
W?

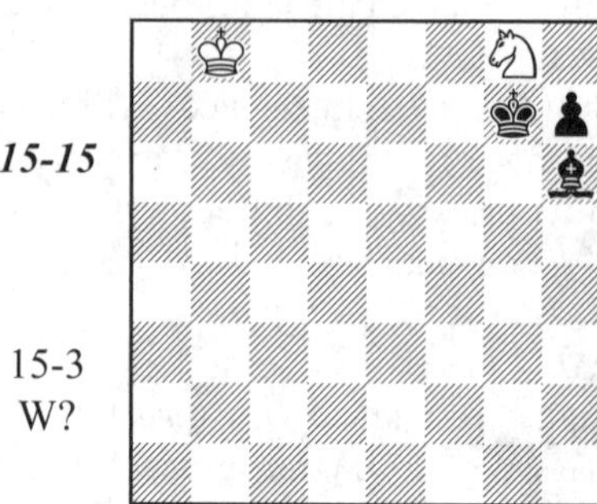

15-16

15-4
W?

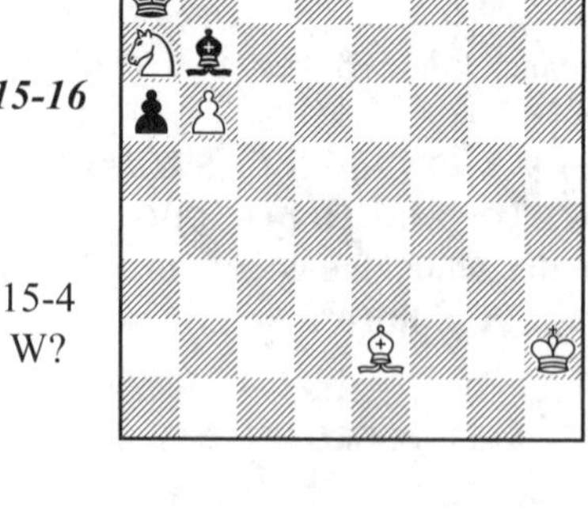

15-17

15-5
W?/Play

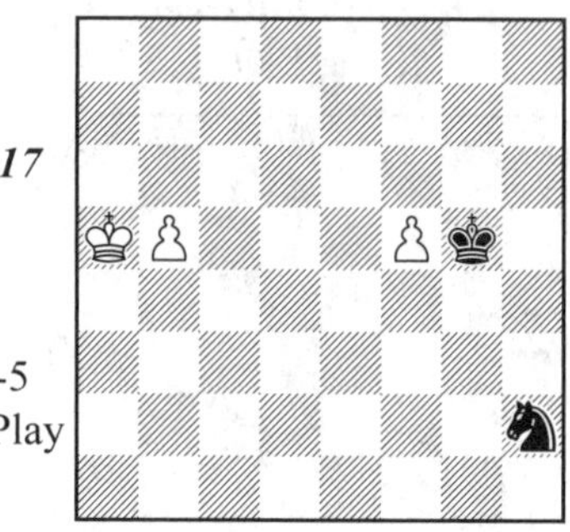

Pawn Power

In middlegames, with many pieces in play, pawns can seldom be promoted. In endgames, however, the main issue is usually the creation of passed pawns and their advancement to promotion. Therefore, the importance of pawns increases in endgames; they become more valuable fighting units, sometimes as strong as pieces or even much stronger.

Gufeld – Kavalek
Marianske Lazne tt jr 1962

15-18

B

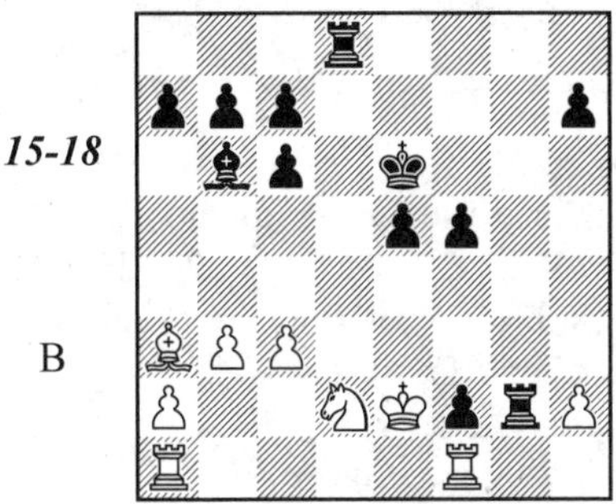

Black obviously stands better but he must beware of the move ♘c4. After an exchange of the b6-bishop, the important f2-pawn will be lost. To maintain it, Kavalek decides on an exchange sacrifice, intuitively sensing that his pawns will be stronger than the white rook.

1...♖×d2+!!

Emms suggested another solution to the problem: 1...e4! 2 ♘c4 (2 ♖ad1 ♖d3! 3 ♘c4 ♖g1 is no better) 2...f4 3 ♘×b6 f3+ 4 ♔e3 ♔f5! (this zwischenzug is the point: 5...♖d3# is threatened) 6 ♖ad1 ♖×d1 7 ♖×d1 ♖g1! 8 ♔×f2 ♖×d1 9 ♘c4 ♖a1 with an easy win.

2 ♔×d2 e4 3 ♗f8

The following curious line, also by Emms, shows the mighty energy of connected passed pawns: 3 h4 f4 4 c4 ♗d4 5 ♖ad1 f3 6 ♔c2 e3 7 ♖×d4 e2 8 ♖dd1 ♖g1! 9 ♖g1 fg♕ 10 ♖×g1 f2 −+.

3...f4 4 b4!

15-19

B?

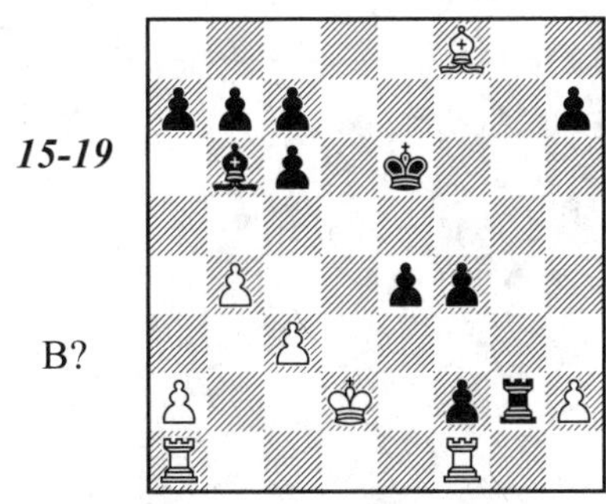

4...♖g5!!

White has prepared 5 ♗c5 in order to interfere with the powerful c5-bishop. To prevent this, Kavalek sacrifices another exchange.

4...e3+ looks tempting, and if 5 ♔e2 then 5...♔f5 (△ 6...♔e4) 6 ♔f3 ♖×h2 (△ 7...♖h3+) 7 ♖h1 e2! 8 ♔×e2 f1♕+! 9 ♔×f1 ♖×h1+ (Bologan). However White has a better defense: 5 ♔d3! f3 6 c4! e2 7 c5 ♖×h2 (7...♖g1? 8 ♖×g1 fg♕ 9 ♖×g1 f2 fails to 10 ♖g6+! hg 11 ♔×e2) 8 ♗g7! (8...♔f7 was threatened) with an eventual draw.

5 ♗c5 ♖×c5! 6 bc ♗×c5 7 ♖ab1 f3

An amazing position! A bishop with pawns turns out to be stronger than a pair of rooks. For example, if 8 ♖h1 then 8...♔e5 9 ♖×b7 e3+ 10 ♔d3 e2 11 ♖bb1 ♗e7! 12 ♔e3 ♗h4 and 13...e1♕.

8 ♖b4 ♔f5 9 ♖d4

The bishop is finally neutralized, but now the black king enters with a decisive effect.

9...♗×d4 10 cd ♔f4! White resigned.

This example demonstrates how dangerous ***connected passed pawns*** can be. In many endings, a ***distant passed pawn*** can be also very important. A fight against it can be a difficult matter, and even if one succeeds in stopping it he often loses control of events on the opposite wing. The possibility of creating a distant passed pawn can often be of decisive importance in evaluating a position.

Lutikov – Gulko
Moscow 1982

15-20

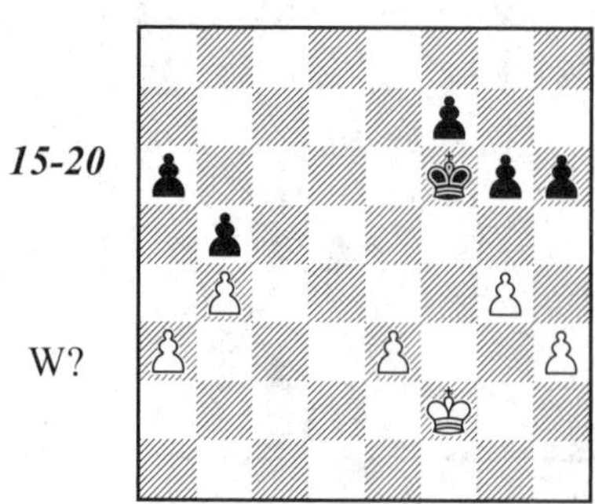

W?

White's only way to a draw was 1 e4! ♔e5 (1...♔g5 2 ♔g3 △ 3 h4+) 2 ♔f3! (rather than 2 ♔e3? g5 3 ♔d3 ♔f4 4 ♔d4 ♔g3 5 ♔e5 ♔×h3 6 ♔f6 ♔×g4–+) 2...g5 (2...♔d4 3 ♔f4=; 2...h5 3 gh gh 4 ♔e3=) 3 ♔e3 f6 4 ♔d3 ♔f4 5 ♔d4 ♔g3 6 ♔d5 ♔×h3 7 ♔e6 ♔×g4 8 ♔×f6=.

This variation is probably rather hard to calculate. An easier task is to come to the conclusion that nothing else is promising. For example, after 1 h4? ♔e5 2 ♔f3 both 2...g5 and 2...f5!? win for Black, e.g. 3 gf (3 g5 h5–+) 3...♔×f5, creating a distant passed pawn.

1 ♔f3? ♔g5!

Again, the evaluation is rather obvious. After 2 ♔g3 f5! 3 gf ♔×f5 or 3 h4+ ♔f6 Black gets a distant passed pawn; otherwise he brings his king to h4, and thereafter widens the beachhead with decisive effect.

2 e4 ♔h4 3 ♔g2 f6!

3...g5? is erroneous in view of 4 e5=. As Naumann has discovered, 3...h5!? 4 gh ♔×h5 also wins, although the process is more complicated than in the actual game: 5 ♔g3 f6 6 h4 g5 7 hg fg (Black has got a distant passed pawn) 8 e5 ♔h6! (the g6 and g4 squares are mined) 9 ♔f3 ♔g7 10 ♔e4 ♔g6! 11 ♔d5 ♔f7!.

4 ♔h2 h5 5 gh ♔×h5 6 ♔g3 g5⊙ 7 ♔h2 ♔h4 (7...g4? 8 ♔g3=) **8 ♔g2 g4** White resigned.

Far-advanced passed pawns are pre-conditions for brilliant combinations based on the promotion idea.

D. Gurgenidze, L. Mitrofanov, 1987

15-21

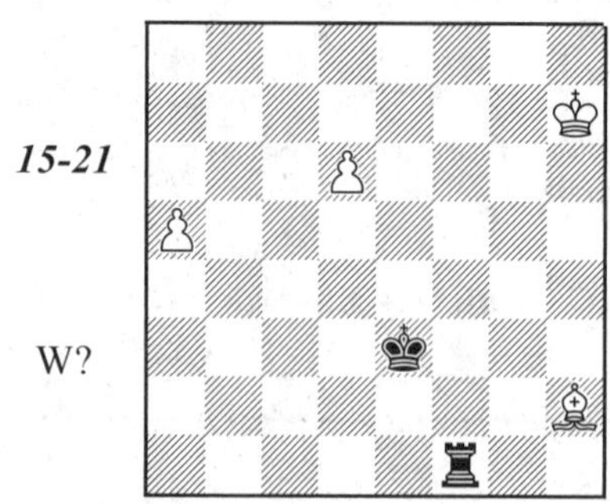

W?

1 a6! ♖a1!

1...♖f8 meets an easier refutation: 2 a7 ♔e4 (2...♖a8 3 d7 ♖×a7 4 ♗g1+) 3 d7 ♖d8 4 ♔g6 (or 4 ♗c7 ♖×d7+ 5 ♔g6). But what should White do now? 2 d7? ♖d1= is useless.

2 ♗g1+!! ♖×g1 3 ♔h8!!

An amazing quiet move. If 3...♖a1(c1), 4 d7 decides, if 3...♖d1(b1) then 4 a7, and if 3...♖f1 then 4 ♔g8!.

3...♖h1+ 4 ♔g8! ♖g1+ 5 ♔f8 ♖h1 (5...♖f1+ 6 ♔e8) **6 d7+–**.

Interference and deflection are standard tactical tools that are helpful for pawn promotion.

Muñoz – Salazar
Novi Sad ol 1990

15-22

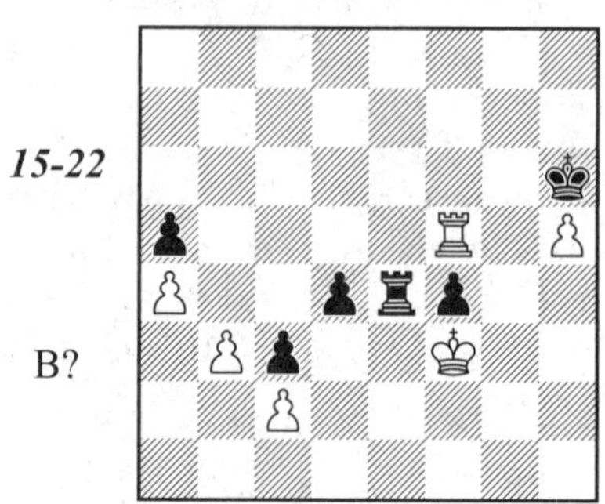

B?

1...d3! 2 cd (2 ♔×e4 dc–+) **2...♖c4!!** (an interference) **3 bc c2 4 ♔×f4 c1♕+ 5 ♔e4 ♕d1** White resigned.

L. Katsnelson, A. Maksimovskikh, 1983

15-23

W

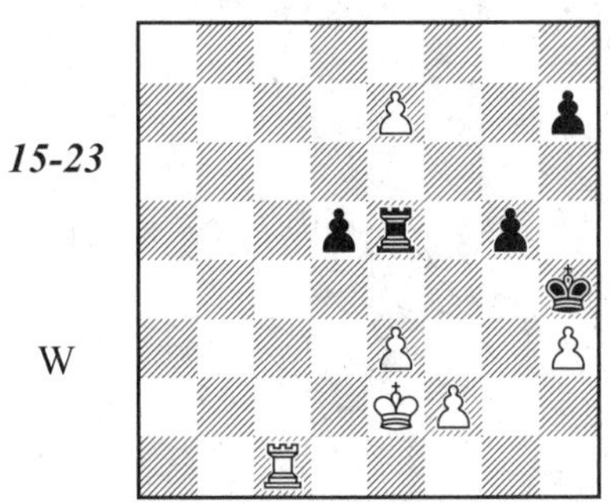

1 ♖c7

With the threat 2 e8♕ ♖×e8 3 ♖×h7#. After 1...h5 2 ♔d3 ♖e4 (otherwise 3 ♔d4 wins easily) both 3 f3 ♖e6 4 f4! gf 5 ef ♖e4 6 ♖b7⊙ ♔×h3 7 f5 and 3 ♖c4!! are decisive. The nice deflection is the main theme of this study; we shall meet it more than once below.

1...♔×h3

2 ♔d3? gives nothing now: 2...♖e4 3 f3 ♖e6=, and a king advance will cost White the important e3-pawn.

2 f4!! gf 3 ♔f3 ♖×e3+ (3...fe 4 e8♕! ♖×e8 5 ♖×h7#) **4 ♔×f4 ♖e4+**

If 4...d4 then 5 ♖c3!! ♖×c3 6 e8♕+−. In case of 4...♖e1 White applies the interference 5 ♖c3+ and 6 ♖e3.

5 ♔f3! h5 (5...♔h2 6 ♖c2+ and 7 ♖e2+−) **6 ♖c1! ♔h4** (6...♔h2 7 ♖c2+) **7 ♖c4!!+−.**

If there is no passed pawn one can often create it by means of a pawn **breakthrough**. The following joke illustrates one of the standard breakthrough techniques.

P. Cathignol, 1981

15-24

W?

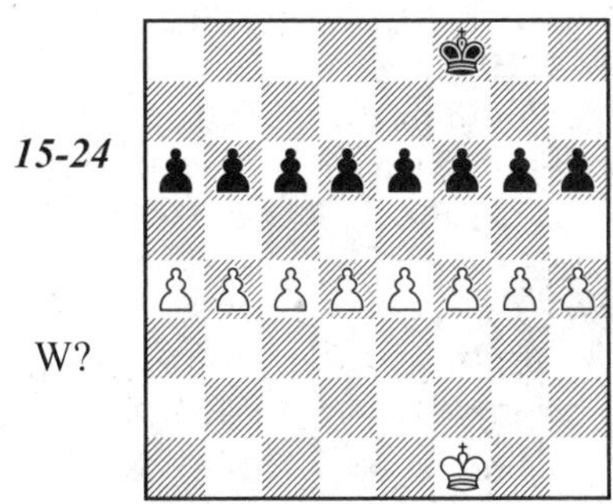

1 d5! ed 2 ed cd

No different is 2...c5 3 a5 ba 4 b5! ab 5 cb etc., as in the main line.

3 a5! ba 4 b5! ab 5 cb ♔e7 6 b6 ♔d7 7 b7 ♔c7 8 g5! fg 9 h5! gh 10 f5 a4 11 f6 a3 12 f7 a2 13 b8♕+! ♔×b8 14 f8♕+.

Sometimes a pawn breakthrough is an elementary tactical tool that brings an immediate decisive effect. But this is not a fixed rule; sometimes a breakthrough results in sharp positions that require deep and precise calculation.

Pillsbury – Gunsberg
Hastings 1895

15-25

W?

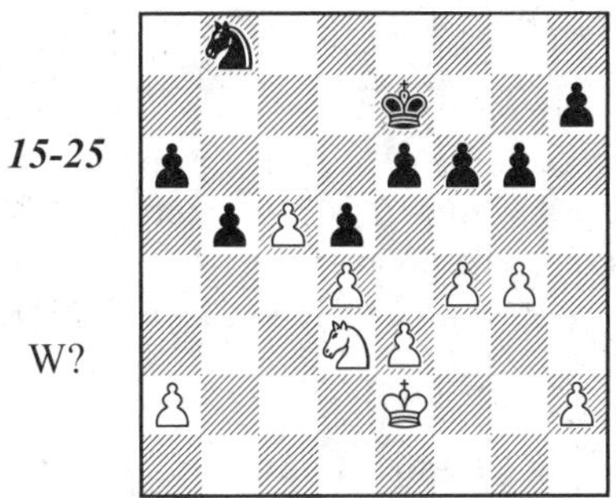

1 f5! (this is not a breakthrough, but an undermining of Black's central pawns) **1...g5!**

Forced, in view of the murderous threat 2 ♘f4. A very promising breakthrough can be found without much effort now, but to calculate it accurately is much harder work. The main line is more than 20 moves long! An additional question, for those who would like to try finding the solution independently: does White's combination work, if the h2-pawn is moved to h3?

2 ♘b4!! a5 3 c6! ♔d6! 4 fe! ♘×c6

Of course, not 4...ab? 5 e7 ♔×e7 6 c7+−.

5 ♘×c6 ♔×c6 6 e4! de 7 d5+ ♔d6 8 ♔e3 b4 9 ♔×e4 a4 10 ♔d4 ♔e7!

The best defense: Black prepares his own breakthrough on the kingside. The continuation in the actual game was much weaker: 10...h5?? 11 gh a3 12 ♔c4 f5 13 h6 f4 14 h7 and Black resigned.

11 ♔c4 b3 12 ab a3 13 ♔c3 f5! 14 gf h5 15 b4 a2 16 ♔b2 g4 17 b5 h4 18 b6 g3 19 hg hg 20 d6+! ♔×d6 21 b7 ♔c7 22 e7 g2 23 b8♕+! ♔×b8 24 e8♕+

If the pawn stood on h3 Black would have created the passed pawn a move earlier; hence White would have lost the game rather than won it.

Tragicomedies

Morozevich – van Wely
Tilburg 1993

15-26

B?

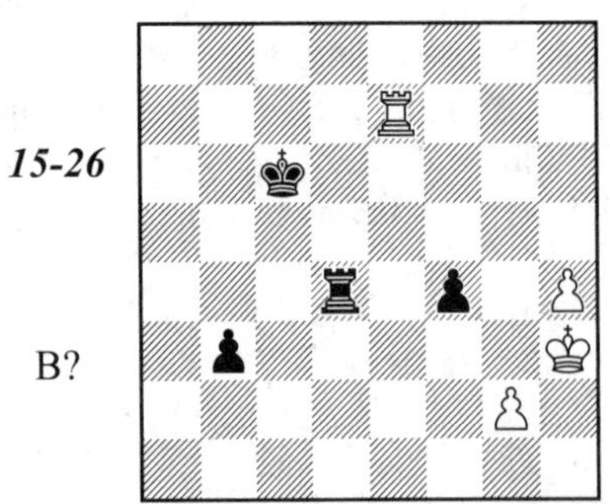

After 1...♖d3+! 2 ♔g4 ♖e3! the b-pawn would have had inevitably promoted, which White's rook could not prevent.

The actual continuation was **1...b2? 2 ♖e1 ♖b4 3 ♖b1** Draw.

Gelfand – Lautier
Belgrade 1997

15-27

W

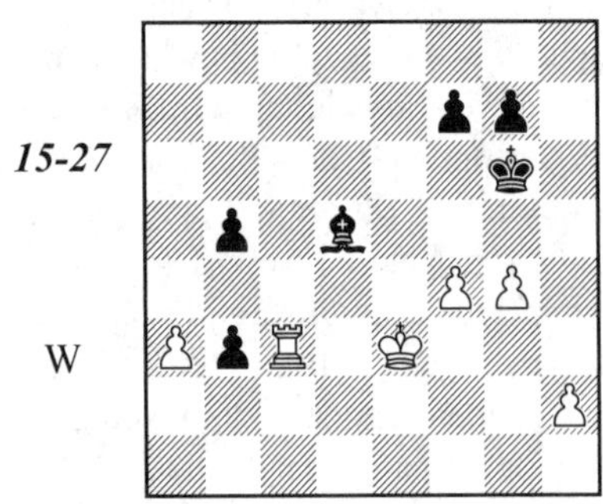

White could have won easily after 1 ♔d2 or 1 ♖c1.

1 ♖c5??

An extremely grave error. White is on the losing side now: 1...b4!! 2 ♖×d5 (2 ab b2; 2 ♔d2 ba 3 ♔c1 b2+) 2...ba 3 ♔d2 a2–+.

1...♗c4?? 2 ♔d2 Black resigned.

Timoshchenko – Stephenson
Hastings 1966

15-28

W?

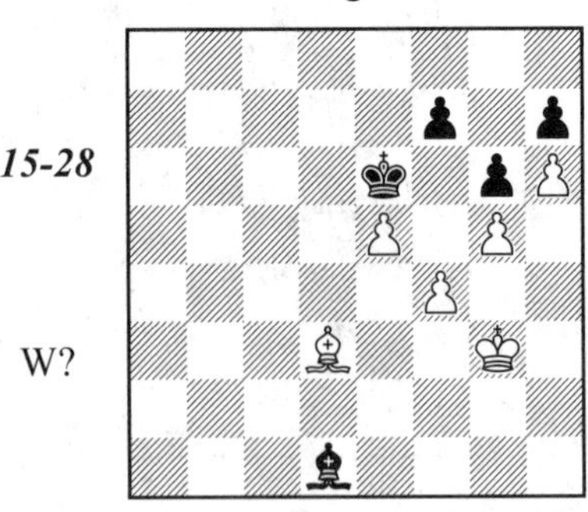

1 f5+! gf (1...♔×e5 2 fg fg 3 ♗×g6+–) **2 ♔f4 ♗g4 3 ♗c2?**

Timoshchenko planned a bishop sacrifice on f7 followed by a breakthrough by one of his pawns to the promotion square. He saw that the immediate 3 ♗c4+ ♔e7 4 ♗×f7? ♔×f7 5 e6+ fails to 5...♔g8! 6 g6 ♗h5!= and decided to play for a zugzwang, making a waiting move. His idea worked successfully in the actual game:

3...♗h3? 4 ♗b3+ ♔e7 5 ♗×f7! ♔×f7 6 e6+ ♔f8 (6...♔g8 7 e7! ♔f7 8 g6+) **7 g6** (7 e7+) **7...hg 8 e7+** Black resigned.

However Black could have saved the game by means of 3...♔e7!. The pawn ending is then drawn: 4 ♗×f5 ♗×f5 5 ♔×f5 ♔e8! 6 ♔f6 ♔f8 7 g6 (the only possible attempt) 7...fg 8 e6 g5! 9 ♔×g5 ♔e7 10 ♔f5 ♔e8 11 ♔f6 ♔f8 12 e7+ ♔e8 13 ♔g7 ♔×e7 14 ♔×h7 ♔f7=. 4 ♗b3 is met with 4...♗h5 5 ♔×f5 (or 5 ♗c4 ♗g6!) 5...♗g6+ 6 ♔f4 ♗b1=.

Another drawing continuation is 4 g6 fg 5 ♗b3 ♔f8! 6 ♔g5 ♗h3! 7 ♗e6 (7 ♔f6 f4 8 e6 ♗×e6 9 ♗×e6 f3 10 ♗d5 f2 11 ♗c4 f1♕+ 12 ♗×f1 ♔g8=) 7...♗f1! (rather than 7...♗g4? 8 ♔f6 ♗d1 9 ♗f7+– or 8...♗h3 9 ♗c8! ♔g8 10 e6 f4 11 e7+–) 8 ♔f6 f4 9 ♗f7 ♗h3 10 ♗×g6 f3 11 ♗×h7 f2 12 ♗d3 ♔g8=.

This last line offers a clue to the correct solution: the breakthrough g5-g6 should be played immediately, when the black king is further from the f8-square.

3 g6!! (or 3 ♗c4+ ♔e7 4 g6!!) 3...fg 4 ♗c4+ ♔e7 5 ♗g8. Black is helpless, for example: 5...♗d1 6 ♗×h7 ♔f7 7 ♔g5 ♗b3 (7...♗h5 8 ♗×g6+ ♗×g6 9 e6+) 8 ♗×g6+ ♔g8 9 ♗×f5 ♔h8 10 ♔f6 ♗c4 11 ♗g6 ♗b3 (11...♔g8 12 ♗f7+!) 12 ♗f7 ♗a4 13 e6 ♔h7 14 ♔g5! ♗b3 15 ♗g6+ ♔h8 16 e7 ♗a4 17 ♔f6 followed with ♔e5-d6-c7-d8, ♗f5-d7 (Dvoretsky).

Exercises

15-29

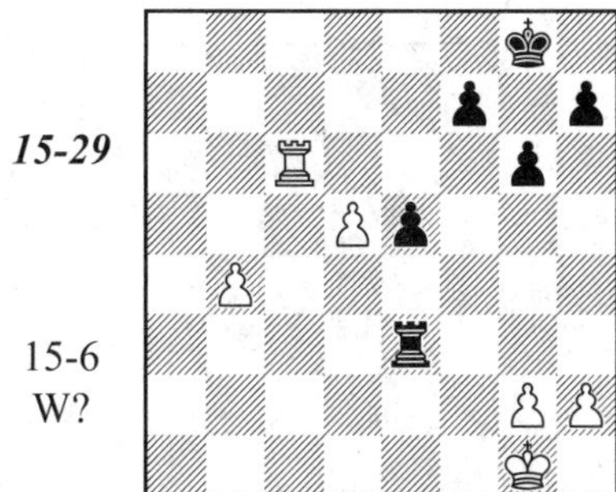

15-6
W?

15-31

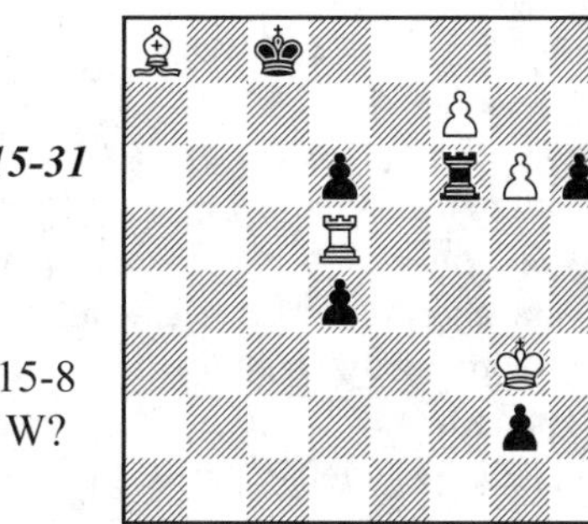

15-8
W?

15-30

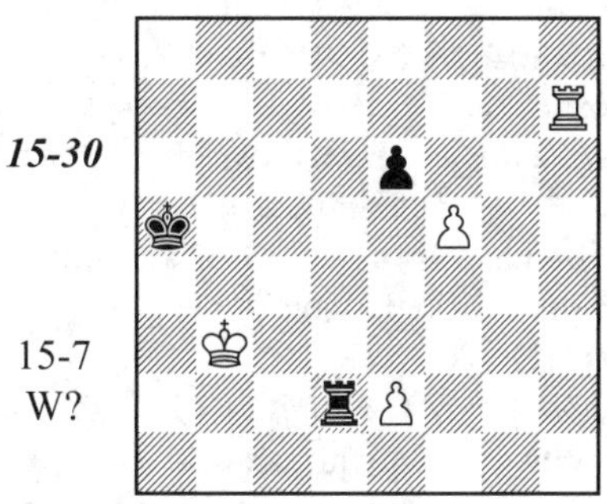

15-7
W?

15-32

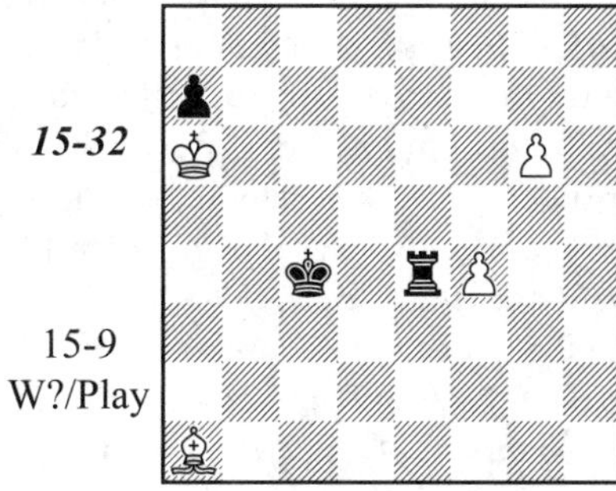

15-9
W?/Play

Zugzwang

Zugzwang is a situation in which each possible move worsens one's position.

Zugzwang is one of the most important endgame tools. It is applicable everywhere: in elementary endgames such as "king and pawn versus king" or "king and rook versus king." In the last case, the checkmating process cannot be successful without a zugzwang technique. And in the most complicated situations that require deep and precise calculation, where the pros and cons of every move can be quite distinct.

Zugzwang is very often reciprocal; both sides try to come to a certain position with the opponent on move. ***Squares of the reciprocal zugzwang are called "corresponding squares."***

The simplest cases of corresponding squares are: ***opposition*** (a correspondence of kings on a file, or rank, or sometimes a diagonal; ***mined squares*** (a pair of corresponding squares); ***triangle*** – a maneuver with the purpose ceding the move to the opponent.

In creating and handling zugzwang situations, ***spare tempi*** can be vitally important. For this purpose it is often useful to keep pawns on their initial positions, in order to have a choice between moving one or two squares when the critical situation arises ("***the Steinitz rule***").

All this is undoubtedly well known to you from the previous chapters. Here we will only take some practical exercise with these ideas.

Zugzwang, whether it has already occurred or can occur soon, is not always evident. Therefore, when seeking a way to the goal, you should ***remember to ask yourselves: how would your opponent play if he were on move?*** This question should be addressed not only to the actual position, but also to positions that arise in calculated lines.

From the next diagram, let us first try the rook exchange: 1 ♖e2+? ♔d5 2 ♖×e5+ ♔×e5 3 ♔f3 ♔d5 4 ♔e3 ♔c4 5 ♔d2 ♔d5 6 ♔d3 c4+ 7 ♔e3 ♔e5 – a draw, because Black maintains the opposition.

The consequences of 1 c4? are harder to calculate. Black plays 1...♔e3 2 ♖d3+ ♔e2 (3...♖e4+ is threatened) 3 ♔f4 ♖h5 4 ♔e4 ♖g5. So how do we strengthen the position? White

A. Seleznev, 1923

15-33

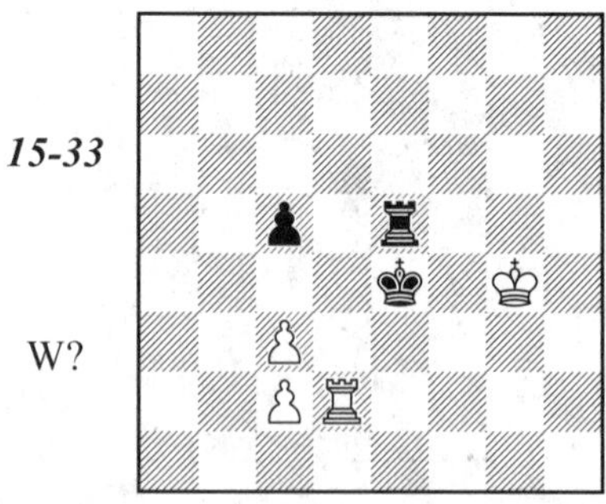

W?

can get the d5-square for his king by means of 5 ♖d6 ♖h5 6 ♖e6 ♔d2 7 ♖e5, but after 7...♖h4+ 8 ♔d5 ♔×c2 9 ♔×c5 ♔d3 10 ♖d5+ ♔c3 his last pawn is lost.

But what if Black is on move? He will naturally play 1...♔e3 but White can easily prevent it by moving his rook away. All Black's moves other than this will only worsen his position.

1 ♖d1!⊙ ♖e6

He cannot play 1...♔e3? 2 ♖e1+, while after 1...c4 White wins by means of 2 ♖e1+ ♔d5 3 ♖×e5+ ♔×e5 4 ♔g5! (a flank opposition) 4...♔e4 5 ♔f6+– (outflanking).

2 ♖e1+ ♔d5 3 c4+! ♔d6 4 ♖×e6+ ♔×e6 5 ♔f4 ♔f6 6 ♔e4 ♔e6 7 c3⊙ +–

Finally, the decisive factor was White's spare tempo that had arisen during the earlier fight.

R. Réti, 1923

15-34

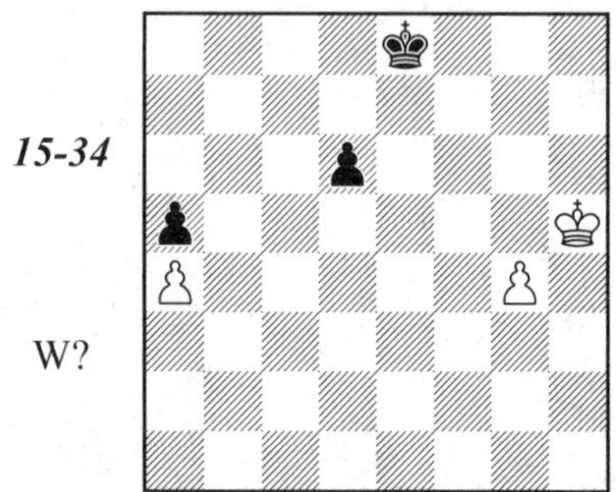

W?

One should discover the minefields here: these are g6 and e7. Actually, in case of 1 ♔g6? ♔e7!⊙ 2 ♔f5 ♔f7⊙ White would win if the d6-pawn did not exist, or if it stood on d5. In the chapter on pawn endings we learned to evaluate these situations instantaneously: the queenside pawns are in the "normal" position while the kingside gives White an extra tempo because his king stands in front of the pawn. But with the pawn on d6 it is a draw because White must spend a tempo capturing it: 3 ♔e4 ♔g6 4 ♔d5 ♔g5 5 ♔×d6 ♔×g4 6 ♔c6 ♔f5 7 ♔b6 ♔e6 8 ♔×a5 ♔d7 9 ♔b6 ♔c8=. Or 2 g5 d5 3 ♔h7 (3 ♔f5 ♔f7= leads to the "normal" position – the white king stands aside the pawn) 3...d4 4 g6 d3 5 g7 d2 6 g8♕ d1♕=.

1 ♔h6? does not win, either: 1...♔f7 2 ♔h7 ♔f6 3 ♔h6 ♔f7 ("pendulum") 4 g5 (4 ♔g5 ♔g7 5 ♔f5 ♔f7=) 4...♔g8 5 ♔g6 d5 6 ♔f5 ♔g7= (the "normal" position again).

1 ♔g5! ♔f7 (1...d5 2 ♔f5+–) **2 ♔f5⊙ ♔e7 3 ♔g6!**

The decisive zugzwang! If 3...♔e6 then 4 g5 d5 5 ♔h7 d4 6 g6+–.

3...d5 4 ♔f5 ♔f7 (4...♔d6 5 g5+–) **5 ♔e5+–**.

R. Réti, 1928

15-35

W?

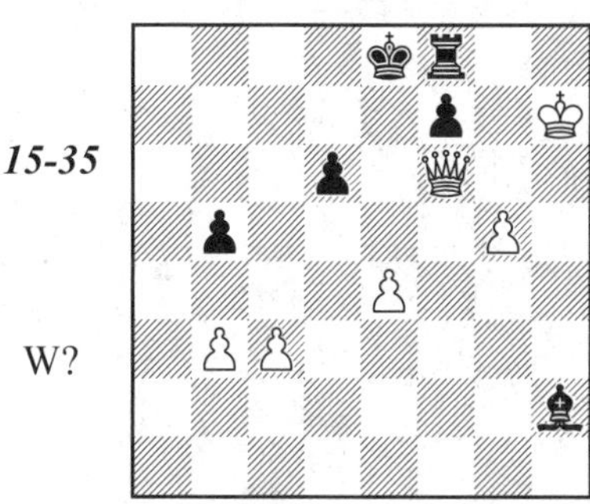

White has a material advantage but his king is badly placed. 1 g6? is erroneous in view of 1...♗e5.

After 1 ♔g7? ♗e5 White is in zugzwang: 2 c4? ♗×f6+ 3 gf b4⊙ –+; if 2 b4 then 2...♗h2(g3). The same position would be reached, but with Black on move, so White adopts a triangular maneuver with his king.

1 ♔h6! (♔h5-g4 is threatened) **1...♗e5 2 ♔g7! ♗h2**

After 2...♗×f6+ 3 gf Black is in zugzwang, he loses in spite of his extra rook.

3 c4 bc (3...b4 4 c5+–) **4 e5!!**

The decisive argument in the fight for the turn to move in the main zugzwang position. 4 bc? ♗e5⊙ –+ is bad.

4...♗×e5 5 bc⊙ ♗×f6+ (5...♗h2 6 c5 ♗e5 7 cd) **6 gf⊙ ♖h8 7 ♔×h8 ♔d7** (the mined fields are g7 and e6) **8 ♔g8! ♔e6 9 ♔g7+–**.

G. Kasparian, 1961

15-36

W?

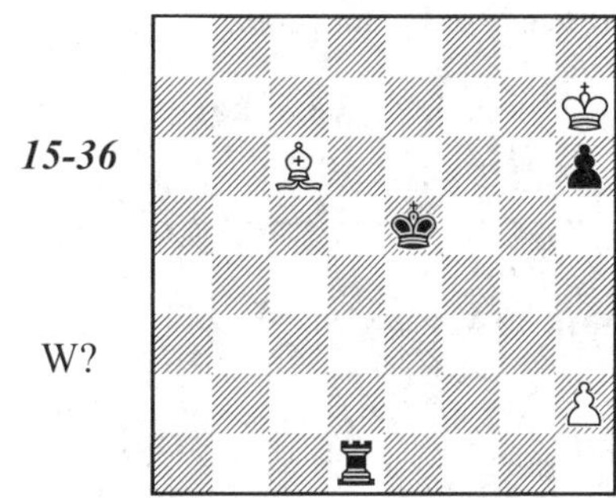

1 ♗e8!

The h6-pawn cannot be captured now: 1 ♔×h6?? ♖d6+. 1 ♗f3? also loses: 1...♖d3! (rather than 1...♖d6? 2 h4! ♔f4 3 ♗h5 ♔g3 4 ♗g6= or 2...♔f5 3 ♗e2!=) 2 ♗g4 (otherwise 2...♖h3) 2...♔f4.

1...♖d8

1...♖d6 2 ♗g6 ♔f6 3 ♔×h6 ♖d4 4 ♔h5= is not dangerous for White.

2 ♗g6! ♔f6 3 ♔×h6

In case of 3 h4? Black wins by means of either 3...♖d4 4 h5 ♔g5 or 4...♖h8+ 5 ♔×h8 ♔×g6 6 ♔g8 h5.

3...♖h8+ 4 ♗h7 ♔f7 5 h3!

"The Steinitz rule" saves White: he can choose between a single or a double pawn move. After 5 h4? ♔f6 6 h5 ♔f7 he would have been set in zugzwang while now the fight ends in a stalemate.

5...♔f6 6 h4 ♔f7 7 h5⊙ ♔f6 Stalemate.

Tragicomedies

Petrosian – Schmid
Bamberg 1968

15-37

B?

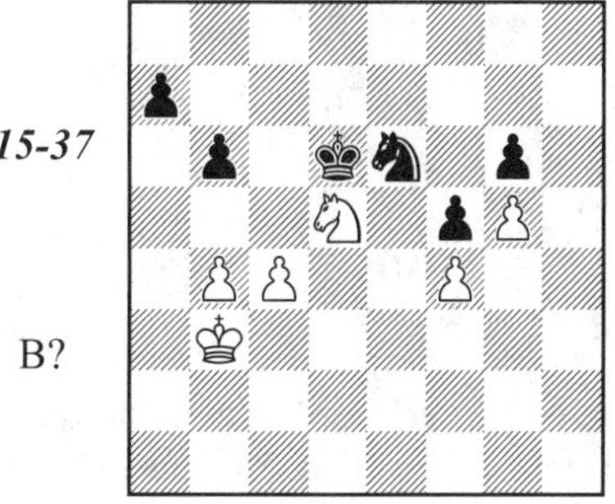

Black could win easily by means of zugzwang: **1...b5! 2 ♔c3** (2 ♘e3 ♘×f4−+; 2 ♘c3 ♘d4+ 3 ♔a3 bc−+) **2...bc 3 ♔×c4 a6!**. Instead of this, Schmid accepted the draw proposal of the world champion.

Zhuravlev – Vasiukov
USSR ch tt, Riga 1968

15-38

B?

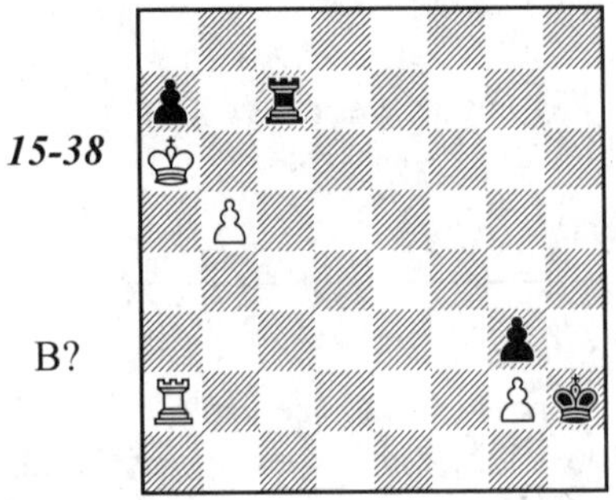

1...♔g1?

Black could win by means of 1...♖f7! (zugzwang) 2 ♔a5 (2 ♖b2 ♖f2 3 ♖b1 ♖a2+ 4 ♔b7 ♔×g2−+) 2...♖f2 3 ♖a4 ♔×g2 4 ♔a6 ♖f7−+.

2 ♖b2?

White does not exploit his opponent's error. He had to leave the a-file with his king: 2 ♔a5! ♖f7 (2...♖c4 3 ♔a6) 3 ♔b4 with a draw, because ♖f2 can be always met with ♖×a7 now.

2...♖f7! 3 ♖c2 ♔h2 (3...♖f2? 4 ♖c1+) **4 ♖a2 ♖f5!**⊙

When the black rook is on f5 or f7, all White's moves can only worsen his position.

5 ♖a5 ♔×g2 6 ♔×a7 ♔h3!

White resigned in view of 7 ♔a6 g2 8 ♖a1 ♖f1−+.

Šahovic – Liberzon
Lone Pine 1979

15-39

W?

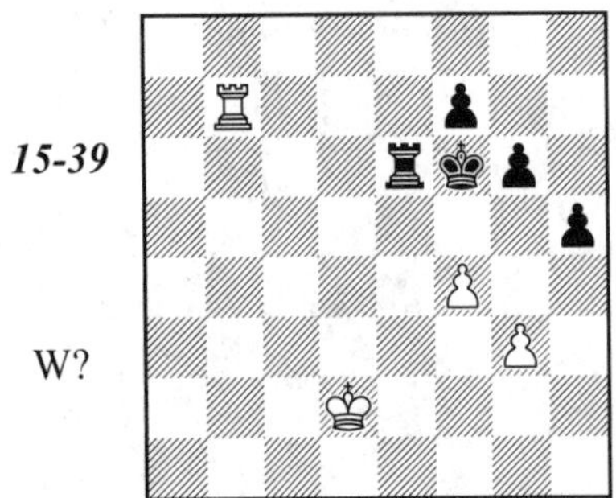

White is in a very dangerous situation. His rook must stand on the 7th or 5th rank to prevent Black's ...♔f5; and his king cannot go to d3 in view of Black's maneuver ♖e1-g1. Meanwhile Black plans ...♖e4 and ...h5-h4.

The key to this position is a reciprocal zugzwang that arises when the black rook stands on e4 and the white – on a5. The reason can be seen from the following line: 1 ♖b5! ♖e7 2 ♖c5 (rather than 2 ♖a5?) 2...♖e4 3 ♖a5! h4 4 ♔d3! ♖b4 5 ♔c3! (5 gh? loses to 5...♖×f4 6 h5 g5) 5...♖b1 6 gh ♖f1 7 h5 ♖×f4 8 hg fg 9 ♔d3 ♖f5 10 ♖a1 ♖e5 11 ♖f1+ (or 11 ♖g1) with a draw. If the black rook could occupy the a4-square White could not have saved this ending.

The actual remainder of the game was:

1 ♖a7? ♖e4?

Neither opponent sees the correspondence between the a5- and e4-squares. After 1...♖e7! 2 ♖a5 ♖e4! White is in zugzwang: 3 ♖b5 h4 4 ♔d3 ♖a4 5 gh ♖×f4 6 h5 g5−+, or 3 ♖a7 h4 4 ♔d3 ♖b4 5 ♔c3 ♖b1 6 gh ♖f1 7 ♖a4 ♔f5−+.

2 ♖a5= h4 3 ♔d3 ♖b4 4 gh?? (4 ♔c3! ♖b1 5 gh=) **4...♖×f4−+ 5 h5 g5 6 ♖a6+ ♔g7 7 h6+ ♔h7 8 ♔e3 f6** White resigned.

Exercises

15-40

15-10
W?

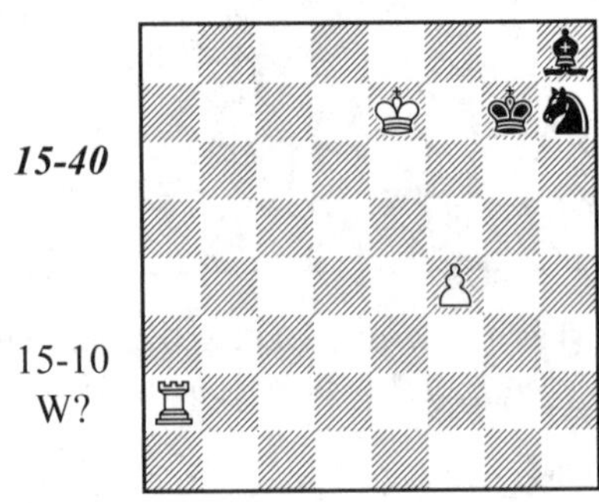

15-41

15-11
W?

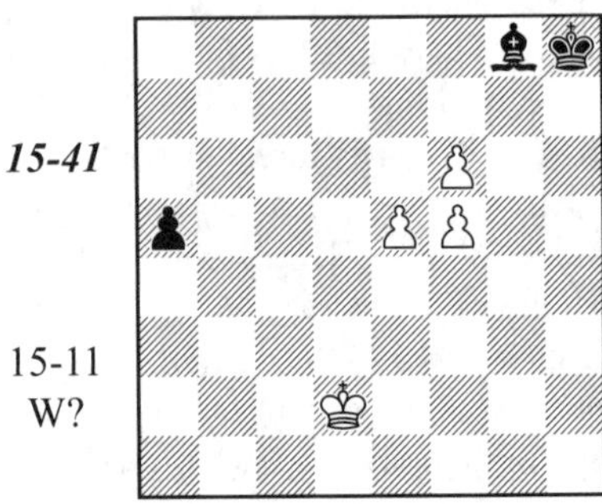

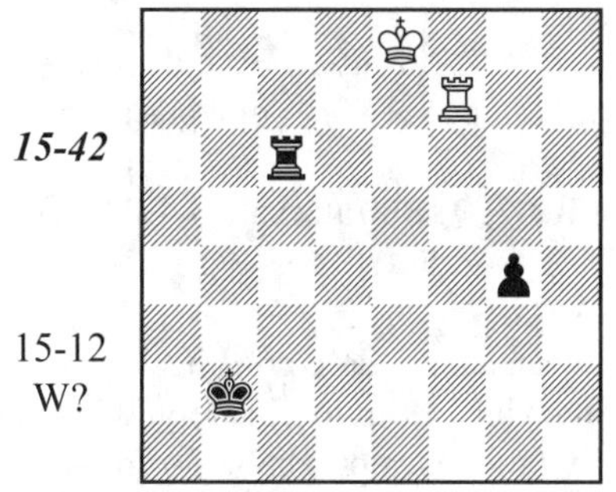

15-42

15-12
W?

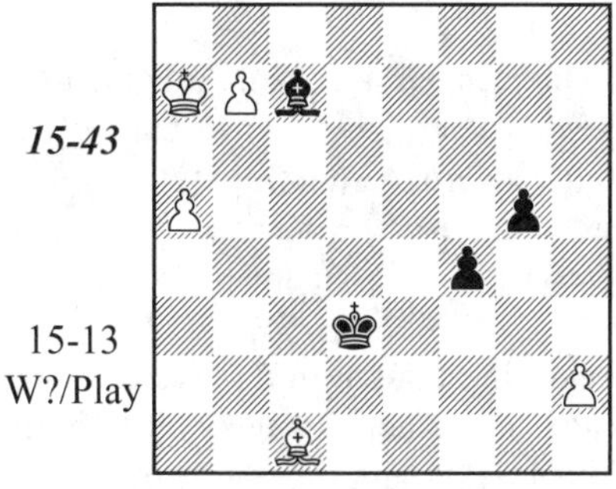

15-43

15-13
W?/Play

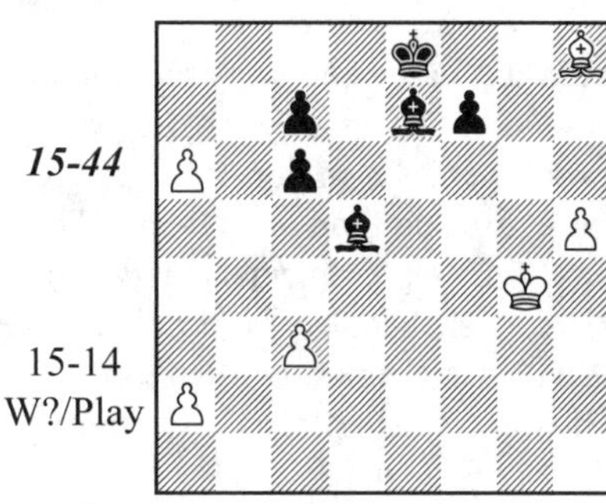

15-44

15-14
W?/Play

Fortresses

We have discussed the construction of a fortress in several chapters (opposite-colored bishops, a rook versus a minor piece, a queen versus a rook, a bishop versus pawns). These fortresses were mainly elementary and known to theory. Here we shall look at the problem more widely. You will discover new types of fortresses, together with my own simple classification.

A Fortified Camp

We define this as a situation in which a king, with or without the assistance of pieces or pawns, is successfully defending a small territory (as a rule, in a corner) and cannot be ousted. Almost all the theoretical fortresses that are already known to you belong in this category.

I add only a single, more complicated example here.

F. Simkhovich, 1926

15-45

W?

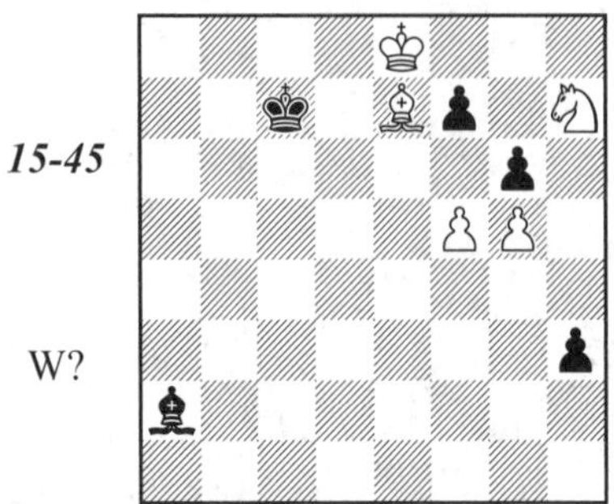

The h3-pawn will inevitably be promoted. White's only chance for a successful defense consists in building a fortress: f5-f6 and ♔f8-g7. But for building a reliable fortress he needs to place his bishop on h6. Otherwise Black brings his king to f5, takes the knight with his queen and captures the g5-pawn, winning. The question is whether White can perform this task in time.

The natural 1 f6? loses: 1...h2 2 ♔f8 h1♕ 3 ♔g7 (3 ♔g8 ♔d7 4 ♗f8 ♕a8! △ ...♔e6-f5−+) 3...♔c6 4 ♘f8 ♕h4 5 ♘h7 ♔d5 6 ♗a3 ♔e4 7 ♗b4 ♔f5 8 ♗d2 ♕f2 9 ♗c1 ♕e1 10 ♗a3 ♕h1 followed with 11...♕×h7+.

1 ♗f6! ♔d6 (1...h2? 2 ♗e5+) **2 ♗e7+ ♔c6**

The king has been forced to occupy a square on the h1-a8 diagonal. This is precisely what White wanted. Simkhovich included the moves 2...♔e5 3 ♗d8 ♔d6 4 ♗e7+ and only now 4...♔c6. But after 2...♔e5? White has a simpler draw: 3 fg fg 4 ♔d7=.

3 f6! h2 4 ♗f8! (rather than 4 ♔f8? h1♕ 5 ♔g8 ♕h2 6 ♗f8 ♕b8! 7 ♔g7 ♔d7 etc.) **4...h1♕ 5 ♗h6=**

The queen cannot deliver a check from a8, and the white king comes to g7 safely. White has successfully built an impregnable fortress.

A Pawn Barrier

Even a huge material advantage sometimes cannot be exploited when a pawn barrier lies across the chessboard. A king (or, as it may happen in exceptional cases, a king and other pieces) cannot overcome the barrier, and therefore there is no win.

We saw this situation in the exercise 7/15 (in the chapter on bishop versus knight), in the annotation to 4 ♔b3!. The alternative possibility led to a gain of a piece and to ... an obvious draw caused by erecting a pawn barrier that the king could not overcome.

The following curious example is taken from a game between two leading chessplayers of their time.

Chigorin – Tarrasch
Vienna 1898

15-46

W

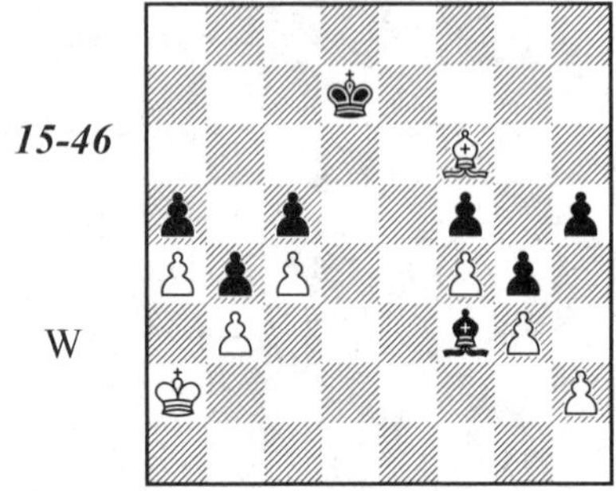

Chigorin offered a draw, and Tarrasch unexpectedly rejected this offer. Then Chigorin took his bishop away from the board and suggested his opponent to try to win with an extra piece. Tarrasch immediately accepted the draw proposal. Actually, his king cannot invade White's position, while his bishop alone cannot accomplish anything.

Keres – Portisch
Moscow 1967

15-47

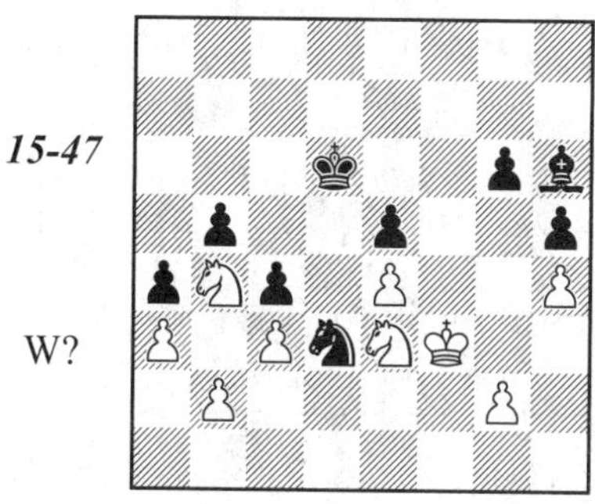

W?

The b2-pawn is attacked. In case of an exchange on d3, the black king gets an open road into White's camp via the white squares: 1 ♘×d3? cd 2 g3 (2 ♘d1 ♗c1 △ ...♔c5-c4-b3 −+) 2...♔c5 3 ♔f2 ♗×e3+ 4 ♔×e3 ♔c4 5 ♔d2 ♔b3 −+.

1 ♘d1! ♗c1 2 ♔e2!

Obviously, 2...♗×b2? 3 ♘×b2 ♘×b2 4 ♔d2= yields nothing, but why can't Black take the pawn with his knight? This was Keres' idea.

2...♘×b2? 3 ♘×b2 ♗×b2 4 ♔d2 ♗×a3 5 ♔c2. How does one exploit two extra pawns? Black's bishop is locked, White intends to move his king from c2 to b1 and back. If 5...g5 then 6 g3!. If Black brings his king to c5 or a5, White gives a knight check from a6 (resp. c6) and plays back to b4. Finally, if Black exchanges his bishop for the knight, his king will be unable to cross the barrier, so both passed pawns, at a4 and c4, will be useless.

Portisch recognized this clever trap and chose **2...♘c5! 3 ♔f3 g5!**; this allowed him to exploit his positional advantage later on.

L. Pachman, 1953

15-48

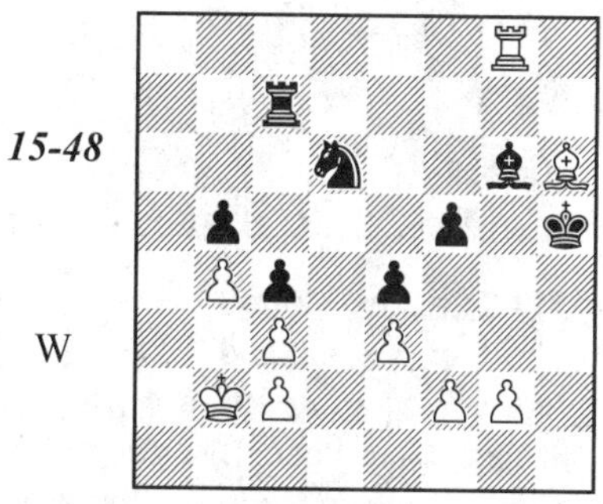

W

1 ♗f4 ♖c8! 2 g4+! fg 3 ♗×d6!!

In case of 3 ♖×g6? ♔×g6 4 ♗×d6 g3! Black wins by invading with his king via the white squares. However 3 ♖×c8!? ♘×c8 4 ♗g3= is an alternative solution that the author has not observed. Black may gain the c3-pawn with his knight, but then ♔d2 and c2-c3 follows, and no further progress can be achieved. The two black pieces, the king and bishop, cannot overcome the pawn barrier.

With the rook, it is precisely the same.

3...♖×g8 4 ♗g3!=.

Tragicomedies

Kengis – Yuneev
USSR 1989

15-49

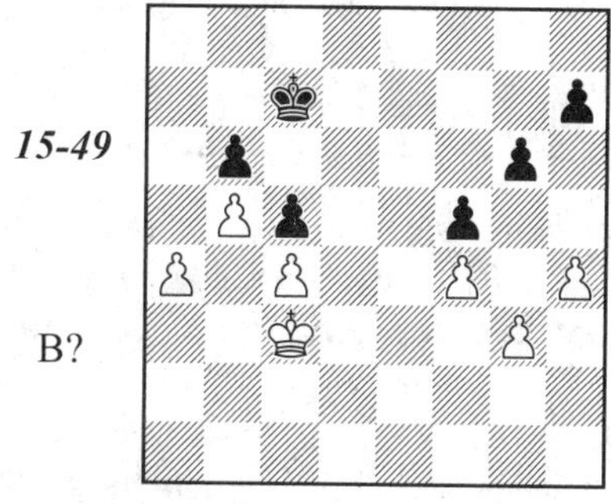

B?

Black had to complete the building of his barrier with 1...h5!=. However, Yuneev thought that this could be postponed.

1...♔b7?? 2 h5! gh 3 ♔d3 h4

Black obviously counted only on 4 gh? h5=.

4 ♔e3! hg 5 ♔f3 Black resigned.

A. Petrosian – Hazai
Schilde jr 1970

15-50

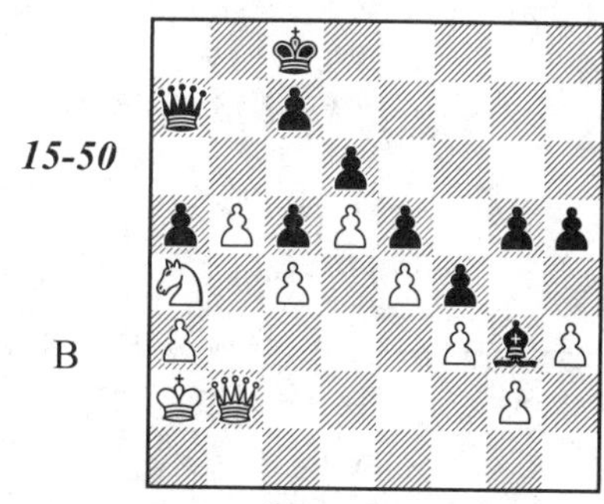

B

Black is strategically lost. He tries his last chance, and the trap suddenly succeeds.

1...♕b6!? 2 ♘×b6+??

Unjustified greed. After 2 ♕d2! followed by, say, ♔b3, ♘b2, ♔a4, ♘d3-c1-b3, White could have gained the a5-pawn and won the game.

2...cb (△ 3...h4=) **3 h4 gh 4 ♕d2 h3! 5 gh h4**

Draw. Neither the king nor the queen can overcome the barrier.

So. Polgar – Smyslov
London 1996

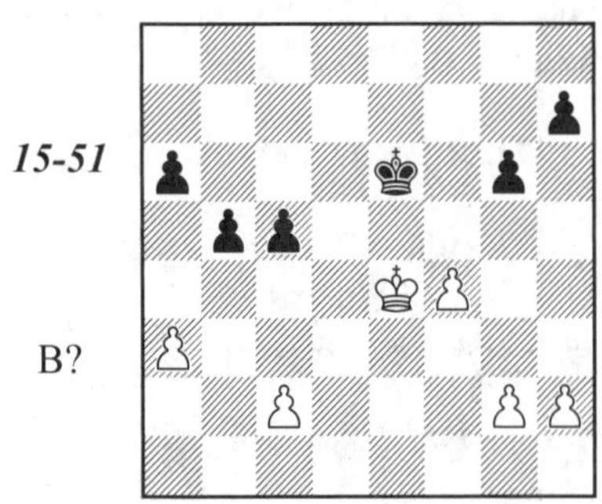

15-51 B?

White's king is more active but still White stands worse. After ...a6-a5-a4 his king will be forced out of the center in view of Black's threat to create a passed pawn.

1...a5?

A technical error – 1...h5! would have been much stronger. By this temporary prevention of g2-g4 (the move White should play in all cases), Black could have gained the decisive tempo: 2 g3 (2 h3 h4–+) 2...a5 3 h3 a4 △ 4...b4–+.

2 g4! a4 (2...b4 3 a4! c4 4 ♔d4 c3 5 ♔c4 ♔d6 6 ♔d4=) **3 ♔d3 b4** (3...♔d5 4 c3 or 4 c4+ bc+ 5 ♔c3) **4 ab??**

An error in return. After 4 c4!! b3 (4...bc 5 ♔×c3=) 5 ♔c3 h5 6 h3 Polgar could have achieved a draw because the black king could not invade White's position.

4...a3 5 ♔c3 cb+ 6 ♔b3 ♔d5 White resigned.

Exercises

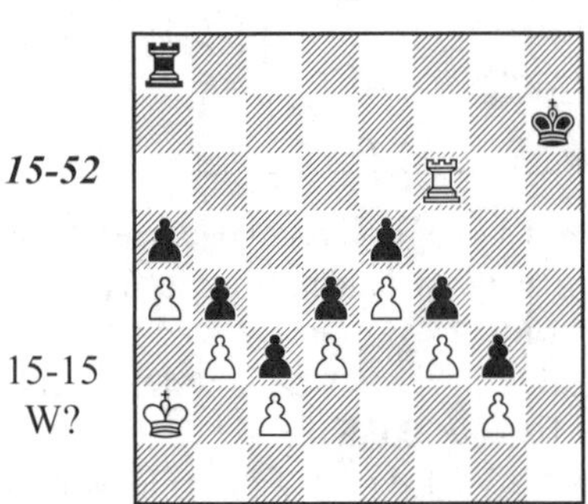

15-52 15-15 W?

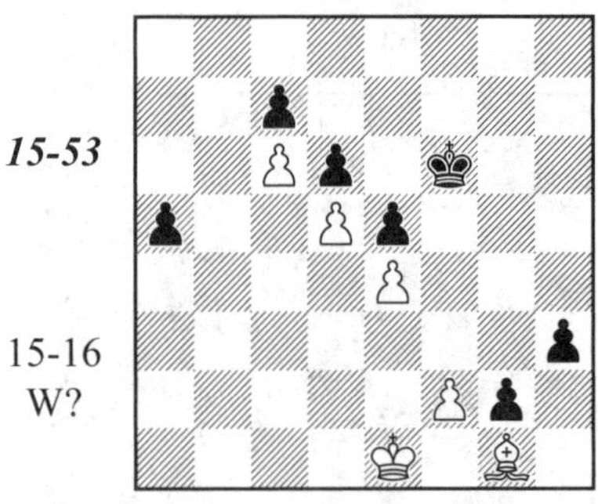

15-53 15-16 W?

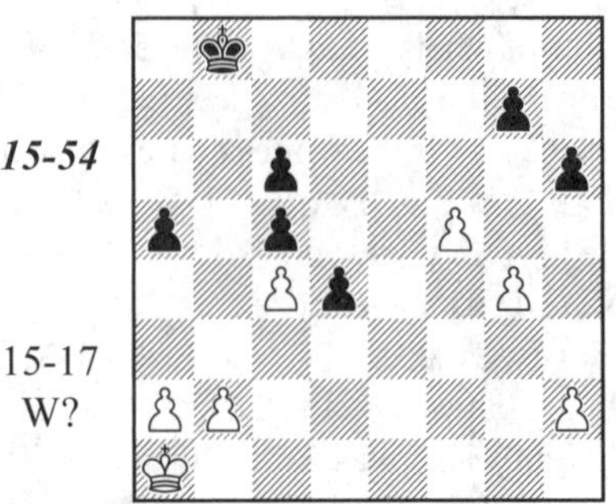

15-54 15-17 W?

An Imprisoned King

Sometimes the hostile king can be "caged" on an edge of the board. Without its participation the remaining pieces may be unable to achieve any success.

V. Smyslov, 1998

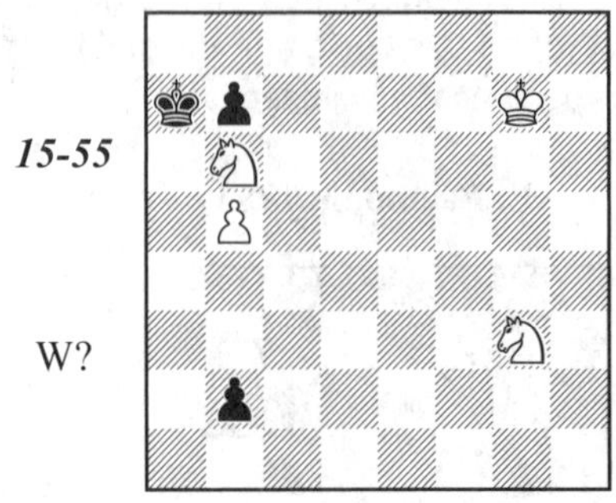

15-55 W?

1 ♘d5! b1♕ 2 b6+ ♔b8

If 2...♔a6 then 3 ♘e2! and 4 ♘ec3=. The black king is locked on a6 and a5, while the queen cannot checkmate alone. Black could have won if he managed to put White in zugzwang by stalemating his king. For example, 3...♕f1 4 ♘ec3 ♕f5 5 ♔h6?? ♕g4 6 ♔h7 ♕g5 7 ♔h8 ♕g6–+, but after 5 ♔g8! he cannot manage this.

The queen is denied of the important f6-square, or after 5...♕d7 6 ♔f8 (6 ♔h8?? ♕f7–+) 6...♔a5 7 ♔g8, the e7-square. 5...♕g6+ also gives nothing: 6 ♔f8! ♕h7 7 ♔e8 ♕g7 8 ♔d8 ♕f7 9 ♔c8=.

3 ♘h5! ♕g1+ 4 ♔f7! ♔c8 5 ♘hf6 ♔d8 6 ♔e6!=

Here again the draw is obvious because the black king cannot leave the edge. After 6 ♔f8? ♕g6!⊙, however, White should have released the king. Zugzwang is the main danger that in all similar situations, but it can be mostly avoided in practice.

Even a knight alone can arrest a king. If Black played his king to a8 on move 2, while the white knight was on d7 and his king on an adjacent square, the second knight would not have been needed.

P. Pechenkin, 1953*

15-56

B

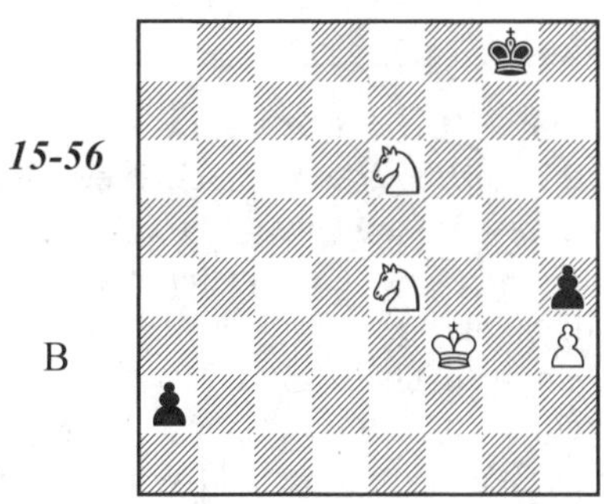

After 1...a1♕ 2 ♘4g5 the black king would have been caged as in the previous example.

1...♔f7!? 2 ♘6g5+ ♔g6

The king is free, but White manages to save himself by creating a fortified camp around his own king.

5 ♔g2! a1♕ 6 ♘f3 ♔f5 7 ♘fd2=

The black king cannot go farther than f4 and e2, while the queen cannot come close enough to the white king to deny him of the free squares in the corner; therefore the draw is inevitable.

Here is another example of this theme, a much more difficult and impressive one.

K. Behting, 1906

15-57

W

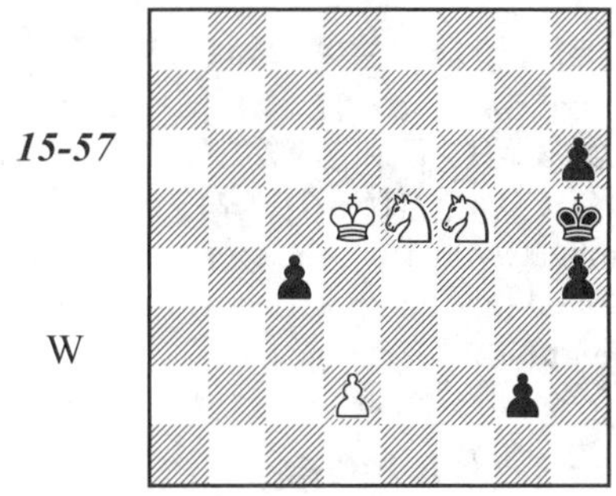

White cannot stop the pawns:

1 ♘f3? h3 2 ♘e3 h2–+;

1 ♘xh4? ♔xh4! 2 ♘f3+ ♔g3 3 ♘g1 h5–+;

1 ♘g7+? ♔g5 2 ♘e6+ ♔f6 3 ♘f3 h3–+.

Hence his only hope is to create a fortress. The process of building it starts with an apparently senseless king move.

1 ♔c6!! g1♕

If 1...h3 (1...♔g5? 2 ♘f3+) then 2 ♘g3+ ♔h4 3 ♘e2 h2 4 ♘f3+ ♔h3 5 ♘xh2 ♔xh2 6 ♔c5 g1♕+ 7 ♘xg1 ♔xg1 8 ♔xc4=.

2 ♘xh4! ♕h1+ (2...♔xh4 3 ♘f3+) **3 ♘hf3=**, and the black king is locked on the edge of the board.

Both 1 ♔xc4? and 1 ♔d6? would have made the plan impossible because Black could give a zwischenschach on move 2, so that his queen was brought away from any knight fork.

Locking in with knights is just one of several methods of immobilizing the hostile king.

Reshevsky – Fischer
Los Angeles m (11) 1961*

15-58

W?

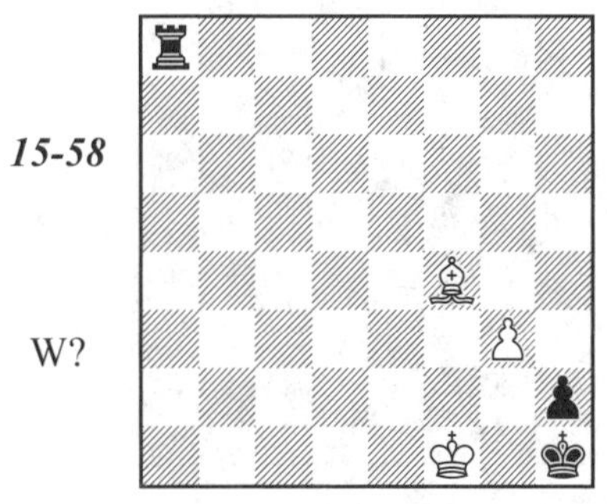

Fischer, in his annotations to the game, wrote that White loses in view of 1 ♔f2 ♖a2+ 2 ♔f1 ♖a3! 3 ♔f2 ♖f3+! 4 ♔xf3 ♔g1 5 ♗e3+ ♔f1–+. However Murey demonstrated a rather simple way to a draw, based on locking in the king.

1 ♗e3!! ♖a1+ 2 ♔f2 ♖a2+ 3 ♔f1! (3 ♔f3?? ♖a3−+) **3...♖a3 4 ♗b6 ♖f3+** (4...♖×g3 5 ♔f2) **5 ♗f2! ♖f7 6 g4 ♖g7 7 ♗b6 ♖×g4 8 ♔f2! ♖g6 9 ♗a7 ♖f6+ 10 ♔g3=**, and the king cannot get away from the corner. Kling and Horwitz found the final position as long ago as the middle of the 19th century.

Exercises

15-59

15-18
W?

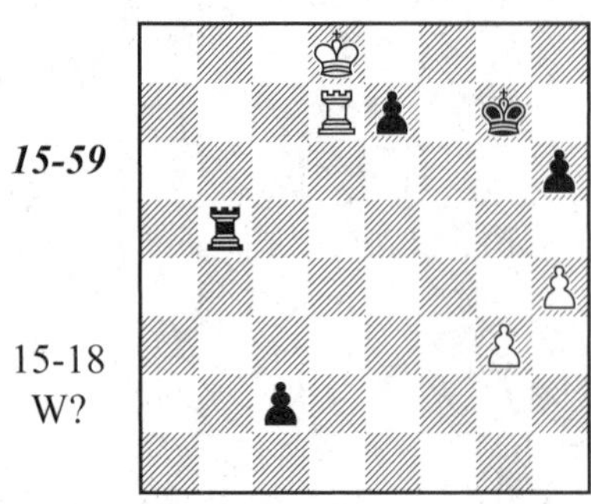

15-60

15-19
W?

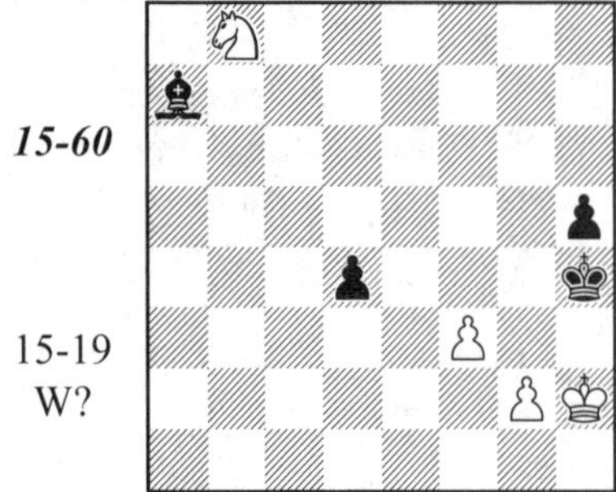

15-61

15-20
W?

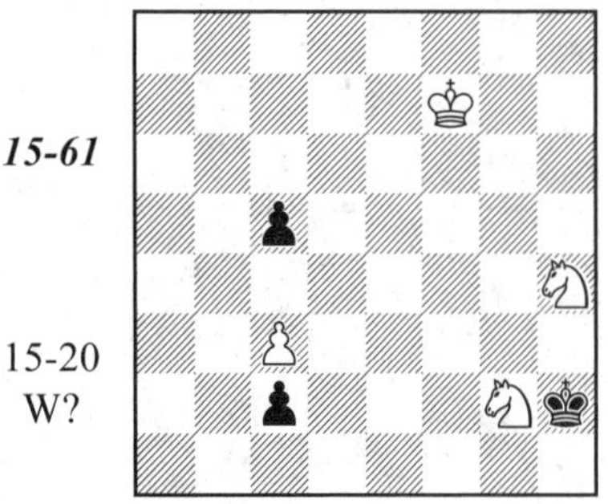

An Imprisoned Piece

Any piece, not just a king, can be "imprisoned."

Chess composers, by the way, use the word "blockade" for such cases. I prefer to avoid it because this word has a different sense when referring to practical chess.

Kobaidze - Tsereteli
USSR 1970

15-62

B

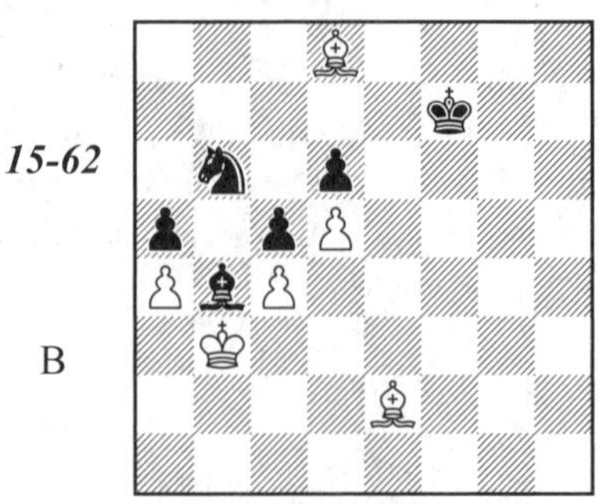

1...♔e8! 2 ♗×b6 ♔e7 Draw.

The white bishop is locked in forever; it can only be given away for a pawn. Without its support, White's king and light-squared bishop are unable to do anything.

In case of 1...♘a8 2 ♗h5+ ♔f8 3 ♔c2 Black would have played ...♘b6! sooner or later anyway, in order to parry the threat of White's king coming to e6.

A. Gurvich, 1952

15-63

W?

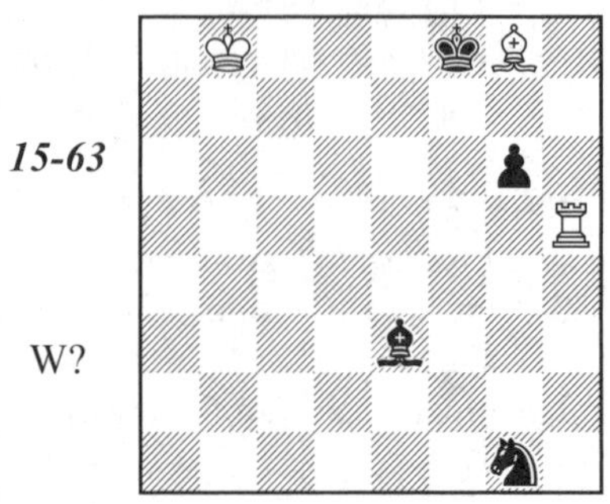

1 ♖h4?! ♔×g8 2 ♖g4 ♔g7 (2...g5? 3 ♔b7 △ 4 ♖g3=) 3 ♔b7! is seemingly strong. If 3...♔f6?, White holds by means of permanently pursuing the bishop: 4 ♖g3 ♗c5 (4...♗f2 5 ♖g2, 4...♗d4 5 ♖g4 ♘f3 6 ♖f4+) 5 ♔c6 ♗a7 6 ♔b7=. But 3...♔h6!! is much stronger: 4 ♖g3 ♗c5! 5 ♔c6 ♗d4! 6 ♖g4 (6 ♔d5 ♗a7−+) 6...♘f3! 7 ♖f4 (without a check!) 7...♘e5+ 8 ♔d5 ♗g1!, and

Black manages to move the pieces away from attacks: 9 ♔×e5 ♗h2–+ or 9 ♖f1 ♗h2 10 ♖h1 ♘g4–+.

The correct method is to keep the bishop rather than the rook, in order to use it for locking in the black knight on g1.

1 ♖h8! ♔g7 2 ♗h7! g5 3 ♗f5!! ♔×h8 4 ♗g4 ♔g7 5 ♔c7 ♔f6 6 ♔d6 ♗c1 7 ♔d5 ♗a3 8 ♔e4(d4) ♔e7 9 ♔d5! ♔d8 10 ♔c6! ♗b4 11 ♔b7! ♔e7 12 ♔c6 ♔f6 13 ♔d5=

Unfortunately for Black his king is also locked, in addition to the knight.

Even as a strong piece as a queen can sometimes be immobilized.

Ree – Hort
Wijk aan Zee 1986

15-64

B?

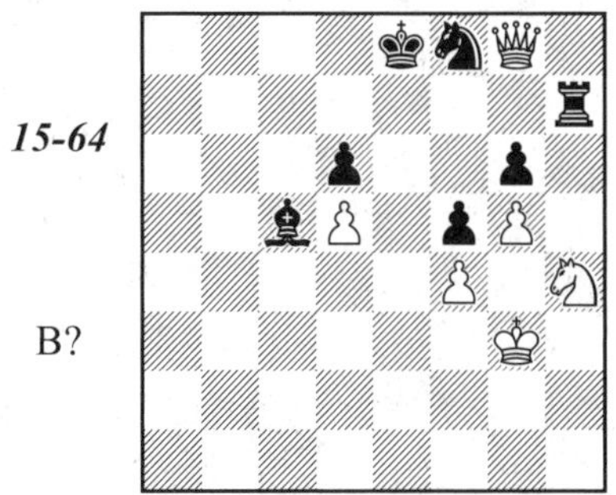

After 1...♗f2+? 2 ♔×f2 ♖×h4 Black is most probably lost: 3 ♔g3 (another possible method is 3 ♕g7!? ♖×f4+ 4 ♔g3 ♖g4+ 5 ♔f3 with the threats 6 ♕f6 and 6 ♕c7) 3...♖h7 4 ♔f3 followed by the king's march to c6.

1...♖×h4!! 2 ♔×h4 ♗d4! 3 ♔g3 ♔e7 4 ♔f3 ♗a1

Draw. The queen has no square to go to.

Exercises

15-65

15-21
W?

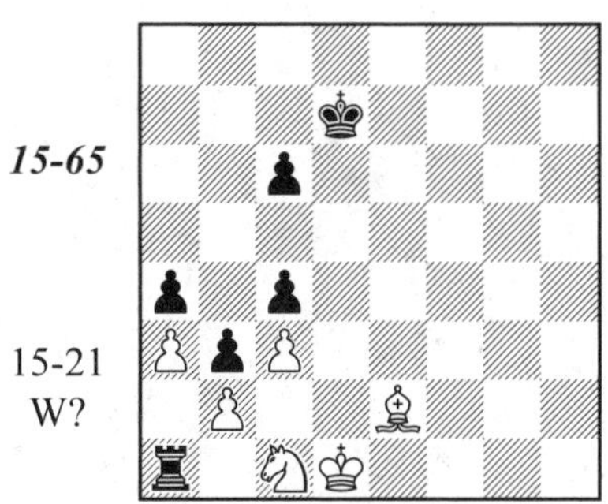

15-66

15-22
W?

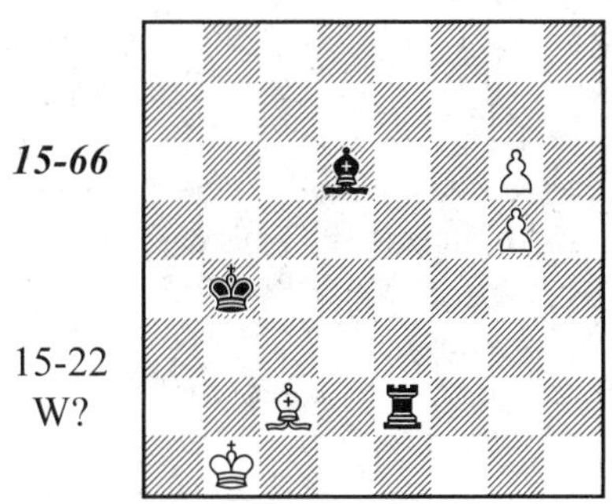

Binding

Utilization of a material advantage can sometimes be impossible because one piece of the stronger side is pinned or must protect an important square (another piece, or pawn).

Deutsche Schachzeitung, 1889

15-67

W

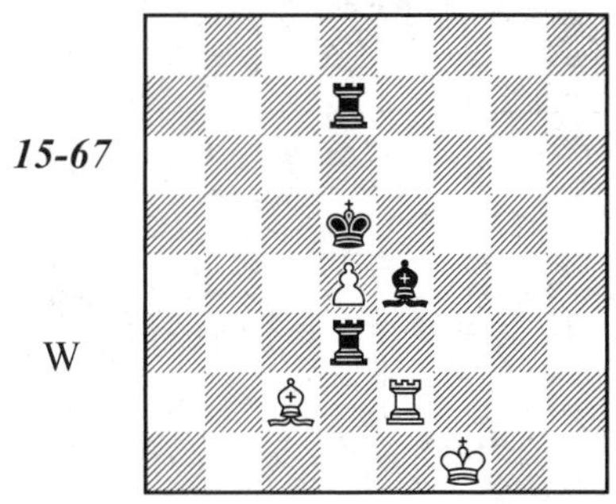

1 ♖×e4! ♔×e4 2 ♔e2 ♖7×d4 3 ♗b1=

One of Black's rooks is pinned; another rook together with the king must protect it. Therefore Black has no win in spite of his huge material advantage.

Vaganian – Georgadze
Erevan zt 1982

15-68

B?

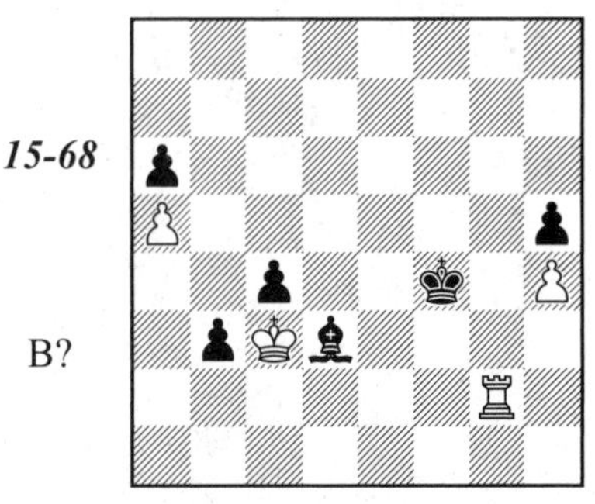

It is not easy for Black to find an acceptable

move. Both 1...♔f3? 2 ♖g5 and 1...♗c2? 2 ♖g5 ♗d1 3 ♖g6 lose a pawn. 1...♔e4? is not much better in view of 2 ♖g5 ♗e2 3 ♖g6 (with the threat 4 ♖×a6 b2 5 ♖b6+−) 3...♗d3 4 ♖h6+−.

Georgadze finds the only good possibility: he drives his king ahead to help his passed pawns.

1...♔e3! 2 ♖g5 b2! 3 ♔×b2 ♔d2 4 ♖c5 (4 ♖g2+ ♗e2) Draw.

After 4...♗e2 White cannot make progress because his rook must watch the passed c-pawn.

In case of 2 ♖g3+ (instead of 2 ♖g5) the simplest reply is 2...♔f4! 3 ♖g5 ♗e2 4 ♖g6 ♗d3=, and White can play neither 5 ♖×a6? b2 nor 5 ♖h6? ♔g4. However 2...♔e2 does not lose, either: 3 ♖g5 ♔d1! (3...b2? 4 ♖g2+) 4 ♖×h5 ♔c1 5 ♖g5 ♗e2 6 ♖g1+ ♗d1 7 ♖g2 ♗f3! (the squares h5 and h2 are mined: 7...♗h5? 8 ♖h2⊙+−) 8 ♖h2 ♗h5⊙=.

Exercises

15-69

15-23
W?

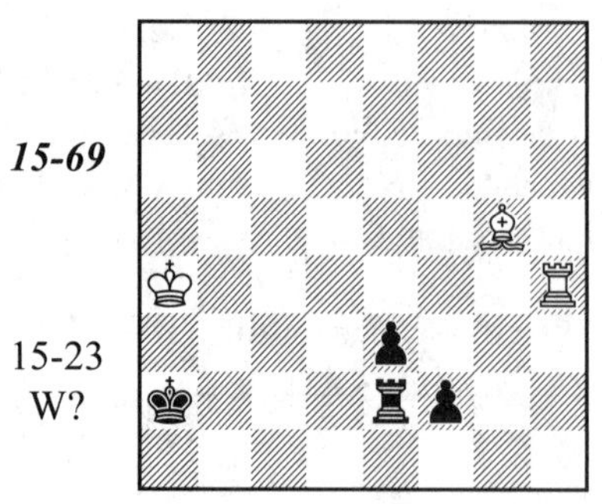

15-70

15-24
W?

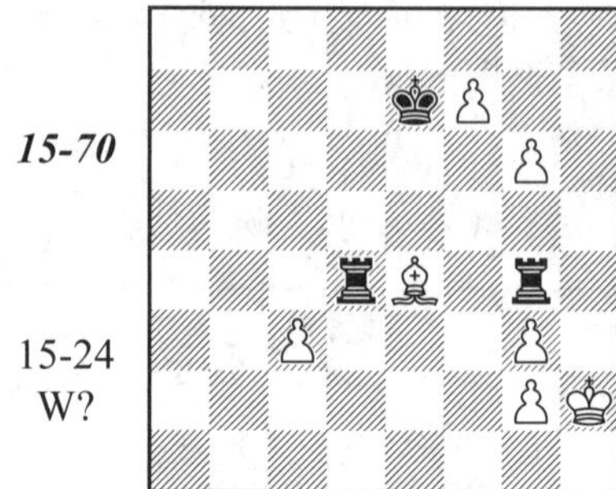

Stalemate

Another important defensive resource, besides building a fortress, is stalemate. It should be taken into account without regard to material balance, as stalemate situations can arise quite suddenly.

Polovodin – S. Ivanov
Leningrad ch 1984

15-71

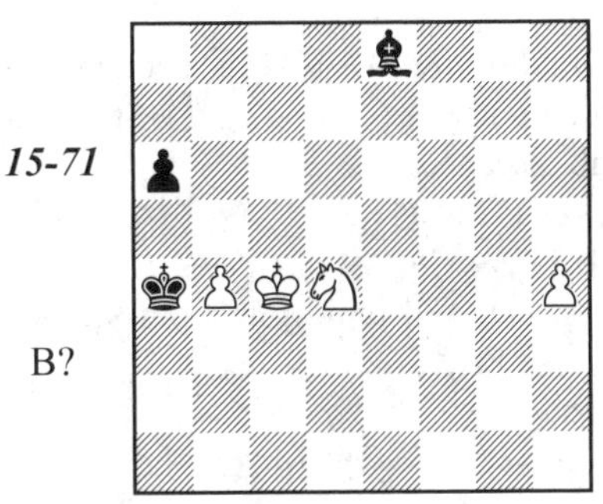

B?

1...a5!!=

Black would have been quite helpless without this resource, for example 1...♗h5? 2 ♔c5 ♗g4 3 ♘c6 ♗e2 4 ♘a5 ♗h5 5 ♘c4 ♔b3 6 ♘b6 △ ♘d5-f6(f4). Now, however, 2 b5 ♗×b5+! 3 ♘×b5 leads to a stalemate and 2 ba ♔×a5 – to a drawn endgame.

V. Smyslov, 2000

15-72

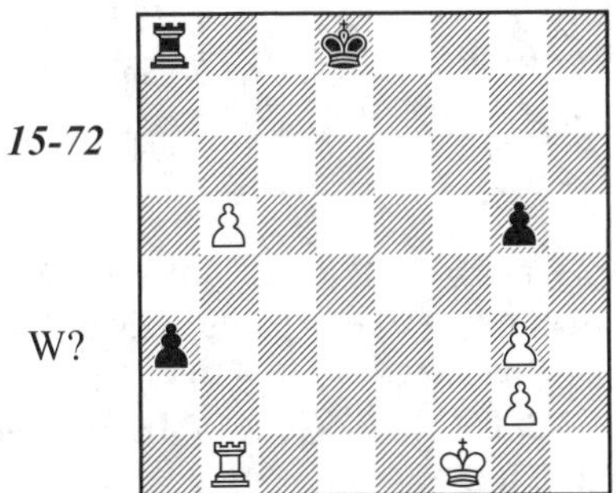

W?

1 ♔e2 looks quite natural, but after 1...♔c7 2 ♔d3 ♔b6 3 ♔c4 (3 ♔e4 ♖a5–+) 3...a2! 4 ♖a1 g4 White is lost (5 ♔b3 ♔×b5 6 ♖×a2 ♖×a2 7 ♔×a2 ♔c4–+).

Playing for a stalemate is his salvation.

1 b6! (the threat 2 b7 forces Black to push his pawn to a2) **1...a2 2 ♖a1 ♔c8 3 g4! ♔b7 4 g3 ♔×b6 5 ♔g2 ♔b5 6 ♔h3 ♔b4 7 ♖×a2!=**.

Goldstein – Shakhnovich
Moscow 1946

15-73

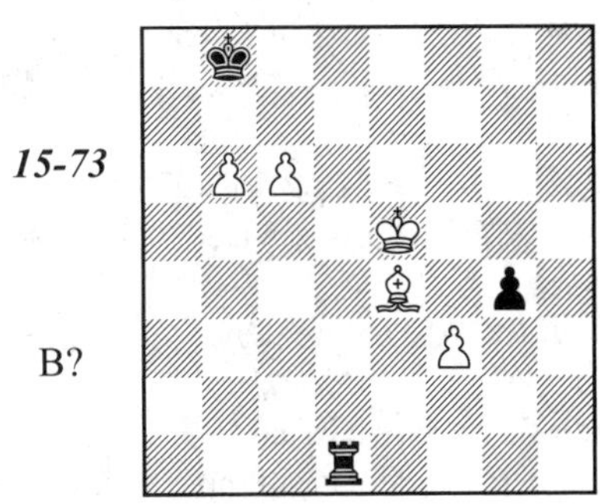

B?

1...gf!

1...g3? is erroneous: 2 c7+ ♔c8 3 ♗f5+ ♖d7 4 ♗h3 g2 5 ♗×g2+–.

2 ♗×f3

If 2 c7+ ♔c8 3 ♗×f3 (3 ♗f5+ ♖d7=) then 3...♖c1 4 ♔d6 ♖c6+!.

2...♖d7!!

Only this nice move holds the game. At first I thought that 2...♖c1 3 ♔d6 ♔c8! is also sufficient for a draw. For example, 4 ♗d5 (4 c7 ♖c6+!) 4...♖c2 5 ♗e6+ ♔b8 6 ♔d7 (6 c7+ ♔b7 7 c8♕+ ♖×c8 8 ♗×c8+ ♔×b6) 6...♖d2+ 7 ♔e7 ♖c2 8 ♔d6 ♖c1 9 ♗d5 ♔c8!, or 4 ♗e2 ♔b8! 5 ♔d7 (5 ♗a6 ♖d1+) 5...♖c2! (5...♖c3? 6 ♗a6) 6 ♗d3 ♖c1!. A reciprocal zugzwang: Black loses if it is his turn to play, but now White is on move.

However grandmaster Karsten Müller found the following winning way for White: 4 ♗g4+ ♔b8 5 ♔d7 ♖c3(c2) 6 ♗f5 ♖c4 (Black must beware of 7 ♗e4; in case of 6...♖c1 7 ♗d3 we have the reciprocal zugzwang position from above, but with Black to play) 7 ♗e6 ♖c5 8 ♗b3⊙. And wherever the rook goes along the c-file, 9 ♗d5 will be decisive.

3 ♔e6 ♖b7!! Draw.

G. Kasparian, 1963

15-74

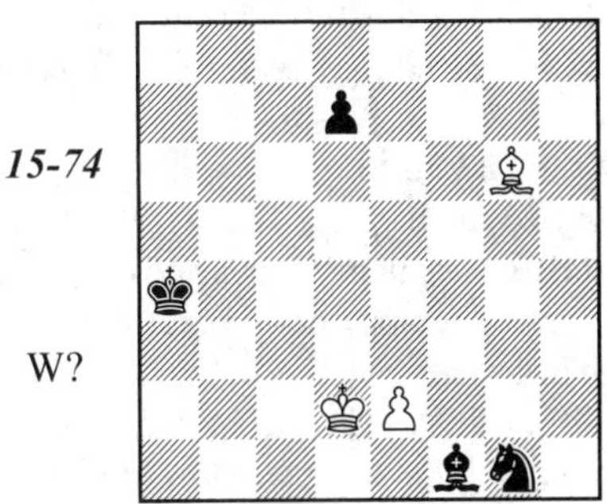

W?

White's attempts to gain any piece back fail: 1 ♔e1? ♗×e2 2 ♔f2 ♘h3+ 3 ♔×e2 ♘f4+ or 2 ♗c2+ ♔b4 3 ♔f2 ♘f3! 4 ♔×e2 ♘d4+. Therefore he chooses another plan: attacking the d-pawn.

1 ♔e3! ♗×e2 (1...♗h3? 2 ♔f2=; 1...♗g2? 2 ♗c2+ and 3 ♔f2=; 1...♘h3? 2 ♗e8=) **2 ♗f5! d6**

Both 2...♗b5 3 ♔f2 ♘e2 4 ♗×d7 and 2...d5 3 ♗e6 ♗c4 4 ♔f2 ♘e2 5 ♗×d5 lead to an immediate draw.

3 ♔d4! (4 ♔d5 is threatened) **3...♗f3 4 ♗e4 ♘e2+**

White's threats are parried (5 ♔d5? ♘c3+), but an unexpected stalemate in the center of the board saves him now:

5 ♔c4!! ♗×e4 Stalemate.

Or 5...♗h5 6 ♗c6(c2)+ and 7 ♔d5=.

A situation can arise when the defender has only one mobile piece, and if it can be sacrificed, a stalemate occurs. Even though the opponent rejects the Greek gift, "***the desperado***" continually offers itself for capture.

To escape from the pursuit of a "desperado queen" is almost impossible. With a rook in the "desperado" role, everything depends on the specific circumstances.

A. Frolovsky, 1989

15-75

W?/Play

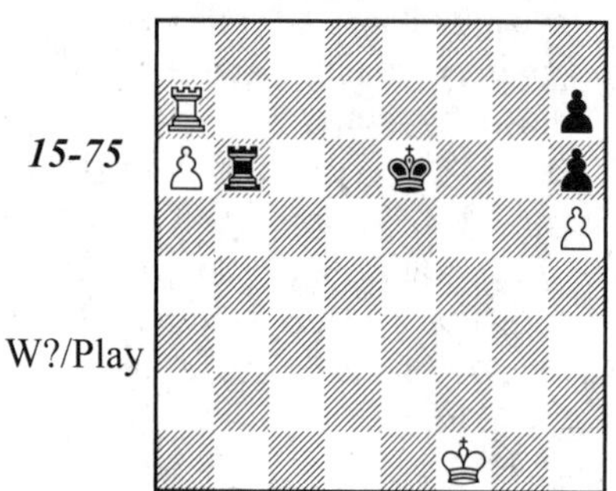

1 ♖a8!

1 ♖×h7? ♔f5 2 a7 ♖a6 leads to a draw. It seems now that Black may well resign in view of the threat 2 a7.

1...♖b1+ 2 ♔g2!!

This move can be played only if White has discovered Black's stalemate idea and evaluated it well enough. The apparently natural 2 ♔e2? misses a win because of 2...♖a1 3 a7 ♔f6!! 4 ♖f8+ ♔g7 5 a8♕ ♖e1+! (a desperado rook) 6 ♔f2 (6 ♔d2 ♖d1+) 6...♖f1+ 7 ♔g2 ♖f2+! (7...♖×f8!? is also good enough for a draw) 8 ♔g3 ♖f3+ 9 ♔g4 ♖f4+.

2...♖a1 3 a7 ♖a2+

After 3...♔f6 4 ♖f8+ ♔g7 5 a8♕ the desperado rook is curbed immediately: 5...♖g1+ 6 ♔h2!, and there are no checks anymore, because the queen keeps the squares g2 and h1 under control.

4 ♔g3! ♖a3+ 5 ♔f4 ♖a4+ 6 ♔e3 ♖a3+ (6...♔f6 7 ♖f8+ ♔g7 8 a8♕ ♖a3+ 9 ♔f4! +−) **7 ♔d4!**

The final subtlety. 7 ♔d2? is erroneous: after 7...♔f6! 8 ♖f8+ ♔g7 9 a8♕ ♖d3+! the white king cannot escape.

7...♔f6 (7...♖a4+ 8 ♔c5 ♔f6 9 ♔b6 ♖b4+ 10 ♔a5) **8 ♖f8+ ♔g7 9 a8♕ +−**

The checks will rapidly run out 9...♖d3+ 10 ♔e5 ♖e3+ 11 ♔f4.

In practical chess, the rook is the most frequent kind of desperado, but other pieces can also play the role.

H. Weenink, 1918

15-76

W?

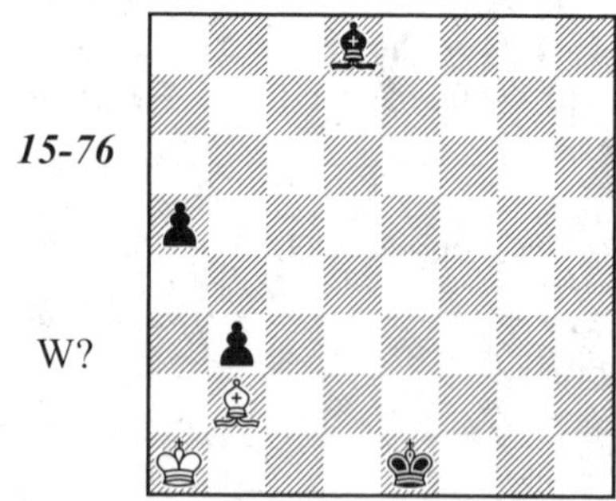

1 ♗c3+ ♔d1 (1...♔e2? 2 ♗×a5=) **2 ♔b1!**
2 ♗×a5? fails to 2...♔c2−+, while after 2 ♔b2? Black wins by means of 2...a4 3 ♔a3 ♔c2.

2...a4 3 ♗f6! ♗c7 4 ♗e5! ♗b6 5 ♗d4! ♗a5! 6 ♗c3! a3!

The only possible attempt to avoid a stalemate or a permanent pursuit.

7 ♗×a5 a2+ 8 ♔a1!

8 ♔b2? loses to 8...a1♕+! 9 ♔×a1 ♔c2 10 ♗c3 ♔×c3.

8...♔c2 9 ♗c3! ♔×c3 Stalemate.

Tragicomedies

Trabattoni – Barlov
La Valetta 1979

15-77

W?

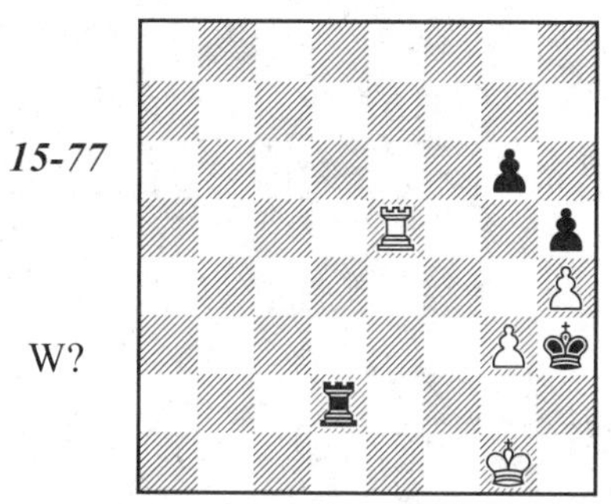

A simple stalemate combination could have led to a draw: 1 ♖e6! ♖g2+ 2 ♔h1 ♖×g3 3 ♖×g6!. White played **1 ♖g5?** with the same idea, but after **1...♖g2+ 2 ♔h1 ♖f2! 3 ♔g1 ♖f6!**, instead of the desired stalemate, a reciprocal zugzwang arose.

4 ♖a5 ♖f3 5 g4 ♖g3+ 6 ♔h1 ♔×g4 7 ♖a4+ ♔h3 White resigned.

Zapata – Vaganian
Thessaloniki ol 1984

15-78

B?

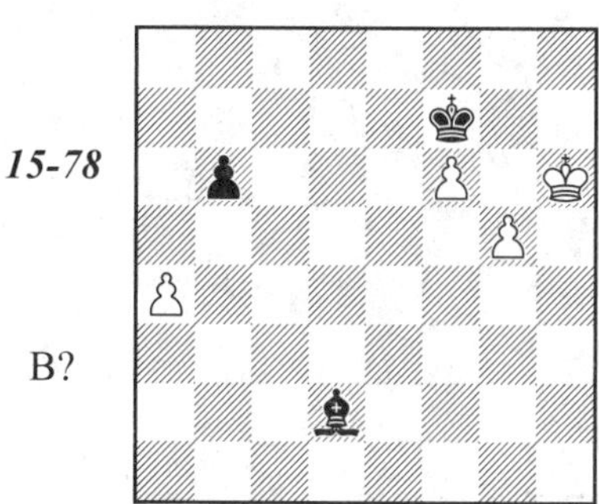

1...♗c3?

As Vaganian demonstrated the waiting move 1...♗c1! wins for Black. The main line is then 2 ♔h5 ♗b2 3 ♔g4 (3 ♔h6 ♗×f6–+) 3...♔g6 4 ♔f4 ♗c1+ 5 ♔e5 ♗×g5 6 ♔d6 ♗d2! 7 ♔e7 (7 ♔c6 ♗a5) 7...♗b4+ 8 ♔e6 ♗c3 9 f7 ♗b4!–+ (rather than 9...♔g7? 10 ♔e7 ♗b4+ 11 ♔e8⊙ ♗c5 12 ♔d7 ♔×f7 13 ♔c6=).

Another winning continuation is 1...♗e3 2 ♔h5 ♗c1 (in case of 2...♗d4? 3 ♔g4 ♔g6 4 ♔f4 Black's bishop is placed too close to the white king) 3 ♔h6 ♗d2! (the bishop will occupy the optimal b4-square because of this triangular maneuver) 4 ♔h5 ♗c3 5 ♔g4 ♔g6 6 ♔f4 ♗b4!? (after 6...♗d2+ 7 ♔e5 ♗×g5 we transpose to the Vaganian line) 7 ♔e5 (7 ♔g4 ♗d2⊙) 7...♔×g5 8 f7 ♔g6 9 ♔e6 ♔g7 10 ♔d7 ♔×f7 11 ♔c6 ♗a5–+ (Inarkiev).

2 a5??

White misses the saving resource: 2 g6+! ♔×f6 3 a5! ba 4 g7 ♔f7 5 ♔h7 ♗×g7=. Zapata has hit on the stalemate idea but the transposition of moves is fatal for him.

2...ba 3 g6+ ♔g8! White resigned.

Another tragicomical incident happened in the same Greek town four years later.

Hickl – Solomon
Thessaloniki ol 1988

15-79

W?

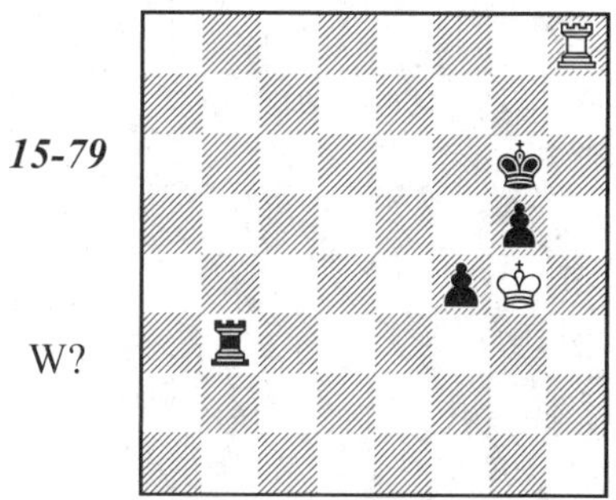

1 ♖g8+ ♔f6 2 ♖f8+??

2 ♖g6+! led to a stalemate; the spectators saw this possibility, but the players overlooked it.

The game was adjourned here. An elementary win was possible after 2...♔e7 or 2...♔g7, but Black decided to repeat moves to be "on the safe side" and sealed **2...♔g6??**.

The captain of the Australian team ordered his player Solomon, to look satisfied, to go back to the hotel immediately, and to stay silent. Hickl did not suspect that his opponent could have sealed such a move and did not want to return for a hopeless resumption, so he resigned the next morning at breakfast.

Many cases of miraculous salvation through stalemate can be mentioned. I want to add just one more.

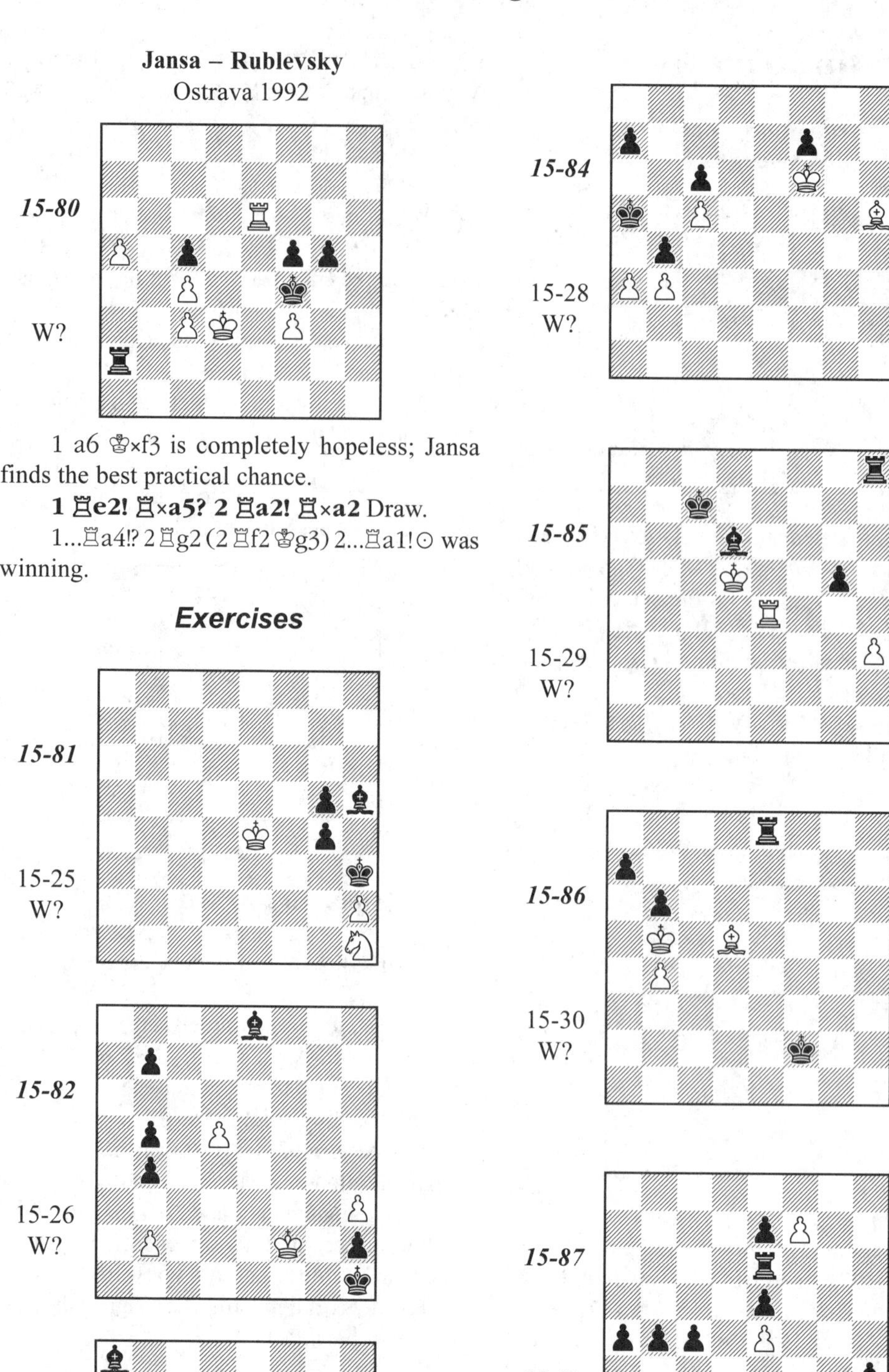

Jansa – Rublevsky
Ostrava 1992

15-80

W?

1 a6 ♔×f3 is completely hopeless; Jansa finds the best practical chance.

1 ♖e2! ♖×a5? 2 ♖a2! ♖×a2 Draw.

1...♖a4!? 2 ♖g2 (2 ♖f2 ♔g3) 2...♖a1!⊙ was winning.

Exercises

15-81

15-25
W?

15-82

15-26
W?

15-83

15-27
W?

15-84

15-28
W?

15-85

15-29
W?

15-86

15-30
W?

15-87

15-31
W?/Play

Checkmate

The aim of chess is checkmate. But a mating net can hardly be made when only a few pieces remain on the board. First one should obtain a considerable advantage by means of a pawn promotion. Therefore, as has been mentioned already, creation and advance of passed pawns is the main theme of endgames.

However king attacks are possible in endgames, too. They happen relatively seldom but are almost always sudden, because our thoughts are occupied with other topics and mate threats can be easily overlooked.

Simagin – Bronstein
Moscow ch 1947

15-88

B

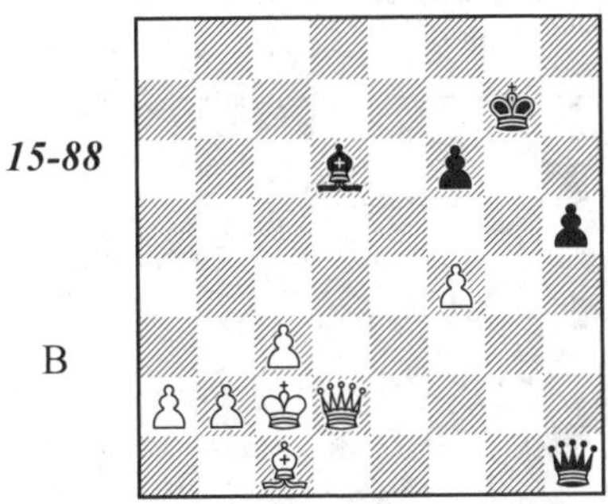

1...♕e4+ 2 ♔d3 ♕g2+ would have led to an easy draw. However, Bronstein decided to force a draw by means of a bishop sacrifice in order to rapidly advance his passed pawn.

1...h4? 2 ♕×d6 ♕g2+ 3 ♔b3 h3 4 ♕d7+! ♔g8 (4...♔g6 5 f5+ ♔h5 6 ♗f4+–) **5 f5 h2**

It might well seem that White can only give perpetual check. These illusions were dispelled by the following pretty stroke.

6 ♗g5!! h1♕

If 6...fg then 7 f6 with an inevitable mate; after 6...♕×g5 7 ♕c8+ ♔g7 8 ♕c7+ the h-pawn is lost.

7 ♕e8+ ♔g7 8 ♕g6+ ♔f8 9 ♕×f6+ ♔g8 10 ♕d8+ ♔g7 11 ♕e7+

Another way to a mate was 11 ♗f6+ ♔f7 12 ♕e7+ ♔g8 13 ♕e8+ ♔h7 14 ♕h8#.

11...♔g8 12 ♕e8+

Black resigned on account of 12...♔h7 13 ♕g6+ ♔h8 14 ♗f6# or 12...♔g7 13 f6+ ♔h7 14 ♕f7+ ♔h8 15 ♕g7#.

The queen is a powerful piece, so it is no wonder that its presence on the board is often dangerous for the hostile king. But a mating net can also sometimes be achieved with more modest forces.

Moldoyarov – Samochanov
cr 1974

15-89

W?

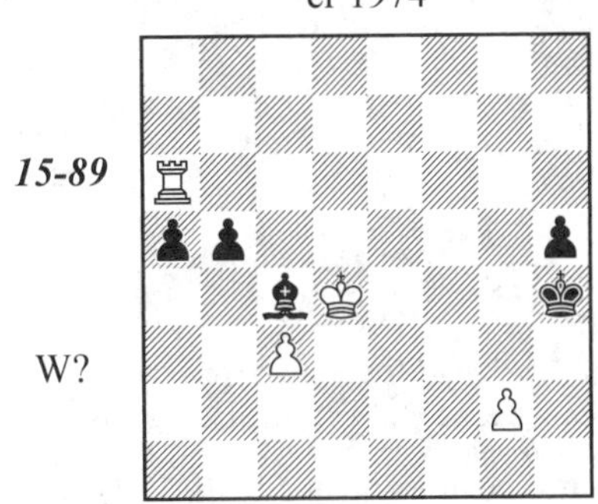

1 ♖g6!

White plays for a mate. 1 ♖×a5? ♔g3 leads to a draw.

1...a4 2 ♔e3 a3 3 ♔f4 a2 4 ♖g3! ♗e6 5 ♖h3+! ♗×h3 6 g3#.

S. Kaminer, 1925

15-90

W?

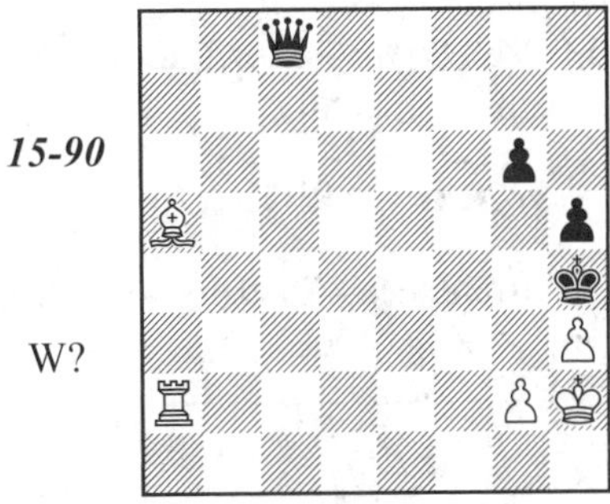

Unlike the previous examples, here one feels that the black king is in danger. Paradoxically, White must immediately give up his strongest fighting unit to successfully conduct the attack.

1 ♖c2!! ♕×c2

Black must accept the sacrifice. If 1...♕b8+ then 2 ♗c7 ♕f8 3 ♖c5! ♕×c5 4 ♗d8+ and 5 g3#. 1...♕f8 2 ♖c4+ ♔g5 3 ♗d2+ ♔f6 4 ♖f4+ is also bad. Other queen retreats are met with 2 ♖c5, cutting off the king's escape.

2 ♗d8+ g5 3 ♗a5!

An amazing position: a bishop proves stronger than a queen. 4 ♗e1+ is threatened. Black will be checkmated immediately in case of 3...g4

4 ♗d8# or 3...♕d1 4 g3#, while after 3...♕f2 4 ♗c7 he is put in zugzwang.

3...♕e2 4 ♗c7! (△ ♗g3#) **4...♕f2 5 ♗d6!**⊙ (rather than 5 ♗e5? g4) **5...♕f4+ 6 g3+! ♕×g3+ 7 ♗×g3#**.

L. Kubbel, 1940

15-91

W?

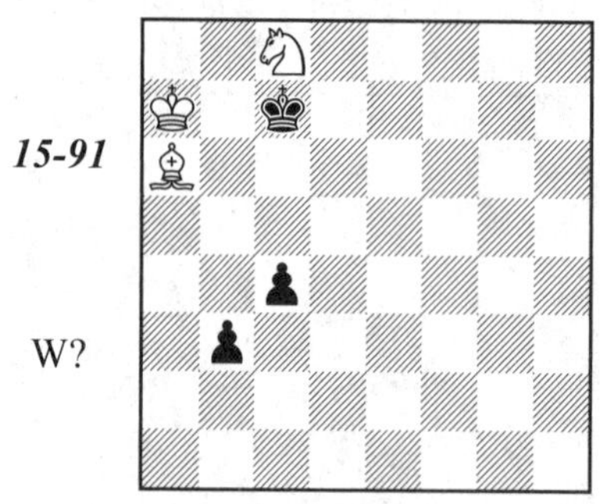

Does this position belong here? Is there any semblance of mating ideas, or is the only question whether White can safely block the black pawns? Let us see:

1 ♘b6 b2 2 ♘d5+ ♔d6 3 ♘c3 ♔c5 4 ♘b1! ♔b4 (if 4...♔d4 then 5 ♗c8! c3 6 ♗f5+– – a barrier) **5 ♔b6 c3**

Both 5...♔b3 6 ♗c8 ♔c2 7 ♗f5+ and 6...c3 7 ♔b5 are no better.

6 ♗d3 ♔b3 7 ♔b5 c2 8 ♗c4#

It is checkmate after all!

Tragicomedies

Pilskalniece – Berzinš
Riga 1962

15-92

B

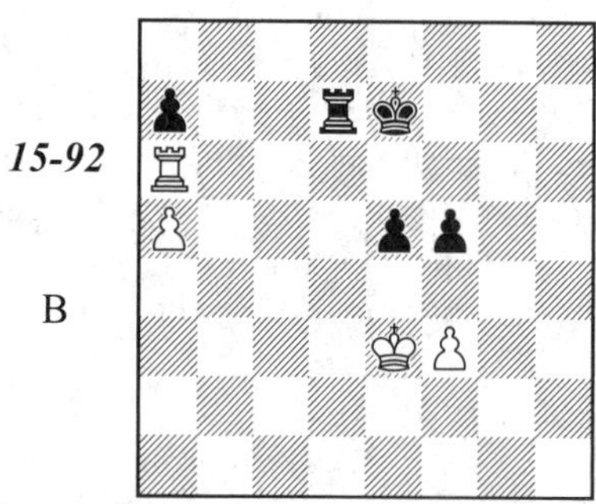

The position is drawish; the extra pawn has no influence because of the activity of White's rook.

1...f4+!? 2 ♔e4??

Black's rather primitive trap is successful. White could have held the balance after 2 ♔e2!.

2...♖d6!

White resigned. After 3 ♖×a7+ ♔e6 the mate 4...♖d4# can be postponed only by means of a rook sacrifice. The pawn endgame is hopeless: 3 ♖×d6 ♔×d6 4 a6 ♔e6 5 ♔d3 ♔d5⊙ 6 ♔c3 (6 ♔e2 ♔c4) 6...e4.

Exercises

15-93

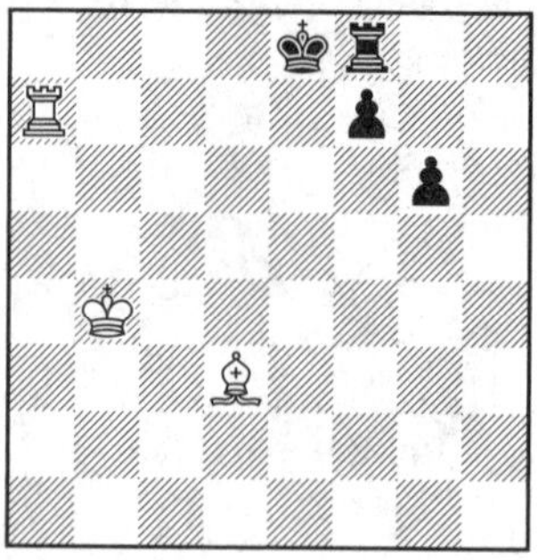

15-32
W?

15-94

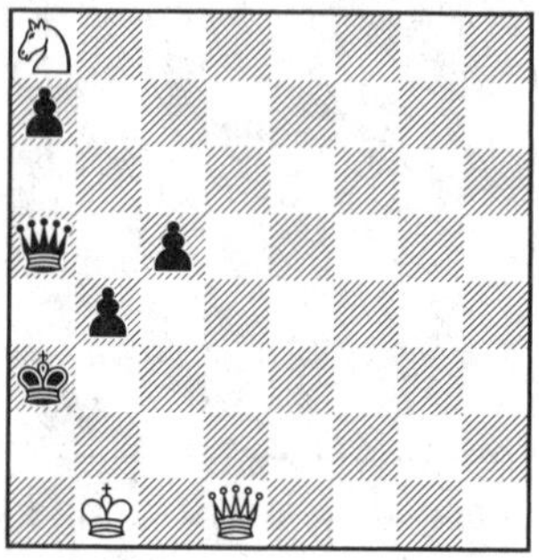

15-33
W?

15-95

15-34
W?

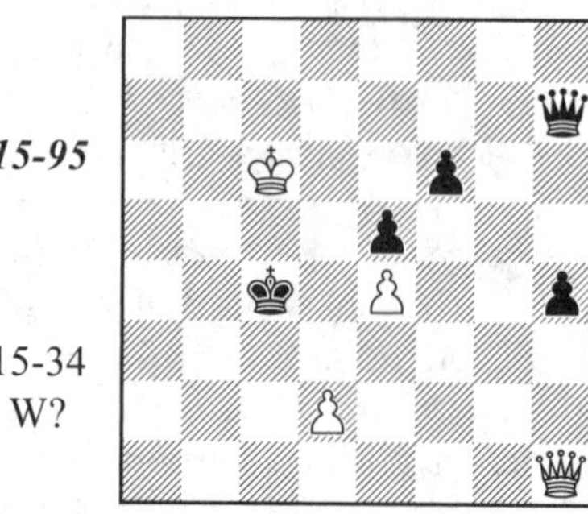

15-96

15-35
W?

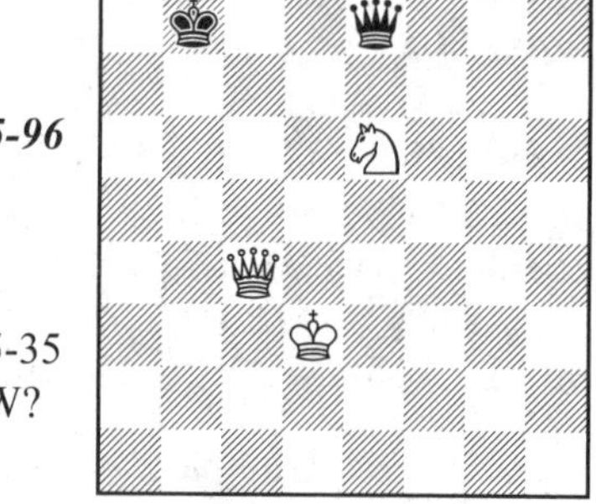

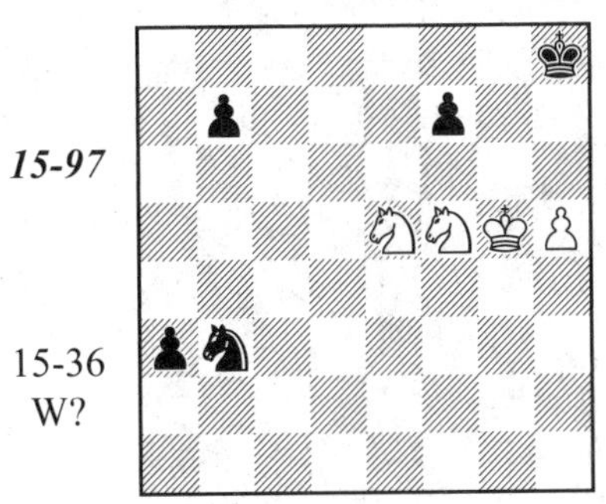

15-97

15-36
W?

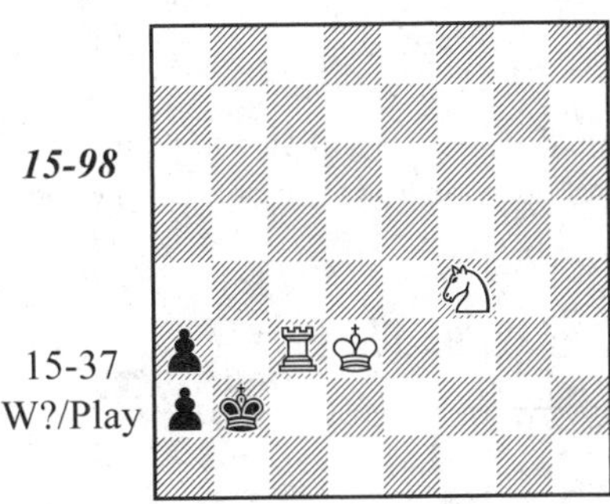

15-98

15-37
W?/Play

Domination

We use the word "domination" to name the technique that involves trapping an enemy piece by taking control of all of its flight squares. This method is applicable not only in endgames. Botvinnik was of the opinion that a clever play for domination, in all stages of the game, is a characteristic feature of the chess style of the 12th World Champion Anatoly Karpov.

Domination can be implemented in many ways. One can catch and eliminate an enemy piece or simply deprive it of all moves. Sometimes one can just make important squares inaccessible to certain pieces in order to prevent their interference in the main events on the board.

Please visualize some endgames with an extra exchange: catching a lonely knight when it is separated from its king, or a win with a rook versus a bishop when a king is in a dangerous corner, or the Elkies position (diagram 11-20).

Perhaps a knight is caught the most often because it is the least mobile piece.

Al. Kuznetsov, 1955

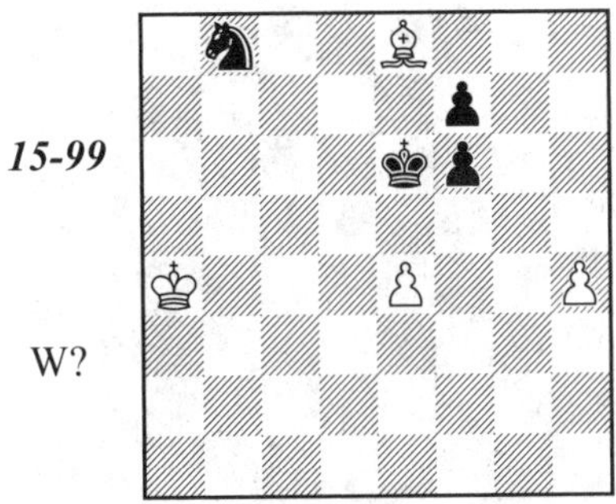

15-99

W?

1 h5 f5 2 h6 ♔f6 3 ef ♘a6 4 ♔b5!
To prevent liberation of the knight, White must sacrifice his bishop.

4...♘c7+ 5 ♔c5!

After 5 ♔c6? ♘×e8 (a reciprocal zugzwang) 6 ♔d7 Black holds: 6...♔×f5! 7 h7 ♘f6+. White must lose a tempo in order to get the same position with Black to move.

5...♘×e8

5...♘a6+ 6 ♔c4 ♘c7 7 ♗c6 ♘a6 8 ♔b5 ♘c7+ 9 ♔b6 ♘e6 10 fe fe 11 ♗e8! e5 12 ♔c5+–.

6 ♔c6⊙ +–.

The cases when weaker pieces dominate stronger ones are, of course, the most impressive.

J. Sulz, 1941

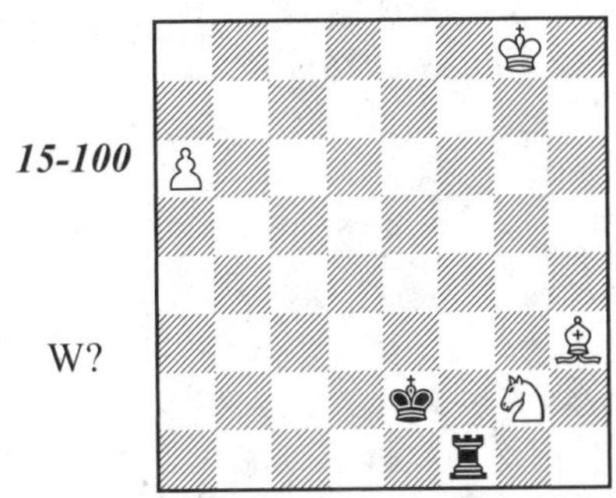

15-100

W?

White cannot win by "normal" means because Black attacks the a-pawn with his rook and king in time. For example, 1 ♗c8? ♔d3 2 ♗b7 ♖a1 3 ♘f4+ ♔c4=, or 1 ♗d7? ♖a1 2 ♗b5+ ♔f3 3 ♘h4+ ♔e4=, or 1 ♘h4? ♖a1 2 ♗c8 ♔d3 3 ♘f5 ♔c4=.

1 ♘f4+!! ♖×f4 2 ♗d7!+–

A striking situation: all paths to the a-file and to the 8th rank are closed for the rook on an open board (2...♖f3 3 ♗g4; 2...♖f1 3 ♗b5+; 3...♖f6 3 a7 ♖a6 4 ♗b5+).

An equally sudden and striking capture of a rook on an open board is the point of the next study:

Y. Bazlov, 1997

15-101

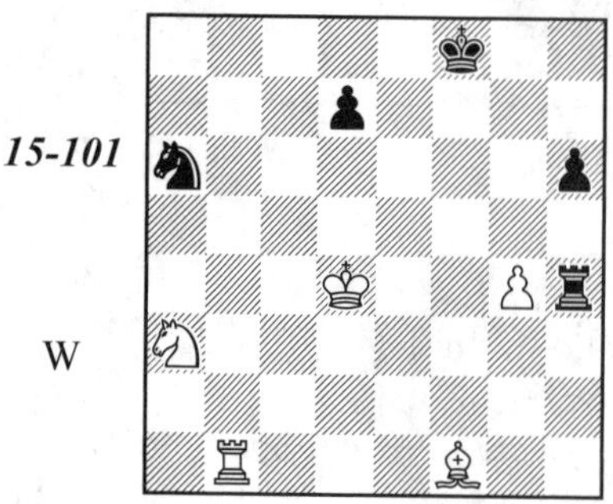

W

1 ♗e2!

1 ♗×a6? ♖×g4+ and 2...♖a4 is an immediate draw.

1...h5 2 ♔e5! hg

Again, 3 ♗×a6? enables Black to gain the piece back: 3...♖h5+ and 4...♖a5. Of course, White may try to do without capturing on a6 and proceed with 3 pieces against 2. Nobody has analyzed such positions seriously, but some (though not many) practical examples confirm that winning chances exist. However, White has a more forceful method at his disposal.

3 ♖f1+! ♔e7 4 ♗×a6 d6+! (4...♖h5+? 5 ♖f5+–) **5 ♔d4! g3+ 6 ♔c3! ♖a4**

15-102

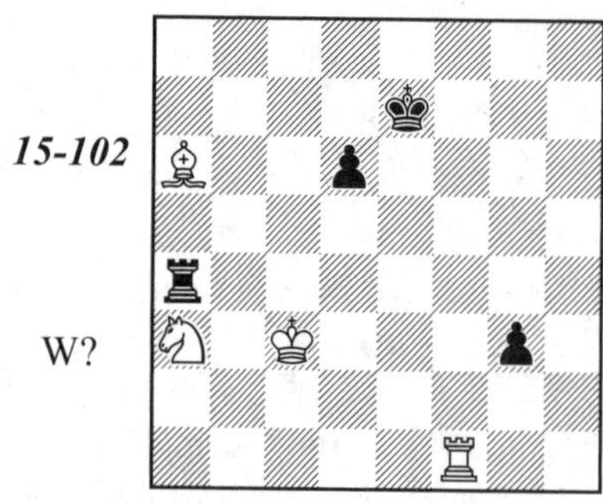

W?

7 ♘c2!! ♖×a6 8 ♘b4!

The rook has no refuge from knight forks.

8...♖a3+ (8...♖a8 9 ♘d5+) **9 ♔b2! ♖a4** (9...g2 10 ♖e1+) **10 ♔b3 ♖a8 11 ♘d5+**, and the rook is lost.

Even a queen can sometimes be caught.

L. Kubbel, 1914

15-103

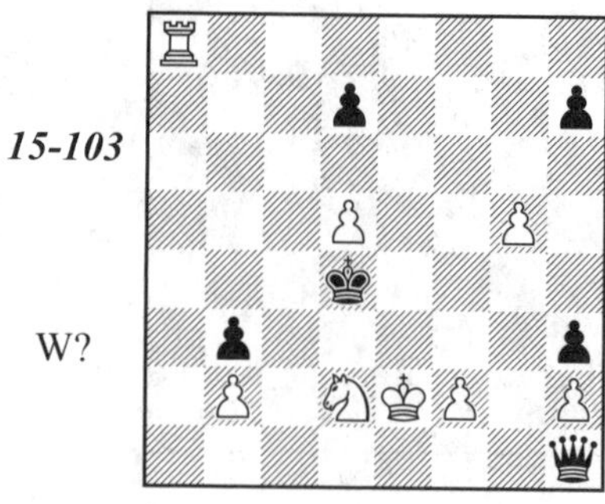

W?

1 g6! (1 ♖a1? ♕g2!) **1...hg** (1...♕g2 2 gh ♕g4+ 3 ♘f3+) **2 ♖a1! ♕g2**

Here and later on the rook cannot be captured in view of a knight fork with loss of the queen. In case of 2...♕×d5 the queen will be lost after 3 ♖a4+ ♔e5 4 ♖a5!. But now the same mechanism works on the kingside.

3 ♖g1! ♕×d5 4 ♖g4+ ♔c5 5 ♖g5!+–.

Y. Afek, 1997

15-104

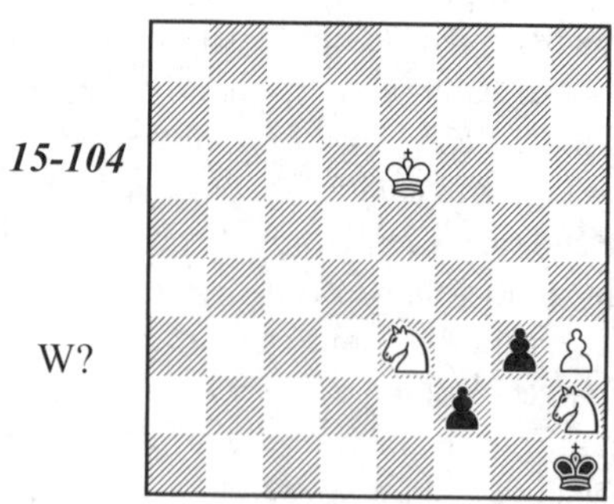

W?

After 1 ♘hg4? Black holds by means of 1...f1♕! 2 ♘×f1 ♔g2! 3 h4 ♔×f1 4 h5 ♔e2! 5 h6 g2=.

1 ♘hf1! g2 2 h4!! g1♕ 3 ♔f7!⊙ +–.

Exercises

15-105

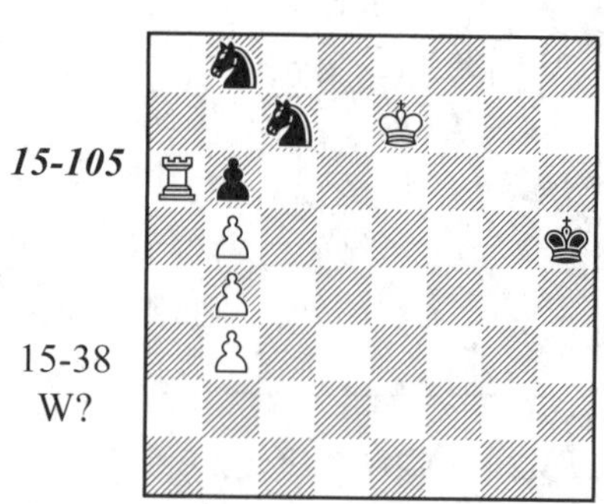

15-38
W?

15-106

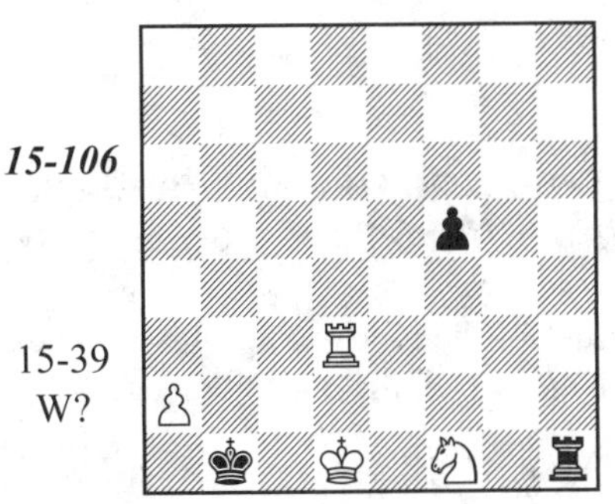

15-39
W?

15-108

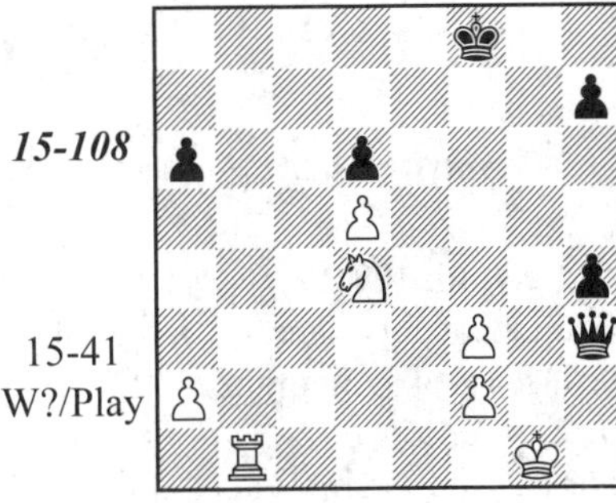

15-41
W?/Play

15-107

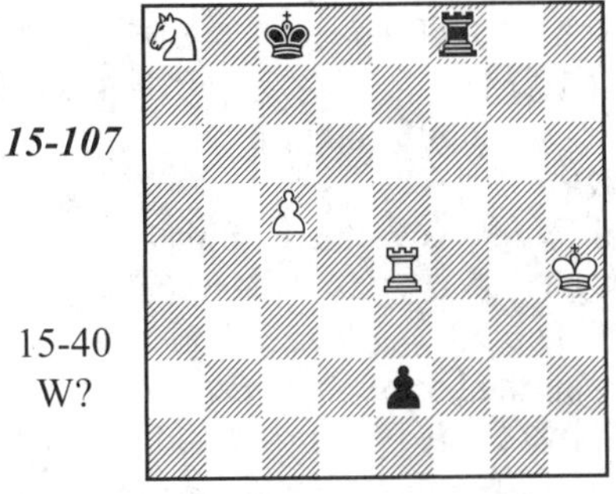

15-40
W?

15-109

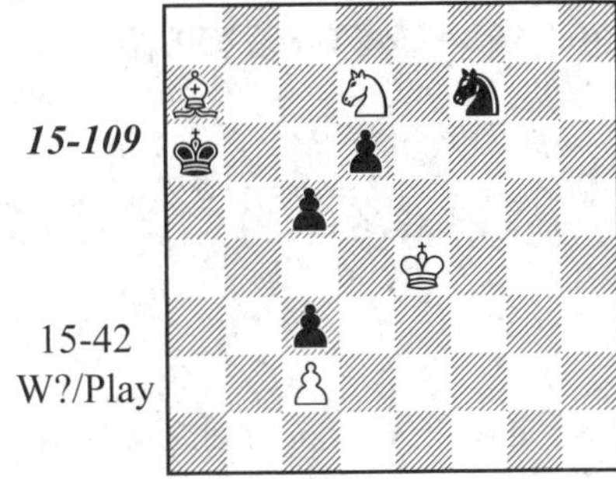

15-42
W?/Play

Chapter 16

SOLUTIONS

Chapter One

1/1. C. Salvioli, 1887

The solution of this exercise is based on the ideas we discussed at diagram 1-7.

1...b4! 2 c4 b3!

2...♔a5? loses to 3 ♔b3 ♔a6 4 ♔xb4 ♔a7 5 ♔b5 ♔b7 6 a3! ♔c7 7 ♔a6 ♔c6 8 a4! ♔c7 9 ♔a7 ♔c6 10 ♔b8!.

3 a3 (3 ab+ ♔b4 and 4...b5=) **3...♔a5 4 ♔xb3 ♔a6 5 ♔b4 ♔a7! 6 ♔b5 ♔b7**

Here White has only one spare tempo while in the line 2...♔a5? he had two.

7 a4 ♔c7 (7...♔a7?? 8 a5+−) **8 ♔a6 ♔c6 9 ♔a7 ♔c7! 10 ♔a8 ♔c8=**.

1/2. H. Weenink, 1924

1 ♔e4 ♔g4

How should White continue? If he managed to pass the move to his opponent he could force a favorable pawn exchange on the kingside (2...♔g5 3 ♔e5 ♔g4 4 ♔f6! etc.). But how can this be done? 2 ♔e5 is useless: 2...♔g5! (2...♔g3? 3 ♔f5) 3 ♔d4 ♔h4!. The only chance is to threaten the b5-pawn!

2 ♔d5! ♔h5! (2...♔f5 3 ♔d4 and Black loses the opposition) **3 ♔c6!**

After 3 ♔c5 ♔g5! Black still maintains the opposition, while capture of the pawn leads to a draw: 4 ♔xb5? ♔g4 5 ♔c5 ♔g3 6 b5 ♔xg2 7 b6 f3=. But what can Black do now? To maintain the opposition, 3...♔g6 is required, but the king is too far from the g2-pawn then and 4 ♔xb5 wins. Otherwise White seizes his coveted opposition and then transforms the distant opposition into the close one by standard means (an outflanking).

3...♔g5 4 ♔c5! ♔g4 5 ♔d6! ♔h5 6 ♔d5! ♔h4 7 ♔e6 ♔g5 8 ♔e5 ♔g4 9 ♔f6 ♔g3 10 ♔f5+−.

1/3. E. Somov-Nasimovich, 1936

1 ♔g3!

1 ♔g1? is erroneous in view of 1...♗b6 2 ♖h5+ ♔g6 3 ♖h2 ♖xf2 4 ♖xf2 a5 5 ♔f1 ♗xf2 6 ♔xf2 a4−+. Now 1...♗b6 can be met with 2 ♘d3!.

1...♖xf2! 2 ♖h5+! ♔g6 3 ♖d5 ♗b6 4 ♖d6+ ♔f5 5 ♖xb6 ♖xf3+! 6 ♔g2!! ab 7 ♔xf3=

Because of the pretty tempo-loss on move six, White has seized the opposition.

1/4. N. Grigoriev, 1933

1 ♔a6 (of course, not 1 b6? ♔b7=) **1...♔b8** (1...f4 2 b6+−) **2 g3!**

The hasty 2 b6? misses the win: 2...♔c8! (△ 3...cb) 3 b7+ ♔b8 4 g3 c5 5 ♔b5 ♔xb7 6 ♔xc5 ♔c7 7 ♔d5 f4! 8 gf ♔d7=; Black saves the game by seizing the opposition.

2...♔a8

Another defensive method also does not help: 2...♔c8 3 ♔a7 ♔d8 4 ♔b8! (an opposition!) 4...♔d7 5 ♔b7 ♔d8 (5...♔d6 6 ♔c8+−) 6 ♔c6 (an outflanking!) 6...♔c8 7 ♔d5 ♔b7 8 ♔e5 ♔b6 9 ♔xf5 ♔xb5 10 g4 c5 11 g5 c4 12 ♔e4! (we shall see this method - decoying the hostile king into a check - more than once in this book) 12...♔b4 13 g6 c3 14 ♔d3! ♔b3 15 g7 c2 16 g8♕+.

3 b6 ♔b8 4 ♔b5! (4 b7? c5 5 ♔b5 ♔xb7=) **4...♔b7 5 bc ♔xc7 6 ♔c5 ♔d7 7 ♔d5+−**

This time White has seized the opposition, therefore the pawn sacrifice 7...f4 is senseless.

1/5. An Ancient Problem

The white king must come closer to the black one, maintaining the opposition. And, when this is impossible, to outflank along the c-file. In fact, all this is an algorithm that we know already – a transformation of a distant opposition into a close one.

1 ♔a2! ♔b8! 2 ♔b2! ♔a8 (2...♔a7 3 ♔a3! ♔b7 4 ♔b3) **3 ♔c3! ♔b7** (3...♔a7 4 ♔c4!) **4 ♔b3! ♔a7 5 ♔c4 ♔b8 6 ♔b4 ♔a8 7 ♔c5 ♔b7 8 ♔b5 ♔a7 9 ♔c6 ♔b8** (9...♔a6 10 ♖a1#; 9...♔a8 10 ♔c7) **10 ♔b6 ♔a8 11 ♖c8#.**

1/6. M. Dvoretsky, 1976 (based on the themes of an Estrin - Gusev ending, Moscow 1963).

If Black postpones the transition to the pawn

ending, playing 1...f4?! (with the idea 2 ♔e2 ♖×d7 3 ♖×d7? ♔×d7 4 ♔d3 ♔e7!, and Black seizes the opposition when the white king enters the 4th rank) he will have serious troubles in the rook-and-pawn endgame after 2 ♖c2+! ♔×d7 3 ♖c5 ♖g8 4 ♔e2. He should focus on the task at hand and calculate the following forced drawing line:

1...♖×d7! 2 ♖×d7

2 ♖c2+ ♔d6 3 ♖c5 ♔e6 4 ♖c6+ ♖d6 is not dangerous for Black.

2...♔×d7 3 f4! g4!

After 3...gf? 4 ♔f3 ♔e6 5 ♔×f4 ♔f6 6 g3 White creates a distant passed pawn that will be decisive. We shall discuss this sort of position later.

4 g3!

16-1

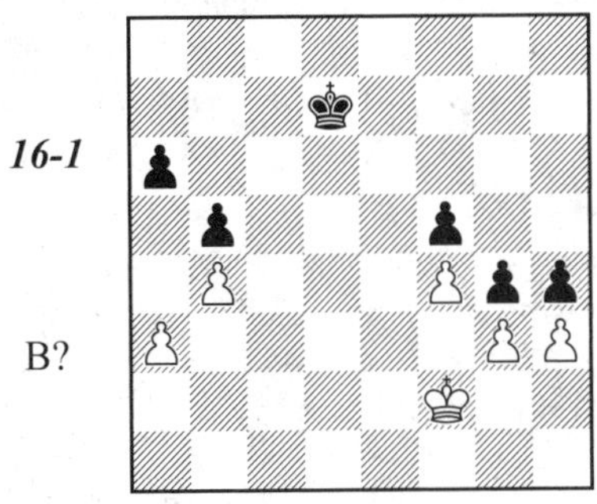

B?

4...gh!!

4...hg+? loses to 5 ♔×g3 gh 6 ♔×h3 ♔e6 7 ♔h4 ♔d5 (the pair of mined squares are g5 - e4) 8 ♔h5! ♔d4 9 ♔g6! ♔e4 10 ♔g5+–.

5 gh ♔e6 6 ♔g3 ♔f6 7 h5 (7 ♔×h3 ♔g6=) **7...♔g7 8 ♔×h3 ♔h7! 9 ♔g3 ♔g7**

The h4- and h6-squares are mined. White cannot win because 10 ♔f3 ♔h6 11 ♔e3? ♔×h5 12 ♔d4 ♔h4! 13 ♔d5 ♔g3 14 ♔e5 ♔g4⊙ is bad.

1/7. Taimanov - Botvinnik, USSR ch tt, Moscow 1967

1...♖g4! 2 ♖×g4 (2 ♖×a6 ♖×h4–+) **2...hg 3 ♔g2 g5!**

3...♔f6 4 ♔g3 ♔f5? (it is not too late for Black to play 4...g5!) is erroneous: 5 e4+! ♔×e4 6 ♔×g4 e5 7 ♔g5 ♔f3 8 ♔×g6 e4 9 h5=.

4 h5

4 ♔g3 ♔g6 5 ♔×g4 does not help: 5...gh 6 ♔×h4 ♔f5 7 ♔g3 ♔e4 8 ♔f2 a5!? (rather than 8...♔d3 9 ♔f3 e5? 10 a3=) 9 ♔e2 a4 10 a3 e6! 11 ♔d2 ♔f3 12 ♔d3 e5⊙ –+.

4...♔g7 5 ♔g3

16-2

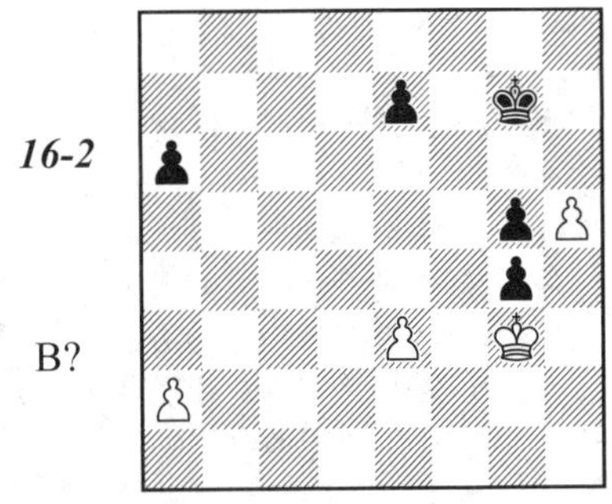

B?

5...♔h7!

The situation is very much like that in the game Alekhine – Yates (diagram 1-22). 5...a5? would have been a grave error in view of 6 ♔×g4 ♔h6 7 e4 and it is Black who is put in zugzwang.

6 ♔×g4 ♔h6 7 e4

White resigned in view of 7...a5 8 a4 e5 9 ♔f5 ♔×h5 10 ♔×e5 g4 11 ♔f4 ♔h4 12 e5 g3 13 e6 g2 14 e7 g1♕ 15 e8♕ ♕f2+ 16 ♔e5 ♕e2+, winning the queen.

1/8. N. Grigoriev, 1920

The c3- and e3-squares are obviously corresponding.

The white king will break through to e3 in order to set the d-pawn in motion; the black king will confront him from the f3-square. The reciprocal zugzwang arises when the kings are on d2 and f3, so another pair of corresponding squares is defined. The third pair – c2 and f4 – is adjacent with those already known. Finally, we come to the squares b3 and b2, which can be used for ceding the move because the single square (f3) corresponds to them.

1 ♔c2!

Rather than 1 d4? ♔e4 2 ♔c3 ♔f5! 3 ♔d3 ♔f4=.

1...♔f4! 2 ♔b3(b2)! ♔f3 3 ♔b2(b3)!⊙ ♔f4 4 ♔c2! ♔e5

4...♔e3? is quite bad in view of 5 ♔c3⊙, 4...♔f3 5 ♔d2⊙ is also inferior.

Now we must discover a new subtlety: there is a reciprocal zugzwang when the kings are on d2 and d4, so the mined square d2 should be avoided.

5 ♔d1! (5 ♔d2?! ♔d4 6 ♔e2? ♔c3=) **5...♔d5 6 ♔e2 ♔d4 7 ♔d2 ♔e5! 8 ♔e3 ♔d5 9 d4 ♔c4**

Black's only hope is to attack the b4-pawn. His pawn would promote simultaneously, but unfortunately the new queen is immediately lost.

10 ♔e4 ♚×b4 11 d5 ♚c5 12 ♔e5 b4 13 d6 b3 (13...♚c6 14 ♔e6 makes no difference) **14 d7 b2 15 d8♕ b1♛ 16 ♕c7+ ♚b4 17 ♕b7+**

It is worth mentioning that 11...♚a3 (instead of 11...♚c5) 12 d6 b4 does not save Black – a queen versus knight pawn endgame is winning. But if we shift the initial position one file to the right, then Black, with the bishop pawn against the queen, holds. We shall discuss this sort of position later.

1/9. B. Neuenschwander, 1985

1 ♔h4? with the idea 2 g5, for example 1...♚h6? 2 g5+ ♚h7 3 ♔g4+– or 1...f6? 2 g5!+–, does not win in view of 1...g6! 2 ♔g5 ♚g7! (rather than 2...gh? 3 gh and White creates a distant passed pawn) 3 ♔f4 f6!=.

The natural plan is an attack against the d5-pawn, but it should be conducted very carefully. White must take Black's counterplay (g7-g6) into account.

1 ♔f5? is erroneous in view of 1...♚h6 and White is in zugzwang. 2 ♔e5 is met with 2...♚g5 3 ♔×d5 ♚×g4=, and 2 ♔f4 – with 2...g6! 3 hg (3 ♔e5 gh 4 gh ♚×h5 5 ♔×d5 f5=) 3...♚×g6 4 ♔e5 ♚g5 5 ♔×d5 ♚×g4=.

However Black could have had serious difficulties if he was on move when the kings were on f5 and h6. We come to the conclusion that these squares are mined.

1 ♔f4! ♚h6 2 ♔f5!⊙ f6!□ 3 ♔e6 ♚g5 4 ♔f7! ♚h6

4...♚×g4? 5 ♔×g7 ♚×h5 (5...f5 6 h6) 6 ♔×f6 was bad, but what should White do now? The answer is rather simple: he uses triangulation in order to pass the move to Black.

5 ♔e7! (rather than 5 ♔e8? g6) **5...♚g5 6 ♔f8! ♚h6** (6...g6 7 ♔g7!+–) **7 ♔f7⊙ ♚h7 8 ♔e6 ♚h6 9 ♔×d5+–.**

1/10. R. Réti, 1929

First let us try 1 ♔c6 g5! 2 ♔b7 (2 hg h4–+); Black wins by means of 2...g4! because his pawn promotes with check. Now we notice that if the black king is on f6 White may play ♔c6 because he exchanges on g5 with check, avoiding Black's promotion on g1.

White cannot prevent ...g6-g5, but does this move invariably win? Assume that the black king has just taken the white pawn on g5 and White has replied with ♔g3. Now we calculate: 1...♚f5 2 ♔h4 ♚e5 3 ♔×h5 ♚d5 4 ♔g4 ♚c5 5 ♔f3 ♚×b5 6 ♔e2 ♚c4 7 ♔d2 ♚b3 8 ♔c1 with a draw. White has made it just in time! This means that he would have lost if his king were slightly further away from the h5-pawn (say, on f3).

We know enough to define the corresponding squares. The most simple reciprocal zugzwang is with the kings on f4 and f6: Black, if on move, cannot achieve anything, while otherwise White is lost: 1 ♔e4 g5–+ or 1 ♔g3 ♚e5–+.

The correspondence between the e5- and f7- squares is less evident. Actually, if Black is on move, 1...♚e7 is met with 2 ♔d5 ♚f6 and now 3 ♔c6!=, profiting from the fact that the black king is unfortunately placed on f6. But what if White is on move? If 1 ♔f4 then 1...♚f6–+, while after 1 ♔d5 Black wins by means of 1...g5! 2 hg ♚g6 3 ♔e4 (3 ♔c6 h4) 3...♚×g5 4 ♔f3 ♚f5.

Using the neighborhood principle, the third pair of corresponding squares is g7 - e4. When the black king is on e7, White plays ♔d5.

1 ♔d5! (1 ♔e6? g5–+; 1 ♔e5? ♚f7⊙–+) **1...♚f7**

Or 1...♚g7 2 ♔e4! ♚f6 3 ♔f4 ♚e7!? 4 ♔e3!=, rather than 4 ♔e5? ♚f7⊙–+ or 4 ♔g5? ♚f7 5 ♔f4 ♚f6⊙–+.

2 ♔e5! ♚e7 3 ♔d5! ♚f6 (3...♚d7 4 ♔e5 ♚c7 5 ♔d5!=) **4 ♔c6! g5 5 hg+ ♚×g5 6 ♔b7=.**

1/11. M. Zinar, 1987

While both kings travel to the queenside they must be aware of the pair of mined squares c4 - d6. If the white king should arrive safely at d3, a drawing situation with untouchable pawns arises. However, we should take into account the utmost importance of the potential reciprocal zugzwang position with the kings on e4 and f6 that may occur. Analyzing all this, we discover the correspondence of the squares f4 - g6 and g4 - h6 and come to the conclusion that an anti-opposition takes place here.

1 ♔g5? ♚g7 2 ♔f5 ♚f7 3 ♔e4 (3 ♔e5 ♚e7⊙–+) 3...♚f6!⊙ 4 ♔d3 (4 ♔f4 c4 5 ♔e4 c3 6 ♔d3 ♚e5–+) 4...♚e5 5 ♔c4 ♚d6⊙–+;

1 ♔g4? ♚h6!! 2 ♔f5 (2 ♔f4 ♚g6 3 ♔e5 ♚f7) 2...♚g7 3 ♔f4 ♚g6! 4 ♔e5 ♚f7! 5 ♔e4 ♚f6⊙–+;

1 ♔g3!! ♔h6! 2 ♔g4! ♔g7! 3 ♔f3! (3 ♔f4? ♔g6! −+) **3...♔g6 4 ♔f4! ♔f7 5 ♔e3! ♔f6 6 ♔e4!⊙ ♔e7 7 ♔d3 ♔d7 8 ♔c3=**.

1/12. A. Troitsky, 1913

White must eliminate the g2-pawn: after the premature 1 a4? ba 2 ba ♔g3! 3 a4 h5 his king will be checkmated.

However, after 1 ♔×g2? ♔g5 2 a4 ba 3 ba the black king enters the square of the a-pawn and arrives in time to hold the 8th rank: 3...♔f6! 4 a4 ♔e7! 5 a5 (or 5 ♔f3) 5...♔d8, etc.

1 f6! gf 2 ♔×g2! ♔g5 3 a4 ba 4 ba ♔f5

The 8th rank is not available anymore; Black must use the 5th rank. However, White creates barriers to this route, too.

5 a4

5 d6? cd 6 a4 is premature in view of 6...♔e6! 7 c6 dc 8 a5 ♔d7.

5...♔e5 6 d6! (rather than 6 c6? d6!) **6...cd 7 c6! dc 8 a5 ♔d5 9 a6+−**.

1/13. Gustavson - Bata, cr 1985

1 ♔g8!! (1 h5? ♔f7! −+) **1...♔×f5** (1...c4 2 h5) **2 ♔g7! ♔g4** (otherwise 3 h5=) **3 ♔g6! ♔×h4 4 ♔f5=**

None of this actually happened. Even though the game was played by mail, White failed to find the saving maneuver and resigned!

1/14. T. Gorgiev, 1928

1 g4+! ♔g5! (1...♔×g4 2 ♔g6 c5 3 h4=) **2 ♔g7!**

The premature 2 h4+? loses to 2...♔×h4! 3 ♔g6 ♔×g4 4 ♔f6 ♔f4 5 ♔e6 ♔e4−+.

2...c5 3 h4+! ♔×g4 (3...♔×h4 4 ♔f6) **4 ♔g6! ♔×h4 5 ♔f5=**.

1/15. N. Grigoriev, 1937

1 h3 c5 2 ♔b1 c4 3 ♔a2

Black's king cannot join his pawns in time, so he counts on the Réti idea!

3...c3

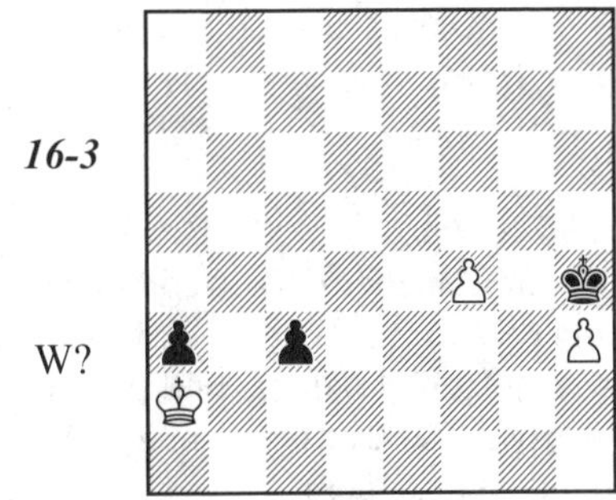

16-3

W?

4 ♔b3!!

After 4 ♔×a3? Black holds by means of the Réti maneuver: 4...♔g3! 5 f5 ♔f4! 6 f6 ♔e3 7 ♔b3 ♔d3 8 f7 c2 9 f8♕ c1♕=. By postponing the pawn capture, White gets the same position but with his king on a more favorable square: a2 instead of a3.

4...a2□ 5 ♔×a2 ♔g3 6 f5 ♔f3

If 6...♔f4 then 7 f6 ♔e3 8 f7 c2 9 f8♕ c1♕ (the pawn is promoted without check) 10 ♕h6+, winning the new queen.

7 ♔b1!+−

Another advantage of the king's position on a2! The Réti idea could have worked after both 7 f6? ♔e2! and 7 ♔b3? ♔e4!.

1/16. Lickleder - Dvoretsky, Germany tt 1997

1...♕×e4! 2 de a5!

White resigned in view of 3 c3 d3 4 c4 a4−+ or 3 ♔b3 c5 4 ♔c4 (4 c3 d3; 4 c4 ♔e6⊙) 4...a4 5 c3 a3 6 ♔b3 d3−+.

2...c5? would have been a grave error in view of 3 c3!. Now 3...d3? loses to 4 c4 a5 5 ♔c3, 3...dc+ 4 ♔×c3 a5 is an obvious draw, while after 3...a5 4 cd cd 5 ♔b3 White is threatening to eliminate all the queenside pawns; however, Black still has a draw: 5...g5!! 6 fg ♔e6 7 ♔c4 ♔e5 8 g6 ♔f6 9 ♔×d4 ♔×g6=.

1/17. Ravikumar - Nielsen, Esbjerg 1980

Black has a single way to a draw.

1...♔b7! (△ 2...dc) **2 a6+** (2 cd cd=; 2 b6 cb!=) **2...♔a7! 3 b6+ ♔×a6! 4 bc ♔b7 5 cd ♔c8=**

All other moves lose.

1...dc? 2 b6 c4 (2...cb 3 a6 c4 4 d6 c3 5 d7 ♔c7 6 a7+−) 3 a6 c3 4 a7+ ♔b7 5 bc+−;

1...♔c8? 2 a6! △ 3.b6+−;

1...♔a7? 2 b6+ ♔b7 (2...cb 3 cd+−) 3 bc+−;

1...♔a8? (this was played in the actual game) 2 b6 ♔b7 3 bc ♔×c7 4 cd+ Black resigned.

1/18. M. Rauch

The winning method is not complicated: White should pass the move to his opponent by means of triangulation. Then he will be able to advance his pawns, so that they can decide the fight without the king's help.

1 ♔f1! ♔d3 2 ♔g2 ♔d4 3 ♔g1! ♔d3 4 ♔f1⊙ ♔d4 5 ♔e2⊙ ♔d5 6 ♔e3 ♔d6 7 f4 ♔d5 8 b4+– (the pawn square has reached the edge of the board).

1/19. Bologan – Vokác, Ostrava 1993

The game continued 1 ♗×g2? hg 2 ♔b7 g1♕ 3 a7. As we know from the discussion at diagram 1-62, White is lost here: the black king comes in time to arrange a mating attack.

3...♕b1+ 4 ♔a8 ♕c2 (4...♕h7 would have made the process shorter) 5 ♔b7 ♕b3+ 6 ♔a8 ♕c4 7 ♔b7 ♕b5+ 8 ♔a8 ♕c6+ 9 ♔b8 ♔d6! White resigned.

Baron has shown that White could hold the draw by retaining his bishop.

1 ♔b8! g1♕ 2 a7 ♕g8+ 3 ♔c7 (3 ♗c8? ♕b3+ 4 ♗b7 h2–+) **3...♕f7+ 4 ♔b6!=**.

1/20. A. Botokanov, 1985

1 ♔f6? ♔g3 2 ♔g5 ♔×g2 3 ♔×h4 ♔×f3 would be bad, as Black's king would get to the queenside first.

1 ♔f7! ♔g3 2 ♔g8! ♔×g2 (2...h3? 3 gh ♔×h3 4 ♔f7+–) **3 f4 h3 4 f5 h2 6 f6 h1♕ 7 f7**, and there is no win for Black, for example: 7...♕h6 8 f8♕ ♕×f8+ 9 ♔×f8 ♔f3 10 ♔e7 ♔e4 11 ♔d6 ♔d4 12 ♔c6 ♔c4 13 ♔b6 ♔×b4 14 ♔×a6 ♔c5 15 ♔b7 b4 16 a6 b3 17 a7 b2 18 a8♕ b1♕+ 19 ♔c8! (but not 19 ♔c7? ♕h7+, and mate is forced) 19...♕f5+ 20 ♔b8! ♕f4+ 21 ♔a7!=.

1/21. A. Troitsky, 1935*

1 ♔e5!

1 ♔c5? loses after 1...♖d8 2 e7 ♖e8 3 ♔d6 (3 ♔×c4 g3 or 3...e3 4 ♔d3 ♔f2) 3...e3 4 ♖×c4 g3 5 ♖e4 ♔f2.

1...e3 (1...♖d8 2 ♔×e4=) **2 ♖×c4** (2 e7? e2–+) **2...e2 3 ♖×g4+**

3 ♖e4? ♔f2 4 e7 e1♕ 5 ♖×e1 ♔×e1 6 ♔f4 ♖f3+ 7 ♔e4 ♔e2–+.

3...♔f2 4 ♖e4 (4 ♖f4+ ♖f3 5 ♖e4 is equivalent) **4...♖e3! 5 ♖×e3 ♔×e3 6 e7 e1♕**

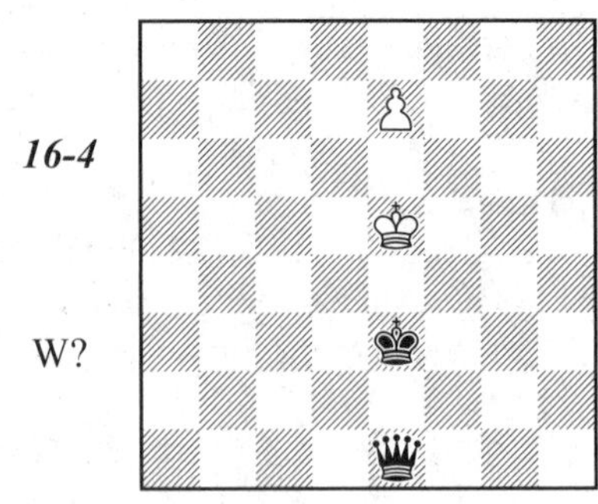

7 ♔e6! ♔f4+ (7...♔d4+ 8 ♔d7!=) **8 ♔f7!=**.

1/22. J. Timman, 1988

After 1 ♔b3? ♔d5 2 ♔b4 ♔e5 3 ♔b5 ♔×f5 4 ♔a6 ♔e6 5 ♔×a7 f5 an endgame of "queen versus rook pawn" arises. The black king is close enough to the queenside to arrange checkmate: 6 a4 f4 7 a5 f3 8 a6 f2 9 ♔b8 f1♕ 10 a7 ♕b5+ 11 ♔c7 ♕d7+ 12 ♔b8 ♔d6 13 a8♕ ♕c7#.

1 a4! a5

After 1...♔d5 2 ♔b4 White has an extra tempo in comparison with the previous annotation.

2 ♔d3!

2 ♔b3? ♔d4 is quite bad. Black is at the crossroads now. The line 2...♔d5 3 ♔c3 ♔e5 4 ♔c4 ♔×f5 5 ♔b5 leads to a mutual promotion, while after 2...♔b4 the white king will be able to attack the f6-pawn.

2...♔b4 3 ♔d4 ♔×a4

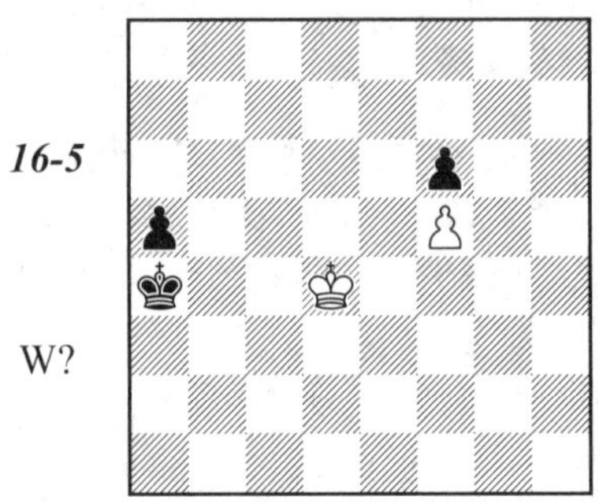

4 ♔c4!!

A necessary subtlety! It is important to push the black king as far away as possible from the f-pawn. The straightforward continuation 4 ♔d5? loses to 4...♔b5! 5 ♔e6 a4 6 ♔×f6 a3 7 ♔e7 (unfortunately he cannot go to g7 because Black then promotes with check) 7...a2 8 f6 a1♕ 9 f7 ♕g7 10 ♔e8 ♔c6 11 f8♕ ♕d7#.

4...♔a3 5 ♔d5 a4 6 ♔e6 ♔b4 7 ♔×f6 a3 8 ♔e7! a2 9 f6 a1♕ 10 f7=

When on b4, the black king is not dangerous anymore!

1/23. Salwe - Flamberg, Petersburg 1914

One's first impression might be that Black wins in every way, but this is far from so. Only the pretty move **1...♘h4!!** decides, as was actually played.

After 2 ♔×h4 ♔b4 Black promotes first and prevents White from promoting.

Black cannot create a similar situation by means of 1...♔b4? 2 ♔×f3 a5. White plays 3 ♔e3 ♔b3 4 ♔d2, either coming with his king to c1 or forcing the black king to occupy the b2-square and interfering with the a1-h8 diagonal.

1...♘e5+ 2 ♔f5 ♔b4? also does not win (2...♘f3! 3 ♔g4 ♘h4! is necessary) 3 h4 a5 4 h5. All lines lead to a drawn endgame of "queen versus rook pawn." For example, 4...♘f7 5 ♔g6 ♘h6 6 ♔×h6 a4 7 ♔g7! a3 8 h6 a2 9 h7 a1♕+ 10 ♔g8=, or 4...♘d7 5 h6 ♘f8 6 ♔f6 a4 7 ♔f7! (7 ♔g7? ♘e6+ 8 ♔f6 a3−+) 7...♘h7 8 ♔g6! (8 ♔g7? ♘g5−+) 8...♘f8+ 9 ♔f7!=.

1/24. A. Khachaturov, 1947

(after N. Grigoriev, 1930)

Who finishes first in the coming breathtaking pawn race? White can win only if he promotes with check.

1 f5! ♔c5 2 h5!

Rather than 2 f6? ♔d6 and the black king enters the square of the h-pawn.

2...g3 3 ♔e1!

This is essential for postponing an eventual check from the d-pawn till as late as possible.

3...d4 4 f6! ♔d6 5 h6!

White's technique is becoming clear. First the f-pawn is advanced, threatening to promote with check (its mission is to decoy the black king to the 8th rank), thereafter comes time for the h-pawn. If 5...d3 now (without check!) then 6 f7 ♔e7 7 h7.

5...g2 6 ♔f2 d3 7 f7! ♔e7 8 h7 g1♕+ 9 ♔×g1 d2 10 f8♕+! ♔×f8 11 h8♕+

1/25. J. Moravec, 1950

This exercise will be easy if one recollects the study by Timman (diagram 1-63).

1 ♔d5!!

Rather than 1 ♔×d6? e4 2 c4 e3 3 c5 e2 4 c6 e1♕ 5 ♔d7 ♕d1+! 6 ♔c8 ♕g4+.

1...♔f3 (1...♔g3 2 ♔e4 △ 3 c4=) **2 ♔×d6! e4 3 c4 e3 4 c5 e2 5 c6 e1♕ 6 ♔d7! ♕d1+ 7 ♔c8!** with an inevitable 8 c7=.

1/26. E. Dvizov, 1965

1 ♔f6? is enough for a draw only: 1...♔g8! 2 g6 b3! 3 h6 b2 4 h7+ ♔h8 5 g7+ ♔×h7 6 ♔f7 b1♕ 7 g8♕+ ♔h6.

1 ♔g6!! ♔g8

1...b3 2 ♔f7 b2 3 g6 b1♕ 4 g7+ ♔h7 5 g8♕+ ♔h6 6 ♕g6+! ♕×g6 7 hg c3 8 g7 c2 9 g8♕ c1♕ 10 ♕g6#.

2 h6 b3

After 2...c3 White checkmates as in the previous note: 3 h7+ ♔h8 4 ♔f7! c2 5 g6 c1♕ 6 g7+ ♔×h7 7 g8♕+ ♔h6 8 ♕g6#.

Now not a queen, but a pawn checkmates:

3 h7+ ♔h8 4 ♔h6! b2 5 g6 b1♕ 6 g7#.

1/27. N. Grigoriev, 1931

1 h4!

White should keep the black pawns in the shape of a compact structure that can be comfortably attacked by his king. The premature 1 ♔f7? misses the win: 1...g5! 2 ♔g7 ♔b3 3 ♔×h7 ♔c4 4 ♔g6 g4! 5 ♔g5 ♔d5 6 ♔×g4 ♔e6 7 ♔g5 ♔f7=. Now, however, White arrives in time: 1...♔b3 2 ♔f7 ♔c4 3 ♔×g7 h5 4 ♔g6 ♔d5 5 ♔×h5 ♔e6 6 ♔g6+−. 1...h6 2 h5 is also hopeless for Black. But the fight is still not over.

1...h5!

With the idea 2 ♔f7? g5 3 hg h4=. However if the a2-g8 diagonal remains open, the white pawn promotes with check.

2 ♔f8! g6 3 ♔e7!+−

The only way to attack the g-pawn without fearing 3...g5. From f7, the king interferes along the diagonal, while from g7, with his own pawn.

1/28. N. Grigoriev, 1932

1 ♔f5! ♔e3 2 ♔e5 c6!

The only possibility to resist. 2...♔d3? 3 ♔d5 ♔c3 4 ♔c5 loses immediately.

3 a4 ♔d3 4 a5 c5 5 a6 c4 6 a7 c3 7 a8♕ c2

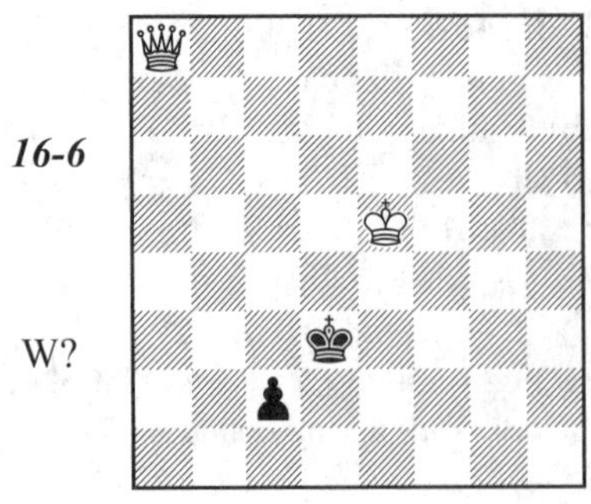

16-6

W?

Black is close to salvation, for example:

8 ♕a3+? ♔d2 9 ♕a2 ♔c3!= (9...♔d1? 10 ♔d4 c1♕ 11 ♔d3+–);

8 ♕e4+? ♔d2 9 ♕d4+ (9 ♕d5+ ♔e1!) 9...♔e2 (9...♔c1 is also possible) 10 ♕c3 ♔d1 11 ♕d3+ ♔c1 12 ♔d4 ♔b2 13 ♕e2 ♔a1!= (rather than 13...♔b1? 14 ♔c3! c1♕+ 15 ♔b3+–).

Nevertheless White can win this position in the following way:

8 ♕d5+!! ♔e3

8...♔c3 9 ♕d4+ ♔b3 10 ♕a1+–; 8...♔e2 9 ♕a2! ♔d1 (9...♔d3 10 ♕b2 ♔d2 11 ♔d4) 10 ♔d4! c1♕ 11 ♔d3+–.

9 ♕g2! c1♕ (9...♔d3 10 ♕g5+–) **10 ♕g5+**

A similar finale happened in the study by Elkies (diagram 1-64).

1/29. J. Speelman, 1979

With 1 ♔e5? White forces the opponent to open the way for the king to one of the pawns. However the line 1...♔d7! 2 ♔f6 (2 ♔d5 is useless in view of 2...♔c7 or 2...h5) 2...♔c6 3 h4 ♔b5 4 h5 ♔×a5 5 ♔g7 b5 leads only to a draw.

Notice that White has missed by a single tempo to promote first and then win the hostile queen. Thus the same zugzwang position but with the pawn on h4 (rather than h3) would have been winning.

After 1 h4? ♔f7 2 h5 h6 this goal cannot be reached because it is Black who seizes the opposition. White must act more subtly.

1 ♔g5! ♔f7 2 ♔h6 ♔g8 3 h4 ♔h8 4 ♔h5!

After 4 ♔g5? ♔g7 it is Black again who holds the opposition. Another line that does not work is 4 h5? ♔g8 5 ♔g5 ♔f7 (or 5...♔g7 6 h6+ ♔f7 7 ♔f5 ♔e7 8 ♔e5 ♔d7 9 ♔f6 ♔d6! 10 ♔g7 ♔e7 11 ♔×h7 ♔f7=) 6 ♔f5 (6 ♔f4 ♔e6) 6...h6=.

4...♔g8 (4...♔g7 5 ♔g5) **5 ♔g4!**

White seizes the distant opposition and, by means of the usual outflanking procedure, transforms it into close opposition.

5...♔f8 6 ♔f4 ♔e8 7 ♔g5!

Rather than 7 ♔e4? ♔d7! and Black holds: 8 ♔f5 ♔c6= or 8 ♔d5 h5=.

7...♔f7 8 ♔f5 ♔e7 9 ♔e5⊙

White has successfully achieved his goal and, due to zugzwang, breaks through to one of Black's pawns.

9...♔d7 10 ♔f6 ♔c6 11 .h5 ♔b5 12 ♔g7 ♔×a5 13 ♔×h7 b5 14 h6 b4 15 ♔g7! b3 16 h7 b2 17 h8♕ b1♕ 18 ♕a8+ ♔b4 19 ♕b8+.

1/30. Yermolinsky – Komarov, USSR 1986

It is no easy matter to utilize the extra pawn to win. White found a superb solution: he opened the way for his king to the queenside.

1 f4+!! gf+ 2 ♔f3! fe 3 fe! ♔d5 4 ♔f4 ♔e6 5 e4 fe 6 ♔×e4

Black resigned. White captures the c4-pawn unimpeded and advances his pawn to c6, achieving the position from Fahrni - Alapin (diagram 1-27).

Let us consider another attempt to make progress: the triangulation technique.

1 ♔g2 ♔d5 (1...♔e6? 2 e4+–) 2 ♔h3 ♔e6! After 2...♔e5? 3 ♔g3⊙ White's idea turns out to be successful: 3...♔e6 4 f4 g4 5 f3 gf 6 ♔×f3 ♔d5 7 e4+ fe+ 8 ♔e3+–.

a) 3 f4?! gf 4 ef ♔d5! 5 f3 ♔c5 6 ♔h4 ♔b5 7 ♔g5 ♔a4! 8 ♔×f5 ♔b3 9 ♔g6 (9 ♔e4) 9...♔×c3 leads to a queen-and-pawn endgame with an extra pawn for White. 4...♔f6? is erroneous in view of 5 ♔h4! ♔g6 6 f3⊙ ♔h6 7 ♔g3 ♔h5 8 ♔f2 ♔h4 9 ♔g2 ♔h5 10 ♔g3⊙ ♔g6 11 ♔f2 ♔h5 12 ♔e3 ♔h4 13 ♔d4 ♔g3 14 ♔e5 ♔×f3 15 ♔×f5 ♔e3 16 ♔e5+–. 5 ♔g3? is less accurate, White can achieve only the same queen-and-pawn endgame as above: 5...♔g6! 6 ♔h4 (6 ♔f3 ♔h5 7 ♔e3 ♔g4 8 ♔d4 ♔×f4 9 ♔×c4 ♔f3 10 ♔d5 ♔×f2 11 ♔e5 ♔e3=) 6...♔h6 7 ♔h3 ♔g7! 8 ♔g2 ♔f6(f7)! 9 ♔f3 ♔e6 10 ♔g3 ♔d5 11 f3 ♔c5 12 ♔h4 ♔b5 13 ♔g5 ♔a4!? etc.

b) 3 e4?! fe 4 fe ♔e5 5 f3 ♔f4 6 e5! (6 ♔g2 g4 7 fg ♔×g4=) 6...♔×f3 (6...♔×e5? 7 ♔g4 ♔f6 8 f4+–) 7 e6 g4+ 8 ♔h2 (8 ♔h4) 8...♔f2 9 e7 g3+ 10 ♔h3 g2 11 e8♕ g1♕ 12 ♕f7+ and 13 ♕×c4. Again, White has an extra pawn in the queen-and-pawn endgame, and again it is not clear whether this advantage is sufficient for a win.

c) The best option is a return to the plan by Yermolinsky: 3 ♔g3! ♔e5 4 f4+!! gf+ 5 ♔f3! +−. Nevertheless, as grandmaster Naer has demonstrated, an "alternative solution" exists: White should play e3-e4 when the king is standing on h2 (rather than on h3 as in the "b" line).

1 ♔h2! ♔e6 (1...♔d5 2 ♔g2⊙) **2 e4! fe 3 fe ♔e5 4 f3 ♔f4 5 ♔g1!! g4 6 e5! ♔×e5 7 fg ♔f4 8 ♔f2+−**.

1/31. J. Moravec, 1952

1 ♔f7 ♔d6 2 ♔f6 ♔d5! 3 ♔f5 a5 4 e4+ ♔c6!

Black applies the Grigoriev zigzag.

5 e5!

Of course not 5 ♔e5? (△ 6 ♔d4) 5...♔c5! 6 ♔f6 a4 7 e5 a3 and Black promotes with check. 5 ♔g6? is also erroneous in view of 5...a4 6 e5 ♔d5! 7 ♔f5 a3 8 e6 ♔d6! 9 ♔f6 a2−+.

5...a4 (5...♔d7 6 ♔e4=) **6 e6 a3 7 ♔g6!**

A similar zigzag saves White.

7...a2 8 e7 ♔d7 9 ♔f7=.

1/32. I. Gabdrakipov, 1985

In this study we can see the both kinds of zigzags again.

1 ♔d3 (1 g4? c5=) **1...♔b3 2 ♔d4! ♔b4**

2...h5 does not help: 3 g4! hg 4 h5 c5+ 5 ♔e3!.

3 g4 (rather than 3 ♔e3? ♔c5!=) **3...c5+ 4 ♔e3! c4 5 g5!**

After 5 ♔d2? c3+ 6 ♔c2 ♔c4 White has no win: 7 g5 hg 8 h5 (8 hg ♔d5=) 8...g4= or 7 h5 ♔d4 8 g5 ♔e5 9 g6 ♔f6=. One should know this drawing position with a pawn minus; a reminder will be given in the chapter devoted to the protected passed pawn.

5...hg 6 h5!

After 6 hg? Black holds by means of a zigzag: 6...c3 7 g6 ♔a3! 8 ♔d3 ♔b2 9 g7 c2=.

6...c3 7 h6 ♔b3 8 h7 c2 9 ♔d2! ♔b2 10 h8♕+.

1/33. V. Kondratiev, 1985

1 ♔a6 ♔e2 2 ♔a5!

The squares b5 and d3 are mined. 2 ♔b5? loses to 2...♔d3⊙ 3 ♔b4 c6! 4 ♔×a4 c5.

2...♔d3 3 ♔b5⊙ c6+ 4 ♔b4⊙

Of course not 4 ♔×c6? ♔c4! −+. Now Black has no waiting move ...c7-c6, and his king is forced to leave the comfortable d3-square. Then White finally takes the a4-pawn and holds by means of a pendulum.

4...♔d4 5 ♔×a4 c5 6 ♔b3 ♔d3 7 ♔b2! ♔d2 8 ♔b3=.

1/34. N. Grigoriev, 1931

The attack against the b7-pawn comes too late: 1 ♔g5? ♔c2 2 ♔f6 ♔d3 3 ♔e5 ♔c4 4 ♔d6 ♔b5 5 ♔c7 ♔a6⊙. The only hope is to meet ...♔×b6 with ♔b4. The trail should be blazed with awareness of the fact that the black king will try to out-shoulder his colleague.

1 ♔g3! ♔c2 2 ♔f2! ♔d3 3 ♔e1! ♔c4 4 ♔d2 ♔b5 5 ♔c3 ♔×b6 6 ♔b4=.

1/35. N. Grigoriev, 1925

1 ♔f6? ♔g4 2 ♔×f7 ♔f5! is hopeless. On 1 ♔d5? f5 2 ♔c6 f4 we get a lost "knight pawn vs. queen" endgame. White's only hope is to keep the black king locked on the h-file until Black advances his f-pawn close enough to the white king.

1 ♔f5! ♔h4 2 ♔f4 ♔h3 3 ♔f3 ♔h2 4 ♔f2 f6 (forced) **5 ♔f3 ♔g1 6 ♔e4 ♔f2**

The king has blocked the way of his own pawn, so White's attack against the b6-pawn arrives in time. But 6...♔g2? would have been even worse than this: the white king eliminates the f-pawn and has enough time for a return to the queenside: 7 ♔f5 ♔f3 8 ♔×f6 ♔e4 9 ♔e6+−.

7 ♔d5! (7 ♔f5? ♔e3−+) **7...f5 8 ♔c6 f4 9 ♔×b6=**.

1/36. A. Gerbstman, 1961

1 g7! (1 b7? ♖c2+!) **1...♖c2+**

Or 1...♖g2 2 b7 with the same result.

2 ♔b8! ♖g2 3 b7 ♖×g7 4 ♔a8! ♖g8+! (4...♖×b7 Stalemate) **5 b8♕ ♖×b8+ 6 ♔×b8 ♔b6**

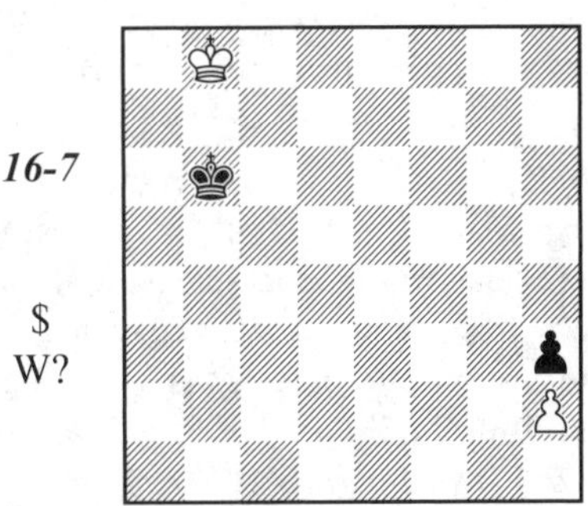

7 ♔c8?? would have been a grave error now: 7...♔c6! (shouldering!) 8 ♔d8(b8) ♔d5 and the white king fails to reach f2.

7 ♔a8! ♔c6 8 ♔a7! ♔d5 9 ♔b6 ♔e4 10 ♔c5 ♔f3 11 ♔d4 ♔g2 12 ♔e3 ♔×h2 13 ♔f2=.

1/37. H. Adamson, 1915

The straightforward 1 ♔d7? fails: 1...♔b6 2 ♔e6 ♔c5 3 ♔f5 ♔d4 4 ♔g6 ♔e3 5 ♔×h6 ♔f4=. White must keep the black king locked on the edge, choose a proper moment for luring the pawns closer, and only then go to the kingside. Very subtle play is required for accomplishing this plan.

1 ♔c7! ♔a6 2 ♔c6 ♔a5 (2...♔a7? 3 g4! ♔b8 4 ♔d7! ♔b7 5 ♔e6+–) **3 ♔c5 ♔a4 4 ♔c4 ♔a3 5 ♔c3 ♔a2 6 ♔c2!**

It is still early for a pawn advance: 6 g4? ♔b1= or 6 g3? ♔b1 7 ♔d2 ♔b2 8 g4 ♔b1! (rather than 8...♔b3? 9 ♔d3!+–) 9 ♔d3 ♔c1!=. If 6....♔a1, then 7 g4 ♔a2 8 ♔d3 wins. 6...h5 is also bad: 7 ♔d3 ♔b3 8 ♔e4 ♔c4 9 ♔f5.

6...♔a3

16-8

W?

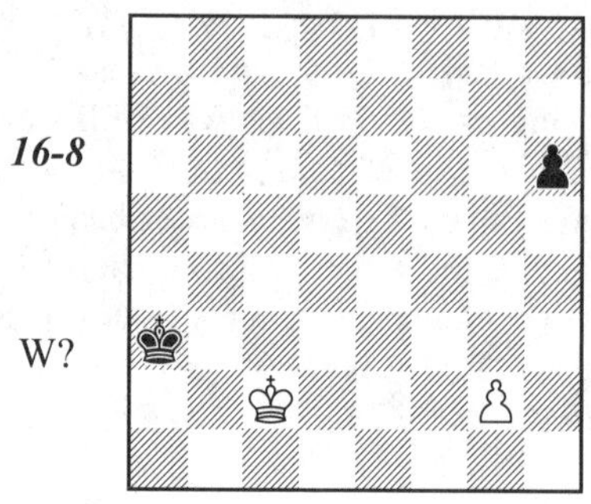

7 g3!!

Rather than a hasty 7 g4? in view of 7...♔b4 8 ♔d3 ♔c5 9 ♔e4 ♔d6 10 ♔f5 h5! 11 gh ♔e7=.

7...♔a4!?

This continuation is perhaps more clever than the author's solution 7...♔b4 (7...♔a2 8 g4+–; 7...h5 8 ♔d3 ♔b4 9 ♔e4 ♔c5 10 ♔f5) 8 ♔d3 ♔c5 9 ♔e4⊙ ♔d6 10 ♔f5 ♔d5 (10...♔e7 11 ♔g6) 11 g4+–.

8 ♔c3!

After 8 ♔d3? ♔b4 9 ♔e4 ♔c5 a position from the previous variation arises. How strange it may seem, this is a reciprocal zugzwang and, with White on move, the outcome is only a draw: 10 g4 ♔d6 11 ♔f5 h5!= or 10 ♔f5 ♔d4=.

8...♔b5 9 ♔d4 ♔c6 10 ♔e5! (10 ♔e4? ♔c5!⊙=).

10...♔c5 (10...♔d7 11 ♔f6+–) **11 g4+–.**

1/38. L. Prokeš, 1944

(after H. Mattison, 1929)

1 ♔f6!

Both 1 ♔f7? ♔h7 2 g4 g5⊙ 3 ♔f6 h5= and 1 g4? g5 2 ♔f6 h5= are erroneous.

1...♔h7 2 g4 g5 (2...h5 3 g5+–) **3 ♔f7⊙ h5 4 h4! ♔h6** (4...gh 5 g5; 4...hg 5 hg) **5 ♔f6+–.**

1/39. J. Behting, 1905

1 ♔e1!! ♔g2 (1...♔h2 2 ♔f2! ♔h3 3 ♔f3⊙ ♔h2 4 g4) **2 g4 fg 3 f5 g3 4 f6!** (4 h6? gh 5 f6 ♔h2=) **4...gf 5 h6 f5 6 h7 f4 7 h8♕ f3 8 ♕a8+–**

If the white king had gone to e2 on move one, the move 7...f3 in the main line would have been check, with a draw after 8 ♔e3 f2. Another alternative 1 ♔f2? also leads to a draw: 1...♔h2 2 ♔f3 ♔h3⊙=.

1/40. T. Kok, 1939

The standard pawn breakthrough does not work immediately: 1 c5?! dc 2 b5? (2 bc bc 3 dc ♔f3=) 2...cd+. White must prepare it, but how? Of the many king retreats, only one leads to success.

1 ♔d2!! ♔f3 (1...b5 2 d5! cd 3 cb; 1...d5 2 b5! cb 3 cd; 1...c5 2 dc dc 3 bc bc 4 ♔e3) **2 c5! bc** (2...dc 3 b5! cb 4 d5) **3 d5! cd 4 b5+–**

All other first moves draw or even lose.

1 b5? cb (1...c5!–+ is even more simple) 2 ♔b4 (2 cb d5–+) 2...bc 3 ♔×c4 ♔f3 4 ♔d5 b5–+;

1 ♔b2?! ♔f2 2 c5 bc 3 d5? cd 4 b5 d4 5 b6 d3–+;

1 ♔c2?! ♔f3 (1...c5=) 2 c5 bc! 3 d5? cd 4 b5 ♔e2 5 b6 d4 6 b7 d3+ and 7...d2–+;

1 ♔d3?! ♔f3 2 c5 bc! 3 d5 cd 4 b5 c4+ 5 ♔d4 c3! 6 ♔×c3 ♔e3=;

1 d5?! c5! (1...cd? 2 ♔d4! dc 3 ♔×c4 ♔f3 4 ♔d5+–) 2 bc bc 3 ♔b3 ♔f3 4 ♔a4 ♔e4 5 ♔b5 ♔d4 6 ♔c6 ♔×c4 7 ♔×d6 ♔b4 8 ♔e7 c4=.

1/41. Guliev - Tukmakov,

Nikolaev zt 1993

1 ♗×e5!

1 a4? ♘c4∓ △ 2...♘b6.

1...de 2 a4!

This is how White should have played. However, the remainder of the game was 2 ♔e3?? ♔d6 3 ♔e4 c4 4 a4 c3 5 ♔d3 ♔×d5, and White resigned. One tragicomedy more!

2...♔d6 3 a5 c4

If 3...♔×d5 then 4 a6! △ 5 b6+– – we have seen a similar conclusion in the game Capablanca – Ed. Lasker. But Black cannot avoid it.

16-9

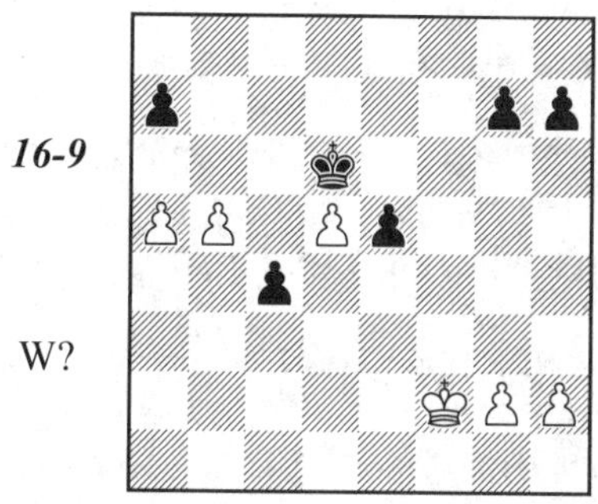

W?

4 a6!

4 b6? leads only to a draw: 4...a6! 5 ♔e3 ♔d7 6 ♔e4 ♔d6 7 b7 ♔c7 8 ♔×e5 c3 9 d6+ ♔×b7 10 ♔e6 c2 11 d7 c1♕ 12 d8♕.

4...♔c5 5 d6! ♔×d6 6 b6+–.

1/42. K. Rothländer, 1893

Black, if on move, holds by means of 1...f5!.

1 f5+! ♔×f5 (1...♔g5 2 f6!+–) **2 h4 ♔f6** (2...♔e5 3 ♔g4 f6 4 h5 ♔e6 5 ♔f4+–) **3 ♔f4 ♔g6 4 ♔g4 ♔h6 5 h5 f6**

5...♔h7 6 ♔g5(f5) is the same.

6 ♔f5 ♔×h5 7 ♔×f6 ♔g4 8 ♔e5 ♔f3 9 ♔×d5! ♔e3 10 ♔c4⊙ +–.

1/43. W. Bähr, 1935

White has seized the opposition and his king will inevitably break through to one of the wings.

1...♔e7! 2 ♔e3! ♔f7!

Black gives away the a-pawn. If he plays 2...♔d7? and gives away the h-pawn, White wins: 3 ♔f4 ♔d6 4 ♔g5 ♔e5 5 ♔×h5 ♔f5 6 ♔h6 ♔f6 7 h5 ♔f7 8 ♔g5 ♔g7 9 ♔f5, because his a-pawn is above the middle line.

3 ♔d4 ♔f6! 4 ♔c5 ♔e5 5 ♔b6 ♔d6 6 ♔×a6 ♔c6 (6...♔c7 is playable, too) **7 ♔a7 ♔c7 8 a6 ♔c8 9 ♔b6 ♔b8=**

A "normal position" has arisen.

1/44. W. Bähr, 1935

After **1 ♔c2! ♔b4 2 ♔d3 ♔×a4 3 ♔c4⊙** (if White were on move here he would have been lost) **3...a6 4 ♔c5!** (4 ♔c3? ♔b5+–) **4...♔a5 5 ♔c4 ♔b6 6 ♔b4=** we come to a familiar drawing position.

1 ♔a3? (hoping for 1...a5? 2 ♔b2 ♔b4 3 ♔c2 ♔×a4 4 ♔c3 ♔b5 5 ♔b3=) meets a refutation: 1...♔c3! 2 a5 ♔c4 3 ♔a4 ♔c5! (3...a6? 4 ♔a3 ♔b5 5 ♔b3 ♔×a5 6 ♔c4 ♔b6 7 ♔b4=) 4 a6 ♔b6 5 ♔b4 ♔×a6 6 ♔c5 ♔b7 (6...♔a5⊙ is even stronger) 7 ♔b5 ♔c7. The a7-pawn is standing above the key diagonal f1-a6, so Black disposes of a decisive tempo.

1/45. M. Zinar, 1982

1 e5? is erroneous; after 1...♔d5 2 ♔f4 ♔e6 3 ♔e4 ♔e7= the count of the reserve tempi is 1:1, therefore the position is drawn. When the pawn is on e4, however, White has two spare tempi instead of one (his pawn is 2 squares from e6) - a favorable situation for him.

1 ♔f3? does not work, either: after 1...♔b3 2 e5 ♔×a3 a drawn endgame with queen versus rook pawn arises. However, this endgame is winning when the king is standing on the e-file. From all this, the winning plan can be constructed: White must pass the move to the opponent by means of triangulation.

1 ♔e2! ♔d4 2 ♔f3 ♔c4 (2...♔e5 3 ♔e3 ♔e6 4 ♔d4 ♔d6 5 ♔c4+–) **3 ♔e3⊙ ♔b3 4 e5 ♔×a3 5 e6 ♔b2 6 e7 a3 7 e8♕ a2 8 ♔d2 a1♕ 9 ♕b5+ ♔a3 10 ♕a5+ ♔b2 11 ♕b4+ ♔a2 12 ♔c2+–.**

1/46. N. Grigoriev, 1936

Black has the distant opposition and is planning to transform it into close opposition by means of an outflanking at the appropriate moment. White's only hope is the drawn Dedrle position (diagram 1-139), but how it can be achieved?

1 ♔c2! ♔c8! (1...♔c7? 2 ♔c3=) **2 ♔d2** (rather than 2 g5? hg–+) **2...♔d8 3 ♔e2!**

It is still too early to push the king ahead: 3 ♔e3? ♔e7 4 ♔f3 (4 g5 hg 5 ♔f3 ♔e6–+) 4...♔d6! 5 g5 h5–+, as we know, the white king must go to d4 in this position.

3...♔e8

16-10

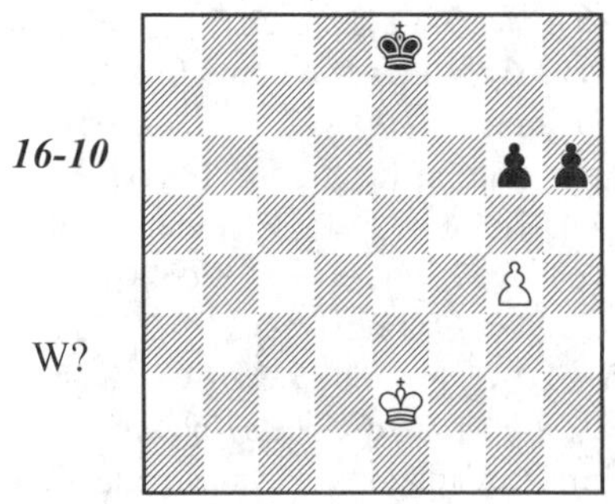

W?

Black is ready to outflank: 4 ♔d2? ♔f7! or 4 ♔f2? ♔d7!, while 5 g5 is still impossible in view of 5...hg.

4 ♔f3! ♔d7

4...♔f7 5 ♔f4 ♔f6 6 g5+! hg+ 7 ♔g4=; 4...♔e7 5 ♔e3!=

5 g5!! h5 6 ♔e3! ♔c7 (6...♔d6 7 ♔d4; 6...♔c6 7 ♔e4 ♔c5 8 ♔e5) **7 ♔d3! ♔b7 8 ♔e3! ♔a6 9 ♔e4!** etc.

1/47. V. Chekhover, 1951

The king must enter the square of the c-pawn (1 fg?? c3–+). The immediate 1 ♔f2? is erroneous in view of 1...gf 2 ef c3 3 ♔e3 ♔d5 4 f5 ♔c4. The d4-pawn must stay protected and passed.

1 f5+! ♔×f5

Black's counterplay on the queenside fails now, e.g. 2 ♔f2 ♔e6? 3 ♔e2 c3 4 ♔d1 ♔d5 5 ♔c1! (the squares c2 - c4 are mined) 5...♔c4 6 ♔c2 ♔b4 7 d5 ♔c5 8 ♔×c3 ♔×d5 9 ♔b4, and the white king controls key squares. But defensive resources are not exhausted: the black king can enter the fight via the kingside as well after ...g5-g4!.

The natural continuation 2 ♔f2? gives only a draw after 2...g4! 3 hg+ ♔×g4 4 ♔e2 (4 ♔e1 ♔f3 5 ♔d2 c3+ or 5 d5 ♔×e3 6 d6 c3 7 ♔d1 ♔f2 8 d7 e3=) 4...c3⊙ 5 ♔d1 (5 d5 ♔f5=) 5...♔f3 6 d5 ♔×e3 7 d6 ♔f2=.

Notice that Black would have been lost if he had been on move in the position with the king on e2 and the pawn on c3. From this fact, we define the corresponding squares and choose the most precise route for the king.

2 ♔f1!! c3 (2...g4 3 hg+ ♔×g4 4 ♔f2! c3 5 ♔e2⊙) **3 ♔e1! g4 4 hg+ ♔×g4 5 ♔e2!⊙ c2** (5...♔g3 6 d5; 5...♔f5 6 ♔d1) **6 ♔d2 ♔f3 7 d5 c1♕+ 8 ♔×c1 ♔×e3 9 d6 ♔f2 10 d7 e3 11 d8♕+–.**

1/48. Hernandez - Ferragut, Cuba 1998

Question number one: where do we place the pawns? If 1 g7? ♔f7 2 ♔e3 ♔g8 3 ♔f4, with the idea 3...♔h7? 4 ♔f5 e3 5 ♔e6+–, Black responds with 3...♔f7! and the king's march does not win 4 ♔g5 e3 5 ♔h6 e2 6 ♔h7 e1♕ 7 g8♕+ ♔×f6 8 ♕g6+ ♔e7=.

If the pawn is on f7 and the black king on f8, ♔×d5! wins. But the immediate 1 f7+? does not lead to this position because Black has 1...♔g7! 2 ♔e3 ♔f8 3 ♔f4 ♔g7=.

1 ♔e3! ♔f8 2 f7! ♔g7 3 ♔d4⊙ ♔f8 4 ♔×d5! (if 4 ♔e5 then 4...♔e7) **4...e3 5 ♔e6 e2** (5...♔g7 6 ♔e7) **6 ♔f6 e1♕ 7 g7#.**

1/49. N. Kopaev, 1947

1 ♔b6!

Both 1 ♖h5? ♔d8 and 1 ♖g5? ♔c7! yield nothing.

1...♔d8 (1...♖×h6? 2 ♖g5+–) **2 ♖g5 ♔e8 3 ♖g8+ ♔f7 4 ♖g7+ ♖×g7 5 hg!**

We have forcibly reached a pawn endgame with White's far-advanced passed pawns.

5...e5 6 ♔c5 e4 7 ♔c4!

An important subtlety, the upcoming king assault works only when the black king is standing on g8. At this moment White must plan how to reach the inevitable zugzwang position with Black on move. 7 ♔d4? d5 8 ♔e3 ♔g8 9 ♔f4 ♔f7⊙ leads only to a draw: we have already seen this position in the previous exercise, in the 1 g7? line.

7...d6!? 8 ♔c3! (8 ♔d4? d5=) **8...♔g8 9 ♔d4 d5 10 ♔e3 ♔f7 11 ♔f4⊙ ♔g8 12 ♔g5!** (12 ♔f5?! ♔f7!) **12...♔h7** (12...e3 13 ♔g6 e2 14 f7#; 12...♔f7 13 ♔h6 e3 14 ♔h7+–) **13 ♔f5! e3 14 ♔e6 e2** (14...♔g8 15 f7+ ♔×g7 16 ♔e7) **15 ♔f7 e1♕ 16 g8♕+ ♔h6 17 ♕g6#.**

1/50. N. Grigoriev, 1932

White's king is in the square of the b-pawn, but if he approaches it Black will create another passed pawn on the f-file at cost of his d5-pawn. For example, 1 ♔g3 b5 2 ♔f3 b4 3 ♔e2 f5 4 ♔d3 b3! 5 ♔c3 d4+! 6 ed f4 7 d5 f3 8 d6 f2 9 d7 f1♕ 10 d8♕ ♕c1+ 11 ♔b4 ♕e1+! 12 ♔a4 ♕a1+! 13 ♔×b3 ♕b1+ 14 ♔c3 ♕c1+ 15 ♔b4 ♕b1+! 16 ♔a5 (16 ♔c5 ♕c2+) 16...♕f5+ with a draw.

So the strongest plan is to rush the king over to his own passed pawns.

1 e4!!

The straightforward 1 ♔g3? b5 2 ♔f4 (there is no time for 2 e4 already, in view of 2...b4!) 2...b4 3 ♔f5 leads only to a draw: 3...b3 4 ♔e6 b2 5 h8♕+ ♔xh8 6 ♔f7 b1♕ 7 g7+ ♔h7 8 g8♕+ ♔h6 and the black queen defends the g6-square where White would have liked to checkmate. Therefore the b1-h7 diagonal must be closed.

1...de

1...d4 is even worse in view of 2 ♔g3 b5 3 ♔f4 b4 (3...d3 4 ♔e3) 4 ♔f5 with checkmate.

2 ♔g3 b5 3 ♔f4 e3

We already know that Black will be checkmated from g6 after 3...b4 4 ♔f5! etc. For this reason, he tries to distract the white king from the kingside.

4 ♔×e3 b4

After 4...f5 5 ♔f4! (5 ♔d4? f4) 5...b4 6 ♔e5! b3 7 ♔e6 b2 8 h8♕+ ♔×h8 9 ♔f7 the black pawn on f5 is as treacherous as the e4-pawn: it cuts his own queen off from the g6-square.

5 ♔d4! f5

Unfortunately, this is forced: after 5...b3 6 ♔c3 f5 7 ♔×b3 the king remains in the square of the f-pawn.

6 ♔e5! b3 (6...f4 7 ♔e6!) **7 ♔e6 b2 8 h8♕+ ♔×h8 9 ♔f7 b1♕ 10 g7+ ♔h7 11 g8♕+ ♔h6 12 ♕g6#.**

1/51. A. Troitsky, 1900*

After 1...♔g4? the main line of the study arises. White builds a stalemate shelter on the queenside: 2 a5! ♔×h5 (2...♔f4 3 ♔f2=) 3 ♔d2 ♔g4 4 ♔c2 h5 (or 4...♔f3 5 ♔b2 ♔e3 6 ♔a3 ♔d3 7 ♔a4 ♔×c3 8 a3=) 5 ♔b2 h4 6 ♔a3 h3 7 ♔a4 h2 8 a3 h1♕=.

But 1...a5?? is even worse because White manages even to win after 2 ♔e3 ♔g4 3 ♔e4 ♔×h5 4 ♔f5⊙ ♔h4 5 ♔e6.

However, Rubenis has refuted the study, yet Black nevertheless can win.

1...♔f4!! (△ 2...a5) **2 a5 ♔e4! 3 ♔d2**

3 ♔f2 ♔d3 is hopeless. After 3 a3 ♔f4 Black's king can simply steal the kingside pawns, because the road to the refuge does not exist anymore.

3...♔f3 4 ♔c2 ♔e3 5 ♔b2 ♔d3 6 ♔a3 ♔×c3 7 ♔a4 ♔d2 8 a3 c3−+ – there is no stalemate!

1/52. N. Grigoriev, 1934

1 b4!

Of course, not 1 ♔g5? c5 (or 1...♔d4) with a draw.

1...♔d4

At first glance everything is quite simple. White's pawns protect themselves after c2-c3; he must just go to the kingside for the h7-pawn and come back.

Actually, however, the problem is much more complicated than that. Black has an unexpected idea: to play ...c7-c5 and to answer b4-b5 with ...c5-c4. Then he gets a stalemate shelter on c5 for his king. We continue the analysis and come to see that, with this pawn configuration, the outcome depends on the flank opposition after capturing the h-pawn.

The superficial move 2 c3+? enables Black to win the fight for the opposition and to achieve a draw: 2...♔d5! 3 ♔g5 c5 4 b5 c4 5 ♔h6 ♔d6 6 ♔×h7 ♔d7 7 ♔h6 (7 ♔g6 ♔e6 8 ♔g5 ♔e5 9 ♔g4 ♔e6) 7...♔d6 8 ♔h5 ♔d5 9 ♔h4 ♔d6! 10 ♔g4 ♔e6 11 ♔f4 ♔d6 12 ♔e4 (12 ♔f5 ♔d5 13 ♔f6 ♔d6) 12...♔c5! (Black's defensive plan!) 13 ♔e3 (13 ♔e5 Stalemate) 13...♔d5! 14 ♔f3 ♔e5 15 ♔g4 ♔e6! etc.

2 ♔e6!

White must take the d5-square away from the black king.

2...h6 3 c3+!

3 ♔f5? is premature: 3...c5 4 b5 ♔d5! 5 ♔g6 c4 6 ♔×h6 c3= or 6 c3 ♔e5 7 ♔×h6 ♔d6! and Black holds the opposition again.

3...♔c4 4 ♔e5!

It is important to entice the pawn to h5. 4 ♔f6? c5 5 b5 ♔d5 6 ♔g6 c4 7 ♔×h6 ♔d6!= is erroneous.

4...h5 5 ♔f5 c6!? 6 ♔g5 ♔d5 7 ♔h4!

An obligatory loss of a tempo - after 7 ♔×h5? c5 8 b5 c4 it is again White who is in a zugzwang.

7...c5 (there is nothing else) **8 b5 c4 9 ♔×h5**

White has won the fight for the opposition! The rest is standard (approaching with the help of outflanking).

9...♔d6 10 ♔h6! (10 ♔g4? ♔e6=) **10...♔d5** (10...♔d7 11 ♔h7 or 11 ♔g5 ♔e6 12 ♔g6) **11 ♔g7! ♔e6 12 ♔g6+−.**

1/53. Yermolinsky – I. Ivanov,
USA ch, Parsippany 1996

1 g5!

With this move, White not only gets a spare tempo (h3-h4) but also deprives the black king of the important f6-square.

The actual game continuation was 1 gf? gf 2 ♔e2 ♔e7 3 ♔d3 h5 4 ♔×d4 h4 5 ♔d3 Draw.

1...♔f7 2 ♔e2 ♔e7 (2...♔e6 3 ♔d3 ♔d5 4 e6 ♔×e6 5 ♔×d4⊙) **3 ♔d3 ♔e6 4 ♔×d4 ♔d7**

Now White should sacrifice the e-pawn and occupy the corresponding square d4 when Black captures it; this will put Black in zugzwang.

5 ♔c3 ♔e6 6 ♔c4⊙ ♔d7 7 e6+! ♔e7 8 ♔d3⊙ ♔×e6 9 ♔d4⊙ ♔f7 10 ♔e5 ♔e7 11 h4⊙ +–

If Black tries 1...♔g7 (planning 2...h5), the simplest is 2 e6! ♔f8 3 ♔e2 ♔e8 4 ♔d3 ♔e7 5 ♔c4!⊙ ♔×e6 6 ♔×d4⊙, transposing into the main line.

1/54. E. Post, 1941

A breakthrough is threatened (1 f4? b5! 2 cb c4), therefore the white king must enter the square of the c-pawn. The move 1 ♔g5 seems illogical because it creates no threat (2 ♔×g6 or 2 f4 will be still met with 2...b5). 1 ♔g4 (△ 2 f4) speaks for itself, the breakthrough fails thereafter and the black king must run to the kingside. But let us look what can happen:

1 ♔g4 ♔b8! 2 f4 ♔c7 3 f5 gf+ 4 ef ♔d7 5 f6! ♔e6 6 ♔g5 ♔f7 7 ♔f5. Black is in zugzwang, but his spare tempo 7...b6! saves him: the white king must go to an unfavorable square (g5).

8 ♔g5 d5 9 cd c4 10 d6 c3 11 d7 c2 12 d8♕ c1♕+ the pawn promotes with check.

Seeking for an improvement for White, we come back to 1 ♔g5. Yes it creates no threat but still, how should Black react? 1...♔b6 is bad in view of 2 ♔×g6! (the black king is an obstacle for ...b7-b5), the same reply follows after 1...♔a6 (if 2...b5 White takes the pawn with check). If 1...♔b8 then 2 f4! b5 3 f5 gf 4 ef and the f-pawn promotes first with check. What remains is the waiting move 1...b6, but then Black lacks the highly important spare tempo.

1 ♔g5!! b6□ 2 ♔g4! ♔b7 3 f4 ♔c7 4 f5 gf+ 5 ef (White has created a distant passed pawn) **5...♔d7 6 f6!**

A mistake would be 6 ♔g5? d5 7 cd c4 8 ♔f4? (8 f6=) 8...b5! 9 ab a4 10 b6 c3! 11 ♔e3 a3! 12 b7 ♔c7 13 f6 c2!–+. This technique of decoying the king into a check is already known to us from Khachaturov's study (exercise 1/24).

6...♔e6 7 ♔g5 ♔f7 8 ♔f5⊙ d5 9 cd c4 10 d6 c3 11 d7 c2 12 d8♕ c1♕ 13 ♕e7+ with checkmate.

1/55. Randviir - Keres, Pärnu 1947

1...♔b5!

In case of 1...♔b6? 2 ♔c4 a5 3 a4⊙ Black is forced to waste his spare tempo before the critical moment arrives: 3...h6. Thereafter both 4 d6 ♔c6 5 d7 ♔×d7 6 ♔×c5 and the more simple continuation 4 ♔d3 ♔c7 5 ♔c3! lead to a draw ("untouchable pawns").

2 a4+ (2 ♔c3 c4 3 ♔d4 c3! 4 ♔×c3 ♔c5–+) **2...♔b6 3 ♔c4 a5!** (3...h6? 4 a5+) **4 d6**

4 ♔d3 loses immediately: 4...♔c7 5 ♔c3 ♔d6 6 ♔c4 h6⊙.

4...♔c6 5 d7 ♔×d7 6 ♔×c5 ♔e7

The king goes to the kingside to create the threat ...h7-h5 (so that White has no time to attack the a5-pawn). 6...♔e8 is also playable; White responds with 7 ♔d4! (rather than 7 ♔d5? ♔e7!⊙).

7 ♔d5 ♔f7 8 ♔e4 (8 ♔d6 h5)

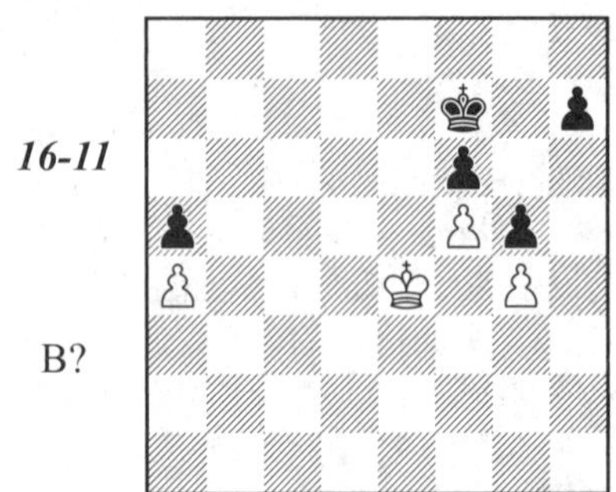

16-11

B?

8...h5? is premature here: 9 gh ♔g7 10 ♔f3 ♔h7 11 ♔g3= ("untouchable pawns"). But how should White proceed if he is on move? If 9 ♔e3(f3) then 9...♔e7 10 ♔e4 ♔d6 11 ♔d4 h6⊙ (this is what the spare tempo is needed for!). If 9 ♔d4(d5) then 9...h5 10 gh ♔g7–+ (or 9...♔g7 △ 10...h5–+).

8...♔f8!⊙

Thus, the move is passed to the opponent. The f8-square is equivalent to f7 in all aspects (two steps to both d6 and h6). 8...♔g7 is less precise: 9 ♔f3! ♔g8 10 ♔e3! ♔f7 11 ♔e4!.

9 ♔e3 ♔e7! 10 ♔e4 ♔d6 11 ♔d4 h6⊙ 12 ♔e4 (11 ♔c4 ♔e5 12 ♔b5 h5 13 gh

♔×f5 14 ♔×a5 g4) **12...♔c5 13 ♔e3 ♔d5**

Almost everything wins now. For example, 13...♔b4 14 ♔d4 ♔×a4 is good enough.

14 ♔d3 ♔e5 15 ♔e3 h5 16 gh ♔×f5 17 ♔f3 ♔e6

17...g4+ 18 ♔g3 ♔g5 is also strong: 19 h6 ♔×h6 20 ♔×g4 ♔g6 (the f-pawn is standing above the c1-h6 diagonal).

18 ♔g4 ♔f7 19 ♔f5 ♔g7 White resigned.

Chapter Two

2/1. A. Troitsky, 1906

1 ♔f3!

Rather than 1 ♔f2? ♔h1 2 ♘g3+ ♔h2 3 ♘e4 ♔h1 ⊙, and White fails to checkmate. As we already know, a knight cannot "lose" a tempo.

1...♔h1 2 ♔f2 ♔h2 3 ♘c3

The goal is the f1-square. It can also be reached via ♘d4-f5-e3-f1.

3...♔h1 4 ♘e4 ♔h2 5 ♘d2 ♔h1 6 ♘f1⊙ h2 7 ♘g3#.

2/2. L. Kubbel, 1934

White can exchange rooks by force if he attacks the knight. But first, in order to make this endgame drawn, the h-pawn should be enticed to h3.

1 ♖b7! h6

1...♖h3? 2 ♖b1, and there is no 2...♘c2?? in view of 3 ♖b3+.

2 ♖b6 h5 3 ♖b5 h4 4 ♖b4!

Attacking the h-pawn with the king is not justified: 4 ♔g2? ♖f4 5 ♔h3 ♘c2 6 ♖h5 ♘e3 7 ♖×h4 ♖f3#.

4...h3 (4...♘c2 5 ♖×h4 ♘e3 6 h3=) **5 ♖b1 ♘c2 6 ♖b3+ ♔e2 7 ♖×f3 ♔×f3 8 ♔h1(f1)=.**

2/3. P. Faragó, 1943

1 h7? ♖g5 2 h6 ♘c6 3 a7 ♘e5(d8) loses immediately, hence White's initial move is forced.

1 ♔g7 ♖g5+ 2 ♔f6!

2 ♔f7? is erroneous: 2...♖f5+ 3 ♔g7 ♔e7 4 h7 ♖f7+ 5 ♔g6 ♖f8 6 ♔g7 ♖h8! 7 h6 ♘c6 8 a7 ♘e5 9 a8♕ ♖×a8 10 h8♕ ♖×h8 11 ♔×h8 ♔f7 12 ♔h7 ♘d7 13 ♔h8 ♘f8 14 h7 ♘g6#. Checkmating the white king in the corner with the knight is Black's goal in all cases, while White has to find a way to avoid this sorrowful outcome.

2...♖g8

2...♖×h5 3 ♔g7 ♔e7 4 h7 leads to nothing, for example: 4...♖h3!? 5 h8♕ ♖g3+ 6 ♔h6!= (rather than 6 ♔h7? ♔f7–+).

3 h7!

The king prefers to stay on f6 where it deprives the black knight of the important e5-square. After 3 ♔f7? White cannot hold the game anymore: 3...♖e8! (the rook will be sacrificed in the corner only when the white pawn comes to h7) 4 h7 ♖h8 5 h6 ♘c6 6 a7 ♘e5+! 7 ♔f6 ♔d6! 8 ♔g7 ♔e7, and we have already seen what follows. By the way, another winning method exists: 8...♔e6 9 a8♕ ♖×a8 10 h8♕ ♖a7+!? 11 ♔g8 ♘g4 12 ♔f8 (12 h7 ♘h6+ 13 .♔f8 ♖a8+ 14 ♔g7 ♘f5+ and 15...♖×h8) 12...♘f6, and White has no satisfactory defense against the threat 13...♖f7#.

3...♖h8 (3...♖a8 4 ♔g7=) **4 h6!** (rather than 4 ♔g7? ♔e7 5 h6 ♘c6–+ again) **4...♘c6**

16-12

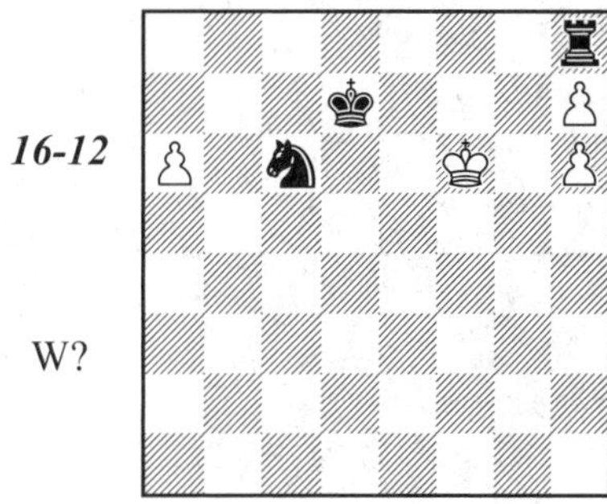

W?

5 a7!

Before White sends his king to the corner he wants to get rid of the a-pawn (5...♘×a7 6 ♔g7=). Of course, Black does not take the pawn but his knight cannot go to e5; it must occupy a less favorable square.

5...♘e7 6 ♔g7

6 a8♕? is premature: 6...♖×a8 7 ♔g7 ♘f5+.

6...♔e6 7 a8♕! ♖×a8 8 h8♕ ♖×h8

White's last opportunity for a mistake: 9 ♔×h8? ♔f7 10 ♔h7 (we know this position from exercise 2/1) 10...♘c6 11 ♔h8 ♘e5 12 ♔h7 ♘d7 13 ♔h8 ♘f8 14 h7 ♘g6#.

9 h7!=.

2/4. Mankus - Fokin, Vilnius 1977

If Black had time to block the pawn by playing 1...♘d6 he would have stood better.

1 d6! ♘×d6 2 ♗d5±

White's next move is 3 ♗×b7!, and the bishop cannot be captured because White promotes after 3...♘×b7 4 a6. But White still has an obvious advantage even if Black does not take the bishop. In this sort of open position, with a distant passed pawn as well, a bishop is much stronger than a knight.

2...♔f8 3 ♗×b7! ♔e7 4 ♗d5 f5 5 h4 h6 6 ♔f1 ♔d7 7 ♔e2 ♘b5 8 ♔d3 ♔d6 9 ♗f7 ♔c5 (9...g5 10 ♔c4 ♘c7 11 ♗g6) 10 ♗×g6 ♘d6 11 a6 ♔b6 12 ♗×f5! and White won (if 12...♘×f5 then 13 ♔e4 and 14 ♔×e5 is decisive).

2/5. N. Grigoriev, 1932

The knight cannot arrive at h2 in time — at the most, it can only prevent a promotion by taking the h1-square under control. Then White's only hope is to create a barrier that will make it difficult for the black king to approach.

1 ♘g6? h3 2 ♘f4 h2 3 ♘e2+ ♔d2! 4 ♘g3 ♔e1 −+ does not work. Let us try another route.

1 ♘f7! h3 2 ♘g5!

2 ♘d6? fails to 2...♔d3 3 ♘f5 ♔e2! 4 ♘g3+ ♔f2 −+.

2...h2 3 ♘e4+

16-13

B

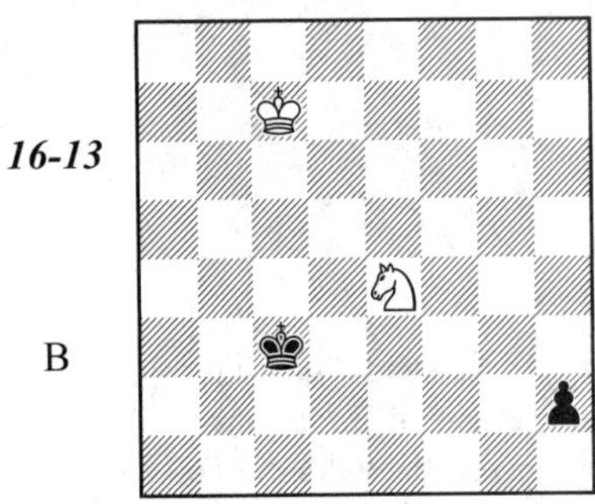

Where should the black king go? After 3...♔d3?! 4 ♘g3! a barrier arises, as we already know. If 3...♔d4 then 4 ♘g3? is bad: 4...♔e5! 5 ♔c6 ♔f4 6 ♘h1 ♔f3 and the white king fails to come to f2, but White has 4 ♘f2! ♔c3 (both 4...♔e3 and 4...♔e5 are met with 5 ♘g4+) 5 ♔d6 ♔d2 6 ♔e5 ♔e2 7 ♘h1 ♔f3 8 ♔d4 ♔g2 9 ♔e3 ♔×h1 10 ♔f2=.

3...♔c2 4 ♘g3!

4 ♘f2? ♔d2 leads to the line from the previous annotation, but with an extra tempo for Black.

4...♔d1 5 ♔d6 ♔e1 6 ♔e5 ♔f2 7 ♔f4=.

2/6. D. Gurgenidze, 1970

(after N. Grigoriev, 1934)

White can easily parry the threat to the h7 knight: by means of approaching the b5-pawn with his king, e.g. 1 ♔b3(a3) ♔f7 2 ♔b4 ♔g7 3 ♔×b5 ♔×h7 4 ♔c4=. However Black has a more dangerous plan, namely 1...♔e6! and if 2 ♔b4 then 2...♔f5 3 ♔×b5 h5 −+. Since the white king fails to enter the square of the h-pawn after 1...♔e6 the task of fighting against it must be taken by the knight: 2 ♘f8+. It is highly important to foresee its entire route, because the correct first move can only be discovered in this way.

1 ♔a3!!

Only here, to keep the b3-square free. Both 1 ♔b3? ♔e6! and 1 ♔b2? ♔f7! are losing.

1...♔e6! 2 ♘f8+! ♔f5 3 ♘d7 h5 4 ♘c5 h4 5 ♘b3!!

5 ♘d3? h3 6 ♘f2 h2 7 ♔b4 ♔f4 −+.

5...h3 6 ♘d2 h2 (6...♔f4 7 ♘f1=) **7 ♘f1 h1♕ 8 ♘g3+.**

2/7. Stangl - Schneider, Berlin 1992

In the actual game, White played 1 ♘g7?. The position after 1...♗f6 2 ♘×h5 ♗d4! (△ 3...♔d3) is definitely lost: White cannot prevent Black's king march to the queenside pawns.

3 c5 ♗×c5 4 ♘f6. In case of the more stubborn 4 ♘g7!? ♔d3 5 ♘e6 both 5...♗e3 6 ♘d8 ♔c4 7 ♘c6= and 5...♔c4 6 ♘g5 ♔b4 (6...f2 7 ♘e4) 7 ♘×f3 ♔×a4 8 ♘d2 ♔b4 9 ♔e2= are useless. As Müller has demonstrated, Black wins after 5...♗e7! 6 ♔f2 ♔e4 7 ♘c7 ♗h4+ 8 ♔f1 ♔d4 9 ♘b5+ ♔c4 10 ♘d6+ ♔b4 11 ♘f5 ♗f6 12 ♔f2 ♔×a4 13 ♔×f3 ♔b3 −+.

4...♔d4 5 ♘d7 ♔d5 6 ♔e1 ♗d4 7 ♔d2 ♔c4 8 ♘b8 ♔c5 9 ♘d7+ ♔b4 10 ♘b8 ♔×a4 11 ♘c6 ♗b6 12 ♘e5 f2 13 ♔e2 ♔b3 14 ♘f3 a4 15 ♘d2+ ♔b4 White resigned.

White can advance his c-pawn in order to gain the bishop for it. It looks highly risky but should be checked, because the alternative is completely hopeless.

1 c5! ♗g3 2 c6 h4 3 c7 ♗×c7 4 ♘×c7 h3 5 ♘d5+ ♔d4 (5...♔e4 6 ♘f6+ ♔f5 7 ♘h5=) **6 ♘e7!**

16-14

B

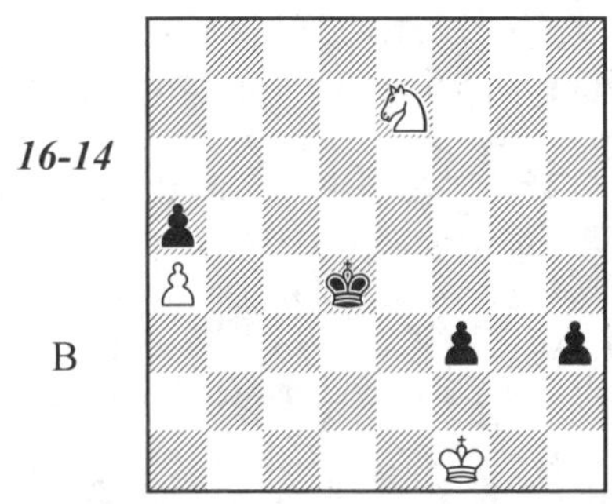

6...h2 (6...♔e4 7 ♔g1!=) **7 ♘f5+ ♔c4 8 ♘g3 ♔b4 9 ♔f2 ♔×a4 10 ♔×f3 ♔b3 11 ♔g2 a4 12 ♘e2 ♔b2** (12...a3 13 ♘c1+) **13 ♘f4** (we know this drawing position from the Grigoriev's study) **13...♔c3!?** (13...a3 14 ♘d3+) **14 ♘d5+!** (14 ♘e2+? ♔d2!−+) **14...♔b3 15 ♘f4! a3 16 ♘d3=** (Dvoretsky).

2/8. I. Horowitz, I. Kashdan, 1928

White's barrier is not effective: Black plans 1...♔b4 followed with ...a5-a4-a3. For example, 1 ♔e7? ♔b4 2 ♔d6 a5 3 ♔d5 a4 4 ♘c4 ♔b5!⊙ 5 ♔d4 ♔b4 6 ♔d3 ♔b3=.

A better place for the knight should be investigated.

1 ♘b3!! ♔b4 2 ♘a1+−

This barrier is solid enough. An advance of the a-pawn gives Black nothing now: if ...a4-a3 then ♘c2+ with ba to follow.

We should also explore the attempt to overcome the barrier from the side. As we shall see it takes too much time.

1...♔c4!? 2 ♘a1! ♔d3 3 ♔e7 ♔d2 4 ♔d6 a5 (4...♔c1 5 b4! ♔b2 6 ♔c6!, rather than 6 ♔c5? ♔c3!⊙=) 5 ♔c5 a4 (5...♔c1 6 b3 ♔b2 7 ♔b5) 6 ♔b4 ♔c1 7 ♔a3 (7 ♔c3) 7...♔b1 8 ♘b3!+−.

2/9. Tal - Böök, Stockholm 1960*

Black's king must go to the hostile pawns but 1...♔d4 is met with the fork 2 ♘e6+. An advance of the g-pawn enables White to fix the kingside: 1...g6? 2 g5! hg 3 hg a4 4 ♔c1! ♔d4 5 ♘e6+ ♔e5 6 ♘f8 ♔f5 7 ♘h7+−, or 1...g5? 2 hg hg 3 ♔c1 (3 ♘e4+ ♔b2 4 ♘×g5 a4 5 ♘f3 a3 6 ♘d4 a2 7 ♘c2 is also strong) 3...♔d4 4 ♘d7! ♔e4 5 ♔b2 ♔f4 6 ♘f6 ♔e5 7 ♘h5+−.

Let's study 1...♔d4? more attentively. We can see that Black loses here, too: 2 ♘e6+ ♔e5 3 ♘×g7 ♔f4 4 g5 hg 5 h5 ♔e5 6 ♘e8! (△ 7 h6) 6...♔f5 7 ♘d6+ ♔f6 8 ♘e4+ and 9 ♘g3+−, or 5...g4 6 h6 g3 7 ♔e2!+−.

However, the last line gives us a tip to the correct solution: first the white king should be diverted to the queenside.

1...a4!! 2 ♔c1

After 2 ♘×a4+ ♔d4 neither the knight nor the king can help the pawns in time.

2...a3 (2...♔d4 is also possible already) **3 ♔b1 ♔d4 4 ♘e6+ ♔e5 5 ♘×g7 ♔f4 6 g5 hg 7 h5**

16-15

B?

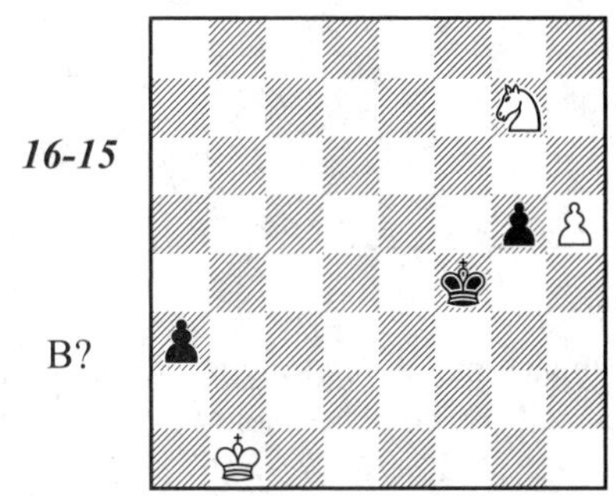

7...g4! 8 h6 g3 9 ♘e6+ (9 ♘h5+ ♔g5) **9...♔f5! 10 h7 g2 11 ♘d4+ ♔g6=**.

Chapter Three

3/1. H. Rinck, 1920

1 ♘e7 is met with 1...♘d7 △ 2...♘f6, and 1 ♘f6 fails after 1...♘c6 △ 2...♘e7. A gain of the knight for the g-pawn gives White nothing; he should try to deflect the knight from the passed pawn, exploiting the fact that Black's king is misplaced.

1 ♘e7! ♘d7 2 ♘c6+ ♔b6

In case of 2...♔a6, the deflecting knight sacrifice decides: 3 ♘b8+! ♘×b8 4 g7. And now, again, the same technique rapidly leads to the goal:

3 ♘×e5! ♘f6 4 ♘d7+! ♘×d7 5 e5+−.

3/2. Szabó - Grószpéter, Kecskemet 1984

1 ♘d2! ♘×d2

He must accept the knight sacrifice because both 1...♘e5 2 ♔×b6 and 1...h4 2 ♘×c4 h3 3 ♘e3 (△ 4 ♘f1) 3...h2 4 ♘g4+ are quite bad.

2 a5 (2 ♔×b6? h4)

In this position, the game (it was played in a team competition) was adjudicated and White was awarded a win. The main line is instructive and nice:

2...ba

2...h4 3 ab h3 4 b7 h2 5 b8♕ h1♕ 6 ♕h8+

2...♘c4 3 a6 ♘d6 (3...h4 4 ♔b8) 4 ♔xb6 h4 5 ♔c5! (5 ♔c6? h3; 5 ♔a5? ♘c4+; 5 a7? ♘c8+ 6 ♔c5 ♘xa7 7 b6 ♘c6!) 5...♘c8 6 b6+-.

3 b6 ♘c4 4 b7 ♘e5

16-16

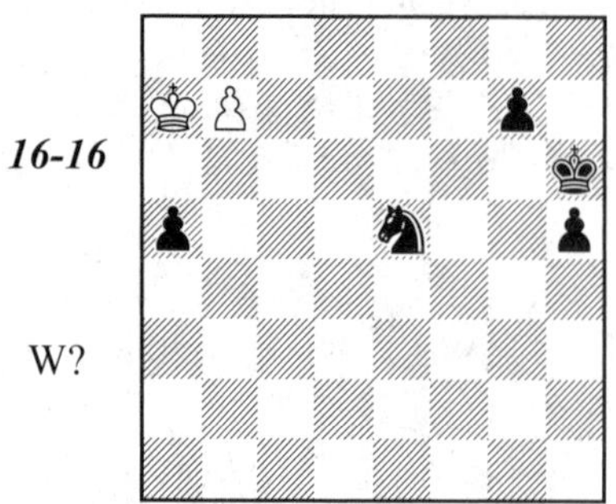

W?

5 ♔b8!!

An unusual move: the king interferes with his own pawn! The natural looking 5 ♔b6? is erroneous: 5...♘d7+ 6 ♔c6 (6 ♔c7 ♘c5) 6...♘b8+ 7 ♔c7 a4! (it makes no sense for Black to repeat moves 7...♘a6+ 8 ♔b6 ♘b8) 8 ♔xb8 a3 with two extra pawns in the resulting queen-and-pawn endgame.

5...♘c6+

5...a4 6 ♔c7+-; 5...♘d7+ 6 ♔c8!+-.

6 ♔c7 ♘b4 7 ♔b6+-.

3/3. Bonner - Medina, Haifa ol 1976

The goal is achieved by means of a knight sacrifice followed by pawn breakthrough to the promotion square.

1...♘c3! 2 bc a4 3 cd cd-+

White resigned after 4 c3 a3.

3/4. Vilela - Augustin, Prague 1980

1 ♔c5!

A shouldering! 1 a5? does not work in view of 1...♔d6! 2 a6 ♘e5!=.

1...f5 (1...♘e5 2 a5 ♘d7+ 3 ♔c6!+-) **2 a5 f4 3 a6 f3 4 ♘c4!+-**

4 a7? f2 5 a8♕ f1♕ 6 ♕e8+ ♔f5!= leads only to a draw. Now, on the contrary, the white knight holds the f-pawn while the a-pawn cannot be stopped.

The remainder was 4...f2 5 ♘d2 ♘f6 6 ♔c6! (6 a7? ♘e4+) 6...♘e4 7 ♘f1 and Black resigned.

3/5. Timman - Ree, Amsterdam 1984

1 ♘f5?! suggests itself, but what to do after 1...♘g2 ? In case of 2 g6? ♘f4 3 g7 ♘h5+ 4 ♔f7 ♘xg7 5 ♔xg7 ♔c4 the knight cannot arrive in time to prevent an exchange of queenside pawns. The tempting deflecting knight sacrifice 2 ♘e3+? ♘xe3 3 g6 is refuted by means of 3...♔d6! 4 g7 ♘d5+ 5 ♔f7 ♘e7. As Müller has discovered, White still wins after 2 ♘e7+! ♔d6 (2...♔c4 3 ♔e5 ♘h4 4 ♔f4+-) 3 g6 ♘f4 4 a4 ♘xg6 5 ♘xg6 a5 6 b5 ♔c5 7 ♔e5 ♔b4 8 ♔d4 ♔xa4 9 ♔c4.

But playing for zugzwang wins much more simply.

1 a4! b5 2 a5⊙ ♔c4 3 ♘f5 ♘g2 4 ♔e5! Black resigned.

3/6. V. Halberstadt, 1949

To achieve success, one must remember the "triangulation" technique.

1 ♔g5!! ♔a7

If 1...♔b8 then 2 ♔f6 ♔c8 (2...♔c7 3 ♘e6+) 3 ♔g7 ♘d7 4 ♘xd7 ♔xd7 5 ♔f7+-.

2 ♔f5

The tempo is lost, and Black is in zugzwang.

2...♔b6 3 ♘d7+! ♘xd7 4 e6+-

1 ♔f5? misses the victory: after 1...♔a7! it is White who is in zugzwang. 2 ♘d7 does not win here in view of 2...♘xd7 3 e6 ♘b6! 4 e7 ♘c8, while 2 ♔f6 is met with 2...♔b6=.

3/7. Cvetkovic - Stefanovic, Porec 1987

Thanks to the distant passed a-pawn, the white king is placed closer to the kingside than his opponent. But how does he save the pawns from annihilation by the black knight? This mission is far from simple.

1 ♘xh7? ♘xh2 △ 2...♘f1=;

1 ♔d4? ♘xh2 2 ♔e3 ♘g4+ 3 ♔f3 ♘f6=;

1 h4? ♘xg3 2 ♔d4 ♘e2+ 3 ♔e3 (3 ♔e5 ♘g1 △ 4...♘f3=) 3...♘c3 4 ♘xh7 ♘d5+ 5 ♔f3 ♔xa4 6 ♘f8 ♘e7, and White cannot activate his king in time: 7 ♔e3 (7 ♔e2 ♔b4 8 ♔d3 ♔c5) 7...♘d5+ 8 ♔e2!? ♘xf4+ 9 ♔f3 ♘h5 10 ♘xg6 ♔b5 11 ♘e7 ♔c5 12 ♘xf5 ♔d5 13 ♔g4 ♔e5=

The last line can be improved: if White takes a single step with his h-pawn instead of a double. In that case, the king gets an additional route: via h4.

1 h3!! ♘xg3 2 ♔d4! (2 ♔d5? ♘e2 3 ♔e5 ♘g1=) **2...♘e2+**

If 2...♔xa4 then 3 ♘xh7 △ 4 ♘f8+-. After 2...♘h5, 3 ♔e5 decides (rather than 3 ♔e3? ♘f6).

3 ♔e3 ♘c3 4 ♘xh7 ♘d5+ 5 ♔f3 ♔xa4 6 ♘f8

16-17

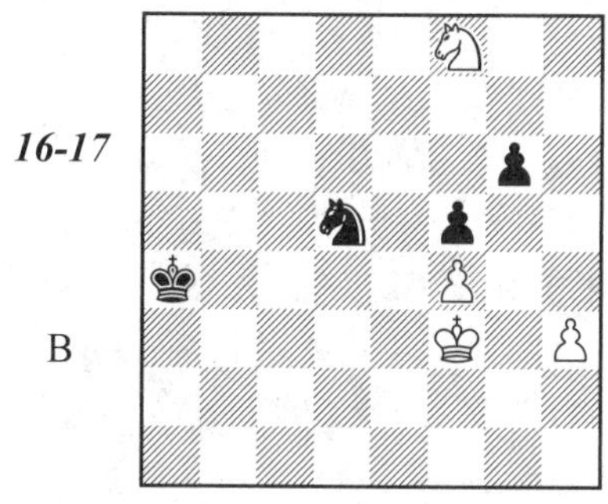

B

6...♘e7 is hopeless now: 7 ♔g3! ♔b4 8 ♔h4 ♔c4 9 ♔g5 ♔d5 10 ♘×g6.

The game continued 6...♔b5 7 ♘×g6 ♔c5 8 ♔g3! (the king must be activated) 8...♔d6 9 ♔h4 ♔e6 10 ♔g5 ♘c3 11 ♘f8+ ♔f7 12 ♘d7 ♘e4+ 13 ♔×f5, and White had two extra pawns.

Chapter Four

4/1. O. Frink, 1923

1 ♗d7!! ♔e3 2 h4 ♔e4 (2...♔f4 3 ♔d4+–) **3 h5 ♔e5 4 h6 ♔f6 5 ♗e8!+–**.

4/2. G. van Breukelen, 1969

Is it possible to prevent the black king's march to the corner? Yes, if White manages to discover the reciprocal zugzwang positions and reach them with Black to move.

1 ♔d7!! ♔f4 2 ♔e8! ♔g5 (2...♔f5 3 ♔f7) **3 ♔e7!⊙ ♔g6 4 ♔f8⊙ ♔h6** (4...♔f6 5 ♗f7) **5 ♔f7 ♔g5 6 ♔g7+–**

1 ♔d6? leads only to a draw: 1...♔f4 2 ♔e7 (2 ♔e6 ♔g3!=) ♔g5⊙ 3 ♔e8 (3 ♗e6 ♔g6=; 3 ♔f7 ♔h4=) 3...♔f6! (or 3...♔h5!) 4 ♔f8 ♔g6⊙, because both zugzwang positions arise with White on move.

4/3. A. Gerbstman, 1928

1 b6 ab

1...♔c6 2 ♗e7! ab (2...♔b7 3 ♗d8+–) 3 a6 is the same.

2 a6 ♔c6 3 ♗e7!

Thanks to the threat of 4 ♗d8, White distracts the king to c7 gaining a supremely important tempo. The straightforward 3 ♗×d6? does not give more than a draw: 3...b5 4 ♗c5 ♔c7 5 ♗a7 b4 6 ♔d3 ♔c6 7 ♔c4 b3 8 ♔×b3 ♔b5=.

3...♔c7 (3...b5 4 ♗d8 d5 5 ♔d3 b4 6 ♔d4⊙ +–) **4 ♗×d6+! ♔c6 5 ♔d3 b5 6 ♗c5 ♔c7 7 ♗a7 ♔c6 8 ♔c3+–**.

4/4. V. Smyslov, 1999

1 ♘f1! ♗×f1 (1...c2 2 ♔d2 ♗×f1 3 f4!!) **2 f4!!**

White's goal is the elementary fortress that we know already. 2 d5? ♗g2 3 d6 ♔f7 loses.

2...♗g2 (2...gf? 3 a7+–) **3 ♔d1!**

3 a7? is erroneous in view of 3...♗f3!–+.

3...♗e4 4 a7 ♔f7 5 d5!

White uses his passed pawns to distract the bishop from protecting his own pawns. The last two moves can be transposed.

5...♗×d5 6 ♔c2 ♔e6 7 ♔×c3 ♔d7 8 a8♕ (or 8 ♔d4 ♔d6 9 a8♕) **8...♗×a8 9 ♔×c4=**

White has only one remaining thing to do: to return his king to g1.

4/5. H. Weenink, 1922

Black's hopes to build an elementary fortress, e.g. 1 ♗h7? ♔c3 2 ♔b5 ♔d4 3 ♔c6 ♔e5 4 g6 (4 ♔d7 g6!=) 4...♔e6 5 ♗g8+ ♔e7=.

White can gain the missing tempo by means of a bishop sacrifice followed by shouldering in the arising pawn endgame, but the straightforward attempt 1 ♔b4? ♔×c2 2 ♔c4 does not win 2...♔d2 3 ♔d4 ♔e2 4 ♔e4 ♔f2 5 ♔f4 (5 ♔f5 ♔g3 6 ♔g6 ♔g4=) 5...♔g2 6 ♔g4 g6 7 ♔f4 ♔h3=.

1 ♗b1!!

A brilliant move! After 1...♔c3 the bishop is better placed on b1 than on h7: 2 ♔b5 ♔d4 3 ♔c6 ♔e5 4 ♔d7 g6 (4...♔f4 5 g6+–) 5 ♔e7, and the black king cannot step to f5.

1...♔×b1 also loses: **2 ♔b3 ♔c1 3 ♔c3 ♔d1** (3...♔b1 4 g6+–) **4 ♔d3 ♔e1 5 ♔e3 ♔f1 6 ♔f3.**

4/6. E. Somov-Nasimovich, 1935

The rook must go back from g8, but where? Only a deep precise calculation can tell.

If 1 ♖f8+? then 1...♗f5 2 g8♕ h1♕+ 3 ♔a2 ♕d5+! 4 ♕×d5 cd. The d-pawn can be stopped by means of 5 ♔b1 d2+ 6 ♖×f5+ ♔×f5 7 ♔c2, but the pawn ending turns out to be losing: 7...♔e5 8 ♔×d2 ♔d4 and if 9 b3 then 9...a3–+ (rather than 9...ab? 10 b5=).

1 ♖h8! d2 2 g8♕ d1♕+ 3 ♔a2 ♕b3+! 4 ♕×b3 ab+

16-18

W?

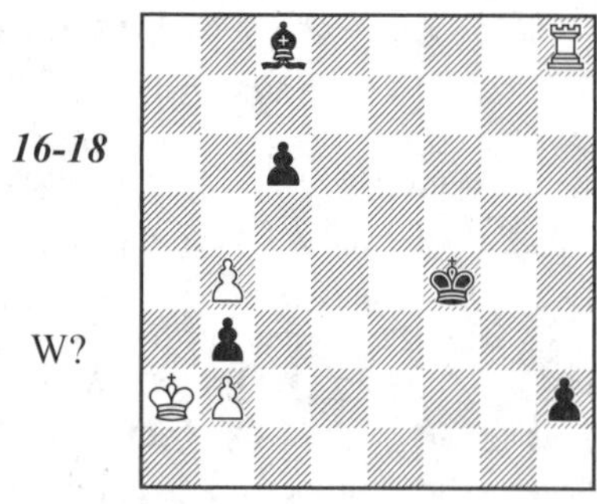

16-19

W?

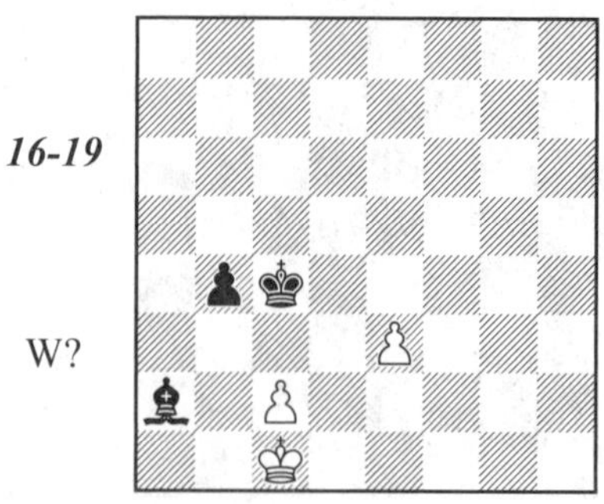

5 ♔a3!!

In case of 5 ♔×b3? ♔g3 6 ♖×h2 (forced – otherwise 6...♗h3–+) 6...♔×h2 7 ♔c4 ♗a6+! (7...♔g3? 8 ♔c5 ♗d7 9 ♔d6 ♗e8 10 ♔e7 ♗h5 11 ♔d6 ♗f3 12 ♔c5 and 13 b5=) 8 ♔c5 ♗b5 White is lost. 5 ♔a1? ♔g3 6 ♖×h2 ♔×h2 7 b5 c5! is also useless.

5...♔g3 (△ 6...♗h3) **6 ♖×h2 ♔×h2 7 b5! cb**

7...c5 makes no sense in view of 8 ♔×b3=. Now the drawing pawn structure is built, and all that remains to do is a king retreat homewards.

8 ♔b4! ♔g3 9 ♔c3 ♔f2 10 ♔d2=.

4/7. H. Seyboth, 1908

1 ♗c5? ♗h2 2 f4 gf (△ 3...♗g3+) 3 ♗f2 loses to 3...♗f4! 4 c5 ♗g5! (△ 5...♗h4–+) 5 ♗g3+ ♔d8 6 ♔f2 ♗e3+. In order to stop the menacing g2-pawn White must give all his pieces and pawns away.

1 d6+! ed 2 ♗×d6+! ♔×d6 3 c5+ ♔×c5 4 ♗f1! gf♕+ 5 ♔×f1 ♗h2 6 f3! g3 (6...gf 7 ♔f2) **7 ♔g2** (or 7 f4) with a draw.

4/8. P. Kiriakov, 1997

1 c4! (otherwise 1...♗a2–+) **1...b4!** (1...bc? 2 ♔d2=) **2 ♔d1!**

White must "lose" a tempo. After 2 ♔d2? ♔c5 he is put in zugzwang. 3 ♔c1 ♗a2 4 c3 bc is hopeless, while 3 e4 loses to 3...♔d4! (rather than 3...♗a2? 4 c3).

2...♔c5 3 ♔d2!

Now it is Black who is in zugzwang, and it may seem that the fight is over 3...♔×c4 4 ♔c1 or 3...♗a2 4 c3! b3 5 ♔c1=. However Black still has resources.

3...♔×c4 4 ♔c1 ♗a2

5 ♔d2!!⊙

The "obvious" 5 ♔b2? is met with 5...♗b3!! 6 cb+ ♔d3 with a winning pawn endgame. Now, however, Black cannot avoid the Ponziani position.

5...♔b5 6 c3! b3 7 ♔c1=.

4/9. V. & M. Platov, 1911

1 h5! gh

1...♔×d3 2 hg fg 3 ♘c5+! (or 3 ♘b4+!) and 4 e6+–.

2 g6! fg 3 e6 ♗a3 4 ♘b4!! ♗×b4 5 a4

"Pants"! Yes the black king is in the square of the a-pawn, but his own pawns and bishop are obstacles on his way ("obstacles" is a method that we have seen when studying pawn endgames.

5...♔d4 6 a5 ♔c5 7 e7+–

5...♔×d3 does not help: 6 a5 d4 7 a6 ♔e2 8 a7 d3 9 a8♕ d2 10 ♕a2 ♔e1 (10...♔e3 11 ♕b3+) 11 ♔g2! d1♕ 12 ♕f2#.

4/10. M. Lewitt, 1933

1 ♔e4 ♗d8

The first move was obvious, but what to do now? The bishop plans to go to f6, 2 ♔f5 will be met with 2...♗b6. 2 ♔e5 (hoping for 2...♗c7+? 3 ♔d5+–) suggests itself, but Black has a defense: 2...♗g5! 3 h7 ♗c1 4 ♔d5 ♗×b2 5 ♔c6 ♗e5! 6 b6 ♔a6⊙=. We come to the conclusion that this zugzwang is reciprocal: Black's bishop is overburdened, but how can we reach this position with Black to play?

2 b6!! ♔a6! (2...♗×b6 3 h7; 2...♔×b6 3 ♔f5) **3 ♔e5! ♗g5 4 h7 ♗c1 5 ♔d6! ♗×b2 6 ♔c7!** (△ 7 b7) **6...♗e5+ 7 ♔c6⊙ ♗d4 8 b7 ♔a7 9 ♔c7+–**.

4/11. Minev - Dukanovic, Belgrade 1977

The "pawns in the crosshairs" method is applicable here.

1...Bc1! 2 h7 (2 g6+ Ke7 or 2...Kg8) **2...Kg7 3 g6 Bb2** (3...Kh8 4 f6 Bb2 5 f7 Ba3 6 Ke6 Kg7= is also playable) **4 Ke6** (the threat is 5 f6+ Bxf6 6 h8Q+ Kxh8 7 Kxf6) **4...Kh8! 5 f6 Bxf6 6 Kxf6** Stalemate

In the actual game, however, Black decided to wait, thinking that White will play g5-g6 anyway. But this idea failed.

1...Bc3? 2 h7! Kg7 (2...Bb2 3 f6) 3 Ke6! Kxh7

3...Kh8 does not help: 4 f6 Bb2 5 Kf7 (or 5 Ke7) 5...Bc3 6 Ke8! (6 g6? Bxf6=) 6...Bb2 (6...Kxh7 7 Kf7) 7 f7 Ba3 8 f8Q+ Bxf8 9 Kxf8 Kxh7 10 Kf7 Kh8 11 Kg6! Kg8 12 Kh6+–.

4 Kf7 Kh8 5 g6 Bb2 6 f6 Black resigned.

4/12. Azmaiparashvili - Shirov,
Madrid 1996

White's pawns are very dangerous; this can be seen from the following line: 1...Ke6? 2 Kg5 Bc6 3 f4! Be4 4 g4 (△ 5 f5+) 4...Bh7 (4...Kd7 5 Kh6!) 5 h5 a5 6 Kh6 Be4 7 Kg7+–.

Black should prevent f2-f4 by placing his bishop on f3, where the bishop will keep the advancing g- and h-pawns in the crosshairs.

1...Bc6!! 2 Kg5 Bf3! 3 Kf5 Kd5 4 g4 Kd6 5 h5 Kd5 6 Kf4 Bd1 7 Kg5 Bf3!=

White cannot make any progress because 8 h6? Be4 9 f4 Bh7! loses. The remainder was 8 Kf4 Bd1 9 Kg5 Bf3 10 Kf4 Draw.

Chapter Five

5/1. S. Tarrasch, 1921

Black cannot prevent White's pawns from taking one step forward: for this purpose, the bishop should have gone to c6. Therefore he must try to reach the basic drawing position with the pawns on the 5th rank (the bishop on f7 or g8, the king on d7).

1...Bb5? is erroneous in view of 2 Bb4+! (rather than 2 Bg3+? Ke7! 3 d5 Be8 4 e5 Bf7=) 2...Ke6 (2...Kc7 3 d5 Be8 4 e5 Bf7 5 e6) 3 d5+ Ke5 4 Bc3+ Kd6 5 Kd4 Be8 6 e5+. Black misses a single tempo in all these lines.

1...Bc4! 2 Bg3+ Kc6!

Of course not 2...Ke6? 3 Kd2 and 4 Kc3 planning the king's march to c5. As soon as the black king leaves e6 White plays d4-d5, and the bishop fails to come to f7.

3 Kf4 Bg8 4 Ke5 Kd7 5 d5 Bh7!

Pawns in the crosshairs: Black does not let the white king to go to f6. In the meantime, 5...Bf7 6 Kf6 Ke8! 7 Bf4 Bg8 is less precise but still good enough for a draw.

6 Kf4 Bg6 7 e5 Bf7!=.

5/2. Schöneberg – Starck,
DDR ch, Weimar 1968

Black's intentions are obvious: ...Ke5-f6 followed with ...e5-e4. This plan can be parried only by a king assault on d5 (similar to diagram 5-5). But prior to it White should get rid of his own b5-pawn, which only snarls his plans (positional factors are more important than pawns!).

1 b6!! Bxb6

Attempting to save a tempo by ignoring the b6-pawn fails: if 1...Ke5, then the simplest is 2 Kf3 Kf6 3 Ke2 e5 4 Kd3 Bxb6 5 Kc4, but 2 b7 Ba7 3 Kf3 Kf6 4 Ke2 e5 5 b8Q!! Bxb8 6 Kd3 e4+ 7 Kd4 is also playable.

2 Kf3 Ke5 3 Ke2! Kf6 4 Kd3 e5 5 Kc4 e4 6 Kd5 e3

In case of 6...Kg6 (with the idea 7...e3 8 Ba6 Kh5), both 7 Ke5 Bc7+ 8 Kd4= and 7 Kc4 f4 8 Kd5! e3 9 Bg4= are good.

7 Ba6

The draw is obvious now, e.g.: 7...g4 (7...Kg6 8 Be2) 8 hg fg 9 Ke4 (9 Bf1?? g3) 9...Kg5 10 Kd3! Kh4 11 Ke2 Kg3 and now either 12 Bc8 or 12 Kf1 Kh2 13 Bb7.

In the game, however, White failed to tackle the problem he was faced with.

1 Kf3? Ke5? (1...Bb6! was winning) 2 Bd7? (he could have saved the game with 2 b6! again) 2...Bb6!–+ 3 Ke2 Kf6.

The pawn is stopped on b5 where it blocks the important a6-f1 diagonal, so the king's march is not possible anymore: 4 Kd3 e5 5 Kc4 e4 6 Kd5 e3–+.

4 Kf3 e5 5 Bc6 Ke6 6 Bb7 e4+

This gain of the bishop leads to a quick finish. Black could have won in another way, too: 6...Kd6!? followed with ...Kc5-d4, as in the theoretical positions we have studied.

7 Bxe4 fe+ 8 Kxe4 Bf2

8...Bc7 9 b6 Bb8 (9...Bxb6?? 10 h4!=) 10 Kf3 (10 h4 g4) 10...Kf5 11 Ke3 Kg6–+ is equivalent.

9 b6 Kd6 10 Kf5 Bh4 White resigned.

Before we abandon this example, I want to draw your attention to another defensive possibility: a pawn sacrifice on the kingside.

1 h4?! gh

1...g4? seems to lead to a draw: 2 h5 Be3 3 Kf1 f4 4 Ke2 (rather than 4 h6? f3 5 h7 g3−+, but 4 Kg2!? is playable: 4...Ke5 5 h6 f3+ 6 Kg3 B×h6 7 b6 Kf5 8 B×e6+! K×e6 9 b7 f2 10 b8Q) 4...Bd4 5 Kd3 f3 (△ 6...g3) 6 Bb7 Bg7 7 Be4! (7 b6? Kc5 8 B×f3 gf 9 b7 Be5−+) 7...Kc5 8 Ke3 Bh6+ 9 Kf2= △ 10 Kg3.

2 Kh3 Bf2!? 3 b6

In case of 3 Kg2 Bb6 4 Kh3 Black can choose between 4...Bd8 5 b6□ B×b6 and 4...Ke5!? 5 K×h4 Kf6 6 Kg3 e5 7 Bb7 e4 8 Kf4 Bc7+ 9 Ke3 Ke5.

3...B×b6 4 K×h4

16-20

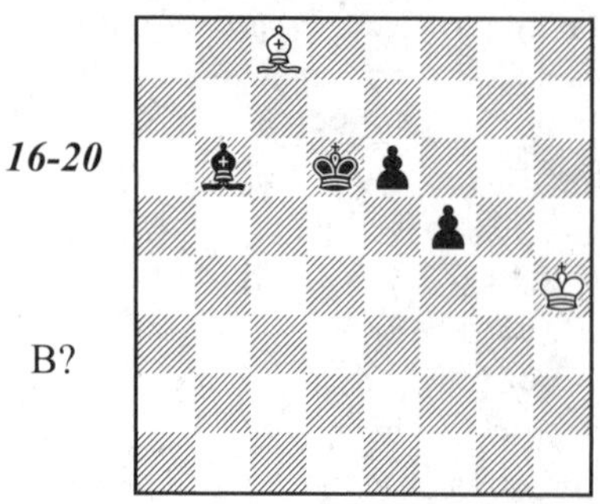

B?

Can Black win here? Frankly, I started the analysis of 1 h4 mainly to answer this question.

4...Ke7!

The incautious move 4...Ke5? allows White to save the position by means of 5 Kg5! (△ Kg6-f7). The same technique as in the 1 b6!! line, the king attacks the pawns from the rear!

5 Kg5 Kf7! 6 Kf4

If 6 Ba6 Be3+! 7 Kh4 then either 7...e5 or 7...Bf4, but by no means 7...Kf6?? 8 Kg3 e5 9 Kf3 and 10 Bd3=.

6...Kf6 7 Kf3 e5 8 Bb7

To play ...e5-e4, Black must bring his king to d4, but before that, as we already know, he should take control of the f4-square by transferring his bishop to h6.

8...Bc5 9 Bd5 Bf8!

White has two alternative defensive policies: one is waiting, another involves the king transfer to d3.

A) 10 Bc6 Bh6 11 Bb7 Ke7 12 Bc6 Kd6 13 Bb7 Bg5! 14 Ba8 Kc5 15 Bb7 Kd4−+. Notice the premature 13...Kc5? (instead of 13...Bg5!) allows White's salvation: 14 Bc8! e4+ 15 Ke2! (rather than 15 Kf2? f4 16 Bh3 Kd4! 17 Bg2 Kd3) 15...f4 16 Bh3! f3+ (otherwise 17 Bg2 leads to a basic drawing position) 17 Kf2, and there is no defense from Bh3-g4×f3.

B) **10 Ke3 Bh6+ 11 Kd3 Kg5 12 Bg2**

This plan is familiar to us from the previous exercise. However it fails here due to zugzwang.

12...Kf4 13 Bh3 e4+ 14 Ke2 Bf8 15 Kf2 Bc5+ 16 Ke2 Kg5!⊙ (but not 16...Ke5 17 Bg2 f4?? 18 Bh1=) **17 Bg2 Kg4 18 Kf1 Kg3 19 Bh1 Kh2 20 Bg2 Bd4**⊙ **−+.**

5/3. A. Chéron, 1957

1...Bc7!

The diagonal b8-h2 is quite long, but only two squares are available for the bishop: b8 and c7. Both 1...Bd6? 2 Kf5 Kd4 3 Ke6 Kc5 4 Kd7+− and 1...Bh2? 2 Kf5 Kd4 3 f4+− are bad.

2 Kf5 Kd4! 3 Ke6 (3 f4 Ke3) **3...Kc5 4 Kd7 Kb6** (the king "maintains the zone" quite successfully) **5 Be8 Bb8! 6 Ke6 Kc5 7 Kf5 Kd4 8 Kg4 Ke3 9 Bh5 Bc7!=.**

5/4. A. Norlin, 1922

White's king wants to go to f8, to help his pawn that is stopped by the black bishop, but Black then advances his pawn, deflecting the white bishop from the c7-pawn.

The principle of "the single diagonal" is helpful here. White should transfer his bishop to a5, where it will protect the c7-pawn and hold the black one. For this purpose, he must first protect the c7-pawn with the king, and thus prevent ...a7-a5-a4 (with the pawn on a4 it is a draw, e.g. 1 Kc5? a5! 2 Kb5 a4 3 Kb4 Kc8=).

1 Kc3! Bf7 2 Kb4 Be6 3 Be5!

The bishop should now clear the d6-square. 3 Kc5?! is inaccurate in view of 3...Bb3! with the threat 4...a5.

3...Kc8!?

If 3...Bf7 then 4 Kc5 Kc8 (4...a5 5 Kb5; 4...Bb3 5 Kd6 Kc8 6 Bc3) 5 Kc6! (6 Bc3 is threatening) 5...Be8+ (5...a5 6 Kb5) 6 Kd6 Bf7 7 Bc3! and 8 Ba5.

4 Kb5!

The author's line 4 Kc5 Bb3! 5 Kb5! Kb7 6 Kb4! and 7 Kc5 is a little bit slower than this.

4...Kb7 (5 Ka6 was threatening) **5 Kc5 Bb3 6 Kd6** (△ 7 Kd7) **6...Kc8 7 Bc3!**

White has carried out his plan. With his next move he places the bishop on a5 and then advances his king to f8.

5/5. Berezhnoy – Gusev, Rostov-Don 1972

1...♔e6!

The king runs to the h-pawn, reaching the first defensive position. But can the bishop prevent a creation of another passed pawn on the queenside?

2 h5 ♔f7 3 h6 ♔g6 4 ♗f4 ♔h7 5 ♔b6

16-21

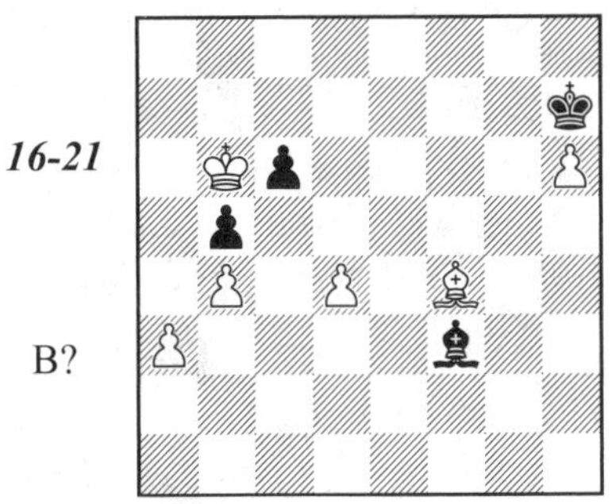

B?

5...♗d5!

The game continued 5...♗e4?? 6 ♔a5 ♔g6 (6...♗c2 7 d5!+–) 7 a4 ba 8 ♔xa4 ♔f7 9 b5, and Black resigned.

6 ♔a5 ♗b3!

White has no win. 7 a4 ba 8 b5 cb 9 ♔xb5 a3 is useless – the a-pawn will deflect the bishop from protecting his own pawn.

It is worth mentioning that reaching the first defensive position is the only correct plan for Black. Yes, after 1...♗e2 the immediate 2 d5 cd 3 ♔xd5 does not succeed in view of 3...♗d1! 4 ♗d6 (4 ♔c5 ♗a4=) 4...♔e8 5 ♔e6 ♗b3+ 6 ♔f6 ♗d1=. But White plays 2 ♗f4 ♗f3 3 ♗e5, and 3...♔e6! is quite necessary here, because the prolonged passive policy 3...♗e2? loses to 4 d5 cd 5 ♔xd5 ♗d1 (5...♔e7 6 ♔c5, planning ♔b6-a5 and a3-a4+–) 6 ♔c5 ♔e6 (6...♗a4 7 h5 ♔e6 8 h6) 7 ♔xb5! ♔xe5 8 ♔c6! (shouldering in the most precise way) 8...♗f3+ 9 ♔c7 ♗e2 10 a4+–.

5/6. Tringov – Smyslov, Reykjavik 1974

The f2-pawn must go forward, but where?

The game continued 1 f4? ♗g1! 2 ♔d3 ♗h2 3 ♔e3 ♔f6.

Black has chained his opponent to the defense of the f4-pawn and now directs his king to b2. White has no answer to this simple plan. By the way, the bishop has gone to h2 (rather than c7) in order not to interfere with the king when it steps to d6.

4 ♗a2 ♔e7 5 ♗g8 ♔d6 6 ♗f7 ♔c5 7 ♗a2 (7 ♗e6 ♔b4 8 ♔d3 ♗xf4 9 ♔c2 ♗e5! 10 ♗xf5 a2–+) 7...♔b4 8 ♔d4 ♗xf4 9 ♔d5 ♗g3 10 ♔d4 f4 White resigned.

In endings with opposite-colored bishops, the defender should keep his pawns on the squares of his bishop's color. Therefore **1 f3!** suggests itself, having in mind the first defensive position. The bishop can protect kingside pawns easily when the king stands on b3 (if ...♔f4 then ♗e6!, and if ...f5-f4 then the bishop goes to g4). The question is whether White can build this setup in time.

1...♔f6 2 ♔d3 ♔e5!

The eventual consequences of 3 ♔c2 ♔f4 4 ♔b3 (4 ♗e6? ♔xf3 5 ♗xf5 a2) 4...♔xf3 (4...♗c5? 5 ♗e6=) 5 ♔xa3 are not so easy to calculate right now. After the apparently natural 5...f4? White's king comes to the kingside in time: 6 ♔b3 ♔g3 7 ♔c2 f3 (7...♔xh3 8 ♔d3 △ ♗d5, ♔e2=) 8 ♔d3 ♔xh3 (8...♗b6 9 ♗d5; 8...f2 9 ♔xd4) 9 ♔xd4 ♔g3 (9...♔g2 10 ♗d5) 10 ♔e3 f2 (10...h3 11 ♗d5 f2 12 ♔e2=) 11 ♗f1=.

However Black can successfully apply the "shouldering" technique we have already seen in pawn endgames: 5...♔e3!! 6 ♔b3 ♔d2! 7 ♗d5 (7 ♗e6 f4 8 ♗g4 ♔e3 9 ♔c2 f3 10 ♔d1 ♔f2 11 ♗e6 ♔g1–+) 7...f4 8 ♗c6 ♗b6 9 ♗d5 ♔e2! (△ ...f3-f2) 10 ♗c4+ ♔f2 11 ♔c2 f3 12 ♔d1 (12 ♗d5 ♔e2) 12...♔g1, winning.

The alternative 3 f4+? ♔xf4 4 ♔xd4 does not help, either: 4...♔g3 5 ♔e3 f4+ 6 ♔e2 f3+ 7 ♔f1 ♔xh3 8 ♔f2 ♔g4–+.

But the position is drawn after all! White should make a waiting move, for example **3 ♗g8!**, and Black turns out to be in zugzwang (a unique case: the stronger side is in zugzwang in a sharp fight for tempi in the forthcoming race).

16-22

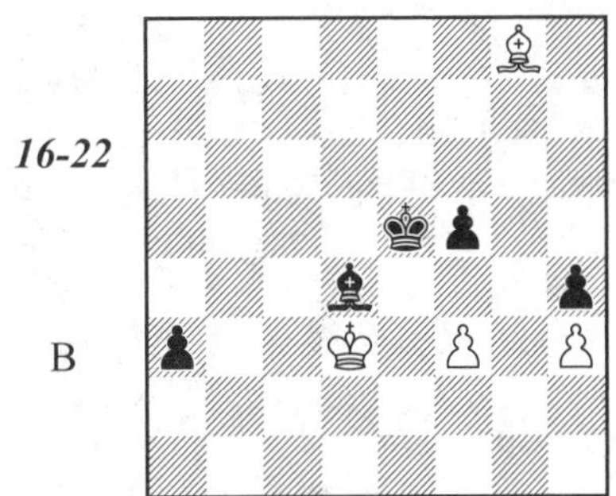

B

If the bishop retreats from d4 White can transpose into the first defensive position: 4 ♔c2 ♔f4 5 ♗e6! ♔xf3 6 ♗xf5, and 6...a2 is not dangerous for him anymore, while after **3...♔f4!? 4 ♔xd4 ♔xf3** the king is placed worse on f3 than on g3 (see the line 3 f4+?), and this circumstance allows White's salvation: **5 ♗d5+! ♔g3 6 ♔e3 f4+** (6...♔×h3 7 ♔f3, locking the king on the h-file) **7 ♔e2 f3+ 8 ♔f1! ♔×h3 9 ♔f2 ♔g4 10 ♗×f3+** (analysis by Dvoretsky).

I want to mention that Nikolay Minev, when annotating this endgame for the *Encyclopaedia of Chess Endings*, was very close to revealing the secrets of this position: he analyzed 3 ♗a2 ♗g1 4 ♔c3 ♔f4 5 ♗d5 ♔g3 6 ♔b3 f4–+. Of course, instead of 5 ♗d5? White has to play 5 ♗e6!= ("pawns in the crosshairs!").

At the training session for young Russian players I led in the spring of 2001, my apprentices suggested another defensive plan for White: 1 ♔f3 ♔f6 2 ♗a2 ♔e5 3 ♗g8 ♗c5 4 ♗a2. The king cannot now go to d4 in view of 5 ♔f4, therefore Black must play 4...♗f8 with the idea of 5...♗h6 and only then, finally, 6...♔d4. White responds with 5 ♔e3! ♗h6+ 6 ♔d3, closing the way to the black king. However after 6...♔f4 (7...♔f3 was threatened) 7 ♗d5 ♗f8 (the bishop wants to go to c5 in order to attack the f2-pawn) 8 ♔c2 ♗c5 9 ♔b3 ♗×f2 10 ♔×a3 Black wins by the familiar "shouldering" technique: 10...♔e3!! 11 ♔b3 ♔d2!.

5/7. Simagin – Janssen, wchsf cr 1967

The second defensive position is present. According to the rules, a road for the king to the h5-pawn should be paved, but how does one do so? The straightforward attempt 1 ♔b2 ♔b6 2 ♔a3 ♗g5 3 ♔a4 ♗h6 4 a3 ♗g5 5 b4 ab 6 ab cb 7 ♔×b4 allows Black to build an unassailable fortress by means of 7...♗d2+! 8 ♔b3 ♔c5.

The breakthrough a2-a3 and b3-b4 (followed with c4-c5) should be carried out when the king is on d3. The bishop belongs on a4 where it deprives the black king of important squares and holds Black's eventual passed b-pawn that soon appears.

1 ♗f7! ♗f8 2 ♗e8 ♗h6 3 a3 (△ 4 b4) **3...♗f8**

If 3...♔b6 then 4 ♔d3 (△ ♔e4-d5) 4...♔c7 5 b4! ab 6 ab cb 7 c5 b3 (7...♗f8 8 ♔c4 b3 9 ♗a4 b2 10 ♗c2+–) 8 ♔c3 (or 8 ♗a4 b2 9 ♗c2+–) 8...♗f8 9 c6+–.

4 ♗a4!⊙ ♔b6 (in case of 4...♗h6 or 4...♔d6, 5 b4 is decisive) **5 ♔d3** (△ ♔e4-d5) **5...♔c7**

16-23

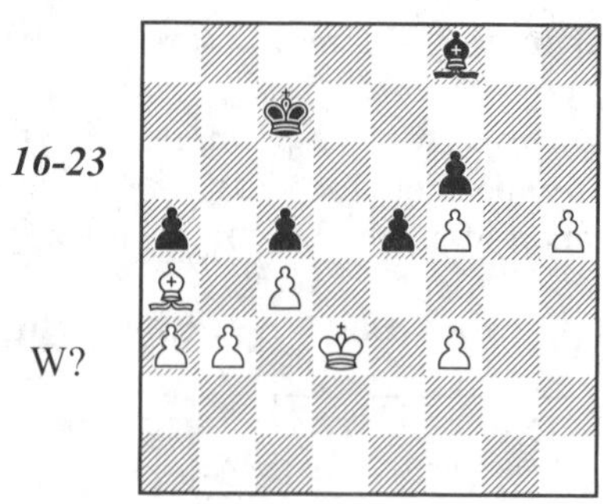

W?

6 b4! ab 7 ab cb 8 c5!

Black resigned because of 8...♗×c5 (8...b3 9 ♔c4 b2 10 ♗c2) 9 ♔c4 ♗f8 (9...♔d6 10 h6) 10 ♔d5 ♔d8 11 ♔e6+–.

Other winning methods for White are not apparent. I tried 6 ♔e4 (instead of 6 b4) 6...♔d6 7 f4 ef 8 ♔×f4 ♗h6+ 9 ♔e4. The idea works in case of 9...♗d2? 10 b4! ab 11 ab cb 12 ♔d4 ♗h6 (12...♗c3+ 13 ♔d3) 13 c5+. But Black's defense can be improved: 9...♗c1! (strangely enough, this is a reciprocal zugzwang!) 10 ♗b5 (10 b4 ab 11 ab cb 12 ♔d4 ♗b2+!; 10 ♗e8 ♔e7 △ 11...♗×a3) 10...♔e7! (△ ♗×a3) 11 b4 ab 12 ab (12 a4 b3 13 ♔d3 ♔d6 also leads to a draw) 12...♔d6!=.

Chapter Six

6/1. L. Centurini, 1847

1 ♗h4

The bishop wants to go to b8; if it manages to get there the fight will be over immediately. So Black tries to prevent it.

1...♔b5! 2 ♗f2 ♔a6

If White now directs the bishop to c7 then the black king returns to c6 in time. After 3 ♗e3 ♗d6! 4 ♗g5 ♔b5 5 ♗d8 ♔c6, there is no sense in 6 ♗e7 ♗h2, because the white bishop cannot enter the g1-a7 diagonal immediately. But if the black bishop occupies some other position, White could have won the decisive tempo by means of deflection.

3 ♗c5!⊙ ♗e5 4 ♗e7 ♔b5 5 ♗d8 ♔c6 6 ♗f6! ♗h2 7 ♗d4 △ ♗a7-b8+–.

6/2. Zviagintsev – Chernin, Portoroz 1997

White wins if he manages to advance the pawn to b6 and to penetrate to a7 with his king. Black's initial move 1...♔f6? allowed White to carry out this plan unhindered.

2 b5 ♔e7 3 b6 ♗e2 4 ♗c6! ♔d6 (4...♔d8

5 ♗b5 ♗×b5 6 ♔×b5+–) 5 ♗b5 ♗f3 6 ♔a6 ♔c5 7 ♗f1.

Black resigned. The king transfer to the rear of the white king (7...♔b4 8 ♔a7 ♔a5) cannot help here because the a6-c8 diagonal, where the bishop will be forced, is too short.

As Zviagintsev has demonstrated, Black could have held the game.

1...♗e2! 2 ♗a6 ♗f3 3 b5

If 3 ♗f1 then 3...♗c6! (rather than 3...♔f6? 4 b5 ♔e7 5 ♔a6+–) 4 ♔b6 ♗e8 5 ♔c7 ♔f6 6 ♔d6 ♗a4 7 ♗c4 ♗e8 8 ♗d5 ♗b5 9 ♔c5 ♗e8 10 ♗c6 ♗h5 11 b5 ♔e7 12 b6 ♔d8=.

3...♔f6 4 b6 ♔e7 5 ♗f1

5 ♗c8 ♔d8 6 ♗f5 ♗b7 or 6...♗e2 gives nothing - the king cannot come to a7.

5...♗b7 6 ♔b5 ♔d8

6...♔d6 is also playable, but after 7 ♗h3 he must retreat anyway: 7...♔e7□.

7 ♗h3 ♔e7 8 ♔c5 ♔d8 9 ♔d6 ♗f3 10 ♗e6 ♗b7!=

A position of reciprocal zugzwang has arisen, with White on move (see diagram 6-3).

6/3. Y. Hoch, 1977

The initial moves are easy to find.

1 ♔d8 ♗b7 2 c7+ ♔a7 3 ♗c6! ♗a6 4 ♗×b5 ♗b7

16-24

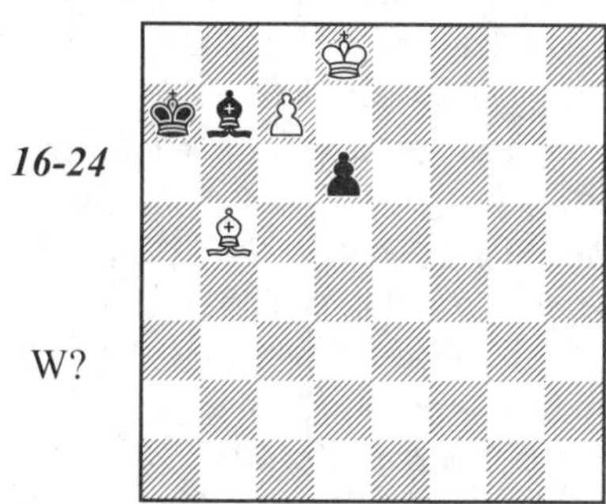

W?

5 ♗c6!!

But here precise calculation is required to the end. Only then will the reason for this zwischenzug will be clear.

5...♗a6 6 ♗d7 ♔b6 (6...d5 7 ♗c8 ♗f1 8 ♗b7 ♗h3 9 ♗c6 d4 10 ♗d7+–) **7 ♗c8 ♗f1 8 ♗b7 ♗h3**

Now White should bring his bishop to d7 as soon as possible (before the black king comes to d6).

9 ♗g2! ♗e6 (9...♗g4 10 ♗f3!; 9...♗f5 10 ♗e4!) **10 ♗d5! ♗h3 11 ♗f7 ♔c5 12 ♗e8** △ ♗d7+–

Black's d6-pawn caused his death, because it stood in the way of his own king. If White did not find the correct continuation on the fifth move Black could have gotten rid of the pawn:

5 ♗d7? ♔b6 6 ♗c8 ♗g2 (or 6...♗d5) 7 ♗a6 ♗h3 8 ♗f1 ♗e6! 9 ♗c4 d5! 10 ♗×d5 ♗h3 11 ♗f7 ♔c5 12 ♗e8 ♔d6=.

6/4. J. Sulz, 1948

White has a clear plan: to drive the black bishop off the a3-f8 diagonal and create an interference on f6. Black's only hope is the advance of his h-pawn because his king cannot come to f5 in time. The hope is not completely groundless, as can be seen from the line 1 ♗h4? h5! 2 ♗e7 ♗a5! 3 ♗f8 ♗d8 4 ♗g7 h4 5 ♗f6 h3! 6 ♗×d8 h2 7 e7 h1♕=.

1 ♗e1!!

A subtle zwischenzug that provides the important b4-square to the bishop in the future.

1...♗c5 2 ♗h4 h5! (2...♔d5 3 ♗e7 ♗b6 4 ♗f8 ♗d8 5 ♗g7 ♔e4 6 ♗f6+–) **3 ♗e7 ♗b6 4 ♗b4! ♗d8 5 ♗a5!**

This is the point! The black bishop is forced out from the comfortable d8-square.

5...♗g5 6 ♗c3 h4 7 ♗f6 ♗×f6 (7...h3 8 e7) **8 ♔×f6 h3 9 e7+–**.

6/5. I. Agapov, 1981

The task of utilizing the material advantage is rather difficult here because the white king is out of play forever. For example, the straightforward attempt 1 c7? ♔h4 2 c8♕ ♗×c8 3 ♗×c8 ♔g3 leads to a draw. ***Connected passed pawns are often impotent when they are fixed on squares of their bishop's color.***

1 g3!

Now 2 c7+– is threatened. Black prevents the pawn advance with a pinning technique, similar to the Capablanca – Janowsky ending we have seen already.

1...♗d5! 2 ♗a8! (△ 3 c7 ♗e6 4 ♗b7+–; 2 f4? is erroneous in view of 2...♔g4 3 ♗c8+ ♔×g3=) **2...♗e6!** (2...♗×f3? 3 c7 ♗g4 4 ♗f3+–) **3 c7 ♗c8**

16-25

W?

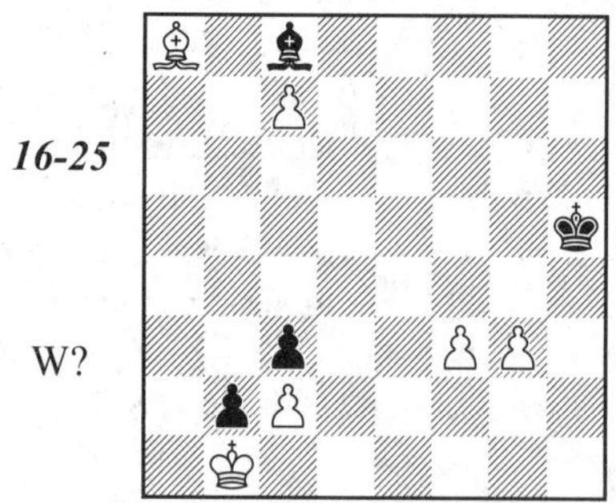

What to do now? In case of 4 f4? ♔g4 5 ♗e4 ♗d7, White cannot make any progress.

We might consider the idea of a bishop sacrifice on h3 with the interference g3-g4 to follow. But this plan is difficult to carry out, because Black can respond with a king march to the c7-pawn. For example, 4 ♗e4? ♔g5 5 ♗d3 ♔f6! 6 ♗f1 (6 f4 ♔e7=; 6 g4 ♔g5 7 ♗f5 ♗a6=) 6...♔e7 7 ♗h3? ♗×h3 8 g4 ♔d7−+.

Hence the bishop should be transferred to e8 first, so that Black will be forced to defend the h5-square in order to avoid the bishop exchange ♗h5-g4. And only when the black king is at the utmost distance from the queenside, can the main plan be successful.

4 ♗c6! ♔g6!? 5 ♗e8+ ♔g5 6 ♗f7!⊙ ♔h6 (6...♗d7 7 ♗c4 ♔f6 8 ♗a6) **7 ♗c4!**

There is no other winning way: 7 f4? ♔g7 8 ♗h5 ♔f6 9 g4 ♔e6 10 g5 ♔e7!!⊙ (10...♔f5? 11 ♗g4+; 10...♔d6? 11 g6 ♔×c7 12 g7 ♗e6 13 f5) 11 ♗g6 (11 ♗f3 ♔d6=) 11...♔d6= gives only a draw.

7...♔g6 8 ♗f1 ♔f6 9 ♗h3! ♗×h3 10 g4+−.

6/6. Lasker – Bogatyrchuk, Moscow 1935

White cannot do without e3-e4. The game continued 1 e4? d4! 2 ♗c4 ♗b7 3 ♔g5 ♗c8 4 ♔f4 ♔d7 5 ♔f3 ♗b7 6 ♔e2 ♗c8 7 ♔d3 ♗b7 8 ♔×d4 ♗c8 9 ♔e3 ♗b7 and a draw was agreed. In the final position, White's own e4-pawn only causes him trouble because it closes the important h1-a8 diagonal. Without this pawn, White would have had the upper hand. So the correct plan is a king transfer to d4 prior to the advance e3-e4.

1 ♔g5! ♔f7 2 ♔f4

As N. Grigoriev demonstrated, 2 ♗g6+! ♔e7 3 ♔f4 would have been even more precise. However, even with an active king, Black is faced with severe problems.

2...♔g7 3 ♔f3 ♔h6 4 ♔e2 ♔g5 5 ♔d2 ♔g4 6 ♔c3 ♔g5 7 ♔d4 ♗b7 8 e4!

16-26

B

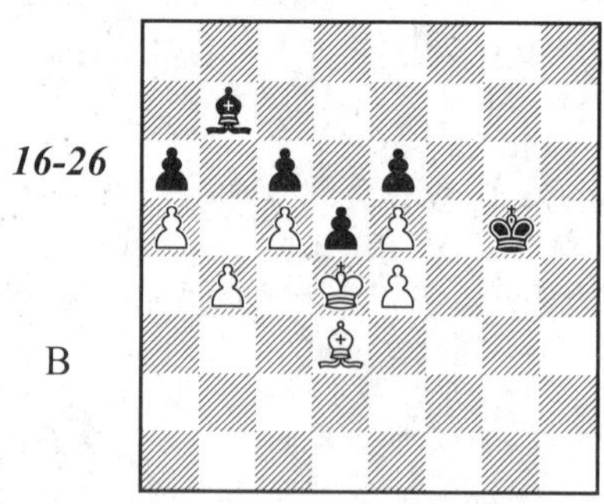

If 8...♗c8 now, then 9 ed ed 10 ♗f1 ♔g6 11 ♔d3 ♔g5 12 ♔e3⊙ ♔g4 (12...♔g6 13 ♔f4; 12...♗b7 13 ♗h3) 13 e6+−.

8...de 9 ♗×e4 ♔h5 10 ♔d3 ♔g5 11 ♔e3⊙ ♔h6

11...♗a8 12 b5! ab 13 a6 b4 14 ♗c2 △ ♗b3+−;

11...♔g4 12 ♗g6 ♔g5 13 ♗f7! ♔f5 14 ♔d4 ♗c8 15 ♗e8 ♗b7 16 ♗d7⊙ +−.

12 ♔f4 ♔g7 13 ♔g5 ♔f7 14 ♔h6 ♔e7 15 ♔g7⊙ ♗a8 16 b5! ab 17 a6+−.

6/7. Stefanov – Beliavsky, Bucharest 1980

Beliavsky has calculated quite well that, after the exchange of dark-squared bishops, he will be able to create a solid barrier against White's king.

1...♗e5+! 2 ♗×e5 ♔×e5 3 ♔d3

If 3 c7 ♗b7 4 ♗d3 (△ ♗f5) then 4...♔d6 5 ♔d4 ♗c8! (5...♔×c7 is less strong, but Black perhaps can survive after 6 ♔e5 ♗f3 7 ♔f5 ♔d6 8 ♔×g5 ♔e5) 6 ♗f5 ♗×f5 7 gf ♔×c7 8 ♔e5 ♔d7 9 f6 g4 10 ♔f4 ♔e6 11 ♔×g4 ♔×f6=, or 6 ♗e2 ♗e6(d7)=.

3...♗d5 4 ♔e3 ♗e6 5 ♗f3 ♗c8=

White cannot utilize his extra pawn. The defense is successful mainly because all of White's pawns are on the squares of their own bishop's color.

6 ♗d1 ♗e6 7 ♔f3 ♗d5+ 8 ♔g3 ♔d6 9 ♗e2 ♗e6 10 ♗d3 ♗d5 11 ♔f2 ♗e6 12 ♔f3 ♗d5+ 13 ♔e3 ♗e6 14 ♗e2 ♔e5 15 ♗f3 ♗c8 16 c7 ♔d6 17 ♔d4 ♗d7 18 ♗e2 ♗c8 19 ♔e4 ♗d7 20 ♔d4 ♗c8 Draw.

Chapter Seven

7/1. P. Seuffert, 1856

A reciprocal zugzwang arises with the bishop on d4 and the king on b5 or d5. We have discussed an almost identical position, only moved one file to the right (diagram 7-2), where Black could successfully avoid a zugzwang. Here he fails to do so.

1 ♗c3! ♔b6□ 2 ♗a5+! ♔b5 3 ♗d8 ♔c5 4 ♗g5 ♔b5

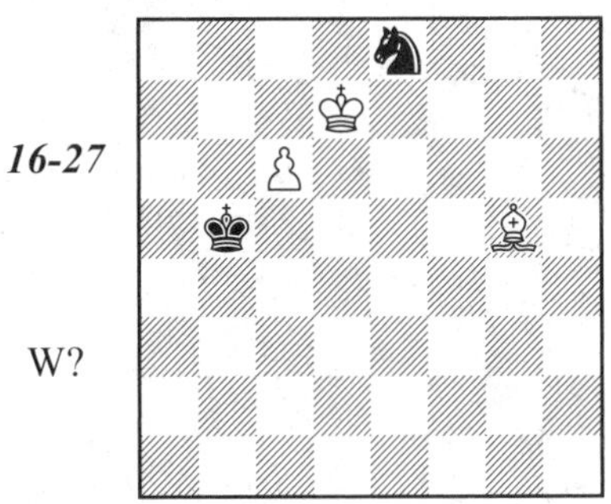

16-27

W?

5 ♗h4!⊙

This waiting move did not exist in the above-mentioned case: the edge of the board was closer.

5...♔c5 6 ♗f2+ ♔d5 7 ♗d4⊙ ♘d6 8 c7+–.

7/2. L. Katsnelson, 1979

1 ♔b1!

The line 1 g4? ♔c2 2 ♘f2 ♗e3 3 ♘e4 ♔d3 or 2 ♘b2 ♗g7 is hopeless. But, if White had no pawns in the last case, he could have saved the game because of a stalemate: 3 ♔a2. This tactical idea can serve as an anchor, because White cannot avoid a zugzwang anyway.

1...♗g5 (1...♗d2 2 g4 ♗g5 3 g3) **2 g4 ♗d2 3 g5! ♗×g5 4 g4**

After 4 g3? ♗h6 5 g4 ♗g5!⊙ 6 ♔a1 ♔c2 White is lost because he has failed to get rid of his own pawn in time.

4...♗h6 5 g5! ♗×g5 6 ♔a1 ♔c2 7 ♘b2! ♗f6 (7...c3 8 ♘a4=) **8 ♔a2 ♗×b2** Stalemate.

7/3. J. Kling, B. Horwitz, 1851

1 ♘c3 ♗b5!!

Only this subtle move, suggested by Chéron, saves Black. After 1...♗e8? 2 ♘d5⊙ he loses because of the unlucky placement of his king in the corner. For example, 2...♗b5 3 ♘b4 (△ 3 ♘c6) 3...♗e8 4 ♘c6⊙, or 2...♔a7 3 ♘b4⊙ ♔a8 4 ♘c6⊙.

2 ♘d5 (2 ♘×b5 Stalemate) **2...♔a7 3 ♘b4 ♗e8!⊙ 4 ♘c6+ ♔a6=.**

7/4. A. Kalinin, 1974*

The bishop is ready to hold the pawn from either diagonal. If it occupies the a3-f8 diagonal then White must interfere by means of ♘e7 before the black king can prevent this. From g7, the bishop can only be driven away by the knight from f5.

There is a single (and unusual) way to solve both these problems in time.

1 ♘g2!! ♗b4+

If 1...♗g7 then 2 ♘h4!, and 3 ♘f5 cannot be prevented. 1...♔g6 also loses, to 2 ♘h4+ ♔g5 3 ♘f5! ♗b4+ 4 ♘d6. Finally, 1...♗b2 2 ♔e8 ♗a3 transposes to the main line of the solution.

2 ♔e8 ♗a3

In case of 2...♔g7 3 ♘f4 ♔f6 Black loses the bishop: 4 ♘d5+.

3 ♘f4(e3) ♔g7 4 ♘d5+– (△ 5 ♘e7).

7/5. A. Troitsky, 1924

1 ♗a3! f5 2 d5!

The black knight should not occupy the d5-square, as 2 a5? ♘f6 3 a6 ♘d5 leads but to a draw.

The initial moves cannot be transposed: 1 d5? cd 2 ♗a3 d4! 3 ♔g2 (3 a5 d3 4 ♗b4 ♘e7) 3...f5! 4 a5 ♘f6 5 a6 ♘d5=.

2...cd 3 a5 ♘f6 4 a6 ♘e8 (4...♘d7 5 ♗c5! ♘×c5 6 a7+–) **5 ♗d6! ♘×d6 6 a7+–.**

7/6. J. Marwitz, 1937

1 ♗d3!!

Both 2 e6 and 2 ♗c4 are threatened. The premature attempt 1 e6? misses the win: 1...♘e2+ 2 ♔f1 g2+! 3 ♗×g2 ♘g3+ and 4...♘f5=.

1...♔b7 (1...♘×d3 2 e6+–) **2 ♗c4!**

The knight is corralled, but the fight is still not over yet.

2...♔b6 3 ♔g2 ♔c5 4 ♔×g3!

After 4 e6? ♔d6 the knight releases itself via d3 or e2, because the bishop is overworked between the two diagonals.

4...♔×c4 5 e6 ♘e2+ 6 ♔h2!!+–

The knight fails to stop the pawn after this move, while after 6 ♔g4? it could do so successfully: 6...♘c3 7 e7 ♘d5 8 e8♕? (8 e8♘= is relatively better) 8...♘f6+.

7/7. L. Katsnelson, L. Mitrofanov, 1977

The bishop clearly dominates the knight. White's hopes are based on the reduced material on the board and on the Réti idea that we have discussed in the chapter on pawn endgames.

1 ♔c7!

Both 1 c7? ♗d6 2 ♔b7 ♗×c7 3 ♔×c7 ♔h3 and 1 ♔b7? ♗d6 2 ♔b6 ♗×h2 (2...♔h3) 3 ♔b5 ♗c7 4 ♔c4 g3 lose.

1...b2

An immediate draw results from 1...♗b4 2 ♔b6 ♗d6 3 ♔b5 ♔h3 (3...♗×h2 4 ♔c4) 4 ♔c4 ♔×h2 5 ♔×b3 g3 6 ♘e3=. The consequences of 1...♗c5!? are less obvious: 2 ♔d7 ♗b6 3 ♔e6 ♔h3 (3...♗c7 4 ♔d5 △ ♔c4=) 4 ♔f5 (the king must move away from the b3-pawn because the threat 4...♔×h2 should be prevented) 4...♗c7 5 ♘f2+ (a safer alternative is 5 ♔e4! ♔×h2 6 ♔d3 followed with 7 ♘e3).

16-28

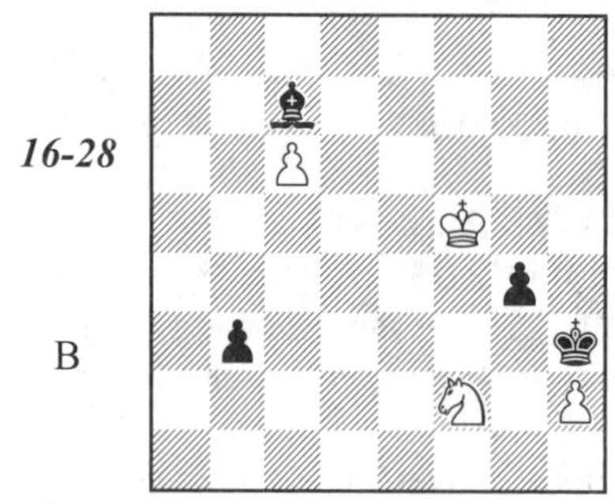

B

a) 5...♔×h2 6 ♘×g4+ ♔g1 7 ♘e5! b2 8 ♘f3+ ♔f2 9 ♘d2 ♔e2 10 ♘b1=;

b) 5...♔h4 6 ♘d1! ♗×h2 7 ♔e4! ♗c7 8 ♔d3 g3 9 ♘e3 ♔g5 10 ♔c3=;

c) 5...♔g2 6 ♘d3! ♔f3 7 ♘e5+! ♔e3 8 ♘c4+ ♔d4 9 ♘b2 ♗×h2 10 ♔×g4=.

2 ♘×b2! (2 ♘c3? ♗b4–+) **2...♗×b2 3 ♔d6 ♗c1 4 ♔e5 ♔g5** (the only way to stop the c-pawn) **5 ♔e4 ♗f4 6 h4+! gh 7 ♔f3 ♔f5 8 ♔f2 ♗h2 9 c7=**.

7/8. Chekhover – Lasker, Moscow 1935

Black stands better (his bishop is obviously better than the knight) but he must play accurately. For example, after 1...♗b2? 2 a4 ♔b6 3 ♔e1 ♔a5 4 ♔d2 ♔b4 5 ♔c2 White manages to defend his queenside in time. In case of 1...♔c6?! 2 ♔e1 b5 3 ♔d2 ♗b2 Black must take 4 b4! ♗×a3 5 ♔c3 a5 (he has nothing else) 6 ba into account.

1...b5! 2 ♔e1 ♗b2! 3 a4 ba 4 ba ♔c6

Black cannot eliminate the a4-pawn (4...♔b6 5 ♔d2 ♔a5? 6 ♔c2 ♗e5 7 f4 ♗d6 8 ♔b3=), therefore the king goes to the center.

5 ♔d2 ♔c5

If **6 ♔c2** then **6...♗d4! 7 f3 ♔c4! 8 ♘×d4 ♔×d4 9 ♔b3 a5!–+**

The game continued 6 ♘c3 ♔b4 7 ♘b5 a5

7...a6!? 8 ♘d6 ♔×a4 9 ♘×f7 (9 ♔c2 ♘e5) 9...♔b3 was probably more precise. As Müller indicates, White could have answered the text with 8 ♔d3! because 8...♔×a4 9 ♔c4 traps the king on the edge of the board, making it extremely difficult for his opponent to make the most of his advantage.

8 ♘d6 ♔×a4 9 ♔c2 ♗e5 10 ♘×f7 ♗×h2 11 ♘d8 e5 12 ♘c6 ♗g1 13 f3 ♗c5 14 ♘b8 ♔b5 15 g4 ♗e7 16 g5 fg 17 ♘d7 ♗d6 18 ♘f6 ♔c4!. White resigned in view of 19 ♘×h7 ♗e7.

7/9. Korchnoi – Polugaevsky,

Buenos Aires cmsf (13) 1980

After 1 gf ♗×f5, 2 ♘d4 loses to 2...♗b1 while 2 e4 de 3 ♘e3 ♗e6 leaves Black with an obvious advantage. 1 ♔g3 fg 2 fg ♔f6 3 ♘d4 ♔e5 (or 3...♗e8) is also favorable for Black. Korchnoi finds the best defensive possibility.

1 f4!! fg

After 1...gf?! 2 g5! fe+ 3 ♔×e3 White, in spite of being a pawn down, seizes the initiative due to his dangerous g5-pawn and the black central pawns that are blocked on squares of their bishop's color.

2 fg

The position is roughly even, the g5-pawn offers White enough counterplay. If 2...♗f5 3 ♘d4 ♗b1 then 4 ♔g3 (rather than 4 ♘c6+ ♔d6 5 ♘×a5? ♔c7, winning the knight) 4...♗×a2 5 ♘c6+ ♔d6 6 ♘×a5 ♗b1 (4...♔c7? is bad in view of 7 e4! de 8 g6+–) 7 ♘b7+.

The remainder of the game was: 2...♔e6 3 ♘d4+ ♔e5 4 ♔g3 ♗e8 5 ♔×g4 ♔e4 6 ♔g3! ♔×e3 7 ♘f5+ ♔d2 8 ♔f4 ♔c3 9 ♔e5 d4 10 ♘×d4 ♔b2 11 ♘e6! ♔×a2 12 ♘c5 (we know this technique of protecting a pawn with a knight) 12...♔b2 13 ♔f6 ♔c3 14 g6 ♗×g6 15 ♔×g6 a4! 16 ba ♔c4 17 ♘e4 b3 18 ♘d2+ ♔b4 19 ♘×b3 ♔×a4 Draw.

7/10. Spassky – Botvinnik,

USSR ch tt, Moscow 1966

What can White do against a march of the black king to the a2-pawn? Botvinnik indicated the correct defensive plan: White should hold the enemy king on the edge by posting his own king to c2, while the knight must block the passed pawn from e2.

1 ♘f1! ♔c3 2 ♘g3 e3 3 ♔d1 ♔b2 4 ♘e2 ♔×a2 5 ♔c2, and White has built a indestructible fortress.

Instead of 1...♔c3, Black has a more poisonous possibility: 1...♗c7!?, creating difficulties for a knight march to a2. But White manages to hold in this case, too: 2 ♘e3 ♗f4 3 ♘g4 (3 ♘c4?! ♔c5) 3...♗g5 (3...♔c3 4 ♘f6 ♔b2 5 ♘d5! ♗d6 6 ♔d1 ♔×a2 7 ♔c2 ♔a3 8 ♘e3 ♗f4 9 ♘f5 e3 10 ♘d4=) 4 ♘f2 ♔e5 5 ♘g4+ ♔f5 6 ♘f2 ♗c1 7 ♘h3 ♗b2 8 ♔e3! ♔e5 9 ♔e2 ♗d4 10 ♘g5 ♔f5 11 ♘f7 (analyses by Averbakh).

In the game, however, 1 ♘c4? was played. Here the knight is placed too far away from e2, thus the defensive plan that we have discussed does not work, and no other plan exists.

1...♔c3 2 ♔d1 ♗d4 (△ 3...♔d3) 3 ♔e2 e3 4 ♘a5 (the pawn ending after 4 ♘×e3 ♗×e3 is lost) 4...♔b2 5 ♘c6 ♗c5 6 ♘e5 ♔×a2 7 ♘d3 ♗e7 White resigned.

7/11. S. Kozlowski, 1931

1 ♘d7+! ♔c7 2 ♘f8!

The only way to imprison the bishop.

2...♔d8

2...♔d6 3 ♔g4! ♔d5 4 ♔h5! (detour around the mined g5-square) 4...♔e5 5 ♔g5⊙ ♔e4 6 ♔h6+–;

2...♔c8 3 ♔f4 ♔d8 4 ♔g5 ♔e8 5 ♔h5! +–.

3 ♔f4 ♔e8 4 ♔g5 ♔×f8 5 ♔h6⊙ +–

An amazing position: Black is lost in spite of his extra bishop!

7/12. M. Liburkin, 1947

1 ♘c6+ ♔b7!

After 1...♔a8 2 ba ♔b7 3 ♘d8+ ♔×a7 4 ♘f7+– White's task would have been simpler.

2 ba ♔a8 3 ♔f7! ♔b7

16-29

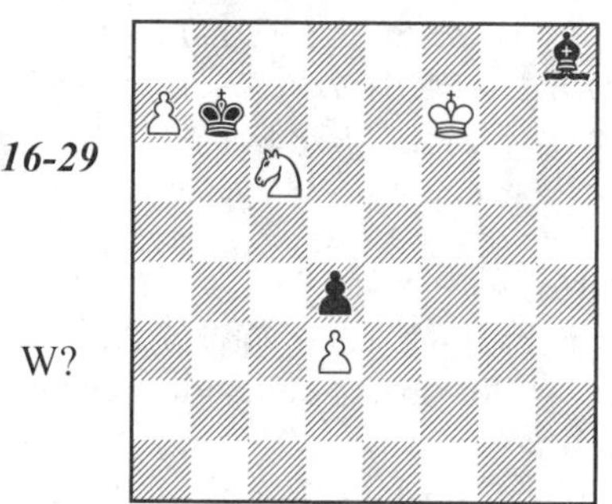

W?

4 a8♕+!! ♔×a8 5 ♔g6⊙ ♔b7 6 ♘d8+ ♔b6 7 ♘f7 ♔b5 8 ♘×h8+–.

7/13. Gerusel – Kestler,
BRD ch, Mannheim 1975

1...b5!–+

Otherwise White plays 2 a4 and eventually a4-a5. After the technically perfect solution in the game, he is devoid of any counterchances.

2 ♔g3 ♔f5 3 ♗d2 ♘f6 4 ♗c1 ♘h5+ 5 ♔h4 ♘f4 6 ♗d2 g5+ 7 ♔g3 ♘e2+ 8 ♔f2 ♘×d4, and Black won.

7/14. Popa – Galic, Bucharest 1938

White would have gladly brought his knight to a6, but there is no way to that square. If he attacks the c7-pawn the bishop will protect it. Black is not afraid of zugzwang because he has two squares for his king: f6 and g6.

White cannot do without a king transfer to the queenside. The black king can only reach c8; White places his king on a8 and drives Black away with a knight check from a7.

1 ♔d3! ♔f7 2 ♔c4 ♔e8 3 ♔b5 ♔d8 4 ♔a6 ♔c8 5 ♔a7! ♗f6 6 ♘e4 ♗e7 7 ♔a8! ♗d8 8 ♘c3 ♗f6 9 ♘b5+–

The remainder of the game was 9...e4 10 fe ♗e5 11 ♘a7+ ♔d8 12 ♔b7 ♗c3 13 ♘b5 ♗a5 14 ♘×d6 (the simple 14 ♘d4 △ ♘e6+ was good enough, too) 14...cd 15 e5 ♗c7 16 e6 ♗a5 17 e7+ ♔×e7 18 c7 ♗×c7 19 ♔×c7 Black resigned.

7/15. Botvinnik – Eliskases, Moscow 1936

Generally, it is useful to press Black even more by advancing the pawn to c6. However the immediate 1 c6? was met with 1...♗d3 2 ♔c3 b5!, and White had to accept the draw because the line 3 ♘d4 ♗c4 4 ♘e6 ♗×d5 5 ♘×c7? (5 ♘d4=) 5...♗×c6 is senseless.

After the game, Botvinnik found the correct solution: the advance c5-c6 should have been prepared by means of **1 ♔c3!**

A) 1...♗d3 2 ♘d4 bc (2...b5 3 ♘e6+–) 3 bc dc 4 ♘b3 c4. The pawn ending that results after 5 ♘a5 ♗f1 6 ♘×c4? ♗×c4 7 ♔×c4 ♔e7⊙ is drawn (the corresponding squares are c5 – d7, d4 – d6, c4 – e7; the correspondence is favorable for Black now, and White cannot cede the move to him). However 5 ♘d4! ♗f1 6 ♘b5 ♔e7 7 ♘×c7 ♔d6 8 ♘b5+ ♔×d5 9 ♘d4 wins.

B) 1...♗b7 2 c6 ♗c8 (2...♗a6 3 ♘d4 △ ♘e6) **3 ♘d4 ♔e7**

A try for zugzwang seems attractive now: 4 ♘b5 ♔d8 5 ♘a7. Black responds with 5...♝a6! 6 b5 ♝c8 7 ♔d4⊙ ♔e7 8 ♘×c8+ ♔d8 9 ♘a7 ♔e7=, and it suddenly becomes clear that Black has built a fortress, so the extra knight cannot be utilized.

4 ♔b3!

Planning a king transfer to b5 followed by a knight sacrifice on b6. Another winning method was suggested by Inarkiev: 4 b5! ♔d8 5 ♘c2 ♔e8 6 ♘b4 ♔e7 7 ♘a6 ♔d8 8 ♔c4 and Black is in zugzwang.

4...♔d8 5 ♔a4 ♔e7 6 ♔b5+− △ ♘c2-a3-c4×b6.

Chapter Eight

8/1. A. Troitsky, 1912

1 de ♖c1+ 2 ♔f2!

In case of 2 ♔g2? ♖×h1 3 ♔×h1 ♔c6 the knight is unable to protect the e-pawn.

2...♖×h1 3 e7 ♖h2+ 4 ♔f3

4 ♔e3? is erroneous in view of 4...♖h5!=. First of all, White should eliminate the f6-pawn.

4...♖h3+ 5 ♔f4 ♖h4+ 6 ♔f5 ♖h5+ 7 ♔×f6 ♖h6+ 8 ♔f5!

Rather than 8 ♔e5? ♖h1 9 ♘f6 ♖h8 10 ♘d7+ ♔c7 11 ♘f8 ♖h1=.

8...♖h5+ 9 ♔f4 ♖h4+ 10 ♔f3 ♖h3+ 11 ♔e2 ♖h2+ 12 ♔d3 ♖h3+ 13 ♔d4 ♖h4+ 14 ♔d5 ♖h5+ 15 ♔d6

16-30

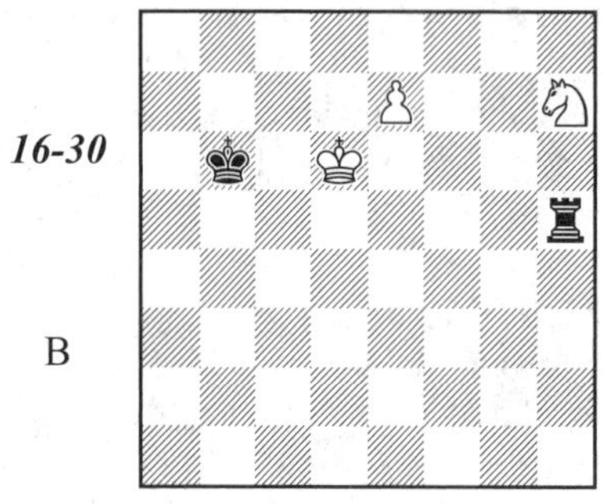

B

15...♖h6+

If 15...♖h1 then 16 ♘f6 ♖e1 17 ♘d7+ and 18 ♘e5+−.

16 ♘f6! ♖×f6+

16...♖h8 17 ♘d7+ and 18 ♘f8+−.

17 ♔d5 ♖f5+ 18 ♔d4 ♖f4+ 19 ♔d3 ♖f3+ 20 ♔e2+−

The king had to take two tours — up and downstairs!

8/2. J. Moravec, 1913

1 ♔h7!!

In case of 1 ♔×g7? h4 2 ♔g6 h3 3 ♔g5 h2 4 ♔g4 h1♕ White is forced to play 5 ♖a1+ (5 ♔g3?? ♕h8). Therefore the g7-pawn should be left alone.

1...h4

After 1...g5!? 2 ♔g6 g4, the primitive 3 ♔×h5? g3 4 ♔g4 g2 5 ♔h3 ♔h1! leads only to a draw. In order to avoid stalemate, the h5-pawn should not be captured: 3 ♔g5!!.

2 ♔g6 h3 3 ♔g5 h2 4 ♔g4 h1♕

4...g5!? 5 ♔g3 h1♘+ 6 ♔f3 g4+ 7 ♔×g4 ♘f2+ 8 ♔f3 does not help because the knight will be caught soon (see diagram 8-5).

5 ♔g3+−.

8/3. P. Benko, 1980

The line 1 ♔c3? a1♕+ 2 ♔b3 ♕a8!−+ is clearly unacceptable. By analogy with the previous exercise, 1 d5 ed 2 ♔c3 (2...a1♕+? 3 ♔b3+−) seems attractive, inasmuch as after 2...a1♘? 3 ♖h4 the knight is lost: 3...♔a2 4 ♖d4 ♔a3 5 ♖×d5 ♘b3 6 ♖b5+−. But Black manages to hold after 2...d4+! 3 ♔b3 a1♘+!.

The winning method is known from pawn endgame theory – a “half-stalemate.”

1 ♖h1+ ♔b2 2 ♖a1! ♔×a1 3 ♔c2! e5 4 d5 e4 5 d6 e3 6 d7 e2 7 d8♕ e1♘+ (7...e1♕ 8 ♕d4+) **8 ♔b3** (8 ♔c3 ♘d3 9 ♕b6) **8...♘d3 9 ♕d4+!**.

8/4. V. Sokov, 1940

The routine 1 ♔e7? misses a win in view of 1...♔b4! 2 ♖e1 (otherwise 2...♔c3) 2...a5 3 ♔d6 a4, and the black king applies a shouldering to the white opponent. The move ...♔b4! should be prevented.

1 ♖b1!! ♔a2

1...a5 2 ♔e7 a4 3 ♔d6 ♔a2 4 ♖e1 a3 5 ♔c5 ♔b2, and here both 6 ♖e2+ ♔b1 (6...♔b3 7 ♖×e3+) 7 ♔b4 a2 8 ♔b3+− and 6 ♔b4 a2 7 ♖e2+ ♔c1 8 ♖×a2 ♔d1 9 ♔c3+− are strong.

2 ♖e1! a5 3 ♔e7 ♔b3

We know already what happens after 3...a4 4 ♔d6.

4 ♔d6!

Rather than 4 ♖×e3+? ♔b4 5 ♔d6 a4 6 ♖e4+ ♔b5! with a draw (shouldering again!).

4...a4

4...♔b4 5 ♔d5 a4 6 ♔d4 a3 7 ♖b1+.

5 ♔c5 a3 6 ♖×e3+ ♔a4

6...♔b2 7 ♔b4 a2 8 ♖e2+ ♔b1 9 ♔b3+–.

7 ♔c4 a2 8 ♖e1 ♔a3 9 ♔c3+–.

8/5. Y. Averbakh, 1980

1 ♔e6! e4 2 ♖g5!!+–

Only this move wins. White places his rook behind the passed pawn with tempo and, after Black moves his king out of the way, the white king outflanks him from the opposite side.

2...♔d2(d3) 3 ♖d5+! ♔c2 4 ♖e5! ♔d3 5 ♔f5!;

2...♔f2(f3) 3 ♖f5+! ♔g2 4 ♖e5! ♔f3 5 ♔d5!;

2...♔e2 3 ♔e5 e3 4 ♔e4.

The premature 1 ♖g5? leads only to a draw after 1...♔f4! 2 ♔f6 e4. 1 ♔d6? is also erroneous: 1...e4 2 ♖g5 ♔d3(d2)!, as well as 1 ♔f6? e4 2 ♖g5 ♔f3(f2)!, because the outflanking technique cannot be applied.

8/6. N. Kopaev, 1954

Being well armed with the experience of previous examples, we can find White's initial move, perhaps, almost automatically.

1 ♖f7+! ♔g3!?

If 1...♔e3 then 2 ♖g7! ♔f4 3 ♔f7 g4 4 ♔g6! g3 5 ♔h5+–.

2 ♔e7 g4 3 ♔e6!

3 ♔f6? is bad in view of 3...♔f4!! (shouldering) 4 ♔g6+ ♔e3!=.

3...♔h2 4 ♔f5

4 ♔e5 is also playable, while the check 4 ♖h7+?! is premature in view of 4...♔g2 5 ♔f5? (the only winning method is 5 ♖f7!! g3 6 ♔e5 here) 5...♔f3! 6 ♖a7 g3 7 ♖a3+ ♔f2 8 ♔f4 g2=.

4...g3 5 ♔g4 (5 ♖h7+ and 5 ♔f4 are equivalent) **5...g2 6 ♖h7+ ♔g1 7 ♔g3 ♔f1 8 ♖f7+ ♔g1 9 ♖f8**

Almost every move is good here, for example 9 ♖a8 or 9 ♖g7, but by no means 9 ♖f2?? ♔h1! and a stalemate saves Black.

9...♔h1 10 ♖h8+ ♔g1 11 ♖h2+–.

8/7. P. Rossi, 1961

1 ♖h6+ ♔g3 2 ♖g6+ ♔h3 3 ♖g1! hg♕+ 4 ♔×g1 ♖a8 (4...♔g3 5 f8♕ ♖a1+ 6 ♕f1+–) **5 ♔f2!**

The incautious move 5 e6? would have allowed Black to draw by means of attacking the white king, pressed to the edge of the board: 5...♔g3 6 ♔f1 ♔f3 7 ♔e1 ♔e3 8 ♔d1 ♔d3 9 ♔c1 ♔c3 10 ♔b1 ♖b8+.

5...♖f8 6 e6 ♔g4 7 ♔e3+– △ 8 e7.

8/8. Bowden – Duncan,
Britain ch tt 1996/97

The remainder of the game was 1 ♖f7+? ♔g2 2 ♔×e4 g3 3 ♖h7 (if 3 ♔f4, Black's reply is the same) 3...♔h2!, and White resigned.

He had to make a waiting move.

1 ♖h8! e3 (it will soon be obvious that the same consequences result from 1...♔g2 2 ♔×e4 g3 3 ♔e3) **2 ♖f8+ ♔g2**

In case of 2...♔e2, White has a draw only after 3 ♖h8! ♔d2 4 ♖a8! or 3...♔f2 4 ♖f8+ ♔g1 5 ♔×e3 h2 6 ♖a8! (6 ♖h8? g3) 6...g3 (6...h1♕ 7 ♖a1+ ♔g2 8 ♖×h1 ♔×h1 9 ♔f4=) 7 ♖a1+ ♔g2 8 ♔f4=.

3 ♔×e3 g3

As may be seen, White has gained a tempo rather than lost it, because his king is placed better on e3 than on e4.

4 ♖h8! ♔h2 (4...h2 5 ♔f4=) **5 ♖g8! g2 6 ♔f2=.**

8/9. L. Mitrofanov, B. Lurye, 1983

Black's pawns are advanced far enough, but his king is badly placed, so White has at least a draw. The question is whether he can win.

1 ♖g3+ ♔h8!

In case of 1...♔h7, the solution is simple: 2 ♔f6! b2 (2...♔h8 3 ♖g7) 3 ♖g7+ ♔h8 4 ♖b7 a3 5 ♔g6+–.

2 ♖g6!! b2 3 ♖b6 a3 4 ♔f7 ♔h7

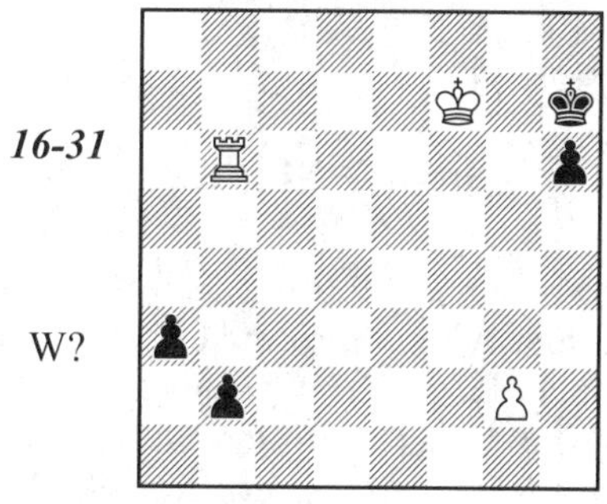

16-31

W?

5 g4!! a2 6 g5! hg 7 ♖×b2 a1♕ 8 ♖h2#.

8/10. R. Réti, 1929

The rook should attack a kingside pawn, but which one?

In case of 1 ♖f8? f3 2 ♖f4 b4 3 ♖×g4 b3 4 ♖g1 f2 5 ♖f1 b2 the black pawns are too close to each other, therefore White loses: 6 ♔g7 ♔d4

7 ♔f6 ♔d3–+.

1 ♖g8! g3 2 ♖g4 b4 3 ♖×f4 b3 4 ♖f1 g2 5 ♖g1 b2 6 ♔g7 ♔d4 7 ♔f6 ♔e3 8 ♖b1! ♔d3 9 ♖g1!=.

8/11. V. Chekhover, 1949

Certainly one of the pawns will be promoted. 1 ♔e6? ♔e2 2 ♖g2 ♔e3 (2...h4) 3 ♖×f2 ♔×f2 4 ♔f5 ♔g3 is hopeless. So what to do?

1 ♔g8!! h4 2 ♖h7 h3 3 ♖×h3 ♔g2 4 ♖h7! f1♕ 5 ♖g7+, and the black king cannot escape from checks.

8/12. J. Ullmann, 1928*

The same problem that we had in the previous exercise. Both 1 ♖×a3? ♔b2 and 1 ♔e3? ♔d1 2 ♖d7+ ♔e1 3 ♖c7 a2 lose at once.

1 ♔f3!! ♔d2 2 ♖d7+ ♔c3

2...♔e1 is useless in view of 3 ♖e7+ ♔f1 4 ♖h7.

3 ♖c7+ ♔b3 4 ♔e2(e3) (4 ♖b7+? ♔a4 5 ♖c7 a2–+) **4...a2 5 ♔d3! ♔b4**

5...a1♕ 6 ♖b7+ ♔a3 7 ♖a7+ ♔b2 8 ♖×a1=.

6 ♖b7+ ♔c5 7 ♖a7! ♔b6 (7...c1♕ 8 ♖c7+) **8 ♔×c2! ♔×a7 9 ♔b2=.**

8/13. R. Réti, 1928

1 ♔f2!

The standard method 1 ♔×g2? ♔e4 2 ♔f2 lets Black survive after 2...e1♕+!! (2...♔d3? 3 ♔e1⊙+–) 3 ♔×e1 ♔d3⊙ 4 ♖a1 ♔c3 (△ ♔b2) 5 ♖c1 ♔d3.

1...♔e4 2 ♔×e2 ♔d4 3 ♖g1! ♔e4 (3...♔c3 4 ♔e3+–) **4 ♖e1! ♔d4** (4...♔f4 5 ♔f2+–) **5 ♔d2+–.**

Chapter Nine

9/1. N. Kopaev, 1953*

The unlucky placement of the king kills Black (with the king on h7 it would have been a draw); in addition, his rook is too close to the f-pawn. But it is by no means easy for White to exploit these disadvantages.

1 ♔f6! ♖c6+ 2 ♔e5 ♖c8

If 2...♖c5+ then 3 ♔d6 ♖c8 4 ♖e1! ♔g7 5 ♖e8+–. With a rook on b8, the saving check 5...♖b6+ exists.

3 ♖g6!! ♔h7 4 ♖c6! ♖a8 5 ♔f6

The rook protects the king from side checks. Black is helpless against the maneuver ♖e6-e8.

9/2. N. Kopaev, 1958

1...♔f6!

Black should take measures against strengthening White's position after ♔e8 and e6-e7. If 2 e7+ now, then 2...♔f7=.

1...♖b1? loses to 2 e7 ♖b7+ 3 ♔e6 ♖b8 4 ♖d6 and 5 ♖d8+–.

2 ♖c6 ♖e2 (2...♖d1+? 3 ♔e8) **3 ♖d6 ♖e1 4 ♖d2** (△ 5 ♖f2+) **4...♖a1!**

Only now, when the white rook has abandoned both the a-file and the 6th rank, does Black undertake the side attack.

5 ♖f2+ ♔g7 6 e7 ♖a7+ with a draw.

9/3. Hector – Krasenkov, Ostende 1990

Black would have gladly abandoned the corner with his king but 1...♔h7? loses forcibly: 2 ♔f8+ ♔h6 3 ♖e6+! ♔h7 (3...♔g5 4 f6 ♔f5 5 ♖b6 ♖a8+ 6 ♔g7+–) 4 f6+–.

So he should follow a waiting policy.

1...♖a1! 2 ♖e2!

The game continued 2 f6?! ♔h7! with a drawn position we already know (3 ♔f8+ ♔g6 4 f7 ♔f6! 5 ♔g8 ♖g1+). White could have set his opponent much more difficult problems.

2...♖a7+ 3 ♔g6 ♖g7+ (a passive defense 3...♖a8 loses) **4 ♔f6 ♖g1**

The rook dares not to come back to the long side: 4...♖a7?? 5 ♖e8+ ♔h7 6 ♖e7+.

5 ♔e7 ♖g7+

16-32

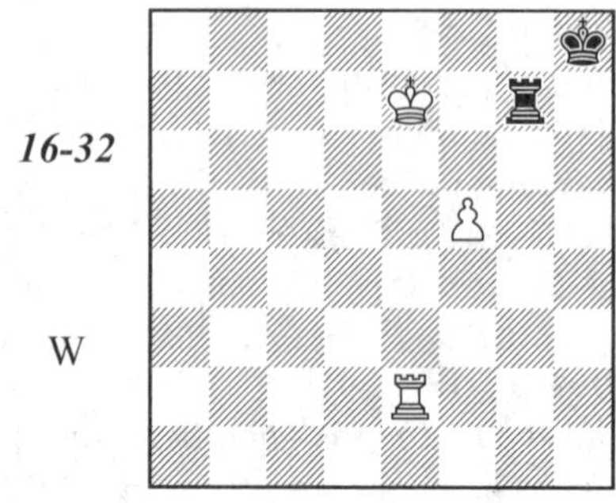

W

6 ♔e8 ♖a7! 7 ♔f8

If 7 f6 then 7...♔g8! (7...♖a8+? 8 ♔f7 ♖a7+ 9 ♔g6+–) 8 ♖g2+ ♔h7 9 f7 ♖a8+, and the checks from the long side save Black.

7...♖a8+ 8 ♔f7 ♖a7+ 9 ♖e7 ♖a1

The initial position has arisen again.

10 ♖e2 ♖a7+ 11 ♔g6 ♖g7+ 12 ♔f6 ♖g1 13 ♔e7 ♖g7+

Having returned to the diagrammed position, White tries another possibility.

14 ♔d6!? ♖f7!

This subtle defense saves the game. After 14...♖a7? 15 ♖e8+ ♔h7 16 ♖e7+ or 14...♖g1? 15 f6 ♔g8 16 ♔e7 Black was lost.

15 ♖e8+ (15 ♔e6 ♖a7=) **15...♔g7 16 ♖e7 ♔f6=**.

9/4. Vukic – Müller, Varna 1975

Black holds by means of transferring his king to the short side.

1...♔f8! 2 ♖b6 (2 ♔×f6 ♖a6+; 2 ♖b8+ ♔e7 △ ...♖g4+) **2...♖f4!**

2...♖g4+!? 3 ♔×f6 ♔g8 4 ♖b8+ ♔h7 is less accurate but still playable. If we shift this position by one file to the left, White should have won. Here, however, Black holds because of the fact that he has two files (a- and b-) for his rook to stay far away from the white king. The white rook occupies one of them, but Black can use the remaining one: 5 ♔e6 ♖e4+ 6 ♔f7 ♖a4=.

3 ♔×f6 (3 ♖×f6+ ♔g8 4 ♖a6 ♖g4+) **3...♔g8 4 ♖b8+ ♔h7 5 ♔e6** (5 ♖f8 ♖a4) **5...♔g7=**

Black chose the erroneous continuation 1...♖a6? 2 ♔g7!+−. The f-pawn will be lost anyway and the king will forever remain on the long side where it only obstructs his own rook. The remainder was 2...♖c6 3 ♖b8+ ♔e7 4 ♖b1 ♖a6 5 ♖e1+ ♔d8 6 ♔f7 ♔d7 7 ♖d1+ ♔c7 8 ♔e7 Black resigned.

9/5. Rohde – Cramling,

Innsbruck wch jr 1977

This position was deeply analyzed by Kopaev in 1955. White wins, although with some hard work. When playing it, one should beware of slipping into theoretically drawn endings. Rohde was probably ill prepared theoretically and failed to avoid an error.

1 ♔e6! (of course not 1 ♔f6? ♖e1!=) **1...♔f8** (1...♔d8? 2 ♖h8+ ♔c7 3 ♔e7+−) **2 ♖f7+!**

An important zwischenschach to impair Black's king position. Both 2 ♖a7? ♖e1! and 2 ♖h8+? ♔g7 3 ♖a8 ♖e1! draw immediately.

2...♔g8

2...♔e8 3 ♖a7 ♔f8 4 ♖a8+ ♔g7 5 ♔e7 ♖b1 6 e6 is hopeless for Black. When we were discussing diagram 9-8 we stated that the white rook is ideally placed on a8. This is the position White wants in this ending, and he can achieve it - provided that he plays correctly.

3 ♖d7!

Rather than 3 ♖a7? ♖e1! (3...♔f8? 4 ♖a8+ ♔g7 5 ♔e7+−) 4 ♔f6 (4 ♔d6 ♔f8!) 4...♖f1+ 5 ♔e6 (unfortunately there is no 5 ♔e7?? ♖f7+ – this is why the white rook should be placed near the king) 5...♖e1=.

The move 3 ♖c7?! is much less precise, however it does not miss the win after 3...♖e1 4 ♔f6! ♖f1+ 5 ♔e7 ♖a1 6 ♖c2 ♖a7+ 7 ♔f6 ♖f7+ 8 ♔e6 ♖a7 9 ♖d2!.

3...♖e1 4 ♔f6! ♖f1+ 5 ♔e7! (the flaws of the disadvantageous position of the black king on g8 tell for the first, but not for the last time in this ending) **5...♖a1!**

The occupation of the long side is the most stubborn defensive method. White's task would have been much easier after 5...♖f7+ 6 ♔d6 ♖f8 (6...♖f1 7 e6 ♖d1+ 8 ♔e7 ♖a1 9 ♖d2+−) 7 e6 ♖a8 8 ♔e5! (8 ♔e7? ♔g7=) 8...♔f8 9 ♔f6+−.

16-33

W?

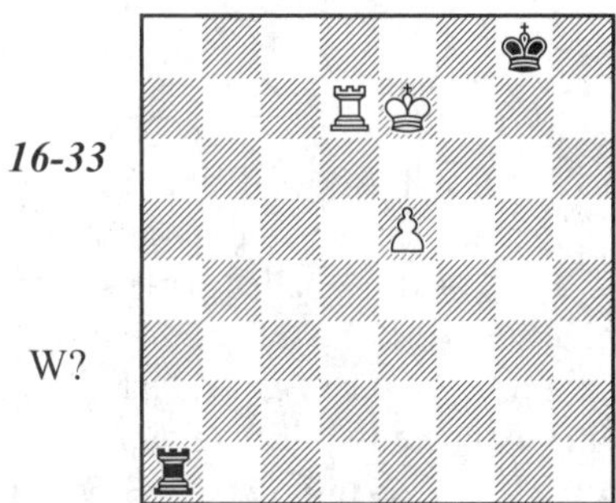

The game continued 6 e6? ♔g7 (see diagram 9-7, the line 2...♖a1) 7 ♖d6 (△ ♔e8+−) 7...♖a8! with a drawn position.

6 ♖d2! ♖a7+ (the threat was 7 ♖g2+) **7 ♔f6 ♖f7+** (forced) **8 ♔e6 ♖f1**

Unfortunately for Black, the rook must leave the long side because 8...♖a7 9 ♖d8+ ♔g7 10 ♖d7+ is bad. White immediately occupies the a-file.

9 ♖a2! ♔g7 (9...♖e1 10 ♔f6! ♖f1+ 11 ♔e7 ♖f7+ 12 ♔d6+−; 9...♔f8 10 ♖a8+ ♔g7 11 ♔d6+−) **10 ♖a7+**

It is still not too late for a mistake: 10 ♔e7? ♖f7+ 11 ♔d6 ♖b7 12 e6 ♖b6+ 13 ♔d7 ♖b7+ 14 ♔c6 ♖b1 15 ♖f2 ♖a1!=, or 12 ♖a6 ♔f7= (12...♖b8=).

10...♔g6 (10...♔f8 11 ♖a8+ ♔g7 12 ♔d6) **11 ♖a8 ♔g7 12 ♔e7** (12 ♔d6 is equivalent) **12...♖f7+** (12...♖b1 13 e6 ♖b7+ 14.♔d6) **13 ♔d6 ♖b7 14 e6 ♖b6+ 15 ♔d7 ♖b7+ 16 ♔c6 ♘e7 17 ♔d6+−**.

9/6. Arencibia – Vladimirov, Leon 1991

The game continued 1 ♖c5? ♔b4 2 ♖c1 c5 3 ♖b1+ ♔a3 4 ♖c1 ♖d5, and White resigned. The reason for the defeat is the same as in the Kochiev - Smyslov and the Tal - I. Zaitsev endings: the poor position of the king on e2.

Another erroneous possibility is 1 ♖a6?, expecting 1...♔b4? 2 ♔e3! ♔b5 3 ♖a1=. But Black plays 1...♔c3!, putting White into zugzwang. In case of 2 ♔e3 ♖e6+ the white king is driven one more file further from the pawn; after 2 ♔e1 ♔b4 3 ♔e2 ♔b5 4 ♖a1 c5 the king fails to leave the 2nd rank in time. All that remains is 2 ♖b6, but then 2...♖d2+ 3 ♔e3 c5–+ follows. If the rook were on a6, a check from a3 would have saved the game.

1 ♔e3! ♔b4 2 ♖a1 c5 3 ♖b1+ ♔a3 4 ♖c1=, and if 4...♖d5 then 5 ♔e4.

9/7. Spiridonov – Shamkovich,
Polanica-Zdroj 1970

The natural looking 1 ♖b6? meets a brilliant refutation 1...♖f4!! 2 ef a2 3 ♔f3 ♔h5 4 ♖a6 b3–+. The line 1 ♔d2? ♖f2+ 2 ♔c1 a2 is hopeless; the same may be said about 1.♔d3? ♖f2 2 ♔c4 ♖b2 ("self-propelled pawns") 3 e4 a2 4 e5 ♔g5. Finally, if 1 e4? then the simplest is 1...♖b7 2 ♔d2 b3 3 ♔c1 b2+ 4 ♔b1 ♖b3 △ 5...♖c3–+. Only one possibility remains:

1 ♖a4! ♖b7 2 ♔d3(d2) ♔g3 3 ♔c2 (△ 4 ♔b3=) **3...b3+ 4 ♔b1 a2+ 5 ♔b2=**

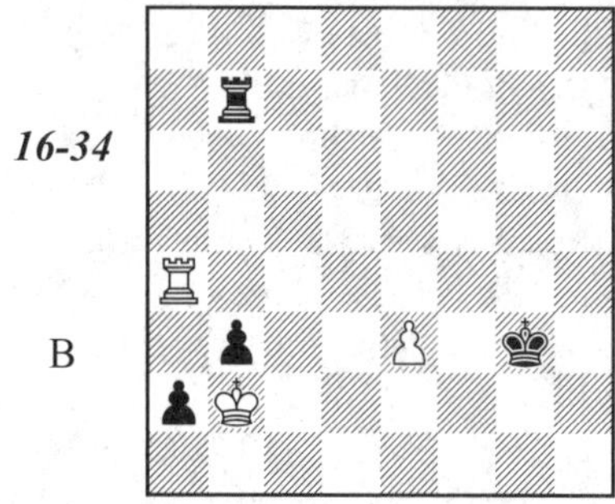

This is a theoretical draw (even without the e3-pawn) – as we know from our analysis of Kasparian's position.

9/8. G. Kasparian, 1948*

In case of 1...♔e6? 2 h4 ♔f6 3 h5 ♔g7 4 ♖h7+ ♔g8 (see diagram 9-53) 5 ♔a2!! White wins. Black must redirect his king to the opposite wing in order to utilize the unfavorable position of the white king on the edge.

The tempting 1...♖g2?! 2 h4 ♔c4 is probably losing after 3 ♔b1! ♔b3 4 ♔c1 ♔c3 5 ♔d1 ♔d3 6 ♔e1 ♔e3 7 ♔f1 ♖f2+ 8 ♔g1 ♔f3 9 h5 ♖g2+ 10 ♔h1! (10 ♔f1 ♖h2). For example: 10...♔f2 11 ♖h7 ♔g3 12 ♖f7! (rather than 12 g7? ♔f2 △ 13...♖g4) 12...♖h2+ (12...♖a2 13 ♔g1 ♖a1+ 14 ♖f1 ♖a2 15 ♖b1+–) 13 ♔g1 ♖×h5 14 g7 ♖g5 15 ♖f2! ♔h3+ 16 ♔h1+–. If 10...♖g4 then White does not play 11 ♖h7?! ♖g5! and he is in zugzwang: 12 g7? (12 ♖h6) 12...♖g4 13 ♔h2 ♖g2+ with a perpetual check, but 11 ♖h8! ♖g5 (11...♔f2 12 ♖f8+) 12 ♖h7! instead, and it is Black who is in zugzwang: 12...♖g4 13 ♖f7+ winning (analysis by Leitao and P. H. Nielsen).

1...♔c4! (△ 2...♔b3) **2 ♔b2 ♖g2+ 3 ♔a3**

3 ♔c1 ♔c3 4 ♔d1 ♔d3 5 ♔e1 ♔e3 6 ♔f1 ♔f3 7 h4 ♖h2 8 ♔g1 ♖g2+ (9...♖a2 10 h5 ♖a1+ 11 ♔a2 ♖a2+ 12 ♔h3 ♖a1=) 9 ♔h1 ♔f2= (9...♖g4=).

3...♖g3+ 4 ♔a4 ♖g1 5 ♔a5

5 ♖h4+ ♔d5 6 ♖g4 ♖×g4+ 7 hg ♔e6=.

5...♔c5 6 ♔a6 ♔c6 7 ♔a7 ♔c7 8 ♔a6 (8 ♖h7+ ♔d6 9 ♖b7 ♔e6=) **8...♔c6=**.

9/9. Beliavsky – Azmaiparashvili,
Portoroz 1997

Of the six possible king retreats, only one is correct, but which one?

1...♔d4? is quite bad: 2 ♖f1 followed with 3 ♔×h3. Or 1...♔f4(f3)? 2 ♖a1 ♖a6 3 f6 (the f-pawn cannot be captured because, after the rook exchange, the king is beyond the square of the a5-pawn).

The game continued 1...♔d2? 2 ♖e5 ♔d3 hoping for 3 ♔×h3? ♔d4 4 ♖b5 ♔c4=. However Beliavsky responded with 3 a6! ♖×a6 4 ♔×h3, and Black was lost: the king is on the long side, and can be cut off from the pawn not only vertically, but horizontally as well. The remainder was 4...♔d4 (4...♖a4 5 ♔g3) 5 ♖e6 ♖a8 6 ♔g4 ♖g8+ 7 ♔f4 ♔d5 8 ♖a6 (8 ♖e1 was also good here – a frontal attack does not help because the pawn has crossed the middle line) 8...♖g1 9 f6 ♖f1+ 10 ♔g5 ♔e5 11 ♔g6 ♖g1+ 12 ♔f7 ♖b1 13 ♔g7 ♖g1+ 14 ♔f8 ♔f5 15 f7 ♖e1 16 ♔g7 ♖g1+ 17 ♔h7 Black resigned.

Let's look at 1...♔f2?. Here 2 ♖e5? is not good anymore, because after 2...♔f3 3 ♖b5 ♔g4 the h3-pawn is protected and White cannot strengthen his position. Therefore, he plays 2 ♖a1! ♖×f5 (2...♖a6 3 ♔×h3+–) 3 a6 ♖f8 4 a7 ♖a8 and cuts the black king off horizontally by 5 ♖a3! in order to slow its march to the a7-pawn. The following line shows what happens then: 5...♔e2 6 ♔×h3 ♔d2 7 ♔g4 ♔c2 8 ♔f5 ♔b2 9 ♖a6! ♔b3 10 ♔e6 ♔b4 11 ♔d6! ♔b5 12 ♖a1 ♔b6 13 ♖b1+ ♔a6 14 ♔c7! ♖×a7+ 15 ♔c6+–.

Now – the correct solution!

1...♔d3!! 2 ♖f1

In case of 2 ♖d1+, 2...♔e4? is bad in view of 3 ♖f1+–. The simplest is 2...♔e3, but 2...♔e2 is also playable: 3 ♖d5 ♔f3= or 3 ♖a1 ♖×f5 4 a6 ♖f8 5 a7 ♖a8 6 ♖a3 ♔d2= (here Black has an extra tempo in comparison with 2...♔f2).

2...♔e2 3 ♖f4! ♔e3 4 ♖a4 ♖×f5 5 a6 ♖f8 6 a7 ♖a8 7 ♔×h3 ♔d3 8 ♔g4 ♔c3 9 ♔f5 ♔b3 10 ♖a1 ♔b4 11 ♔e6

16-35
$

B?

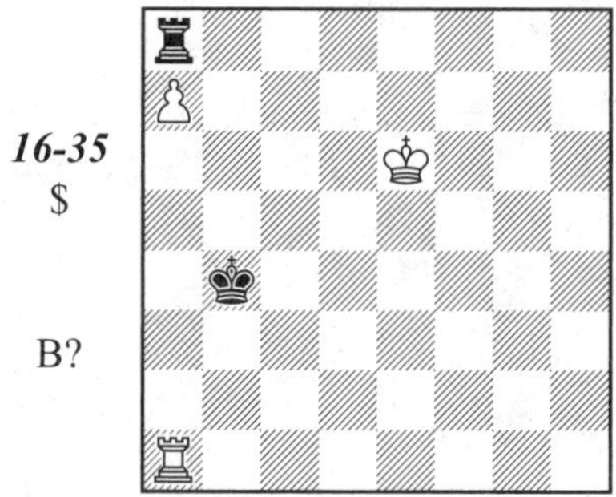

11...♔c5!

This case of shouldering is familiar to us from the analysis of the Kasparov – Short ending. 11...♔b5? is bad: 12 ♔d6! ♔b6 13 ♖b1+ – this is precisely what results from 1...♔f2?.

12 ♔d7 ♔b6 13 ♖b1+ ♔c5! 14 ♖b7 ♖h8=.

9/10. Beliavsky – Radulov,
Leningrad 1977

1...g3? 2 ♖g6 g2 3 ♔b3 ♖f4 (3...♔f2 4 ♔b4=) 4 a6 leads to a draw. The white pawn is advanced far enough, so Black has no time either for utilizing the fact that the white king is cut off along the 4th rank (4...♔f2 5 a7) or for interfering by 4...♖g4.

1...♖f5!

It is important to chain the white rook to defense of the pawn. If 2 ♔b3 g3 3 ♔b4 g2 4 ♖g6, the bridge technique is decisive: 4...♖f4+ △ 5...♖g4.

2 ♖a8 g3 3 a6 ♖f6! 4 a7 ♖f7! White resigned.

9/11. D. Gurgenidze, 1987

1 c3!!

As soon becomes clear, 1 c4? loses. In the upcoming rook versus pawn endgame, White plays for a stalemate, therefore the c-pawn should be left to be captured by the black king.

1 ♖e1? is very bad in view of 1...♖f8+!. However, after Inarkiev's suggestion 1 ♖e7!? (with the idea of 1...♖f8+ 2 ♔e6) Black seems to have no win, for example 1...♖b8 2 ♖a7+ ♔b1 3 g4 ♔×c2 4 ♖a2.

1...♖f8+! 2 ♔g6 ♔b3 3 ♖×b2+ (3 ♖e1? ♖g8+ △ ...♖×g2–+) **3...♔×b2 4 g4 ♔×c3 5 g5 ♔d4 6 ♔h7! ♖f7+!?** (the last trap) **7 ♔h8!**

Rather than 7 ♔h6? ♔e5 8 g6 ♖f1 9 g7 ♔f6–+.

7...♔e5 8 g6 ♖f8+ 9 ♔h7 ♔f6 10 g7 ♖f7 11 ♔h8 ♖×g7 Stalemate.

9/12. V. & M. Platov, 1923

1 e6

After 1 ♖b7+? ♔a6 2 e6 Black holds by means of 2...c5+! 3 ♔c3(d3) (3 ♔e5? d6+) 3...♖f5!?.

1...♖f6

If 1...♖f8 then 2 ♖×d7 f3 (2...♖e8 3 ♔e5) 3 ♖b7+! ♔a6 (3...♔a4 4 ♖f7 ♖d8+ 5 ♔c4) 4 ♖f7 ♖d8+ 5 ♔c5 ♖×d2 6 e7 ♖e2 7 ♔×c6 f2 (7...♖c2+ 8 ♔d7 ♖d2+ 9 ♔e8 f2 10 ♔f8+–) 8 ♖×f2! ♖×e7 9 ♖a2#.

2 ♖b7+!

This zwischenschach is necessary. The gain of a rook for a pawn in the line 2 ed? ♖d6+ 3 ♔e5 ♖×d2 4 ♔e6 f3 5 ♖c8 ♖e2+ 6 ♔d6 ♖d2+ 7 ♔c7 c5= brings only a draw.

2...♔a6

After 2...♔a4 3 ed ♖d6+ 4 ♔c5 ♖×d2 an interference on the d-file decides: 5 ♖b4+ △ 6 ♖d4.

3 ed ♖d6+

3...♖f8 4 ♖c7 ♖d8 5 ♔c5 f3 6 ♔d6 f2 7 ♖×c6+ and 8 ♖c1+–.

4 ♔c5 ♖×d2

16-36

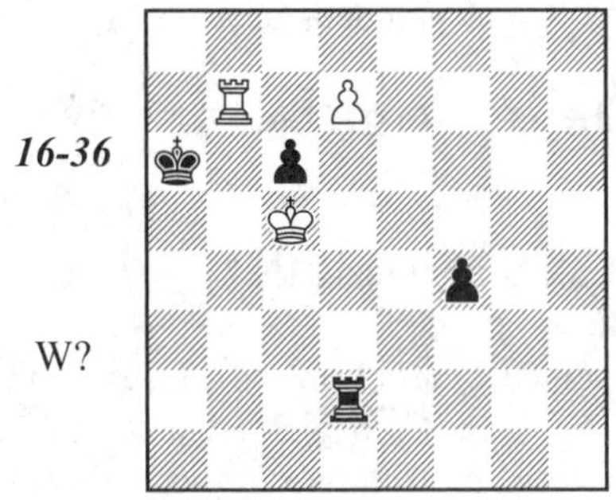

W?

5 ♖b2!

White improves the position of the rook with tempo, utilizing the fact that 5...♖×d7 is impossible in view of 6 ♔×c6. 5 ♖b3? is erroneous: 5...f3! 6 ♔×c6 (6 ♖×f3 ♔b7=) 6...♖c2+ with a draw.

5...♖d3

Black cannot create a fortress with a rook against a queen: 5...♖×b2 6 d8♕ ♖c2+ 7 ♔b4 ♖b2+ 8 ♔c4 ♖b5 9 ♕c7+–. 5...♖d1 is also bad: 6 ♔×c6 ♖c1+ 7 ♔d6 ♖d1+ 8 ♔c7 ♖c1+ 9 ♔d8 f3 10 ♖d2!+–.

6 ♖b3!

The rook occupies the 3rd rank in order to prevent an advance of the f-pawn. 6 ♔×c6? is premature: 6...♖c3+ 7 ♔d6 ♖d3+ 8 ♔c7 ♖c3+ 9 ♔d8 ♖e3! (rather than 9...f3? 10 ♖d2!+–) 10 ♖d2 ♔b7=.

6...♖d2 7 ♔×c6 ♖c2+ 8 ♔d6 ♖d2+ 9 ♔c7 ♖c2+ 10 ♔d8 ♖e2!? (with the idea 11 ♖d3? ♔b7) **11 ♖f3!**

Black must protect the pawn, but his rook will be too close to the white king.

11...♖e4 12 ♔c7 ♖c4+ 13 ♔d6 ♖d4+ 14 ♔c6! ♖c4+ 15 ♔d5+–.

9/13. Petrosian – Karpov,

USSR ch, Moscow 1976

In case of 1...♔h6? White wins similarly to Lasker's study: 2 f7 ♔h7 (2...♖a1 3 ♔g8) 3 h6 ♔×h6 (3...♖a1 4 ♖×c2) 4 ♔g8 ♖g1+ 5 ♔h8 ♖f1 6 ♖c6+ ♔h5 7 ♔g7 ♖g1+ 8 ♔h7 ♖f1 9 ♖c5+ ♔h4 10 ♔g7 ♖g1+ 11 ♔h6 ♖f1 12 ♖c4+ ♔h3 13 ♔g6 ♖g1+ 14 ♔h5 ♖f1 15 ♖c3+ ♔g2 16 ♖×c2+.

1...♔h8! 2 f7 ♖a1!

He must begin the counterattack immediately! Otherwise White plays 3 h6, and the black king is denied the important g7-square.

16-37

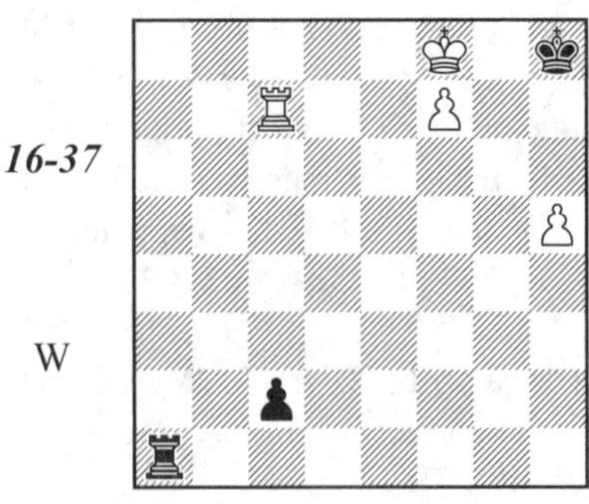

W

3 ♔e7

The king has a refuge from vertical checks: h6. However, Black manages to hold because of a stalemate!

3...♖e1+ 4 ♔f6 ♖f1+ 5 ♔g6 ♖g1+ 6 ♔h6 c1♕+! 7 ♖×c1 ♖g6+!=

In the actual game, 3 ♖×c2 was played (instead of 3 ♔e7). Black forced the white king far away from the pawns with a series of side checks: 3...♖a8+ 4 ♔e7 ♖a7+ 5 ♔f6 (5 ♔e6 ♖a6+ 6 ♔d7 ♖a7+ 7 ♖c7 ♖×c7+ 8 ♔×c7 ♔g7=) 5...♖a6+ 6 ♔g5 ♖a5+ 7 ♔g4 ♖a4+ 8 ♔g3 ♖a3+ 9 ♔g2 ♔g7 10 ♖f2 ♔f8 11 ♖f5 ♖a6!

11...♖a7? loses to 12 h6 ♖a6 (12...♖×f7 13 h7) 13 ♖h5.

12 ♔g3 ♖h6 13 ♔g4

Draw, in view of 13...♖h7.

9/14. Yakovich – Savchenko, Rostov 1993

1 ♖g1!!=

1 ♔h2? ♖a4! 2 ♔g3 ♔h5–+ is bad. Now White impedes Black's king activation in time, for example 1...♔h5 2 ♔h2 ♖a4 3 ♖g5+.

1...♖×a5 2 ♔h3 ♖a8 3 ♖g3 ♖e8 4 ♖g1 ♖e6 5 ♖g3 ♖f6 6 ♖g2 ♖f8 (6...f4 7 ♔g4 f3 8 ♖f2=) 7 ♖g1 (7 ♖g5) 7...f4 8 ♔g2 f3+ 9 ♔f2 ♖f5 10 ♖g4 ♔h5 11 ♖a4 Draw.

White could also successfully apply another defensive method: the occupation of the 8th rank with his rook: 1 ♖e8! ♖×a5 (1...♔h5 2 ♖h8+ ♔g4 3 ♖h6) 2 ♖h8+ ♔g7 3 ♖b8=.

9/15. G. Levenfish, V. Smyslov, 1957

This position resembles the ending Tarrasch – Chigorin but the solution is completely opposite.

Black holds with **1...♖a1!** (△ 2...a2) because White cannot remove the f-pawn from the 3rd rank in time, for example: 2 ♔f4 a2 3 ♖a4 ♔f6 4 ♖a6+ ♔g7 5 g5 ♔f7 6 ♔f5 ♖f1 7 ♖a7+ ♔g8! 8 ♖×a2 ♖×f3+ 9 ♔g6 ♖f8=.

The attempt 1...♖b2? loses after 2 ♖a4 a2 3 ♖a6 (rather than 3 ♔f4?? ♖b4+) 3...♔f7 4 f4 or 4 g5 etc.

9/16. Bernstein – Zuckerman, Paris 1929

The main question is, which pawn should be advanced first?

1 h6!

Bernstein played 1 g6? a2 2 ♔g2 ♖b1! 3 ♖×a2 ♖b5 4 ♖a8+ ♔g7 5 ♖a7+ ♔g8 6 ♖h7, and now 6...♖b3! could have led to a draw à la Kasparian (see diagram 9-53). Instead of this, Black played 6...♖g5+?? and lost.

1...a2

Both 1...♔f8 2 ♖a8+ ♔f7 3 h7 and 1...♔h8 2 ♔g2 ♖a2+ 3 ♔f3 ♖a1 4 g6 are quite bad.

2 ♔h2! (2 ♔g2? ♖b1 3 ♖×a2 ♖b5=) **2...♖b1 3 ♖×a2 ♖b5 4 ♖g2 ♔h7**

16-38

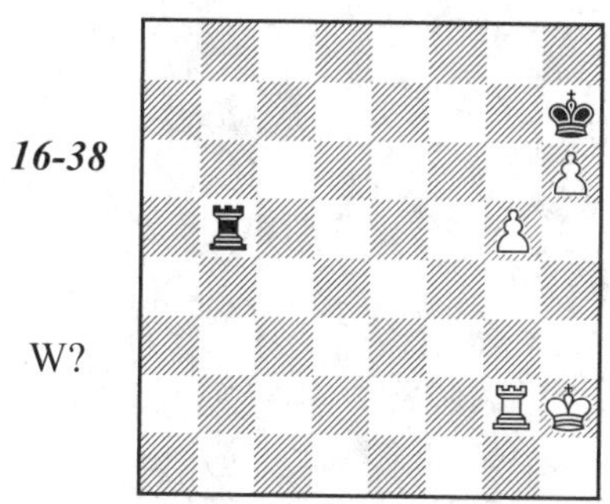

W?

5 g6+!

But surely not 5 ♔h3? ♔g6 arriving at the Kling and Horwitz drawn position.

5...♔g8 6 ♖g3! ♖a5 7 ♖b3 ♖h5+ 8 ♖h3 ♖g5 9 h7+ (9 g7 ♔h7 10 ♖g3 is equivalent) **9...♔h8 10 ♖g3 ♖h5+ 11 ♔g2 ♔g7 12 ♖h3 ♖g5+ 13 ♔f3 ♖f5+ 14 ♔g4 ♖f8 15 ♔g5+–.**

9/17. Mednis – Djukic, Nis 1977

1...♖a8+! (an important zwischenschach that entices the white king to the b-file; 1...g3? 2 b7 ♖f8 3 ♖b2! △ ♔a6-a7 is bad for Black) **2 ♔b5 g3**

Mednis chose 3 b7 ♖f8! 4 ♖c2 (if 4 ♔a6, the same reply follows) 4...♖f2!

Amusingly, the standard exchange proposal saves Black even in such an apparently hopeless situation. In case of 5 b8♕ ♖×c2 6 ♕a8 the simplest is 6...♖×g2=. A waiting tactic is also possible: 6...♖f2 7 ♔c4 ♔g1 8 ♔d3 ♔h2 9 ♔e3 ♔g1 10 ♕d5 ♔h1= (rather than 10...♔h2? in view of the zugzwang after 11 ♕f3!).

5 ♖c4 ♖f8 6 ♖c8 ♖f2 7 b8♕ ♖b2+ 8 ♔c4 ♖×b8 9 ♖×b8 ♔×g2 10 ♔d3 ♔f2 11 ♖f8+ ♔e1! Draw.

As grandmaster Pal Benko demonstrated, White could win after **3 ♖b2!** (instead of 3 b7) **3...♖f8 4 ♔c4! ♖f2 5 ♔c3 ♖f7 6 b7 ♖×b7 7 ♖×b7 ♔×g2 8 ♔d2!+–** (8...♔f2 9 ♖f7+, and the king cannot go to e1).

Black can try 5...♖f8!? (instead of 5...♖f7) 6 b7 ♖b8 7 ♔d4 ♔g1 8 ♔d5 ♔h2 (8...♖×b7 9 ♖×b7 ♔×g2 10 ♔e4+–) 9 ♔c6 ♖f8!, hoping for 10 ♔c7 ♖f7+ 11 ♔b6? (11 ♔d6? ♖×b7=) 11...♖f2!=. However, after 10 ♔d6! he is in zugzwang, for example 10...♔g1 (10...♖g8 11 ♔c7 ♖g7+ 12 ♔b6 ♖g8 13 ♔a7+–) 11 ♔c7 ♖f7+ 12 ♔b6 ♖f2 13 ♖b1+ (or 13 ♖b3), winning.

Grandmaster Karsten Müller has proven that even after **3 b7 ♖f8!** White still can win: instead of 4 ♖c2?, he should play **4 ♖a2! ♖f2 5 ♖a4 ♖f8 6 ♔c6 ♔×g2 7 ♖a8 ♖f6+ 8 ♔c5 ♖f5+ 9 ♔c4 ♖f4+ 10 ♔c3! ♖f3+ 11 ♔d2 ♖b3 12 b8♕+–.**

9/18 Yusupov – Malaniuk,
USSR ch, Moscow 1983

1...♖f8! (△ ♖f4) **2 ♔c2!**

Yusupov ably prevents Black's plans. If 2...♖f4? then 3 ♖×f4 gf 4 g5 ♔e2 (4...♔e3 5 ♔d1!) 5 g6 f3 6 g7 f2 7 g8♕ f1♕ 8 ♕c4+ is decisive.

2...♔g3!

The king frees the way for the future of the upcoming passed f-pawn.

3 a4

16-39

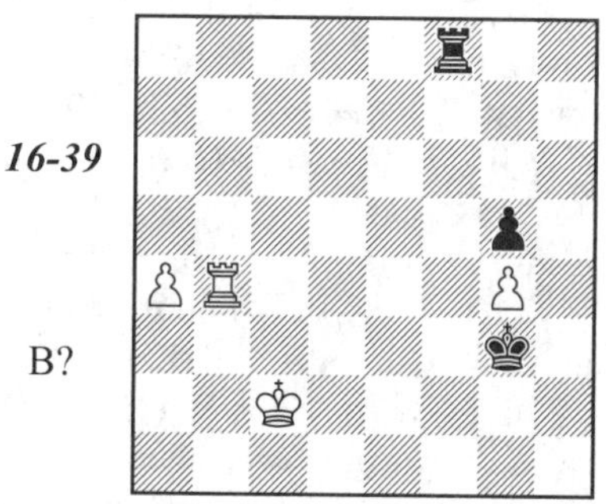

B?

The game continued 3...♖f4? 4 ♖×f4 gf 5 g5 f3 6 g6 f2 7 g7 f1♕ 8 g8♕+ ♔h4 11 ♕d8+!. Black resigned because he could not prevent a queen exchange: 11...♔g4(h5) 12 ♕d1+ or 11...♔g3(h3) 12 ♕d3+. As can be easily seen, after 8...♔h2 or 8...♔h3 the white queen gives a pair of checks and enters the d-file with a forced exchange to follow.

After the game, Malaniuk expressed the opinion that a frontal attack could have saved him: 3...♖a8!? 4 ♔b3 ♔f3 5 ♖d4 ♔g3 6 ♔b4 ♖b8+ 7 ♔c5 ♖a8 8 ♔b6 ♖b8+ 9 ♔c6 ♖a8 10 ♔b7 ♖a5 11 ♔b6 ♖a8 12 a5 ♖b8+ 13 ♔c6 (13 ♔a7? ♖b1=) 13...♖a8 14 ♖a4 ♖×a5 15 ♖×a5 ♔×g4. Of course, this would not work: in the final position, both 16 ♔d5 and 16 ♖a8 ♔f3 17 ♖f8+! ♔e3 18 ♖g8! ♔f4 19 ♔d5 g4 20 ♔d4 ♔f3 21 ♔d3 g3 22 ♖f8+ wins for White.

Black's play can be improved in this line, if he abandons his frontal attack in timely fashion, for the basic plan in such positions: repositioning the rook to f4: 10...♖f8! (instead of 10...♖a5?) 11 a5 ♖f4= (as given by Müller).

Salov and Ionov discovered the same idea in a different setting: they proposed giving a series of checks from the side (similar to the Taimanov - Averbakh endgame), to drive White's king into an inferior position, before offering the exchange of rooks on f4.

3...♖f2+!? 4 ♔c3 ♖f3+ 5 ♔b2 (5 ♔d2 ♖f2+ 6 ♔d1 ♖a2 7 ♔c1 ♖f2) **5...♖f4! 6 ♖×f4 gf 7 g5 f3 8 g6 f2 9 g7 f1♕ 10 g8♕+ ♔h4**

White can no longer trade queens, so the game should end in a draw.

9/19. Stein - Vaganian,
Vrnjacka Banja 1971

1...♖a5? 2 ♔c7 would be very bad. In such situations, Black's hopes usually lie in active kingside counterplay. Vaganian decided to break up the opposing pawn chain with ...h7-h5!.

1...♔g7 2 ♔c8 h5! 3 gh g5!= (the best defense, however 3...gf 4 ♔b8 ♖a5 5 ♔b7 ♖e5! may not lose, either.) 4 ♔b8 ♖a5 5 hg (5 ♔b7 ♖×f5 6 ♔b6 ♖f4!=) 5...fg 6 ♖b7+ (6 ♔b7 ♖×f5=) 6...♔h6 7 f6 ♖×a4 Draw.

White's play was not best. He could have played 3 ♔b8! ♖a5 4 fg. In Lubomir Ftacnik's opinion, the position after 4...hg 5 ♖×g4 f5 6 ♖g5 ♖×a4 7 h5 f4 8 h6+ ♔×h6 9 g7 ♔×g5 10 g8♕+ ♔h4, is drawn; however, the computer endgame tablebase says White must win.

Ftacnik also looked at the line 4...♔×g6 5 ♔b7 ♖e5 6 ♔b6 ♖e6+ 7 ♔c5 ♖e5+ 8 ♔d6 hg 9 ♖×g4+ ♔h5 10 ♖c4 ♔g6, and showed that a draw is inevitable after 11 ♔c6 f5 12 ♔b6 ♖e6+ 13 ♔b5 ♖e8 14 a5 ♖a8+. Yet, the simple 11 ♖c5! allows White to get both his pawns to the 5th rank for free, which obviously leads to a win.

So Vaganian's plan would probably not have saved the game had his opponent reacted properly. Far more effective is the unexpected tactical idea found thirty years later by Irina Kulish: to play for stalemate!

1...gf 2 gf ♔h5! followed by 3...h6 and 4...♖×a4!.

9/20. Eliseevic – Pytel, Trstenik 1979

After 1...a5? 2 ♖×e6 ♖e4 (△ ...♔f7) 3 ♖e7 ♔f8 4 ♖a7 ♖×e5 5 ♔f2 Black's extra pawn does not offer him any real winning chances. The only promising possibility is to place the rook behind the distant passed pawn.

1...♖f4+! 2 ♔g1 (2 ♔e2 ♖e4+ and 3...♖×e5) **2...♖f7!** (rather than 2...♖f8 3 ♖a7!=).

16-40

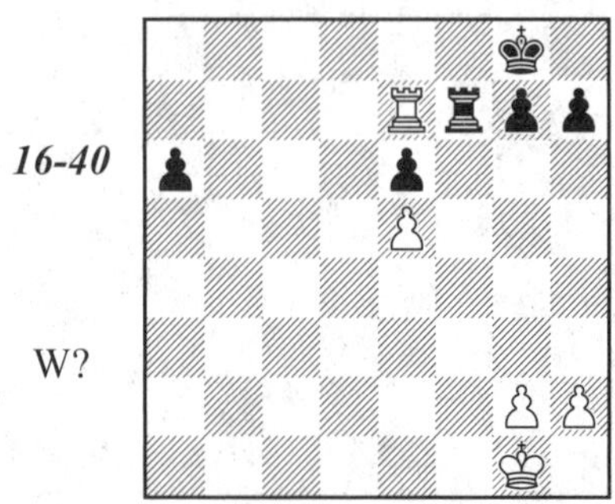

W?

In the game, Black's plan was completely successful.

3 ♖×e6 ♖a7 4 ♖d6 a5 5 e6 ♔f8 6 ♖d3 ♔e7 7 ♔f2 ♔×e6 8 ♔e3 a4 9 ♖a3 ♔d5 10 ♔d3 ♔c5 11 ♔c3 ♔b5 12 ♔b2 ♔c4 13 ♖g3 a3+! 14 ♔a2 ♔d4 15 ♖h3 h6 16 ♖g3 g5 White resigned. 17 h4 is met with 17...♖a5, and if 18 ♖b3 then 18...♔e4 19 ♖b6 ♔f4 20 ♖×h6 g4 △ 21...♔g3−+.

White should have defended his position more actively. Prior to blocking the passed pawn with his rook, he had enough time to gain one of the kingside pawns.

3 ♖e8+! ♖f8 4 ♖×e6 ♖a8 5 ♖e7 (5 ♖d6 is worse in view of 5...♖a7!?) **5...a5 6 e6 a4 7 ♖d7 ♔f8** (7...a3 8 e7) **8 ♖f7+ ♔e8 9 ♖×g7 ♖a5 10 ♖c7 a3 11 ♖c1 a2 12 ♖a1 ♔e7 13 ♔f2 ♔×e6 14 ♔e3** Black still stands better, but a draw seems very likely.

9/21. Fernandez Garcia – Kotronias,
Dubai ol 1986

The game continued 1...♖a3?? 2 a6 ♖a2 3

a7 ♖a3 (3...♔g4 4 ♖f8 ♖×a7 5 ♖×f6+–) 4 f3!+–, and we already know the rest from the ending Unzicker – Lundin.

A draw could be reached after **1...g5! 2 hg fg 3 a6 ♔g6 4 ♔f1** (△ 5 a7 ♔g7 6 f4+–) **4...g4=**. 1...♔e6!? 2 a6 ♔f7 3 ♔f3 (3 ♖a7+ ♔e6) 3...♔g7 was also playable.

9/22. Kholmov – Timoshchenko,
USSR chsf, Pavlodar 1982

As Kholmov discovered after the game, he could have obtained a draw after **1 ♔h2!** △ 2 g3 (see diagram 9-131).

However, he actually played 1 ♖a4+? ♔c3! (2...♔b3 was threatened) 2 ♖a8, and after 2...f5! his position became lost. Black's winning plan is simple: the pawn comes to f4, the king attacks the h4-pawn and, when this pawn is dead, Black gets a passed f-pawn.

3 ♖a7 (3 ♔h2 f4) 3...f4+ 4 ♔h2 ♔d4 5 ♖a4+ ♔e5 6 ♖a3 ♔f5 7 ♖a6 ♔g4 8 ♖×g6+ ♔×h4 9 ♖a6 ♔g5 10 ♖a8 h4 11 ♖g8+ ♔f6 12 ♖a8 h3! 13 gh f3 14 ♖a3 ♔e5 White resigned.

9/23. Yusupov – Timman,
Linares cmsf (7) 1992

Where should White place his rook, at the side of his passed pawn or behind it?

The winning move was **1 ♖e4!**. Here the rook protects only one pawn but at the first appropriate opportunity it will go to the 5th rank where it holds everything. For example, 1...♔f5 2 ♖e5+ ♔f6 (2...♔g4 3 ♖g5+) 3 a5+–, or 1...♖a5 2 ♔e3 ♖d5 3 ♖e5!. Black has no arguments against a king march to the queenside.

The actual continuation was 1 ♖a1?? ♖a5! (he should block the pawn as early as possible) 2 ♔e3 e5!.

This is the point: one pair of pawns is exchanged immediately, another will be exchanged soon (...g6-g5), and too few pawns remain on the board.

3 ♔e4 (3 fe+ ♔×e5 4 ♔d3 ♔d5 5 ♔c3 ♔c6 6 ♔b4 ♖e5=) 3...ef 4 ♔×f4 (after 4 gf the white pawns are vulnerable) 4...♔e6 5 ♔e4

He probably should have tried 5 ♖e1+ ♔f6 6 ♖e4 g5+ 7 ♔e3, but this position is also drawn. 5...g5! 6 hg ♖×g5 7 ♔f3 ♖a5, and a draw was soon agreed.

9/24. Taimanov – Chekhov, Kishinev 1976

White wants to play e3-e4+, and then slowly improve his position with a2-a4, f2-f3, ♔g4, ♖b5 etc. And although objectively White's advantage is insuffiecient to win, Black should still avoid passive defense.

1...♖d3! 2 ♖×b6

White could have tried 2 a4!? ♖a3 3 ♔f3⊙, but after 3...g4+! 4 ♖×g4 b5! 5 ab ♖b3 a drawn endgame with two pawns versus one would have arisen.

2...♖a3=

The white rook must occupy a passive position. After 3 ♖b2 ♖a4 a draw was agreed.

I worked with Valery Chekhov as his coach from 1973 until 1975, and our collaboration was crowned with his victory in the World Junior Chess Championship. All of my students firmly absorbed the most important principles of playing endgames. Therefore, for Chekhov, the utilization of the pawn sacrifice to activate the rook was just a simple technical device.

9/25. Larsen – Kavalek,
Solingen m (7) 1970

Kavalek chose 1...♔g7?? 2 ♖c4 ♖a7 (2...♖b3 3 ♖×a4 ♖×g3 4 ♖g4+). Against such a passively placed rook, White wins without trouble, and the remainder of the game confirms this generalization.

3 ♔c3 h5 4 ♔b4 ♔g6 5 ♖c6+ ♔g7 6 ♖c5 ♔h6 7 ♔b5 (△ ♖c4) 7...♖e7 8 ♔×a4 ♖e3 9 g4 hg 10 hg ♖e4+ 11 ♔b5 ♖×g4 12 a4 ♖g1 13 a5 ♖b1+ 14 ♔c6 ♖a1 15 ♔b6 ♖b1+ 16 ♖b5 ♖f1 17 a6 ♖f6+ 18 ♔a5 ♖f7 19 ♖b6+ ♔g5 20 ♖b7 ♖f1 21 a7 ♔h6 22 ♖b6+ ♔g7 23 ♖a6 Black resigned.

He had to keep the rook active, responding to ♖c4 with the counterattack ...♖b3!, for this purpose Black should take measures against a rook check from g4.

1...♔f7 seems natural, as the king goes closer to the center. White could respond with 2 g4, intending 3 h4 and 4 ♖c4. If 2...♔e6 3 h4 ♔d5 then 4 g5! △ 5 ♖g3 followed with either 6 ♖g4 (attacking the a4-pawn) or 6 h5 (the rook behind the passed pawn). However, Black has a powerful reply as indicated by Müller: 2...h5! 3 gh (3 g5 h4; 3 ♖c4 ♖b3) 3...♔g7 4 h4 ♔h7 5 ♖c4 ♖b3! 6 ♖×a4 ♖f3. This is the standard drawing situation with a- and h-pawns: the king blockades one of the pawns (or in this case – both at once, which is unimportant), while the rook attacks the other from the side, while not letting the enemy rook off the a-file.

White's play can be strengthened by the in-between check 2 Rf3+!. If 2...Kg6?, then 3 Rf4 (now that Black can't play 3...Rb3 4 R×a4 R×g3 5 Rg4+), and on 2...Ke6 there comes 3 g4 followed by 4 h4, retaining the advantage – with the king in the center, the ...h7-h5 pawn sacrifice would be ineffective.

1...h5!!

The only defense, but sufficient. 2 Rc4 is useless now: 2...Rb3! 3 R×a4 R×g3=. If 2 h4 then 2...Rg7! △ ...Rg4=, and from g4 the rook attacks the g3-pawn, protects the a4-pawn and prevents White's king march across the 4th rank.

2 g4 can be met by 2...h4!=, fixing a target for counterattack (the h3-pawn): 3 Rc4 Rb3 ⇄. But 2...hg 3 hg Kg7 does not lose, either: 4 Rc4 Rb3! (activity at any price!) 5 R×a4 Rg3 6 Kb2 Rg2+ 7 Kc3 Rg3+.

As can be seen, after 1...h5! Black's rook remains active in all lines, and this circumstance saves him.

9/26. Kovacevic – Rajkovic,
Yugoslavia 1983

1...g4+? 2 Kf4 is hopeless. In the game, Black resigned after a single move: 1...gh? 2 gh, in view of 2...Rg7 3 a4 (△ 4 a5 ba 5 Rc5#) or 2...Ra8 3 Rc7 R×a3 4 Rd7+.

Instead of being persecuted, the black king could have become a dangerous attacking piece!

1...f4!! 2 gf (2 ef K×d4; 2 hg fe 3 K×e3 Rg7 4 Rb3 R×g5 5 R×b6 R×g3+ 6 Kf2 R×a3=) **2...g4+! 3 Ke2 Ke4=**

16-41

W

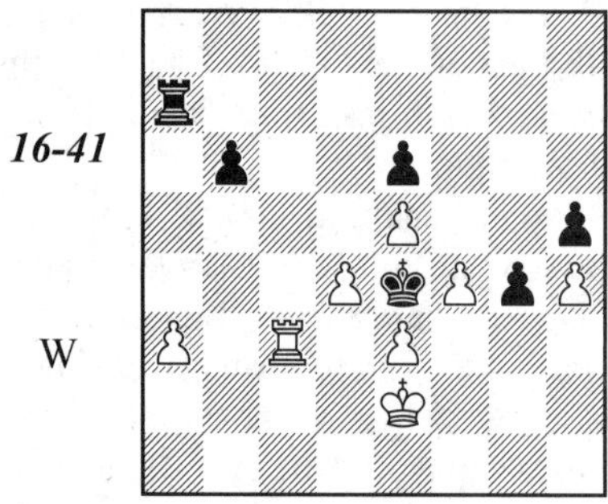

The king's activity fully compensates Black for his deficit of two pawns.

9/27. Kozlovskaya – Carvajal,
Rio de Janeiro izt 1979

The king must take part in the fight against the passed pawns.

1...Rc2! 2 c6 Ke7! 3 R×e5+ Kd6∓

The king has arrived at the center and firmly blocked the pawns. White should play carefully to avoid grave problems.

In the actual game, however, Black was too greedy.

1...R×a3? 2 Rc1!

The rook goes behind the passed pawn that is farthest from the black king and therefore the most dangerous.

2...Ke8 3 c6 Kd8 4 c7+ Kc8 5 d6. Black resigned in view of 5...Rd3 6 Rc6 △ 7 Rb6 or 7 R×a6.

9/28. Obukhov – Ibragimov, USSR 1991

White's passivity 1 Rh1? caused a quick loss: 1...h3 2 Rh2 a6⊙ 3 Kg4 (3 Kg5 Rg8+ 4 Kf5 Rg3) 3...Kf6 4 R×h3 R×h3 5 K×h3 d5! White resigned.

His only correct plan was to activate the rook!

1 Rb1! h3 2 Rb7+ Kf8□

White had undoubtedly considered this line, but failed to find out how it should have been continued. In fact, 3 Rb8+? fails to 3...Kg7 4 Rb7+ Kh6–+ and 3 Kf6? to 3...Rh6+ 4 Kg5 h2–+. If 3 Kg6? then 3...Rh4! decides: 4 f5 h2 5 Rb8+ (5 f6 Rg4+ or 5...Rh6+) 5...Ke7 6 f6+ Kd7 7 f7 h1Q–+. But one more possibility exists:

3 Kg5!! h2 (3...Rg8+?? 4 Kf6+–) **4 Rb8+ Kg7 5 Rb7+** with a perpetual check.

9/29. Browne – Biyiasas,
USA ch, Greenville 1980

The way to a draw is to activate the king.

1...Kc5! 2 Rh7 b6 3 Rc7+ (3 Rb7 Re3) **3...Kb4 4 Rc6 K×b3 5 R×b6+ K×c4=**

Another way, suggested by Benko, also exists: 1...Kc7! 2 Rh7+ Kc8 3 Kf6 b6 4 Re7 Rh3! 5 Ke6 Rh6+ (precisely the same defensive idea as in Savon - Zheliandinov, diagram 9-210).

Black played 1...Re3? instead, allowing 2 Rc8!, so that his king was locked in on the queenside. If 2...R×b3, then 3 Ke6 is decisive.

2...Re5+ 3 Kf6 Re3 4 c5+! dc 5 d6 Rd3 6 Ke7 Re3+ 7 Kd8

Black resigned in view of 7...R×b3 8 d7 Re3 9 Rc7 △ 10 Kc8+–.

Chapter Ten

10/1. Zahrab, IX century

1 ♖e3 ♘g1 2 ♔f5!

The mined squares for the kings are f4 and d4. The premature 2 ♔f4? ♔d4⊙ misses the win: 3 ♖e1 ♘h3+ 4 ♔g3 ♘g5 5 ♔f4 ♘h3+.

2...♔d4 (otherwise 3 ♔g4) **3 ♔f4**

It is Black who is in zugzwang now!

3...♔c4 4 ♔g3 ♔d4 5 ♖e1+–.

10/2. Duz-Khotimirsky – Allakhverdian, Erevan 1938

1 g6! ♘×g6 2 ♖h6!

The game continued 2 ♖g5? ♘f4 3 ♖g8 ♘e6! (△ ...♔f4, ...♘g5=) 4 ♖g6 ♘f4 5 ♖g8 ♘e6 Draw.

2...♘e5 3 g5 ♘f7 4 ♖h5! (4 ♖g6? ♔g4=) **4...♘e5** (4...♔g4 5 g6) **5 g6!+–** (Kromsky, Osanov).

A good idea is to study White's alternatives and discover new positions where a rook and a pawn cannot beat a knight.

After 1 ♖h6 ♘f7! 2 ♖a6? (2 ♖h5!) 2...♘×g5 3 ♖a4 ♔f3 4 ♔c2 ♘e6 5 ♔c3 ♘g5 the white king cannot come closer to the pawn. If White plays 6 ♖c4 and directs the king around the rook along the 5th rank, Black comes with his king to h4 and attacks the pawn in time. For example, 6...♔g3 7 ♔b4 ♔h4 8 ♔c5 ♘h3 9 ♔d5 ♘f2 10 ♔e5 ♔g5=.

Another attempt can be 1 ♖h1? ♔×g4 2 ♖g1+ ♔f5 3 ♔e2 ♘g6 4 ♔e3 ♘h4 5 ♖g3 ♘g6 6 ♔d4 ♘f4 7 ♔c4

16-42

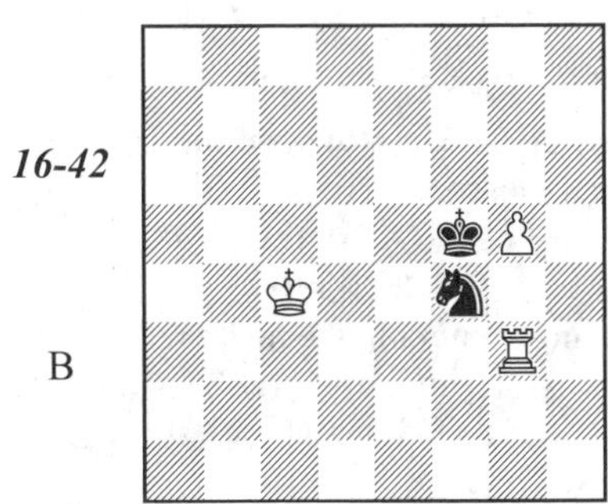

B

Now the simplest defensive plan is to force the pawn advance to the 7th rank. The edge of the board will then be an obstacle to invasion by the white king.

7...♘e6!? 8 g6 ♔f6 9 ♖g4 ♘g7 10 ♔d5 ♘f5 11 ♔c5 ♘e7! (rather than 11...♘g7? 12 ♔d6 ♘f5+ 13 ♔d7 or 11...♔g7? 12 ♔c6! ♘e7+ 13 ♔d6 ♘×g6 14 ♔e6!) 12 g7 ♔f7 13 ♖g5 ♘g8 14 ♔d5 ♘e7+ 15 ♔e5 ♘g8, and White cannot make any progress.

The waiting policy is also good: 7...♘g6 8 ♔d5 ♘f4+ 9 ♔d6 ♘g6 10 ♖g1 ♘h4! 11 ♔e7 ♔g6 12 ♔e6 ♘f3=. In this line, 10...♘f4? (instead of 10...♘h4!) loses: 11 ♔e7 ♔g6 12 ♖g3! ♘h5 13 ♖g4! ♘g7 14 ♔d6! (14 ♖g1? ♘f5+ 15 ♔e6 ♘d4+ and 16...♘f3=) 14...♔f5 15 ♖g1 ♘h5 16 ♔e7 ♔g6 17 ♔e6 ♘f4+ 18 ♔e5+–.

10/3. P. Benko, 1986

The white king has already invaded the black camp, therefore Black's idea is to attack the pawn rather than to create a fortress. He will even readily sacrifice his knight for the pawn.

In case of 1 ♖h4? ♘b2! 2 ♔d7 c4 3 ♖h5+ (3 ♔c7 ♘a4 4 ♖h3 ♘×c3!=) 3...♔e4 4 ♔c6 Black holds by means of 4...♘d1! 5 ♖h3 ♔f5!! 6 ♔c5 ♔g4, driving the rook back from the 3rd rank. White should take this idea into consideration in all lines.

1 c4+! ♔e5 2 ♖g4!!

The apparently natural 2 ♖h4? could, after 2...♘b2? 3 ♔d7 ♘×c4 4 ♖×c4 ♔d5, lead to the position from the famous study by Réti (diagram 8-10), where White wins: 5 ♖c2(c3)!! c4 6 ♖c1! ♔c5 7 ♔c7⊙. However, Black has an adequate defense: 2...♘e1! 3 ♔d7 ♘f3 4 ♖g4 ♔f5=.

2...♘b2

2...♘e1 is already useless here: 3 ♔d7+–.

3 ♖h4!

Rather than 3 ♔d7? ♔f5 4 ♖h4 ♔g5 5 ♖e4 ♔f5=.

3...♘×c4 (3...♔f5 4 ♔d6+–) **4 ♖×c4 ♔d5 5 ♖c1! c4 6 ♔d7! ♔c5 7 ♔c7⊙** (7 ♔e6? ♔d4!=) **7...♔b4** (7...♔d4 8 ♔b6) **8 ♔d6+–.**

10/4. A. Seleznev, 1920

On 1 ♖d7? ♘e6 2 ♖e7 ♘c5+ 3 ♔b4 ♔b7 Black has a comfortable draw. To achieve success, some combinational spirit is necessary!

1 c5! ♘e6 (1...dc 2 ♖d7 ♘e6 3 ♖e7+–) **2 cd! ♘×d8 3 dc ♘b7! 4 c8♖!** (4 c8♕? - stalemate) **4...♘×a5 5 ♖c5 ♘b7 6 ♖c6#.**

10/5. L. Kubbel, 1925 (corrected by A. Chéron)

1 d7 ♖a8!

Hopeless is 1...♖a1+ 2 ♔e2 ♖a2+ 3 ♔f3 ♖d2 4 ♘f6 (△ 5 ♘d5) 4...♖d6 5 ♔g4 followed by 6 ♔f5 and 7 ♔×e5, and if the pawn is defended by the king from d4, then 7 g4 or 7 ♔g6.

2 ♘h6! (but not 2 ♘e7? ♔c5 3 ♘c8 ♖a1+ 4 ♔e2 ♖a2+) **2...♔d3!** (2...♖d8 3 ♘f7 ♖×d7 4 ♘×e5+) **3 f3** (3 ♘f7?? ♖a1#) **3...♔e3 4 ♘f5+ ♔d3 5 ♘e7! ♔e3** (5...♖d8 6 ♘c6 ♖×d7 7 ♘×e5+) **6 ♘d5+! ♔d3 7 ♘c7! ♖d8 8 ♘e6 ♖×d7 9 ♘c5+**.

10/6. S. Tkachenko, N. Rezvov, 1997

1 d7!

1 ♘e6+? is erroneous: 1...♔e3 2 d7 ♖a4+ 3 ♔b7 ♖b4+ 4 ♔c7 ♖c4+ 5 ♔d6 ♖c1 6 ♘c5 ♖d1+ 7 ♘d3 ♔×e2=.

1...♖a4+ (1...♖d4? 2 ♘e6+) **2 ♔b7 ♖b4+ 3 ♔c6!**

3 ♔c7 is useless, as after 3...♖c4+ White must go back to the b-file (4 ♔d6? ♖d4+).

3...♖b8 (3...♖c4+? 4 ♔b5 ♖d4 5 ♘e6+) **4 ♔c7! ♖a8! 5 ♔b7 ♖h8!**

There is no other square on the 8th rank for the rook: 5...♖d8? 6 ♘e6+, or 5...♖g8? 6 ♘e8.

16-43

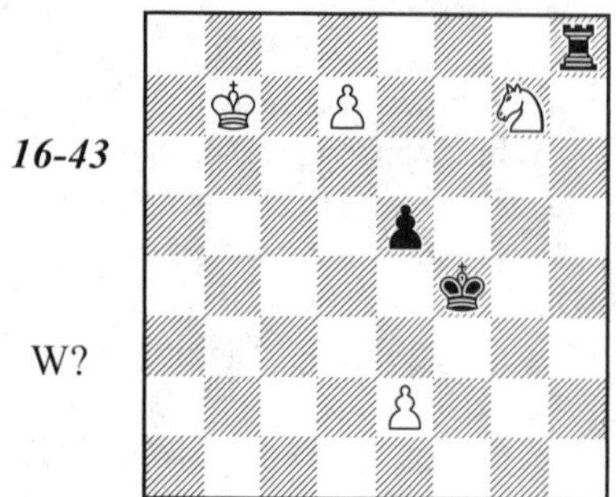

W?

6 e4!!

A difficult move to find! Nothing can be gained by 6 ♘e8? ♖h7 7 ♔c6 ♖×d7 8 ♔×d7 ♔e3=.

6...♔f3!?

The pawn cannot be captured in view of the knight fork: 6...♔×e4 7 ♘e8 ♖h7 8 ♘f6+. If 6...♔g5 then 7 ♘e8 ♖h7 8 ♔c6 ♖×d7 9 ♔×d7 ♔f4 10 ♘d6(f6). Finally, 6...♔e3 (△ 7...♖d8) fails to 7 ♔c7 ♖a8 8 ♘f5+! ♔×e4 9 ♘d6+ and 10 ♘c8.

7 ♔c6! (7 ♔c7? ♖a8! 8 ♘f5 ♖a7+ 9 ♔c6 ♖×d7) **7...♖d8**

If 7...♖a8 then 8 ♘f5 ♔×e4 9 ♘d6+ △ ♘c8.

8 ♘e6 ♖×d7 9 ♘g5+! ♔g4 10 ♔×d7 ♔×g5 11 ♔e6! (11 ♔d6? ♔f6=) **11...♔f4 12 ♔d5⊙ +–**.

Chapter Eleven

11/1. V. Platov, 1925

1 ♔f5! ♔g8 2 ♖a4!!

The only way to victory is to utilize the bad position of the bishop. After 2 ♔g6? ♔f8 the black king slips away from the dangerous corner.

2...♗e1 (2...♗g3 3 ♖g4+; 2...♗f2 3 ♔g6 ♔f8 4 ♖f4+; 2...♗d8 3 ♖a8; 2...♗e7 3 ♔g6) **3 ♔g6 ♔f8 4 ♖f4+!** △ 5 ♖e4+–.

11/2. J. Vancura, 1924

1 ♔f6? ♗e4 leads to the Cozio drawing position. White wins if he prevents the black bishop's entering the b1-h7 diagonal.

1 ♖g4! ♗b5 (△ ...♗d3) **2 ♖d4! ♔h7 3 ♔f6+–**

The rook completely dominates the bishop. The rest is simple: 3...♗c6 4 ♔g5 ♔h8 (4...♗b5 5 ♖d5 ♗c6 6 ♖e5 ♗a4 7 ♖e7+ ♔h8 8 h7) 5 ♖c4 ♗d5 6 ♖c8+ ♗g8 7 ♖e8 ♔h7 8 ♖e7+ ♔h8 9 ♔g6 ♗c4 10 h7+–.

11/3. J. Vancura, 1924

1 ♔g5!!

But, of course, not 1 ♔h6? ♗e4! 2 ♖a7 ♗b7!= and not 1 ♖a7? ♗e4+! (1...♗b7?? 2 ♔h6⊙) 2 ♔h6 ♗b7 3 ♖a4 ♗e4!=.

1...♗g2 (1...♔×h7 2 ♖h4+; 1...♗c6 2 ♖c4 ♗d5 3 ♖d4 △ 4 ♔h6) **2 ♖g4 ♗f3** (2...♗h3 3 ♖b4 or 3 ♖f4) **3 ♖f4+–**

The rook has abandoned the a-file, so the king may come back to h6.

11/4. Y. Roslov, 1996*

If 1 ♔f2? ♗d5 2 ♔e3 ♔f7 3 ♔d4 ♗b3, the game comes to the Del Rio position. To avoid it, only tactical measures will do.

1 f7+! ♔e7 2 ♖d6!! (rather than 2 ♖h8? ♗a6+! 3 ♔f2 ♔×f7) **2...♗h1**

Amazingly enough, the bishop cannot find a refuge from rook attacks: 2...♔f8 3 ♖d8+ ♔×f7 4 ♖d7+; 2...♗c8 3 f8♕+ ♔×f8 4 ♖d8+; 2...♗f3 3 f8♕+ (or 3 ♖f6).

3 ♔g1 ♗e4 (3...♗b7 4 ♖d7+!) **4 ♖e6+!**.

11/5. Stoliar – Bobotsov, Albena 1973

The position after 1...♗e3? 2 ♖e2 f4, like all similar situations with the pawn on the square of bishop's color, is lost.

The game continuation 1...♗g1? is also erroneous: 2 ♖e2+ ♔f6 (2...♔d6 3 f4! △ 4 ♔d3,

5 ♖e5) 3 ♔d5 ♗a7 4 ♖e8! ♗f2 5 f4! Black resigned.

1...♗g3! (Also possible is 1...♗h4) **2 ♖e2+ ♔f6**

Timman showed that 2...♔d6! 3 ♔d4 ♗f4 (or 3...♗h4 △ ...♗f6+) is also sufficient to hold the draw. However, White can just transpose moves and force the king to retreat to f6: 2 ♔d4!? ♗e5+ 3 ♔c5 ♗d6+ 4 ♔c6 △ 5 ♖e2+ (Müller).

3 ♖g2 ♗c7 4 ♔d5 ♗b8 5 ♖g8 ♗h2!

Black's last move was given by Pfrommer. Timman had examined 5...♗c7? 6 ♖f8+ ♔g5 7 ♔e6 ♔f4 8 ♖f7! (rather than 8 ♖×f5+? ♔e3 9 ♖c5 ♗g3! 10 ♖c3+ ♔f4 11 ♔d5 ♗f2 △ ♗e3=) 8...♗b6 (8...♗b8 9 ♖b7) 9 ♖×f5+ ♔e3 10 ♖f7 △ 11 f4+−.

6 ♖f8+ (6 ♖h8 ♗g3!) **6...♔g5 7 ♔e6 ♔f4 8 ♖×f5+ ♔e3=** (△ 9...♗f4).

11/6. Moiseev – Botvinnik,
USSR ch, Moscow 1952

If 1...♖c3+ 2 ♔e4! (2 ♔f2 ♔f4−+) 2...♖g3 3 ♗h3, Black is in zugzwang. The solution will be clear if we realize that the zugzwang is reciprocal.

1...♖c7!!⊙ 2 ♗h3

2 ♔e4 ♖e7 3 ♔e5 ♖e8⊙ is also bad. The remainder of the game was 2 g4 ♖c3+ 3 ♔g2 h3+ 4 ♔h2 ♔h4 5 g5 ♖c2+, and White resigned.

2...♖c3+ 3 ♔e4 ♖g3!⊙ 4 ♔e5 ♖e3+

The black king takes the key f4-square under control, invades on g3, and an exchange sacrifice decides.

11/7. A Theoretical Position

This example can be found in many theoretical treatises, given with a wrong or, at least, an imprecise evaluation.

1 b4!

1...a5= should be prevented. Now this move loses a pawn: 2 ba ba 3 ♔c5 a4 4 ♔b6 ♔c8 5 ♖g4+−. 1...♗f3 2 a4 ♗e4 3 a5 ba 4 ba is also hopeless for Black (see diagram 11-23).

Another continuation, 1 ♖g4!?, also deserves attention: 1...♗f3 (1...♗b1 2 ♔c6! ♗×a2 3 ♖g7+−) 2 ♖f4, and if 2...♗g2 then 3 b4, planning a2-a4-a5.

1...♗c2!?

If Black manages to place his bishop on a4 he achieves a draw. The same outcome results from 2 ♔c6 ♗e4+ 3 ♔b5 ♗d3+ 4 ♔a4 ♗c2+ 5 ♔a3? a6!= (diagram 11-35). This means that White's next move is obligatory.

2 b5!+−

2...♗e4 3 a4 ♗d3 (3...♗f3 is equivalent) 4 ♔d5! ♗f5

16-44

W

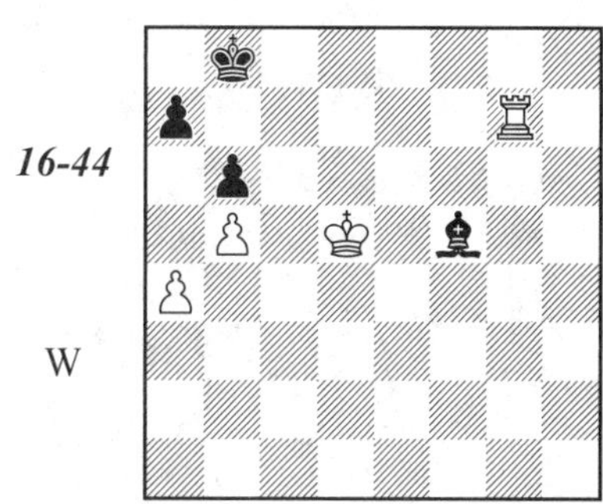

The diagrammed position is known from Ljubojevic – Keene, Palma de Mallorca 1972 (with reversed colors and wings). Books on theory say it is a draw. We know from the Khalifman - Leko ending that this is not so. The winning plan is simple: White brings his king to b4 and plays a4-a5, arriving at the Elkies position, so the most rapid progress can be achieved after 5 ♔c4!.

The players and the annotators ignored this plan because they did not know that the Elkies position is winning. Keene tried to invade with his king to c6, failed to do so, and a draw was agreed.

5 ♖g5 ♗d3 6 ♖g3 ♗c2 7 ♖g2 (7 ♖e3? ♗×a4! 8 ♔c6 a6 9 ♔×b6 ♗×b5=) 7...♗d3 8 ♖f2 (8 ♖d2 ♗g6! 9 ♖e2 ♗h5 10 ♖f2 ♔c7! 11 ♖f6 ♗e8! 12 ♖f5 ♗g6) 8...♔b7 9 ♖f7+ ♔b8 10 ♖e7 ♗f1 11 ♖e8+ ♔b7 12 ♖e7+ Draw.

After 12...♔b8, White still could have played 13 ♖e1! ♗g2+ (13...♗d3? 14 ♔c6) 14 ♔c4+−.

11/8. Georgadze – Yusupov,
USSR ch, Vilnius 1980

After the inevitable exchange of queens, it is very important for White to also exchange the a5-pawn. Thereafter he will be able to build a fortified camp on the kingside, following one of the models: diagram 11-29 or diagram 11-34.

This aim could be achieved by means of **1 a3!! ♕e5** (1...♖×c2? 2 ♕d3+) **2 ♕×e5 ♖×e5 3 b4** with a high probability of a draw.

The game continued 1 ♗d3? ♕e5 2 ♕×e5 ♖×e5 3 ♗c4 ♖e3!, and 4 a3 ♔e7 5 b4 did not make sense anymore in view of 5...a4!. Black has a winning position.

4 a4 ♔e7 5 h4 ♔d6 6 g3 ♔c5 7 ♔h3 ♔b4 8 ♔g4 ♖×b3! 9 ♗b5 ♔c5 (△ 10...♖×b5) 10 ♗e8 ♖b8 11 ♗d7 ♔d6 12 ♗f5 ♔e5 13 ♗d7 g6 White resigned.

Chapter Twelve

12/1. Shmirin – Novikov, USSR 1982

1...f5! 2 a5 (White has nothing else) **2...♛g7+!**

White resigned because his queen will either be lost (3 ♔f3 ♕b7+) or traded.

12/2. Matokhin – G. Kuzmin, USSR 1970

1...f6+! 2 ♔g4 (2 ♕×f6 ♕g3#) **2...♛g2+ 3 ♕g3 f5+ 4 ♔f4 e5+!**

White resigned in view of 5 de ♕d2#.

12/3. L. van Vliet, 1888

1 ♕b4!⊙ ♛h1

1...♕d5 2 ♕a4+ ♔b6 3 ♕b3+! ♕×b3 4 b8♕+;

1...♕f3 2 ♕a4+ ♔b6 3 ♕b3+!;

1...♕g2 2 ♕a3+ ♔b6 3 ♕b2+!

2 ♕a3+ ♚b6

Or 2...♔b5 3 ♕b2+ ♔c4 4 ♔a7+–.

3 ♕b2+ ♚c7

If 3...♔c5 then 4 ♔a7 ♕h7 5 ♕b6+ and 6 ♔a6+–. In case of 3...♔a6, the following familiar tactical device decides: 4 ♕a2+ ♔b6 5 ♕b1+!. When the black king is on c7, the same idea of winning the queen works diagonally.

4 ♕h2+!! ♛×h2 5 b8♕+.

12/4. L. Kubbel, 1936

1 ♕h1+! (1 ♕g1? ♕c7!) **1...♚g4 2 ♕e4+ ♚h3 3 ♕e6! ♛c7(f8) 4 ♕d6!+–.**

12/5. L. Kubbel, 1929

Both 1 ♕g1? ♔e4 and 1 ♕f1+? ♔e4 2 ♕c4+ ♔f3 3 ♕d3+ ♔f4! (3...♔f2? 4 ♕e3+ ♔f1 5 ♔g3+–) 4 ♕e2 e4 give nothing.

1 ♕g2! (△ 2 ♕g4#) **1...f5**

1...e4 is quite bad: then 2 ♕g3+ ♔f5 3 ♕g5#.

2 ♕e2! (△ 3 ♕e3#)

Rather than 2 ♕f1+? ♔e4 3 ♕c4+ ♔f3 4 ♕d3+ ♔f2! (4...♔f4? 5 ♕e3#) 5 ♕e3+ ♔f1, and 6 ♔g3?? loses to 6...f4+.

2...e4 3 ♕e1! (△ 4 ♕g3#) **3...♚e5 4 d4+!** and 5 ♕×a5.

Chasing after the king has suddenly resulted in catching the queen.

12/6. Ermolin – Petriaev, USSR 1971*

After 1 ♔g1? ♕e5 White is in serious trouble. A nice combination helps him.

1 ♕f2!! ♛×f2 (1...ef - Stalemate) **2 g3+** and Black cannot avoid stalemate.

12/7. Szily – Ozsváth, Hungary ch 1954

The game continued: 1...♕c1? 2 ♕f7+ ♔e1 (if 2...♔e2 3 ♕×g6 ♕f4+ 4 ♔g1 ♕e5 then 5 ♕d6!=, rather than 5 ♕×c6? ♕a1+ 6 ♔h2 ♔f2 with an inevitable mate) 3 ♕×g6 ♕f4+ 4 ♔g1 ♕f1+ 5 ♔h2 ♕c4 6 ♕×c6 e3 7 ♕d6, and the game equalized.

Why did Black not push his passed pawn? Presumably, he calculated the line **1...e3! 2 ♕c4+** (2 ♕f7+ ♕f2 3 ♕×g6 ♕f4+ 4 ♔h1 e2 5 ♕d3 ♔f2 6 ♕c2 ♕g5–+) **2...e2 3 ♕f4+ ♛f2 4 ♕c1+**

16-45

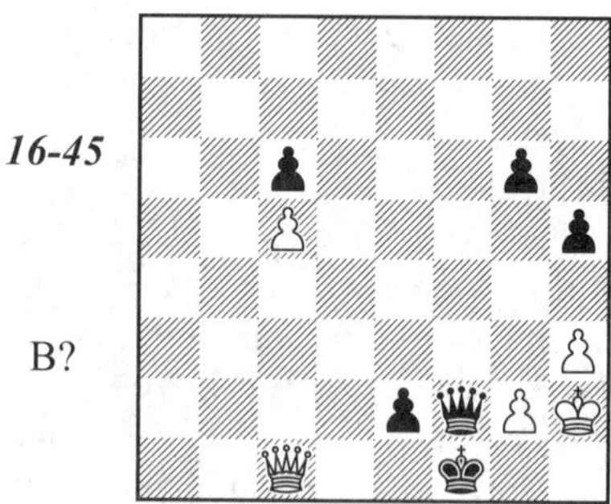

B?

...and came to the conclusion that it leads to a perpetual check: 4...e1♕ 5 ♕c4+ ♕fe2 6 ♕f4+ ♕1f2 7 ♕c1+ etc.

However, underpromotion to a knight could prevent the perpetual check: **4...e1♘!! 5 ♕c4+ ♛e2 6 ♕f4+ ♘f3+! 7 ♕×f3+ ♛×f3 8 gf ♚f2–+.**

12/8. Ehlvest – Topalov, Novgorod 1995

After 1...♔c8?? 2 ♕g4+ ♔c7 a draw was agreed, in view of 3 ♕d1=.

1...♚c7!

1...♔c6 is less precise: after 2 ♕a4+ he should go back (2...♔b6 3 ♕b4+ ♔c7!) because 2...♔c5? 3 ♕a5+ ♔c6 4 ♕a8+ leads to a perpetual check. While the outcome of the complicated duel between the king and queen in the line 2...♔c7 3 ♕a7+ ♔d8 4 ♕b6+ ♔e7 5 ♕f6+ ♔d7 is hard to foresee.

2 ♕e7+ (2 ♕c3+ ♔d8) **2...♔c6 3 ♕e8+ ♔c5 4 ♕f8+ ♔d4−+**

The king has broken through into the opposite camp where he can both find a refuge from checks and support his passed pawn.

12/9. Kharitonov – Ivanchuk,
Frunze 1988

1 ♕e7!+−

White has completely tied down his opponent, having deprived the black queen of the e8- and d7-squares. Now he plans to combine threats to the king with an advance of his queenside pawns.

1...h5 (otherwise g3-g4 and h4-h5-h6) 2 ♔g2 ♕c8 (2...♔h8 3 ♕f8+ ♔h7 4 ♕f7+ ♔h6 5 ♕g8 ♕c3 6 ♕×e6) 3 b4 ♕c6 4 a3 ♕c8 5 a4 ♕c6 6 ♕f6! ♔h7 (6...♕e8 7 b5) 7 ♕f7+ ♔h6 8 ♕g8 ♕c3 9 b5 ♕f6 10 ♔g1?!

Quicker progress could be achieved with 10 ba ♕f3+ 11 ♔g1 ♕d1+ 12 ♔h2.

10...ab 11 ab d4 12 ed ♕×d4 13 ♕×e6 ♕d1+ 14 ♔h2 ♕f3

If 14...♕e2, White does not play 15 ♕b6 ♔h7! (△ 16...e3). He has 15 ♕f6! ♔h7 16 b6!, and if 16...e3 then 17 ♕e7+.

15 ♕b6 Black resigned.

12/10. Adorján – Orsó,
Hungary ch, Budapest 1977

1 ♕d3!

A multipurpose move, White threatens a queen invasion to h7 and prevents ...b6-b5.

1...♕h1!

A prophylactic move 1...♕a4 allows a pawn advance on the kingside: 2 g4 and 3 f5.

2 ♕h7 ♕×h5 3 ♕×g7 ♕g6 4 ♕f8+ ♔b7 5 g4! h5?!

He cannot play 5...♕d3? in view of 6 ♕×f7+ ♔a6 7 ♕×e6. If 5...♕×g4? then 6 ♕×f7+ ♔a6 (6...♔b8 7 ♕f8+ and 8 ♕×h6+−) 7 ♕f8! h5 (7...♕h3 8 ♕c8+ ♔a5 9 ♕d7 a6 10 f5! ef 11 e6+−) 8 ♕c8+ ♔a5 9 ♕d7 ♔a6 10 b4! cb 11 ab (△ ♕c8#), and the king escapes from the checks to a4.

The move 5...a5!? is harder to refute. Both 6 f5? ef 7 ♕e7+ ♔c6(c8) 8 ♕e8+ ♔c7! (the queen cannot go to d7) and 6 ♕e7+? ♔a6 7 ♕d7 (7 f5 ♕×g4) 7...♕e4! are useless. A stronger alternative is 6 ♕e8!? with the idea 7 f5 ef 8 ♕d7+. For example, 6...♕×g4? 7 ♕×f7+ ♔a6 8 ♕f8! ♕f3!? 9 ♕c8+ (9 ♕×h6? a4=) 9...♔a7 10 ♕d7+! ♔a6 11 ♕×e6 ♕×f4 (11...a4 12 ♕d5) 12 ♕d5 ♔a7 13 e6+−.

However Black has a better continuation: 6...♔c7! 7 ♕e7+ ♔c8(c6) 8 ♕d6 ♔b7 9 ♕d7+ ♔a6 10 ♕e8 (10 f5 ♕×g4=) 10...♕e4!=.

Another drawing possibility existed, as well: 5...♔a6!? 6 ♕c8+ ♔a5 7 ♕b7 (7 ♕d7 ♔a6 8 f5 ♕×g4=) 7...a6 8 ♕f3 ♕c2=.

So we see that White could not win against an accurate defense. However his plan is absolutely correct because Black is now faced with serious problems.

6 f5! ef 7 ♕e7+ ♔a6

Or 7...♔c6 8 ♕e8+ ♔c7 9 gh! ♕×h5 10 e6+−.

8 b4! cb 9 ab b5 (his only defense against a mate)

16-46

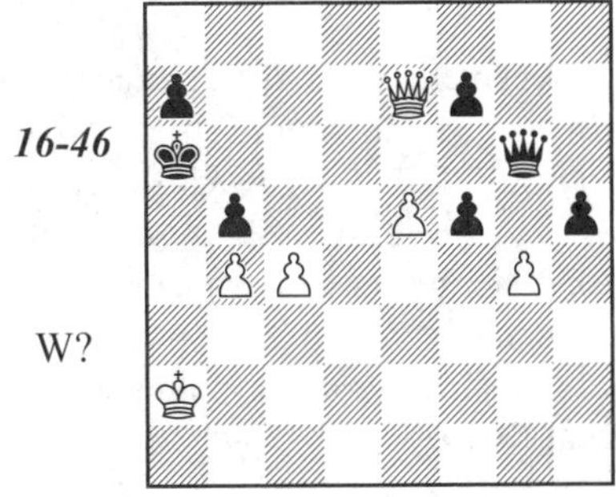

W?

Unfortunately, White went astray at the last moment. After 10 ♕d6+? ♔b7! there was no win. The remainder of the game was 11 ♕d7+ ♔b8 12 ♕×b5+ ♔c8 13 ♕e8+ ♔c7 14 ♕e7+ ♔c8 15 ♕e8+ ♔c7 16 ♕e7+ ♔c8 17 g5 f4 18 ♕e8+ ♔c7 19 ♕e7+ ♔c8 20 ♕c5+ ♔b7 21 ♕d5+ ♔b8 22 ♔a3 ♕×g5 23 ♕d6+ ♔c8 Draw agreed.

The winning continuation was **10 e6!! ♕×g4** (10...fe 11 ♕d7!; 10...♕×e6 11 ♕×e6+ fe 12 gh f4 13 h6 f3 14 h7 f2 15 h8♕ f1♕ 16 ♕c8+ ♔b6 17 c5#) **11 ♕d6+** (11 cb+ ♔b6 12 ♕c5+ ♔b7 13 ♕d5+ ♔b8 14 ef+− was equivalent) **11...♔b7 12 ♕d7+ ♔b8** (otherwise he will be checkmated) **13 ♕×b5+ ♔c7 14 ♕d7+ ♔b8 15 ♕d8+ ♔b7 16 ♕d5+ ♔c7 17 ef+−.**

Chapter Thirteen

13/1. L. Prokeš, 1938

1 ♖h8? loses after 1...♕a3+ 2 ♔b7 ♕×b2+ 3 ♔a7 ♕b6+! (but surely not 3...♕×h8? 4 c8♕+ ♕×c8 Stalemate) 4 ♔a8 ♕×c7 5 ♖h5+ ♔c4 6 ♖h4+ ♔c3 7 ♖h3+ ♔c2, and checks are exhausted.

1 ♖d8! ♕h6+ 2 ♔b7 ♕b6+ 3 ♔a8! ♕×c7 4 ♖d5+ ♔b6

The king can be forced to go to the 6th rank only when the white rook is on the d-file (there is no use in 4...♔c4 5 ♖d4+ etc.).

5 ♖b5+ (5 ♖d6+ is also good) **5...♔a6 6 ♖b6+!** with stalemate or perpetual check.

13/2. A. Chéron, 1950

After 1 ♕a8? ♔b4 White cannot prevent the Guretzky-Cornitz drawing position (diagram 13-20). For example, 2 ♕f8 (2 ♕a6 ♖c4+ 3 ♔d5 b5=) 2...♔b3 3 ♕b8 (3 ♕f3+ ♔b4 △ 4...♖c4+ and 5...b5=; 3 ♔d3 ♖c3+ △ 4...b5=) 3...b5 4 ♔d4 ♖c4+.

The correct method is **1 ♕b7!**, holding the black pawn on the 6th rank. After 1...♖g5, Chéron analyzed 2 ♕d7+ ♔a6 3 ♕c8+. A quicker alternative is 2 ♔d4! ♖c5 (2...♖g4+ makes White's task easier because his king crosses the 5th rank immediately: 3 ♔e5 ♖g5+ 4 ♔f6 ♖c5 5 ♔e6) 3 ♕a8!, achieving the winning position from diagram 13-19.

13/3. V. Khenkin, 1982

If White is on move, **1 ♕h6+ ♔g8 2 ♕h3 ♖e1 3 ♔h6 g5!** followed with 4...♖e6+ leads to the Dedrle drawing position (diagram 13-27).

If Black is on move, all rook retreats lose: 1...♖f2? 2 ♕h6+ ♔g8 3 ♕h4 ♖e2 4 ♔h6+−, or 1...♖f3? 2 ♕h6+ ♔g8 3 ♕h1! ♖e3 4 ♔h6+−.

After **1...f6+! 2 ♔h4,** 2...♖f3 is tempting, because Black, after the forced continuation 3 ♕e7+ ♔h6 4 g5+ fg+ 5 ♕×g5+ ♔h7, is close to the drawn Guretzky-Cornitz position (diagram 13-17): all he needs is to play ♖f5 when the king is on the 7th or the 8th rank. However he fails to reach it: White plays 6 ♕e7+ ♔h6 7 ♕e5! ♔h7 8 ♕c7+ ♔h6 9 ♔g4 ♖f5 10 ♕e7!⊙ ♖h5 11 ♕f8+ ♔h7 12 ♕f7+ ♔h6 13 ♕g8 ♖g5+ 14 ♔f4 ♖f5+ 15 ♔e4, forcing the black king ahead and achieving the winning position from diagram 13-19 (Dvoretsky).

2...g5+! 3 ♔g3 ♖f4 4 ♕f7+ ♔h6

16-47

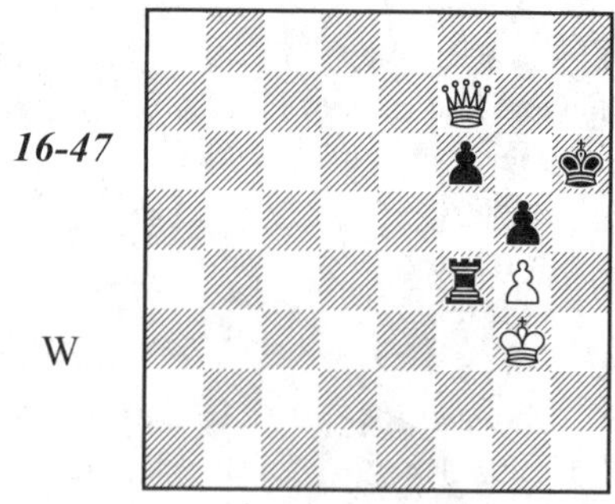

W

His unfavorably placed king betrays White. 5 ♕g8 ♖f1 is useless. The king can break through to freedom only by **5 ♔g2!?**, but after **5...♖×g4+ 6 ♔f3 ♖f4+** (6...f5!? Dvoretsky) **7 ♔e3 ♖h4! 8 ♕×f6+ ♔h5 9 ♕g7** (9 ♕f7+ ♔h6 △ 10...♖f4) **9...♖f4** the Guretzky-Cornitz drawing position (diagram 13-20) arises.

Summing up, Black holds no matter who is on move.

13/4. L. Katsnelson, 1971

1 ♖e6 ♘c4+ 2 ♔b5!

Both 2 ♔b7? ♖g7+ △ 3...♖e7−+ and 2 ♔a6? ♖g6!−+ are erroneous.

2...♘e5! 3 ♖×e5 ♖g5! 4 ♗f5! ♖×f5! 5 ♖×f5 e1♕ 6 ♖×f8+ ♔h7 7 ♖f7+!

7 ♖f3? is premature in view of 7...♕f1+ △ 8...♕×g2. He should decoy the king to the g-file first.

7...♔h6 8 ♖f6+ ♔h5 9 ♖f5+ ♔g4 10 ♖f3 (the g2-pawn is indirectly protected) **10...♕c1**

16-48

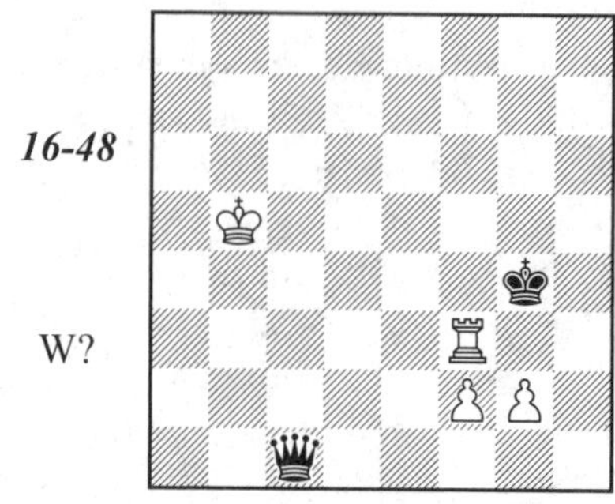

W?

The outcome of the fight now depends on whether Black succeeds in stalemating the white king, putting him in zugzwang. This danger is quite real as the following analysis shows:

11 ♔a4? ♕b2 12 ♔a5 ♕b7 13 ♔a4 ♕b6 14 ♔a3 ♕b5 15 ♔a2 ♕b4 16 ♔a1 ♕d2 17 ♔b1 ♔g5! 18 ♔a1 ♕c2⊙ −+.

11 ♔b6? ♕c4 12 ♔a5 ♕c5+ 13 ♔a4 ♕b6 etc.

11 ♔b4! ♕c6 12 ♔b3 ♕c5 13 ♔b2 ♕c4 14 ♔b1 ♚g5 (14...♕e2 15 ♖g3+ with a perpetual check: the king cannot step on the e-file) **15 ♔b2 ♚h6 16 ♖h3+!** (16 ♔b1? ♕f1+) **16...♚g6 17 ♖f3!=**.

Chapter Fourteen

14/1. Beliavsky – Miles,
Thessaloniki ol 1984

1...c2! 2 ♘e3+ ♚d2 3 ♗×c2 ♜c8!, and White cannot prevent 4...♖c3=, with a draw.

In the game, Black played 1...♖h8? which might not be losing; however, this severely complicates his defense, and increases the likelihood of new errors.

2 ♗e4 ♔e1 (2...♖h1!?) 3 ♘a3?! (3 ♔e3! was stronger.) 3...♔d1? (Karsten Müller indicates that 3...♔d2! 4 f5 ♖h4!, or 4 ♘c4+ ♔d1! 5 f5 ♖h4! would have saved Black.) 4 f5 ♖h7 5 ♔f4 and with his pieces coordinated, White won easily.

14/2. H. Aloni, 1968

The active rook on the 7th rank ensures White's advantage. However, he must play energetically, otherwise Black limits the mobility of the rook with ...♘f7.

The idea of the rook sacrifice on b7 comes instantly as we have seen this idea already, see diagrams 2-9 and 2-14. However the immediate 1 ♖×b7? ♘×b7 2 a6 is refuted with 2...♘d6 3 a7 ♘c4+ and 4...♘b6.

If 1 ♔d4?! then 1...♔d6 (1...♘f7? 2 ♔c5 △ ♔b6) 2 f5 ♗g4 (2...♗f3), and 3 ♖×b7? ♘×b7 4 a6 is erroneous again, this time because of 4...c5+! 5 ♔e4 (5 ♔e3 ♘a5!) 5...♔c6! △ 6...♘d6+.

1 f5+! ♚d6! (1...♔×f5? 2 ♖d7) **2 ♔f2!!**

The rook sacrifice is still premature: 2 ♖×b7? ♘×b7 3 a6 ♘a5! 4 ba (4 a7 ♘c4+) 4...♔c7. The subtle king move makes it inevitable. The chosen square for the king is determined by the necessity to control e2 and f3 (2 ♔f4? ♗e2!).

2...♝b3

16-49

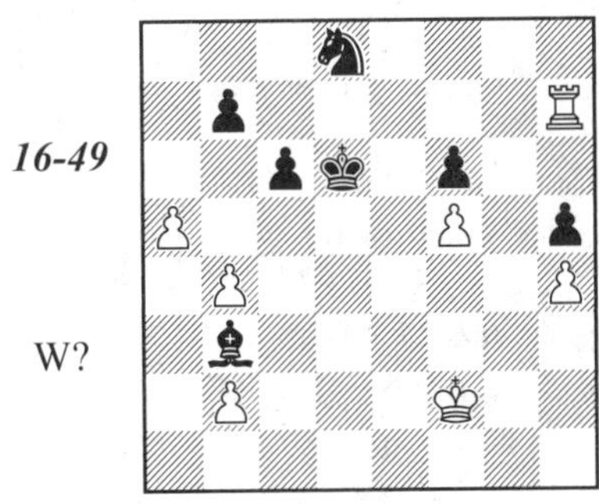

W?

3 ♖×b7!

The other pawn is less valuable: 3 ♖×h5? ♘f7 4 ♖h7 ♔e7 △ 5...♔f8 or 5...♗c2.

3...♝c4 (3...♘×b7 4 a6+–) **4 ♖h7!?**

4 ♖a7!? c5 5 a6 is also strong, for example 5...cb 6 ♖b7! (rather than 6 ♖a8 ♘c6 7 a7 ♗d5! and the pawn cannot be promoted) 6...♗d5 (6...♘×b7 7 a7) 7 ♖×b4 or 7 ♖b6+ with a decisive advantage.

4...♞f7

Both 4...♗f7 5 a6 ♔c7 6 a7 ♔b7 7 ♖h8 and 4...♔e5 5 ♖d7! are hopeless.

5 ♖×h5 (5 ♔e3!?) **5...♚e5**

Or 5...♔e7 6 ♖h7 ♔f8 7 ♔e3 ♔g8 8 ♖×f7+–.

6 b3! ♝b5 7 ♖h7 ♞d6 8 h5 ♞×f5 (8...♔×f5 9 ♖g7) **9 h6 ♚e6 10 ♖b7! ♞×h6 11 ♖×b5! cb 12 a6+–**.

14/3. G. Nadareishvili, 1954

1 ♗g1 ♚g3 2 ♘c6! ♚g2

White survives after 2...f5 3 ♘d4 ♔g2 (3...f4 4 ♘e2+) 4 ♘e2 (rather than 4 ♘×f5? ♔×g1 5 ♘d4 ♔f2–+) 4...♔f1 (4...♔f3 5 ♘d4+) 5 ♘f4=.

The black pawn will inevitably be promoted; White's only way to salvation is to reach the Karstedt position.

3 ♗d4! h2 (3...f5 4 ♗e5=) **4 ♗×f6 h1♛ 5 ♗b2! ♛h5 6 ♘d4 ♛a5+ 7 ♔b1!** (rather than 7 ♔b3? ♔f2 8 ♔c2 ♕a2!–+) **7...♛a4 8 ♗a1=**.

14/4. G. Kasparian, 1969

Materially, it is a draw, but White's pieces are divided and one can hardly see how he can avoid the loss of a piece:

1 ♖g3? ♕f4+ 2 ♖g4 ♕h6+ 3 ♔g3 ♕e3+ 4 ♔h2 (4 ♔g2 ♕e2+) 4...♕f2+ 5 ♖g2 ♕h4+

6 ♔g1 ♕e1+ and 7...♕xb1;

1 ♖f3? ♕h2+ 2 ♖h3 ♕f2+ 3 ♔h5 (3 ♖g3 ♕f4+) 3...♕c5+ 4 ♔h6 (4 ♔h4 ♕b4+; 4 ♔g6 ♕b6+) 4...♕c1+;

1 ♔h3? ♕c8+ 2 ♔h4 ♕f8!−+;

However an unusual way to salvation exists:

1 ♔g4! ♕c8+ 2 ♔f3!! (2 ♔h5? ♕c5+; 2 ♔h4? ♕f8!−+) **2...♕b7+ 3 ♖d5!!=**

White's pieces cooperate now, a capture of any piece will cost Black the queen.

14/5. Yermolinsky – Kaidanov,
USA ch, Long Beach 1993

The threat ♖g5+ should be neutralized. Black played 1...♔g7? because he failed to see the killing reply: after 2 ♖g5+ ♔f8 White has 3 ♖g6! with a decisive doubling of the rooks in the f-file. The game continued: 3...e5 4 ♖gf6 e4 5 ♖xf7+ ♔g8 6 ♖e7 (having gained a pawn, the rooks regroup for attacking another pawn) 6...♕d3 7 ♖f4 e3 8 ♖fe4 ♕c2+ 9 ♔h3 ♕c8+ 10 g4 ♕c1 11 ♖xe3 ♕h1+ 12 ♔g3 ♕g1+ 13 ♔f4 ♕f2+ 14 ♔g5 ♕d2 15 ♔g6 Black resigned.

The correct defense was **1...♕d7! 2 ♖g5+ ♔h7!**⩲ (rather than 2...♔h6? 3 ♖f6+ ♔h7 4 ♖g4 e5 5 ♖g5+−). White cannot gain a pawn: if 3 ♖f6 then 3...♕e7.

14/6. G. Zakhodiakin, 1967

1 g7! ♕g6+ 2 ♔h1 ♕xg7 3 ♖f4+ ♔h5 4 ♖f5+ ♔h4 (if 4...♔h6, the same reply follows)

16-50

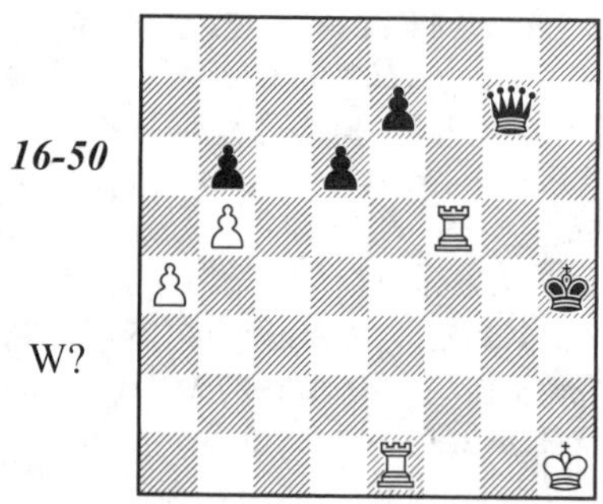

W?

5 ♖ee5!! de 6 ♖f2!+−

White gains the queen for the rook and wins by means of the breakthrough a4-a5.

Inarkiev noticed that the quiet move 1 ♔h1!? is also strong enough for a win, for example 1...♕c3 (1...♕b3 2 ♖f2+−) 2 ♖e2 ♔h5 3 ♖g2 ♕e1+ 4 ♔h2 ♕e5+ 5 ♔g1 ♕d4+ 6 ♖ff2+−.

Chapter Fifteen

15/1. N. Grigoriev, 1932

1 ♔f5!

Shouldering! 1 h5? is erroneous in view of 1...♔g4 2 h3+ ♔h4⊙, the same holds for both 1 h3? ♔g3 2 h5 ♔h4⊙= and 1 ♔g5? ♔g2 2 h5 ♔h3⊙ 3 ♔g6 ♔g4!=.

1...♔g2 2 h5 ♔h3 (if 2...♔f3, the same reply follows) **3 ♔g5!⊙ ♔xh2 4 ♔g6+−**.

15/2. B. Breider, 1950

How to fight against the distant passed pawn (a4)? The knights cannot cross the h3-c8 diagonal, which will be occupied by the black bishop, while the king is placed hopelessly far away. However he comes to the opposite wing in time, utilizing the Réti idea.

1 ♘f5! ♗c8 2 ♔g3! ♗xf5

If 2...d3, White has 3 ♘e6! (rather than 3 ♔f2? ♗xf5−+ or 3 ♘e3? a3−+) 3...d2 (3...♗xe6 4 ♘d4! ♗c8 5 ♔f2=; 3...a3 4 ♘ed4=) 4 ♘e3 ♗xe6 5 ♔f2 a3 6 ♔e2 a2 7 ♘c2=. Another resource is 3 ♘d6! d2 4 ♘e4!, forcing 4...d1♘!=.

3 ♔f4! ♗c8 4 ♘e6! ♗xe6 (4...d3 5 ♔e3 ♗xe6 6 ♔xd3=) **5 ♔e5! ♗c8 6 ♔xd4=**.

15/3. N. Rezvov, V. Chernous, 1991

1 ♔c7!

After 1 ♘e7? ♗f4+ 2 ♔b7 ♔f6 an attempt to bring the king to h1 fails because of shouldering: 3 ♔c6 ♔e5! 4 ♔c5 ♗g5 5 ♘d5 h5 with a winning endgame.

1...♗g5!

The line 1...♗f4+ 2 ♔c6 ♔g6 3 ♔d5 ♔f5 4 ♘f6! h6 5 ♔d4 ♗e5+ 6 ♔e3= is not dangerous for White.

2 ♔d6 ♔g6

3 ♔e5? loses now to 3...♔h5! 4 ♔f5 ♔h4 5 ♔e4 ♔g4!.

3 ♔e6!!⊙

16-51

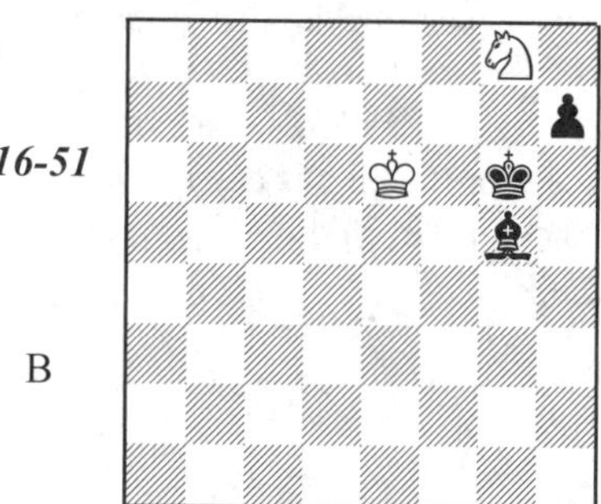

B

White saves himself by chasing two birds at once. In case of 3...h5 4 ♔e5 his king arrives at h1 safely.

3...♔h5

But now he runs in the opposite direction.

4 ♔f7! ♔g4 5 ♘h6+! ♗×h6 6 ♔g8=.

15/4. O. Pervakov, 1991

The king must hasten to help the b6-pawn.

1 ♔g1!!

We have already mentioned that the laws of Euclidean geometry are not valid on the chessboard: the king's path to c5 along the fractured line (via g1) is by no means longer than the direct route via g3.

In case of 1 ♔g3? ♗d5 (△ 2...♔b7) 2 ♗×a6 (2 ♘c8 ♔b7 3 ♗g4 a5 4 ♔f4 a4=) 2...♗b7 3 ♗c4! ♗h1!, Black holds. For example, 4 ♘c8 (or 4 ♔h2 ♗f3! 5 ♔g3 ♗h1!) 4...♔b7 5 ♗e6 ♔a6! 6 ♔f4 ♗b7 7 ♗c4+ (7 ♔e5 ♗×c8) 7...♔a5=.

The cunning reason behind White's initial move is becoming clear: the black bishop is now denied the important h1-square.

1...♗d5

1...a5 2 ♘b5 is absolutely bad. If 1...♔b8 2 ♔f2 a5 then the simplest reply is 3 ♔e3, but 3 ♘b5 ♗d5 (3...♗a6 4 ♘d6) 4 ♘c3 ♗b3 5 ♗f3 a4 6 ♘b1 ♗e6 7 ♔e3 ♗c8 8 ♔d4 is also playable.

2 ♗×a6 ♗b7 3 ♗c4! (3 ♗d3 ♗d5!) **3...♗f3** (3...♗e4 4 ♘b5!+−) **4 ♔f2** (the crucial tempo!) **4...♗h1 5 ♗e6** (or 5 ♘c8 ♔b7 6 ♗e6) **5...♔b7 6 ♘c8 ♔a6**

If 6...♔c6!? (hoping for 7 ♔e3? ♔c5 △ 8...♗b7=) then 7 ♗g4! ♔c5 8 ♗f3 ♗×f3 9 ♔×f3 ♔c6 10 ♔e4 ♔b7 11 ♔d5 ♔×c8 12 ♔c6 ♔b8 13 b7+−.

7 ♔e3 ♗b7 8 ♗c4+! ♔a5 9 ♔d4 ♗×c8 10 ♔c5

The rest is simple. The king goes to c7 and Black loses because the a6-c8 diagonal is too short.

10...♗b7 11 ♗b5 ♗c8 12 ♔c6 ♔b4 (12...♗d7+ 13 ♔c7 ♗c8 14 ♗f1⊙) **13 ♗f1 ♗g4 14 ♗g2 ♗c8 15 ♔c7 ♔c5 16 ♗f1⊙+−.**

15/5. P. Benko, 1981

1 ♔b6!!

1 b6? ♘f3(g4) 2 b7 ♘e5 leads to an immediate draw. Therefore White applies keener tactics; his king will fight on two fronts simultaneously, supporting both passed pawns.

1...♘g4! (1...♔×f5 2 ♔c7+−) **2 ♔c7! ♘e3!** (2...♘f6 3 ♔c6+−) **3 ♔d7!** (rather than 3 ♔d6? ♔×f5=) **3...♘c4** (3...♘d5 4 ♔d6 ♘b6 5 ♔e6+−) **4 ♔e6**

This position resembles the ending Svidler - Anand (diagram 15-11), does it not? But while in that case the fight was over when the king joined the f-pawn, here it only enters the most crucial phase.

4...♘b6 5 f6 ♔g6 6 ♔e7!

6 f7? is erroneous: after 6...♔g7 7 ♔e7 ♘d5+! there is no win. Therefore White triangulates to cede Black the turn to move.

6...♘d5+ 7 ♔d6! ♘b6 (7...♘×f6 8 b6+−) **8 ♔e6!⊙ ♔h7**

A weaker reply is 8...♘c8 9 f7 ♔g7 10 ♔d7 ♘b6+ 11 ♔e8+−, while now immediate attempts to promote the f-pawn will fail. So the king first goes to another wing and only then returns to the kingside.

9 ♔e7! ♘d5+ 10 ♔d6 ♘b6 11 ♔c6! ♘c4 12 ♔d7! ♔g6 (12...♘b6+ 13 ♔e8!+−) **13 ♔e7!** (13 ♔e6? ♘b6) **13...♘e5** (13...♘b6 14 f7+−) **14 b6+−** (or 14 ♔e6+−)

Generally, a knight is a speedier runner than the king is, but one can get an opposite impression from this ending.

15/6. Yudasin – Kramnik,

Wijk aan Zee cm(3) 1994

A winning line was **1 ♖c8+! ♔g7 2 b5 ♔f6 3 ♖e8!** (cutting the king off), and one of the pawns promotes: 3...♖b3 4 d6, or 3...♖d3 4 b6.

The zwischenschach is necessary: after the immediate 1 b5? Black holds by means of 1...♔f8!.

Yudasin's 1 d6? was also weak: 1...♔g7! 2 b5 ♔f6 3 d7+ ♔e7 4 ♖d6 ♔d8 led to a draw.

15/7. H. Rinck, 1906

1 f6 ♖×e2

Both 1...♔b5 2 ♖h8 ♖d7 3 ♖e8 and 1...♖d4 2 ♖e7 ♖e4 3 ♖e8 are hopeless. But now 2 ♖h8? ♖f2 3 ♖f8 ♔b6 4 f7 ♔b7 5 ♔c4 ♖f5= does nothing. An interference decides in White's favor.

2 ♖h5+! ♔b6 3 ♖f5!+−.

15/8. A. Maksimovskikh, 1977

Simple ideas do not work: 1 ♔×g2? ♖×g6+ 2 ♔h3 ♖f6 3 ♖×d6 ♖×f7=, or 1 f8♕+? ♖×f8 2 ♔×g2 ♖f6=.

1 ♔h2! g1♕+! 2 ♔×g1 ♖×g6+ 3 ♖g5!! ♖×g5+ (3...♖f6 4 ♖g8+) **4 ♗g2! ♖f5 5 ♗h3 ♔d8 6 ♗×f5 ♔e7 7 ♗g6!+−**

Rather than 7 ♗e6? h5=. The bishop protects his own pawn and holds the h6-pawn along the same h5-e8 diagonal, while the king will take care of Black's central pawns.

15/9. H. Mattison, 1927

1 ♗e5!

Both 1 f5? ♔d5 2 f6 ♔e6 △ 3...♖f4= and 1 g7? ♖e8 2 f5 ♔d5 3 ♔×a7 ♔d6 4 ♗f6 ♔d7 △ ...♖g8, ...♔e8-f7= are erroneous.

1...♖e2 2 g7 ♖g2 3 ♗f6 (4 ♗g5 is threatened) **3...♖g6**

16-52

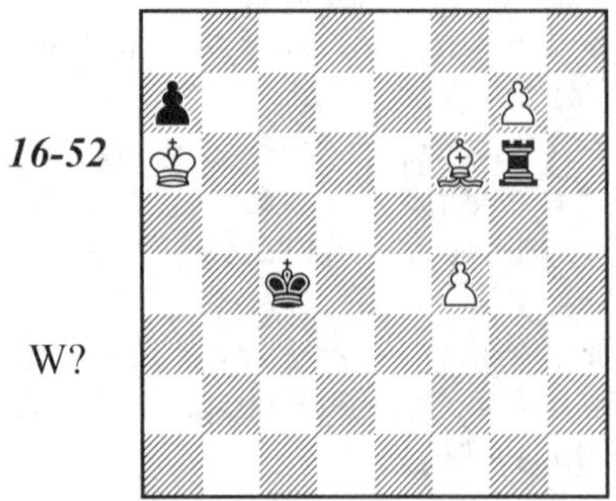

W?

4 ♔b7!!

He cannot lose time on capturing the pawn: 4 ♔×a7? ♔d5 5 f5 ♖g2 6 ♔b8 ♔d6! 7 ♔c8 ♖a2! 8 ♔b7 ♖g2=. 4 ♔a5? ♔d5 5 f5 ♖g2 6 ♔a6 ♔d6= is also useless.

4...♔d5 5 f5 ♖g2 6 ♔c8!

The king should leave the 7th rank. White is not afraid of 6...♔d6 7 ♔d8+−. An advance of the a-pawn does not bother him, either: 6...a5 7 ♔d8 a4 8 ♔e7 a3 (8...♔e4 9 ♔e6) 9 ♗a1 a2 10 f6+−.

6...♔e4 7 ♗g5! ♖×g5 8 f6+−

If the king is on c7 the bishop sacrifice does not work: 8...♔f5 9 f7 ♖×g7−+.

15/10. G. Zakhodiakin, 1930

1 ♖g2+? ♔h6 2 ♔f7 ♘f6! 3 ♖g6+ ♔h5 4 ♖×f6 ♔g4 5 f5 ♔g5 leads to a draw.

1 ♖a6! ♔g8

1...♘f8 2 f5 ♔g8 (2...♘h7 3 ♖g6#) 3 ♖a8 ♗g7 4 f6+−.

2 ♖a8+! ♔g7 3 ♖×h8! ♔×h8 4 ♔f7⊙ +−.

15/11. M. Liburkin, 1947

1 e6 a4 2 ♔d1!

After 2 ♔c3? a3 White is in a zugzwang: 3 ♔b3 (3 ♔c2 ♗h7) 3...♗h7 4 e7 ♗g8+ 5 ♔×a3 ♗f7=. The same zugzwang results from 2 ♔c1? a3 (3 ♔b1 ♗h7=).

2...a3 3 ♔c1!⊙ ♔h7 4 ♔b1

Only now, when the black king has deprived his own bishop of the h7-square, White may move his king closer to the pawn. Equally good is 4 ♔c2 ♔h6 5 ♔c3⊙ +−.

4...♔h6 5 ♔a1!⊙ a2 6 ♔b2!⊙ ♔h7 7 ♔×a2+−.

15/12. N. Grigoriev, 1937

1 ♖f5!!

A deep and a difficult introduction; White foresees the reciprocal zugzwang position that soon arises.

1...g3

1...♔c3 2 ♖g5 ♖c4 3 ♔f7 ♔d3 4 ♔g6 ♔e3 5 ♔h5 ♔f3 6 ♔h4 ♖f4 7 ♖a5 g3+ 8 ♔h3=.

2 ♖g5 ♖c3 3 ♔f7 ♔c2 4 ♔g6 ♔d2 5 ♔h5 ♔e2 6 ♔h4 ♔f2 7 ♔h3 ♖f3 (the threat is 8...♖f8−+) **8 ♖g4!**

16-53

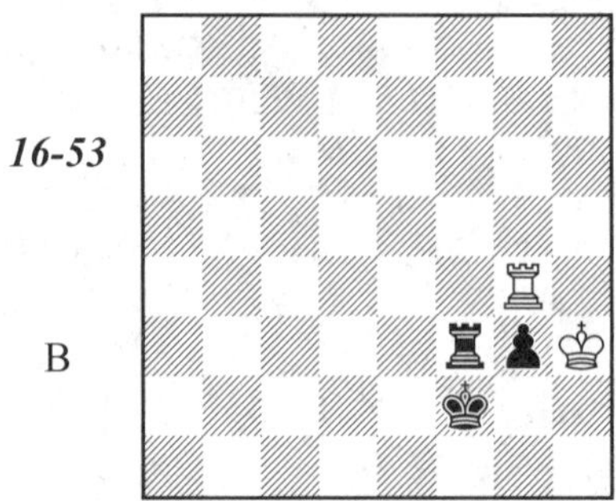

B

The aforementioned zugzwang position! If White were on move he would be lost.

8...♖f8 (8...♖a3 9 ♖g8 ♖f3 10 ♖g4!) **9 ♖f4+! ♖×f4** Stalemate.

In case of 1 ♖f4? g3 2 ♖g4 ♖c3 3 ♔f7 ♔c2 4 ♔g6 ♔d2 5 ♔h5 ♔e2 6 ♔h4 ♔f2 7 ♔h3 ♖f3 it was White who was set in zugzwang: 8 ♖g5 ♖f8−+ or 8 ♖a4 g2+.

Also bad is 1 ♖g7? ♖c4 because the king can go neither to f7 nor e7 and will be cut off from the pawn: 2 ♖g5 ♖f4!−+ or 2 ♔d7 ♖e4! 3 ♔d6 ♔c3 4 ♔d5 ♔d3−+. 1 ♖f1? loses to 1...g3

2 ♖g1 (2 ♔f7 ♖c1) 2...♖c3 3 ♔f7 ♔c2 4 ♔g6 ♔d2 5 ♔g5 ♔e2 6 ♔h4 ♔f2.

15/13. O. Duras, 1906

1 ♗a3! (2 ♗c5 is threatened) **1...♔c4 2 ♗e7! f3 3 ♗d8! ♗×h2** (3...f2 4 ♗×c7 f1♕ 5 b8♕+–) **4 ♗b6**

The bishop has successfully stopped the f-pawn but Black has also succeeded in stopping White's pawns.

4...♔b5 (4...g4 5 a6 ♔b5 leads to a transposition of moves) **5 a6 g4 6 ♗f2 ♗c7**

16-54

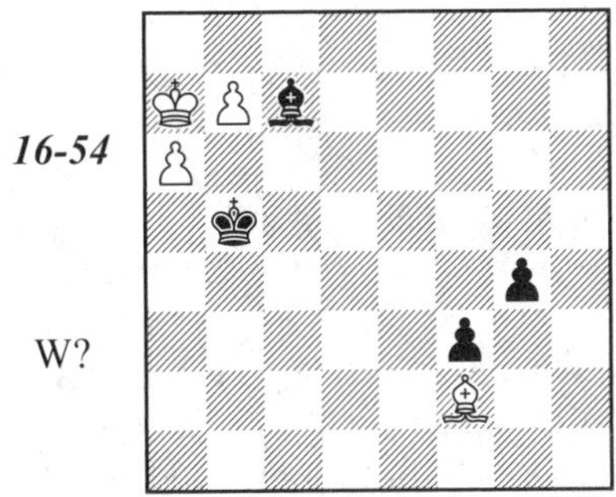

W?

7 b8♕+! ♗×b8+ 8 ♔b7! ♔a5

The black bishop cannot be moved. To put Black in zugzwang, White should deprive the black king of the a5-square.

9 ♗h4 (or 9 ♗g3) **9...♔b5 10 ♗e1⊙ g3 11 ♗×g3 ♗×g3** (11...♔a5 12 ♗h4 ♔b5 13 ♗e1⊙) **12 a7 f2 13 a8♕ f1♕ 14 ♕a6+**, and the black queen is lost.

15/14. N. Riabinin, E. Markov, 1993

White should first completely tie down his opponent. Both 1 a7? c5 and 1 c4? ♗e6+ are not strong enough.

1 h6! f6! 2 h7 ♔f7 3 c4! ♗e6+ 4 ♔h5 ♗c8 (4...♗c5? 5 ♗×f6+–) **5 a7 ♗b7 6 c5! ♗a8**

16-55

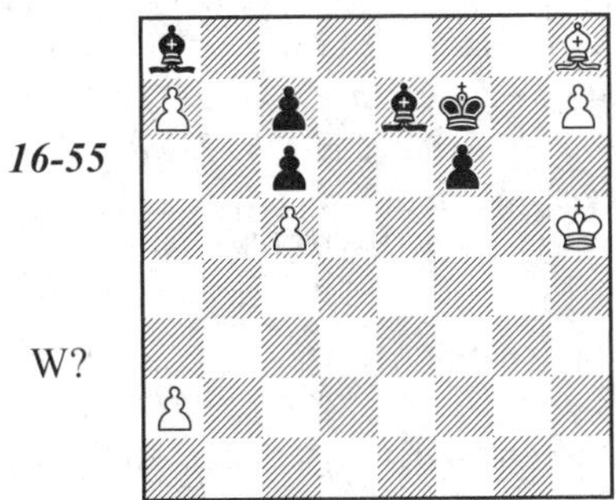

W?

White must now decide whether the a-pawn should make a single or a double step forward. Generally, it wants to go to a6 in order to deprive the light-squared bishop of moves and to put Black in zugzwang. But deeper insight shows that White should get rid of his a7-pawn in order to free this square. This consideration explains the next move.

7 a3!!

7 a4? leads only to a draw: 7...♗b7 8 a5 ♗a8 9 a6 ♗f8 10 ♗×f6 ♗g7=.

7...♗b7 8 a4 ♗a8 9 a5 ♗b7 10 a8♕! ♗×a8 11 a6⊙ ♗f8□ (11...♗d8 12 ♔h6 △ 13 ♗g7+–) **12 ♗×f6 ♗g7 13 ♗×g7 ♔×g7 14 ♔g5 ♔×h7 15 ♔f6 ♔g8 16 ♔e7 ♔g7 17 ♔d7(d8) ♔f7 18 ♔c8!**

White should not take the pawn: 18 ♔×c7? ♔e7 19 ♔b8 ♔d7 20 ♔×a8 ♔c8 21 ♔a7 ♔c7=.

18...♔e7 19 ♔b8 ♔d7 20 ♔×a8 ♔c8 21 a7⊙ +– (or 21 ♔a7⊙ +–).

15/15. J. Hašek, 1937

How to defend the position against the threat of the rook invasion along the h-file? 1 ♖e6? ♖h8 2 ♖×e5 ♔g6 is hopeless.

1 ♔b1! ♔g7 2 ♖h6!! ♔×h6 3 ♔c1 ♔g5 4 ♔d1 ♖h8 5 ♔e2 ♖h2 6 ♔f1 ♖h1+ (6...♖×g2 7 ♔×g2 ♔h4 8 ♔g1 ♔h3 9 ♔h1 g2+ 10 ♔g1=) **7 ♔e2**, and the rook cannot remain on the 1st rank in view of stalemate.

If Black plays 1...♖h8, then 2 ♖f8!! ♖×f8 3 ♔c1 leads to the same drawn position.

15/16. V. Chekhover, 1948

1 ♗h2? loses to 1...a4 2 ♔d2 a3 3 ♔c2 ♔g5 4 f3 (4 f4+ ef 5 e5 a2 6 ♔b2 f3 7 ed f2–+) 4...a2 5 ♔b2 g1♕ 6 ♗×g1 ♔f4 7 ♗h2+ ♔×f3 8 ♔×a2 (8 ♗×e5 de 9 d6 h2–+) 8...♔×e4! (rather than 8...♔g2? 9 ♗×e5=) 9 ♔b3 ♔×d5. The solution is quite unexpected: White should build a fortified camp with a bishop against a queen!

1 f3! a4 2 ♔f2!! a3 3 ♔g3 a2 4 ♔×h3 a1♕ 5 ♔×g2 ♕b2+ (5...♔g5 6 ♗e3+ ♔h4 7 ♗f2+) **6 ♗f2 ♔g5 7 ♔g3**

16-56

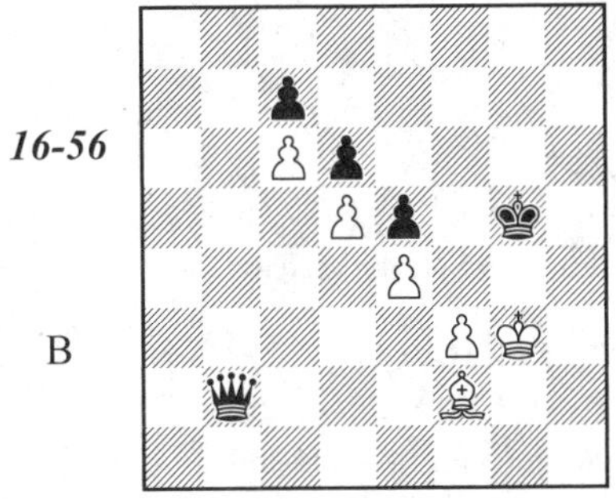

B

It becomes clear that a breakthrough on the kingside is a difficult matter. A king march to the queenside is senseless because the a7-square is not available: the white bishop controls it.

7...♕c1 8 ♗a7! (the only square for the bishop) **7...♕f4+ 9 ♔g2 ♕d2+ 10 ♔g3!=.**

15/17. Kozlov – Nevmerzhitsky,
USSR 1964

A pawn breakthrough does not work: 1 h4? ♔c7 2 g5 hg 3 hg (3 f6 gf 4 h5 g4 and the white king will be checkmated) 3...♔d6 4 f6 gf 5 g6 ♔e7–+. 1 ♔b1? ♔c7 2 ♔c2 ♔d6 3 ♔d3 ♔e5 is quite bad; if 1 a3? ♔c7 2 b4 then 2...cb 3 ab d3! 4 ♔b2 a4! 5 h4 d2 6 ♔c2 a3–+.

1 a4!! ♔c7 2 b4!! cb (2...ab? even loses) **3 c5! ♔d7 4 h4 ♔e7 5 g5 hg 6 hg=**

The pawn barrier is built; the b- and d-pawns cannot promote without support from the king.

15/18. G. Zakhodiakin, 1949

The c-pawn cannot be halted in view of a decoying rook sacrifice, for example 1 ♖×e7+? ♔f6 2 ♖c7 ♖b8+ 3 ♔d7 ♖b7!–+.

1 ♖c7! ♖b8+ 2 ♔×e7 ♖b7! 3 ♖×b7 c1♕ 4 ♔e6+ ♔g6 (4...♔g8 5 ♖b8+ ♔g7 6 ♖b7+) **5 h5+! ♔×h5 6 ♖g7 ♕f1** (the threat is 7...♕f8–+) **7 ♔e7!=**

The black king is padlocked and cannot be released.

15/19. A. Troitsky, 1910

1 ♘c6 d3 2 ♘×a7!! d2 3 ♘b5 d1♕ 4 ♘c3! ♕d6+ 5 ♔h1=

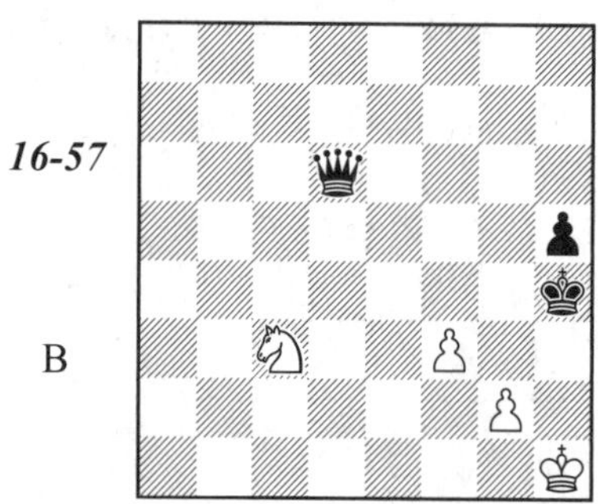
16-57

B

The knight inevitably goes to e4 and immobilizes the black king (5...♔g3? is impossible because of 6 ♘e4+ and 7 ♘×d6).

15/20. E. Zakon, 1953

1 ♘f3+! ♔h1! 2 ♘g1!! c1♕

Whichever knight Black takes, his e-pawn will be stopped: 2...♔×g2 3 ♘e2= or 2...♔×g1 3 ♘f4 ♔f1 4 ♘d3 ♔e2 5 ♘c1+ ♔d2 6 ♘a2=.

3 ♘e2 ♕f1+ 4 ♘gf4=.

15/21. F. Simkhovich, 1927

1...♖b1 and 1...♖a2 are threatened.

1 ♗g4+ ♔d6 2 ♗f5! ♖a2 3 ♘×a2!! ba 4 ♔c1 a1♕+ 5 ♗b1= (followed with ♔c2-c1-c2).

15/22. C. de Feijter , 1941

1 g7 ♖e1+! (1...♖e8 2 ♗h7=) **2 ♗d1!**

Rather than 2 ♔a2? ♗e5–+.

2...♖e8 (2...♖×d1+? 3 ♔c2) **3 ♗h5! ♖g8 4 ♗f7 ♖×g7 5 g6=.**

15/23. A. Troitsky, 1898

1 ♖f4? (hoping for 1...♖e1? 2 ♖f3=) fails because of 1...♖d2! 2 ♖f3 ♖d4+ 3 ♔b5 ♖d5+.

1 ♖h1! ♖e1 2 ♖f1!! ♖×f1 3 ♗×e3

The black rook is condemned to protect the pawn and the king fails to come and help it.

3...♔b2 4 ♔b4 ♔c2 5 ♔c4 ♔d1 6 ♔d3 ♔e1 7 ♗d2+ ♔d1 8 ♗e3=.

15/24. F. Simkhovich, 1940

The defensive plan is uncomplicated: White must keep both black rooks in the crosshairs, not allowing them to leave the 4th rank. The only question is, from which square should the bishop begin the attack?

1 ♗f5! ♖c4 (1...♖g5 2 g7! ♔×f7 3 g8♕+ ♔×g8 4 ♗e6+ and 5 cd) **2 ♗e6! ♔f8 3 ♔h3 ♖ge4 4 ♗d5! ♖a4 5 ♗c6! ♖ec4 6 ♗b5! ♔g7 7 ♔h2! ♖g4 8 ♗d7!=** etc.

1 ♗f3? loses to 1...♖a4! 2 ♗d1 ♔f8!⊙ 3 ♔h3 ♖a1! 4 ♗×g4 ♖h1#.

15/25. L. Kubbel, 1926

1 ♘g3? is bad in view of 1...♔×h2! (1...♗g6+? 2 ♔e3 ♔×h2 3 ♔f2=) 2 ♘×h5 g3–+.

1 ♔e3! ♔×h2 2 ♔f2! (△ 3 ♘g3=) **2...♔×h1 3 ♔g3⊙ ♔g1** Stalemate.

15/26. J. Møller, 1916

1 b3!+–

The bishop is fighting against the passed pawns on two diagonals and is therefore unable to get the upper hand ("pants").

The inaccurate 1 d6? (or 1 h4?) allows Black to hold by locking in his own bishop for the sake of a stalemate: 1...b3! 2 h4 b4 3 h5 ♗a4! 4 h6 b5=.

15/27. L. Prokeš, 1938

1 ♖a2+! ♔b7 2 ♖g2!! fg 3 b5!⊙ =

This combination resembles that from the Goldstein – Shakhnovich ending. Here, precisely as in that case, another defensive plan (to keep the rook behind the bishop pawn) fails, for example 2 b5 ♔b8 3 ♖a6 ♗d5 4 ♖×b6+ ♔c7 5 ♖f6 f2+ 6 ♔f1 ♗c4+ 8 ♔g2 ♗×b5 and the king goes to the kingside. Unfortunately for White, the corner square (h1) is of the same color as the black bishop, so a rook sacrifice for two pawns does not help.

However, as Mrkalj has demonstrated, another solution exists: 2 b5 ♔b8 3 ♖c2! ♗e4 4 ♖c3 ♔b7 5 ♔f1=. Black cannot make any progress: his king is confined to the queenside and the bishop is chained to defense of the f3-pawn.

15/28. J. Gunst, 1966

1 a4 a6!

It may seem that Black can take refuge in a stalemate defense but, in fact, White wins because he can subvert Black's plan with a series of precise moves.

2 ♔f5! f6 3 ♔g4! f5+ 4 ♔h3! f4 5 ♗e2 f3 6 ♗×a6! f2 7 ♔g2+–.

15/29. D. Przepiórka, 1926*

Here, as in the Zapata - Vaganian ending, finding the stalemate idea is not enough, a precise order of moves also needs to be chosen.

1 h4! gh

1...♖×h4 2 ♖×h4 gh 3 ♔e4 h3 4 ♔f3 ♔d7 5 ♔f2 ♗h2 6 ♔f3=.

2 ♖c4+! ♔d7

Black may also try 2...♔b6!? 3 ♔×d6 h3, but White holds by means of 4 ♖c1 (or 4 ♖b4+! ♔a5 5 ♖b1) 4...h2 5 ♖b1+! (rather than 5 ♖h1? ♖h5! 6 ♔e6 ♔c5 7 ♔f6 ♔d4 8 ♔g6 ♖h8 9 ♔f5 ♔e3 10 ♔g4 ♔f2–+) 5...♔a5 6 ♖h1 ♖h5! 7 ♔e6 ♔b4 8 ♔f6 ♔c3 9 ♔g6 ♖h8 10 ♔g5 ♔d3 11 ♔f4! (11 ♔g4? ♔e3 12 ♔g3 ♖g8+ 13 ♔h3 ♔f2 14 ♖×h2+ ♔f3–+) 11...♔e2 12 ♔g3 ♖g8+ 13 ♔f4! ♖g2 14 ♖a1=.

3 ♖×h4!=

The try to avoid the 2...♔b6 line by means of a transposition of moves 1 ♖c4+? ♔d7 2 h4 is refuted with 2...♖×h4! 3 ♖×h4 gh 4 ♔e4 h3 5 ♔f3 ♔e6 6 ♔f2 ♗h2! 7 ♔f3 ♔f5–+.

15/30. J. Fritz, 1965

1 ♔a6 ♖e7 2 ♗b7!

2 b5? ♔e3 3 ♗b7 ♔d4 4 ♔×a7 ♔c5 is bad. But now 2...♔e3 is not effective already: 3 ♔×a7 ♖e6 (3...b5 4 ♔b6 ♔d4 5 ♗c6=) 4 ♔a6 ♔d4 5 ♔b5 and 6 ♗c6=.

2...♖×b7 (with 3 ♔×b7? a5–+ in mind)

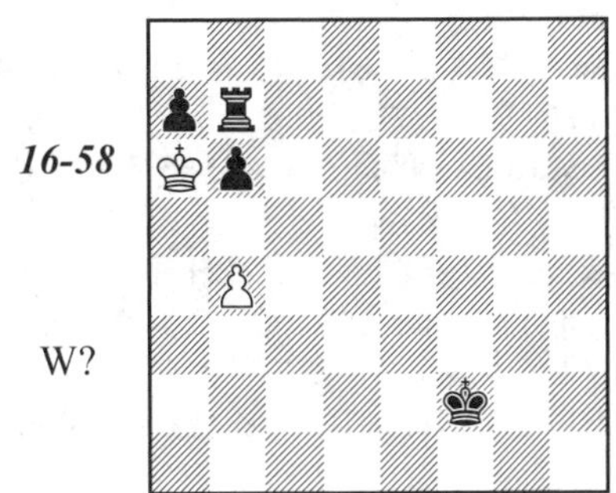

16-58

W?

3 b5!!

A nice quiet move! Any rook retreat along the 7th rank results in a stalemate, while 3...♔e3? even loses: 4 ♔×b7 ♔d4 5 ♔×a7 ♔c5 6 ♔a6⊙.

3...♖b8 4 ♔×a7 ♖h8 5 ♔×b6=.

15/31. D. Gurgenidze, 1980

1 f8♕? loses to 1...♖f6+ 2 ♕×f6 ef 3 ♖×a4 c3 4 ♖×b4 c2 5 ♖c4 c1♕ 6 ♖×c1+ ♔×c1 7 ♔g3 ♔d2 8 ♔×h3 ♔e3 9 ♔g4 ♔×e4 10 h4 f5+ (or 10...♔d5). Only a play for stalemate promises chances of salvation.

1 ♖a1+! ♔d2 2 ♖d1+!

A necessary zwischenschach. If 2...♔×d1 then 3 f8♕ ♖f6+ 4 ♔e3! ♖×f8 Stalemate.

2...♔c2! 3 ♖h1!!

This fantastic move is the point of White's idea. With the king on d2, the idea does not work: 2 ♖h1? ♖f6+ 3 ♔g1 ♔e2! 4 f8♕ ♖g6#.

3....b3! 4 f8♕ ♖f6+ 5 ♔g1! b2! (5...♖×f8 Stalemate) **6 ♕b8 ♖b6!**

The rook sacrifice is the only possibility to continue to fight for the win. When the rook is on the f-file, the queen becomes a desperado, while no other file can be used for the rook in view of 7 ♔f2.

7 ♕×b6 b1♕+ 8 ♕×b1+ ♔×b1 9 ♔f2+ ♔b2 10 ♔e2 a3 11 ♔d2 a2

16-59

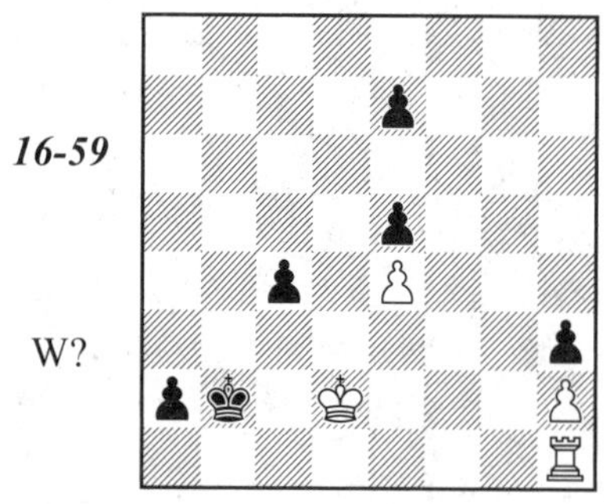

W?

12 ♖a1!

In case of 12 ♖g1? a1♕ 13 ♖×a1 ♔×a1 14 ♔c3 ♔b1 15 ♔×c4 ♔c2, the black king has enough time to attack the h2-pawn: 16 ♔d5 ♔d3 17 ♔×e5 ♔e3 18 ♔f5 ♔f3 (18...e6+ 19 ♔e5 ♔f3 is also possible) 19 e5 ♔g2–+. Therefore White tries to arrange a stalemate again, but this time to the black king!

12...c3+ 13 ♔d3 (13 ♔d1 is equivalent) **13...e6**

There is no sense in 13...♔×a1 14 ♔c2 e6 15 ♔c1 c2 16 ♔×c2 Stalemate. After 13...c2 14 ♔d2 c1♕+ 15 ♖×c1 a1♕ 16 ♖×a1 ♔×a1, 17 ♔c2? ♔a2 18 ♔c3 ♔b1! 19 ♔c4 ♔c2–+ is bad (see the previous note). The king should be directed to the h-pawn: 17 ♔e3! ♔b2 18 ♔f3 ♔c3 19 ♔g4 ♔d3 20 ♔×h3 ♔×e4 21 ♔g2! ♔d3 22 ♔f2! ♔d2 23 ♔f3 ♔d3 24 ♔f2 (a pendulum) 24...e4 25 ♔e1 ♔e3 26 h4 ♔f4 27 ♔e2=.

14 ♖×a2+

14 ♖g1 c2 15 ♔d2 a1♕ 16 ♖×a1 ♔×a1 17 ♔c1!= is also playable.

14...♔×a2 15 ♔c2!

It is important to gain the opposition (15 ♔×c3? ♔a3 16 ♔c4 ♔b2–+).

15...♔a1 16 ♔×c3 (16 ♔c1? c2 17 ♔×c2 ♔a2–+) **16...♔b1 17 ♔b3=**

The black king cannot leave the 1st rank because the reserve tempo (...e7-e6) is already spent.

15/32. J. Hašek, 1929

After 1 ♔c5? f5 the position is drawn. A sudden bishop sacrifice decides.

1 ♗f5!! gf 2 ♔c5 f6 3 ♔d6 ♖g8 4 ♔e6 ♔f8 5 ♔×f6+–.

15/33. L. Kubbel, A. Troitsky, 1936

1 ♕c1+ ♔a4 2 ♕c4! ♕d8 3 ♕a6+ ♕a5 4 ♘b6+! ab 5 ♕c4!⊙ +–.

15/34. H. Rinck, 1906

1 ♕b1! (△ 2 ♕b5+ ♔d4 3 ♕d5#) **1...♔d4 2 ♕b3!! ♕×e4+ 3 ♔d6**

4 ♕c3# is threatened. If 3...♕h1 then 4 ♕c3+ ♔e4 5 ♕c6+.

3...♕a8 4 ♕e3+ ♔c4 5 ♕c3+ ♔b5 6 ♕b3+ ♔a6 7 ♕a4+ ♔b7 8 ♕b5+ ♔c8 (8...♔a7 9 ♔c7+–) **9 ♕d7+ ♔b8 10 ♕c7#.**

15/35. H. Rinck, 1917

The initial attacking moves are easy to find.

1 ♕c7+ ♔a8 2 ♕a5+ ♔b7 (2...♔b8 3 ♕b6+) **3 ♘c5+ ♔b8** (3...♔c6 4 ♕a4+; 3...♔c8 4 ♕a8+) **4 ♕b6+ ♔c8 5 ♕b7+ ♔d8**

16-60

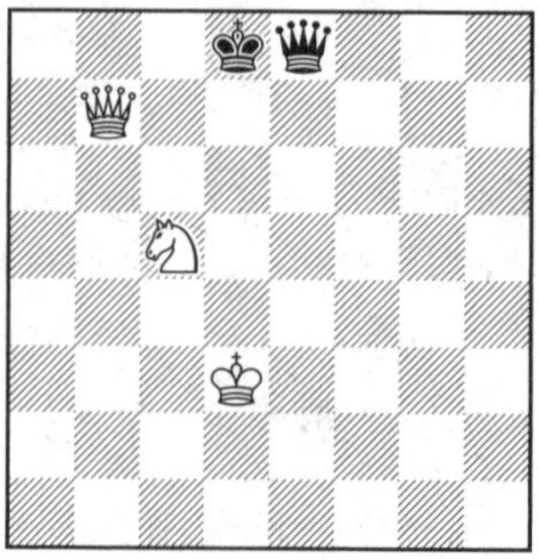

W?

However no success can be achieved by means of new checks. The solution of this position is a zugzwang:

6 ♔d2!!+–.

15/36. Zakharov – Petrushin, USSR 1973

The a-pawn cannot be stopped (for example, 1 ♘e3? ♘d4!–+ or 1 ♘×f7+? ♔h7! 2 ♘e3 ♘d4!–+). White's chances are only in a kingside attack.

Zakharov chose 1 ♘e7?. He had 1...a2?? 2 ♔h6!+– or 1...♔h7? 2 ♘d5 (△ 3 ♘f6+; 3 ♘c3) in mind. However, Petrushin replied with 1...f6+! 2 ♔×f6 ♔h7 3 ♘f5 a2 4 ♘g6 ♘d4!. A careless 4...a1♕+? 5 ♔f7 could lead to a perpetual check (♘f8-g6+), while after the move actually played White had to resign.

According to Gufeld's comments in *Chess Informant*, White could have achieved a draw by means of 1 ♔f6 a2 2 ♔×f7 a1♕ 3 ♘g6+ ♔h7 4 ♘f8+. However Nunn indicated that this is wrong – Black could win after 1...♔g8! 2 ♘e7+ (2 ♘h6+ ♔f8) 2...♔h7 3 ♔×f7 a2 4 ♘f5 ♘c5! (4...a1♕? 5 ♘d7= or 5 ♘g6=) 5 ♘g6 ♘d7 6 ♔e7 a1♕.

Grandmaster Nunn found a win for White

in the initial position:

1 ♔h6!! ♔g8 (1...a2 2 ♘e7! △ ♘×f7#; 1...f6 2 ♘f7+ ♔g8 3 ♔g6 a2 4 h6 a1♕ 5 h7+) **2 ♘d7!** (the threat is 3 ♘e7+ ♔h8 4 ♘e5) **2...f6** (2...♔h8 3 ♘f6 △ ♘d6+−) **3 ♔g6 a2 4 ♘h6+ ♔h8 5 ♘×f6 a1♕ 6 ♘f7#.**

15/37. A. Troitsky, 1910

1 ♖c2+

The line 1 ♔d2? a1♕ 2 ♘d3+ ♔a2! (rather than 2...♔b1? 3 ♖c1+ ♔a2 4 ♘b4+ ♔b2 5 ♖×a1 ♔×a1 6 ♔c1⊙ a2 7 ♘c2#) 3 ♘c1+ ♔b1! 4 ♖b3+ ♕b2+ only leads to a draw.

1...♔b3!

1...♔b1 is bad: 2 ♘e2(d5) a1♕ 3 ♘c3+ ♕×c3+ 4 ♔×c3 a2 5 ♖b2+.

2 ♖c1 a1♕! (2...♔b2 3 ♔d2 a1♕ 4 ♘d3+ ♔a2 5 ♘b4+ ♔b2 6 ♖×a1 ♔×a1 7 ♔c1⊙ +−) **3 ♖×a1 ♔b2**

16-61

W?

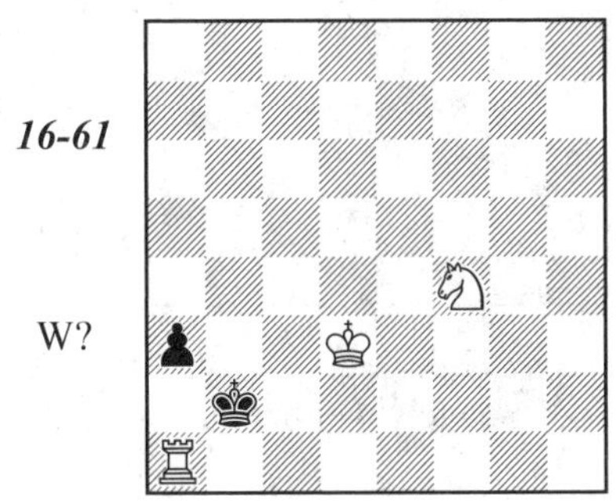

4 ♖f1!!

The only correct place for the rook retreat, as becomes clear from further events.

4...a2 5 ♔c4! a1♕ 6 ♘d3+ ♔a2 7 ♘b4+ ♔b2 8 ♖f2+ ♔b1

He has no 8...♔a3? 9 ♘c2+; in case of 8...♔c1 White wins by means of 9 ♘a2+ ♔b1 10 ♔b3. If the white rook stood on e2, Black could save the game with 8...♔c1 9 ♘a2+ ♔d1.

9 ♔b3+−

If the rook was on g2 or h2, Black could parry the mate threat with 9...♕a7 or 9...♕a8 respectively. Now, however, he cannot do it: the knight controls the a6-square.

15/38. F. Bondarenko, Al. Kuznetsov, 1971*

False ideas are 1 ♖×b6? ♘d5+ or 1 ♖a7? ♘×b5 2 ♖b7 ♘c6+ 3 ♔d7 ♘cd4 4 ♖×b6 ♔g5 and Black can hold without much effort.

1 ♖a8!! ♘×a8 2 ♔d8 ♔g5 3 ♔c8+−

The king alone gains the upper hand against two knights!

15/39. J. Fritz, 1953 (corr.)

1 a3!! ♖×f1+ 2 ♔e2 ♖f4 (2...♖h1 3 ♖d1+; 2...♔c2 3 ♖d2+) **3 ♖b3+ ♔a2 4 ♖b4!+−**

In the composers first version, a bishop stood on f1 rather than a knight. But if so, White can win mundanely because the black king is too unfavorably placed: 1 ♖f3 ♔×a2 2 ♔c2.

15/40. A. Kuriatnikov, 1981

1 ♖e7!!

The line 1 ♘b6+? ♔b7 2 ♔g3 (2 ♖×e2 ♖f5) 2...♔c6 3 ♘a4 ♔b5! △ 4...e1♕ leads to a rapid draw. 1 ♖×e2? ♔b7 is also unpromising. As we soon shall see, the rook belongs on e1 in this sort of position.

1...e1♕+

2 ♘b6+ was threatened. If 1...♖f4+ then 2 ♔g3 ♖c4 3 ♘b6+ ♔d8 4 ♘×c4 ♔×e7 5 ♔f2+−. In case of 1...♔d8, White wins by means of 2 ♖×e2 (the king cannot go to b7) 2...♔d7 3 ♘b6+ ♔c6 4 ♖e5 ♖f1 5 ♘c8 ♖c1 6 ♘e7+.

2 ♖×e1 ♔b7 3 ♘b6!

Rather than 3 ♖a1? ♔c6 4 ♖a5 ♖f5 5 ♖a6+ ♔b7 6 ♖a5 ♔c6=.

3...♖f5 (3...♔c6? 4 ♖e6+ or 4 ♖e5) **4 ♘d7 ♔c6**

4...♖d5 5 ♖e6! ♔c7 6 c6 ♖d6 7 ♖×d6 ♔×d6 8 ♘e5+−.

16-62

W?

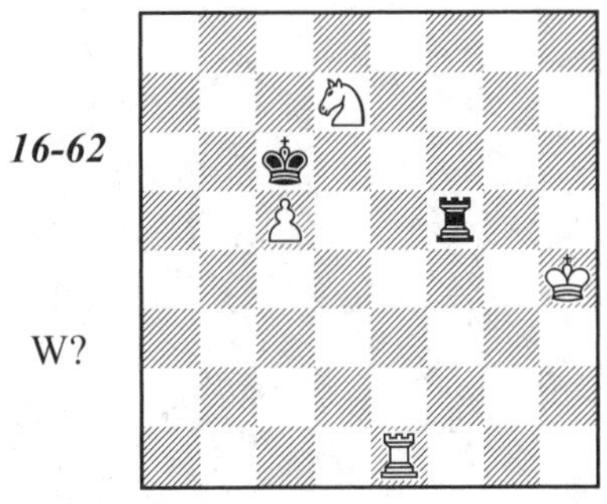

5 ♖d1? is useless now: 5...♖d5! 6 ♖×d5 ♔×d5 7 ♔g5 ♔c6=. It is an unexpected trapping of the rook that decides.

5 ♘e5+! ♔×c5 6 ♔g4!+−

This is why the white rook went to e1! After 1 ♖×e2? the black rook would have had a safe square (f1) in the final position.

15/41. V. & M. Platov, 1905

1 ♘e6+ ♔e8 2 ♖b8+ ♔e7!

In case of 2...♔d7? 3 ♖f8! (with the threat 4 ♘g5) White obtains his coveted position immediately, while now he cannot play 3 ♖f8? in view of 3...♕×e6! –+.

3 ♖b7+! ♔e8

An inferior alternative is 3...♔f6 4 ♖f7+! ♔e5 5 a4 a5 6 ♖f8⊙ +–.

4 ♖f7!!

The rook is untouchable in view of the knight fork; White deprives the black queen of the f5-square and creates a threat (5 ♖f8+ ♔e7 6 ♘g5 +–).

4...h6 5 ♖f8+!

After 5 ♖f4? ♔e7! 6 a3 a5 7 a4 ♔e8! 8 ♖f8+ ♔d7!⊙ White cannot make any progress because he has already spent his reserve tempo on the queenside.

5...♔d7 (5...♔e7 6 ♘f4+–) **6 a3! a5 7 a4⊙ ♔e7 8 ♘f4+–.**

15/42. G. Zakhodiakin, 1948

1 ♗b8 ♔b7?!

Inarkiev has found that 1...♔b5! is much stronger than this. For example, 2 ♔d5 ♘g5! 3 ♘f6 (3 ♗×d6 ♘f3 followed with 4...♘e1 or 4...♘d4) 3...♘f3 4 ♘g4!? ♔b4 (4...♘e1? 5 ♘e3 ♔b4 is erroneous in view of 6 ♗×d6 ♔a3 7 ♗g3! ♘×c2 8 ♘×c2 ♔b2 9 ♘e1 +–) 5 ♘e3 ♔a3 6 ♗×d6 ♔b2 and 7...♘e1(d4)=.

2 ♔d5 ♔c8 3 ♔c6!

After the inaccurate 3 ♔e6? Black holds thanks to an attack against White's only pawn: 3...♘g5+! 4 ♔×d6 ♘f3 △ 5...♘d4=.

3...♘d8+ 4 ♔×d6 ♔b7!

White has fallen into zugzwang and cannot maintain his extra pawn. 5 ♔d5 ♔c8 6 ♔d6 ♔b7 leads to a repetition of moves, while after 5 ♔×c5? ♔c8 6 ♔d6 ♔b7! the brilliant idea seen below does not work.

5 ♘e5!! ♔×b8 6 ♔d7 ♘b7 7 ♘c6+ ♔a8 8 ♔e6! c4 9 ♔d5!⊙ +–

16-63

B

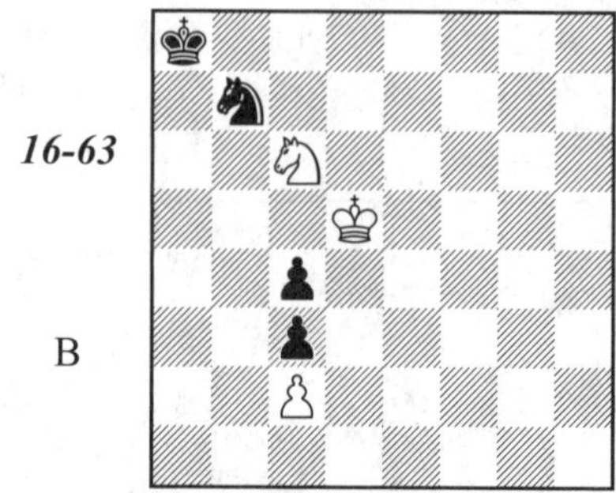

A picturesque position: Black, with his extra pawn, is completely without moves.

BIBLIOGRAPHY

Listed here are books used, to a greater or lesser extent, in writing this book. To a considerable degree, however, the book is based on my extensive collection of endgame positions and analyses, gathered over many years of coaching (my "exercise filing-cabinet" being a part of it), so that I can hardly recall all the primary sources for the positions and analyses included here.

Some of the books listed here are recommended to my readers; these have short synopses appended. Among the rest are some good works, some mediocre and even some obviously poor. Perhaps I should have pointed these out specifically, to warn my readers against buying them. However, in my experience, the least competent authors are often the most vocal and argumentative. I do not want to lose time, either my publisher's or my own, in pointless squabbles with them in chess periodicals or on the Internet.

Please do not think that I recommend some of my earlier works here out of immodesty. I have never written a book unless I was convinced that I had some important ideas to share with my potential readers, plus some fitting examples to illustrate these ideas, examples which have proven their worth over years of actual chess training. Perhaps it is this approach that has made my books useful to chessplayers of the most varied qualifications, from amateurs to the world's leading grandmasters.

The approach taken by some authors seems far less productive to me. Sometimes they even write quite frankly, in their prefaces, that they have first chosen a subject, often one quite new to them, and only then started searching for appropriate examples. Within the limited period of a book's actual writing, it is quite difficult to make a deep investigation into the selected subject plus to collect original and high-quality illustrations.

This list is divided into several sections for clarity. The classification is somewhat arbitrary, since some books fit several descriptions.

ENDGAME HANDBOOKS

These are books that give a more or less systematic presentation of the whole of endgame theory, or at least some of its chapters. The most complete is undoubtedly the Yugoslavian *Encyclopaedia of Endgames*, but most readers feel more comfortable when thoughts are represented verbally rather than symbolically.

Averbakh, Yuri (editor), *Shakhmatnye okonchaniya*, 2nd edition (in 5 volumes), Fizkultura I Sport (FiS), Moscow, 1980-1984. A high-quality monograph written by Yuri Averbakh in co-operation with other Soviet endgame authorities. The authors took several earlier endgame handbooks (by R. Fine, M. Euwe, A. Chéron) as starting points and added a great deal of their own creative work, correcting old analyses and providing many new examples.

Levenfish & Smyslov, *Teoriya ladeinykh okonchanii*, 3rd edition, FiS, Moscow, 1986. A classic on the most important parts of endgame theory.

Müller & Lamprecht, *Fundamental Chess Endings*, Gambit Publications Ltd., London, 2001.

Panchenko, Alexander, *Teoriya i praktika shakhmatnykh okonchanii*, Ioshkar-Ola, 1997.

Various authors, *Encyclopaedia of Endgames* (in 5 volumes), Chess Informant, Belgrade, 1982-1993.

Villeneuve, Alain, *Les Finales* (in 2 volumes), Garnier, Paris, 1982-1984.

ANALYTICAL COLLECTIONS

I appreciate this sort of book very much, because they bring much fresh material, not borrowed from other authors. In addition, their examples are usually well-analyzed and sometimes even well-generalized and explained.

Dvoretsky, Mark, *Shkola vysshego masterstva 1 – Endshpil*, 2nd edition, Kharkov, Ukraine, Folio,

2001. (In English: *School of Chess Excellence 1 – Endgame Analysis*, Edition Olms, Zürich, 2001 In German: *Geheimnisse gezielten Schachtrainings*, Edition Olms, Zürich, 1993.) This was my first book; it was published in 1989 in Russian under the title *Iskusstvo analiza* (The Art of Analysis). In 1991, Batsford Publishers translated it into English under the title *Secrets of Chess Training*; the book then received the British Chess Federation "Book of the Year" award. The new editions, both Russian and English, are considerably corrected and enlarged. The book contains only original endgame analyses by me and my pupils; on this basis, I explain the most important endgame ideas and methods of improving one's chess strength in general, not merely in playing endgames.

Grigoriev, Nikolai, *Shakhmatnoe tvorchestvo N. Grigorieva*, 2nd edition, FiS, Moscow, 1954. The first edition was compiled by Konstantinopolsky and the second by Bondarevsky. Grigoriev was a classic analyst of the endgame, pawn endgames in particular. The book contains his numerous studies, analytical works, and tutorial materials.

Korchnoi, Victor, *Practical Rook Endings*, Edition Olms, Zürich, 2001. The outstanding grandmaster makes an extremely deep investigation of rook endgames from his own games. However, one should realize that the book is complicated, and designed for players of advanced skill.

Lutz, Christopher, *Endgame Secrets*, Batsford, London, 1999.

ENDGAME MANUALS

Amazingly enough, I have not yet found a single endgame manual which I could recommend wholeheartedly to my pupils (the wish to fill this gap stimulated me to write this book). Most existing books are either elementary and useful for novices only, or are useless methodologically, or do not cover endgame theory fully (in this case, they are mentioned in the next section).

Alburt and Krogius, *Just the Facts!*, Chess Information and Research Center, New York, 2000.

Averbakh, Yuri, *Chto nado znat' ob endshpile*, 3rd edition, FiS, Moscow, 1979.

Soltis, Andrew, *Grandmaster Secrets – Endings*, Thinker's Press, Davenport, Iowa, 1997. The book is original and fresh, with a good collection of examples, but the author's pedagogical concepts do not inspire my trust.

BOOKS ON VARIOUS ENDGAME THEMES

In this section of the index, various books are mentioned. Their quality depends not so much on the subject as on the competence of the author, his ability to underline and to explain the most important and instructive ideas.

Beliavsky & Mikhalchishin, *Winning Endgame Technique*, Batsford, London, 1995.

Beliavsky & Mikhalchishin, *Winning Endgame Strategy*, Batsford, London, 2000.

Benko, Pal, *Chess Endgame Lessons* (2 volumes), Self-published, 1989, 1999. Grandmaster Pal Benko is a great connoisseur of endgames and a renowned study composer. The book is a compilation of his monthly columns in the American *Chess Life* magazine. Both theoretical endgames and practical cases from various levels, from amateur to grandmaster, are analyzed.

Nunn, John, *Tactical Chess Endings*, Collier Books, New York, 1988.

Speelman, Jonathan, *Endgame Preparation*, Batsford, London, 1981. Some important endgame problems and concepts are analyzed, such as zugzwang, the theory of corresponding squares, pawn structure and weak pawns, an extra outside passed pawn, an extra pawn with all pawns on one wing, etc.

Speelman, *Analysing the Endgame*, Batsford, London, 1981.

BOOKS ON ENDGAME TECHNIQUE

As I have already mentioned in the preface, general endgame technique (and, particularly, the technique of exploiting an advantage) is beyond the scope of this book, although its important principles are described here more than once. A more systematic presentation of endgame technique can be obtained from the books named below.

Dvoretsky & Yusupov, *Tekhnika v shakhmatnoi igre*, 2nd edition, Folio, Kharkov, Ukraine, 1998. (In English: *Technique for the Tournament Player*, Batsford, London, 1995. In German: *Effektives Endspieltraining*, Beyer Verlag, 1996.) One of the main themes of the book is the problem of technique, although there are also chapters on other subjects, such as methods of improving one's endgame play, theory of certain types of endgame, etc.

Mednis, Edmar, *Practical Endgame Lessons*, David McKay, New York, 1978. This book was later refined and published under a new title; unfortunately, I have not seen the new version yet. The author's views on basic endgame techniques seem at first sight very different from mine and Shereshevsky's, but in fact they are very close to ours. This book is perhaps not so deep as Shereshevsky's, but is more attractive and accessible.

Shereshevsky, Mikhail, *Strategiya endshpilya*, FiS, Moscow, 1988. This book has already been mentioned in the preface. The author explains the main principles of endgame technique and gives numerous illustrative examples.

ENDGAME MATERIALS IN VARIOUS PUBLICATIONS

Only the most important of the many sources I have used are mentioned here.

Belavenets, Sergey, *Master Sergey Belavenets*, FiS, Moscow, 1963. The book includes tutorial lectures on endgames that Belavenets had prepared shortly before the 2nd World War (in which he was killed). The lectures are very good, and gave me (and later, Shereshevsky) an impetus to prepare our own tutorial materials on endgame technique.

Dvoretsky, Mark, *School of Chess Excellence 3 – Strategic Play*, Edition Olms, Zürich, 2002. (In Russian: *Shkola vysshego masterstva 3 – Strategiya*, Folio, Kharkov, Ukraine, 1998. In German: *Geheimnisse der Schachstrategie*, Edition Olms, Zürich, 1999.) The first and largest part of the book is dedicated to various aspects of positional play; the second part handles positions with limited material, mainly problems of technique.

Nunn, John, *Secrets of Practical Chess*, Gambit, London, 1998. This relatively small book contains practical advice on many problems important for a practical player. The endgame section of the book is, in my opinion, slightly below the level of other chapters, but the professional and intellectual level of Nunn's work as a whole is so high that I can recommend it without reservation to every chessplayer, whatever his level.

Shereshevsky, Mikhail, *The Soviet Chess Conveyor*, Sofia, 1994.

Chess Informant

Chess magazines: *64*, *Shakhmaty v SSSR*, *New in Chess*, etc.

INDEX OF PLAYERS

Numbers in **bold** denote that the player named first had White. Numbers in brackets denote that the respective diagram was discussed or mentioned again later in the text.

INDEX OF COMPOSERS AND ANALYSTS

A diagram number in **boldface** denotes a position stemming from the given composer or analyst. If a name is merely mentioned in the text, normal type is used. Annotators of their own games are not indicated, nor are those whose names are, for whatever reason, omitted from the text (for example, the author's own analytical corrections and additions are often not named). Double names (e.g. "Platov, Vasily & Mikhail" or "Levenfish, Grigory & Smyslov, Vasily") are included in the index only when the book contains more than one study or analysis by that duo.

INDEX OF STRATEGIC AND TACTICAL TECHNIQUES

When a tool is a particular case of a more general tool (for example, "mined squares" is a particular case of corresponding squares), it is not mentioned in the list of the more general case. Many positions are found in more than one list because several different tools are used in them.